EDWARDIAN FICTION

AN OXFORD COMPANION

EDWARDIAN FICTION

AN OXFORD COMPANION

SANDRA KEMP, CHARLOTTE MITCHELL
DAVID TROTTER

Oxford New York
OXFORD UNIVERSITY PRESS
1997

Oxford University Press, Great Clarendon Street, Oxford OX2 6DP
Oxford New York
Athens Auckland Bangkok Bogota Bombay Buenos Aires
Calcutta Cape Town Dar es Salaam Delhi Florence Hong Kong
Istanbul Karachi Kuala Lumpur Madras Madrid Melbourne
Mexico City Nairobi Paris Singapore Taipei Tokyo Toronto
and associated companies in
Berlin Ibadan

Oxford is a trade mark of Oxford University Press

Published in the United States by
Oxford University Press Inc., New York

British Library Cataloguing in Publication Data
Data available

Library of Congress Cataloging in Publication Data
Kemp, Sandra.
Edwardian fiction: an Oxford companion/Sandra Kemp, Charlotte Mitchell, David Trotter.
Includes bibliographical references (p.).
1. *English fiction—20th century—Dictionaries.* 2. *English fiction—20th century—Bio-bibliography—Dictionaries.*
3. *Great Britain—History—Edward VII, 1901–1910—Dictionaries.*
I. Mitchell, Charlotte. II. Trotter, David, 1951– III. Title.
PR881.K39 1997
823′.91209—dc21 [B] 96–37878
ISBN 0–19–811760–4

1 3 5 7 9 10 8 6 4 2

Typeset by Pure Tech India Ltd, Pondicherry
Printed in Great Britain by
Bookcraft Ltd,
Midsomer Norton, Somerset

ACKNOWLEDGEMENTS

The book could not have been written without the help of many other people. We should like particularly to thank our research assistants, Mrs Gillian Cochran and Ms Anna Snaith. Professor John Sutherland gave us a high standard to emulate with his own *Longman Companion to Victorian Fiction* (1988) and provided consistent support. Dr Philip Horne contributed the entry on Henry James and checked our references to that writer. Dr Charles Mitchell read the typescript and made many helpful comments. Mrs Kathryn Metzenthin printed out many drafts at inconvenience to herself. Ms Frances Whistler of Oxford University Press was supportive over a long period of time. Many other friends gave helpful advice, including Mr Henry Berens, Professor Simon Frith, Lady Violet Powell, and Mrs Julian Watson.

Among the many librarians and archivists who helped us we would like to mention the staff of the British Library, the London Library, the India Office Library, the Family History Center at the Church of Jesus Christ of Latter Day Saints, Exhibition Road, and the Principal Registry at Somerset House. For help, sometimes repeated help, with specific problems we are grateful to Ms Carol Ibrahim of the University of London Archives Department; Miss Carol Bowen of University College London Records Office; Ms Patricia Methven of the King's College, London, Archives; Ms Juanita Cutler of the Archives Department, Royal Holloway and Bedford New College; Mr Richard Williams of Birkbeck College Library; Ms Helen Cordell of the Library of the School of Oriental and African Studies; the Secretary of the Guild of the Cheltenham Ladies' College; Miss L. Storey of the Theosophical Society in England; Mr Peter Traynor, Group Archivist of the Prudential Corporation PLC; K. W. Dickins of the Sussex Archaeological Society; Ms Hazel Bannister of the Society of Authors; Mr Charles Wright of the Fabian Society; J. V. Stemp, Librarian of Lady Margaret Hall, Oxford; Ms Pauline Harris, Librarian of Somerville College, Oxford; Dr. David Smith, Librarian and Archivist of St Anne's College, Oxford; Miss Maria Croghan, Librarian of St Hilda's College, Oxford; Miss Deborah C. Quare, Librarian of St Hugh's College, Oxford; the Research Secretary of the United Reformed Church History Society; Ms Helen Cordell and Ms Anna Allott of the School of Oriental and African Studies; the staff of the Salvation Army Heritage Centre; Mrs Paula Lucas of the Royal Geographical Society; the staff of Bradford Central Library; Mrs J. M. Cook of Tonbridge School Library; Ms Patsy Conway of the Membership Department of the Zoological Society of London; Mr Michael Bott of the University of Reading Library; Mr Michael Meredith of the Eton College Library; the Curator of Bateman's; and Ms C. Coates, Librarian of the Trades Union Congress.

Of the people who kindly responded to enquiries about individual writers we should thank Dr G. Krishnamurti of the 1890s Society; Ms Jane Fenoulhet of the Department of Dutch, University College London ('Maarten Maartens'); Sir Jack Boles (Hugh Clifford); the Earl of Verulam and Mrs David Lascelles (H. V. Prichard); the late

Acknowledgements

Lady Acland (Eleanor Cropper); Mrs Angela Hesselgren, Mrs Veronica Goodenough, and Lt.-Col. Peter Pender-Cudlip (Mrs Pender Cudlip and W. P. Drury); Mrs E. E. Roach (Edith C. M. Dart); Lady Harrod (Frances Harrod); Mr Brian Mitchell (Beatrice Heron-Maxwell); Mr Richard Lawrence (Rosamond Napier); Professor Virginia Blain (Mrs Edward Kennard); Miss Maria Pakenham, Mr John Saumarez Smith, and Mrs Handasyde Buchanan ('Handasyde'); Lt. and Mrs F. R. A. Turnbull ('Lucas Cleeve'); Mrs G. S. Legge and Mrs Jane Day (A. E. J. Legge and Margaret Legge); Mr Meirion Bowen of Sir Michael Tippett's office (Mrs Henry Tippett); Caroline Belgrave of Curtis Brown (Mrs Fred Reynolds); the Earl of St Germans ('Ellova Gryn'); and Miss Patricia Herbert of the British Library's Oriental and India Oice Collections (Mrs Chan-Toon).

Contents

INTRODUCTION

What were the Edwardians about, when they turned to fiction? As writers—and publishers—what territories did they stake out, in subject-matter, genre, and readership? And as readers, what novels of their own period did they rate highly or read eagerly? Clearly, their choices were not necessarily those we would make now, nor as narrowly selective. Asked by *The Bookman* to list the books of 1906 which had interested him most, H. G. Wells replied:

> Pardon a telegraphic style. No single dominant book this year, but a shower of admirable ones—*Joseph Vance* struck me as a book that would have made a great reputation in Victorian times—*The Old Country* (Newbolt) I found charming—I re-read Hudson's *Crystal Age* with zest—*Sir Nigel* (Doyle), a ripping good story with a delightful clear brightness of detail—some of Conrad's best in *The Mirror of the Sea*—*The Home of Islam*, a happy recovery for Pickthall—the early part of *The Workaday Woman* is the best I've read of Miss Hunt—I was interested by the unconscious verity of Bennett's *Whom God Hath Joined*—and there were lots more.
>
> P.S.—Was *The Golden Bowl* (James) in 1906? If so, put it first of all.[1]

Wells was, in fact, two years late in trying to include *The Golden Bowl*—the only book he mentions which is still read at all widely today, and James's last completed novel—and it is interesting that it seemed so immediate to him in 1906. It might have been a subtly different work had it actually appeared in that year, for James as a writer was by no means indifferent to his own literary and cultural context. One of the major services offered by a reference book of this sort is to revitalize that context, revealing the diversity of literary work that surrounded, competed with, and influenced the writing and publication of what we now see as solitary masterpieces. All the writers named by Wells have entries in the present book, as do some 800 others—constituting a flourishing literary scene which is the particular province of this *Companion* to Edwardian fiction.

As the *Companion* shows, in the actual year of *The Golden Bowl*'s publication, 1904, this context consisted not only of Conrad's *Nostromo*, Chesterton's *The Napoleon of Notting Hill*, E. F. Benson's *The Challoners*, and Hall Caine's *The Prodigal Son*, but also of a mass of work by less canonical authors. Angela Brazil broke through into popularity with her first schoolgirl novel, *A Terrible Tomboy*; the prolific L. T. Meade produced ten or so novels in different popular genres; W. E. Norris, a friend of James's, published *Nature's Comedian*; and H. O. Sturgis—another friend—*Belchamber* (after James's criticism of this Sturgis never wrote fiction again).

If one turns back to Wells's list (and books genuinely from 1906), it is noticeable that the writers who are still widely read today—Conan Doyle, Conrad, Hudson, and

[1] *The Bookman*, 31 (Jan. 1907).

Bennett—were all then in mid-career; as the titles show, the ideas and genres which they were pursuing were not necessarily those that made their subsequent reputations. Doyle rated his historical romances such as *Sir Nigel* more highly than his Sherlock Holmes stories—an opinion not shared by readers then or now. Conrad's *The Mirror of the Sea* is a collection of essays. Hudson's *The Crystal Age* (actually 1887) was utopian science fiction, strongly influenced by Samuel Butler's *Erewhon* (1872) and already rather eclipsed by the runaway success of his *Green Mansions* (1904): his best-remembered books, the non-fictional *A Shepherd's Life* and the autobiographical *Far Away and Long Ago*, were yet to come (1910 and 1918). Bennett's novel *Whom God Hath Joined* was his contribution to the then-popular 'marriage-problem' genre.

What begins to be apparent here is the shape not only of literary reputations but of literary careers, something that can be explored further with the aid of a *Companion*. The Bennett example is indicative: he is best known today for the novels set in the 'five towns', based on the Potteries area of the midlands—his characteristic fictional territory, first established as early as 1902 in *Anna of the Five Towns*, and deepened and broadened in later novels from *The Old Wives' Tale* (1908) onwards. *Whom God Hath Joined* belongs with *Sacred and Profane Love* (1905), another sensational tale, to a transitional phase during which he experimented with a range of genres. To explore that phase is to witness the formation, out of diverse elements, of a literary personality which now seems immutable, and which we probably think of as something both possessed and recognized by the writer since birth.

Such an exploration also illuminates the significance of genre in that process of formation: the fresh imaginative opportunities offered to the writer by different sets of literary conventions, and the varied relationships with different sets of readers that they involve. Wells's list demonstrates in microcosm the sheer generic diversity of the novel in the Edwardian period. The writers he names provide examples of new genres and of work in more than one genre (and indeed the combining of fiction with quite different creative fields, in the case of William De Morgan, the ceramic designer who turned to fiction in his mid-sixties with *Joseph Vance*, and Henry Newbolt, poet and promotor of English studies).

As an example of a new genre, Violet Hunt's *The Workaday Woman*, which Wells rightly praises, is one of many Edwardian novels to describe the lives of independent working women—as few before the period had done. Marmaduke Pickthall divided his novels between those set in England and those in exotic, often oriental, locations, as did writers such as Robert Hichens and A. E. W. Mason; unlike them he also developed two distinct styles of writing, so that works in the different settings might be by different writers. Needless to say, *The Home of Islam* is in the exotic vein, which Wells presumably considered a 'recovery' from the preceding English novel, *Brendle* (1905). As Pickthall moved in this way between the domestic and the exotic, as Bennett moved from 'marriage problem' melodrama to light-hearted fantasy to sober realism, as Doyle moved from the detective story to historical romance, so they deepened and extended the scope of narrative fiction. In this *Companion*, we have attempted to draw out the importance of genre by thematic entries which act as signposts to the numerous writers who employed them (see list on page xxiii).

We have chosen to begin our survey at 1900 and to conclude it at 1914, less from a prior commitment to any particular definition of Edwardianism than from a sense that this is a period of enormous interest and almost unprecedented literary activity, and at the same time one that has been largely neglected in the current literary-historical record. There is in any case no consensus as to when the 'Edwardian era' began and ended: it is variously viewed as running from the Boer War (1899–1902) to the First World War (1914–18), or comprising simply Edward VII's reign (1901–1910), or something in between. Nor, as a literary term, is 'Edwardian' as well established as, say, 'Romantic' or 'Augustan', implying rather an existence between two other periods, 'Victorian' and 'Modern'. Although it has been used to clarify the preoccupations and techniques of a particular group of writers, in fact no event (symbolic or actual) marks the beginning of Edwardian fiction, and no significant début: the great figures—Wells, Bennett, Conrad, Galsworthy—had all published their first work under Victoria. What we have found more interesting to explore is the very diversity of the period's transitional position, exemplified in the *Companion* by entries such as Walter Besant's *The Fourth Generation* (1900) and Joyce's *Dubliners* (1914)—the one a late novel of an ageing Victorian, the other the first work of fiction by one of the earliest and most significant Modernists.[2]

The attributes usually associated with the period are worth examining, however. Edwardianism has usually been understood, or mythologized, in socio-economic terms. 'This oozing, bulging wealth of the English upper and upper-middle classes', as Orwell described it; an atmosphere of 'eating everlasting strawberry ices on green lawns to the tune of the Eton boating song'.[3] The supposed evanescent charm of the era is captured in the cynical urbanity and malicious wit of Saki's short stories, and in Vita Sackville West's *The Edwardians* (1930), which takes as its field of action the characteristically Edwardian scene, a country house party in 1905. One has only to list some of the country houses of Edwardian fiction—Howards End, Friars Pardon, Holmescroft, Overdene, Pendragon—to see how heavily the imagination of the era was invested in landed property. The country house was one definition of England itself.

At the same time, another powerful account of the Edwardian era, namely the recognition of suburban humanity as an irreversible feature of modern England, appears in the fiction of Bennett, Wells, and Galsworthy. Bennett's 'Simon Fuge' is a moving meditation on metropolitan and provincial values. It portrays a small suburban town and conveys affectionate sympathy for the urban middle class. 'Not to everyone is it given to take a wide view of things—to look over the far, pale streams, the purple heather, and moonlit pools of the wide marshes . . . To most it is given to watch assiduously a row of houses, a back-yard,' remarks Galsworthy in *The Country House* (1907).[4] Wells's *Tono-Bungay* (1909), like Forster's *Howards End* (1910) and Galsworthy's *Fraternity* (1909), describes the life of the urban poor. *Tono-Bungay* is a graphic depiction of the anonymity of the modern city, and of modern life and character including the business worlds of commerce and advertising. Subject-matter of this sort was accompanied by a terror of the increasingly dispossessed working class. In

[2] For detailed studies of Edwardian fiction see John Batchelor, *The Edwardian Novelists* (Duckworth, London, 1982); Jefferson Hunter, *Edwardian Fiction* (Cambridge, Mass., Harvard University Press, 1982); Anthea Trodd, *A Reader's Guide to Edwardian Fiction* (Brighton, Harvester, 1991).

[3] George Orwell, 'Such, Such Were the Joys', in *Collected Essays, Journalism and Letters*, ed. Sonia Orwell and Ian Angus (New York, Harcourt Brace Jovanovich, 1968), iv. 357.

[4] John Galsworthy, *The Country House* (London, Heinemann, 1907), pp. 133–4.

Forster's *Howards End* Margaret Schlegel describes the threat of the urban poor as 'odours from the abyss'.[5] Leonard Bast, in the novel, lives on the edge of that abyss, an exemplary victim of urban poverty. The metaphor of the abyss is also frequently used in Arthur Morrison's low-life adventure story *The Hole in the Wall* (1902).

More poignantly, Chesterton wrote of 'This strange indifference . . . this strange loneliness of millions in a crowd'.[6] Such inner qualms were perhaps responsible for the Edwardians' obsession with their health. Tennis, sea-bathing, hot water after meals, and mind-cures were among the panaceas of the moment. 'Sandow's Exercises', named after Eugene Sandow, an Englishman who made a career for himself in America in the 1890s as a 'body-builder', were the fashion among Edwardian suburban men. William James has fun at the expense of these claims in *The Varieties of Religious Experience* where he refers to the 'Gospel of Relaxation', the 'Don't Worry Movement', and those who say 'Youth, Health, Vigour' as they dress themselves every morning. Arnold Bennett, himself a hypochondriac, also exploited the market for 'health', with his books *Mental Efficiency* (1911) and *How to Live on Twenty-Four Hours a Day* (1908).[7]

The impact of the growth of the cities, and in particular the spread of middle-class suburbs, changed the social, cultural, political, and literary maps. Edwardian fiction considers the city as a significant social and political fact: the new opportunities it offers as well as the dehumanization of the urban middle class and poor. In 'The Fallow Fields of Fiction', Bennett speaks of dining in an Italian restaurant in Victoria Street, then wandering out in search of fictional material 'with the intention of perceiving London as though it were a foreign city'.[8] In the guise of Richard Remington, Wells declares that 'London is the most interesting, beautiful and wonderful city in the world to me, delicate in her incidental and multitudinous littleness, and stupendous in her pregnant totality: I cannot bring myself to use her as a museum or an old bookshop.'[9]

Firmly ensconced in Bloomsbury, Virginia Woolf was to sneer at the Edwardian writers' preoccupation with material and social forces (what she called the fabric of things): 'Every sort of town is represented, and innumerable institutions; we see factories, prisons, workhouses, lawcourts, Houses of Parliament; a general clamour, the voice of aspiration, indignation, effort and industry, rises from the whole; but in all this vast conglomeration of printed pages, in all this congeries of streets and houses, there is not a single man or woman whom we know.'[10] But the restlessness and rapid change of the period is graphically presented by this very kaleidoscopic content of the fiction, which includes material as diverse as bloomers, telephones, telegrams, bicycles, trains, the growth of the Labour Party, and the appearance of militant suffragettes, the Fabians, homosexuality, the drop in wages, strikes, the inability of the authorities to cope with the London slums, the inefficiency of the management of the Boer War, the myth of the navy, the excesses of commerce and advertising, the fear of invasion, the English Hymnal, scientific development, realism, mysticism, symbolism, and psychical

[5] E. M. Forster, *Howards End* (London, Edward Arnold, 1910), p. 115.

[6] Chesterton, *The Napoleon of Notting Hill* (London, John Lane, 1904), p. 149.

[7] See Batchelor, *The Edwardian Novelists*, pp. 7–8.

[8] Repr., in *The Author's Craft* (London, John Lave, 1928), pp. 65–6.

[9] H. G. Wells, *The New Machiavelli* (London, John Lane, 1911), p. 283.

[10] Virginia Woolf, 'Mr Bennett and Mrs Brown', *Nation and Athenaeum* 34 (1 Dec. 1923), repr. in *The Author's Craft*, p. 270.

research. Marie Corelli's automobile apocalypse, *The Devil's Motor* (1901), provides a graphic symbol for the times—the offence to Edwardian sensibilities presented by the motor car's revaluation of the speed of life.[11]

Edwardianism is frequently distinguished from Modernism by its supposed assertion of continuity and tradition—in contrast to what is considered the 'modern' resisting of the past and assertion of a new identity—but the fiction of the period often belies this. A significant number of characters in Edwardian novels view change, not permanency, as the essential social fact of their time—among them Wells's Dick Remington (*The New Machiavelli*), and George Ponderevo (*Tono-Bungay*), Galsworthy's Richard Shelton (*The Island Pharisees*), and even Bennett's Edwin Clayhanger (*Clayhanger* and *Hilda Lessways*)—and define their relation to change by a conscious *choice* of old or new roles. Moreover, the rapid socio-economic developments of the period made the ideology of the Victorian novel, with its leaning towards people and houses, no longer tenable or desirable to many Edwardian writers. As Edmund Gosse put it:

> I am tired of the novelist's portrait of a gentleman, with gloves and hat, leaning against a pillar, upon a vague landscape background. I want the gentleman as he appears in a snap-shot photograph with his every-day expression on his face, and the localities in which he spends his days visible around him.[12]

However, here again the large generalizations of conventional histories of the period are undermined if one looks across the range of writing, high and low. For example, in terms of topography ('localities'), a number of authors stop writing of adventures abroad and start writing of the experience of coming home: from the Congo to the home counties; from the probing of heroic acts abroad to the cultivation of English virtues at home. Kipling, for example, precisely fits this paradigm in his movement from *Kim* to *Puck of Pook's Hill*; so does Conrad in moving from *Lord Jim* to *The Secret Agent*. On the other hand, no sooner had Kipling transferred out of India than a group of other writers transferred in, making it not only their own but a rather different place from the one portrayed in his writing. This group included many women, among them Ethel M. Dell, Maud Diver, 'O. Douglas', Sara Jeanette Duncan, K. M. Edge, Alice Perrin, Flora Annie Steel, and Patricia Wentworth. Clearly the aims of these writers varied, as did their level of achievement; but they continued to examine, as Kipling had done, though now through female protagonists, the nature and limits of a heroism put to the test in foreign places.

If the exotic locations were an established theme, the influx of women writers, and of women as central subjects of fiction, was something new. Where the fiction was located on home ground, the women were discovered in the flats and boarding-houses of Britain's cities. Henry James called them 'The contemporary London female, highly modern, inevitably battered'.[13] A notable feature of late-nineteenth-century Britain was the increase in numbers of middle-class working women. (For example, in 1861 nearly 80,000 were employed as teachers in England and Wales; by 1911 there were 183,000. Over the same period, the number of women employed as clerical workers rose from 279 to 124,000.) No longer the background to, or interrup-

[11] See Hunter, *Edwardian Fiction*, p. 46.

[12] *Questions at Issue* (1893), p. 31.

[13] *The Wings of the Dove* (London, Archibald Constable, 1902), p. 48.

tion of, lives supposedly shaped by romantic longing and fulfilment, work itself became the basis of female identity—and Edwardian writers were the first to give serious attention to women at work.

To be sure, the professions chosen by and for Edwardian heroines often involved plenty of scope for creativity: artist, writer, musician. But women doctors, nurses, teachers, journalists, secretaries, even the odd travel agent, became visible in fiction in a way they had never been before. Working-class careers are harder to find, but—and this in itself marks a change—they do exist. The second major polemical focus of Edwardian feminist fiction, which emerged after the foundation of the Women's Social and Political Union in 1903, was the campaign for the vote. The degree of economic and sexual independence achieved by women during the Edwardian era outstripped and rendered obsolete the 'traditional' narrative forms which had on the whole consigned them to dependence. To make either work or political commitment, or both, the theme of a novel was to put into question narrative fiction's traditional reliance on wedlock as a guarantee of formal closure. These novels have not only a new subject-matter, but a new shape.

There were other respects in which the emergence of new themes—and the dominance in the bestseller lists of women writers handling them—marked out the fiction of the period, not just from that of an earlier era, but also from what followed. Sometimes this writing can be seen at its most radical when it was on an entirely different tack from the Modernism of the 1920s. First, there were the marriage problem novels that dominated serious Edwardian fiction, some of which carried a powerful feminist slant. Maud Churton Braby, who wrote marital advice books as well as novels, was not alone in observing 'a spirit of strange unrest' among married women; she advocated better sex education for girls, a 'preliminary canter' for women before marriage, and 'wild oats' for wives. Further, a striking number of Edwardian female writers topped the bestseller lists in popular romance (a market dominated by Marie Corelli, Baroness Orczy, Florence Barclay, Ethel M. Dell, Elinor Glyn, and others) and children's literature—again, genres that have tended to be eclipsed by radical Modernist experiments in form. Frances Hodgson Burnett and E. Nesbit were the bestselling writers of children's fiction—a genre that allowed them to explore surreptitiously their predicament as women. The appeal of Burnett's *The Secret Garden* (1911) lies in the heroine's discovery of a garden, if not a room, of her own. The motif of the Secret Garden (Never Never Land, Enchanted Place) was a persistent one in children's literature of the period. It is as if this desire to lavish more attention on children arose partly because of the uncertainties of the adult public world—as an attempt to gain for and from children the sense of security that the outside world could not provide. Arcadian writing for children was also clearly part of a general tendency towards idyllic ruralist fantasy among many English authors of the pre-war period.

Anxiety—a favourite theme of cultural and literary historians of the period, and undoubtedly a thread that runs through some important Edwardian texts—is another idea that may be re-evaluated in the light of the material in this *Companion*. G. E. Moore approached his moral philosophy with the question, 'What is Good?', and Edwardians anxiously pondered it: what was good, what was right, where duty lay, what the direction of man should be. Some critics have felt that the key to the period was the devalued and directionless state in which the early twentieth century hero found himself.[14] Yet, as the *Companion* demonstrates, there are many Edwardian novels which, while fully acknowledging the difficulty of the times, have at their centre a hero whose state is neither devalued nor directionless: Jerome K. Jerome's *Paul Kelver* (1902), Arthur Morrison's *The Hole in the Wall* (1902), Haldane Macfall's *The Masterfolk* (1903), Leonard Merrick's *Conrad in Quest of His Youth* (1903), K. C. Thurston's *John Chilcote, M.P.* (1904), John Law's *George Eastmont, Wanderer* (1905), Marmaduke Pickthall's *Brendle* (1905), E. V. Lucas's *Over Bemerton's* (1908), Philip Gibbs's *The Individualist* (1908), Hilaire Belloc's *A Change in the Cabinet* (1909), George Meredith's *Celt and Saxon* (1910), J. D. Beresford's *The Early History of Jacob Stahl* (1911), Oliver Onions' *In Accordance with the Evidence* (1912), Constance Holme's *The Lonely Plough* (1914), and W. Kineton Parkes's *Hardware: A Novel in Four Books* (1914). C. F. Masterman's undeniably sombre account of *The Condition of England* (1909) has often been seen as as the epitome of Edwardian anxieties. It is less often noticed, however, that Masterman saw a cause for hope in the playful buoyancy of writers like W. E. Henley, Rudyard Kipling, and Robert Louis Stevenson. Max Beerbohm astutely observed that, while seriousness and frivolity remain segregated in Matthew Arnold's writing, they coexist inextricably in Bernard Shaw's. Beerbohm himself, but also Shaw, Wells, Chesterton, Belloc, Baring, Saki, and Joyce, among others, characteristically treat the most serious issues with malicious humour. The Edwardian 'gospel of fun' was part of a widespread social change which transformed Victorian hostility to mere entertainment and made recreation a mass industry in Britain. Can one imagine a more anxious monarch than Victoria, or a more insouciant one than Edward VII? Chesterton's fiction exemplifies this doctrine to perfection. It was Chesterton who in *The Flying Inn* scathingly parodied the fashionable invasion scare stories which have since been taken to epitomize Edwardian paranoia; and who in an essay published in 1908 wrote his own defence of his whimsical discussion of weighty theological and philosophical matters: 'It is an equally awful truth that four and four makes eight, whether you reckon the thing out in eight onions or eight angels, or eight bricks or eight bishops, or eight minor poets or eight pigs.'

Between the decline of the three-volume novel in 1895 and the outbreak of the First World War lay twenty years in which fiction was the most important section of the leisure industry. It was not only that the new novel became cheaper (6*s*. for a single volume as opposed to a first edition in three volumes at 31*s*. 6*d*), it ceased to be considered a luxury item; smaller and more convenient to handle, it could be read by a larger proportion of a wider variety of people in all sorts of different places. Changes in the market for fiction made possible the diversity we have spoken of. Writers sought out new and more narrowly defined readerships. They identified and addressed their readers by creating new characters (jockeys, diplomats, spies, journalists, housewives, anarchists, international criminals, dictators, aesthetes), new points of view, and new sub-genres, such as Ruritanian romance. Like the secret gardens of children's literature, Ruritania provided Edwardian writers with a territory that was at once familiar and unfamiliar; one which was European yet exotic, where magical transformations

[14] See Batchelor, *The Edwardian Novelists*, ch. 1, which characterizes Edwardianism as an age of anxiety, of 'contracting moral horizons' and 'epistemological crisis'.

might occur and political experiments succeed or fail. The most commercially successful Edwardian adaptation of the genre was Elinor Glyn's *Three Weeks* (1907), in which a fundamentally upright but aimless young Englishman is regenerated by an encounter with a princess. Ouida's *Helianthus* (1908), set in an imaginary European country, combines the genre with another potent theme of the period, the threat of German militarism. Distant echoes of Ruritania can be heard as far afield as George Meredith's astringent *Celt and Saxon* (1910).

At times, for example in Magnay's *Count Zarka* (1903), Ruritanian romance intersected with the kind of spy fiction written by E. Phillips Oppenheim and others which features tortuous diplomacy in exotic locations. Spy fiction had become established as a bestselling genre in Britain at the turn of the century, and has, roughly speaking, kept its generic shape ever since. What distinguishes it from other types of sensational fiction (crime fiction, historical romance, etc.) is its political agenda. This agenda had been set by George Chesney's *The Battle of Dorking* (1871), the first of many stories about the invasion and conquest of Britain. By 1900, however, two further developments had decisively altered the character of the genre: during the 1880s the accelerating pace of technological change added a new dimension to Great Power rivalries; and during the 1890s the popular press and popular magazines became insatiable in their pursuit of sensational material. In the early years of the century, the industrial and military rivalry between Britain and Germany intensified dramatically. It really did seem as though the two great European powers had locked themselves into a battle for global hegemony. At one point in Erskine Childers's *The Riddle of the Sands* (1903), the narrator, Carruthers, gets hold of some German journals whose 'rancorous Anglophobia' is a chilling reminder of the threat facing his country. The general consequence of such chilling reminders was an epidemic of spy fever. From Childers through the ultra-sensational tales of Le Queux and E. Phillips Oppenheim to John Buchan's *The Thirty-Nine Steps* (1915), Edwardian writers devised a new kind of hero: one who would adequately represent a nation which, though sunk in decadence, was still sound at heart, and likely to respond to the scent of battle. They found that hero in the amateur agent or accidental spy, the sleepy young Englishman whose complacency is shattered when he stumbles across some fiendish plot; contending with the unsportsmanlike conduct of his enemies and the disbelief of his friends, he learns what it is like to be temporarily an outsider; the rites of passage regenerate him morally and provoke political awakening.

Real war was also explored in fiction. The Boer War may be an unfashionable subject now but it also demands an entry in a *Companion* of this kind, because it was an event which brought individual and collective identities into focus, and one whose consequences for the literature of the period have never been studied systematically. Surveying the contemporary novel in 1911, H. G. Wells suggested that the Boer War marked the dividing line between the assurance of Victorian fiction and the doubting, sceptical note of Edwardian fiction.[15]

Cracks in Edwardian confidence can also be detected in other kinds of writing. If Ruritanian romance and spy fiction kept the sinister at a safe distance by associating it with an imaginary elsewhere, fantasy, like the horror story, envisaged its intrusion

[15] 'The Scope of the Novel', in *Henry James and H. G. Wells*, ed. Leon Edel and Gordon N. Ray (Urbana: Illinois University Press, 1958), p. 145.

closer to home. Some notable Edwardian fantasies are laboratory experiments which observe, to comic, tragic, or polemical effect, what happens when normality is disrupted by the arrival of a supernatural being or overturned by a supernatural act for example, in F. Anstey's *The Brass Bottle* (1900), Marie Corelli's *The Life Everlasting* (1911), and H. G. Wells's, *The Sea Lady* (1902). Equally characteristic of the period was the peopling of recognizable landscapes with fairy tribes, in the work of Lord Dunsany, Dermot O'Byrne, James Stephens, and M. Urquhart. Closer to mainstream domestic realism were stories about the transfer of minds, bodies, or even parts of bodies, and tales which imagine the eruption of the past (historical or legendary) into the present.

Edwardian writers pooled ideas, argued about techniques, and sometimes collaborated. The advent of the literary agent as an intermediary between author and publisher gave a new kind of cohesion and professionalism to the literary life. The Edwardian period marked the transition between the Victorian era, when publishers were still in some respects mediators between authors and printers, and the contemporary mass-audience, multimedia publishing business. Arnold Bennett, for example, went to J. B. Pinker's agency in 1901 when he was earning only £2 10*s*. per 1,000 words. The literary agent Arthur Addison Bright committed suicide in 1906 after swindling J. M. Barrie out of £16,000. By then it had become clear that the business of exploiting copyrights had become too complicated (and time-consuming) for authors to handle themselves. In the first decades of the twentieth century, it was possible for writers like Bennett to enjoy the kind of lifestyles that were to be associated with film stars in the 1920s and 1930s.

The development of a mass reading public and a vastly increased demand for books and magazines at the turn of the century also led to debate about the nature of the reader. Edwardian writers were constantly speculating about the nature of the audiences they addressed, and their perception of the needs and demands of their readers created an awareness of fine demarcations of genre and sub-genre. Writers frequently switched genres. Literariness and polemic were not then regarded as mutually exclusive, and many writers moved happily enough between the two, or combined both in the same book. A number sought to bridge the increasing gap between up-market and down-market readerships by combining a self-consciously literary style with an interest in social and aesthetic theory and with sensational subject-matter: these include Charles Marriott, W. Kineton Parkes, John Masefield, May Sinclair, John Collis Snaith, Benjamin Swift, and Hugh Walpole. Similar conclusions could probably also be drawn about bestselling fiction. Many popular writers developed a main line in one genre and a sideline in another. For example, Baroness Orczy's historical romances earned her fame and fortune, but she also wrote less successful detective stories; with Arthur Conan Doyle it was the other way round. It is generic promiscuity, rather than specialization, which characterizes the careers of many bestselling writers who either began or flourished during the Edwardian period: for example, Alice and Claude Askew, Guy Boothby, L. T. Meade, Louis Tracy, Edgar Wallace, H. B. Marriott Watson, and Roma White.

Generic promiscuity, inventivenesss in new genres and new authorial voices, the exploration of new themes and the exploitation of new audiences—above all, the vigour and zest that these writers brought to the fiction of the period—have made the compiling of this Edwardian *Companion* particularly enjoyable. In the course of it, we have rediscovered obscure authors (not all of them, in the publisher's phrase, 'unjustly neglected', but all meriting a place here alongside their more celebrated peers whose unforgetable novels they help contextualize). We have read or reread some 800 novels (not all of which, in the end, won their authors a place in the book). Doing so has brought into a new sharpness of focus the themes and preoccupations of the era, the new prospects offered by changes in the literary market-place—not least the great increase in writing for and by women, who make up nearly half the author entries in the *Companion*—and the sheer diversity of its literary aims and achievements. We hope that users of this book will feel some of the same pleasure, and perhaps surprise, that we have experienced during the course of writing it.

Books Frequently Consulted

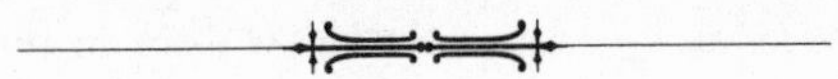

Anderson, Patricia J., and Rose, Jonathan, *British Literary Publishing Houses* 1820–1880 (Detroit, Gale Research, 1991).

Blain, Virginia, Clements, Patricia, and Grundy, Isobel (eds.), *The Feminist Companion to Literature in English: Women Writers from the Middle Ages to the Present* (London, Batsford, 1990).

Burke, Sir Bernard, and Burke, Ashworth P., *A Genealogical and Heraldic History of the Landed Gentry of Great Britain* (London, Harrison & Sons, 1906) (and later editions).

——*A Genealogical and Heraldic History of the Peerage and Baronetage* (London, Harrison & Sons, 1914) (and later editions).

Chevalier, Tracy (ed.), *Twentieth-Century Children's Writers* (Chicago and London, St James Press, 1989).

Cross, Nigel, *The Royal Literary Fund* 1790–1918: An Introduction to the Fund's History and Archives, with an Index of Applicants (London: World Microfilms, 1984).

Daims, Diva, and Grimes, Janet, with Robinson, Doris, *Towards a Feminist Tradition: An Annotated Bibliography of Novels in English by Women,* 1891–1920 (New York, Garland, 1982).

Grimes, Janet, and Daims, Diva, with Robinson, Doris, *Novels in English By Women* 1891–1920: A Preliminary Checklist (New York, Garland, 1981).

Hoehn, Matthew, OSB, *Catholic Authors: Contemporary Biographical Sketches* 1930–1947 (Newark, NJ, St Mary's Abbey, 1948).

——*Catholic Authors: Contemporary Biographical Sketches* (Newark, NJ: St Mary's Abbey, 1952).

Houghton, Walter E., Houghton, R. E. and Slingerland, J. H. (eds.), *The Wellesley Index to Victorian Periodicals* 1824–1900 (5 vols., Toronto, University of Toronto Press London, Routledge, 1966–89).

Plarr, Victor G. (ed.), *Men and Women of the Time: A Dictionary of Contemporaries* (London, George Routledge, 1900).

Ritchie, John et al., (eds.), *Australian Dictionary of Biography* (12 vols. and index, Melbourne, Melbourne University Press, 1966–91).

Robinson, Doris, *Women Novelists* 1891–1920: An Index to Biographical and Bibliographical Sources (New York, Garland, 1984).

Rose, Jonathan, and Anderson, Patricia J. *British Literary Publishing Houses* 1881–1965 (Detroit, Gale Research, 1991).

Sullivan, Alvin, ed., *British Literary Magazines*, 3 volumes, London: Greenwood Press 1984.

Short titles

We have referred in the text to the following books by short titles:

Ashley	Mike Ashley, *Who's Who in Horror and Fantasy Fiction* (London, Elm Tree Books, 1977).
Black	Helen C. Black, *Notable Women Authors of the Day* (Glasgow, D. Bryce, 1893).
Bleiler	Everett F. Bleiler, with the assistance of Richard J. Bleiler, *Science-Fiction: The Early Years* (Kent, Oh., Kent State University Press, 1990).
Brown	Stephen J. Brown, SJ, *Ireland in Fiction: A Guide to Irish Novels Tales Romances and Folklore*. Vol. i, (Dublin and London, 1919; repr. Shannon, Irish University Press, 1969); vol. ii, by Brown and Desmond J. Clarke (Cork, Royal Carbery Books, 1985).
DNB	*The Dictionary of National Biography* ed. Leslie Stephen and Sidney Lee (21 vol., Oxford, Oxford University Press, 1885–1909, and supplements to 1993).
Keating	Peter Keating, *The Haunted Study: A Social History of the English Novel*, London: Secker & Warburg, 1989.
Krishnamurti	G. Krishnamurti, *Women Writers of the 1890s* (London, Henry Sotheran, 1991).
Kunitz and Haycraft	Stanley J. Kunitz and Howard Haycraft (eds.), *Twentieth-Century Authors: A Biographical Dictionary of Modern Literature* (New York, H. W. Wilson, 1950); supplemented by Stanley J. Kunitz and Vineta Colby (eds.), *Twentieth Century Authors: First Supplement* (New York, H. W. Wilson, 1955).
Reilly	John M. Reilly (ed.), *Twentieth-Century Crime and Mystery Writers* (London and Basingstoke, Macmillan, 1980).
Sutherland	John Sutherland, *The Longman Companion to Victorian Fiction* (Harlow, Longman, 1988).
Wolff	*Nineteenth-Century Fiction: A Bibliographical Catalogue Based on the Collection Formed by Robert Lee Wolff* (5 vol., New York, Garland, 1981–6).
Who Was Who	*Who Was Who 1897–1990* (7 vols, and index, London, A. & C. Black, 1920–91).

Abbreviations

CH	Companion of Honour
DBE	Dame Commander of the Order of the British Empire
DD	*Divinitatis Doctor* (Doctor of Divinity)
DSC	Distinguished Service Cross
FRGS	Fellow of the Royal Geographical Society
HAC	Honourable Artillery Company
ILP	Independent Labour Party
JP	Justice of the Peace
KBE	Knight Commander of the Order of the British Empire
KC	King's Counsel
KCB	Knight Commander of the Order of the Bath
KCMG	Knight Commander of the Order of St Michael and St George
KCSI	Knight Commander of the Order of the Star of India
KG	Knight of the Order of the Garter
Kt.	Knight
LRCP	Licentiate of the Royal College of Physicians
MB	*Medicinae Baccalaureus* (Bachelor of Medicine)
MD	*Medicinae Doctor* (Doctor of Medicine)
MP	Member of Parliament
MRCS	Member of the Royal College of Surgeons
MVO	Member of the Royal Victorian Order
OGPU	Soviet counter-intelligence agency 1922–34
NCCL	National Council for Civil Liberties
OUDS	Oxford University Dramatic Society
PEN	international association of writers (Poets, Playwrights, Editors, Essayists, Novelists)
QC	Queen's Counsel
RAMC	Royal Army Medical Corps
RTS	Religious Tract Society
VAD	Voluntary Aid Detachment (for nursing)
WSPU	Women's Social and Political Union

Note To The Reader

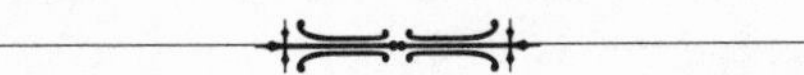

The *Companion* surveys fiction in English, published principally but not exclusively in Great Britain and Ireland between 1 January 1900 and 31 December 1914. American writing in the period would require another book even bigger than this, and is excluded here. In the Edwardian period the literature of Canada, the African colonies, British India, Australia, and New Zealand was widely read in Britain, and much of it was published in London. It is part of our picture. Although in describing the careers of individual writers we have referred to earlier and later work we have focused on their Edwardian output. We have not included any novels and stories, however important, which though written in the period were published later: hence the omission of an entry on E. M. Forster's *Maurice* (1971) written 1913–14, and the absence of Wyndham Lewis (1884–1957) and Olive Schreiner (1855–1920).

The *Companion* consists of four kinds of entry arranged in a continuous alphabetical sequence:

1. *Thematic entries* on the following genres and topics, which give background material and also point the reader towards relevant author and title entries, by listing important books and authors who specialized in particular genres. They describe our response to the exploration of Edwardian fiction, while offering signposts for others to follow:

Boer War fiction
crime fiction
Empire
exoticism
family sagas
fantasy fiction
feminist fiction
historical romance
horror stories
illustrations
invasion scare stories
literary agents
marriage problem fiction
political fiction
publishing
regional fiction
Ruritanian romance
science fiction
spy fiction
suburban fiction

2. *Author entries* on over 800 individual writers, mostly British, with some Canadians, South Africans, Australians, and New Zealanders, and a handful of Americans, such as Henry James, Mrs Hugh Fraser, and H. O. Sturgis, with marked English affiliations. We have deliberately excluded many minor children's writers, many colonials who made little impact in London, and many writers who published only occasionally.

These author entries are headed by the name the author published under most often in our period. Where authors changed the names under which they published, acquired titles, or adopted pseudonyms, they are listed under the form most often used in their publications of 1900–1914. An index on p. xxix lists the alternative forms, including the real names of pseudonymous authors, and the maiden/married names of women writers who married during the period. Writers better known by names used outside the period (F. M. Hueffer, Arthur Firbank) are cross-referenced under the more familiar forms. Listing writers under the names and pseudonyms they used in the period can be revealing: for example, initials conceal gender; military and other titles project an authorial persona. To save space, initials have, wherever possible, been expanded with square brackets to give the full name: L[eonard] S[idney] Woolf. Where the name on the title-page differs in a more complicated way from the author's original name, the publication name is followed by a colon and the author's real name. We have included wherever we could the dates of marriages, because they often indicate women's changes of name.

The entries consist of an outline biography and an attempt to place the Edwardian fiction in relation to the whole literary career. Wherever appropriate we have given cross-references which give the author's connections in the literary world or place his or her fiction in the context of similar work. Though these entries are roughly similar in format, they vary a good deal in length and in the kind of research they incorporate. In bringing to light many minor fiction-writers of the period, we have often had to do primary research to establish basic facts (dates of birth and death, real name, sex) and have deliberately expanded on interesting figures. In contrast, entries on major writers tend to be factual, on the grounds that readers can consult innumerable books devoted exclusively to them, and are more likely to consult the *Companion* for facts than analysis of such writers, as, say, Henry James or D. H. Lawrence.

3. *Title entries* on novels or volumes of short stories, which give the full title and subtitle, the date of first publication (in London unless stated otherwise), and the name of the publisher. They also summarize the plots and sometimes comment on other interesting features (such as literary quality, publishing history, or relationship to a particular genre). There are upwards of 250 such entries, representing a wider sample of fiction than is discussed in most studies of the period. They have been selected on various grounds: works of major authors, bestsellers, characteristic works of minor authors, works typical of the period in various ways. While working on the *Companion* we have been struck by the way certain motifs recur in the fiction of the period, for example: eugenics, impersonation, dishonour, spiritualism, divorce. Anyone wishing to chart the treatment of such topics in Edwardian fiction, both highbrow and low-brow, should find these entries (along with the briefer descriptions of books in our author entries) invaluable.

4. *Periodical entries* which briefly describe the character and history of some important magazines and journals of the period.

CHRONOLOGY

	British fiction	Other books and cultural events	Historical events
1900	*Lord Jim* *Love and Mr Lewisham* *The Half-Hearted* *The Cardinal's Snuff-Box* *The Visits of Elizabeth* *The Fourth Generation*	Sigmund Freud (1856–1939), *The Interpretation of Dreams* (first English translation 1913). Edward Elgar (1857–1934), *The Dream of Gerontius*. 22 June: Opening of the Wallace Collection, London. Max Planck (1858–1947) proposes quantum theory.	27 February: foundation of the Labour Representation Committee, forerunner of the Labour Party. 28 February: relief of Ladysmith; 17 May: Mafeking night in London. Boxer Rising in China.
1901	*Kim* *The First Men in the Moon* *Our Friend the Charlatan* *Anna Lombard* *The Black Mask* *The Hero* *The House with the Green Shutters* *The Inheritors*	Nobel prize for Literature won by R.-F.-A. Sully Prudhomme (1839–1907). Thomas Mann (1875–1955), *Buddenn-brooks* (first English translation 1924). George *Gissing, *By the Ionian Sea*. A. P. Chekhov (1860–1904), *The Three Sisters* (first English translation 1920). Foundation of Abbey Theatre, Dublin, to perform Irish plays.	22 January: death of Queen Victoria; Edward VII succeeds. 22 July: Taff Vale case makes trade unions liable for damage during strikes. 16 December: Guglielmo Marconi (1847–1937) sends the first trans-atlantic radio message
1902	*The Four Feathers* *The Hound of the Baskervilles* *Youth* *The Wings of the Dove* *Anna of the Five Towns* *Haunts of Ancient Peace*	Nobel prize for Literature won by Theodor Mommsen (1817–1903). William James (1842–1910), *The Varieties of Religious Experience*. Claude Debussy (1862–1918), *Pelléas et Mélisande*.	31 May: Peace of Vereeniging ends Boer War. 11 July: A. J. Balfour (1848–1930) becomes Conservative Prime Minister.
1903	*Lady Rose's Daughter* *The Ambassadors* *The Way of All Flesh* *The Riddle of the Sands* *Conrad in Quest of his Youth* *The Masterfolk*	Nobel prize for Literature won by Björnstjerne Björnson (1832–1910). G. E. Moore (1873–1958), *Principia Ethica*. Frederick Delius (1862–1934), *Sea Drift*. Thomas Traherne (1636–1674), *Poetical Works*, first published from rediscovered manuscript. Edwin S. Porter (1869–1941), *The Great Train Robbery*, film.	Orville Wright (1871–1948) makes the first aeroplane flight at Kitty Hawk, North Carolina, with the help of his brother Wilbur (1867–1912). Foundation of Women's Social and Political Union. Some Conservatives agitate for tariff reform.
1904	*The Garden of Allah* *Nostromo* *Hadrian the Seventh* *The Napoleon of Notting Hill* *The Golden Bowl* *The Prodigal Son*	Nobel prize for Literature won by Frédéric Mistral (1830–1914). Max Weber (1864–1920), *The Protestant Ethic and the Spirit of Capitalism* (first English translation 1930). Freud, *The Psychopathology of Everyday Life* (first English translation 1914). Paul Cézanne (1839–1906), *The Bathers*. J. M. Synge (1871–1909), *Riders to the Sea*.	February: Russo-Japanese War begins. 8 April: England and France sign an *entente cordiale*. 24 October: Dogger Bank incident leads to tension with Russia.

	British fiction	Other books and cultural events	Historical events
1905	*The Four Just Men* *Where Angels Fear to Tread* *Kipps* *The Return of Sherlock Holmes* *The Scarlet Pimpernel* *Ayesha* *The Hill*	Nobel Prize for Literature won by Henryk Sienkiewicz (1846–1916). Havelock Ellis (1859–1939), *Studies in the Psychology of Sex* (1897–1910). G. B. Shaw (1856–1950), *Major Barbara* performed. Fauvist movement in Paris. Albert Einstein (1879–1955) publishes his theory of relativity.	27 May: defeat of Russians by Japanese in the naval battle of Tsushima. 15 September: war ended by Treaty of Portsmouth. Mutiny on the Russian battleship *Potemkin*. December: Balfour resigns. Jewish pogroms in Russia.
1906	*The Man of Property* *Puck of Pook's Hill* *The Viper of Milan* *The Invasion of 1910*	Nobel prize for Literature won by Giosuè Carducci (1835–1907). Lord Acton (1834–1902), *Lectures in Modern History*. Launch of the Everyman Library. Upton Sinclair (1878–1968), *The Jungle*.	January: Liberal party elected with big majority: Sir Henry Campbell-Bannerman (1836–1908) becomes Prime Minister. February: Launch of HMS *Dreadnought*. Trade Disputes Act reverses effect of Taff Vale case.
1907	*The Secret Agent* *The Longest Journey* *Three Weeks* *The Convert* *The Grim Smile of the Five Towns*	Nobel prize for Literature won by Rudyard *Kipling. Edith Wharton (1862–1937), *Madame de Treymes*. Pablo Picasso (1881–1973), *Les Demoiselles d'Avignon*. James *Joyce, *Chamber Music*. Henry Adams (1838–1918), *The Education of Henry Adams*.	Deceased Wife's Sister's Marriage Act passed. M. K. Gandhi (1869–1948) begins civil disobedience in South Africa. Anglo-Russian *entente*.
1908	*The Wind in the Willows* *The Old Wives' Tale* *A Room with a View* *Maurice Guest* *The Blue Lagoon* *The Great Amulet* *The Individualist*	Nobel prize for Literature won by Rudolf Eucken (1846–1926). Foundation of Women Writers' Suffrage League. First International Congress of Psychoanalysis meets in Vienna. Riots in Dublin over the play, *The Playboy of the Western World* (1907) by J. M. Synge, regarded as insulting Irish women.	Imprisonment of Emmeline Pankhurst (1858–1928) for suffrage agitation. Young Turk rebellion in Turkey. H. H. Asquith (1852–1928) succeeds Campbell-Bannerman as Prime Minister. Boy Scouts movement founded. Model T Ford, the first mass-produced motor car, launched in US.
1909	*Tono Bungay* *The White Prophet* *The Glimpse* *Maudie*	Nobel prize for Literature won by Selma Lagerlöf (1858–1940). Thomas Hardy (1840–1928), *Time's Laughingstocks*. A. C. Bradley (1851–1935) *Oxford Lectures on Poetry*. George *Meredith, *Last Poems*. D. W. Griffith (1875–1948), *A Corner in Wheat*, film. Sergei Diaghilev (1872–1929) brings the *Ballets Russes* to Paris.	1 January: Old Age Pensions Act (1908) comes into force. Constitutional crisis in Britain over powers of the House of Lords. Force-feeding of suffragettes on hunger strike.
1910	*Howards End* *Clayhanger* *The Book of Wonder* *Rebel Women* *The Caravaners* *The Holy Mountain*	Nobel prize for Literature won by Paul von Heyse (1830–1914). First Post-Impressionist Exhibition in London. Bertrand Russell (1872–1970) and A. N. Whitehead (1861–1947), *Principia Mathematica*, 3 vols. (1910–13). Alexander Scriabin (1872–1915), *Prometheus*.	6 May: Edward VII dies and George V succeeds. 22 October: conviction of H. H. Crippen for uxoricide.

	British fiction	Other books and cultural events	Historical events
1911	*The White Peacock* *Under Western Eyes* *Hilda Lessways* *Zuleika Dobson* *The Secret Garden* *Suffragette Sally* *In a German Pension*	Nobel prize for Literature won by Maurice Maeterlinck (1862–1949). Eleventh edition of *The Encylopaedia Britannica.* The Camden Town Group formed. Ezra Pound (1885–1972), *Canzoni.* Erik Satie (1866–1925), *Parade.*	1 July: Agadir incident increases tension with Germany. 18 August: Parliament Act limiting powers of House of Lords passed. December: conquest of South Pole by Roald Amundsen (1872–1928). Sun Yat-Sen (1866–1925) ends Manchu empire in China.
1912	*The Chronicles of Clovis* *The Trespasser* *The Way of an Eagle* *A Derelict Empire* *The Devil's Wind*	Nobel prize for Literature won by Gerhart Hauptmann (1862–1946). Publication of first volume in the series *Georgian Poetry*, ed. Edward Marsh (1872–1953). Edith Wharton, *The Reef.* C. G. Jung (1875–1961), *The Psychology of the Unconscious* (first English translation 1916).	14 April: sinking of the SS *Titanic.* 5 July: National Health Insurance Act (1911) comes into force. Anti-suffragette 'Cat and Mouse Act' passed. Marconi corruption scandal smears Liberal politicians. 30 April: Irish Home Rule Bill passes House of Commons. Agitation in Ulster against Home Rule.
1913	*Sons and Lovers* *Chance* *Sinister Street* *Trent's Last Case* *The Third Miss Symons* *The Coryston Family* *Fortitude*	Nobel prize for Literature won by Rabindranath Tagore (1861–1941). Willa Cather (1876–1947), *O Pioneers!* Marcel Proust (1871–1922), *Du côté de chez Swann* (first English translation 1922). The Armory Show brings Impressionism and Post-Impressionism to New York. The *New Statesman* founded.	End of first Balkan War February: news reaches Europe of death of Captain Scott (1868–1912) in Antarctica. A suffragette dies throwing herself under the King's horse at the Derby. Panama Canal completed. The House of Lords reject the Irish Home Rule Bill.
1914	*The Ragged Trousered Philanthropists* *Dubliners* *The Prussian Officer* *The Black Peril*	G. B. Shaw, *Pygmalion* performed. Maxim Gorky (1868–1938), *Childhood* (first English translation 1915). Robert Frost (1874–1963), *North of Boston.* Charlie Chaplin (1889–1977), *Tillie's Punctured Romance*, film.	28 June: assassination of Archduke Franz Ferdinand (b. 1863) by Gavrilo Princip (1893–1918). 4 August: Britain declares war on Germany. Welsh Church Disestablishment Act.

Index To Pseudonyms And Changes Of Name

This index includes the real names of pseudonymous authors included in the *Companion*, changes of name (for example on marriage), some multiple names, and a few other cases where confusion seemed possible. There are cross-references in the main text where authors included published fiction under more than one name in the period.

Acland, Eleanor: see Eleanor *Cropper
Agresti, Olivia: see 'Isabel *Meredith'
Allhusen, Beatrice: see B. M. *Butt
Anethan, Eleanora Mary d' see Baroness Albert *d'Anethan
Angeli, Helen: see 'Isabel *Meredith'
Angell, B. M.: see 'H. Ripley *Cromarsh'
Arnim, Mary Annette von: see '*Elizabeth'
Arthur, Mary Lucy: see 'George David *Gilbert'
Ash, Georgina: see 'Raymond *Jacberns'
Askwith, Ellen: see Mrs Henry *Graham
Atkins, Francis Harry: see 'Fenton *Ash'
Back, Blanche: see 'Derek *Vane'
Baillie-Weaver, Gertrude: see 'G. *Colmore'
Baily, Helen Marion: see May *Edginton
Baker, Louisa Alice: see '*Alien'
Barber, Margaret Fairless: see 'Michael *Fairless'
Barclay, Marguerite: see 'Oliver *Sandys'
Barrett, Alfred Walter: see 'R. *Andom'
Barstow, Emma: see Baroness *Orczy
Barton, Robert Eustace: see 'Robert *Eustace'
Battersby, Henry: see 'Francis *Prevost'
Bax, Arnold: see 'Dermot *O'Byrne'
Bayly, Ada Ellen: see 'Edna *Lyall'
Beauchamp, Kathleen: see 'Katherine *Mansfield'
Bedford, Jessie: see 'Elizabeth *Godfrey'
Beith, John Hay: see 'Ian *Hay'
Bell, John Keble: see 'Keble *Howard'
Bickerstaffe-Drew, Francis: see 'John *Ayscough'
Binstead, Mary: see Mary *Openshaw
Blake, Mrs Muirson: see Jean *Delaire
Blanco White, Amber: see Amber *Reeves
Bland, Edith: see 'E. *Nesbit'
Blaze de Bury, F.: see 'F. *Dickberry'
Blount, Melesina Mary: see 'Mrs George *Norman'
Blunt, Sibell: see Countess of *Cromartie
Blunt-Mackenzie, Sibell: see Countess of *Cromartie
Booth, Eliza Margaret Jane: see '*Rita'
Bowden, Kathleen: see 'Katherine *Mansfield'
Bright, Mary Chavelita: see 'George *Egerton'
Brown, George Douglas: see 'George *Douglas'
Brown, Thomas Alexander: see 'Rolf *Boldrewood'
Brownlow, Maude Annesley: see Maude *Annesley
Buchan, Anna: see 'O. *Douglas'
Buchanan, Emily Handasyde: see '*Handasyde'
Burghard, Sidney Groves: see 'Ridgwell *Cullum'
Burnett, Ivy Compton: see Ivy *Compton-Burnett
Caffyn, Kathleen: see '*Iota'
Campbell, Margaret Gabrielle: see 'Marjorie *Bowen'
Castle Smith, Georgina: see '*Brenda'
Caulfeild, Kathleen Mary: see K. M. *Edge
Churton, Maud: see Maud Churton *Braby
Clairmonte, Mary Chavelita: see 'George *Egerton'
Clerihew, E.: see E. C. *Bentley
Clifford, Elizabeth: see Mrs Henry *de la Pasture
Comfort, Bessie: see Bessie Marchant
Conan Doyle, Arthur: see A. Conan *Doyle
Cory, Annie Sophie: see 'Victoria *Cross'
Cory, Vivian: see 'Victoria *Cross'
Cory, Winifred: see Winifred *Graham
Costanzo, Margaret Gabrielle: see 'Marjorie *Bowen'
Cotes, Mrs Everard: see Sara Jeannette *Duncan
Cox, Denis: see D. H. *Dennis
Coxon, Muriel: see Muriel *Hine
Craigie, Pearl: see 'John Oliver *Hobbes'
Creed, Mary Louisa: see Louise *Mack
Cross, Ada: see Ada *Cambridge
Daniell, Emily Hilda: see E. H. *Young
De Bathe, Emilie Charlotte: see Lillie Langtry
De Jan, Winifred: see Winifred *James
De La Cherois-Crommelin, May: see May *Crommelin
De La Ramée, Marie Louise: see '*Ouida'
De Sélincourt, Anne: see Anne Douglas *Sedgwick
Dill, Mildred: see 'Andrew *Merry'
Dillon, Dora Amy: see 'Patricia *Wentworth'
Dobbin, Gertrude: see Gertrude *Page
Douglass, Norman: see Norman *Douglas
Drower, Ethel May Stefana: see E. S. *Stevens
Dunkerley, Elsie Jeannette: see 'Elsie J. *Oxenham'
Dunkerley, William Arthur: see 'John *Oxenham'
Dunn, Gertrude: see 'G. *Colmore'
Ely, George Herbert: see 'Herbert *Strang'
Emery, Florence: see Florence *Farr
Everest, Hope: see 'Austin *Clare'
Everett, H. D.: see 'Theo *Douglas'
Felkin, Ellen Thorneycroft: see Ellen Thorneycroft *Fowler
Fifield, Salome: see Salome *Hocking
Fitzgerald, Ménie Muriel: see Ménie Muriel *Dowie
Ford, Thomas Murray: see 'John *Le Breton'
Foster, Annie Edith: see 'J. E. *Buckrose'
Frankau, Julia: see 'Frank *Danby'
Gates, Marie: see 'G. N. *Mortlake'

A

ABBOTT, J[ohn] H[enry] M[acartney] (1874–1953) married (1926) Katherina WALLACE. Born at Haydonton, New South Wales, into an influential family, he was educated at the King's School, Parramatta, and briefly at the University of Sydney before going to work on a family sheep farm and beginning to write; he contributed his first articles to the Australian *Bulletin* in 1897. In January 1900 he enlisted in the ranks in the 1st Australian Horse to fight in the *Boer War; he was commissioned in May and invalided home in October. From this experience he wrote *Tommy Cornstalk: Being Some Account of the Less Noticeable Features of the South African War from the Point of View of the Australian Ranks* (1902), a book which became the model for subsequent portrayals of the ordinary Australian fighting man. Success as a freelance journalist (his articles, stories and sketches 'of my own people in peace and at war' were collected in *Plain and Veldt*, 1903) took him to London, where he became a regular contributor to the *Daily Telegraph* and the *Spectator*, and published *An Outlander in England: Being Some Impressions of an Australian Abroad* (1905), the semi-autobiographical **Letters from Queer Street: Being Some of the Correspondence of the Late Mr John Mason* (1908), on the seamier side of London, and the travelogue, *The South Seas: Melanesia* (1908). In 1909 Abbott returned to Australia to write a sensational novel, *The Sign of the Serpent*, before concentrating on historical novels about pioneer life in New South Wales, such as *The Governor's Man* (1919), *Castle Van: A Romance of Bushranging on the Upper Hunter in the Olden Days* (1920), *Ensign Calder* (1922), and *Sydney Cove* (1923). Though prolific, Abbott was often in financial difficulty throughout his life, and ceased writing in 1948; he died at Rydalmere Mental Hospital.

ACKWORTH, John, *pseud.*: Frederick R. SMITH (1845–?1919). A Methodist minister, he chronicled the dreary existence of the workers in Lancashire's mills. *Clog Shop Chronicles* (1896) was well received and followed by a sequel, *Dixie Dent* (1899). Further tales on similar topics were collected and published in *The Mangle House* (1902). *The Minder: The Story of the Courtship, Call and Conflicts of John Ledger, Minder and Minister* describes the increasing popularity of Methodism and almost certainly draws on Smith's own experience. It is effectively characterized by its title and subtitle. John Ledger is minder and minister to Lancashire mill-hands, and the novel opens with the clatter of clogs on a flagged sidewalk. Its chapter titles reflect its essentially Victorian tone: 'A Race for a Pulpit', 'Sallie Turns the Tables on Her Lover', 'A Staggering Complication', 'A Bank Smash and a Proposal', etc. Other works include *Beckside Lights* (1897) and *The Scowcroft Critics* (1898)—both collections of short stories, *The Making of The Million* (1899), *The Coming of the Preachers: A Tale of the Rise of Methodism* (1901), *From Crooked Roots* (1903), *Old Wenyon's Will* (1904), and *The Partners* (1907). Smith also published religious works including *Life's Working Creed* (1909), an interpretation of St James's Epistles.

Actions and Reactions, Rudyard *Kipling, 1909, Macmillan. A collection of eight stories and poems more notable for their variety of theme and genre than for any common argument other, perhaps, than that of the chorus line of 'The Puzzler': 'But the English—ah the English—they are quite a race apart.' In 'An Habitation Enforced', a restless American couple find themselves slowly being embedded in the life of the English landed gentry. 'Garm—a Hostage' celebrates the relationship of a dog and a British soldier. 'The Mother Hive' describes the naïve reaction of young bees to the invasion of a wax-moth. 'With the Night Mail' ('A story of 2000 AD. Together with extracts from the magazines in which it appeared') imagines a future in which 'dirigibles' sail through the air like ships through the sea. 'A Deal in Cotton' brings together familiar Kipling characters (Strickland, Stalky and company) to hear of young Adam Strickland's first experiences as an Assistant-Commissioner in Africa. 'The Puzzler' is a comic moral fable about a colonial administrator, a Law Lord, an organ-grinder's monkey, and the 'Ties of Common Funk'. 'Little Foxes' is a witty account of how the creation of a full-scale hunt in Ethiopia becomes an essential part of colonial administration there. Most substantially, 'The House Surgeon' is the unsettling story of a house less haunted by a ghost than pervaded by depression, by 'that horror of great darkness which is spoken of in the bible'.

ADAIR, Cecil: see E. *Evereth-Green.

ADAMS, Arthur H[enry] (1872–1936) married (1898) Lilian PATON. Born at Lawrence, Otago, New Zealand, he graduated from Otago University and began to study law before abandoning it for journalism, serving as war correspondent during the Boxer Rebellion in China. He began by publishing verse. *Tussock Land: A Romance of New Zealand and the Commonwealth* (1904) appeared in T. Fisher Unwin's First Novel Library; its heroine is part-Maori, and foreshadows a race of New Zealanders drawing strength from both colonist and colonized. His later fiction is about Australia, where he lived from 1898 and worked on the Sydney *Bulletin* from 1906; it includes *The New Chum and Other Stories* (1909), *Galahad Jones* (1910), whose hero is a bank clerk who persuades his daughter's lover to pretend to love a dying girl, and *A Touch of Fantasy: A Romance for Those Who Are Lucky Enough to Wear Glasses* (1912). He wrote libretti for the Australian composer Alfred Hill (1870–1960), including one for the opera *Tapu* (1903). *A Man's Life* (1929) is fictionalized autobiography.

ADAMS, Mrs Leith: Bertha Jane GRUNDY (d. 1912) married, first (1869), Andrew Leith ADAMS (d. 1882) and, secondly (1883), Robert Stuart de Courcy LAFFAN (1853–1927). A solicitor's daughter, born in Cheshire, she worked on *All the Year Round* from 1880, and contributed serials to it. Her novels include *Nancy's Work: A Church Story* (1876), *Aunt Hepsy's Foundling* (1881), *Geoffrey Stirling* (1883), *Garrison Romance* (1892), and *Colour Sergeant No. 1 Company* (1894), which ran to six editions. She shared the interest of her second husband, a clergyman, headmaster, and social reformer, in widening the educational horizons of the working classes, and ardently campaigned to this end. Her concern for women's issues is evident in *Bonnie Kate: A Story From A Woman's Point-of-View* (1891), a novel of the New Woman school of the 1890s. Undeserved misfortune is a recurrent theme in *Cruel Calumny and Other Stories* (1901): in the title story, Dr Crosbie kills Alice Deacon's drunken, violent husband, and marries her, but their lives are ruined by malicious gossip. *The Dream of Her Life* (1902) includes six sentimental tales of childhood and romance. The title story tells of Edna Gray's love for Dennis Halkett, which is thwarted by his marriage and subsequent death. The theme of lost dreams sets the tone for the volume as a whole. The first part of *The Vicar of Dale End* (1906), 'The Descent into Hell', describes the Reverend Lawrence Amphlett's disintegration after his son takes to crime; the second part, 'Resurgam', leads up in true Adams style to his beautiful and redemptive death. Her later publications include *Poems* (1907), *Dreams Made Verity: Stories, Essays and Memories* (1910) and *Book of Short Plays and A Memory* (1912).

ADCOCK, A[rthur] St John (1864–1930) married (1887) Marion TAYLOR. Born in London, he trained as a lawyer, but from 1893 he devoted himself to literature full-time; before and after this he published short stories, poems, and essays in various periodicals. His first book, *An Unfinished Martyrdom and Other Stories* (1894), was followed in 1896 by *Beyond Atonement*. *East End Idylls* (1897) contains evocative accounts of life in the slum districts of London, showing the influence of Arthur *Morrison. *In the Image of God* (1898), a sequel, and *The Consecration of Hetty Fleet* (1898) also have vivid descriptions of the dingy, dark side of London life. His three publications in 1900—*The Luck of Private Foster, In the Wake of the War*, and *Songs of War*—share a common martial theme. *In the Wake of the War* is a collection of serio-comic stories, of a mildly patriotic cast, about low-life characters caught up in the *Boer conflict; perhaps the most interesting, because the most unusual, concerns a Boer barber in London who narrowly escapes being beaten up. Adcock became editor of the **Bookman* in 1908, published prolifically (more than thirty books by 1930), and lived comfortably in Hampstead, London. *Love in London* (1906), *A Man with a Past* (1911), and *Seeing it Through* (1915) are typical works. Other publications are *Famous Houses and Literary Shrines of London* (1912) and *Modern Grub Street and Other Essays* (1913); his *Collected Poems* were published in 1929. Some of his most accomplished works were his long poems where a satirical edge is evident. Yet the *Times* obituary considers him 'too kindly and humorous, and too essentially humble to be a true satirist'. Adcock died at home in Richmond, Surrey; his *London Memories* was published posthumously in 1931.

Adventures of Brigadier Gerard, The, A. Conan *Doyle, 1903, John Murray. Doyle's second collection of stories from the **Strand Magazine* about the French soldier with, in Napoleon's words, 'the thickest head and stoutest heart' in his army. Inspired by French accounts of the Napoleonic wars, and in particular by *The Memoirs of Baron de Marbot* (published in English in 1892), and designed to ease the discontent left among Doyle's readers by the death of Sherlock Holmes, this volume continues where the first, *Exploits of Brigadier Gerard* (1896), left off. In 'How the Brigadier Lost His Ear', Gerard takes the place of a female prisoner who is to be punished (by Venetian terrorists) for fraternization; in 'How the Brigadier Slew the Fox', Gerard infiltrates an English foxhunt (in Spain), gets to the fox first, and slices it in two with his sword. In 'How the Brigadier Triumphed in Britain', Gerard, a prisoner, gets involved in a duel and is adjudged a gentleman; in 'How the Brigadier Bore Himself at Waterloo', Gerard finds and foils a plot to kill Napoleon; in 'The Last Adventure of the Brigadier', Gerard plots to rescue Napoleon from St Helena but gets there just as he dies. As Owen Dudley Edwards remarks, the 'laughable and loveable' Gerard, who reveals his vanity and courage, his stupidity and integrity, in his quite unselfconscious conceit, remains a highly enjoyable hero, one who combines the glamour of the cavalryman with the fatalism of the footsoldier, one whose virtues (as a Frenchman fighting against the British) were taken by Doyle to be those of all soldiers and not just a matter of national pride.

AGNEW, Georgette: Alexandra Georgette CHRISTIAN (d. 1957) married (1889) Philip Leslie AGNEW (1863–1938). Brought up in Egypt, she was the author of three lightweight romances in the period, and one earlier. The heroes of *The Countess* (1905) and *The Bread upon the Waters* (1911) are country squires who fall in love, respectively, with a lady tenant and with an actress. In the more adventurous *The Night That Brings out Stars* (1908), the orphaned daughter of the British consul in Rome returns to London, is briefly married to an Irish journalist, and thereafter struggles to make a living for herself and her young niece. Agnew's style is characterized by Dickensian mannerisms. She also published verse, and, as 'Nevin Halys', a poem and some plays in the 1930s. Her husband was chairman of Bradbury, Agnew & Co., the printers and owners of *Punch*.

AGNUS, Orme, *pseud.*: John C. HIGGINBOTHAM (d. 1919). Although born in Cheshire, Higginbotham lived throughout his adult life at Wareham in Dorset, where he was a schoolteacher. He specialized in the depictions of rural life that were so popular at the turn of the century. *Love in Our Village* (1900) describes the idyllic side of village life seen through the eyes of a convalescent from London. It owes much to the works of Thomas Hardy (1840–1928), but a more ebullient tone predominates. The narrator of *Jan Oxber* (1900), a 'plain writing-body' who has retired for health reasons to Barleigh, an 'inland village of Wessex', tells five stories about local life. The title story concerns Jan Oxber, a wheelwright's son, expert mechanic, and champion athlete who is wrongly imprisoned for poaching and on his return becomes a local hero when he takes on and defeats the womanizing squire, Deverill. The Barleigh peasants have been taught for the first time that they have 'rights as men that only dastards dare not claim'. Other stories concern drunkenness, shrewishness, and religious dissent. Oxber's female counterpart in Barleigh legend is the heroine of *Sarah Tuldon* (1903) and *Sarah Tuldon's Lovers* (1909). The *Daily News* said that the former 'resembles Mr Thomas Hardy's work in presenting the dialect and rustic characters of a Wessex village'. Agnus's fiction was not confined exclusively to rural subjects. In *Minvale: The Story of a Strike* (1906), the Revd Donnimore's arrival in Minvale, a manufacturing town, coincides with the unionization of the workers under the influence of a Dissenting minister, Matthew Lemmer. Donnimore's increasing sympathy for the strikers leads him into conflict with the town's leading entrepreneur, Mr Slayter, whose daughter he loves. The moral regeneration of marriage is set, in a manner reminiscent of the 'Condition of England' novels of the 1840s, against the pointless violence unleashed by class conflict. *The Prime Minister* (1908) also treats a *political subject, but in a more sensational manner. There is a crisis in the House of Commons, the Prime Minister is sent for to save the situation, but refuses to rise, knowing that to open his mouth would be to convict himself of murder: in the Ladies' Gallery sits the wife he had deserted as a young man, whose son-in-law, the husband of his own daughter, he murdered to prevent exposure. She does not know him as Prime Minister, but would recognize his voice. Agnus makes it clear that he is no ordinary scoundrel, but motivated by patriotism and a belief in himself as a man of destiny.

ALBANESI, E. Maria: Effie Adelaide Maria HENDERSON (1859–1936) married Carlo ALBANESI (d. 1926). Born in Australia, she was the author of more than 100 penny and sixpenny romances under the pseudonym 'Effie Adelaide Rowlands' and of more than sixty under her own name. One of her earliest publications was the anonymous *Margery Daw* (1886); she went on turning out fiction until her death. Her heroines tend to be variations on the roguish, indomitable type embodied by Becky Sharp (in *Vanity Fair*, 1848, by W. M. Thackeray, 1811–63). *Capricious Caroline* (1904) is a pretty, charming, selfish widow who lives and dresses well, flirts, 'keeps things up', and in the end disposes both of the benefactor who has supported her and of the rake who would ruin her. *The Brown Eyes of Mary* (1905) are trained on her decaying ancestral home, now occupied by newcomers. *The Invincible Amelia* (1909) comes to a thoroughly good end. Albanesi herself, it seems, did not. In applying to the Royal Literary Fund in 1912 and 1914 she cited the iniquity of her publishers, her ill health, and that of one of her two daughters, as well as the fact that her husband, a music teacher and later a professor at the Royal Academy of Music, suffered during the war from the prejudice against foreigners. She herself suffered from neuralgia and there were family strains because, as her doctor wrote to the Fund, 'Signor Albanesi is one of the most highly nervous men I have met'. An obituary in the *Times* (17 Oct 1936) observed that 'the sentimental interest which characterized her work was the reflection of her own warm-hearted and affectionate nature'. A great sadness was the death of her daughter, a young actress who starred in *East of Suez* by Somerset *Maugham in 1922 and died in the following year: her mother published a memoir, *Meggie Albanesi* (1928).

Albany Review, The, (1903–1908) (also known as the *Independent Review*) appeared monthly between 1903 and 1907. Founded by G. M. Trevelyan (1876–1962) and other Cambridge Apostles, it reflected Cambridge intellectual humanism, particularly in its essays and reviews. Contributors included E. M. *Forster, Gilbert Murray (1866–1957), Havelock Ellis (1859–1939), and Ramsay MacDonald (1866–1937), as well as *Wells and *Chesterton. Lytton Strachey (1880–1932) was a regular contributor—his first published essay, 'Two Frenchmen', appeared in the first issue.

ALCOCK, Deborah (1835–1913). Daughter of a Church of Ireland clergyman, Archdeacon of Waterford, she lost her mother and only sister when she was a baby, and became entranced by history at an early age. Her evangelical father, to whom she was devoted, disapproved of fiction, and made her turn her first story into a biography of Gustavus Adolphus. Later, encouraged by Elizabeth Rundle-Charles (1828–96), she began a successful series of anonymous Protestant *historical novels for children. Her great success was the *The Spanish Brothers: A Tale of the Sixteenth Century* (1871); many of her subsequent works appeared as 'by the Author of *The Spanish Brothers*'; after 1890 she put her name to them. Though not extraordinarily prolific, she continued to publish into the twentieth century; her last works include *Not for Crown or Sceptre* (1902), *Under Calvin's Spell* (1902), and *Robert Musgrave's Adventure: A Story of Old Geneva* (1909). Her life was uneventful; she had poor health, spent her life in a round of charities, and moved from Ireland to England in 1891, living at Bournemouth. There is a biography (1914) by Elisabeth B. Bayly.

ALDINGTON, Mrs A. E.: Jessie May GODFREY married Albert Edward ALDINGTON (d. 1921). The wife of a Dover solicitor, she benefited from the vogue for *regional fiction, confining herself more or less exclusively to Kentish village life. Works in the period include *Love Letters That Caused a Divorce* (1905), *'Meg of the Salt-Pans'* (1909), *The King Called Love* (1913), *A Man of Kent* (1913), and *Love Letters to a Soldier* (1915). She also published two volumes of verse (1907, 1917) and contributed to *Cassell's*. According to her son,

Richard Aldington (1892–1962), and his biographers, she was socially ambitious, domineering, affected, alcoholic, and vulgar; he portrayed her as Mrs Winterbourne in *Death of a Hero* (1929), and blamed her for the unhappiness of his parents' marriage and their money troubles.

ALIEN, *pseud.*: Louisa Alice DAWSON (1858–1926) married (*c.*1894) —— BAKER. During her youth in New Zealand, Louisa Dawson wrote for the *Otago Witness* under the pseudonym 'Alice'. She emigrated to England in 1894, married, and adopted the pseudonym 'Alien'. She complained to a New Zealand magazine in 1903 that in Britain 'a story with an English setting is of three times the value in London, commercially, of one with a colonial background'. Her novels are melodramatic *marriage problem novels, studies of romantic passion generally set against a New World (i.e. New Zealand) backdrop, and she was greatly encouraged by the example of Olive Schreiner (1855–1920). *The Untold Half* (1899) charts the convoluted love-lives of a group of colonists. *The Devil's Half Acre* (1900) explores the consequences of extreme emotion in its study of religious fanaticism and homicide in the goldfields of New Zealand. *Another Woman's Territory* (1901) dwells again upon the moving force of great passions: a talented but unfulfilled novelist, Howard Grey, travels the New Zealand outback in search of inspiration, and finds a devoted wife, Caroline; when he weakly allows himself to become attracted to another woman, Geraldine Ward, the passions aroused between woman and woman seem more powerful than those aroused between man and woman. In the novel's crucial encounter, Caroline tells Geraldine that a woman, in 'remembering her own womanhood' (that is, in renouncing an unworthy desire), 'grants another woman her rights'. Baker described her fiction as denouncing 'any sort of marriage that does not give a trinity of union, body, soul and mind'. Her other works include *Looking Glass Hours* (1899), which was written with '*Rita', *Not in Fellowship* (1902), *His Neighbour's Landmark* (1907), *A Double Blindness* (1910), and *A Maid of Mettle* (1913).

ALLEN, F. M: see Edmund *Downey.

Amateur Gentleman, The: A Romance, Jeffery *Farnol, 1913, Sampson Low. Farnol's second novel reworks the plot of his first, *The *Broad Highway*, with additional scenes of London high and low life. Barnabas Barty, son of a champion boxer turned innkeeper and a runaway lady, is left the fortune his uncle has made in Jamaica and sets off to London to become a gentleman. He has barely started his journey when he rescues a maiden in distress, Lady Cleone Meredith, from the evil Sir Maurice Carnaby. Barnabas falls in love and is thereafter embroiled in the world of the dissolute Regency aristocracy, a world of fashion, debts, boxing, duels, racing, gambling, and the Bow Street Runners. Barnabas sees off his enemies, sees through London society, and leaves the city to enjoy his new status as a married landed gentleman. This time out the plot is a little creaky and the characters even more sentimentalized, but the popular success of the Farnol formula was now assured.

Ambassadors, The, Henry *James, 1903, Methuen. Lambert Strether, the middle-aged editor of a heavyweight New England journal, is sent to Paris by his patron and possibly future wife, Mrs Newsome, to bring her son, Chad, home to Woollett, Massachusetts, and to the family business. A romantic entanglement is thought to have Chad kept in Europe. *En route* through England, Strether meets Maria Gostrey, an American expatriate living in Paris, who serves initially as an enticing taste of Europeanized sophistication, and subsequently as an ally and confidante. Arriving in Paris, Strether is enchanted by the change in Chad, now no longer an uncultured 'pagan', and by his friends. The latter include a dilettante artist, Little Bilham, and the beautiful Madame de Vionnet, whose daughter, Jeanne, Chad is vaguely supposed to be in love with. Chad's friends do little to enlighten Strether about the real nature of his relationship with Madame de Vionnet, and Strether, assuming no more than a benevolent moral influence, blesses it by suspending his mission and starting to enjoy life. In a scene sometimes said to epitomize the novel, he exhorts Little Bilham to 'Live all you can'. So convinced is he by his own doctrine that Mrs Newsome despatches a second embassy, in the shape of her formidable daughter, Sarah Pocock, and her vulgar husband, Jim. Sarah is impressed neither by Paris nor by Madame de Vionnet's influence, and orders Chad and Strether home. Strether urges Chad to stay, fully recognizing, as he does so, the consequences for himself. When, quite by chance, Strether encounters Chad and Madame de Vionnet on the river outside Paris, it becomes apparent to him that they are lovers. Knowing that he has been deceived, he none the less keeps faith with his perception of the beauty of the relationship, and advises Chad not to betray it. Chad, however, has begun to revert to paganism. Deciding that his education in life is now over, he prepares to return to Woollett, having arranged a marriage for Jeanne. Strether will follow him, even though Woollett now holds little for him, and Maria Gostrey beckons. If the novel's ostensible theme is an innocent American's efforts to decipher European customs and codes—'A study of the New England conscience', as one reviewer put it, 'subjected to the hot-house atmosphere of the Parisian *Vie de Bohème*'—the mystery for the reader is Strether, and his resolve not to have got anything out of the affair for himself.

AMBER, Miles: See Ellen *Cobden.

ANDOM, R., *pseud.*: Alfred Walter BARRETT. Born in London, he was a journalist, assistant editor of the *Literary World*, and from 1900 editor of *Scraps*, a comic penny weekly. Barrett's whimsical 'Troddles' stories were well received in the 1890s and 1900s. Characteristic is *Lighter Days with Troddles* (1907), in which the narrator, Bob, and his friends Murray, Wilks, and Troddles purchase a barge: there are many puns on the term 'lighter' and chapters with headings like 'In Which Troddles Gets in Difficulties, and We Get into the Mud'. *The Strange Adventure of Roger Wilkins* (1895) is a *Wellsian story about the transfer of personality. In *The Identity Exchange: A Story of Some Odd Transformations* (1902), the narrator comes across a personality swap-shop: he becomes, among other things, a judge, a pirate, and a professor, in each case leaving the original possessor of the identity exchanged in a state of considerable confusion. *Neighbours of Mine* (1912) is an affectionate, occasionally satirical tale of *suburban life in the tradition of *The Diary of a Nobody* (1892). 'Now and again the author conveys a moral, discreetly,' the blurb soothes, 'but generally he is content to be extravagantly amusing in depicting adventures which are sufficiently out of the ordinary to be termed "singular".'

Anglo-Saxon Review, The: *A Quarterly Miscellany* was published in ten issues between June 1899 and September 1901. Founded by the recently widowed, American-born society figure Lady Randolph Spencer Churchill (1854–1921), mother of Winston *Churchill, and published by John Lane, it was designed to be the most opulent (200 pages per issue) and, at a guinea a time, the most expensive magazine of its day. The idea was to make money out of Lady Randolph's rich friends and acquaintances in Britain and the USA. The *Review* was genuinely miscellaneous, combining historical documents, memoirs, and military anecdotes, with articles on music, art, and 'collectibles' (by Shaw and *Beerbohm among others), and each issue included poetry, drama, a short story, and literary criticism. Literary contributors included Henry *James, Stephen Crane (1871–1900), George *Gissing, and Algernon Swinburne (1837–1909), and the *Review* published the original call for a National Theatre by William Archer (1856–1924). The *Review* took on a particularly imperialist tone in the context of the *Boer War and eventually ceased publication when, as John Lane had warned, it became clear that there was not a large enough rich readership to support such an expensive venture.

Anna of the Five Towns: *A Novel*, Arnold *Bennett, 1902, Chatto & Windus. Bennett's second novel, the first set in the Five Towns, was conceived in February 1896, begun in September 1896, and finished in May 1901. 'I am absorbed in the Potteries just now,' he wrote in February 1900, 'a great place, sir, and full of plots. My father's reminiscences have livened me up considerable.' Bennett's father had suffered a breakdown in November 1899, and was to die in January 1902; the focus of the novel is paternal authority. Ephraim Tellwright exercises a tyrannical miserliness which oppresses and crushes his two daughters, 12-year-old Agnes and 21-year-old Anna. Anna inherits money from her mother, but is prevented by her father from putting it to constructive use. She is courted succesfully by Henry Mynors, a smoother version of her father, but implicated increasingly in the plight of her feckless tenants, Titus and Willie Price. Anna rebels by burning a bill of exchange the Prices have forged, but she cannot save them from bankruptcy. Titus's disgrace and suicide brings her closer to Willie, but the scandal forces him to emigrate. After declaring her love for Willie, Anna marries prosperous, respectable, bland Henry Mynors.

Anna Lombard, 'Victoria *Cross', 1901, John Long. A bestselling story of passion and self-denial told by Gerald Ethridge, Assistant Commissioner at Kalatu in the British Raj. Rather like Carruthers, in Erskine *Childers's *The *Riddle of the Sands* (1903), Ethridge has a brilliant career but an empty life. At a dance, he meets Anna Lombard, a general's daughter, serious-minded, educated in England, and beautiful in an English way. It is love at first sight. Before he can propose, Gerald receives orders to transfer to Lihudi, a desolate outpost in Burma. Visiting the Lombards to say goodbye to Anna, he finds her asleep in the garden wearing a semi-transparent cambric gown which exposes her neck but, 'of its own will, apparently', closes over the 'softly rising and falling bosom': 'I stood entranced, letting my eye travel reverently over the sleeping form.' Feeling that he cannot ask Anna to share his life in Lihudi, Gerald decides not to wake her, and instead leaves a passionate letter and a keepsake. Lihudi is hell on earth: hot, swampy, malarial. Women throw themselves at him (including a snake girl who sports a wreath of pythons). All around him, white men go mad in *Kiplingesque fashion or native in *Conradian fashion. After a year, he is recalled to Kalatu. Anna greets his return rapturously, and they become engaged. But she does not want to marry immediately. Passing beneath her bedroom window one afternoon, Gerald hears her declaring passionate love to another man *in Hindustani*. During his absence, she has been sexually enthralled by a humble but ravishingly beautiful Pathan, Gaida Khan and has secretly married him. Unable to accept her proposal of a *ménage à trois* ('Englishmen do not share their wives'), Gerald enters the wilderness of self-denial. When Gaida Khan contracts cholera, Gerald nurses him faithfully. When he dies, Gerald marries Anna, and will not sleep with her as long as she is carrying another man's child. The balance of self-denial shifts, however, when Anna, in a fit of bitter remorse, suffocates the child. After a year of atonement, they at last meet on an equal footing, and live happily ever after. Cross added an indignant preface to later editions. 'I endeavoured to draw in Gerald Ethridge a character whose actions should be in accordance with the principles laid down by Christ... It is a sad commentary on our religion of today that a presumably Christian journal, the *Daily Chronicle*, should hold this Christ-like conduct up to ridicule and contempt, stigmatise it as "horrid absurdity", and declare that for such qualities a man ought to be turned out of the service.'

ANNESLEY, Maude married —— BROWNLOW. She contributed to the *Fortnightly Review*, the *Westminster Gazette* and to daily papers, and published ten volumes of fiction 1908–23. Her main line was in restless daughters and wives. Characteristic are *This Day's Madness* (1909), the heroine of which becomes involved with a spineless musician and a great experimental scientist after her dull husband dies in an accident; *Wind Along the Waste* (1910), about the double life led by a beautiful red-haired artist in Paris; and *All Awry* (1911), about a baronet's daughter who wishes she was a man, goes to sea as an assistant purser, is shipwrecked, and falls in love with her companion in adversity. In *The Sphinx in the Labyrinth* (1913), the double life is led by a man who loves both his invalid wife and the young woman who comes to stay with them: the interest lies in the wife's gradual acceptance of the situation. Annesley's fiction tends to the lurid, and she also developed a sideline in tales of the paranormal. In one, a mysterious stranger leads the clairvoyant heroine towards *The Door of Darkness* (1908); in another, *Shadow Shapes* (1911), a terminally ill man tries to hypnotize his wife into dying when he does (fortunately there is a doctor at hand to counter-hypnotize her into staying alive). She also published *The Wine of Life* (1903) and *Nights and Days* (1912), a collection of short stories. *My Parisian Year* (1912) is a chatty account of French social habits, in a series to which I. A. R. *Wylie contributed *My German Year* and Richard *Bagot *My Italian Year*; it indicates that Annesley lived in Paris.

Ann Veronica: *A Modern Love Story*, H. G. *Wells, 1909, T. Fisher Unwin. Ann Veronica Stanley is a vibrant, intellectually adventurous young woman stifled by her parents' middle-class *suburban life. She refuses to submit to her father's views of women or to marry his idea of an appropriate suitor, and runs away, taking a room in London. There she joins the Fabian Society, and takes part in the suffrage campaign, enduring arrest and imprisonment for civil disobedience. She has, meanwhile, enrolled as a biology student at the Central Imperial College, which Wells seems to think preferable to politics. 'Contrasted with the confused movements and presences of a Fabian meeting, or the inexplicable enthusiasm behind the suffrage demand, with the speeches that were partly egotistical displays, partly artful manoeuvres, and partly incoherent cries for unsoundly formulated ends, compared with the comings and goings of audiences and supporters that were like the eddy-driven drift of paper in the street, this long, quiet, methodical chamber shone like a star seen through clouds.' She has two suitors: Manning, a florid poetaster wrapped in the Age of Chivalry, who idealizes her; and Ramage, a middle-aged womanizer with an invalid wife, who lends her money and tries rather clumsily to seduce her. But she falls in love with her biology teacher, Capes, and tells him that she means to have him. They take a blissfully illicit holiday together in Switzerland. The final chapter is set four years after their return: Mr and Mrs Capes, as they now are, entertain a group of guests which includes Ann Veronica's father and aunt. The heroine's intellectual and sexual forwardness aroused considerable controversy. The **Spectator* (20 November 1909) published a vitriolic denunciation entitled 'A Poisonous Book', while in 1910 one Canon Lambert told the Hull Public Libraries Committee that he 'would as soon send a daughter of his to a house infected with diphtheria or typhoid' as put the novel in her hands (it was promptly removed from local library shelves). But the reviewer for the **Nation* pointed out that Wells had in fact devoted most of his 'extraordinary ironic power' to 'savage, destructive criticism' not of ancient customs but of 'modern emancipators'. Wells's affair with Amber *Reeves was one source for the plot.

ANSTEY, F., *pseud.*: Thomas Anstey GUTHRIE (1856–1934) was born in London, son of a successful military tailor, and was educated at King's College School, London, and Trinity Hall, Cambridge. He was called to the Bar in 1880 but never practised, taking to authorship and quickly gaining success with his comic novel of a father and son changing places to the discomfiture of the former: *Vice Versa, or, A Lesson to Fathers* (1882). In *The Brass Bottle* (1900), Horace Ventimore, talented but unsuccessful architect, receives a commission from Professor Anthony Futvoye, an eminent archaeologist and the father of the woman he is in love with, to purchase at auction an antique brass bottle containing a genie, Fakrash-el-Aamash, who once dwelt in the Palace of the Mountain of the Clouds above the City of Babel in the Garden of Irem. *Fantastic adventures ensue before Ventimore, now well on his way to fame and fortune, disposes of the bottle by stuffing it into a kitbag, weighting it with coals and dropping it into the Thames. Anstey made £8,000 from the novel, which was both dramatized and filmed, and probably influenced E. *Nesbit in her genie books. *In Brief Authority* (1915) was conceived and partly written before war broke out, and its facetiousness modulates somewhat unconvincingly at the end into a sombre stoicism. From 1886 Guthrie wrote a column, 'Voces Populi', for *Punch*; he remained on the staff until 1930. Besides comic sketches and essays, he also wrote other fantasy stories, and had a second great popular success with a play, *The Man from Blankley's* (1901) (adapted from a sketch published in 1893) which satirized nineteenth-century snobbery. Guthrie continued writing until his death, but, as he makes clear in his posthumous autobiography, *A Long Retrospect* (1936), he felt most comfortable satirizing the middle-class mores of the Victorian age. His brother, Dr Leonard Guthrie (1858–1918), published *Hospital Sketches*.

ANTROBUS, C. L: Clara Louisa ROGERS (1846–1919) married (1871) Arthur John ANTROBUS (d. 1872). Born in Grantham, the daughter of a surgeon, she was brought up in Bowdon, Cheshire, which she described in *Quality Corner: A Study of Remorse* (1901) under the name 'Ringway'. She began writing as a widow when she left the north for London: her first novel was *Wildersmoor* (1895). She told an interviewer from the **Bookman* (July 1901) that 'when a book or short tale is finished [she cut it]... remorselessly—generally to half its original length'. She went in for romances of (mostly northern) country life. Characteristic are *The Wine of Finvarra and Other Stories* (1902) and *The Stone Ezel* (1910), about an ancient monument on a Lancashire moor which has witnessed a series of family tragedies and the rhapsodies of a young artist. Her obituary in the *Times* (12 Feb. 1919) observes that she 'excelled in presenting sad and wistful aspects of life'.

Ape's-Face, Marion *Fox, 1914, John Lane. Elegant *horror story set on the Wiltshire downs, where the Unknown lurks. Armstrong, a 40-something historian and biographer, discovers that the papers of John Morton, an Elizabethan swordsman and philosopher, are in the possession of his descendant, Mr John Delane-Morton, who lives with his sister Ellen, his sons Godfrey and Arthur, and his daughter Josephine, in an old house at the foot of the downs. Visiting this odd ménage in order to study the papers, Armstrong becomes increasingly fascinated by Josephine, nicknamed 'Ape's-Face' on account of her looks. She appears to have access to a mysterious force which is to be felt on the downs and occasionally around the house. His researches, and the visions granted to Josephine, suggest that the force is a 'blood toll' extorted by the ancient conquered race which once occupied the area. Throughout history, the curse has set brother against brother, brother against sister, in the Morton family. In this instance Godfrey and Arthur, rivals for the favours of a flirtatious young woman artist who is staying at a farm up on the downs, are only prevented from killing each other by Josephine's last-minute intervention. Meanwhile the wheelchair-bound Ellen has been revealed as a hyperactive witch. After attempting to murder her brother in his bed, she dies, and the curse is lifted. Although the situations involving Ellen are somewhat theatrical, the story is raised above the ordinary by its integration of a poetics of landscape into the tale of horror.

APPLETON, G[eorge] W[ebb] (1845–1909) married Georgiana SCHUYLER. An American by birth, Appleton published twenty-two novels between 1878 and 1910. His favourite topic was the involvement of sturdy professional men in arcane upper-class intrigue. In *The Lady in Sables* (1904), a beautiful unknown collapses outside the front door of the house in Richmond where Dr Williams lives with his sister; and we soon discover that the doctor's father belongs to an anarchist secret society. In *The Duchess of Pontifex Square* (1907) a doctor is summoned to attend an ageing Italian duchess who has been driven into seclusion by her scheming relatives; he finds a second and much younger duchess to marry.

Arbiter, The: *A Novel*, Mrs Hugh *Bell, 1901, Edward Arnold. In this thoughtful novel about the interlocking of personal and political lives, Lady Gore, reduced to the status of an incurable invalid by rheumatic fever, creates an active life for herself by developing a strenuous sympathetic interest in the activities of her husband, Sir William, a Liberal MP, and her daughter, Rachel. This interest is the making of Sir William: 'It was she who infused into his life every possibility beyond the obvious.' When Lady Gore dies, and Rachel marries Francis Rendel, private secretary to his Tory opponent, Lord Stamfordham, the Foreign Minister, Sir William is reduced to near-helplessness. He becomes involved in a mining company, The Equator, Ltd, whose survival depends on the completion of a trans-African railway. He weakly allows an ambitious journalist, Robert Pateley, to inspect and publish a secret map depicting the route of the railway. Rendel, to whom the map has been entrusted, takes the blame. Sir William dies, and Rachel suffers a stroke. The denouement occurs at a German spa where the main protagonists have gathered. Pateley reveals to Rachel that it was her father, not her husband, who betrayed the secret; she in turn tells Lord Stamfordham, who promptly reinstates Rendel.

ARNOLD, Edwin Lester [Linden] (1857–1935) married, first, Constance BOYCE, and, secondly (1919), Jessie BRIGHTON. Son of the poet and Oriental specialist Sir Edwin Arnold (1832–1904), he was educated at home and at Cheltenham College. After attempts at cattle-farming in Scotland and arable farming in Travancore, a previously uncharted region of India, Arnold returned to England to write. His best-remembered work *The Wonderful Adventures of Phra the Phoenician* (1890), a *fantasy concerning reincarnation and time-travel, sold well and ran to several editions (including one in 1910). *The Constable of St Nicholas* (1894) is a spirited *historical tale about the Knights of Rhodes. The time-travel device was again employed in *Lepidus the Centurion: A Roman of Today* (1901) but with less success: Louis Allanby encounters Lepidus, a Roman who resembles him closely, and ends by acquiring some of his superior characteristics. *Lieut. Gulliver Jones* (1905) is a Martian adventure. Arnold travelled and cruised extensively with his father, and these experiences gave rise to such works as *A Summer Holiday in Scandinavia* (1877) and *On the Indian Hills* (1881).

ARNOLD, Mrs J. O.: Adelaide Victoria ENGLAND married (1883) John Oliver ARNOLD (1858–

1930). The daughter of a mining engineer, she published ten novels between 1911 and 1928, mostly of a moorland-and-ancient-superstitions sort. *Fire i' the Flint* (1911) is the Hardyesque tale of a morris-dancing country girl who captivates two young men on a walking tour, and must choose between them when she becomes a London sensation. *Megan of the Dark Isle* (1914) is set on Anglesey: the heroine, a child of nature, marries an adventurer who is ensnared by the local witch-temptress. Reviewers thought it unnecessarily gruesome. Her husband was professor of metallurgy at Sheffield University.

ASH, Fenton, *pseud.*: Francis Harry ATKINS (1840–1927). Born in Oxford, he trained as an engineer, and published boys' books in periodicals and in volume form, including *The Radium Seekers, or, The Wonderful Black Nugget* (1905), in which two boys discover a new kind of radium which enables them to fly to South America, where they discover a lost race. The lost-race motif also appears in *By Airship to Ophir* (1911) and *The Black Opal* (1915). Martians figure in both *A Son of the Stars* (*c.*1907) and *A Trip to Mars* (1909). Atkins also wrote, as 'Frank Aubrey', works including *King of the Dead: A Weird Romance* (1903), a fantasy about a white master-race in Brazil, reminiscent of the work of H. Rider *Haggard.

ASHDOWN, Clifford: see R. Austin *Freeman.

ASHTON, Helen [Rosaline] (1891–1958) married (1927) Arthur JORDAN. The daughter of a KC, she worked as a VAD during the First World War, and afterwards, believing that there would be a shortage of doctors, trained at London University (MB, B.Ch.) and was a houseman at the Great Ormond Street Hospital for Children. However, she ceased to practise after marrying a barrister. She was author of twenty-four novels to 1954. The earliest, *Pierrot in Town* (1913) and *Almain* (1914), are both about bohemian life in London. The former treats the social and sexual round quite deftly. Its main characters are: an elderly scientist weary of science; his younger, embittered wife; her admirer, a novelist (described by one reviewer as 'something between a vampire and a hermit crab'); a brilliant Jewess; her cold-blooded admirer; and the hero, an ambiguous outsider, half-English, half-French. They are all left at the end very much as they were at the beginning. *Dr Serocold* (1930) was probably her most popular work. Several of her later novels, such as *William and Dorothy* (1938), *Parson Austen's Daughter* (1949), and *Letty Landon* (1951), are fictionalized biographies of writers; she also published, with Katherine Davies, *I Had a Sister: A Study of Mary Lamb, Dorothy Wordsworth, Caroline Herschel, Cassandra Austen* (1937).

ASHTON, Teddy: see Allen *Clarke.

ASKEW, Alice and Claude : Alice J. de C. LEAKE (d. 1917) married (1900) Claude Arthur Cary ASKEW (d. 1917). Neither of these writers published anything alone. As a team, their output was prolific, almost in the L. T. *Meade league: over ninety novels, many published in sixpenny and sevenpenny series, between 1904 and 1918. A favourite topic was the innocent young woman surprised or lured into marriage by a more or less unsatisfactory foreigner, who could be anything from an unscrupulous Frenchman, as in *Eve—and the Law* (1905), to a *Boer farmer, as in *Alice of the Plains* (1906), or a Maharajah, as in *The Englishwoman* (1912). Sometimes the unscrupulous foreigner is played, so to speak, by the sinful metropolis, as in *Lucy Gort* (1907) or *Gilded London* (1914). The Askews diversified into other popular genres: *The Baxter Family* (1907) is a *suburban tale, while *The Premier's Daughter* (1905) involves scandal in high *political life and strange cries in the night. *The Shulamite* (1904) is about English and Boer life in South Africa. During the First World War they undertook relief operations in Serbia, which gave rise to *The Stricken Land: Serbia as We Saw It* (1916). They died together (leaving two orphan children) when the boat they were travelling on was torpedoed by a submarine in the Mediterranean; her body was washed ashore in Corfu, where the Archbishop of Serbia conducted the funeral. Claude Askew was an FRGS.

ASTOR, William Waldorf: see under **Pall Mall Magazine*.

At the Villa Rose, A. E. W. *Mason, 1910, Hodder & Stoughton. In the first of his three books featuring Inspector Hanaud of the Sûreté, Mason sought (in F. Tennyson *Jesse's categories) 'to combine the *crime story which produces a shiver with the detective story which aims at a surprise'. Based loosely on real cases (a wealthy French widow found murdered in her villa, her maid drugged, gagged, and bound nearby; an English shopkeeper murdered for jewels that the thieves then cannot find), and drawing for procedural detail on the memoirs of French policemen, *At the Villa Rose* features a detective who, Mason had decided, 'should be first of all a professional, secondly as physically unlike Sherlock Holmes as he could possibly be'. (Hanaud is a short, broad man who looks like a 'prosperous comedian'. His Watson in this book is Julius Ricardo, a fussy English dilettante 'with a passion for entertaining interesting people'.) While the detective story as such ends in the middle of the book, when the villains are unmasked (the remainder of the book explains what really happened), it is significant in the history of detective fiction—more directly, fairly, and teasingly than Conan *Doyle, Mason challenges the reader to guess the solution to a murder mystery from the clues provided.

Athenaeum, The, was published between 1828 and 1921, when it merged with the **Nation*. In the 1830s it became the biggest circulation magazine in Britain, and remained a widely read weekly title for the rest of the century. Under the proprietorship of Sir Charles Wentworth Dilke, 2nd Bt. (1842–1911), and the editorship (1871–1900) of Norman McColl (1843–1905), it maintained its broad approach, covering both the arts and the sciences, reviewing both books and the proceedings of the learned societies, and becoming perhaps the most influential journal of late Victorian literary criticism. Its regular reviewers included Theodore Watts-Dunton (1832–1914), Edmund Gosse (1849–1928), Andrew *Lang, W. E. Henley (1849–1903) and Walter Pater (1839–94); scholarly reviewers included Henry Sweet (1845–1912) and Henry Sidgwick (1838–1900). In this century, under the editorship (1919–21) of John Middleton Murry (1889–1957), the *Athenaeum* followed a less mainstream path, publishing stories by Katherine *Mansfield and Virginia *Woolf, for example, and poetry by Wilfred Owen (1893–1918) and T. S. Eliot (1888–1965).

AUBREY, Frank: see Fenton *Ash.

AUSTIN, Alfred (1835–1913) married (1865) Hester Jane HOMAN-MULOCK. Born at Headingley, near Leeds, son of a wool-merchant and a magistrate, he was educated at St Edward's King and Confessor School, Everton (1843–1849), Stonyhurst College, Oscott, and London University (BA 1854). He was called to the Bar in 1857, travelled in Italy, and stood unsuccessfully in 1865 as Conservative candidate for Taunton. From the mid-1860s he contributed regularly to periodicals, writing, for instance, on foreign affairs for the *Quarterly Review*. From 1866 to 1896 Austin was a leader-writer and occasional foreign correspondent for the *Standard*. In 1883 he became joint editor (1887–93 sole editor) of the *National Review*, a staunchly conservative publication. He was appointed Poet Laureate in 1896. According to the diary of Wilfred Scawen Blunt (1840–1922), the appointment was 'a ridiculous one, for with the exception of three sonnets Austin has never written anything in the smallest degree good'. Some argue that Austin was given the post as a reward for services rendered to the Tory party, others that there was little competition for it. He was a prolific writer whose output included not only lyrical, dramatic, and narrative poetry but also political and critical essays, an autobiography (in two volumes), and sentimental novels. Austin's greatest success arose not from his poetry but from his passionate prose—writing about English countryside and gardens—especially his own, Swinford Manor in Kent. *The Garden That I Love* (1894, 1907) and *In Veronica's Garden* (1895), both written in journal form, were resounding successes, and influenced many garden writers of the time, including *'Elizabeth'. **Haunts of Ancient Peace* (1902) is an evocation of Englishness in the aftermath of the *Boer War. Austin listed his recreations in *Who's Who* as 'riding, gardening and fishing'. This love of outdoor life is evident in his best work; his failures are chiefly due to his inability to handle abstract philosophical themes and ideas within epic and dramatic forms. The unsympathetic *Times* obituary (3 June 1913) concluded that 'as a poet it would be untrue to say that Austin ever ranked high in the opinion of skilled judges, though his verse was fairly popular with the general public'. His *Autobiography* (1911) is astoundingly self-congratulatory. His wife was a sister of Mrs Arthur *Kennard.

AVERY, [Charles] Harold (1867–1943) married (1898) Winifred ALLEN. The son of a JP, he was born at Headless Cross in Worcestershire and attended New College, Eastbourne. Avery's writing career took off in the 1890s ; his steady output invariably featured tales of schoolboy skill and daring on the playing fields and the translation of these worthy virtues to the fields of war. *Frank's First Term, or, The Making of a Man* (1896) is a typical Avery title. In 1897 he made the first of many contributions to the *Boy's Own Paper*. Other works are *Head of the School* (1912), *Line Up!* (1918), and *Caught Out* (1919). Characteristic is *Highway Pirates, or, The Secret Place at Coverthorne* (1904) whose narrator, Sylvester Eden, describes events which took place during his childhood, when he became mixed up with convicts, was cast away at sea, and discovered a secret passage leading to the house of his friend Miles Coverthorne. In *Firelock and Steel: A Story of the Good Old Days* (1906), set in 1808, young Bob Gilroy helps his father, a returned convict, to hide from the authorities. Though over age, Avery volunteered for service at the outbreak of the First World War.

Ayesha: *The Return of She*, H. Rider *Haggard, 1905, Ward Lock. In this sequel to *She* (1887), the heroic Leo Vincey and his foster father (and faithful scribe) L. Horace Holly pursue their vision of the nature goddess to the mountainous regions off the map beyond Tibet and play out again the story of the Egyptian priest Kallikrates (Leo), his seduction by the witch-princess Amenartas (Atene), and the revenge of the goddess Isis through her priestess, Ayesha, who wins eternal life in leading Kallikrates to his death. This time round Leo resists Atene, and conquers Ayesha through the plain strength of his human desire, but is killed by the power of her kiss. Perhaps Haggard's most successful integration of the male adventure story (plenty of physical violence, suffering, and suspense—the Ordeals of the Death-Hounds, the Mountains, and the Precipice) with a rich, legend-based *fantasy (a precursor of much later fantasy writing). From his imperialist perspective, it seems, the East is more unproblematically a source of wisdom than Africa, though Haggard's view of woman-as- nature (unlike his passionate celebration of Leo's masculinity) is even more ambiguous than in *She*: 'Ayesha was still woman enough to have worldly ambitions, and the most dread circumstance about her superhuman powers was that they appeared to be unrestrained by any responsibility to God or man.'

AYRES, Ruby M[ildred] (1883–1955) married (1909) Reginald William POCOCK. The daughter of an architect, she married an insurance broker. Her first book, *Castles in Spain* (1912), is one of the large class of romances narrated by a disillusioned middle-aged bachelor. Her many later works—she is said to have been able to write 15,000 to 20,000 words a day—include *Richard Chatterton, V. C.* (1915), *Paper Roses* (1916), *For Love* (1918), *The One who Forgot* (1919), *The Woman Hater* (1920), and *The Love of Robert Dennison* (1920). An obituary in the *Times* (15 Nov. 1955) attributes to her the remark: 'First I fix the price. Then I fix the title. Then I write the book.' True or not, it indicates her reputation. To literary historians she is best known as partly inspiring P. G. *Wodehouse's character Rosie M. Banks, author of *Mervyn Keene, Clubman, All for Love, Madcap Myrtle, A Red, Red Summer Rose, Only a Factory Girl, The Courtship of Lord Strathmorlick, The Woman Who Braved All*, and other works, mentioned first in the collection *The Inimitable Jeeves* (1923).

AYSCOUGH, John, *pseud.*: Francis Browning Drew BICKERSTAFFE (1858–1928) who changed his surname (1879) to BICKERSTAFFE-DREW, and was created (1909) a Papal Count and a Knight of Malta. The son of a Church of England clergyman, he converted to Roman Catholicism while an undergraduate at Oxford (where he added his mother's name to his own). He was ordained as a Catholic priest in 1884, served as a chaplain to the forces, and was ennobled for service as a Private Chamberlain to the Pope. His contemporary and *historical romances vary considerably in subject-matter and tone, and draw on both his military and his religious interests. The **Times Literary Supplement*, while applauding the good humour of *Admonition* (1903), described it as 'rather a patchwork: Scene i., a Country Vicarage; Scene ii., Syracuse, the household of Princess von und zu Rumpelstiltzchen; and "Admonition"—that is, the young lady's name who tells the tale—begins as the vicar's sister teaching the choir and ends as a peeress in her own right.' *Monksbridge* (1906), set in provincial England in the mid-nineteenth century, concerns the assimiliation of a widow, Mrs Auberon, and her three children, Eustace, Peterkin, and Sylvia, an exceedingly competent 17-year-old, into the local community. *Dromina* (1909) is the story of an Irish chieftain, Dermod M'Morogh, and his family, in the years following the death of

George III in 1820. *Mezzogiorno* (1910) concerns the transcontinental romantic adventures of Gillian Thesiger, daughter of a nomadic landscape painter, who has no country or formal education but a gift for languages and splendid copper-coloured hair. *Hurdcott* (1911) reverts to the early nineteenth century and the West Country (William Hazlitt, 1778–1830, and Charles Lamb, 1775–1834, have walk-on parts). *Gracechurch* (1913) is a ruminative tale of local life in the eponymous small town. Dedicating it to the Bishop of Clifton, Ayscough remarked that 'The thread on which these Gracechurch papers are strung together is stronger than any of consecutive narrative working towards the climax of a plot, for it is the simple and indestructible one of love for the dear old place and the kind, dear people who lived there.'

B., T., *pseud.*: see A. C. *Benson.

BACCHUS, George (1873–1945). Born in St Leonards, Sussex, the son of a former officer in the Austrian army, he was educated at Clifton College (where he set a record for running 440 yards which still stood in 1948) and Exeter College, Oxford. He became a journalist, and the authorship of the pornographic novels **Maudie* and **Pleasure Bound 'Afloat'* is attributed to him. Both his younger brothers were killed as stretcher-bearers in the First World War: it is possible that their Austrian birth made enlisting impossible.

BAGOT, Richard (1860–1921) was the son of a Guards officer; his mother was a niece of the 5th Duke of Northumberland. Educated privately, he became private secretary to Sir Frederick Napier Broome (1842–96), Governor of Western Australia (1882–3). He converted to Roman Catholicism in 1881, but was highly critical of its institutions and practices. In his *Casting of Nets* (1901) the nets in question are those cast in the staunchly Protestant village of Abbotsbury by the staunchly Catholic wife of the local landowner. 'The courage of the author is undisputed, and the ability and force with which he has denounced the unwarranted intrusion of the priest in domestic affairs cannot be overlooked,' the **Spectator* commented rather grimly. In the same year, after having published pieces unsympathetic to Vatican politics, Bagot renounced his title as Knight of Honour of the Order of Malta. *The Just and the Unjust* (1902) also dwells on the turmoil arising from religious principles. Much of his later life was spent in Italy, about which he wrote such books as *The Lakes of Northern Italy* (1907) and *Italians of Today* (1912) and articles exploring the place of Italy in international affairs. For his services to Italy he was made a Grand Officer and Commendatore of the Order of the Crown of Italy in 1917. In the year before his death he inherited the family estate in Westmorland. *Donna Diana* (1902) is set in Rome, and concerns the romance, much impeded by intrigue, between the (Catholic) Italian heroine and a young (Protestant) Englishman who once saved her cousin's life. *Love's Proxy* (1904) has a rather more orthodox preoccupation with class and with sexual morality: the heroine is torn between her elderly husband, whom she starts by pitying and ends by loving, and a dashing politician. *The Passport* (1905) returns to Rome, and another troubled courtship, this time between two Italians. *A Roman Mystery* (1899) is a tale of hereditary insanity.

BAILEY, H[enry] C[hristopher] (1878–1961) married (1908) Lydia Haden Janet GUEST. Born in London, he was educated at City of London School and Corpus Christ College, Oxford. After graduating in 1901 with a First in Classics, Bailey spent his writing career on the staff of the *Daily Telegraph*, where he served as both theatre critic and war correspondent before ending up as a leader writer. His first novel, *My Lady of Orange* (1901), was published while he was still a student, the first of a series of *historical novels. *Raoul, Gentleman of Fortune* (1907) concerns the adventures of a Nostromo-like vagabond mercenary in the Dutch war of liberation against Spain. The publisher's advertisement describes the hero as 'a good deal less than a saint, but a very human man with a highly individual outlook on life'. 'We should imagine that the author has "struck oil" with Raoul,' the *Daily Telegraph* murmured, 'we shall certainly be glad to hear of him again.' *The God of Clay* (1908) is Napoleon Bonaparte, and although the novel invites us to suspend judgement, its sympathies are clearly with the man who brought 'order and law' to the 'blood-smirched chaos' of the French Revolution. Other historical novels are *Colonel Stow* (1908), *Storm and Treasure* (1910), *The Lonely Queen* (1911), *The Gentleman Adventurer* (1914), and *The Highwayman* (1915). Bailey was best known, though, as a *crime novelist, with a long series of short stories and novels featuring Reggie Fortune, pathologist and gourmet, beginning with *Call Mr*

Fortune (1920). In their day Bailey's detective stories were regarded as clever and civilized, placing him among the mystery élite, but they have dated badly: the hero seems too mannered. Bailey also created a second detective, Joshua Clunk (*Garstons*, 1930), whose appeal has not survived at all; he and Fortune meet in *The Great Game* (1939).

BAILLIE-SAUNDERS, Margaret: see Margaret Baillie *Saunders.

BAIN, Francis William (1863–1940) married (1890) Helen Margarita BLANDFORD (d. 1931). The son of a historian, he was educated at Westminster School (where he was head boy) and Christ Church, Oxford; he became a Fellow of All Souls College, Oxford. He had published fiction, for example *Dmitri* (1890), a *historical romance set in Russia, before his decision, which rather surprised his friends, to take in 1892 a job in the Indian educational service as professor of history and economics at the Deccan College, Poona. A brilliant teacher, he rose to become its principal, studied Sanskrit, and was inspired to write *exotic fables and fiction about India, usually purporting to be 'translated from the original manuscript', of which *In the Great God's Hair* (1904), *A Heifer of the Dawn* (1904), *A Draught of the Blue* (1905), and *A Syrup of the Bees* (1914) are characteristic. His *Indian Stories* were collected in thirteen volumes (1913–20). He also published on economics and history.

BAKER, Amy J[osephine] (b. ?1895) married Maynard CRAWFORD. Born at Richmond, Surrey, she was educated at St Katherine's School, Wantage, and married an army officer. She published forty volumes of romantic fiction to 1955, the earliest of which, *I Too Have Known* (1911) and *The Impenitent Prayer* (1913), are set in England and South Africa.

BAKER, James (1847–1920) married Agnes Anne HALLETT. A lecturer, educationist, novelist and travel-writer, he was tutored by his father, a Somerset teacher and publisher, and became a journalist. His great love of travel inspired his writing: for his work on Bohemia he was given the Great Silver Medal of Prague. He reported on Bohemian education for the Department of Education, and was the author of *A National Education to National Advancement* (1904). Other non-fictional publications include *A Plea for Power for the Church of England* (1906) and *Literary and Biographical Studies* (1908). His Victorian fiction consisted of tame melodramas and *historical romances for the juvenile market. *A Double Choice* (1901) concerns the arrival in Netherleigh-on-Sea of a German governess, Hilda Jordan, and the simultaneous rise to journalistic fame of one of the town's most prominent citizens, Geoffrey Lowther; they eventually marry. *The Inseparables* (1905) is set in nineteenth-century Oxford and Egypt. Robert Lyndeley works for the Egyptian Scientific Association. Two women, Edith Assheton and the glamorous Lady Ruth Walgrave, move in and out of his life; he marries Edith, deciding that his attraction to Lady Ruth is not true love. Baker's memoirs appeared as *Reminiscent Gossip of Men and Manners* (1913). He was a Fellow of the Royal Historical and Royal Geographical Societies.

BALFOUR, Andrew (1873–1931), KCMG (1930), married (1902) Grace NUTTER. A pioneer of preventive medicine, Balfour was the son of an Edinburgh doctor. He was educated at George Watson's College and at Edinburgh University (MB, 1894, MD, 1898) and Strasburg University. He travelled the world during his period of service as a naval surgeon. Balfour was involved in research at Caius College, Cambridge during the 1890s (DPH 1897). He was decorated for his service as a field surgeon during the *Boer War. His experiences during this period inspired a series of short stories for **Chambers' Journal* which was later published as *Cashiered* (1902). After his marriage he resumed his research work in Khartoum at the Wellcome Tropical Research Laboratory, leaving only to enlist in 1913. In 1915 he was made temporary lieutenant-colonel of the RAMC. From 1923 he was director of the London School of Hygiene and Tropical Medicine. In his youth he wrote *historical romances inspired by R. L. Stevenson, such as *By Stroke of Sword* (1897) and *To Arms: Being Some Passages from the Early Life of Allan Oliphant, Chirurgeon, Written by Himself* (1898). What distinguishes the latter from other contemporary historical romances is the pastiche of eighteenth-century English. Oliphant, who has survived the defeat of Bonnie Prince Charlie, remembers his part in the earlier uprising of the prince's father. *Gentleman Jerry, or, How The Kraal Was Saved* (1899) and *The Golden Kingdom: Being an Account of the Quest for the Same as Described in the Remarkable Narrative of Doctor*

Henry Mortimer (1903) show the influence of Rider *Haggard. The stories are mostly of the stiff-upper-lip variety, but with an underlying current of interest in miscegenation. His obituary in the *Times* states that 'he stood throughout the long years of his service to his fellows, unmoved by success and unflinching in the face of opposition and danger'.

Ball and the Cross, The, G. K. *Chesterton, New York 1909, London 1910, Wells, Gardner. A heady mix of fable and thesis which the *Daily News* described as a 'theological farce' and the *Times* as a 'philosophic romance' of 'Gargantuan hilarity'. Professor Lucifer arrives in London in an airship and before departing deposits his passenger, Michael, a holy man from Bulgaria 'almost entirely covered with white hair', on the top of St Paul's Cathedral, where they decide that the ball and cross symbolize their respective faiths, materialism and Christianity. This fable frames a picaresque tale about the interminable duel between a James Turnbull, the editor of *The Atheist*, and Evan MacIan, who sees what he takes to be an insulting reference to the Virgin Mary displayed in the window of the editorial office, and immediately smashes it with his stick. The duel gets under way in the back garden of a curiosity shop in St Martin's Lane, from whose owner the duellists have purchased a couple of swords. It continues, despite the vigilance of the police, all over the country, and beyond. At one point, a car accident supervenes. The combatants hear a woman calling, and run towards her. She is a Swedenborgian. They drive back to London in her car, accumulating further material for heated debate as they go. Their adventures conclude in the garden of a lunatic asylum in Margate, where Michael, after attempting 'in a voice like a silver trumpet' to convert passers-by in the street, has been confined. The asylum burns down, and Michael, after marrying MacIan to the Swedenborgian, goes singing down a corridor of flames. As usual, Chesterton's high spirits and serious purpose won over the reviewers, though the *Times* did point out that the narrative abounds in stock characters and incidents 'curiously suggestive of the very journalism which Mr Chesterton never wearies of denouncing'.

BALL, Hylda: see under Kathlyn *Rhodes.

BANCROFT, Francis, *pseud.*: Frances Charlotte SLATER (b. 1870) Born at Carnarvondale, Cape Colony, South Africa, one of twelve children of a farmer, she and her five sisters were well educated for the period. She came to England and had some success with her novels about South African affairs, such as *Of Like Passions* (1907) and *The Veldt Dwellers* (1912), but, owing partly to the bankruptcy of her publisher, she was reduced, according to a letter addressed by M. P. *Willcocks to the secretary of the Royal Literary Fund, to living on bread and rice in Paignton, Devon. As 'Francis Bancroft' she published in all eighteen novels between 1906 and 1933. The South African poet and bank manager Francis Carey Slater (1876–1958) was her nephew and used her as an intermediary in dealings with English publishers. His volume of stories, *The Sunburnt South* (1908), is unusual for its date because Slater, who spoke Xhosa, used native African myths in his writing.

BANNERMAN, Helen: Helen Brodie Cowan WATSON (1862–1946) married (1889) William Burney BANNERMAN (1858–1924). The most famous work of this children's writer, *Little Black Sambo* (1899), was a nursery fixture in the 1900s. She was one of seven children of a scientist and a minister in the Free Church of Scotland. As a child she lived in Madeira (though she went to school in Edinburgh), but after the family's money was lost her father had to return to the ministry. In 1874 she became engaged to a researcher for the Indian Medical Service, and, after receiving an external degree in literature and language from St Andrew's University, she married and moved to India, where she lived until 1918. *Little Black Sambo* was originally written for Bannerman's own four children, as a letter to them in Edinburgh, and the book contained her own drawings. An instant success, it was followed by *Little Black Mingo* (1901) and *Little Black Quibba* (1902). The young hero of *Pat and the Spider* (1904) rescues a butterfly from a spider's web, and in return is taught how to alter his own size by crawling through a bamboo shoot. After several metamorphoses and some hair-raising jungle adventures, he runs 'gaily home to tea'. Bannerman's stories are now thought to epitomize a particular sort of patronizing racism; at the time, the most striking thing about them was usually held to be the authenticity of the threat contained in her jungle and its beasts. There is a biography by Elizabeth Hay (1981).

Barbara Rebell, Mrs Belloc *Lowndes, 1905, William Heinemann. A novel about the tendency of one generation to repeat the mistakes of another. When dandyish Richard Rebell is accused of cheating at cards, he and his wife, Adela, a famous beauty, seek refuge in France, where they are supported by a generous benefactress, Madame Barbara Sampiero (she too has a dark secret, in the shape of a love-child by Lord Bosworth, a cabinet minister). Their daughter, also Barbara, marries a distant relation, Pedro Rebell, the half-Spanish owner of a plantation in the West Indies. The marriage is unhappy. When Madame Sampiero is paralysed by a stroke, Barbara is summoned to her home, Chancton Priory, to nurse her. There she encounters Oliver Boringdon, Mrs Sampiero's land agent, and James Berwick, Lord Bosworth's nephew. James sold his soul when he married an older woman for her money. His wife has since died, decreeing, in what is by no means the only distant echo of *Middlemarch* (1872) by George Eliot (1819–80), that he will lose the fortune he has inherited from her if he remarries. Barbara and James fall in love. Oliver Boringdon also loves her, and is loved unrequitedly by Lucy Kemp, daughter of an 'Indian Mutiny' hero. Knowing that he will lose all prospect of a political career if he marries, James persuades her to become his mistress (they will meet at a château in France). At the last moment, remembering the less than salutary outcome of Lord Bosworth's affair with Madame Sampiero, they draw back. They are rewarded for their renunciation when both Pedro Rebell and Lord Bosworth die, the latter leaving everything to James. They marry. Lucy Kemp is left hoping that Oliver will get over his disappointment.

BARCLAY, Armiger: see under 'Oliver *Sandys'.

BARCLAY, Florence L.: Florence Louisa CHARLESWORTH (1862–1921) married (1881) Charles Wright BARCLAY (1853–1926). She was born at Limpsfield, Surrey, the daughter of a Church of England clergyman. Maria Louisa Charlesworth (1819–80), the Evangelical children's writer, was her aunt. In 1870, her father moved to an east London slum parish, St Anne's Limehouse, where he was assisted by the young and wealthy Charles Barclay, whom Florence married at 18. The Barclays moved to Little Amwell, in Hertfordshire, where Charles served until his retirement in 1921. Florence was profoundly devout, an accomplished musician, a keep-fit fanatic, and the mother, eventually, of eight children. She began writing to pass the time while recovering from a severe illness. *Guy Mervyn*, the first of her twelve novels, was published under the pseudonym 'Brandon Roy' in 1891. Her career was transformed by the runaway success of *The *Rosary* (1909), which sold upwards of 150,000 in its first year; this too had mostly been written, in 1905, while she was recovering from illness. The novel deftly if precariously combines romantic and religious passion. It was said of her that she could always 'damp the glowing embers of the flesh with an aptly-chosen quotation from Nehemiah or Habakkuk'; she made sure that her commitment to romance did not obscure her commitment to the Christian faith. In 1909 she toured America with her sister Maud, who had married a son of William Booth (1829–1912), of the Salvation Army, lecturing on 'Palestine and the Bible'; the following year, she was back again, this time as the author of *The Rosary*, to advertise *The Mistress of Shenstone* (1911), the first of a series of novels cut more or less to the same pattern, which was later filmed with Pauline Frederick in the starring role. In *The Following of the Star: A Romance* (1911), a marriage of convenience between an heiress and an African missionary, both vowed to celibacy, turns into one of passion; as elsewhere in Barclay's novels, the medium of the transformation is an awakening to motherhood which enables the heroine to treat her temporarily incapacitated husband as a child well before she has a child by him. *The Upas Tree* (1912) also has a hero who travels to central Africa, though this one is a novelist in search of material, not a missionary, and a marriage regenerated by the nurturing of a childlike husband and by the birth of a child. In *A Broken Halo* (1913) the roles are reversed, and a husband is regenerated morally and spiritually by his growing ability and desire to nurture his childlike wife, whom he calls his Little White Lady. Since her family was already well off, Barclay devoted a large proportion of her literary earnings to charitable work; though she did buy a motor car, which enabled her to fulfil even more lecture engagements. A biography, *The Life of Florence L. Barclay: A Study in Personality* (1921), by 'one of her daughters', makes her seem like the heroine of one of her own novels. Her later years were spent at Overstrand in Norfolk.

BARCLAY, Mrs Hubert: Edith Noël DANIELL (1872–1952) married (1890) Hubert Frederick BARCLAY (1865–48). She was born in India. Her father became Chief Constable of Hertfordshire; she married an army officer (a nephew of Florence L. *Barclay's husband) and lived at Berkhamsted. She was president of the Mothers' Union 1919–25. Her five novels in the period are all anodyne romances. In *Trevor Lordship* (1911) a marriage begins in cool courtesy and ends in passion. In *A Dream of Blue Roses* (1912) a French girl comes to England, renounces a fortune, and finds happiness. *East of the Shadows* (1913) is slightly more lurid: when a man loses his memory after an accident, his fiancée marries another; twenty-two years later, he mistakes her niece for her.

BARING, Maurice (1874–1945). Fourth son of the 1st Lord Revelstoke, the banker, he was educated at Eton College and Trinity College, Cambridge, and served in the diplomatic service from 1898 to 1904. He then worked as the *Morning Post*'s correspondent, first in Manchuria during the Russo-Japanese War (1904–5), and then in St Petersburg. He converted to Roman Catholicism in 1909. His early adventures are described in the autobiography *The Puppet Show of Memory* (1922). A brilliant linguist, he published *Landmarks in Russian Literature* (1910) and travelled extensively in Russia, China, and Turkey. He was the author of two volumes of short stories in the period, and later fiction. Those collected in *Orpheus in Mayfair and Other Stories and Sketches* (1909) range from impressions of high society to *Wellsian *fantasies. Of the twelve included in *The Glass Mender* (1910), one had appeared previously in the **English Review*, and five in the *Morning Post*, which suggests that Baring had his eye both on an élite and on a mainstream readership: they are mostly of the whimsical once-upon-a-time variety. *Dead Letters* (1910) was the first of a series of imaginary comic sketches involving historical characters collected as *Unreliable History* (1934). He published several children's books, including *Forget-me-not and Lily of the Valley* (1905), as well as plays and verse. He was a close friend of 'Vernon *Lee'. Parkinson's disease was diagnosed in 1936, and the rest of his life was spent in painful decline. There is a biography by Emma Letley (1991).

BARING, Max, *pseud.*: Charles MESSENT (b. 1857) was the author of a volume of short stories (1896) and six later volumes of fiction which are mostly Dickensian tales of village life. *A Doctor in Corduroy* (1905) features a rough-diamond vet; *The Shattered Idol* (1907) and *Joanna and His Reverence* (1910), muscular but priggish clergymen.

BARING-GOULD, S[abine] (1834–1924) married (1868) Grace TAYLOR (d. 1916). The son of a landowner, educated at Clare College, Cambridge, Baring-Gould was squire of the parish of Lew Trenchard in Devon from 1872, and its rector from 1884. He also published more than 150 books between 1857 and 1920 including novels, religious works (such as the sixteen-volume *Lives of the Saints*, 1897–8), travel books, folklore, poetry, hymns, and a biography of another literary clergyman, R. S. Hawker (1803–75). He is best remembered now as the author of 'Onward Christian Soldiers', but his novels, often set in Devon, were widely read in their day. His fictional canon also shows a wide range of styles. *Royal Georgie* (1901) is the story of two of the Prince of Wales's ex-cronies who, on his appointment as regent in 1811, find themselves condemned to exile in bleakest Devon, and of the young girl who is supposedly the niece of one of them, but may have royal blood in her veins: character proves more important than the possession of pedigree. *Nebo the Nailer* (1902) is a contemporary tale after the fashion of George *Gissing's *Demos* (1886) or Mrs Humphry *Ward's *Marcella* (1894) which juxtaposes idle but well-meaning aristocrats with dedicated but impetuous working-class radicals. As so often, the real enemy turns out to be the middle-class or lower-middle-class exploiter. *In Dewisland* (1904) is a Welsh romance with an undercurrent of riot and random violence.

BARLOW, Jane (1857–1917) was the daughter of a Church of Ireland clergyman who was professor of history at, and later vice-provost of, Trinity College, Dublin. An enthusiastic Irish Nationalist from childhood, she contributed to *Hibernia*, and published verse and sixteen volumes of fiction between 1892 and 1917, many of which are collections of Irish tales such as *Irish Neighbours* (1907) and *From the Land of the Shamrock*

(1901). Her career as a writer of short stories was encouraged by Sir William Robertson Nicoll (see *publishers). *Flaws* (1911) is a novel about the rebellion of a daughter against her oppressive family. There is a moving tribute by her friend Katharine *Tynan in the **Bookman* (June 1917), describing her as 'one of those good gifts which Anglo-Ireland gives to the foster-country, one of those sprung of the English colonists who become in time more Irish than the Irish'.

BARR, Robert (1850–1912) married (1876) Eva BENNETT. Born in Scotland, he moved to Canada at the age of four. His output was prolific; much of his early work was journalistic in nature. Barr was headmaster of Windsor Public School in Canada until 1876, when he married and began to write for the *Detroit Free Press*. He was both a colourful and a conscientious young journalist. His obituary in the *Times* illustrates Barr's gusto: 'he crossed a frozen river, more than a mile wide, leaping from ice-floe to ice-floe in order to give his paper early and exclusive information about a sensational murder on the other side of the frontier.' He was made an honorary member of the Iroquois tribe of Indians. He started a London-based version of the paper with John *Oxenham. In 1892 Barr founded the **Idler*, an illustrated paper for men, co-edited by Jerome K. *Jerome. Barr was well known for spoofs like *The Adventures of Sherlaw Kombs* (1892). *The Face and the Mask* (1894) is a collection of short stories which display a tendency to tease his readers with unexpected twists in the plot. An ironic attitude pervades all his novelistic endeavours—a fact supported by his rather fanciful romantic comedies and his concentration on verve rather than veracity in his *historical fiction. Occasionally this mocking streak fades and more serious views emerge. *The Mutable Many* (1897) is about a strike. The *Times*'s obituary (22 Oct. 1922) describes it as 'probably the best informed story of its kind ever written'. *Jennie Baxter, Journalist* (1898) is his sprightly contribution to New Woman fiction. In 1903 he completed *The O'Ruddy*, an unfinished novel by Stephen Crane (1871–1900). The strong emphasis on story-line in Barr's work culminates in his depiction of a swaggering French detective in *The *Triumphs of Eugene Valmont* (1906), long before Agatha Christie (1891–1976) thought of Hercule Poirot. Much of Barr's work is formulaic; he was a professional writer with an eye to commercial success. An inveterate London clubman, he was associated with many well-known literary figures such as Rider *Haggard and Conan *Doyle. According to his obituary he was 'a most genial companion and [an] exceptionally entertaining raconteur'. Other works, many of them *historical romances, include: *The Strong Arm* (1900), a medieval romp set in the Rhineland at the time of the Crusades and written in the spirit of Sir Walter Scott (1771–1832) (who had at one time considered *The Strong Arm* as a possible title for *Rob Roy*, 1817); *The Victors: A Romance of Yesterday Morning and This Afternoon* (1902), which has the unusual setting, for English fiction of the period, of the University of Michigan at Ann Arbor; *Over the Border* (1903), a story about the Earl of Strafford, Chief Minister to Charles I, and his daughter's involvement, after his execution, in Royalist politics; *Stranleigh's Millions* (1909), six episodes demonstrating the generosity of the eponymous millionaire; and *The Sword Maker* (1910), which returns to the Rhineland in the Middle Ages, to the reopening of the river for trade, and the consequent enrichment of the city of Frankfurt. Barr died at Woldingham in Surrey.

BARRETT, Frank (1848–1926) married Joan——. This novelist and inventor started his writing career at the age of 18 as a literary critic. He was also an accomplished potter. He published sensational *historical romances and *crime novels. *Breaking the Shackles* (1900) is a detective story with well-drawn prison scenes. All his work displays a tendency towards a swift-moving plot, sometimes reflected in a truncated literary style. His narratives are very often written in the first person, perhaps to heighten tension and pathos. *Hidden Gold* (1904) is the story of an honest, puritanical, and penniless carpenter, Philip Brooke, and his daughter, Iris. Brooke finds some gold coins buried in a ruined abbey, and, thinking of his daughter's future, appropriates them. Once he has made his fortune, he reburies twice the amount of his original haul. These coins are found by his daughter's suitor, Harold Grandison: they enable him to marry Iris, and thus find his true 'hidden gold'. *The Error of Her Ways* (1905) concerns a love triangle: Thomas Clifford loves Sylvia Harrowgate, who becomes engaged to another man, who turns out to be a thief and a bigamist; violence ensues, leaving Thomas with brain damage; a miraculous operation cures him on the last page, and he recognizes his beloved, who now sees the error of her ways. In *The Obliging Husband* (1907), a haberdasher, John Goodman, leaves his business to his apprentice, Robin Fairfellow, on the condition that Robin marries his unruly daughter, Margaret. The beautiful and ambitious Margaret begins to consort with men above her station. Robin, however, remains faithful, and she is forced to acknowledge his virtues when one of her admirers attacks him. The fable ends with a reconciliation. Barrett published more than fifty fictional works as well as three plays and numerous articles for periodicals. His wife also published some fiction in the 1890s and 1920s.

BARRIE, J[ames] M[atthew] (1860–1937), OM (1922), created (1913) 1st Baronet, married (1894) Mary ANSELL (*c*.1862–1950) (divorced 1909). Seventh of eight surviving children of a handloom weaver, Barrie was born at Kirriemuir, Forfarshire. His second brother, their mother's favourite child, died when Barrie was 6, and she turned the force of her personality on him, encouraging him to write. He resolved to make up to her for the son she had lost, and later celebrated her in *Margaret Ogilvy*, 1896. He was brought up in the Free Church of Scotland, and educated at Glasgow Academy (where his brother Alexander was a teacher), Forfar Academy, Dumfries Academy, and Edinburgh University. He was given his first job as leader-writer on the *Nottingham Journal* in 1883, but lost it when the owners, the Bradshaw brothers (see Mrs Albert S. *Bradshaw) decided to economize in 1884 by sacking him. His charming, quaint sketches of Scottish life, collected as *Auld Licht Idylls* (1888), were published in the *St James's Gazette* from 1884, and their success encouraged Barrie to go to London in 1885. He had his first literary success with the sentimental melodrama, *The Little Minister* (1891), and his first theatrical success with a farce produced as *The Lifeboat* in 1892. Barrie's future wife was an actress in the cast. *Sentimental Tommy* (1896), a Kailyard novel, brought Barrie both critical appreciation and mass sales; **Tommy and Grizel* (1900), his last novel for adults, was a sequel. In the late 1890s he was a prominent figure in literary circles, with his own cricket team, the Alhakbarries (in which Conan *Doyle and 'Charles *Turley' played). Barrie's remarkable impact on the London stage in the 1900s began with *Quality Street* (1901) and *The Admirable Crichton* (1902), which combined his own taste for whimsical romance with the contemporary interest in social issues. The play *Peter Pan, or, The Boy Who Wouldn't Grow Up* (1904) grew out of Barrie's friendship with the five Llewelyn Davies brothers; with it are associated the novels *The Little White Bird* (1902) and *Peter and Wendy* (1911), and in 1912 Barrie arranged that a statue of Peter Pan should be put up, at his expense, in Kensington Gardens (to which he had a private key). In 1897 Barrie had met the beautiful Sylvia Llewelyn Davies, daughter of the novelist and cartoonist George du Maurier (1834–1896), a barrister's wife with several small boys, whom he saw in Kensington Gardens. He became mawkishly devoted to both mother and sons, and when the father, who had tolerated him, died young of cancer in 1907, Barrie seems to have largely assumed financial responsibility for the family. In the same year, the agitation against the Lord Chancellor's decision not to grant a licence for the play *Waste* by Harley Granville-Barker (1877–1946) brought the Barries into contact with the secretary of the committee, Gilbert *Cannan. In 1909 Barrie discovered his wife's adultery with Cannan, and she announced her wish for a divorce. Shortly afterwards Sylvia Llewelyn Davies was diagnosed as having cancer: she died in 1910, and Barrie took in the five boys, aged between 6 and 17. The eldest, George, was killed in the war; his favourite, Michael, drowned while at Oxford in 1921. As the others grew up and left home Barrie developed a last devoted attachment to a married woman, his secretary, Lady Cynthia Asquith (d. 1960). If some of his plays—most famously *Peter Pan*, *Alice-Sit-by-the-Fire* (1905), *Dear Brutus* (1917), the familiar tale of what goes wrong when people get their wishes, and the supernatural tale *Mary Rose* (1920)—are glutinously sentimental, others, such as the feminist *What Every Woman Knows* (1908) and the one-act comedy *The Twelve Pound Look* (1910), have a satirical edge which reflects the influence of Oscar Wilde (1856–1900) and G. B. Shaw (1856–1950). If Barrie believed, nostalgically, that all men were really little boys, all women really mothers, he could be surprisingly sharp about the men and women who did not live up to their appointed roles.

BARRY, John Arthur (1850–1911). Born in Devon, he joined the merchant navy at the age of 13. In 1875 he travelled to Australia where he went in for gold-digging and sheep-herding amongst other occupations and eventually settled in Sydney, about which he wrote *Old and New Sydney* (1902). He worked for the *Times* from 1884, including a stint as foreign correspondent, and wrote romantic adventure stories in his free time, which include *Steve Brown's Bunyip and Other Stories* (1893) with introductory verses by *Kipling, *Against the Tides of Fate* (1899), the short stories *Red Lion and Blue Star* (1902), *Sea Yarns* (1910), and *South Sea Shipmates* (1913). He died in Sydney.

BARRY, Dr William: William Francis BARRY (1849–1930). Born in London, he was educated at Hammersmith Training School, Sedgeley Park School, and Oscott College. In 1868 he went to the English College in Rome and the Gregorian University there; and he was ordained a Catholic priest in 1873. He returned to England to take the Chair of Philosophy and Church History at Olton Theological College, and later went to Oscott, his old school, as Professor of Theology. He lived at Dorchester-on-Thames in Oxfordshire 1883–1907; then at Leamington until he moved back to Oxford in 1928. He was well read in the classics and fluent in several European languages. His novels often handled controversial topics: *The New Antigone* (1887) is a sprightly assault upon the fashionable breakaway concepts of socialism, atheism, free thought, sexual openness, and rights for women. *Arden Massiter* (1900) portrays a youthful English socialist's entanglement in Italian revolutionary politics. Barry's wit is well exercised in his attack upon the Celtic Revivalists in *The Wizard's Knot* (1901). *The Dayspring* (1903) is a combination of *crime novel, sentimental romance, and history of the Paris Commune. A young Irishman escapes to Paris under the false name of Henry Guiron after shooting a tyrannical landlord. He becomes involved in the Commune, but eventually decides to sail for America, which holds a truer prospect of a 'world of freedom', with his fiancé, the Comtesse de Montalais. The novel's flimsy realism attracted the scorn of the **Times Literary Supplement*. 'Nor is it the habit of surgeons to give "a leap of exultation" the moment they have operated successfully—not even on the other side of the Channel.' Barry has been dubbed the creator of the English Catholic novel. Yet his obituary in the *Times* (16 Dec. 1930) considered his fiction less powerful than his journalism. 'Had his style been equal to unravelling the burden of his knowledge, he would have become more than a publicist and all-round writer.' From 1875 onwards he contributed regularly to the *Dublin Review*, as well as the **Contemporary Review*, the *Edinburgh Review*, and the **Nineteenth Century*. He also wrote non-fiction such as *The Papal Monarchy* (1902). *Memories and Opinions* (1926) is autobiographical. Barry was created Notary Apostolic by Pius XI in 1923; he died in Oxford.

BARTRAM, George published two volumes of verse (1900, 1913) and six volumes of fiction between 1897 and 1914, mostly *historical romances set in the English provinces in the early nineteenth century: *The Longshoremen* (1903) features smugglers, *Lads of the Fancy* (1906) sporting squires.

BATEMAN, May [Geraldine Frances] was educated at the Anglo-French College, South Kensington, London, and was the *Daily Express*'s correspondent during the *Boer War. She was associated with Lady Knightley of Fawsley (d. 1913) in editing the *Imperial Colonist*, and contributed to *Good Housekeeping* and *Harper's Bazaar*. She was at one time the object of Oswald *Crawfurd's attentions. *The Altar of Life* (1898) is a novel about a woman who marries a soldier who has apparently been dishonoured. The hero of *The Glowworm* (1901) is another soldier whose childhood sweetheart marries a cheat; later he kills her sooner than let her face a fate worse than death at the hands of marauding Indian natives. *Farquharson of Glune* (1908) is a drama of *political life featuring an ambitious young politician, the clever woman who wants to shape his career, and the dim one he marries.

BATTERSBY, H. Francis: see 'Francis *Prevost'.

BAYNTON, Barbara: Barbara Jane LAWRENCE (1857–1929), married, first (1880), Alexander FRATER (divorced 1890), secondly (1890), Thomas BAYNTON (*c.*1820–1904), and, thirdly (1921), Rowland George ALLANSON-WINN (1855–1935), who succeeded (1913) as 5th Baron HEADLEY. Born in Scone, New South Wales, she was educated at home. Though she later claimed that her father was an officer in the Indian army, he seems to have been a carpenter. She advanced her social position by marriage to the son of the farming family for whom she was working as a governess. He ran away with a servant in 1887; she moved to Sydney, married an elderly surgeon, and began publishing stories and journalism. She travelled to England, where she was encouraged by Edward Garnett (1868–1937), who helped her to have *Bush Studies* (1902) accepted by Duckworth. It was followed by *Human Toll* (1907). These two works, drawing on Baynton's own experience of the oppressed life of a farmer's wife on a remote station, are considered important in that they represented a female challenge to the image of life in the outback. Garnett reviewed the latter in the **Bookman* (Mar. 1907), calling it 'a work of genius indisputably, disconcertingly sinister, extraordinarily actual' and praising her exposure of 'the terrible earthiness of human instinct . . . the determining force of a mean environment, the gauntness and squalidness of decivilised Australian life'. By careful investment of the proceeds of her second husband's estate in antiques and stocks she became rich and a well-known literary hostess in Australia and London. She left her third husband within a few years of marriage and lived in Australia thereafter.

Beasts and Super-Beasts, *'Saki', 1914, John Lane. A collection of three dozen of 'Saki''s brief tales, most but by no means all of which feature real or imaginary animals. The stories are comic, but cruel. Some are uncanny, tragic, mocking fairy tales, others (like 'The Open Window') are spoofs. Throughout his stories 'Saki' uses irony and black comedy as a means of distancing or deflecting emotion. He was above all a dazzling stylist who applied his incisive wit and epigrammatic brilliance to the quirky preoccupations of his age. His characters range from effete youths to articulate duchesses. There is something Wildean about his elegant displays of cynical repartee, as in the conversation between the two women in 'Fur'. But the best-known stories in this collection, 'The Story-Teller' or 'The Lumber Room', for example, concern the revenge of imaginative children on their unloving, humourless guardians, in which stupidity is humiliated, pomposity discomfited, and misunderstandings exploited. Throughout *Beasts and Super-Beasts*, 'Saki' satirized society from the point of view of artistocratic Toryism. His stories evoke the evanescent charm of the Edwardian era, beneath which lurk macabre and disturbing undercurrents. He anticipates a dominant mood of the 1920s: cynical urbanity and malicious charm.

Beau Brocade: *A Romance*, Baroness *Orczy, 1908, Greening, and 1907, P. J. B. Lippincott, Philadelphia. The story is set on Brassing Moor, in Derbyshire, in the aftermath of the defeat of the Young Pretender in 1745. The blacksmith John Stich is sheltering Philip James Gascoyne, 11th Earl of Stretton, who is suspected of Jacobite sympathies, although in fact he remained loyal to King George, and has letters to prove it. The hunt is also on for the local Robin Hood, a highwayman known as Beau Brocade. The beefily villainous Sir Humphrey Challoner plans to steal the exculpatory letters from Gascoyne's devoted sister, Patience, who has promised to take them to the king in London; he will use them to obtain her hand in marriage. Challoner's lawyer, Master Millachip, tricks Beau Brocade, now revealed as Captain Jack Bathurst, into holding up Patience's coach. The highwayman is so enchanted by her beauty that instead of robbing her he invites her to dance by moonlight on the moor, while Challoner, lurking nearby, seizes this opportunity to grab the letters. Eventually, both Gascoyne and Bathurst are captured, and taken before the Duke of Cumberland. However, Bathurst in turn has tricked Challoner into releasing the letters, which prove Gascoyne's innocence. Bathurst receives a royal pardon (the officer he was cashiered for striking has since proved a villain), and is reunited with Patience. The story extends Orczy's interest in the definition of gender. Beau Brocade, as his name rather firmly indicates, is foppish; but his foppery, like the Scarlet Pimpernel's, conceals an unmistakeable manliness.

BECKE, [George] Louis (1848–1913) married——. Born at Port Macquarie in New South Wales, the son of an English South Sea trader, he was sent to sea in 1869 to learn the rudiments of commodity trading. Later he worked as a journalist in Sydney before he came to Britain in 1896. Becke became a celebrated exponent of swashbuckling sea stories. He drew heavily upon his own colourful adventures as a youth (he was once tried for piracy upon the high seas alongside Captain Bully Hayes, an American buccaneer). *By Reef and Palm* (1894) was his first novel. He collaborated with Walter Jeffrey on

First Fleet Family (1896). Journalistic in tone, it is an authentic record of the territory of New South Wales in the early eighteenth century. *The Mutineers* (1898), again written with Jeffrey, is an *historical romance relating the mutineers' exploits aboard the *Bounty* and their subsequent settlement on Pitcairn Island. Twentieth-century film versions of the *Bounty* episode owe much to it. *The Adventures of a Supercargo* (1906) recalls his eventful boyhood in New South Wales. Reviewing *Notes from My South Sea Log* (1900), the *Times* caught the essential appeal of Becke's sub-Stevensonian stories about the Pacific Islands. 'Mr Becke paints them for us as they were of old. He shows us the natives not quite converted and the seas not quite policed, and the wastrels wandering from isle to atoll.' *Tom Wallis* (1900) is a swashbuckler featuring the Australian equivalent of one of G. A. *Henty's youthful heroes. Somewhat surprisingly, it was published in London by the Religious Tract Society: reviewing *The Ebbing of the Tide* (1896), the *National Observer* had suggested that Becke was 'of the fleshly school, but with a pathos and power not given to the ordinary professors of that school'. *Tessa* and *The Trader's Wife* are two novellas published in a single volume in 1901: the first celebrates, through the love of a young and friendless woman for an intrepid (and much older) seafarer, the spirit of empire ('Go through a file of Australian newspapers from the year 1806 to the year 1900 and you will see how unknown Englishmen have died, and are dying, in those wild islands, and how as they die, by club, or spear, or bullet, or fever, how easily the young hot blood of other men of English race impels them to step into the vacant places'); in the second, a sea captain arranges for his unfaithful wife to be marooned on a desert island with her villainous lover. *Breachley, Black Sheep* (1902) is the first-person rogue's narrative of an Australian Tom Jones; *Helen Adair* (1903) the story of a reformed rogue, a woman transported to Australia as a convict who ends up marrying her honest sea-dog employer after the death of his vain and shallow wife. The **Times Literary Supplement* praised the former as the kind of narrative demanded by the new interest in 'world politics and world geography', a demand which the old type of 'studio-made' romance could no longer satisfy; and subsequently condemned the latter as, in effect, a studio-made romance. *The Adventures of Louis Blake* (?1909) has the more comic tone of Becke's semi-autobiographical accounts of boyhood. During the final years of his life he suffered from recurrent bouts of malaria and was a chronic alcoholic. He died in Sydney. Becke was a curious and colourful character who listed as his recreations in *Who's Who* 'sea-fishing, shooting and ethnology'. The warm and informative obituary in the *Times* (19 Feb. 1913) concludes that 'his special gift was one which gave him a place in the company, if not quite of Mr *Conrad, at any rate of Mr Cutcliffe *Hyne and Mr *Bullen—the gift of picturesque and graphic portrayal from his own experiences of seafaring life in the uttermost parts of the world'.

BEDFORD, H. Louisa collaborated with E. *Everett-Green on several children's books, and herself published twenty-five volumes of pious juvenile fiction between 1896 and 1915, including *Maids in Many Moods* (1912): the maids leave England for New Zealand, and their moods are mostly romantic.

BEERBOHM, [Henry] Max[imilian] (1872–1956), Kt. (1939), married, first (1910), Florence Kahn (d. 1951), and, secondly (1956), Elisabeth Jungmann (d. 1959). The son of a corn merchant, he was educated at Charterhouse and at Merton College, Oxford. Half-brother of the actor-manager Sir Herbert Beerbohm-Tree (1853–1917), Beerbohm made an immediate impact on the London bohemian scene of the 1890s, with his essay in praise of artifice, 'A Defence of Cosmetics', which appeared in the first issue of the *Yellow Book* in 1894, a year after he had left Oxford without a degree. He became a prominent fin-de-siècle figure as an essayist—his first book, boldly entitled *The Works of Max Beerbohm* (1896), collected his seven published essays—, parodist in *A Christmas Garland* (1912), caricaturist (specializing in drawings of literary, political, and theatrical celebrities), and dandy. He was a disciple of Oscar Wilde (1856–1900), most obviously in his Regency fairy tale, *The Happy Hypocrite*, published in the *Yellow Book* in 1896. With the passing of the *Yellow Book* and its successor, the *Savoy*, Beerbohm began writing for the more staidly middle-class *Daily Mail*, and in April 1898 he succeeded G. B. Shaw (1856–1950) as theatre critic for the *Saturday Review*, a job he held until 1910, when he went to live at Rapallo in Italy with his first wife; *Around Theatres* (1924) was his own selection of his reviews. During the Second World War he returned to Britain and became a successful broadcaster. Beerbohm's only novel, **Zuleika Dobson, or, An Oxford Love Story* (1910), was an elegant and extravagant memoir of Oxford life and the London literary scene in the 1890s, with shades of '*Ouida', whom he much admired, in the characterization of the beautiful adventuress laying all low before her. Beerbohm's literary importance is partly as a witness (in words and drawings) of Edwardian England. His satirical reminiscence of literary figures such as 'Enoch Soames' and 'Savonarola Brown' in *Seven Men* (1919) is an astute and witty dissection of the tactics used by would-be artists in the modern, commercial world of letters; and his caricatures of the prominent writers of the time equally capture the absurdity of literary fame. As a young man he enjoyed the shock value of the 1890s literary scene—the dandyism, aestheticism, and decadence—but his own status was always detached, ironic, and elusive, involving a refusal to delineate distinctions between fact and fiction, memory and imagination. As he writes in his second collection of essays, *More* (1899), 'Well! For my own part, I am a dilettante, a *petit maître*. I love best in literature delicate and elaborate ingenuities of form and style.'

BEGBIE, [Edward] Harold (1871–1929) married Gertrude SEALE. Born in Suffolk, fifth son of a Church of England clergyman, he tried to become a poet, but after various rebuffs became instead a very popular journalist and political commentator. His first job was on the staff of the *Globe*. He was the author of a number of books for children. His adult fiction is anodyne and diverse, with a consistent emphasis on the steadying effects of religion. *Racket and Rest* (1908), for example, features a young woman from the chorus line who rises to be a star of musical comedy, deserts her suburban husband and their child, falls in with a dissolute man-about-town, and is eventually redeemed through the pious influence of her husband's widowed mother. *The Challenge* (1911) is that presented by India to the young wife of a dull civil servant: spirituality enables her to meet it. Other challenges involve an unhappy marriage, in *The Cage* (1909); alcoholism, in the bestselling *Broken Earthenware* (1909); and the Romanizing methods of the 'Secret Society of Nicodemus', in *The Priest* (1906). Begbie held the view that the Church of England was in danger from its Anglo-Catholic wing. His first novel, *The Curious and Diverting Adventures of Sir John Sparrow, Bart.* (1902), is a light-hearted treatment of a favourite Edwardian theme: the dangers of open-mindedness. The hero, an amiable baronet, a Don Quixote in modern London, flirts successively with vegetarianism, theosophy, the 'natural life', and Zionism. *The Distant Lamp* (1913) is a *historical romance about the children's crusade. Begbie also published *On the Side of the Angels* (1915), controverting Arthur *Machen's claim that the legend of the Angels of Mons derived from a story written by Machen. The German novelist Ernst Jünger (1895–) praised in his diary (17 Sept. 1942) the discussion of alcoholism as a spritual weakness in Begbie's *Broken Earthenware* (1909). Like *'Saki' Begbie wrote a political satire in the form of a parody of *Alice in Wonderland*; Begbie's, which was written with J. S. Ransome and M. H. Temple as 'Caroline Lewis', was called *Clara in Blunderland* (1902). He also sometimes published anonymously.

Belchamber, H. O. *Sturgis, 1904, Constable. A critique of fashionable society. 'Sainty' Belchamber, heir to a fortune and an estate, is a man with radical sympathies. Outclassed in all the gentlemanly pursuits by his younger brother, Arthur—'He rode, as he ate rice pudding, because he had to'—he feels a certain relief when he is crippled in a riding accident. Disability is the perfect excuse to leave the responsibilities of wealth and privilege to Arthur. Bullied at Eton, blissfully happy at Cambridge, Sainty is pitched back on his 21st birthday into the social whirl. The misdemeanours of the fast set appal him. Arthur is trapped into a disastrous marriage to a music-hall artiste, and disavowed by their puritanical mother. Instead of happily yielding to Arthur, Sainty must now bend all his efforts to preventing the actress from becoming the next Duchess. His ugliness and his principles make it hard to find a wife. Cissy Eccleston accepts him; but on their wedding night she makes it plain that she will not sleep with him, and, desperate to avoid the scandal of a divorce, Sainty agrees that they should lead separate lives. She proceeds to dissipate his fortune, and soon embarks on an affair with Sainty's cousin, Claude Morland. Cissy has a child by Claude, which she passes off as Sainty's. This child becomes his only consolation. When the child dies tragically, Cissy declares that she is going to leave him for Claude. Claude, however, has other ideas, and is already engaged to a wealthy heiress. Cissy and Sainty cannot escape each other. *Belchamber* was Sturgis's third novel. After withering criticism from Henry *James, he never wrote another. It may simply be that he tried too hard. The novel's wit, for example, is punctuated by some remarkably portentous chapter-openings: 'The world is like a huge theatrical company in which half the actors and actresses have been cast for the wrong parts,' and so on.

BELL, Mrs Hugh, or (after 1904), BELL, Lady: Florence Eveleen Eleanore OLLIFFE (1851–1930), DBE (1918), married (1876) Thomas Hugh BELL (1844–1931), who succeeded (1904) as 2nd Baronet. Born in Paris, where her father served as physician to the British Embassy, she married a businessman who owned a colliery in north Yorkshire; by his first wife he was father of the Arabic scholar and traveller Gertrude Bell (1868–1926). Bell wrote books for both adults and children many of which contained advice on parlour games and pastimes for adults as well as children. *French-Without-Tears* (1895–7) was a very popular series of textbooks. *Pauline's First Reading Book About Tom & Jane & Their Naughty Friend* (1912) is one of her story-books for children. She also wrote several plays, such as *Time Is Money* (1905) with Arthur Cecil, and *The Way the Money Goes* (1910). The promiscuity of the heroine of her New Woman novel, *The Story of Ursula* (1895), was considered immoral by the reviewers. *Miss Tod and the Prophets* (1898) is more light-hearted, concerning an ageing spinster who seeks the 'good life' before a meteorite obliterates the planet, and is left in dire financial straits when the predicted collision does not happen. *The *Arbiter* (1901) is a more serious study of marital breakdown and reunion. Other novels include *The Dean of St Patrick's* (1903), *Down with the Tariff! A Tale of Free Trade* (1908), and *The Good Ship Brompton Castle* (1915). In 1907 Lady Bell conducted a survey of working-class families in Middlesbrough, published as *At the Works: A Study of a Manufacturing Town*. Her collected essays and articles 1894–1922 were published as *Landmarks* (1929). She was a great friend of Elizabeth *Robins (though they disagreed about female suffrage), who describes in a tribute in the *Times* (17 May 1930) 'following her through the black streets and alleys of a coal-mining community, where doors flew open and women and children rushed out to meet the wife of the ironmaster...'

BELL, R[obert] S[tanley] Warren (1871–1921) married (1905) Edithe M. BARRY. Born at Long Preston, Yorkshire, in 1871, Bell was the son of a Church of England clergyman and the brother of 'Keble *Howard'. He was educated at St John's School, Leatherhead, read for the Bar, and worked in a school before taking to literature. Bell was editor (1899–1910) of *The Captain: A Magazine for Boys and Old Boys*, a publication designed to feature articles to entertain rather than edify boys. Frank *Swinnerton described it as full of 'stories and articles fit to be read by the self-respecting of tender years'. There, and in other magazines such as the *Gem* and *Chums*, he published boys' school stories of the usual type. Later he tried to earn his living as a playwright. Bell wrote many flimsy comic novels for adults, including *The Cub in Love* (1897), *The Papa Papers* (1897), *Batchelorland* (1899), and *Love the Laggard* (1901). The latter is the comic tale of a bright young socialite spurning an eligible millionaire. Later works in a similar mould include *Jim Mortimer* (1904), *The Duffer* (1905), *Cox's Cough Drops* (1906), *Green at Greyhouse* (1908), and *Dormitory Eight* (1914). In 1915 he applied to the Royal Literary Fund for a grant.

Bella Donna: *A Novel*, Robert *Hichens, 2 vols., 1909, William Heinemann. Mrs Ruby Chepstow, heroine of a gruesome divorce case, 42 years old, but a subtle actress, decides to 'let the ugly side of her nature run free with a loose rein, defiant of the world'. She manages to captivate Nigel Armine, younger brother of Lord Harwich. He thinks he is the man to reclaim her; she thinks he will succeed to his brother's title. He owns some land in Egypt, and the scene switches to that favourite location for *exotic tales. On the boat out, they run across Mahmoud Baroudi, a physically and mentally 'compelling' Turco-Egyptian millionaire, who secretly hates the British and regards women from an 'Oriental' point of view. Ruby is duly compelled by Baroudi, and sets about disposing of her husband by means of a menu of subtle poisons. In the nick of time he is rescued by an equally compelling physician, who is in Egypt on vacation, and to whom we were introduced in the novel's opening sentence. 'Doctor Meyer Isaacson had got on as only a modern Jew, whose home is London, can get on, with a rapidity that was alarming. He seemed to have arrived as a bullet arrives in a body.' In desperation, Ruby confesses her love for Baroudi, and announces that she will once again let the ugly side of her nature run free by throwing herself at him. Baroudi, however, in his 'Oriental' way, has lost interest in her, and dismisses her brusquely. She stumbles off alone into the desert.

BELLOC, [Joseph] Hilaire [Pierre René] (1870–1953) married (1896) Elodie Agnes HOGAN (d. 1914). Born in France of a French father and an English mother, and obliged to spend eighteen months as a conscript in the French army, Belloc was educated at the Oratory School and Balliol College, Oxford, but always felt alienated from the English establishment. He began his professional writing career as a versifier, publishing in 1896 both *Verses and Sonnets* and the deliciously cruel *The Bad Child's Book of Beasts*, illustrated by his Oxford friend Lord Basil Blackwood (1870–1917). The latter parody of Victorian moral texts had a number of sequels—*More Beasts for Worse Children* (1897), *A Moral Alphabet* (1899), *Cautionary Tales* (1907), and *More Peers* (1911). *Danton* (1899) was the first of his many biographical studies of the French Revolution; *The Path to Rome* (1902), an account of Belloc's walk to the city from France, was the first of his European travel books. In 1900 Belloc met G. K. *Chesterton, who shared his anti-imperialist view of the *Boer War, and they began collaborating on political essays and speeches (a double act nicknamed by G. B. Shaw the Chester–Belloc). Belloc was the Liberal MP for Salford, 1906–10 (while working as chief book-reviewer for the *Morning Post*), but by 1910 had become disillusioned by party politics (his own political views were spelt out most clearly in *The Servile State*, 1912), and in 1913 he founded (with G. K.'s brother Cecil Chesterton, 1879–1918) a political weekly, the *New Witness*, which was gleefully hostile to the Liberal establishment and prominent in uncovering the Marconi corruption scandal of 1912. Belloc's major impact on the public, though, came as a commentator on the First World War in *Land and Water* (a magazine dedicated to war coverage), where his reputation was that of a lucid, confident, inspiring patriot. Belloc had once hoped to become a history don at Oxford (and believed that his Catholicism was held against him) and he regarded his historical work as his most important writing, that least driven by the exigencies of the market. In such books as *The French Revolution* (1911) and *Europe and the Faith* (1920) (as well as in his travel books) Belloc developed his argument that the Catholic Church was the dynamic, spiritual centre of European history, an argument he believed to be essentially alien to the Protestant, commercially minded British. This belief also informed his contempt for the British political establishment, for Jewish financiers, for the effete middle classes, a contempt more powerfully expressed in his essays (collected in such volumes as *On Nothing*, 1908; *On Everything*, 1909; *On Anything*, 1910; *On Something*, 1910; and *On*, 1923) than in his rather crudely satirical novels (often illustrated by Chesterton): **Emmanuel Burden, Merchant* (1904), **Mr Clutterbuck's Election* (1908), *A *Change in the Cabinet* (1909), *Pongo and the Bull* (1910), and *The *Girondin* (1911). *The Green Overcoat* (1912) is one of Belloc's slighter fables. A psychology professor is setting off for home after a party when he realizes that his overcoat is missing. The devil tempts him to borrow a striking green coat, which the professor vows to send back as soon as he gets home. On his way there, though, he is kidnapped by two men who have been lying in wait for the coat's owner. The professor, removed from his familiar social world and his usual psychological certainties, is forced to define himself and to prove who he is (and is not). Belloc's best-natured books were his accounts of his travels, such as *The Old Road* (1904) and *The Pyrenees* (1909); but, ironically, his most enduring have been verses for children. Mrs Belloc *Lowndes was his sister. There is a biography by A. N. Wilson (1984).

Beloved Vagabond, The, W. J. *Locke, New York, 1906, London, 1907, John Lane. A coming-of-age novel, which exuberantly celebrates the romance of bohemianism. The 'unwashed urchin' narrator, son of a drunken London washerwoman, is taken into service by the eccentric philosopher Paragot, manager of the bohemian Lotus Club, and renamed Asticot. He proceeds to live the vagabond European life, as Paragot returns to his native France and takes up with the travelling peasant musician Blanquette and the dog Narcisse. In the course of their travels the group meet Paragot's long-lost love, Joanna Rushworth, now Comtesse de Verneuil.

It is revealed that Paragot, born Gaston de Nerec, had sacrificed his love to save the honour of her father. After the death of the Comte de Verneuil and her discovery of the true story of his actions, Gaston and Joanna are re-engaged, but he is now unable to live conventionally and flees England for French rural life and marriage to Blanquette. Meanwhile, Asticot becomes a successful Parisian artist. The novel's bohemianism is half-hearted, indeed covertly puritanical: Paragot may be irreverent and absinthe-soaked, but he is also an old Rugbeian and a brilliant architect.

Benefactor, The: *A Tale of a Small Circle*, Ford Madox *Hueffer, 1905, Brown, Langham. Hueffer's second novel. George Moffat is an idealist—the novel he is writing, *Wilderspin*, about the discovery of America, is 'full of the open air, of the sea; yes, certainly of romance; of kindness, too, and a certain good-hearted braveness'—whose good works cause either resentment or unhappiness in those he helps and eventually ruin his life too. Having long ago lost his wife, who objected to his coterie of young men, and given up his career as a poet because he was too busy helping other people start theirs, Moffat now loses his latest protégé, the novelist Hailes, who bleeds him dry and is taken up by his sister-in-law (thus causing a rift between Moffat and his brother), and has to declare bankruptcy because of his generosity. In a final disaster Moffat, trying to cure his friend, the half-mad Reverend Brede, of his guilt complex, encourages him to return to ministerial work. Brede goes completely mad in the middle of a sermon, and Moffat, who is in love with Brede's daughter Clara, feels obliged to renounce his happiness with her, too.

BENNETT, [Enoch] Arnold (1867–1931) married (1907) Marie Marguerite SOULIE (b. 1874) (legally separated 1921). Born at Hanley, Staffordshire, eldest of six children of a solicitor who had formerly been a potter and a schoolmaster, he was brought up as a Wesleyan Methodist and educated at the Burslem Endowed School, the Middle School, Newcastle under Lyme, and an art school. He went into his father's office in 1885, and three years later moved to a London solicitors. He began working as a freelance journalist, and in 1893 began to write for the weekly journal *Woman*; he later wrote for the *Academy*. In these early years he owed a good deal to the encouragement of Eden *Phillpotts, with whom he worked on various abortive theatrical projects. In 1903 he went to live in Paris and there married a Frenchwoman; they returned to England in 1912, and adopted one of his orphan nephews in 1915. After the failure of his marriage he lived from 1922 with a former actress, Dorothy Cheston (1891–1978), who took the name Bennett by deed poll: they had a daughter in 1926. The epitome of the twentieth-century professional writer, Bennett had published by the time of his death thirty-seven novels, seven collections of short stories, fifteen plays, thirteen works of non-fiction, an autobiography, four volumes of essays, five volumes of letters, five travel books, and three volumes of journals. He had also served as director of the Ministry of Information during the First World War. Of his books, the most important are the series of novels which bring to life turn-of-the-century urban experience in the 'Five Towns' region around Stoke-on-Trent: **Anna of the Five Towns* (1902), **Leonora: A Novel* (1903), *The *Old Wives' Tale* (1908), **Clayhanger* (1910), **Hilda Lessways* (1911); and *These Twain* (1916). Much of his best work was semi-autobiographical—most notably his first novel, *A Man From the North* (1898). He always combined his career as a novelist with that of literary journalism. He was, in particular, a prolific and influential book-reviewer (most notably in the 'Books and People' series for the *Evening Standard*, 1926–31), in which role he represented a robust defence of middle-class taste. As a novelist Bennett was most influenced by French writers like Gustave Flaubert (1821–80), Émile Zola (1840–1902), and Guy de Maupassant (1850–93); his journals were inspired by those of the de Goncourt brothers, Edmond (1822–96) and Jules (1830–70). This appears in his aim of being 'true to life' through the use of social detail, through the narrative emphasis on the drab, the squalid, and the mundane, and is most obvious, perhaps, in some of the short stories collected in *Tales of the Five Towns* (1905), *The *Grim Smile of the Five Towns* (1907), and *The *Matador of the Five Towns* (1912). Bennett was an exceptionally versatile writer, even by Edwardian standards. He also published novels in a sensational vein, such as **Sacred and Profane Love: A Novel in Three Episodes* (1905), and **Whom God Hath Joined* (1906), a *marriage problem novel; light comedies, such as **Buried Alive: A Tale of Three Days* (1908), *The *Card: A Story of Adventure in the Five Towns* (1911), and its sequel, *The *Regent: A Five Towns Story of Adventure in London* (1913), *A *Great Man: A Frolic* (1904), and **Helen with the High Hand: An Idyllic Diversion* (1910); and a fantasy, *The *Glimpse: An Adventure of the Soul* (1909). Opposite the title-page of *The Regent*, there is a list of Bennett's fiction which distinguishes between the novels and short story collections described above, and a group of 'Fantasias'. The latter include the essentially pot-boiling romances he produced with great facility in the wake of the very successful *The *Grand Babylon Hotel: A Fantasia on Modern Themes* (1902): *The Gates of Wrath: A Melodrama* (1903); *Teresa of Watling Street: A Fantasia on Modern Themes* (1904); *The Loot of Cities: Being the Adventures of a Millionaire in Search of Joy: A Fantasia* (1905); *Hugo: A Fantasia on Modern Themes* (1906); *The Sinews of War: A Romance of London and the Sea* (1906); *The *Ghost: A Fantasia on Modern Themes* (1907); *The City of Pleasure: A Fantasia on Modern Themes* (1907); *The Statue* (1908); and *The Price of Love: A Tale* (1914). *Lord Raingo* (1926) was a political novel. He also wrote plays, most successfully *Milestones* (1912), written with Edward Knoblock (1874–1945). In her 1925 critique of the work of Bennett and his fellow 'materialists', *Galsworthy and *Wells, Virginia Woolf (1882–1941) wrote that 'they write of unimportant things . . . they spend immense skill and immense industry making the trivial and the transitory appear the true and the enduring.' For Bennett (who regarded himself as a socialist), people are the product of their material and social environment; the task of the novelist is, therefore, to describe that environment as precisely as possible, without passing moral or aesthetic comment.

BENSON, A[rthur] C[hristopher] (1862–1925) was the eldest of the three writing sons of Edward White Benson (1829–96), the prominent Victorian churchman who became Archbishop of Canterbury in 1883. A. C. Benson himself went to Eton College and King's College, Cambridge, and followed an academic career, first as a master at Eton and then, from 1904, as a Fellow of Magdalene College, Cambridge (of which he was Master 1915–25). However, his published work (some sixty books between 1890 and 1925) was hardly academic—his most scholarly work was his two-volume life (1898) of his father—rather, it was belles-lettres, comfortable and readable reflections on life, art, and literature. Forrest *Reid remembered that in 1905 'everybody was reading, or had read, *The Upton Letters*, which had been published anonymously, though of course the authorship was known at Cambridge. I hadn't read them and was uninterested. "Is it a book there is any necessity to read?" [someone asked,] unluckily putting the question to . . . Benson, who . . . replied with perfect urbanity, "Not in the least." ' Published under the pseudonym 'T. B.', *The Upton Letters* purport to be the letters addressed by a middle-aged bachelor schoolmaster to a male friend (a family man dying abroad), containing reflections on his reading, the modern novel, modern life, and the pros and cons of classical education. *Watersprings* (1913) has a Cambridge don as hero. Fortyish, cheerful, competent, he has never had any close relationships, or written his book on the psychological significance of religious celibacy, until he feels strangely attracted to Jack Sandys, a handsome undergraduate. His passion is displaced onto Jack's sister, whom, after some conventional delay, he marries. Both are seeking spiritual consolation; their child dies; they trust in a larger hope. Such collections as *From a College Window* (1906) and *Beside Still Waters* (1907) gave him a significant literary reputation (and income), though he is probably best known now as the author of 'Land of Hope and Glory', the words sung to March No. 1 of *Pomp and Circumstance* by Sir Edward Elgar (1857–1934). Benson's diaries, and letters to such friends as Henry *James and Edmund Gosse (1849–1928), suggest that in private he had a caustic wit which rarely appears in his public output. James called him 'big and red and rough as to surface . . . but . . . ever so refined inwardly.' He encouraged the young Hugh *Walpole. He was a depressive, a note which appears in the stories in *The Hill of Trouble and Other Stories* (1903) and *The Isles of Sunset* (1905). He published more fiction after the First World War. He was a shareholder in the publishing firm Sidgwick & Jackson, founded by his cousin Frank Sidgwick (d. 1939), brother of Ethel *Sidgwick.

BENSON, E[dward] F[rederic] (1867–1940). Brother of A. C. *Benson and R. H. *Benson, he was educated at Marlborough College and

King's College Cambridge, and worked as an archaeologist in Greece and Egypt (1892–5). The commercial success of his first novel, *Dodo* (1893), a comedy about high society, whose brilliant heroine was allegedly based on Margot Tennant (1864–1945), later Countess of Oxford, led him to writing fiction full-time; thereafter he published a book a year. Many of these reflect the demands of the market—short sentimental tales, historical romances, school and college stories such as *David Blaize* (1916) and its two sequels, novels about the corrupting effects of money on marriage and morality (as in *Money Market* (1898) and *Mammon and Co.* (1899), and ghost stories. *The Princess Sophia* (1900) is a *Ruritanian romance; *The Challoners* (1904) is a sentimental tale about an austere, repressed clergyman, Sidney Challoner, whose beautiful, talented son and daughter disappoint him bitterly, one by becoming an acclaimed pianist and a convert to Catholicism, the other by falling in love with an atheist. *The *Climber* (1912) is another novel of modern English life. His Mapp and Lucia series, published between 1920 and 1935, are probably E. F. Benson's best known works. Comic novels about the genteel rivalries of ladies in the English provinces, they are mostly set in the country town of Tilling, based on Rye in Sussex, where Benson lived, in Henry *James's former house, and of which he was mayor (1934–7). *As We Were* (1940) is a memoir of his Victorian youth.

BENSON, R[obert] H[ugh] (1871–1914). Younger brother of A. C. *Benson and E. F. *Benson, he was educated at Eton College and Trinity College, Cambridge. When he was 11 their father became Archbishop of Canterbury. At Cambridge he began to read for the Indian Civil Service, but failed his exam and instead studied theology; he was ordained in the Church of England in 1895, while working at the Eton Mission in the East End of London. He became an Anglican monk in 1898. In 1903, after a decade of doubt and introspection, he converted to Roman Catholicism. His religious views were expressed in a series of somewhat lush historical novels and contemporary studies. *The King's Achievement* (1905) is a *historical romance set in the reign of Henry VIII and concerns two brothers, Ralph and Chris Torridon, one of a worldly, the other of a mystical, disposition. Ralph becomes a henchman of Thomas Cromwell and dies in jail. With *The Sentimentalists* (1906), Benson, as the **Times Literary Supplement* pointed out, exchanged the Reformation for the twentieth century, the 'oak settle' for the 'chintz-covered sofa'. The anti-hero, Christopher Dell, sentimentally tries out attitudes without ever believing any of them. Two men compete to reveal his true self: Dr Rolls, a sinister 'doctor of souls', and the more sympathetic Father Richard Yolland, who has loved Christopher since their student days. Benson's novels became increasingly didactic. *The Lord of the World* (1908) is set in Europe in the twenty-first century, when the tyranny of socialism and the religion of humanity is only opposed by an underground Catholic Church; the climax is Apocalypse. *The Necromancers* (1909) expounds a theory of spiritualism, while *The Conventionalists* (1908) is little more than a religious tract. But there had always been a strain of doctrinaire mysticism in his writing: *Light Invisible* (1903), for example, consists of a series of conversations between a visionary priest and an extremely patient listener. Two novels published in 1912 indicate the limits of Benson's achievement: *Come Rack! Come Rope!*, concerns the persecution of Catholics in Derbyshire between 1579 and 1588; *The Coward* is a **Four Feathers*-type tale about a man whose rigid family traditions label him a coward, but who in fact displays plenty of less orthodox moral courage. *The Mirror of Shalott* (1907) is a collection of ghost stories recounted to each other by a group of priests. Benson was a friend and supporter of Fr. *Rolfe, until the Roman Catholic authorities put a stop to his association with so controversial a figure. In 1911 he became Private Chamberlain to Pius X.

BENTLEY, E[dmund] C[lerihew] (1875–1956) married (1902) Violet BOILEAU (d. 1949). Educated at St Paul's School and Merton College, Oxford, Bentley was President of the Oxford Union (1898) and was called to the Bar in 1902. But he became instead a highly successful journalist, working for the *Daily News* 1902–12 and as a leader-writer for the *Daily Telegraph* (1912–34). His lasting fame is as the inventor of the light verse epigram, the Clerihew. This form—a witty combination of two rhymed couplets, purportedly biographical—first appeared in his *Biography for Beginners* (1905), illustrated by his friend G. K. *Chesterton. His only fiction in this period is the classic detective story **Trent's Last Case*

(1913), which was both an ironic commentary on the genre itself and an excellently plotted mystery. Philip Trent, the artist detective, later appeared in short stories and a less distinguished novel, *Trent's Own Case* (1936). Bentley wrote an autobiography, *Those Days* (1940). The writer and cartoonist Nicolas Bentley (1907–1978) was his son.

BERESFORD, J[ohn] D[avys] (1873–1947) married Beatrice ROSKAMS. The son of a Church of England clergyman, he was educated at Oundle School and trained as an architect, practising for some years before going to work in advertising. As a child he had infantile paralysis, and was lame for the rest of his life. He did not become a full-time writer until quite late, at 40. He was thereafter highly prolific, usually producing a couple of volumes a year. Dorothy Richardson (1873–1957) described him as 'a mildly intellectual collector of new thought-systems in each of which, in turn, he would for a while feel himself possessed of steering-gear'. During the First World War he expressed pacifist views. He was a friend and supporter of D. H. *Lawrence. His first two books appeared in the same year: *The Hampdenshire Wonder* (1911) is a fantasy about a boy who wishes (as Beresford had as a child) to be as full of knowledge as the *Encyclopaedia Britannica*, and is mysteriously murdered. *The *Early History of Jacob Stahl* (1911) is the first volume of the trilogy continued in *A Candidate for Truth* (1912) and *The Invisible Event* (1915). These books, clearly written under the influence of H. G. *Wells's **Tono-Bungay* and Samuel *Butler's *The *Way of All Flesh*, reflected Beresford's own experience. In *Goslings* (1913) a plague has struck the East and Europe, killing almost all the men, resulting in social breakdown, only alleviated by the arrival of a boatload of Americans. His greatest success was *The *House in Demetrius Road* (1914), a meticulous study of the shifting relationships between the three inhabitants of a suburban villa. Beresford was a craftsman who attempted to explore philosophical ideas through carefully organized fictions.

BESANT, Walter (1836–1901), Kt. (1895), married (1874) Mary Garrett FOSTER-BARHAM (d. 1904). The son of a Hampshire merchant, he attended grammar school in his home town of Portsea and in Stockwell, then studied at King's College, London, and Christ's College, Cambridge, before going to Mauritius as Senior Professor at Royal College (1861–67). On his return, Besant was appointed Secretary of the Palestine Exploration Fund (a post he held until 1885). He was subsequently honorary secretary. He regularly contributed to the *Daily News* from 1868 to 1874. In 1871 he collaborated with E. H. Palmer (1840–82) on a historical piece, *Jerusalem: The City of Herod and Saladin*. Another joint project, this time with James Rice (1843–82), the editor of *Once a Week*, produced *Ready-Money Mortiboy* (1872), a bestselling novel and the first of fourteen volumes of fiction written by the pair. Rice had been chiefly responsible for the story-lines of their joint works; after his death Besant's novels show a shift to a broader canvas that emphasized historical and sociological perspectives, for example *Dorothy Forster* (1884), a tale of Jacobite insurrection, and *For Faith and Freedom* (1888), about Monmouth's rebellion. *The *Fourth Generation* (1900) is a novel deeply influenced by Henrik Ibsen (1828–1906), which depicts the labyrinthine nature of the child–parent relationship. One of his last novels, *The Alabaster Box* (1900), portrays the son of a loan-shark whose conscience leads him to try and atone for his father's unscrupulous treatment of impoverished Londoners. Many consider *Dorothy Forster* Besant's best fictional work. His obituary in the *Times* (11 June 1901) calls it 'a capital story' although it 'does not re-create an epoch the way Scott or Thackeray would, nor does it take possession of the reader as the works of a great master [would]'. *All Sorts and Conditions of Men* (1882) and *Children of Gibeon* (1886) highlight social ills in the East End of London and clearly demonstrate Besant's desire for social reform. He was the guiding spirit behind the foundation of 'The People's Palace' in 1887—a centre to promote education and recreation in London's East End community, which later became Queen Mary's College, London. The establishment in 1884 of the Society of Authors was a great personal achievement for Besant. He had long campaigned for legal and financial rights for authors and the elevation of their work to the status of a profession. In May 1890 Besant was the founding editor of the *Author*, the Society's periodical. He also wrote *The Society of Authors: A Record of Its Actions from Its Foundation* (1893) and *The Pen and the Book* (1899). In 1894 he commenced a work in emulation of *A Survey of London* (1598, 1603) by John Stow (1525–1605). Although he did not live to complete the *Survey* himself, the project was continued and published between 1902 and 1912. G. E. *Mitton was his assistant. Other later works include *Beyond the Dreams of Avarice* (1895), *The Orange Girl* (1899), *The Lady of Lynn* (1901), and *No Other Way* (1902). In *Who's Who* Besant rather whimsically listed 'looking on' as his major pastime. He died at home in Hampstead, London. The theosophist Annie Besant (1847–1933) was his sister-in-law.

BETHAM-EDWARDS, M[atilda Barbara] (1836–1919). Born at Westerfield in Suffolk, daughter of a gentleman farmer, she was a cousin of Amelia Ann Blanford Edwards (1831–92), the writer and Egyptologist, and was named after her mother's sister, Mary Matilda Betham (1776–1852), miniature-painter and author of *A Biographical Dictionary of the Celebrated Women of Every Age and Country* (1804). Although she attended school for a while Edwards was largely self-taught; she scoured the 'small but priceless' library at home. There was an unhappy period as a teacher in a seminary at Peckham, south London. She then went to Württemberg to study German and later to Frankfurt, Heidelberg, Vienna, and Paris. Her first book, *The White House by the Sea* (1857), was very popular. For a year after her father's death in 1864 she ran the family farm. In 1865 Edwards moved to London, where she met George Eliot (1819–80), who became a friend. *The Lord of the Harvest* (1899) contains many passages of poetic, evocative description of the East Anglian countryside. The novella records the ancient, often pagan, rituals associated with harvest. The following year *A Suffolk Courtship* was published, in which Edwards draws upon her own struggles to manage the family farm. The title is self-explanatory , the protagonists being 30-year-old Kezia Kersey and timid farmer Jack Foulger. Chapters tend to start with sentences like 'It is difficult for modern folk to appraise that talismanic charm, the spell of the fiddle in old-world country places.' *Mock Beggars' Hall: A Story* (1902) is another farming tale which concludes that the eponymous hall is well named, since we are all, rich and poor alike, beggars on this earth. She also wrote factual books about France, French literature, and the French countryside for which she had a lifelong passion, and was made *officier de l'instruction publique de France* in 1891. She also published *Poems* (1907), *Reminiscences* (1898), and *Mid-Victorian Memories* (1919). She was a Nonconformist of anti-clerical opinions. She was awarded a Civil List pension of £100, and obtained £200 from the Royal Literary Fund in 1907 to pay the doctor's bills after an operation for cancer. The *Times*'s obituary (7 Jan. 1919) concludes that 'she had no inconsiderable popularity as a novelist, though her fiction lacked the highest distinction'. She died at her home at Hastings, Sussex.

Better Sort, The, Henry *James, 1903, Methuen. Many of these eleven stories feature artists or reflect on the meaning of art in a commercial society. In 'The Beldonald Holbein', a woman who chooses ugly maids to offset her own carefully preserved beauty is mortified when her latest companion is taken up by painters as a perfect image from Holbein. In 'The Tone of Time' a woman commissions an imaginary picture of a husband she might have had; the painting turns out to be a vivid portrait of the man she and the painter had both loved years before. In 'The Special Type' a married man displays a woman as his mistress to goad his wife into divorcing him; she does, and, as he always intended, he marries someone else altogether. His discarded 'mistress', who loves him, takes as her payment for her help his portrait, so they can, at last, be alone together. In 'Broken Wings', a painter and writer, mutually attracted for years but in awe of each other's success, discover by chance that they both make their living, in fact, as hacks. In 'Flickerbridge' and 'The Papers', James attacks popular journalism and the craving for publicity; in 'The Birth Place' he mocks the use of literary reputation as a tourist attraction; in 'The Story in It' he debates the nature of literary appeal. 'The Two Faces' and 'Mrs Medwin' are slightly sour society anecdotes. But the centrepiece of this collection is 'The Beast in the Jungle', one of James's finest stories. John Marcher is told by his friend May Bartram to expect life to spring something unusual on him, like a beast out of the jungle. The years pass, they occasionally meet, nothing much happens to him. She remarks that she has identified the beast but that he will never know it. Later still she falls ill and suggests that she would live for him if she could, but dies. Returning some time later to the cemetery Marcher witnesses the uncontrollable grief of another mourner, and realises that May had loved him for himself but that he had been too self-centred to notice. He was destined to be the one man in the world to whom nothing happened—love was what might have happened; what had happened was that it didn't.

Beyond the Rocks: *A Love Story*, Elinor *Glyn, 1906, Gerald Duckworth. The novel marks a transition in Glyn's career from the first-person comedy of manners to third-person sexual romance. Blonde, blue-eyed (earlier heroines had had her own red hair and green eyes) Theodora Fitzgerald marries a rich elderly Australian, Josiah Brown, in order to repair her aristocratic father's fortunes, and tries her hardest to be a good wife. At Versailles, where the first part of the book is set, she meets a man of her own class, the handsome and well-bred Lord Bracondale, and falls in love with him. They continue to meet in England, on the country-house circuit, and Theodora decides that they must part. She writes a long, passionate letter of farewell, and a short note to her husband telling him that she will return to London. Her sworn enemy, Morella Winmarleigh, who resents her success with Lord Bracondale, switches the letters. Bracondale and Josiah both behave with great dignity, the former retiring to Alaska to shoot bears, accompanied by a bust of Psyche, Josiah dying slowly of a broken heart. The book received a mixed critical reception but enjoyed solid sales. It was filmed in 1922, with Gloria Swanson as Theodora and Rudolph Valentino as Lord Bracondale. Some liberties were taken with the original. Instead of dying unobtrusively of a broken heart, Josiah is brutally murdered while on safari in Africa. There are also some rather unexpected shots of Lord Bracondale galloping across the desert in a burnous, the studio having decided to introduce some unused sequences from Valentino's previous film, *The Sheik*.

BINDLOSS, Harold (1866–1945). Born in Liverpool, Bindloss spent more than a decade at sea and in Britain's various colonies, particularly in Africa, then settled in London in 1896 and began a career as a journalist. His first published book was a non-fictional account of African life, *In the Niger Country* (1898), but thereafter he used his experiences as the basis for stories of colonial adventure. Amazingly prolific (publishing two or three novels a year throughout the first decades of the century) his yarns have convincing geographical detail, and thus he supplied the continuing demand for credible imperial romance with such books as *The Concession-Hunters* (1902): 'Where Government official, scientific explorer, and capitalist's servant have followed and finished, the unknown, and sometimes rascally, adventurer has usually pointed the way.' The adventurer in question, Alexander Cummings, discovers a mahogany forest on the west coast of Africa and persuades a British company to invest in it. The resulting story is down-market *Conrad, with a full complement of desolate outposts, jungle-fever, steamers, and bullets-against-spears skirmishes. Bindloss juggled his frontiers skilfully: *His Master Purpose* (1903) has a Canadian setting, as does *The Impostor* (1905). *The Liberationist* (1908) returns to Portuguese West Africa, where red-faced Anglo-Saxon master purpose is contrasted with Iberian indolence. His other books include *A Wide Dominion* (1899), *Ainslie's Ju-Ju* (1900), *The Gold Trail* (1910), and *The Wastrel* (1913).

BINSTEAD, Arthur M[orris] (1861–1914) married ——. Born in London and educated there in private schools, he was co-editor of the *Sporting Annual*, and contributed to the *Sporting Times* a long series of sketches as 'Pitcher', collected in such volumes as *Pitcher in Paradise* (1903). He also founded and edited *Town Topics* in 1912. Other works include *Gal's Gossip* (1899), *More Gal's Gossip* (1901), and *Mop Fair: Some Elegant Extracts from the Private Correspondence of Lady Viola Drumcree* (1905). His *Collected Works* were published in two volumes (1927).

BIRMINGHAM, George A., *pseud.*: James Owen HANNAY (1865–1950) married (1889) Adelaide Susan WYNNE (d. 1933). An Ulsterman, he was educated at Haileybury and at Trinity College, Dublin; he graduated and was ordained deacon in 1887, priest in 1888. He was Rector of Westport, Co. Mayo from 1892 to 1913, where he scandalized his Protestant parishioners by learning Irish and joining the Gaelic League; he left after they boycotted him for political reasons. He was a friend of L. *Macmanus. He toured America and served as a chaplain in the First World War; later he worked as a clergyman in Kildare, Budapest, Somerset, and, from 1934, in London. His early fiction is passionate both in its defence of Irish national identity and in its attacks on the delusions generated by the pursuit of that identity. *The Seething Pot* (1905) and *Hyacinth* (1906) are both satires, the latter the picaresque tale of a young man, the son of a Protestant vicar in the west of Ireland, who proceeds to Trinity College, Dublin, where he approves the character but decries the aims and methods of a political agitator clearly based on Maud Gonne (1866–1953). He subsequently becomes a *Boer sympathizer, a traveller in woollens, and a curate in England who is drawn back to a sterile life in Ireland by mere nostalgia. In *Benedict Kavanagh* (1907), satire frequently lapses into glum polemic. The hero is the illegitimate son of a follower of Parnell, brought up by a Protestant clergyman, who achieves very little in life, and finally retires to a property left him by his mother in Co. Galway, where he is to dedicate himself to reforming the feckless villagers. *The Bad Times* (1909), about the Land League controversy of the 1870s and 1880s, remains indignant. But Birmingham tended increasingly to divert Irish themes into popular genres. *The Northern Iron* (1907) is a *historical romance set during the 1798 Rebellion. **Spanish Gold* (1908) is a florid, amusing adventure story. He also published some works of religious history under his own name.

BIRRELL, Olive M[ary] (1848–1926). Daughter of the minister of the Pembroke Baptist chapel at Wavertree, Liverpool, she devoted her life to social work. Her obituary in the *Times* (17 Feb. 1926) states that her fiction reveals her 'acquaintance with the trials and heroism of humble folk, among whom she laboured with self-sacrificing zeal'. The bulk of it is Victorian, but her last works are still of interest. **Love in a Mist* (1900) contains an unusual portrait of young working women, while *Nicholas Holbrook* (1902) is about a politician who owns slum property in a provincial town. Augustine Birrell (1850–1933), Liberal politician and author of a once-popular volume of literary essays, *Obiter Dicta* (1884), was her brother.

BLACK, Clementina [Maria] (1853–1923). At the age of 22 she assumed responsibility for her invalid father (formerly the town clerk of Brighton) and six younger siblings, and she was in her late 20s before she could devote much time to her own interests. In the early 1880s she moved to Bloomsbury, London, to live with her sisters, one of whom, Constance (1861–1946), married the critic Edward Garnett (1868–1937) and was an important translator of Russian fiction. Black found a job at the nearby London Museum and became interested in socialist, especially Fabian, politics, becoming secretary of the Women's Protective and Provident League (1886–8). She created the Consumers' League to root out low-wage-paying employers and initiated an 'Equal Pay' resolution at the Trades Union Congress of 1888. She and Frances Hicks founded the Women's Labour Bureau, building upon the rallying of women workers she had carried out during the 1880s. Further consolidation led to the Women's Industrial Council in 1894 (she was later its president). Her novel *An Agitator* (1894) relates the story of a socialist strike organizer who is wrongly incarcerated. Workers' and, more particularly, women's rights are discussed in *The Princess Desirée* (1896), and *The Pursuit of Camilla* (1899). *Caroline* (1908) is a costume drama which begins in 1774, when, before the impressionable eyes of young Caroline Dalyngrange, the dashing Gilbert Hardy, an admiral's nephew, rescues a mare from a blazing stable; ten years on, after Hardy has been falsely accused of running smuggled goods and of attempting to carry her off, she accepts his proposal of marriage. *The Linleys of Bath* (1911) is the biography of an eighteenth-century family. Black went on campaigning for women's rights well into the early twentieth century. In 1907 she published *Sweated Industry and the Minimum Wage. The Makers of our Clothes: A Case for Trade Boards* (1909), written with Adèle, Lady Meyer (d. 1930), was a more specific challenge to the profits of the industrialists: a through inquiry into working conditions and wages in the clothing trades—especially skilled needlework done for very poor return. In 1915 Black edited *Married Women's Work* for the Women's Labour League. She also translated from French and German and published *Kindergarten Plays (in Verse)* (1903).

Black Mask, The, E. W. *Hornung, 1901, Grant Richards. A second outing for the hyper-elegant A. J. Raffles, man-about-town, thief and 'finest slow bowler of his generation'. The first collection of tales, *The Amateur Cracksman* (1899), had ended with Raffles's cover blown: charged with stealing a priceless pearl aboard a steamer in the Mediterranean, he dives overboard somewhere near the Isle of Elba, and is presumed drowned. His faithful companion and chronicler, Bunny Manders, is put away for a spell in Wormwood Scrubs, and thereafter reduced to poverty. After a stormy romance in Italy, and an even stormier encounter with the Neapolitan branch of the Mafia, the Camorra, Raffles returns to London disguised as Mr Maturin, a bedridden Australian pensioner, and looking a great deal the worse for wear. He is reunited with Bunny when he advertises for a 'nurse and constant attendant', and they resume their criminal career with some success. The eight episodes which make up *The Black Mask* are the mixture as before, with as much emphasis on panache (though with intensifying suggestions of fallibility) as on the logistics of crime. In 'The Wrong House', Raffles and Bunny break into a boarding-school, are discovered, and make their escape on bicycles: 'the most sporting night we ever had in our lives'. The fallibility which overtakes Raffles is as much moral as physical. The outbreak of the *Boer War shows him the light. 'There was less crime in England that winter than for years past; there was none at all in Raffles. And yet there were those who could denounce the war!' He realizes that 'he had had his innings; there was no better way out'. The amateur cracksmen enlist in a cavalry regiment, and Raffles unmasks an enemy spy before being killed by a sniper's bullet. The third and final collection of Raffles stories, *A Thief in the Night* (1905), was something of an afterthought.

Black Peril, The, George Webb *Hardy, 1914, Holden & Hardingham. The publishers' advertisement announces *The Black Peril* as an 'outspoken work'—'The relations between the Black and White races are strongly displayed. A purposeful novel which should awaken the moral conscience of the Nation'—and its two epigraphs maintain the note of strenuousness. The first, from the Rt. Revd C. Gore, Bishop of Oxford, points out that statesmen 'do not know what to make of the Black Peril, and the Nationalist movement in China, India, and Africa'. The second is from W. E. Gladstone (1809–98): 'Corruption there must be, wherever there is not the utmost publicity.' Around these two themes, of the Black Peril (i.e. sexual relations between blacks and whites) and of the role of the press in pursuing corruption and injustice, Hardy built a somewhat exiguous narrative. Raymond Chesterfield, an Oxford-educated, widely travelled radical journalist, arrives in the South African colony of 'Zutal' (presumably Natal) and founds a campaigning newspaper which advocates racial, though not social, equality: 'To each individually according to his merits, his education, and his standing as a man—that is our view as regards both black and white.' Chesterfield lives at a boarding-house run by an alcoholic parson and his disaffected aristocratic wife, where his fellow-lodgers provide between them a variety of responses to his journalistic essays, and a romantic interest, in the shape of Mary Rosebery, a serious-minded 'modern' woman who has come to South Africa to get over a misplaced engagement. Chesterfield becomes convinced that it is his duty to expose the sexual threat posed to white women by the black men whom they take into their houses as servants—a threat the authorities seem determined to play down. His campaigning articles are condemned as obscene and he is thrown into gaol. Mary, who has herself been harassed by a black servant, returns to England, while Chesterfield writes fiery letters from gaol to an English friend denouncing the prison regime. Several years later, after his release, he too returns to England, and is reunited with Mary. The novel is remarkable for the passion of its commitment to racial equality—a commitment which in the end, however, baulks at the prospect of interracial marriage.

BLACKWOOD, Algernon [Henry] (1869–1951) was educated at Wellington College, by the Moravian Brotherhood, and briefly at Edinburgh University. He had an early interest in Buddhism. Although the child of upper-class parents (his father was Financial Secretary to the Post Office, his mother the widow of the 6th Duke of Manchester), Blackwood left Britain for North America in 1889, aged 20, and supported himself with numerous jobs including journalism on the New York *Evening Sun* and the *New York Times*. He returned to England in 1899, and became a full-time writer following the publication of his first collection, *The *Empty House and Other Ghost Stories* (1906); **John Silence* (1908) features a 'Psychic Doctor', a Sherlock Holmes of the occult. Blackwood lived in Switzerland from 1908 to 1914, served as an undercover agent during the First World War, and afterwards lived in Kent. From 1934 he worked for the BBC and became famous as 'the Ghost Man'. Blackwood's supernatural tales reflect both his journalistic experience of urban low life and his romantic belief in the mystical effect of nature;

his recurring theme is that ordinary people possess extraordinary powers. *Jimbo* (1909) is about the salutary influence of fantasy, and the stupidity of those who try to eliminate it by associating it in children's minds exclusively with terror. When Jimbo suffers a head-wound, he is trapped in a fantasy world which his governess has thoughtlessly peopled with monsters. The **Times Literary Supplement* thought the novel, 'in all sobriety, Shelleyan'. *The Education of Uncle Paul* (1909) continues the theme by exploring the re-education of a 45-year-old man in the value of childhood's 'vivid creative thought'; it is dedicated to 'all those children between the ages of eight and eighty who led me to "the crack"; and have since journeyed with me through it into the land "between yesterday and tomorrow"'. Another favourite theme was 'intellectual mysticism', either of a Faustian and necromantic flavour, as in *The Human Chord* (1910), or with pantheist and orientalist leanings, as in some of the stories collected in *Pan's Garden* (1912), or in *The Centaur* (1911), which is well supplied with epigraphs from (among others) William James (1842–1910), Walt Whitman (1819–92), Edward Carpenter (1844–1929), Henri Bergson (1859–1941), and F. W. H. Myers (1843–1901). In the latter, O'Malley, an Irishman with a roving newspaper commission in the Caucasus, encounters a Russian mystic whose psychic conflicts re-enact the dawn of the world when the Centaurs battled the Lapithae. There is a culminating vision in the mountains of central Asia. *Episodes Before Thirty* (1923) is an autobiography.

Blast: *The Review of the Great English Vortex* was published in two issues in 1914 and 1915. It was the outlet for a circle of young London artists, who had briefly formed the Rebel Art Centre, grouped around Percy Wyndham Lewis (1884–1957). He founded the magazine, recruited its contributors, designed its distinctive, dramatic graphics and layout, and wrote most of its manifestos and slogans. Lewis's most significant collaborator was Ezra Pound (1885–1972), who contributed his own poetry and the label 'Vorticism', which enabled Lewis to differentiate his movement from Futurism, with which it had much in common—the attack on nineteenth-century tradition, the interest in modern-day speed and light, violence and movement, the use of abstraction, the pursuit of publicity. Given its origins, *Blast* was, not surprisingly, organized around its artwork, but literary items in the first issue included an extract from Ford Madox *Hueffer's *The Good Soldier* (1915) and a feminist short story by Rebecca West (1892–1983), 'Indissoluble Matrimony'; and in the second, 'Preludes' and 'Rhapsody on a Windy Night' by T. S. Eliot (1888–1965).

BLATCHFORD, Robert [Peel Glanville] (1851–1943) married (1880) Sarah Crossley (d. 1921). He was born in Maidstone, Kent, the son of two actors; his father, a staunch Tory, named him after the Prime Minister Sir Robert Peel, 2nd Bt. (1788–1850). Blatchford, whose father died when he was 2, always maintained that he was educated 'nowhere', being taught by his mother as best she could as she travelled to find work in the theatre. At 14 he was apprenticed to a brushmaker, but, dissatisfied, left to join the army. Deeply influenced by his years in the 103rd Regiment of the Dublin Fusiliers (1871–77, and again for a short period in 1878; he reached the rank of sergeant), he expressed his affection for the army in the novel *Tommy Atkins of the Ramchunders* (1895). Blatchford worked for a while as a clerk in Northwich, before starting as a journalist on *Bell's Life in London* during 1885. The following year he moved to Manchester's *Sunday Chronicle*, which he left in 1891 because his socialist views were unacceptable to the proprietor. With his brother and fellow-journalists Alexander Mattock Thompson (1861–1948) and Edward Francis Fay (d. 1896) he raised £400 and founded a socialist weekly, the *Clarion*. The first issue appeared in December 1891. Blatchford wanted to expose the evils of the industrial north of England and to inform a new audience of the possibilities of bringing about social reform free from the jargon of the Marxists and the trade unionists. He often used the pseudonym 'Numquam' for his journalism. His 'Merrie England' articles epitomize this plain-speaking approach to what he called 'the labour problem'. These were collected and published under the title *Merrie England: A Series of Letters on the Labour Problem, Addressed to John Smith of Oldham, a Hard-Headed Workman, Fond of Facts* (1893), which sold 30,000 one-shilling copies. A penny edition followed and had sold 750,000 copies by the end of 1895. Yet such tremendous popular success did little to impress the Labour Party. In 1909 Ramsay MacDonald (1866–1937) dismissed *Merrie England* as simplistic: 'it was like a man fully explaining a motorcar by describing a wheelbarrow'. Rifts emerged for other reasons too. Blatchford's military training was deep-rooted, and he could not grasp the olive-branch mentality of the international socialists. His patriotism outweighed his socialism; he once said, 'I am ready to sacrifice Socialism for the sake of England, but never England for the sake of Socialism.' He had been in favour of the *Boer War, and in his column in the *Daily Mail* advocated action against Germany. Blatchford described himself late in life as a 'Tory democrat'; certainly he was not a common or garden socialist; his views were more akin to those of William Morris (1834–96) than to those of Karl Marx (1818–83). He was always a writer rather than a politician; a writer deeply concerned about the lot of the working classes. The Education Act of 1870 had created a fresh new audience which necessitated the shift away from the standard promulgations of the Victorian press. Blatchford was one of the first to make this shift; he fought passionately to empower the working people of Britain by making information accessible to them. His fiction includes *A Son of the Forge* (1894) and his best novel *The *Sorcery Shop: An Impossible Romance* (1907). Non-fiction includes *Britain for the British* (1902), *Not Guilty: A Plea for the Bottom Dog* (1905), and *As I Lay A-Thinking* (1927). He died at Horsham in West Sussex.

BLISSETT, Nellie K. published eight novels between 1896 and 1905. *Beggars' Luck* (1905) and *The Silver Key: A Romance of France and England 1669–70* (1905) are *Weymanesque *historical romances, while *The Bindweed* (1904) is *Ruritanian.

BLOUNDELLE-BURTON, John [Edward] (*c*.1848–1917) married Frances CHURCHMAN (d. 1910). After being educated for the army he travelled in North America and became a naval correspondent and special correspondent for the *Standard* newspaper. He also worked for the *World*. He was the author of numerous volumes of fiction between 1886 and 1915, mostly *historical romances with an emphasis on seafaring and derring-do, although he did write some modern novels. According to his obituary in the *Times* (12 Dec. 1917), he published more than sixty novels, which mostly came out first in serial form; the *British Library Catalogue* lists only thirty-four: no doubt some never made it between hard covers. Examples include *A Vanished Rival: A Story of To-Day* (1901), *A Woman from the Sea: A Romance of '93* (1907), and *Fortune's Frown: A Romance of the Spanish Fury* (1913).

Blue Lagoon, The: *A Romance*, H. de Vere *Stacpoole, 1908, T. Fisher Unwin. On his final voyage, a red-faced, superstitious old sailor (and old soak), Paddy Button, finds himself, after shipwreck, in a dinghy with two 8-year-old cousins, Dick and Emmeline Lestrange. They land on a paradisial South Seas island, and when, after preliminary adventures, Button falls into an alcoholic stupor and dies, the children are left to their own inevitable devices. According to one reviewer, their 'innocent mating' is 'as fresh as the ozone that has made them strong'. Indeed, their lovemaking is spontaneous, and all over before either of them realizes that it has begun. Only after the event do they begin to take an erotic interest in each other. 'Her breasts, her shoulders, her knees, her little feet, every bit of her he would examine and play with and kiss.' Made visible by Dicky's desire, Emmeline's body becomes the emblem of that desire. After a while, they are parents before they have stopped being children. The book's enduring appeal lies in its exhibition of sex without sexuality, and its recreation of a lost paradise—nothing intrudes upon the lovers' mutual absorption except poor old Paddy, and a handsome set of stone idols. The novel gave rise to several films.

Blue Review, The, was published in three issues in May, June, and July 1913, as a supplement/successor to *Rhythm*, the magazine founded in 1911 by John Middleton Murry (1889–1957) while he was an Oxford undergraduate. The sub-editors were Gilbert *Cannan, Frank *Swinnerton, and Hugh *Walpole. The first issue had a cover by Max *Beerbohm, and stories by Katherine *Mansfield and D. H. *Lawrence ('The Soiled Rose'). Otherwise the *Review* was undistinguished in both its criticism and its poetry.

BLUNDELL, Margaret: see under 'M. E. *Francis'.

BLUNDELL, Mary: see 'M. E. *Francis'.

BLUNDELL, Mrs Francis: see 'M. E. *Francis'.

BLYTH, James (1864–1933) was educated at King Edward VI's School, Norwich, and Corpus Christi College, Cambridge, and was the author of more than fifty volumes of fiction between 1904 and 1921. In 1908, for instance, he published

The Weaning, with T. Werner Laurie; *The Smallholder*, with Everett & Co.; *Rubina*, with John Long; *The Diamond and the Lady*, with Digby, Long & Co.; and (the only non-fiction he wrote) a collection of letters written by the poet and translator Edward FitzGerald (1809–83) to an old fisherman in Lowestoft, also with John Long. *The Smallholder* and *The Diamond and the Lady* make an interesting pair, in that they offer generically distinct treatments of the same theme, village life in Norfolk: the first, whose coarseness offended reviewers, is a realistic tale about a town-dweller's return to the land, the second a routine *crime story. Blyth also collaborated with Barry *Pain on *The Shadow of the Unseen* (1907) and *The Luck of Norman Dale* (1908).

BODKIN, M[atthias] McDonnell (1850–1933) married (1885) Arabella NORMAN. The son of a Galway doctor, he was educated at Tullabeg Jesuit College before attending the Catholic University as an exhibitioner. He subsequently studied law, was called to the Irish Bar, and was a County Court judge in Clare 1907–24. He was Nationalist MP for North Roscommon 1892–5. He is best known for a series of *crime stories: *Paul Beck: The Rule of Thumb Detective* (1899), *Dora Myrl: The Lady Detective* (1900), *The Capture of Paul Beck* (1909), and *Young Beck: A Chip Off the Old Block* (1911). To begin with, Dora Myrl, his female detective, radiates independence; she carries a small revolver and can pick a lock with a hairpin. But in *The Capture of Paul Beck* she meets Bodkin's other protagonist, Paul Beck, the 'greatest detective alive'. Although they are on opposite sides, and she pursues her side vigorously, often by means of some strenuously independent bicycling, she eventually assumes a subservient role. The 'capture' that matters for her is not of the criminal, but of the hero in marriage. Dora does have the consolation of producing the next generation of detectives, in the shape of Young Beck. Bodkin's other fiction includes some passionate *historical romances including two about the uprising of 1798 (*Lord Edward Fitzgerald*, 1896, and *The Rebels*, 1897), *A Madcap Marriage* (1906), *Recollections of an Irish Judge* (1914), and *When Youth Meets Youth* (1920). He also wrote, as 'Crom a Boo', *Poteen Punch* (1890) a collection of Irish after-dinner stories. He died in Dublin.

Boer War. The war declared by the Boer Republics on 11 October 1899 gave the British, in Rudyard *Kipling's words, 'no end of a lesson'. Expected to be over by Christmas, it dragged on until 1902. It was the costliest (over £200 million) and bloodiest (22,000 British, 25,000 Boer, and 12,000 African lives) Britain fought between 1815 and 1914. For many British writers, the Boer War was just the latest in a long series of small colonial wars which served as up-to-date settings for traditional coming-of-age sagas. See, for example: J. H. M. *Abbott, *Tommy Cornstalk* (1902); A. St John *Adcock, *The Luck of Private Foster* (1900); Captain F. S. *Brereton, *With Rifle and Bayonet: A Story of the Boer War* (1900); Mrs B. M. *Croker, *The Old Cantonment and Other Stories of India and Elsewhere* (1905); G. A. *Henty, *With Roberts to Pretoria* (1902); E. W. *Hornung, *The *Black Mask* (1901); Anna *Howarth, *Nora Lester* (1902); Fergus *Hume, *A Traitor in London* (1900); Bertram *Mitford, *Aletta: A Tale of the Boer Invasion* (1900); Hume *Nisbet, *The Empire Makers* (1900); Morley *Roberts, *Taken by Assault* (1901); Gordon *Stables, *On War's Red Tide* (1900); John Strange *Winter, *Blaze of Glory* (1902). Two public-school novels of the period end with heroic deaths in South Africa: B. and C. B. *Fry's *A Mother's Son* (1907) and Horace Annesley *Vachell's *The *Hill* (1905). However, the difficulties (indeed, the humiliating setbacks) the army experienced in subduing a numerically and logistically inferior enemy gave focus and dramatic expression to widespread anxieties about Britain's ability to fulfil its imperial destiny. A number of writers (J. H. M. Abbott, Andrew *Balfour, Erskine *Childers, Winston *Churchill, A. G. *Hales, Rudyard *Kipling, 'Francis *Prevost', Edgar *Wallace) witnessed the war at first hand and harboured few illusions about its conduct (Hales's *Driscoll, King of Scouts*, 1901, for example, contains sharp criticism of the British army's organization and tactics). Some commentators blamed the class system, others the degeneration of the race. Some (Hilaire *Belloc, G. K. *Chesterton, 'Vernon *Lee', L. *Macmanus, George *Meredith, 'Robert *Tressall') doubted the imperial destiny itself. Silas *Hocking and Edna *Lyall published passionately anti-war novels. J. H. M. Abbott, in **Letters from Queer Street* (1908), 'Austin *Clare', in *The Tideway* (1903), '*Handasyde', in *For the Week End* (1907), W. Somerset *Maugham, in *The *Hero* (1901), and H. G. *Wells, in *The Passionate Friends* (1913), described the moral and social indiscipline produced by experience of war. Major Ferdinand *Peacock's *When the War Is O'er* (1912) is a good deal sunnier. Depictions of the home front were on the whole fairly bleak. See, for example: A. St John Adcock, *In the Wake of the War* (1900); Robert *Cromie, *Kitty's Victoria Cross* (1901); W. L. *George, *The Making of an Englishman* (1914); 'Lucas *Malet', *The *Far Horizon* (1906); Compton *Mackenzie, **Sinister Street* (1913–14). Even a writer like 'Richard *Dehan', whose bestselling *The *Dop Doctor* (1910) defined the war as the catalyst of individual and collective regeneration, knew that there had been plenty to regenerate. Charles *Gleig's *When All Men Starve* (1899), in which the Boers and the Germans join forces against the British, and Guy *Boothby's *A Cabinet Secret* (1901), about the kidnap of the general appointed to lead the British forces in South Africa, are among the earliest of the many warnings about international conspiracy to be uttered in Edwardian *spy fiction (see also *political fiction). However, Alfred *Austin's **Haunts of Ancient Peace* (1902) was to offer some reassurance in its celebration of enduring English virtues. Perhaps the strangest Boer War novel of all is Ménie Muriel *Dowie's **Love and His Mask* (1901), whose heroine corresponds with a major-general in the South African field force in the hope of establishing, at a healthy distance, an ideal friendship. Surveying the contemporary novel in 1911, H. G. Wells suggested that the Boer War marked the dividing-line between the assurance of Victorian fiction and the doubting, sceptical note of Edwardian fiction.

BOLDREWOOD, Rolf, *pseud*.: Thomas Alexander BROWN (1826–1915), who changed his surname (1860s) to BROWNE and married (1861) Margaret Maria RILEY. Born in London, son of a shipmaster who emigrated to Sydney in 1831, he was educated at Sydney College and in 1844, after his father's ruin, became a rancher, which he remained, with varying success, until 1869. In 1871 he was made police magistrate, and in the following year was commissioner, at the new and unruly gold-fields at Gulgong. He served as magistrate in various stations until his retirement in 1895. He wrote from about 1870, beginning early in the morning before the day's work began. Of his best-known work, he told a friend 'I am also writing a rather sensational novel in the *Sydney Mail* called "Robbery Under Arms". A man with eight children and a limited income must do all he can to supplement the income.' It was published serially 1882–3 and in England in 1888 with great success. Browne used his pseudonym for a series of novels and stories that reflected his experiences as a squatter and magistrate in the Australian gold-fields. His later works include *The Ghost Camp* (1902) and *The Last Chance* (1905). His eldest daughter Rose published, as 'Rose Boldrewood', *The Complications at Collaroi* (1911).

BOLDREWOOD, Rose: see under 'Rolf *Boldrewood'.

BONE, David W.: see under Gertrude *Bone.

BONE, Gertrude: Gertrude Helena DODD (1876–1962) married (1903) Muirhead BONE (1876–1953), Kt. (1937). Daughter of a Wesleyan minister who had once been a blacksmith, she was brought up in Glasgow, where her brother, Francis Dodd (1874–1949), met her future husband at Garnett Hill School: both were to be prominent figures in the early twentieth-century revival of etching; her son, Stephen Bone (1904–1958), was also an artist; Ford Madox *Hueffer mentions Muirhead Bone in *Return to Yesterday* (1931) as one of the 'group of serious and advanced individuals' in the circle of Richard Garnett (1835–1906). They were friends of *Conrad. Her first published fiction was *Provincial Tales* (1904); the first of her three novels was *Women of the Country* (1913), a gentle, meticulously observed story about an unmarried, middle-aged cottager, Ann Hilton, and the interest she takes in a pretty young woman, Jane Evans, who is seduced and made pregnant by the squire and dies in the local infirmary. It is notable for its decisive but unsensational focus on the experience of women: the male characters have walk-on parts only. Muirhead Bone's brother, David W. Bone, an officer in the merchant navy, was the author of some nautical fiction, including *The Brass-Bounder* (1910).

Book of Wonder, The: *A Chronicle of Little Adventures at the Edge of the World*, Lord *Dunsany, 1912, William Heinemann. Twelve of these fifteen tales were reprinted from the *Sketch*, two from the *Saturday Review*. Their subject-matter is as fantastic and exotic as that of Dunsany's earlier collections, but the language is much less bejewelled with archaism. Indeed, the narrative often tips over into self-parody with a sudden change of register, as if to suggest that Dunsany's characteristic style has become rather absurd. *The Arabian Nights* is evoked in the stories which are, as with the earlier tales, parables of the relation between man and the universe. In 'The Bride of the Man-Horse' a young centaur comes of age and seeks a bride, the offspring of sphinx, lion, and centaur. Desire overcomes the fear of death. In 'The Tale of Thangobrind' a sordid transaction of money and flesh (a stolen jewel to be exchanged for a woman) leads a shifty jeweller to a horrible end. 'Miss Cubbidge and the Dragon of Romance' is about an MP's conventional daughter who is captured by a dragon and lives happily in the land of romance. 'The Wonderful Window' is about a romantic young clerk who buys a window through which he sees a medieval city. Ten of the stories were written to explain illustrations provided by S. H. Sime (1867–1941) (who had collaborated with Dunsany since his first book came out), reversing their normal practice.

Bookman, The, (1891–1934) was founded by William Robertson Nicoll (1851–1923), editor of the *British Weekly*. A. St John *Adcock became editor in 1908. It was conceived to popularize literature by offering a monthly read at *6d.* a time to people with limited finance. As a journal for 'Book buyers, Book readers, and Book sellers', the *Bookman* combined reviews with short items of news about book people and essays on general literary subjects, as well as many illustrations. There were also special issues on particular authors. It was highly successful in commercial terms, and a useful source of income to writers as diverse as W. B. Yeats (1865–1939), A. E. W. *Mason, Walter Pater (1839–94), J. M. *Barrie, Edward Thomas (1878–1917) and Arthur Ransome (1884–1967). If, between the wars, the *Bookman* was eventually unable to compete for readers with newspapers and radio, it had successfully established a definition of literary interest as that which combines an equal concern for past and present authors, for 'high' and 'low' fiction, and for a literary knowledge that included news about publishers and booksellers as well as about authors.

Books (1906–7) was launched by the *Daily Mail* in 1906 in direct competition to the **Times Literary Supplement* (which had started in 1902). It adopted much the same format (longish reviews covering a range of titles) but despite its distinguished editors—first Edmund Gosse (1849–1928) then Archibald *Marshall—and regular contributions from Ford Madox *Hueffer, the *Mail*'s supplement ceased publication in 1907. Quite a large proportion of Marshall's short autobiography is devoted to detailing the inaccuracies in Hueffer's account of his association with the paper in his *Return to Yesterday* (1931).

BOOTHBY, Guy [Newell] (1867–1905) married Rose Alice BRISTOWE. He was born in Adelaide, the son of an Australian politician, and was educated in England from 1874 until he returned to Australia in 1883. After his return to Australia he served as private secretary to Adelaide's mayor and wrote several lacklustre plays, as well as undertaking a trek from the north to the south coast of the continent, described in *On the Wallaby* (1894). In 1894, once he had again settled in England, he devoted himself to the steady production of unpolished but exciting popular fiction. During his career he received advice and encouragement from *Kipling. His most successful works were the series of Gothic tales with Mediterranean settings about the warlock-like genius, doctor, and necromancer Dr Nikola: *A Bid For Fortune, or, Dr Nikola's Vendetta* (1895), *Dr Nikola* (1896), *Dr Nikola's Experiment* (1899), and **Farewell Nikola* (1901). *The Maker of Nations* (1900) shows Boothby at his light-hearted best—love ousts politics from a young revolutionary's heart. In *A Millionaire's Love Story* (1901), the millionaire George Kilvert loves Cecilia Cardew, a violinist, who travels and performs with a mysterious pianist, Gravbowski. Kilvert dissuades Cecilia from suicide. When Gravbowski, who was loved by and who then abandoned her mother, is murdered, Cecilia shields the killer. She marries Kilvert. *My Indian Queen* (1901) is a *historical romance: the story of Sir Charles Verrinder, whose dramatic loss of wealth and status prevents him from marrying his fiancée, Cicely Henderston. He travels to India to earn another fortune, and finds her waiting for him when he returns. Robert Walpole (1676–1745) has a small part. *The Curse of the Snake* (1902) features satanic possession by a somewhat lethargic serpent, in an Australian and Far Eastern setting. *My Strangest Case* (1902) begins quite promisingly in a seedy hotel in Singapore: three Englishmen find treasure in Burma; one of them robs the others, and is hunted across England and the Continent by an incompetent detective, Fairfax (who none the less gets the girl, and is last seen settled in his conservatory with a soft felt hat on his head and a pipe in his mouth). The origins of *A Brighton Tragedy* (1905) are to be found as far afield as Colombia: a roving Englishman, Eric Anstruther, has rescued a young Colombian heiress from an importunate admirer and brought her to England, where she is falsely accused of murder; a famous detective called Dexter offers genial assistance. *A Royal Affair and Other Stories* (1906) is a mixed bag of tales set in Australia, England, Japan, and America. The hero of the title story is an adventurer who takes part in a revolution, and, like Marlow in Joseph *Conrad's **Heart of Darkness*, is asked by a friend to convey a message to his beloved in the event of his death: the latter turns out to be a German queen. In *A Bid for Freedom* (1904), another of Boothby's 'rolling stones', the rakishly handsome Roger Gavesson, rescues the beautiful Lady Olivia Belhampton from the levantine wiles of His Majesty the Sultan of Madrapore. Two earlier novels, *The Woman of Death* and *A Maker of Nations* (both 1900), had implicated other laconic wanderers in, respectively, a Parisian secret society and a South American revolution. The **Times Literary Supplement* described *A Queer Affair* (1903) as 'one of Mr Boothby's naïve tales—about Lord Lavington's engagement to a Dulwich young lady and the mysterious murder of her father'. Boothby's writing is a generic melting-pot. The *Times* (26 Feb. 1905) described it as 'frank sensationalism carried to its furthest limits'. He died, a successful and wealthy writer, at home in Boscombe, Bournemouth, after a severe bout of 'flu.

BOSANQUET, Edmund published five novels about social and sexual dilemmas between 1911 and 1914. *A Society Mother* (1911) and *Catching a Coronet* (1913) are distinctly upper-crust. In *The Woman Between* (1912), an astute young financier deserts a typist for the daughter of a simple country magnate; in *The Dice of Love* (1914), the hero must choose between his charming cousin and the vulgar daughter of a vulgar baronet. *Mary's Marriage* (1914) is a little more complex: a woman's much older husband asks her to marry his cousin after his death, in order to carry on the family name.

Bosom Friends: *A Seaside Story*, Angela *Brazil, 1910, Thomas Nelson. Eleven-year-old Isobel Stewart comes with her poor but genteel widowed mother (her father was killed in the *Boer War) to Silversands for a summer holiday. Her mother is also hoping for a reconciliation with her father-in-law, Colonel Stewart, of the Chase, who disapproved of his son's marriage. Isobel becomes bosom friends with her namesake, the pampered and snobbish Isabelle Stuart, and they join with a number of other holiday-making children to form the United Urchins' Recreation Society. The children have a series of seaside adventures, culminating in the discovery and possession of their own desert island, while Isobel comes painfully to realize that Isabelle is essentially selfish and fickle. Isobel charms her unknowing grandfather (who wrongly believes Isabelle to be his grandchild). The moral contrast between the true and false Isobels is a familiar Brazil theme, but *Bosom Friends* (which is not confined by a school setting) is also surprisingly sharp in its observation of the different layers of the English middle class and of how social distinctions are expressed by tastes in furnishing, clothes, and leisure.

BOTTOME, Phyllis (1882–1963) married (1917) Ernan FORBES-DENNIS. Daughter of an American clergyman and an English mother, as an adolescent she lived in Long Island, but she returned to Europe when tuberculosis put an end to her stage ambitions, and took to writing instead. Her first novel, *The Master Hope* (1904), an exuberant love story, was written when she was 17. After its publication she divided her time between winters in England and summers in Italy. Her husband became passport control officer in postwar Vienna, and during her stay there she fell under the spell of Alfred Adler (1870–1937), whose biography she wrote. Much of her later fiction draws on Adlerian psychology and depicts Austrian families. Her short stories were collected as *Strange Fruit* (1928). The subtitle of *Raw Material: Some Characters and Episodes among Working Lads* (1905) is self-explanatory. The lads include the rebellious but affectionate charges of Nurse Briggs: Harry Holt, nicknamed 'The Chitter', who works on a barge, and Bill Badgers, an apparently incorrigible 16-year-old who turns over a new leaf. *Broken Music* (1907) is a sombre story about unfulfilled promise. Jean d'Ucelles, brought up in provincial France by an English aunt after his parents die, moves to Paris in order to train as a musician. There he mixes with wealthy bohemians, thinks of becoming a hermit, wins and loses love, and is reduced to abject poverty. Only in the final scene, hearing his ex-lover sing, does he realize that he too is capable of making music: albeit a 'broken' music, since there can be no beauty without suffering. *Search for a Soul* (1948), *The Challenge* (1952), and *The Goal* (1962) are autobiographical.

BOWEN, Marjorie, *pseud.*: Margaret Gabrielle CAMPBELL (1886–1952) married, first (1912), Zeffirino Emilio COSTANZO (d. 1916), and, secondly (1917), Arthur L. LONG. Born at Hayling Island, Hampshire, she was the elder daughter of Mrs Vere *Campbell, and spent an unhappy childhood in great poverty after her parents' separation. She grew up in a bohemian household, in which she taught herself to write and paint, eventually studying at the Slade School of Art in London and in Paris. Her first book was published when she was 16, and thereafter, as 'Marjorie Bowen', she wrote to earn money to support her family. She married partly to escape from her mother and sister, and lived in Italy until she was able to bring her baby back to England in 1915, where it soon died. She had another child before returning alone to Italy to nurse her dying husband. There she fell passionately in love with a doctor, who later wrote and told her that he was dying and that she must marry another man. She did so, with moderate success, but 'did not achieve that home which had been her dream since she was a child . . . The toil was incessant, the labour seemed without reward.' Her peak year for production was 1928: seven books. Her *historical romances were strong in plot and spectacle, the best-known being *The *Viper of Milan* (1906). *Black Magic: A Tale of the Rise and Fall of Antichrist* (1909), which the **Times Literary Supplement* called 'Pope Joan in masquerade', is the tangled history of a refractory young nun, Ursula, an 'effeminate and hysterical artist', Dirk, and a diabolic Pope. In this story of witches, violence, and mayhem, the heroine robs the Church, bribes the college of cardinals, and works hard to excommunicate an emperor. Other titles include *The Glen o'Weeping* (1907), *The Sword Decides* (1908), *The Rake's Progress* (1912), and *A Knight of Spain* (1913). *The Debate Continues* (1939) is a harrowing but interesting autobiography. She also wrote as 'George Preedy', 'Robert Payne', 'Joseph Shearing', and 'John Winch'.

BOWER, Marian published sixteen volumes of fiction 1893–1934. *Marie-Eve* (1903) is a society novel with a flavour of Russian intrigue. *The Wrestlers* (1907) concerns the conflict between husbands and wives, and between Germany and Poland. *Skipper Anne: A Tale of Napoleon's Secret Service* (1913) has a French aristocrat sent to an English country house to spy on his cousins. She contributed to the *National Review.*

BOYD, Mary Stuart: Mary KIRKWOOD (1860–1937) married (1880) Alexander Stuart BOYD (1854–1930). Brought up in Glasgow, she married an artist, who illustrated several of her books. As well as contributing to periodicals such as the *Graphic* and *Black and White* she published three travel books and eight volumes of fiction, all in this period. She attempted a number of popular genres. *With Clipped Wings* (1902) is a gentle comedy of manners set in a village and featuring the usual suspects (retired naval officer, old maid, ladies' man, etc.). *Backwaters* (1906) is a loss-of-memory mystery set on the Thames. *Her Besetting Virtue* (1908) moves from a Bloomsbury boarding-house to a coastal resort, *The Glen* (1910) from the West Highlands to London. The former strongly suggests that romance will never flourish in the kind of boarding-house which was a staple of Edwardian *feminist fiction: no sooner has the heroine reached the coastal resort (Budcombe, Devon) than she encounters a mysterious and eminently personable baronet. Boyd also wrote a travel book as 'Paxton Holgar'. The Boyds emigrated to Auckland, where she became first president of the League of New Zealand Penwomen.

BRABY, Maud Churton: Maud CHURTON (d. 1932) married Percy BRABY (*c.*1867–1924) Born in China, educated at an Anglican convent in England, and later in Germany, she married a London solicitor. She published her first story at 17, and persisted in attempts to get into journalism against rebuffs, telling the **Bookman*'s interviewer (May 1910): 'I remember . . . the editor of *Black and White* explaining to me with the utmost gentleness that there were no vacancies on his staff for persons aged eighteen who could do "everything"!' She became a successful interviewer, admired by the great editor W. T. Stead (1849–1912), and said that she published her first book anonymously in 1903 'with an authoress who has now become famous'. (It is tempting to identify the authoress as the sex-novel specialist Gertie de S. *Wentworth-James, and the novel as *Confidences: Being Six Months in the Lives of Melisande and Geraldine*, published in 1903 by 'M. C. and G. de S. W.', but the evidence is slight.) Braby said that 'once an idea really takes hold upon her she can do her writing anywhere, even in the nursery with her three children, whose ages range from six months to six years'. Her first novel under her own name was **Downward: A 'Slice of Life'* (1910), which belongs to the group of novels about unmarried mothers; it was followed by *The Honey of Romance* (1915). She also wrote two superficially feminist but fundamentally conservative marriage manuals, *Modern Marriage and How to Bear It* (1909) and *The Love-Seeker: A Guide to Marriage* (1913), which strive to achieve a compromise between modern ideas of independence and old institutions of marriage and motherhood. She contributed to the *Times*, the *Tatler*, the *Daily Mail*, and the **English Review*.

Bracknels, The: *A Family Chronicle*, Forrest *Reid, 1911, Edward Arnold. Young Denis Bracknel is the odd, sensitive son of a philistine family. His father is a self-made man, a Belfast merchant, and a dogmatic bully; his mother is weak and frightened, his older brother, Alfred, a coarse waster, his sisters Amy and May foolish flirts. Enter Hubert Rusk, Denis's tutor, just down from Cambridge, and the immediate object of Amy's and May's attentions. He slowly takes to Denis's oddities, even after the discovery that he is a moon-worshipper. He is due to take Denis abroad when Mr Bracknel dies of a heart attack while having a row with Alfred about stolen money. Denis is finally pushed over the edge and hangs himself.

BRADBY, G[odfrey] F[ox] (1863–1947), the son of an eminent Victorian headmaster, was educated at Rugby School and Balliol College, Oxford, and became a schoolmaster at Rugby in 1888, retiring in 1920. As a young man he lost an eye, and in old age he became almost totally blind. His satirical school story, *The Lanchester Tradition* (1913), set in a thinly disguised Rugby, is about the attempts of a new headmaster to recapture the spirit of the founder in the teeth of conservative opposition. He wrote a dozen other volumes of mildly adventurous fiction between 1904 and 1929, including *The Marquis's Eye* (1905), in which a solid young Englishman exchanges his bad eye for one belonging to the eponymous marquis, with the melancholy consequence that he sees the world as a Frenchman, and *When Every Tree Was Green* (1912), about five children who live with their grandparents while their parents are away in India. He also published verse (a tribute in the *Times*, 8 July 1947, said 'his monologues in the manner of Browning are something that no one else has achieved with equal success') and literary criticism.

BRADDON, M[ary] E[lizabeth] (1835–1915) married (1874) John MAXWELL (1820–1895). One of the more remarkable figures in late Victorian fiction, author of numerous bestselling novels, poetry, plays, and short stories, she also edited magazines (**Temple Bar*, *Belgravia*, and the *Mistletoe Bough*) and contributed regular sketches and comments to *Punch*, the *World*, and *Figaro*. Her father, a shady solicitor, deserted the family when she was a child, and she first began to make her own living as an actress, taking to the stage aged 19 under the name 'Mary Seyton'. She gave this up to be a writer, producing in quick succession a stage comedy, her first novel, *Three Times Dead* (1860), and her first book of poems, *Garibaldi and Other Poems* (1861), a commission from a wealthy admirer of the Italian nationalist. She lived with a magazine publisher, who became her manager and publisher, and had five children with him (1862–1870) before the death of his insane wife enabled them to marry. The editor of the *Times*, John Delane (1817–1879), was her first cousin; the novelists W. B. *Maxwell and Gerald *Maxwell were her sons. Her name was made in the 1860s by a series of sensation novels, including *Lady Audley's Secret* (1862), *Aurora Floyd* (1863), and *John Marchmont's Legacy* (1863). In the first and most celebrated of these a golden-haired 'angel in the house' turns out to be a mad murderess. *The Doctor's Wife* (1864) draws heavily on *Madame Bovary* (1857) by Gustave Flaubert (1821–80). For the rest of her long life Braddon wrote plays, novels, and stories as the market required— *historical and social novels, society novels, short sensation stories, and children's novels. Her thirteen twentieth-century novels include *The *Infidel: A Story of the Great Revival* (1900) and *The *Conflict* (1903). Her interest in the work of Émile Zola (1840–1902) led her to pursue her own form of naturalism in portraying female sexual emotion, and *Dead Love Has Chains* (1907) has a more tragic feel than the run of her sensation fiction. *The Green Curtain* (1911) is a leisurely biographical study of George Godwin, a Shakespearian actor who achieves great triumphs on the Regency London stage after a very rough provincial apprenticeship. Clearly inspired by the life of Edmund Kean (1787/90–1833), also drawing on Braddon's own stage experiences as a young actress and on her continuing love of the theatre, it is something of an elegy for her own career as well as for that of Godwin: the green curtain is the final curtain. She was for many years one of the bestselling writers in English, and, since she was married to her publisher, her circumstances were unusual. W. B. Maxwell points out that, by the time he took over as her manager after his father's death, 'All her books were in her own hands, including the first issue of each new novel and the subsequent cheaper editions. "The Author's Edition" was unceasingly selling and reprinting... in fact she was her own publisher. She bought the paper, gave orders to printers and binders, and finally sent the bound and wrappered books to Simpkin, Marshall, and Company for distribution.' There is a biography by Robert L.Wolff, Jr. (1979).

BRADSHAW, Mrs Albert S.: Annie CROPPER (d. 1938) married Albert Septimus BRADSHAW (d. 1914). Brought up in Nottingham, she was married to the owner of the *Nottingham Journal*, who gave J. M. *Barrie his first job. A vegetarian, anti-vivisectionist, feminist, and elocutionist, she published fourteen volumes of fiction from 1885, including *The Rags of Morality* (1911). She also performed and published recitations.

BRAMAH, Ernest, *pseud.*: Ernest Bramah SMITH (1868–1942) married (1897) Lucie Maisie BARKER. Born near Manchester and educated at Manchester Grammar School, Smith started life *c.*1887 as a farming pupil and farmed himself for about four years without making it pay, an experience described in his first book, *English Farming: Why I Turned It In* (1894). He wrote a column about farming in the *Birmingham News*; this led to his drifting into journalism, and from 1892 he seems to have earned his living from his pen, with some family money. He is probably best known for his Kai Lung stories, mock-Chinese tales with a twist, collected in seven volumes between *The *Wallet of Kai Lung* (1900) and *Kai Lung Beneath the Mulberry Tree* (1940). Smith also created a blind detective in **Max Carrados* (1914). *What Might Have Been: The Story of a Social War* (1907) was initially published anonymously; when reissued under his pseudonym it was entitled *The Secret of the League*. Britain is governed disastrously by socialists and people fly with artificial wings: the situation is saved by unionization of the rich and a property qualification for voters. The Carrados stories were staples in British magazines in the 1910s and 1920s, and the hero remains an attractive figure as a self-deprecating master of reason, putting his blindness to ingenious use. Smith was a journalist on a provincial newspaper and worked as secretary to Jerome K. *Jerome; afterwards he was on the staff of Jerome's magazine *To-day*. Like his character Carrados, he was an expert numismatist.

Brass Bottle, The, 'F. *Anstey', 1900, Smith, Elder. In this comic *fantasy Horace Ventmore, a struggling and rather proper young architect on holiday in France, falls in love with Sylvia, daughter of the self-important orientalist Professor Futvoye. Back in London the professor asks Horace to attend an auction, but he fails to buy anything except a brass bottle. This contains a Jinnee, Fakrash-al-Aamash, who is so grateful for his release that he promises Horace that 'I shall never cease to study how I may most fitly reward thee for thy kindness towards me'. Unfortunately the Jinnee's ideas of fitness are hardly appropriate to contemporary London life and Horace is left 'a ruined and discredited man, with a client who probably supposes I'm in league with the devil; with the girl I love, and might have married, believing I have left her to marry a Princess; and her father unable ever to forgive me for having seen him as a one-eyed mule'. Order is restored when the Jinnee is resealed in the bottle, having wiped the memory of Horace's exotic wealth and fame from everyone's memory. The book's humour lies in the determination of all the characters to treat the most *outré* events as somehow explicable in terms of good and bad manners.

BRAZIL, Angela (1869–1947) was born in Preston, Lancashire, the youngest of four children of a cotton manufacturer, and was educated at the junior school of Manchester High School and at Ellerslie College, Manchester, where she boarded, and became head girl. Her experience there (as explained in her autobiography, *My Own Schooldays*, 1927) can be seen to underlie her success as an author of school stories for girls. She also attended Heatherley's art school in London (with Baroness *Orczy), and began her career as an illustrator of children's books. *The Mischievous Brownie*, four plays for children, came out in 1899, but her breakthrough book was *A *Terrible Tomboy* (1904, with illustrations by Brazil and her sister Amy). Her first school story was *The Fortunes of Philippa* (1906); though it heralded such a rush of boarding-school stories it owes much to a Victorian precursor, *Six to Sixteen* (1875) by Mrs J. H. Ewing (1841–1885). It was followed by *The Third Class at Miss Kaye's* (1908), *The Nicest Girl in the School* (1909), **Bosom Friends: A Seaside Story* (1910), and nearly fifty other novels, which became staples of girls' reading for the next fifty years or more. It was Brazil who established the conventions of the girls' school story—the jolly-hockey-sticks good nature, the suspicion of foreigners and deviousness (usually linked), the clear social hierarchies, and the passionate but unsexualized female friendships. Her heroines begin as outsiders but are gradually integrated into the group; as tomboys, but learn to accept the ideology of femininity; and as adolescents, but are left on the verge of adulthood. For whatever reasons, stories of this closed female world appealed widely to readers who knew nothing else about boarding-schools at all. Much similar work was done by writers such as L. T. *Meade and Mrs George de Horne *Vaizey.

BRENDA, *pseud.*: Georgina MEYRICK (1845–1933) married (1875) Castle SMITH (1849–1936) and later used the surname CASTLE SMITH. Daughter and wife of London solicitors, Georgina Castle Smith was a prolific author of children's books between 1873 and 1932, many of which, including her big success, *Froggy's Little Brother: A Story of the East End* (1874), were street Arab tales like Silas K. *Hocking's *Her Benny* (1879). But in the twentieth-century 'Brenda' did publish two novels for adults: a fictionalized tract for working-class women, *Mary Pillenger* (1912), and *The Secret Terror* (1909), a temperance tale about an upper-class woman alcoholic, in which it is claimed that 'the drug habit—morphia and cocaine—[is] rampant in society.'

Brendle, Marmaduke *Pickthall, 1905, Methuen. As the story begins, Cyprian Wells, 23-year-old Liberal candidate, arrives in Brendle, a market town somewhere in the Home Counties. He is greeted by the local magnate, John Ashford, a brewer, who takes him home and introduces him to his three daughters, vivacious Clara and Kate and languid Mabel. Although he wins the election, and eventually Mabel's hand in marriage, his tale, of high *political life and fashionable London society, is no more than a frame for the central conflict between the tyrannical but fair-minded brewer and his talented, irresolute son, Hammond. Determined to defy his father, but not really knowing how, Hammond, who has some skill as a furniture designer and interior decorator, goes into business in partnership with a carpenter, Joe Nunn. They open a shop just outside the gates of his father's brewery. The path to independent success proves a stony one, but Hammond is the kind of person people go out of their way to help and protect. Mabel's colourful friend, Stephanie Revel, rejects Hammond for an officer, Major Fred Bathurst, and he marries instead Jenny, Joe Nunn's pretty but rather clinging daughter. Cyprian Wells defects to the Tories over the Irish Home Rule issue, and Ashford is elected in his place. Ashford dies as Lord Brendle, leaving a complicated will which reveals that his primary advantage in his long struggle with his son was a sense of humour. Hammond has to admit defeat. 'A crestfallen figure entered the room, the same which Cyprian had seen come into the brewer's garden on the day when he first met Mabel. Now, as then, the whole appearance of the man drooped, suggesting a plant in a foreign soil.'

BRERETON, Captain F. S.: Frederick Sadleir BRERETON (1872–1957) married, first (1898), Ethel Mary LAMB (d. 1948), and, secondly (1953), Isobel Jessie MURDOCH. Brereton published nearly fifty boys' books between *With Shield and Assegai: A Tale of the Zulu War* (1900) and *Trapped in the Jungle* (1945). Like his model, G. A. *Henty, he wrote indifferently about modern and historical battles, as a brief list of early titles shows: *With Rifle and Bayonet: A Story of the Boer War* (1900), *In the King's Service: A Tale of Cromwell's Invasion of Ireland* (1901), *The Dragon of Pekin: A Tale of the Boxer Revolt* (1902). He also worked other well-worn seams of boys' fiction: *The Great Aeroplane: A Thrilling Tale of Adventure* (1911), *King of Ranleigh: A School Story* (1913), and *Roughriders of the Pampas: A Tale of Ranch Life in South America* (1909).

Broad Highway, The: *A Romance of Kent*, Jeffery *Farnol, 1910, Sampson Low. George Vibart bequeaths £20,000 to one nephew, Sir Maurice Vibart, a celebrated Regency rake, 'in the fervent hope that it may help him to the devil within the year'; £10 (for the purchase of a copy of Zeno or any other Stoic philosopher) to the other, Peter Vibart, the narrator; and a further £500,000 if either marries Lady Sophia Sefton within the year. In Book I, Peter sets off on a walking tour through Kent and Surrey which involves picaresque encounters with footpads, pickpockets, pugilists, duellists, Peninsula War veterans, and chambermaids. At the beginning of Book II, the beautiful Charmian Brown bursts into his cottage in the middle of a violent storm, pursued by a man, whom Peter eventually overpowers. Thereafter Charmian keeps house for him, while he earns his living as a blacksmith. They fall in love, although Peter's bookish paranoia prevents him from trusting her fully. Her mysterious assailant reappears: it is Sir Maurice, whom she had run away with, and then run away from. Sir Maurice is found shot near the cottage. Thinking that Charmian is responsible, Peter takes the rap, and then escapes from prison. Making his way to London, he is reunited with Charmian, who reveals that she had nothing to do with Sir Maurice's death, and that the actual murderer has confessed. Charmian is Lady Sophia Sefton in disguise. A subplot involving a jealous blacksmith, Black George, who thinks that Peter is trying to seduce his woman, Prudence, provides plenty of scope for low-life episodes. The first of Farnol's many romances set in Regency England, it is immediately striking for its sheer vitality—once the hero hits the road in Chapter II there is never a dull moment. This book is still a rollicking read, with the narrator taking an unexpected interest in the reader-pleasing devices of his own narrative.

Broken Road, The, A. E. W. *Mason, 1907, Smith, Elder. A familiar theme of *Empire fiction—the folly of educating 'the native'—is explored with more sympathy than usual, and with some understanding of the hypocrisy of the British. Shere Ali, son of the ruler of Chiltistan on India's north-eastern frontier, is sent to Eton and Oxford for his education. There he becomes best friends with Dick Linforth, son and grandson of men who have given their lives to building a road opening up these north-eastern territories. As young men, both Linforth and Shere Ali fall in love with the beautiful widow Violet Oliver. Shere Ali returns to India to find himself now part of an inferior race and, in particular, is made to realize the impossibility of his marrying a white woman. In his bitterness he reverts to his Muslim faith, joins with rebels against his father's pro-British rule, and leads an uprising along the frontier. The insurrection is put down; Shere Ali flees but is hunted down by Linforth and brought back to India in humiliation. Linforth himself has become a harder, wearier man—his love of Violet has also been doomed by her flirtation with Shere Ali. The road is now being completed, but only for military reasons.

BROOKE, E[mma] F[rances] (1845–1926 or ?1859–1926) was the daughter of a North Country industrialist and attended Newnham College, Cambridge, before settling in Hampstead in 1879. She had connections at the London School of Economics and compiled analytical surveys of women's working conditions in both Britain and Europe, such as *A Tabulation of European Factory Acts, in so far as They Relate to the Hours of Labour and Special Regulations for Women and Children* (1898). Her first noteworthy fictional work was the anonymously published *A Superfluous Woman* (1894), which charts a woman's struggle to come to terms with her own individuality and sensuality—feelings her upbringing had taught her to repress: 'as to her own nature, of that she had heard nothing; passion she had been taught, was an offensive word, an unlady-like allusion . . .'. *Transition* (1895) tells of an intelligent young woman's bid for an independent life in London and her subsequent conversion to socialism, a plot which parallels Brooke's own move south and political awakening. *Life the Accuser* (1895) explores the lives of three woman: one emancipated, one narrow-minded, and the third a compromiser, who is faithful to an unfaithful husband for her own convenience rather than out of a sense of duty. *The Engrafted Rose* (1900) reveals the militancy of Brooke's sexual politics. She was interested in the dilemma faced by women whose truer awareness of themselves led, in a sense, to ostracization, raising at least as many problems as it solved. Brooke was a more political writer than

'George *Egerton', and is one of the best New Woman novelists. *The Poet's Child* (1903), set in a bleak northern landscape, chronicles the marriage of Amabel to Lord Wynspeare of Wandisforth and her subsequent affair with a poet, whose children she bears. Wynspeare dies, the poet leaves, Amabel struggles on. Her faith in her children is ultimately vindicated. 'Poetic feeling is the inspiration of the story,' the *St James's Gazette* reported. *The Twins of Skirlaugh Hall* (1903) are Laura and Letitia, born in 1850 to the Redeburnes of the eponymous Hall, in the Dale of Brackenholme: Laura is beautiful and cruel, Letitia barely survives her birth, but grows up morally sound and triumphs in the end. The **Times Literary Supplement* compared *The Story of Hauksgarth Farm* (1909) to an Icelandic saga. Set in Westmorland, in 1830, it concerns old George Whinnery, his daughter Silence, his witch-like stepdaughter Nanna, and his stepson Silver. Brooke died at a nursing-home in Weybridge.

BROSTER, D[orothy] K[athleen] (1878–1950) was educated at Cheltenham Ladies' College and at St. Hilda's College, Oxford, where she read history. After working in the Franco-American Hospital in France during the First World War, she became secretary to the Regius Professor of History at Oxford before retiring to Sussex. Her first novels, *Chantenelle* (1911) and *The Vision Splendid* (1913), were written with Gertrude Winifred Taylor, but she is best known for her trilogy about the 1745 rebellion in Scotland: *The Flight of the Heron* (1923), *The Gleam in the North* (1927), and *The Dark Mile* (1929). *The Vision Splendid* is a *historical novel about the Tractarian Movement: Tristram Hungerford and Charles Dormer are converts; Tristram falls in love with Horatia Grenville, who goes a step further and marries a French Catholic.

BROUGHTON, Rhoda (1840–1920). One of the most popular and controversial of Victorian novelists, Broughton was the daughter of a widowed Church of England clergyman, and raised bookishly in an Elizabethan manor house in Staffordshire, which supplied the setting for much of her fiction. Her early literary efforts were encouraged by J. S. Le Fanu (1814–73), whose wife was related to her mother. Orphaned in 1863, she lived first with her sister and then, after her sister's death, with her cousin. She became friendly with a number of notable figures, including Mark Pattison (1813–84), widely believed to be depicted unflatteringly in her novel *Belinda* (1883), Anne Thackeray Ritchie (1837–1919), and Henry *James. A noted conversationalist, she incorporated a great deal of witty dialogue into novels whose main theme was the conflict between love and duty. She made her reputation with sexually provocative sensation novels, publishing in 1867 two novels, *Cometh Up as a Flower* and *Not Wisely But Too Well*, which were immensely popular and controversial depictions of the emotional and sexual experiences of young girls, one of whom is made to marry for money a man who disgusts her, the other who has her life ruined by a male flirt. The tomboyish, forthright heroines and the colloquial, witty dialogue were variously celebrated and execrated by critics. She is also a fairly unusual example of a novelist who, having established her success in the era of the three-volume novel, found that the change to shorter fiction after 1894 suited her style better. The heroine of *A Beginner* (1894) writes a sexually provocative sensation novel, and brings shame to her family. *Foes in Law* (1900) is a satirical account of Victorian family life. Broughton's Edwardian career offers an interesting insight into the evolution of the 'fast' heroine. *Lavinia* (1902) confronts one of the frank but genteel tomboys who had been the staple of her earlier successes with the familiar choice between love and duty. The heroine lives with her well-bred, impoverished uncle, and her two cousins, one a soldier who dies in the *Boer War, the other a sensitive philosophical type who thinks himself a coward and is in love with her. The arrival of a gallant convalescent starts her on a course of dangerous comparisons. In the end, she resists temptation. Sexual energy is in effect displaced onto a minor (and contrastingly parvenu) character, Miss Feodorovna Prince, of Prince's Candles, who not only offers herself to the successful general of the hour but positively glories in the deed. *A Waif's Progress* (1905) replaces the tomboy-model (frank, genteel) with the waif-model (demurely deceitful, classless). For much of the novel, this modernized heroine flirts mercilessly with her guardian. Broughton clearly thinks hard about disposing of his elderly wife, to clear the way, but in the end refrains. Thereafter, in novels like *Mamma* (1908) and *The *Devil and the Deep Sea* (1910), Broughton assiduously sought winds to sail closer to. But reviewers tended to think that she was no longer quite up to it. *Between Two Stools* (1912), for example, about a woman bound to the sofa of a tyrannical invalid husband while loving and being loved by another, was compared unfavourably, from the point of view of sensation, to W. B. *Maxwell's *The Guarded Flame* (1906). 'I began my career as Zola,' Broughton noted. 'I finish it as Miss Yonge.'

BROWN, Campbell Rae was a dramatist, specializing in comedy, who was also the author of topical verse, including the once-celebrated recitation 'Kissing Cup's Race' and some fiction, mostly about horse-racing, including *The Avenging Kiss* (1912), *The Devil's Shilling* (1897), *The Great Newmarket Mystery* (1909), *Kissing-Cup the Second: Being a Racing Romance* (1910), and *Sport and the Woman* (1911).

BROWN, Vincent (d. 1933) published thirty-one volumes of fiction between 1898 and 1933. His Edwardian fiction consists mostly of arch accounts of clerical, sexual, and clerico-sexual scandal. In *The Sacred Cup* (1905), the normally tolerant and sympathetic vicar of Lamberfield refuses the Lord's Supper to an unrepentant sinner. *The Irresistible Husband* (1911) has to do with entanglements at a Scottish 'hydro'. In *The Clergy House: A Story for a Quiet Hour* (1914), a curate absconds with the wife of a scoundrel, who promptly reforms himself.

BRYANT, Marguerite (1870–1962) married (1901) Philip W. MUNN (d. 1949). She published seventeen volumes of fiction between 1895 and 1926. The heroine of *Anne Kempburn, Truthseeker* (1910) seeks the truth by becoming secretary to two leading figures in the Labour movement. Bryant was born in Chippenham, and wrote plays for the Women's Institute.

BRYDEN, Henry Anderson (1854–1937) married Julia WRIGHT (d. 1934). The son of a solicitor, he was educated at Cheltenham College, then studied law. Although he took articles he never practised as a solicitor but turned instead to literature. Bryden was a talented amateur sportsman (he represented England in the rugby union side of 1874 and broke the amateur mile record the following year). He also travelled widely in Norway, Spain, Portugal, France, the Canaries, and Morocco. His move to South Africa during the 1890s greatly influenced his subsequent fiction. Titles include: *Tales of South Africa* (1896), *An Exiled Scot* (1899), *From Veldt Campfires* (1900), *Don Duarte's Treasure* (1904), and *The Gold Kloof* (1907). Bryden was keenly interested in natural history and outdoor pursuits, particularly hunting and fishing, and published many essays, articles and books on these topics, such as *Hare-Hunting and Harriers* (1903) and *Nature and Sport in Britain* (1904).

BUCHAN, John (1875–1940), CH (1932), created (1935) 1st Baron TWEEDSMUIR of ELSFIELD, married (1907) Susan Charlotte GROSVENOR (1882–1977). Born in Perth, Scotland, son of a Presbyterian minister, Buchan spent his early childhood in Fife. He was educated at Hutcheson's School, Glasgow, and the University of Glasgow (where, like George *Douglas, he studied Classics under Gilbert Murray, 1866–1957). In 1895 he won a scholarship to read history at Brasenose College, Oxford. At Oxford he was President of the Union and won history and poetry prizes, as well as writing a couple of novels, publishing in the *Yellow Book*, reading manuscripts for the publisher John Lane, and writing a history of Brasenose. After leaving Oxford Buchan studied law, supporting himself by writing for the **Spectator* and *Blackwood's Magazine*. He qualified as a barrister in 1901 but instead of practising went to South Africa as private secretary to the High Commissioner, Lord Milner (1854–1925). In 1906 he became chief literary adviser to the *publisher Thomas Nelson. During the First World War he was a war correspondent for the *Times* in France and then worked in the Ministry of Information. Buchan's great vitality enabled him to combine his professional duties with his writing, despite bad health. He was Conservative MP for the Scottish Universities 1927–35 and Lord High Commissioner to the General Assembly of the Church of Scotland 1933–35. Ennobled on his appointment as Governor General of Canada in 1935, he served in Montreal until his death.

Buchan's zest for *historical romance is revealed in his sympathetic biography, *Walter Scott* (1932); and the works of R. D. Blackmore (1825–1900) and Robert Louis Stevenson (1850–94) had a profound influence upon his fiction. It defies the naturalism, realism, and concern for the inner life of characters which predominate in the early twentieth-century novelists. The key concepts are the hero (and the potential for the heroic in all of us) and civilization, defined in imperialistic, ethnocentric terms. The typical

Buchan hero is an ordinary man who is ennobled by the part he plays in foiling extraordinary threats to the security of Great Britain, and British rule—i.e. 'civilization' as defined by Buchan. Lewis Haystoun in *The *Half-Hearted* (1900) single-handedly rescues Kashmir, British India (perhaps even the British Empire itself) from the treacherous Russians and Afganistanis. In **Prester John* (1910) the young Scots storekeeper David Crawfurd struggles against great odds to avert a native uprising in southern Africa planned by the black preacher John Laputa, who is, however, quite sympathetically drawn and emerges favourably in comparison with Hendriques, a treacherous Portuguese trader. Richard Hannay, Buchan's best-known hero, averts national disaster by preventing confidential naval information falling into enemy (German) hands in *The Thirty-Nine Steps* (1915). Another popular, though in some respects atypical, Buchan hero is Sir Edward Leithen, who made his first appearance in 'Space,' a short story in *The Moon Endureth* (1912). In *The Power-House* (serialized during 1913 and published in 1916) Leithen shares the burden of protecting 'civilization' from hostile forces. *A Lodge in the Wilderness*, published anonymously in 1906, is one of Buchan's most intriguing works. Neither a romance nor an adventure story, it is a serious attempt to define the 'cryptic faith' of imperialism following the Tories' resounding defeat in the general election that year. The novel concerns the attempt to rationalize the idea of 'Empire'. Many modern readers find it difficult to sympathize with his imperialist attitudes: 'I blush today to think of the stuff I talked... God forgive me, but I think I said I hoped to see the day when Africa would belong once more to its rightful masters' (*Prester John*). This is a serious handicap because so many of the plots hinge on threats to imperial stability. Buchan's novels have been seen as latter-day tales of George and the Dragon: something familiar, reliable, and dearly loved threatened by the unknown and the incomprehensible, and thus compared with the Fu Manchu stories of 'Sax *Rohmer', which play upon hidden fears and rely upon the sanctuary of stereotypes. Women play little part in Buchan's fictional world; when they act at all it is in the wings rather than centre stage, as, for instance, Mary Hannay does in *The Three Hostages* and *The Island of Sheep* (1934). *Huntingtower* (1922) introduced the series character Dickson McCunn. His autobiography, *Memory Hold-the-Door* (1940), and an interesting last novel with a Canadian setting, *Sick Heart River* (1941), were published posthumously. O. *Douglas was Buchan's sister; his wife published five novels from 1937; and her mother, Caroline Grosvenor (d. 1940), published three novels 1906–11. There is a biography by Andrew Lownie (1995).

BUCKROSE, J. E., *pseud.*: Annie Edith FOSTER (1868–1931) married Robert Falconer JAMESON (d. 1925). Born in Hull and educated there and in Dresden, she was the author of forty volumes of fiction, mostly about middle-class life in Yorkshire, between 1903 and 1932. The titles and subtitles of *A Little Green World: A Village Comedy without a Plot and without a Problem* (1909) and *Down Our Street: A Provincial Comedy* (1911) give a fair idea of the scope and tone of her Edwardian fiction. In *Love in a Little Town* (1911), Celia Bassingdale, granddaughter and heiress of Cope of Cope's Complete Cleanser, is sent into temporary poverty so that her fiancé can demonstrate that he loves her for herself rather than her money, and emerges from it with a second and much better fiancé. Jameson also published *The Browns* (1912); contributed to *Good Housekeeping*; and was an enthusiastic member of the Church of England. Her husband was a timber merchant.

BULLEN, Frank T[homas] (1857–1915) married (1878) Amelia GRIMWOOD. A writer and public lecturer, Bullen was born at Paddington, north London, of working-class parents. He was abandoned on his parents' separation and looked after by an aunt. When she died Bullen had to learn to fend for himself. He did attend Westbourne School, Paddington, until 1866 but left to work as an errand boy at the age of 11. In 1869 he took up the position of cabin-boy on a ship, the *Arabella*, under his uncle's command. As a teenager Bullen signed on for the crew of the *Cachalot* while it was docked in Massachusetts; it was to be the setting for his best book, *The Cruise of the Cachalot* (1898), a tale of whale-fishing. Bullen worked his way up to the rank of chief mate before he left in 1883 to work as a clerk at the London Meteorological Office. In 1899 he took up a post at the *Morning Leader*. Encouraged by enthusiastic praise from the editor of the **Spectator*, Bullen decided to leave London and concentrate on his writing career. In 1908 his great popularity culminated in an invitation to York

House to read some of his tales to the young princes; he was awarded a Civil List pension in 1912. A deeply religious man all his life, he claimed to have read the Bible from cover to cover twenty-five times. A warm obituary in the *Times* (2 Mar. 1915) observes that 'few men have managed to get more of the salt spray of the sea suggested in their writings, and fewer still have combined with the ability to spin a good yarn a genuine and almost evangelical fervour of religious conviction'. *Deep-Sea Plunderings: A Collection of Stories of the Sea* (1901) is self-explanatory, and indeed characteristic in many ways of Bullen's output. Among the twenty-four stories collected are tales about crusty seafarers (comical cooks, in particular) and the perils of the seas (the South Seas, in particular), essays on whales and cuttlefish, and a passionate defence of the Royal Navy ('the outposts of our Empire, the piquets of our power'). *A Whaleman's Wife* (1902) is dedicated to Theodore Roosevelt (1858–1919), and concerns a strapping New England farmhand who ships on a whaler and gets to see the world. *Beyond* (1909) is also about whaling. There are pirates and the inevitable cuttlefish, and vivid descriptions of the factory-ship at work. 'The last case, emptied of its contents, had been cut away, and the *Titan* wallowed amidst a sleek scum that smoothed the sea for a square mile around her, a monument of greasy affluence.' In later life Bullen began to hold public lectures to supplement the income from his novels and articles. His *Recollections* relates his experiences during this phase of his life. Bullen's health became increasingly fragile as he grew older, and he died in Madeira.

BULLOCK, Shan F. (1865–1935) married (1889) Emma MITCHELL (d. 1922). As a youth Bullock showed no desire to farm his father's considerable land holdings around Crom in Co. Fermanagh. He attended Farra School, Co. Westmeath, and King's College, London; and lived in London after graduation, moving to Surrey after his marriage. Bullock began to publish fiction in the early 1890s, mostly about the Fermanagh area of Ireland, a border between the Protestant north and Catholic south. The sketches collected in *Irish Pastorals* (1901) are comic or pathetic in tone, but *The Squireen* (1903) reflects the contemporary interest in narratives of moral degeneration. The squire in question is a spendthrift and roué who marries into a tough, bible-thumping clan of Orangemen even though he loves another woman. At first, he reforms, and becomes a model husband. Then their child dies, and he begins to disintegrate, finally going mad. *The Red Leaguers* (1904), *Dan the Dollar* (1905), and *The Cubs* (1906) all have Irish subjects. But Bullock's greatest success in the Edwardian period came with two novels which are in effect ethnological studies of English *suburban life, **Robert Thorne: The Story of a London Clerk* (1907) and *A Laughing Matter* (1908). The heroine of the latter has descended into suburbia from the landed gentry, but conducts herself in a frank and sturdy manner, and clearly wins the author's approval through her inability to understand the novels of George *Meredith. Bullock's absorption in suburban life never amounted to approval: both novels promote the broader and deeper opportunities available on the frontiers of Empire. *Hetty: The Story of an Ulster Family* (1911) marked his return to Irish subject-matter. *The Loughsiders* (1924), a late work, is generally taken to be his most accomplished. In 1913 he published *The Race of Castlebar* with the Hon. Emily Lawless (d. 1913).

BURGIN, G[eorge] B[rown] (1856–1944) married (1893) Georgina Benington (d. 1940). Born in Croydon, he was educated at Totteridge Park Public School in north London. His first job was as private secretary to General Valentine Baker (1827–87), known as 'Baker Pasha'. On his return from his travels with Baker in Asia Minor in 1885, Burgin took up journalism. He wrote for and was a sub-editor for the **Idler* until 1899. Burgin also contributed to the *Bookseller* and later became the literary editor for the *Daily Express*. Burgin was also general editor of the 'New Vagabond' fiction series. He was a Fellow of the Institute of Journalists, vice-president of the Dickens Fellowship, and secretary of the Authors' Club (1905–8). Burgin's tales are light-hearted in tone and the earlier ones were often first serialized by **Pearson's Magazine*. His publications include *The Man Who Died* (1903), *A Simple Savage* (1909), and *Diana of Dreams* (1910). He published over ninety novels between 1894 and 1938.

Buried Alive: *A Tale of These Days*, Arnold *Bennett, 1908, Chapman & Hall. Priam Farll, a reclusive painter in his 50s, takes on the identity of his dead valet, Henry Leek—and marries the woman Leek was due to meet through a matrimonial agency, Alice Challice. Alice 'could have been nothing but the widow of a builder in a small way of business well known in Putney and also in Wandsworth. She was every inch that.' Farll lives a perfectly contented life with her in Putney, until his fortune suddenly evaporates, and he is forced to resume his career as a painter. His abilities are still intact, and a noted connoisseur, who has recognized his style but thinks it a forgery, makes a fortune by buying his works at a low price through a small dealer and selling them in America as the genuine article. An American purchaser, suspecting fraud, brings a legal action; but Farll's obstinate shyness prevents him from conclusively proving his real identity. This is a gentle social comedy, as though H. G. *Wells had decided to write about a *Jamesian artist-hero. Frank *Harris, then editor of *Vanity Fair*, and a recent acquaintance of Bennett's, thought it 'admirably written and delightfully humorous; but why make the incidents improbable, why rob yourself of the help which a real skeleton affords? The humour would have been seen as clearly in a true tale and would have been, I cannot help but think, more effective.'

BURLAND, [John Burland] Harris (1870–1926) or J. B. HARRIS-BURLAND. The son of a major-general in the army, he was educated at Sherborne School. Prevented by ill health from going to the Royal Military College, Sandhurst, and taking up a career in the army, he trained at a theological college, intending to become a clergyman, before again changing his mind and going to Exeter College, Oxford, where he won the Newdigate Prize of 1893 with his poem 'Amy Robsart'. After becoming an actor for a year he became a secretary of various public companies. Then between 1903 and 1925 he published some twenty-five volumes of sensational *crime and adventure fiction, including *Dr Silex* (1905), in which a lost race of Norman supermen flourishes near the North Pole.

BURMESTER, Frances G. Brought up in Essex, she lived much of the time in Italy and elsewhere on the Continent. She published six novels between 1902 and 1916, some of which inject a welcome bizarreness into stock themes. The heroine of *A November Cry* (1904) is a farmer-novelist. The hero, who takes her shooting, and is loved by her, was the publisher's reader who wrote sarcastic comments in the margin of her rejected manuscript. He dies tragically, halfway through a confession, in November. The hero of *Davina* (1909) marries a woman he does not love but whom he has permanently disfigured with a blow from a hockey-stick; the no-nonsense heroine pulls him through. In *A Bavarian Village Player* (1911), a village mystic chosen to play Christ in a passion play finds himself unable to abandon the role, and proceeds to Rome to preach the gospel, where he comes to a sticky end. On the whole, Burmester's more formulaic novels, such as *Clemency Shafto* (1906), a society shocker involving stolen jewels, were not well received. This author is probably to be identified with the Frances Georgina Burmester, spinster, who died in Hammersmith in 1940.

BURNETT, Frances Hodgson: Frances Eliza HODGSON (1849–1924) married, first (1873), Swan Moses BURNETT (*c.*1847–1906) (divorced 1898), and, secondly (1900), Stephen TOWNESEND (1859–1914) (separated 1902). Burnett grew up in Manchester, one of five children in a middle-class family. The death of her father, an ironmonger, in 1853 meant a decline in family fortunes; when she was 15 they moved to Tennessee, where her mother had a brother. There she began writing for money. After a long engagement she married a doctor; they went to live in Paris, so that he could study, and then in Washington. The heroine of her first novel, *That Lass o' Lowrie's* (1877), set in the industrial north of England, is a working-class girl who marries a mining engineer: the move from rags to riches (or sometimes riches to rags and back to riches) was to be a recurring feature of Burnett's plots; it made her name on both sides of the Atlantic. Her best novel for adults, *Through One Administration* (1883), was a study of a failed marriage in a political setting in Washington. After the triumph of *Little Lord Fauntleroy* (1886) she spent increasing amounts of time in Europe, and in 1889 she met Townesend, a doctor and would-be actor, a lame duck whose career she promoted, and who did secretarial work for her both before and after their brief marriage (into which he may have blackmailed her). After parting from him she was renaturalized an American citizen in 1905. The elder of her two sons died in Paris in 1890 aged 15; she never got over it. She wrote three classic children's novels: *Little Lord Fauntleroy* (1886),

*A *Little Princess* (1905), and *The *Secret Garden* (1911). *Sara Crewe, or, What Happened at Miss Minchin's* (1887) was the basis (via a stage version) of *A Little Princess. The Lost Prince* (1915) is about the restoration of a boy prince to his kingdom: a sort of *Ruritanian **Kim*, it is far less powerful than *The Secret Garden. The *Making of a Marchioness* (1901) and *The *Shuttle* (1907) are novels for adults in which true love triumphs over the marriage market. The latter, like *T. Tembarom* (1913), also uses the 'international theme'. Her interest in spiritualism is reflected in her two last novels, *The Head of the House of Coombe* (1922) and *Robin* (1922). A good deal of the very large income she made from writing came from her dramatizations and original plays. There is a biography by Ann Thwaite (1974).

BUTLER, Samuel (1835–1902) was born in Nottinghamshire, the son of a Church of England clergyman, and educated at Shrewsbury School and St John's College, Cambridge. Butler is a figure in the Victorian rather than Edwardian literary scene; he also composed music and exhibited paintings at the Royal Academy. He spent 1860–4 as a colonist in New Zealand, an experience which informs his most popular novel, *Erewhon, or, Over the Range* (1872), a utopian satire in which crime becomes illness and illness crime, and babies choose their own parents. It reflects Victorian debates about progress, science, and religion (the latter topic is further explored in the sequel, **Erewhon Revisited*, 1901). In the sequence of works which began with *The Fair Haven* (1873) Butler was one of the more eloquent and persuasive critics of Darwin's theory of natural selection, arguing for intention, a life-force in natural history, an argument influential at the turn of the century. Butler challenged scholarly conventions in articles like 'The Authoress of the Odyssey' (1897) and 'Shakespeare's Sonnets Reconsidered' (1899), in which he suggested that their object was a young plebeian. His significance for Edwardian literature, though, rests on the posthumously published novel, *The *Way of All Flesh* (1903). The history of a family through four generations, it seemed remarkably modern in its treatment of the continuing effects of inherited traits and its understanding of the repressons and ambiguities involved in the relations of fathers and sons.

BUTT, B[eatrice] M[ay] (1856–1918) married (1876) William Hutt ALLHUSEN (1845–1923). Born in Scotland, she married a sportsman and adventurer. Her earliest writings are short stories for *Blackwood's Magazine*. Her Victorian fiction, from *Miss Molly* (1876) to *Keith Deramore* (1893), is largely concerned with the psychology of devoted women divided, for various reasons, from the object of their affections. Her Edwardian novels are broader in scope. *The Great Reconciler* (1903) is set partly in South Africa during the *Boer War, and parallels emotional and political conflict. In *Dan Riach, Socialist* (1908), a baronet who in his youth had been a disciple of Dan Riach and the lover of Riach's niece becomes, as a captain of industry, his opponent, and leaves the niece for another woman. Some of Allhusen's works appeared as by 'The Author of *Miss Molly*'. She died in Hindhead.

BYATT, Henry was a playwright who lived at Lancing and produced fictional accounts of the past, present, and future of England which are uniform in their paranoia, if nothing else. *Land O' Gold* (1907) is a melodramatic tale of county society in the 1850s and 1860s; *The Flight of Icarus* (1907) concerns a 'King of the Jews' who rules the land from his 'palace' in Park Lane; *Purple and White: A Romance* (1905) is set in 1980, when the German Kaiser of the day has fallen in love with an English girl. *The Real Man* (1909) involves an exchange of identities, after a motor accident, between a millionaire and his double, a feckless adventurer who starts to develop public-spiritedness. A reviewer described Byatt's novels as being of the 'tedious-lively type'.

CAINE, [Thomas Henry] Hall (1853–1931), KBE (1918), CH (1922), married (1882) Mary CHANDLER (d. 1932). Born at Runcorn, Cheshire, son of a ship's smith of Manx family, Caine lived for some years as a child with relations on the Isle of Man. He left school in Liverpool at 14 and studied architecture, but ill health led him to return to Man as a schoolteacher. Later he worked in Liverpool as a builder's clerk, and as a journalist, writing on architecture. His great stroke of good fortune was to attract the attention of D. G. Rossetti (1828–82) by sending him a lecture he had given on Rossetti's poetry. Three years later, in 1881, Caine went to live in Rossetti's house in London, working as a leader-writer on the *Liverpool Mercury* (partly owned by Egerton *Castle), in which his first novel, *The Shadow of a Crime* (1885), was serialized. He made his name, however, with *The Deemster* (1887), set on Man in the eighteenth century. His vision of Manx life, riddled with illegitimacy and superstition, seems to have been rather resented by the islanders, but it appealed to the public. His novels seemed daring in their account of sexual passion, and profound in their conception of human destiny. In interviews Caine claimed that the central motive of all his books was 'the idea of justice, divine justice, the idea that righteousness always works itself out, that out of hatred and malice comes love'. The plots of his novels were based on the Bible: *The Deemster* on the parable of the prodigal son, *The Bondman* (1890) on Jacob and Esau, *The Scapegoat* (1891) on Eli and Samuel. Caine occupies an important place in the publishing history of the novel. His novels circulated all over the English-speaking world, and were widely translated. He played a significant role in the abandonment of the three-decker by allowing *The Manxman* (1894) and subsequent novels to be published immediately in one six-shilling volume. He observes in his memoirs that he probably earned more than any dead writer, and Samuel Norris in his (1947) study suggests that Caine may have earned more from subsidiary than from book rights. His novels were serialized, dramatized (often by himself) and filmed. He also wrote plays; one for Henry Irving (1838–1905) about Muhammad was stopped by the Lord Chamberlain at the insistence of Indian Moslems. After 1895 Caine lived in Greeba Castle on the Isle of Man, where no income tax was levied; when he died there he left nearly £250,000. Norris argues that in his early days he was read because he seemed excitingly coarse; he was soon overtaken in this respect. The Manx novels were received with admiration in literary circles; by the twentieth century he was selling better than ever but his pretensions to prophetic wisdom were increasingly mocked. George Saintsbury (1845–1933) objected in the *Fortnightly Review* (January 1895) to the monotony of theme (two men in love with the same woman), the overuse of stormy weather coinciding with stormy passion, and the ranting sentimentality of tone. Many found Caine personally ridiculous; he had a high, balding forehead and cultivated an alleged resemblance to Shakespeare by growing a pointed beard. He published in this period *The *Eternal City* (1901), *The *Prodigal Son* (1904), *The *White Prophet* (1909), *The Woman Thou Gavest Me* (1913), and an autobiography (1908). An unfinished life of Christ was posthumously published by his sons (1938).

CALDERON, George [Leslie] (1868–1915) married (1900) Katherine RIPLEY née HAMILTON. Fifth son of the painter Philip Hermogenes Calderon (1833–98), he was educated at Rugby School and Trinity College, Oxford. He was called to the Bar (1894) and then, less conventionally, went to St Petersburg for two years (1895–97), working as a foreign correspondent and English teacher. He subsequently worked in the British Museum Library's Slavonic section (1900–3) and collected material for a projected book on Eastern European folklore. He was influential in bringing Russian literature to the attention of British critics; he translated Chekhov plays and published *The Russian Stage*

(1912). His own series of plays began with *The Fountain* (1909). Earlier, however, he had published two novels. *The Adventures of Downy V. Green, Rhodes Scholar at Oxford* (1902) is a sequel to *The Adventures of Mr Verdant Green* (1853) by 'Cuthbert Bede' (i. e. Edward Bradley, 1827–89), in which an American descendant of the original green newcomer is gulled. *Dwala* (1904) is a satire about an anthropoid ape, the Missing Link, who learns to talk, comes to London as 'Prince Dwala', becomes Prime Minister, is unmasked, and dies of consumption. It is one of the most amusing of the many novels of this period which express anxiety about British political institutions by condemning the ease with which rich newcomers (especially Jewish, South African, or other foreign millionaires) could buy political power and social advancement in England. Calderon was an enthusiastic opponent of women's suffrage, and published two books on the issue. He enlisted in the First World War as an interpreter, was commissioned, and was killed during the Dardanelles campaign. A nostalgic memoir (1921) by Percy Lubbock (1879–1965) speaks warmly of Calderon's charm and ability. 'Thickly as his path was strewn with books half written, schemes of all sorts projected and abandoned, [his] own work went forwards through everything, though the second half of the book might be replaced by a political campaign, and the campaign itself, after a round or two, lead into the production of a play.'

Call, A: *The Tale of Two Passions*, Ford Madox *Hueffer 1910, Chatto & Windus. Clever, lazy Robert Grimshaw, a bachelor ambivalently in love with two women, Pauline Lucas and Katya Lascarides, resolves the dilemma by marrying Pauline off to stupid, maddeningly honourable Dudley Leicester—or partly resolves it, since he is too lazy, or too clever, to complete the equation by marrying Katya. The consequences of his scheming are brought home to him when he sees Leicester entering the house of an old flame, Etta Stackpole, now Lady Hudson. That evening, Leicester answers the phone at the Hudson mansion, pretending to be the butler, but is recognized by a caller who refuses to give his name. Knowing that his secret is shared, but not who shares it, he becomes increasingly paranoid, suspecting blackmail at every turn. Katya Lascarides eventually resolves his obsession by producing the man who made the fatal call: Robert Grimshaw, of course. Her price is Grimshaw's hand in what looks like being a far from happy marriage. The themes of the novel—idleness, unbreakable reserve, guilt, the failure of social and moral codes to encompass sexual feeling—have often been related to Hueffer's own experience. The pairing of a clever, lazy man with a stupid, energetic one was a favorite narrative device (see **Mr Fleight* and *The Good Soldier*, 1915). Reviewing *A Call* in the **New Age*, Arnold *Bennett suggested that 'Mr Hueffer owes something to Mr Henry *James, and perhaps also he has learnt from Mr James some of the charming grace which is displayed in the construction of the book. It is a mild novel. It deals with tragic matters, but deals with them mildly. It does not engross, and probably is not meant to engross. It induces reverie and reflection.' In his journal, he was not so kind. 'Slick work, but not, I fear, really interesting. He doesn't get down to the real stuff.'

Call of the Blood, The, Robert *Hichens, 1906, Methuen. Hermione Lester, 34, plain but characterful, marries Maurice Delaney, a beautiful younger man with Italian blood. They honeymoon in Sicily, where, in the course of a particularly energetic dance, Maurice's blood is 'called'. 'The dancing faun was dimly aware that in his nature there was not only the capacity for gaiety, for the performance of the tarantella, but also a capacity for violence which he had never been conscious of when he was in England.' When Hermione goes off to nurse an intellectual friend, the novelist Emile Artois, who has fallen sick while on a visit to Egypt, Maurice falls in love with a fisherman's daughter, Maddalena. He seduces her, and is killed, **Nostromo*-style, by the fisherman. The novel shows how Italy had become, for some Edwardian writers (compare E. M. *Forster), an *exotic place of vivid and often brutal awakenings.

CALTHROP, Dion Clayton (1878–1937) married (1898) Mary Violet ——. His father was an actor who died in 1888, and his mother was the daughter of Dion Boucicault the elder (?1820-90), the playwright and actor. Brought up by a bachelor uncle, he was educated at Colet Court, St Paul's School, and Calderon's Art School, and became an illustrator, stage designer, and playwright who published twenty-eight volumes of fiction to 1936. In *Everybody's Secret* (1909) a fastidious bachelor adopts his illegitimate daughter, and complications ensue when his best friend marries her mother. Calthrop also collaborated with Haldane *MacFall and published non-fiction on costume and gardening and an autobiography, *My Own Trumpet* (1935), in which he mentions lean times after the First World War.

CAMBRIDGE, Ada (1844–1926) married (1870) George Frederick CROSS (1844–1917). Born at Wiggenhall St Germains in rural Norfolk, she was the daughter of a gentleman farmer who was at law with his brothers over his father's will, and who by the time of her marriage had become a commercial traveller. She was educated by governesses, one of whom abused her, probably sexually, and spent a few months at boarding-school. She published poetry and fiction, pious in tone, before departing for Australia on marriage to a clergyman. There has recently been a revival of interest in her subsequent writing: novels dealing with the life of the Australian middle class, especially its women, and verse protesting at sexual injustice and the female predicament. Both fiction and poetry have been reprinted in Australia. She often dwells in her fiction on the financial and social difficulties of the Anglican clergyman's family; and she wrote copiously and in response to commercial pressures. Two of her five children died young and she suffered from persistent ill health. Both she and her husband felt exiled, though on revisiting England in 1908 and 1912–17 she expressed her loyalty to Australia, where she returned after his death. She was president of a women writers' club. Novels such as *Sisters* (1904) and *A Platonic Friendship* (1905) tend to use the obvious differences between Australia and England to establish other, more abstract distinctions (between rough and smooth, for example, or passion and matrimony). *The Making of Rachel Rowe* (1914) suggests that on the whole she preferred the rough to the smooth. A young Australian girl comes to England and marries a swindler who turns out to have several existing wives. The experience proves the making of her. She and her young boy are eventually rescued by the Australian doctor who had always loved her, and taken back to Australia. Cambridge published two volumes of autobiography (1903, 1912).

CAMERON, Mrs Lovett: Caroline Emily SHARP (1844–1921) married (1867) Henry Lovett CAMERON. Born in Walthamstow, Essex, the daughter of a businessman, she was sent to Paris aged 6 to learn French, and then to a boarding-school. She did not write until encouraged by her husband, who was parliamentary agent to the Treasury. A long series of melodramatic novels followed *Juliet's Guardian* (1877). *In A Grass Country* (1885) reached a ninth edition. Her practice is to titillate the reader by approaching sexual sin and tragedy and then retreating to romance: in *Bitter Fruit* (*c*.1914) a painter's engagement is threatened by the appearance of a former mistress, who cries, 'Would she have been taught to condone *your* offence and to forgive *your* past, whilst she would recoil with horror from mine?' But by the end she has been conveniently burned to death and the lovers live happily ever after. The heroine of *Remembrance* (1904) has a worldly mother who tries to part her from her low-born lover and force her to make a marriage of convenience and fails. She also wrote *The Man Who Didn't, or, The Triumph of a Snipe Pie* (1895), one of the many ripostes to *The Woman Who Did* (1895, by Grant Allen, 1848–99). It is an unsympathetic picture of a New Woman, who fails to take her lover away from his boring wife. Her brother-in-law, the African explorer Verney Lovett Cameron (1844–94), published a number of adventure stories for boys in the 1880s.

CAMPBELL, Frances published seven romances between 1900 and 1907, with widely varied settings. *Two Queenslanders and Their Friends* (1904) is about children in the Australian bush. In *A Pillar of Dust* (1905), the general in command of a penal settlement in Queensland has two nephews, a bad one, who lives in his household, and a good one, who is a convict; the former is unmasked, the latter vindicated. *The Measure of Life* (1906) consists of Irish sketches of a mystical tendency. *A Shepherd of the Stars* (1907) is a desert romance, frivolous rather than torrid, drawing on Campbell's own travels in Morocco, recounted by the spinster guardian of two nieces. Campbell was her married name. She may have been an Australian, since she contributed a weekly letter to the *Brisbane Courier* and the *Queenslander*.

CAMPBELL, Mrs Vere: Josephine Elisabeth ELLIS married Vere Douglas CAMPBELL (d. *c*.1905). Daughter of a Moravian clergyman, she was educated at school in Germany. She was the mother of 'Marjorie *Bowen', who portrays her unfavourably in her autobiography as extravagant and unstable. According to the daughter, the Campbells separated when their children were young; their first child died 'under deplorable circumstances in a London lodging'. To support herself and her two daughters she wrote plays and published eight novels between 1899 and 1910, while living in great poverty in bohemian circles in London. Bowen commented that her work 'dealt entirely with her own experiences of passion and poverty. She wrote again and again of misunderstood and wronged women and the various attractive, but faithless, men who had crossed their path.' She also writes of her 'bitter death that was the direct outcome of her frustrated, unfortunate life'. *Ferriby* (1907) is set in a northern manor house occupied by a family of decayed gentlefolk; wild weather and fierce arguments are followed by murder. *For No Man Knoweth* (1910) begins in Brittany among fisher-folk, who likewise are of the school of Hall *Caine; but the scene is transferred to London bohemia when a fisherman's widow elects to train as an artist, and some touches draw on 'Victoria *Cross''s *Five Nights* (1908).

CANDLER, Edmund (1874–1926) married (1902) Olive Mary TOOTH. The son of a doctor, he was educated at Repton School and Emmanuel College, Cambridge. He became a teacher in Darjeeling, and in 1900 professor of English Literature at a college in Madras; in his vacations he travelled widely in the Far East. He contributed to various periodicals, and was the *Daily Mail* correspondent on an expedition to Tibet, where he had his hand amputated after a fight. Subsequently he did more teaching and worked as a war correspondent in Mesopotamia during the First World War. His fiction consists of a collection of short stories *The General Plan* (1911), and *Sidi Ram: Revolutionist* (1912) and its sequel *Abdication* (1922), which deal unsympathetically with the militant Indian nationalist movement, and suggest that conflict between Indians and their rulers is instinctive, and the *Empire itself is doomed. In the story 'A Break in the Rains' two English lovers steal a sacred statue and experience the horror of India until they return it. He also published an autobiography, *Youth and the East* (1924), in which he reflects with unusual self-consciousness on the colonial experience and its literary dimension: '*Kipling was a provocation and a challenge. I believe that the very hideousness of the picture in such tales as "At the End of the Passage", or "The City of Dreadful Night" was part of the lure of the East.'

CANNAN, Gilbert (1884–1955) married (1910) Mary BARRIE née ANSELL (*c.*1862–1950). Born in Manchester, one of nine children of a shipping clerk, he was educated at Manchester Grammar School and King's College, Cambridge. After a brief period as a barrister he became dramatic critic of the *Star* and honorary secretary of the Society for the Abolition of Censorship. G. B. Shaw (1856–1950) caricatured him as Gilbert Gunn in *Fanny's First Play* (1911): 'Gunn is one of the young intellectuals: he writes plays himself. He's useful because he pitches into the older intellectuals who are standing in his way.' He began an affair with J. M. *Barrie's wife. His first novel, *Peter Homunculus* (1909), concerns the difficulties of a clever young man encountering older and more sophisticated women in literary society. Its title declares what was to prove a lasting dedication to the *Bildungsroman*, or novel of development. David Brockman, the lead homunculus in Cannan's second novel, *Devious Ways* (1910), also becomes, inexplicably and after an unpromising start, a prominent figure in London society. He marries, suffers from mental unrest, discovers that he has 'come by' a religion, kisses a countess who is not his wife, then settles down. Barrie petitioned for divorce in 1909 and the defendants married in the following year. Cannan's translation of Romain Rolland's *Jean Christophe* (10 volumes, 1889–1912), appeared 1910–13 and doubtless influenced the conception of the semi-autobiographical Lawrie Saga, consisting of *Little Brother* (1912), **Round the Corner* (1913), *The Stucco House* (1917), *Three Pretty Men* (1916), *Time and Eternity* (1919), and *Annette and Bennett* (1922). *Little Brother* (1912) betrays an increasing literary self-consciousness. The character and career of Stephen Lawrie, scion of a notable Scottish family, have the makings of a good novel, the **Times Literary Supplement* pointed out, 'but they are not worth the elaborate machinery invented for them'. In 1914 Cannan wrote a preface to a translation of M. P. Arzibashev, *Sanine* (1907), defending it, especially its treatment of sex and its nude bathing scene. 'What is society? What is it but the accumulated emanations of fear and timidity and shyness that beset human beings whenever they are gathered together? . . . Love is rare; physical necessity is common to all men and women . . .' These ideas are important in *Round the Corner*, which was praised by Henry *James in 'The Younger Generation' (1914) and had a significant impact on the literary world. H. G. *Wells noted the debt to *The *Way of All Flesh*; 'You handle a parson as well as Samuel *Butler . . . but with more sympathy and humanity.' Cannan, now at the height of his reputation, became a close friend of D. H. *Lawrence. Several plays were produced before the First World War, and he also published some short stories and *Old Mole* and *Old Mole's Novel* (both 1914). The former is a ludic and satirical story about a middle-aged schoolmaster, Herbert Jocelyn Beenham, who joins a group of strolling players, marries a young (and already pregnant) servant-girl, and, having shed his pedagogic preconceptions and adjusted to the real world, disappears rather than hinder her sexual fulfilment. The latter airs Cannan's views on marriage and war. However, during the war his marriage collapsed and he began to show signs of mental instability; a further blow was the elopement of his girlfriend, Gwen Wilson (d. 1982), with Henry Mond (1898–1949), later Lord Melchett, son of the owner of the **English Review*. For a few years afterwards he travelled (promoting Lawrence's work in America) and went on translating and writing fiction and drama. *Mendel* (1918) is a novel based on the life of Mark Gertler (1892–1939). But in 1924 he was certified insane, and spent the rest of his life in lunatic asylums; he died in Holloway Sanatorium. There is a biography (1978) by Diana Farr.

CAPES, Bernard E[dward] J[oseph] (1850?–1918) married (1889 or earlier) Rosalie ——. Capes was a journalist, editor of the *Theatre* (c.1880–97), whose first novel was published in 1898. In the next twenty years he wrote ghost, adventure, and *crime stories many of which were published in magazines. In an article on plots in the **Cornhill Magazine* (July 1900), he lists various preposterous ideas for novels which he has rejected; the ones he used were no less intricate. *The House of Many Voices* (1911) is set in an English house-party and has far too many characters, each one of whom has a misunderstanding to reveal or a past to disentangle, with the help of a magic diamond and a pair of young lovers. *Love like a Gipsy: A Romance* (1901) begins in the American War of Independence and hinges on a changeling who is the missing heir. *Loaves and Fishes* (1906) and *Bag and Baggage* (1913) are collections of short stories reprinted from periodicals; in the second there is a story about a bullet-proof vest. His writing is lively, witty, and lightweight. After he died G. K. *Chesterton wrote a touching preface to his last book *The Skeleton Key* (1919): 'He had a mind of that fertile type which must always leave behind it . . . a sense of unfinished labour . . . He carried on the tradition of the artistic conscience of Stevenson; the technical liberality of writing a penny-dreadful so as to make it worth a pound.' He died in Winchester. His sister Harriet Mary Capes (1849–1936), translator and author of children's books, was a friend of *Conrad, who dedicated *A *Set of Six* (1908) to her.

Captain Desmond, V. C.: *A Novel*, Maud *Diver, 1907, Edinburgh and London, William Blackwood. The first of Diver's many robust tales about life on the North-West Frontier of India. The frontier, it is made plain, requires a very special gallantry from men, and a very special stoicism from women. Theo Desmond, VC, has plenty of the former, and a wife, Evelyn, singularly lacking in the latter. The alarms and excursions of frontier life ('By Jove! A mad pariah! I must go and see what's up') frighten and depress her; but merely invigorate Honor Meredith, a general's daughter who has arrived to visit her brother. Evelyn drifts into debt, and flirts with the district superintendent of police, Owen Kresney, a '*pukka* bounder', villainous because half-caste. Honor, who has fallen in love with Theo, selflessly steers Evelyn back onto the straight and narrow (she has the 'true woman's passion—to protect and help'). At the last moment, a Muhammadan fanatic murders Evelyn, leaving Honor free to marry Theo. Diver revised the book substantially in 1914. The Desmonds have a supporting role in her next novel, *The *Great Amulet* (1908).

Caravaners, The, *'Elizabeth', 1909, Smith, Elder. Part of von Arnim's long-running campaign against Prussian philistinism and arrogance, and, more slyly, the obtuseness of her first husband, Count Henning August von Arnim-Schlagenthin. The narrator, Baron Ottringel, an artillery officer, is persuaded by his Anglophile wife to undertake a caravanning holiday in Kent and Sussex with a German acquaintance and her English friends. Hunger, fatigue, rain, and the rudeness of the natives exhaust the Baron's patience; meanwhile, his unflagging self-importance exhausts the patience of the other members of the group, who drop off one by one. The Baron's opinions are conveyed in an idiom and tone derived unmistakeably from *The Diary of a Nobody* (1892) by George (1847–1912) and Weedon Grossmith (1854–1919); the haughty Baron, like Henning von Arnim, is a petit bourgeois at heart. The joke is a good one, if a little over-extended, and accommodates serious preoccupations. The Baron's assumption that mighty Prussia will one day conquer decadent Britain—'I hope never to see it again,' he remarks of the Medway bridge, 'unless officially at the head of my battalion'—leaves a sour taste; as does his persecution of his wife, who has been encouraged to rebel by the example of her English companions. The book sold well, and inspired a brief vogue for caravanning.

Card, The: *A Story of Adventure in the Five Towns*, Arnold *Bennett, 1911, Methuen. Edward Henry (Denry) Machin, a solicitor's clerk, adds his own name to the list of those invited to a municipal ball given by the Countess of Chell, and distinguishes himself by dancing with the Countess herself. Thereafter, his ability to improvise and his instinct for grand gestures carry him through a variety of commercial and matrimonial enterprises. The former include moneylending, tourism, the 'Five Towns Universal Thrift Club', and the newspaper business; the latter a honeymoon in Switzerland. Denry eventually emerges as Mayor of Bursley. When one councillor wonders whether he is identified with any great causes, another replies crushingly that he is identified with 'the great cause of cheering us all up'—a neat enough description of Bennett's cause, too. Bennett, however, did not think cheering everyone up the only aim in life. In his journal (2 Mar. 1909) he recorded that he had finished *The Card* the previous day. 'Began it on Jan. 1, I think. 64,000 words. Stodgy, no real distinction of any sort, but well invented and done up to the knocker, technically, right through.' The book's cheerfulness and virtuosity earned it a warm reception. Dixon Scott (?1891–1915), writing in the *Manchester Guardian*, caught something of its appeal. 'It is the gayest exposition. Nothing is ever done "off" on Mr Bennett's stage; we see exactly what Denry does and how he does it; how (for instance) fishing a scrap of chocolate out of a glass of lemonade and perceiving its precise relation to Llandudno he converts it into a cool five hundred pounds. *Toujours l'audace!*' Bennett wrote a sequel, *The *Regent* (1913).

Cardinal's Snuff-Box, The, Henry *Harland, 1900, John Lane. Travelling in Italy the English novelist Peter Marchdale meets Beatrice, Duchess of Santangiolo, who reminds him irresistibly of the heroine of his *A Man of Words*. She affects not to know he is the author of the work, published under a pseudonym. He falls in love. '"What a woman it is," said Peter to himself, looking after her. "What vigour, what verve, what *sex*! What a woman!"' However, it takes the intervention of her cousin, Cardinal Udeschini, who leaves his snuff-box on Peter's copy of the novel, to bring them together. When he returns the snuff-box, Peter meets Beatrice in the garden, and declares both his identity and his love. Like its hero, the man of words, *The Cardinal's Snuff-Box* is elegant and oblique; it never quite renders the vigour and verve, let alone the 'sex', attributed to its heroine.

CAREY, Rosa Nouchette (1840–1909) was born at Stratford-le-Bow, London, the sixth of seven children of a shipbroker. She was educated at home and at the Ladies' Institute, St John's Wood, where she was a great friend of the feminist writer Mathilde Blind (1841–96). But this friendship was, Carey told Helen Black, 'interrupted by the divergence of their religious opinions'. The profits of Carey's novels supported a sister, a nephew, and two nieces who lived with her. She also gave a home from about 1875 to the deaf poet Helen Marion Burnside (1841–1923), at one time a colleague on the staff of the *Girls' Own Paper*. Her fiction is unpretentious romance addressed to women and girls. She was High Church, and has been seen as a follower of the older Anglo-Catholic novelists Elizabeth Sewell (1815–1906) and Charlotte M. Yonge (1823–1901); however, the less intellectual Carey altogether lacks their interest in doctrine, and it is doubtful whether a Dissenting reader of her fiction could have found much to object to in her advocacy of churchgoing and unselfishness. This may help to account for her wide appeal: her first novel, *Nellie's Memories* (1868), sold over 52,000 copies. It is also relevant that on the whole she deals with problems confronting women of the urban or suburban middle class rather than the rural gentry. She writes with sympathy about uncongenial homes, wasted talents, and frustrated energies, but resolves her novels with romance. The heroine of *No Friend like a Sister* (1906) is a career woman who uses her private means to start a successful nursing-home, but her two sisters, lacking her vocation, find happiness in marriage. The *British Library Catalogue* also credits Carey with four other novels under the pseudonym 'Le Voleur', but Jane Crisp, in her bibliography (1989), states that evidence for this is lacking. The last of these, *The Champington Mystery* (1900), is a murder mystery. A private detective, ex-Scotland Yard, reveals that the murdered woman had been blackmailing the heroine's father with evidence that he married her and not the heroine's mother. But we discover that she had been married before, that her first husband murdered her, and consequently that the heroine is legitimate and can happily marry her lover.

CAREY, Wymond, *pseud.* According to the **Bookman* (July 1905) this was 'a *nom de plume* which conceals... the identity of a well-known Oxford Don'. He was rumoured to be a historian, but no further suggestion can be made. His four novels (1902–7) are *Weymanesque *historical romances; they include *Monsieur Martin: A Romance of the Great Swedish War* (1902) and *No. 101* (1906), which is about the career of the Marquise de Pompadour.

CARNIE, Ethel (1886–196?) married (*c.*1916) Edwin HOLDSWORTH. She worked in a Lancashire cotton mill from the age of 9. 'I always hated the mill and wanted to get away from it,' she told an interviewer from the *Yorkshire Observer* (5 April 1932). Her break came when her *Songs of a Factory Girl* (1910) attracted the attention of Robert *Blatchford, who gave her a job on a new paper he was starting in Manchester, the *Woman Worker*. When it folded 'it felt like a ship going down, and I took the line of least resistance and went back into the factory again. But it was only for about a year.' She published in 1913 both a novel, *Miss Nobody*, and a collection of children's fables, *The Lamp Girl and Other Stories*. In the title-story a downtrodden princess who lights the lamps for her proud sisters marries the good prince. The hero of 'The Blind Prince' recognizes the inequality around him and starts a commonwealth. After the First World War her sketches and tales appeared in the *Sunday Worker*, and ten more volumes of fiction, including her best-known novel *This Slavery* (1925), were published between 1917 and 1931. She also contributed stories to the *Yorkshire Weekly Post* and the *Shipley Times*. From 1917 she published as Ethel Holdsworth; her husband published verse written 'in the scanty leisure of a working man's life', according to her preface to his *Poems from My Drawer Corner* (1926). Her novel *Helen of Four Gates* (1917) was filmed. In 1932 she was living in Barnoldswick and hoping to finish her eleventh novel by the autumn. In fact she published nothing more.

Carnival, Compton *Mackenzie, 1912, Martin Secker. Jenny Raeburn, a dancer at the Oriental Palace of Varieties, falls in love with Maurice Avery, a dilettante, who eventually tires of her. She is then, after a brief and mostly scornful involvement in the suffrage campaign, seduced by a libertine pornographer, Jack Danby. Her mother, despairing of her, goes mad and dies. Then Jenny is introduced to Zachary Trewhella, a Cornish farmer, who saves her from Danby and takes her to live on his farm, where she gives birth to a son, Frank. Trewhella turns out to be a bully and ferociously jealous. When a penitent Maurice approaches Jenny, he tracks the couple along the cliffs, and shoots her, wrongly supposing her to be unfaithful. Self-conscious and over-elaborate, the novel made Mackenzie's name; it was adapted for the stage in November 1912, and filmed for the first time in 1915. The problem with it is that the heroine is, as Henry *James pointed out in his 1914 essay on 'The New Novel', 'too minute a vessel of experience for treatment on the scale on which the author has honoured her—she is done assuredly, but under multiplications of touch that become too much, in the narrow field, monotonous.' *Coral: A Sequel to Carnival* appeared in 1925.

CARR, Mrs Comyns: Alice Laura Vansittart STRETTEL (1850–1927) married (1873) Joseph William Comyns CARR (1849–1916). Born in Taplow, daughter of a Church of England clergyman, she was a goddaughter of Charles Kingsley (1819–75). Her father was chaplain in Genoa throughout her childhood, and she was educated at home and at a boarding-school in Brighton. She married an art critic and playwright, later editor of the *English Illustrated Magazine*, and published fiction, mostly run-of-the-mill romances, from 1881. *John Fletcher's*

Madonna (1905) is set in a Genoese *palazzo* and an Elizabethan country house. The hero goes to Italy to buy an Old Master, and marries the owner's daughter. In *By Ways That They Knew Not* (1910) a newly engaged man discovers that his first wife is alive and that he has a little daughter. Carr also designed costumes for her great friend Ellen Terry (1847–1928); her *Recollections* appeared in 1925.

CARREL, Frederic (1869–1928) was possibly an American, though he seems to have lived and worked in England, and was a member of the Authors' Club and contributor to the *Fortnightly Review*, the *Nineteenth Century*, and *Scientific Progress*. He was also the author of twelve novels (1895–1914), of which the most successful (to judge by the number of editions) was *The Adventures of John Johns* (1897), a satire on the speedy rise to social and financial success as a newspaper editor of Frank *Harris. Subsequently Carrel published sometimes under his own name, sometimes as 'the author of *The Adventures of John Johns*'. These novels are distinguished for eccentricity rather than literary merit. *Houses of Ignorance* (1902) appeared with a portentous foreword: 'I do not offer this book as a novel in the ordinary sense of the word, but as a story... dealing with the broader instincts of life from an ethical standpoint, in harmony with the scientific spirit.' The novel is in stilted dialogue and concerns the struggle between worldly self-interest, personified by Agnes Alexander, and humanitarianism, personified by her sister Clara Maxwell, who enquires at one point, 'Do you not think that we have a sense which makes us suffer when we contemplate an act which is against the welfare of the greater number?' Agnes has married for social advancement, while pregnant by a lover, and forces her weak husband to desert the Liberal cause for the Conservative. *2010* (1914) is a futuristic novel of eugenicist tendency in which the great scientist Caesar Brent invents a 'cytoplasmic bonnet' which gives humanity all the wisdom of the past and inaugurates a period of peace and prosperity. Unfortunately European women go barren, and Brent is obliged to invent a selective poison to defeat the attempt of the 'Orientals' to take over the world.

CARYL, Valentine, *pseud.*: see Valentina *Hawtrey.

CASSIDY, James, *pseud.*: Edith Mary STEANE (b. 1861) married —— STORY. This New Zealand writer published four novels under this pseudonym during this period, which include a historical romance, *Black Humphrey: A Story of the Old Cornish Coaching and Kidnapping Days* (1911), and two volumes of sentimental stories about humble life, *Love Is Love: Tales and Episodes* (1903) and *A Bridge of Fancies: Tales and Episodes* (1909). *Father Paul* (1908) is something of an oddity. A single-minded Roman Catholic priest raises a slum child, with consequences that he does not anticipate at the outset. There is a curious episode on the Atlantic island of 'Sanduna' where a band of people have retired to pursue the simple life. She also published, as E. M. Story, verse, criticism, and New Zealand history.

CASTLE, Egerton and Agnes: Egerton Smith CASTLE (1858–1920) married (1883) Agnes SWEETMAN (*c.*1860–1922). Egerton Castle was born in London, the grandson of the founder of the *Liverpool Mercury*, of which he became part-owner. He was educated at the Lycée Condorcet in Paris, at the Universities of Paris and Glasgow, at Trinity College, Cambridge, the Inner Temple, and Sandhurst. He worked on the **Saturday Review* 1885–94. He was an expert on fencing, publishing several works on its history and acting as captain of the British epée and sabre teams at the Olympic Games 1908. He was on the council and managing committee of the Society of Authors. He published four novels on his own and thirty-five, mostly *historical, in collaboration with his wife. Their best-known works seem to have been *The Bath Comedy* (1900) and its sequel, *Incomparable Bellairs* (1903), which describe intrigues in Georgian Bath; it was their vision of late eighteenth-century England populated with duelling highwaymen and flirts which was communicated to the next generation by Georgette Heyer (1902–74). *Diamond Cut Paste* (1909) has a contemporary setting and describes the farcical attempts of his family to disentangle an elderly married general from a designing woman. They also wrote a series of books about their house and garden at Hindhead in Surrey, where they were neighbours of Grant Allen (1848–99) and Conan *Doyle: *Our Sentimental Garden* (1914), *A Little House in War Time* (1915), and *The Third Year in the Little House* (1917). Agnes Castle was born of a Irish Catholic family, the youngest of four daughters of whom the second, Mary, wrote as M. E. *Francis, and the third, Elinor Sweetman, was a poet. She published one short and curious quasi-historical novel on her own, *My Little Lady Anne* (1896): an old servant describes the forced marriage of a retarded young girl who dies of fright.

Celestial Omnibus, The, *and Other Stories*, E. M. *Forster, 1911, Sidgwick & Jackson. By 1911 Forster had become, especially since the success of **Howards End* (1910), a writer to be reckoned with. But the stories collected here derived from the very beginning of his career. They were the fruit of his travels in Italy (1901–2) and Greece (1903), and rather dutifully assemble *fin-de-siècle* themes of a homoerotic slant: notably the celebration, popularized by *Sketches and Studies in Italy and Greece* (1874, 1898) by John Addington Symonds (1840–93), of a single male figure as *genius loci*. Forster said that he had found himself 'sitting down' on the topic of 'The Story of a Panic' as though it were an anthill, in a valley north of Ravello, in May 1902: a 'vision' of the god Pan terrifies a group of tourists, including the obtuse narrator, but transforms one of their number from a sulky 14-year-old to an assertive, sensuous free spirit. In the title-story, respectable, pompous Mr Bons ('snob' reversed) talks knowledgeably about literature and art but is nonplussed when, courtesy of the 'celestial omnibus', he meets the heroes of literature and the great writers of the past. Other stories fantasize about paganism, or about alternative worlds where all men are brothers. But the suspicion remains that Forster is very much at home in English suburbia, where his irony can take hold on *petit bourgeois* dummies like Mr Inskip ('ink-sipid'?), in 'The Other Kingdom'.

Celt and Saxon, George *Meredith, 1910, Constable. Long meditated, and long in the writing, but left incomplete at his death, the novel frames Meredith's enduring preoccupation with national identity—'an ideal of country, of Great Britain, is conceivable that will be to the taste of Celt and Saxon in common'—within a love affair. The quick-witted, fanciful Patrick O'Donnell, educated by the Jesuits in Paris, has inherited an estate in Ireland and desires to see the world a little before settling down to manage it. He visits Earlsfont, in Wales, the seat of Edward Adister, whose daughter Adiante was once engaged to his elder brother, Philip, a soldier, in order to discover Adiante's address on the Continent and plead with her on his brother's behalf. Adiante, however, has married the sinister Nikolas Schinderhannes, a Middle European prince with *Ruritanian political and military ambitions, and wishes to sell two estates inherited from her grandmother in order to raise money for her husband's enterprises. Patrick is present when Adister discusses the problem with his lawyer, Mr Camminy, and his niece, Caroline; he also obtains possession of a miniature of the lady herself. In Chapter 8 the scene switches to the London home of Patrick's cousin, Captain Con O'Donnell, a fiery Nationalist who is happily married to an older and unbendingly English woman, Adister's sister. Chapter 11 introduces a new character, the Liberal MP John Mattock, a self-made man, a 'thorough stout Briton and bulldog for the national integrity', whose equally sturdy young daughter, Jane, helps run the family laundry ('We're aiming at steam, you know'), and soon falls in love with Patrick. Richard Rockney, a radical (and radically patriotic) journalist, an Englishman with an Irish wife, makes his debut during a raucous dinner party, and thereafter provides the focus for a leisurely and wide-ranging discussion of the state of the nation. Chapter 17 brings Patrick's sister Kathleen to England, accompanied by Father Boyle, and Mr Colesworth, whom Patrick had met on the Continent; by this time, it turns out, Schinerhannes's adventure has come to a bloody end, and Adiante returned to her father's house to recuperate; Philip, meanwhile, has been wounded in battle, and Captain Con elected to Parliament. The novel is characteristic of Meredith not only in its theme but in its serio-comic tone: 'humour in its intense strain has a seat somewhere about the mouth of tragedy, giving it the enigmatical faint wry pull at a corner visible at times upon the dreadful mask'. Meredith's aim, as always, was to steer a course between romance and naturalism. 'The theme is chosen and must be treated as a piper involved in his virtue conceives it: that is, realistically; not with Bull's notion of the realism of the butcher's shop and the pendent legs of mutton and blocks of beef painted raw and glaring in their streaks, but with the realism of the active brain and heart conjoined.'

CHALLACOMBE, Jessie: Jessie WORSFOLD (1864–1925) married (1891) William Allen CHALLA-

COMBE (d. 1951). Brought up in Dover, she spent most of her life as the wife of a Church of England clergyman in New Malden. She was a prolific author of children's fiction for the SPCK.

Chance: *A Tale in Two Parts*, Joseph *Conrad, 1913, Methuen. Meeting the newspaper magnate Gordon Bennett (1841–1918) in Ceylon in 1909 (a chance encounter, suitably enough), Hugh *Clifford persuaded him to serialize Conrad's next novel, and to buy the book in advance. Conrad had begun and abandoned *Chance* (then a short story called 'Dynamite') as early as 1898, but now completed it with relative ease between June 1911 and March 1912. 'It's my *quickest* piece of work,' Conrad told his *literary agent, J. B. Pinker: 'About 140 thousand words in 9 months and 23 days.' Boosted by the serialization, by an energetic publicity campaign and favourable reviews, by chapter headings (for the first and last time in Conrad's *œuvre*), by a happy ending, and by a dust-jacket which shows a man in uniform placing a shawl around the shoulders of an attractive young woman seated in a deck-chair, the book sold very well indeed: 10,000 copies in the first few months, 13,200 in two years. And yet its genesis, themes, incidents, and narrative method are essentially Conradian. Flora de Barral, daughter of a confidence man and swindler, currently in jail, is bullied by her governess, a woman of 'ungovernable passions' who seems 'avid' for pleasure, and persuaded that she is an 'utterly common and insipid creature'. Rescued by her neighbours, the discreetly lesbian Mrs Fyne and her 'pedestrian' husband, she contemplates suicide, but is prevented by Mrs Fyne's brother, Captain Roderick Anthony, son of a famous but unpleasant and sexually incontinent poet, Carleon Anthony. Roderick marries Flora, and removes her to his ship, the *Ferndale*, but declines to consummate the marriage because he has been led to believe that she does not love him. There they are joined by Flora's newly released father, who becomes insanely jealous of Roderick and resolves to murder him. Powell, second mate of the *Ferndale*, sees de Barral pouring poison into Roderick's brandy. Thinking Flora the culprit, Roderick says he will put her off at the next port. She replies that she does not want to leave him, and they are reconciled. De Barral, his plot foiled, drinks the fatal brandy. Later, the *Ferndale* is involved in a collision, and Roderick Anthony goes down with it, leaving Flora free to marry Powell. The story is told by Powell to Marlow (also of **Youth*, **Heart of Darkness* and **Lord Jim*, but a lot grumpier), who tells it to the anonymous narrator: a process Henry *James, in his 1914 essay on 'The New Novel', likened to buckets of water passed along a chain of firemen, and to the overlapping shadows cast by aeroplanes flying in formation. Parallels can be drawn with other novels by Conrad, notably *Victory* (1915), and with James's *The Turn of the Screw* (1898), which also involves a governess and an innocent young girl called Flora. Mr Fyne is said to have been modelled on H. G. *Wells, Carleon Anthony on Coventry Patmore (1823–96), and de Barral, in part, on Ford Madox *Hueffer. Why, then, was so idiosyncratic and complex a novel so successful? It may be that, as in the case of John Fowles's *The French Lieutenant's Woman* (1969), the narrative technique and the Hardyesque emphasis on coincidence served somehow to enhance the fundamental simplicity of the heroic vision: a woman in danger from corrupt urban sophisticates, but regenerated by a sojourn aboard a mobile Eden (the *Ferndale*) crewed by more or less noble savages (Powell, Anthony).

Change in the Cabinet, A, Hilaire *Belloc, 1909, Methuen. This nicely sardonic but inconsequential satire on parliamentary democracy is set in 1915. Dim, impecunious George Demaine is to succeed clever but shady Sir Charles Repton, who has been elevated to the House of Lords, as Warden of the Court of Dowry: an office with responsibility for all aspects of maritime commerce. Repton goes mad; Demaine goes missing. In Swiftian fashion, the madness takes the form of compulsive candour, while Demaine's adventure brings him into eye-opening contact with working people. In the end, the 'inveterate hope of the governing class that a gentleman can always get out of a hole' is fulfilled by Repton's recovery and Demaine's rescue. Government returns to deception as usual. The Prime Minister of the day has a Private Secretary, Edward Evans, whose job is to square the press, which he does with authentic creepiness.

CHANNON, E. M.: Ethel Mary BREDIN (1875–1951) married (1904) Francis Granville CHANNON (1875– after 1944). Born at Rathdowney, Ireland and educated at St Leonard's College and Cheltenham Ladies' College, she married an assistant master at Eton College. In her first novel, *The Authoress* (1909), Venetia Conway befriends and makes presentable plain and stupid Vivia Mortlake, because the man she loves has fallen in love with Vivia after reading her book. Vivia finally confesses that the real authoress is her cousin Blanche and dies in Venetia's arms. Channon's second novel also focuses on a woman in love with the idea of being a writer. In *Miss King's Profession* (1913) Petronella King leaves her real duties to her mother and sister and writes magazine stories. Her error is pointed out to her first by her best friend and then by the vicar, both of whom turn out to have written far better novels than she: her real vocation is matrimony (with the vicar). Many of Channon's later books were school stories for girls and romances; thirty-six titles (1909–36) are listed in the *British Library Catalogue*.

CHAN-TOON, Mrs M.: Mabel Mary Agnes COSGROVE (d. before 1922) married, first (*c.*1893), SAN HTUN AUNG and, secondly, —— WOODHOUSE-PEARSE. The little that is known about this writer is intriguing, though her fiction is more remarkable for subject-matter than style. An Englishwoman, she married a Burmese barrister and lived in Rangoon before returning to England, where she wrote fiction about the difficulties of interracial marriage and other subjects and remarried after his death. Most of the information about her career derives from the brief introduction to the 1922 publication of a manuscript play, *Love of the King: A Burmese Masque*, sent to her in 1894 by Oscar Wilde (1854–1900), with whom she had apparently been long acquainted, their parents being friends. In the letter which enclosed the play he describes it as 'the outcome of long and luminous talks with your distinguished husband in the Temple and on the river, in the days when I was meditating writing a novel as beautiful and as intricate as a Persian praying-rug. I hope that I have caught the atmosphere.' Chan Toon refers to his trial in her novel *Mrs Helen Wyverne's Marriage* (1912). As Mabel Cosgrove she published *What Was the Verdict?* (1892); and, as 'Mimosa', *Told on the Pagoda: Tales of Burma* (1895). As 'Mrs Chan-Toon' she published six volumes of fiction 1905–14, the first of which was the almost certainly autobiographical *A Marriage in Burmah* (1905), the tale of a disastrous marriage between an English girl and a Burmese lawyer brought up in Europe, which the preface states was designed to 'show... how vast is the gulf that divides the Eastern from the Western'. He turns out vulgar, a liar, and an alcoholic; she leaves him and an unloved baby to return to England. Her second novel, *Love Letters of an English Peeress to an Indian Prince* (1912), concerns an imaginary and high-flown love affair between an Englishwoman and Nana Sahib. *Leper and Millionaire* (1910) is another *marriage problem story. Her first husband was a barrister of the Middle Temple, and, it is said, a nephew of the King of Burma; he is probably also to be identified with the author of a textbook on pawnbroking law (1872), *The Nature and Value of Jurisprudence: Roman Law and International Law* (1888), *Leading Cases on Buddhist Law* (1899), and *The Principles of Buddhist Law* (1903). If he was dead by the time of her second marriage it cannot have been he, but perhaps a son and namesake, who was 'constitutional adviser' in Burma in the 1940s.

CHARTRES, A. Vivanti: Anita VIVANTI (1868–1942) married (1892) John CHARTRES. She was born in London; her father was an Italian nationalist exile and her mother, Anna Lindau, a German writer. After an unsettled adolescence spent between Switzerland, England, and the United States, she became an actress, singer, and poet. The elderly poet Giosuè Carducci (1835–1907) became infatuated with her; their correspondence has been published (1951). She married an American journalist. Her novel *The Devourers* (1910) was published in English, her verse and later novels in Italian. The 'devourers' in question are men and women of genius, and particularly children of genius (Vivanti's own daughter, Vivien, was a gifted musician). Nancy, child of an English father and an Italian mother, is a genius, turning out from an early age poems which earn widespread admiration. She remains unaware of the tyranny exerted over others (notably her mother) by the demands of her genius. Her mother's cousin, Nino, who has had a long affair with an actress, falls in love with her. The actress gives him up so that he may marry Nancy and save her from the handsome but unscrupulous Aldo. Nancy, however, chooses Aldo, only to find that a bad marriage destroys talent. She herself becomes the mother of a child genius, Anne Marie, a gifted musician. What Vivien Chartres thought of these dire warnings about the effects of precocity is not known. She died tragically in bombing in 1941. Persecuted as a Jew, Vivanti herself was confined with other English citizens in Arezzo. She died in Turin.

CHESNEY, Weatherby, *pseud.*: see C. J. Cutcliffe *Hyne.

CHESSON, Mrs W. H.: Eleanor HOPPER (1871–1906) married (1901) Wilfrid Hugh CHESSON (1870–1952). Born in Exeter, the daughter of an Indian Army officer, she went to school in Kensington and began to publish verse in 1887. As Nora Hopper she published prose (one Irish myth) and verse in the *Yellow Book* from 1894, and she is best known as a poet of the Celtic revival. Although she wrote children's books, and her *A Northern Juliet* was serialized in the girls' periodical *Atalanta*, the only novel of hers which reached volume form was *The Bell and the Arrow: An English Love Story* (1905). It is set in an English village, and traces from childhood the love affairs of two couples. Margaret fancies she loves her adopted brother, a tramp's son, but marries a rich man. The brother marries a quiet girl who understands him; the knowledge that she is pregnant ends Margaret's attempt at being unhappily married. Despite the banality of its plot, the novel's minor characters have some force. The harrowing story told by Chesson's Royal Literary Fund file makes it seem likely that she wrote a novel because verse paid so badly, since she was now the breadwinner. Her application in 1905 was supported by G. K. *Chesterton, E. V. *Lucas, and Edward Garnett (1868–1937). The latter wrote that her husband had had 'a complete mental breakdown and is now suffering from persistent spiritualistic delusions'. In the following year she gave birth to a daughter and died of puerperal fever, leaving three small children, on whose behalf Lucas applied again. W. H. Chesson was a literary critic who published two novels in the 1890s; a colleague of Garnett's at T. Fisher Unwin, he recommended to him the manuscript of *Conrad's *Almayer's Folly.*

CHESTERTON, G[ilbert] K[eith] (1874–1936) married (1901) Frances BLOGG (d. 1938). Chesterton was born in Kensington, where his great-grandfather had started an estate agency. His father was cultivated, Liberal, and Unitarian; he did not work in the family business because of poor health. Chesterton went to St Paul's School (1887–92) where he made friends with E. C. *Bentley. An eccentric boy with a habit of scribbling drawings, he became an art student at the Slade (1893–5) instead of going to university, but while there he was able to attend lectures on English literature at University College London. He worked for the publisher T. Fisher Unwin (1895–1901) and during this time began to develop a career as a journalist, writing reviews, art criticism, and political commentary. His anti-imperialist beliefs were shaped by opposition to the *Boer War; his famous objection to the 'deaf and raucous Jingoism' of 'my country right or wrong'—'it is like saying, "My mother, drunk or sober" '—was published in the *Speaker* (26 May 1901). As early as the collection of articles published as *The Defendant* (1901) he championed popular culture. A permanent job reviewing for a Liberal paper, the *Daily News*, in 1901 enabled him to marry; after 1905 he was paid £350 a year to write a weekly column in the *Illustrated London News* (continued till his death), some of which were collected as *All Things Considered* (1908). *Heretics* (1905) enunciated his own philosophical position in sketches of his contemporaries, including Shaw, *Kipling, and *Wells. Through his brother Cecil Chesterton (1879–1918) he had connections with the Fabian Group. It was in the pages of the Fabian Arts Group's magazine the **New Age* that the famous controversy with *Belloc, *Wells, and G. B. Shaw (1856–1950) took place during 1907–9. He also contributed to the *Eye-Witness* (1911–12), run by his brother and Hilaire *Belloc, and its successor, the *New Witness* (1912–23), which he took over when Cecil went to war and which became *G. K.'s Weekly* (1925–36). His novel *The *Ball and the Cross* (New York 1909, London 1910) was serialized in the Christian Social Union's magazine *Commonwealth* during 1905–6. His other fiction during this period consists of *The *Napoleon of Notting Hill* (1904), *The *Club of Queer Trades* (1905), *The *Man Who Was Thursday: A Nightmare* (1908), *The *Innocence of Father Brown* (1911), **Manalive* (1912), *The *Wisdom of Father Brown* (1914), and *The *Flying Inn* (1914). In the First World War he published a few works of propaganda, and ceased to contribute to the Socialist *Daily Herald* because of its pacifist stance. His career as prolific journalist, essayist, novelist, commentator on politics, ethics, and religion, poet, and illustrator continued till his death. He became a Roman Catholic in 1922. His autobiography was published posthumously (1936). 'John Keith *Prothero' was his sister-in-law.

CHILDERS, [Robert] Erskine (1870–1922), DSC (1916), married (1904) Mary Alden OSGOOD (d. 1964). Born in London, Childers was 6 when his father, an orientalist, died of tuberculosis. His mother, herself infected, retreated to a home for incurables and sent her five children to her father in Ireland; she died eight years later. Childers was educated at Haileybury and Trinity College, Cambridge, but his childhood home was in Co. Wicklow. He served with the HAC in the *Boer War, and published a memoir of his experience and two historical works on the episode. His only novel, *The *Riddle of the Sands: A Record of Secret Service Recently Achieved* (1903), grew out of his hobby of sailing small yachts in the North Sea in his holidays. He was Clerk in the House of Commons 1895–1910 but, converted to the cause of Home Rule for Ireland, resigned in order to agitate publicly. In the First World War he fought in the Royal Naval Air Service. He settled in Ireland in 1920 and was elected to the Dáil Éireann in the following year. He became a close adherent of Éamon de Valera (1882–1975). Vehemently opposed to partition, he was an awkward secretary to the Irish delegation at the London conference negotiating independence. He wrote in his diary that Arthur Griffiths 'says I caused the European War and now want to cause another'. In the civil war which followed he fought against the Free State army, and was arrested at his old home in 1922 by forces of the Provisional Government. He had a gun, and since possession of a lethal weapon was a capital crime he was summarily court-martialled and shot. His elder son became the fourth President of Ireland (1973–4). There is a biography by Andrew Boyle (1977).

Children of the Dead End: *The Autobiography of a Navvy,* Patrick *MacGill, 1914, Herbert Jenkins. The novel describes the odyssey of a young Irish labourer, Dermod Flynn, who travels to Scotland to pick potatoes and subsequently works as a platelayer and navvy. He starts to read the works of John Ruskin (1819–1900) and Thomas Carlyle (1795–1881) at the Carnegie Library in Glasgow, and soon discovers socialism, organizing a railway strike. He submits stories of navvying life to a London paper, and is eventually taken on to the staff. His success is contrasted with the tragic failure of his intermittent companion, Norah Ryan, who gambles her money away and eventually resorts to prostitution. The novel is notable primarily for the robust speech of two 'gypsies of labour' Flynn encounters on his travels, Moleskin Joe and Carroty Dan. The term 'gypsy' gives the game away. These are the wise vagrants, the hedgerow prophets, of High Romantic tradition: their nearest contemporary equivalents are Brum and New Haven Baldy in W. H. *Davies's *The Autobiography of a Super-Tramp* (1908), or the more pious, and more static, hero of 'Michael *Fairless' *The Roadmender* (1902).

Chippinge, Stanley J. *Weyman, 1906, Smith, Elder. A swashbuckler with the usual supply of melting maids, crabbed Machiavels, and divided loyalties; set, unusually, in England at the time of the first Reform Bill. Arthur Vaughan is an ardent reformer bound by ties of allegiance to the old order (whose representatives he is continually rescuing from enflamed mobs). The density of historical reference, particularly to the Bristol riots of 1831, and the fact that the hero's dilemma does reflect a real if limited inquiry into the nature of democracy, give the narrative additional substance. Indeed, it turns rather neatly on the abolition of the very *ancien régime* which was the favourite resource of historical novelists like Weyman.

CHOLMONDELEY, Mary (1859–1925) was the third of eight children and eldest of five daughters, and was educated at home by a governess. Her father, a nephew of the poet Reginald Heber, Bishop of Calcutta (1773–1833), was a clergyman whose family were landed gentry. Late in life he inherited his childhood home and had to sell it. The life of the country house and the landowner's obligations were favourite themes of his daughter's. Her mother, paralytic and depressive, was fascinated by science; her daughter wrote 'she ought to have been a bachelor professor in a whitewashed laboratory, instead of the invalided mother of many children'. Until her father's retirement to London in 1896 Cholmondeley lived at Hodnet in Shropshire; some account of this life appears in her memoir *Under One Roof: A Family Record* (1918). Her first novel, *The Danvers Jewels* (1887), was published anonymously; she was encouraged by Rhoda *Broughton, a family friend. Her major success was *Red Pottage* (1899), which sold 18,000 copies in three weeks. *Moth and Rust* (1902) is a collection of stories. *Prisoners—Fast Bound in Misery and Iron* (1906) is a melodramatic novel beginning with a *crime passionnel* in Italy; the scenes in an English country house are wittier and more plausible. There is a harrowing scene of a mother dying: '"With men it is take, take, take, until we have nothing left to give."' A. E. *Benson, according to his brother E. F. *Benson, was one of several bachelor friends of Cholmondeley offended by the book. She was accused of libel, and prefixed a disingenuous disclaimer to her next collection, *The *Lowest Rung* (1908). *Notwithstanding* (1913) deals with the fashionable theme of dishonour. Cholmondeley published another volume of short stories, *The Romance of His Life* (1921), but her last years were unproductive, spent in a long and painful illness. There is a biography by Percy Lubbock (1928) and a bibliography by Jane Crisp (n. d.). Her sister Essex was the mother of the novelist Stella Benson (1892–1933).

Chronicles of Clovis, The, '*Saki', 1912, John Lane. A. A. Milne (1882–1956), introducing the Bodley Head reprint of 1937, recalled discovering 'Saki', and particularly his glamour, in the *Westminster Gazette* in the early years of the century. 'While we were being funny, as planned, with collar-studs and hot-water bottles, he was being much funnier with werwolves and tigers... Even the most casual intruder into one of his sketches, as it might be our Tomkins, had to be called Belturbet or de Ropp, and for his hero, weary man-of-the-world at seventeen, nothing less thrilling than Clovis Sangrail would do.' Today the world-weariness looks more like a snobbish preoccupation with the upper crust of the upper crust. But 'Saki' 's accounts of country-house parties, tiger-shoots, anarchist outrages and magical transformations are so wonderfully sly and heartless that it is difficult to resist them for long. Particularly irresistible is 'The Background', about a man who has the Fall of Icarus tattooed across his torso and consequently becomes a work of art, much debated by scholars and critics.

CHURCHILL, Winston [Leonard] SPENCER (1874–1965), KG (1953), OM (1946), married (1908) Clementine Ogilvy HOZIER (1885–1977), created (1965) Baroness SPENCER-CHURCHILL of CHARTWELL. The statesman was the author of one novel, **Savrola* (1900). He was awarded the 1953 Nobel prize for Literature for his historical writings. He is not to be confused with the American historical novelist Winston S. Churchill (1871–1947).

CLARE, Austin, *pseud*.: Wilhelmina Martha JAMES (*c*.1845–1932) was the eldest daughter of the eight children of a Church of England clergyman, rector of Kirkhaugh, Northumberland. Her large output includes much children's fiction and many religious tracts for the SPCK between 1868 and 1931. Her adult fiction includes *The Tideway* (1903), in which a *Boer War veteran is tempted to cheat another man for the sake of a woman, and *Randall of Randalholme: A Tynedale Tragedy* (1904), set, like other works, in her native Northumberland and the border country. Her most popular book seems to have been *The Carved Cartoon: A Picture of the Past* (1874), a historical novel for children about the sculptor Grinling Gibbons (1648–1720), which was dramatized, and which Marghanita Laski (1915–88) called 'the best historical children's book I know'. She lived in Bootle, Lancashire, and also published as 'Hope Everest'.

CLARKE, [Charles] Allen (1863–1935) married first, (late 1880s) Lavinia PILLING (d. after a few months) and, secondly, Eliza TAYLOR (d. 1928). Born during the cotton famine caused by the American Civil War blockade, at Bolton, Lancashire, the eldest of nine children of two textile workers, Clarke devoted his life to writing for and about the working class. At 13 he began part-time work at a mill in Bolton, while still attending some classes at school. He was later a pupil teacher, and taught until at 21 he managed to get into the fringes of journalism. He worked on the *Bolton Evening News* until 1890, when he started his own weekly, the *Labour Light*. In the following year this was replaced by a lighter paper, the *Bolton Trotter* (1891–2), in which was serialized Clarke's first novel, *The Knobstick* (1893), based on the strike of Bolton engineers in 1887. He then worked for the *Cotton Factory Times* and as editor of the *Blackpool Echo* (1896–1900) and *Northern Weekly* (1900–6). He started another vehicle for his humorous writing, *Teddy Ashton's Journal* (1896–1908), which reached a circulation of 30,000. His book *The Effects of the Factory System* (1899) attacked the half-time education which he had himself received, and led to a correspondence with L. N. Tolstoy (1828–1910), who had it translated into Russian, and proposed also to translate Clarke's novels. Clarke stood unsuccessfully as ILP/SDF candidate for Rochdale in 1900. After the drowning of his son in 1899 he became a convert to spiritualism; he was also interested in Maude Egerton *King's revival of rural crafts. Clarke's copious output includes non-fiction, Lancashire topography and history, and humorous sketches, many published under the pseudonym 'Teddy Ashton'. His fiction in this period includes the anti-Imperialist *Starved into Surrender* (1904), in which a wicked Russian prince resolves to bring down the degenerate British empire by buying up all the corn in England and blockading the ports, which leads to starvation, revolution, and the establishment of a utopian commonwealth, and *Lancashire Lads and Lasses* (1906), in which a mill-owner's son falls in love with a mill girl whose father was swindled by his father; he is nearly hanged for parricide but all is revealed and the novel ends with a wedding and a chorus of congratulation.

CLARKE, Isabel C[onstance] (d. 1951). Born near Plymouth, she was the daughter of an army officer who became professor of military law at the Staff College, Camberley. He dictated his books to her, and she graduated from this, through submitting entries to magazine competitions, to authorship. She travelled widely and lived in Rome for twenty-six years before the Second World War, which she spent mostly in Jamaica. She wrote biographies of women writers including Elizabeth Barrett Browning (1806–61) and Maria Edgeworth (1767–1849), and fifty-six volumes of melodramatic fiction between 1897 and 1950. Their outstanding characteristic is a devoted commitment to Roman Catholicism. In *By the Blue River: A Novel* (1913), set in North Africa, the heroine's son is kidnapped by Arabs who try to convert him to Islam. He defies their torture and their arguments and eventually becomes a monk. *Fine Clay* (1914) is about a little boy whose dead mother was Catholic but who is being brought up as his heir by his fiercely Protestant English grandfather. Although beaten and tyrannized from the age of 4, he secretly says his rosary every night, converts when he is 21 and becomes a priest. Expatriate life in Italy and Tunisia plays a large part in Clarke's fiction.

Clayhanger, Arnold *Bennett, 1910, Methuen. After the critical and commercial success of *The *Old Wives' Tale* (1908), *Clayhanger* set the seal on Bennett's reputation as the laureate of the commonplace. It is a *Bildungsroman* describing the youth and young manhood of Edwin Clayhanger, whom we first see as he is on the point of leaving school at the age of 16. His father, Darius, is a printer in the Five Towns whose life has been shaped by early experience of the workhouse: a triumphantly self-made man, he will not tolerate criticism of himself, or any sign of weakness in others. The conflict between father and son is also a conflict between eras: between Victorian thrift and (somewhat tentative) Edwardian pleasures, the latter consisting chiefly of the purchase of books and the desire to become an architect. After a short-lived rebellion, Edwin settles down into the family business, which he takes over after his father's breakdown and death. His decline into bachelordom is halted by the appearance, and then abrupt disappearance (to marry a man who turns out to be a bigamist and swindler) of the secretive, provocative Hilda Lessways. The critic who praised the novel's 'physical verity' probably came as close as anyone to defining its appeal. Bennett's triumphal progress from New York to Chicago ensured that it was widely noticed in America. **Hilda Lessways* (1911) describes some of the same events from a different perspective, while *These Twain* (1916) chronicles Hilda's marriage to Edwin. A somewhat inferior fourth volume, *The Roll-Call* (1919), features George Edwin Cannon, Hilda's son by her first husband.

CLEEVE, Lucas, *pseud.*: Adeline Georgiana Isabella WOLFF (1860–1908) married (1885) Howard KINGSCOTE (1845–1917). Wolff's father was a diplomat and Conservative politician, Sir Henry Drummond Wolff (1830–1908), and her grandfather, the Revd. Joseph Wolff (1795–1862), a rabbi's son who became a famous Anglican missionary. In *Who's Who* she wrote: 'Educ: The School for Scandal. AA Oxford Univ. Chequered and varied career, great traveller and linguist.' It seems that she was not at any of the women's colleges at Oxford; possibly she attended extension lectures, or this may be a joke. She married an army officer stationed in India and bore three children in the late 1880s. As 'Mrs Howard Kingscote' she published two books from her Indian experience: a collection of Indian folk-tales (in collaboration, 1890) and a book of advice on childrearing in India (1893). In 1895, as 'Lucas Cleeve', she burst into more controversial areas with *The Woman Who Wouldn't*, one of the many responses to *The Woman Who Did* (1895) by Grant Allen (1848–99). She reverses the situation of that novel (in which a man and a woman are lovers without being married) by having a heroine who refuses to sleep with her husband. Her novel is thus far more titillating than Allen's; the plot makes explicit what is usually implicit in romantic fiction, the postponement of sexual fulfilment. *The Woman Who Wouldn't* is perhaps the earliest example of the use of the plot of the unconsummated marriage which was to become a staple of twentieth-century romantic fiction, and was used by Elinor *Glyn in *The Reason Why* (1911) and Joseph *Conrad in **Chance* (1914). Kingscote declares in the second edition of *The Woman Who Wouldn't* that the first sold out in three weeks; evidently it caused a stir, since she also deplores 'the exaggerated and narrow-minded, not to say uncultivated and badly-expressed reviews of my book in some of the inferior newspapers, criticisms which amount almost to libel'. Not all her subsequent novels were in the same vein: *Lazarus* (1897) describes the impact of the Crucifixion on the followers of Christ; Lazarus wants to marry Mary Magdalene but she is killed by the jealous daughter of Caiaphas. *Our Lady of Beauty* (1904) is a *historical novel about Agnes Sorel (1422–50). However the theme of desire and power in sexual relationships persists in her work, which deteriorated in quality as her output increased. In *What a Woman Will Do* (1900) a woman allows herself to be divorced so that her husband can marry a rich woman; by the end the two women have united against him. The heroine of *Duchinka* (1908) is a Russian princess won by her husband at cards; he is too high-minded to sleep with her until they acknowledge their love in the last chapter. Here the plot of *The Woman Who Wouldn't* is being exploited simply for effect; analysis of sexual politics has been abandoned. The *British Library Catalogue* credits Kingscote with the amazing total of fifty-six novels published between 1900 and 1911 alone. She died at Chateau d'Oex in Switzerland, where she had been living apart from her husband.

CLERKE, Ellen Mary (1840–1906). The daughter of an Irish Catholic bank manager with a keen interest in chemistry, Clerke was born in Ireland but travelled much in Italy. She lived with her sister Agnes Mary Clerke (1842–1907), a well-known astronomer. Ellen Clerke contributed many articles on Italian and German literature to English periodicals. She also published verse and one novel, *Flowers of Fire* (1902). Esme Zaroiska is the daughter of a patriotic Polish nobleman. A sinister prince, long ago spurned by her mother, gets the father imprisoned in order to trick the daughter into marrying him. Esme, about to sacrifice herself, discovers his perfidy, flings herself at the Czarina's feet, wins her father's freedom, and marries her Italian lover. There is a memoir (1907) of the Clerke sisters by Lady Huggins.

CLIFFORD, Hugh [Charles] (1866–1941), KCMG (1909), married, first (1896), Minna A'BECKETT (d. 1907) and, secondly (1910), Mrs Henry *De La Pasture. Clifford's father was a general, a VC, of a grand Roman Catholic family, and lived abroad because of a scandalous affair with a servant girl. Clifford went to a Catholic school, Woburn Park, and joined the Malay Civil Service in 1883. He rose to be Governor of North Borneo (1899–1901), Colonial Secretary of Trinidad and Tobago (1903–7) and of Ceylon (1907–12), and Governor of the Gold Coast (1912–19), of Nigeria (1919–25), of Ceylon (1925–7), and of the Straits Settlements (1927–8). He clung to an ideal of benevolent imperialism untainted by commerce, while emphasizing the strains of the clash of culture in fiction about both native Malayan life and the experience of the white man in the colonies. He has been claimed as a significant precursor of and influence on his friend *Conrad, who praised his work, for its truth rather than its art, in a review of Clifford's *Studies in Brown Humanity* (1898). His Edwardian fiction includes *Sally: A Study, and Other Tales of the Outskirts* (1904) and *Saleh: A Sequel* (1908), both of which deal with the predicament of a Malayan raja educated in England; *Bush-Whacking and other Sketches* (1901); *A Free-lance of To-day* (1903), a novel set in Sumatra, which bears signs of the influence of Rider *Haggard; and *Malayan Monochromes* (1913). The first of the latter collection descibes a colonial governor who returns, as Clifford did, to his first posting at the end of his career. Many of his stories were first contributed to *Blackwood's*, **Temple Bar*, the *Graphic*, and other magazines. His first wife was the only child of Gilbert à Beckett (1837–91), the *Punch* writer. Clifford was afflicted periodically with manic depressive illness, which led to early retirement. From 1931 to his death he was confined in a convent at Roehampton. There is a biography by Harry A. Gailey (1982).

CLIFFORD, Mrs W. K.: Sophia Lucy Jane LANE (1849–1929) married (1875) William Kingdon CLIFFORD (1845–79). Lucy Clifford was born in London and brought up in Barbados, the daughter of a colonial administrator, and was left a penniless widow with two small children. Her husband was a distinguished mathematician and philosopher who had many influential friends. They (including 'George Eliot', 1819–80) helped her get a Civil List pension of £80 annually and a Royal Literary Fund grant of £200. Having already published an untraced anonymous novel, she took to literature. Her *Anyhow Stories* (1882) for children have been praised by Alison Lurie in *Don't Tell the Grown-Ups* (1990); her first known novel, *Mrs Keith's Crime* (1885), about infanticide, had reached four editions by 1888. *Aunt Anne* (1892) is the story of an unsuccessful marriage beween a middle-aged woman and a young man. *A Woman Alone: Three Stories* (1901) comprises three linked stories about loneliness. The first woman adores a difficult husband who lives apart from her; the third loves but cannot marry because she murdered her first husband. *Woodside Farm* (1902) has a worldly villainess whose attempts to prevent the heroine's marriage are drastic and unsuccessful. The idyllic rural setting of the heroine's childhood is contrasted with London's nasty sophistication. In the short stories of *The Modern Way (Eight Examples)* (1906) the theme is again marriage and the individual in modern society. Clifford was a friend of both Henry *James and Elizabeth *Robins. She was a prominent figure in literary circles for many years, but by 1920 appeared ridiculous to Virginia Woolf (1882–1941), who described her vitriolically: 'black velvet, morbid, intense, jolly, vulgar—a hack to her tips . . . If I could reproduce her talk of money, royalties, editions, and reviews, I should think myself a novelist . . .' Clifford's daughter Ethel, later Lady Dilke (d. 1959), published verse.

Climber, The, E. F. *Benson, 1908, William Heinemann. This is an unambitious but well-judged rewriting of *Vanity Fair* (1848) by W. M. Thackeray (1811–63). Benson's Becky Sharp and Amelia Sedley are Lucia Grimson and Maud Eddis, who meet, not at a private school but, in true Edwardian fashion, at Girton College, Cambridge. Orphaned Lucia lives with maiden aunts in provincial Bisham, where cricket and tennis matches constitute excitement. She entraps Lord Edgar Brayton, whom she knows Maud to be in love with, and uses him as the means of a rapid social ascent. The meticulous, conservative Brayton, who founds a Shakespeare society and always observes the speed limit, is soon outpaced by Lucia's fast set. Maud, meanwhile, has married Brayton's fatally easygoing friend Charlie Lindsay. Lucia realizes that she has fallen in love with Lindsay, and decides that she must have him, too, whatever the cost to Edgar and Maud. She deceives herself as ruthlessly as she has deceived others. Edgar's anticlimactic qualities serve him well when he finds Charlie and Lucia together. Charlie returns to Maud, Lucia to the surviving maiden aunt. Benson's novel does not have anything like the sweep of Thackeray's, but it surveys the 'vanity fair' of Edwardian high society thoughtfully and amusingly.

CLOUSTON, J[oseph] S[torer] (1870–1944) married (1903) Winifred CLOUSTON. Clouston's father was a mental specialist in Edinburgh, of an Orcadian family; his mother was American. He was born in Cumberland, where his father was then medical superintendent of the Cumberland and Westmorland Asylum, educated at Merchiston and Magdalen College, Oxford, and called to the Bar in 1895. He lived in Orkney, where he took part in local politics and published several works on its history and antiquities. His first novel, *Vandrad the Viking* (1898), is a solemn *historical adventure describing the coming of Christianity to Orkney. It was followed by the much more successful *The Lunatic at Large* (1899), which was had reached its sixth impression by 1902, a farcical and picaresque account of the adventures of a man who undertakes to look after a patient with brain fever. Clouston wrote many sequels to this book, including *Count Bunker* (1906), whose German hero speaks in broken English throughout. *The Adventures of M. D'Haricot* (1902), an early Victorian adventure, and *Tales of King Fido* (1909), a *Ruritanian romance, are both in Clouston's facetious, slapstick style. He was a prolific writer and continued to publish novels until 1941.

Club of Queer Trades, The, G. K. *Chesterton, 1905, Harper. The five stories in the collection concern a club whose members have all invented the method by which they earn their living. One runs an Adventure and Romance Agency, another in an Organizer of Repartee, a third a Professional Detainer, a fourth an estate agent who specializes in 'arboreal villas', a fifth an author who has invented a new language in order to test his theory of language acquisition, and will speak no other. In pursuit of their specialisms, these men come into contact with the narrator, Swinburne, and two of his friends, Basil and Rupert Grant, one a retired judge, the other a private detective with a 'romantic interest' in London life. Basil Grant turns out to be President of the Club: on retiring from the Bench, he set up a Voluntary Criminal Court to settle 'purely moral differences'. The stories, illustrated by Chesterton himself, are as flimsy as they are witty; but they derive from a vivid sense of the unknowability of urban experience. 'It's only a social fiction,' the Professional Detainer remarks of his occupation. 'A result of our complex society.'

CLYDE, Constance, *pseud.*: Constance McADAM (b. 1872). Born in Scotland, she was taken as a child to Otago, New Zealand, was educated at Dunedin, and became a journalist in New Zealand before moving to Queensland, Australia. Dorothea, the heroine of her only novel, *A Pagan's Love* (1905), which was published in London in T. Fisher Unwin's First Novel Library, similarly travels from New Zealand to Australia. Her experience of an unconsummated love affair with a married man is contrasted with that of Ascot Wingfield, a self-supporting woman writer who has elected to have an illegitimate child. The social issues which are raised by Dorothea's emotional education are discussed with humour and skill; there is much detail, of historical interest, in the New Zealand and Australian settings.

COBB, Thomas (1854–1932) married Emily MOON (d. 1931). The son of a tailor, he left school at 12 and went into his father's business, where he worked for twenty years. When more than thirty he began a second career as a prolific hack writer: he was to publish seventy-eight novels between 1889 and 1932, and claimed also to have written 300 short stories. He was one of those interviewed in the **Bookman* (Jan. 1909) about Hall *Caine's complaint in his autobiography that he had struggled in his early days as a writer on £300 a year. Cobb, without declaring that it was his own experience, but with an undercurrent of bitterness, said that there were novelists, known to thousands through the circulating library system, who had never earned as much as £300 a year. His own novels range from society romance in *The Friendships of Veronica* (1905) and *Lady Gwendoline: A Novel* (1902) to a straighforward school story about a boy in disgrace for stealing who vindicates himself, *Masterman's Mistake* (1913). In *The Chichester Intrigue* (1908) the mystery is whether a girl or her aunt is being blackmailed for having had an affair with an actor. According to his obituary in the *Times* (16 Jan. 1932) Cobb had lately adapted to 'the growing vogue of detective fiction' by writing a series about an Inspector Bedison.

COBBAN, J[ames] MacLaren (1849–1903) married (1881) Harriet BOTTOMLEY (b. 1858). Born in Aberdeen and trained at New College, London as a Presbyterian minister, Cobban had to give up university and his career because of his father's death, and took a job in a boarding school in north London. From about 1877 he became a miscellaneous writer and journalist. His first novel was *The Cure of Souls* (1879), which he sold to Chatto for £20, and which was thought to show a promise Cobban, dogged by ill health and poverty, never fulfilled. He applied for Royal Literary Fund grants in 1882 and 1887, supported by Edmund Gosse (1849–1928) and Ford Madox Brown (1821–93). He worked for W. E. Henley (1849–1903) on the staff of the *National Observer* (1889–91) and also contributed to *Chambers', Cassell's, Black and White*, and the **Strand*. The publication of *A Reverend Gentleman* (1891) seems to have encouraged him to give up journalism. He became a prolific author of adventure and *crime stories, and wrote a biography (1901) of the then celebrated general Earl Roberts (1832–1914). *Cease Fire! A Story of the Transvaal War of '81* (1900) was probably also an attempt to cash in on the new interest in South Africa. The Boer characters are stupid and malign. The hero is a young Englishman who has abandoned his training as a Methodist minister, and meets a beautiful girl in a green veil in the middle of the veld, who turns out to be an Irish spy. *The Last Alive* (1902) hinges on a millionaire's will, which is to enrich the last of his friends to survive. Another illness and more doctors' bills necessitated another application to the Royal Literary Fund in 1903, and his widow had recourse to the Fund again after his death.

COBDEN, Ellen [Melicent] (*c.*1848–1914) married (1885) Walter Richard SICKERT (1860–1942) (divorced 1899). She was the daughter of the radical politician Richard Cobden (1804–65). Her novel *Wistons* (1902) is about the tragic experiences in society of two daughters of a Sussex farmer and a gypsy. This was written under the pseudonym 'Miles Amber' and opened the First Novel Series started by her brother-in-law, the *publisher T. Fisher Unwin. *Sylvia Saxon: Episodes in a Life* (1914), which appeared under her own name, featured a spoilt heiress struggling with marital difficulties and social questions. She separated from her painter husband in 1896 when he told her he had been unfaithful to her since their marriage. The printer T. J. Cobden-Sanderson (1840–1922) was another of her brothers-in-law. There is a brief impressionistic memoir of Ellen Cobden by Desmond MacCarthy (1920).

COKE, Desmond [Francis Talbot] (1879–1931). His father was a major-general in the army; his mother, Charlotte Coke (1843–1922), was a journalist on women's magazines who also published advice books as 'Mrs Talbot Coke'. He was educated at Shrewsbury School (where he was head boy) and University College, Oxford. After being invalided out of the army in the First World War he became briefly a schoolmaster at Clayesmore, an experimental school near Winchester. Before the war he wrote a series of popular comic novels about school and university life. Some of these, such as *The Bending of A Twig* (1906), which is about Shrewsbury, and *The House Prefect* (1908), are tales of honour regained not unlike those of the young P. G. *Wodehouse. Others are burlesques of the genre. *The Chaps of Harton: A Tale of Frolic, Sport and Mystery at Public School* (1913) is ostensibly attributed to 'Belinda Blinders', though Coke's name is on the title-page. The feminist Belinda presumes to write about a boy's school and of course gets it all wrong. Snobbishness, misogyny, and chauvinism also mark more conventional novels such as *Beauty for Ashes: A Comedy of Caste* (1910). Humphry is about to inherit an impoverished landed estate, and a foolish girl tells him he ought rather to be doing social work in the East End, which he does. By the end he realizes he cannot alter the person he is, and goes back to the country.

COLE, Robert W[illiam] is described by Bleiler as the author of 'the first real space opera, filled with space battles, invasions, and escalating weapons'. This was *The Struggle for Empire: A Story of the Year 2236* (1900), in which Earth battles with the planet Kairet for control of the universe. He also wrote an effective *invasion scare story, *The Death Trap* (1907), in which Britain narrowly escapes defeat by Germany, because of the corrupt and incompetent government, but the real winners are the Americans, who corner world trade while the European nations destroy each other. Cole published two other novels, both comic. *His Other Self* (1906) concerns the adventures of a reformed rake subject to relapses into his old identity. *The Artificial Girl* (1908), in which a young man dresses up as a girl and takes his sister's place at school, struck the critics as faintly improper.

COLE, Sophie (1862–1947) was born in Clapham, South London, and educated at private schools. She wrote in *Who's Who* that she began to write for pleasure and 'continued to do so as a means of living'. Mills & Boon published almost all the sixty-three novels she wrote between 1908 and 1944. Cole's main interest was London topography and local history, on which she wrote several works of non-fiction, and this gives some flavour to her romances for working girls. *A Wardour Street Idyll* (1910), the story of a typist who marries her antique-dealer employer, has a detailed scene in the Victoria and Albert Museum. The heroine of *Patience Tabernacle* (1914) is the daughter of a bank clerk and loves the upstairs lodger, an artist; they go together to see the house of Thomas Carlyle (1795–1881).

COLERIDGE, C[hristabel] R[ose] (1843–1921) was born in Chelsea. She was the granddaughter of S. T. Coleridge (1772–1834); her father was a Church of England clergyman. Her aunt Sara (1802–52) and uncle Hartley (1796–1849) also wrote poetry, and her only sibling was the literary scholar E. H. Coleridge (1846–1920). M. E. *Coleridge was a second cousin once removed. However, the chief literary influence on Coleridge was the Anglo-Catholic novelist and children's writer Charlotte M. Yonge (1823–1901), who was related to M. E. Coleridge and the other descendants of S. T. 's elder brother James, but was no blood relation of her own. She described her 1903 biography of Yonge as 'the first piece of literary work of any consequence which I have ever done without the help of her criticism and sympathy'. Part of a circle of younger women centred on Yonge (see 'Esmé *Stuart'), with some of whom she participated in five collaborative novels, she was first joint editor with Yonge (1891–4), then sole editor (1894–9), of the *Monthly Packet*, a High Church periodical for girls. She was editor of *Friendly Leaves*, magazine of the Girls' Friendly Society (for Anglican working-class girls) (1890–1917). Coleridge's father retired to Torquay in 1880, and she lived there for the rest of her life. Her first novel, *Lady Betty* (1869), is a historical work for children. Her novels are aimed at young women; they deal with domesticity and religious duty. But she is also much preoccupied with the themes of family reputation and personal honour. The hero of *The Winds of Cathrigg* (1901), a novel set in Westmorland, becomes head of a gentry family falling in the world. They are in debt, his father has been discreditable, his uncle is disgraced, he is guilty of quarrelling with his father, and wrongly accused of murdering him. He contrives to overcome these obstacles, inherit a fortune, and marry, but Coleridge is concerned to discriminate between the different effects of shame, guilt, and dishonour. She emphasizes nuances of class distinction, which are the subject of her last novel, *Miss Lucy* (1908). The heroine is left penniless, marries the gamekeeper, and lives happily with him until her children grow up. Their new employer's wife turns out to have risen in the world as Lucy has sunk.

COLERIDGE, M[ary] E[lizabeth] (1861–1907) was a great-great-niece of the poet, and was born and lived throughout her life in London. Her father held a legal post and taught his daughter Hebrew. She also learned Latin, German, French and Italian; attending lectures at the Ladies' Department of King's College, London. As an adult she was one of several women who read Greek literature with the ex-schoolmaster and poet W. J. Cory (1823–92) at his house in Hampstead. Her early ambition was to be a painter. Inspired by reading L. N. Tolstoy (1828–1910) to work with the poor, she held a class for girls at her home, then after 1895 taught English literature once a week at the Working Women's College. Robert Bridges (1844–1930) read her poems in manuscript and persuaded her to publish them; two volumes appeared in 1896 and 1897 under the pseudonym 'Anodos', taken from the hero of *Phantastes* by George MacDonald (1824–1905). In Bridges' collected essays there is an appreciation of her work. She is an occasional and idiosyncratic writer, sometimes praised and often neglected. Edith Sichel (1862–1914) observes in the memoir prefixed to a collection of her prose (1910) that 'in her writing she showed the same wilful love of mystification that she showed in her life'. The novels are fantastic, obscure, but memorable. Her first novel was *The Seven Sleepers of Ephesus* (1893); the *historical romance *The King with Two Faces* (1897) gave her a reputation; it was followed by *The Fiery Dawn* (1901). She published an early story *The Shadow on the Wall* (1904) to raise money for charity. Her last novel was *The *Lady on the Drawingroom Floor* (1906). Much of her small body of surviving work consists of sketches, reviews, and stories published in the **Monthly Review*, the **Cornhill*, the **Times Literary Supplement* and the *Monthly Packet*, collected in *Non Sequitur* (1900) and *Gathered Leaves* (1910). Her *Collected Poems* were edited by T. Whistler (1954). At her death she left unfinished a medieval romance and her life of Holman Hunt (1827–1910) was published posthumously (1908).

COLLINGWOOD, Harry, *pseud.*: William Joseph Cosens LANCASTER (1851–1922) married (1878) Keziah Hannah Rice ——. Born in Weymouth, the son of a naval officer, and educated at the Royal Naval College, Greenwich, Lancaster was too short-sighted to enter the navy and became a marine engineer. He was a prolific author of nautical tales for boys from 1878. His novels are mostly recounted by the central character, typically a boy midshipman who unexpectedly finds himself in command of a ship, and displays exemplary and resourceful behaviour during various incredible adventures. By the end he has found a fortune in jewels and returns home a hero. *Overdue, or, The Strange Story of a Missing Ship* (1911) is set on a hijacked emigrant ship headed for Australia whose passengers try to set up a socialist utopia in the South Seas.

Through Veld and Forest: An African Story (1914) has the usual rather dull narrator; its plot is derived from Rider *Haggard. *With Airship and Submarine: A Tale of Adventure* (1908), set on a ship which can both dive and fly, is equally indebted to Jules Verne (1828–1905); it is a sequel to Lancaster's *The Log of the 'Flying Fish'* (1887). 'I think our boys' books of adventure are best, like *Treasure Island*, or books by *Henty, or Kingston, or Collingwood. I used to *love* them,' wrote D. H. *Lawrence (28 Mar. 1916).

COLLINGWOOD, William Gershom (1854–1932) married (1883) Edith Mary ISAAC (d. 1928). The son of a painter, Collingwood went to Liverpool College and on a scholarship to University College, Oxford. He studied art at the Slade, and was for twenty years secretary to John Ruskin (1819–1900). He was Professor of Fine Art at University College Reading, and wrote a textbook on sketching. He also published a biography of Ruskin and some editions of his works, several books on the antiquities and topography of the Lake District, and, in the 1890s, *historical novels about tenth-century Norsemen in the area. *Dutch Agnes, Her Valentine* (1910), his only Edwardian novel, is set in seventeenth-century Coniston. His son, the philosopher and historian R. G. Collingwood (1889–1943), describes in his autobiography (1939) a childhood in a bookish and artistic household, where his father taught him Latin from the age of 4 and Greek from 6.

COLMORE, G., *pseud*.: Gertrude RENTON (?1860-1926) married, first (1882), Henry Arthur Colmore DUNN (divorced) and, secondly (1901), Harold Baillie WEAVER or BAILLIE-WEAVER (d. 1926). She was the sixth daughter of John Thomson Renton of Bradstone Brook (evidently a man of some means, since he made a settlement on her in 1879) and was educated at school in Frankfurt and in London and Paris. Her first novel, *Concerning Oliver Knox* (1888), is the story of a spectacularly unsuccessful marriage. The heroine is forced by her husband to bring up his mistress's son in place of her own; he contrives that her son should become an idiot. Discovering this, she brings about the death of the other boy, only to have it revealed that the mistress had swapped the children as babies. *A Ladder of Tears* (1904) continues the note of feminist feeling, the criticism of marriage and materialism, but has a mystical note. The heroine has by the end resolved to devote her life to her backward stepsons. *Priests of Progress* (1908) is anti-vivisectionist propaganda; three doctors are judged by their response to the issue. One devotes his life to it and, despite the loss of worldly prosperity, gains happiness with the heroine. Some of the most interesting passages discuss the experience of the poor in hospitals; she vividly suggests that a patriarchal and autocratic system bears harshly on its victims. She is now remembered for **Suffragette Sally* (1911). Weaver's twenty-two titles include volumes of stories, verse, and novels. Both her husbands were barristers, and she and her second husband were theosophists, anti-vivisectionists, members of the ILP, and keen suffragists. She was a member of the Fabian Society from 1907. There is another writer, with whom she is not to be confused, named Gertrude Dunn (b. 1884), who published three novels in the late 1920s.

COLVILL, H[elen] H[ester] (1854–1941) was born in Winchmore Hill, the daughter of an army officer; both her parents were of Irish birth. She published five novels between 1880 and 1894 as 'Katharine Wylde' and under her own name translated the work of Grazia Deledda (1875–1936), and published four novels 1905–28, including *The Incubus* (1910), in which the neglected intellectual daughter of divorced parents searches for her sister and finds her vulgar, sensual, and dying, in Egypt. She also wrote a biography of St Teresa of Avila (1909).

Combined Maze, The, May *Sinclair, 1913, Hutchinson. A tale of *Jamesian renunciations set in the 1880s in a *suburban world of the kind created by Arnold *Bennett and H. G. *Wells. John Randall Fulleymore Ransome, Ranny for short, is the son of a 'weedy, parched, furtively inebriate' chemist and his long-suffering and rather prim wife, and lives with his parents in Wandsworth High Street. A furniture dealer's 'inexpensive and utterly insignificant clerk', he is also a fitness fanatic with a moral and physical distaste for flabbiness. At the Polytechnic Gymnasium, he meets a pretty, sympathetic shop-girl, Winny Dymond. Together they feature in the Combined Maze, an intricately choreographed and faintly mystical gymnastic exercise. However, Winny's friend, the sensuous Violet Usher, seduces Ranny, and persuades him to marry her. They set themselves up in a villa, and have a child. As Violet degenerates into a 'suburban odalisk', Winny selflessly holds the family together, baking steak pies and looking after the child. When Violet elopes with Ranny's friend Leonard Mercier, a man of all-round flabbiness, it seems as though Ranny will be able to marry Winny. Violet, however, abandoned by Mercier, and by a subsequent lover, returns home. If Ranny does not take her back, she will soon be on the streets. Ranny and Winny renounce each other.

COMPTON, Herbert [Eastwick] (1853–1906). The son of an officer in the Honourable East India Company's Service, Compton was educated at Malvern College. In *Who's Who* he called himself 'novelist, biographer, and writer on Georgian, Indian historical, canine and fiscal subjects'. He wrote romantic military novels with historical and exotic settings, as well as real-life accounts of travel and exploration. *Kipling selected his *The Military Adventurers of Hindustan* (1892) as one of the Hundred Best Books for Boys. *A Fury in White Velvet* (1901) is set in north India, where a young officer falls in love with a widowed princess who wanders around accompanied by a snow leopard. *The Undertaker's Field, or, Murder Will Out* (1906) is a romance set in Kent about a poor girl who is at her wits' end for money and finds true love and buried treasure on the last page. But Compton's enthusiasm for the colonial past gives the book some flavour: they are living in a house which is literally an old ship which a sea dog ancestor of hers has pulled up onto dry land and in which he has hidden the jewels of an Indian princess.

COMPTON-BURNETT, I.: Ivy Compton BURNETT (after 1901 COMPTON-BURNETT) (1884–1969), DBE (1967). James Compton Burnett, a homeopathic doctor, had five children by his first wife and seven (of whom Ivy was the eldest) by his second wife. He died in 1901 and his widow hyphenated the family surname. Compton-Burnett went to school at Addiscombe College, Hove, and Howard College, Bedford, and read classics at Royal Holloway College (1902–6). It is acknowledged that the oppressive Edwardian households which are the settings of the series of novels she wrote between *Pastors and Masters* (1925) and *The Last and the First* (1971) were inspired by the unpleasant atmosphere in this large family ruled by her tyrannical mother, who died in 1911. There was tragedy: her brother Guy died of pneumonia in 1905; her brother Noel was killed in action in 1916, whereupon his wife attempted suicide; and her two youngest sisters poisoned themselves together in the following year. After her mother's death Ivy took her place as the family tyrant, and her sisters refused to live with her after 1915; she was, however, to achieve some domestic happiness with the art historian Margaret Jourdain (d. 1951), with whom she lived after 1919. She published only one novel before the First World War: **Dolores* (1911). She once observed, 'I do not feel that I have any real or organic knowledge of life later than about 1910.'

Conflict, The, M. E. *Braddon, 1903, Simpkin, Marshall, Hamilton. A rambling throwback to the days of the three-decker, this novel could well serve as a brief history of fashions in sensational fiction from 1860 to 1900. It begins like one of the high Victorian melodramas which made Braddon's name. Walter Arden, the youngest son of a peer, bookish but no milksop, saves his landlady's daughter from the wiles of a satanic seducer, Colonel Konstantin Melville. When Melville turns his attention to Arden's sister, Lady Mary Selby, and lures her to Paris, Arden follows them, and tracks them through dens of iniquity disguised as a monk. To save Mary's honour, he challenges Melville to a duel, and kills him, though not before the dying man has promised to haunt him for the rest of his days. The novel thus incorporates the fascination with satanism and reincarnation popularized by Marie *Corelli in the 1890s. Braddon, however, has further strings to her bow. For Arden meets Rachel Lorimer, daughter of a wealthy engineer, who goes in for East End philanthropy in a manner popularized by the novels of another bestselling contemporary, Mrs Humphry *Ward. Arden becomes her devoted assistant, but she refuses to marry him because he is not a true believer. Dismayed by rejection, Arden sets off on a prospecting trip in the Yukon perhaps a Rider *Haggard touch, with an Anglo-American explorer called Archer Stormont. They take with them a working-class socialist, Michael Dartnell, who has been imprisoned for manslaughter but is now reformed. Dartnell contracts fever, and reaches the point of death before enjoying a miraculous recovery. However, he returns to life transformed. He has lapsed back into his bestial, criminal self, and promptly attempts to murder Arden, who narrowly escapes with his life when Dartnell plunges down a rapid. The pattern is repeated, with a glance at *Jane Eyre* (1847) by Charlotte Brontë (1816–55), when Arden, back in London and married to Rachel, who has apparently agreed to overlook his agnosticism, encounters an elegant, saintly churchman, St Just. St Just falls in love with Rachel, but nobly retires to his yacht. Nursing the sick in Naples, he contracts tuberculosis, and, when all seems lost, recovers miraculously. But he too has relapsed. A saint no more, he pursues Lady Mary, as Manville had done, and murders her when she refuses him. Then he kidnaps Rachel, who leaps out of a window to escape him. She survives, he spits blood and dies (completely, this time). Arden, meanwhile, has renounced materialism and found happiness. Haunted no longer by Manville, he establises a model industrial estate in Hertfordshire. It has been said that Braddon's later work is less sensational, more psychological. *The Conflict* suggests, rather, that she simply integrated 'psychological' forms of sensation, notably those developed by Corelli and Ward, into the type of high Victorian melodrama she herself had patented.

CONNOR, Ralph, *pseud.*: Charles William GORDON (1860–1937) married Helen KING. Born in Glengarry, Ontario, and educated at High School, St Mary's, Ontario, Toronto University, and Knox's College, Toronto, he became a minister like his father and eventually Moderator of the General Assembly of the Presbyterian Church of Canada. He was ordained at the age of 30 and became a missionary among the lumberjacks and miners of the Rocky Mountains. In 1894 he took a ministry at Winnipeg; he remained based there for the rest of his life. His first publications were articles for the *Westminster Magazine*. His pseudonym was the result of a mistake; he meant to use 'Cannor' (from Can. Nor. West Mission) but his editor changed it to Connor and added 'Ralph'. He had great success with his two first novels, *Black Rock, A Tale of the Selkirks* (1898) and *The Sky Pilot* (1899)—a colloquialism for 'clergyman'. His 'Glengarry' series began with *The Man From Glengarry: A Tale of the Ottawa* (1901) in which young Ranald Macdonald has to learn not to seek vengeance on his father's murderer. He saves the murderer's life, becomes prosperous through invincible probity and marries happily. *The Patrol of the Sun-Dance Trail* (1914) begins 'High upon the hillside in the midst of a rugged group of jack pines the Union Jack... marked the headquarters of Superintendent Strong, of the North-west Mounted Police, whose special duty it was to preserve law and order along the construction line of the Canadian Pacific Railway Company.' The Mounties keep down the trouble brewed by Frenchmen and Indians.

CONRAD, Joseph: Jozef Teodor Konrad NALECZ KORZENIOWSKI (1857–1924), naturalized a British citizen (1886) as Joseph CONRAD, married (1895) Jessie Emmeline GEORGE (1873–1936). Conrad was born in the Ukraine, which had been annexed by Russia from Poland in 1793; his father was a Polish patriot politically at odds with the Russian authorities. His early childhood was spent in internal exile in Russia; his mother died in 1865. After 1867 father and son lived in Lwow, a part of Poland under Austrian rule. Apollo Korzeniowski was highly cultivated, had translated Shakespeare into Polish, and imbued Conrad with a love of French literature; he died in 1869. Partly under the influence of childhood reading of the novels of Frederick Marryat (1792–1848), and after overcoming some difficulties because he was a Russian subject liable to military service, Conrad became a merchant seaman in 1874. Four years later he joined a British ship, and in 1886 he qualified as a master mariner. His voyages took him to Australia and the Far East; in 1890 he was employed for a few months by the Société Anonyme Belge pour le Commerce du Haut-Congo, and made the journey up the Congo which was an inspiration for *Heart of Darkness* (published with *Youth*, 1902). He began his first novel, *Almayer's Folly*, while staying in London in 1889; it was finished in 1894, in which year he settled in England, and published in 1895, having been read for publication by Edward Garnett (1868–1937) (see under Olive *Garnett), who was to be a great friend and supporter for many years and was portrayed as Lea in *The *Inheritors* (1901). He also made friends with Ford Madox *Hueffer, with whom he collaborated on three novels, *The Inheritors*, **Romance* (1903), and *The Nature of A Crime* (published in the **English Review*, 1909, and in book form 1924). The favourable reviews of **Lord Jim* (1900) led him to call himself 'the spoiled child of the critics', but authorship was insecure and Conrad contemplated returning to the sea. There were permanent financial worries, exacerbated by the frequent illnesses of himself, Jessie, and their two sons, which intermittently plunged Conrad into depression and nervous breakdown. Though he borrowed money from his friends, Hueffer for instance, and from his *literary agent, J. B. Pinker (1863–1922) and received several unusually large grants from the Royal Literary Fund (£300 in 1902, £200 in 1904, £200 in 1908), the Royal Bounty Fund (£500 in 1905–6), and the Civil List (£100 p. a. from 1910) as well as the support of a number of eminent fellow authors, the Conrads were always hard up, and writing was slow. In 1905 Henry *Newbolt proposed that Conrad should declare himself bankrupt. Much of his energy went into the short stories published in *_Typhoon and Other Stories_ (1903) and *_'Twixt Land and Sea_ (1912). Even so the years of struggle produced a number of major works: *_Nostromo: A Tale of the Seaboard_ (1904), _The *Secret Agent: A Simple Tale_ (1907), and *_Under Western Eyes_ (1911). The turning-point in Conrad's finances came with the serialization of *_Chance_ in the Sunday issue of the _New York Herald_ (Jan.–June 1912). Lucrative in itself, the success of this introduced Conrad's novels to the American market. Whereas _Under Western Eyes_ sold 4,112 copies in its first two years, the English edition of _Chance_, delayed to 1914 because of a strike, sold 13,000 copies in the same period. _Victory_ (1915) sold 11,000 copies in the first three days. By 1917 Conrad felt able to resign his Civil List pension. Two months before his death he declined a knighthood, and he left £20,045. His autobiography, _Some Reminiscences_, is valuable though not invariably accurate (1912). There is a chronology by Owen Knowles (1989) and a biography by Frederick R. Karl (1979), who is editing the letters with Laurence Davies (1983–).

Conrad in Quest of His Youth: _An Extravagance of Temperament_, Leonard *Merrick, 1903, Grant Richards. This is a picaresque tale of 37-year-old Conrad Warrener, who is released from drudgery by a legacy and decides to revisit old haunts and acquaintances. He tracks down a companion of twenty-two years ago, Mary Page, in Tooting; she is now a vulgar, snobbish suburbanite (shades of Arthur Clennam and Flora Flinching, in _Little Dorrit_, 1855–7). More elusive, more tantalizing, is Mrs Adaile, whom he had fallen in love with when he was 17, at a hotel in Rouen, and now finds in a hotel in Ostend. He attempts to revive his passion for her; she humours him to the extent of agreeing to come to his room. When she gets there, he is fast asleep. She leaves a note which reads '_Dreamer_! Goodbye. There is no way back to Rouen.' At this point, the novel itself abandons its recital of disillusionments and begins to dream. Conrad falls in with Lady Rosalind Darlington, who is also trying to find a way back to her lost youth (spent, like Merrick's own, on the stage). The book ends as the affair is about to turn serious. The conclusion drawn, that 'a man is young as often as he falls in love', perhaps explains why J. M. *Barrie compared it to _A Sentimental Journey_ (1768) by Laurence Sterne (1713–68).

Contemporary Review (1866–). Founded, in an attempt to bridge the gulf between secular and religious reading, as a monthly and Church of England equivalent of the secular and liberal _Fortnightly Review_, and edited (1870–77) by J. T. Knowles (1831–1908), founder of the Metaphysical Society, who left to found the *_Nineteenth Century_. The magazine devoted extensive space to art and music, but the dominant tone of scholarly Christianity was clearly evident in the reviews, textual criticism of the Bible, and its consideration of the relationship between philosophy, science, and religious issues and problems. Knowles opened the _Review_ to the debates of the Society and also published more speculative and conflicting articles by scientists, atheists and Catholics. He brought in Cardinal Manning (1808–92), Matthew Arnold (1822–88), W. E. Gladstone (1809–98), T. H. Huxley (1825–95), John Ruskin (1819–1900), and Herbert Spencer (1820–1903). Percy William Bunting (1836–1911) assumed the editorship in 1882, and the review became more specifically activist, a platform for social reform and political liberalism. Bunting also increased the coverage of foreign events. English journalists who now contributed included W. T. Stead (1849–1912) and E. J. Dillon (1854–1933). Bunting increasingly directed the journal along more strictly Liberal lines and this link between _Contemporary_ and the Liberal party remains characteristic of it today.

Convert, The, Elizabeth *Robins, 1907, Methuen. The novel of Robins's successful play, _Votes for Women_. Vida Levering, a society beauty, is converted to the cause, and to a broader sympathy for the underprivileged, by her experience, first as an observer then as a participant, of the suffrage campaign. She even uses her guilty secret, an dead illegitimate child, to gain the support of the child's father, Geoffrey Stonor, a rising Tory politician. The book is notable chiefly for its detailed and explicit attention to politics, and particularly to sexual politics. Much of the action takes place at suffragette meetings, with argument and counter-argument (or heckling) expounded at great length. One militant carries a dog-whip because she knows that the campaigners will be subjected to sexual harassment ('unholy handling'). Claims that the militants are sexless non-women are countered by the claim that they alone possess a true 'sex pride', a true interest and faith in women.

CONYERS, Dorothea: Dorothea Spaight BLOOD-SMYTH (1869–1949) married, first (1892), Charles CONYERS (1867–1915) and, secondly (1917), John Joseph WHITE (1863–1940). Born a member of the Protestant landed gentry in Co. Limerick, Conyers wrote: 'the bad times fell on Ireland when I was very small. I can remember going to church and seeing a fox nailed on the door.' Her father died when she was a child, and there was less money and no more hunting for a while. She married an army officer and moved with him round England and Ireland. He was killed in action; and with her second marriage she returned to a big house in Co. Limerick. She was a prolific author of cheerful romances, in which the subjects of Ireland and hunting recur. Her first book was *The Thorn Bit* (1900). *Lady Elverton's Emeralds* (1909) is a *crime story with hunting passages; *For Henri and Navarre* (1911) a *historical tale. *The Boy, Some Horses and A Girl: A Tale of An Irish Trip* (1903) has comic Irish servants and a competition among three men to win an heiress with a desirable house and stableyard in the west of Ireland. Conyers's *Sporting Reminiscences* (1920) are the best source of information on her career.

COOKE, W[illiam Joseph] Bourne (1869–1935) married Rose Ethel ——. A journalist, living in Edwalton, near Nottingham, he published fiction 1902–34. Cooke specialized in *historical romances such as *Her Faithful Knight* (1908), set in Nottingham and Leicester during the English Civil War, and *The Cragsman: A Story of Smuggling Days* (1913). *Bellcroft Priory* (1910) is an old-fashioned Gothic tale which opens in 1795 with the murder of a young farmer in the ruins of an old priory. Cooke also published contemporary stories such as *The Canon's Daughter* (1902) and *Madam Domino* (1907), the heroine of which, loved by two ill-natured men, marries each of them in turn. It looks as though he turned to historical romance after the failure of these contemporary stories.

COOPER, Edward H[erbert] (1867–1910). Born at Newcastle under Lyme, the son of a landowner, Cooper went to University College, Oxford. He was an active Liberal Unionist, and after 1896 a journalist working in Paris for the *New York World* and *Galignani's Messenger.* In 1901 he visited Finland and wrote about its politics. He returned to London and was special reporter on the *Daily Mail* (1903–6). Though crippled from childhood, he loved hunting, and described his recreations in *Who's Who* as 'horse-racing, children's parties'. His interest in children led him to work with the movement for legislation to protect children from cruelty and to write a number of children's books, most notably a Carrollesque series about a little girl called Wyemarke. *The Twentieth Century Child* (1905) is non-fiction; it includes some stories written by small children. Cooper is sentimental about children, but also practical; he writes sympathetically about the conflict between the ideology of motherhood and the movement for the education and enfranchisement of women. The fascination with children and racing give a distinct flavour to his novels. His first was the semi-autobiographical *Geoffory* [*sic*] *Hamilton* (1893). *The Eternal Choice* (1901) is a novel about English high society, which hinges on an elderly and religious millionaire's deliberations about which of his relations should be his heir. *The Marquis and Pamela* (1908) is a light romance, with many racecourse scenes.

CORBETT, Mrs George: Elizabeth Burgoyne —— (1846–1930) married (probably by 1869) George CORBETT (d. 1912). Born in Wigan, she began contributing to the family budget by writing for the *Newcastle Chronicle* in the early 1880s. Her husband, a marine engineer, was sometimes unemployed or absent at sea, and not highly paid. By the turn of the century she had moved from Newcastle to the London suburbs, where she lived by writing serial fiction for such periodicals as the *Sunday Companion* and *Home Chat*, so that her list of published novels does not reflect the extent of her output. Like several such writers, she was badly hit by the First World War, and made repeated applications to the Royal Literary Fund. Her most interesting work is *New Amazonia: A Foretaste of the Future* (1890). In this feminist utopia disease has been abolished and publishers eliminated. Her novel *The Marriage Market: A Series of Confessions Compiled from the Diary of a Society Go-Between* (1905) is narrated by Irene, Lady Canby, who is unhappily married to a spendthrift and contracts to arrange marriages for money. It tries to be light-hearted but expresses a hideous vision of the world. Corbett also wrote *crime novels and nautical novels.

CORELLI, Marie, *pseud.*: Mary MACKAY or MILLS (1855–1924). Probably the bestselling of all Victorian novelists, and an umistakable if increasingly mocked presence in the Edwardian era, she was born plain Mary Mills, the daughter of Charles Mackay (1814–89), then editor of the *Illustrated London News*, who married her mother six years later, his first wife having died in 1859. The family lived at Box Hill, in Surrey, where George *Meredith was a neighbour. In 1876 her mother died, and Bertha Vyver, a childhood friend, joined the household: she was to become Corelli's lifelong companion. Corelli devised her Italianate name with a view to a musical career, but it went well enough with the confected *exoticism which was to become the staple of her literary career. She was no beauty, but, as Sutherland puts it, 'vain to the point of mania', and routinely pretended to be younger than she actually was. Her first novel, *A Romance of Two Worlds* (1886), set the tone of her work: the heroine-narrator encounters in a visionary dream the magician Heliobas. Psychic travel, with a hint of pseudo-science, was to be her main theme. The sequel, *Ardath: The Story of a Dead Self* (1889), which Corelli thought her best novel, lands Heliobas in Babylon, 5,000 years before the birth of Christ. W. E. Gladstone (1809–98) called on her in that year, and the derision her fiction had begun to attract seemed to have little effect on its universal appeal. *The Sorrows of Satan* (1895), about a young novelist who makes a pact with the Devil, was a huge success; Rupert Brooke (1887–1915) thought it the funniest novel he had ever read. Corelli introduced herself as 'Mavis Clare', a popular but misunderstood authoress. Bestseller followed bestseller. She was now selling about 100,000 copies of her books per year, and was thought to be earning £10,000 for each. She began to take herself very seriously indeed, both as a writer and as a social theorist. *The Mighty Atom* (1896) is a violently sarcastic attack on 'Self-styled Progressivists who by Precept and Example assist the infamous Cause of Education without Religion'. *The Master Christian* (1900) is a plea for world peace issued 'in the name of Christ', whose spokeswoman she clearly took herself to be. However, her health collapsed in 1897, and the death of her half-brother Eric in 1898 almost provoked a breakdown. In 1901 she moved with Bertha Vyver to Stratford-upon-Avon, claiming kinship with William Shakespeare, and keeping a gondola on the river. Her Edwardian fiction includes *Temporal Power* (1902), *The Treasure of Heaven* (1906), and the thoroughly characteristic *The *Life Everlasting* (1911). Its success is hard to explain. All her novels are poorly plotted and hysterical in tone. But it may have been precisely their unselfconscious, muddled well-meaningness which found a response in self-consciously muddled, well-meaning readers. 'The unrivalled vogue of Miss Marie Corelli', wrote Arnold *Bennett in 1901, 'is partly due to the fact that her inventive faculty has always ranged easily and unafraid amid the largest things.' Ten years later, however, the vogue was over. In 1911, the *literary agent J. B. Pinker told 'Martin *Ross' that middle-class readers were finally getting 'beyond' Corelli. The exoticism peddled by the bestselling romances of new writers like Elinor *Glyn and Ethel M. *Dell was sexual rather than spiritual. Corelli was a spent force.

CORNFORD, L[eslie] Cope (1867–1927). A journalist and short-story-writer, Cornford published in **Outlook*, the **Pall Mall Magazine*, and **Longman's Magazine*. He was a friend of W. E. Henley (1849–1903), for whom he worked on the *National Observer* (Max *Beerbohm christened Henley's circle of journalist admirers 'the Henley Regatta'). He was naval correspondent of the *Morning Post* from 1901 and from 1906 worked on the Standard. Between 1896 and 1927 Cornford published a biography of Henley, various textbooks and works on maritime and military history, and several volumes of fiction. *The Last Buccaneer, or, The Trustees of Mrs. A* (1902) is a *historical romance about pirates, in which Captain Morgan plays a part.

Cornhill Magazine, The, (1860–1975) was a monthly, founded by the publisher George Smith (1824–1901) to provide serial fiction for family reading among reviews and articles. W. M. Thackeray (1811–63) was its first editor, and his son-in-law Leslie Stephen (1832–1904) edited it between 1871 and 1882. Stephen retained the bias toward serialized fiction but also devoted significant space to the literary essay. Although Stephen himself was at the forefront of the intellectual conflicts of his day, he kept the *Cornhill* free from discussion of religion, morals or politics. The novelist James Payn (1830–98) succeeded Stephen as editor; in an attempt to augment diminishing subscriptions he halved the price and decreased the literary essays, restoring the bias towards fiction. But the *Cornhill* could not compete with the sixpenny papers and Payn resigned in 1896. George Smith wished to continue publishing the unprofitable paper; he appointed John St Loe Strachey (1860–1927) as editor in July 1896 and restored the cover price to a shilling. Under Strachey the magazine became more military and nationalistic, with more space given to memoirs, autobiographies, and diaries. Strachey moved to the **Spectator* eighteen months later, and Smith's son-in-law Reginald Smith (1857–1916) took over the editorship. With his death in 1916 the magazine was taken over by the *publishers John Murray, who published it as a quarterly. The *Cornhill* sparked off a string of lookalikes, including **Temple Bar.*

Coryston Family, The, Mrs Humphry *Ward, 1913, Smith, Elder. Begun in December 1912 and completed by May 1913, the novel was coloured by the events of April 1913, when Mary Ward's son, Arnold, almost bankrupted the family through his compulsive gambling. It began as a story about a tyrannical wife and ended as a story about a mother destroyed by the disobedience of her sons. Lady Coryston is the widow of a weak, amiable man of letters; despising him, she has always worshipped her father, a politician and 'comrade of Dizzy'. She has four children, three of them sons. The eldest defies family tradition by entering Parliament as a Radical. She disowns him. The second son will have nothing to do with the inheritance, which thus falls to the third, also an MP. But the third son also turns against his mother, falling in love with the daughter of her most hated political enemy. She suffers a stroke, and dies. The novel was a commercial and critical failure; but Ward's portrayal of a resilient, embittered matriarch stands comparison with Hugh *Walpole's *The *Duchess of Wrexe* (1914).

COSTELLO, Pierre.: see Heath *Hosken.

COSTELLOE, Ray: Rachel Mary COSTELLOE (1887–1940) married (1911) Oliver STRACHEY (1874–1960). The stepdaughter of Bernard Berenson (1865–1959) and niece of Logan Pearsall Smith (1865–1946), she was educated at Kensington High School, Newnham College, Cambridge, and Bryn Mawr, and married one of the brothers of Lytton Strachey (1880–1932). *The World at Eighteen* (1907) describes the attempts of a young English-educated American girl living with her mother and a bookish uncle in Italy to disentangle herself from an engagement to an obnoxious man who despises emancipated women. Strachey's life was devoted to the cause of women's suffrage and emancipation. Her most famous book, *The Cause* (1928), is a history of the suffrage movement. She also published *Causes and Openings for Women* (1935), several biographies of women, and two other novels (1923, 1927).

Cottage Pie: *A Country Spread,* Neil Lyons, 1911, John Lane. These arch stories about village life in Sussex and Buckinghamshire attempt a *Kiplingesque fidelity to local custom and idiom. The book was withdrawn from libraries when the National Vigilance Association denounced it for obscenity. It is hard to know why it might have caused offence. On one occasion, the narrator feeds strawberries, Alec D'Urberville fashion, to the village beauty—'just as I was popping the third one (such a whopper, too) between her interesting lips, Perkin chanced to look up from his plate'—and they subsequently retire to dally, while Perkin mows the lawn. But that is the summit of offensiveness. The ban provoked Austin Harrison (1873–1928), the editor of the **English Review,* to denounce a reading-public which lapped up Elinor *Glyn but was shocked by the investigations ('clean, moral, and even helpful') of a writer like Lyons (Feb. 1911). Harrison concluded by asking the President of the NVA 'Whether he thinks *Cottage Pie* to be more injurious to the youth of England than the lavish, beautiful, and astonishing display of women's under-garments—stays, chemisettes, pantalettes, and what not—to be found in the innumerable illustrated magazines—features which I have heard one excellent old gentleman friend of mine declare to be among the best things in the magazines?'

COTTERELL, Constance [A. M.] was the daughter of George Cotterell (1839–98), who reviewed fiction and poetry in the *Academy* and edited the *Yorkshire Herald*. She published eight novels between 1889 *and* 1933 and contributed to the New York *New Illustrated Magazine*, the *Yellow Book*, and **Temple Bar*. In this period she wrote *The Virgin and the Scales* (1905) and *The Honest Trespass* (1911). The heroine of the former marries her guardian, who has really loved her since childhood although she has twice prevented him running off with a married woman. In the latter, a young wife whose husband is in a madhouse gradually yields to to an earlier (and unworthy) suitor.

Country House, The, John *Galsworthy, 1907, William Heinemann. Horace Pendyce, the owner of Worsted Skeynes, is an autocrat of the old school whose 'instinctive belief in precedent' forms the basis of his main moral quality: 'the power of making a decision'. His son George, a gambler and man about town, has an affair with a beautiful married woman, Mrs Helen Bellew. Horace, unyielding as ever, wants to disinherit him. But his wife Margery, the representative, like Mrs Wilcox in E. M. *Forster's **Howards End* (1910), is of another England, an England of 'gentleness' and 'balance', and intervenes to resolve the dispute. Galsworthy makes some attempts to encompass the Condition of England: for example, by juxtaposing consumptive seamstresses with the good-for-nothing members of George's club (the Stoics). But his own view is uncomfortably like the view from the club window. He satirizes something he himself rather enjoyed: the ceremony of Edwardian upper-class life. Like Horace Pendyce, he loved dogs: when he wants to reveal Pendyce's anguish, he shows him treading on his favourite dog three times in the course of one chapter. *The Country House* was not as successful as *The *Man of Property*, to Galsworthy's chagrin.

Country of the Blind and Other Stories, The, H. G. *Wells, 1911, Thomas Nelson. Published at a time when Wells had more or less ceased to write short stories, the collection had, as he himself pointed out in a preface which traced the evolution of the genre through the 1890s and 1900s, a 'definitive' aspect. He said that, starting as it did with his first published story and finishing with five which had not previously appeared between hard covers, it included all the stories he wanted anyone to read again. His account of their creation emphasizes the note of audacious *fantasy which colours the whole collection. 'Little men in canoes upon sunlit oceans would come floating out of nothingness, incubating the eggs of prehistoric monsters unawares; violent conflicts would break out amidst the flower-beds of suburban gardens; I would discover I was peering into remote and mysterious worlds ruled by an order logical indeed but other than our common sanity.' Wells recognized that such an order had already been to some extent established in the midst of common sanity by the power of science: in 'The Cone' and 'The Lord of the Dynamo', industrial technology is conceived as a vengeful deity claiming its sacrificial victims. In 'The Stolen Bacillus', an anarchist gets hold of a test-tube containing what he thinks is the cholera bacillus, but is in fact only a drug which turns people blue. The other 'order' sometimes erupts in the form of mutant plants ('The Flowering of the Strange Orchid') or animals ('In the Avu Observatory', 'Aepyornis Island', 'The Sea-Raiders', 'The Valley of the Spiders', 'The Empire of the Ants'). Sometimes it is to be found in hidden, recessed worlds ('The Door in the Wall', 'The Country of the Blind'). Sometimes it is entered or created by feats of magic or telecommunication ('The Remarkable Case of Davidson's Eyes', 'The Crystal Egg'). The collection is remarkable also for a diversity which reflects some of the uses to which the short story had already been put, and anticipates subsequent developments. 'Miss Winchelsea's Heart', for example, is an almost *Forsterian story about a momentous visit to Rome; while 'The Late Mr Elvesham', a chilling story about an elderly scientist who exchanges his body for that of a penniless student, recalls the work of R. L. Stevenson (1850–94) and foreshadows that of Franz Kafka (1883–1924).

COURLANDER, Alphonse (1881–1914) married Elsa HAHN. Born at Hampton Wick, he was educated at Whitgift Grammar School and abroad. He published seven novels between 1904 and

1912, and at the time of his early death was regarded as a promising young writer. Some of his fiction is influenced by that of Thomas Hardy (1840–1928). *The Taskmaster* (1904) is set among bricklayers near Salisbury; *Seth of the Cross* (1905) is about the disillusionment of a Wiltshire roadmender with literary pretensions. *Mightier than the Sword* (1912) has some interesting discussion of the life of Fleet Street journalists. The hero, Humphrey Quain, progresses from a provincial reporter to a special correspondent, shedding various women as he goes, and dies in a French riot.

COX, Sir Edmund C., Bt. (1856–1935) married (1891) Ella Marion BORRODAILE. The son of a Church of England clergyman who was author of many textbooks on history and theology, he was educated at Marlborough College and at Trinity College, Cambridge, which he left without taking a degree. He joined the Indian Service in 1877 and rose to become Deputy Inspector-General of Police in the Bombay Presidency, of which he published a history (1887); his other works include fiction and non-fiction about crime in India. He is best known for *John Carruthers, Indian Policeman* (1905) and its sequel *The Achievements of John Carruthers* (1910). He also wrote *The Exploits of Kesho Naik, Dacoit* (1912), recounted by Krishna, an Indian police constable and the dedicatee of *John Carruthers*. Cox states that he 'thought out these stories in Hindustani and Mahratti; and . . . endeavoured to give them an English rendering'. His uncle and father had both unsuccessfully laid claim to a baronetcy; Cox himself inherited this claim and is often (incorrectly) described, on his title-pages and elsewhere, as 'Sir Edmund Cox, 15th Bart.'. He published his memoirs, *My Thirty Years in India* (1909).

CRAVEN, Lady Helen: see Lady Helen *Forbes.

CRAVEN, Priscilla: see under W. Teignmouth *Shore.

CRAWFURD, [John] Oswald [Frederick] (1834–1909) married, first, Margaret FORD (d. 1899), and, secondly (1902), Amelia BROWNE née von FLESCH BRUNNINGEN. The son of a diplomat, Crawfurd was educated at Eton College and Merton College, Oxford, which he left without a degree. He went into the Foreign Office and was British consul in Oporto 1866–90. His first wife was the daughter of Richard Ford (1796–1858), the leading British expert on Spanish history and topography, and Crawfurd emulated his father-in-law by publishing books on Portugal, sometimes using the pseudonym 'John Latouche'. As 'John Dangerfield' he wrote three novels in the 1870s; and as 'George Windle Sandys' *Don Garcia in England* (1879). He was director and managing director of Chapman & Hall, and the first editor of *Chapman's Magazine of Fiction*, whose opening volume (1895) includes work by George *Gissing, Violet *Hunt, Flora Annie *Steel, and Mary E. Wilkins Freeman (1852–1930). He was also first editor of the *New Quarterly Magazine* (1873). He engaged in a wide variety of miscellaneous literary work, editing anthologies and writing books on bridge. He collaborated with 'Anthony *Hope' and Mrs Alfred Hunt (1831–1912) on *Dialogues of the Day* (1895). He was the lover of the latter's daughter Violet Hunt, and he is generally blamed for infecting her with the syphilis of which she died. During his affair with her, lasting most of the 1890s, he also had affairs with the wife of the *publisher Frederic Chapman and with his future second wife, Mrs Ralph Browne, and (according to Hunt) attempted to seduce the novelist May *Bateman. After his first wife's death Amelia Browne (known as 'Lita') obtained an uncontested divorce from her husband in 1902, and married Crawfurd. Afterwards they lived mostly abroad and he died in Montreux. Barbara Belford's biography of Hunt (1990) notes that after resigning from Chapman & Hall Crawfurd was short of money, and described what he was writing as 'mostly rot'. *The Sin of Prince Eladane* (1903) is a verse drama set in Britain as the Romans depart. *The League of the White Hand* (1909) describes the actions of a society devoted to opposing 'that growing and pestilent form of collectivism which chooses to call itself Socialism'. The League's agenda is aristocratic, anti-millionaire, anti-union, and pro-suffragette; its tactics include kidnapping. The secret society was fashionable in thrillers of the time; the immediate influence was perhaps Edgar *Wallace, *The *Four Just Men* (1905).

CRESWICK, [James] Paul (1866–1947) married (1893) Maude Lavinia MORRIS. He was born in Kingston-on-Thames, the son of an art-dealer, and was great-nephew of the well-known Victorian actor William Creswick (1813–88). He went to South Lambeth Grammar School, and then, from the age of 16 (1882), worked for the Prudential Assurance Company, after 1910 as a departmental manager. He was a great supporter of its magazine, *Ibis*, to which he contributed fiction and verse. He took up writing in his spare time in 1890. He founded and edited a short-lived periodical *The Windmill: An Illustrated Quarterly* (1898) in which he published creepy, fragmentary, soft-centred, sub-Wildean pieces. There is a story of his in the *Quarto* (1897), which was started to publicize painters from the Slade. Of his *The Temple of Folly*, Edward Garnett (1868–1937), the publisher's reader, commented: 'he has piled Anthony *Hope on Stanley *Weyman, put in a dash of *Q and invented some brave mannerisms a la *Crockett, and lo and behold we have a very typical story of adventure.' Creswick wrote several *historical romances for children: the boy hero of *With Richard the Fearless* (1904) discovers he is the son of Richard the Lionheart but keeps it a secret to marry Blondel's sister. *In A Hand of Steel, or, The Great Thatchmere Mystery* (1907) is another boy's book; large pieces of plot are taken from Conan *Doyle's Sherlock Holmes stories. *Idols of the Flesh* (1909) is a melodrama about a publisher who falls in love with a working-class girl, who gives him up at his mother's demand. The atmosphere of squalid tragedy is characteristic of Creswick's adult fiction. He served in the First World War. On his retirement from the Prudential in 1925 he went to live in Hove, where he became a member of the town council.

crime fiction. A single problem defines crime fiction during the Edwardian period: the problem of of Sherlock Holmes. From the first appearance of Arthur Conan *Doyle's amateur detective in A *Study in Scarlet* (1887), it had been apparent that the most effective way to shape and articulate the reading public's fascination with mysteries of a criminal nature was to imagine crime as a transcendence of the normal order of things which could only be countered by the transcendent genius of the lone investigator. In his 'Defence of the Detective Story' (1901), G. K. *Chesterton suggested that detective fiction was a 'popular realisation of the poetry concealed in city life'. The writer of such fiction, he went on, 'should be regarded as the poet of the city, and the detective as a romantic hero, the protector of civilization'. What distinguishes the Edwardian period is the development of a wide variety of detectives who occupy Holmes's position as protector of civilization, while being in every other respect as unlike Holmes as possible. The period saw the debut of: a metaphysical detective, *Chesterton's Father Brown, in *The *Innocence of Father Brown* (1911); a forensic-scientist detective, R. Austin *Freeman's Dr John Thorndyke, in *The *Red Thumb Mark* (1907); an Anglo-Indian detective, Sir Edmund *Cox's John Carruthers, in *John Carruthers, Indian Policeman* (1905); an ex-Anglo-Indian detective, with a terrific eye for poisons, Robert *Cromie's John Hedford, in *The Romance of Poisons* (1903); a foreign detective, A. E. W. *Mason's Hanaud, in **At the Villa Rose* (1910); a comic foreign detective, Robert *Barr's Eugene Valmont, in *The *Triumphs of Eugene Valmont* (1906); a blind detective, Ernest *Bramah's Max Carrados, in **Max Carrados* (1914); a gruff detective, 'Dick *Donovan''s Fabian Field, in *The Triumphs of Fabian Field, Criminologist* (1912); a down-to-earth barrister detective, Arthur *Morrison's Martin Hewitt, in *Martin Hewitt, Investigator* (1894); a genealogist detective, in A. C. *Fox-Davies's Dennis Yardley, in *The Mauleverer Murders* (1907); a female detective, Baroness *Orczy's Lady Molly, in **Lady Molly of Scotland Yard* (1910); and an entire family of detectives, the Becks, in M. McDonnell *Bodkin's *Paul Beck: The Rule of Thumb Detective* (1899), *Dora Myrl: The Lady Detective* (1900), and *Young Beck: A Chip Off the Old Block* (1911). Most Edwardian writers of detective fiction chose to work within the form perfected by Doyle: the series of self-sufficient episodes which makes possible a subtle dialectic between the invariable and the variable, between the familiarity of the hero or heroine whose presence guarantees that the mystery will be resolved, and the unfamiliar mysteries which require resolution. The other major development in the period was of the story or novel in which the criminal is either the hero or heroine, as in E. W. *Hornung's Raffles stories, *The Episodes of Marge: Memoirs of a Humble Adventuress* (1903) by H. Ripley *Cromarsh, Carlton *Dawe's *The Black Spider* (1911), Ethel M. *Dell's *The Swindler and Other Stories* (1914), May *Edginton's *Brass* (1910) and *The Adventures of Napoleon Prince* (1912), Valentina *Hawtrey's *In the Shade* (1909), Roy *Horniman's *Israel Rank: The Autobiography of a Criminal* (1907), G. Sidney *Paternoster's *The Motor Pirate* (1903), E. Livingston *Prescott's

Knit by Felony (1903), K. O'B. and H. V. Prichard's *The Chronicles of Don Q* (1904), *Chicane* by 'Oliver *Sandys' (1912), and Margaret *Baillie-Saunders's *Lady Q* (1912); or the object of fascinated sympathy, as in Marie Belloc *Lowndes's *The Lodger* (1913). Appropriately enough, perhaps, it concluded with E. C. *Bentley's **Trent's Last Case* (1913), which is both a skilfully plotted mystery and an ironic commentary on the genre itself. Edwardian writers who at one time or another turned their hand to crime fiction include: Frank *Barrett, Guy *Boothby, Bernard *Capes, Rosa Nouchette *Carey, Thomas *Cobb, J. MacLaren *Cobban, Dorothea *Conyers, Mrs George *Corbett, Mrs Philip Champion *De Crespigny, H. Burford *Delannoy, J. S. *Fletcher, Major A. *Griffiths, 'Headon *Hill', Fergus *Hume, Mrs Robert *Leighton, William *Le Queux, Ivy *Low, Robert *Machray, Arthur W. *Marchmont, L. T. *Meade, E. Phillips *Oppenheim, Edwin *Pugh, Sax *Rohmer, M. P. *Shiel (with L. *Tracy), George *Sims, and Edgar *Wallace.

Crock of Gold, The, James *Stephens, 1912, Macmillan. Stephens's second and most famous novel, a prose fantasy developed out of pieces he had written for the Irish nationalist newspaper *Sinn Féin*. Setting and characterization are self-consciously Irish: two philosophers, one married to the Grey Woman of Dun Gortin, the other to the Thin Woman of Inis Magrath, who live in the middle of a wood; their (oddly *Kiplingesque) children; a gang of leprechauns who lose and attempt to recover the crock of gold; the gods Pan and Angus Og (the god of love and divine imagination) who compete for Caitilin Ni Murrachu, 'the most beautiful girl in the world'; and an assortment of farmers, tinkers, and comic policemen. The novel can be read as an irreverent commentary on Irish nationalism and the repressive effects of religion and the law, and on the Irish literary revival, with its paraphernalia of gods and ceremonies. It ends with the restoration of lost people and objects.

CROCKETT, S[amuel] R[utherford] (1860–1914) married (1887) Ruth Mary MILNER. Born at Balmaghie, Kirkcudbrightshire, Crockett was the illegitimate son of a farmer's daughter. He won a bursary Edinburgh University, and took a job as a tutor, travelling round Europe. He then studied theology at New College, Edinburgh. While there he kept himself by reviewing in the *Manchester Guardian*. He was ordained a minister in the Church of Scotland in 1886, and was minister of Penicuik until he resigned in 1895. By that time he was famous as a member of the then fashionable 'kailyard school' of Scots sentimentalism; his best-known story being 'The Stickit Minister', about a dying farmer who has given up his career in the Church for an ungrateful brother, which gave its name to a collection of 1893. There were a number of sequels. By 1899 all his novels had been translated into Swedish. However, by the Edwardian period Crockett had become a hack, and he turned out a mass of *historical fiction and children's books, including a number of retellings for children of the novels of Walter Scott (1771–1832). Between 1900 and 1914 he published no fewer than thirty-six novels for adults. The bulk of these are historical romances set in Galloway in the time of the Stuarts: *Raiderland* (1904), *The Moss Troopers* (1912), *The Dew of Their Youth* (1910), *Silver Sand* (1914). But Crockett also had a fondness for French history, as he demonstrated in *The *White Plumes of Navarre* (1906), *Anne of the Barricades* (1912), set in the Paris Commune, and *A Tatter of Scarlet: Adventures and Episodes of the Commune in the Midi,* 1871 (1913). *Deep Moat Grange* (1908), in Northumberland, is where a mail robber and murderer keeps a family of mad women, the tale being narrated by the son of a well-to-do shopkeeper who loves his granddaughter. There is a substantial residue of 'kailyard' humour and pathos in *Young Nick and Old Nick: Yarns for the Year's End* (1910) and *Love in Pernicketty Town* (1911), a romance about a provincial schoolmaster which includes a tearful death scene. Crockett died at Avignon.

CROKER, Mrs B. M.: Bithia Mary SHEPPARD (?1849–1920) married (1870) John Stokes CROKER (1844–*c.*1910). The only daughter of a Church of Ireland clergyman in Co. Roscommon who died when she was 7, Croker was educated at Rockferry, Cheshire, and in Tours. Her husband was also Irish, and an officer first in the Royal Scots then in the Royal Munster Fusiliers. She went with him to Madras immediately on marriage. They were afterwards stationed in Burma and, after a return to England, in Bengal. Her popular Anglo-Indian romances began with *Proper Pride* (1880); her husband was on half-pay in the early 1880s and no doubt the money she earned was welcome. *The Company's Servant: A Romance of Southern India* (1907) is about a disgraced gentleman who has become a guard on an Indian railway. His best friend is an opium-smoking Englishman reminiscent of *Kipling's McIntosh in 'To Be Filed For Reference'. Needless to say, the hero is restored to respectability and prosperity. *Katherine the Arrogant* (1909) is an English romance about the predicament of a penniless girl who takes a job as a maid and falls in love with a married man. *The Old Cantonment and Other Stories of India and Elsewhere* (1905) includes a *Boer War tale and one about the transmigration of souls. Croker's novels are witty and fast-moving. Wolff quotes from the extant correspondence with her *literary agent Morris Colles, which shows her getting as much as £1,650 for a novel of 100,000 words such as *The Spanish Necklace* (1907). In this story Hester Forde, a shy young heiress, is driven from her home by tyrannical servants and takes to touring the Continent with a chaperone. The action mostly takes place in Spain, where Hester is wooed by a dashing Spanish noble, Paul de Sarazin, the necklace of the title being no more than a perfunctory excuse for their mutual involvement. Croker told Helen Black that she sometimes worked for ten or twelve hours a day. On her husband's retirement in 1892 they went to live in Co. Wicklow, but she moved to Folkestone before her death.

CROMARSH, H. Ripley, *pseud.*: Bryan Mary Julia Josephine DOYLE (1877–1927) married Charles Cyril ANGELL (*c.*1875–1937). Youngest of the five sisters of Arthur Conan *Doyle, she was named after her mother's friend Dr Bryan Waller, and brought up on his estate near Kirkby Lonsdale in Westmorland. She married the son of a neighbouring clergyman, himself a clergyman and lived with him in London (1906–12), at Leven, Scotland (1912–19), and then at Dunkerton, Somerset until her death. She published two novels under the pseudonym and a volume of verse (1918) as 'B. M. Angell'. *The Episodes of Marge: Memoirs of a Humble Adventuress* (1903) suffers from a failure to control the tone; Marge begins as a cheerful, resourceful thief, who conceals her class origins in a way common in fiction at the time, but the book then dissolves into sentimental melodrama. *The Secret of the Moor Cottage* (1907) is also amateurish work, a mystery set in eighteenth-century Yorkshire.

CROMARTIE, Countess of: Sibell Lilian MACKENZIE (1878–1962) succeeded (1893, confirmed 1895) as Countess of CROMARTIE, married (1899) Edward Walter BLUNT (1860–1949), who changed his name (1905) to BLUNT-MACKENZIE. She published seven volumes of fiction 1904–14 and then another four novels 1924–35. In *Out of the Dark* (1910), an aristocratic Englishwoman, holidaying in the Scottish Highlands, hankers for a 'frankly Pagan sense of sacrifice', and is promptly swept off her feet by an ancient Phoenician potentate who emerges from a Celtic barrow. Reviewing *Sword-of-the-Crowns* (1910), a translation, the *Manchester Guardian* complimented Cromartie on her 'vigorous rendering of an exciting Oriental wonder-tale'. Another wonder-tale, *Sons of the Milesians* (1906), mingles ancient Irishman with ancient Greek. She was a niece of Lady *Napier of Magdala.

CROMARTY, Deas, *pseud.*: Elizabeth Sophia FLETCHER (1850–1918) married (1874) Robert Addison WATSON (1845–1921). The daughter of a Wesleyan minister, and wife of a minister in the Free Church of Scotland, she published religious works and fiction under her maiden name and novels set in Scotland and Yorkshire. Her first novel was *Crabtree Fold* (1881). She contributed to various religious periodicals, including the *British Weekly*, the *Christian Leader* (of which, with her husband, she was editor), and the *Speaker*. She was interested in other religions, though confident of the superiority of her own. The last of the five novels she published as 'Deas Cromarty', *Lauder and Her Lovers: A Novel of the North* (1902), is dedicated 'To the Heart of Scotland which still beats for Liberty and the Ideal' and set in a Scots village whose castle has been sold by the heir to a self-made man. The novel is much concerned with the Scots idea of family and has an inheritance plot which depends on a clandestine marriage and a concealed birth. The heroine is universally attractive, and on inheriting the castle marries the Free Church clergyman. Watson left at her death, like Hall *Caine and M. P. *Shiel, an unfinished life of Christ, which was edited by her husband, who added a short memoir, and published as *The Heir of All Things* (1919).

CROMIE, Robert (1856–1907) was the son of a doctor in Clough, Co. Down, and was educated at the Royal Belfast Academical Institution. He was on the staff of the *Northern Whig* newspaper in Belfast. In 1895 he published an ingenious terrorist novel, *The Crack of Doom* (the genre became popular, in the wake of various assassinations, in the 1880s). Herbert Brande, a crazed anarcho-scientist, invents a kind of atom bomb. He means to detonate two bombs simultaneously in Labrador and the South Seas. The hero sabotages one expedition; the other 'has not returned, nor has it ever been definitely traced'. *Kitty's Victoria Cross* (1901) is a romance about the life of two middle-class Protestant girls in rural Ireland. Kitty's lover is killed and she is given his VC; she marries another Englishman, and her friend Nannie an American. Cromie collaborated with T. S. Wilson (possibly the physician Theodore Stacey Wilson, 1861–1949) on a series of *crime stories, originally published in *Black and White*, whose hero is Surgeon-Colonel John Hedford, late of the Indian Medical Service, who is brilliant at spotting little-known poisons. These were collected as *The Romance of Poisons: Being Weird Episodes from Life* (1903).

CROMMELIN, May: Maria Henrietta DE LA CHEROIS-CROMMELIN (1850–1930) belonged to a family of impoverished Irish gentry, Huguenot in origin, living in a castle in Co. Down. In her childhood they were absentees because of the political unrest. She had foreign governesses. After the death (1885) of her father, who 'had rigid ideas on feminine dependence and subordination', she moved to a flat in London and earned her living by her pen. Her two applications to the Royal Literary Fund (1891, 1909) paint a depressing picture of her life; she had poor eyesight, was swindled out of money, and had to cope with a drunken brother-in-law. Her novels are sometimes described as 'by the author of *Queenie*' (1874), her first novel. She also published travel books, and some of her novels have *exotic settings; she is supposed to have done research in Moroccan harems for *Kinsah: A Daughter of Tangier* (1899). The heroine of *A Woman-Derelict* (1901) has amnesia, and recovers to find her husband has remarried. She goes and nurses a madwoman, who murders her; the treatment is sentimental and melodramatic. Crommelin's literary efforts were not treated very seriously. The title-story of *One Pretty Maid and Others* (1904) is, like *Esther Waters* (1894), the biography of a housemaid, and the **Athenaeum*'s reviewer wrote snootily, 'It is, in design and execution, a very different work from Mr. George *Moore's—how different may perhaps best be indicated by our conviction that every housemaid in the country would find it interesting.' One of Crommelin's cousins married John *Masefield.

CROPPER, Eleanor [Margaret] (*c.*1880–1933) married (1905) Francis Dyke ACLAND (1874–1939) who succeeded (1926) as 14th Baronet. Born into an upper-class family, she studied art and published, as 'Margaret Burneside,' *The Delusion of Diana* (1898) and, under her own name, *In the Straits of Hope* (1904), a novel of artistic life and love in Chelsea. Some details of her upbringing and her life as the wife of a Liberal politician and Devonshire landowner are described in the memoir of her childhood and that of a daughter who died young, published posthumously as *Goodbye for the Present* (1935). After the First World War she published one more novel, *Dark Side Out* (1921), set in Westmorland, where she had been brought up. She and her husband were friends of E. M. *Forster.

CROSS, Victoria, *pseud.*: Annie Sophie CORY (1868–1952), also known as Vivian CORY or Vivian Cory GRIFFIN, was born at Rawalpindi in Punjab. Her father Arthur Cory (*c.*1830–1903) was an officer in the Bengal army, decorated at the siege of Lucknow, author of an oriental romance in verse *The Re-Conquest* (1865, 1868), who resigned from the army in 1876, publishing in the same year a study of the Russian threat to India, critical of British policy. He was briefly (*c.*1879–81) editor and joint managing proprietor of the *Civil and Military Gazette* in Lahore (his successor gave *Kipling his first job), but founded in the early 1880s the *Sind Gazette* in Karachi. His daughters probably grew up in the isolated European community there, though it is known that the second went to school in England. The eldest, Isabel Edith Tate, née Cory, succeeded her father as editor. The second, Adela Florence (called 'Violet') Nicolson, née Cory (1865–1904), published from 1901, as 'Laurence Hope', three bestselling volumes of erotic, orientalizing verse, notorious as the *Indian Love Lyrics*. The career of the third sister is poorly documented, but she became one of the most infamous of the New Woman writers of the 1890s. Her first publication seems to have been 'Theodora: A Fragment' published as 'Victoria Cross' in the *Yellow Book* 4 (Jan. 1895), which the *Birmingham Daily Post* called 'a full-blooded fragment of passion'. It describes a few days in which sexual desire wells up between a man and a woman; the reader is left ignorant as to the outcome. Cory's first novel, which came out in the same year, was to be published as *Consummation*, but John Lane renamed it *The Woman Who Didn't* in order to cash in on the notoriety of *The Woman Who Did* (1895) by Grant Allen (1848–99). The author's name is given as 'Victoria Crosse'. It describes an unconsummated love affair on a boat between an Indian officer and an unhappily married woman. They part, and she returns to her duty. It was followed by novels which came far closer to pornography, such as **Anna Lombard* (1901). Oscar Wilde (1854–1900), according to Frank *Harris, said that 'if one could only bed Thomas Hardy with Victoria Cross he would have had some real light with which to show off his little keepsake pictures of starched ladies'. Another successful sex novel was *Five Nights* (1908) which describes an open sexual relationship between a painter and his cousin. She will not marry him, lest he should feel caged, and leaves him when she gets pregnant so that he shall not see her 'broken, distorted, hideous'. Early on she models Phryne for him; he warms up his studio 'like a hothouse' and determines 'to let her discard the drapery as she liked ... I should simply watch her, and at some moment during the unveiling she would fall naturally into ... some pose ... which might give me my inspiration.' The title was no doubt intended to extinguish **Three Weeks* (1907). Cory can be agreeably irreverent; early on in *The Night of Temptation* (1912) we are told that 'whoever it was who wrote 'Home, Sweet Home' one feels the author must have been an orphan and brought up at a school'. The novel describes the affair between a young woman painter and her rich, older lover. As in *Five Nights*, childbirth is seen as degrading and marriage as a weapon against men which the emancipated woman is too high-minded to use. Her last book was *Martha Brown M. P.: A Girl of To-Morrow* (1935), a futurist fantasy in which England is ruled by women and men have become dependent, weak, and whining. As in many of Cory's novels, the argument is conducted at a preposterous, trivial level, but she none the less deals entertainingly with crucial areas of sexual and social politics. She seems to have lived from at least 1910 with her mother's brother, Heneage Mackenzie Griffin (1848–1939), travelled with him, and assumed his surname. Sewell Stokes describes in *Pilloried* (1928) meeting the two of them in Menton, where she told him her father had left her to the uncle in his will and that together they had been twice round the world. However, at her father's death she was a successful novelist of 35; the arrangement must have been voluntary. She told Stokes that *Anna Lombard* had sold six million copies. Griffin died at Lugano in Switzerland, leaving her about £100,000. She went on living there, and died in hospital in Milan.

Crossriggs, Mary and Jane *Findlater, 1908, Smith, Elder. Alexandra Hope, a clever, spirited, and sharp-tongued young woman, lives in genteel poverty in the east Scottish village of Crossriggs (an hour by train from Edinburgh) with her father, an impractical dreamer, and her sister, a widow with five children. Since childhood Alex Hope has loved the local gentleman scholar Robert Maitland, but he has married the more attractively feminine Laura. To supplement the meagre family income, Alex takes a job reading to the blind, irascible snob Admiral Cassilis, and meets his young grandson, Van Cassilis. Van falls in love with Alex but realizes, bitterly, that she is in love with Maitland, and marries the bold, bad Dolly Orranmore, but then, aware of her corrupting effect on him, drowns himself. Alex acts as companion to a rich aunt, who leaves her a substantial fortune, enough to enable Alex and her father to set out on a world trip—for him a lifetime's ambition, for her a new start. *Crossriggs* is partly a lightly told vignette of Scottish village life at the turn of the century, sharp in its observation of local values and prejudices, and partly a despairing exploration of the lonely situation of an articulate and emotional woman who lacks the conventional romantic appeal of either femininity or wealth.

CROUCH, Archer Philip (b. 1857/8) graduated from Keble College, Oxford in 1879 and contributed articles on foreign news and history to *Blackwood's* and the *Cornhill* in the 1890s. His eight novels tend to be set in *exotic locations: Tibet, South America, West Africa. *Nellie of the 'Eight Bells'* (1908), however, is set in Portsmouth during the Napoleonic wars. A naval lieutenant falls in love with a barmaid and discovers she is really the squire's granddaughter; her wicked lawyer uncle has concealed the evidence. The hero of *A Modern Slavedealer* (1901) sets out plant rubber in West Africa. Although early on the heroine shoots a wild boar which is about to gore him, when they are both captured by her cousin whose plantation is worked by slaves she appeals to his chivalry and he comments: 'in spite of the type of heroine so popular in modern novels, the large majority of men still regard the simile of the ivy and the oak as best expressing the ideal relations of the sexes.'

Crump Folk Going Home, Constance *Holme, 1913, Mills & Boon. Holme's first novel is a spirited melodrama set in Westmorland, in which the writer's love of the county and its cultural peculiarities is rather more convincing than her stiff-upper-lipped characters' love for each other (the book includes, among other local scenes, emotionally intense descriptions of a sheepdog trial and a wrestling contest). The title alludes to a village saying about the rooks returning to roost behind Crump Hall, in their 'haven of immemorial tranquillity'. Immemorial tranquillity—that is, a 'fantastical harbouring of terrible tradition and drear belief'—characterizes the Lyndesay clan. The book begins with the death of Stanley 'Slinkin' Lyndesay, Master of Crump, when it is revealed that, despite his official engagement to Deborah Lyndesay, daughter of the Crump steward, he is already married to Nettie Stone, a horse-dealer's daughter. By the end of the novel, Deborah is engaged to the new Master of Crump, the noble Christian 'Lakin' Lyndesay; his embittered mother has been crushed to death by the great Crump cedar tree; Nettie has returned to her true love, Dixon of Dockerneuk; impetuous cousin Lionel 'Larrupin' Lyndesay has finally won the hand of would-be New Woman, Verity Cantacute, and immemorial tranquillity looks set to resume its sway.

CUDLIP, Mrs Pender: Annie Hall THOMAS (1836–1918) married (1867) Pender Hodge CUDLIP (d. 1911). Born in Aldeburgh, Suffolk, the daughter of a lieutenant in the Royal Navy in charge of the coastguard station, she was educated at home and wrote novels from 1862. Her early books were considered shocking in their account of the sexual feelings of girls, and often bracketted with those of Florence Marryat (1838–99), a lifelong friend, their fathers being old colleagues and neighbours. In *The Cross of Honour* (1863) she observes 'a writer whose highest aspiration it is to be amusing, must not linger in the woeful and solemn paths of fiction too long'. She was immensely prolific; the publisher William Tinsley (1831–1902) remembered her as capable of turning out a three-volume novel in six weeks; it is not surprising that her books are remarkably slapdash. She edited *Ours: A Holiday Quarterly* (1878–?). Her husband was a High Church clergyman who, apart from a period in Paddington, London (1873–81), held livings in Devon and Cornwall; from 1884 to 1911 he was vicar of Sparkwell, Devon. Her last five novels came out 1900–5, and in her later years she was in financial distress, applying to the Royal Literary Fund in 1907 and 1908. In the latter year she stated that the highest offer she had received for her latest novel was £15.

CULLUM, Ridgewell, *pseud.*: Sidney Groves BURGHARD (1867–1943) married (1898) Agnes Winifred MATZ. He was born in London and left England aged 17. In the next thirty years he travelled very widely, writing in *Who's Who*: 'joined earlier gold rush in Transvaal, and later passed some years trading in the remote interior of Africa; saw much service in the Kaffir Wars; later on . . . travelled through the far north-west of Canada . . . fur-hunting and trading; ultimately spent many years cattle ranching in the State of Montana and adjoining states; took part in some of the later Indian risings.' In 1904 he settled in England and began to write Westerns, which were cheaply reprinted in large quantities. Kunitz and Haycraft refer to 'the huge success of his first literary sallies'. *The Devil's Keg* (1903) had sold 25,000 copies by 1909. The hero of *The Night-Riders: A Romance of Western Canada* (1906) has been to 'an essentially athletic public school' and is therefore able to defeat a sinister blind ranch-owner (who turns out to be a cattle thief by night) and marry his beautiful daughter. *The Sheriff of Dyke Hole: The Story of a Legacy* (1909) describes the search for a millionaire's lost daughter; she turns out to be a highway robber but reforms, and the sheriff marries her. *The Son of His Father* (?1915) describes the attempts of a millionaire's son to gain his father's respect by getting the better of him in a land deal. *The Way of the Strong* (1914) is a tale of romance, skulduggery, and wheat production set on the American prairies; a woman's love for a tough-minded millionaire is at first obstructed but eventually clarified and perfected by her promise to raise her dead sister's illegitimate son. Burghard seems to have assumed the name of Cullum in ordinary life; he died at Torquay.

Cunning Murrell, Arthur *Morrison, 1900, Methuen. This is a jocular tale of old salts, smugglers, pugilists, and witches set in the Essex marshes at the time of the Crimean War, inspired by historical records of real people and events. Mrs Martin and her niece, Dorrily, live apart from the villagers of Hadleigh—her husband was in the Revenue Service; her son (now at sea fighting the Russians) is a coastguard. When disasters begin to afflict the feckless Banham family, the local sage, Cunning Murrell, diagnoses witchcraft, and throws suspicion on Mrs Martin. Meanwhile their landlord, Simon Cloyes, is involved in a gin-smuggling scheme. When John Martin is killed at sea, it seems that Dorrily will be obliged to marry unpleasant young Sim Cloyes, if only for the sake of her unhappy and oppressed mother, but with the help of Stephen Lingood, the village smith (who loves her), and an ancient sailor, Roboshobery Dove (who honours John), and following Cunning Murrell's unfortunate involvement in Cloyes's smuggling operation, Mrs Martin is publicly cleared of witchery, the Cloyes are captured by the coastguard, and Dorrily is free to marry Stephen. A perfunctory tale, it is most interesting for its portrait of Murrell, a man whose 'wisdom' is clearly the result of his hard and systematic work observing and noting down everything he can about his neighbours, but whose belief in witchcraft, devilry, and magic is never presented as anything but sincere.

CURTIS, Marguerite published five novels 1908–13. Her first novel, *The Bias* (1908), at least had the virtue of originality. It concerns an experiment conducted on the unconscious person of an orphan girl by a psychologist who thinks that the bias of women is towards evil and a doctor who takes the opposite view. *Oh! For an Angel* (1911), about an evangelist with mysterious powers to do both good and evil, reveals an intelligent interest in the nature of faith. Her other novels in the period are *Marcia: A Transcript from Life* (1909), *The Dream Triumphant* (1912), and *The Dividing-Line* (1913).

CUSHING, Paul, *pseud.*: see R. A. *Wood-Seys.

D

DAHLE, T[homas] T[heodore] (1867–1910). Born in Norway, he moved to Hull in early life and became a journalist. *The Notions of a Nobody* (1893) is a collection of humorous sketches originally published in the *Leeds Times*. In his only novel, *The Tragedy of Three* (1900), a politician falls in love with and marries a pure young girl without telling Esma Allison, with whom he has been having an affair for ten years. The consequent débâcle is made the vehicle for a discussion of sexual and social mores. At the end Esma nobly renounces him.

DALE, Darley, *pseud.*: Francesca Maria STEELE (1848–1931). Born in Dalston, London, the daughter of an insurance company official, she went to Bedford College, University of London. She lived in Jersey from 1874 to 1884 and then moved to Gloucestershire. From her father's death in 1884 to her mother's in 1902 she supported the latter, since her father had lost everything except his pension in the failure of a bank. At the time of her application to the Royal Literary Fund in 1914 she was also supporting her sister. She became a Roman Catholic in 1887. Under her pseudonym she published children's books and adult fiction from 1878 including *Brother Francis* (1904) and *The Daughters of Job* (1902). The heroines of the latter are the rector's daughters, Jemima, Kezia, and Kerenhappuch, who develop careers as, respectively, journalist, secretary, and cook, but eventually dwindle into marriage. Steele published under her own name historical and biographical works of a religious kind such as *The Life and Visions of St. Hildegarde* (1914) and *The Convents of Great Britain and Ireland* (1924).

DALE, Lucy: see under G. M. *Faulding.

DANBY, Frank, *pseud.*: Julia DAVIS (1861–1916) married (1883) Arthur Frankau (d. 1904). Davis's father was a Jewish painter, reduced by the demands of rearing nine children to becoming a photographer. Her journalist sister, Eliza Aria, states in her memoirs that they were brought up 'strictly in the Jewish faith'. After a Jewish day school they had lessons with Laura Lafargue (1845–1911), daughter of Karl Marx (1818–1883), while her husband was imprisoned. In the financial straits after their father's death Julia earned money doing church embroidery and addressing envelopes, and wrote some art-historical works. Through her brother James (?1839–1907), who wrote lyrics and a few novels as 'Owen Hall' (i.e. 'owing all'), and who started a periodical called *Pan*, she met Oscar Wilde (1854–1900) and was introduced to journalism. In 1887 she published *Dr. Phillips: A Maida Vale Idyll*, a novel about a Jewish doctor who has an affair with a Gentile governess and murders his wife, which was held by some to libel Jewish middle-class society, and (according to the *Bookman*, July 1903) a 'well-known London physician ... caused the book to be suppressed by legal means'. Frankau's husband was prosperous, a partner in a firm of wholesale cigar merchants, and she entertained literary London, including George *Moore, who was first a friend and then an enemy. *A Babe in Bohemia* (1889) out-Zola'd Zola: Lucilla Lewesham, a young girl brought up by her decadent father and his shrieking mistress, escapes moral contamination but not hereditary epilepsy. The book was savagely denounced in the press and banned by Mudie's Library. **Pigs in Clover* (1903) is a satire on the excesses of *nouveaux riches* and decadent aristocrats in Edwardian London; its theme is reminiscent of *The Massereenes* by '*Ouida' (1897). But some of the characters are Jewish, and there is an interesting portrait of a suicidal South African woman novelist. The characteristically racy *Baccarat* (1904) concerns the French wife of an English lawyer who returns to France on holiday and loses her fortune and her reputation at the tables. *The Heart of a Child: Being Passages from the Early Life of Sally Snape, Lady Kidderminster* (1908) is another social comedy, about a chorus girl who marries an aristocrat, in which the Jewish theme is less important. It contains lively scenes of work in a fashionable dressmaker's shop, and of backstage life. In the preface to the posthumously published *Mothers and Children* (1918) her son Gilbert Frankau (1884–1952) expressed the view that her work suffered because she devoted so much time to her children: 'to no woman is it granted that she achieve supreme success both as mother and as artist.' Meeting her in 1911, Arnold *Bennett found her 'very chic'—and thoroughly ashamed of her novels. Her son Gilbert and his daughter Pamela Frankau (1908–67) were also novelists.

D'ANETHAN, Baroness Albert: Eleanora Mary HAGGARD (1860–1935) married (1886) Albert D'ANETHAN (d. 1910). Youngest daughter of a Norfolk landowner, she was sister of H. Rider *Haggard, Andrew *Haggard, and Arthur *Haggard, and married a Belgian diplomat who served in Japan 1873–5 and 1893–1910. Her rather dull Japanese diaries appeared as *Fourteen Years of Diplomatic Life in Japan* (1912), and she also published eight volumes of fiction 1897–1926, including *It Happened in Japan* (1906) and *The Twin-Soul of O'Take'San* (1914). *Two Women* (1909) consists of the diaries of a mother and daughter, tyrannized by an odious father (because in fact the girl is not his daughter), who forces the latter to marry a millionaire. They travel to Japan, which spins the story out with guidebook descriptions, before the mother dies and the daughter is reunited with the millionaire. Women must submit to humiliation for society to survive.

Dan Russel the Fox: *An Episode in the Life of Miss Rowan*, E. Œ. *Somerville and 'Martin *Ross', 1911, Methuen. Katherine Rowan and Jean Masterman, holidaying in Aix-les-Bains with a languid cousin, Ulick Adare, meet Mrs Lily Delanty, a spirited Irish widow, and agree to rent a house from her in Ireland. There they become embroiled with the overbearing master of hounds, Fitz-Symons, and his shy, passionate brother, John Michael. Between blood-curdling rides across country, Katherine and Lily fall in love with John Michael. When the hunt breaks up, however, he quarrels with his brother and leaves for America. Lily marries a dense Englishman, Fanshawe, while Katherine returns to the Continent with Jean. Darker than the 'Irish R.M.' stories, the novel still has plenty of good gallops.

Dark Flower, The, John *Galsworthy, 1913, William Heinemann. This is a chronicle of the three ages of a sculptor and intermittent amorist, Mark Lennan. In the first section, 'Spring', young Lennan, a student at Oxford, falls in love with Anna Stormer, the wife of his classics tutor, a woman seventeen years his elder. The Stormers invite him to join them on a climbing-trip in the Alps, and subsequently visit him at his guardian's house in Devonshire, where the relationship with Anna, passionate but unconsummated, ends. Seven years later, in 'Summer', Lennan follows Olive Cramier, a woman his own age married to an older, brutal man, to Monte Carlo, where she is travelling with her aunt and uncle, Colonel and Mrs Ercott (patently modelled on the Assinghams in *The *Golden Bowl*). On their return, Lennan rows Olive up the Thames and, as far as one can tell, seduces her. However, her husband has followed them, and hurls himself into the boat, sending Olive to a watery grave. In the final section, 'Autumn', Lennan is 46, successful, and married to Sylvia Doone, an insipid blonde, who has been trying to attract his attention throughout the previous 'Spring' and 'Summer'. He is strongly attracted to yet another dark, passionate siren, Nell Dromore, the daughter of a schoolmate, but resists. Galsworthy began the novel in 1912, and finished it, after numerous revisions, on 4 June 1913. This might indicate that he had difficulty with its sensationalism, and also, perhaps, its autobiographical content: 'Autumn' incorporates feelings aroused by (and, it has been said, incidents from) his affair with a young actress, Margaret Morris. The deficiency lies in Lennan's amorousness, which is pronounced but almost wholly intransitive. Perfectly ordinary desires are treated as though they were extraordinary, and Lennan is made to seem extraordinary simply because he controls them.

DART, Edith C[harlotte] M[aria] (*c.*1871–1924). Daughter of a prosperous builder in Crediton, Devon, she was educated at home, where she lived till her death. Her niece observes that owing to ill health she was 'exempt from all domestic or garden chores [and] seemed to spend all her time in her oak-panelled "den", where she had quite a considerable library'. Her great friend was M. P. *Willcocks, who lived nearby in Exeter. She published five novels between 1908 and 1920 and two volumes of verse. In her first novel, *Miriam* (1908), a farmer's granddaughter becomes companion to the squire's wife and fights against a scheming upstart lawyer. *Rebecca Drew* (1910) concerns the marriage between the last surviving member of a once great family and a feckless bohemian. In *Likeness* (1911) a hardworking typist discovers herself to be identical to a millionaire's daughter who asks her to go to a ball in her stead. Dart contributed to periodicals including *Country Life*, the **English Review*, and the **Pall Mall Magazine*.

DAVIDSON, Lillias Campbell was born in Brooklyn, New York. Davidson's earliest work seems to have been an article in *Blackwood's* in 1882; she wrote *Hints to Lady Travellers* (1889) and *Handbook for Lady Cyclists* (1896) and fourteen novels between 1900 and 1916. *The Confessions of a Matchmaking Mamma* (1901) is a light-hearted comedy about a widow with eight daughters. *Those Berkeley Girls* (1902) is about two penniless girls who sink their pride and set up a teashop. By the end a millionaire has married one of them and arranged a series of teashops to give employment to such girls in all classes. The heroine of *A Girl's Battle* (1904) discovers her brother has been embezzling money and persuades him to own up and take a job in London. She types, and they have a tiny flat in a working-class district; eventually she marries a philanthropic doctor. Davidson's last book, *Children of Liberty* (1935), her first since 1914, is a fictionalized biography of Samuel Verplanck, who lived during the American War of Independence. As a young woman in the 1880s Davidson shared a flat with Ménie Muriel *Dowie and Alice Werner (1859–1935); Werner was also a journalist, who published some fiction including *Chapenga's White Man: A Story of Central Africa* (1901), about a naughty little African boy who saves a white man's life, and she later became an anthropologist and professor of Swahili at London University. Ethel F. *Heddle described their ménage in *Three Girls in a Flat*.

DAVIES, W[illiam] H[enry] (1871–1940) married (1923) Helen Matilda PAYNE (*c.*1900–79). He was born in Newport, Monmouthshire. Apprenticed to a picture-frame maker, he left England for America and became a tramp. He lost his leg below the knee in an accident during a trip to Canada in 1899. After that he returned to London and, while living in a doss-house in Newington Butts, tried to become a writer, starting with a blank-verse tragedy. He paid £19 for the publication of his first volume of poetry, *The Soul's Destroyer* (1905), and sent it to various literary men. The book attracted the attention of Edward *Thomas, who became a friend and patron. *The Autobiography of a Super-tramp* (1908) made his name. Davies was awarded a Civil List pension in 1911. The rather feeble novel *A Weak Woman* (1911) is cast in autobiographical form, and depicts the hardships of a literary life. The tale is told in an artless, curiously uninterested way by the son of a businessman; he has two sisters, good Lucy and foolish, drunken Maud. He comes to London to become a painter, is swindled, and meets Henry Soaring, a would-be writer who is being harshly treated by patrons, editors, and publishers, and who eventually marries Lucy. After the First World War Davies wrote another novel, *Dancing Mad* (1927), many more volumes of poetry, and some autobiographical prose, including a book based on the experiences of his wife, whom he had met at a bus stop, a pregnant country girl, which was published after her death as *Young Emma* (1980). He retired to Gloucestershire in 1931 and died there. There is a biography by Richard J. Stonesifer (1963).

DAWE, [William] Carlton [Lanyon] (1866–1935). Born in Adelaide, Australia, he lived in England after 1892. He was the author in the 1890s of some interesting works of fiction drawing on his extensive travels in the Far East, dealing with the predicament of colonial civil servants and the problems of interracial marriage. By the twentieth century, however, he had settled down to turning out thrillers and romances; he published in all seventy-four novels between 1890 and 1936. In *A Morganatic Marriage* (1906) a briefless barrister falls in love with a Spanish princess who is about to be forced to marry an Italian duke who already has a morganatic wife. They marry secretly, but are deceived into parting; when the duke dies she comes back to him. *The Plotters of Peking* (1907) is a series of stories about an Englishman at the Imperial Chinese court; the sinister Empress is trying to destabilize her weak son's government. All the characters talk in flowery pseudo-Chinese, as in *The *Wallet of Kai-Lung* by 'Ernest *Bramah'. *The Black Spider* (1911) and *The Crackswoman* (1914) are both about single women who become society jewel thieves; each falls in love and repents; the latter ends up nursing the French Foreign Legion. The similar, pretty, penniless, middle-class girl who recounts *The Confessions of Cleodora* (1908) becomes the mistress of an elderly roué; her story ends in romance. Dawe died in Bristol.

DAWSON, A[lec] J[ohn] (1872–1951). Born in Wandsworth, he was apprenticed very young to a Glasgow shipping company, but jumped ship in Melbourne because of 'the really rather extraordinary brutality of a Peterhead second mate'. His experiences on the run were evoked in his novel *Daniel Whyte* (1899). In Australia he was at various times a cowman and a tramp, then editor for a year of the *Bathurst National Advocate*. In the early 1890s he travelled widely in the Far East, Africa, and Europe, and became a journalist. In 1894 he settled down in London as a short-story-writer. He wrote *Leeway* (1896) as 'Howard Kerr'. In order to get the right atmosphere for *Bismillah* (1898) he 'lived for four months entirely on the Koran and the Old Testament and Burton, reading not a single line of anything else', according to an interview in the **Bookman* (Jan. 1901). He edited the *Standard of Empire* 1908–13. He and his brother Ernest (d. 1960), a former Burma magistrate, were friends of *Conrad. Dawson wrote fifteen novels between 1897 and 1930, and several volumes of short stories. The stories in *African Nights' Entertainment* (1900) are mostly set in Morocco, and concerned with interracial sexual attraction; however, in 'The Treatment of Brierly' a Nigerian barrister marries an English school-girl, and the reader is advised if he is 'a good, innocent, racial-equality person... do not read this story'. It is evident that while Dawson is ready to glamorize Moors he finds nauseating the thought of a white woman marrying a black African. *Kipling's stories, especially 'Kidnapped', are an obvious influence on the collection. *The Message* (1907) is an *invasion scare novel, with delightful illustrations by H. M. Brock (1875–1960); the Germans overrun England, but are beaten back with the help of Canada and South Africa.

DAWSON, Coningsby [William] (1883–1959) married (1918) Helen WRIGHT-CLARK née CAMPBELL. Born in High Wycombe, one of the six children of William James *Dawson, he read history at Merton College Oxford, and emigrated to America with his parents in 1905. After a year at theological college in New York he decided against joining the Methodist ministry, and worked first as a journalist and then for the publisher George H. Doran 1910–13. He served with the Canadian forces in the First World War, and published several reminiscences of this experience. *The House of the Weeping Woman* (1908) is set in London, where a businessman's son wants to become a great writer; he lives with his friend Lancaster, an altruist who seeks to emulate Christ, keeping his house open to all comers. In the end Lancaster dies; and art is abandoned for Christianity. *The Road to Avalon* (1911) is a pseudo-medieval, Arthurian tale, apparently indebted to Maurice *Hewlett, but forming a Christian allegory. *The Garden Without Walls* (1913), which Kunitz and Haycraft call 'a somewhat sultry and poetically written romance, [which] was a best-seller', describes the emotional adventures of Dante Condover, who is in love with a married American, Vi, has a pure stepsister, Ruthita, and desires a beautiful, amoral dancer, Fiesole. By the end he has lost all three, and analyses his problem as a conflict between his puritan conscience and his pagan temperament.

DAWSON, William James (1854–1928) married (1879) Jane POWELL. Born at Towcester, Northamptonshire, Dawson was the son of a Wesleyan Methodist minister. He went to Kingswood School, Bath, and Didsbury College, Manchester, training as a Wesleyan minister, and followed that profession from 1875 to 1892, when he resigned and for twelve years was minister of the Quadrant Congregationalist Church in Highbury. 'Fate had made me a preacher; my own secret aim was to make myself a writer.' He worked as a journalist and gave public lectures on literary subjects as well as writing novels, theology, and critical works. In about 1904 he emigrated to America. His novel *Masterman and Son* (1909) is about the struggle between an unscrupulous, self-made builder and his Oxford-educated son, and might be compared to Marmaduke *Pickthall's **Brendle* (1905). After the father is ruined and dies the son acknowledges that he had guts. Dawson's autobiography (1925) gives an interesting account of his intellectual influences; he was an early admirer of Emily Dickinson (1830–86). Coningsby *Dawson was his son.

DAWSON-SCOTT, C. A.: Catherine Amy DAWSON (1865–1934) married (1896) Horatio Francis Ninian SCOTT (d. 1922). She was born in Dulwich and educated at the Anglo-German College in Camberwell. She had an unhappy childhood; both her parents were alcoholics, her mother died young, and her stepmother was unsympathetic. They were supported financially by their family; her paternal grandfather had a pottery business. At 18 she went out to work as a secretary-companion to an elderly blind professor who taught her Latin and Greek; in 1889 she published *Sappho*, an epic poem on women's rights. After leaving home with her sister she became a friend of the *publisher William Heinemann, who published some of her verse, and moved in London literary circles, to her great pleasure. After marriage to a doctor she ceased to publish for a while. Her first novel, *The Story of Anna Beames* (1907), was the beginning of a new period. Its 35-year-old heroine keeps house for her brother, rector of a small English village. There is an asylum nearby, run by two of her brothers, who employ Stephen Barclay as steward and odd job man. Barclay has led an adventurous life, and is a thorough scoundrel. Anna approaches him in order to rescue her servant and godchild from his attentions. She achieves her aim, but falls under his spell. He seduces her, promising marriage. Her brothers intervene (one of them has evidence which might convict Barclay of murder). After a few months of squalid marriage, Anna dies giving birth prematurely (her husband has pushed her down some stairs). The burial service is read by a curate who offered her happiness too late. *The Agony Column* (1909) is almost as grim. Frances Morgan, who lives in Bath with her middle-aged soldier husband, is an idealist immune to everyday joys and sorrows. She meets a young Jew who shares her asceticism, but will neither wreck his life by eloping with him nor spare her own by renouncing him altogether. Like many of Dawson's novels, it is partly set in north Cornwall. This was the first in a trilogy, 'Some Wives', of which the second was *Madcap Jane* (1910) and the third *Mrs Noakes: An Ordinary Woman* (1911), but the characters do not recur. Mrs Noakes is followed through fifty years of supporting a weak, drunken husband. In 1909 Dawson-Scott moved back to London and established something of a literary salon in Southall, where she had a great influence on the career of Charlotte Mew (1869–1928). In 1912 her Elizabethan tragic novel, *Ulalia*, was refused by Heinemann. Dawson's point of view is feminist and ironic; her dialogue and characterization are good; some of her later work was influenced by Dorothy Richardson (1873–1957). Her postwar novels make a deliberate attempt to record Cornish dialect and customs. During the First World War she discovered her husband's adultery, and was granted a decree nisi in 1920; two years later he committed suicide. After his death she became a keen spiritualist and published two books on the subject. Although her writing has individuality and force Dawson-Scott's chief claim to fame is undoubtedly the fact that in 1921 she founded International PEN. She requested in her will that no biography of her should be written; however, her daughter, Marjorie Watts, has published one (1987) and also a history of the early years of PEN (1971).

DEAKIN, Dorothea published some fairly tedious comedies of village or country house life, all in this period, including *The Smile of Melinda* (1903), *The Poet and the Pierrot* (1905), *'Georgie'* (1906), *Tormentilla* (1908), *The Young Columbine* (1908), and *The Goddess Girl* (1910). The standard Deakin figure is the heroine of boyish charm whose lover calls her a 'good sport' and whose mission in life is to upset the rector's wife.

DEAN, Ellis may have been a nurse, since her romantic fiction includes *The New Matron* (1906) and *A Raw Probationer* (1905). The latter is a first-person coming-of-age narrative about a young nurse who in her first posting encounters a tyrannical head nurse, an untidy room-mate and an overdose of laudanum, and triumphs over them, partly through the sense of duty which persuades her to volunteer for service in a military hospital in Egypt, partly through marriage and motherhood. *A Strange Honeymoon* (1908) is a South Seas tale.

DEANE, Mary [Bathurst] (d. 1940) was the daughter of the Revd John Bathurst Deane (1797–1887), Rector of St Helen's with St Martin's, London, whom she depicted as the central character in *Kinsfolk* (1891); other ancestors appear elsewhere in her fiction. Her earliest publication seems to have been a historical tale, 'The Duke's House', in the *Dublin University Magazine* (Dec. 1873). She also contributed to **Temple Bar*, edited a book of Deane genealogy (1899), and wrote eleven novels for children and adults between 1878 and 1920. *The Rose-Spinner* (1904) is set in Georgian Somerset, *The Other Pawn* (1907) in mid-Victorian Bath; both are love stories. *Treasure and Heart* (1903) is about an orphaned English child adopted by an Italian art-dealer; the mystery of her parentage and her love affairs provide the plot, against a background of the life of English expatriates in Italy. Deane's sister Eleanor was P. G. *Wodehouse's mother.

DEARMER, Mabel: Jessie Mabel WHITE (1872–1915 married (1891) Percy DEARMER (1867–1936). The daughter of an army surgeon, she was educated at home and at Herkomer's School of Art, Bushey. In the memoir prefixed to *Letters from a Field Hospital* (1915), Stephen *Gwynn speaks of a 'lonely childhood' and a 'precocious and uneasy girlhood, fevered with ambition', in which she advanced extreme socialist views in opposition to a conservative stepfather. She married young a poor clergyman, a member of the Fabian Society, and to help pay the bills contributed stories and pictures to the *Yellow Book*. She also illustrated children's books, and wrote novels and plays for adults and children. The *Spectator* called *The Noisy Years* (1902) 'A faithful and charming picture of childhood in the present day'. *The Alien Sisters* (1908), set largely in Cornwall, describes the marriage between far-from-spotless Sir Raymond Templeton and Elizabeth Grahame, a pure young woman whose girlhood has been spent 'in preparation for the disillusion of marriage'. Sir Raymond fathers one daughter, Ruth, by his wife, and another, Rose, by his rapacious and embittered mistress, Rosalie de Winton, whom we first see attended by a leering elderly admirer, raining blows on her 3-year-old daughter (brutality topped only by her laughing account of the death of an over-affectionate dachshund). *The Difficult Way* (1905) also concerns a marriage entered into in all innocence. Other fiction includes *The Orangery: A Comedy of Tears* (1904), *Brownjohn's* (1906), and *Gervase* (1909). Dearmer's husband was a clergyman and hymnologist who wrote extensively on church music and ecclesiastical art. She died of enteric fever while working in a hospital in Serbia during the First World War.

DEASE, Alice [Mary Frances] (*c.*1874–1949) married (1915) Philip Charles CHICHESTER (1865–1930). The tenth daughter of an Irish Catholic landowner in Co. Westmeath, she wrote about local folklore, and published fiction with the Catholic Truth Society. Her work includes *The Beckoning of the Wand: Sketches of a Lesser Known Ireland* (1908) and *The Lady of Mystery* (1913), a novel about a young Catholic baronet who buys back the seat of his Irish ancestors. The love interest involves one of the many girls in the fiction of this period whose identity has been lost in a railway accident.

DE CRESPIGNY, Mrs Philip CHAMPION: Rose KEY (*c.*1860–1935) married (1878) Philip Augustus CHAMPION DE CRESPIGNY (1850–1912). The daughter of an admiral, she was brought up in Greenwich and other naval postings, and received a rather scientific education, strongly Low Church. She married young, and her husband retired to the New Forest, where she painted landscapes and seascapes for sale, since they had financial worries, exhibiting until 1929. *From Behind the Arras* (1902), published in T. Fisher Unwin's First Novel Library, is set in eighteenth-century France. Except that the narrator is a young girl rather than a middle-aged man, it much resembles the *historical romances of Stanley J. *Weyman, but its plot is based on the 'tomboy tamed' pattern then fashionable in fiction for girls. *The Mischief of a Glove* (1903) is similar but set in the reign of Bloody Mary, with some anti-Catholic feeling. Many of her later novels, however, are *crime stories. After her husband's death she became an enthusiastic convert to spiritualism and was honorary principal of the British College of Psychic Science. Her memoir, *This World and Beyond* (1934), contains some biographical details and description of intellectual influences, as well as many accounts of occult experiences.

DEEPING, [George] Warwick (1877–1950) married Maude Phyllis MERRILL. Born in Southend, the son of a country doctor, educated by a tutor and at Merchant Taylors' School, Trinity College, Cambridge, and the Middlesex Hospital Medical School, Deeping qualified as a physician but only practised for a year. His two earliest novels, *Uther & Igraine* (1903) and *Love Among the Ruins* (1904), are Arthurian romances, sentimental medieval pastiche, rather in the manner of Maurice *Hewlett. *Mad Barbara* (1908) is set in the reign of Charles II; the hero's father has murdered Barbara's father because he is having an affair with her mother; when Barbara discovers this she is locked up as mad. Samuel Pepys helps a stepbrother to rescue her. *The Return of the Petticoat* (1909) expresses some of the contemporary anxieties about class and gender roles. An Australian woman wishes she were a man and asks an English doctor to cut off her breasts; he suggests a 'light bandage' instead. She sets up as a farmer, but after an accident is nearly unmasked by Tom, who works for her. Realizing she is in love with him, she again asks the doctor's advice and he sends her to a superb beautician—of whom the heroine comments: 'women who have the real power do not go and howl at Westminster.' Newly dressed, electrolysed, fortified with feminine arts, she returns to the farm as her own sister. Class barriers are hard to overcome, but after Tom has lost an arm she reveals herself to him and they acknowledge their love. Deeping's great success, however, came with the publication of the heart-warming melodrama *Sorrell and Son* (1925). Deeping knew of and resented highbrow condemnation of his work, commenting to Kunitz and Haycraft: 'A negative cynicism seems to me to be a form of cowardice.... I like... people who do the work of the world without remembering to be self-consciously clever...' He served in the First World War with the RAMC at Gallipoli, in Egypt, and in France. He lived at Weybridge, Surrey.

DEHAN, Richard, *pseud.*: Clotilde Inez Augusta Mary GRAVES (1863–1932). Born at Buttevant, Cork, the daughter of an army officer, she studied at the Royal Female School of Art, Bloomsbury, and became an actress and journalist. She published novels, as Clo Graves, from 1887, and also wrote verse, pantomimes, and plays. Her living was precarious and she applied to the Royal Literary Fund in 1905 and 1910. But her great success came with the publication, as 'Richard Dehan', of *The *Dop Doctor* (1910), and thereafter her pseudonym appeared on the title-page, sometimes below her own name. *Between Two Thieves* (1912), like its predecessor, is an epic romance with the backdrop of war, fast-moving and melodramatic. The hero's career, which ranges from the circle of Napoleon through the Crimean War, is based on that of Jean-Henri Dunant (1828–1910), founder of the Red Cross. He falls in love with a thinly disguised version of Florence Nightingale (1820–1910), but they cannot marry, as she has sworn on her mother's deathbed not to marry a Roman Catholic. (Graves herself converted to Roman Catholicism in 1896.) Her earlier work under her own name includes *Maids in a Market Garden* (1894), a farcical novel about some single women who use their capital to embark on a cooperative market garden in Cornwall. There is feminist feeling in the book, in which the hardships of genteel poverty are exposed, but the finale is a series of prosperous marriages which will in future exempt the heroines from the necessity of earning their livings. After 1928 Graves lived in a convent at Hatch End.

DELAIRE, Jean (1888–?) married H. W. Muirson BLAKE. Born in France and educated privately, she described herself as the founder of the philosphical circle of the Lyceum Club, and of the first Christian lodge in the Theosophical Society, and was interested in health reform. She contributed to the *Theosophical Review and Health and Efficiency*, and was editor of the *Christian Theosophist*. She also published six volumes of fiction and several works on religion. *Alsatian Tales* (1902) describes the oppression of francophile Alsatians under German rule. The stories are saccharine and melodramatic: a little girl dies of exposure because the German teacher threatens her; a man who has deserted to join the French army is killed visiting his dying mother. The book was reprinted in 1914 as *The Germans in Alsace. Around A Distant Star* (1904) is much odder and shows the interest in religion which appears in the non-fiction. Two boys go on a space rocket to a distant planet, meet a strange monkey race, and are nearly seduced by a woman lily. They then focus their telescope on the Holy Land in the time of Christ. The narrator comes back to earth, leaving his companion behind to convert the monkeys to Christianity and colonize.

DE LA MARE, Walter: Walter John DELAMARE (1873–1956), CH (1948), OM (1953), who changed his name to DE LA MARE, married (1899) Constance Elfrida INGPEN (*c.*1863–1943). He was born at Charlton, near Woolwich, the sixth of seven children of an official in the Bank of England who died in 1877, was brought up in Forest Hill, went to St Paul's Cathedral Choristers' School, and worked for the Anglo-American Oil Company as a book-keeper (1890–1908). His first publication was a story, 'Kismet', accepted by the *Sketch* in 1895. There were many rejection slips, four children born quickly after marriage on a clerk's salary, then gradual recognition, encouragement from the *literary agent H. P. Pinker, from Henry *Newbolt, who published his poems in the **Monthly Review*, and from Edward *Thomas, who reviewed his *Poems* 1906 favourably. In 1908 Newbolt secured him a bounty of £200 from the Civil List, and he gave up his job for reviewing and writing full-time. During 1911–14 he also worked for Heinemann as a publisher's reader. From 1911 he had an emotional entanglement with the literary editor of the *Saturday Westminster Gazette*, Naomi Royde-Smith (d. 1964). He was unusual in that his preoccupation with the sensibility of the child; and the fact that much of his work was aimed at child readers did not prevent his achieving a serious literary reputation, though it has affected the evaluation of his poetry. His first book was *Songs of Childhood*, poetry written for children, published under the pseudonym 'Walter Ramal' in 1902. His first novel *Henry Brocken: His Travels and Adventures in the Rich, Strange, Scarce-Imaginable Regions of Romance* (1904), is a Quixote tale in which a traveller encounters figures from legend and literature: Lucy Gray, Jane Eyre (now Jane Rochester), Bottom, Gulliver, the Sleeping Beauty, Annabel Lee, Criseyde, and others. In its evocation of a lonely child's exploration of books, it anticipates the essay introducing de la Mare's famous anthology of poetry for children, *Come Hither* (1923). *The Three Mulla-Mulgars* (1910) is a novel for children, about three monkeys, facetious in the manner of *Kipling's **Just So Stories* (1902), but in its complex theology also drawing on his *Jungle Book* (1894). *The *Return* (1910) is a novel for adults about a man losing his identity. After the First World War de la Mare published one other adult novel, *Memoirs of a Midget* (1922), and many more short stories and volumes of verse for all ages. He was awarded a Civil List pension of £100 p.a. in 1915, and also inherited in that year a third share of the estate of Rupert Brooke (1887–1915), which the vast posthumous success of Brooke's *1914 and Other Poems* (1915) made a secure maintenance. He died at Twickenham. There is a biography by Theresa Whistler (1993).

DELANNOY, H. Burford published seventeen volumes of fiction between 1897 and 1931, mostly *crime stories such as *The Margate Murder Mystery* (1902), a story narrated by the protagonists in the manner of Wilkie Collins (1824–89), and *Dead Man's Rooms* (1905), about the sensational events which occur in a young lawyer's rooms and which include murder committed by a 'strong woman'. There is a distinctive frenzy about Delannoy's melodramas. *In Mid-Atlantic* (1904) opens with one survivor of a shipwreck observing to the other that there is not room for both of them on the life-raft. *Beaten at the Post* (1907) concerns the machinations of a villainous doctor at the deathbed of Mr Grey of Greystones. *The Money-Lender* (1907) mysteriously punctuates the rise of a financier with savagery on a desert island. In *A Studio Model* (1909), the beautiful and virtuous heroine is persecuted by a famous painter.

DE LA PASTURE, Mrs Henry: Elizabeth Lydia Rosabelle BONHAM (1866–1945), CBE (1918), married, first (1887), Henry Philip Ducarel DE LA PASTURE (1841–1908) and, secondly (1910), Hugh *CLIFFORD. The daughter of a diplomat, she was born in Naples. Her novels deal with affairs of the heart among the upper middle class in England, dwelling repeatedly on the discrepancy between romantic anticipation and prosaic reality. Her young, inexperienced, and slightly stupid heroines display to the reader their embarrassments, tragedies, and follies. The heroines of both *Deborah o'Tods* (1897) and *Catherine of Calais* (1901) hold idealized pictures of the older men who have married them. Sometimes the difficulties her heroines face are social: they marry out of their class. *The Grey Knight* (1908) is about a romance between two middle-aged people; only when they have each been disillusioned about the other can they marry. Often, as in *The Lonely Lady of Grosvenor Square* (1907), some of the characters are French. Its heroine is brought up on a Welsh farm and transplanted to Grosvenor Square, where she commits various social enormities before marrying a duke. De La Pasture's writing is bitter, witty, and snobbish; although her view of marriage is so dark she never proposes any alternative occupation for women. Her most cheerful work is *The Unlucky Family* (1907), a comic children's book about a large family who inherit a country house. Both her husbands belonged to upper-class English Roman Catholic families. She was awarded the CBE for humanitarian work in the Gold Coast, where Hugh Clifford was governor. The elder of her daughters by her first marriage was 'E. M. Delafield' (1890–1943), who is thought to have drawn on personal experience in describing the autocratic mothers in her novels.

DELL, Ethel M[ary] (1881–1939) married (1922) Gerald Tahourdin SAVAGE (1883–1958). She was born in Streatham. Her father, who worked in an insurance company, had abandoned the Roman Catholic faith to marry her mother. She was educated by her mother and at Streatham College for Girls; the family lived near Sevenoaks and after 1898 in Kent. She wrote copiously, and her father had some of her tales privately printed. In 1901 she published some stories in magazines. By 1910 she had completed a novel which, after having been rejected by eight *publishers, came out as *The *Way of an Eagle* (1912) in T. Fisher Unwin's First Novel Library; one of the spectacular bestsellers of its day, this tale of passion in India had twenty-seven printings by 1915 and at one point represented half of the publisher's turnover. *The Keeper of the Door* (1915) and *By Request* (1927) are sequels to it. Remarkably, although Dell had some cousins who were brought up in India, and read the novels of Flora Annie *Steel, Maud *Diver, Alice *Perrin, F. E. *Penny, and *Kipling, she herself not only had never visited the country but in all her life left England only once, for the south of France. When her husband's regiment was posted to India, she made him resign his commission. Some of her information about India derived from the *Illustrated London News*. The novel brought her a large income—her biographer mentions £20,000 a year after the First World War—and there was a move to a large house near Guildford. She led a rather reclusive life, with sentimental friendships with other women. She was fanatical about privacy, and they were much troubled by her fans. Although her income from writing was the sole support of the household, she was in the habit of writing at night. In about 1929 she developed breast cancer and underwent a mastectomy; a recurrence of cancer killed her. Her second novel, *The Knave of Diamonds* (1913), which also sold very widely, is about the relationship between an unhappily married woman and a man who is supposed to be depraved and unreliable. She is pure, and repels his attempt at seduction. The use of scenes of physical violence to raise the erotic temperature is a hallmark of Dell's style; the heroine's husband beats both the Knave and her. Widowed, she marries the Knave, who has been purged by suffering and love. Like Nick Radcliffe, the hero of *The Way of an Eagle*, the Knave is not physically attractive but small and ugly. Dell's heroines magnanimously overcome repulsion in a way which symbolizes their willingness to reconcile feminine virtue with masculine desire. They forgive transgression, such as the attempted seduction; they forgive deceit and crime: in the title-story of *The Swindler and Other Stories* (1914) the hero is a thief. There is a biography by Penelope Dell (1977).

DE MORGAN, William [Frend] (1839–1917) married (1887) Mary Evelyn PICKERING (*c.* 1857–1919). He was born in Gower Street, London, and went from University College School to University College London, where his father was professor of mathematics. While at the college he took art lessons, and in 1859 he left for the Royal Academy School, where he made friends with the Pre-Raphaelites. He spent most of his life as an innovative and brilliant designer and manufacturer of ceramics, especially tiles, and stained glass. However, in 1906 he published **Joseph Vance*. Here and in his later novels De Morgan emulates Charles Dickens (1812–1870) in the comic and sentimental use of working-class settings, and the use of a child's-eye view of class distinctions (De Morgan could quote pages of Dickens's novels by heart). Joseph Vance loves the daughter of his first benefactor, but marries another woman; this theme recurs in *It Can Never Happen Again* (1909), whose hero is prevented from marrying the woman he loves because the Deceased Wife's Sister's Marriage Act 1907 has not yet been passed. The heroine of *Alice-for-Short* (1907) is a little orphan adopted by an artist. As she grows up, a mystery surrounding the haunted house they lived in is revealed, Alice's ancestry is disentangled, and she marries the artist after his first wife's death. With their genial humour and complicated plots, the books inspired affection in contemporary readers but De Morgan is now remembered for his tiles rather than for the novels of his old age. After his death his wife, who was a painter, completed and published (1919, 1920) the last two of his novels.

DENNIS, D. H., *pseud.*: Denis COX published five novels of widely varying emphasis in the period: *Moths and the Maid* (1909), *Soul of the Snows* (1910), *The Spell of the Lotus* (1911), *Crossroads* (1913), and *The Widow of Gloane* (1914). The first of these is partly about young people at an engineering works, partly about married life abroad. The last, written in a slangy style, concerns the troubled marriage between a wealthy woman addicted to spiritualism and gambling and a not-so-wealthy man addicted to literature and motoring. In *The Spell of the Lotus*, an Englishman engaged to a bishop's daughter goes to Japan, discovers a supposed Japanese ancestry, and marries a Japanese woman; meanwhile the bishop's daughter marries and divorces an Englishman, before herself deciding to visit Japan. The whole thing is rounded off by an Anglo-Japanese war.

DE PRATZ, Claire (d. 1934). Of French family, but born and partly brought up in England, she moved to Paris as a young woman and studied at the Sorbonne. After two or three years teaching adult evening classes, she became for eight years a teacher of English Language and Literature at a *lycée* for women, then General Inspectress of Public Charities at the Ministry of the Interior. This information is derived from the description of herself in *France from Within* (1912). Like that book, her novels set out to explore the differences between the two cultures, especially as they affect the education, marriage, and employment of women. *Elizabeth Davenay* (1909) describes the predicament of a French feminist, a teacher, young, pretty, and educated in England. She interviews a prostitute, deplores the double standard in sexual morality, and helps set up a feminist newspaper. Discussing the emancipation of women with an English suffragist friend, she argues that the English are too mealy-mouthed to recognize the central importance of sex; feminists cannot be expected simply to abstain. But she has to give up her own lover: 'he is still strongly imbued with all the old ingrained and backward ideas concerning the relations between men and women.' *Eve Norris* (1907) is similar in its Paris and London settings, themes, and conclusions. *The Education of Jacqueline* (1910) and its sequel, *Pomm's Daughter* (1914), describe the upbringing of girls in France. Pratz was the correspondent of *Le Petit Parisien* and the *Daily News*, and contributed to the *Woman's World* while her friend Oscar Wilde (1854–1900) was its editor; she saw him in Paris shortly before his death.

Derelict Empire, A, 'Mark *Time', 1912, William Blackwood. A 'fantasy' dedicated to the British elector, 'in the hope that ten years hence the assumptions from which it starts may still be wholly imaginary'. A Socialist government has abolished the House of Lords, granted Ireland Home Rule, extended suffrage to all adults of both sexes, nationalized the railways and the mines, reduced the armed forces drastically, taxed land heavily, and introduced old-age pensions. One consequence is rebellion in India. Captain Maurice Wardlaw, of the Fortieth Punjab Lancers, is appointed commander of the British army in India, the only force capable of holding the country together. He takes over the chaotic National Assembly, and foils assassinations and invasions. Kaiser Wilhelm, impressed by his resoluteness, offers protection from Russia and Japan in return for favourable trade terms. Wardlaw's loyalty is strained to the limit, but he agrees; it is the only way to save India. The novel is an interesting illustration of the belief, widely held in right-wing circles, that Britain would have to Prussianize itself in order to defeat Prussia in the war which, by 1912, seemed inevitable. There is some action of the stiff-upper-lip variety. The only wound Wardlaw suffers during his campaigns proves on inspection to be 'little more than a deep scratch, requiring no treatment beyond a sprinkle of boracic acid powder and a cold-water bandage. These simple remedies having been applied, [he] sat down to a late breakfast.'

DE SAIX, Tyler, *pseud.*: see H. de Vere *Stacpoole.

DE SÉLINCOURT, Hugh (1878–1951) married (1907) Janet Mabel WHEELER. Educated at Dulwich College and University College, Oxford, de Sélincourt became the drama critic of the *Star* (1910–12) and the literary critic of the *Observer* (1911–14); he went on reviewing for the latter for many years. His fame rests on the fact that, himself the captain of a village cricket team, he wrote a classic fictional account of one, a book much loved by enthusiasts for the game, *The Cricket Match* (1924). But he began his career before the First World War, and his early novels focus on the sexual and social problems of his generation. *A Boy's Marriage* (1907) describes the emotional career of Beverley Teruel, an innocent boy whose parents encourage him to marry very young. Ignorant about sex, he is appalled to find out that his father had a premarital affair, is discouraged on his wedding night by his wife's timidity, and finally dies young. De Sélincourt's sixth novel, *A Daughter of the Morning* (1912), the first of a trilogy, descibes the sexual awakening of a woman, the epitome of upper-middle-class decorum. She falls in love with a married artist who is not brave enough to consummate their affair; this contrasts with their servants, who deal with a similar situation in a more flexible and sensible way. The literary critic Ernest de Sélincourt (1870–1943) was his brother and also taught him at Oxford; another brother married Anne Douglas *Sedgwick.

DE VAURIARD, G. Specialized in comic sexual and social melodramas. In *The Sibyl of Bond Street* (1907) an adventuress descends on her three elderly female cousins, who have hitherto lived a blameless village life. *The House of the Majority* (1909) is partly about the partnership between a pair of charlatan spiritualists and partly about a lodging-house servant with psychic powers who falls in love with her sworn enemy, a rich Sheffield mine-owner and politician. The heroine of *Mated in Soul* (1912) is staying with her husband in a Sicilian hotel when she sees her soulmate sitting across the room. Even though he is wearing an 'unbecoming suit of chocolate brown tweed' and a scarlet tie, she immediately leaves her husband, who soon reasserts himself by very nearly running the soulmate down in his motor car. There is a question as to the paternity of the child she eventually bears. De Vauriard also published *The Lily and the Rose* (1914).

Devil and the Deep Sea, The, Rhoda *Broughton, 1910, Macmillan. Broughton said that she had begun her long career controversially, as a kind of Zola, and would end it tamely, as a kind of Charlotte Yonge; but she did not go *that* quietly. In this novel, published when she was 70, two people with something to hide meet in Rapallo. John Greene is recovering from a motoring accident, Susan Field from an emotional accident. Just as they are falling in love, Greene is recognized by, of all people, a chauffeur, who hails him as Bill Street and seems to want to recall their days in the servants' hall. Susan is horrified ('She had pursued him—pursued a footman with her attentions!'). Greene alias Street disappears, only to reappear a few months later, considerably mended, on the French Riviera. He explains that he was turned out of doors by his brutal father and forced to earn his living for a year and a half as a footman, before coming into a fortune. Just as she is on the point of revealing *her* secret, Susan is approached by Mr Cresswell, an elderly friend of Greene's father, whom he insists on referring to as Tom Rutland. Cresswell reveals that Rutland Junior is an 'unmitigated young blackguard' who disguised himself as a footman in order to conduct a liaison with a married woman, and received his injuries leaping from her bedroom window—an achievement hardly matched by Susan's confession that her father is a convicted embezzler. The novel ends with Susan about to choose between the devil Rutland has shown himself to be and the deep sea of a loveless existence. After all, the one thing about Rutland which is authentic is his fortune.

Devil in London, The, George R. *Sims, 1908, Stanley Paul. Millionaire Alan Fairfax decides to spend a part of his fortune exploring the contemporary 'Babylon' of London. He befriends an old French woman, Blanche d'Artigny, and she gives him a magic ring, which she had from an Indian raja, and which enables the possessor the summon the Devil. In Chapter 47 of *Dombey and Son* (1848), Charles Dickens (1812–1870) had asked for a 'good spirit' who would 'take the house-tops off' and 'show a Christian people what dark shapes issue from amidst their homes, to swell the retinue of the Destroying Angel as he moves forth among them!' The Devil himself peforms this function for Alan Fairfax, conducting him to vile haunts where he encounters the Destroying Angel's full retinue: alcoholics, gamblers, white slavers. The climax of the tour is a visit to an East End opium den patronized by well-to-do upper-middle-class women. The Devil also describes a Morphia Club for women, the 'Rosalind', which required members to dress in male attire, and which closed when the president insisted that they should all wear their hair cut short. The only beacons of light in the modern Babylon are Dr Barnardo's Homes. Fairfax falls in love with a beautiful mission sister. Blanche d'Artigny dies, and the Devil is able to reclaim his ring.

Devil's Garden, The, W. B. *Maxwell, 1913, Hutchinson. William Dale, postmaster in a

Hampshire village, discovers that his wife has been seduced by the local MP, Barradine. He manages to kill Barradine without arousing suspicion, and eventually becomes a prosperous farmer and captain of the local fire brigade. He dreams of seducing Norah, a young servant; but before he can do so, an orphanage endowed by Barradine burns down, taking most of the fire brigade with it. The novel was banned by the circulating libraries. Maxwell wrote to the *Times* (9 Sept. 1913) to protest. He admitted that *The Devil's Garden* was 'outspoken', but felt confident that 'no-one, man, woman, or child, will be the worse for reading it'. Two days later, Clement Shorter (1857–1926), editor of the *Sphere* and literary man about town, took up the issue. He was not in favour of state censorship, but did object to one of Dale's fantasies about Norah, in which they both dance naked in a stream. Maxwell replied that the passage had been read out of context; Dale is half-mad, and anyway never yields to temptation.

Devil's Wind, The, 'Patricia *Wentworth', 1912, Andrew Melrose. The novel has the same plot as Maud *Diver's **Captain Desmond, V. C.*, this time set during the Indian Mutiny. Captain Richard Morton marries a pampered beauty, Adela Lauriston, and carries her off to Cawnpore, where she fails to measure up to the rigours of frontier life. They are joined by Adela's straight-arrow friend, Helen Wilmot. When Cawnpore surrenders to the 'mutineers', Richard and Helen escape together, and fall in love. Adela is less fortunate: she is saved from an ignominious death by an equally ignominious marriage to Francis Manners, a half-caste, once a suitor for her hand, now an ally of his uncle, Dhundoo Punth, the local potentate. Adela, cast off by Manners, surfaces again just as Richard and Helen are about to marry. Fortunately she is on her last legs, and the ceremony need not be delayed for too long. The novel is notable for the hatred directed against people of mixed race: fat, jaundiced Dhundoo Punth and greasy Francis Manners, who has inherited his uncle's unspeakable 'oriental' vices.

DICKBERRY, F., *pseud.*: F. BLAZE DE BURY, probably Fernande BLAZE DE BURY. Four novels by this writer are listed in the *British Library Catalogue*, of which the first and much the most successful was *The Storm of London* (1904), whose hero, the Earl of Somerville, wakes up one morning to discover that no one has any clothes any more. It is a satire on the falsity of society—all classes are identical. With everyone naked, it is possible to set up cooperative canteens and so on. In the end he wakes up; he has been ill, but his fiancée has heard his dream and shares his vision of the future. *Phantom Figures* (1907) is another witty novel of high society about an adulterous love affair which is finally ended by the malevolence of the man's wife. It seems likely that this writer is to be identified with the Fernande Blaze de Bury who contributed articles on Prévost and Zola to the *Scottish Review* in 1899 and 1900; even if not, s/he was probably related to the French man of letters Ange-Henri Blaze de Bury (1813–88) and his Scots wife, Marie Pauline Rose Stuart (1813/14–94).

DICKENS, Mary Angela (?1863–1948) was one of the seven daughters (she had one brother) of Charles Dickens, Jr. (1837–1896), and the author of eight novels published between 1891 and 1912. *The Debtor* (1912) is about becoming a Roman Catholic (Dickens was herself a convert). Mary Chichester is a widow who was married to a monster and is bravely running a teashop. When she falls in love she feels she is at last going to enjoy herself. While her fiancé is in America for six months she develops heart disease. Cured by a miracle, she converts; he is incredulous and disapproving; they break it off. *The Wastrel* (1900) is about a rich man who has frittered away his life. He is swindled out of his fortune and divorced for adultery of which he is innocent; it is the making of him. In 'For Her', in *Unveiled and Other Stories* (1906), a widower confesses he has killed his wife to her best friend, who has lured him into making love to her, whereupon she shoots him dead. Although not in her grandfather's league, Dickens is good at such strong scenes, and her novels are well constructed.

DICKSON, Harris published eight novels between 1901 and 1916, all *Weymanesque *historical romances, including *The Black Wolf's Breed* (1901), set in France and Canada during the reign of Louis XIV, *The Siege of Lady Resolute* (1902), set in France and Louisiana during the reign of Louis XIV, and *Gabrielle, Transgressor* (1906), set in eighteeenth-century New Orleans, whose heroine loves an Arab but is eventually persuaded to return to her convent. Other titles include *She*

That Hesitates (1903), *The Duke of Devil-May-Care* (1905), and *The Kavanels* (1905).

DIEHL, Alice M.: Alice Georgina MANGOLD (1844–1912) married (1863) Louis DIEHL (*c.*1837–1910). She was born in Essex, daughter of a German musician and an English mother who also taught music and had rather grander social connections. Her parents had money troubles and were not happily married; on her father's side there was a family tendency towards clinical depression. Though she was brought up as a Unitarian, she converted to Roman Catholicism in 1861. In that year she made her debut, and became a professional pianist of some celebrity, of whom Berlioz allegedly said, 'Si elle ne s'en approchait pas, c'est le piano qui marcherait vers elle'. She also taught music privately and at the North London Collegiate School for Girls. She retired from public performance in 1872. Her husband was an orchestral violinist when she married him; he also wrote music, but had poor health and became a complete invalid in the 1890s. Her first novel was *The Garden of Eden* (1882); she published thirty-seven more, the last in 1912. The heroine of *The Desborough Mystery* (1903) marries a man whom she thinks her dead fiancé's identical twin—or were they swapped? Yes, they were, but worse—there were identical triplets. *A Lovely Little Radical* (1907) is a novel about the transgression of class barriers; the squire's niece marries a tenant's son, who becomes a famous tenor. Her novels recur continually to the triumph of (musical) genius over adversity. In *A Born Genius* (1909), a young musician who has been brought up as a colonel's son throws in his lot with some gypsies, but still becomes a great composer. When not regretting in fiction her abandoned musical career, Diehl wrote fluent, agreeable, neatly triangular romances. *A Man in Love* (1903) concerns the relations between a peer, his land agent, who comes to grief, and the land agent's sister, whom he marries; *The End of a Passion* (1907), those between an impoverished country clergyman who goes blind, his daughter, and the other clergyman who comes to his aid by offering literary collaboration. Diehl's autobiography (1908) is embittered: when she describes a visit to women's colleges in Cambridge she writes 'Not only was I deeply interested in all schemes to render females women instead of dolls, but I was still under the delusion that . . . at least one of my three daughters [would] have laudable ambitions in the direction of some sort of unselfish work.' However her six applications to the Royal Literary Fund between 1904 and her death indicate the causes of the low quality of her work and the gloom of her autobiography. She explained 'I have written four novels in a twelvemonth'; she was the sole support of a household camping in a tumbledown house near Ilchester, her seven children being variously afflicted with epilepsy and madness.

DIVER, Maud: Katherine Helen Maud MARSHALL (1867–1945) married (?1896) Thomas DIVER (1860–1941). Born at Murree in north India, the daughter of an officer in the Indian army, she was brought up in India and Ceylon, although educated in England. She was a lifelong friend of *Kipling's sister Trix Fleming. She left Ceylon for England on her marriage to Diver, who had risen from the ranks to become an officer in the Royal Warwickshire Regiment. Her first publication was the successful romantic novel **Captain Desmond, V. C.* (1907), which contrasts two Englishwomen in India in the 1880s, one selfish, one admirable. *The *Great Amulet* (1908) was also a success. The many non-fiction works which Diver wrote about India, especially *The Englishwoman in India* (1909), make similar points about the dangers of worldliness and frivolity for middle-class women freed from domestic chores in a rootless community. The hero of *Candles in the Wind* (1909) falls in love with an Englishwoman who has been deceived into marrying a half-caste doctor. The situation is only resolved when the doctor dies nobly in an epidemic. *Lilamani* (1911) (published in America as *The Awakening*) is the story of a high-caste Indian girl, trained as a doctor, who marries an Englishman. Their happiness is threatened by his family in England, and by his horror of the thought of a half-caste son. By the end, however, he saves her from drowning herself, and is reconciled to the prospect of a son uniting 'the spirituality of the East, the power and virility of the West'. In a sequel, *Far to Seek* (1920), Diver qualifies her approval of mixed marriage by arranging that the Desmonds (from *Captain Desmond*) should prevent the son marrying his Indian cousin and diluting his English blood any further. If Anglo-Indian novelists divide into those who just use the *exotic setting to lend colour and excitement (like Ethel M. *Dell and B. M. *Croker) and those who seek, at least ostensibly, to instruct the reader in the complexities of the situation (like Flora Annie *Steel and Sara Jeannette *Duncan), Diver falls into the second class. A romantic imperialist, she also wrote a good deal of journalism and several biographies of Anglo-Indians.

Divine Fire, The, May *Sinclair, 1904, Archibald Constable. This blockbuster romance features a poet of indeterminate class and determinate genius: *Gissing's themes are given the Ethel M. *Dell treatment. Savage (a name, not an attribute) Keith Rickman, a semi-cockney bookseller's son, is sent down to Devonshire to catalogue the superb private library built up by Sir Joseph Harden and now owned by his son, Frederick. There he meets Frederick's daughter, Lucia, who recognises him as the young poet recently 'discovered' by her cousin, Horace Jewdwine, a languorous literary editor. Rickman's speciality is neo-classical verse drama; his love of classical literature enables him to bridge, momentarily, the 'social gulf' which separates him from Lucia. However, he is soon separated even further by his implication in a scheme to purchase the library for much less than its value. Estranged from Lucia, from his father, and from a succession of patrons and friends, he struggles to redeem the library from an amiable but grasping moneylender, while not sacrificing his genius to journalism, or to three predatory women (in descending moral order, a dancer, a gold-digger, and a prostitute). The divine fire burns at a low ebb, but is finally rekindled, after more than 600 pages, by reunion with Lucia. The irony is that a book which denounces the commercialization of literature became itself a bestseller. Sinclair travelled to America to promote it, and met President Theodore Roosevelt (1858–1919), an ardent admirer. She does not seem to have entered fully into the spirit of celebrity. Mark Twain (1835–1910), placed next to her at dinner, thanked her afterwards for 'a remarkably interesting silence'. Nor was she unaware of the book's defects; she wrote nothing else remotely like it.

DIXIE, Lady Florence: Florence Caroline DOUGLAS (1855–1905) married (1875) Alexander Beaumont Churchill DIXIE (1851–1924) who succeeded (1872) as 11th Baronet. She was a daughter of the 7th Marquess of Queensberry, and thus aunt of Lord Alfred Douglas (1870–1935). Her first publication was a travel book about Patagonia (1880). As a result of the success of this she was appointed war correspondent for the *Morning Post* during the Transvaal war; while there she became a supporter of Cetewayo and published several books about Africa. She was an advanced Liberal, although opposed to the Irish Land League, and agitated for women's suffrage and dress reform. A keen sportswoman in early life, she became, like many feminists of the 1890s, a fanatical opponent of blood sports and vivisection. She died at her house near Annan in Scotland. *Little Cherie, or, The Trainer's Daughter: A Racing & Social Novel* (1901) is a romance set in racing circles, featuring an attempt to poison the favourite for the Hunt Cup. Lord Cairnsmore saves the life of his racehorse trainer's daughter and falls in love with her; by the end his fiancée Lady Irene has given him his freedom and gone off to establish a co-operative utopia in Zululand. *The Story of Ijain: The Evolution of a Mind* (1903) is fictionalized autobiography, in which she appears as Lady Ijain Dugald, who, like Dixie herself, has a twin brother whose different education she envies. Similarly, Lady Isa Delamere, née Dhugla, the heroine of *Izra: A Child of Solitude* (1906) (which was advertised as a sequel to *Ijain*) is an idealized self-portrait. The beautiful wife of an unsympathetic fox-hunting baronet, she has another life dressed as a boy, in which she travels the world (like Haroun-al-Raschid) relieving the poor and advocating socialism and women's rights. Woman-to-boy transvestism had also figured in Dixie's best-known work, the feminist novel *Gloriana, or, The Revolution of 1900* (1890).

DIXON, Ella [Nora] Hepworth (1857–1932). The seventh child of William Hepworth Dixon (1821–79), editor of the *Athenaeum, she was born in London and educated there and in Heidelberg and Paris. On her father's death his family were left in financial difficulty, and applied to the Royal Literary Fund. The experiences of a penniless, fatherless girl trying to make a living writing are evoked in her best-known work, the autobiographical New Woman novel *The Story of a Modern Woman* (1894). Dixon trained as an artist in Paris, but worked mainly as a journalist, editing the *Englishwoman's Review. One Doubtful Hour* (1904) is a collection of well-turned stories about financial and romantic problems besetting middle-class women. In the first tale a 30-year old spinster caught in the 'degrading, unceasing pursuit of the possible husband' commits suicide. Others are more light-hearted.

DOKE, Joseph J[ohn] (1863–1913) married (1886) Agnes H. BIGGS. The son of a Baptist minister at Chudleigh, Devon, he was prevented by ill health from following his elder brother to a death as a Baptist missionary in the Congo, but became a Baptist preacher, travelling in search of warm climates for the benefit of his lungs. He lived at various times in India, the Holy Land, Chudleigh, Bristol, and, from 1894, in New Zealand. In 1907 he went as minister to Johannesburg, where he made his mark on history as an associate of M. K. Gandhi (1869–1948) in the Passive Resistance movement. He wrote an authorized biography of Gandhi (1909). In July 1913 he set out on a mission to evangelize in the upper Congo, and died as a consequence of exertion, on the return journey. His fiction includes *The Secret City: A Romance of the Karroo* (1913), a *Haggardesque tale of an Egyptian culture surviving among Bushmen.

Dolores, I. *Compton-Burnett, 1911, ?William Blackwood. A tale of self-sacrifice and ecclesiastical disputes. Dolores, daughter of the Revd Cleveland Hutton and his first wife, whose funeral is described in Chapter 1, leaves the village of Millfield, Yorkshire, to attend a teachers' college in Oxford. Her four years at the college culminate in 'days of hope'. But the hope is dashed when her father recalls her to tutor his children by a second wife: hers is to be a life lived in the background of other people's lives. (Compton-Burnett read classics at Royal Holloway College, London, and subsequently returned home to Hove to teach her younger sisters.) Released from this duty by an uncle's benevolence, Dolores returns thankfully to Oxford, only to discover that Sigismund Claverhouse, a playwright she loves and reveres, has resolved to marry her shallow, pretty friend Perdita. Nine months later Perdita dies in childbirth, and Dolores resumes her role as spiritual companion and amanuensis. Sigismund, whose eyesight is failing, begins to reciprocate her love. Then her stepmother dies, and she leaves him in order to take care of her father. She rejects an Oxford don, Soulsby, who has long admired her, when she realizes that her younger sister, Sophia, is in love with him. On a brief visit to Oxford she is reunited with Claverhouse, but a final bout of self-denial carries her home once more, only to discover that her father is about to marry for a third time and no longer has any need for her. She accepts a job at the teachers' college. 'George Eliot' (1819–80) presides over the narrative; but Compton-Burnett's heroine does not have the fire of Maggie Tulliver or Dorothea Brooke, and her portrait of a provincial community, although ecclesiastically spirited, is in other respects meagre.

DONOVAN, Dick, *pseud.*: James Edward MUDDOCK (1843–1934), who also called himself Joyce Emmerson MUDDOCK, later PRESTON MUDDOCK or PRESTON-MUDDOCK (Preston was his mother's maiden name) married (perhaps first, *c.*1868) —— and, ?secondly (*c.*1880), Eleanor RUDD. Born at Southampton, the son of a sea captain, he was educated at home and at school in Cheshire, where he came to like 'being whacked'. When he was 8 his father went to work in the East and his mother went home to her family in Lancashire. Summoned by his father to India, he arrived in Calcutta having 'not yet completed my fourteenth year' early in 1857, on the eve of the Indian Mutiny. The consequent dissolution of the East India Company blighted his hopes of employment, and he returned to England in 1859, travelled in Australia and the Far East, and after various vicissitudes drifted into journalism. He was in London in the late 1860s, a friend of Mayne Reid (1818–83), G. A. Sala (1828–95), Tom Hood, Jr. (1835–74), and Blanchard Jerrold (1826–84), and a member of the Savage Club. He was already producing cheap fiction (such as *A False Heart*, 1873) and claimed to be an early exponent of syndication. He was Swiss correspondent of the *Daily News* (*c.*1881–7) and author of guidebooks to Switzerland, and later lived in Dundee, working on the staff of the *Dundee Weekly News*. It was there, in 1888, that he began to write the 'Dick Donovan' books, mostly *crime stories and thrillers, which proved lucrative. Muddock himself, like A. Conan *Doyle, affected to despise this side of his work, and preferred writing the *historical romances which he published under his own name. As 'Dick Donovan' he was much in debt to Doyle, as is apparent in *The Triumphs of Fabian Field, Criminologist* (1912), in which the gruff, brainy expert takes a new stimulant drug to discover a missing heiress who affects him as no other woman has before. Not all the 'Dick Donovan' books are thrillers: *A Wild Beauty* (1909) is an Irish story about a man who bets he will marry the prettiest girl in Connaught, and does. 'Dick Donovan' and E. Way Elkington, *The Rich Man* (1912) is a rather confused attempt at a non-feminist *marriage problem story, in which a returned colonist falls in love with a woman whose husband does not understand her. His novels as Muddock include many historical fictions, some of which draw on his experiences in the Indian Mutiny, and *In the Red Dawn: A Manchester Tale* (1904), a feeble mystery melodrama in which two children have been stolen by gypsies and swindled out of their inheritance. His fiction is poor stuff; but his autobiography (1907) has interesting passages on the Mutiny and on London literary bohemia in the 1870s. Muddock made several applications to the Royal Literary Fund, giving his name in 1874 and 1875 as James Edward Muddock, in 1899 as James Joyce Edward Emmerson Muddock, and in 1915 as James Edward Preston Muddock. In 1874, 1899, and 1915 his date of birth is 1843, in 1875 it is 1841. The record suggests a near-bankruptcy at the turn of the century, and a period of low water during the First World War. In 1900 the words 'by my present wife I have eight children' imply at least two marriages.

Dop Doctor, The, 'Richard *Dehan', 1910, William Heinemann. Asked to pick a 'book of the year' for 1910, Arnold *Bennett wrote instead about the grounds upon which such a selection might be made. No book would stand much of a chance, he reckoned, unless, like E. M. *Forster's **Howards End*, it had been 'talked about' by the 'right people'. But was this the appropriate criterion? What about *The Dop Doctor*, which had 'sold very well indeed throughout the entire year', but not, as far as he knew, been talked about by the right people? It is an epic *Boer War romance set before, during, and after the siege of Mafeking (which appears as 'Gueldersdorp'). Owen Saxham, a brilliant young doctor, is falsely accused of performing an abortion and has to give up his Harley Street practice. He hides himself away in Gueldersdorp, where he earns a reputation as a drunkard. If this were a naturalist novel, he would be well on his way to perdition. However, the town is besieged by the Boers, and the challenge revitalizes Saxham, who becomes right-hand man to the infinitely sagacious commanding officer (modelled none too loosely on Robert Baden-Powell, 1857–1941). Inspired by his new responsibilities, he begins the bitter struggle against alcoholism. After many complications, he wins the love of Lynette Mildare, an inmate of Gueldersdorp convent who was brutally raped when scarcely more than a child by a renegade Englishman. Her faith in Saxham at once secures and softens his redemption. The most important of the many sub-plots concerns the parallel regeneration of the lower classes, in the shape of a cockney couple who redeem their urban fecklessness when under fire. The slum novel is thus the second genre to be inverted, its anti-heroes converted into heroes. Unflinchingly prurient, not to mention racist and sexist, *The Dop Doctor* is one of the most exuberant of Edwardian adventure stories. The regenerations are as crucial to its effect as the rapes and bombardments.

DORRINGTON, Albert (1868–after 1919) married——. Born in Birmingham, he stated to the Royal Literary Fund that he had 'known no other profession than that of literature'. In the ten years before 1914 he was earning £400 a year; the war reduced this to £50 a year, with the consequence that he, his wife and three daughters were evicted from their house in Bournemouth. He also applied to the Society of Authors and the Professional Classes War Relief Council for support. His first book was *And the Day Came* (1908), in which an Australian girl is seduced by a debauched and eccentric English aristocrat; her lost baby reappears as a Roman Catholic priest. 'I've been hunting for a little god that escaped from some pitchblende, Tony!' begins *The Radium Terrors* (1912), which must be an early example of a novel hinging on the theft of radioactive material by a sinister foreign gang, in this instance Japanese. It was first published in the *Scrap Book* (Jan.–Aug. 1911). Dorrington wrote several other unremarkable novels, not all thrillers.

DOUDNEY, Sarah (1843–1926) was born in Portsmouth and educated in Southsea. She published two poems in *All the Year Round* while Dickens was editor, and stories in the *Churchman's Shilling Magazine* in 1870. She subsequently wrote a great many school stories and morally uplifting romances for girls and young women, and a quantity of religious verse, including a once popular hymn, 'Sleep On Beloved'. Her work is pure and dull; much of it was published by the Religious Tract Society and the Sunday School Union. *Silent Strings* (1900) describes the life of the five children of a doctor: the clergyman sacrifices the woman he loves because his brother wants her; the selfless eldest daughter looks after their selfish old father; the pretty girl marries a rich squire and the emigrant inherits a fortune. The plot of *One of the Few* (1904) is less predictable; a successful woman writer who has not married is described with some sympathy. At the end she marries the man whom she might have wasted her life propping up. *Shadow and Shine* (1906) describes three girls whose love affairs are nearly disastrous: one marries the right man after her fiancé is murdered, the second is happy when her lover comes back to her, and the third decides to be a useful spinster. Doudney's conventional girls' fiction is comparable to that of Rosa Nouchette *Carey or Emma Marshall (1830–99).

DOUGALL, L[ily] (1858–1923). Born in Montreal and brought up in Canada and the US, she was one of the six daughters of John Dougall (1808–86) a Quebec businessman who founded and edited the *Montreal Witness*, a fanatically Calvinist, anti-Catholic, anti-French, anti-Irish, evangelical and Sabbatarian temperance newspaper, and later founded similar daily and weekly papers in New York City. He was succeeded as editor by the eldest of his three sons. Lily Dougall moved, aged 20, to Edinburgh, where she lived with an aunt and attended lectures at the University. In this way she taught herself Greek. Her novel *Beggars All* (1891) was successful enough to encourage her to write another ten novels in the next ten years. The mainspring of her life was religious; she published several theological works, including the anonymous and controversial *Pro Christo et Ecclesia* (1900) and with her friend and companion Mary Sophia Earp she organized religious conferences at the house at Cumnor, near Oxford, where she lived from 1911. She also published a volume of verse (1919) in collaboration with the novelist Gilbert Sheldon. *The Earthly Purgatory* (1904) is set in Georgia, after the American Civil War, where a dispossessed Southern gentleman whose wife has left him lodges with two New England spinsters. It is a mystery about revenge and retribution. *The Spanish Dowry: A Romance* (1906) is told by a querulous boy cripple, whose uncle and guardian is just another such gentleman, with a mysterious past and a missing wife, whose problems are sorted out by the end.

DOUGLAS, George, *pseud.*: George Douglas BROWN (1869–1902) was born at Ochiltree, Ayrshire, the son of a farmer who refused to marry his mother, Sarah Gemmell. So Gemmell, a farm worker, struggled to bring her son up on her own. She desperately wanted him to escape the fate of most of his schoolfellows: a working life spent down Ayrshire's coalmines. He attended his local village school and the Coylton Parish School, where the schoolmaster spotted Brown's potential; he managed to obtain a place for Brown at Ayr Academy. Brown studied there from 1881 to 1887. At the Academy, William Maybin (to whom Brown would later dedicate *The *House with the Green Shutters*) encouraged his evident talents in English and the classics. In 1887 he matriculated at Glasgow University (he won a bursary). His brilliance was quickly spotted by the professor of Greek, Gilbert Murray (1866–1957), whose assistant he became. He gained a first-class degree and was sent to Balliol College, Oxford, in 1891. Brown did not excel at Oxford, partly because of his mother's grave illness (she died in 1893). But he had at least decided where his future lay, and settled in London to earn his living by teaching and working as a publisher's reader. He did a good deal of reviewing and wrote (as 'Kennedy King') a book for boys, *Love and a Sword* (1899). In the closing years of the 1890s he had spent an increasing amount of time on a piece set in the fictitious Scottish village of Barbie. This later developed into *The House with the Green Shutters* (1901), published under the name 'George Douglas', which was an instant success and had run to five editions by June 1902. (The royalties he earned gave him the only respite from financial hardship that he ever knew.) The novel's central theme is the tragedy in family life, but Brown's chief aim was to draw a realistic picture of life in rural Scotland, to obliterate the 'sentimental slop' of *Barrie and *Crockett and Watson (i.e. 'Ian *MacLaren'), and others of the Kailyard school. Brown died unexpectedly of pneumonia in Muswell Hill. He is not to be confused with Lady Gertrude Georgiana Douglas (1842–93), sister of Lady Florence *Dixie, who also published novels as 'George Douglas'.

DOUGLAS, Norman: George Norman DOUGLASS (1868–1952), who changed his surname (*c.*1908) to DOUGLAS, married (1898) Elizabeth Louisa Theobaldina FITZGIBBON (*c.*1876–1916) (divorced 1904). He was born at Thüringen and spent his childhood there and in Scotland. His mother was half-German, half-Scots; his father, the son of a Scots laird, died when his son was 6. He followed his elder brother to Uppingham (1881–2), which he hated, and then to Karlsruhe Gymnasium (1883–9). After four years in London he became an attaché at the British Embassy in St Petersburg (1894–6), but fled Russia for the Bay of Naples, allegedly in fear of the male relatives of his pregnant mistress. He married the daughter of his mother's sister; his wife's nephew, the novelist Constantine FitzGibbon (1919–1983), wrote a biography of Douglas (1953). Douglas divorced her for adultery and moved to Capri, but after a financial crisis in about 1907 had to sell the house. In London he became a contributor and after 1912 assistant editor of the *English Review*, during which period he made friends with *Conrad, Edward Garnett (1868–1937), and D. H. *Lawrence. However, after being arrested in November 1916 on a charge of molesting a 16-year-old boy Douglas left England. Thereafter, except for a brief period in England during the Second World War, he lived in Italy and France. In 1946 he went back to Capri, where he died. With his wife he wrote, as 'Normyx', *Unprofessional Tales* (1901), of which he claimed that eight copies only were sold. The novella 'Nerinda', which was published separately in the same year and can confidently be ascribed to Douglas himself, is the diary of an English tourist in southern Italy who becomes obsessed with one of the bodies at Pompeii. He ends by murdering the caretaker in order to smash the cast of the girl and drown himself with her bones. This volume was followed by three idiosyncratic and erudite topographical works: *Siren Land* (1911), *Fountains in the Sand* (1912), and *Old Calabria* (1915), which gave him a reputation. Douglas's first novel *South Wind* (1917), set on a thinly disguised Capri, had a great success. He did not publish much more fiction, and his later works of travel, history, and autobiography are of uneven quality, since they were sometimes written in response to what Douglas called in *Looking Back* (1934) 'one or other of the financial cataclysms which have enlivened my earthly sojourn'. There is a biography by Mark Holloway (1976).

DOUGLAS, O. *pseud.*: Anna BUCHAN (1878–1948) was born at Pathhead, Fife, the only daughter of a minister in the Free Church of Scotland; she had four brothers, of whom the eldest was John *Buchan. She went to school in Glasgow, at Hutcheson's Grammar School and Queen Margaret College. In her autobiography (1945) she describes a cheerful, bookish, Calvinist childhood. In 1907 she went to India to visit one of her brothers who was working there and on her return published *Olivia in India: The Adventures of a Chota Miss Sahib* (1913), an epistolary novel which she later described as 'a book in which practically all the incidents were true and in which the characters could all recognise themselves and each other'. Olivia, in love with her correspondent, does not regret returning home. Before the book was published the brother in India was dead; another was killed in the First World War. Buchan spent most of her life keeping house for a third brother, Walter, the town clerk of Peebles, with occasional visits to John's more glamorous household. She describes her mother struggling with John's thrillers, but liking to read the works of 'O. Douglas', which, in Buchan's own words 'were pure and almost as sweet as home-made toffee'. Her autobiography is deprecating about their value, and she comments wryly of her writing: 'nobody minded interrupting me. I had not even a room of my own.' Some of her novels (such as *The Setons*, 1917) evoke the atmosphere of the plain-living and high-thinking household she was brought up in.

DOUGLAS, Theo, *pseud.*: Henrietta Dorothy HUSKISSON married Isaac Edward EVERETT (d. 1904). The daughter of an officer in the Royal Marines, she married a Stafford solicitor and after his death retired to Worcestershire. The first man to be run over by a train, William Huskisson, MP (1770–1830), was her great-uncle. She was the author of twenty volumes of fiction, mostly ghost stories, published between 1896 and 1920. *A White Witch* (1908) is set in seventeenth-century Oxford; predatory women feature in its plot, as generally in Everett's fiction. *The Grey Countess* (1913) is a beautiful Russian princess who pretends to be her own sister, but is found out after murdering to keep her secret. *Malevola* (1914) is a vampire story with an anti-feminist streak: Rose does not want to marry and goes to stay with an interesting foreign lady, who grows plump and rosy as Rose gets paler and thinner; fortunately she is rescued in time and marries after all. The association of feminism, lesbianism, and death is made quite clear. Reviewers tended to praise the 'atmosphere' of her *historical romances, but, despite the preponderance of female narrators, identified the author as a man. *White Webs* (1912) is set on the Sussex coast in 1746, in the aftermath of Bonnie Prince Charlie's defeat: the white webs are those woven by the loom, and by Jacobite conspiracy.

DOWIE, Ménie Muriel (1866–1945) married, first (1891), Henry NORMAN (1858–1939), Kt. (1906), created. (1915) 1st Baronet (divorced 1903), and, secondly (1903), Edward Arthur FITZGERALD (1871–1931). Dowie was born in Liverpool; her father was a merchant and her mother was a daughter of Robert Chambers (1802–1871), the Edinburgh publisher and author of *Vestiges of the Natural History of Creation*, so she was a cousin of Violet *Tweedale; another cousin married Barry *Pain; her sister married Allan *Monkhouse. Dowie was educated in Liverpool, Stuttgart, and France. She contributed a series of travel articles to the *Fortnightly Review* which were published as *A Girl in the Karpathians* (1891), and stories to the *Yellow Book*, collected as *Some Whims of Fate* (1896). During her first marriage she also wrote for the *Daily Chronicle*, of which Norman was assistant editor from 1895. Her novel *Gallia* (1895) was a scandalously advanced account of sexual selection, denounced along with *Jude the Obscure* in a famous article, 'The Anti-Marriage League', by Margaret Oliphant (1828–97) in *Blackwoods* (Jan. 1896); it was followed by *The Crook of the Bough* (1898), set in the Balkans, which she thought her best book. **Love and His Mask* (1901) is a *Boer War novel. Dowie's authorial tone is that of a woman of the world, *au fait* with aristocratic habits—her heroine is living on 'a tiny jointure of £500 a year'. Her scenes of social comedy are amusing.

The much more conventional *Things About Our Neighbourhood* (1903), originally published as a serial in *Country Life*, is a fictionalized gardening book/sketches of middle-class rural life. Her second marriage to a rich army officer and mountaineer put an end to Dowie's career as a novelist, and, if the account in Berta *Ruck's autobiography is to be trusted, she led an extravagantly luxurious life as a society hostess, travelling widely and dressing exquisitely. She died in Tucson, Arizona.

DOWNEY, Edmund (1856–1937) was born in Waterford and educated at the Catholic University School and St John's College Waterford. On first coming to London he got work, through his cousin, the novelist Richard Dowling (1846–98), for the *Hornet, Funny Folks, the Weekly Dispatch*, and other obscure periodicals. During 1879–84 he worked for the publishers Tinsley Bros. in London; then started his own firm, Ward & Downey, later Downey & Co. His autobiography (1905) gives some account of the life of a hack writer and publisher in the 1880s. His first volume of fiction was made up of sea stories published separately elsewhere, *Anchor Watch Yarns* (1884). *Clashmore* (1903) is set in Waterford and its neighbourhood. Lord Clashmore's nephew and the son whom he does not acknowledge discover he has been kidnapped to conceal the existence of buried treasure; at the end all is revealed and they marry the two heroines. *Dorothy Tuke* (1905) is a captain's orphan daughter; of the two officers in charge of her ship, one is a villain and she marries the other. As 'F. M. Allen' Downey published twelve volumes of fiction from 1887, of which the last, *London's Peril* (1900) is an *invasion scare story, remarkable only in that it is the French (rather than the Germans) who are digging a tunnel from Cap Gris Nez to Hampstead. They are foiled in time. Downey also wrote a study (1906) of the novelist Charles Lever (1806–72). The list of the publications of Downey & Co. includes several reprints of early nineteenth-century Irish fiction, for example works by William Carleton (1794–1869), Gerald Griffin (1803–40), J. Sheridan Le Fanu (1814–73), and Samuel Lover (1797–1868).

Downward: *A 'Slice of Life'*, Maud Churton *Braby, 1910, T.Werner Laurie. Dolly Fitzgerald, an actress, is seduced and abandoned by the weak but charming Theodore Walter. Four years later, living in seclusion in a Kentish village, Dolly tells her story to the local doctor, Arthur Jocelyn, who promptly tries to take advantage of her. Rebuffed, he betrays Dolly to her most eligible suitor, Godwin Leigh, an earnest social reformer. Leigh, like Angel Clare in Thomas Hardy's *Tess of the D'Urbervilles* (1891), is appalled to discover that she is no longer 'pure'. This time, however, the 'pure woman' triumphs, becoming engaged to her faithful lawyer, Dacre Hamilton. The novel is notable for a preface by Edward Garnett (1868–1937) which staunchly defends the New Woman novel which had flourished since the early 1890s. It would be a mistake, Garnett argued, 'for masculine critics to try and freeze the "sex novel" out of existence, and say, in icy tones, to women writers, "Why is your art so immature, so biased, so over-emotional?" The sex novel, even when it is not good art, is a document, a piece of polemics, a special diagnosis of a state of social unrest of a vast class of women who are placed in a radically false situation to men by the defects of our social organization.'

DOYLE, A. Conan: Arthur Ignatius Conan DOYLE, later CONAN DOYLE (1859–1930), Kt. (1902), married, first (1885), Louise HAWKINS (d. 1906) and, secondly (1907), Jean LECKIE. Doyle came of an Irish Roman Catholic family; his father was an unsuccessful and alcoholic clerk in the Board of Works and his uncle, Richard Doyle (1824–83), was an artist who worked on *Punch*. He was educated at Stonyhurst, at a Jesuit school at Feldkirch, Austria, and at Edinburgh University (1876–81), where he read medicine. He worked as a ship's doctor, then practised in Plymouth and Southsea until 1890. In 1885 he was awarded a doctorate by Edinburgh University for a dissertation on syphilis. He began to publish stories in 1879. His first book, *A Study in Scarlet* (1887), introduced Sherlock Holmes to the world; but it was not until the short stories featuring the great detective were published in the **Strand Magazine* (1891–2) that he became famous. Doyle's own view was that his best work lay in his historical novels, such as *Micah Clarke* (1889), set during Monmouth's rebellion, *The White Company* (1891) and the linked *Sir Nigel* (1906), romances of chivalry in the tradition of Walter Scott (1771–1832) and Charles Kingsley (1819–75), set in fourteenth-century England. A series of stories about a pompous Napoleonic soldier began with *The Exploits of Brigadier Gerard* (1896) and continued with *The *Adventures of Brigadier Gerard* (1903). *Rodney Stone* (1896) is set among Regency pugilists and *Uncle Bernac* (1897) during the French Revolution. Another recurring character was Professor Challenger, who appeared in the science fiction novels *The *Lost World* (1912), *The Poison Belt* (1913), and *The Land of Mist* (1926) and also in the short stories 'When the World Screamed' (1928) and 'The Disintegration Machine' (1929). The novel *Beyond the City* (1892) discusses the new feminism and *The Stark–Munro Letters* (1895) draws on Doyle's medical experience. Doyle was for many years one of the best-paid short-story-writers in England. As a public man he defended several unfashionable causes out of high principle. Roger Casement (1864–1916), became a friend during the campaign against Belgian atrocities in the Congo, converted Doyle to Home Rule, although he had stood as a Liberal Unionist candidate in the 1900 election. Doyle was one of the few people who continued to help financially with Casement's defence after the revelation of his homosexuality. He behaved with a similar indifference to public opinion in campaigning against the false imprisonment of George Edalji and Oscar Slater, and in espousing the cause of spiritualism and publicly avowing his belief in fairies. He was president of the Divorce Law Reform Society and was knighted for medical services during the *Boer War. Among the vast quantity of secondary literature on Doyle and Holmes the biographies of the former by Julian Symons (1979) and Owen Dudley Edwards (1983) are useful. Doyle's sister Bryan wrote novels as 'H. Ripley *Cromarsh'; his sister Constance married E. W. *Hornung.

DRAKE, Maurice (1875–1923) married (1897) Alice WILSON. His father was a glass-painter in Exeter, and he went to the grammar school in Teignmouth. He published books on stained glass and six novels between 1906 and 1924. *The Salving of a Derelict* (1906) was selected from over 600 manuscripts as winner of a *Daily Mail* £100 prize. The hero is the derelict, the son of a fraudulent financier, who works as a merchant seaman and falls in love with the daughter of one of his father's victims, who reforms him. *WO2* (1913), his most successful book, is also about the disreputable young captain of a boat; this one discovers a German plot. The mixture of *crime novel afloat and *invasion scare story is reminiscent of Erskine *Childers's *The *Riddle of the Sands* (1903). The books are adventure/romance for boys and young men; they are given some individuality by the lively first-person narratives and settings in bleak northern seas. Drake lived in Exeter Cathedral Close.

Dream and the Business, The, 'John Oliver *Hobbes', 1906, T. Fisher Unwin. This is a tragi-comic tale about the romantic involvements of four youngish people: Jim Firmalden, the son of a Congregational minister, who follows in his father's footsteps; his sister Sophy; Lessard, a beautiful, brilliant composer and singer who is in love with Sophy; and Tessa, Lady Marlesford, who flirts with Firmalden and is obsessed by Lessard. Complications ensue: Lessard offends Mr Firmalden, and loses Sophy; Tessa remains faithful to her husband, and dies in childbirth. But the novel's motive force is the clash between two faiths: Sophy's passionate Nonconformism and Tessa's passionate Catholicism. *The Dream and the Business* was Mrs Craigie's last novel, and at times she seems more interested in the conversations being conducted than in those conducting them: this is particularly true of a long discussion about Ireland between William Ewart Gladstone (1809–98) and a Nonconformist clergyman. The cover design, by Aubrey Beardsley (1872–98), showing a grim woman in a swirling red dress, and apparently some pain, gives it an 1890s feel.

DRUMMOND, Hamilton (1857–1935) was Irish but lived in Lincoln. He published a volume of verse in 1893; his first novel, *Gobelin Grange* (1896), was followed by thirty-four volumes of fiction, of the adventure-story class, to 1934. In *On Behalf of the Firm* (1903) a Spanish-speaking clerk is sent to Haiti to deal with a bad debt, his predecessor having being shot. He frustrates the firm's sinister Jewish rival and comes home covered in glory, having cleared the name of his fiancée's father. The book is racist, full of comments like 'where black rules white, the white has scant chance of justice'; but its attempt to endow commerce with the glamour of imperialism is comparatively unusual in fiction. *Room Five* (1905) is a problem novel: two men are found dead in a hotel room; one has committed murder and suicide, but which? We are given the background but we have to decide for ourselves. *The Chain of Seven Lives* (1906), which is linked to *Room Five* at the end, is a novel beginning in Italy in the time of Albertus Magnus (1206–80), based on the idea of a series of lives linked together through history.

DRURY, Major W. P.: William Price DRURY (1861–1949) married (1900) Marguerite PENDER CUDLIP (d. 1950s). Born in Devonport of a naval family, he was educated at Brentwood School, Plymouth College, and Chatham, and went into the Royal Marines. He also studied painting at the Plymouth College of Art. He worked in the Naval Intelligence department from 1900, and the rise in salary enabled him, after a twelve-year engagement, to marry an actress, the daughter of the novelist Mrs Pender *Cudlip. Shortly afterwards he was invalided out of the service, and much of their later life was spent in Cornwall, though they also travelled in India and South America. In the years before the First World War he, like Rudyard *Kipling, William *Le Queux, and others, was an enthusiastic supporter of Lord Roberts (1832–1914), who argued that Britain was unprepared for war. Drury travelled the country lecturing for the cause, and became chief organizer of the National Service League. He used to write standing up, and was also the author of several successful plays; his many novels include ship-board comedies, horror, adventure, and boys' books. *The Tadpole of an Archangel* (1904) is a collection of stories about the services and the colonies which uncomfortably resemble *Kipling's work, even down to the facetious, mock-biblical tone of the narrative voice, full of archaisms and inversions. *Long Bow and Broad Arrow* (1911) is even preceded by a poem about the Union Flag, including the verse:

> For now have we bred lesser men to work our undoing—
> Pale, lank-haired effetes, who shamble like apes to their wooing,
> Who toy at the tee, with croquet and badminton trifle,
> *While the grim Alien mendeth his aim with the* rifle.

Drury's entertaining autobiography (1926) speaks in passing of nervous breakdowns and periods of low water. Between 1929 and 31 he was mayor of Saltash in Cornwall, and he died in that town.

Dubliners, James *Joyce, 1914, Grant Richards. A collection of fifteen short stories which seemed to contemporary readers to strike new heights (or depths) of literary realism. The stories, all set in Dublin, are very roughly arranged according to four phases or aspects of human development: childhood; adolescence; mature private life; and mature public life. 'The Sisters' describes the response of a young boy, the unnamed narrator, to the death of Father James Flynn, a learned and eccentric priest who had been his mentor and had been nursed, during his final days, by his two sisters. In 'An Encounter', the narrator and his friend Mahony, playing truant, meet a tramp and sexual pervert as learned and eccentric in his way as Father Flynn. In 'Araby', it is the young boy who fantasizes, about a bazaar, which he finally reaches just as it is on the point of closing. The theme of unrealized or half-realized fantasy carries over into the first of the stories of adolescence, 'Eveline', about a young woman who cannot quite find the courage to elope with a glamorous sailor. In 'After the Race', Jimmy, the 26-year-old son of a 'merchant prince', desperate for a patina of cosmopolitanism, fritters his allowance away on motor racing and gambling. 'The Two Gallants', Corley and Lenehan, are approaching the point where they will have nothing more to aspire to: their performance as men of the world, impressive in its own way, enables them to hide from themselves, for the time being, the depth of their own degradation. In 'The Boarding House', a lodger is trapped into marrying the landlady's daughter, while in 'A Little Cloud' a clerk meets an old friend who has become a successful journalist in London, and is forced to acknowledge that his marriage is a prison. 'Counterparts' concerns the 'indignities' of professional and domestic life, relieved only by an act of insubordination reenacted at epic length in the pub. The protagonists of 'Clay' and 'A Painful Case' are both spinsters: one an overseer at the Dublin by Lamplight laundry and professional maiden aunt, the other a cashier and student of Friedrich Nietzsche (1844–1900) whose self-dissociation—'he lived at a little distance from his body, regarding his own acts with doubtful side-glances'—is emblematic of the 'moral paralysis' Joyce discerned in Dublin life. 'Ivy Day in the Committee Room' anatomises the boozy, sentimental hypocrisy of Irish nationalist politics, while the events described in 'A Mother' take place during a patriotic concert: Mrs Kearney upsets the committee by demanding that her daughter be paid in full. In 'Grace', a habitual drunkard is persuaded to go on a retreat with three of his friends. Joyce described the style in which these fourteen stories were written as a 'scrupulous meanness'. But in 'The Dead', the last and longest story in the collection, it finally modulates into lyricism, as Gabriel Conroy, a prosperous, genial, liberal-minded Dubliner, is both mortified and reinvigorated by the revelation that his wife, Gretta, had once been passionately in love with a young man, Michael Furey, who died for her.

Duchess of Wrexe, The, *Her Decline and Death: A Romantic Commentary*, Hugh *Walpole, 1914, Martin Secker. A Forsyte-ish saga concerning the Beaminster clan, whose head, the Duchess, a decrepit but still fearsome autocrat, inhabits a gloomily expressive mansion in Portland Place. The Duchess's granddaughter, Rachel, marries her favourite, Roddy Seldon, a sturdy but dim country squire. 'He hated this mixing of the classes, this perpetual urging of the working man to think.' Finding him too conventional, she falls for Francis Breton, a one-armed and somewhat half-hearted explorer. Breton is also loved by Lizzie Rand, the family secretary, an ultra-efficient 'typewriter g[illegible]'. Roddy Seldon is thrown from his horse, and partly paralysed. Realising that he is a better man than Breton, Rachel falls in love with him, and their marriage is confirmed by the birth of a child. The novel aspires to *Galsworthian or *Forsterian social commentary, but Walpole's talent was for romance rather than realism: two of the more plausible characters—the weak prodigal, Francis Breton, and Arkwright, a brooding frontiersman—are at their happiest without a roof over their heads.

DUDENEY, Mrs Henry: Alice WHIFFIN (1866–1945) married (1884) Henry Ernest DUDENEY (d. 1930). She was educated at Hurstpierpoint, and adopted Sussex as her home in 1911. During the First World War she moved to Lewes. According to an interview in the *Sussex County Magazine* (Dec. 1926) 'the loss of our first little baby compelled me to find some occupation in which to lose myself. I became visiting secretary to Sir Wemyss Reid [1842–1905], the head of Cassells, and was thrown at once into the literary atmosphere.' She began by writing stories, which were always her forte. She published fifty volumes of fiction between 1898 and 1937, which mostly deal with sex problems and domestic life among the working and lower middle classes. Her view of the predicament of women and the relationship of the sexes is extremely pessimistic;

and she paints a dark picture of the life of rural agricultural labourers. Reviewers sometimes compared her to Thomas Hardy (1840–1928). Chrismas, the heroine of *What a Woman Wants* (1914), is one of fourteen children of a poor farmer; the women of her family lead a life of drudgery and privation at the hands of the men, but none of them is able to establish an independent life. In her short stories, for example in *A Country Bunch* (1905) and *A Sense of Scarlet* (1909), she shows women bitter and deformed by lack of opportunity, but also humorous and resourceful; at her best she is an English counterpart of Mary E.Wilkins Freeman (1852–1930). Dudeney's husband devised puzzles professionally. Her diaries (1910–45) are in the East Sussex Record Office.

DUNCAN, Sara Jeannette: Sarah Janet DUNCAN (1861–1922) married (1890) Everard Charles COTES (1862–1944). She was born at Brantford, Ontario, the daughter of a merchant, was educated at Toronto Normal School, and trained as a teacher. However, she soon moved to journalism, and by the age of 24 was writing editorials for the Washington *Post*. In 1886 she became the first woman reporter hired by the *Toronto Globe*. She turned her experiences on a world tour in 1888–90 into a very successful travel book *A Social Departure* (1890), which had sold 16,000 in the US alone by 1903 and made her world-famous. She married an English museum official in India; he later resigned and became editor of the *Indian Daily News*, and later still a freelance journalist; they lived in India, in Simla and elsewhere, for twenty-five years before returning to England, where she died. *Forster visited her in Simla, and when in *A Passage to India* (1924) he has an Anglo-Indian lady talk Hindustani in the imperative because she only knows how to address servants he repeats a point made by Cotes in *The Burnt Offering* (1909). Her early work, including some of her journalism and travel writing, makes use of the international theme. The influence of W. D. Howells (1837–1920), who was a friend, and Henry *James, whose prose style she imitated, can be felt in such novels as *An American Girl in London* (1891) and *Cousin Cinderella* (1908) (about a Canadian girl in London). However, the recent revival of interest in Cotes's work is a result of her focus on the Edwardian empire. Canadian critics have been particularly interested in *The Imperialist* (1904), and students of British India in her several novels about Anglo-Indian problems. The last of these, *The Burnt Offering*, describes the effect of the visit of a British Labour MP and his daughter to India at a time of political unrest (probably inspired by the 1907 visit of Keir Hardie). Cotes suggests that their well-meant interventions actually inflame the situation; and her hero is a gentlemanly official who loves the MP's daughter and dies preventing an assassination. The novel is not optimistic about democratic self-government for India, but nor is it simply pro-imperialist. *On the Other Side of the Latch* (1901) describes a period spent living in the garden of her Simla house in the attempt to cure herself of tuberculosis.

DUNSANY, Lord: Edward John Moreton Drax PLUNKETT (1878–1957), succeeded (1899) as 18th Baron DUNSANY, married (1904) Beatrice CHILD VILLIERS (1880–1970). Dunsany was born in London into the Anglo-Irish ascendancy. Sir Horace Plunkett (1854–1932), Unionist politician and pioneer of agricultural cooperatives, was his uncle, and briefly his guardian. He served with the Coldstream Guards in the *Boer War and conceived a lifelong interest in Africa. After his return and his marriage he lived between London and Dunsany Castle, Co.Meath, until after the Second World War, when he went to live in Kent. In Ireland he was a friend and supporter of W. B. Yeats (1865–1939) and other figures in the Irish literary renaissance. His first book, *The Gods of Pegāna* (1905), is a series of myths about cruel, wanton, imaginary gods, written in a mannered style, full of biblical rhythms and poetic diction, whose conception was influenced by the orientalizing play *The Darling of the Gods* (1902), by David Belasco (1859–1931) and John Luther Long (1861–1927). The book was illustrated in black and white by S. H. Sime (1867–1941), with whom he continued to collaborate closely for many years. Dunsany paid for the publication: he never had to again. *Time and the Gods* (1906) is a sequel, containing more myths of Pegana, and includes 'The Cave of Kai' a parable about art and memory. All King Khanazar's wise men cannot restore to him the happy past; only the harper can revive the memory and make Khanazar's warlike deeds immortal. Many later writers were to imitate this model of a short story set in a *fantasy world. *The Sword of Welleran*

(1908) includes for the first time stories in which human beings appear. Other collections are *A Dreamer's Tales* (1910), and *The *Book of Wonder* (1912). *The Glittering Gate*, produced at the Abbey Theatre, Dublin, in April 1909, was the first of a series of successful plays. For a decade he was immensely popular as a playwright on both sides of the Atlantic. Dunsany wrote at great speed, without revising—he once observed: 'I try sometimes to explain genius to people who mistrust or hate it by telling them it is doing anything as a fish swims or a swallow flies, perfectly, simply, and with absolute ease. Genius is in fact an infinite capacity for not taking pains.' After the First World War he gradually abandoned his early, ornate style, and wrote some full-length novels, including *The Curse of the Wise Woman* (1933), his most autobiographical work, in which an old man looks back on a childhood in Co. Meath, across the barrier of the Troubles and the religious and cultural divide. *The Travel Tales of Mr Joseph Jorkens* (1931) was the first of five volumes of tall stories recounted by a club bore. Both *My Talks with Dean Spanley* (1936) and *The Strange Journeys of Colonel Polders* (1950) are novels about characters who remember living as dogs. Dunsany wrote three volumes of autobiography (1938, 1944, 1945) and there is a biography by Mark Amory (1972). He died in Dublin.

E

Early History of Jacob Stahl, The, J. D. *Beresford, 1911, Sidgwick & Jackson. A *Bildungsroman* in five books, each named after a shaping influence on Jacob's life. As a result of a sequence of accidents, baby Jacob, son of a German-Jewish commercial traveller and his simple Irish wife, is propelled out of his pram, crashes into the gutter, and injures his spine: for the first fifteen years of his life he is not allowed to put his feet to the ground. Jacob's brother, Eric, is solid and serious; he, by contrast, represents 'an untidy, heterogeneous collection of qualities with nothing to bind them together'. When his mother dies he is adopted by his aunt, Hester Stahl, and lives with her in a cottage at Ashby Sutton. Gradually he learns to overcome his handicap, and by the age of 17 he can walk with the aid of a stick. His father dies, leaving much more money to Jacob than to Eric, which widens the existing temperamental division between the brothers. He becomes articled to an architect, and falls in love, rather like the hero of H. G. *Wells's **Tono-Bungay* (1909), with the daughter of the local landowner, Madeline Felmersdale, and follows her to London. He finds work, and is introduced to women and drink by a (momentarily) idolized colleague, Tony Farrell. Under the influence of another colleague, the talented Owen Bradley, he begins to read more widely in science and philosophy. He also moves in Bohemian circles, falling in love with the widowed, and frighteningly intellectual, Lola Wilmot, a freelance illustrator. They marry. Lola, however, turns out to be a woman with a past, a divorcee rather than a widow, and the marriage deteriorates. Reunion with Madeline, now a wife and mother, does not raise his spirits. The last chapter finds him in Cornwall, deserted by his wife, practically bankrupt, contemplating the Atlantic, and resolved to become a writer. His subsequent experiences form the subject of *A Candidate for Truth* (1912) and *The Invisible Event* (1915). *The Early History* is in many respects conventional, but notable both for the relatively detailed account it provides of the hero's employment as an architect and for its unsentimental attitude to his physical disability. 'His lameness was not drawback to him, it did not hamper him in the life he led, his pallor was due not to ill-health but to the texture of his skin, that look of suffering was the result of his childhood's experience, it did not express his thought, his real feeling; it was no indication of mental or physical trouble.'

ECCLES, Charlotte [O'Conor] (1863–1911) was born in Roscommon, Ireland, and educated at Upton Hall, near Birkenhead, and at convents in Paris and Germany. She published in Irish periodicals before moving to London and working as a journalist. She published two volumes of fiction in the period: the first, *Aliens of the West* (1904), is a collection of stories about Irish provincial life; the second, *The Matrimonial Lottery* (1906), is a comic novel about a failing literary weekly, the *Comet*, which is put back on its feet when the editress marries money and a title. Eccles published an earlier comic novel, about a boarding-house, *The Rejuvenation of Miss Semaphore* (1897), as 'Hal Godfrey'. Some of her work, including a translation from Polish, appeared only in America. She was incapacitated after a stroke in 1908, and she and the devoted sister who nursed her were several times relieved by grants from the Royal Literary Fund.

ECCOTT, W. J. published nine novels, all *Weymanesque *historical romances, with Blackwood between 1904 and 1918. *His Indolence of Arras* (1905) and *A Demoiselle of France* (1910) are both set in the court of Louis XIV. Subsequent novels include *The Mercenary: A Tale of the Thirty Years' War* (1913). He also wrote a treatise on income-tax law (1932).

EDGAR, George (1877–1918) married Jeannie HOWARD. Born in Warrington, he became a reporter on the *Liverpool Gazette* and other provincial papers before coming to London in 1900 to try his luck as a freelance reporter and short-story-writer. His first novel, the popular *The Blue*

Bird's Eye (1912) is about prize-fighting, and he wrote it only because he made a rule never to refuse any offer of work. Encouraged by its success, he wrote another seven volumes of fiction, including *The Pride of the Fancy* (1914).

EDGE, K[athleen] M[ary] (d.1946) married (1903) Charles Trevor CAULFIELD (1863–1947). One of three daughters of an Irish barrister who became an Indian judge, she was married to a general in the army and published four novels 1902–12. The first two, *Ahana* (1902) and *The After Cost* (1904), are notable for their violent and occasionally gruesome treatment of the delicate issue of relations between English people and Eurasians in India. *The Shuttles of the Loom* (1909), which appeared as 'by K. M. Edge (Mrs C.T. Caulfield)', is more conventional. Its hero is an official in the Indian Civil Service, a strong silent man who falls in love and dies in a cholera epidemic. *Through the Cloudy Porch* (1912) concerns the blurring of genetic rather than racial distinctions. The heroine, the long-suffering wife of a contemptible cavalry officer stationed in South Africa, discovers that her husband is in fact her half-brother, and finds happiness after she has left him. Caulfield was a non-militant but enthusiastic member of the NUWSS.

EDGINTON, May: Helen Marion EDGINTON (1883–1957) married (1912) Francis Evans BAILY (d. 1962). As a young contributor to the *Royal Magazine* she married one of the editorial staff; they separated in 1930. She published more than fifty volumes of humorous and romantic fiction to 1955. Her opening gambit was a strong line in morally dubious protagonists. In *The Weight Carriers* (1909), a woman from a poor background marries a rich and adoring husband whom she despises for his physical and moral cowardice. The success of E. W. *Hornung's Raffles stories had made roguish heroes fashionable, and Edginton cashed in with *Brass* (1910), about a vagabond who finds a happy home despite his involvement in bigamy and murder, and *The Adventures of Napoleon Prince* (1912), about a criminal in the grand style. *The Sin of Eve* (1913) followed, and then her most successful book, *Oh! James! The Story of a Man Who Tried to Prove the Goodness of the World* (1914). The man (dis)-proving the goodness of the world is an entrepreneur who cannot stop making money. His thrifty wife will not let him spend it, so he establishes a number of impecunious young ladies in homes of their own, with impecunious young men watching over them unseen, and visits each of them in turn: the world puts an obvious construction upon this innocent philanthropy. She also co-authored several plays, one of which became the popular musical *No! No! Nanette*. Her husband was the author from 1921 of a long series of popular romantic novels, mostly under his own name, some as 'Susan French'; his memoirs hardly mention her, though they speak of the extreme difficulty of picking up the pieces after three years' separation during the First World War.

EGERTON, George, *pseud.*: Mary Chavelita DUNNE (1859–1945) married, first (1891), George Egerton CLAIRMONTE (d. 1901) (divorced 1901) and, secondly (1901), Reginald Golding BRIGHT (1874–1941). She was born in Melbourne, eldest of six children of an improvident Catholic Irishman who had been cashiered from the army, and at 14, after her mother's death in Ireland, went to Germany as a pupil-teacher; later she worked as a nurse. In the 1880s she became companion to the widow of the novelist G. J. Whyte-Melville (1821–1878), who was married (perhaps bigamously) to a shady and drunken American named Henry Higginson. In 1887 Higginson and Dunne eloped together, probably with some of Mrs Whyte-Melville's money, to Norway, where he died in 1889, leaving her with some property there. This episode was later used by her in her novel *The Wheel of God* (1898). Her stay in Scandinavia was at least profitable from an intellectual perspective—she gained a good knowledge of both Norwegian and Swedish, and therefore was able to read the works of August Strindberg (1849–1912), Henrik Ibsen (1828–1906), Björnstjerne Björnson (1832–1910), and Knut Hamsun (1859–1952) just as they were beginning to gain favour (often in bad translations) in London. She had a brief affair with Hamsun, but settled in Ireland in 1891 with Clairmonte, a work-shy, impecunious Canadian, and adopted her pseudonym on their return to London during 1892. Her *Keynotes* (1893) was recommended to Elkin Matthews and John Lane for publication by Richard *Le Gallienne. It sold 5,000 copies in Britain and the USA in its first year and prompted a special 'Keynote' series. It was followed by other collections: *Discords*, (1894), *Symphonies* (1897), and *Fantasias* (1898). 'A Lost Masterpiece' appeared in the *Yellow Book* I and 'The Captain's Book' in Volume VI. She parted from Clairmonte after the birth of their son in 1895; he died soon after their divorce. **Rosa Amorosa* (1901) is based upon her letters to a anonymous Norwegian lover. Shortly after this affair she married Bright, the *Sun*'s drama critic. When his brother Arthur Addison Bright, the theatrical agent, proved to have been swindling his clients (J. M.*Barrie lost £30,000) and committed suicide in 1906, Golding Bright sorted out the mess and set up as an agent himself, with his wife's help. Egerton tried writing for the theatre (she successfully translated and adapted plays), but her own plays were not well received. She turned to journalism. Ibsen was a formative influence, and the impressionism of Hamsun and Björnson is reflected in her literary style. Her semi-realistic, semi-impressionistic approach to women's sexuality was exhilarating even to a *fin-de-siècle* readership. The moving force behind Egerton's work was an awareness that in literature 'everything had been better done by man, than woman could hope to emulate'. This view (a curious mixture of the traditional and the avant-garde in its partial admission of defeat) led her to believe that the woman writer had best strike out on new ground, on 'the terra incognita of herself, as she knew herself to be'. In *Keynotes* Egerton's strong desire to communicate the true nature/experience of women is made explicit. Men she says must become aware that 'an untamed, primitive savage temperament... lurks in the mildest, best woman'. Egerton's obituary in the *Times* (13 Aug. 1945) considers any association of her work with that of the New Woman writers quite ill-founded since 'beyond the fact that in most of them a woman, either wife or mistress, is misunderstood, any suggestion of sex warfare is absent'. Her final work of note was again a collection of short stories, *Flies In Amber* (1905). Her only child was killed in the First World War. She died in Crawley. Her letters were edited by Terence de Vere White (1958).

Egoist, The: *An Individualist Review*, was published from January 1914 to December 1919. It originated in the feminist journal *Freewoman*, launched by Dora Marsden and Harriet Shaw Weaver in 1911. In June 1913, under the influence of Ezra Pound (1885–1972) and John Gould Fletcher (1886–1950), Marsden and Weaver took over the editorship and changed its name to *New Freewoman*, which under Pound's literary direction began to take an interest in philosophy and new poetry and fiction. At the end of 1913, *New Freewoman* changed its name to the *Egoist*, which while still concerned with issues facing the 'new woman' was now focused on 'advanced' literature and art, on writers such as 'HD' (1886–1961), Marianne Moore (1887–1972), William Carlos Williams (1883–1963), D. H. *Lawrence, and James *Joyce. The *Egoist* serialized *A Portrait of the Artist as a Young Man*, and published parts of *Ulysses*. T. S. Eliot (1888–1965) succeeded Richard Aldington (1892–1962) as literary editor in 1917 and developed in its pages the critical arguments that culminated in 'Tradition and the Individual Talent', which appeared in its final issue.

ELIZABETH or 'The Author of *Elizabeth and Her German Garden*', *pseud.*: Mary Annette BEAUCHAMP (1866–1941) married, first (1891), Graf Henning August von ARNIM-SCHLAGENTHIN, (d. 1910) and, secondly (1916), John Francis Stanley RUSSELL (1865–1931), who succeeded (1878) as 2nd Earl RUSSELL (legally separated 1919). Born in New Zealand, youngest of six children, she moved with the family from Sydney to London in 1870. She picked up education from her brothers' tutors, and went at 16 to Queen's College School in Acton, where the family lived for much of her childhood. She met Graf Henning von Arnim, the recently widowed son of a disgraced and exiled German diplomat, in 1889 on holiday in Rome. In 1896 they moved to Nassenheide in Pomerania, an estate confiscated from Arnim's father, which had recently been returned. Their marriage was troubled by the difference of age and nationality, and by her distaste for repeated childbearing. She found an escape in writing fiction, including an early draft of *The Pastor's Wife*. Her enthusiasm for gardening led to a gift of Alfred *Austin's whimsical, sketchy, precious, quasi-fictional book *The Garden That I Love* (1894), which was an important exemplar for the book which, literally, made her name, *Elizabeth and Her German Garden* (1898), which, published in September, was reprinted eleven times and earned her £10,000 by the end of the year. It was a thinly disguised account of her life in Pomerania, contrasting the author's creative freedom in her garden with the stifling social conventions indoors, and as 'The Author of *Elizabeth and her German Garden*', Arnim produced three further accounts of her life in Germany, *The Solitary Summer* (1899), *The April Baby's Book of Tunes* (1901), and *The Adventures of Elizabeth in Rügen* (1904). Other novels ranged more widely and satirically across German society: *The Benefactress* (1901), **Fraulein Schmidt and Mr Anstruther* (1907), *The Governess* (1909). *The *Caravaners* (1909) drew on a real caravanning holiday taken in the wet summer of 1907 in Kent and Sussex, in the course of which they were joined by E. M.*Forster and visited Alfred Austin and H. G.*Wells. In later novels such as *The Pastor's Wife* (1914), *Vera* (1921)—a frightening account of marriage to a man who is charming until crossed, based on her life with Russell—, *The Enchanted April* (1923), and *Mr Skeffington* (1940), Arnim drew on her experiences after returning to England. In 1909 a crisis in Henning von Arnim's finances had necessitated the sale of Nassenheide and a move to England. Soon afterwards he died, and she sold the German property and invested it in Switzerland, whence she escaped after the outbreak of the First World War, and was renaturalized an Englishwoman in September 1914. An affair with Wells in 1910–12 was followed by a disastrous, short-lived marriage to the elder brother of Bertrand Russell (1872–1970). After the war she lived between England and Switzerland, where she renewed her friendship with Katherine *Mansfield, whose father was her first cousin. In the 1920s she had an affair with a much younger man, A. S. Frere (1892–1984), later a successful publisher. In 1939 Arnim moved to the USA, where she died. She published an autobiography, *All the Days of My Life* (1936). Through all her work Arnim provided an unsentimental account of domestic life, one sensitive to the play of power in the household and its often oppressive effects. There is a biography by Karen Usborne (1986). Two minor Edwardian novelists tried to imitate the success of her first novel: Sybil Gwendolen Spottiswoode (later Aitken, later Lamb, b. 1879) who published as 'The Author of *Marcia in Germany*' (1908) and Anne Topham (b. 1874), who published as 'The Author of *Daphne in the Fatherland*' (1912).

Elizabeth Visits America, Elinor *Glyn, 1909, Duckworth. A sequel to *The *Visits of Elizabeth* (1900). After quarrelling with her husband, Harry, Elizabeth joins a party of friends who are touring America (or at least its fashionable and picturesque sections), as Glyn herself had recently done. Harry, meanwhile, is shooting game in Africa. Elizabeth has a minor romance with a mining engineer from Nevada, and gets caught in a hold-up, before being reunited with Harry. The main narrative device of the original *Visits*, Elizabeth's ingenuous frankness, will not work here, since she is now a marchioness with two children. What takes its place is a commentary on America and Americans. 'Elizabeth still patronises, still accepts hospitality with her quizzing little nose in the air, is "very British" and says and does things which are not always in good taste,' the *Globe* observed. Glyn was by now more or less alienated from her spendthrift husband, and writing was her only source of income.

ELKINGTON, E. Way: see under 'Dick *Donovan'.

ELLIOT, Anne. Her first novel was the anonymous *Dr. Edith Romney* (1883). Several of her eleven subsequent novels were published as 'by the author of *Dr. Edith Romney*'; the three last are *A Martial Maid* (1900), *Mansell's Millions* (1903), *The Memoirs of Mimosa* (1912): all are commonplace romances set in English country society. Mansell is a millionaire who returns to rescue his family from decline.

ELLIS, Mrs Havelock: Edith Mary Oldham LEES (1861–1916) married (1891) Henry Havelock ELLIS (1859–1939). The only daughter of a landowner, she was organizer of the Fellowship of the New Life (among whose members the Fabian Society had originated) when she met Ellis, the pioneer sexologist. They shared an enthusiasm for the teaching on ethics and marriage of James Hinton (1822–75). Together they lived for some time in Cornwall, setting of several of her works. Soon after their marriage, which was consciously undertaken on progressive lines (they were to be financially independent and live in separate establishments), her lesbianism became apparent. This, and their various mutual jealousies, are treated in some detail in Ellis's *My Life* (1940). She died of diabetes. *My Cornish Neighbours* (1906) and *The Imperishable Wing* (1911) are collections of tales about humble life which incorporate a good deal of dialect. *Attainment* (1909) concerns a Cornish doctor's daughter who wants to see the world. She moves to London, settles in a flat, works among the poor, and helps found a Brotherhood of the Perfect Life. There is much reforming talk of a 'visionary' kind, but in the end she decides that love is the only thing which matters, goes home, and marries. Her first volume of fiction, *Seaweed: A Cornish Idyll* (1898), later revised as *Kit's Woman* (1907), about the wife of a crippled Cornish miner who has a child by another man, is probably her best-known work.

Emmanuel Burden, Merchant, *of Thames St. in the City of London, Exporter of Hardware: A Record of his Lineage, Speculations, Last Days, and Death,* Hilaire *Belloc, 1904, Methuen. Emmanuel Burden, wealthy owner of a hardware company, is a widower with rather dissolute son, Cosmo. I. Z. Barnett is an unscrupulous financier who realizes he can make a killing out of the newly 'pacified' African territory of the M'Korio Delta if he can control the only colonial traders there, Burden and his friend, the shipowner Abbott. Barnett's plan is to sell a rather desolate place as a source of untold wealth. Playing on Burden's patriotism, and exploiting his own hold on the debt-ridden Cosmo, Barnett and his friends persuade Burden to join the M'Korio Delta Syndicate. Abbott (whose views match Belloc's own, not least his anti-semitism) refuses to join such a corrupt venture, and when Burden realizes his new partners are determined to ruin Abbott, he at last revolts against Barnett's scheme. He saves his soul but is physically wearied and soon dies. His son inherits the business and is fully committed to the aims of the M'Korian Syndicate. Belloc's basic argument, that the decent but weak and naïve British businessman is no match for the cunning international capitalist, is given bite by his use of an unctuous, hypocritical narrator, and by his satirical account of the parts played by the self-deceiving aristocracy, Church, and press in the creation of economic bubbles.

Empire. There is, of course, nothing specifically Edwardian about the interest in Empire which became an important element of British fiction from the middle of the nineteenth century onwards. The three writers who are often said to have defined the fictional frontiers of Empire—Joseph *Conrad, Rider *Haggard, and Rudyard *Kipling—all began to publish before the turn of the century; the writer who is often said to have heralded the dissolution of those frontiers, E. M. *Forster, did not turn his attention to them until after 1914. Nevertheless, the Edwardian years did witness a number of significant developments in the representation of Empire. There was, for example, a new, or newish, sense of the far-flung territories ruled by white men as a kind of gigantic playground, a laboratory for the processing of 'rough diamonds', a vast cabinet of (mostly living) curiosities: a sense evident above all in the work of Louis *Becke, Hugh *Clifford, R. B. Cunninghame *Graham, and W. H. *Hudson, but also in that of Harold *Bindloss, Archer Philip *Crouch, 'Ridgewell *Cullum', A. J. *Dawson, 'Sydney Carlyon *Grier', Colonel A. F. P. *Harcourt, G. A. *Henty, Bart *Kennedy, 'G. B. *Lancaster', Basil *Lubbock, Bertram *Mitford, F. Frankfort *Moore, Hume *Nisbet, Edward *Noble, Gilbert *Parker, Arthur *Paterson, Major Ferdinand *Peacock, Charles E. *Pearce, Clive *Phillipps-Wolley, Gordon *Stables, 'Herbert *Strang', 'Joan *Sutherland', 'John Strange *Winter', and P. C. *Wren. So secure were the conventions of colonial picaresque that they could withstand near-parody, in the work of Arthur Conan *Doyle and Edgar *Jepson, and the incorporation of a woman's point of view, in the work of Beatrice *Grimshaw, 'M.*Hamilton', Flora Annie *Steel, and others. An equally important development was an increasing focus on the connections between Empire and commerce, evident in novels by Hilaire *Belloc, Harold Bindloss, Hamilton *Drummond, Ernest *Glanville, and C. J. Cutliffe *Hyne; and, of course, Conrad's **Nostromo* (1904). The opening chapter of H. Rider *Haggard's *The Yellow God* (1911), an African romance, is entitled 'Sahara, Limited'. Here and there, in Leonard *Woolf's *The *Village in the Jungle* (1913), or in stories and novels by Francis William *Bain, Cecil *Lowis, and Marmaduke *Pickthall, there is evidence of an effort to understand the point of view of the colonized. But easily the most explosive issue investigated by Edwardian fiction of Empire, and one which tended to reinstate fairly rapidly the point of view of the colonizers, was that of sexual relations between people of different races. Anxiety about miscegenation is the main preoccupation of novels by, *inter alia*, Mrs *Chan-Toon, 'Victoria *Cross', A. J. *Dawson, Maud *Diver, K. M. *Edge, Percival *Gibbon, M. T. *Hainsselin, Anna *Howarth, V. I. *Longman, Norma *Lorimer, 'Allan *McAulay', A. E. W. *Mason, 'Elinor

*Mordaunt', Ethel *Savi, and 'Patricia *Wentworth'. Even George Webb *Hardy's *The *Black Peril* (1914), which is passionately anti-racist in most respects, still baulks at the thought of sexual contact between the races. There were also apocalyptic warnings about political rather than sexual collapse, such as D. *Gerard's *The Blood-Tax* (1902) and *A *Derelict Empire* (1912), by 'Mark *Time'. Even bestsellers like Mason's *The *Four Feathers* (1902) and *The *Broken Road* (1907) were far from sanguine about the individual and collective benefits of colonization to the colonizers; though Edgar *Wallace, in **Sanders of the River* (1911), was both sanguine and sanguinary. Equally significant for the future of the British novel was the emergence of a large number of writers who had either been born and raised in, or who had emigrated to, the white colonies. Australia led the way, with J. H. *Abbott, E. Maria *Albanesi, Guy *Boothby, Ada *Cambridge, Frances *Campbell, Carlton *Dawe, Miles *Franklin, Mary *Gaunt, Nat *Gould, A. G. *Hales, Lillias *Hamilton, Winifred *James, Louise *Mack, Hume *Nisbet, Mrs Campbell *Praed, 'Henry Handel *Richardson', Douglas *Sladen, William S. *Walker, and I. A. R. *Wylie. But New Zealand could claim Arthur H. *Adams, *'Alien', H. Louisa *Bedford, 'James *Cassidy', B. L. *Farjeon, Fergus *Hume, 'G. B. *Lancaster', 'Katherine *Mansfield', and Hugh *Walpole. 'Constance *Clyde' was born in New Zealand, but emigrated to Australia, as does the heroine of her only novel, *A Pagan's Love* (1905); H. B. Marriott *Watson was born in Australia, and moved with his family to New Zealand during his early childhood. Canada could claim Robert *Barr, 'Ralph *Connor', L. *Dougall, Sara Jeannette *Duncan, L. M. *Montgomery, Gilbert *Parker, and Charles G. D. *Roberts, while the South African colonies produced 'Francis *Bancroft', Sir Percy *Fitzpatrick, George Webb *Hardy, Anna *Howarth, Basil *Marnan, and Gertrude *Page. W. H. *Hudson was born in Argentina, Annie E. *Holdsworth in Jamaica, Mrs Archibald *Little in Madeira, W. J. *Locke in British Guiana, '*Saki' in Burma, and M. P. *Shiel in Monserrat. Many of these writers are now studied in the context of their respective national literatures.

Empty House, The, *and Other Ghost Stories*, Algernon *Blackwood, 1906, Eveleigh Nash. The pattern of these ten entertaining but unremarkable stories is set by the title story. Jim Shorthouse arrives in a seaside town on a weekend visit to Aunt Julia to find that she has acquired the keys to the local haunted house. They explore the house at night, and witness the ghostly re-enactment of the murder (of a servant-girl by a stableman) which caused its haunting. Shorthouse also appears in 'A Case of Eavesdropping', 'With Intent to Steal', and 'Skeleton Lake: The Strange Adventures of a Private Secretary', without acquiring any noticeable identity. Locations include 'The Wood of the Dead', a couple of lodging-houses, and the Canadian wilderness. 'Keeping His Promise' rather effectively features an Edinburgh student cramming for an examination.

The End of the Tether: see **Youth: A Narrative and Two Other Stories*.

English Girl, An: *A Romance*, Ford Madox *Hueffer, 1907, Methuen. When his millionaire father dies, Don Kelleg becomes the 'richest citizen in the world'. His parents were British, and had emigrated to America. He himself has been educated at an English school and university, yet remains an American. He is engaged to an English girl, Eleanor Greville, who owes her placid self-assurance to an ancient lineage. Of artistic temperament, hostile to his father's values, he regards his fortune as a burden 'too heavy for a man that hopes for heaven'. They travel from Canterbury to New York with a view to extensive philanthropy. His father had got his start by swindling a barber, Kratzenstein, out of a copper mine. Don tracks the man down in New York and offers to make reparation. But Kratzenstein angrily refuses charity: he wants Don to manipulate the stock market on his behalf. Appalled by the extent of corruption and philistinism in America, Don resolves to give up the unequal struggle and return to England, where he proposes to live the modest life of a gentleman-artist. But no sooner have they settled in England than Don's American impulses and loyalites reassert themselves. He announces his intention to return once again to America, and do what he can with the power which has been entrusted to him, the power of great wealth. Eleanor declines to accompany him, and they separate for ever. The novel develops a theme which preoccupied a number of Edwardian writers: the tragedy of a fluid temperament. In this case, the fluidity is provided by the hero's Anglo-American background and upbringing. Eleanor's father, who accompanies them on their initial trip to America, is one of the wise observers who often feature in Hueffer's novels. *An English Girl* was the first of his books to receive an extensive, and extensively favourable, review: from the Liberal politician C. F. G. Masterman (1873–1927), in the *Daily News* (28 Sept. 1907).

English Review, The (1908–1937) was published from 1908 to 1937, when it merged with the *National Review.* Founded by Ford Madox *Hueffer as an alternative to the established Edwardian literary journals, the first issue of the *English Review* featured poetry and stories by Thomas Hardy, *Conrad, Henry *James and H. G.*Wells, and Hueffer's skill as editor was to attract contributors from different literary generations. (His major discoveries were Norman *Douglas, Ezra Pound, Wyndham *Lewis, and D. H.*Lawrence). Ford was not a good businessman, though, and was replaced as editor by Austin Harrison (1873–1928) in December 1909, after the magazine was bought by the Liberal industrialist Alfred Mond (1868–1930). Harrison, who edited the magazine till 1923, preserved the *Review*'s literary standards and internationalism, if with less sense of a critical edge. Thereafter, despite the enterprising literary editorship (1931–5) of Douglas Jerrold (1893–1964), the *Review* drifted into conservatism.

Englishwoman's Love-Letters, An, Laurence *Housman, 1900, John Murray. This bestseller was at first published anonymously. 'It need hardly be said,' begins the preface to the first edition, 'that the woman by whom these letters were written had no thought that they would be read by any one but the person to whom they were addressed.' Housman's achievement was to maintain the note of disingenuousness for a further 300 pages. 'It is you who make me think so much about myself, trying to find myself out,' the heroine writes in her second letter to an unnamed lover. 'I used to be more self-possessed, and regarded it as the crowning virtue: and now—your possession of me sweeps it away, and I stand crying to be let into a secret that is no longer mine. Shall I ever know *why* you love me? It is my religious difficulty; but it never rises into a doubt.' This fake religiosity was one reason for the book's success, enabling the reviewer in *Vanity Fair* to observe that the author of the letters was evidently 'a woman of great parts, of very refined sense . . . We remember nothing in literature quite so full of passionate human appeal as Letter LXXVII.' Another reason was its lack of individualizing content. The letters contain a smattering of gossip and some description of a visit to Italy, but little else. No explanation, apart from innate nobility, is given for the lovers' decision to separate. Readers and reviewers were thus able to project onto the book whatever feelings they wanted to. 'It is a loud cry,' the *Daily Mail* commented, 'not merely of one intoxicated and torn heart, but of the claim of inner and true emotion to be still the greatest force of life; the one thing worth having—worth living for, longing for, dying for.' Housman himself thought it poor stuff, and both Barry *Pain and the muck-raking journalist T. W. H. Crosland (?1868–1924) published parodies.

Erewhon Revisited Twenty Years Later, *Both by the Original Discoverer of the Country and by His Son*, Samuel *Butler, 1901, Grant Richards. Higgs, the narrator of *Erewhon* (1872) (the sequel is narrated by his son) returns to the country, a topsy-turvy world where sickness is punished and crime cured and where young people attend universities of unreason, after twenty years, and is distressed to find that the Erewhonians were so wonder-struck by his ascent into heaven by balloon at the end of *Erewhon* that he has become the object of a religious myth—his sayings are treasured, his relics preserved, and a temple is being built for his cult, Sunchildism. The novel satirizes the exploitation of credulity in the characters of professors Hanky and Panky, and plays with with Christian parallels (Higgs discovers that Yram, the gaoler's daughter who loved him, has subsequently had a son, Geroge).

ESLER, E. Rentoul: Erminda RENTOUL (?1860–1924) married (1883) Robert ESLER. She was born in Ireland, the daughter of the Revd Alexander Rentoul, DD, MD, of Manor Cunningham, Donegal. She was educated at Nimes, France, in Berlin, and at Queen's University, Belfast, where in 1879 she was awarded a First Honour certificate. She married a doctor and scientific writer and settled in London, where she contributed to the **Cornhill* and *Sunday at Home*. Esler's works are portraits of rural life, set in both England and Ireland. *The Wardlaws*

(1896) is considered one of her best novels. Other publications include *The Awakening of Helena Thorpe* (1902), *The Maid of the Manse* (1895), and *The Trackless Way: The Story of a Man's Quest for God* (1903). Her romances are old-fashioned and earnest. Indeed, *The Trackless Way*, about a Presbyterian minister in Ireland, contained altogether too much religion for some reviewers. She listed among her recreations in *Who's Who* 'conversation with people of individual mind'.

Eternal City, The, Hall *Caine, 1901, William Heinemann. Romantic melodrama set amidst the somewhat confusing background of turn-of-the-century Rome and the struggles between Church and State, between royalists and republicans. The three main protagonists are David Rossi, a young, Christ-like, 'anarchist' deputy; the machiavellian prime minister, Baron Bonelli; and his beautiful ward, Donna Roma. Rossi and Roma discover that they knew each other as young children in London, the natural daughter and adopted son of a Roman aristocrat in political exile. They fall in love but are prey to the cunning machinations and brutal power of the Baron, which even reach up to the Pope (who turns out to be Rossi's father!). Using the apparent treachery of Donna Roma (whom he had been grooming since childhood as his own wife), Bonelli seems to see off the threat of both Rossi's Republican movement and his love for Roma, but in a struggle over her honour the Baron is himself killed by the deputy. Roma takes the blame, is imprisoned, and becomes a national heroine. The king abdicates and a republic is declared, but Rossi's triumph is muted by Roma's plight. Thanks to the Pope, the couple are reconciled but she almost immediately dies of an inherited incurable disease.

EUSTACE, Robert, *pseud.*: Robert Eustace BARTON (1868–1943), LRCP (1897), MRCS. Educated at University College Hospital Medical School, Barton became a London physician and later was medical director of a mental hospital in Northampton. He collaborated with L. T. *Meade on five *crime novels 1898–1902, and with Gertrude *Warden on *The Stolen Pearl: A Romance of London* (1903). His role, no doubt, was to supply the medical evidence. Dorothy L. Sayers (1893–1957) regarded his work with Meade as innovative in its use of medical pathology in crime fiction. She began correspondence with him while collecting early crime stories for an anthology, and this led to his providing the plot of a novel which appeared over both their names as *The Documents in the Case* (1930). He seems to have done little of the writing of the novel, although he did publish novels alone: *A Human Bacillus: The Story of a Strange Character* (1907) and *The Hidden Treasures of Egypt: A Romance* (1925). These are no ordinary shockers. *The Stolen Pearl* concerns the hypnotic influence exerted by a Russian doctor over his fashionable patients, with disastrous consequences. *A Human Bacillus* is even odder: the hero is a boy of Anglo-Portuguese parentage, whom we first meet at public school, and whose startling scientific achievements occupy the rest of the story.

EVERETT-GREEN, E[velyn] (1856-1932). Born in London, daughter of the artist George Pycock Everett-Green (d. 1893) and the historian Mary Anne Everett-Green (1818–95), she went to Gower Street Preparatory School and Bedford College, London (Reid Scholarship 1872–73). She studied music at the London Academy and worked as a nurse in London for a while. In her late 20s she moved to the country and began to write wholesome fare for youthful readers published by the Religious Tract Society; her first children's books were published as 'H. F. E.'. Much of her work consists of romantic adventures in historical settings aimed at a readership of teenage girls. Her output from the 1880s until her death was truly prodigious; over 200 titles under her own name alone. In *Olivia's Experiment* (1901), a widow whose two young children have died resolves to raise a foundling boy left on her doorstep; he goes to the dogs, but redeems himself during the *Boer War. Everett-Green cultivated the spirit of place. In *Dufferin's Keep* (1905), new money, in the shape of Lady Alys Lorraine, restores the fortunes of an old landed family, and is in return validated through marriage. In The *Magic Island: Being the Story of a Garden and Its Master* (1906), the garden, on an island in the middle of a river, is owned and governed by a Prospero-like 'Master', Sir Richard Knollys, and visited by the heroine, Arielle, a combination of Ariel and Miranda, who eventually falls for Knollys's nephew, Philip. Another favourite topic, colourfully rehearsed in *Married in Haste* (1907) and *The Evolution of Sara* (1911), was successful marriage between a young woman and a much older man. There are very faint echoes of the woman's movement in *The House of Silence* about a young genius who is loved by his secretary, Silence Desart, but has to endure marriage to a beautiful American heiress and tragedy before he can be brought to recognize Silence's worth. During the latter half of her life Everett-Green mainly lived abroad, in Madeira and elsewhere. She also published fiction as 'Cecil Adair', such as *Cantacute Towers* (1911), *Gabriel's Garden* (1913), *Mist Pool* (1915), and *The Cactus Hedge* (1919), and, as 'E. Ward', *A Pair of Originals* (1892) and *Patricia Pendragon* (1911). She collaborated with H. Louisa *Bedford on several works in the 1890s. Tame as Everett-Green's fiction is, her *publishers, the Scots firm Thomas Nelson & Sons, made her tone down a kissing scene.

exoticism. It is probably true to say that far-away places, and the unsettling and transforming experiences which are traditionally held to take place there, have always played an important part in narrative fiction. Literature and travel are cognate activities of mind. But the emergence during the 1880s of new forms of romance, as an alternative to the domestic realism which had since the early years of the century dominated the market for fiction, gave the exotic a distinctively modern flavour and significance. The writers associated with the new romance—Robert Louis Stevenson (1850–94), Rider *Haggard, and Rudyard *Kipling—had achieved immense popularity, while still addressing matters of considerable moral, social and even geopolitical weight. No wonder Joseph *Conrad launched his career in the 1890s with exercises in (admittedly jaundiced) exoticism. One can get some idea of what a career in exoticism of the sober variety might look like—Conrad without the metaphysics, so to speak—by studying the short stories of his friend Hugh *Clifford, who also wrote about the Far East. Writers who tried to keep the metaphysics in would include Robert Cunninghame *Graham and W. H. *Hudson, who both wrote primarily about South America. But the latter had only take one short step aside from his psychologically and sociologically informed traveller's sketches to produce, in **Green Mansions* (1904), a florid bestseller. For it was chiefly in the realm of bestselling fiction that exoticism made its mark in the Edwardian period. Old-style sensation novels, such as those of 'Marie *Corelli' or Florence *Barclay, still tended to insist on an awakening that was as much spiritual as sexual. Exoticism permitted a much franker, if far-fetched, portrayal of sexual awakening. The landmarks were Robert *Hichens's *The *Garden of Allah* (1904), Elinor *Glyn's **Three Weeks* (1907), H. de Vere *Stacpoole's *The *Blue Lagoon* (1908), and Ethel M. *Dell's *The *Way of an Eagle* (1912). The first of these is set in the North African desert, the third in the South Seas, the fourth on the North-West Frontier of India; and, although *Three Weeks* is set in a hotel in Geneva, the crucial event occurs on a tiger-skin rug. The formula which evolved from the success of these novels and others like them was an exclusive focus on personal experience, on the introduction of an emotionally inhibited hero or heroine into a world supposedly without inhibitions. The world invented in such books was often not only sexually permissive, but violent. 'Oriental' thuggery and cunning, a minor theme in nineteenth-century sensation novels, became a major theme in the work of such writers as K. M. *Edge, Flora Annie *Steel, and Louise *Gerard, who was hailed as a promising newcomer on the strength of lurid accounts of West African horrors. To some extent, the settings of exotic tales were interchangeable; but an implicit hierarchy of exoticism did begin to emerge. In Rider Haggard's **Ayesha* (1905), the sequel to *She* (1887), the scene switches from Africa, by that time a much-explored fictional territory, to the mountainous regions beyond Tibet, the source, perhaps, of yet more potent mysteries. It is to the East Asian wilderness that Guy *Boothby's psychic superman retires at the end of **'Farewell, Nikola'* (1901). Although India frequently featured in such fiction, it was a place where, for the British writer and reader, the personal might prove hard to disentangle from the political. Writers like Robert Hichens and, later, E. M. Hull, author of *The Sheik* (1919), who did not want politics to get in the way of mating, consequently preferred the French territories of North Africa. Additions were sometimes made to the map of exoticism, notably Japan, in the work of the Baroness *d'Anethan, 'D. H. *Dennis', Mrs Hugh *Fraser, Sadi *Grant, 'George *Griffith', Major Arthur *Haggard, 'Clive *Holland', 'G. N. *Mortlake', and H. Grahame *Richards. Also of particular interest were territories which appeared to represent a mixture of the familiar and the unfamiliar, the

'European' and the 'Oriental'. Italy became a place of sexual awakening and outbreaks of violence, not only for E. M. *Forster in *A *Room with a View* (1907), but for Richard *Bagot in *Donna Diana* (1902), 'Marjorie *Bowen' in *The Viper of Milan* (1906), Rhoda *Broughton in *The *Devil and the Deep Sea* (1910), Hall *Caine in *The *Eternal City* (1901), Rider Haggard in *The *Wanderer's Necklace* (1914), Robert Hichens in *The *Call of the Blood* (1906), and Mrs Henry *Tippett in *The Power of the Petticoat* (1911). Rose *Macaulay vainly tried to persuade her readers, in *The *Furnace* (1907), that it was not really that exciting. Similarly, it was the hybridity of Spanish identity, part-European, part-Moorish, which attracted Stephen *Gwynne. The exoticism of Egypt had a lot to do with its marginal or intermediate geographical and cultural position. Hall Caine, H. H. *Colvill, Joseph J. *Doke, 'Robert *Eustace', Elinor Glyn, 'M. *Hamilton', Robert Hichens, A. C. *Inchbold, Norma *Lorimer, Rachel Swete *Macnamara, Gilbert *Parker, Kathlyn *Rhodes, Douglas *Sladen, and Marmaduke *Pickthall were among those who could not resist.

FAIRLESS, Michael, *pseud.*: Margaret Fairless BARBER (1869–1901), who took the name DOWSON. She was born in Yorkshire, the daughter of a lawyer, and educated at home and at school in Torquay and outer London. She had a spinal weakness, and though she trained as a nurse and at various times looked after a sick relation, worked as a parish nurse, and did social and medical work in the East End of London, these activities were interrupted and finally ended by debilitating illness. In her youth she had had lessons in modelling; after her period in the East End she convalesced in a remote cottage where she befriended tramps. H. Rider *Haggard, whose brother was married to her sister, writes of her in his memoirs as talented but erratic, now 'under the sway of a Low Church mania', then 'equally High Church', next 'with difficulty restrained from starting off alone to become a missionary in China'. In the last phase of her life, when she had been informally adopted into the family of her woman doctor (Mary Emily Dowson, b. 1848, author of theological works as 'William Scott Palmer'), had taken their name, and was living as an invalid with them in Cheyne Walk, she took up modelling again and then began to compose fictionalized books of religious experience, published posthumously to great success. *The Gathering of Brother Hilarius* (1901), set in the Middle Ages, features a peripatetic monk and his rise to the position of prior. *The Roadmender and Other Papers*, a collection of reflective essays, was written during the last twenty months of her life as she lay bed-ridden. It was first serialized in the *Pilot* before its complete publication in 1902. It draws upon Barber's own feelings of detachment from 'the road of life'. It was in its thirty-first edition by the end of 1912 and had sold 250,000 copies by 1922. All her books were published posthumously; others were *The Grey Brethren and Other Fragments in Prose and Verse* (1905) and *Stories Told to Children* (1914), edited by M. E. Dowson. Her *Complete Works* were published in 1932.

FALKNER, J[ohn] Meade (1858–1932) married (1899) Evelyn Violet ADYE. Born in Wiltshire, the son of a Church of England clergyman, and educated at Marlborough College, he graduated in history from Hertford College, Oxford, in 1882. Soon afterwards he became tutor to the sons of Sir Andrew Noble (1831–1915), one of the owners of Armstrongs, the armament manufacturers. Noble subsequently made Falkner his private secretary; he then became an employee of the company, and rose eventually to be chairman of its board of directors (1915–20). Falkner was an enthusiastic antiquarian and local historian, writing guidebooks to Oxfordshire and Berkshire. He was an expert on the medieval history of Durham (where he lived), honorary librarian to the Dean and Chapter of Durham, and honorary reader in palaeography at Durham University. He published three Gothic novels which reflect his feeling for the romance of the past and his knowledge of ecclesiastical architecture and heraldry: *The Lost Stradivarius* (1895), concerning an old violin which when played releases the evil spirit of a previous owner; *Moonfleet* (1898), a tale of smugglers; and *The *Nebuly Coat* (1903). Hugh *Walpole, who had been a small boy in Durham, remembered' watching Falkner's heavy body lumbering up the Durham street, myself eaten up with wonder, amaze and ambition.... All the Cathedral set were shocked to their skins by *The Nebuly Coat*. I love the man to this day. He was a real abnormal romantic.'

family sagas. Nineteenth-century novelists like Sir Walter Scott (1771–1832), Honoré de Balzac (1799–1850), and Anthony Trollope (1815-82) wrote series of novels which, since they sometimes took as their subject the development of specific families through two or more generations, might justly be regarded as 'family sagas'. But the increasing prominence in the final decades of the century of Social Darwinism, with its emphasis on genetic explanations of social and moral behaviour, gave the term a sharper focus.

Émile Zola's (1840–1902) Rougon-Macquart novels (1871–93) analysed the effects of heredity and environment on the members of a single family, tracing the passage of a genetic 'flaw' down the legitimate line of the Rougons and the illegitimate line of the Macquarts. Sociological (or rather bio-medical) theory determined the very shape of these narratives. Henry *James pointed out that each section of the long chronicle was '*physiologically* determined by previous combinations'. In each generation the inherited flaw topples an individual life into a downward spiral of disease, alcoholism, poverty or madness. This downward spiral was one of the ways in which late nineteenth-century novels, in Europe and America, spoke about individual and social development. Edwardian sagas (some single-volume, some multi-volume) extended and refined the downward-spiral plot, tending on the whole to suggest that decline could be reversed or ameliorated by the exercise of integrity and will-power. The hero of Walter *Besant's *The *Fourth Generation* (1900) concludes that 'the liability to temptation—the tendency—is inherited, but the necessity which forces a man to act is not inherited; that is due to himself.' The major Edwardian examples of the genre are Arnold *Bennett's Clayhanger saga, J. D. *Beresford's Jacob Stahl saga, Gilbert *Cannan's Lawrie saga, John *Galsworthy's Forsyte saga (only the first volume of which, *The *Man of Property* (1906), was published in the period), and E. *Nesbit's Bastable saga. Cannan's Lawrie saga was strongly influenced by his translation (1910–13) of Roman Rolland's (1866–1944) *Jean Christophe* (1889–1912). Critics compared Ethel *Sidgwick's *Promise* (1910) and *Succession: A Comedy of the Generations* (1913) with *Jean Christophe*. Notable one-volume sagas include Samuel *Butler's *The *Way of All Flesh* (1903), Valentina *Hawtrey's *Rodwell* (1908), Constance *Holme's **Crump Folk Going Home* (1913), Lady *Napier of Magdala's *To the Third and Fourth Generations* (1913), Forrest *Reid's *The *Bracknels* (1911), and Hugh Walpole's *The *Duchess of Wrexe* (1914). D. H. *Lawrence's *The Rainbow* (1915) might be seen as (among other things) an ironic commentary on the assumptions which underpinned the genre.

fantasy. If romance emerged during the nineteenth century as an exotic rival to domestic realism, then fantasy emerged, in the work of Hans Christian Andersen (1805–75), Lewis Carroll (1832–98), Charles Kingsley (1819–75), George Macdonald (1824–1905) and others, as its domestic rival. The Edwardian period witnessed a greater degree of specialization, so that a small number of insistent preoccupations and tropes recur again and again. While *exoticism and *Ruritanian romance kept the paranormal at a safe distance by associating it with a mythical elsewhere, fantasy, like the *horror story, envisaged its intrusion closer to home. Some notable Edwardian fantasies are laboratory experiments which observe, to comic, tragic, or polemical effect, what happens when normality is disrupted by the arrival of a supernatural being or overturned by a supernatural act: *The *Brass Bottle* (1900) by 'F. *Anstey', G. K. *Chesterton's *The *Ball and the Cross* (1909), *The *Life Everlasting* (1911) by 'Marie *Corelli', C. E. *Lawrence's *Much Ado About Something* (1909), Constantine *Ralli's *The Strange Story of Falconer Thring* (1907), Stephen *Reynolds's *The *Holy Mountain* (1910), and H. G. *Wells's *The *Sea Lady* (1902). Max *Beerbohm described **Zuleika Dobson* (1911) as a 'fantasy', and there are perhaps grounds for thinking of the heartless heroine as an alien being. Fantasy had always played an important part in children's fiction, and Edwardian writers such as Helen *Bannerman, W. A. *Fraser, Kenneth *Grahame, Rudyard *Kipling, Beatrix *Potter, Charles G. D. *Roberts, and '*Saki' developed a distinctive line in anthropomorphic animals. Equally characteristic of the period was the peopling of recognizable landscapes with fairy tribes, in the work of Lord *Dunsany, 'Fiona *Macleod', 'Dermot *O'Byrne', James *Stephens, and 'M. *Urquhart'. Closer to mainstream domestic realism were stories about the transfer of minds, bodies or even parts of bodies—*The Identity Exchange* (1902) by 'R. *Andom', G. F. *Bradby's *The Marquis's Eye* (1905), Henry *Byatt's *The Real Man* (1909), Walter *de la Mare's *The *Return* (1910), Sir William *Magnay's *A Poached Peerage* (1909), Barry *Pain's *An Exchange of Souls* (1911), Mrs H. H. *Penrose's *Something Impossible* (1914)—and stories which imagine the eruption of the past (historical or legendary) into the present: Edwin *Arnold's *Lepidus the Centurion* (1901), the Countess of *Cromartie's *Out of the Dark* (1910), Walter de la Mare's *Henry Brocken* (1904) and *The*

Return (1910), E. M. *Forster's *The* **Celestial Omnibus and Other Stories* (1911), Mrs Aylmer *Gowing's *By Thames and Tiber* (1903), Ford Madox *Hueffer's **Mr Apollo* (1908), Rudyard Kipling's **Puck of Pook's Hill* (1906) and **Rewards and Fairies* (1910), **Louis Norbert: A Twofold Romance* (1914) by 'Vernon & Lee', E. *Nesbit's *The* **Story of an Amulet* (1906), Henry *Newbolt's *The Old Country: A Romance* (1906), Mrs Campbell *Praed's *The Body of His Desire: A Romance of the Soul* (1912), and Margaret *Woods's *The Invader* (1908). A number of writers made polemical points through the invention of utopias or dystopias: R. H. *Benson, in *The Lord of the World* (1908); Robert *Blatchford, in *The* **Sorcery Shop: An Impossible Romance* (1907); Samuel *Butler, in **Erewhon Revisited* (1901); G. K. *Chesterton, in *The* **Napoleon of Notting Hill* (1904); Joseph *Conrad and Ford Madox *Hueffer, in *The* **Inheritors: An Extravagant Story* (1901); Allen *Clarke, in *Starved into Surrender* (1904); James Elroy *Flecker, in *The Last Generation: A Story of the Future* (1908); Horace *Newte, in *The Master Beast* (1907); Thomas A. *Pinkerton, in *No Rates and Taxes: A Romance of Five Worlds* (1902); Constantine Ralli, in *Vanessa: A Romance of the New Century and the New World* (1904); Ralph *Straus, in *The Dust Which Is God* (1907); Richard *Whiteing, in *All Moonshine* (1907). Fantasy proved well adapted to the short-story form, as in *Pope Jacynth and Other Fantastic Tales* (1904) by Vernon Lee, George *Raffalovich's *The Deuce and All* (1910), and H. G. Wells's *The* **Country of the Blind and Other Stories* (1911). Although they do not involve little green men, the pornographic stories attributed to George *Bacchus are certainly a form of fantasy.

'Farewell, Nikola', Guy *Boothby, 1901, Ward Lock. The last of the 'Nikola' books and the only one to be published in the period. The sinister doctor makes his first appearance in *A Bid for Fortune, or, Dr Nikola's Vendetta* (1895) as an immaculately dressed dinner host with a black cat perched inscrutably on his shoulder. He retains to the end of the series both his necromantic powers and his penchant for vendetta. Here he is encountered living in a crumbling palazzo in Venice by some old adversaries, Sir Richard and Lady Hatteras, who are accompanied by Miss Gertrude Trevor and her admirer, Lord Glenbarth. Nikola takes them on a tour of the hidden Venice (including, to establish the Doctor's beyond-the-law credentials, a sanctuary for Russian Nihilists); when Gertrude Trevor falls ill, he restores her to health. All the time, he weaves his spells on the company, and on a South American, Don Jose de Martinos, who promptly loses a fortune in the casino and the remnants of his sanity. It turns out that Don Jose is Nikola's long-lost stepbrother, who had tormented him horribly when he was a child and is thus his current object of revenge. After pleas from Hatteras and, to greater effect, Gertrude Trevor, Nikola spares Don Jose and retires to a monastery in Eastern Asia. Gertrude marries Lord Glenbarth.

Far Horizon, The, 'Lucas *Malet', 1906, Hutchinson. Dominic Iglesias, son of a Spanish anarchist, devotes his life to the care of his saintly mother. After her death, he moves to a *suburban lodging-house where he is exposed, for the most part happily, to the psychopathology of everyday petit bourgeois life. The story begins with his dismissal, at the age of 55, from his position as head clerk in a City bank. Immediately, his horizons broaden. He befriends Poppy St John, a resting actress with few moral scruples and a fine collection of toy spaniels, and invests money in the career of a fellow-lodger, De Courcy Smith, an aspiring playwright and accomplished drunkard. His responsibilities intensify when it emerges that Smith and St John, with whom he has fallen in love, are (estranged) husband and wife, and that she is the mistress of his ex-employer's son. However, he has by this time had his glimpse of the 'far horizon': the true (Catholic) faith. His religious conviction enables him to tolerate the increasingly loutish Smith, as well as a good deal of detrimental suburban gossip, while finding time to rescue his old firm from the consequences of bad management. Smith commits suicide, thus liberating Poppy St John, whose triumphant return to the stage coincides with Iglesias's death from heart disease. The story is set during the period of the *Boer War, and includes some compelling descriptions of turn-of-the-century London.

FARJEON, B. L.: Benjamin FARJEON (1833 or 1838–1903), who assumed the additional name Leopold, married (1877) Margaret JEFFERSON. Born in Whitechapel to a poor family of orthodox Jews, Farjeon decided at 13 to become a writer aged after reading *The Caxtons* (1849) by Edward Bulwer-Lytton (1802–1873). He worked on the *Noncomformist* as a printer's devil, at 4*s*. a week for a twelve-hour day. A sympathetic schoolmaster and an obliging bookseller helped with his education. At 17 he quarrelled with his parents over religion, borrowed £50 from an atheist uncle, and went to Australia. He even started a newspaper on the emigrant ship. There and subsequently in New Zealand, where he worked on the *Otago Daily Times*, he achieved moderate prosperity, began to write fiction, and dignified himself with the middle name Leopold. He had the ability, unusual among novelists, of being able to compose fiction in the act of setting it up in type. He sent a novel to Charles Dickens (1812–1870), whose very temperate letter of encouragement inspired Farjeon to return to London, where he spent the rest of his life as a quite successful and very prolific novelist, playwright, and journalist. Some of his early novels (which combine social criticism and melodrama in the Dickens tradition) achieved some critical success. But by the turn of the century his day was over, and his last novels are not distinguished. *The Pride of Race* (1901) is about a rich Jew who makes his son into a gentleman. In *The Mystery of the Royal Mail* (1902) Mabel loves the feckless Stephen but must marry his rich brother Andrew to save her father from ruin. There is a fraud, Andrew suspects her of adultery, and they part; only at the end is it revealed that Stephen stole the money, Mabel is guiltless, and the next generation can live happily ever after. *The Mesmerists* (1900) was published in a format proclaiming its originality: a novel and a play on the same subject between two covers. The plot depends on hypnotism, blackmail, and young love; the setting is Switzerland. Eleanor Farjeon (1881–1965), children's writer, Joseph Jefferson Farjeon (1883–1955), playwright, and Herbert Farjeon (1887–1945), playwright and critic, were his children.

FARNOL, [John] Jeffery (1878–1952) married, first (1900), Blanche V. W. HAWLEY (divorced 1938) and, secondly (1938), Phyllis CLARKE. Born in Birmingham, Farnol was the son of a brassfounder, and his first job was in that trade, but he lost it by hitting the foreman for calling him a liar. He then attended Westminster School of Art. He moved to America in 1902, and earned his living painting stage scenery and selling short stories. His first novel *The *Broad Highway* (1910), full of nostalgia for the English countryside, was written in America but published in England, where it proved successful. *The *Amateur Gentleman* (1913) is another Regency romance. Some of Farnol's novels are set in the eighteenth or nineteenth centuries; others in a mythical Middle Ages, which gave him the chance to describe fights in armour, of which he was a collector. His immediate model was probably Maurice *Hewlett, who also both worked in a Spenserian mode (*The Forest Lovers*, 1898) and wrote sprightly Regency social comedies (*The Stooping Lady*, 1907). Compared to other *historical novelists such as Stanley J. *Weyman and Agnes and Egerton *Castle, Farnol is vague about historical detail and depends more on erotic tension to animate his fiction. His heroes tend to be strong, silent and lacking in self-confidence. They resort to violence when rejected by his high-spirited heroines, who then crumple adoringly in response. Sententious peasants, prophetic fools and loyal retainers appear repeatedly; the style is marked by facetious humour and lavish use of stock archaisms.

FARR, Florence [Beatrice] (1860–1917) married (1884) Edward EMERY (*c*.1861–1938) (divorced 1895). Born in Bromley, Kent, the daughter of a physician and Assistant Registrar-General at Somerset House, she was educated at Cheltenham Ladies' College and Queen's College, Harley Street. After a brief, unsuccessful stint as a teacher, she went on the stage, first as 'Mary Lester' and then under her own name. She married an actor, but lived with him for only four years. She is now remembered for her affair with George Bernard Shaw (1856–1950) and her friendship with W. B. Yeats (1865–1939). Like the latter, she was a member of the Order of the Golden Dawn, and a good deal of her energy went into esoteric studies. Later, in 1902, she joined the Theosophical Society. Shaw complained that she did not pursue her career with enough concentration, but she was admired as an actress: she played Rebecca West in the first English performance of *Rosmersholm* in 1891, and was Louka in *Arms and the Man* (1894). She wrote the incidental music for Yeats's *Cathleen ni Houlihan* (1902) and for the translation of Euripides' *Hippolytus* by Gilbert Murray (1866–1957). She worked with Yeats on developing methods of chanting verse and gave performances of her technique. In 1907 she wrote a series of articles in the *New Age*. She also wrote two novels. In *The Dancing Faun* (1894), which came out in the Keynotes series, a New Woman shoots an unreliable actor who is supposed to be based partly on Emery and partly on Shaw. *The Solemnization of Jacklin* (1912), for whose publication she paid, also treats the difficulty of mature relationships between men and women. 'To me,' Farr states in the preface, 'the work of making the mind clear by first-hand experience is the holy alchemy of life. I call it solemnization; but I recognize it also under the mark of levity.' Jacklin solemnizes herself by divorcing one husband, marrying another, and then returning to the first. In 1912 Farr left England to become lady principal of a girls' school in Ceylon. Soon after retiring in 1916 she developed breast cancer; a mastectomy was followed by a relapse.

FAULDING, Gertrude Minnie (1875–1961). Born in London, she was educated in Switzerland and Germany and read modern languages at Somerville College, Oxford. She worked as a language coach and published, as well as verse and prose for children, two adult novels, both in collaboration with Lucy Dale, who later published history books. The first of these, *Time's Wallet* (1913), although not original in form or style, is of interest in that the characters are young, intellectual, progressive Liberal women. It is a correspondence between two women in their late 20s who have been at Somerville together (like the authors) and undertaken social work in Stepney. They discuss politics, women's lives, Bergson, and love affairs; and finally Nell (who writes children's books) makes Nan admit she is in love with the doctor who has gone to South America to forget her: all ends happily and conventionally.

Felix: *Three Years in a Life*, Robert *Hichens, 1902, Methuen. Felix Wilding, a handsome but rather dim 18-year-old from the provinces, arrives in London to make a life for himself and instead falls in love with an older married woman, Mrs Ismey, who, he eventually realizes, has an expensive morphia habit to keep up, sometimes with the help of his infatuation. Mrs Ismey has been introduced to the pleasures of morphia by the strong-willed Lady Caroline Hurst, who regularly injects not only herself but her maid and even her dog. While pining for her, Felix signs on at a 'school of journalism' run by the Dickensian Samuel Carringbridge, disciple of Macaulay and Froude, where he befriends the humbly aspiring Paul Chalmers (a precursor of Leonard Bast in E. M. *Forster's **Howards End*, 1910). Felix has a particular fondness for Mrs Ismey's beautiful arms; when she prepares to take off her long white gloves he has almost to be helped from the room. But he soon discovers that her hands are filthy—a result, he will learn, of the carelessness induced by her worsening addiction. All is revealed at the end of a tense holiday on the south coast, during which she keeps losing her 'cigarette-case'. Felix's mother falls ill. He can either stay with her while she undergoes major surgery, or accompany Mrs Ismey to Paris for a cure, as he had promised. He chooses his mother. Aleister Crowley (1875–1947) maintained in his autobiography that Hichens had based the shady chemist patronized by Mrs Ismey on E. P. Whineray, who 'knew all the secrets of London'.

feminist fiction. A significant proportion of the work published by women writers during the Edwardian period can best be considered as the second of three waves of feminist fiction which helped to determine the nature and scope of modern feminism: the first being the New Woman novels and stories of the 1890s, the third the self-consciously experimental modernist writing of the 1920s. The New Woman fiction of the 1890s turned on two issues: higher education and marriage. Its main impact stemmed from its imagining of a new freedom for women within, and sometimes beyond, marriage. In a famous polemic of 1896, Mrs Margaret Oliphant (1828–97) characterized the New Women writers as members of an 'anti-marriage league'. By that time, however, the impact of anti-marriage arguments was already beginning to wear off. On the whole, those arguments are by no means prominent in the later work of the New Women writers who continued to publish in the Edwardian period: Mrs Leith *Adams, Clementina *Black, E. *Brooke, Mary *Cholmondeley, Ella Hepworth *Dixon, Sarah *Grand, '*Iota'. Exceptions to the rule are Lady Florence *Dixie's *Izra: A Child of Solitude* (1906), Ménie Muriel *Dowie's **Love and His Mask* (1901), and **Flies in Amber* by 'George *Egerton'. (1905). As the impact of anti-marriage arguments wore off, or rather was diverted into a separate genre, the *marriage problem novel, another fundamental preoccupation emerged to take their place: economic independence. A notable feature of late-nineteenth-century Britain was the increase in the numbers of middle-class working women. In 1861 nearly 80,000 women were employed as teachers in England and Wales; by 1911 there were 183,000. Over the same period, the number of women employed as clerical workers rose from 279 to 124,000. The proportion of the total workforce holding white-collar jobs increased from 7. 6 per cent in 1861 to 14. 1 per cent in 1911; the proportion of women workers in those jobs increased from 5 per cent to 16. 4 per cent. For these women, labour was not only a means of survival but a source of dignity and independence. In *Women and Labour* (1911), the bible of the contemporary women's movement, Olive Schreiner argued that women must gain access to the new opportunities created by social and technological developments; those developments, she said, were the 'propelling force' behind the women's movement. Work became one of the two major themes of Edwardian feminist fiction. No longer the background to, or interruption of, lives shaped by romantic longing and fulfilment, work became itself the basis of identity. To be sure, the professions chosen by and for Edwardian heroines often involved plenty of scope for creativity: artist, writer, musician. But women doctors, nurses, teachers, journalists, secretaries, even the odd travel agent, became visible in fiction in a way they had never been before. Working-class careers are hard, but (and this in itself marks a change) not impossible to find. Edwardian writers who gave serious attention to women at work include Georgette *Agnew, Maude *Annesley, Helen *Ashton, Jane *Barlow, Olive *Birrell, Clementina *Black, M. McDonnell *Bodkin, Marguerite *Bryant, Mrs Vere *Campbell, Mary *Cholmondeley, 'Constance *Clyde', Ray *Costelloe, 'Victoria *Cross', 'Darley *Dale', Edith C. M. *Dart, Lillias Campbell *Davidson, C. A. *Dawson-Smith, Ellis *Dean, 'D. H. *Dennis', Claire *de Pratz, Sarah *Doudney, 'George *Egerton', Mrs Havelock *Ellis, Gertrude Minnie *Faulding, Mary and Jane *Findlater, Miles *Franklin, Walter M. *Gallichan, Louise *Gerard, Katharine Bruce *Glasier, Eleanor Hughes *Gibb, Lady *Gilbert, Maude *Goldring, Mrs Harold E. *Gorst, Francis *Gribble, Mabel Barnes *Grundy, Cicely *Hamilton, Helen *Hamilton, Lillias *Hamilton, 'M. *Hamilton', Mrs Mary *Hamilton, Marie *Harrison, Frances *Harrod, Ethel F. *Heddle, Jessie Leckie *Herbertson, Violet *Hunt, C. J. Cutcliffe *Hyne, A. M. *Irvine, Sheila *Kaye-Smith, Annesley *Kenealy, Arabella *Kenealy, Flora *Klickmann, Rosamond *Langbridge, Margaret *Legge, M. *Little, Ivy *Low, Mrs Belloc *Lowndes, Louise *Mack, Ethel Colburn *Mayne, F. M. *Mayor, Gladys *Mendl, 'Isabel *Meredith', Viola *Meynell, Jean *Middlemass, Florence *Montgomery, L. M. *Montgomery, 'Elinor *Mordaunt', Horace W. C. *Newte, Frederick *Niven, Alfred *Ollivant, A. *Perrin, Margaret *Peterson, John *Randal, Amber *Reeves, Mrs Baillie *Reynolds, W. Pett *Ridge, E. Gallienne *Robin, Berta *Ruck, Margaret Baillie *Saunders, Adeline *Sergeant, W. Teignmouth *Shore, Constance *Smedley, G. B. *Stern, Netta *Syrett, Violet *Tweedale, Katharine *Tynan, Nora *Vynne, Mrs Wilfrid *Ward, M. P. *Willcocks, 'Dolf *Wyllarde', and F. E. Mills *Young. The second major polemical focus of Edwardian feminist fiction, which emerged after the foundation of the Women's Social and Political Union in 1903, was the campaign for the vote. Significant suffragette fiction includes: Elizabeth *Robins, *The *Convert* (1907); Evelyn *Sharp, *Rebel Women* (1910); Annie S. *Swan, *Margaret Holroyd* (1910); 'G. *Colmore', **Suffragette Sally* (1911); Constance E. *Maud, **No Surrender* (1911). To make either work, or political commitment, or both, the theme of a novel was to put into question narrative fiction's traditional reliance on wedlock as a guarantee of formal closure. These novels have not only a new subject-matter, but a new shape. They are sometimes as radical in their implications as the writing of the female modernists, who, although more innovative formally, had on the whole little to say about work and political commitment. Of course, the radicalism of Edwardian feminist fiction should not be overstated. Many writers preferred to suspend the wedlock plot temporarily rather than to abolish it, allowing their heroines a brief professional or political canter before they reimposed the curb. But there were other ways to alter the balance of narrative forces within a novel or story. Arnold *Bennett said that in **Hilda Lessways* (1911), the second volume in the Clayhanger tetralogy, he wanted to convey 'the multitudinous activities of the whole [female] sex, against a mere background of masculinity'. The title of Agnes Grozier *Herbertson's *A Book Without a Man!* (1897) refers not to the novel itself, but to a novel written by one of the characters. However, a number of Edwardian writers came closer to achieving this ideal than Bennett: *Patricia, a Mother* (1905) by *'Iota', **Queer Lady Judas* (1905) by *'Rita', *Diaries of Three Women of the Last Century* (1907) by 'Evelyn *St Leger', Gladys *Mendl's *The Roundabout* (1911), Gertrude *Bone's *Women of the Country* (1913), Gertrude Minnie Faulding's *Time's Wallet* (1913), F. F. *Montresor's *The Strictly Trained Mother* (1913), Mrs Henry. *Dudeney's *What a Woman Wants* (1914), and May *Sinclair's *The Three Sisters* (1914). These novels anticipate the often noticed emphasis on women in later stories by 'Katherine *Mansfield'. Another strategy was to include in an otherwise traditional wedlock plot a minor character whose uncompromising independence the heroine admires but does not in the end want for herself. Examples would be Dorothy Edge in Olive *Birrell's **Love in a Mist* (1900), Lady Sarah Dorminster in Dowie's *Love and His Mask*, Mary Skelton in Penance (1901) by 'Leslie *Keith', Miss Adam in Mrs L. B. *Walford's *Stay-at-Homes* (1903), Eleanor West in Adeline *Sergeant's *Accused and Accuser* (1904), Ascot Wingfield in *A Pagan's Love* (1905) by 'Constance *Clyde', Jehane Bruce in Violet Hunt's *The Workaday Woman* (1906), Rosamund Ilbert in Rose *Macaulay's *Abbots Verney* (1906), Anne Yeo in Ada *Leverson's **Love's Shadow* (1908), Josie Lawrence in Ethel Colburn Mayne's *The Fourth Ship* (1908), Jane Mattock in George *Meredith's **Celt and Saxon* (1910), Margaret Rossiter in Willcocks's **Wings of Desire* (1912), and Lizzie Rand in Hugh *Walpole's *The *Duchess of Wrexe* (1914). The Edwardian period has often been presented as a hiatus in the development of feminist fiction. This is not the case.

FENN, Geo[rge] Manville (1831–1909) married (1855) Susanna LEAKE. Born in Pimlico, London, Fenn was educated at private schools and at the Battersea Training College for Teachers (1851–4). He taught in a school in Lincolnshire, and worked as a tutor and then as a printer. He founded *Modern Metre*, a magazine devoted entirely to poetry which failed in its first year (1862). A project for a local paper also failed. But in 1864 Dickens accepted a sketch for *All the Year Round* and other editors followed his lead. Fenn's sketches of working-class life, contributed to the *Star*, were collected as *Readings by Starlight*. In 1867 Fenn published two novels for children, and it was in this field that he became famous. He continued to work as a journalist and edited *Cassell's Magazine* and *Once a Week* in the 1870s. After 1881 he devoted himself to the production of fiction, including many boys' books which show Fenn's interest in natural history and science. A good example of his work in this vein is *Devon Boys* (1886). Set in north Devon in the 1750s, it describes the adventures of three boys who catch fish in a weir, discover a silver-mine by playing with gunpowder, are shown how to smelt it, get involved in smuggling, and have various narrow escapes from death. Fenn wrote a biography of his old friend and rival in this field, G. A. *Henty. There are, however, many adult novels among the just over a 100 volumes of fiction he published from 1866 onwards. In *The Cankerworm: Being Episodes of a Woman's Life* (1901) Lady Inveraigh is threatened with exposure by the villainous officer who deceived her as a 15-year-old schoolgirl with a false marriage. Fortunately, her husband forgives her for having married him without revealing her past, and a loyal old friend produces her long-lost son who is in love with her stepdaughter. Of the four tales in *The Bag of Diamonds and Three Bits of Paste* (1900) the most remarkable is the anti-feminist 'Eve at the Wheel: A Tale of Three Hundred Virgins' (originally published in *Fenn's Christmas Annual*, 1885). A ship carrying emigrant women to Australia is wrecked, and the doctor and the mate find themselves on a desert island with 300 women, led by a virago who attempts to take charge. However, since the men have the only guns, all the women are frightened of snakes, the virago is soon enslaved by love, and two loyal women are in love with the two officers, they do not have as much difficulty as might be expected in asserting the authority invested in them by both God and man.

Fifth Queen and How She Came to Court, The, Ford Madox *Hueffer, 1906, Alston Rivers. The Katharine Howard trilogy, Hueffer's first masterpiece, combines beautifully rendered romantic atmosphere with a profound meditation on the limits and pleasures of power. *The Fifth Queen* concerns Katharine's education in *Realpolitik*. Arriving at Greenwich Palace with her ruffianly cousin, Thomas Culpepper, in the middle of a riot, she soon loses sight of both him and the familiar world, and eventually succumbs to the vertigo of conspiracy (Hueffer's subject, as ever, is doubt, anxiety, incomprehension). Hueffer, who had been researching a biography of Henry VIII for several years, regarded his reign as the start of the modern world. In the trilogy, the King hovers uncertainly between Katharine, the idealistic upholder of the old faith, of feudal values, and Thomas Cromwell, the Lord Privy Seal, a religious and political reformer, a calculating if doggedly loyal exponent of 'kingcraft'. Hueffer declined to adjudicate between Puritanism and Catholicism, on the grounds that 'it will remain to the end a matter for dispute whether a practicable or an ideal code be the more beneficial to humanity'. The trilogy does not force any conclusion on the reader. *The Fifth Queen* was a modest success, selling 2,850 copies, and was followed by *Privy Seal: His Last Venture* (1907), which describes Cromwell's career and ultimate downfall, and *The Fifth Queen Crowned: A Romance* (1908), which concludes with Katharine's execution. Hueffer's aim, R. A. Scott-James observed in a review of the final volume of the trilogy in the *Daily News*, 'has nothing in common with that of the too well-known writers of roystering, gushful romance, who take a few historical facts and set them in a ridiculous halo of knight-errantry and heroic love and villainous intrigue. Nor, to put it on a higher plane, is his aim the same as that of a Walter Scott, who aims at showing the panorama and romantic movement of history. His object is nothing less than to combine the qualities of *historical romance with those of the modern school of realists and psychological novelists.' Joseph *Conrad called the trilogy the 'swan song of historical romance', adding, a little ambiguously, 'and frankly, I am glad to have heard it'.

FINDLATER, Mary [Williamina] (1865–1963) and Jane [Helen] (1866–1946) were the second and third daughters of the Free Church minister at Lochearnhead, Perthshire, where they were born. Their mother, Sarah Borthwick, wrote some religious works in collaboration with her sister Jane. They were educated by governesses, one of whom was the botanist and suffragist Annie Lorrain Smith (1854–1937). From childhood they were singularly devoted to each other, and Mary is supposed to have broken off her engagement on realizing that marriage would part her from Jane. Life at the manse was simple and restricted, but their father's death in 1886 meant severe isolation and indigence. Jane's first novel *The Green Graves of Blairgowrie* (1896) was written on paper discarded by the grocer. (She wrote as 'Jane Helen Findlater'; they wrote together as 'Mary and Jane Findlater'.) After its publication, the sisters' writing supported themselves, their mother and sister Sarah, called Mora, who worked as a nurse and suffered from mental illness. The sisters also had considerable social success in Edwardian literary circles; their many friends in England and America included Ellen Terry (1847–1928), Mary *Cholmondeley, and Mrs William James (1849–1922). They moved to the south of England for the sake of their mother's health, and lived in Cornwall and Devon until settling at Rye after the First World War. During the Second World War they retreated to Scotland once more. Mary Findlater's first novel was *Over the Hills* (1897). As well as collaborating with each other on six volumes, of which the first was *Tales That Are Told* (1901) and the most famous, **Crossriggs* (1908), the sisters wrote *The Affair at the Inn* (1904) and *Robinetta* (1911) with 'Allan *McAulay' and the American novelist Kate Douglas Wiggin (1856–1923). Jane's novel *The Story of a Mother* (1902) begins in the household of an autocratic and puritanical Church of Scotland minister, with a beautiful wife and a rebellious teenage son. Lord Ruxton is attracted to both the latter, and befriends the son. After the minister's death the boy disappears. He reappears, after seventeen years as a slave, to discover his mother married to Lord Ruxton. The themes of disillusionment, especially with marriage, and resentment at the restrictiveness of Scots life, especially for women, are typical of the sisters' work, as is the emphasis on small daily pleasures (nature, climate, food, children). Mary's *The Rose of Joy* (1903) is a more accomplished novel, which successfully contrasts a series of Scots households, in each of which women have difficult parts to play. The heroine makes an unsuccessful marriage which turns out to be invalid, and her child dies, but she finds fulfilment in art. The sisters' fiction explicitly rejects the idea that a single life is a wasted life. *Penny Monypenny*

(1912), a joint work, is an analysis of the upbringing and education of a young girl. She falls in love with her cousin Lorin, who is weak in health and erratic in temperament. He drifts into an affair with the West Indian wife of a neighbour and Penny's heart is broken. Her widowed mother has brought her up to make a love-match because she was herself disappointed, but has neglected to educate her for any career other than marriage. When Penny throws herself into social work and acquires external interests her problem is resolved. By the end both she and her mother have married and thrown off the past. There is a biography, drawing on unpublished correspondence, by Eileen Mackenzie (1964).

Finer Grain, The, Henry *James, 1910, Methuen. The five stories are on familiar Jamesian themes: modernity and tradition, the power of self-deception, the unpredictability of a talent for moral perception. In 'The Velvet Glove', John Berridge, an American writer on a European tour, encounters in a Parisian salon a glamorous English lord and his enchanting consort. He is disconcerted to find that the goddess writes trashy novels under the pen-name of Amy Evans. Still, he can hardly believe his luck when she invites him for an intimate drive, followed by supper at her house. But her motire is simply to persuade him to write a preface for the American edition of her latest effort, *The Velvet Glove*. 'Mora Montravers' concerns a *suburban couple, Sidney and Jane Traffle, their niece, Mora, and the painter she has taken up with, Walter Puddick. Mora turns out to be rather more worldly-wise than her anxious advisers; but the real surprise is the resoluteness and wisdom displayed by the wispy Jane. In 'A Round of Visits', Mark Monteith returns to New York after discovering that he has been swindled by his stockbroker, Phil Bloodgood; his round of visits implicates him in the suicide of another fraudster, Newton Winch. In 'Crapy Cornelia', the fogeyish White-Mason visits the *nouveau riche* Mrs Worthingham with a view to proposing to her. There he encounters a friend of his youth, recently returned to America, Cornelia Rasch. Beside Mrs Worthingham, Cornelia seems impossibly dowdy, but her presence reminds him of all that he would miss in a relationship with the latter: a shared sensibility, a shared history. In 'The Bench of Desolation', Herbert Dodd is threatened with a breach-of-promise suit when he transfers his affections from Kate Cookham to Nan Drury. He agrees to pay her £400, even though he believes that she doesnot care about him and has indeed been carrying on with another man. He raises £270, but the effort drains him, as does marriage to the nagging Nan. Kate Cookham reappears, and bestows £1,260 on the startled Herbert. She had taken his money, and done with it what he would never have done, because she really did love him. As in the comparable 'The Beast in the Jungle', in *The *Better Sort* (1903), a man recognizes, too late, a woman's superior insight.

FINNEMORE, E[mily] P[earson]: Eliza Emily PEARSON (b. 1863) married John *Finnemore. *From a Welsh Hillside* (1923) is a collection of short stories, some by him, some by her. Many of her eighteen volumes of fiction 1898–1909 were published by the Christian Knowledge Society and aimed at a juvenile audience. The *Spectator* review of *A King of Shreds and Patches* (1898) compared her with Mary E. Wilkins Freeman (1852–1930). It is a Hardyesque tale which follows the career of George Paxton, whose father has declined into poverty and drunkenness, from boyhood to early manhood. 'Old William Towel is one of the best rustics we know in fiction,' remarked the *Manchester Guardian*. *Tally* (1904), set in the early nineteenth century, has a similar feel. It is the story of the doomed love between a tailor's daughter, Tally Patson, and the local squire, Jack Stannion, whose philandering leads to his ruin; when he commits murder, Tally brings him to justice.

FINNEMORE, John (1863–1915) married E. P. *FINNEMORE. He wrote many textbooks and adventure stories for boys such as *A Captive of the Corsairs* (1906), *The Wolf Patrol: A Tale of Baden-Powell's Boy Scouts* (1908), *Three School Chums* (1907), biographical collections for children, and several volumes in the series 'Peeps at Many Lands' such as *Japan* (1907) and *Holland* (1912). The death-date is included on the assumption that he is the John Finnemore, author, of Tyissa, Llanfarian, Cardigan, who died 17 December 1915, the executrix being his widow, Eliza Emily Finnemore.

FIRBANK, Arthur [Annesley Ronald] (1886–1926). The son of a Welsh landowner and MP, grandson of a miner who made a fortune in the railway boom, Firbank was brought up in Kent. He was sent briefly to Uppingham and to an army crammer near Buxton. He began writing as a child, and as a schoolboy he collected the autographs of popular novelists, including 'Marie *Corelli', 'F. *Anstey', E. F. *Benson, and Mrs Edward *Kennard. He was sent to Tours for a year (1902–3) and travelled in Spain. He went up to Trinity Hall, Cambridge, in 1906. By this time he had published (as 'Arthur Firbank') two stories, 'La Princesse aux Soleils' and 'Harmonie' in *Les Essais* (Nov. 1904, Feb. 1905) and the volume containing the two short stories, *Odette d'Antrevernes (1905). While at Cambridge he published 'The Wavering Disciple' and 'A Study in Opal' in *Granta* (Nov. 1906, Jan. 1907). He converted to Roman Catholicism in 1907 and left Cambridge in 1909, without taking a degree, with some idea of trying to obtain employment in the Papal Guard. He spent the First World War in retirement in Oxford writing. *Vainglory* (1915) was the first of his books to be signed 'Ronald Firbank'. Subsequently he travelled: a visit to Haiti in 1922 provided material for the novel *Prancing Nigger* (1924). Perhaps his most celebrated novel is *Valmouth: A Romantic Novel* (1919): several works were published after his death from pneumonia. There is a biography (1969) by M. J. Benkovitz.

FIRBANK, Ronald: see Arthur *Firbank.

First Men in the Moon, The, H. G. *Wells, 1901, George Newnes. The novel, which Wells described as an 'imaginative spree', began life as a series of three interconnected short stories published in the **Strand* in 1900. The narrator, Bedford, an aspiring playwright, encounters Cavor, the inventor of a moon vehicle. The editor of the *Strand*, Greenhalgh Smith, was sufficiently impressed to commission further instalments, which are more didactic in tone. When they land, the travellers are captured by a tribe of moon-dwellers, the Selenites. The leading Selenite, the Grand Lunar, subjects Cavor to a penetrating interrogation; like the King of Brobdingnag in Swift's *Gulliver's Travels* (1726), he cannot comprehend what seems to him the folly of human arrangements. The travellers escape, but only one, Bedford, makes it back to earth. The remainder of the book consists of fragmentary messages from Cavor, who is still stranded on the moon. The messages die away 'into the Unknown—into the dark, into that silence that has no end'. The book was a considerable success. Wells thought it 'probably the writer's best "scientific romance"', chiefly on account of its close conformity to the astronomical knowledge and theory of the time.

FITZPATRICK, Sir Percy: James Peter FITZPATRICK (1862–1931), Kt. (1902), who changed his name to James Percy FITZPATRICK and married (1889) Elizabeth Lillian CUBITT (d. 1923). Born at King William's Town, Cape Colony, the son of an Irish Catholic judge in the South African Supreme Court, he was educated at Downside Abbey in England and at St Aidan's School, Grahamstown. After stints as bank clerk, storekeeper, transport-rider, and newspaper editor, he became prominent in the mining industry and in South African politics. He sought to reconcile the antagonism between Boer and British settlers and to create a unified South Africa. He is remembered for *Jock of the Bushveld* (1907). In this bestselling classic of *Empire fiction, FitzPatrick celebrates the dangerous and beautiful veld and its effect on those who travel it, such as the brave but drunken Jim Makokel, the Zulu who has fought at Isandhlwana and Rorke's Drift, and the narrator himself, who matures from ignorant boy to wise hunter in the course of the book.

FLANEUSE, *pseud.* Twenty volumes of fiction were published under this name between 1910 and 1930, ten of which were dated 1913 and published by A. M. Gardner & Co.; later titles have other publishers. The earliest in the *British Library Catalogue*, *Guilty Splendour* (1910), is ascribed to 'the author of *Chaos* etc.'. It is the story of an engaged couple who decide that marriage may destroy their love and so live together; she becomes a chorus girl, marries another, is found out by her forgiving husband, and lives happily ever after. This improving tale is a peg on which to hang much suggestive discussion of female sexual desire but little open description of sexual relations. The heroine of *Scored!* (1913) takes it on herself to revenge the wrongs of women by making fools of a series of men, and ends by falling in love and committing suicide. The pseudonym appears either as 'Flaneuse' or 'Flâneuse'. Works by Maud H. *Yardley and Elinor *Glyn were advertised together with the works under this name, which may cover the identity of more than one writer.

FLECKER, [Herman] James Elroy (1884–1915) married (1911) Helle SKIADARESSI. Born in Lewisham, London, the son of a Church of England clergyman, he was educated at Dean Close School, Cheltenham (of which his father was headmaster), Uppingham School, Trinity College, Oxford, where he read classics, graduating in 1906, and Caius College, Cambridge, where he studied oriental languages as a preparation for the consular service. He worked in Constantinople from 1910, and later in Beirut, but his service was interrupted by bouts of illness. In May 1913 he retired to Switzerland, where he died of tuberculosis. He is remembered for his verse and verse dramas: *Forty-Two Poems* (1911), *The Golden Journey to Samarkand* (1913), *Hassan* (1922). However, he also published two prose *fantasies in the period. *The Last Generation: A Story of the Future* (1908) is a dystopian vision of a world dominated by a tyrant, King Harris, and a contraceptive, Smithia. *The *King of Alsander* (1914) might be said to represent the swan-song of another popular Edwardian genre, the *Ruritanian romance.

FLETCHER, J[oseph] S[mith] (1863–1935) married Rosamond *LANGBRIDGE. Born in Halifax, the son of a Nonconformist minister, Fletcher went to Silcoates School. He was a journalist who contributed notes on rural life to the *Leeds Mercury*, the *Star*, the *Morning Leader*, *Vanity Fair*, and the *Daily Mail*. Between 1893 and 1898 he wrote leaders on the *Leeds Mercury*. *When Charles the First Was King* (1892), his first novel, was an old-fashioned *historical romance. He was a prolific author of local history and novels to 1935; he also wrote dialect poetry. Many of his later works are crime stories, and Kunitz and Haycraft state that they enjoyed some vogue in America because they were admired by President Woodrow Wilson (1856–1924). *Morrison's Machine* (1900) is the story of a young inventor whose unscrupulous employer takes advantage of his breakdown from overwork to claim the credit for his new machine. The inventor's loyal sister, her fiancé, and a crusading newspaper editor contrive to foil his scheme; the inventor recovers and the employer dies in the witness-box. In *The Three Days' Terror* (1901) Britain is held to ransom by a sinister group called the Dictators who have an effective extermination machine. *Mr. Poskitt* (1907) is a series of sentimental dialect sketches about a jolly, retired Yorkshire farmer, originally published in the *Daily Mail*, the *London Magazine* and *Cassell's Magazine*; it includes 'He Goes to a Wedding', 'An Old Fashioned Christmas', and 'He Plays Cricket'.

FLOWERDEW, Herbert (1866–1917) married (1890) Florence WATTS (b. 1863). Born at York, Flowerdew went to Nottingham High School. He published fourteen novels between 1897 and 1914. He stated in *Who's Who* that his recreation was the invention of mechanical toys. His widow's application to the Royal Literary Fund indicates that, never a prosperous writer, he found it difficult to sell his work after the First World War broke out, and at which stage he suffered a nervous breakdown. He went insane and may even have committed suicide. *Retaliation: A Novel* (1901) is an unsubtle exploration of class and gender issues. The hero is the descendant of a Roundhead, and when the squire's son kisses his sister he kisses the squire's daughter. Much later in London he is a well-known young author, his silly sister is still encouraging the young squire, and he himself embarks on an ill-thought-out campaign to seduce the squire's daughter, without realizing that she is far more oppressed than himself, penniless and fighting off an odious arranged marriage. *The Woman's View: A Novel About Marriage* (1903) is a *marriage problem tale with a complicated plot drawing attention to the inaccuracy with which the marriage laws relate to how people, especially women, feel about marriage. Valerie marries a fortune-hunter, and discovers he had a wife who was alive when they were married but is now dead. Philip, who has always loved her, tells her she is free, but she still feels married, and remarries her husband. He beats her and her baby dies as a result, so Philip rescues her. The husband sues for divorce on grounds of adultery, and so she is once more free, though she has not committed adultery. She marries Philip to save his political career, but refuses to sleep with him, as she still has a husband alive. Her cousin, who is in love with Philip, tells her she must: Valerie then responds by telling him to get an annulment and going back to her husband. As in *Retaliation*, Flowerdew sacrifices plausibility for the sake of his thesis. Flowerdew published an article, 'A Substitute for the Marriage Laws' in the *Westminster Review* (September 1899).

Flying Inn, The, G. K. *Chesterton, 1914, Methuen. The story opens on an island in the eastern Mediterranean, where Captain Patrick Dalroy, an Irish adventurer forced to resign his commission in the English navy on account of his Fenian sympathies, and now self-styled King of Ithaca and last opponent in Europe of Turkey's power, has been forced to accept a humiliating peace by the representative of the Great Powers, Lord Ivywood. On his return to England, Ivywood sets out to Moslemize the country, and passes an Act abolishing all inns except a very few, which remain as curiosities. Wherever an inn-sign still stands, alcohol can be sold lawfully. Dalroy visits his old friend, Mr Humphrey Pump, landlord of the 'Old Ship' at Pebbleswick, at the moment when Ivywood arrives with the police to evict him for contravening the law. Dalroy, a man of great strength, tears up the inn-sign, and he and Pump go forth, like Don Quixote and Sancho Panza, with a keg of rum, an enormous cheddar cheese, and the inn-sign, on an odyssey which concludes with the insurrection of the English people and the defeat of the Moslem army Ivywood has been gathering on his estate. *The Flying Inn* at once derides the contemporary vogue for *invasion scare stories and attacks some familiar targets. As the **Times Literary Supplement* pointed out, it 'dresses up in a vague allegory Mr Chesterton's favourite ideas that England is going to the dogs, that the good old religion is dead, that Asiatics are getting too much influence, and that we shall not be ourselves again till the good old English countryside is what it used to be and old-fashioned inns, not tied to brewers, are kept by "mine hosts" of the "Tabard" description, and the good old, bluff old, hardy old, sturdy old English spirit, with its mine of country lore and its contempt for books, once more takes the lead to the confusion of aesthetes, politicians, poets, Jews, and sentimentalists'. But once the adventures of the sign get under way, punctuated by Dalroy's doggerel songs, satire becomes subordinate to the pleasures of invention. As the *Observer* put it, Chesterton 'either abolishes liquor in Great Britain for the sake of pointing the inconveniences of Turkish domination, or else hands over this country to the Porte for the sake of depriving it of beer'.

Following Darkness, Forrest *Reid, 1912, Edward Arnold. Narrative of the adolescence of Peter Waring, a celebrated art critic, supposedly edited by one of his friends, Owen Gill. Peter is the gifted, clumsy son of David Waring, a puritanical teacher who runs a school in Newcastle, Co. Down, and whose wife left him some years before; he has the run of Derryaghty, a nearby house belonging to the recently widowed Mrs Carroll. Recognizing Peter's gifts, Mrs Carroll plans to send him to university at her own expense. Derryaghty, with its splendid library, its portraits, and its attic full of exotic lumber, feeds Peter's mysticism, and his dissatisfaction. An acute attack of scarlatina, around the time of his 16th birthday, marks a watershed in his life. 'The memory of my convalescence is a strange one, for it came at a time when certain physical changes were taking place within me, and I seemed to myself to be somehow different from what I had been before I fell ill.' Mrs Carroll invites two young relations, Katherine and Gerald Dale, to visit Derryaghty for the summer. Peter is attracted to Katherine, and fascinated by the more complex and consistently ironical Gerald. At the end of the summer, he moves to Belfast, to lodge with his unglamorous uncle and aunt, George and Margaret McAllister, who keep a shop, while he attends school. His fastidiousness is tested to the limit by their son, whose room he shares, and whose 'licentious imagination' encompasses boxing-matches and pornographic photographs. At school he becomes friendly with a fellow-pupil, Owen Gill, and invites him to Newcastle for part of the next summer. Owen is an alarming success with Katherine. Owen departs, but Peter can no longer conceal from himself that she is indifferent to him. Uncle George, meanwhile, has accused him of corrupting young George. Appalled by the squalor which surrounds him, and feeling a complete failure, Peter tries to kill himself by staying out all night in a storm. He falls ill on schedule, but is nursed back to health by Mrs Carroll. She at least will never abandon him. The novel was dedicated to E. M. *Forster, and revised in 1937 as *Peter Waring*.

Food of the Gods, The, H. G. *Wells, 1904, Macmillan. Wells later described the book, with a portentousness belied by its deft comic touches, as 'the most complete statement of the conception that human beings are now in violent reaction to a profound change in conditions demanding the most complex and extensive readjustments in the scope and scale of their ideas'. Two cautious and incompetent scientists, Mr Bensington and Professor Redwood, discover a miracle nutrient which they name Herakleophorbia. Purchasing an experimental farm in Kent, they breed giant chickens (and, inadvertently, due to the sloveliness of their research assistants, Mr and Mrs Skinner, giant wasps, earwig and rats). Then they start administering the food to their own children and, again inadvertently, to Mrs Skinner's grandson, Albert Edward Caddles. The children grow into a race of giants, who envisage a reformed world under their benevolent control. Wells describes brilliantly the violent reaction to this terrifying new possibility. 'And since it is easier to hate animate than inanimate things, animals more than plants, and one's fellow men more completely than any animals, the fear and trouble engendered by giant nettles and six-foot grass blades, awful insects and tiger-like vermin, grew all into one great power of detestation that aimed itself with a simple directness at that scattered band of great human beings, the Children of the Food.' A Tory politician, John Caterham, harnesses that 'power of detestation'. He suggests that the Children of the Food should be transported to a reservation in North America or Africa. The Children refuse to submit. 'We will scatter the Food; we will saturate the world with the Food.' The book combines the narrative *élan* of Wells's early scientific romances with the allegorical scope of his subsequent 'fiction about the future'.

FORBES, Lady Angela: Angela Selina Bianca ST CLAIR-ERSKINE (1876–1950) married (1896) James Stewart FORBES (1872–1957) (divorced 1906) and resumed her maiden name by deed poll (1929). Elinor *Glyn claimed to have based the heroine of *The *Visits of Elizabeth* (1900) on Lady Angela, whose photograph appears facing the title-page. Much the youngest of her upper-class family, she married an army officer and had two daughters, but the marriage broke down. 'Quite frankly, I am afraid it was a commercial rather than a literary instinct which prompted me to first take up my pen,' she wrote in her memoirs (1922). *The Broken Commandment* (1910) was 'banned by the libraries' and the reviewer in the *Times* called it 'a compound fracture of the seventh commandment'. Its heroine, Lady Peggy Dennison, finds sex with her husband John repellent, so he becomes a spendthrift. Edgerton, a businessman, gives John a job and then forces Peggy to be his mistress. This is a success: Peggy learns about current affairs, John about business life. Then Peggy is sexually awakened by a man unhappily married to a rich woman, who finds out and blackmails him into returning to her. John consoles the bereft and pregnant Peggy. Self-consciously advanced about sex and marriage, the novel, though implausible, is written with some verve. Forbes was a member of the 'Souls' circle and published later novels, two volumes of pot-boiling memoirs (1922, 1934) and non-fiction such as *How to Dress* (1926). Her sister Millicent, Duchess of Sutherland (1867–1955), a close friend of 'Anthony *Hope', published a novel (1899) about socialist agitators during a strike, and volumes of short stories in 1902 and 1925. Their brother, the 5th Earl of Rosslyn (1869–1939), went on the stage, playing the first Arthur Gower in *Trelawny of the Wells* (1898); he was grandfather of the playwright Nell Dunn (b. 1936).

FORBES, Lady Helen: Helen Emily CRAVEN (1874–1926) married (1901) Ian Rose-Innes Joseph FORBES (1875–1957). The daughter of the 3rd Earl of Craven, she was a Roman Catholic and educated at home. She wrote three novels as 'Lady Helen Craven', starting with *Katherine Cromer* (1897), and six under her married name. *It's a Way They Have in the Army* (1905) is a denunciation of the system of promotion by favour in the army, told as the story of an earl's daughter who marries an army officer and goes with him to India, where she endures the vulgarity of his colleagues and their wives. *The Bounty of the Gods* (1910) and its sequel *The Polar Star* (1911) trace the fortunes of Frazco Ximantes, son of a noble Spanish father and an English mother. He and his brothers are brought up by their Yorkshire squire uncle, but Frazco, torn between various influences, after various emotional entanglements, becomes a great singer, and *déclassé*. In the sequel he marries an earl's daughter and their son inherits the Yorkshire estate. The themes are religion, class, and sex. In the second book, Frazco's wife's ignorance about sex and her awakening are treated openly and sympathetically. Forbes's characterization and plots are conventional, but her dialogue is intelligent and humorous. Her two sons became priests and two of her four daughters nuns.

FORBES, The Hon. Mrs Walter R. D.: Eveline Louisa Michell FARWELL (1866–1924) married (1888) Walter Robert Drummond FORBES (1865–1929). Educated at home, she published nine novels between 1889 and 1918. *A Gentleman* (1900) is set in English high society in Italy, London, and Australia. Raymond has been brought up as an English gentleman, and only when he wishes to marry a peer's beautiful daughter is it revealed that his widowed mother has paid for this by her earnings as a fashionable dressmaker. His allies get him a job in Australia, where in a very short space of time he makes good and marries his inamorata. The theme of dress is quite artfully integrated into the analysis of class distinctions: Forbes really concludes that money is the crucial factor, and does not seem unduly disturbed. The plot suggests parallels with *Mrs Warren's Profession* (1898) by G. B. Shaw (1856–1950) and Jeffery *Farnol's *An *Amateur Gentleman*. *Dumb* (1901) is a badly constructed novel about an unsuccessful marriage; its plot takes in a Scottish castle, the Swiss Alps, and the North-West Frontier of India. Aileen Conyngham marries quickly and regrets at length, until her husband dies, and she can express her love for another man. The best scenes satirize a proud Scots family. Forbes was fond of single-word titles like this, e. g. *Blight* (1897), *Unofficial* (1902), and *Nameless* (1909). The last is set between Scotland, London, and Africa, but finds its two heroines in Tullymore House, where a philosophical lady novelist called 'Cecil Grey' has installed herself as a guest of Sir Philip and Lady Ierne Lynford, and Tullymore Village, where the carpenter's daughter marries tragically. Forbes also published articles on palmistry in the *New Review*.

FORD, Ford Madox: see Ford Madox *Hueffer.

FOREMAN, Stephen lived in Cork, Ireland, and was the author of a volume of verse (1895) and three novels. *The Overflowing Scourge* (1911) is the story of a wicked Irish judge and the consequences of his sins. The **Times Literary Supplement* was surprised by the number of references to hell, and the *Irish Book Lover* observed that it was 'not written *virginibus puerisque*'. *The Fen Dogs* (1912) is dedicated to the memory of Abraham Thornton, who was charged with murder in 1817, and became the last man to assert his right to trial by battle. Set in the period of the Napoleonic wars, it concerns two soldiers, one of whom deserts before Corunna and brings home a Spanish maiden. *The Terrible Choice* (1913) features an alcoholic husband who masters his vice out of respect for his wife.

FORESTIER-WALKER, Clarence [Francis] (1857–1907) married (1891) Blanche Lancaster CLARK (d. 1933). Third of the eight sons of a baronet, he wrote six novels between 1900 and 1908. He published two translations from French, of which *The Romance of the Harem* (1901) is a curious account of harem life, ostensibly from personal knowledge, though richly implausible, which argues that women are happier immured. His novel *The Silver Gate* (1902) is also about the oppression of women. Evelyn escapes from her father into an unhappy marriage; when she is widowed she is blackmailed, but a noble friend shoots the blackmailer dead. *The Chameleon* (1908) is about an orphaned girl, living with a kind, mannish woman cousin, who makes friends with a beautiful Russian princess, Marie. When the heroine becomes pregnant, Marie behaves wonderfully well; later she becomes obsessively jealous of Sir Cosmo Grantley, and commits suicide when he finally elopes with the girl. The novel hints constantly at lesbianism, without ever dealing with it openly.

FORREST, R[obert] E[dward Treston] (d. 1914) married Mary Evangeline WILD. He was the elder son of an officer in the Bengal Artillery who was awarded the VC for defending the magazine at Delhi in 1857 and died soon afterwards. His mother took her children (who also included the historian of British India, Sir George Forrest, 1845–1926) home to England to be educated. Robert Forrest worked in the Irrigation Branch of the Indian Office of Public Works and designed canals; he was also interested in Indian antiquities and contributed to the Asiatic *Quarterly Review*. After retirement he published novels including *Eight Days* (1891) and *The Sword of Azrael* (1903), both of which are heart-rending *historical romances about the Indian Mutiny from the Anglo-Indian point of view.

FORSTER, E[dward] M[organ] (1879–1970), CH (1953), OM (1959), was registered at birth as 'Henry Morgan FORSTER' but by mistake was christened and always afterwards known as 'Edward Morgan'. His father, an architect, was descended from members of the high-minded, rich, influential Clapham Sect; his mother was the daughter of a poor artist, and had been trained as a governess and patronized by Marianne Thornton (1797–1887), who was aunt to Forster's father and whose biography he published in 1957. The year after Forster's birth his father died of tuberculosis. His mother went to live at Stevenage, where Forster grew up, surrounded by solicitous women. She moved to Tonbridge, so that he could go as a day-boy to the public school there, in 1893. He then went to King's College, Cambridge, where he was influenced by G. Lowes Dickinson (1862–1932) and Roger Fry (1866–1934) and joined the 'Apostles'. At this time he met several of those who were later to form the 'Bloomsbury Group'. On graduating, uncertain of his career, he travelled in Italy (1901–2) with his mother, an experience he found liberating in a way which colours his first novel, **Where Angels Fear to Tread* (1905), and several of the short stories of this period. On his return he began to give classes at the Working Men's College in London. He travelled again in 1903 in Italy and Greece, and on his return contributed to the *Independent Review* (later the *Albang Review), which started in October. In 1905 he spent a period, as Hugh *Walpole did after him, as tutor to the daughters of '*Elizabeth' in Pomerania, which, despite her autocratic ways, he enjoyed. After the publication of his Cambridge novel, *The *Longest Journey* (1907), he spent the summer with 'Elizabeth' and her daughters on the caravanning trip on which she gathered material for *The *Caravanners*. *A *Room with a View* (1908), on which he had been working since 1902, increased his reputation, and **Howards End* (1910) was still more successful. *The *Celestial Omnibus and Other Stories* (1911) was illustrated by Roger Fry. In 1912 he wrote a few chapters of *Arctic Summer*, a novel which was never completed. In 1912–13 he travelled to India, where he visited Sara Jeannette *Duncan. The conception of *Maurice* (completed 1914, published 1971), a novel in which Forster wrote explicitly about homosexual experience, was affected by his meeting with Edward Carpenter (1844–1929), author of *The Intermediate Sex* (1908). Early in the First World War there was an abortive project for a book about Samuel *Butler. He spent 1915–19 in Alexandria, working for the Red Cross, where he made friends with the poet C. P. Cavafy (1863–1933), one of many writers whose work he championed. This period was important for him emotionally: he had a love affair with an Egyptian tram conductor which was more satisfactory than the earlier awkward passions for men of his own class, such as H. O. Merriman and Syed Ross Masood (1889–1937). On his return to England he worked at literary journalism and became a member of the Memoir Club, to which many Bloomsbury Groupers belonged. He spent 1921–22 in India as secretary to the Maharajah of Dewas Senior. On the return journey he was already working on the novel published as *A Passage to India* (1924). Its success, coinciding with a legacy from an aunt, meant that henceforward he felt well off. His 1927 Clark Lectures at Cambridge, published as *Aspects of the Novel*, reached a wide audience; he also broadcast for the BBC on literary subjects. A long and possibly unconsummated relationship with a policeman, Bob Buckingham, gave him emotional stability from the 1930s to his death. He refused a knighthood in 1945, and accepted in 1946 an honorary fellowship at King's College, Cambridge, which was his home for the rest of his life. He was devoted to the cause of freedom and free speech, twice serving as President of the National Council for Civil Liberties, and trying to prevent both *The Well of Loneliness* (in 1928) and *Lady Chatterley's Lover* (in 1960) from being banned. There is a fine biography by P. N. Furbank (1977, 1978).

FORSTER, R[obert] H[enry] (1867–1923) married (1912) Margaret Hope PAYNE. Born near Newcastle upon Tyne, the son of a mining engineer, he went to Aysgarth School, Harrow School, and St John's College, Cambridge. He was called to the Bar in 1892. *The Newcastle Daily Chronicle* commented, 'As Mr Hardy knows Wessex, as Mr Crockett knows Galloway, and as Mr Blackmore knew Exmoor, so does Mr Forster know Northumberland.' Forster was an expert on Romano-British archaeology, who wrote verse and sentimental, faintly facetious, historical novels set in the Scots Borders. *Strained Allegiance* (1905) is the diary of Cuthbert Belton during the 1715 rebellion. He is Church of England, and has some fascinating cousins who are Roman Catholic, one of whom he eventually marries. The plot is heavily indebted to *Waverley* (1814) by Walter Scott (1771–1832). *The Arrow of the North* is set in the same area in the reign of Henry VII.

Fortitude: *Being a True and Faithful Account of the Education of an Explorer*, Hugh *Walpole, 1913, Martin Secker. Walpole's fifth novel, and the one intended to establish his claim to seriousness, is a leaden refashioning of Dickens's *David Copperfield* (1850). Peter Westcott, raised by a brutal drunken father and a neurotic mother on the Cornish coast, finished at a scarcely less intimidating public school in Devon, never has his troubles to seek. Escaping to London after a furious quarrel with his father, he finds work in a bookshop owned by a mysterious but unfailingly boisterous foreigner, Emilio Zanti. After seven years he has met his future wife, the pretty but empty-headed Clare Rossiter, sustained a literary friendship with a consumptive fellow-boarder, Norah Minogue, and completed his first novel. The modest success of the novel enables him to marry. Thereafter it is downhill all the way. The marriage fails, as do his next two novels. Norah dies, after declaring her love and exhorting him to struggle on. The reviewers declared that Walpole was a deep-dyed romantic, rather than the realist he supposed himself to be. But the curious thing about Peter Westcott, who is consistently characterized as an 'Explorer', not a 'Stay-at-home', is his inertness. Zanti's bookshop is the setting for an anarchist plot, complete with bombs and soulful Russians, which he fails to notice, never mind take part in. He is so boring that his wife elopes with his best friend, the Steerforthian Jerry Cardillac. Still, *Bennett and *Galsworthy were polite about the novel, while Henry *James prevaricated charmingly.

FOULIS, Hugh: see Neil *Munro

Four Feathers, The, A. E. W. *Mason, 1902, Smith, Elder. Harry Feversham, a sensitive young man forced to follow the family tradition of military service, resigns his commission, ostensibly because of his engagement to Ethne Eustace, but in fact because he has heard that his regiment is shortly to be sent to Egypt, where it is likely to see action. When his brother-officers, Trench, Willoughby, and Castleton, realize his motive, they send him three white feathers to mark his cowardice; dismissing him, Ethne adds a fourth. Confiding only in an elderly and sympathetic friend of his father, Lieutenant Sutch, Harry sets off for Egypt to win back the respect of his friends. Castleton is killed in battle, but Harry earns the gratitude and admiration of Willoughby and Trench by performing acts of great bravery. Meanwhile, his devoted friend, Jack Durrance, unaware of Harry's disgrace, courts Ethne, and wins her after he has been blinded by sunstroke. The love that Ethne feels for him is in fact pity, and as soon as the feathers have been returned, he withdraws, leaving her, and the glory, to Harry. Mason's achievement is to combine a story of enablement with a story of disablement. Harry Feversham redeems himself, and carries off all the available prizes. Jack Durrance goes blind, and loses everything. The novel is as definite and incontestable about loss as it is about gain, refusing to allow enablement to supersede or conceal disablement. In its most moving scene, Durrance, now blind, retires to his study—which, as befits a man of action, is more of a gun-room—and runs his hands over the trophies which make the room 'a gigantic diary'. The final scene is not of Feversham's triumph, but of Durrance leaning over the rail of a steamer anchored in Port Said, picturing to himself 'the flare of braziers upon the quays, the lighted portholes, and dark funnels ahead and behind in the procession of the anchored ships'.

Four Just Men, The, Edgar *Wallace, 1905, Tallis Press. The four just men are Gonsalez, Poiccart, and Manfred, wealthy citizens of the world who have pledged themselves to revenge injustices which the law has overlooked, and Thery, a thuggish Spanish peasant whom they have hired for a particular job. This is to prevent the British Parliament passing a bill which would permit the extradition of aliens, if necessary by assassinating the minister responsible, the Foreign Secretary, Sir Philip Ramon. Wallace's interest is not in the Just Men's politics, but in their methods: the expertise, the ruthlessness, the meticulously observed protocol of warnings. The police take every possible step to protect Sir Philip. But he is none the less murdered at the exact moment and in the exact place predicted by the assassins. This, then, is not a whodunnit but a how-could-they-possibly-have-done-it. The first edition concludes with an invitation to readers to solve a mystery which the book itself does little to clear up.

Fourth Generation, The, Walter *Besant, 1900, Chatto & Windus. A shorter version of this, Besant's most ambitious novel (and his personal favourite), was published in the *Humanitarian* in 1899. It opens with an old man pacing the terrace of a dilapidated country house in Buckinghamshire. He is Algernon Campaigne. For seventy years, since the unsolved murder of his brother-in-law and best friend, Langley Holme, in 1829, and his wife's death on the same day, he has not uttered a word to anyone. The mysterious event which drove him into silence appears to have laid a curse on the subsequent three generations of the family: accident, suicide, bankruptcy, unfortunate marriage, a catalogue of sins and crimes. The narrative follows the efforts of the old man's great-grandson, Leonard Campaigne, a rising lawyer and politician, to unravel the mystery. Leonard is an honourable man, and entirely ignorant of the stain on the family honour, but proud and self-absorbed. The nature and extent of the stain is brought home to him by the arrival of a stream of importunate and untrustworthy relatives: Uncle Fred, a drunken conman who has returned from Australia to float a bogus company on the Stock Exchange; Uncle Christopher, apparently a successful barrister, but in fact the writer of other men's after-dinner speeches; a cousin, Algernon, a bohemian wastrel; and another cousin, Sam Galley-Campaigne, a down-at-heel solicitor anxious for a share of the 'accumulations' from their great-grandfather's estate. With the help of Constance Ambry, an independent young woman living in the flat opposite his, Leonard establishes that the patriarch himself committed the murder, after a vicious quarrel with his brother-in-law, and has been expiating his sin ever since. When Constance, who is in fact Langley Holme's great-granddaughter, confronts the old man, he confesses, and then dies. Leonard emerges from the experience a better man, and Constance, who had earlier declined his offer of marriage, admits that she fallen in love with him. The novel's seriousness derives from its treatment of the inheritability of moral and social characteristics, a topic much debated at the time. Leonard concludes that 'the liability to temptation—the tendency—is inherited, but the necessity which forces a man to act is not inherited; that is due to himself'. The novel combines the plot of a crime story with Dickensian motifs: Algernon Campaigne's life has been arrested as abruptly and completely at the moment of trauma as Miss Havisham's, in *Great Expectations* (1861); Sam Galley-Campaigne bears a striking resemblance to the turbulent petit bourgeois blackmailers of *Bleak House* (1853).

FOWLER, Edith Henrietta (1865–1944) married (1903) William Robert HAMILTON (1869–*c.*1953). Younger and less well-known sister of Ellen Thorneycroft *Fowler, her novels similarly deal with the romantic problems of high-minded, politically active, Christian members of the upper class. *For Richer For Poorer* (1905) is a *Little Lord Fauntleroy* tale, about a young girl who reforms a selfish old clergyman by believing that he embodies every Christian virtue. In *Patricia* (1915) a girl brought up in a careless bohemian household is writing the life of her father, an unscrupulous journalist, and includes some disloyal letters written by the dead Lord Wellingborough. Before the book comes out she has fallen in love with his son and successor, an Evangelical clergyman. His forgiveness of her is both an image of Christ's mercy and an opportunity for this Cinderella to become a peeress. As in her sister's novels, the combination of snobbishness and spirituality is actieved with considerable polish. The way that publication of a book becomes an act of transgression for which the heroine must atone is borrowed from her sister's *Concerning Isabel Carnaby* (1898). Fowler herself wrote an extremely devout biography (1912) of their own father and, in the 1890s, three witty children's books. She was married to a Church of England clergyman.

FOWLER, Ellen Thorneycroft (1860–1929) married (1903) Alfred Laurence FELKIN (1856–1942). The elder daughter of the Liberal politician H. H. Fowler (1830–1911), created (1908) 1st Viscount Wolverhampton, she was brought up in the Church of England, although her father was the first Methodist to be made a peer: many of her novels have Nonconformist settings. Her first and successful novel, *Concerning Isabel Carnaby* (1898), describes the attempts of an ambitious young man from a provincial and Dissenting household to woo a clever but worldly society girl. Christian Liberal in her social attitudes, Fowler's heroines are usually too talkative and self-confident for their own good. Isabel Carnaby breaks off her engagement because she doesn't care to be dictated to, but by the end, well chastened, has asked for the hero's forgiveness. A sequel, *In Subjection* (1906), articulates even more clearly the message that radical politics should not lead to radical sexual politics. Isabel, now married, goes wrong when she tries to obtain her husband a job without consulting him; her protégée, a half-Indian girl, only realizes she loves her gentle husband when, deceived by her male disguise, he beats her up. *Kate of Kate Hall* (1904), written in collaboration with her new husband, a schools inspector, takes *The Taming of the Shrew* as a model of the ideal sexual relationship. The merits of Fowler's books are their humour and lively dialogue. Many are set in government circles.

FOX, Marion [Inez Douglas] (b. 1885) married (1914) Stephen Burman WARD. Born in Aldershot, daughter of an army officer, she published seven volumes of fiction 1910–28. *The Seven Nights: A Journey* (1910), her first novel, is a medieval romance set against the background of the Peasants' Revolt. *The Hand of the North* (1911) and *The Bountiful Hour* (1912) are *historical romances, the former set in London and Northumberland in Elizabeth's reign, the latter in Olney during the life of William Cowper (1731–1800). **Ape's-Face* (1914), set in Wiltshire, takes the historical imagination as its subject-matter. Fox lived in Paris.

FOX-DAVIES, A[rthur] C[harles] (1871–1928) married (1901) Mary E. B. CROOKES. A barrister, born in Bristol and educated in Yorkshire, Fox-Davies was in his time one of the greatest experts on English heraldry and genealogy, and edited *Burke's Peerage* and *Dod's Landed Gentry.* He also wrote novels, many of which are *crime stories which reveal his preoccupations. In *The Mauleverer Murders* (1907) the controller of the Russian secret service advises Dennis Yardley, the famous English detective, 'My friend, if you desire to succeed in your profession, I strongly advise you to study genealogy.' In fact it turns out that the elaborate and romantic inheritance plot is a false trail: Colonel Mauleverer's five sons have been murdered one by one not so that the Duchess of Merioneth can claim the throne of the Czars but because her maid, the Colonel's cast-off mistress, wants revenge on him for having her (and his) twin sons shot in a court martial. In *The Dangerville Inheritance: A Detective Story* (1907) Yardley turns up again, along with the brilliant barrister, Ashley Tempest, who has married the Duchess. The mysterious Lord Dangerville calls them in when he receives threatening letters: by the end he is revealed as a woman in disguise. Fox-Davies's preposterous plots depend a good deal on women being mistaken for one another, being identical, or, as it were, interchangeable. *The Testament of John Hastings* (1911) draws on his experience fighting the 1910 election at Merthyr Tydvil against Keir Hardie (1856–1915).

FRANCIS, M. E., *pseud.*: Mary SWEETMAN (1859–1930) married (1879) Francis Nicholas BLUNDELL (1853–84). The sister of Agnes *Castle, she was born into a landowning Catholic family living near Dublin, and educated by governesses and in Brussels. The novelist Walter Sweetman (1830–1905) was her uncle. Her husband was a younger son of a old Lancashire recusant family who lived at Crosby, near Liverpool, and he took her to live there. The Ireland of her youth, the Lancashire of her married life, and the Dorset of her retirement provided backgrounds for many of her fifty-two volumes of fiction, some of which were published with the pseudonym alone, some with the explanatory 'Mrs Francis Blundell'. *The Manor Farm: A Novel* (1902) is about two cousins in a farming family, Beulah and Reuben, who rebel against the family order that they should marry, but then fall in love after all. *Christian Thal: A Novel* (1903) is set mostly on the Continent, and attempts to express the relation between 'artists' and the rest of society. Juliet is the impressionable daughter of a professor, and falls in love with a brilliant young musician. *Dorset Dear* (1905), *Simple Annals* (1906), and *Stepping Westward* (1907) are collections of short stories (or 'Country Idylls') with Dorset subjects. Like all pastoral, Francis's novels introduce and resolve class conflict. In *Wild Wheat* (1905), a well-to-do yeoman takes a job as underkeeper out of love for the young lady of the hall; in *Galatea of the Wheatfield* (1909), a young undergraduate, Gerald Bannister, courts a milkmaid, Tabitha Bolt. *Lychgate Hall* (1904) is a *historical romance set in the North Country in the early years of the eighteenth century. The **Times Literary Supplement* felt that there could be little wrong with a romance 'when it is told by a sturdy lad with a horse of his own and the first chapter is entitled "The Stranger"'. Like *The Wild Heart* (1910), the novel was serialized in the Weekly Edition of the *Times*. Her output was tremendous; other works from the first decade of the twentieth century are *Fiander's Widow* (1901), *North, South and Over the Sea* (1902), *The Manor Farm* (1902), *Margery of the Mill* (1907), *Hardy-on-the-Hill* (1908), and *The Tender Passion* (1910). Blundell continued to publish novels after the First World War, and also collaborated with her daughters Margaret Blundell (1882–1964) and Agnes Blundell (1884–1966).

FRANKLIN, [Stella Maria Sarah] Miles (1879–1954). Born at Talbingo, New South Wales, eldest child in a downwardly mobile farming family, she was educated at home and at Thornford Public School. Until she was 10 she lived in the outback, described in her memoir *Childhood at Brindabella* (1963). She tried teaching and nursing before finding her career with the success of her first novel, the innovative and subversive **My Brilliant Career* (1901). Written at the age of 16, it describes a girl's successful struggle against a conventional marriage. A sequel, *My Career Goes Bung*, was written in 1902, rejected by the publisher on the grounds that its portrait of literary society in Sydney was libellous, and was not published until 1946. Franklin, who objected to the assumption that her first novel was wholly autobiographical, refused to allow it to be republished in her lifetime. *Some Everyday Folk and Dawn* (1909) is another idiosyncratic feminist novel, dedicated to 'English *men* who believe in votes for *women*', pointing out that her Australian women characters have had the vote since 1902. The invalid actress narrator lodges with Dawn's grandmother and observes how women are exploited by men and invite their own subjection. Another lodger commits suicide and the women unite to tar her seducer. The novel ends rather lamely, though, with Dawn's marriage to a rich man. Franklin left Australia for America in 1906, where she worked in the women's trade union movement, leaving for England in 1915. She published *The Net of Circumstance*, in London, as 'Mr and Mrs Ogniblat L'Artsau', in the same year. In 1917 she served in a medical unit in the Balkans. She returned to Australia in the late 1920s, where she wrote novels both under her own name and under the pseudonym 'Brent of Bin Bin', and became an important supporter of Australian literary culture, not least in bequeathing her estate to found the literary prize which bears her name.

FRASER, Mrs Hugh: Mary CRAWFORD (1851–1922) married (*c*.1872) Hugh FRASER (d. 1894). She was born in the American expatriate community in Rome. Her father, the sculptor Thomas Crawford, died in 1857; she was brought up by her mother, a sister of Julia Ward Howe (1819–1910) and a devoted attendant at the American Episcopal Church who unsuccessfully tried to prevent her children from converting to Roman Catholicism, as Fraser did in 1884. She was educated at the school kept by the novelist Elizabeth Sewell (1815–1906) at Bonchurch in the Isle of Wight. Fraser married an attaché at the British embassy in Rome and went with him to China in 1874. From 1888 until his death they were in Japan, an experience which she put to good use in her fiction and non-fiction. Her half-sister, Margaret Chanler, wrote in her memoirs (1934) 'he died as Minister to Japan, leaving her with two sons to educate and very little money. She eked out her widow's pension by writing.' In *The Stolen Emperor: A Tale of Old Japan* (1903) a strong regent controls a figurehead child emperor, who is kidnapped by a rebellious chieftain in love with his beautiful mother. She smuggles the baby emperor out of the stronghold with the help of a loyal peasant girl, and word is sent to the regent, who meanwhile has been overcome with avuncular and chivalrous loyalty. *A Little Grey Sheep: A Novel* (1901) concerns a misunderstood child who grows up into a violent passionate man who makes tragedy for the woman he loves. *The Golden Rose* (1910) was written with J. I. Stahlmann, with whom she also collaborated on two other novels. It concerns the attempts of a beautiful German widow to bring up her daughter Rose in perfect happiness. But Rose falls in love with a young prince, who deceives her into making an irregular marriage, then repudiates her, whereupon she becomes a nun. Her mother has neglected to make religion the centre of both their lives. Her son John Crawford Fraser was the author of *Death the Showman* (1901); she collaborated with him, and also with Hugh C. Fraser, probably her other son, on fiction and non-fiction. The best-selling American novelist F. Marion Crawford (1854–1909) was her brother; they were both friends of Henry *James.

FRASER, W[illiam] A[lexander] (1859–1933) married (1889) Jessie Maud BARBER. A Canadian novelist and inventor, he was born in Nova Scotia of Scots parents and educated at Westchester. He worked as a mining engineer in India, Burma, and Canada, before taking to writing and broadcasting animal stories. *Thoroughbreds: A Sporting Novel* (1903) is concerned with horse-racing in America. The plot hinges on a sinister banker trying to ruin the honest trainer by drugging horses with cocaine; the climax is when the trainer's lovely daughter disguises herself as a jockey in order to win the crucial race. *Mooswa and Others of the Boundaries* (1900) is a series of derivative animal stories (after *Kipling) about Mooswa the Moose, protector of the Boy who is the son of the Hudson's Bay Company's factor in a remote area of Canada.

Fraternity, John *Galsworthy, 1909, William Heinemann. This is a complex, laconic 'Condition of England' novel about relations between the classes. Stephen and Hilary Dallison, the one a lawyer, the other a poet and critic, are upper-class men in early middle age whose peace of mind has been sufficiently secured by wealth and status for them to acknowledge a residue of 'self-consciousness', lingering doubts about the world and their place in it. They are married to two sisters, Cecilia and Bianca Stone, whose father, Sylvanus Stone, is a cranky advocate of universal brotherhood. Sylvanus remarks that each member of the upper classes has a 'shadow' in the lower, a sinister double. In this case the shadows are Mr and Mrs Hughs, a violent ex-soldier and his seamstress wife, and a young model called Ivy Barton. Hilary Dallison and Ivy Barton fall in love, but in the end cannot surmount the barrier of class. Stephen and Cecilia's daughter, Thyme, inheriting her grandfather's social conscience, leaves home in order to assist the efforts of her cousin, Martin Stone, a doctor and sanitary reformer, but rapidly loses heart. In both cases, the instinct of class-consciousness proves more powerful than the forces which might undermine it: love, 'the Social Conscience'. By the end of the novel, Hilary has left Bianca, but not for Ivy, while Thyme has returned home in defeat. Meanwhile old Sylvanus Stone has gone quietly mad. Galsworthy's treatment of the relations between the classes is bleaker than E. M. *Forster's in **Howards End* (1910)

Fraulein Schmidt and Mr Anstruther: *Being the Letters of an Independent Woman*, *'Elizabeth', 1907, Smith, Elder. A young Englishman, Roger Anstruther, comes to improve his German under an impoverished professor in Jena (he envisages a career in the Foreign Office), and falls in love, at the very last moment, with the daughter of the house, Rose-Marie. He returns to England. The book consists of Rose-Marie's letters to him, which reveal, after initial exhilaration, a dawning disillusionment, as she realises that he would prefer a more advantageous match to an Englishwoman, Nancy Cheriton. Resigned to her fate, Rose-Marie lapses into witty, confiding, well-read, morally acute friendship. The problem is the speed with which she evolves from a wide-eyed adolescent, in her first letters, to a sardonic woman of the world who reveres Wordsworth and Thoreau, and who sees through Roger's pathetic strategies and self-delusions immediately. The reason for this startling metamorphosis is that Arnim was drawing on her own experience with William Stuart, a young Englishman who had fallen in love with her while acting as tutor to her children. Having read the novel, Stuart, by that time a don at Cambridge, fell back in love with its author, as Anstruther had done with her mouthpiece, Rose-Marie. Arnim researched it by disguising herself as an English governess and offering her services to a professor in Jena. All would have gone well had not the son of the house, a young man of 20, become infatuated with her and asked her to marry him. She arranged for her husband to send a telegram which read 'Children ill. Come at once.'

FREEMAN, R[ichard] Austin (1862–1943) married (1887) Annie Elizabeth EDWARDS (d. 1948). Youngest of the five children of a tailor, he at first worked in a chemist's shop then was apprenticed to an apothecary; he then studied at Middlesex Hospital, and qualified as a doctor in 1887. He went to work in the Gold Coast (now Ghana) as Assistant Colonial Surgeon, until he was invalided home with black water fever in 1891. His ill health persisted, and in 1896 he retired to Broadstairs. He was Assistant Medical Officer at Holloway Prison in 1900. In 1903 he settled in Gravesend and did some private tutoring, becoming a self-employed writer in 1919. His earliest works were short stories written with J. J. Pitcairn under the pseudonym 'Clifford Ashdown', which appeared in volume form in 1902 as *The Adventures of Romney Pringle*. The chief influence on his *crime fiction was undoubtedly his fellow physician, A. Conan *Doyle. His detective, Dr Thorndyke, who first appeared in *The *Red Thumb Mark* (1907), is a fantasy of scientific rationalism, to whom no inanimate object fails to reveal its story. Both a lawyer and a doctor, and having at his side the indispensable Polton, photographer and technician, he is seen repeatedly to triumph over ignorant and unscientific opponents, whether policeman or criminals. And Freeman is credited with the invention of the inverted detective story, in which the murderer is known to the reader, in a series of stories for **Pearson's Magazine* (1912), of which the first was 'The Case of Oscar Brodski', about a murdered diamond merchant. Freeman also published four non-detective novels, including *The Golden Pool: A Story of a Forgotten Mine* (1905), a *Haggardesque tale which derives its local colour from the 'picturesquely horrible rites of the Sakrobundi fetish of North Ashanti'. He was a member of the council of the Eugenics Society and author of *Social Decay and Degeneracy* (1921), and there are many references in his fiction to race theories current at the time. In 'A Sower of Pestilence' (published in *The Puzzle Lock*, 1925) Thorndyke deduces that the same criminal has been responsible for two unconnected crimes, and explains, 'the agent in each was evidently a moral imbecile who was a professed enemy of society. Such persons are rare in this country, and when they occur are usually foreigners, most commonly Russians, or East Europeans of some kind.' Freeman served in the RAMC in the First World War. There is a biography by Oliver Mayo (1980).

FRITH, Walter (?1857–1941) married (1898) Maud LAW née HILL. The son of the painter W. P. Frith (1819–1909), and the brother of Mrs J. E. *Panton, he was educated at Harrow School, Trinity Hall, Cambridge and the Inner Temple (1880). He became a barrister, and was the author of numerous plays between 1889 and 1911. He also wrote three novels, only one of which falls into this period: *The Tutor's Love Story* (1904). It is written in the first person by a discontented tutor whose father's financial ruin has brought to an end his prospects as a barrister. He muses sententiously on the materialism and snobbishness of the world, but by the end is looking hopefully at a future of hard work and consoling his bereaved loved one.

FRY, B. and C. B.: Beatrice HOLME-SUMNER (d. 1946) married Charles Burgess FRY (1872–1956). The famous cricketer and his wife wrote one novel, *A Mother's Son* (1907). A widow brings up her son to be a true Englishman. He is head boy of his public school, an amateur jockey while at Oxford, plays cricket for England, marries, fathers a child, and goes off to fight in the *Boer War, knowing he must die young. Fry's own career was similarly heroic and exemplary to his generation: he went to Repton School and Wadham College, Oxford, where he was senior scholar. He played for England at both cricket and soccer and at one time held the world record for the long jump. Later the Frys ran a training-ship for boys entering the navy. He also wrote many books on cricket, one on diabolo (1907), and an autobiography (1939).

Furnace, The, Rose *Macaulay, 1907, John Murray. This uneventful, elliptical story is about a brother and sister, Tommy and Betty Crevequer, who lead a carefree, hand-to-mouth, mildly artistic existence in Naples. Wilfully indefinite and androgynous, they have no function in life other than that of the perpetual 'go-between'. The arrival of Tommy's schoolmate Warren Venables, with his novelist mother, goofy sister, and tantalizing cousin, promises (or threatens) to break the spell: to remould them in the 'furnace' of adult relationship. But nothing happens. 'So, sick-hearted, the Crevequers had looked at the old ways which so clogged them, which would possibly (why not?) always clog them, clinging heavily like mire; and at the new ways which they were seeking wearily, with no heart, with "too late" echoing in their souls like a knell.'

FURNISS, Harry (1854–1925). Born in Wexford and educated at the Royal Hibernian Academy Schools in Dublin, he settled in London at the age of 19 and became an illustrator, contributing to the *Illustrated London News*, the *Graphic*, and *Punch*. He exhibited at the Royal Academy from 1875. *Poverty Bay: A Nondescript Novel* (1905), which he both wrote and illustrated, is a first-person narrative about a rich orphan who finally marries an actress and retires from materialistic, snobbish, thieving London society.

G

GALLICHAN, Walter M[atthew] (1861–1946) married, first, Ada E. WHITE, secondly, Norah Kathleen MUTCH, and, perhaps also C. Gasquoine *HARTLEY. Born at St Helier, Jersey, he was privately educated in Reading. He became a contributor to the *National Reformer* and the *Free Review*, and the author of *How to Love: The Art of Courtship and Marriage* (1915), *Modern Woman and How to Manage Her* (1909), *Women Under Polygamy* (1914), *Our Invisible Selves: An Introduction to Psychoanalysis* (1921), *The Poison of Prudery: An Historical Survey* (1929), *Sexual Apathy and Coldness in Women* (1927), *The Sterilisation of the Unfit* (1929), guidebooks, and other books on health, personal relationships, fishing, and ornithology. His two Edwardian novels rather belie the fearsomely anthropological and psychotherapeutic tendency of his non-fiction. The conflict in *The Conflict of Owen Prytherch* (1908) is indeed between man and wife, as well as between minister and congregation, but the reconciliations are thoroughly sentimental. Even more gushing is *A Soul from the Pit* (1907), about an innocent young woman from a Welsh farm who is lured to London by a wicked procuress, saved by the influence of a cheerful lady journalist, and loved by an artist. Gallichan also published as 'Geoffrey Mortimer'; he was awarded a Civil List pension in 1934.

GALLON, Tom (1866–1914) was born in London and educated privately. He became a clerk, and a schoolmaster, then secretary to the mayor of a provincial town, before illness led to him giving up work and becoming a tramp. In 1895 he began to 'hunt for stray guineas in Grub Street'. He was the author of many music-hall sketches and some fiction. *The Kingdom of Hate: A Romance* (1899) and *Rickerby's Folly* (1901) are 'Mysteries of London' adventures which make much of the exciting but dangerous anonymity of the city. In the former, Bernard Aubanel, one of a group of bored young men hanging around on a hot June night, undertakes for a modest wager to charm his way into the first house he sees which is showing a light—and duly finds himself caught up in a *Ruritanian conspiracy involving an evil count and a beautiful princess. *The Second Dandy Chater* (1901) is a Dickensian tale, set in the Essex marshes, about a man who takes the place of his murdered twin brother and undoes the wrong done by his malevolent double. Equally Dickensian, and equally preoccupied with impersonation, is *The Dead Ingleby* (1902), about a man who passes as a respectable member of English society while also running a district in Italy through a gang of comic opera bandits. *The Great Gay Road* (1910) returns to favourite themes (prodigal sons, usurpers), and provides further evidence in its low-life scenes of Gallon's debt to Dickens.

GALSWORTHY, John (1867–1933), OM (1929), married (1905) Ada Nemesis Pearson GALSWORTHY née COOPER (?1864–1956). The son of a solicitor and businessman, he was born at Kingston Hill, Surrey, and educated at Harrow School and New College, Oxford; he seemed set for a conventional upper-middle-class career (he was admitted to the Bar in 1880, and worked for his father's business). But both in his private life and in his literary work he reacted against the bourgeois conventions of his upbringing, and the impact of the twentieth century on the structure and ideology of the middle-class Victorian world and its children are repeatedly the subject of his work. The most striking event in his personal life is the fact that in 1895 he began an affair with Ada Galsworthy, who had married his cousin Arthur in 1891 (and who ceased to live with her husband when he left to fight in the *Boer War). A version of this story is the central feature of the plot of *The Forsyte Saga*. Galsworthy's early works of fiction, written as 'John Sinjohn' (the short stories of *From the Five Winds*, 1897, and *A Man of Devon*, 1901; the novels *Jocelyn*, 1899, and *Villa Rubein*, 1900) were essentially autobiographical and unsuccessful, but he was able to give the themes of work and emotion a more satisfying narrative shape (with help from Edward Garnett, 1868–1937) in *The *Man of Property* (1906), a critique of London middle-class life and the emotionally corrupting effects of property, developed through the shifting family relationships of the Forsytes. His first work under his own name was *The *Island Pharisees* (1904); other Edwardian fiction includes *The *Country House* (1907), **Fraternity* (1909), *The *Patrician* (1911), *The *Dark Flower* (1913), and the short stories of *A Commentary* (1908) and *A Motley* (1910). Galsworthy returned to the Forsyte family in 1918, and wrote eight additional novels in the Forsyte Saga, which was completed in 1932, having traced the lives of two generations of Forsytes from 1886 till the end of the 1930s. As the story unfolds the character of the family patriarch, Soames Forsyte, shifts from villain to hero, reflecting Galsworthy's own movement from critique to celebration of the propertied class. Following the success of *The Man of Property* and until he resumed the Forsyte Saga Galsworthy was best known as a playwright, with a series of dramas that used the stage as a setting for the exploration of various social problems: *The Silver Box* (1906) addressed inequities in the judicial system; *Strife* (1909) focused on labour/management issues; *Justice* (1910) exposed prison conditions effectively enough to lead to prison reform. Both as a novelist and as a playwright, Galsworthy was concerned to provide a moral critique of society: on the hand to expose the public and private effects of materialism and convention and, on the other, to suggest the liberating value of art and literature. His critique was developed in the form of the family history of the Forsytes and of the dramatic realism of his plays. The narrative was left to make the critical points, ironically rather than directly, and the effect is such that, in the end, Galsworthy is clearly part of the world he is criticizing. He refused a knighthood in 1918 and was awarded the Nobel prize for Literature in 1932. There is a biography by James Gindin (1987).

Garden of Allah, The, Robert *Hichens, 1904, Methuen. An early example of desert romance, a genre which became immensely popular after the First World War with the success of *The Sheik* (1919) by 'E. M. Hull'. Domini Enfilden, a young and fervently Catholic Englishwoman travelling in Algeria, meets and marries a mysterious Russian, Boris Androvsky. Disappointingly, Boris turns out to be a renegade monk. Appalled by his betrayal of God, Domini packs him off back to his monastery, and brings up their child on her own. Like most desert romances, the novel relishes polarity. Topographically, it is divided between city and desert, civilization and barbarism. The barbaric men who inhabit the desert are all man, mighty, muscular, and iron-willed. It is at their hands alone that the half-woman who sets out from the decadent city (described in full) will become all woman. Still, the polarity between Domini and Boris is softened by her Amazonian mannishness and his fumbling hesitancy. Boris, as befits a monk, is clumsy and virginal. Domini teaches him the ways of the world, initiates him. At first, it seems that marriage will put an end to this role-swapping and re-establish Boris as master. But when he confesses that he has betrayed God, and the confession reduces him to a second childhood, Domini takes charge again. In a final assertive stroke, she conceals from him the fact that he is to be a father; she herself will be the only creator, the only authority. She retires to an Edenic walled garden on the edge of the desert. The polarities of male and female, city and desert, collapse. Hichens's frothy mysticism makes room for a confusion of genders and cultural stereotypes which later examples of the genre were rigorously to exclude.

GARNETT, Olive: Olivia Rayne GARNETT (1871–1958). Born in Primrose Hill, London, she was one of the six children of Richard Garnett (1835–1906), keeper of printed books in the British Museum. She was educated at Queen's College, Harley Street, which she left in 1889; in the following year the family moved into the British Museum. She was the author of *Petersburg Tales* (1900) and *In Russia's Night* (1918), fiction reflecting her deep interest in Russia and revolutionary politics. She was in love with the revolutionist S. M. Stepniak (1851–1894) (depicted as Nekrovitch in *A Girl Among the Anarchists* (1903) by 'Isabel *Meredith'), who was married and had been exiled in England since 1884. When he was run over by a train she cut off her hair in mourning and suffered from depression. She was briefly engaged in 1897 to an architect, Alfred Powell (1865–1960), and in later life she became a great admirer of Henry *James. On her father's dying intestate she had to leave her Hampstead home and live with her youngest brother in Kew. Her interesting diaries 1890–5 have been edited by Barry C. Johnson (1989, 1993). Edward Garnett (1868–1937), the *publisher and critic, a friend and supporter of Barbara *Baynton, Joseph *Conrad, W. H. *Hudson, D. H. *Lawrence, Henry *Lawson and many other novelists, was her brother; he was married to Constance Garnett (1861–1946), the most important translator of Russian fiction at this period, and a sister of Clementina *Black. His essay 'The Sex Novel' prefaced Maud Churton *Braby's **Downward*; he edited and prefaced numerous other works and was author of the novels *Light and Shadow* (1889) and *The Paradox Club* (1888), some plays, and volumes of literary criticism. There is a biography of Edward Garnett by George Jefferson (1982). Their elder brother was married to Mrs R. S. *Garnett.

GARNETT, Mrs R. S.: Martha ROSCOE (1869–1946) married (1896) Robert Singleton GARNETT (1866–1932). The daughter of a solicitor, she was educated at Queen's College, Harley Street, Miss Norton's School, Holly Hill, and Newnham College, Cambridge. She published two novels in the period. *The Infamous John Friend* (1909) is a *historical romance about a thoroughly sympathetic and thoroughly unprincipled spy for Napoleon. *Amor Vincit: A Romance of the Staffordshire Moorlands* (1912), set in the 1850s, is a melancholic and occasionally brutal confection out of Emily Brontë (1818–1848) and Thomas Hardy (1840–1928). She also wrote *Samuel Butler and His Family Relations* (1926). She and her sister-in-law and friend from schooldays, Olive *Garnett, took part in a demonstration in favour of women's suffrage in February 1907 and were jeered at by the crowd. Her husband was a lawyer and translator.

GARVICE, Charles (?1854–1920). Little is known about the life of the man who became one of the most prolific and successful of Edwardian authors. His first publication was a volume of verse (1873). This was followed in 1875 by a three-decker, *Maurice Durant*, dedicated to the actor Henry Irving, which was a dismal failure: so dismal, in fact, that for more than twenty years Garvice confined himself to journalism and magazine stories. Journalism brought him modest wealth and status. He purchased a farm in north Devon which was later to feature in *A Farm in Creamland: A Book of the Devon Countryside* (1911). It was the unexpected success in America of *Just a Girl* (1898) which encouraged him to resume his career as a novelist. After that he was unstoppable, often reworking themes and episodes from his magazine stories. One obvious talent was the ability to encapsulate a story in a snappy metaphoric title: *A Coronet of Shame* (1900); *In Cupid's Chains* (1903); *The Rugged Path* (1903); *Linked by Fate* (1905); *Love, the Tyrant* (1905); *The Gold in the Gutter* (1907); *In Wolf's Clothing* (1908); *Barriers Between* (1910); *His Guardian Angel* (1912); *Love in a Snare* (1912); *The Loom of Fate* (1913); *The Woman's Way* (1914); *The Waster* (1919). Garvice's novels were invariably melodramatic, and invariably straightforward in their moral attitudes: a crucial factor with the large Nonconformist reading public. There is really no point in describing or summarizing any of them. Readers bought or borrowed a 'Garvice', rather than a novel, and he never let them down. His sales were phenomenal. Douglas *Sladen, Garvice's friend and neighbour, thought that his career was the most remarkable literary success on record, with more than six million copies of his books sold worldwide by 1913. His reward was a house in fashionable Richmond and a cottage on the Thames to add to the Devon farm. He was a member of several clubs, and the president or chairman of numerous institutes and societies. He died at Richmond. Edgar *Jepson tells in his memoirs a story of how Garvice lured away Ford Madox *Hueffer's secretary 'and paid her to put the Literature into his work for him, for he felt sure that, working so much with [Hueffer], she must have caught it from him'.

GAUNT, Mary [Eliza Bakewell] (1861–1942) married (1894) Hubert Lindsay MILLER (d. 1900). Born at Indigo, Victoria, Australia, daughter of a judge and governor of goldfields, she was educated at Grenville College, Ballarat, and the University of Melbourne, but left the latter after a year. Instead she became a writer, and made enough money to travel to England and India. Her short marriage to a doctor left her with a small income, and in 1901 she moved to London to be nearer the literary market-place. As well as novels, of which the first was *Dave's Sweetheart* (1894), she published a series of travel books about journeys to far-flung spots, including *Alone in West Africa* (1911) and *A Woman in China* (1914). *Every Man's Desire* (1913) begins when practical 29-year-old Janey Walters, a teacher at St Agnes' School for Poor Girls in Liverpool, is kissed by Hugh Gresham, a man she does not love and who does not love her. Her awakening is completed by marriage and an African journey. Gresham goes to the bad. He has already gone native, marrying, some time before, the sister of an African chief. Janey returns to England with her secret love, the stalwart Adam Ramsay. In the 1920s Gaunt moved to Italy, where she lived until she fled to France after the outbreak of the Second World War. She died at Cannes.

George Eastmont, Wanderer, 'John *Law', 1905, Burns & Oates. George Eastmont, born into a military and landowning family of Tory convictions, drops out—'it was difficult to class his dress, which reminded one of a country house, a smoking-room, and a political meeting'—and discovers Socialism, under the influence of a charismatic militant, Dick Charleston. He becomes a popular speaker and, in the hope of acquainting himself further with the people, marries Julia Hay, daughter of a small farmer in Essex. They live in an Artizans' Block in the East End of London. Eastmont's militancy is defined against the Fabianism of an East End priest, the Revd Edgar Podmore, and a philanthropic spinster, Mary Cameron. He takes part in a riot, is convicted, and jailed for two weeks, during which time his wife, by now exposed as irredeemably vulgar and peevish, dies from an overdose of morphia. During a bitter dock strike, Eastmont seeks the help of an old patron, Cardinal Loraine, whose intercession ensures the triumph of the strikers. Exhilarated by this success, Charleston decides that the way forward lies through trade unionism and parliamentary politics rather than direct action. Eastmont, who wants to 'bring the Social millennium about by a *coup-de-théâtre*', takes himself off to Australia, where he studies the Land Question as clerk to the Blackheath Labour Settlement. Involvement in an election convinces him of the futility of parliamentary politics. He inherits his grandfather's estate (without the title), and determines to run it on democratic and economically progressive lines. Podmore, meanwhile, has married Mary Cameron, and moved to a mining community. Eastmont, though still personally unfulfilled, has wandered to some effect. The novel ends with the death of Cardinal Loraine. Dedicating it to the memory of Cardinal Manning, 'with whom the author was associated during the great dock strike of 1889', Margaret Harkness added that it contained her experiences of and thoughts about the Labour movement.

GEORGE, W[alter] L[ionel] (1882–1926) married, first (1908), Helen PORTER (d. 1914), secondly (1916), Helen Agnes MADDEN (d. 1920), and, thirdly (1921), Kathleen GEIPEL. Although British by parentage, George was born and lived in Paris until he was 23, only learning English at 20. He came to England in 1905 to work in an office, but turned to journalism and became foreign correspondent of various London papers. His first novel, *A Bed of Roses* (1911), is the story of a penniless young widow who, under the strain of keeping body and soul together, 'sinks below her class in manners', as the **Times Literary Supplement* put it, 'and then in morals'. Its frank treatment of prostitution earned George some notoriety, and enough money to enable him to become a full-time novelist. *The City of Light* (1912) concerns the romantic adventures of a Parisian clerk, Henri Duvernoy, who rebels against his stultifyingly bourgeois father and mother by marrying a woman they disapprove of, the daughter of a bankrupt speculator and a mildly disreputable actress. There are some lively music-hall scenes and a number of Anglo-French comparisons. *The Making of an Englishman* (1914) is dedicated to the first young Frenchman who called the author John Bull and the first young Englishman who called him Froggy. Beginning on the night of the relief of Mafeking during the *Boer War, it celebrates, through the gradual Anglicization of a young Frenchman, an Englishness pondered and measured, rather than taken for granted. His other titles include *Israel Kalisch* (1913), and *The Second Blooming* (1914). George's novels reflected his interest in pacifism, feminism, and labourism, and he also wrote political tracts: *Engines of Social Progress* (1907), *Labour and Housing at Port Sunlight* (1909), *Women and Tomorrow* (1913), and *The Intelligence of Women* (1917).

GERARD, D[orothea Mary Stanislaus] (1855–1915) married (1886) Julius LONGARD de LONGGARDE. Born to an upper-class Scots Catholic family, at Rochsoles, near Airdie in Lanarkshire, Scotland, she was educated at home and at the convent of the Sacré Cœur at Riedenburg in the Austrian Tyrol. After her mother's death when

Dorothea was 15 she lived with her elder sister, E. *Gerard, at Brzezany in Galicia, where she met her husband, an Austrian officer. She began her career by publishing, in collaboration with her sister, a novel each year between 1880 and 1885 as 'E. D. Gerard'. Her first novel on her own was *Orthodox* (1888); and she maintained a high and usually competent level of production throughout the Edwardian period: opposite the title-page of *Restitution* (1908) there is a list of thirty-three books 'by the same author'. Her romances usually convey a message. *The Blood-Tax* (1902) is a pamphlet about national defence disguised as a novel: an impressionable young Englishman goes to Germany to manufacture bicycles, is appalled by German militarism, and returns to England with a scheme for conscription and the drilling of schoolboys. The message was more often moral than political. In *Holy Matrimony* (1902), about the early married life of two sisters, one of whom has married for love, the other for money, the polemical motive is displaced onto the narrator, a German Baroness who advocates the simple life (for other people) and has published a pamphlet on *The Death of Luxury. The Eternal Woman* (1903) is also concerned with the ethics of courtship: the woman in question marries a man for his money and then falls in love with him. Gerard sidestepped her own didacticism, but not her preoccupation with ethical dilemmas, in *The Bridge of Life: A Novel Without a Purpose* (1904); an eminent doctor uses an oriental poison to put terminally ill patients out of their pain. *Made of Money* (1904) and *The Three Essentials* (1905) hammer away at the theme of the insignificance of material possessions, a theme which receives its most complicated and sententious treatment in *Restitution*. A young woman inherits a large estate in Lithuania which was her grandfather's reward for helping to suppress the Polish uprising of 1863. We soon discern in the distinguished-looking stranger seen lurking in the park, with a wistful eye bent on the house, the son of its original owner, to whom restitution is clearly due. About this time, Gerard began to inject an element of explicit *fantasy into her fiction. In *The Improbable Idyll* (1905), an ineffectual suburban family emigrates to Austrian Poland, where they buy a farm and are steadily fleeced until the arrival of a strong silent Englishman. The *Itinerant Daughters* (1907) are bored and restless, and agree to exchange families. *The Red-Hot Crown: A Semi-Historical Romance* (1909) is *Ruritanian. In *The Grass Widow* (1910), a Russian revolutionary marries and deserts two women in succession. On the whole, the diverse settings of Gerard's novels—India in *The Inevitable Marriage* (1911), the seamy side of Viennese life in *The Waters of Lethe* (1914)—were effortlessly homogenized by the consistency of the sentiment. An article by Helen Black (1896) describes her living with her husband and daughter in a remote region of Galicia, seeing scarcely anyone except Polish and Jewish peasantry. She was also the author of *The Austrian Officer at Work and at Play* (1913).

GERARD, [Jane] E[mily] (1849–1905) married (1869) Miecislaus de LASZOWSKI (d. 1905). Elder sister of D. *Gerard, she too was educated in a convent at Riedenburg, and excelled in her studies of languages, particularly German; for some years she was the German literature reviewer for the *Times*. She too (as did also a third sister, Anne) married an Austrian officer; her husband became a lieutenant-general. When, after Dorothea's marriage, they stopped writing novels together, she too published fiction on her own (although not in the same quantity or with the same success) of which the three last titles, *The Extermination of Love: A Fragmentary Study in Erotics* (1901), *The Heron's Tower* (1904), and *Honour's Glassy Bubble: A Story of Three Generations* (1906), fall into this period. The second of these is a *historical romance set in Germany in the eighteenth century, the third an anti-duelling novel set in Hungary at the castle of an arrogant duellist who calls himself Attila XXXVII. She also published *The Land Beyond the Forest: Facts, Figures and Fancies from Transylvania* (1888).

GERARD, [Amelia] Louise (1878–1970). The daughter of a Nottingham soap manufacturer, she started writing after leaving Nottingham High School. She was at first hailed as a promising addition to the ranks of sensational writers, and one can see why. *The Golden Centipede* (1910) deals luridly with West African horrors, notably the eponymous creature, which hangs menacingly on the heroine's arm. *The Hyena of Kallu* (1910) is the sultan of a West African tribe which emerges periodically from the bush to rob and murder Europeans; he is also, as it turns out, a public-school man and the rightful Earl of Agleton. The heroine of *A Tropical Tangle* (1911) has a strange experience in the London fog, whose consequences only become apparent when she goes out to West Africa to work as a nurse in Ashanti. *The Swimmer* (1912) tackles one of the favourite themes of Edwardian *feminist fiction: the struggle to become a writer. Lisle Thornton, orphaned daughter of a gentleman artist who married a lodging-house keeper, is reduced to menial occupations, but eventually achieves success through her writing and marries a doctor whom she had first known, many years before, as a lodger. Gerard's other novel in the period is *Flower-of-the-Moon* (1914). She published twenty-three titles in all to 1936, all with Mills & Boon. She was an enthusiastic traveller and an FRGS.

GERARD, Morice, *pseud.*: John Jessop TEAGUE (1856–*c*.1929). Educated at Emmanuel College, Cambridge, he was ordained as a Church of England clergyman in 1880. He served in Devon parishes 1884–1905, later in Croydon and London. He published some sixty volumes of fiction between 1890 and 1924, most of which, like *One of Marlborough's Captains* (1912) and *The Gate of England: A Romance of the Days of Drake* (1914), are *historical romances of the school of G. A. *Henty, in which honest soldiers and sailors triumph over rogues and foreigners. The outbreak of the First World War prompted the **Times Literary Supplement* to notice in the latter 'the same forces operative as chance is now bringing vividly into action'. Teague's other novels are romances with an interest in class. The heroine of *Ruth Gwynnett, Schoolmistress* (1905) is the foster-child of a Cornish coastguard, who unearths a distinguished aristocratic father. In *Dr Manton* (1907), a strong silent professional man rescues an heiress in distress.

Getting of Wisdom, The, 'Henry Handel *Richardson', 1910, William Heinemann. Laura Tweedle Rambotham is the daughter of a widow living in comparative poverty in a small town in the Australian outback, and the eldest of four children in a tight-knit family. As the book opens, she is about to enrol in the select Melbourne Ladies College, where wisdom of various kinds is to be got. After a bruising induction which cruelly exposes her naïvety, she learns to conform, and doggedly achieves a measure of academic and social success. An important part of the book's charm is its ability to grasp the precariousness of success, particularly in friendship. Laura's first date, with a friend's cousin, Bob, who is supposedly 'gone' on her, proves a disaster. Desperate to repair the damage to her reputation, she assiduously nurtures a crush on the school curate, Robby Shepherd, a married man and thus a suitable object of universal infatuation. A weekend spent with his family secures her standing in the school. His sourness rapidly disillusions her, but she is none the less able to hint strongly at a romance. Her stories are exposed as pure fabrication when another girl, Mary Pidwall, stays with the Shepherds. It takes her some time to recover from this setback, and from the expulsion of another girl, the devoted Chinky, who has stolen money in order to buy her a ring. Gradually, however, she works her way back into favour, and is invited to join the Literary Society. Obsession with an older girl, Evelyn, distracts her from her work, but she does pass her final examinations. She leaves school uncertain of her future but exhilarated by the freedom of adulthood.

Ghetto Comedies, Israel *Zangwill, 1907, William Heinemann. 'Over all Zangwill's work', wrote his friend Thomas Moult, 'broods tragedy—tragedy in the Greek, the true sense. It was instinctive in him to feel tragedy passing everywhere.' But, as the Zangwill scholar Maurice Wohlgelertner notes, he also 'adored the comic spirit', seeing it as a necessary part of literary realism, and published the collection, *Ghetto Comedies*, to coincide with the reissue of *Ghetto Tragedies* (1893), explaining in his introduction that he could not make 'the usual distinction between tragedy and comedy'. As the heroine of 'The Hirelings' puts it, 'With us Jews, tears and laughter are very close', and the fourteen stories here cover both the tragic and comic consequences of Jews' individual and collective self-deception, of their attempts to evade the reality of their situation as Jews. In 'The Model of Sorrows', for instance, a painter searches for a model for his portrait of Christ and finds the necessary image of 'haunting sadness and mystery' in a streetwise petty criminal. In 'The Hirelings' a concert pianist, returning from a failed US tour, meets a rich American and her maid, a Jewess with whom he falls in love. Inspired by her to play old synagogue songs, he enchants her mistress, who offers to take him back to America and guaranteed success. Faced with the choice between this and the London ghetto, he chooses the former. In 'Samooborona', the hero, David, seeks to rouse a Russian Jewish community to prepare a military defence against the advancing pogrom, but it is too divided by sectarian differences, and the town is duly destroyed. As the Jews are at last united in death, David, aware of the irony of the gesture, turns his gun on himself.

Ghost, The: *A Fantasia on Modern Themes*, Arnold *Bennett, 1907, Chatto & Windus. A pot-boiling occult tale of interest primarily for the light its composition throws on the contemporary market for fiction. It arose from Bennett's realization, as the editor of *Woman*, that he was paying literary syndicates large amounts of money for work he could do better himself. 'As an editor, I knew the qualities that a serial ought to possess. And I knew specially that what most serials lacked was a large, central, unifying, vivifying idea . . . There are no original themes; probably no writer ever did invent an original theme; but my theme was a brilliant imposture of originality. It had, too, grandeur and passion, and fantasy, and it was inimical to none of the prejudices of the serial reader.' Bennett claimed that he wrote the twelve instalments in twenty-four days, composing in his head as he walked to work in the morning, and knocking out 2,500 words after he came home in the evening. He made sure to put in 'generous quantities of wealth, luxury, feminine beauty, surprise, catastrophe, and genial incurable optimism'. He finished on 23 January 1899, and felt able to record in his journal that the result was, 'of its kind, good stuff, well written and well contrived'. The syndicate he had approached paid him £75 for it, and it appeared as 'Love and Life' in *Hearth and Home*, a magazine to which he contributed regularly, beginning on 17 May 1900. Although he contracted with Chatto & Windus in February 1902 to publish the serial in book form, he soon became dissatisfied with it, and, sure that he could make it 'very striking & thrilling indeed, & at the same time good', resolved to rewrite it. This he did in October and November 1906, and the book finally appeared in 1907, to mixed reviews (though the *New York Times* counted it among its Best Books for Summer Reading). Sales did not rise above 3,000 until 1910. The ghost, incidentally, is a faultlessly dressed apparition who dogs the footsteps of a young doctor who is pasionately in love with a famous singer, Rosa Rosetta: when Rosa casts herself before it in 'the ecstacy of a sublime appeal', it waves its hand reluctantly, and disappears.

Ghost-Stories of an Antiquary, M. R. *James, 1904, Edward Arnold. The first collection of James's ghost stories, designed, as he puts it in the preface, to make their readers 'feel pleasantly uncomfortable when walking along a solitary road at nightfall, or sitting over a dying fire in the small hours'. M. R. James had nothing of Kipling's or Blackwood's fascination with the causes of ghostly apparitions (in particular, the states of mind in which ghosts are seen). His tales veer more towards horror. The eight stories in this collection reflect James's own scholarly interests, drawing on his knowledge of the trappings of research into paleography, medieval art, and church history. James adapted themes from folklore and legend, myth and ballad, and his stories are constructed from such traditional elements, to which an air of conviction is appended by the addition of footnotes, translations, and (genuine) bibliographical references. Scholars and clerics are the protagonists (or victims) as well as narrators of the supernatural visitations and horrible spectres. But, as in all of James's stories, plot is of paramount importance, and character is reduced to a minimum of simplicity and transparency. Place is crucial throughout (in James's words 'prolific in suggestion'), and everyday objects are imbued with ghastly possibilities. James's blend of the quiet scholarly atmposphere, old towns and flat landscapes (particularly East Anglia) and inexplicably malevolent forces has become the very type of the English ghost story.

GIBB, Eleanor Hughes: Eleanor —— married Hughes GIBB. Three of her four publications in the period—*The Soul of a Villain* (1905), *Through the Rain* (1906), and *His Sister* (1908)—are novels of domestic suffering and redemption. In the first, a financier woos a squire's daughter, and then his widow, and comes good in the process; in the third, a woman remains passionately committed to her bacteriologist brother through unhappy marriage and divorce. *Gilbert Ray* (1914) is something of a departure, though no less conventional in its way : a Cambridge mystic becomes a Christian Socialist, plunges into work among iron-workers in the north of England, and is killed during a labour riot.

GIBBON, [Richard] Percival (1879–1926) married ——. Born at Trelech, Carmarthenshire, the son of a clergyman, he was educated at a Moravian school in Koenigsfeld, Baden. He went to sea and worked on British, American, and French merchant ships before becoming a journalist, a war correspondent, and a contributor of short stories to periodicals. Gibbon went in for tales of far-flung adventure which take a lively interest in racial and sexual politics. *Souls in Bondage* (1904), set in a small town on the South African veld, is largely concerned with the difficulties confronting people of mixed race. The heroine of *Margaret Harding* (1911) is a cultivated English girl who is sent to South Africa to cure her lungs and makes friends with the orphan son of a rebel Kaffir king who has been educated in England as a doctor and now finds himself rejected by both races. Gibbon's most intriguing invention was the middle-aged female narrator. *The Vrouw Grobelaar's Leading Cases* (1905) is a collection of stories told by a wealthy and formidable Boer widow with a 'discriminating taste in corpses'. Even more striking is *The Adventures of Miss Gregory* (1912): twelve widely dispersed episodes involving a cheerful, vigorous, intelligent 50-year-old whose intimidating grey-tweed skirt is equipped with a revolver pocket. *Salvator* (1908) might be read as Gibbon's ironic comment on his own globe-trotting propensities. The heroine is engaged to a heroic Austrian baron, who leaves her to pursue his real passion, the reform of the Portuguese colony of Mozambique; she marries a dull squire instead. But the author's evident admiration for the heroic baron leaves little room for irony. *The Second-Class Passenger and Other Stories* (1913) is certainly far-flung in setting and emphasis. He also published the official record of the surrender of the German fleet and a volume of verse about Africa.

GIBBS, A[rthur] Hamilton (1888–1964) married (1919) Jeannette PHILLIPS. The youngest brother of Philip *Gibbs and Cosmo *Hamilton, he was educated (1901–1905) at the Collège de St Malo in Brittany. He then took a job with a firm of assayers and refiners of precious metals before being sent at the expense of his brother Cosmo to St John's College, Oxford (1907–9). There he founded the magazine *Tuesday Review*, in which he published the sketches collected as *The Compleat Oxford Man* (1911). On graduating, Arthur Gibbs became Cosmo's secretary, taking on various duties including acting in his plays, travelling to America to act in *The Blindness of Virtue*. In the First World War he served in France, Egypt, and Serbia, winning the Military Cross, and between tours of duty writing up his experiences in *Gunfodder* (1919). After the war he returned to the USA, married a lawyer and writer, and settled at Lakeville, Massachusetts. He became an American citizen in 1931. His novels, which answered the middlebrow call for fiction to treat ethical dilemmas in tones of moral neatness, includes *Cheadle and Son* (1911), *The Hour of Conflict* (1913), *The Persistent Lovers* (1914), and a series of bestsellers, *Soundings* (1925), *Labels* (1926), *Harness* (1928), and *Chances* (1930).

GIBBS, Philip [Armand Hamilton] (1877–1962), KBE (1920), married (1898) Agnes Mary ROWLAND (d. 1939). Fifth of the seven children of a civil servant in the Board of Education who disapproved of public schools and had published fiction, he was educated at home. Cosmo *Hamilton was his elder brother, A. Hamilton *Gibbs his younger brother, and their sister Helen Hamilton Gibbs published five novels 1928–37. He began his literary career in Cassells, the publishers, before joining, for brief periods, the *Daily Mail*, *Daily Express*, *Daily Chronicle* and, as literary editor, the *Tribune*. His first novel, *The *Street of Adventure* (1900) was about journalism, the second, *The *Individualist* (1908) about *politics. *Intellectual Mansions, S. W.* (1910) was rendered a failure when suffragette leaders bought up the edition and bound it in their colours. John le Dreux, a young doctor, and his sister, Margaret, escape provincial life by moving into a mansion block in South London. Their neighbours speak 'a language of allusions, of literary and artistic slang, which seemed to belong to some inner society of intellectuals, with secret code words and ideas'. The woman John falls in love with, Phillida Fraquet, becomes increasingly involved in the suffrage campaigns, much to the distress of her resoundingly self-absorbed husband, Raymond. Raymond, an advocate, though so far not an exponent, of free love, persuades Margaret to elope with him to Paris. They are forestalled by Phillida's heroic death during a suffrage riot. Her dying word, breathed into John's ear, is 'Glad', and her sacrifice earns the commendation of the *Times* itself. All the novel earned from the **Times*

Literary Supplement was the contemptuous remark that 'there are wild and turbulent scenes, and a tragedy which is supposed to make the nation take the movement seriously'. Gibbs continued as a freelance journalist before joining the *Daily Chronicle* as a special correspondent, reporting on a variety of events and activities but increasingly used to cover foreign conflicts. On the outbreak of the First World War he became war correspondent for the *Chronicle*, one of the five accredited reporters with the Allied Forces (for which he was knighted in 1920) and responsible for some of the finest war reportage. His own experiences are described in both fictional (*The Middle of the Road*, 1923) and non-fictional terms (*Realities of War*, 1920). Gibbs continued as a journalist after the war (reporting from Russia in 1921, for example), but left the *Daily Chronicle*. He briefly edited the *Review of Reviews* in 1920-1, and increasingly wrote as a commentator on international affairs, and as an advocate of world peace. His books include, *Beauty and Nick* (1914), *The Soul of War* (1915), *Battle of the Somme* (1916), *Now It Can Be Told* (1920), *Adventures in Journalism* (1923), and *Young Anarchy* (1926). He was a Roman Catholic, and in 1919 became the first journalist ever to interview the Pope. His son Anthony Gibbs was the author of fourteen novels 1925–50.

GIBERNE, Agnes (1845–1939). Born in India, daughter of an army officer, she was educated privately, and began writing at the age of 7. She was the author of a large quantity of tracts and fiction for adults and children published from 1864, and of a long series of popular science books. Her later books include *The Rack of This Tough World* (1902), a commonplace thriller focused on a family taint which is redeemed by self-sacrifice, and *Polly, the Postmaster's Daughter* (1911). Her first few works appeared either anonymously or as by 'A. G.' She lived in Eastbourne.

GIBSON, L[ettice] S[usan] (b. 1859). She published four novels, all in the period: *The Freemasons* (1905), *Burnt Spices* (1906), *Ships of Desire* (1908), and *The Oakum Pickers* (1912). The second of these is occult: a tempestuous beauty returns after death to haunt the Gray's Inn chambers of a man who rejected her in favour of an anodyne rival, and is eventually exorcised by a clairvoyant doctor. The oakum picked in the fourth is picked not in gaol but in the prison of an unhappy marriage.

GILBERT, George David, *pseud.*: Mary Lucy ARTHUR (*c.*1882–1919). The daughter of a doctor of Irish family, she spent her life at Keymer, Sussex, and died young rather suddenly. She published *historical romances like *In the Shadow of the Purple* (1902), about George IV and Mrs Fitzherbert, *The Baton Sinister: A Study of a Temperament and a Time*, 1674–1686 (1903), about Monmouth's rebellion, and *The Island of Sorrow* (1903), about robert Emmet and the Irish rebellion of 1798, which struck reviewers as unusually well-researched, and a little indigestible.

GILBERT, Lady: Rosa MULHOLLAND (1841–1921) married (1891) John Thomas GILBERT (1829–1898), Kt. (1897). The daughter of a Belfast doctor, she was educated at home and studied art in South Kensington. Her husband was an Irish historian; she lived as a widow in Dublin. Some of her early short stories were printed in *All the Year Round*. She published a novel, *Dunmara*, under the pseudonym 'Ruth Murray' in 1864, and subsequently a large number of novels set in rural Ireland which featured strong, independent female characters and were Catholic and nationalist in feeling. In *Cynthia's Bonnet Shop* (1900) two poor Irish sisters open a milliner's shop in London to support their invalid mother; the heroine of *A Girl's Ideal* (1908) is an American heiress trying to spend her fortune for the good of Ireland; *The Return of Mary O'Murrough* (1910) is about a girl who returns from the US to Killarney to find her lover imprisoned by the unfair legal system; *The Tragedy of Chris* (1903) has the usual setting in rural Ireland, but gains an additional breadth from excursions into the Dublin slums, and to London, where the 'tragedy' of Chris's disappearance occurs. Gilbert also published verse including *Spirit and Dust* (1908) and *Dreams and Realities* (1916). Her sister Clara Mulholland published several books for children and young girls, of a pious Catholic cast, including *Terence O'Neill's Heiress* (1909). Gilbert's early career was fostered by Father Matthew Russell, SJ (1834–1912), who edited the *Irish Monthly* and whose brother was married to another of her sisters.

GILCHRIST, R[obert] Murray (1868–1917) spent his boyhood in Sheffield, Yorkshire, and was educated at the Royal Grammar School there. He worked for a while with W. E. Henley (1849–1903) on the *National Observer*. Gilchrist was a great lover of the Peak District (*The Peak District*,

1911) and its inhabitants; this passion spills over into his fictional works. Characteristic in this respect are the stories collected in *Natives of Milton* (1902). Sometimes, as in *The Labyrinth* (1902), which involves secret marriage, robbery, murder, the House with Eleven Staircases, and the Abode of the Leper, Gilchrist gave his Peak District stories an eighteenth-century setting (reviewers took the novel's title to refer as much to its narrative method as to its subject). But his fictional world is timeless, except when invaded, as it is in *Damosel Croft* (1912), by a novelist in a motor car. There are signs that he meant it to be classless, too. In *The First Born* (1911), a landowner allows his first but humbly born grandson into the inheritance. *Weird Wedlock* (1913) is a melodrama with ghostly overtones. *The Gentle Thespians* (1908) marks something of a departure: two eighteenth-century queens of the stage, widowed after happy marriages, assemble a young company from among the 'quality' and tour the country, enjoying a hearty outdoor life. Gilchrist also published in the period *Beggar's Manor* (1903) and *The Secret Tontine* (1912). He was a friend of Hugh *Walpole, who thought his books underrated, and wrote about him in *The Apple Trees* (1932).

Girondin, The, Hilaire *Belloc, 1911, Thomas Nelson. The action begins in Bordeaux on 8 August 1792 and ends at the battle of Valmy on 21 September 1792. Georges Boutroux, the scapegrace nephew of a wealthy wine merchant who has joined a revolutionary club, leads an angry mob to his uncle's door and then, a little later, kills the sentry they have posted there in a duel. Thereforward he is pursued by Republicans and Royalists alike. After a number of picaresque adventures, he enlists in a cavalry regiment and goes to war against the Republic's enemies. War turns out to mean aimless marches and counter-marches in the pouring rain. Georges misses his chance at glory, dying on the day of the battle as a result of wounds suffered in a traffic accident. The novel's demystifications are reminiscent of *The Red Badge of Courage* (1895) by Stephen Crane (1871–1900). This is *historical romance without the romance.

GISSING, Algernon (1860–1937) married (1887) Catherine BASELEY (1859–1937). Born in Wakefield, west Yorkshire, son of a chemist and botanist, he was the younger brother of George *Gissing, and attained only minor success as a regional novelist. He shared their father's interest in botany and natural history, and was also an expert on the life and work of Samuel Johnson (1709–84). He trained as a solicitor, and practised briefly in Wakefield. Perhaps spurred on by his brother's literary successes of the 1880s, Algernon published his first novel, *Joy Cometh in the Morning: A Country Tale*, in 1888, the first of many to dwell upon matters bucolic. It sold less than 400 copies. Several more novels with rural settings, were to follow: *Both of This Parish* (1889), *A Village Hampden* (1890), and *A Moorland Idyll* (1891). George *Meredith influenced *A Masquerader* (1892). The sales of the novel were poor but Gissing continued to produce lacklustre work until 1899, when *A Secret of the North Sea*, a melodrama set on the Northumberland coast, was favourably received. Thereafter he turned out Hardyesque tragedies, one or two, such as *One Ash* (1911), set in Wessex, but the majority in Northumberland. Characteristic of this vein are *The Keys of the House* (1902), about a 16-year-old boy torn between his austere parson father and a mother who left home in search of social success, and returns without having found it; and *The Dreams of Simon Usher* (1907), about a dogged Yorkshire factory lad who finds refuge among the farmers and traders of a Northumberland fishing village, and is ambiguously befriended by a wealthy older woman, before falling in love with the daughter of the local magnate. Critics tended to complain about the lack of any organic connection between theme and setting. The herdsman in *The Herdsman* (1910) delivers lectures on archaeology; and, as one reviewer pointed out, 'Kensington Gardens would have supplied all the necessary sheep.' Gissing did make some effort to broaden the scope of his fiction. *An Angel's Portion* (1903), for example, is a fantastically complicated story about the illegitimate daughter of a baronet who inherits his property, much to the indignation of his second wife, and who marries one man, her father's honest factotum, while secretly in love with another, who has married her husband's sister. *Second Selves* (1908) attempts a Meredithian treatment of weak egotism: the hero takes part in a village fête while his father lies dying in the vicarage, commits forgery to clear himself of undergraduate debts, marries a humble girl under compulsion from her brother, and ends up as a farm labourer. *The Unlit Lamp* (1909) is a *historical romance set in early-nineteenth-century Gloucestershire: at one point the hero decides to pay a visit to William Wordsworth (1770–1850). But none of these initiatives seems to have paid dividends, and Gissing returned in *The Top Farm* (1912) to bleak landscapes and bleaker marriages. One of his last books was *The Letters of George Gissing to Members of his Family* (1927), co-edited with their sister Ellen. He has a thick file in the archives of the Royal Literary Fund: 'Always of a nervous and retiring temperament he has found the stress of modern commercialism more than he could fight against,' commented one supporter. He died at home at Bloxham, near Banbury.

GISSING, George [Robert] (1857–1903) married first, (1879), Marianne Helen HARRISON (1858–1889) (separated 1882) and, secondly (1891), Edith Alice UNDERWOOD (1867–1917) (separated 1897). Born in Wakefield, Yorkshire, the eldest of five children of a chemist and amateur botanist who died in 1870, he was educated there and, from 1870, at a Quaker boarding-school at Alderley Edge, where he was unhappy. In 1872 he got an exhibition to Owens College, Manchester, but was expelled in 1876 for stealing and went briefly to prison. He spent a year, 1876–77, in America, picking up a living writing and teaching, then came back to London and existed in the same way, in great poverty. It is not clear when he began to live with the woman who became his first wife, whether he had known her before he left for America, or whether she was involved in any way with his early theft. They parted by early 1882; she seems to have been ill and they were very poor, partly because Gissing used some money he had inherited to pay for the publication of his first novel, *Workers in the Dawn* (1880). In 1880 he began to tutor the sons of Frederic *Harrison; he later taught other boys, which gave him a reasonable total income of more than £150 p. a. by 1884 In 1885 he gave up tutoring to devote himself full-time to literature; in the late 1880s he travelled in France, Italy, and Greece for the first time. He had an interest in foreign literature unusual among English novelists of his generation 'My masters are the novelists of France and Russia,' he wrote to a friend. In 1891 he moved to Exeter, where he married another working-class girl; he was soon complaining of domestic difficulties, compounded by the birth of two sons and his own increasing lung trouble. Edith Gissing was to die in a lunatic asylum. *New Grub Street* (1891) provides a vivid picture of the sheer grind and poverty of the lives of the vast majority of professional writers in London by the end of the 1890s, and also indicates Gissing's own frustration with his career (approaching his 33rd birthday, he had already published eight novels; they had been well received critically but not commercially, and it was not clear why this situation should change). His early fiction concerned London proletarian life; other examples are *The Unclassed* (1884), *Demos: A Story of English Socialism* (1886), *Thyrza* (1887), and *The Nether World* (1889). Slowly their critical reputation (and that of *The Odd Women*, 1893, which addressed the dilemmas facing the New Woman of the 1890s) was matched by sales, and by the end of the decade Gissing had made enough money from writing to be relieved of the daily anxieties of the market-place. He left his second wife by travelling to Siena in 1897, where he wrote a study of Dickens, then on to Calabria, about which he wrote *By the Ionian Sea: Notes of a Ramble in Southern Italy* (1901). Soon after his return to England in 1898 he met Gabrielle Fleury (1868–1954), a cultivated Frenchwoman who wanted to translate *New Grub Street*. In May 1899 he moved to France, where they lived together as man and wife (for the benefit of the Fleury family) but did not at first tell the Gissing family. He died at Ispoure in the south of France. *The *Private Papers of Henry Ryecroft* (1903) is a semi-autobiographical celebration of freedom from poverty and of literature as a source of pleasure. **Our Friend the Charlatan* (1901) and **Will Warburton: A Romance of Real Life* (1905) was finished in France. His unfinished novel, *Veranilda: A Romance* (1904), draws on his travels in the Mediterranean in the last phase of his life. A volume of short stories, *The *House of Cobwebs* (1906), was also published posthumously. Though an admirer of Charles Dickens (1812–80), of whom he published a critical study in 1898, Gissing was also influenced early in his career by French naturalism, exploring the physical and cultural representation of the lower middle classes less in terms of melodrama than in terms of prosaicism, reflected in both his writing style and gloomy view of love. Gissing's career as a literary man is treated fictionally by his old friend Morley *Roberts in *The Private Life* *of Henry Maitland* (1912), a book which helped to create several myths about Gissing's life. After his death an annual Civil List pension of £74 was awarded to his two sons during their childhood.

GLANVILLE, Ernest (1856–1925). Glanville's mother and journalist father left Devon for South Africa before he was born, and he was educated in Graham's Town; on completing his studies there he spent some time diamond-mining before following in his father's footsteps. The *Times* and other London papers took his commentaries on the Zulu War during 1879. From the early 1890s until the close of the following decade Glanville lived in England writing novels with South African backdrops, including *The Lost Regiment* (1901), *The Inca's Treasure* (1902), and *The Diamond Seeker* (1902). *A Rough Reformer* (1905) concerns the exploits of Westmacott Vane, whose business is to promote companies on an Imperial scale, and none too scrupulously, and whose pleasure is to develop agricultural schemes for the benefit of the tenants on his country estate.

GLASIER, Katharine BRUCE: Katharine Saint John CONWAY (1867–1950) married John BRUCE GLASIER (d. 1920). Under her maiden name she published *Husband & Brother* (1894), in which two New Women conspire against a literary man, the husband of one and the brother of the other: the emancipation of women is promoted, free love deplored. The sister runs away and becomes a journalist in London, resists seduction, and trains as a nurse. *Tales from the Derbyshire Hills : Pastorals from the Peak District* (1907) is a collection of tearful love stories reprinted from periodicals and sold in aid of the ILP. She and her husband were activists in the ILP and the International Socialist movement; they were pacifist and anti-nationalist. She edited the *Labour Leader* and worked for the Women's Labour League, among other causes campaigning for baths to be provided for miners at the pithead. *Dolly-logues* (1926) started life as a series of women's columnns written in 1919 for the journal of the Birmingham branch of the ILP and originally entitled 'A Socialist Dolly Dialogues: With Apologies to Anthony *Hope'. They are very different from *The Dolly Dialogues* (1894), the story of a young socialist typist's attempt to prove that drudgery is unnecessary by working for some relations. She shows them that their house is not labour-saving, lectures them on theosophy and socialism, and ends by falling in love with their gassed, disillusioned, shell-shocked son.

GLEIG, Charles (b. 1862). A retired commander in the Royal Navy, he was editor of the *Naval and Military Record* from 1890 to 1893. As a novelist he specialised in comic nautical fiction, such as *The Middy of the Blunderbore* (1909), *The Nancy Manoeuvres* (1910), and *Contraband Tommy* (1911), but tried his hand at other genres as well. *When All Men Starve* (1898) is an *invasion scare story in which the Boers and the Germans gang up against the British. *Julian Winterson, Coward and Hero* (1908) is a **Four Feathers*-style story about a young man pitchforked into the navy by his crusty admiral father, and out again by his commanding officer when he runs away during an engagement on the west coast of Africa; he dies redemptively. *A Woman in the Limelight* (1912) concerns two middle-aged bachelors who enter engagements which come to nothing and fall back on friendship.

Glimpse, The: *An Adventure of the Soul*, Arnold *Bennett, 1909, Chapman & Hall. The central part of the novel originated as a short story which *Black and White* declined to publish because, according to Bennett, it was 'much too good, too spiritual'. He began to extend it into a novel on 18 May 1909, finishing in mid-August. In the first part Morrice Loring, a wealthy music critic, returns home from a concert at the Rutland Galleries, a 'retreat for the dilettante', to host a dinner party for his sister, Mary, the quiet, capable widow of a stockbroker, and his best friend, Johnnie Hulse, a libertine ex-soldier. During the course of the evening, his Catholic, pleasure-loving wife, Inez, lets slip that she has been having an affair with Hulse. Loring suffers a heart attack, and, as his spirit is leaving his body, Inez places a penny and a half-crown on his eyelids, and ties up his jaw. He spends the second part of the novel in a trance like death, awaking (a genuine Bennett touch) to hear the half-crown roll off his eye-socket onto the floor. The trance has offered him a vision of an aesthete's paradise, which turns out to be the sterile echo of his own egotism; he returns from it convinced that a sympathetic understanding of other people is the key to happiness. When he reawakens, he discovers that Inez, thinking him dead, has committed suicide. The third and final part describes the coroner's inquest and Morrice's resumption of his old life. He does not, in all honesty, seem greatly changed by his experience, and hands Mary over to Hulse as though nothing had happened. The interest of the novel lies in its attempt to incorporate the *fantastic into the kind of realism Bennett had made his own in *The *Old Wives'* Tale (1908). Frank *Harris told Bennett that all the time the hero was enjoying his glimpse of the next world he was wondering what the wife and the lover were doing in this. At the time, Bennett thought the first and third parts of the book as good as the best he could do. But H. G. *Wells said after Bennett's death that it was 'a glimpse into an empty cavern in his mind'.

GLYN, Elinor: Elinor SUTHERLAND (1864–1943) married (1892) Clayton Louis GLYN (1857–1915). The second child of parents whose pretensions to aristocratic birth were not matched by their income (her father was an engineer), she lived, after her father's death in 1865, with her grandparents in Canada before returning to Jersey when her mother remarried. She disliked her stepfather and became an avid reader and writer. Elegant, proud, and poor, she rejected various suitors before marrying a country squire from Essex, who turned out to be a gambler and drinker. Their neighbour Daisy, Countess of Warwick (1861–1938), half-sister of Lady Angela *Forbes, became her close friend and launched her in high society. Glyn started writing for the social pages of various publications, and published her first novel, *The *Visits of Elizabeth* in 1900, followed by *The Reflections of Ambrosine* (1902), and *The *Vicissitudes of Evangeline* (1905), light, anecdotal accounts of society life. *Beyond the Rocks* (1906) marked the transition in her career from first-person comedy of manners to third-person sexual romance. Gilbert *Parker gave her advice on dealing with her publisher, Duckworth. Her breakthrough book was **Three Weeks* (1907), a romantic melodrama of exotic seduction, which reversed the usual formula by having an Englishman seized by a mystery foreign lady, and featured what became the Elinor Glyn trademark, tiger-skin rugs. The book was a huge success, translated into every European language, and Glyn followed it with other romances similarly lush and daring in their descriptions of female sexuality, such as **His Hour* (1910), *The Reason Why* (1911), **Halcyone* (1912), *These Things* (1915), and *The Career of Katherine Bush* (1917). After discovering in 1908 that her husband had been living on his capital for years, she became the family breadwinner and quickened her rate of production. In 1913 he decamped to Constantinople. Like 'John Oliver *Hobbes' she had some sort of romance with Lord Curzon (1859–1925), to whom she never spoke again after he married for the second time, without telling her, in 1917. During the First World War she went to France as a war correspondent, and in 1920 she became a figure in Hollywood (advising on sex appeal and set decoration as well as writing scripts) and made a great deal of money, of some of which she was relieved by unscrupulous agents. Her daughters encouraged her to turn herself into Elinor Glyn Ltd in order to prevent such exploitation, with partial success, and in 1929 she moved back to England. By this time she had become interested in spiritualism. She produced two unsuccessful films at Elstree, and, once again was forced to churn out fiction to pay her debts. She remained until her death one of the biggest-selling authors in Britain, but such was her extravagance that her family doled out money to her in cash, and for the last eight years of her life she never signed a cheque. There is an autobiography, *Romantic Adventure* (1936), and a biography by Anthony Glyn (1968).

GODFREY, Elizabeth, *pseud.*: Jessie BEDFORD (1854?–1918). Her main line was in offbeat and rather serious-minded romances. *The Winding Road* (1902) and *The Cradle of a Poet* (1910) both have heroes afflicted with *Wanderlust*, the latter being the poetic son of a quarry-owner whose girlfriend becomes a famous dancer. The Bridal of Anstace (1906) is a more demure version of Robert *Hichens's bestselling *The *Garden of Allah* (1904). The heroine marries a Greek count. It turns out that his first wife is still alive. He retires to a monastery, she to a fishing village. Godfrey's non-fiction includes *Home Life Under the Stuarts* (1903), *Social Life Under the Stuarts* (1904), and a biography, *A Sister of Prince Rupert* (1909)

Golden Bowl, The, Henry *James, New York, 1904; Charles Scribner's Sons, London, 1905, Methuen. A dense and complex analysis of moral, emotional, sexual, and social allegiance, based on a story so slender that James himself was able summarize it in one sentence: 'the Father and the Daughter, with the husband of one and the wife of the other entangled in a mutual passion, an intrigue.' Adam and Maggie Verver, the (widowed) father and the daughter, are wealthy Americans living in London. He is a collector of fine objects, and has collected for his daughter a charming but impoverished Italian, Prince Amerigo. It is from the Prince's point of view that we watch events in the run-up to the wedding; the main event being the arrival on the scene of his former lover, and Maggie's friend, Charlotte Stant. Later, Charlotte marries Adam, while still very clearly in love with Amerigo. Maggie finds out about their continuing affair when she buys for her father a golden bowl which, it turns out, Charlotte had once thought of buying for Amerigo, as a last present to her lover before his wedding. The final sections of the novel, told from her point of view, show her efforts to disentangle Charlotte from Amerigo without alarming her father, to whom she remains extraordinarily close. At the end, Adam and Charlotte return to America, where he is to open a museum: one of the prime exhibits being, in a sense, his tamed wife. The novel is famous for its obliqueness, but all the main characters are, at one time or another, and in various combinations, ambitious, vain, predatory, and ruthless. Reviewers tended to cling like drowning men to the perspective provided by Colonel and Mrs Assingham, close friends of the Ververs, who function as a kind of chorus.

GOLDIE, Valentine F. TAUBMAN published two volumes of verse (1911, 1914) and nine rather syrupy novels between 1905 and 1923. The hero of *Nephele* (1912) is a solitary musician who falls in love with a woman first heard singing in the still woods at night. *The Declension of Henry d'Albiac* (1912) is at once more topical and more incisive. The hero is a wealthy young idler, thoroughly conventional, and engaged to a very similar young woman, who falls under the spell of a thoroughly unconventional widow, a vegetarian and suffragist. The twist is that the suffragist exploits her femininity far more effectively than the doll-like society woman. 'Declension' was Arnold *Bennett's term, in **Hilda Lessways* (1911) and elsewhere, for physical and moral deterioration. Little is known about Goldie, except that he was the only son of a remarkable and forceful character, Sir George Dashwood Taubman Goldie (1846–1925), founder of Nigeria and a key figure in the scramble for West Africa.

GOLDRING, Maude published four novels in the period, all set in provincial backwaters. *Dean's Hall* (1908) is an understated account of Yorkshire West Riding life in the early nineteenth century. *The Downsman: A Story of Sussex* (1911) has a more theatrical plot, and a fine outburst by a socialist at a garden party. *The Wonder Year* (1914) is about the dullness of provincial life, and the women who want to escape it: one of them succeeds as a writer in London. Goldring also published a volume of verse (1914), with a preface by Katharine *Tynan, and a biography of Charlotte Brontë (1915).

GORDON, Samuel (1871–1927). Although born at Buk in Prussia, Gordon came to England at the age of 13, attended the City of London School, and read Classics at Queen's College, Cambridge (BA, 1893). His novels are deeply involved with Jewish concerns, notably the aim of maintaining a separate identity for Jewish communities. His early works include *In Years of Transition* (1897), *A Handful of Exotics* (1897), *A Tale of Two Rings* (1898), *Daughters of Shem* (1898), and *Lesser Destinies* (1899). Gordon's most accomplished work is *Sons of The Covenant: A Tale of Anglo-Russian Jewry* (1900), whose production was supported by the Jewish Publication Society of America (which had invited Israel *Zangwill to write *The Children of the Ghetto*, 1892). It depicts the lives and careers of two brothers and explores the nature and position of Jewish communities in the East End and West End of London. *Unto Each Man His Own* (1904) follows the fortunes of Ellen Devereux, a devout Christian who converts to Judaism when she marries Arthur Clauston (formerly Abraham Clausenstein). The main focus is on relations with the West End set, represented by the Louissons, and on the irreparable racial and spiritual antagonism between the Jewish and Christian communities. *The Ferry of Fate* (1906) is about Russian Jewry and Russian bureaucracy. Gordon did on occasion depart from Jewish themes. *The Queen's Quandary* (1903) is a *Ruritanian romance about a country called Transmontany. The **Times Literary Supplement* summarized *The New Galatea* (1908) succinctly: '(1) Noyce Manseigh, a country parson's daughter, is the cold virgin who, to help him with his work, marries (2) Horace St George, artist, who, being starved in his affections, deteriorates in his work, and is loved by, but does not yield to, (3) Hetty Hillary, his model, who eventually is the means of bringing husband and wife together.' Gordon listed his recreation in *Who's Who* as 'doing nothing and doing it well'.

GORST, Mrs Harold E.: Nina Cecilia Francesca KENNEDY (1869–1926) married Harold Edward GORST (1868–1950). Educated at home, she was a novelist and playwright who married a journalist who also wrote plays. She published six novels in the period, mostly relentless studies of the deprivations of slum and suburban life. In *The Light* (1906), an orphan is seduced, gives birth to a blind child, spends two years in the workhouse, finds employment as a drudge in a London lodging-house, a waitress in a suburban restaurant, and at a laundry whose owner harasses her; the light is that shed by her child, who has been brought up in a peaceful village. *The Thief on the Cross* (1908) concerns another daughter of the slums, while *The Leech* (1911) is the voluble, bullying Mrs Barnes who comes to live with her sister-in-law in the London suburbs. Her husband's memoirs appeared as *Much of Life Is Laughter* (1936). He wrote the novel *Furthest South: An Account of the Startling Discovery made by the Wise Antarctic Expedition* (1900) and collaborated with Gertrude *Warden on *Compromised: A Tale* (1905) from their earlier play.

GOULD, Nat[haniel] (1857–1919) married (1886) Elizabeth Madelin RUSKA. Born in Manchester, the son of a tea merchant, and educated privately in Southport, he tried his father's trade and farming before becoming a journalist on the *Newark Advertiser* in about 1878. He went to Australia in 1884, worked on different newspapers, married in Brisbane, and began to write novels. The first, *The Double Event* (1891), began as a newspaper serial; it had vast sales in volume form and was the first of 130 bestselling novels about the world of horseracing. He contracted, first with Routledge and then, in 1903, with John Long, to supply four novels and a short story every year, which he did. In 1895 he came back to England with his family. As well as novels he published books about Australian life such as *Town and Bush* (1896) and some memoirs: *The Magic of Sport: Mainly Autobiographical* (1909). He died at Bedfont, Middlesex, leaving twenty-two novels to be published posthumously at the rate of five a year.

GOWING, Mrs Aylmer: Emilia BLAKE (1846–1905) married (1887) William GOWING. The daughter of a Dublin QC, she married an actor whose stage name was Walter Gordon, and worked as an actress and elocutionist; she also did recitations. She published verse and recitations from 1874, plays, and fiction. She published three novels of a *fantastic tendency in the period: *As Caesar's Wife* (1902), *By Thames and Tiber* (1903), and *A King's Desire* (1904). The half-English, half-Italian heroine of *By Thames and Tiber* gets lost in the Roman catacombs, and dreams, for half the book, of the sacrifice of a martyr ancestress in the days of Nero. *A King's Desire* is Saharan and *Ruritanian: the monarch of a tiny German state loves an Englishwoman of mysterious parentage.

GRAHAM, Mrs Henry: Ellen PEEL (1863–1962), married, first (1890), Henry GRAHAM (d. 1907) (separated 1900) and, secondly (1908), George Ranken ASKWITH (1861–1942), KCB 1911, created (1919) 1st Baron ASKWITH. She was born into an upper-class family; her mother died at her birth and her stepmother was uncongenial. She was educated at home in north Wales; at 25 she left for Australia in charge of her brother, whose mental illness took the form of making indiscriminate sexual advances to fellow-passengers. Unhappy at home, she married, to get away, an army officer who turned out to be an alcoholic, and took to journalism to help make ends meet after their separation. Her second husband was a barrister and politician. She ran canteens in the First World War and subsequently did much charitable and public work. She published two novels in the period: *The Tower of Siloam* (1905), a romance of London and country society, and *The Disinherited of the Earth* (1908), a grim tale about the degeneration of a child raised by a libertine father and narrowly moralistic mother. Betty Askwith's *A Victorian Young Lady* (1978) is a memoir by her daughter, drawing on diaries from 1886.

GRAHAM, [Matilda] Winifred [Muriel] (*c.*1875–1950) married (1906) Theodore J. CORY. Educated at home, she published a large volume of fiction from 1900 onwards, mostly sensational, some of it polemical. *Angels and Devils and Man* (1904) features a professor who unmasks villainy by thought-reading. *Christian Murderers* (1908) is an attack on Christian Science. *The Love Story of a Mormon* (1911) concerns the attempted abduction of an English girl by a Mormon agent. She also published several volumes of self-aggrandizing autobiography and non-fiction about spiritualism (of which she was in favour) and the Mormon Church (which she was against). An obituary in the *Times* (6 Feb. 1950) observed: 'from the beginning her dramatic and sentimental fictions came easily and flowingly from an ardent if not very exacting or self-critical fancy'.

GRAHAM, R. B. CUNNINGHAME: Robert BONTINE (1852–1936), who changed his name (1883) to Robert Bontine CUNNINGHAME GRAHAM on his father's death, married (1878) Gabrielle Marie de LA BALMONDIERE (*c.*1860–1906). The son of a Scots laird who went mad, he was at Harrow for a short time but at 17 went to South America (his maternal grandmother was Spanish and had taught him the language). During the 1870s he made several journeys between England and South America; his ostensible aim was to retrieve the family fortunes by various commercial schemes, in Paraguay, Uruguay, Argentina, and Brazil, including horse-dealing and trading in maté, none of which was successful. He later lived with his wife in Texas and Mexico (1879–81). After his father's death they went to live in Scotland, and Graham embarked on a career in politics. In 1886 he was elected Radical Liberal MP for North-West Lanark, an industrial suburb of Glasgow, on a platform of land reform and shorter working hours. He became notorious for his socialist opinions, especially after 'Bloody Sunday' (13 Nov. 1887), a riot in Trafalgar Square in which Graham was knocked down by a policeman and spent six weeks in jail for unlawful assembly. The episode is described in the novel *News from Nowhere* (1891) by William Morris (1834–96). In 1892 Graham failed to be elected as Labour candidate for the Camlachie division of Glasgow. He was a friend of Keir Hardie (1856–1915) and an important figure in the labour movement, joining the ILP in 1893; he campaigned on behalf of many oppressed groups, including chain-makers, dockers, match-girls, American Indians, and Africans threatened by imperialist expansion. In the late 1890s he began a third career as a writer. He had an aversion to the Kailyard school, 'those awful McCrocketts, and Larens' (i. e. S. R. *Crockett and 'Ian *Maclaren'), expressed in an article reprinted in *The Ipané* (1899), the first of a series of collections of short fictions and sketches drawing on his experiences of South American and Scotland. It was followed by *Thirteen Stories* (1900), *Success* (1902), *His People* (1907), *Faith*, (1909), *Hope* (1910), *Charity* (1912), and *A Hatchment* (1913). *Faith* is representative. It contains eighteen short stories, some of them little more than travel sketches, set in South America, North Africa, Spain, Scotland, and London. Not very much happens: a nun adopts a wounded bird as a pet; a saintly anarchist dies peacefully; a Moorish soldier employed by the British consulate at Fez buries his young son; a blind Arab placidly undergoes an unsuccessful eye operation performed by a German surgeon; a Spanish sailor loses his way in the Scottish mists; a bill-sticker publishes a pamphlet denouncing Queen Victoria as a Messalina; an English painter philosophically visits a Spanish brothel and a German spa. There is some violence. But Graham's ability to describe landscape, and enter into the ways of life of a wide range of men and women, is genuinely impressive. The record of places seen and people observed or talked to constitutes an implicit autobiography. 'Everything a man writes brings sorrow to him of some kind or other,' Graham comments in his preface. By the time of *A Hatchment* his sketches had abandoned any pretension to sustained narrative and settled into elegiac contemplation of the last traces of a disappearing world: crumbling English mansions, legendary Scottish outlaws, a 'West' (mostly South American) that was no longer 'Wild'. What remains interesting in Graham's work is how he uses his experiences of other cultures to cast an estranged eye on British culture and politics. He also wrote travel books and a number of historical studies of the Spanish presence in South America. His handwriting was notoriously difficult to decipher and his printed works are consequently full of errors. His literary career was fostered by Edward Garnett (1868–1937); he was a close friend of W. H. *Hudson, and of *Conrad, who is thought to have been indebted to Graham for some of the background to **Nostromo* (1904). Graham's anti-imperialist essay 'Bloody Niggers' compares the Roman and British empires in a way analogous to the opening of **Heart of Darkness* (1902). G. B Shaw (1856–1950) gives a romantic sketch of Graham and acknowledges a debt to him in the notes to *Captain Brassbound's Conversion* (1901). During and after the First World War, which he spent in South America buying horses for the army, Graham continued to publish fiction, history, and travel books. In 1929 he became first president of what was to become the Scottish Nationalist Party. He died in Buenos Aires. Graham's exotic career made a deep impression on his contemporaries; he combined aristocratic ancestry with revolutionary opinions and glamorous appearance and manner. There is a biography by Cedric Watts and Laurence Davies (1979). His wife Gabrielle, known as Gabriela, born in Chile of a French father and a Spanish mother, was translator and author of some mystical works, and after her death Graham edited her *The Christ of Toro and Other Stories* (1908).

GRAHAME, Kenneth (1859–1932) married (1899) Elspeth THOMSON (d. 1946). Born in Edinburgh, son of a lawyer, he was educated at St Edward's School, Oxford, and spent two years in the office of a parliamentary agent before, denied the opportunity of going to university, he joined the Bank of England as a clerk in 1879. His mother had died when he was 5; and his father sent the children to her mother in Berkshire, and himself abandoned his legal career in 1867 for a life as an English teacher in France, never seeing or writing to his children again. This double bereavement and loss of adult company encouraged the children to live in a world to themselves. Kenneth Grahame rose to become secretary of the Bank in 1898, and retired for health reasons in 1908. Meanwhile he had begun a parallel career writing reviews and sketches in the *National Observer*, edited by W. E. Henley (1849–1903), and in the *Yellow Book*, collected in *Pagan Papers* (1893) and *The Golden Age* (1895). *Dream Days* (1898) is a sequel to the latter with the same child characters. His marriage was not happy. Grahame's best-known work, *The *Wind in the Willows* (1908), began as a series of letters to his only child Alastair (1900–20), who was run over by a train as an undergraduate; it may have been a suicide. Grahame and 'Anthony *Hope' were first cousins.

GRAND, Sarah, *pseud.*: Frances Elizabeth Bellenden CLARKE (1854–1943) married (1870) David Chambers McFALL (1832–1898). Born in Northern Ireland, the daughter of an alcoholic naval officer who died when she was 7, she married at 16 a much older, widowed army doctor with two young sons, who worked in an asylum for prostitutes with venereal disease. With him she travelled to the Far East, where they lived for five years in the 1870s. After 1875 they settled at Warrington, Lancashire. The marriage was unhappy and the money from the success of her second novel, *Ideala: A Study of Life* (1888), which addressed the issues of mismarriage and female sexuality (her first, *Two Dear Little Feet*, had been published in 1880), enabled her to move to London, where she lived with her stepsons while her husband stayed in Lancashire. McFall joined the Writers' Suffrage League, and became an active suffragette. Her essays and lectures on female education, marriage laws, the double sexual standard, and so forth, were published as *Modern Man and Maid* (1898). In about 1920 she moved to Bath, where she stayed. In 1923 her friend the bookbinder Cedric Chivers was elected mayor and asked her to act as mayoress: she thus became a prominent figure in the city. Her literary importance was as a New Woman novelist (she coined the term) in the 1890s, with her feminist trilogy, *Ideala*, the bestselling *The Heavenly Twins* (1893), which dealt with the issue of venereal disease, and *The Beth Book* (1897), in which she explored the problems of female desire and the dilemmas of the woman artist. *Adnam's Orchard* (1912) is a 640-page epic whose concluding words are 'End of Prologue'. The prologue is Adnam's youth: the vividness of youthful perception had always been McFall's strong suit as a writer. When his father dies, Adnam's elder brother inherits the family farm, and he sets out for London in Farmer Hallbin's gig. The world, especially sections of London society, becomes his orchard. 'All the modern problems flourish here—one or two of them a little damaged by long service,' the **Times Literary Supplement* reported, 'all the cries and causes'. *The Winged Victory* (1916) addressed the issue of land reform. It was intended to form, with *Adnam's Orchard*, part of a trilogy which was never completed. Other works are *Babs the Impossible* (1900) and *Emotional Moments* (1908). She was on good terms with Haldane *MacFall, who was her stepson.

Grand Babylon Hotel, The: *A Fantasia on Modern Themes*, Arnold *Bennett, 1902, Chatto & Windus. A romance in the manner of 'Anthony *Hope', set in the distinctly *Ruritanian Grand Babylon Hotel in the Strand. An American multi-milionaire, Theodore Racksole, buys the hotel, reputedly the finest in Europe, when his daughter, Nella, is refused a beefsteak and a bottle of Bass. An intrigue develops. Prince Eugen must borrow £1 million from a Jewish financier, Mr Sampson Levi, aided by his youthful uncle, Prince Aribert, and impeded by agents of the King of Bosnia. There is a death, a suicide attempt, a secret passage, a trip to Ostend, a mysterious lady in a red hat, and a skirmish in the wine cellar. Nella falls for the dashing Aribert to conclude this elegant pot-boiler. *The Grand Babylon Hotel* was the second serial Bennett wrote after his arrival in London (the first being *The* **Ghost*). He completed it in fifteen days sometime during 1900, and sold the rights to the Tillotson syndicate for £100. It appeared in the *Golden Penny* from 2 February 1901, and subsequently all over the provincial press, accompanied by lavish advertisement in railway stations up and down the land. Tillotson sold the world book rights to Chatto & Windus for £80. Bennett himself referred to its 'mechanical ingenuities' and 'surface glitter'; but, as so often in his lightweight comedies, the hero's impudence and ingenuity provide an absorbing, implicit parallel to his own. Some reviewers preferred the descriptions of hotel business to the Ruritanian entanglements.

Grand Magazine, The, (1905–1940) was published monthly. Launched by George Newnes as yet another competitor for the *Strand*, it featured the same mix of popular fiction, anecdotal essays, and humorous verse, and drew on much the same pool of writers, including Conan *Doyle and George Bernard Shaw.

GRANT, Sadi published nine volumes of fiction from *A New Woman Subdued* (1898) to 1916, including *Folly at Cannes* (1902), a very lightweight tale of a vicar's daughter in the south of France, seduced into a false marriage by a wicked peer; *A Japanese House-Party* (1904); and *Lobelia of China* (1907).

GRAVES, Clo: see 'Richard *Dehan'.

GRAY, Maxwell, *pseud.*: Mary Gleed TUTTIETT (1847–1923). A surgeon's daughter, Tuttiett was born at Newport, Isle of Wight and was still living there, supporting her invalid parents, at the time of her first application to the Royal Literary Fund in 1893. At that time complications of asthma, rheumatism, and weak lungs had prevented her from walking for ten years. She later went to live in Ealing, and applied again unsuccessfully for relief in 1920. She wrote under a male pseudonym and was a keen advocate of women's rights. Her most widely known novel (which she later developed into a highly successful stage play) is *The Silence of Dean Maitland* (1886). In *The Great Refusal* (1906) Adrian Bassett refuses not only the fortune accumulated by his father, Sir Daniel, a self-made millionaire, but his fiancée, Lady Isobel Mostyn. A spell in a university settlement in the East End of London, during which he contracts typhoid, opens his eyes to the dangers of inequality. Thereafter, disinherited, his engagement annulled, be drives a van, works in a jam factory, edits a newspaper, becomes secretary to a cabinet minister, and founds a community called the Brotherhood of the Golden Rule on the East Coast of Africa. In *Something Afar* (1913) Ronald Leith, a lugubrious bank clerk, inherits a fortune and decides to revisit Lugano, the scene of his first love. However, Gray's work was by this time beginning to seem distinctly old-fashioned, and the success of *The Silence of Dean Maitland* a long way off. The **Times Literary Supplement* complained that *Unconfessed* (1911) read like a novel written in the 1880s.

GRAY, Rowland, *pseud.*: Lilian Kate ROWLAND-BROWN (1863–1959). The daughter of a barrister, she was educated in Cambridge and Fontainebleau, and became a journalist, contributing to the **Times Literary Supplement, Nineteenth Century,* the *Church Times,* and other periodicals. She was High Anglican. She published a number of anodyne romances, such as *The Unexpected* (1902), about the experiences of a well-connected governess in a parvenu family, and *Green Cliffs* (1905), about an eventful holiday on the Brittany coast. *Surrender* (1909) is a little out of the ordinary: two middle-aged women both fall in love with younger men, one a soldier, the other a doctor; one renounces her love, the other is doomed to frustration.

GRAYDON, William Murray (1864–1946) published fourteen books for boys from 1897, including *The Fighting Lads of Devon, or, In the Days of the Armada* (1900), *The Jungle Trappers: A Tale of the Indian Jungle* (1905), *Lost in the Slave Land, or, The Mystery of the Sacred Lamp Rock* (1902), *On Winding Waters: A Tale of Adventure and Peril* (1902), *With Cossack and Convict: A Realistic Story* (1903), and *With Musketeer and Redskin: A Tale of*

New Plymouth (1904). It is probable that other works were published serially.

Great Amulet, The, Maud *Diver, 1908, Blackwood. The surgingly romantic story of a mismatched couple whose love for each other, shallow at first, ripens and blossoms under pressure. Eldred Lenox is a puritanitical Scots artilleryman serving on the North-West frontier of India. His wife, Quita, is a vivid, whimsical artist. They discover their incompatibility on the day of their wedding and decide to separate, as they would have done in a New Woman novel. Eldred becomes addicted to work and opium, Quita to art, independence, and flirtation. But, as this is not quite a New Woman novel, Eldred is regenerated by an arduous expedition into the mountains north of Kashmir, Quita by motherhood ('a triumph of the essential woman over mere line and curve'). The Desmonds from **Captain Desmond, V. C.*, monumentally constant to each other and the Empire, form the background to Eldred and Quita's turbulent self-renewal.

Great Man, A: *A Frolic*, Arnold *Bennett, 1904, Chatto & Windus. This is the story of the unexpected rise to literary prominence of the naïve but well-meaning draper's son Henry Shakspere [*sic*] Knight, despite the best efforts of his cynical cousin Tom, who continually distracts him, with sweets as a child, with wine, women and gambling as a grown-up. The plot gives Bennett an opportunity to satirize various aspects of the publishing business (literary agents, book and magazine publishers, booksellers, reviewers, etc.), and to mock popular taste in sentimental romance in his descriptions of Knight's world-wide bestsellers, *Love in Babylon*, *A Question of Cubits*, and *The Plague-Spot*. Bennett began writing the novel in December 1903, and finished it, after an interruption of five weeks, on 13 March 1904, when he described it in his journal something which began as farce and ended as 'rather profound satire'. When a brief notice in the *Pall Mall Gazette* misrepresented it, Bennett wrote to the editor to complain, with the result that the magazine printed a much longer review praising the author's 'gentle sarcasm against the fiction-reading public'. According to Bennett, it was greatly appreciated by Charles *Marriott, Eden *Philpotts and H. G. *Wells, among others.

Green Mansions: *A Romance of the Tropical Forest*, W. H. *Hudson, 1904, Duckworth. In this best-selling eco-romance, the mansions in question are the forests of western Guiana, close to the foot of the Parahuari mountains, where Abel Geuvez de Argensola, a political refugee from Venezuela, abandoning his search for gold and his literary ambitions, has settled with a tribe of Indians. Exploring the edges of a forest which the natives regard as haunted, Abel becomes aware of an invisible presence with a voice like a bird's. The presence, recognizing his harmlessness, materializes as 'a girl form, reclining on the moss among the ferns and herbage, near the roots of a small tree . . . she was small, not above four feet six or seven inches in height, in figure slim, with delicately shaped little hands and feet.' This is Rima, last survivor of a lost tribe, who has been brought up by an old man, Nuflo, after her mother's death. Abel and Rima fall in love and, learning from the old man that her mother came from a district called Riolama, set off with Nuflo to find her mother's people. Her mother's people do not exist. On the way back, Rima easily outstrips her companions, who arrive days later to discover that the Indians have caught her and burnt her to death. In revenge, Abel persuades a neighbouring tribe to massacre them. Plunged into despair by her death and its aftermath, he becomes a hermit. Eventually, recovering her bones, he sets off for the coast, and arrives in Georgetown 'wasted almost to a skeleton by fever and misery of all kinds, his face blackened by long exposure to sun and wind'. The story mixes *exoticism with detailed observation of spiders, snakes, grubs, centipedes, and moths (one cannot imagine Rider *Haggard bothering to describe anything smaller than an elephant).

GRIBBLE, Francis [Henry] (1862–1946) married, first, Maria Evertje Aleida SCHANZE (d. 1928) and, secondly (1937), Minnie Maud BATTELL. Gribble was born at Barnstaple, Devon, son of a banker, and educated at Bedford Grammar School, Chatham House, Ramsgate, and Exeter College, Oxford, graduating in 1884 with a first-class degree in classics. He taught classics at Warwick Grammar School before moving to London in 1887 to take up a journalistic career. He was the first editor of *Phil May's Annual* and was a frequent contributor to the *Fortnightly Review*. He began to publish fiction in the

1890s, some of it sensational, like *The Red Spell* (1895), about the Paris Commune, some of it realistic, like *Sunlight and Limelight: A Story of the Stage Life and the Real Life* (1898), about provincial repertory theatre. His most notable Edwardian novel is *The Pillar of Cloud* (1906), which concerns a boarding-house for women who earn their living as clerks, typewriters, daily governesses, and so on. They form a Way Out Club, where they plot their escape from servitude. Some make it, some do not. Gribble was no feminist. His workaday women seem unable to prosper through their own efforts alone, or through mutual support. But he did insist that they should not rely too much on men, and he did emphasize the idea of female community by tracing the individual destinies of a *group* of women. *Double Lives* (1911) is a contrastingly good-humoured, whimsical tale of a brilliant Oxford student's social and amorous conquests in fashionable London. Gribble also published travel books and biographies, such as *The Love Affairs of Lord Byron* (1910), *The Life of Emperor Francis Joseph* (1914), and *The Romantic Life of Shelley* (1911). Like many other writers of his generation, he worked in the Ministry of Information during the First World War. *Seen In Passing* (1926) is a memoir.

GRIER, Sydney Carlyon, *pseud.*: Hilda Caroline GREGG (1868–1933). Born in Gloucestershire, daughter of a consumptive Church of England clergyman, Gregg received a private education before completing a BA course at London University; she then worked as a teacher. She and her mother, who died in 1913, lived together in Eastbourne. Her first short story was accepted by the *Bristol Times* in 1886. Gregg's two great passions were India and royalty. *The Power of the Keys* (1907) is set in a medical mission in northern India. The skills of two English nurses prove useful when India is invaded by the 'Scythians'. The novel is a *roman-à-clef* warning of the dangers of complacency and maladministration. *The Path to Honour* (1907), set in the 1840s in a Native State on the borders of India, is more straightforwardly romantic. Two soldiers, action man Robert Charteris and the scientific Henry Gerrard, are rivals for Honour Cinnamond, who initially prefers to reform rather than to adore them: one wins honour, the other Honour. In *The Prince of the Captivity* (1902), neither the prince nor his captivity is of much consequence. Attention centres on Felicia Steinherz, a heartless American heiress who becomes in some mysterious way a European queen, on a good-natured Englishman, Lord Usk, and on the impulsive, simple-minded Princess Helene of Schwarzwald-Molzau. In *The Heir* (1906) Maurice Teffany, a young Cambridge man, is informed by a patriotic enthusiast, Professor Panagiotis, that he is heir to a rather vaguely specified 'Empire of the East'. He sets off with his sister to stake his claim, and on the way encounters a young lady who turns out to be a rival claimant. Teffany also features in *The Heritage* (1908) and *The Prize* (1910). *The Great Pro-Consul* (1904) is a diary-memoir intended to present Warren Hastings as he appeared to his intimates from 30 June 1777 to 3 December 1818, and Gregg warned off the reader who expected a *historical romance. She later edited *The Letters of Warren Hastings to His Wife* (1915). She died in Eastbourne. The *Times* obituary (26 June 1933) saw her as both an accomplished story-teller and a sensitive, skilled writer: 'Life under various conditions in different parts of the world was what inspired her stories, and in all of them there was the same realistic touch, the unlaboured attention to seemingly careless detail, the same power of seeing through the eyes of widely differing races.'

GRIFFIN, E. Aceituna: Editha Aceituna—— (1876–1949) married Robert Chaloner GRIFFIN. The wife of an army officer, she contributed to the *Ladies' Pictorial* and the *Daily Mail* and published thirteen novels between 1906 and 1939, of which the earliest, both commonplace romances, are *Lady Sarah's Deed of Gift* (1906) and *The Tavistocks* (1908). The former is the autobiography of a flirt; the latter concerns two sisters whose husbands are absent abroad, and who react in different ways.

GRIFFITH, George, *pseud.*: George Chetwynd GRIFFITH-JONES (d. 1906). The son of a Church of England clergyman, he set out as a young man to travel the world and claimed to be thus entirely self-educated. He made his way by taking whatever work was available (sailor, sundowner, stockrider, teacher, journalist) before becoming a writer of sensational and often futuristic tales. His *The Outlaws of the Air* (1895) influenced H. G. *Wells's *The War in the Air* (1908). In *Angel of the Revolution: A Tale of the Coming Terror* (1893), which set the pattern for much of his later work, Richard Arnold, an engineer whose design for an airship has been rejected by the British government, enlists in the Brotherhood, an international secret society led by Natas, a Russian Jew who has suffered terribly at the hands of the Tsarist police. Arnold builds airships for the Brotherhood, which uses them to foment and regulate a world war between Britain, Germany, and Austria, on one hand, and France, Russia, and Italy, on the other. Although in theory neutral, the Brotherhood brings America into the war on the side of Britain and Germany, and thus ensures their triumph. *A Honeymoon in Space* (1901) is about the travels of an English lord and an American girl to the Moon, Mars, Venus, and Saturn: *Criminal Croesus* (1904) also has science fiction elements, this time submarine. *The Stolen Submarine: A Tale of the Russo-Japanese War* (1904) has a large cast of millionaires, princesses, forgers, and blackmailers. When the action switches to the war in the East, an aerial ship and a submarine wreak terrible damage. In *The World Peril of 1910* (1907)—1910 was the year in which, according to William *Le Queux and others, Britain would be invaded by one or other Continental power—the coming terror takes the form of a comet which is destroyed in the nick of time by a projectile fired from a gigantic cannon. Griffith-Jones also wrote sensational stories about high society. *The White Witch of Mayfair* (1902) is an orgy of blackmail and murder featuring an adventuress called Lena Castello who eventually commits suicide. The *Mayfair Magician* (1905) is a criminal scientist with hypnotizing eyes. Other novels in the period include *Brothers of the Chain* (1900), *Captain Ishmael: A Saga of the Seven Seas* (1900), *The Justice of Revenge* (1901), and *Miss Nitocris: A Phantasy of the Fourth Dimension* (1906).

GRIFFITHS, Major A.: Arthur George Frederick GRIFFITHS (1838–1908). Born at Poona, India, the son of an army officer, he was educated at King William's College, Isle of Man. He joined the 63rd Manchester Regiment in February 1855, saw the fall of Sebastapol during the Crimean War, and served in Nova Scotia and Toronto. He rose to the rank of brigade-major during his term in Gibraltar (1864–70). While stationed there he edited the *Gibraltar Chronicle* (1864), contributed to other journals, and was military correspondent for the *Times*. Griffiths retired in May 1875, was appointed to the Prison Service, and eventually became Inspector of Prisons (1878–96) and a well-known penologist. He represented Britain at an international conference on criminal anthropology in Geneva in 1896. He edited (1901–4) the *Army and Navy Gazette*, and at other times *Home News*, the *Fortnightly Review*, and the *World*. Griffiths popularized criminology with a series of sensational works: *Secrets of the Prison House* (1893), *A Prison Princess* (1893), *Criminals I Have Known* (1895), *Mysteries of Police and Crime* (1898), and *The Brand of the Broad Arrow* (1900). His reminiscences, *Fifty Years in the Prison Service* (1904), shed an interesting light on Victorian penology. The knowledge gained during his prison work was put to good use in a series of highly popular *crime stories. *The Rome Express* (1896) was one of his most successful books; other detective novels were *In Tight Places* (1900), *Tales of a Government Official* (1902), *The Silver Spoon* (1903), and *Thrice Captive* (1908). Military tales such as *The Queen's Shilling* (1873), *The Thin Red Line* (1900), and *Before the British Raj* (1903) were far less popular. *Agony Terrace* (1907) is the name of a remote room in the select Cynosure Club, a 'place of penitence' where many secrets are revealed and scandals rehearsed. Captain Macgregor, who has helped to resolve some of them, provides a selection. Griffiths also wrote serious historical works, including a contribution to the official *History of the War in South Africa (1889–1902)* (4 vols. 1906–10).

GRIMSHAW, Beatrice [Ethel] (1871–1953) was born at Cloona, Co. Antrim and educated at Caen, Normandy, Victoria College, Belfast, and Bedford College, London. She became a journalist in Dublin and an enthusiastic bicyclist, holding the women's 24-hour world record. She next worked as a journalist in London, and then contrived to fulfil her dream of world travel by exchanging free tickets from shipping companies for free publicity. From 1906 she lived in the Pacific and travelled widely in New Guinea, Borneo, the Solomon Islands, and elsewhere. She published more than thirty volumes of fiction from 1897. Her Edwardian output is very much an offshoot of her travels in the South Pacific: *Vaiti of the Islands* (1906), *When the Red Gods Call* (1911), *Guinea Gold* (1912), *The Sorcerer's Stone* (1914). The focus of the latter is an immense diamond belonging to a wizard, but critics found something to admire in the terse Australian narrator and his companion, a fat French anthropologist. Her autobiography is *Isles of Adventure: From Java to New Caledonia but Principally Papua* (1931). An obituary in the *Times* (1 July 1953) comments: 'Though far from insensible of the picturesque aspects of life in the South Seas, Miss Grimshaw deprecated the exaggerated romanticism which has often represented the islands as being given over to alchoholic libations, passionate dalliance and garlands of flowers.'

Grim Smile of the Five Towns, The, Arnold *Bennett, 1907 Chapman & Hall. Most of these stories, focused on the Potteries' bourgeoisie, are little more than dressed-up anecdotes (an honest manufacturer sacrifices himself and his enterprise to the whims of an idle younger brother; two brothers who have not spoken to each other for a decade are made fools of by the woman over whom they quarrelled; a burgher's self-arranged burglary goes wrong; a man casually returns to his wife twenty years after walking out on her), and four feature the insufferably coy *'adventures' of rich young Vera Cheswardine. But this collection also contains Bennett's finest story, 'The Death of Simon Fuge', a moving meditation on the meaning of art, on the relationship between metropolitan and provincial values, and on the fact that no man is a prophet in his own country. Like Maupassant's 'Le Rosier de Mme Husson', which it closely resembles, 'Simon Fuge' is almost plotless. The story is structured through a series of visits, and the reader's attention is engaged instead by the light-hearted, ingenious narration. Loring, an employee of the British Museum, *en route* to purchase some china in the Five Towns, reads the obituary of a past acquaintance, Simon Fuge, during his train journey. As it happens Kynpe is Simon's home town, and during his visit, Loring discovers the discrepancies between Fuge's reputation abroad as artist and amorist, and the reality (particularly with reference to Fuge's account of a romantic night in his youth with two beautiful sisters). By contrast, in his meetings with the local inhabitants of Kynpe, Loring discovers art and culture where he least expects it—in the heart of a small suburban town—and Bennett's skill in this story is to show that delight in the arts, and in living, exists in places other than big cosmopolitan cities. 'The Death of Simon Fuge' conveys affectionate sympathy for the urban middle class, and a sense of the significance to be found amidst the humdrum routines of daily life.

GROSSMAN, Edith Searle: Edith Howitt SEARLE (1863–1931) married (1890) Joseph Penfold GROSSMAN. Born in Victoria, Australia, she moved with her family to New Zealand in 1878, and was educated at Invercargill Girls' High School and Christchurch Girls' High School. In 1881 she went with a scholarship to Canterbury College, where she started as one of only four women. She published her first novel, *Angela* (1890), in New Zealand as Edith Searle; her three later novels appeared in London. *In Revolt* (1893), its sequel, *The Knight of the Holy Ghost* (1907), and *The Heart of the Bush* (1910) are interesting feminist novels with an admixture of nostalgia for a lost rural idyll. In the latter novel hero and heroine retreat to a remote farm.

GRUNDY, Mabel [Sarah] Barnes published twenty-three romances to 1946 which are notable mainly for their extraordinary cheerfulness. *A Thames Camp* (1902) is a wife's gossipy diary of outings on the Thames and at the seaside, written 'only for women who love the river'. *The Vacillations of Hazel* (1905) provided a mild test for Grundy's cheerfulness, and *Marguerite's Wonderful Year* (1906), about a wife crippled immediately after her wedding, a sterner one, confidently met. Grundy continued to name her books after their heroines: *Hilary on Her Own* (1908), *Gwenda* (1910), *The Third Miss Wenderby* (1911), *Patricia Plays a Part* (1913), and, as though to underline the point, *'Candytuft—I Mean Veronica'* (1914). Hilary is a modern young woman who earns her living as a secretary in medical circles; Patricia an heiress travelling incognito.

GRYN, Ellova, *pseud.*: see **Three Weeks.*

GUBBINS, Nathaniel, *pseud.*: Edward Spencer MOTT (1844–1910). Born in Lichfield, Staffordshire, he was educated at Eton College and the Royal Military College, Sandhurst, and served with the army in India and Burma between 1862 and 1867; he left to pursue a theatrical career. His subsequent (and varied) writing career included a post on the *Sporting Times*, contributions to the *Allahabad Pioneer*, the *Pall Mall Gazette*, the *Lady's Pictorial*, and *Baily's Magazine*. Mott wrote operettas, pantomimes, and burlesques, as well as light fiction such as *Pink Papers* (1899), *The Flowering Bowl* (1899), *The Great Game* (1900), *Bits of Turf* (1901), and *Dead Certainties* (1902), all of which were concerned either with the racing world or with the seamy side of society. He also wrote cookery books as 'Edward Spencer', and memoirs, *A Mingled Yarn: The Autobiography of E. S. Mott* (1898).

GULL, Ranger: Cyril Arthur Edward Ranger GULL (1876–1923) married ——. Son of a Church of England clergyman, he was educated at Denstone and at Oxford University, before joining the literary staff of the *Saturday Review* in 1897. He worked on other literary magazines and the *Daily Mail* before becoming a full-time writer of fiction, both under his own name and as 'Guy Thorne'. He was a prolific author of *horror and mystery novels which sometimes have a redeeming bizarreness. The *Terror by Night* (1912) is a noiseless, anarchist motor car equipped with a pneumatic gun which is to be aimed at the House of Commons. *When Satan Ruled* (1914) is a sensational *historical romance set in the days of Pope Paul III and Benvenuto Cellini, with a background of Satanism and Black Masses. He told the **Bookman* (Nov. 1911) that he had based *The Drunkard* (1912) 'largely on the actual notes of a brilliant man of letters now deceased'. Much his best-known book, however, is **When It Was Dark*, which, his obituary in the *Times* (10 Jan. 1923) notes, 'formed the subject of sermons by popular preachers, headed by the Bishop of London, and . . . had a sale of over half a million copies'.

GUTTENBERG, Violet. Her three novels in the period include a commonplace mystery, *The Power of the Palmist* (1903), and two thoughtful stories about the dilemmas of Jewishness. *Neither Jew Nor Greek: A Story of Jewish Social Life* (1902), dedicated to 'Marie *Corelli', concerns a Jewish girl who marries the parson's son. *A Modern Exodus* (1904) is a futuristic tale about the marriage of a Jewish woman and an English aristocrat, which prompts the prime minister of the day to pass a Jews' Expulsion Bill: the result is a proposal for a settlement in Palestine, but the prime minister has second thoughts in the final chapter, and the Act is repealed.

GWYNNE, Paul, *pseud*. Ernest SLATER (d. 1942) was editor of the *Electrical Times*, *L'Ingénieur Industriel*, and *El Ingeniero Industriel*, and author of five novels in this period, which draw on the knowledge of Spain and Mexico he acquired on engineering projects; he also wrote some travel books. The theatrical plots of *Marta* (1902) and *The Bandolero* (1904) are pegs on which to hang essays about Spanish 'character', the interest lying in a people who are at once European and non-European, alike and utterly alien. *Nightshade* (1910) was written to illustrate his opinion that through electricity 'we are getting into touch with something much more palpitating than has ever before been dreamt of, and this has no reference to mesmerism, telepathy, second-sight, theosophy, or any other 'sophy extant' (*Bookman* July 1910).

GWYNN, Stephen [Lucius] (1864–1950) married (1889) Mary Louisa GWYNN (d. 1941). Son of a Church of Ireland clergyman, he was educated at St Columba's College, Dublin (of which his father was warden), and Brasenose College, Oxford. His mother was the daughter of the Irish nationalist William Smith O'Brien (1803–64). After teaching classics at Bradfield, at Sheffield University, and at St Columba's, he came to London in 1896 and worked as a journalist, where he made friends with Mabel *Dearmer and Evelyn *Sharp. He was particularly interested in West African politics, although he wrote copiously on literary and other topics. In 1904 he moved back to Ireland, and was Nationalist MP for Galway City 1906–18. He joined up as a private soldier in the First World War, and rose to the rank of Captain. He also edited many volumes of memoirs and literary classics, and wrote verse, guidebooks, travel books, biographies, and fiction. The title story in *The Glade in the Forest and Other Stories* (1907) is a whimsical tale about two men fighting a duel, which is stopped by a beautiful actress. Other fiction includes *John Maxwell's Marriage* (1903) and *Robert Emmet: A Historical Romance* (1909). *Experiences of a Literary Man* (1926) is an autobiography. His wife, who was his first cousin, published *Stories from Irish History Told for Children* (1904).

Hadrian the Seventh: *A Romance*, Fr. *Rolfe, 1904, Chatto & Windus. Arrogant, hedonistic George Arthur Rose, once an unsuccessful candidate for holy orders, is suddenly accepted into the bosom of the Church, hurried to Rome, and elected Pope, to general amazement. 'His utter lack of personal swagger or even dignity, His habit of rolling and smoking continual cigarettes, His natural and patently unprofessional manner, offended many outsiders who only could think of the Pope as partaking of the dual character of an Immeasurably Ambitious Clergyman and a Scarlet Impossible Person.' Once installed, Rose does not actually *do* very much, which may be the novel's weakness. He hobnobs with Kaiser Wilhelm II, issues incomprehensible Epistles to the nations of the earth, and has the walls of his palace covered in brown packing paper. The background to his brief reign is the rise of socialism and anarchism in Europe. An English socialist, Jeremy Sant, thwarted in his plans to exercise influence over the Pope through an old flame, resorts to newspaper calumny. Rose is able to rebut all the charges, but Sant murders him in desperation.

HAGGARD, Lt.-Col. Andrew, DSO: Andrew Charles Parker HAGGARD (1854–1923) married, first (1883), Emily Isabella CHIRNSIDE (divorced) and, secondly (1906), Jeannette Ethel FOWLER née —— (d. 1957). The fifth son of a Norfolk landowner, he was the elder brother of H. Rider *Haggard, Arthur *Haggard, and Baroness Albert *d'Anethan. Educated at Westminster School, he entered the 25th Regiment (King's Own Borderers) in 1873, served in India and Egypt, and joined the Egyptian army in 1883, winning the DSO at the battle of Ginness. He published novels, history, and verse from the late 1880s to the 1920s. Much of his non-fiction chronicles the amorous history of the French court; he also wrote about Madame de Staël (1766–1817) and the women of the French Revolution. He emigrated to British Columbia, where he lived on Vancouver Island and explored the wilderness in search of game, but returned to England to die of bronchitis at St Leonards. *A Persian Rose Leaf* (1906) is set in the Sudan, and glorifies the role played by the English officers of the Egyptian army in the wars of the 1880s. Lord Rothiemay is young, rich, and disillusioned with women. He fights nobly (Haggard is keen on battle scenes), is captured and nursed back to health by a beautiful Shia Muslim called Fatima, and marries her. He subsequently returns to England, thinking she is dead and has betrayed him; only when he is on the brink of contracting a loveless marriage does she confront him in London, where they agree to live happily ever after.

HAGGARD, Major Arthur: Edward Arthur HAGGARD (1860–1925) married (1887) Emily CALVERT (d. 1924). Seventh and youngest son of a Norfolk landowner, brother of H. Rider *Haggard, Andrew *Haggard, and Baroness Albert *d'Anethan, he was educated at Shrewsbury School, Pembroke College, Cambridge, and the Royal Military College, Sandhurst. He joined the King's Shropshire Light Infantry in 1884 (later transferring to the Army Service Corps and then the militia) and retired from the army in 1904. In 1908 he helped found the Veterans' Corps, and Rider Haggard wrote in his diary that his exertions on its behalf had brought on his death from kidney disease. His first novel was *Only a Drummer Boy* (1894) published under the pseudonym 'Arthur Amyand'; his later work appeared under his own name with the pseudonym in brackets. As Captain Arthur Haggard he published *The Kiss of Isis and The Mystery of Castlebourne* (1900), two long stories. The first borrows the setting, Egypt in the 1880s, from his brother Andrew, while its plot (an English girl is the reincarnation of Isis) owes more than a little to Rider Haggard's *She* (1887). The second tale opens with a statement about our ignorance of psychology; for Haggard spiritualism and the supernatural afford the means of exploring these areas. A ghost is revealed in a photograph.

Malcolm the Patriot (1907) is a strongly imperialist and Conservative tale of a boy who, though dispossessed of his father's estate by a wicked uncle, grows up to make good and become a great statesman.

HAGGARD, H[enry] Rider (1856–1925), Kt. (1912), married (1880) Mariana Louisa MARGITSON (d. 1943). The sixth son of a Norfolk landowner, he was educated at Ipswich Grammar School, being deemed too stupid to go to public schools like his brothers, and at a crammer in London. His paternal grandmother was Jewish; his mother, who came of an Anglo-Indian family with some Indian blood, had published verse. Andrew *Haggard and Arthur *Haggard were his brothers; his sister Mary wrote novels under her married name as Baroness Albert *d'Anethan; another brother married a sister of 'Michael *Fairless'. In 1875, aged 19, he went out to South Africa, scene of much of his later fiction, as secretary to the Governor of Natal. He was then attached to the mission which resulted in the annexation of the Transvaal in 1877. There he met M'hlopekazi (d. 1897), a Swazi of royal family, who appears, much romanticised, as Umslopogaas in several of his novels, and of whom he wrote in his memoirs, 'the face might have served some Greek sculptor for the model of that of a dying god'. While he was in Africa his first love, Lily Jackson (later Archer, d. 1909), married another man. Haggard rose to be Master of the High Court of the Transvaal (1877–9), but, disliking the political situation, became briefly an ostrich farmer and then returned to England for good in 1881, and trained as a barrister at Lincoln's Inn. However, like so many barristers of the period, he found literature more rewarding, and his third novel, *King Solomon's Mines* (1885), written in six weeks, was so immensely successful that he never practised. The tale of the discovery of an unknown African tribe and a cache of huge diamonds, it gave rise to a powerful myth of Empire and inspired hundreds of imitations. Haggard himself wrote many sequels and connected tales, from *Allan Quatermain* (1887) to *Allan and the Ice-Gods* (1927). Another series began with the even more popular *She* (1887), continued in **Ayesha, or, The Return of She* (1905), *She and Allan* (1921), and *Wisdom's Daughter* (1923). Like many men of the upper middle class, Haggard had some doubts about his career as a novelist, writing in his memoirs, 'at the bottom of my heart I share some of the British contempt for the craft of story-writing'. He discussed the subject with *Kipling, who 'pointed out... that all fiction is in its essence an appeal to the emotions, and that this is not the highest class of appeal'. After *She* he thought to write a serious novel about the South African political débâcle which he had witnessed, but *Jess* (1887) never sold like its predecessor. He returned to romance, and researched *Cleopatra* (1889) in Egypt and *Eric Brighteyes* (1891) in Iceland. But *Beatrice* (1890) was a modern novel about sexual relationships, and *Dr. Therne* (1898) was written to combat a scare about vaccination. *Pearl Maiden* (1903) is about the martyrdom of the first followers of Christ, and was written after Haggard's tour of Palestine in a serious attempt at historical accuracy. Of *Fair Margaret* (1907), an *historical romance set in the reign of Henry VII, the publishers, Hutchinson, promised: 'There is plenty of fighting and hair-breadth escapes on sea and land and the whole book is in the author's most popular vein.' See also **Red Eve* (1911). Hugh *Walpole commented in the *Dictionary of National Biography* that Haggard was lucky to write at a time 'when romance was taken seriously by criticism as a legitimate inspiration for art'. His early novels were indeed received respectfully, but by the end of his career their quality had declined and fashions had changed. By the time of his death, and for years afterwards, his fiction was derided as escapist, imperialist schoolboy fantasy. However, more recently Haggard's novels have been the object of much critical attention, as prejudices against the supernatural and the imperial elements have both faded, and it has been again possible to appreciate the power with which his plots image the anxieties of the period. Some critics have suggested that the triangular relationships in his novels reflect a conflict between his affection for his wife and his unsatisfied passion for Lily Archer, who continued to figure in his imaginative life, and whom he supported emotionally and financially after her husband ruined her health, embezzled her fortune, and fled the country (husband and wife allegedly both died of syphilis). Apart from Africa and the Empire, Haggard's great interest was agriculture. His wife inherited an estate in Norfolk, where they lived, and Haggard wrote *The Farmer's Year Book* (1899) from personal experience. *Rural England*

(1902) and *The Poor and the Land* (1905) were the products of research in England and the colonies. It was for this side of his work that he was knighted. He stood unsuccessfully as Unionist candidate for East Norfolk in 1895. After the First World War he devoted much time to the welfare of ex-servicemen. An autobiography, *The Days of My Life* (1926), was published posthumously.

HAINSSELIN, M[ontague] T[homas] (1871–1943) married Eva Mary Henrietta ——. Born at Devonport and educated at Plymouth Grammar School, Hainsselin graduated (1893) from Oxford University as a non-collegiate student (this was cheaper) and was ordained as a Church of England clergyman in 1896. He was Vicar of Mount Morgan, Queensland, 1897–1902, and then, following his elder brother, he became a chaplain in the Royal Navy. His Edwardian novels are light fiction. *The Isle of Maids: A Romance of the Mediterranean* (1908) is about two men marooned on a Greek island whose only other inhabitants are four upper-class Greek girls on holiday wearing antique costume, whom they contrive to save from brigands (*Phroso* (1897) by 'Anthony *Hope' probably influenced this). The hero of *Markham of Mohistan: A Romance of Bombay and Beyond* (1909) is too humble to propose to Lady Evelyn but saves her brother from disgrace by taking the blame for the seduction of a Eurasian. He disappears, saves the British Empire from the Young India party, saves Evelyn from assassination, and is rewarded when the brother confesses all on his deathbed. During the First World War Hainsselin published a series of semi-fictional propagandist books about the work of the Navy, beginning with *In the Northern Mists: A Grand Fleet Chaplain's Note Book* (1916).

HALCOMBE, Charles. J. H. (b. *c.*1865) married LIANG Ah Ghan. Halcombe went to Australia aged 15 and became a sailor. He claimed to have been twice shipwrecked and through a mutiny before he was 21. At 20 he became a contributor to the *Globe*, and went to Africa, an experience described in *Travels in the Transvaal* (1899). He arrived in Shanghai in 1887 and briefly joined the staff of the *North China Daily News* before getting a job in the Imperial Maritime Customs, in the course of which employment he lived for the next six years in various Chinese ports. This is recounted in his travel book *The Mystic Flowery Land* (1896). He wrote three novels, two of which have Chinese settings; the last, *Children of Far Cathay* (1906), published in Hong Kong, is illustrated with posed photographs. The hero, Herbert Montrose, is jilted, becomes a missionary in China, marries a Chinese girl, and ends up fighting in the civil war. Halcombe's preface to the novel stresses the mutual sympathy between China and Japan, and his own desire to give an accurate picture of Chinese life. He lived in Herne Bay.

Halcyone, Elinor *Glyn, 1912, Duckworth. Dedicated to Sir Francis Jeune (1843–1905), High Court judge and classical scholar, who had encouraged Glyn's self-education, the novel, one of her least sensational, was said to be her personal favourite. Orphaned Halcyone La Sarthe lives with two impoverished maiden aunts at La Sarthe Chase, lavishing devotion on a bust of Aphrodite she has found in the attic. A retired professor, whom she nicknames Cheiron, takes a cottage outside the gates and is persuaded to give her an extensive classical education. She meets one of his pupils, John Derringham, an ambitious and self-centred young Tory politician. Years later, they meet again. Derringham needs to marry money, and is wooing an American widow, Mrs Cricklander, whose hired companion prepares a daily digest of culture, thus enabling her to hold her own in relentlessly classicizing company, and to impress Derringham, himself a fine scholar. Halcyone falls for Derringham. 'She was no more herself, but had come to dwell in him.' They become secretly engaged. Hurrying to meet her one evening, Derringham tumbles into the ha-ha and knocks himself out. Distressed at his failure to keep the rendezvous, Halcyone flees to London. Derringham is nursed back to health by Mrs Cricklander, and awakens to find himself engaged to her. Heartbroken, Halcyone flees to Italy, with Cheiron and the bust of Aphrodite. Mrs Cricklander discovers that the government is about to fall and, not wishing to finance a mere leader of the opposition, transfers her affection to a Radical. Derringham pursues Halcyone to Italy, finding her at the top of a tower in Perugia. Derringham was based on Lord Curzon (1859–1925), whom Glyn had loved passionately, Cheiron on her friend F. H. Bradley (1846–1924), the leading metaphysician of the age, and Halcyone on herself. The book was well received by the critics. The *Daily Express* described it as 'eminently Glynesque, albeit less tempestuously than **His Hour*, less amusingly than the famous **Visits of Elizabeth*'. The relative lack of tempestuousness and amusement meant that sales were poor.

HALES, A[da] M[atilda] M[ary] (1878–1957). The daughter of a Church of England clergyman, she was brought up in Brighton and educated at the Villa Lehman, Montreux, and St Hugh's College, Oxford. *Leslie* (1913) portrays a strained sexual relationship between a selfish, ambitious man and his cousin. The characterization, especially of the hero, has a certain distinction; the plot creaks rather. After the First World War Hales published two other novels; she also wrote for children.

HALES, A[lfred Arthur] G[reenwood] HALES (1860–1936) married, first (1886), Emmeline PRITCHARD (d. 1911) and, secondly (1920), Jean REID. Born at Kent Town, Adelaide, the son of a gold-miner, he described his parents as 'staid, respectable, God-fearing folk'. He was educated at grammar schools in Adelaide until he was 13; he was then apprenticed to a carpenter; later he studied assaying at the Ballarat School of Mines. He published his first story in *Frearson's Weekly* at 16, and it was as a journalist that he was to make his name. He also worked as a boxing manager. In 1894 he was in London and, hearing about the gold rush in Western Australia, he returned to found the *Coolgardie Mining Review.* He stood unsuccessfully for the Australian Parliament in 1897. By 1899 he had become the *Daily News* correspondent on the *Boer War; he was then sent to Macedonia and to the Russo-Japanese War. He spent the First World War with the Serbian Army. He claimed to have written for the *Evening News* the world's first report of an air fight. He published verse, travel books, fiction, plays, and books about sport and animals. *Driscoll, King of Scouts: A Romance of the South African War* (1901) contains an extensive criticism of the organization and ethos of the British Army during the *Boer War, especially its snobbishness and unfitness to conduct a guerrilla war. Driscoll, an Irish soldier, becomes a volunteer officer, fights brilliantly, and dies at the same moment as the true-hearted Boer girl he loves.

Half-Hearted, The, John *Buchan, 1900, Isbister. In the Scottish lowlands, Lewis Elphinstone Haystoun, celebrated explorer and author of an influential book about Kashmir, finds himself engaged in a struggle for a seat in Parliament, and the hand of Alice Wishart, with the hard-working, mulish Albert Stocks. Alice almost drowns, and is saved by Stocks rather than the irresolute Haystoun, who immediately accuses himself of terrible weakness. Stocks is returned to Parliament, and proposes to Alice. Meanwhile, news has reached the Foreign Office in London of trouble on the frontiers of India. An indefatigable Russian agent, Constantine Marker, has been stirring up the tribesmen with a view to mounting an invasion. Marker believes that all the European powers apart from Russia are degenerate, ready for the kill. Haystoun, in despair, offers his services as a troubleshooter, and just has time before departing to discover that Alice loves him. Once in Kashmir, his spirits rise. 'Life was quick in his sinews, his brain was a weathercock, his strength was tireless.' He and Marker enter into a deadly rivalry. Realizing where the attack will come, he alerts the British frontier force, and helps foil the invasion. The Russians get him in the end, but he has saved India, and been regenerated in the process. He has mastered his disabling lethargy, and understood the purpose of *Empire.

HALIDOM, M. Y., *pseud.* This pseudonymous author published *Tales of the Wonder Club* (1899) as 'Dryasdust'. A subsequent edition (1903) and ten other ghost stories to 1912 appeared 'by M. Y. Halidom'. His stories are distinguished by a certain zestful gruesomeness. In *Zoe's Revenge* (1908) a murderer is haunted, in colourful locations, by a life-size doll built around the skeleton of the woman he murdered. In *The Poet's Curse* (1911), an American millionaire tries to get hold of Shakespeare's bones, but is thwarted by a curse inscribed on the poet's monument. Ashley suggests that more than one person may have been involved in writing these stories.

HALIFAX, Robert, *pseud.*: Robert Edwin YOUNG (b. 1870) married (*c.*1895) ——. Born in Dalston, London, Young went into the Post Office at about the age of 13 and worked as a telegraphist until retiring (*c.*1903) with a pension of £38 p.a. following a nervous breakdown and the partial failure of his eyesight. He also suffered from chronic insomnia and writer's cramp; his wife had serious gynaecological problems. This is recorded because he applied to the Royal Literary Fund for relief, often in very eloquent terms, describing his struggle 'to keep front curtains clean and opaque—to maintain an appearance of respectability when often short of bare food'. Among those named as helping him were 'Allen *Raine', Arnold *Bennett, and 'W. Pett *Ridge', writers who shared his interest in lower-middle-class and working-class life: he specialized in realistic depictions of life in the East End. Although the distinction of his writing was recognized by reviewers, he made hardly any money out of it, selling the copyrights of *The Gap of Gold* (1906), *The House of Silence* (1907), *The Shadow on Mayfair* (1909), and *The Venturesome Virgin* (1910) for £10 apiece. He published in all fourteen novels (1899-1917). The *Manchester Guardian* wrote of *The Borderland* (1908), 'There is no one writing more truthfully of low London life than Mr. Halifax.' In *A Whistling Woman* (1911) Lydia loves Arthur, who does not want to be bothered with the expense and responsibility of a wife and family. She lives in a sinister house with an eccentric mother who, it later emerges, has been keeping a murderer husband secretly hidden. Halifax evokes uneasy relationships, conversations at cross-purposes, with a good deal of skill. At the end he resorts, however, to the social novel's oldest trick, emigration to the colonies. *The House of Horror* (1911) is a melodramatic thriller which begins when a gentleman saves a woman from being mugged by a foreign detective in London at night.

HAMILTON, Catherine J[ane] (b. 1841). Her father was a Church of England clergyman of Irish birth, and educated her himself at home. She was born in Somerset and brought up in England, but moved to Ireland on her father's death in 1859: many of her novels have Irish settings. Later she moved back to London. *The British Library Catalogue* lists publications between 1880 and 1933. She published her first story, *Hedged with Thorns*, at 25. The Northern Newspaper Syndicate published her serials; she also wrote verse, children's books and plays, and *Women Writers: Their Works and Ways* in two series (1892, 1893) of biographical sketches. Other women writers are included in her *Notable Irishwomen* (1904). Her novel *A Flash of Youth* (1900) concerns a marriage between a lady and a cultivated farmer's son, which ends in tragedy when he flirts with a younger girl of his own class. Someone says of the heroine 'I wonder whether she is a new woman or an old woman': Hamilton doesn't seem to have quite decided. *The Luck of the Kavanaghs* (1912) turns the same marriage across class boundaries into the stuff of hackneyed romance: a poor Irish boy makes a fortune in America and comes back to marry the poverty-stricken gentlewoman he has always loved.

HAMILTON, Cicely: Cicely Mary HAMMILL (1872–1952) who changed her name to Cicely HAMILTON. The daughter of an army officer, she, like *Kipling and many others of her class and generation, spent four years of childhood (from 9 to 13) being brought up by strangers because her parents were abroad. The experience of unkindness from a woman who favoured her own children over the Hammills gave her a lifelong antipathy to sentimental talk about motherhood. She was educated at schools in Malvern and Bad Homburg, so that she could earn a living as a teacher. Disliking institutions, she left teaching after about two years, and lived with a sister in London, translating German, writing, and trying to become an actress. She spent ten years on the provincial stage in 'fit-up' companies. She wrote in her memoirs 'you needed, in those days, to be a bit of a barnstormer to play emotional scenes to a Saturday Tyneside audience—which had come to the theatre with plenty of beer in it, and brought bags of nuts to crack through the show.' Failing to reach the London stage, she concentrated on writing sensational stories for cheap periodicals (preferring them to love stories). She joined the suffrage campaign, though 'my personal revolt was feminist rather than suffragist'. She believed in birth control, equal pay, and an end to the mythologizing of marriage and motherhood. She was one of the founders of the Women Writers' Suffrage League, and joined the WSPU, the Actresses' Franchise League, and the Women's Tax Resistance League. However she maintained her mistrust of institutions and party lines, and later came to see the cult of Emmeline Pankhurst (1857–1958) during the militant suffrage agitation as a 'forerunner of Lenin, Hitler, Mussolini . . . the Leader who could do no wrong!' In the First World War she worked as a hospital clerk and acted in concert parties. After the war she was a contributor to *Time* *and Tide*. Much of her fiction, drama and feminist theory is concerned with the criticism of marriage; her best-known work is *Marriage as a Trade* (1909). The novel *Just to Get Married* (1911) puts her ideas in fictional form. In *A Matter of Money* (1916) an affair between an unhappily married woman and a poor doctor leads to her suicide; she has not realized that he cannot afford to have his career ruined. Hamilton was the author of twenty plays, and published an excellent autobiography (1935).

HAMILTON, Cosmo: Cosmo GIBBS (d. 1942), who changed his name (1898) to HAMILTON (his mother's name) by deed poll. The son of an official at the Board of Education, brother of Philip *Gibbs and A. Hamilton *Gibbs, Hamilton, like *Kipling, William *Le Queux, and W. P. *Drury, was associated with Earl Roberts's National Service League, which campaigned for rearmament in the years before the First World War. He wrote novels and plays 1897–1942 and served in both world wars. *The Blindness of Virtue* (1908), which Hamilton also turned into a play, conceals its prurience with ostentatious good intentions. A clergyman's daughter falls in love with her father's pupil, and he with her, but no one has told her the facts of life, although her father deplores 'the ostrich system of bringing up girls', and she therefore waits in her lover's bedroom and tempts him in all ignorance. Feeble as this plot is as an exploration of the inadequacies of feminine conditioning, Hamilton's attempt to write about sexual desire in a young girl without condemning it or her is interesting. *An Accidental Daughter* (1911) is a love story about a sister and brother who are done out of an inheritance by the sudden appearance of the long-lost daughter of their cousin. The sister schemes to kill the girl and finally commits suicide on being discovered. The brother, more effectively, falls in love with the heiress and marries her.

HAMILTON, Lord Ernest: Ernest William HAMILTON (1858–1939) married (1891) Pamela Louisa Augusta CAMPBELL (d. 1931). The seventh son (and he had seven sisters) of the 1st Duke of Abercorn, he was educated at Harrow School and the Royal Military College, Sandhurst, and became a Captain in the 11th Hussars. He was MP for North Tyrone (1885–92) and wrote novels between 1897 and the 1930s. His main line was *historical romance: *The Outlaws of the Marches* (1897) is set in sixteenth-century Liddesdale; *Mary Hamilton* (1901) is a heart-rending tale of the court of Mary, Queen of Scots; its heroine is betrayed by Darnley and dies. He also published *Strawberry Leaves* by 'A Leaf', and, under the same pseudonym, *A Maid at Large* (1905): these are quite different, being flippant high society romances. There is an unrevealing autobiography (1923). Hamilton's sixth brother, Lord Frederick Hamilton (1856–1928), a retired diplomat, was editor of the **Pall Mall Magazine* and also published novels from 1916.

HAMILTON, Helen was the author of *My Husband Still: A Working Woman's Story* (1914), which argues that a poor woman married to a brute ought to have access to divorce. John *Galsworthy, in a foreword, describes it as 'very skilfully prepared from the journal and *viva voce* account of a working woman, by one who vouches for the substantial truth of the narrative'. Hamilton also published *The Iconoclast* (1917), about the romantic life of a schoolmistress, a play, a travel book, and some verse.

HAMILTON, Lillias (d. 1925). Born in New South Wales of an Australian mother and a Scots father, she qualified as a doctor and practised in Calcutta (1890–4). She was then in charge of the Dufferin Hospital, Calcutta (1893–4) before becoming physician to the Emir of Afghanistan (1894–7). Her novel *A Vizier's Daughter* (1900) draws on the latter experience. Gul Begum is a resilient princess who becomes a hostage and a slave; she battles against circumstance and finally dies saving her widowed employer, with whom she has fallen in love. *A Nurse's Bequest* (1907) describes the working life of a nurse in a hospital twenty-five years previously. The heroine is one of five sisters, is bullied by other nurses for her gentility, but perseveres, and marries a German doctor. Much of the book is spent arguing for a system for the education of pauper children in Homes in the colonies. Hamilton was later (1908–24) Warden of Studley Horticultural College for Women. She died in Nice.

HAMILTON, M., *pseud.*: Mary Spotswood ASH (1869–1949) married (1898) Churchill Arthur LUCK (1866–1952). A native of Derry in northern Ireland, she was married in Lahore, by the Anglican Bishop of Lahore, to an officer in the Indian army, who rose to command the 22nd 'Sam Browne's' Cavalry (Frontier Force) and retired in 1919. She had two sons, one of whom died as a baby in 1907, in which year her husband had a year's leave in England. However, otherwise she probably spent the first twenty years of her marriage in India. She published eighteen underrated novels between 1894 and 1928. Some are set in the dour Ulster of her childhood, such as *Beyond the Boundary* (1902). Elsewhere her subject is the middle-aged woman's second chance at happiness. In the Anglo-Indian *Mrs. Brett* (1913), flighty Judy Brett's sick fiancé is nursed by her subdued mother, who long ago ran away briefly from the odious Mr Brett with a lover. 'Don't you know that every hour of my life I regret having accepted what you called your forgiveness?' says Mrs Brett, who in the end goes back with the fiancé to England and a career as a successful painter. The husband of the heroine of *Cut Laurels* (1905) has been a prisoner in Egypt for eighteen years; meanwhile she has brought up their daughter and made a living as a dressmaker in Belfast. When he is released she has to cope with the renewal of intimacy and the revelation that he has an Egyptian wife and two sons. She makes the best of this situation and is rewarded with happiness. Luck's point of view is agreeably astringent.

HAMILTON, Mrs: Mary Agnes ADAMSON (1883 or 1884–1962) married (1905) Charles Joseph HAMILTON (b. 1878). She was born in Manchester; her father was professor of logic at Glasgow University, her mother a teacher. She was educated at Aberdeen Girls' High School, Glasgow Secondary School and (like her mother) at Newnham College, Cambridge, where she was a Scholar, and whose history she later wrote. She published nine novels, some textbooks on ancient history, biographical studies of prominent figures in the Labour movement and others, and memoirs (1944). Her brief marriage to an economist was not successful. She was Labour MP for Blackburn (1929–31), a delegate to the League of Nations (1929, 1930), a governor of the BBC (1933–7) and an Alderman of the LCC (1937–40). *Less than the Dust* (1912) is set in Canada; its heroine stoically endures a hopeless attachment to her brother-in-law. In *Yes* (1914) women must choose between love and art. Joan Traquair wants to paint; and to do so she must leave her invalid sister to look after their odious father. She resents the fact that her brothers have more education, money, and freedom. After her marriage to a brilliant painter she has to balance the demands of his genius, her identity, and their children. Among Hamilton's later novels was *Murder in the House of Commons* (1931).

HANDASYDE, *pseud.*: Emily Handasyde BUCHANAN (1872–1953) published six volumes of fiction, five between 1903–10 and one in 1939. In *For the Week End* (1907) a married woman and an officer returned from the *Boer War fall in love and flirt high-mindedly through the golden afternoons of three country-house weekends before his death in a horse race. The same atmosphere of luxury, rose petals and unspoken sexual desire suffuses *The Heart of Marylebone* (1910), in which a girl marries a rather conventional millionaire because she needs an operation; as she recovers, she melts his heart and they fall in love.

HANNAN, [Robert] Charles (1863–1922) married (*c.*1890) ——. He was born in Glasgow and educated at Edinburgh Collegiate School and Glasgow University. He joined his father's firm of East India and China merchants and travelled extensively in the Far East, becoming a Fellow of the Royal Geographical Society. He was a fairly successful playwright, who reckoned to earn about £350–£400 p.a., up until the First World War, but by 1916 he was working as a temporary clerk at the Admiralty and making urgent appeals to the Royal Literary Fund. He was the author of nine volumes of fiction 1888–1906, some with Chinese settings. *The Coachman with Yellow Lace* (1902) is a ridiculous costume drama about two women who dress up as a duchess and her coachman to make a fortune, but end by deciding that love is best. *Thuka of the Moon* (1906), influenced by Lord *Dunsany, is an obscure allegorical *fantasy about a superman created by the gods who objects when the perfect woman he has created is taken from him. He dramatized his own novels and those of others, and appears in the published correspondence of Thomas Hardy (1840–1928), trying unavailingly to persuade Hardy to let him work on *Two on a Tower* (1882).

HARCOURT, Colonel A. F. P.: Alfred Frederick Pollock HARCOURT (*c.*1835–1910) married Georgiana Laura ——. An officer in the Indian army, he arrived in India and was commissioned in 1855. He served as Deputy, Commissioner and judge in the Punjab from 1862, and retired in

1889. He was the author of five novels, including *Jenetha's Venture: A Story of the Siege of Delhi* (1899) and *The Peril of the Sword* (1903), in which a love story between a gallant officer and a beautiful widow is set against the background of the siege of Lucknow. There are many scenes of battle and much emphasis on the horrors of the Indian Mutiny. He also published *The New Guide to Delhi* (1866). He retired to England.

Hardware: *A Novel in Four Books*, W. Kineton *Parkes, 1914, T. Fisher Unwin. A coming-of-age story set in a Midlands industrial town, 'Metlingham', which has been shaped by the zeal and enterprise of Richard Astbury, a manufacturer and 'public man of genius'. Thorpe Chatwin, son of a skilled mechanic, an inventor and a disciple of Carlyle, grows up in a world which is still zealous and enterprising but altogether less heroic. His horizons expand rapidly under the aegis of Grammar School and Free Library, and it is not long before he has established a chemistry laboratory in the cellar. But his ambitions are not academic, and a series of jobs, beginning with an unwholesome stint in a metal-stamper's warehouse, results eventually in a position of trust at Hubbard and Son, a wholesaling company. Thereafter his life is largely shaped by rivalries among the local magnates in which matrimonial alliances play a far from insignificant part. Thorpe is torn between sweet-natured, conscientious Mary Hubbard and adventurous, sensual Hetty Sharp, daughter of a commercial and political rival. Hetty marries another man, Ernest Linch, while still in love with Thorpe, and after enjoying in his company a quasi-mystical 'vision' of the god Pan. Mary Hubbard also marries someone else, also unhappily. Thorpe, though far from immune to Hetty's charms, gets on with his work, and enters politics as a local councillor. When Linch dies, he and Hetty marry, and he subsequently defeats her father in a battle over the continued public ownership of the town's electricity supply. They are, in their purposeful if relatively undemanding way, a happy couple. The novel's preoccupations and setting closely resemble those of Arnold *Bennett's Clayhanger tetralogy. But it is franker in its treatment of sexuality, and formally innovative: the fragmentariness of modern urban experience finds an analogy in the division of each book into ten chapters and the subdivision of the chapters into numbered sections.

HARDY, George Webb was the author of The **Black Peril* (1914), an interesting and perhaps semi-autobiographical work about the South African situation. No other work by the author is recorded.

HARDY, Iza Duffus (?1852–1922). The daughter of Sir Thomas Duffus Hardy (1804–1878), Deputy Keeper of Records, by his first wife (not his second, the novelist Lady Hardy, née Mary Macdowell, 1824–1891), she was an only child and a precocious writer, having planned a novel before the age of 15. Her first three novels, *Not Easily Jealous* (1872), *Between the Fires* (1873), and *For the Old Love's Sake* (1875), were published anonymously. After her father's death she and her mother travelled to America, which provided material for several travel-books, such as *Oranges and Alligators* (1886), a description of Florida, and lent colour to many of her unpretentious, well-crafted, rather predictable novels. *A Butterfly: Her Friends and Her Fortunes* (1903) is a pretty girl who marries a rich American instead of her poor English lover Patrick. Patrick's sister Janet comes to live in the beautiful house in Florida, and is abducted by the husband, who is half-caste and therefore unreliable. Mercifully, he is shot in time by an old enemy, Janet marries the Butterfly's brother, and the Butterfly, after a decent interval, Patrick. *The Master of Madrono Mills: A Romance of the Redwoods* (1904) is a Californian tale in which an Englishwoman falsely accused of being a murderess is saved from a flood by the Master, who is 'just what the typical Western man ought to be'. Hardy was interested in hypnotism, and was a friend of the blind poet Philip Bourke Marston (1850–87).

HARKER, L. Allen: Lizzie WATSON (1863–1933) married (1886) James Allen HARKER. Born at Gloucester and educated at Cheltenham Ladies' College, she began her career by publishing short stories in the **Outlook*. Her success dates from the publication of *Miss Esperance and Mr Wycherly* (1908), the story of a Scots household consisting of an elderly lady and a reformed alcoholic, which is disrupted when two small boys come to live there. Far more sentimental than *Cranford* (1855), by Elizabeth Gaskell (1810–65), to which it is indebted, the book belongs to the group of novels for adults about children which were popular at the turn of the century, for example Kenneth *Grahame's *Dream Days* (1898), and to the equally popular class of sentimental books about Scotland. Harker's emphasis on quaint or 'old-fashioned' children is indebted to the work of Juliana Horatia Ewing (1841–85) and Mrs *Molesworth. *Mr Wycherly's Wards* (1912) was a sequel. *A Romance of the Nursery* (1902) and *Concerning Paul and Fiammetta* (1906) are about the lives of the squire's children in an idyllic Cotswold village during the 1870s. They share characters with each other and with *The Ffolliots of Redmarley* (1913) which is a novel for adults about class and marriage. Harker lived in Cirencester, where her husband was professor at the Royal Agricultural College. She also wrote plays with F. R. Pryor, one of which, *Marigold* (1927), ran for eighteen months.

HARLAND, Henry (1861–1905) married Aline MERRIAM. The only son of an American lawyer, he was born at St Petersburg and educated in Rome and Paris and at Harvard Divinity School. Although not Jewish, he began his literary career by writing melodramatic novels of Jewish life in New York under the name 'Sidney Luska'. In 1890 he moved to London and began to publish novels and short stories under his own name. He was literary editor of the *Yellow Book* (1894–97), and thus had an influence on English letters quite out of proportion to the short time he spent in England and the success of his own writing; he contributed personally to each volume. He was famously good company, though Netta *Syrett complained that he and his wife 'were more like spoilt children who can be charming when they are good, than any grown-up people I ever met before or since'. His fiction was precious and by the end rather frivolous, but sold well. By 1904 *The *Cardinal's Snuff-Box* (1900) was advertised as being in its 105th thousand and *The Lady Paramount* (1902) in its fifty-fifth thousand. The latter is set partly in England, partly in Italy. The beautiful young countess of the tiny Italian island of Sampaolo decides that her cousin, an Englishman, has been wrongfully deprived of the title by her, so she contrives an elaborate plan for him to fall in love with her without knowing who she is, which is wholly successful. Another pair of beautiful aristocratic lovers, another Italian setting, more incognitoes, and the same motif of the poor man who scruples, momentarily, to marry a rich girl make up the confection that is *My Friend Prospero* (1904). Harland's wife completed his last novel, *The Royal End* (1909), after his death from tuberculosis.

HARRADEN, Beatrice (1864–1936) was the daughter of an importer of musical instruments, and was educated in Dresden, at Cheltenham Ladies' College, at Queen's College, Harley Street, and at Bedford College, London University. In 1888 she met the novelist Eliza Lynn Linton (1822–98) and became her protegée; Linton disapproved of higher education for women, christened Harraden 'my little B.A.', and described her as 'a frail highly strung little creature, in size and stature like a child'. In Linton's company Harraden met other writers, but she had published only children's fiction before her great success, *Ships That Pass in the Night* (1893), which Theodore Watts-Dunton (1832–1914) read aloud to A. C. Swinburne (1837–1909), and which, reportedly, was the only book found in the room of the dead Cecil Rhodes (1853–1902). In the mid-1890s she went for health reasons to California, and wrote *Two Health-Seekers in Southern California* (1897), in collaboration with W. A. Edwards, and *Hilda Stafford and The Remittance Man: Two Californian Stories* (1897). She was a member of the Women's Social and Political Union and argued for female suffrage in *Our Warrior Women* (1916). Michael Sadleir in the *Dictionary of National Biography* attributes the prevailing sentimentality of her fiction to 'the one tragic experience of her life . . . she fell deeply in love with a man who falsified his clients' accounts and whose body was found not long after in a crevasse on a Swiss glacier'. Talented women attracted to rotters appear in several of her novels including *The Fowler* (1899). *Out of the Wreck I Rise* (1912) is the story of two women who have become emotionally entangled with Adrian Steele, a clever but dishonest man who ultimately commits suicide by throwing himself off a Swiss mountainside. *Where Your Treasure Is* (1918) is a sequel. She was interested in the effect of employment on women's social and sexual identity; **Katharine Frensham* (1903) contrasts a selfish wife and a career girl. Geraldine, the heroine of *The Scholar's Daughter* (1906), has been brought up in an all-male household in the belief that her mother was dead. A brilliant actress appears in the neighbourhood, and

Geraldine confesses that she wants to act rather than work on her father's dictionary. There is a symbolic reconciliation of mind and heart when her parents recognize one another and fall into each other's arms. Harraden was given a Civil List pension in 1930.

HARRIS, Frank: James Thomas HARRIS (1856–1931) married, first (1878), Florence Ruth ADAMS (*c.*1852–1879), secondly (1887), Emily Mary CLAYTON née REMINGTON (*c.*1839–1927), and, thirdly (1927), Helen O'HARA (d. 1955). Harris was born in Galway, Ireland, of Welsh parents; his father a lieutenant in the Royal Navy who had risen from the ranks, his mother the daughter of a Baptist minister. He went to school at the Royal Institution in Belfast and Ruabon Grammar School, Denbigh. He ran away to America aged 15 and worked as a builder, a hotel clerk, and shoeshine boy. There followed a period in the Wild West about which the only evidence is the ghost-written and unreliable *My Reminiscences as a Cowboy* (1930). He then went to Lawrence, Kansas, where in 1874 he enrolled at the state university, and was much influenced by Professor Byron Smith, whose family and friends later went to the trouble of publishing a book to protect his memory from Harris's slanders. He returned to Europe aged 20 and spent a year teaching at Brighton College, where he met his first wife, whom he married in Paris while a student at the university of Heidelberg; soon afterwards he moved to Göttingen (1878–9). When she died within the year, leaving him £500, he travelled in Italy, Greece, and possibly Russia. He was briefly a stockbroker's clerk in London before he obtained some work reviewing for the *Spectator*, became a journalist, and, in an amazing coup of effrontery, got himself made editor of the *Evening News* in 1882. Dismissed in 1886, he became editor of the **Fortnightly Review*, and came to exert great influence in English literary life. During this period of his greatest prosperity he married a rich widow and dined with literary London and high society. Frederic *Carrel's novel *The Adventures of John Johns* (1897) gives some indication of how this meteoric rise appeared to his contemporaries. Harris's marriage broke up in 1894, in which year he bought the *Saturday Review*. Although his conduct towards Oscar Wilde (1854–1900) was criticized by, among others, Robert H. *Sherard, there is no doubt that Harris was a friend and supporter before, during, and after his imprisonment. In 1898 Harris left London and sold the *Saturday Review*, spending the money on a hotel in the south of France, an unsuccessful investment which ended in his being accused of swindling. By the late 1890s he was already living with Nellie O'Hara, later his third wife. Although with hindsight Harris's long descent into scrounging and muck-raking can be seen to date from this period, he retained many admirers. But his journalistic ventures (*Candid Friend*, 1901–2; *Vanity Fair*, 1907–10; *Hearth & Home*, 1911–12; *Modern Society*, 1913–14) became increasingly obscure and scandalous, and he was sent to prison for a report on a divorce suit, an experience which inspired him with a hatred for the British establishment. During the First World War he went to America, and published pro-German articles and *England or Germany* (1915). His biography of Wilde was published in New York (1916, 1918); his pornographic and self-aggrandizing memoirs were privately published in Paris (1922–7). He lived in France from 1923. His first volume of stories came out in 1894; another followed in 1900. His first novel, *The Bomb* (1908), was based on an 1886 scandal in Chicago. Much more popular was *The Man Shakespeare and His Tragic Life Story* (1909), biographical criticism in which Harris's identification with Shakespeare permitted him unbridled speculation, but which had considerable vogue at the time. The best of his fiction is to be found in the short stories, which are often well turned and usually designed pour *épater les bourgeois*. 'The Miracle of the Stigmata' in *Unpath'd Waters* (1913) is about a poor carpenter in Caesarea called Joshua who tries to stop his wife Judith becoming a Christian, arguing that Jesus might not really have died on the Cross. St Paul makes Judith leave him and he is heartbroken and dies; the stigmata on his corpse, which should tell everyone that he is really Christ, are interpreted as proof that he was mistaken. 'An English Saint', in the same volume, is another wry and funny story about a stupid young man at Oxford who acquires a great reputation by his ascetic habits. In the title story of *The Yellow Ticket and Other Stories* (1914) a young Jewish girl in Moscow who wants to be a university student tries to get a prostitute's yellow ticket in order to stay in the city. Biographies include those by Vincent Brome (1959) and Philippa Pullar (1975).

HARRIS, J. Henry set most of his fiction in his native Cornwall. He states in *The Young Journalist: His Work and how to Learn it* (1902) 'I have been a working journalist for thirty-five years.' He was evidently a lobby correspondent, probably for a provincial newspaper. The eleven volumes of fiction he published 1898–1913 are undistinguished and amateurish. In *Penelope Ann: A Cornish Romance* (1909), which is illustrated with posed photographs of Cornish types, he states that the reader will find himself in 'an enchanted region... amongst people of grand intuitions, to whom earth and sea and sky speak no uncertain language'. *A Romance in Radium* (1906), however, is science fiction, in which an alien immortal, Ma-Mylitta, comes to earth and nearly falls in love. Harris's father was a Sunday school teacher, and collected materials on the history of Sunday schools, which the son edited and published.

HARRISON, Frederic (1831–1923) married (1870) Ethel HARRISON (d. 1916). The son of a London merchant, he was educated at King's College School, London (1842–9), Wadham College, Oxford (1849–53), and Lincoln's Inn. He practised as a barrister for about fifteen years after 1858. While at Oxford he had become a convinced Positivist and Liberal, and devoted much of his life to the causes of social and legal reform, serving as President of the English Positivist Committee (1880–1905). He was the author of a large number of ethical, critical, and historical studies. He published his only work of prose fiction in his 70s: *Theophano, The Crusade of the Tenth Century: A Romantic Monograph* (1904), a long *historical novel which attempts to analyse the relationship between Christianity and Islam at this crucial period in the history of Byzantium. Some of the same material appears in his verse drama *Nicephorus: A Tragedy of New Rome* (1906). Harrison was a close friend of Maurice *Hewlett and Thomas Hardy (1840–1928); his help was important to George *Gissing's career. His son Austin Harrison (1873–1928) succeeded Ford Madox *Hueffer as editor of the **English Review*.

HARRISON, Marie was a journalist who wrote studies of the Irish problem (1917) and of Alsace-Lorraine (1918). Her only novel reflects the struggle at this period to find an appropriate fictional medium for the expression of advanced *feminist views. *The Woman Alone* (1914) is about a woman doctor who deliberately has an illegitimate child. Her best friend is a journalist who does not want children, whose husband is also a journalist who is sexually harassed by his woman employer. The ethical and social difficulties of single parenthood and of marriages where the couple both work are intelligently treated.

HARROD, Frances: Frances Marie Désirée FORBES-ROBERTSON (1866–1956) married (1900) Henry Dawes HARROD (d. 1919). The youngest of the eleven children of an art critic, she was the sister of the actor Sir Johnston Forbes-Robertson (1853–1937) and published thirteen volumes of fiction 1888–1934. After training as a painter at the Royal Academy, the Slade, and with Frank Brangwyn (1867–1956), she went to Italy in 1885 to work as a secretary and reader to E. J. *Lee-Hamilton but left, saying she was bored and that he had 'insulted her religious beliefs'. After this episode the letters of his half-sister 'Vernon *Lee' include gossip about her expulsion from art school for being fast, and the statement that 'the young man broke off the engagement mainly from fear of Frankie's temper'. In 1889 she briefly became an actress on the successful tour of the USA led by William Hunter Kendal (1843–1917). Her early books appeared under her maiden name; she continued to publish novels and short stories after her marriage to a fellow of New College. *The Hidden Model* (1901) has an atmospheric setting in an artist's studio, all blue china and shadowy drapery, in which a beautiful girl takes refuge after murdering a man. She is enclosed in his hidden room; he is obsessed with her appearance and her secret; their doomed relationship is effectively conveyed. *The Horrible Man* (1913) was described by the *Saturday Review* as an 'allegory of the rise of the militant female'. Harrod also published *historical fiction. Her only child was the economist Sir Roy Harrod (1900–78).

HARTLEY, C[atherine] Gasquoine (1866 or 1869–1928) married, first, Walter M. *GALLICHAN and, secondly, Arthur D. LEWIS (d. before 1928). Born in Antanarivo, Madagascar, the daughter of a clergyman, she described herself in *Who's Who* as having had almost no education until the age of 16. Despite this she became a teacher, and was headmistress of a school in Eltham 1894–1902. In 1903 she came to London and began to write full-time. Her first novel, *Life the Modeller* (1899), was followed by works on Spain and Spanish art, feminism, sociology, education, and sex education, including *The Primitive Position of Woman in Primitive Society: A Study of the Matriarchy* (1914) and *Sex Education and National Health* (1920). *The Weaver's Shuttle* (1905) is the story of Janet Bevan, who becomes an art student in Paris, resists seduction, marries her childhood friend, and has marital difficulties which are finally purged in a severe illness, after which she is to live happily ever after. It is a patchy novel, not without interest in its depiction of a woman struggling with her sexual identity in a (conventionally drawn) narrow provincial English circle. This book was published as by 'C. Gasquoine Hartley (Mrs Walter Gallichan)' and in *Who's Who* Hartley names her husbands as above. However the novelist Walter M. Gallichan (d. 1946) lists two wives, but not her. He describes himself as 'a pioneer of sex education in England', and in the circumstances it seems likely that they were associated at some period, but perhaps not actually married.

HASLETTE, John, *pseud.*: John George Haslette VAHEY (1881–1938) married Gertrude Crowe ——. He was born and educated in Ireland but went to live in Bournemouth. As 'John Haslette' he published seven novels 1909–1916. *The Mesh* (1912) is set in South America, where the wicked President schemes to obtain the deposits of the English Bank, but is frustrated by the English bank manager who doubles as the love interest. Vahey matured into an accomplished hack writer. As 'John Mowbray' he published fourteen thrillers and school stories for boys 1922–41; as 'Vernon Loder' twenty-two murder stories 1928–38; as 'Walter Proudfoot' four crime novels 1931–33; as 'Henrietta Clandon' seven crime novels 1933–38; and as 'Anthony Lang' five crime novels 1928–30. Under his own name he published verse (1926), a volume of angling stories (1932), and fourteen other volumes of fiction 1925–35.

HATTON, Joseph (1841–1907) married (1860) Louisa Howard JOHNSON (d. 1900). Born in Andover and educated by tutors and at Bowker's School, Chesterfield, Hatton was the son of the owner of the *Derbyshire Times*, and came to London in 1868 to edit the *Gentleman's Magazine*, which he did until 1874. For many years European correspondent of the *New York Times*, he also wrote about America for an English audience. *'The New Ceylon': British North Borneo* (1881) is a study of the colony in which his son was killed. He was a prolific author of syndicated newspaper columns, travel books, plays, and novels. *By Order of the Czar* (1890), a novel about a Jewish woman raped and flogged by the district governor, was banned in Russia. His last two fictions were *In Male Attire: A Romance of the Day* (1900), a long-winded novel (almost certainly written for serial publication) about a Chicago secretary, Zella Brunnen, who disguises herself as a man in order to avenge the death of her English lover, and *A Vision of Beauty* (1902), in which a provincial journalist comes to London and becomes 'the tame slave of a foreign-looking woman' before discovering a complicated intrigue, repenting, and going back to the country town, the county paper, and his true love. W. B. *Maxwell wrote that 'amiability... seemed to flow from him, so that he could not talk to people without linking arms, or patting and pawing them'.

Haunts of Ancient Peace, Alfred *Austin, Macmillan, 1902. A celebration of Englishness in the aftermath of the *Boer War. Four sentimentalists undertake a driving tour of the rural parts of the Home Counties punctuated by amiable discussions about the perils of modern life and the enduring virtues of the English (i.e. the inhabitants of the rural parts of the Home Counties). These virtues, visible in the landscape itself, include individualism and organicism: 'everything in English country life is a growth, not a mechanism.' The almost plotless story incorporates poems by Austin and illustrations (of churches, ruins, etc.) by Edmund H. New (1871–1931).

HAWTREY, Valentina. A friend of 'Vernon *Lee', she published seven novels focusing on women's issues and also the novella *A Ne'er-do-well* (1903) in T. Fisher Unwin's Pseudonym Library under the name 'Valentine Caryl'. Her novel *Perronelle* (1904) is set in fifteenth-century Paris. The heroine, who is the victim, aged 15, of an arranged marriage, leaves her husband, and has an illegitimate child who dies. *Suzanne* (1906) is set about fifty years earlier, and concerns a peasant girl who marries a nobleman. Both books focus on the education and social attitudes which make it impossible for men to treat women other than cruelly. *Rodwell* (1908) is a *family saga, beginning in 1864, about the displacement of a gentry family by the illegitimate son of a farmer's daughter who becomes a prosperous financier. It has the characteristic emphasis on the sufferings of women with unworthy husbands. In *In the Shade* (1909) a murderess is permitted to remarry, have a daughter, and live happily. Hawtrey also worked as a translator.

HAY, Ian, *pseud.*: John Hay BEITH (1876–1952), MC (1916), married (1915) Helen Margaret SPIERS. The son of a Manchester cotton merchant of Scots family, he was educated at Fettes College, Edinburgh, and St John's College, Cambridge, where he graduated (1898) with a second class in the Classical Tripos. He then became a schoolmaster at Fettes, at Durham School, and then at Fettes again until he became a full-time writer in 1912. Schools, along with sport, amateur theatricals, and cruises, became staple features of his fiction (for instance in *The Lighter Side of School Life*, 1914, and *Housemaster*, 1936). His first novel, **Pip: A Romance of Youth* (1907), is a light, comic love story concerned with the definition of manliness, which the **Athenaeum* earnestly recommended to 'anyone who may be suffering from a glut of the "feminism" of the current English imitations of Maupassant'; it was quickly followed by *'The Right Stuff': Some Episodes in the Career of a North Briton* (1908) and *A Man's Man* (1909), *Wodehousian facetious college tales. In the First World War Beith served with the Argyll and Sutherland Highlanders, then with the Machine Gun Corps. His bestselling fictional propaganda, such as *The First Hundred Thousand: Being the Unofficial Chronicle of a Unit of 'K(1)'* (1915), had an impact on American public opinion, and he spent 1916–18 in America in the information bureau of the British War Mission. (In the Second World War he was again employed in War Office public relations.) Beith had published a collection of plays in 1913; in the 1920s he became a prolific playwright, dramatizing his own novels and collaborating with several other writers including Guy Bolton (1884–1979), A. E. W. *Mason, and P. G. *Wodehouse. He continued to turn out a stream of cheerful romantic novels, although none did as well as the first few. He was chairman of the Society of Authors (1921–4, 1935–9) and president of the Dramatists' Club from 1937.

HAY, [Agnes Blanche] Marie (1873–1938) married (1903) Herbert von BENECKENDORFF und von HINDENBURG. She was the granddaughter of an earl; her parents divorced when she was three. She lived in Rome, where her husband was attached to the German embassy, and wrote fictionalized historical biographies. *Mas'aniello: A Neapolitan Tragedy* (1913) sets an imaginary romance against the background of the 1647 rising. *The Winter Queen: The Story of Elizabeth of Bohemia* (1910) was recommended by the *Times* to the lover of fiction. *A German Pompadour* (1906) is based on the career of Wilhelmine von Graevenitz. After the First World War she published one more novel, *The Evil Vineyard* (1923), about a young woman brought up in a narrow upper-class English household who marries an older man, goes to live with him in a haunted house in north Italy, and is torn between him and a younger lover. It apparently attracted the attention of the psychoanalyst C. G. Jung (1875–1961). The biographer and diplomat Alfred Duff Cooper (1890–1954) was her half-brother.

HAYENS, [William James] Herbert (b. 1861) married Jeanie Douglas —— (d. 1933). Chief editor at Collins & Co., the publishers, he lived in Glasgow, edited anthologies, and was a prolific author of textbooks and boys' books between 1895 and 1932. In such works as *Scouting for Buller* (1902) and *The President's Scouts: A Story of the Chilian [sic] Revolution* (1904) he gives the boy reader the medicine of history in the jam of battle and adventure, very much in the manner of G. A. *Henty. In the latter book the hero's father actually exhorts him: 'Live a clean life, my boy... fear God and remember if you don't go straight you'll break your mother's heart.' Unlike Henty, Hayens survived to apply the formula to the First World War in *Midst Shot and Shell in Flanders* (1916). He also wrote school stories: his *Play Up!* series began in 1919. John Keir, in his 1952 history of Collins, observes that Hayens 'came of Devonshire seafaring stock, and with his blue eyes, flowing moustache and greying hair looked more like an old-time Devonshire sea captain than an editor. Even his room, high up in the Glasgow office, was a glass-topped crow's nest approached by steep and narrow stairs which resembled a ship's companionway sufficiently to strengthen the general nautical illusion of his surroundings.'

HAYES, F[rederick] W[illiam] (1848–1918) married, first (1876), Margaret ROBINSON and, secondly (1886), her sister Elise ROBINSON. Born in Cheshire, he went to Liverpool College, and trained as an architect, before becoming a painter, especially of water-colours of north Wales. He published five novels with his own illustrations, 1900–7. *The Shadow of a Throne* (1904) is a romance about the French Revolution which so closely resembles *The *Scarlet Pimpernel* (1905) by Baroness *Orczy that it seems incredible that she had not read it. Hayes has much more elaborate detail about life in Paris under the Terror and uses more real historical characters, but his hero, Noel Dorrington, is an English gentleman, a master of disguise, who dedicates his life to saving the Dauphin and Madame Royale from the guillotine, using methods very similar to those of Sir Percy Blakeney. This was a sequel to Hayes's earlier novels *A Kent Squire* (1900) and *Gwynett of Thornhaugh* (1900), in which ancestors of Dorrington also become entangled in French history. *A Prima Donna's Romance* (1905) is set in modern Greece: in its denouement an operatic diva discovers she is not the daughter of a bandit, as she always imagined, but of her benefactor, a doctor whose pregnant wife the bandit had kidnapped. These highly coloured melodramas seem to sit oddly with Hayes's other, rather serious and progressive interests: he was a member of the Fabian Society, the Society for Psychical Research, the Land Nationalization Society, and the Commons and Footpaths Preservation Society.

Heart of Darkness: see **Youth: A Narrative, and Two Other Stories*

HEDDLE, Ethel F[orster] married W. MARSHALL. The *British Library Catalogue* lists nineteen volumes of fiction 1892–1934, mostly books for girls, by this writer, such as *Colina's Island* (1900), *Carola's Secret* (1903), and *Clarinda's Quest* (1910). She is probably also the author of two novels published in 1927 listed under 'Ethel F. H. Marshall'. Krishnamurti states that Heddle's *Three Girls in a Flat* is based on the experiences of Ménie Muriel *Dowie, Lillias Campbell *Davidson, and Alice Werner (1859–1935).

Helen With the High Hand: *An Idyllic Diversion*, Arnold *Bennett, 1910, Chapman & Hall. A story set, like much of Bennett's work, in the Midlands town of 'Bursley' (i.e. Burslem). Helen Rathbone, a young schoolteacher, alternately bluffs and charms her miserly bachelor step-great-uncle, James Ollerenshaw, into acquiring the barrack-like Wilbraham Hall, and social pretensions to match. He, for his part, is awakened to the pleasures of female company—a knowledge he puts to use by marrying a benevolently scheming widow, Mrs Prockter, 'who by reason of the rare "k" in her name regarded herself as the sole genuine in a district full of Proctors'. Helen, meanwhile, successfully sets her cap at the local Byron, Andrew Dean. A low-key tale which delights in demonstrating that a degree of calculation is by no means inimical to romance. Bennett designed the novel, which first appeared as a serial in various provincial newspapers in 1909, under the title of 'The Miser's Niece', 'to be something which would please the serial public without giving the *serious* public a chance to accuse me of "playing down"—as in "The City of Pleasure", etc.' Some reviewers contrasted the high-handed protagonists of Bennett's lightweight comedies with their relatively passive counterparts in novels like *The *Old Wives' Tale* (1908) and **Clayhanger* (1910).

Helpmate, The, May *Sinclair, 1907, Archibald Constable. Boyishly charming Walter Majendie marries large, beautiful, devout Anne. The day after the wedding, she discovers that he had an affair, seven years before, with the notorious Lady Sarah Cayley. Her passion dies, but she stays with him, trusting to the redemptive power of her own purity. Walter's crippled sister, Edith, a shrewd observer, loves the disreputable Charlie Gorst despite, or because of, his infidelities. When Walter takes up with Charlie's ex-mistress, Anne is placed in a similar position. Can she learn to overcome her desire for martyrdom, her 'moral luxury'? The Majendies separate, but are eventually reconciled. It is not so much that Anne's purity has redeemed Walter as that his love of life has rekindled her passion. Her purity was the problem, not the solution. The novel is funny and sexy, and represents Sinclair's most explicit assault on Victorian values.

HENNIKER, Hon. Mrs Arthur: Florence Ellen Hungerford MILNES (1855–1923) married (1882) Arthur Henry HENNIKER-MAJOR (1855–1912). The daughter of the poet and man of letters Richard Monckton Milnes, 1st Lord Houghton (1809–85), she published nine volumes of fiction 1891–1912. She is best known for her friendship with Thomas Hardy (1840–1928); together they wrote 'The Spectre of the Real', in which a clandestine marriage, regretted by both man and woman, is concealed. He dies, she marries, and her husband commits suicide next morning.

Can a physical and legal relationship be private and secret? This was published in Henniker's *In Scarlet and Grey: Stories of Soldiers and Others* (1896); the other stories are in similar vein, focusing on the tragically sordid sexual encounter, so common in highbrow stories of the 1890s. Hardy tried, in a letter (16 Sept. 1893), to make her write more sympathetically about sexual transgression: 'If you mean to make the world listen to you, you must say now what they will all be thinking & saying five & twenty years hence: & if you do that you must offend your conventional friends.' Similarly, he wrote (29 Sept. 1907), of her *Our Fatal Shadows* (1907), 'Of course I should not have kept her respectable, & made a nice, decorous, dull woman of her at the end, but shd have let her go to the d— for the man... But gentle F. H. naturally had not the heart to do that.' They shared an opposition to vivisection. Henniker's novel *Second Fiddle* (1912) describes the life of a rich, kind, well-meaning woman, whom life persistently disappoints and frustrates. The account of her marriage to a selfish flirt is genuinely poignant. Hardy commented, interestingly, that it belonged to the new fashion for novels covering a whole lifetime. Henniker also wrote plays as 'G. Worlingworth' and succeeded her friend 'John Oliver *Hobbes' as president of the Society of Women Journalists in 1896. Her husband was a Guards officer who transferred to the Territorials and became a major-general.

HENTY, G[eorge] A[lfred] (1833–1902) married, first (1857) Elizabeth FINUCANE (d. 1865) and, secondly (1889 or 1890), Elizabeth KEYLOCK. Born at Godmanchester, near Cambridge, the son of a stockbroker and mine-owner, Henty was a sickly child who spent much of his time in bed reading. He was educated at Westminster School (1847–52) and Caius College, Cambridge, but left the latter in 1853 to volunteer for the Crimean War, where he worked in the Hospital Commissariat. His experiences were turned to good use in *Jack Archer (The Fall of Sebastopol)* (1883). Subsequently he ran field hospitals in the Austro-Italian War (1866), while also acting as a journalist. He was staff correspondent for the *Standard* (1865–1876). The 1870 Franco-Prussian War provided material for *The Young Franc-Tireurs* (1872), the Ashanti War (1873–4) for *By Sheer Pluck* (1883), and the Carlist rising (1874) for *With the British Legion* (1902). A much larger number of his books are, of course, set during wars that he had not witnessed, and draw heavily on the work of historians. Schoolmasters and parents were encouraged to believe that Henty's books were wholesome and instructive; he declared: 'my object has been to teach history and still more to encourage manly and straight living and feeling amongst boys.' His amazing rate of production got under way after he retired from being a war correspondent after the Turco-Serbian War (1876). Many of his later works were dictated to his amanuensis, E. Petit Griffiths. There are interesting details of his financial transactions with Blackie & Son, his publishers, in the study by Guy Arnold (1980). As a publishing phenomenon Henty was remarkable: Blackie printed 3.5 million books, and pirated and American sales must further inflate the number. However, he is no exception to the rule that writers for children were paid much worse than those for adults: he failed to make a fortune and was constantly short of money, losing some in a scheme to build a self-righting boat. He was connected with two unsuccessful boys' magazines, acting as editor of the *Union Jack* (1880–3) and *Beeton's Boys' Own Magazine* (1888–90). His second marriage, to his housekeeper, estranged him from his children. He kept going right up to the end of his life: there are twenty Henty titles dated between 1900 and 1906 including *With Roberts to Pretoria* (1902) and **With Kitchener in the Sudan* (1903). Henty's many imitators include Geo. Manville *Fenn, 'Harry *Collingwood', and Herbert *Hayens.

HERBERT, Alice: Alice Louise Grisewood BAKER (1867–1941) married, first (1889), Walter Humboldt LOW (1864–1895) and, secondly (1896), John Alexander HERBERT (1862–1948). She was the daughter of an officer in the Madras Artillery; her mother died when she was a year old and her father had several children by the governess: according to John Carswell's biography of Herbert's daughter Ivy *Low, he was given to sexually abusing his daughters. Alice, already pregnant, married the writer Low, who was Jewish and a Fabian, and was at that time H. G. *Wells's best friend. After his death she reviewed fiction for the *Saturday Review*, then edited by Frank *Harris. She published a volume of verse (1903) and five novels between 1909 and 1927. The second, *Garden Oats* (1914), is a sharp, funny, and probably autobiographical novel about a girl growing up and getting married, which focuses on the social difficulties of women. Her father seduces her governess and ruins the life of her intelligent and enterprising stepmother; she herself is nearly brought by her own sexual feelings to threaten her happy marriage. Herbert's first husband was was a philologist, translator of the Anglo-Saxon Chronicle and other Old English and Norwegian works; he published many textbooks on English literature. After their marriage he studied for a degree at Cambridge, and they lived in cheap lodgings with their baby daughter, Ivy, while he scraped a living coaching. Herbert's second husband was an official in the manuscripts department of the British Museum; she is supposed to have been unfaithful to him.

HERBERTSON, Agnes Grozier was born in Oslo of Scots family, and specialized in short stories for the *Windsor Magazine* and other periodicals. She wrote many children's books, plays, and poems, including *The Book of Happy Gnomes* (1924), and six novels for adults between 1897 and 1947, starting with *A Book Without A Man!* (1897). The title refers to a novel written by one of the characters and does not describe the book itself. *The Plowers: A Novel* (1906) is about a woman unhappily married to a scientist who is making mysterious inhuman experiments. He dies conveniently so she can marry the man she loves, who believes in the sanctity of life and is the hero of a shipwreck. *The Ship That Came Home in the Dark* (1912) involves a woman substituting herself for a blind man's wife, and was perhaps influenced by the plot of Florence L. *Barclay's immensely successful novel *The *Rosary* (1909). Herbertson lived in Cornwall with Jessie Leckie *Herbertson, who was probably her sister.

HERBERTSON, Jessie Leckie was probably a sister of the above; they lived together at St Cleer in Cornwall and her career appears to follow a similar pattern. She was born in Glasgow. Her first publication was *The Stigma: A Novel* (1905), whose heroine is illegitimate. Her best friend's brother loves her but will not offer a nameless woman marriage and she refuses to be his mistress. She takes refuge with some unfeeling relations and works in a lunatic asylum in which the legitimate daughter of her father is incarcerated. Eventually she marries the local doctor.

It is a novel of the school of *Jane Eyre* (1847) by Charlotte Brontë, (1816–55), about a woman stoically asserting her integrity, but the disadvantages of illegitimacy, both social and internalized, are exaggerated to an implausible extent, without intelligent criticism. Herbertson also wrote *Young Life: A Novel* (1911) and was the author of twenty volumes of fiction of various kinds between 1905–39, many of which are girls' books or children's books.

Hero, The, William Somerset *Maugham, 1901, Hutchinson. After five years in India and South Africa, Captain James Parsons VC returns home to a hero's welcome and the smug provincialism of small-town life in Little Primpton, where 'Marie *Corelli' is worshipped as a minor deity. Infatuation with the entrancing Mrs Pritchard-Wallace, wife of a fellow-officer, has put the charms of his sporty, officious fiancée, Mary Clibborn, whose affection is 'free from anything so gross as passion', thoroughly into context. He breaks off the engagement and, after enduring a good deal of disapproval, escapes to London, where he finds a letter from Mrs Pritchard-Wallace waiting at his club. He destroys the letter without opening it, returns to Little Primpton, and contracts enteric fever. Mary Clibborn nurses him devotedly, and he proposes again in gratitude. But he still cannot bear the thought of marrying her, and flees to London in despair. This time he does see Mrs Pritchard-Wallace, who lets him buy her dinner, then coolly announces that her husband is dead and that she is already engaged to someone else. Thrown back on Little Plimpton, James feels utterly trapped. He shoots himself. The novel is very much of its time in its portrayal of a rebellious young man who fiercely rejects his parents' attitudes and values but has not yet invented any of his own (apart, in this case, from a frank enjoyment of war).

HERON-MAXWELL, Beatrice: Beatrice Maude Emilia EASTWICK (d. 1927) married, first, F. Lane HUDDART and, secondly (1891) Spencer Horatio Walpole Heron HERON-MAXWELL (1855–1907). The daughter of a Cornish MP, she was educated at home, and began to write after being left a widow with two daughters after her first husband's death. *A Woman's Soul* (1900) was published in collaboration with her sister Florence Eastwick. *The Queen Regent* (1903) is a run-of-the-mill romance with *Ruritanian overtones. A millionaire's young widow establishes sovereignty over an island which belongs to her and educates her son to become king. After a good deal of social and political intrigue, her son's well-born but impoverished tutor wins her hand in marriage. Heron-Maxwell contributed fiction to *Tit-Bits* from its inception, to the **Strand*, and to the *Bystander*. Her daughter, Gladys M. Huddart, also published fiction in the 1920s.

HEWLETT, Maurice [Henry] (1861–1923) married (1888) Hilda Beatrice HERBERT. Hewlett's father was a lawyer and man of letters; his mother was the sister of J. T. Knowles (1831–1908), founder and editor of the **Nineteenth Century*. Born at Weybridge and educated at Sevenoaks Grammar School, Palace School, Enfield, and London International College, Hewlett joined a cousin's solicitors' firm in Lincoln's Inn in 1878. Later, in 1888, he was called to the Bar at the Inner Temple. After the success of *The Forest Lovers* (1898) he gave up law. He succeeded his father as Keeper of Lands, Revenues, Records, and Enrolments (1896–1901), acting as the government's expert on medieval law. This enforced an acquaintance with the daily life of the Middle Ages. *The Forest Lovers* was a bestseller, in which medieval romance, in the manner of *The Faerie Queene*, met the Stevensonian revival of *historical romance. The faintly facetious Thackerayan narrator says at the beginning: 'Blood will be spilt, virgins suffer distresses; the horn will sound though woodland glades.' Prosper le Gai falls in love with a low-born girl who turns out to be the long-lost daughter of the countess. Hewlett's Edwardian fiction includes *The Life and Death of Richard Yea-and-Nay* (1900), about the amorous career of Richard the Lionheart, and *The *Queen's Quair* (1904). Hewlett also wrote historical romances about Italy, such as *The Fool Errant* (1905), in which an English Roman Catholic student at Padua University becomes a tramp and marries a beautiful peasant girl. *Bendish* (1913) and *The Stooping Lady* (1907) are both set in high society in early nineteenth-century England. *The Stooping Lady* (1907) (based on an earlier play) is concerned with the impact of revolutionary social views on the upper classes; the heroine reads the work of Tom Paine (1737–1809) and falls in love with a butcher who is executed for treason. The hero of the former, Lord Bendish, is a Byron viewed unsympathetically whose career has been moved forward to the 1830s. Like Stanley J. *Weyman's **Chippinge* (1906), it is a novel set during the Reform Bill crisis which implicitly refers to the Edwardian agitation about constitutional and franchise reform. *Halfway House* (1908), *Open Country* (1909), and *Rest Harrow* (1910) form a trilogy which focuses on the social and sexual problems of modern *marriage. Hewlett's letters were edited by Lawrence Binyon (1926).

HEWLETT, [Henry] William. Brother of Maurice *Hewlett, he was described by Compton *Mackenzie in his memoirs as 'my most intimate friend for many years... He was a heartbreak to his family, but at sixteen one does not realise what those heartbreaks mean and I admired him greatly for what I felt was his resolute stand against the tyranny of convention.' He studied music in Leipzig, but threw it up and returned to board with a family in Baron's Court, where he became engaged to his landlady's daughter and had an affair with her son. For the first years of the century he occasionally worked as an actor. He published twelve novels 1913–38. *Uncle's Advice: A Novel in Letters* (1913) consists entirely of letters addressed to the hero, whose voice is never heard except by implication. The device is amusing enough to sustain a light romance in which a young man sows wild oats and then settles down. The opinions expressed are anti-clerical, snobbish, and misogynistic. *Telling the Truth: A Novel of Analysis* (1913) is a novel of greater pretensions which also aims at revising ideas about sexual morality; the hero is a novelist who falls in love with a married woman. By the end they are living together in Cornwall, where they have developed a personal religion independent of institutions.

HICHENS, Robert [Smythe] (1864–1950). The son of a Church of England clergyman, Hichens was born at Speldhurst, Kent, and educated at Clifton College, Bristol, and the Royal College of Music. His first novel, *The Coastguard's Secret* (1886), sank without trace. He resolved to become an organist, but changed his mind and left the Royal College of Music for a course at a school of journalism. He survived by publishing songs and stories, but (partly because of a long illness) his next novel was not published until he was 30. This was *The Green Carnation* (1894), an anonymous satire on Oscar Wilde (1856–1900) and his circle, written in four weeks, which was immensely popular. Hichens was not a member of the Wilde circle, but had spent a winter in Egypt with Reginald *Turner, and picked up material. He was given the job of music critic of the *World* (formerly occupied by G. B. Shaw, 1856–1950) His next novel, *An Imaginative Man* (1895), he called a 'rather concentrated and sombre book'; versatility, amounting to a failure to fulfil the potential his talents seemed to promise, was to be a permanent feature of Hichens's career. The success of *The Londoners: An Absurdity* (1898), a farcical trifle in the manner of Max *Beerbohm, encouraged him to follow it with *The Prophet of Berkeley Square: A Tragic Extravaganza* (1901), which proved a complete failure. **Felix* (1902) contains much autobiographical material. *The Daughters of Babylon* (1899) was novelized from a play by Wilson Barrett (1846–1904) in eight weeks, for £500. His bestselling, much filmed novel *The *Garden of Allah* (1904) was the fruit of travel in the Mediterranean and North Africa, which provided material for several travel books as well as for fiction. For many years he spent the winter at Taormina in Sicily where he had a house. *The *Call of the Blood* (1906) was set in Sicily, **Bella Donna* (1909) in Egypt. In *The Dweller on the Threshold* (1911) a clergyman dominates his curate hypnotically, taking over his mind in order to make him the medium of communication with the Other Side. In *The Fruitful Vine* (1911), set in high society in Rome, a woman has an affair to give her husband the child he wants. During the First World War a great change in Hichens's life came about when he met John Knittel (1891–1970), a Swiss who later, encouraged by Hichens, became a novelist. Knittel and his wife and children lived with Hichens in England, Switzerland, and North Africa for the next twenty-five years. He spent the Second World War in Switzerland, where he died. He published a tired and unrevealing autobiography, *Yesterday* (1947).

Hilda Lessways, Arnold *Bennett, 1911, Methuen. The second volume in the Clayhanger tetralogy was begun on 6 January 1911 and completed, with characteristic dispatch, by 14 June. It describes the background and adventures of Hilda Lessways, Edwin Clayhanger's future wife. It is a novel about women: Bennett said that he wanted to convey 'the multitudinous activities of the whole sex, against a mere background of masculinity'. It begins in a world emptied of men: Hilda and her mother in Bursley, surrounded by servants, landladies, spinsters. But Hilda desperately wants to prove herself in the masculine world, and does so by working for the ultra-masculine Mr Cannon, first as secretary, then as manager of a Brighton boarding-house. She marries him. He turns out to be a conman and bigamist, and departs, leaving an impoverished Hilda in charge of the boarding-house. She returns to Bursley, and once again meets Edwin Clayhanger. She becomes engaged to him, then discovers that she is pregnant by Cannon, and breaks the engagement. The novel leaves her bloody but unbowed. On the whole, reviewers admired Bennett's ability to describe from a woman's point of view events he had described from a man's point of view in *Clayhanger* (1910). 'It is almost incredible', remarked the *Manchester Guardian*, 'that two novels which have so much material in common should nevertheless possess such an absolute individuality that the effect of reading one is an immediate desire to refer to the other for new light on the situations described by both.'

HILL, Headon, *pseud.*: Francis Edward GRAINGER (1857–1927) married Georgina Eve Marsh ——. The son of a Church of England clergyman, Grainger was born at Lowestoft, Suffolk, and educated at Eton College. He went into the army, travelled, and then became a journalist. He also published about sixty volumes of detective fiction between *Clues from A Detective's Camera* (1893) and *The Mammoth Mansions Mystery* (1926). The hero of *The Spies of the Wight* (1899) is a journalist on holiday who unmasks a German master-spy and seems to be more concerned with his scoop than with the threat to Portsmouth dockyard. The heroine of *The Avengers* (1906) hires a penniless gentleman who is the double of her fiancé in order to contrive the release of the latter from a lunatic asylum. The gentleman, who has fallen in love with her, discovers the fiancé is really mad, and, acting from the highest motives, pretends to be him and marries her himself. Grainger lived at Budleigh Salterton.

Hill, The: A Romance of Friendship, Horace Annesley *Vachell, 1905, John Murray. The novel begins with the arrival of young John Verney at Harrow a couple of years before the outbreak of the *Boer War. The first person he meets is Harry Desmond, a cabinet minister's son, who becomes his idol. Unfortunately, he has a rival for Desmond's affections in the powerful but corrupt Scaife, whose deficiencies seem to be as much social as moral (*his* father is a self-made millionaire). There is a great deal of public-school background, complete with impenetrable slang (some of it glossed in footnotes). The school might be seen as a metaphor for the state of the ruling classes: sound structure, a certain amount of 'dry-rot' here and there ('too many beasts wreck a house, as they wreck a regiment or a nation'). The bestiality, which involves Scaife, seems to be restricted to bridge. 'Thank God,' the Headmaster remarks, 'this is not one of those cases from which every clean, manly boy must recoil in disgust.' After an Eton–Harrow cricket match, in which Desmond and Scaife distinguish themselves, war is declared; both join the army, and leave for South Africa. Desmond dies a heroic death. The slightly younger Verney, still at school, is unconsolable—until he receives a letter from Desmond, written the night before the latter's death, describing him as 'the best friend a man ever had, the only one I love as much as my own brothers—*and even more*'.

Hill of Dreams, The, Arthur *Machen, 1907, Grant Richards. Lucian Taylor dreams of a Roman city beneath the Welsh hills which is more real to him than the humiliations which beset him as a boy and young man living in a provincial market town: philistines who despise his bookishness, children who torture helpless animals, a girlfriend who jilts him, a publisher's reader who plagiarizes the manuscript of his first book. The vision is composed in more or less equal parts of pagan mysticism, reverence for an ancient (Celtic) Britain, and erotic *fantasy. Receiving a legacy of £2,000, Lucian moves to London, where he lives a solitary and increasingly drug-dependent life in a dismal suburb. He publishes a 'slim tale' entitled *The Amber Statuette*, which achieves modest success. But he is finding it harder and harder to put his lurid visions, now of the inferno of urban existence, into words. He dies of an overdose, tended only by a prostitute who had figured in his dreams as a priestess. Written between 1895 and 1897, and presumably rendered unpublishable by the aftermath of the Wilde scandal, the novel is very much of that period, with its ornate projection of an 'outland and occult territory', and its towering denunciations of the hell created by modern civilization.

HINE, Muriel [Florence] (d. 1949) married Sidney COXON. She published thirty-five volumes of romantic fiction between 1910 and 1950, including *Half in Earnest* (1910), about a smooth politician who claims that love is the one great force in the world, and on that basis attempts to seduce two married women, and *The Best in Life* (1918), the story of a half-French girl struggling alone in wartime London, which was made into a film entitled *Fifth Avenue Models*.

HINKSON, H[enry] A[lbert] (1865–1919) married (1893) Katherine *TYNAN. Educated at Dublin High School and Trinity College Dublin (where he was a Scholar), and in Germany, he was called to the Bar of the Inner Temple (1902). After 1914 he was a Resident Magistrate in South Mayo. He converted to Roman Catholicism on marriage, and he wrote novels and short stories between 1895 and 1913. The atmosphere of his fiction is conveyed by the *Pall Mall Gazette*'s response to *The Point of Honour* (1901): 'The spirit of adventure and love of life breathe throughout the book, and to read it is to be carried away for the moment to other times when men were more reckless of the future, and women, if possible, more fair.' *The Wine of Love* (1904) is set in modern Ireland, in which a number of conscientious landowners are struggling against the Land League and a well-meaning but ignorant American millionaire. The combination of hunting scenes and the American point of view is reminiscent of *The American Senator* (1877) by Anthony Trollope (1815–82). The book breathes a spirit of optimism about political and religious affairs which seems in retrospect naïve. His daughter Pamela Hinkson (1900–82) was a novelist. His wife's 1917 application to the Royal Literary Fund states that she was the main support of her family, his income of £427 as RM being inadequate.

His Hour, Elinor *Glyn, 1910, Duckworth. Communing with the Sphinx in the Egyptian desert, recently widowed Tamara Loraine realizes that her life has been 'one long commonplace vista of following leads—like a sheep'. However, her thoughts are interrupted by the sudden appearance of a ruthlessly handsome Cossack, Prince Gritzko Milaslavski. At once repelled and fascinated by Milaslavski, Tamara follows him back to St Petersburg, where a succession of patriotic ceremonies, duels, and gipsy suppers confirms both of these feelings. When they dance, he crushes her to him so tightly that the heavy silver cartridges which adorn his Cossack dress leave red marks on her 'milk white chest'. He kidnaps her, and allows her to believe that he raped her while she lay unconscious in his hunting-lodge. She feels that the only honourable course is to accept his proposal of marriage, while hating him. But his passion, now fully reciprocated, eventually wins her over, and he is able to reveal that in the hunting-lodge he did no more than kiss her feet. The idea that Tamara must fulfil her weakness so that Gritzko can fulfil his strength has overtones of sadomasochism also found in the work of other women romancers like Ethel M. *Dell and, later, 'E. M. Hull'. The interest here lies in the interchangeability of hot Egypt and cold Russia as arenas for emotional and sexual awakening. Like the sheikhs of desert romance, Milaslavski is at once barbarous and broodingly sophisticated.

historical romance. Historical romance was in the Edwardian period, as it had been in the Victorian period, one of the most popular and least honoured of literary genres—only more so. Its popularity can be gauged by the appearance of specialist guides and bibliographies like Jonathan Nield's *A Guide to the Best Historical Novels and Tales* (1902) and Ernest Baker's *A Guide to Historical Fiction* (1914). However, whereas almost all the major Victorian novelists had tried their hand at it, Ford Madox *Hueffer was the only major Edwardian novelist to do so to any great effect, in his Katherine Howard trilogy (1906–8), which Joseph *Conrad called the 'swan song of historical romance'. (Conrad had already collaborated with Hueffer on the distinctly ineffective **Romance* (1903); George *Gissing's *Veranilda* was published posthumously in 1904). In the 1880s, the work of Robert Louis Stevenson (1850–1894) and Rider *Haggard, enthusiastically promoted by Andrew *Lang, had established romance (historical and contemporary) as a serious alternative to domestic realism, and taken it decisively down-market. Historical romance, in the Edwardian era, meant costume drama. A number of writers tried, as Stevenson had, to invoke the authority of Sir Walter Scott (1771–1832); examples include Robert *Barr, *The Strong Arm* (1900), Arthur Conan *Doyle, *Sir Nigel* (1906), and R. H. *Forster, *Strained Allegiance* (1905). But the most successful romancers succeeded by transferring their narratives lock, stock, and smuggler's barrel from the realm of history into the realm of myth: 'Marjorie *Bowen', Egerton and Agnes *Castle, Jeffery *Farnol, Henry Seton *Merriman, Baroness *Orczy, *'Q', and Stanley J. *Weyman. Fiction aimed at the juvenile market followed the same pattern, in the work of Harold *Avery, 'Harry *Collingwood', Geo. Manville *Fenn, John *Finnemore, Herbert *Hayens, G. A. *Henty, Beatrice *Marshall, and Gordon *Stables. This shift of emphasis established the genre at the centre of Edwardian popular fiction. Arthur Conan Doyle and Rider Haggard both thought better of their historical romances than of the contemporary fiction which had made them famous. Writers like R. H. *Benson, Warwick *Deeping, Marie Belloc *Lowndes, John Collis *Snaith, and 'Patricia *Wentworth' launched their careers with historical romances, which they knew would find readers, before branching out in more distinctive directions. A list of Edwardian writers whose reputations rested to a large extent on their efforts in the genre would include J. H. M. *Abbott, 'John *Ayscough', W. Bourne *Cooke, W. Patrick *Kelly, 'Vernon *Lee', John Heron *Lepper, John *Masefield, Flora Annie *Steel, and H. B. Marriott *Watson. A list of Edwardian writers who dabbled in it would include a considerable proportion of all the writers included in this *Companion*. The romancers tended to base their stories on larger-than-life historical personages (Henry VIII, Mary Queen of Scots, Cromwell, the Duke of Marlborough, Napoleon, etc.) or on epoch-making historical events (the Crusades, the English Civil War, the Jacobite rebellions, the American and French Revolutions, the 'Indian Mutiny', etc.). There are one or two unexpected favourites: Henri of Navarre (1553–1610), for example, perhaps on account as much of his divided religious allegiance as of his political and military triumphs (Dorothea *Conyers, *For Henri and Navarre*, 1911; S. R. *Crockett, **White Plumes of Navarre*, 1906; Stanley J. Weyman, *The Abbess of Vlaye*, 1904, *In King's Byways*,

1902). Edwardian writers ransacked European and world history in search of episodes with dramatic potential (the *Times Literary Supplement* described the subject of Weyman's *The Long Night* (1903), Charles Emanuel of Savoy's attack on Geneva in 1602, as 'one of the few stirring themes which English historical novelists have so far left untouched'). But their most substantial successes rested on the recreation not so much of historical personages and events as of charismatic, quasi-mythical figures: the highwayman, the dandy, the buccaneer, the Dumas-derived 'musketeer'. One of the bestselling novels of the period, Orczy's *The *Scarlet Pimpernel* (1905), plays skilfully on the expectations aroused by the figure of the Regency fop (she was anticipated in this respect by F. W. *Hayes, in *The Shadow of a Throne*, 1904). The mythical dimension of historical romance connects it to other popular genres such as *Ruritanian romance and the romance of *Empire (the up-to-date protagonists stray into ancient or time-locked kingdoms). So popular was the genre that writers with a polemical point to make, whether about religion (R. H. *Benson, Mrs P. Champion de *Crespigny), Irish politics (M. McDonnell *Bodkin, S. R. *Keightley, John Heron Lepper, Randal William *McDonnell, P. A. *Sheehan), or the position of women (Valentina *Hawtrey), used it to get their message across. Walter *Besant's historical fiction is mildly libertarian in spirit, while Henry Seton Merriman's advertises the futility of political intrigue and insurrection. Maurice *Hewlett's bestselling *The Forest Lovers* (1898) combined Spenserian with Stevensonian romance in such a way as to evoke both erotic tension and deep-rooted Englishness. It was followed by Coningsby *Dawson's *The Road to Avalon* (1911), Warwick Deeping's *Uther & Igraine* (1903) and *Love Among the Ruins* (1904), and Clemence *Housman's *The Life of Sir Aglovale de Galis* (1905). Doyle's *Sir Nigel* sets nostalgia within nostalgia: its hero's chivalric exploits recreate in a modern (fourteenth-century) setting an older and purer chivalry. However, it would be a mistake to suppose that Edwardian historical romance banished history altogether. Some of the most impressive examples of the genre are those which examine the reform or modernizing of the various *ancien régimes* which had traditionally provided it with its quasi-mythical settings. Ford Madox Hueffer's Katherine Howard trilogy is a case in point, as are two carefully researched novels set in the era of the first Reform Bill: Stanley J. Weyman's **Chippinge* (1906) and Maurice Hewlett's *Bendish* (1913).

History of Mr Polly, The, H. G. *Wells, 1910, Thomas Nelson. 'Mr Polly dreamt always of picturesque and mellow things, and had an instinctive hatred of the strenuous life.' Wells's fat, balding, lethargic anti-hero lives two lives: one shaped by his bilious digestive system, his miserable education, and the boredom of apprenticeship, shopkeeping, and an unfulfilling marriage; the other by imagination. Neither has prepared him for the prospect of bankruptcy. He decides to commit suicide, selects a razor for the purpose, then loses his nerve—but only after he has set light to his house. The episode, superbly described, during which he rescues his neighbour's deaf mother-in-law, both regenerates him and sets a literary standard the rest of the novel cannot quite live up to. He abandons shop and wife, and goes on the tramp, ending up at the idyllic Potwell Inn, where he finds work as an odd job man. He is obliged, contradictorily, to take up the strenuous life, in order to see off the malevolent Uncle Jim, a convicted criminal who has battened onto the inn's widowed owner. But the end of the novel sees the idyll resumed, and the shopkeeping life consigned to history for ever. Lighter in tone than Wells's other Edwardian novels about lower-middle-class insurgency, **Love and Mr Lewisham* (1900) and **Kipps* (1905), and published in the same year as 'Condition of England' novels like Arnold *Bennett's **Clayhanger* and E. M. *Forster's **Howards End*, *The History of Mr Polly* neatly sidesteps the obligation to social analysis by foisting it onto an economist with a pince-nez who sits in the Climax Club writing a book about failed shopkeepers like Mr Polly.

History of Sir Richard Calmady, The: *A Romance*, 'Lucas *Malet', 1901, Methuen. The action begins in 1842, when Sir Richard Calmady brings his young wife, Katherine, back to the ancestral home, Brockhurst. Due to the indiscretion of a seventeenth-century Calmady the house has been laid under a curse, which ensures that the male heirs die young and violently; the curse will only be lifted by the intercession of a Child of Promise, half-angel, half-monster. Sir Richard is duly killed in a riding accident, and his son, also

Richard, born hideously deformed: he has the upper body of a man, but the legs of a dwarf. The boy proves angelic in learning, charm, and looks, monstrous in his rage at incapacity. His mother procures him a child-bride, the prettily vacant Lady Constance Quayle, who is in love with a (six-foot) guardsman. The mysteriously aloof Honoria St Quentin, a friend of Calmady's beautiful, vixenish cousin, Helen Ormiston, intervenes to prevent the match, and Lady Constance gets her guardsman. Thinking that no woman will ever love him, Calmady leaves for the Continent, where five years of bad behaviour culminate in a night of passion with Helen, by this time a married woman, in a villa in Naples. Helen, however, has seduced him in order to avenge herself on Katherine, who had once slighted her. She humiliates Calmady and goads her lover, a French poet, into beating him up. Racked by typhoid and self-recrimination, Calmady is brought back to Brockhurst, where he slowly recovers his strength, develops a new spirituality, and falls in love with Honoria St Quentin, now his mother's constant companion. They marry. He founds a home for the disabled. The curse has presumably been lifted. The novel is notable for the frankness, narrowly avoiding prurience, of its interest in Calmady's disability.

HOBBES, John Oliver, *pseud.*: Pearl RICHARDS (1867–1906) married (1887) Reginald Walpole CRAIGIE (b. *c.*1857) (divorced 1895), baptized a Roman Catholic as Pearl Mary-Teresa (1892). She was born near Boston, and her rich parents moved to London when she was an infant. She went to boarding school near Newbury, Berkshire, and in London and Paris. She married young, had a son in 1890, and left her husband in 1891. The *Times* report of the divorce proceedings states that the 'case is an exceedingly filthy one, and most of its details are utterly unfit for publication in a newspaper'. It seems that Craigie was alcoholic and infected her with venereal disease; he is supposed to have accused her of infidelity with Alfred Goodwin (d. 1892), a professor at University College London, where she had studied Greek, Latin, and English literature. She also abandoned the Congregationalist faith in which she had been brought up for Roman Catholicism. On her return to her parents' house she wrote *Some Emotions and A Moral*, published (1891) in T. Fisher Unwin's Pseudonym Library; it sold 40,000 copies in her lifetime. For the rest of her short life she published almost annually novellas, stories, and plays characterized by their epigrammatic dialogue, settings in high society, and interest in socialism and Roman Catholicism. *The School for Saints* (1897) and its sequel **Robert Orange* (1900), trace the political, amorous, and religious career of Robert Orange (partly J. H. Newman, 1801–90, and partly Benjamin Disraeli, 1804–81), a Catholic convert who becomes a priest when his marriage turns out to be invalid. The heroine of *The Serious Wooing: A Heart's History* (1901) is separated from a mad husband, whose relatives have concealed his death from her, and elects to live openly with her radical lover. Wrongly supposing him to have deserted her, and having discovered that she is a widow, she marries again, only to return to the lover. *The *Dream and the Business* (1906) centres on two lovers who marry the wrong people. *The Artist's Life* (1904) was a volume of essays. Craigie was portrayed as a religious fraud addicted to playing with men's emotions in George *Moore's *Evelyn Innes* (1898) and **Sister Teresa* (1901): he was one of a series of men outraged by her willingness to enjoy passionate friendships while remaining chaste. She resisted her parents' wish that she should remarry after her divorce; her friend Lord Curzon (1859–1925) may or may not have been a suitor. Scandal also connected her with Owen Seaman (1861–1936), who parodied her work in *Punch*: Craigie identified herself as the dying heiress Milly Theale in *The *Wings of the Dove* and Seaman as Densher. She suffered from poor health, and was addicted to sedatives. Like Mrs Humphry *Ward she was a member of the Anti-Suffrage League. She was President of the Society of Women Journalists (1895–6). Her *Life and Letters* (1911) were edited by her father, John Morgan Richards (1841–1918), who bought the *Academy* in 1896. After her death Thomas Hardy (1840–1928), who knew her well, wrote (12 Sept. 1906) to her friend Florence *Henniker: 'to keep three plates spinning, literature, fashion, & the Holy Catholic religion, is more than ordinary strength can stand.' There is a biography by Margaret M. Maison (1976).

HOCKING, Joseph (1860–1937) married (1887) Annie BROWN. Born in Cornwall, the younger brother of the better-known Silas K. *Hocking and of Salome *Hocking, he was first apprenticed to a land surveyor, before training as a

Methodist minister at Crescent Range College, Victoria Park, and Victoria University, Manchester, being ordained in 1884. He then spent two years as minister in a Yorkshire village before travelling in Eastern Europe and the Holy Land in 1887. From 1888 to 1910 he was minister at Woodford Green Union Church, Essex. His first novel was *Jabez Easterbrook* (1891). *The Woman of Babylon* (1906) is a melodramatically anti-Catholic tale about the attempts of a wicked Jesuit priest to convert an entire family in order to secure a fortune for the Church. The father and lover of Joyce Raymond chase all over England trying to find her; she is released from incarceration in a convent to live happily ever after. The plot is related to that of *Le Juif errant* (1844–5) by Eugène Sue (1804–1857). In *The Prince of This World* (1910) Marcus Pendennis offers to marry Esther Stormont and save her from her frivolous, gambling lower self. Only after coming to Cornwall and undergoing a conversion in a Nonconformist chapel does she agree. In *The Wagon and the Star* (1925) twin brothers choose the paths of selfishness and idealism. One marries unhappily for money; the other, a supporter of the League of Nations and the brotherhood of man, gets the girl they both love and a fortune into the bargain. Hocking was prolific, publishing more than eighty books, and this, like others of his later works, such as *Felicity Treverbyn* (1928), though no less moral than the earlier work, are fairly trifling love stories with very predictable plots.

HOCKING, Salome (d. 1927) married (1894) Arthur C. FIFIELD. Sister of Joseph *Hocking and Silas K. *Hocking, she was born at St Stephen in Brannel, Cornwall, where her father was a leader of the local Bryanite Bible Christians. She injured her back as a girl helping with farm work, and thereafter was crippled. After the death of her parents she left Cornwall to live with her brothers. Her early fiction, dating from the 1880s, some of which was published serially in Nonconformist periodicals, is based on her Cornish experience, e.g. *Norah Lang: The Mine Girl* (1886). As 'S. Moore-Carew' she wrote *A Conquered Self* (1894). After her marriage she wrote *Belinda the Backward: A Romance of Modern Idealism* (1905) and *Beginnings* (perhaps not issued in volume form), both of which draw on her acquaintance with 'a group of Russian and Continental Tolstoyan exiles & English followers'. Her husband, who presumably introduced her to these people, says in his memoir of her (1927) that she loved to tease them 'about their almost abysmal ignorance of the country life and pursuits so enthusiastically advocated'. *Belinda* is a comedy set in an experimental community. Fifield had a small progressive publishing business; *Married Love* (1918) by Marie Stopes (see 'G. N. *Mortlake') was one of his most successful books.

HOCKING, Silas K[itto] (1850–1935) married (1876) Esther Mary LLOYD (*c.*1855–1940). Brother of Joseph *Hocking and Salome *Hocking, he was born in Cornwall and became a successful purveyor of rather pious fiction to the Nonconformist market. Silas Hocking's great early success was the 'waif' or 'street Arab' tale *Her Benny* (1879), a tear-jerking, bestselling rags-to-riches story of a destitute orphan in the streets of Liverpool. He sold the copyright for £20—a mistake as it continued to be a staple of the Sunday school prize trade well into the next century. (Later the publisher gave him another £10.) Hocking was a minister (1870–1896) in the United Methodist Free Church, first in Pontypool, then in Spalding, Liverpool, Manchester, and finally, from 1883 to his resignation, in Southport. Later in life he stood unsuccessfully as a Liberal candidate for the House of Commons in two elections (mid-Bucks, 1906; Coventry, 1910). He was editor of *Family Circle* from 1894 and was a founder of the *Temple Magazine: Silas K. Hocking's Illustrated Monthly* (1896–1903) for Sunday reading. Typical of his fiction is *Caleb Carthew: A Life Story* (1884), a novel about a good Christian man, told by his lifelong friend. In this (and in several details of plot) it resembles the bestselling *John Halifax, Gentleman* (1856), by Dinah Craik (1826–87), with the important difference that Hocking deliberately denies his hero the material prosperity with which Mrs Craik rewards her hero's hard work and self-sacrifice. A young working-class boy becomes an architect, twice saves the life of the wicked squire who had seduced his sister, and dies, nursed by his devoted wife (the squire's cousin), full of years and honour, the object of the novelist's warmest approbation. In *The Wrath of Man* (1912) a criminal steals his enemy's baby daughter; she grows up, finds her father, and marries a saintly curate. Hocking published an autobiography (1923), in which he speaks of the influence on him of the novels of George MacDonald (1825–1905), with their expressed disbelief in eternal damnation. Hocking was an enthusiastic opponent of the *Boer War; he was vilified for this and, despite his fame, had difficulty in getting his anti-war novel, *Sword and Cross* (1914), published.

HODGSON, Geraldine E[mma] (1865–1937). Born in Brighton, the daughter of a doctor, she was educated at Newnham College, Cambridge, and became a schoolteacher and lecturer on education. She represented her diocese in the Church of England's House of Laity 1920–29. Her publications include studies of Richard Rolle (*c*.1300–49) and other works on medieval theology and literature, textbooks, a life of J. E. *Flecker (1925), and four novels, 1899–1902, including *Antony Delaval, LL.D.* (1900), whose hero is a psychologist who wants to marry a woman, an expert on Old English verse, who has promised to look after her unpleasant old uncle. *The Parliamentary Vote and Wages* (1909) is a pamphlet arguing for female suffrage.

HODGSON, William Hope (1877–1918) married (1911) Betty FARNWORTH. Second of twelve children of a Church of England clergyman living in Essex, Hodgson was educated abroad and, after being orphaned at 13, joined the merchant navy in 1891, in which he spent nine years and gained the experience of the horrors of the sea which served him well in fiction. He held the record for tying up the escapologist and stuntman Harry Houdini (1874–1926), who took two hours to escape. He ran a School of Physical Culture, teaching judo and muscle development, in Blackburn, was later a photographer, and then a full-time writer. He began to write in 1902, peculiar fiction about ghosts and the unseen, rather uncertain in tone: his first novel, which is important in the history of horror fiction, was *The Boats of the 'Glen Carrig': Being an Account of their Adventures in the Strange Places of the Earth* (1907). It is set on an eighteenth-century shipwreck, whose survivors encounter huge octopus-like sea creatures and horrible carnivorous trees. *The *House on the Borderland* (1908) is set in an Irish house where the supernatural world meets the real one. *The Night Land: A Love Tale* (1912), which he considered his major work, is about lovers who share knowledge of a dream world (as in *Peter Ibbetson*, 1891, by George Du Maurier, 1834–96, and *Kipling's 'The Brushwood Boy', 1898). She dies in childbirth and he goes to the Other Side to bring her back, the whole being recounted by him in extraordinary, stilted, would-be-archaic language, which probably functions to mask the brutality of their relationship. The use of *historical fiction to excuse the depiction of sado-masochistic relationships was already well under way by this date. *Carnacki, the Ghost Finder* is a series of stories (published in the **Idler* in 1910, collected in 1913) about a psychic sleuth: most of the strange phenomena turn out to have natural causes. *Men of the Deep Waters* (1914) and *The Luck of the Strong* (1916) are collections of stories. Hodgson was commissioned in the Royal Field Artillery in 1915, wounded, and gazetted out of the army in 1916 because of an accident in camp; he regained his health and was recommissioned in 1917. He was killed in action near Ypres as a second lieutenant in April 1918. His obituary in the *Times* (2 May 1918) notes: 'He was a notable athlete, a fine boxer, a strong swimmer and an all-round good sportsman.' Two volumes of his verse were published posthumously. Several of his stories were originally published in American magazines, and his later reputation has particularly flourished among American horror enthusiasts: *Out of the Storm: Uncollected Fantasies* (1975) has a biographical introduction by Sam Moskowitz.

HOLDSWORTH, Annie E.: Eliza Ann HOLDSWORTH (1860–1917) married (1898) Eugene *LEE-HAMILTON. Born in Jamaica, daughter of a missionary to the ex-slaves there who returned to England in 1871, she did not go to school. In applying to the Royal Literary Fund she stated that her earliest novels were *Bonnie Dundee* (1887) and *Belhaven* (1889); these were published as by 'Max Beresford'. In the 1890s she published short stories, co-edited the *Woman's Signal* with Lady Henry Somerset (1851–1921), and worked on the *Review of Reviews*. Her first successful novel was *Joanna Traill, Spinster* (1894). After marriage she lived in Florence; a baby daughter died aged 2. As a widow she applied to the Royal Literary Fund, since she had two invalid sisters dependent on her, an annual income of £200, and was afraid of losing her home; but she managed to remain there till her death. *A Garden of Spinsters* (1904) is a series of short stories about single women, associating them with stoic wisdom and the care of children and plants in a way which recalls the stories of New England regionalist writers of the same date, such as Sarah Orne Jewett (1849–1909). *A New Paolo and Francesca: A Novel* (1904) is based on a marriage arranged by the heroine's dead father between her and his heir. Disaster strikes because she loves her husband's twin brother, and he, though he does not realize it until the end, loves and is loved by her cousin, Heriot. The new Paolo and Francesca end by dying on a yacht together, leaving Heriot to look after the baby and his father. Holdsworth writes well about the strained atmosphere; but the plot is unworthy.

Hole in the Wall, The, Arthur *Morrison, 1902, Methuen. After his mother's death, young Stephen Kemp goes to live with his grandfather Nat, who owns a pub in Wapping called 'The Hole in the Wall'. Stephen's father is first mate on a merchantman whose owners, Viney and Marr, conspire to defraud both the company's insurers, by having the ship sunk, and its shareholders, by arranging for Marr to disappear with all the remaining capital. Marr, however, is mugged in a colourful dive off the Ratcliff Highway and dumped in the river, and his pocketbook, containing £810 in banknotes, ends up in Grandfather Nat's possession. Complications ensue. The narrative is divided between a third-person account of events and a child's-eye view palpably modelled on *Treasure Island* (1883) by R. L. Stevenson (1850–1894)—there is even a Blind Pew clone. By the end of the 1890s the brief phase of the slum novel was over. The East End of London was still a point of automatic reference in many novels, but the portrayal of working-class life became increasingly sympathetic and light-hearted, with Dickens the obvious inspiration. Grandfather Nat is a fence and a smuggler, but he has no truck with fraud and murder, and strenuously directs Stephen onto the straight and narrow.

HOLLAND, Clive, pseud.: Charles James HANKINSON (1866–1959) married (1894) Violet DOWNS (d. 1945). Born in Bournemouth, son of a civil engineer who became its first mayor, he went to Mill Hill School and trained as a lawyer before becoming a journalist in London in 1893. He had earlier contributed to several boys' papers, and published *The Golden Hawk* (1888) and *Raymi* (1889). His long list of publications includes many guidebooks and travel books and fourteen novels; he was travel editor of the *Queen* (1937–9) and editor of the *British Congregationalist* (which ran 1906–15). He did propaganda work in both world wars. According to his obituary in the *Times*, he knew Émile Zola (1840–1902) and was a friend of R. L. Stevenson (1850–94). The published letters of Thomas Hardy (1840–1928) include a series of more or less snubbing responses to overtures by Hankinson, including (24 Oct. 1909): 'the scheme for abridging my novels . . . seems to me quite impracticable.' Hankinson's most popular novel was *My Japanese Wife: A Japanese Idyll* (1895), in which the narrator falls in love with a girl in a tea-house, marries her, and takes her home to England. The book was decorated with charming illustrations by Fred Appleyard. *The Lovers of Mademoiselle: A Romance of the Reign of Terror* (1913) is a banal *historical romance in which two aristocratic lovers succeed in escaping the French Revolution.

HOLME, Constance (1880–1955) married (1916) Frederick Burt PUNCHARD (d. 1946). The youngest of fourteen children of a land agent, she married another land agent and lived all her life in Westmorland. Much of Holme's fiction was published in the World's Classics series by Oxford University Press; she was encouraged by the Press's Publisher, Sir Humphrey Milford (1877–1952). Her early novels, such as **Crump Folk Going Home* (1913) and *The *Lonely Plough* (1914), are set among the landowning class; after the First World War she began to write about elderly working people and to experiment with the stream-of-consciousness technique. Her themes are country life, problems of renunciation, femininity, and class. *The Splendid Fairing* (1919) won the Prix Femina–Vie Heureuse. The reticence and control which is apparent in her fiction extended to her relations with the outside world, and considering the power of her work very little is known of her life.

HOLMES, Gordon, *pseud.*: see M. P. *Shiel and Louis *Tracy.

HOLT-WHITE, William Edward Bradden was the author of *The Man Who Stole the Earth* (1909), which has elements of both *science fiction and *Ruritanian romance: John Strong uses his airship to persuade a Balkan king to let him marry his daughter. *The Man Who Dreamed Right* (1910) is a novel about a little man who discovers he can predict the future and becomes a pawn in world diplomacy.

Holy Mountain, The: *A Satire on Tendencies*, Stephen *Reynolds, 1910, John Lane. When Lane accepted *A Poor Man's House*, a documentary record of life in a Devon fishing village, in 1909, Reynolds insisted that Lane also publish the 'satire on tendencies' which had absorbed his attention for a number of years. James Trotman, 'Famous Grocer' and mayor of Trowbury, on the Wiltshire downs, has an unprepossessing son, Alec, whom he plans to apprentice to a colleague in London. Walking on the downs with his shop-assistant girlfriend, Julia Jepp, Alec is carried away by the melancholy of imminent separation and declares that his faith in their love will move mountains—which it promptly does, transporting nearby Ramshorn Hill to Acton. Sir Pushcott Bingley, an entrepreneur and press baron, establishes joint ownership of Holy Hill with Alec, its true creator. Alec takes part in an Empire Mission Revival Meeting at Crystal Palace, where his speech is delivered for him by a 'magnogramophone', and in an Imperial Pageant at the Neapolitan Music-Hall, where he faints when called upon to wave a Union Jack from the crest of a replica mound. Thereafter Sir Pushcott turns his attention to the Holy Hill itself, leasing it to the Church of England and then, when the temple erected on the summit fails to attract a congregation, converting it into a music-hall with a beer garden on the roof. Julia Jepp, meanwhile, is fired for going to the aid of her friend Edith Starkey, who has been convicted of soliciting. The final scene takes place on the roof of the temple, from which Edith has just thrown herself; Julia and Alec, now married, plight themselves to each other, and the intensity of their commitment transports the Holy Hill back whence it came, killing them in the process. The novel may be set in London and Wiltshire, but the literary territory it occupies had already been mapped by H. G. *Wells. Even so, the critique of jingoism and of the gutter press is amusing and effective.

HOPE, Anthony, *pseud.*: Anthony Hope HAWKINS (1863–1933) Kt. (1918) married (1903) Elizabeth Somerville SHELDON (*c.*1885–1946). Hawkins was born at Clapton, where his father was headmaster of St John's Foundation School for the Sons of Poor Clergy. He was educated there and at Marlborough and Balliol College, Oxford, where he was a Scholar, gained a First in Classics (1885), and was President of the Union (1886). In the following year he was called to the Bar of the Middle Temple. He went to live in London with his father, now the vicar of St Bride's, Fleet Street, and became a barrister in 1887. As a briefless barrister he began to contribute to magazines such as the *Illustrated London News* with some success, and in 1890 he paid for the publication of his first novel, *A Man of Mark*, set in an imaginary South American state. He also wrote plays and short stories. He stood unsuccessfully as a Liberal candidate for the House of Commons (South Buckinghamshire, 1892). He had published five novels when the tremendous success of *The Prisoner of Zenda* (1894) and *The Dolly Dialogues* (1894) led him to abandon his legal career for literature. Subsequently he published a long series of novels, many in the '*Ruritanian romance' formula he had single-handedly invented, and in which he had so many less distinguished imitators. *The God in the Car* (1894), a tale of the rise to power of an empire-builder, was generally recognized to be based on the career of Cecil Rhodes, who is supposed to have borrowed it, and returned, it, saying, 'I'm not such a brute as that.' *The King's Mirror* (1899) is a first-person narrative describing an unsuccessful royal marriage. *Tristram of Blent* (1901) has a complicated inheritance plot and a pair of squabbling lovers. In 1903, returning from his second visit to America, Hawkins fell in love with an American girl twenty-two years his junior, whom he married. He moved out of the vicarage, and his rate of production of fiction slowed considerably thereafter. *Sophy of Kravonia* (1906) is the story of the rise of an English peasant girl to be queen of another imaginary Balkan country. In the First World War Hawkins worked in the Ministry of Information, for which services he was knighted. His last novel was *Little Tiger* (1925). He published *Memories and Notes* in 1927. The biography by Sir Charles Mallet (1935) gives interesting details of the large income made by Hawkins from his fiction, of which, in later years, film rights formed a significant part. He was a loyal member and president of the Society of Authors, whose pension scheme he founded. Through his mother, Jane Isabella Grahame,

Hawkins was first cousin to Kenneth *Grahame.

HOPE, Graham, *pseud*.: Jessie Margaret HOPE (1870–1920). Born at Parsloes, Essex, she was the daughter of an army officer and diplomat who had won the VC, and of Margaret Cunninghame Graham, aunt of R. B. Cunninghame *Graham. Invalided from an accident at the age of 3, she recovered as an adult and lived in Oxford, where she researched her *historical novels in the Bodleian Library. She published seven novels between 1901 and 1908. *A Cardinal and His Conscience* (1901) and *The Gage of Red and White* (1904) are romantic historical novels based on the imaginary love affairs of, respectively, Charles, cardinal de Lorraine (d. 1574) and his brother François, duc de Guise (d. 1563) . Hope was Organizing Secretary of the Oxford branch of the Women's Unionist and Tariff Reform Association.

HOPKINS, W[illiam] Tighe (1856–1919) married (1881) Ellen CRUMP (d. 1914). His father was a Church of England clergyman. Although both parents were Irish, he was born in Nottingham and educated at St John's, Leatherhead, and Oundle Grammar School. Mortimer Collins (1827–76) was his wife's stepfather. He wrote novels from 1886, and was especially interested in penal reform, which figures in both fiction and non-fiction. He was on the literary staff of the *Daily Chronicle* and the *Nation*, and edited works by the Irish writer William Carleton (1794–1869). Some of his fiction is set in Ireland. As a result of illness and depression his income, which had been £200 p.a. in 1909–12, was reduced, and in 1913 he applied to the Royal Literary Fund, making four applications over the next five years. In 1918 he sold his house in Herne Bay and went back to live with relations in Ireland. The only fictional work of his in this period is *The Silent Gate: A Voyage into Prison* (1900), a series of stories stressing the psychological effects of imprisonment and detailing the daily life of inmates.

HORN, Kate married George Edward WEIGALL (1860–*c*.1924). The daughter of a Lincolnshire clergyman, she married at 21 an officer in the artillery and went to Malta, setting of several of her novels, for five years soon afterwards. She had written stories from childhood, and won prizes from the *Girls' Own Paper* and *Boys' Own Paper*, but her first success was the publication of a serial in *Cassell's Magazine* in about 1889. She wrote every day in the mornings, but never closed the door on her three children: 'they are never shut out of my room, lest I, in turn, should be shut out of their hearts' (**Bookman*, Dec. 1910). She published twenty-four novels between 1908 and 1927, mostly pastoral romances. Characteristic is *Edward and I and Mrs Honeybun* (1910), about an aristocratic young couple who find themselves penniless and retire to a Suffolk village to live on £200 a year: Mrs Honeybun, who ekes out both the novel's plot and its title, is a thirsty charwoman. Other titles in the period include *Ships of Desire* (1908), *The Love-Locks of Diana* (1911), *Columbine at the Fair* (1913), and *The Flute of Arcady* (1914).

HORNIMAN, Roy (1874–1930) was born in Southsea, the son of a naval officer, and educated there and in Bruges. He went on the stage in 1887 and for a time leased the Criterion Theatre. He wrote a series of plays and film-scripts from 1900 as well as novels and short stories, including *That Fast Miss Blount* (1903), a lively chronicle about the adventures of a naval officer's large family in a seaside town, and *Israel Rank: The Autobiography of a Criminal* (1907), which was the basis for the film *Kind Hearts and Coronets. The Sin of Atlantis* (1900) was an occult novel. He was a keen anti-vivisectionist, a member of several pressure groups for animal rights, and also a member of the British Committee of the Indian National Congress. He was for some time owner of the *Ladies' Review.*

HORNUNG, E[rnest] W[illiam] (1866–1921) married (1893) Constance DOYLE. Born in Middlesbrough, the youngest son of a solicitor, Hornung went briefly to Uppingham, before being sent to Australia (1884–6) in the hope that the climate would cure his asthma. On his return he turned to journalism on the **Strand Magazine* and elsewhere, and to fiction. His first three novels have Australian settings. His success came with *The Amateur Cracksman* (1899), whose nonchalant, cricket-playing, gentleman-burglar hero Raffles was enormously popular, despite the objections of those, like Hornung's brother-in-law Arthur Conan *Doyle, who thought it immoral to glamourize theft. Although both the figure of the hero and his story's narration by an admiring schoolfriend owe something to a popular novel of a previous generation, *Guy Livingstone* (1857), by G. A. Lawrence (1827–76), Raffles's chic combination of brutality and sensitivity was something new which hit the taste of the 1890s: 'The man might have been a minor poet instead of an athlete of the first water. But there had always been a fine streak of aestheticism in his complex composition.' Later we are told: 'He could think of Keats on his way from a felony.' The trick was to be much imitated. The slavish, highly charged relationship between Raffles and Bunny, the narrator, is a key feature of the tales: several commentators, including Graham Greene (1904–91) in a brilliant parody, *The Return of A. J. Raffles* (1975), have pointed to the importance of homosexual feeling in the formula. *The Amateur Cracksman* was followed by two more collections of Raffles stories, *The *Black Mask* (1901) and *A Thief in the Night* (1905), and a full-length novel, *Mr. Justice Raffles* (1909). Gerald du Maurier (1873–1934) made a hit playing Raffles on the stage and there were several films. Hornung's other fiction includes a collection of Australian stories, *Stingaree* (1905), and *Peccavi* (1900), a compelling novel about a clergyman suspended for seducing a parishioner, who, ostracized, rebuilds his burnt church with his own hands. Hornung wrote about his experiences with the YMCA in the First World War in *Notes of A Campfollower on the Western Front* (1919); his only son was killed at Ypres. Hornung died of pneumonia at St Jean de Luz.

horror stories. By the end of the nineteenth century the tale of supernatural horror had begun to fragment into different genres or subgenres, and to some extent the Edwardian period simply saw the consolidation of those genres and sub-genres. Thus, the connection between supernaturalism and *Empire forged by Rider *Haggard in *She* (1887), and by Rudyard *Kipling in stories like 'The Mark of the Beast' and 'At the End of the Passage', was maintained: by Haggard himself, in **Ayesha: The Return of She* (1905); by W. W. *Jacobs, in 'The Monkey's Paw', in *The *Lady of the Barge and Other Stories* (1902); by A. *Perrin, in *Red Records* (1906). Egypt, in the form of relics, plays a major part in Bram *Stoker's **The Jewel of the Seven Stars* (1903). But there were significant new developments. In 'My Own True Ghost Story', in *Wee Willie Winkie* (1888), Kipling has the narrator remark: 'That was more than enough! I had my ghost—a first-hand authenticated article. I would write to the Society for Psychical Research—I would paralyse the Empire with the news!' The narrator is being ironic, and the ghost in question turns out not to be a ghost at all, but the detailed case-studies published in the Society's *Proceedings* did provide a challenge and a resource for writers. The ghost story, as it emerged in the work of Algernon *Blackwood and M. R. *James, constituted something in the nature of a case-study; and the genre further established its hold by becoming, in Kipling and Richard *Middleton, as well as James, an examination and even a defence of Englishness. Blackwood's **John Silence* (1908) features a 'psychic doctor', a white magician, supposedly based on an unidentified member of the Rosicrucian Order of the Golden Dawn, who solves five representative cases to do with werewolf folklore, the belief in 'elementals', the witches' sabbath, the relation of animals to the unseen, and vampirism. Of course, most forms of religious experience presuppose a supernatural order, and a number of late Victorian writers, notably M. E. *Braddon, George MacDonald (1824–1905), Margaret Oliphant (1828–97), and the hugely popular 'Marie *Corelli', used fiction as a means of exploring that order. Their Edwardian successors include Maude *Annesley, E. F. *Benson, John *Buchan, the Countess of *Cromartie, Mrs P. Champion de *Crespigny, Mrs B. M. *Croker, 'Theo *Douglas', Major Arthur *Haggard, Violet *Hunt, Oliver *Onions, Mrs Campbell *Praed, T. W. *Speight, Bram *Stoker, Violet *Tweedale, and Evelyn *Underhill. Hilaire *Belloc, in *The Green Overcoat* (1912), and R. H. *Benson, in *The Necromancers* (1909), took a satirical look at spiritualism. Perhaps the most original experiments in the tale of horror are to be found in Marion *Fox's **Ape's-Face* (1914), William Hope *Hodgson's *The *House on the Borderland* (1908) and *The Night Land: A Love Tale* (1912), and Arthur *Machen's *The *House of Souls* (1905).

HOSKEN, [Ernest Charles] Heath (1875–1934) married (1901) 'Coralie *STANTON'. Born in Norwich, Hosken became a journalist on the staff of the *Daily Mail* and *Associated Newspapers* (1905–20). He published *A Sinner in Israel* (1910) and *Tainted Lives* (1912) as 'Pierre Costello'. The former begins as a serious study of orthodox Judaism in the modern world, but takes a

*Ruritanian turn when the hero is discovered to be the son, not of the Jewish millionaire-philanthropist Lord Solvano, but of the King of Istria. The latter is a murder mystery involving insanity. Hosken published many more novels under his own name in collaboration with his wife between 1904 and 1933: see under 'Coralie *Stanton'.

Hound of the Baskervilles, The: *Another Adventure of Sherlock Holmes*, A. Conan *Doyle, 1902, George Newnes. Sherlock Holmes is called in, three months after the event, to investigate the mysterious death of Sir Charles Baskerville, found in the yew walk of his Dartmoor house with his face contorted into a rictus of terror, and to protect Sir Charles's heir, Sir Henry Baskerville, who has just returned from Canada to assume his inheritance. Legend connects family misfortunes with a sinister hound from hell often heard baying on the moor. Claiming pressure of business, Holmes sends Watson down to Baskerville Hall with Sir Henry and his trusty revolver. The local *dramatis personae* consist of Dr James Mortimer, who is responsible for Holmes's involvement in the case; Stapleton, an entomologist with a beautiful sister (in fact his wife), who soon wins Sir Henry's heart; the eccentric, litigious Frankland, whose daughter, Laura Lyons, had, it transpires, made an appointment with Sir Charles in the yew walk at the exact hour of his death, an appointment she never kept; and Sir Charles's servants, the Barrymores (Mrs Barrymore's brother, an escaped convict, lurks on the moors). The middle section of the novel, consonant with the narrative self-consciousness of the Edwardian period, takes the form of Watson's letters to Holmes in London, and extracts from his diary. Holmes, however, soon puts in an appearance; he, too, has been lurking on the moors, from which vantage-point he penetrates the mystery. The physical separation of Holmes and Watson might serve as a metaphor for the parallelism of their thought-processes, with the great detective always a few steps ahead of his amanuensis, and the reader. Stapleton, it turns out, is himself a Baskerville of a disreputable kind, and stands to inherit if he can dispose of Sir Charles and Sir Henry. He unleashes his great hound, daubed with a warpaint of phosphorus, on Sir Henry, but Holmes and Watson are just in time to save their client. Stapleton disappears into the fearful Grimpen Mire, where he has been keeping the dog. The best-known of the longer Holmes adventures, the novel owes much of its effect to the desolate moorland setting.

House in Demetrius Road, The, J. D. *Beresford, 1914, William Heinemann. Martin Bond arrives in Demetrius Road, in the heart of suburbia, to help Robin Greg, a masterful Scotsman and rising Liberal politician, to write a book on Socialism. Greg's wife, Elsie, is dead, and his sister-in-law, Margaret Hamilton, agrees to run the household and look after his young daughter, Biddie. When Greg leaves for the City in the mornings, the house reveals its 'double personality', becoming a feminine realm presided over by Margaret. Bond falls in love with her. He soon discovers that Greg is an alcoholic. He and Margaret join forces to save Greg from drink. Margaret agrees to marry Greg, even though his slovenliness revolts her. But it is Bond she really wants. Realizing this, Greg dismisses them both from the house. The novel is a tense and subtle study of a distinctly unorthodox emotional triangle.

House of Cobwebs, The, *and Other Stories*, George *Gissing, 1906, Constable. These fifteen short stories, published posthumously, explore one of Gissing's most consistent preoccupations: anxiety. In 'Christopherson', an ageing bibliophile is torn between his desire to preserve his books intact and concern for his wife's health. In 'Humplebee' and 'The Salt of the Earth', clerks have their expectations of an escape from shabby-genteel loneliness raised and then dashed. In 'A Poor Gentleman', the protagonist turns out to be slumming through bitter necessity rather than philanthropic impulse. In 'A Charming Family', a spinster is cheated of her savings. In other stories, immovable objects (the landed gentry, suburban gossip) prove more than a match for the supposedly irresistible forces of emancipation and enterprise. The hero of 'A Lodger in Maze Pond' finds himself unable to break out of a cycle of unsuitable marriages. The stories evoke, with characteristic gloom and perceptiveness, a lower-middle-class existence familiar from Gissing's earlier writing. But things were changing. H. G. *Wells, in particular, had found abundant emancipation and enterprise among the lower middle classes. Gissing seems to have caught something of the new spirit. In 'The House of Cobwebs', a young novelist has his first novel accepted for publication. In 'The Scrupulous Father', as in Wells's *Ann Veronica* (1909), a suburban daughter triumphs over the 'little world of choking responsibilities' created by her father's over-scrupulousness. Other stories concern honest businessmen, a feisty spinster, and a humble schoolmaster who becomes a resoundingly successful publican. The collection includes an introductory essay by Thomas Seccombe (1866–1923), a critic and journalist who had followed Gissing's career closely. Edward Garnett (1868–1937), writing in the *Speaker*, summed up what many reviewers felt to be both the strength and weakness of Gissing's later fiction. 'The cautiousness and reserve of the Englishman, the restrictions that his precise and careful temperament exercises upon his mental outlook, the sterilising effect of uncongenial conditions, a certain pettiness of social horizon—all this Gissing understands admirably, and details with a quiet fatalistic acceptation that enforces on the reader the sense of sharing in the spiritual imprisonment from which so many of his characters suffer.'

House of Souls, The, Arthur *Machen, 1906, Grant Richards. A collection of six (longish) short stories, three of which had been published separately in book form before: *The Great God Pan* and *The Inmost Light* as a single volume in John Lane's Keynotes series, with a cover design by Aubrey Beardsley (1872–98), in 1894; *The Three Impostors*, building on the former's success, in 1895, also from John Lane. *The Great God Pan* announces the main theme of Machen's macabre tales: the god himself is a symbol 'beneath which men long ago veiled their knowledge of the most awful, most secret forces which lie at the heart of all things; forces before which the souls of men must wither and die and blacken, as their bodies blacken under the electric current.' A brain surgeon performs an experiment in 'transcendental medicine' on a simply country girl, who has a brief vision of Pan before going insane; nine months later a daughter is born, whose subsequent career as a diabolic heartbreaker we piece together from the reports of a group of young men about town. *The Three Impostors*, a wonderfully poised set of interlinking tales in the manner of Robert Louis Stevenson's (1850–94) *New Arabian Nights* (1882), also features two young men about town, Phillipps, a scientifically minded ethnologist, and the more enterprising and imaginative Dyson, an apostle of style. These two reappear in one of the new stories, 'The Red Hand', where, in the course of solving a murder mystery, they start to resemble Holmes and Watson (Arthur Conan *Doyle was an admirer of Machen). In *The Inmost Light*, another commonsensical-imaginative pairing comes across another practitioner of transcendental medicine: this one performs occult experiments on his wife, with equally tragic results. 'A Fragment of Life' is an intermittently striking *suburban story, closer in tone and preoccupation to E. M. *Forster than to Stevenson, about a clerk whose banal existence (rendered with utter conviction) is infiltrated first by the grotesque, then by a redemptive vision of an ancient and still mysterious way of life. 'The White People', about a young girl who enters a beautiful and dangerous fairy-land under the tutelage of her nurse, returns to the themes, the settings, and the manner of Machen's early work.

House on the Borderland, The, William Hope *Hodgson, 1908, Chapman & Hall. Classic *horror story, supposedly 'From the Manuscript, discovered in 1877 by Messrs Tonnison and Berreggnog, in the Ruins that lie to the South of the Village of Kraighton, in the West of Ireland.' The discoverers are on a fishing-trip when they unearth the manuscript in the ruins of an old house perched on the edge of a terrifying chasm. It is the last testament of the recluse who lived in the house with his sister, and his dog Pepper. One evening, in a 'strange, heavy, crimson twilight', the recluse is transported in a vision across a flat wasteland to a mountainous arena with a mysterious house comparable to his own at its centre. At the edges of the arena loom mythological monsters. 'The mountains were full of strange things—Beast-gods, and Horrors, so atrocious and bestial that possibility and decency deny any futher attempt to describe them.' Returning from his vision, the recluse finds his house under attack from equally atrocious and bestial 'Swine-creatures' who inhabit a ravine at the far end of his garden. Beating them off, he ventures out to discover their lair: a cave in the side of the ravine which extends all the way to and beneath the house. A second vision transports him through Outer Worlds to the very end of time and space, and to a meeting with his soul mate, and he eventually returns to find Pepper a pile of dust. A second assault ensues, this time from a kind of shapeless green mist which infects him with a fatal disease. The visions are perhaps less impressive than the lucid descriptions of the swine-creatures and the terror they provoke.

House with the Green Shutters, The, 'George *Douglas', 1901, Macqueen. This novel was intended to correct the sentimental view of rural Scottish life promoted by the Kailyard school of the 1890s. The setting is the village of Barbie, in the second half of the nineteenth century. John Gourlay, a self-made man, has cornered the carrying trade and built for himself a house which is the 'material expression' of his hard-won success (and of much greater interest to him than his slovenly, novel-reading wife, Janet, his weak son, John, and practically invisible daughter, Janet). James Wilson, son of the local mole-catcher, returns to the village a wealthy man, establishes a hardware and grocery 'Emporium' and contracts a bitter grudge against the sneering Gourlay (too many jokes about moleskin). Seizing opportunities which Gourlay has arrogantly overlooked, Wilson expands into the carrying trade. Gourlay's business begins to suffer. His son, meanwhile, has enrolled at Edinburgh University, and taken to drink, which proves his downfall. Returning in disgrace to Barbie, he is so tormented by his infuriated and now bankrupt father that he kills him with a poker. 'The fiercest joy of his life was the dirl that went up his arm as the steel thrilled to its own hard impact on the bone.' The two women pass the death off as an accident. But John is haunted by the memory of his father's eyes, and poisons himself. His mother, who is dying of breast cancer, and his consumptive sister follow suit. The house is sequestered. A Scottish *Mayor of Casterbridge* (without the sex), the novel is more resourceful in idiom than in plot. 'You see Scotland in it', Arnold *Bennett commented, 'for the first time in your life.'

HOUSMAN, Clemence [Annie] (d. 1955). The sister of A. E. Housman (1859–1936) and of Laurence *Housman, she lived with the latter first in London, then in Somerset, working as a wood-engraver and writer. Like him she was a keen suffragist; a member of the WSPU, she spent a week in Holloway prison for refusing to pay taxes. She was the author of *The Were-Wolf* (1896), *The Unknown Sea* (1898), and *The Life of Sir Aglovale de Galis* (1905). The last is a pastiche of the *Morte D'Arthur* (1485), referred to as 'the works of him I love so much', set in Shropshire, of which county both Housman and Sir Thomas Malory (*c.*1408–1471) were natives. She became a Quaker.

HOUSMAN, Laurence (1865–1959). Sixth of seven children of whom A. E. Housman (1859-1936) was the eldest, Housman was born in Bromsgrove, where his father was a solicitor, and went to Bromsgrove School and then to art schools in London. There he lived with his sister, Clemence *Housman, and wrote and drew for the *Universal Review.* From 1895 he was art critic of the *Manchester Guardian* for sixteen years. He had a long and varied career as a writer of drama, fiction, and non-fiction. His first book was published in 1894; two years later the popularity of his brother's *A Shropshire Lad* (1896) overshadowed his own verses and tales, until the success of the anonymous *An *Englishwoman's Love-Letters* (1900). This made him more than £2,000, which he called a 'mighty windfall for the worst book I ever wrote'. In 1903 he and W. Somerset *Maugham edited *The Venture: An Annual of Art and Literature.* He suffered as a playwright from the censorship of the Lord Chamberlain: his play *Bethlehem* (1902) was banned and privately produced, as was *Pains and Penalties* (1911), about the Queen Caroline affair. The series of plays collected as *Victoria Regina: A Dramatic Biography* (1921–33) were banned until 1936, though they had meanwhile had a vogue in the USA from their association with the Abdication Crisis. Housman's novels include *John of Jingalo: The Story of a Monarch in Difficulties* (1912) and its sequel, *A Royal Recovery* (1914). In the first, a satire on the Liberal government's manipulation of the Constitution, a king realizes the absurdity of his situation and tries to reform the country. Humorous sub-plots call for a reform of ideas about sexual morality and social reform. *Sabrina Warham: The Story of Her Youth* (1904) is a preposterously Hardyesque but rather moving novel, set on the coast of Dorset, about the intellectual daughter of a drunken schoolmaster who discovers her husband has seduced a peasant girl. After his death she marries her earthy farmer cousin, David. After the First World War, in which he was a pacifist, Housman went to the USA and lectured with

Henry Nevinson (1856–1941) for the League of Nations. He was a member of the Men's League for Female Suffrage and published *Articles of Faith in the Freedom of Women* (1910); he joined the ILP in 1919. He went to live with his sister at Street in Somerset, and became a Quaker in 1959.

HOWARD, Keble, *pseud.*: John Keble BELL (1875–1928) married (1911) ——. The third of twelve children of a Church of England clergyman, Bell was brought up at Henley-in-Arden, and went to Oxford as an unattached student with the aim of becoming a clergyman. Later he migrated to Worcester College, Oxford. Disillusioned with the Church, and having failed his degree, he became a schoolmaster and then worked on the *Bicester Advertiser.* He managed to get a job at the Press Association in London, and from there became first assistant editor (1899) then editor (1902–4) of the *Sketch.* His elder brother, R. S. Warren *Bell, the editor of a boys' magazine, the *Captain*, was already a journalist, and Howard changed his name to distinguish himself from his brother. He began to collect his sketches in volume form. One of his great successes was *The *Smiths of Surbiton: A Comedy without a Plot* (1906), to which he wrote two sequels. *My Lord London* (1913) was based on the career of Viscount Northcliffe (1865–1922), who was in America at the time of its publication but managed to have it suppressed, partly by excluding reviews of all books with the same publisher's imprint. Bell claims in his autobiography (1927) that it was intended to be laudatory, not derogatory, and that Northcliffe subsequently acknowledged this. Bell was dramatic critic of the *Daily Mail* (1904–8) and afterwards began a career as a playwright. He started the Croydon Repertory Theatre in 1913. His experiences during the First World War, in which he served with the RAF and in the Ministry of Information, are described in *An Author in Wonderland* (1919).

Howards End, E. M. *Forster, 1910, Edward Arnold. Social values and attitudes are dramatized through an encounter between the Schlegel sisters, Margaret and Helen, and their brother, Tibby, who specialize in culture and friendship, and Henry and Ruth Wilcox and their children, Charles, Paul, and Evie, who (with the exception of the mystical Ruth, owner of Howards End) specialize in 'telegrams and anger': that is, commerce, commonsense, and calisthenics. Helen Schlegel falls briefly in and out of love with Paul, and thereafter reacts violently against the Wilcoxes, championing those they have wronged, like the idealistic clerk Leonard Bast and his slatternly wife. Margaret, on the other hand, feels increasingly drawn first to Ruth Wilcox, and then, after the latter's death, to Henry, whom she marries. Complications ensue. Mrs Bast is revealed as Henry's ex-mistress. Helen becomes pregnant by Leonard; Charles kills him in an outburst of familial piety, and is found guilty of manslaughter. Margaret steadfastly holds the crumbling Henry together, and reconciles him with Helen. At the conclusion, Helen and her child play happily in the grounds of Howards End—encircled, however, by the world of telegrams and anger. Selecting his 'book of the year' in 1910, Arnold *Bennett remarked that none had been discussed more avidly by the 'right people' than *Howards End*. The schematic nature of its oppositions, which has kept the right people discussing it ever since, may also be its main weakness.

HOWARTH, Anna (?1854–1943). The daughter of a Church of England clergyman, she was born in London and sent to South Africa on her father's death. There she trained as a nurse at Grahamstown Hospital. She nursed Selina Kirkman, with whom she afterwards lived. The South African settings of her four novels gave them topical interest in England during and just after the *Boer War. In the first, *Jan: An Afrikander* (1897), she wrote about racial miscegenation. *Sword and Assegai* (1899) records the war experience of one of Kirkman's relations. Thelma Gutsche in the *Standard Encyclopaedia of Southern Africa* states that the fourth novel, *Nora Lester* (1902), was unsuccessful 'owing to the glutting of the market with South African material'. It deals with the adventures of two boys who meet in an orphanage in England and emigrate to South Africa; one marries the half-sister of Nora Lester, the other falls in love with her. It has a complicated and old-fashioned inheritance plot. Its interest lies in the background of the struggle between Boer and English colonists; Howarth's attitude is moderately even-handed but basically pro-English. Howarth returned to England (1935) on Kirkman's death.

HUDSON, W[illiam] H[enry] (1841–1922) married (1876) Emily WINGRAVE (*c.*1826–1921). Born near Buenos Aires, Argentina, the son of American parents, Hudson ran wild in childhood, but in his teens became an invalid—he suffered from heart trouble—and a great reader. From 1865 he was employed by the Smithsonian Institute to collect bird specimens.

He left South America for England in 1874, probably with the intention of getting work as a naturalist. By 1875 he was living in a London boarding-house kept by Emily Wingrave, whom he soon married. Hudson's activities were not lucrative: his first real success was *The Naturalist in La Plata* (1892), which was followed by *Idle Days in Patagonia* (1893), and ended his worst struggle with obscurity and poverty and enabled him to spend holidays in the English countryside. Through the resulting sketches of rural life (*Hampshire Days*, 1903; *Afoot in England*, 1909) he became one of the most significant figures in the nostalgic celebration of 'Englishness' which was so powerful at the *fin-de-siècle*, issuing variously in the architecture and gardening of the Surrey school, in the foundation (1895) of the National Trust, in the work of Hudson's friend Edward Thomas (1878–1917) and of Alfred *Austin, and in magazines such as *Country Life*. He began to have more and more influential friends: for instance he was one of the many writers encouraged by Edward Garnett (1868–1937). Morley *Roberts had early introduced him to George *Gissing. R. B. Cunninghame *Graham insisted on the republication of *The Purple Land* (1885; 1922). Thanks to his friend and admirer the statesman Sir Edward Grey (1862–1933) he received (after being naturalized a British subject in 1900) a Civil List pension of £150 in 1901. One of Hudson's principal interests was the Royal Society for the Protection of Birds, which he supported through writing and lecturing and to which he bequeathed most of his money. From 1900 to his death he had a love affair with a member of its staff, Ethelind or Linda Gardiner, author of five thrillers 1885–99. From 1911 Emily Hudson was a rather difficult and exacting invalid, and she entered a nursing-home in 1914; Hudson himself was often ill and depended on the kindness of Margaret Brooke, Ranee of Sarawak (d. 1936). The success of **Green Mansions* (1904) in America from 1916 brought him £200 p.a., and in 1920 he resigned his Civil List pension. In 1918 he published *Far Away and Long Ago*, the autobiography which is probably his best-known work. His fiction includes *El Ombu* (1902), four stories on the theme of human cruelty and remorselessness set in the South American pampas, including 'Marta Riquelme', the harrowing story of a woman being driven mad by outrage, cruelty, and desertion. There is a biography (1982) by Ruth Tomalin. He should not be confused with William Henry Hudson (1862–1918), author of many textbooks on the history of English literature.

HUEFFER, Ford Madox: Ford Hermann HUEFFER (1873–1939), who was baptized (1892) a Roman Catholic with the additional Christian names Joseph Leopold, changed his name by deed poll (1915) to Ford Madox HUEFFER and again (1919) to Joseph Leopold Ford Hermann Madox FORD, married (1894) Elizabeth *MARTINDALE. Born in Merton, London, and educated at a Froebel school in Folkestone and at University College School, Hueffer was brought up in literary and artistic circles. His father was a naturalized German and music critic of the *Times*; his mother was the daughter of the painter Ford Madox Brown (1821–1893); her half-sister, also a painter, was married to William Michael Rossetti (1829–1919), and their two daughters wrote as 'Isabel *Meredith'. Dante Gabriel Rossetti (1828–82) and Ford Madox Brown were the subjects of two of Hueffer's early works. After his father's death in 1889 the family circumstances were straitened and they went to live with his grandfather. He began to write very young; his first novel, *The Shifting of the Fire* (1892), came out when he was 19. He and his wife, Elsie, married against her parents' wishes and set up house in Sussex, an area where they were to live until 1903. There he met Joseph *Conrad, and began to collaborate with him. As well as playing his part in writing *The *Inheritors: An Extravagant Story* (1901), **Romance: A Novel* (1903), and *The Nature of a Crime* (published serially in the **English Review*, 1909, in one volume 1924) Hueffer also supported Conrad financially, psychologically, and practically during this period. In 1903 he moved back to London; his marriage had been going badly, and he had a breakdown in the following year. *The *Benefactor: A Tale of a Small Circle* (1905) was only the second novel he had written unaided. It was followed by the *historical trilogy *The *Fifth Queen and How She Came to Court* (1906), *Privy Seal: His Last Venture* (1907), and *The Fifth Queen Crowned: A Romance* (1908).

An *English Girl: A Romance (1907), *A *Call* (1910), and *Mr Fleight* (1913) were modern novels. Hueffer founded the *English Review* in 1908 but was forced to sell it within the year. In the following year he began an affair with the novelist Violet *Hunt. Divorce was discussed, but in the end Elsie Hueffer petitioned for the restitution of conjugal rights. A court order to pay his wife a smaller sum of money than he was in fact paying her incensed Hueffer so much that he went to Brixton Prison for ten days rather than pay it. After this he and Hunt travelled in Germany, since they hoped that if Hueffer could establish German residence he would be able to divorce his wife. From September 1911 they passed as a married couple. The publication of *The Governess* (1912), a novel which Violet's mother Mrs Alfred Hunt (1831–1912) had left unfinished at her death, for which Violet Hunt provided an ending and Hueffer an introduction, was the occasion of further litigation by Elsie Hueffer, who objected to Hunt's being described as Mrs Hueffer.

Hueffer published in **Blast* (20 June 1914) a tale, 'The Saddest Story', which later metamorphosed into the first part of his most famous novel, *The Good Soldier: A Tale of Passion* (1915). After a period writing propaganda he fought with the Welch Regiment in the First World War, the experience which inspired the Tietjens tetralogy: *Some Do Not—A Novel* (1924), *No More Parades* (1925), *A Man Could Stand Up—A Novel* (1926), and *The Last Post* (1928). By 1919 he had parted from Violet Hunt and gone to live in Sussex with a young Australian painter, Stella Bowen. In 1922 they left for France, where, living at various times in Paris and Provence, Ford (who had changed his name) set up the *Transatlantic Review* (1924–5), in which he published *Joyce. In 1926 he left Bowen and their daughter and went to America, where he obtained a teaching post. After 1930 he lived with another painter much younger than himself, Janice Biala. He died in Deauville. Throughout his life Ford was an immensely prolific author and journalist; as well as novels he wrote many topographical books, works of popular history, and poetry. His works before *The Marsden Case* (1923) are either anonymous or signed Ford Madox Hueffer. There is a biography by Alan Judd (rev. edn., 1990).

HUEFFER, Oliver Madox (1877 or 9–1931) married Zoe PYNE. He was the younger brother of Ford Madox *Hueffer and like him went to Praetorius School and University College School. He published eight volumes of fiction under his own name between 1901 and 1931 and five as 'Jane Wardle' 1907–10. His brother wrote that he had 'run through the careers of Man About Town, Army Officer, Actor, Stockbroker, Painter, Author and under the auspices of the father of one of his fiancées, that of Valise Manufacturer'. Badly wounded in the First World War, he lived afterwards in Versailles. He died of a seizure. *Where Truth Lies: A Study in the Improbable* (1911) is a comedy about a clerk who inherits a title and, kidnapped by mistake, finds himself with a girl who so longs for romance that he tells her he is a burglar. *Hunt the Slipper* (1913) is a caper-novel concerning the adventures of a 76-year-old military man who travels to America to investigate his son's mysterious disappearance. The narrative, like that of *The Moonstone* (1868) by Wilkie Collins (1824–89), is divided among the various colourful protagonists.

HUME, Fergus: Ferguson Wright HUME (1859–1932). Born in England and brought up in New Zealand, Hume was educated at Dunedin High School and the University of Otago. He was called to the New Zealand Bar in 1885. After three years in Melbourne, during which he published the bestselling *Mystery of a Hansom Cab* (1887), he came to England, where he lived for the rest of his life. Having sold the copyright of his first book for £50, he gained nothing from its vast sales, and none of his 135 other novels, almost all thrillers, achieved an equivalent success. His *crime fiction makes much use of his legal training, and shows the influence of the work of Wilkie Collins (1824–89), another lawyer. He had a special fondness for colour in his titles: *The Purple Fern* (1907), *The Yellow Hunchback* (1907), *The Green Mummy* (1908). In the last, Lucy's lover has bought her for £1000 from her sinister old stepfather, an archaeologist who turns out to have committed a murder by mistake. In *The Golden Wang-Ho: A Sensational Story* (1901) two lovers realize that the dead uncle's forebodings were justified when two mysterious Chinamen appear. *The Mother of Emeralds* (1901) is a *Haggardesque novel about the discovery of a lost race in South America. *A *Traitor in London* (1901) is a *Boer War thriller.

HUNT, [Isobel] Violet (1862–1942) changed her surname (1911) to HUEFFER after going through a form of marriage with Ford Madox *HUEFFER. Born in Durham, the daughter of the novelist Mrs Alfred Hunt (1831–1912) and of the painter A. W. Hunt (1830–1896), she was educated at Notting Hill and Ealing High School and brought up in literary and artistic circles. As a young girl she modelled for and had a long affair with the much older married painter George Boughton (1833–1905); this was the first in a long series of unsatisfactory sexual relationships. Hunt wrote about the problems encountered by emancipated New Women of her generation, and she experienced them. She trained as a painter at South Kensington Art School before following her mother's profession instead of her father's. In 1890 she met Oswald *Crawfurd, who was also married and a contemporary of her father's, and fell in love with him. His connection with Chapman & Hall, the publishers, and the magazine *Black and White* fostered her literary career. Her first novel, *The Maiden's Progress: A Novel in Dialogue* (1894), grew out of her contributions to *Black and White*'s dialogue series. Crawfurd serialized her second novel, *A Hard Woman* (1895), in *Chapman's Magazine*. However, he was a confirmed philanderer, who simultaneously conducted other affairs, including one with Lita Browne, whom he married, to Hunt's chagrin, after his first wife's death. There is a story that Hunt heard he had been writing passionate letters to May *Bateman, and found them 'nearly word for word those he used to write to me'. Their romance was over by 1899, but she was still bitter at the time of his remarriage in 1902, and her novel *Sooner or Later: The Story of an Ingenious Ingenue* (1904) vented some of her feelings. From Crawfurd she caught the syphilis which killed her. *A Workaday Woman* (1906) contrasts two working women, a hired companion who wants to marry and a truly independent writer, who 'ought to have been a man'. She became involved with the suffrage movement, and was a member of the WSPU, a founder of the Women Writers' Suffrage League, and a friend of May *Sinclair and Evelyn *Sharp. On the publication of *White Rose of Weary Leaf* (1908) the former wrote to her, 'It seems to me that you've done what Hardy only tried to do when he wrote Tess. It took a woman to do it.' In the same year Hueffer published in the **English Review* three of the tales which later went into *Tales of the Uneasy* (1911). By 1909 Hunt and Hueffer were having an affair. The failure of their scheme to obtain German residence so that Hueffer could divorce his unwilling wife meant that Hunt's cherished respectability could only be maintained with the pretence that a marriage had taken place, and legal action by Elsie Hueffer soon exploded the fiction. Hunt called herself Mrs Ford Madox Hueffer from September 1911; after the First World War and Hueffer's desertion she resumed her maiden name. *The Desirable Alien: At Home in Germany* (1913) was a collaborative fruit of the German trip. *Zeppelin Nights: A London Entertainment* (1916), a series of tales strung together in the manner of the *Decameron*, was another. Her last novel was *Their Hearts* (1921). There was another collection of stories (1925), an autobiography (1926), and a scandalous biography of Elizabeth Siddal (1932) which, as the *Times* obituarist said, 'gave considerable offence to surviving relatives'. Her last years saw a lingering death from syphilis, aggravated by financial problems and quarrels with relations. There is a biography (1990) by Barbara Belford.

HUTCHINSON, A[rthur] S[tuart] M[enteth] (1879–1971) married (1926) Una Rosamond BRISTOW-GAPPER. Born in India, the son of an irascible Indian army general, he was brought home aged 5 to a comfortable suburban life, first in Southsea, then in Totnes. He went to Totnes Grammar School and became a medical student at St Thomas's Hospital before turning to journalism. He was editor of the *Daily Graphic* (1912–16) and the author of fourteen novels 1908–43. His great success was the fourth of these, *If Winter Comes* (1921), whose hero is a good man cheated by his partners; the book is supposed to have sold 750,000 copies in Britain and America. *The Happy Warrior* (1912) deals with the inheritance of a peerage by the wrong heir. Hutchinson's memoir of his childhood (1958) describes the reading and impressions of a bookish, middle-class child. Despite his bestseller, he had financial difficulties in later years.

HUTCHINSON, Horace G.: Horatio Gordon HUTCHINSON (1859–1932) married (1893) Dorothy Margaret CHAPMAN. The son of a general, Hutchinson went to Charterhouse, but had to leave because of poor health which dogged him all his life. Instead he went to the United Services College, Westward Ho!, near his parents' home in Devon. (He was just too old to have overlapped with *Kipling.) While living in

Devon he learnt to play golf, then just rising into popularity. He became one of the best players in England, and published many books which helped to promote the spread of the sport, beginning with his first publication, *Hints on the Game of Golf* (1886). After Corpus Christi College, Oxford (1878–81), Hutchinson began to read for the Bar but his health broke down again. In 1890 he had the idea of becoming a sculptor and studied briefly with G. F. Watts (1817–1904). He gradually drifted into authorship, writing extensively on sport. Several of his twenty-eight volumes of fiction have sporting backgrounds (for example *Bert Edward, The Golf Caddie*, 1903). *A Friend of Nelson* (1902) is a rather dry *historical romance ending before the battle of Trafalgar. In *The Eight of Diamonds: The Story of a Week-End* (1914) a wastrel about to go bankrupt cheats at cards but confesses. Hutchinson was gravely ill for the last eighteen years of his life.

HYATT, Stanley Portal (1877–1914) married Margaret MARSTON (d. 1912). Educated at Dulwich College, he went into a firm of electrical engineers for two years before going to Australia. He worked briefly on a ranch before cabling to his parents for money to come home, where he tried to patent various devices, including a camera and a bicycle brake. He subsequently went with his brothers to South Africa, where big-game shooting life provided him with material when, after various other vicissitudes and the death of one brother from anthrax in Manila, he drifted first into journalism and then into novel-writing. *The Diary of a Soldier of Fortune* (1910) draws on his experience in embryonic Rhodesia.

HYNE, C[harles] J[ohn] Cutcliffe [Wright] (1865 or 6–1944) married (1897) Elsie HAGGAS (d. 1938). Born at Bibury, Gloucestershire, the son of a Church of England clergyman, and brought up in Yorkshire, Hyne was educated at Bradford Grammar School ('a beastly place') and Clare College, Cambridge, where he read Natural Science. Afterwards he 'wrote pot-boilers for the baser Press, and the more evil of the publishers'. He also turned out boys' books, and wrote three serious novels under various names. After four years in London he went to sea, signing on once as a winch-hand, once as a doctor. He later returned and resumed literary life. He claimed to be able to write three 3,000-word stories a day at three guineas each. He was eventually to turn out more than forty-six volumes of fiction (1892–1942), not counting thirteen adventure stories as 'Weatherby Chesney' (1898–1908). *The Lost Continent* (1900) is an account of the ancient lost civilization of Atlantis, supposedly deciphered by Hyne from a wax document. A minor character in his serial *The Great Sea Swindle* grew into the money-spinning character Captain Kettle, around whom several volumes, beginning with *The Adventures of Captain Kettle* (1898), were contrived. *McTodd* (1903) consists of comic sketches whose eponymous narrator is a drunken Scots engineer of xenophobic tendencies; the book is much indebted to *Kipling's boat stories with monologuing, colloquial narrators. This resemblance is heightened by the fact that the publishers, Macmillan, used the typeface and size familiar from their Uniform Edition (1899–1938) of Kipling's works. *Kate Meredith, Financier* (1907) is set in West Africa, and concerns the hero's attempts to disentangle himself from an engagement to a half-caste so that he can marry his partner in a trading firm. Hyne's only son was killed in the First World War. He lived at Kettlewell-in-Craven, Yorkshire. He published a very funny autobiography, *My Joyful Life* (1935).

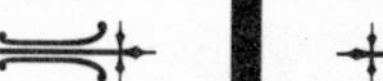

I

IDDESLEIGH, Earl of: Walter Stafford NORTHCOTE (1845–1927), succeeded (1887) as 2nd Earl of IDDESLEIGH, married (1868) Elizabeth Lucy MEYSEY-THOMPSON (d. 1928). Educated at Eton College and Balliol College, Oxford, he served as private secretary to his father in 1867–8 and 1874–7, who at those times was President of the Board of Trade and Chancellor of the Exchequer (and who became Prime Minister in 1885). He was deputy chairman and then chairman of the Board of Inland Revenue 1877–92. As well as editing novels by Benjamin Disraeli (1804–81) and Susan Ferrier (1782–1854), he published five *historical romances in this period, including *Belinda Fitzwarren* (1901), *Charms, or, An Old World Sensation* (1905), and *Ione Chaloner* (1909).

Idler, The, was published monthly from February 1892 to March 1911. Founded as a 'gentleman's magazine' for the newly educated white-collar class by Robert *Barr, it was co-edited by Jerome K. *Jerome, who became sole editor in July 1894 and owner from 1895–7, until forced to sell the magazine to meet the costs of a libel action. It was then edited by Arthur Lawrence and Sidney Sime (the latter was *Dunsany's illustrator) until Robert Barr regained editorial control in 1902. The basic tone of the magazine was urbane; the focus of its regular series (on travel, sport, and theatre), of its humorous essays, and of its interviews with literary personalities, was the gentleman at leisure. The *Idler* made extensive use of short stories, usually of a neat, paradoxical kind rather than experimental or realist (Conan *Doyle, 'O. Henry', 1862–1910, and G. K. *Chesterton were contributors), and serialized fiction (for example by Mark Twain, 1835–1910, and Israel *Zangwill). W. H. *Hodgson's *Carnacki* series appeared in the *Idler* in 1910. Allen *Upward contributed a non-fiction series on 'The Horrors of London'. There is an index to fiction by William B. Thesing and Becky Lewis (1994).

Idolatry, Alice *Perrin, 1909, Chatto & Windus. A British Raj romance along the lines of Maud *Diver given an added dimension by an interest in the clash of religious faiths, and descriptions of the small anxieties attending missionary life. Anne Crivener's father died when she was a baby, and her mother, a 'nobody' (that is, a missionary's daughter), handed her over to her wealthy grandmother before remarrying. The grandmother has now died, having thoughtlessly but not maliciously frittered away a vast fortune, leaving Anne penniless. She discovers that her mother, who has reverted to type and married a missionary, John Williams, is living in the very same part of India to which the nearest eligible bachelor, Captain Dion Devasse, has just been posted. Cynically, she resolves to visit her mother and marry the besotted Devasse, whom she does not love. An engagement ensues, but Anne is increasingly diverted by the magnetism of a selfless and gifted evangelist, Oliver Wray. Wray's main aim in life is to wrest the soul of Ramanund, son of the Rajah of Thanesur, out of the grip of idolatry. Although he and Anne fall in love, she realizes that she will in the end prove an obstacle to his spiritual mission, and, breaking off her engagement to Devasse, returns to England, where, inspired by Wray's example, she rents a tiny flat in London and investigates cases for a charitable association. When Devasse comes back on leave, she is ready to love him. He tells her that Wray has taken his mission to the heathen by roaming among them dressed as a beggar, with little but a stick and a Bible.

illustrations. The history of book illustration has more to do with the history (and technology) of book production than with the history (or aesthetics) of literature as such. The two key technological developments of the late nineteenth century (both related to the invention of photography and the use, after 1896, of photo-engraving) were, first, the declining role of the engraver and, secondly, the improved means of colour reproduction. As Philip James points out in *English Book Illustration 1800–1900* (London, 1967), between 1875 and 1885 the human engraver (who had had great power over book artists: an engraver was needed to translate their pictures into printable blocks) was replaced by photographic and mechanical means of setting and reproduction. By the 1890s commercial wood-engraving was a dead craft. The aesthetic effect of this change in the book production process was twofold: on the one hand, artists now had greater control over the use of their illustrations; on the other, the new reproduction methods (the line-block, for instance) made for the elimination of half-tones and a much greater contrast between full black lines and clear white spaces. Pen and ink draughtsmen like the cartoonist Phil May (1864–1903) and the fantasist Sydney H. Sime (1867–1941), who specialized in illustrating the works of Lord *Dunsany, were obvious beneficiaries of the new technology, but the most important book illustrators of the 1890s represented a more significant trend: a new artistic emphasis on decoration and design. William Morris (1834–96) founded the Kelmscott Press in 1890, to publish not only his own books but also classics (such as the Kelmscott Chaucer). Morris designed founts of type, ornamental letters, and decorative borders; the overall look of his books—the typography, the layout, the binding—was more significant than any particular illustration. Aubrey Beardsley (1872–1898) notoriously illustrated Wilde's *Salome* (1894), Pope's *The Rape of the Lock* (1896), Aristophanes's *Lysistrata* (1896), and Jonson's *Volpone* (1898), but he also acted as art editor of the *Yellow Book* (1894–5) and the *Savoy* (1896), and was as concerned as Morris with books and magazines as objects for design. This approach to illustration was reinforced by the technical possibilities now for using original woodcuts (as in the work of Gordon Craig, 1872–1966) and by the development of lithography and etching as suitable methods for original art. David Bland points out in *A History of Book Illustration* (London, 1958/1969) that whereas in France the *edition de luxe* gave painters an interest in book illustration, in Britain book artists had to deal with cheaper production processes, with the possible decorative effects of black on white. Other important figures in this design movement in British publishing were Charles Ricketts (1831–1931) and Charles Hazelwood Shannon (1863–1937), who in 1893–4 published *Daphnis and Chloe* and *Hero and Leander*, the first books of the new technological era with original woodcuts. Their magazine, the *Dial* (1889), showed the influence of Morris (though pre-dating the Kelmscott Press) and, in turn, influenced Beardsley's magazine work. In 1896 Ricketts and Shannon formed the Vale Press, arguing that 'the illustration ought to give the book the accompaniment of gesture and decoration, perhaps also an added element of visible poetry.' Their first title, in 1896, was an edition of Milton's *Early Poems*. Their approach to book design was shared by Lucien Pissarro (1863–1934), whose Éragny Press, founded in 1894, published French classics decorated with Pissarro's and his wife's wood-engravings; by the Glasgow school associated with Charles Rennie Mackintosh (1868–1928)—most notably Jessie M. King (1876–1949), whose evocative edition of William Morris's *The Defence of Guenevere* appeared in 1904; and Vernon Hill (b. 1887), whose striking art nouveau *Ballads Weird and Wonderful* was published in 1912. One effect of these 'designer' books was to underline the clear distinction now between decorative and 'plain' publishing (and Morris was not alone in believing that the general standards of book illustration and design was declining in the trade press as a result of photographic reproduction methods). Decorative books, that is to say, became special editions, specially produced, and specially priced. The changes in the techniques of colour printing had the same effects. The three-colour process of photographic printing gave illustrators new opportunities to produce 'full autographic' water-colours (printed on specially coated sheets that had to be protected by tissue paper), which they followed up in the production of expensive 'gift books', richly illustrated versions of the classics. Established illustrators like Hugh Thomson (1860–1920), C. E. Brock (1870–1938) and his brother H. M. Brock (1875–1960), and William Nicholson (1872–1949), whose *London Types* (1898) had quatorzaines by W. E. Henley (1849–1903), were joined in these ventures by younger artists. These included Arthur Rackham (1867–1939), whose best-known books were *Rip Van Winkle*, 1905; *Peter Pan in Kensington Gardens*, 1906; *A Midsummer Night's Dream*, 1908; and *A Christmas Carol*, 1915; Edmund Dulac (1882–1953), whose edition of the Brontës' works came out in 1905; William Heath Robinson (1872–1944), who illustrated *Kipling's *The Song of the English* in 1909; and

William Russell Flint (1880–1969), whose *Morte D'Arthur* was issued in 1910–11; and by a new generation of women artists like Evelyn Paul, M. V. Wheelhouse, Eleanor Fortescue Brickdale (1871–1945), and Sybil Towse. These presentation books—familiar, classic stories being used as inspiration for well-known artists with established styles—were marketed in sharp contrast to the other publications which were, by 1900, most systematically exploiting the new means of colour illustration: boys' books and magazines. Colour pictures here (most dramatically as magazine covers) were used to convey spectacular scenes of violent action (or sickly scenes of domestic farewell and loss). In *Five Centuries of Book Illustration* (Aldershot, 1988), Edward Hodnett quotes Kipling commiserating with his friend H. Rider *Haggard: 'What foul illustrations to *Ayesha*. Pity one can't sprinkle lime over illustrators—same as slugs.'

It was left to children's books to integrate high-quality illustrations with the pleasures of ordinary reading. In some cases the author's own illustrations were an essential part of the storytelling, as in Kipling's *Just So Stories*, for example, or in Helen *Bannerman's *Little Black Sambo* series, or, above all, in Beatrix *Potter's books, which, beginning with *The *Tale of Peter Rabbit* in 1902, and making full use of new printing processes and the opportunity to reproduce water-colours, brought a new realism and humour into animal pictures. In other cases commissioned illustrations became inseparable from a book's pleasure (as with the illustrations by Lord Basil Blackwood, 1870–1917, for *Belloc's verse; or those by E. H. Shepard, 1879–1976, for *The *Wind in the Willows*; or H. R. Millar, d. 1935, for the works of E. *Nesbit). Such combinations of words and pictures were becoming rare in adult literature, although there were some Edwardian writers who remained interested in illustration as a literary device. Examples include Max *Beerbohm, whose caricatures were collected in book form (*Twenty-Five Gentlemen*, 1896; *The Poet's Corner*, 1904); G. K. *Chesterton, who provided spoof illustrations for his friend Hilaire Belloc's early novels; and Laurence *Housman, who worked as an illustrator before turning to novels and plays. In general, though, the Edwardian period marked the end of a period of book illustration. Beautiful books were still published (if for collectors rather than readers); thanks to the new technologies, childrens' books had probably never been better illustrated; but readers ceased to find pictures in adult fiction. Magazine serializations might still have an accompanying illustration; book-covers might offer graphic guides to their contents; but by 1920 illustrations had become, in themselves, an indication that a book was meant for children.

In a German Pension, 'Katherine *Mansfield', 1911, Stephen Swift. On 4 June 1909 'Katherine Mansfield' was deposited by her mother, who had travelled from New Zealand for the purpose, in the little Bavarian spa town of Bad Worishofen; on 12 June she moved out of her hotel into the Villa Pension Müller, which was to provide the setting and the title of her first collection of stories. Mansfield's cousin, *'Elizabeth', had already made a successful literary career out of witty assaults on German arrogance, philistinism, and misogyny. In 'Elizabeth''s novels, the Germans are buffoons, albeit buffoons intent on world domination. Mansfield chose the same targets. What distinguishes her account is its preoccupation with the surfaces and apertures of the human body: the border-zone between inside and outside, self and world. The subject of the first story in the collection, 'Germans at Meat', is matter out of place: soup on a waistcoat, a woman who picks her teeth with a hairpin, and a man who cleans his ears with a table napkin. Surfaces and apertures become a contaminated space where self and world mix promiscuously. The story reverts at the end to 'Elizabeth''s territory, with banter about *invasion scares and England's degeneracy. But its bodily emphasis has opened up a margin for the expression of less easily classifiable anxieties. Subsequent stories explore that margin, presenting, among other *frissons*, a tie dunked in coffee and a waiter who cleans his nails with the edge of a concert programme. Equally striking are early manifestations of Mansfield's lifelong preoccupation with umbrellas. Umbrellas are fatally ambiguous: they both separate and conjoin. In one story, an umbrella shields the narrator against the nakedness of fellow sun-bathers; in another, it becomes the excuse for unwelcome intimacies. But Mansfield wasn't only interested in bodily contamination. In 'The Advanced Lady', the narrator encounters a pretentious novelist who is planning a novel about the Modern Woman: the 'real' modern woman, that is, an emblem of spiritual purity, not one of those 'violent creatures' who denies her sex and hides her womanliness under the 'lying garb of false masculinity'. The narrator's escalating derision makes it plain that she has little time for the purity-and-fragrance femininity of the Advanced Lady. The publisher's blurb extolls the 'malicious naïveté' with which Mansfield describes her 'quaint Bavarian people', and she later refused to reissue the collection, deploring its 'youthful extravagance of expression and youthful disgust'. But in fact the malice is not at all (or not all) ill spent.

INCHBOLD, A. C[unnick] published eight novels between 1899 and 1920, including five in the period. Two of these are *historical romances: *The Letter Killeth* (1905), set in Sussex in the early nineteenth century, about the Wesleyan revival; and *Phantasma* (1906), set in Egypt and Syria, about Napoleon and the 'mirage of the Orient'. His contemporary stories ponderously combine sensation and the dramas of religious faith. The heroine of *The Road of No Return* (1909) flees from persecution in Russia to the Holy Land with a company of pilgrims. The heroine of *Love in a Thirsty Land* (1914) is a young French girl immured in a convent in the Holy Land. Inchbold also wrote travel books about Portugal and the Near East.

Independent Review, The: see *The *Albany Review*.

Individualist, The, Philip *Gibbs, 1908, Grant Richards. Alicia Frensham, mistress of Long Stretton village school, is invited to Stretton Hall to meet Stretton Wingfield, nephew of the two unmarried sisters who live there. Wingfield is an explorer and novelist, whose books are 'the work of a revolutionary, of a wandering social atom who had come into touch with the highest and lowest phases of humanity, and who recognised under the veneer of civilisation the primitive conditions and passions of the savage people among whom the writer had lived for a time in Central Africa'. A political and sexual rivalry soon develops between Wingfield and David Heath, son of the local blacksmith, who has been at Oxford on a scholarship. Wingfield compromises Alicia, is knocked down for his pains by Heath, and both men leave the village: Heath to run a settlement in the East End of London, Wingfield to found a third party in Westminster politics, the Independent Democrats, or Individualists. After suffering a breakdown, Alicia moves to London, where she becomes Wingfield's mistress. His weakness destroys both his political faith and his love for Alicia: he reverts to ancestral Conservatism, and marries a woman who is prepared to take on his now extensive debts. He fights a by-election against his old adversary David Heath, the Socialist candidate. Heath triumphs, and is reunited with Alicia. The novel's politics are scarcely profound, but the political and romantic triumph of the working-class protagonist reverses a pattern established in late Victorian novels like George *Gissing's *Demos* (1886) and Mrs Humphry *Ward's *Marcella* (1894).

Infidel, The: *A Story of the Great Revival*, M. E. *Braddon, 1900, Simpkin, Marshall. Set amidst the Methodist movement of the 1750s and 1760s. Antonia Thornton is brought up as a sceptic (and like a boy) by her father William, whom she assists in his work as a hack writer in London. He proposes to sell her to an ageing, rakish Irish peer. Antonia refuses (she is an 'infidel', an atheist, but of high ideals), but when the peer contracts a fatal illness she agrees to marry him out of kindness and pity. On his deathbed, the marriage still unconsummated, she promises not to wed again, and to be buried by his side in his family mausoleum. Now a rich and beautiful widow, she meets a young convert to Wesleyanism and joins him in his work with the poor. She is obliged to reject his lovemaking (because of her promise to her husband) but is converted to a self-sacrificing Christianity by John Wesley (1703–91) himself. She finally dies in Ireland, in her husband's home, from illness contracted during her charitable work. A historical novel, but focusing less on Methodism than on Antonia's personal dilemma (as a passionate young woman sworn to lifelong celibacy) and thus addressing the rather more contemporary question of the relationship between wealth, charity, and sexual sublimation.

Inheritors, The: *An Extravagant Story*, Joseph *Conrad and Ford Madox *Hueffer, 1901, William Heinemann. In this political allegory Hueffer and Conrad champion tradition and individuality against the heartless collectivism of the new politics—the Toryism of Arthur Balfour (1848–1930) against the Social Imperialism of Joseph Chamberlain (1836–1914). Invaders from the Fourth Dimension take over the world, transforming it, according to the fogeyish hero, Etchingham Granger, into 'an immense machine—unconcerned, soulless, but all its parts made up of bodies of men: a great mill grinding out the dust of centuries; a great wine-press.' There is a strange disjunction between the novel's apocalyptic tone and the rather dull slide into dystopia which it actually describes. The authors could not imagine the end of the world, or did not want to. Although both pessimists, neither had much use for the anxiety about cultural decline which so preoccupied contemporary commentators. When the *New York Times Saturday Review* failed to mention that the book was a collaboration, and omitted all reference to Hueffer, Conrad wrote a letter in praise of his collaborator. He pointed out that their satire had been directed not, as the reviewer thought, at English traditions and achievements, but 'at the self-seeking, at the falsehood that had been (to quote the book) "hiding under the words that for ages had spurred men to noble deeds, to self-sacrifice, and to heroism"'. 'Fiction', the letter concluded, 'at the point of development at which it has arrived, demands from the writer a spirit of scrupulous abnegation. The only legitimate basis of creative work lies in the courageous recognition of all the irreconcilable antagonisms that make our life so enigmatic, so burdensome, so fascinating, so dangerous—so full of hope.'

Innocence of Father Brown, The, G. K. *Chesterton, 1911, Cassell. The first collection of stories about Father Brown, the priest-detective who solves problems through his understanding (honed by years in the confessional) of human nature. Father Brown gives the most mundane crime religious significance through his meditations on justice and repentence, just as Chesterton gives the most mundane plots a certain portentousness though his use of atmospheric settings. The first three stories, 'The Blue Cross', 'The Secret Garden', and 'The Queer Feet', are among the best Father Brown tales, and introduce his recurring foil, the master criminal Flambeau. The series as a whole remains entertaining for Chesterton's ability to play tricks of perception, but his mysteries are too clearly plotted in order to suit Father Brown's solutions to be genuine puzzles. The point of the stories, as a number of reviewers acknowledged, lies less in the resolution of mystery than in the exploration of paradox. 'The centre of each', wrote Dixon Scott in the *Manchester Guardian*, 'is some madcap, incredible crime, worked out with a lunatic exactness and intricacy, and then hidden cunningly away in the midst of conspicuously meek and mild accessories—among sweet-shops in Camden Town, placid villas in Putney, policemen and postmen and matter-of-fact porters. This done—solution safe, and relying on his own ready wit to bring the wildest irrelevance to heel—"G. K. C." fairly lets himself go.'

In the Days of the Comet, H. G. *Wells, 1906, Macmillan. Wells here depicts a transformation in human nature caused by a vapour exuded from a comet's tail. Most of the story deals with poverty and jealousy, but one effect of the vapour is that war is declared by Germany against England and France. After the comet's passage, peace is restored, prejudices dissolve, and sexual tensions are relaxed.

Invasion of 1910, The: *With a Full Account of the Siege of London*, William *Le Queux, 1906, Eveleigh Nash. The most sensational of all the *invasion scare stories which were so popular during the period. The story began as another of Alfred Harmsworth's ideas to boost the circulation of the *Daily Mail*. He commissioned Le Queux to write it, after extensive research, and in collaboration with H. W. Wilson (1866–1940), a naval expert, and Field Marshal Earl Roberts (1832–1914), who had campaigned tirelessly for reform and expansion of the army. Le Queux and his collaborators devised a strategically sound invasion route, and presented the scheme to Harmsworth, who found one thing wrong with it: the invaders did not pass through enough places where the *Mail* might actually hope to gain readers. Thereafter ferocious Uhlans galloped into every town of any size from Sheffield to Chelmsford. Special advertisements for the paper carried a map showing which town would be invaded next, while sandwich-men dressed as German soldiers patrolled the streets of London. 'The catastrophe that may happen if we still remain in our present state of unpreparedness', Lord Roberts announced, 'is vividly and forcibly illustrated in Mr Le Queux's new book which I recommend to the perusal of anyone who has the welfare of the British Empire at heart.' The book may have been new, but its ideas were not. The invasion forces assemble on the German North Sea coast behind the East Frisian Islands, as Erskine *Childers had predicted they would in *The *Riddle of the Sands* (1903). They land near Maldon, site of the great battle between the English and Danish raiders in 991. Their tactics involve the usual quota of firing-squads and heartless requisitions. Eventually the English counter-attack and, exercising their mastery of guerilla warfare, overwhelm the invaders. A peace treaty cedes Holland and Denmark to Germany, leaving the British Empire outwardly intact, but inwardly so weakened that only the 'most resolute reforms' accomplished by the 'ablest and boldest statesmen' are likely to restore it to its old position. The German translation (1907) rather pointedly omitted the counter-attack altogether.

invasion scare stories. *The Battle of Dorking* (1871), by Sir George Chesney (1830–95) introduced a new theme into English fiction: humiliating defeat by an army of invasion (in this case, the German army, recent conqueror of France). Chesney was an officer of the Royal Engineers, and his carefully researched and elegantly written cautionary tale had originally been addressed to the respectable middle-class readership of *Blackwood's Magazine*; such was its impact on this readership that the Prime Minister himself, W. E. Gladstone (1809–98), felt compelled to denounce it in a speech at Whitby on 2 September 1871. By 1900, however, two further developments had decisively altered the character of the genre: during the 1880s the accelerating pace of technological change added a new dimension to Great Power rivalries; during the 1890s, the popular press and popular magazines became insatiable in their pursuit of sensational material. The illustrated weekly *Black and White*, launched in January 1891, built its circulation by serializing *The Great War of 189–* (1892), by Admiral Sir Philip Colomb and others. Colonel Frederic Natusch *Maude's *The New Battle of Dorking* (1900) was thus a different creature altogether from its illustrious original. Furthermore, the volatility of European politics meant continuous alterations in the identity of the invader (Chesney suspected the Germans, Maude the French). The visit of the Russian fleet to Toulon in 1893 inspired the aggressive Franco-Russian alliances of *Angel of the Revolution* (1893) by 'George *Griffith' and William *Le Queux's *The Great War in England in 1897* (1894), which went through sixteen editions after it had been endorsed by Lord Roberts, Britain's leading military strategist. In the latter, the French land on the south coast, while in Birmingham Russian troops impale babies on their bayonets. Germany and Italy come to the rescue. 'We spoke of nothing else,' William Somerset *Maugham noted during the war scare provoked by the French annexation of Madagascar in 1894. 'There was a long discussion about the first movements of the war; we talked about what would happen if the French landed an army on the English coast; where they would land; what would be their movements; and how they would be prevented from taking London.' Anti-French stories in the Edwardian period include: Allen *Clarke, *Starved into Surrender* (1904); Edmund *Downey, *London's Peril* (1900); 'Headon *Hill', *Seaward for the Foe* (1903); Max *Pemberton, *Pro Patria* (1901); and Louis *Tracy, *The Invaders* (1901). From 1904 onwards, however, the *entente cordiale* aligned Britain and France against the German threat, at first in fiction, and subsequently in fact. Headon Hill, in *Spies of the Wight* (1899), and Erskine *Childers, to greater effect, in *The *Riddle of the Sands* (1903), were ahead of the field. The Tangier incident of March 1905, engineered by the German Chancellor in the hope of detaching Britain from France, produced a spate of propaganda stories, including Walter *Wood's *The Enemy in Our Midst* (1906) and Robert W. *Cole's *The Death Trap* (1907). Most sensational of all was another collaboration between Lord Roberts and William Le Queux, *The *Invasion of 1910* (1906). This time it is the Germans who impale English babies on their bayonets. In July 1908, an article in the *Quarterly Review* announced that 'what the Spanish danger was to the Elizabethans, what the Gallic danger was to their posterity, that and nothing less nor other is the German danger to this generation'. 1908 saw the publication of, *inter alia*, Coulson *Kernahan's *The Red Peril* and H. G. *Wells's *The *War in the Air*, in which a German air fleet raids New York. Invasion was often presented as the consequence of, and sometimes the punishment for, decadence. In A. J. *Dawson's *The Message* (1907), it provokes in the defeated populace a 'mighty revival of Puritanism, backed by the newly awakened twentieth-century spirit of Imperial patriotism, with its recognition of the duty of loyalty, not alone to country, but to race and Empire'. Significantly, the Puritanism is injected by revivalist preachers from Canada, the Imperial patriotism by a South African 'firebrand': the dying heart of Empire requires a transfusion from its still youthful margins and provinces. Similarly, *When the Kaiser Came* (1913) by '*Saki' seemed to the **Times Literary Supplement* a remarkable departure from the light-heartedness of his previous work. Even *'Elizabeth''s defiantly light-hearted *The *Caravaners* (1909) includes a sombre allusion to the possibility of invasion. 'I hope never to see it again,' a Prussian holiday-maker says of the Medway bridge, 'unless at the head of my battalion.' The only writers who did not manage to keep a straight face were P. G. *Wodehouse, in *The *Swoop! or How Clarence Saved England* (1909), and G. K. *Chesterton, in *The *Flying Inn* (1914). There is an authoritative study of the genre by I. F. Clarke (2nd edn., 1992). See also *spy fiction.

IOTA, *pseud.*: Kathleen HUNT (1853–1926) married (1879) Stephen Mannington CAFFYN (1850–1896). Born in Tipperary, Ireland, she was educated by both English and German governesses and trained as a nurse at St Thomas's Hospital in London. Her husband was a surgeon, writer, and inventor. In 1880 they left for Australia, where Stephen held various medical positions and Kathleen was one of the founding members of the District Nursing Society of Victoria. Both read widely and wrote fiction in their spare time. The success of her husband's novels *Miss Milne and I* (1889) and *A Poppy's Tears* (1890) was matched by that of *A Yellow Aster* (1894) published as 'Iota'. The book was to associate her with the New Women novelists. It was criticized for its feminism and its reliance upon the works of Henrik Ibsen (1828–1906) and Émile Zola (1840–1902); its key character is an emancipated woman of the 1890s. The book explores the tensions and interplay of love and marriage, as well as the ramifications of free thought and free love. Although a further seventeen works were to follow, none rivalled the impact of *A Yellow Aster.* Caffyn continued to write primarily about women, both as oppressors and as oppressed. The hero of *He for God Only* (1903), a parish priest called George Winnington, is devoted to his wife, Joan; but it never occurs to him that she might not be as ready as he is to offer up human desires on the altar of his high spiritual calling. Matters come to a head when his attention to parish business leads indirectly to the death of their child. However, after an interlude of social success in London, husband and wife are reconciled. *Patricia, A Mother* (1905), by contrast, is the story of the struggle between two independent and power-hungry women who need no help from men. The older Mrs Portal is a tyrannical saint who remembers her dead son as saintly, if subdued; the younger Mrs Portal, Patricia, a rebellious redhead, knows better. Penniless Patricia sacrifices herself for her unruly son, Tom, whose love has been bought by his wealthy grandmother. The real conflict is over Patricia herself, whose heart is the only thing her mother-in-law has never conquered, and who ultimately triumphs. There is some evidence that Caffyn's commitment to feminism was beginning to diminish. In *The Magic of May* (1908), the heroine, Eleanor, marries a man she does not love, comes to hate him, through no fault of his, rebels, and is sent back by a bishop to keep her husband's house and bear him children—at which point, she realises that she loves him. The **Times Literary Supplement* expressed surprise that 'Iota', once in the 'vanguard of revolt', should have written a novel intended 'to show that women do not know their own minds in their own special subject [that is, marriage and motherhood], and that until they do they had better take the man's word for it'. Caffyn's later novels do tend to revert to Victorian stereotype. Thus, the heroine of *Whoso Breaketh a Hedge* (1909), the petulantly charming Audrey, is torn between her duty to an adoring mathematician and her love for a soldier who becomes a hero in South Africa. Caffyn died in Turin, Italy, after an operation.

IRONS, Geneviève published five novels in this period and two children's books of Roman Catholic cast, one with a preface by R. H. *Benson. *The Damsel Who Dared* (1909) is the daughter of a Yorkshire clergyman who becomes a Roman Catholic and is cast off by her family. In *The Mystery of the Priest's Parlour* (1911), the hero takes the rap for a crime committed by someone else.

IRVINE, A[my] M[ary] (b. 1866) was the author of several novels about medical life, including *The Specialist* (1904), which features a minor staple of Edwardian fiction, the life-transforming operation. In *Roger Dinwiddie, Soul Doctor* (1907), a doctor famous for the quality of his spiritual nostrums marries the journalist who had found him good copy for her sensational daily newspaper. She also published *The Worst Girl in the School, or, The Secret Staff* (1912), *Nora, the Girl Guide, or, From Tenderfoot to Silver Fish: A Story for Girl Guides* (1913), and later children's books.

IRWIN, H. C.: see 'Mark *Time'.

IRWIN, M[argaret] E[mma] F[aith] (1889–1967) married (1929) John Robert MONSELL. Born in Highgate, she was orphaned as a child and brought up by an uncle who was a classics master at Clifton College, Bristol. She read English at Oxford. Her contemporary stories are frenetically sensational. *How Many Miles to Babylon?* (1913) concerns the adventures of a young girl who begins by going on tomboy excursions with her brother in Cornwall, graduates to midnight escapades at school, is expelled, meets a lonely artist and sits to him in a deserted glen, thereby figuring scandalously in a London gallery as the subject of the picture of the season, marries a man fifteen years older than her, runs away from him, and *still* apparently has some miles to go to Babylon. *Come Out to Play* (1914) is the far from playful tale of the son of a spendthrift who becomes a spendthrift himself and commits suicide. After the First World War she became a bestselling author of *historical novels.

Island Pharisees, The, John *Galsworthy, 1904, William Heinemann. Shelton, a comfortable young man, of traditional upper-middle-class views, background, and education, becomes engaged to Antonia Dennant, young, beautiful, and a suitable match. She sends him away for a three-month probation period and by chance he meets Louis Ferrand, renegade son of a Flemish bourgeois family, who opens Shelton's eyes to a view of Britain from the bottom of the social hierarchy. Confronted with poverty, illness, and despair, Shelton's social conscience is aroused and his milieu becomes unbearable. After much emotional struggle he forsakes both it and Antonia.

J

JACOB, Violet: Violet Mary Augusta Frederica KENNEDY-ERSKINE (1863–1946) married Arthur Otway JACOB (d. 1914–8). Born into a landowning family near Montrose, she married an army officer and spent some years in India, where she became interested in native wild flowers. Her husband was killed in the First World War, and her only son also died in action. *The Sheep-Stealers* (1902), a *historical romance set in Herefordshire in the mid-nineteenth century, was considered a promising debut. It is certainly complicated. A farmer who thinks he has killed a tollgate keeper, the father of the woman he loved and left, in the Rebecca Riot of 1843, goes into hiding. The woman he loved and left finds happiness with the man who is sheltering him, while he finds happiness of a kind with the heartless beauty who has rejected the man hunting him down. He eventually dies redemptively after the original assassin confesses. Jacob followed this up with tales of rural and small town life: *The Interloper* (1904), *The Golden Heart* (1904), and *Irresolute Catherine* (1908). *The History of Aythan Waring* (1908) is the Eden *Philpotts-like story of a woman's fanatical hatred of the man who once rejected her. *Flemington* (1911) is a tale of the Jacobite Rebellion of 1745. Jacobs also published poems, some in Scots dialect. She was a friend of the *Findlater sisters. Edinburgh University gave her an LL D in 1936, naming her as 'a leader in the recent revival of Scottish literature'.

JACOBS, W[illiam] W[ymark] (1863–1943) married (1900) Agnes Eleanor WILLIAMS. He grew up in Wapping in London's docklands, the son of a wharf man, and drew on his experiences of dockside life and people when he began writing. He went to a private school in the City of London and to Birkbeck College, University of London, where he made friends with W. Pett *Ridge. He joined the Civil Service as a boy clerk in 1879, and became a clerk in the Savings Bank department in 1883 where, unwilling to lose a safe job, he remained until 1899. Meanwhile he began writing prose sketches published in *Blackfriars*. In the 1890s he turned to stories, and published in both the **Idler* and the **Strand*. He was an extremely popular writer in his day. His first collection was *Many Cargoes* (1896); a novelette, *The Skipper's Wooing*, came out in 1897; and *Sea Urchins* (1898) was sufficiently successful to allow Jacobs to become a full-time writer. By the time of *Salthaven* (1908) his stories about seafaring and 'barge-world' characters had earned him the status of national treasure. The Jacobs formula included a small number of unvarying ingredients: simple seafaring men in love; women who are too clever for them; sarcastic give-and-take, including jokes about beer and personal appearance; misunderstandings and quandaries; and, at the end, universal happiness. He also wrote stories of horror and the supernatural; the most famous, the much anthologized 'The Monkey's Paw', was first published in *The *Lady of the Barge and Other Stories* (1902). He also wrote plays. 'Quiet, gentle and modest,' wrote the obituarist in the *Times* (2 Sept. 1943), 'he was not fond of large functions and crowds.' 'Ian *Hay', in another tribute (4 Sept.) said that 'he invented an entirely new form of humorous narrative. Its outstanding characteristics were compression and understatement.'

JACOMB, Agnes E., *pseud.*: Agnes Eliza JACOMB HOOD (b. 1866). Born in London, she began her literary career by winning the 250 guinea prize in the Melrose First Novel Competition with *The Faith of His Fathers: A Story of Some Idealists* (1909). She had earlier published journalism and short stories. Four later novels, were published, but to 1914 she published nothing else in volume form.

JAMES, Henry (1843–1916). Born in New York City, he was a grandson of the strict Presbyterian William James of Albany (d. 1832), an Irish immigrant who amassed one of the half-dozen largest fortunes in the United States. His father's generation abstained from business, however, in a 'rupture with my grandfather's tradition and attitude': he was son to Henry James (1811–82), the fifth of William James's eleven children, who had rebelled against his father's moralistic prescriptions and been forced to contest a punitive last will and testament to obtain his share of the estate. James's father used the money to follow his calling as a peripatetic Swedenborgian philosopher and social controversialist, friend of Ralph Waldo Emerson (1803–82) and Thomas Carlyle (1795–1881) among other notable figures of the time, and his five children grew up in a succession of eccentric family homes—New York, Paris, London, Geneva, Boulogne, Bonn, Newport (Rhode Island), and Cambridge (Mass.). Henry James Junior (as he was known till 1883) began in 1864, after a false start at Harvard Law School, his long and influential career as critic, travel writer, dramatist (unsuccessful), autobiographer and, above all, social and psychological novelist. In March 1869 James breakfasted at a Liverpool hotel on his first adult visit to Europe, and, as he wrote much later, 'took up the gage', 'the extraordinary gage of experience that it seemed on the spot to offer'; European reality became a central part of his complex fate, 'this doom of inordinate exposure to appearances, aspects, images'. He met George Eliot (1819–80), John Ruskin (1819–1900), Robert Browning (1812–89), Matthew Arnold (1822–88)—most of the great figures of the British literary establishment. Listening to Tennyson (1809–92) he was surprised that he 'failed to swoon away'; despite his immersion in European life he always retained an American's ironic edge. Late in 1875 James moved to Paris as correspondent of the *New York Tribune*, two weeks before his first novel, *Roderick Hudson*, based on his travels in Italy, came out in book form; he made the acquaintance of Gustave Flaubert (1821–80), Ivan Turgenev (1818–83), Guy de Maupassant (1850–93), Émile Zola (1840–1902), Alphonse Daudet (1840–97), and other notable 'advanced' writers, and wrote *The American* (1877). In December 1876 he settled in London for a heroically protracted campaign of observant participation in European culture: his notorious 107 dinings-out of 1878–9, and his assiduity as a guest at country houses may be seen as a novelist's research, the conscious catching-up of one who lacked the native advantage of Charles Dickens (1812–70), W. M. Thackeray (1811–63), or Anthony Trollope (1815–82). James's first popular (but not financial) success came with *Daisy Miller* (1879), a charming social comedy with a tragic twist, published in Leslie Stephen's *Cornhill*; he had hit his stride. With *The Portrait of a Lady* (1881), he entered a major claim in the George Eliot tradition of the large, serious novel, combining French formal sophistication, English moral psychology, and American serious irony. The 1880s were years of comparative disappointment. The exaggerated claims made for him in 1882 by his compatriot and friend William Dean Howells (1837–1900) as 'chief exemplar' of a new realism, 'a finer art in our day than it was with Dickens and Thackeray', as well as his first fictional portrayals of English society, provoked xenophobic reactions against James (as an American interloper and French cynic) in his host country which lasted for the rest of his career. Between 1890 and 1895 James fruitlessly sought popular success in the theatre with compromised, 'well-made' plays, just too late on the scene to benefit from the example of Henrik Ibsen (1828–1906) and baffled by the success of Oscar Wilde (1854–1900); then returned to the novel with relief and a new experimental excitement derived from his exposure to the 'scenic method'. *The Other House* (1896), *The Spoils of Poynton* (1897), *What Maisie Knew* (1897), 'In the Cage' and 'The Turn of the Screw' (both 1898), *The Awkward Age* (1899), and *The *Sacred Fount* (1901) are the most notable achievements in this period, apart from numerous tales ruefully preoccupied with the fate of cultural values. In these novels and novellas, children and young women and other sensitive, excluded figures frequently struggle to interpret their bewildering experience and make grand sacrifices in complex ironic narratives where action is haunted by the possible other case. In 1897 James both occupied Lamb House, Rye, and bought a typewriter, dictating directly to a secretary; in 1898 he entered an agreement with the *literary agent James Brand Pinker. In the new century James's unique fictional aesthetic reached its ultimate realization in the 'major phase': three great novels of high emotional and intellectual difficulty (for readers as well as protagonists), in which sexual betrayal and deep-laid schemes are dissimulated beneath glamorous, seductive surfaces of civilized good feeling. In order of writing, *The *Ambassadors* (1903), *The *Wings of the Dove* (1902), and *The *Golden Bowl* (1904) represent ever fuller, increasingly active engagements with the intimacies of passion. The titles of critical studies of James enumerate some of the primary concerns: the expense of vision, the ordeal of consciousness, the imagination of disaster, the drama of fulfilment. Here and in his extraordinary travel book about his native land, *The American Scene* (1907), James counts the cost, often tragic, of the civilization he so valued, and confronts the new configurations of the modern world with analytic passion. Between 1906 and 1909, he revised many of his fictions for the 'New York Edition', crowning his critical achievement with prefaces to the volumes which have become famous, or notorious, as complex meditations on the processes of the creative imagination and on the art of the novel. Returns on the Edition were disappointing, and his health suffered. He turned to family biography with *A Small Boy and Others* (1913) and *Notes of a Son and Brother* (1914), but in a magnificently lyrical, improvisatory mode which dramatized the rediscoveries of memory and traced the growth of his own imagination. He never finished *The Middle Years*, about his own early years as a writer, which was published posthumously in 1917. The outbreak of the Great War disturbed him deeply, and his last completed works were associated with the war (*The Sense of the Past* and *The Ivory Tower*, ambitious projected novels, remained fascinating fragments). James's *œuvre* is now being recovered by contextualizing criticism as more actively engaged in dialogue with his times than the traditional image of the remote, abstract 'Master' allowed.

JAMES, M[ontague] R[hodes] (1862–1936). Born at Goodnestone, Kent, son of a Church of England clergyman, he went to Eton College with a scholarship in 1876, and thence as an Eton Scholar to King's College, Cambridge. He was elected a fellow of King's in 1887, Director of the Fitzwilliam Museum, 1893–1908, Vice-Chancellor of the University of Cambridge, 1913–15, and Provost of Eton College from 1918. He died in Eton. A medievalist, palaeographer, and biblical student, he edited a great number of bibliographical and palaeographical works, as well as translating *The Apocryphal New Testament*. But his literary reputation rests on the effectiveness of his ghost stories, **Ghost Stories of an Antiquary* (1904) and *More Ghost Stories of an Antiquary* (1911) in which his tone of slightly fussy scholarship is used to give credibility to tales of the supernatural (these stories, and those from three subsequent volumes, were published in one volume in 1931). He was a lifelong friend of A. C. *Benson.

JAMES, Winifred [Llewellin] married Henry DE JAN. Her fiction includes *Patricia Baring* (1908), the diary from childhood of a warm-hearted, original, independent Australian woman, and *Letters of a Spinster* (1911), which consists of the letters a woman writes from France, Corsica, and Chelsea to a man in a nursing-home in Wimpole Street; its chatty, discursive tone is representative of James's work. She published travel books, essays, and sketches of London life including *Gangways and Corridors* (1936), a description of journeys taken from 1918.

JANE, Fred[erick] T[homas] (1870–1916) married, first (1892) Alice BEATTIE and, secondly (1909), Edith Frances Muriel CARR. Born at Honiton in Devon, he attended Exeter School and at the age of 20 trained as an artist; later he went on to be a naval authority, journalist, and novelist. He was an accomplished illustrator of, for example, *The World's Fighting Ships* (1898), and was naval correspondent for the *Engineer*, the *Scientific American*, and the *Standard*. As a novelist he specialized in *science fantasies reminiscent of the work of Jules Verne (1828–1905), including *Blake the Rattlesnake* (1895), *The Incubated Girl* (1896), *To Venus in Five Seconds* (1897), and *The Violet Flame* (1899). *The Port Guard Ship* (1900) is a more down-to-earth tale of navy life; it was followed by *Ever Mohun* (1901), *The Ought-to-Go* (1907), and *A Royal Blue Jacket* (1908), in which Prince Arthur of Devon, the King's youngest son and an honorary naval lieutenant, finds that Princess Margaret of Texxe Lipstadt will have nothing to do with him unless he proves himself a man, that is, a *real* sailor; he enlists incognito as an ordinary seaman. Jane also published non-fiction such as *The Imperial Russian Navy* (1900) and *The British Battle Fleet* (1912).

JEPSON, Edgar [Alfred] (1864–1938) married (1899) Frieda Bisham HOLMES (divorced 1933). Jepson was born in London, and educated at Leamington College and Balliol College, Oxford. He spent 1890–93 teaching in Barbados, West Indies. Later he became a well-known literary man, and stood in for Frank *Harris as editor of *Vanity Fair* in 1905, with Richard

*Middleton as his secretary. His first published work was *Sibyl Falcon* (1895), a sensationalist work featuring an Amazonian heroine, which he described later as 'a pleasant pirate story, rich in murder'. *On the Edge of the Empire* (1899) was a tale of life on the Indian frontier, written with Captain D. Beames. Like Conan *Doyle, Jepson cheekily took the adventure yarn to the verge of self-parody. *The Dictator's Daughter* (1902) begins: 'I did not go with Kitchener to Khartum; I was already there.' The Earl of Honiton and Vaux is already there because he has been captured by a party of Baggara, who, when communications with his half-brother fail to extract a ransom, enslave him. He is freed by the arrival of Kitchener's expeditionary force, and, aided by a pair of sturdy privates, goes on a revenge spree which culminates in a celebratory 'Wild Hurrah' involving drink and loot. When he returns to England, he does not assume his title, but embarks instead on an adventure involving an infamous figure who was for six weeks the Dictator of Uruguay and who plans to steal and return the crown of a *Ruritanian state called San Stefano. The Dictator has a charming daughter. Jepson commented of this book, 'I have gone on writing it ever since with considerable pleasure.' Jepson's high spirits are also evident in *The Admirable Tinker* (1904), which features a precocious child, son and companion of a wandering baronet, who maroons his father with the woman he is too shy to propose to; and in *The Four Philanthropists* (1907), where the heroes form a 'General Philanthropic Removal Company' to do away with 'captains of industry'. But high spirits certainly did not preclude (indeed, they probably reinforced) a taste for the macabre. In *The Mystery of the Myrtles* (1909), Sir George, returning from the Far East to his suburban residence, hears strange tales about the house next door, the eponymous Myrtles. Pressing through the tangled shrubbery of the Myrtles, he is seized by a hot oppressive air the like of which he has only ever felt once before, on the banks of the Katungoun River in Borneo, where the priests perform their abominable rites. Then he stumbles on a rough-hewn altar, also oddly reminiscent of Borneo. In *The Girl's Head* (1910), Sir John Messiter has no sooner established himself at the family seat at Pyechurch, by Romney Marsh, than he receives a brown paper parcel containing the object alluded to in the title. Jepson also wrote some charming stories for children: *The Lady Noggs* (1906), *Pollyooly* (1911) and their sequels; and wrote under the pseudonym 'E. Edison Page'. He shared Arthur *Morrison's passion for oriental art. His *Memories of a Victorian* (1933), has some amusing anecdotes of the Authors' Club in the 1890s; he also wrote *Memories of an Edwardian and Neo-Georgian* (1937). He was grandfather of the novelist Fay Weldon (b. 1931).

JEROME, Jerome K[lapka] (1859–1927) married (1888) Georgina Henrietta Stanley NESZA. Son of a failed coal owner, he left school at fourteen to take up a clerkship with the London and North Western Railway before becoming a school master and an actor—his first publication, *On the Stage and Off* (1885) recounted his acting experiences, and he continued to draw on theatrical anecdotes in his humorous essays when he became a full-time writer. His most famous book, *Three Men in a Boat* (1889), the comic account of three young men's accident-ridden boating holiday on the Thames, found its humour as much in lower middle-class pretensions as in the farcical set pieces (it was followed by *Three Men on a Bummel*, 1900, about a Black Forest bicycling holiday). Jerome was also a prolific writer of light comedies for the London stage (his best-known play is *The Passing of the Third Floor Back*, 1907). In 1892 he founded the **Idler*, a humorous magazine which he edited with Robert *Barr, and in 1893 he launched *To-Day*, an illustrated weekly. *Paul Kelver* (1902) is an autobiographical *Bildungsroman* which follows the hero's development from childhood bafflement and pain to youthful struggles as an actor and journalist. Its seriousness seems intended to lay at rest Jerome's reputation as no more than a humorist. Jerome also published an autobiography, *My Life and Times* (1926).

JESSE, F. Tennyson: Wynifried Margaret Tennyson JESSE (1888–1958) married (1918) Harold Marsh HARWOOD (d. 1959). Daughter of a Church of England clergyman, she was the granddaughter of Emily Tennyson (d. 1887), sister of the poet and bereaved fiancée of Arthur Hallam (1811–1833). She was born at Chislehurst, Kent, and had an unhappy childhood. She wanted to become a painter and studied art with Stanhope Forbes (1857–1947). But then, in 1909, she changed her first Christian name to 'Friniwyd', started her writing career as a journalist, and came to London. She worked as a reporter for the *Times* and the *Daily Mail* in 1911, and as a reviewer for the **Times Literary Supplement* and the **English Review*. She also wrote *The Mask* (1912) and *The Milky Way* (1913). The latter is a picaresque tale concerning the adventures of two faun-like creatures, Viv and Peter, who meet after a collision at sea. Viv, the narrator, plays many parts: actress, open-air model (she is often found *au naturel*), detective, pavement artist. She is commissioned to illustrate a 'colour book' about Provence, which Peter will write. There is also a baby, which dropped into her arms from the other ship involved in the collision, and which begins to accumulate relatives. It all ends respectably, with a wedding in a City church and a Soho reception. In 1914 Jesse joined the *Metropolitan Magazine* in New York and became its war correspondent and one of the first women to report from the front. Afterwards she turned her hand to a variety of writing—novels (during the war she had published *Beggars on Horseback*, 1915, and *Secret Bread*, 1917), plays (written with her husband), poetry, and reportage (she contributed, for example, to the *Notable British Trials* series). Her best-known novels were written in this later period: *Moonraker* (1927), on Toussaint L'Ouverture, *Lacquer Lady* (1929), set in Burma, and *A Pin to See the Peepshow* (1934) on the Thompson and Bywater murder case. Her husband, a former doctor, became a theatre manager and playwright before going into the family cotton-spinning business. There is a biography (1984) by Joanna Colenbrander.

JESSOP, George H[enry] published six volumes of fiction, including, in this period, *Desmond O'Connor: The Romance of an Irish Soldier* (1914) and *Where the Shamrock Grows: The Fortunes and Misfortunes of an Irish Family* (1911). *His American Wife* (1913) is about a wife who misunderstands her husband, partly because of his absorption in politics, partly because of the notion, spread by a jealous rival, that he married her for her money. Jessop also wrote libretti.

Jewel of the Seven Stars, The, Bram *Stoker, 1903, William Heinemann. The story begins when a young lawyer, Malcolm Ross, is woken in the middle of the night by a knock on his door and a summons to the house of a young woman he has recently met: an attempt has been made on her father's life. He is already deeply in love with Margaret Trelawny, and is dreaming of her when the knock comes. Abel Trelawny has been found lying unconscious beside his safe, having been dragged bleeding from his bed. The safe has not been opened, and there are no signs of forced entry. Trelawny's condition has apparently not been caused by his injuries. The doctors are baffled, but Ross suspects a connection between the attack and the extraordinary collection of Egyptian relics which fills the house. Trelawny returns to consciousness as mysteriously as he left it, and resumes his obsessive quest for power over life and death. He hopes that his knowledge of Egyptian mysteries will enable him to bring back to life one of the most notable adepts of ancient lore, Queen Tera, a 'woman skilled in all the science of her time'. Margaret's cheerful and engaging personality begins to be overlaid by aloofness, and an unusual familiarity with all things Egyptian: she is the agent of or medium for the appearance of the mysterious Queen, whose eventual return from the dead brings destruction. Only Ross survives to tell his cautionary tale. Although an occult tale which clearly appealed to readers of a cabbalistic tendency, *The Jewel of the Seven Stars* is most remarkable for its nervous, expectant rationalism. Trelawny envisages an intellectual renaissance which will combine the discoveries of ancient lore with those of modern science. In the 1903 edition, Queen Tera's return is made possible by the sacrifice of Margaret. Stoker rewrote the story in 1912 for another publisher; in this version, they all live happily ever after.

John Chilcote, M. P., K. C. *Thurston, 1904, William Blackwood. Interesting use of an old standby of sensational fiction, the identity exchange, in the context of parliamentary politics. Two men run into each other in a London fog, one a slave to morphia, the other to boundless ambition. The brilliant career and marriage of John Chilcote, MP, have both been blighted by drug dependence; Loder, a recluse living in Clifford's Inn, is wifeless and careerless. Chilcote persuades Loder to exchange identities with him from time to time. While standing in for Chilcote, who has retired to the country to dry out, Loder is put forward to speak in a crucial debate in the House of Commons, and, primed by his exhaustive study of politics, carries the day. Lost in a daze of ambitious self-absorption, he forgets who he once was. He has also fallen in love with

Chilcote's wife, Eve, who, returning his passion, believes that her marriage has been restored. The crisis approaches when telegrams arrive in Clifford's Inn announcing Chilcote's re-emergence. In the event, however, Chilcote degenerates even further, and dies, leaving Loder to inherit the brilliant career and marriage.

John Silence: *Physician Extraordinary*, Algernon *Blackwood, 1908, Eveleigh Nash. The eponymous hero is the Sherlock Holmes of the occult, a middle-aged, independently wealthy freelance physician: 'the cases that especially appealed to him were of no ordinary kind, but rather of that intangible, elusive, and difficult nature best described as psychical afflictions; and, though he would have been the last person himself to approve of the title, it was beyond question that he was known more or less generally as the "Psychic Doctor".' The volume contains five case-studies narrated by his 'confidential assistant'. In 'A Psychical Invasion', a humorist's experiments with cannabis have rendered him susceptible to demonic possession; the story is much concerned with the sensitivity of animals to the unseen. 'Ancient Sorceries', set in an old French cathedral town, concerns a witches' sabbath and vampirism; 'The Nemesis of Fire', an Egyptian mummy buried amid prehistoric monoliths on a country estate. 'Secret Worship', which, like 'Ancient Sorceries', has a hint of Bram *Stoker's *Dracula* (1897) about it, deposits a stolid English silk merchant in a Moravian school in the depths of the Black Forest where the staff are devil-worshippers. 'The Camp of the Dog', set on a remote Swedish island, concerns werewolf folklore.

JONES, Constance Evan. Her novels are all high-minded studies in emotions impeded by the theatricality of their plots. In *Caprice: A Study in Emotions*, (1905) a husband loves his capricious wife until he is killed in an accident, and she suffers remorse until she too is killed in an accident. In *A Matter of Temperament* (1906) the lovable wife of an unsympathetic sporting baronet adopts a motherless baby from a poor home, who discovers his true origins when he grows up. In *The Ten Years' Agreement: An Experiment in Matrimony* (1907) the woman who insists on a form of marital contract, comes to regret it. She also published *Woman's Looking-Glass: A Spinster's Chronicle* (1909), a volume of verse (1909), and one of prose (1907).

Joseph Vance: *An Ill-Written Autobiography*, William *De Morgan, 1906, William Heinemann. The successful first novel of a 66-year-old ceramic designer, clearly written under the influence of Charles Dickens (1812–70), is narrated by Joseph Vance when an old man, looking back over a life of slow but steady social advancement. Joe's father, Christopher, a builder and shrewd businessman whose ability is 'quenched in beer', wins a contract to clear the drains at Poplar Villa, home of the altruistic Dr Thorpe, a widowed scientist. Thorpe takes the 8-year-old Joe into his household, educates him at public school and Oxford, and watches as he falls in love with his younger daughter, Flossie. Flossie breaks Joe's heart by marrying an Anglo-Indian general, Hugh Desprez. But Joe, whose mastery of mechanics had become apparent at university, sets up in business as an engineer, designing a new type of repeating rifle. He proposes to Flossie's intelligent but plain friend, Janey Spencer, and after a series of misunderstandings, they marry. The marriage is a happy one, but Janey dies tragically, drowned at sea. Heartbroken, Joe travels to Italy with Flossie's younger brother, Beppino, a weak and selfish poet. After their return, Beppino marries an heiress; but it turns out that on the Italian tour he had secretly married and impregnated another woman. He dies on his honeymoon, the other woman dies, and Joe adopts her newborn baby, Cristoforo. To conceal the truth about Beppino, Joe withdraws selflessly to Brazil, and some heroic engineering. Flossie is now a widow, and moves from India to Italy, where she picks up a rumour to the effect that Cristoforo is Joe's own illegitimate child, and writes to him for confirmation or denial. He cannot confirm the rumour without losing Flossie, or deny it without damaging her memories of Beppino. So he breaks off all contact. Eventually, Flossie learns the truth from an old letter of Beppino's, and tracks Joe down in London, where they can at last marry: although the happy ending is revealed only in an appended 'Postscript by the Publisher'. The novel is representative, in its intricate and jocular sentimentality, of a return, after the abrasive slum fiction of the 1890s, to a rather more mellow and complacent depiction of working-class and lower-middle-class life.

JOYCE, James [Augustine Aloysius] (1882–1941) married (1931) Nora Joseph BARNACLE (1884–

1951). Born in Dublin, he was educated at the Jesuit schools, Clongowes Wood and Belvedere College, and University College Dublin. His first published work was an essay on Henrik Ibsen (1828–1906) in the *Fortnightly Review* (Apr. 1900). He lived in Paris after graduating; in 1904, after a return to Ireland, he left permanently for the Continent with Nora Barnacle, moving from Zurich to Pola and finally Trieste, where he taught English. There they lived until the outbreak of the First World War, the family being increased by the birth of a son and a daughter and the arrival of Joyce's brother and sister. His last visit to Dublin was in 1912. The memory of his years in Ireland, his quarrel with his Roman Catholic education, Nora's reminiscences of her childhood and adolescence, and his own vast reading in several languages, while an exile in a foreign country, were all mined for material for his fiction. He evolved a narrative technique which was to become the archetype of modernist fictional form; probably he did more than any other single writer to disturb and discredit the assumptions about characterization, plot, and language on which the novel of European tradition had depended for nearly 200 years. He lived in Zurich during the First World War; in Paris during the 1920s and 1930s, increasingly famous and the centre of a circle of admirers of whom probably the most distinguished was the dramatist Samuel Beckett (1906–1989), and in Zurich again for the last months of his life. In the 1930s his daughter Lucia became mentally ill. His principal works are *Chamber Music* (1907), a volume of lyrical verse; **Dubliners* (1914); *A Portrait of the Artist as a Young Man* (New York 1916), an experimental autobiographical novel and *Bildungsroman*; *Exiles: A Play in Three Acts* (1918); *Ulysses* (Paris 1922); *Pomes Penyeach* (Paris 1927); and a series (published between 1928 and 1937) of fragments from the work in progress (which Joyce, in poor health and increasingly blind, at one point contemplated handing over for completion to James *Stephens), finally published as *Finnegans Wake* (1939). Unpublished works printed after his death include *Stephen Hero: Part of the First Draft of A Portrait of the Artist as a Young Man* (1944) and *Scribbledehobble: The Ur-Workbook for Finnegans Wake* (1961).

Judgment of Eve, The, *and Other Stories*, May *Sinclair, 1914, Hutchinson. Nine stories dedicated to 'The Staff of the Medico-Psychological Clinic'. In her Introduction, Sinclair distinguishes between two types of short story, the condensed novel and the extended sketch, both of which are characteristic of the period. 'The Judgment of Eve', about the courtship and marriage of Aggie Purcell, who prefers an affected solicitor's clerk to a sturdy but dull farmer, and is slowly ground down by the burdensome ordinariness of housekeeping and childbearing, is an example of the first type. 'The Wrackham Memoirs', the story of a daughter's decision to burn the manuscript of her famous father's memoirs, told by a friend of the family, is an example of the second. Sinclair also proclaimed the advantages of the 'method of oblique narrative' in cases where 'certain limitations happen to be the essence of the desired effect' and where 'motives are dubious and obscure'; here 'the interest of the entire performance lies in *how* certain things and certain people appeared to the teller of the tale'. The result is a number of ultra-*Jamesian stories: notably 'The Gift', in which Wilton Caldecott hesitates between two women, one an amiable but shallow socialite, the other a gifted writer. In 'The Fault', a man falls in love with a younger woman, but cannot marry her because the shape of her arms reminds him of his adulterous ex-wife. In 'Return of the Prodigal', an alcoholic who has reformed himself in America, and at the same time become a multi-millionaire, returns to visit his family, but withdraws when he overhears them talking about him in far from complimentary terms. 'Wilkinson's Wife' is about a man who turns out to be devoted to a wife whom everyone thought he merely pitied. 'Miss Tarrant's Temperament' and 'Appearances' are both Jamesian stories about adventuresses with ambiguous motives, one of whom operates at a country house party, the other in a fashionable hotel in Cannes.

Just So Stories for Little Children, Rudyard *Kipling, 1902, Macmillan. Twelve short stories, each having a poem and illustrations by the author. Captions to the illustrations give further details and comments. The series was begun at least eight years previously, while the Kiplings were living in Vermont. The first three were published in *St Nicholas* magazine in 1897–8, where they were introduced by an uncollected preface that explains the title: these were bedtime stories for his daughter Josephine, and

'They had to be told just so; or Effie would wake up and put back the missing sentence.' A further series, written in England, was published in the *Ladies Home Journal* in 1900–2. One story in the book, and all the poems and illustrations, had no prior publication. Mosts of the stories provide fantasy explanations for the characteristics of animals: the whale's throat; the camel's hump; the rhinoceros's wrinkly skin; the leopard's spots; the elephant's trunk; the kangaroo's leaps; the armadillo's swimming and its flexibility; the crab's pincers, and the seasonal shedding of its shell; the cat's independence. Two other stories describe how a prehistoric father and daughter, who resemble Kipling and Josephine, invent reading and writing. The final tale combines biblical characters and Muslim traditions in a story of King Solomon and his wives. Travel is a frequent theme in the poems. The stories, inspired by Aesop and the beast fables of India, use elements from the literature and folk-tales of many lands, but Kipling incorporates such elements into a structure that is all his own. Though the book is ostensibly 'for little children', older readers are catered for in jokes, subtexts, and coded messages of varying complexity, often to be found in the drawings. The stories are written in a style that recalls the earlier fashion for baby-talk in works like *Helen's Babies* (1876) by John Habberton (1842–1921), *Sylvie and Bruno* (1889–93) by 'Lewis Carroll' (1832–1898), and Mrs *Molesworth's *The Adventures of Herr Baby* (1881). Kipling himself had used it in 'Wee Willie Winkie' and 'His Majesty the King' (1888). The version in *Just So Stories* is more sophisticated, recalling Carroll's word-games in *Alice's Adventures in Wonderland* (1865); Kipling is extending a child's grasp of the possibilities in language. *Just So Stories* would be parodied by James *Joyce in *Finnegans Wake* (1939), in the episode of 'The Mookse and the Gripes'.

Katharine Frensham: *A Novel*, Beatrice *Harraden, 1903, William Blackwood. Thirty-seven-year-old Katharine Frensham is left at a loose end when her brother, Ronald, to whom she is very close, marries the pretty but superficial Gwendolen. She meets Professor Clifford Thornton, a brilliant chemist, whose wife, Marianne, has died of a heart attack shortly after a quarrel during which he asked her for a separation. Marianne's scheming friend, Julia Stanhope, believes Clifford is to blame for his wife's death, and poisons his 15-year-old son, Alan, against him. Clifford takes Alan off for a reconciliatory world tour. Meanwhile, Katharine has rather glumly set off to deliver a box of specimens to a pair of Danish botanists, Ejnar and Gerda Ebbesen, who are currently travelling in Norway with Ejnar's aunt, Froken Knudsgaard, Clifford's old governess. Alan's surliness prompts Clifford to cut their tour short, and they too turn up in Norway, where Katharine continues to fall in love with him, while gallantly fending off Julia Stanhope and putting his point of view to Alan. A visit to Peer Gynt's childhood home reveals their mutual longing, but a Hardyesque mislaid letter delays its consummation for a further year. The novel is staunchly feminist, and, in the aftermath of the *Boer War, even more staunchly patriotic.

KAYE-SMITH, [Emily] Sheila (1887–1956) married (1924) Theodore Penrose FRY (1892–1971) who succeeded (1957) as 3rd Baronet. Born in Hastings, the daughter of a doctor, she was educated there and at St Leonards Ladies' College (1896–1905). In her last two years at school she wrote thirteen novels, most of which were historical and much influenced by the works of 'Edna *Lyall'. From schooldays she was interested in religion: her parents belonged to the Church of England (her mother having converted from Presbyterianism) and discouraged her High Church enthusiasm. Another important influence was a series of childhood holidays on Sussex farms. The first of her thirty-one novels is *The Tramping Methodist* (1908), which she sent to the Society of Authors for their advice. For a fee of a guinea they recommended improvements and gave the name of a literary agent. In *Starbrace* (1909) the eighteenth-century setting and highwaymen scenes still show a debt to Lyall. The hero, a gentleman by birth but brought up as a labourer, goes through a painful process of education to become worthy of a squire's daughter, and fails; the coarseness he is unable to exorcize symbolizing sexuality. These early novels of Kaye-Smith's were considered surprising compositions for a young middle-class girl, and caused scandal in Hastings. By the time she wrote *Spell Land* (1910), which describes the failure of a relationship between a farmer and a woman who has left her husband, she had a room of her own to work in her parents' house: 'I was a real author now, entitled to solitude.' *Isle of Thorns* (1913) contains a vivid and original portrait of a woman writer, Sally Odiarne, who tries to become a tramp. She sleeps with Andy Baird, an unreliable circus man who represents sexual and social licence, but is also attracted to the prim and cultivated Raphael Moore. At the end she gives herself up to the police after having knifed Andy. There is clearly a parallel with *Tess of the D'Urbervilles* (1891) by Thomas Hardy (1840–1928), though in characterization and moral atmosphere the novels are worlds apart. Kaye-Smith's Sussex novels were frequently compared by reviewers to Hardy's, and like Eden *Phillpotts, Mrs Henry *Dudeney, and Mary Webb (1881–1927), she is much in his debt, although in her autobiography, *Three Ways Home* (1937), she makes more of the influence at this period of W. L. *George, who gave her advice on plots and planning. With *Sussex Gorse* (1916) she had a greater critical success; her best fiction, such as *Green Apple Harvest* (1920) and *Joanna Godden* (1921), followed soon afterwards. Later books became rather formulaic. She married a High Church clergyman (a converted Quaker of the chocolate manufacturing family, Rowntree).

After several years in various London parishes they both converted to Roman Catholicism in 1929. Thereafter they lived in rural Sussex, farming and ministering to Catholic community there. Kaye-Smith also published two studies (1943, 1950) of the novels of Jane Austen (1775–1817) in collaboration with G. B. *Stern. There is a biography by Dorothea Walker (1980).

KEARY, C[harles] F[rancis] (1848–1917). Born in Stoke-on-Trent and educated at Marlborough College (1862–4) and Trinity College, Cambridge, Keary was an assistant in the coin department of the British Museum (1872–1887). He left the Museum in order to write; his first book, *A Wanderer* (1888), was a collection of bookish reflections published under the pseudonym 'H. Ogram Matuce', signifying *ὁ γραμματεύς*, the literary man. He wrote history, novels, and verse from then until his death and contributed many articles on art, mythology, history, and literature to the most respectable periodicals: he was an expert on early Scandinavian literature and history and Fellow of the Society of Antiquaries. He suffered from asthma and bronchitis and lived much abroad, at Barbizon or in the Pyrenees. George *Gissing, who saw him several times in 1896, called him 'not a man of much account'. His fiction is rather unusual in flavour; the *Times*'s obituarist commented (27 Oct. 1917) that Keary aimed 'at depicting life after the manner of the great Russian writers, in its chaotic reality and avoiding conventional selection and arrangement'. *High Policy* (1902) portrays the English political and social system as encountered by the ingenuous heroine Cynthia, an idealistic Tory. It gives a vivid sense of the clash of mental attitudes and sexual mores. Diverse ideologies, including the belief in the inherited right to rule of the Anglo-Saxon aristocracy, are outlined without authorial endorsement.

KEATING, Joseph (1871–1934) married (1926) Catherine Annie HERBERT. Born of Irish Catholic parents in Mountain Ash, Glamorgan, he worked in a colliery from the age of 12 and went down the pit at 14. He subsequently worked as a pedlar, in the Post Office, as a violinist, as a clerk and then as a reporter. His autobiography, *My Struggle for Life* (1916), chronicles the hardships of a friendless Welshman attempting to become an author. Though **Son of Judith: A Tale of the Welsh Mining Valleys* (1900), of the school of *Germinal* (1885) by Émile Zola (1840–1902), achieved publication after several rejections and made quite a stir, Keating made hardly any money from it. A breakdown was followed by an unsuccessful foray to London in 1904. He worked as a journalist and published short stories under other names. According to his version he was cheated by publishers and literary agents. He returned to London in 1906. The fifteenth publisher accepted *The Great Appeal* (1909), which is set in London high society. Lord Francis Stormont's brilliant political career is ruined when he is falsely accused of adultery; he and his faithful fiancée, the daughter of a newspaper proprietor, retrieve his career by campaigning on a programme to eliminate unemployment by banning child labour and female labour, lessening the hours of work, and raising wages. Despite the fact that *London Opinion* placarded the Strand with sandwich-men proclaiming 'Novelist insults the King', the novel was a complete failure and Keating had to go on living off his short stories. He was in particularly low water in 1911. But the success of *The Perfect Wife* (1913) and the play *Peggy and Her Husband* (1914) restored his fortunes. He went on writing novels and plays until his death and translated Zola's novel *Nana* (1880) in 1926. His brother Matthew Keating (1869–1937) was Nationalist MP for South Kilkenny (1909–18).

KEIGHTLEY, S. R.: Samuel Robert KEIGHTLEY (1859–1949) Kt. (1912) married, first (1892) Gertrude Emily SMITH (d. 1929), and, secondly (1930), Anne VOWELL née ——. Born in Belfast and educated there at Queen's College, Keightley was called to the Irish Bar in 1883. He contested South Antrim as an Independent Unionist (1903) and South Derry as a Liberal (1910). His nine volumes of fiction 1894–1906 include several historical romances. *The Pikemen: A Romance of the Ards of Down* (1903) is about the 1798 Irish rebellion; the narrator is shocked by the brutality of British soldiers into sympathy with the United Irishmen. *A Man of Millions* (1901) is a thriller: Percival Colthurst returns from South Africa with bags of diamonds, to avenge himself on his scheming cousin Christopher, who has married his fiancée. Christopher conspires with Percival's Chinese servant to obtain the jewels, but is murdered.

KEITH, Leslie, *pseud.*: Grace Leslie Keith JOHNSTON (1843?–1929). The fifth daughter (one of eleven children) of the geographer Alexander

Keith Johnston (1804–1871), Johnston was brought up and educated in Edinburgh; she also travelled in Germany. In 1878 she published *A Simple Maiden*, the first of her romantic novels; she wrote more than thirty volumes of fiction, including some children's books, up to 1907. In the late 1880s she was living in Oxford, where 'Sarah *Tytler', who lived in the same boarding-house for a year, found her 'cultured'. *Penance* (1901) is about a woman who saves her jewellery rather than her child in a shipwreck and dies atoning for her crime; there is much detail about rural life in Germany and the professional classes in Scots cities, and a sympathetic portrait of a clever middle-aged spinster who is passed over by the hero in favour of his young ward.

KELLY, W[illiam] Patrick (1848–1915). Brought up in Kilkenny, of Irish Catholic parents, he was educated at Clongowes Wood College, Dublin and the Royal Military Academy, Woolwich. He became an officer in the Royal Artillery, retiring in 1878 as a lieutenant. He lived near Harrogate and was a JP. His first book, *Schoolboys Three* (1895), was based on his own school experiences with the Jesuits in the early 1860s. He wrote nine other volumes of fiction before his death, adventure stories in the manner of Jules Verne (1828–1905), such as *The Cuban Treasure Island* (1903), featuring terrestrial magnetism, and *The Dolomite Cavern* (1899), featuring X-rays; and rather pompous *historical romances set in the distant past: Nineveh in *The Assyrian Bride* (1905), and ancient Egypt in *The Stone-Cutter of Memphis* (1904). In *The Senator Licinius* (1907), the senator's daughter is kidnapped in the dissolute Rome of Caligula; she and her lover eventually become Christians. A probable influence is *Quo Vadis* (1895), set in Nero's court, by the Polish novelist Henryk Sienkiewicz (1846–1916), who had been awarded the Nobel prize for Literature in 1905.

KENEALY, [Mary] Annesley [Flood] (b. 1861). Sister of Arabella *Kenealy, she was born in Wandsworth, trained as a nurse at St Bartholomew's Hospital, and nursed in New York and during the plague in Holland. She then worked on the staff of the *Daily Graphic*, the *Sunday Graphic*, and other Harmsworth newspapers from 1892 to 1900. Her novel *Thus Saith Mrs Grundy* (1911) is supposed to be a true story about a prostitute, one of the most noble women Kenealy ever met. Seduced by an aristocrat, she is then repeatedly deserted by men—the book rails against the cruelty of sexual mores and the legitimacy laws. *The Poodle-Woman: A Story of 'Restitution of Conjugal Rights'* (1913) was the first in the 'Votes for Women' series, suggested by Kenealy to the *publisher Stanley Paul. It is dedicated to 'The Immortal Feminist Cause', and illustrates the unfairness of the laws concerning married women's property and the custody of children in cases of separation and divorce. The heroine is impossibly noble, her husband a monster. Kenealy was on the committee of the Women Writers' Suffrage League. Her novel *A 'Water-Fly's Wooing: A Drama in Black and White Marriages* (1914) indicates that, like her sister Arabella, she was affected by eugenicist theory and opposed miscegenation between black and white races. She also published *The Care of the Sick* (1893) and serials in the *Daily Sketch* and *Sheffield Weekly Telegraph*. She applied to the Royal Literary Fund in 1918, stating that she was dying of heart disease (she also said that she had been born in 1873 and called herself K. Annesley Kenealy).

KENEALY, Arabella [Madonna] (1864–1938). Born at Portslade, Sussex, she was one of the eleven legitimate children of the Irish barrister E. V. H. Kenealy (1819–1880), who was once imprisoned for violence to his illegitimate son, and who was disbarred (1874) for his mad behaviour (perhaps owing to diabetes) while defending the Tichborne Claimant. Kenealy published an admiring biography (1908) of her father. Annesley *Kenealy was her sister; and their brother Alexander Kenealy (1864–1915) became editor of the *Daily Mirror* in 1904. Educated at home and the London School of Medicine for Women, she practised medicine in London and Watford (1888–1894) before retiring from ill health after catching diphtheria. Her first novel, *Dr Janet of Harley Street* (1893), about a female doctor and her protégée, has lesbian overtones. Her later fiction is much concerned with problems of sex and *marriage. In *The Love of Richard Herrick* (1902) Sybilla, a painter, refuses Herrick's offer of marriage because she wants to be independent. He then marries an ordinary girl, who goes mad, and has an affair with a fascinating widow, before the mad wife dies, enabling him to marry the now repentant Sybilla. Eugenicism, sexuality, and feminism are major themes. But some of the stories in the collection

Dr. Smith of Queen Anne Street (1907) are far more conventional treatments of the motif of the woman who doesn't realize what she wants. In 'Bridge and Marriage' a girl must marry a man to whom she owes money. In 'A Mésalliance' Sir Brian is magnanimous to a former fiancée who eloped foolishly with a gamekeeper. *An American Duchess* (1906) is a novel about the decadence of high society; Stella Herbert, a beautiful graduate, is too high-minded to cope and divorces the husband she loves, only to end by wooing him in disguise. Kenealy also wrote non-fiction about medical and sexual issues. Like many feminists of her generation, she was an anti-vivisectionist and interested in the occult. Her books include *The Failure of Vivisection* (1909), *Feminism and Sex-Extinction* (1920) and *The Human Gyroscope: A Consideration of the Gyroscopic Rotation of Earth as Mechanism of the Evolution of Terrestrial Living Forms* (1934).

KENNARD, Mrs Arthur: Ann Homan HOMAN-MULOCK (1844–1926) married (1866) Arthur Challis KENNARD (1831–1903). The youngest daughter (the eleventh of fifteen children) of an Irish landowner who changed his surname from Molloy in 1843, she wrote biographies, contributed articles on historical subjects to periodicals, and published four novels between 1880 and 1900. Some of her work appeared as by 'N. H. Kennard' or 'Nina H. Kennard'. In *The Second Lady Delcombe* (1900) an American heiress marries an impoverished English peer; they do not sleep together until a final reconciliation of New World simplicity and Old World inhibitedness. The Irish problem is a major theme, viewed from a Unionist and aristocratic point of view. She is a wittier and more sophisticated writer than her husband's sister-in-law Mrs Edward *Kennard. In an article, 'Why Women Write', in the *National Review*, (July 1884) she comments that men fear 'that by mental work women may build themselves a rampart, entrenched behind which they are independent agents acting on their own resources'. Her next sister was married to Alfred *Austin.

KENNARD, Mrs Edward: Mary Eliza LAING (*c*.1850–1936) married (1870) Edward KENNARD (1842–1910). Daughter of the railway magnate and MP Samuel Laing (1812–1897), she was brought up in Hampshire and Sydenham, and educated at a school at St Germain. She began by writing stories for her sons after they went to school, collected as *Light Tales* (1886). But her fame and commercial success were to come from the long series of sprightly, romantic sporting novels, mostly about hunting, beginning with *The Right Sort* (1883). However, by the Edwardian period her style had undergone a metamorphosis. It sounds a bitterer note, feminist and progressive in its sympathies. The *Times's* obituarist (9 March 1936) noted that they were far less popular than her earlier novels. *A Son of the Fleet* (1903) is dedicated to a son who was a lieutenant in the navy; it describes the romantic and social difficulties of a young man forced into the navy by his father, with much emphasis on the sordidity of the marriage market. *The Golf Lunatic and His Cycling Wife* (1902) is narrated by an intelligent able woman who is married to a weak man given to flirtation. He is obsessed with golf, she with cycling. Kennard herself became as keen on cycling and motoring as she had been on hunting and salmon-fishing, and the possibility of an autobiographical element cannot be entirely excluded. By the time of her death she was severely crippled and blind. Her husband was the youngest of seven brothers of whom the fourth married Mrs Arthur *Kennard.

KENNEDY, Bart (1861–1930) married (1897) Isobel PRIESTLEY (d. late 1920s). Born in Leeds and brought up in Manchester, he was sent at the age of 6 to work in a cotton mill, under the half-time system, in which children went to school when not working. He worked in mills and machine shops until he was 20, then became a sailor. He wrote in *Who's Who* that he then became 'a labourer and a tramp in the United States; lived and fought with Indians; gold-mined up in Klondyke long before the gold rush; became an opera singer and an actor... drifted into writing.' His fiction is semi-autobiographical, and interesting for its cinematographic, unornamented technique, emphasizing the feelings of the narrator at the passing moment. *A Sailor Tramp* (1902) begins with two drifters in Texas riding trains. One is English and gets work as a docker, then cutting sugar-cane. This was followed by *A Tramp in Spain* (1904) and *A Tramp's Philosophy* (1908). *Slavery: Pictures from the Depths* (1905) is an angry, impressionistic account of the childhood of a working-class boy, left alone by a working mother, with scenes in the workhouse, in the factory, in the militia, which ends with a final vision of workers' revolution. In 1921 he founded a weekly called *Bart's Broadsheet*. In supporting his application to the Royal Literary Fund, A. Conan *Doyle called him 'a man who has narrowly missed greatness' and H. G. *Wells said he had 'a secure place in the mixed treasurehouse of English literature'. He got a grant, even though it was alleged that his wife (who had worked on the *Review of Reviews*) could not keep a female servant in their house in Reigate because he was not to be trusted. After the death of his wife his health failed and he spent his last months in the mental hospital in Haywards Heath, where he died.

KENNY, Louise M. Stacpoole: Louise M. Stacpoole DUNNE (?1885–1933) married T. H. KENNY. A Roman Catholic, the daughter of a doctor in Moymore, Co. Clare, she lived near Limerick and published nine romantic novels for girls between 1905 and 1916, many set in Ireland. Some of her work is unpretending *historical fiction: *Love IS Life* (1910) and its sequel, *The King's Kiss* (1912), are about the adventures of Dymphna Macnamara, an Irish girl at the court of St Germain. Married against her will, she learns to love her husband after all, and resists the advances of Louis XIV. *At the Court of Il Moro* (1911) is set in fifteenth-century Italy. Kenny's other works were hagiographies. She was a member of the Society of Authors from 1911.

KENYON, Edith C. (d. 1925). Born in Doncaster, the daughter of a surgeon, she was brought up there and in north Wales, kept house for her brother, who was also a doctor, in Bradford. She lived in Hastings 1895–8, thereafter in London. She published more than fifty volumes of fiction between 1881 and 1919, many of which are for children, and also translated from German and wrote tracts and biographies. Many of her books were published by the RTS; several of her early novels were published first in New York. In the 1890s she published six titles in collaboration with Richard Gilbert Soans, a writer on religon. Her style is exemplified by *The Wooing of Mifanwy: A Welsh Love Story* (1912). Twins, Mifanwy and Owen, penniless orphans of a bankrupt financier, go to live with their grandfather whom they are surprised to find an old Welsh farmer. Mifanwy falls in love with a farmer's son who becomes a great singer. Non-fiction includes *Scenes in the Life of the Royal Family* (1890) and *Chats with Women on Every-day Subjects* (1908).

KERNAHAN, Mrs Coulson: Mary Jean Hickling GWYNNE (1857–1941) married, first (before 1881), George Thomas BETTANY (1850–1891) and, secondly, Coulson *KERNAHAN. Born in Staffordshire, she was educated by her father, a mathematics master at Taunton College. Then, as a young married woman, she attended classes (1881–4) at University College London. Her first husband lectured in natural science at Girton and Newnham Colleges, Cambridge, and worked as a publisher's hack writing textbooks on physiology, anthropology, and botany. After his death she was left with a baby and girls of 11 and 12. Walter *Besant wrote of her predicament to the secretary of the Royal Literary Fund: 'The usual story—widow & children & tuppence in the house—how familiar to you!' Coulson Kernahan, who was executor of her husband's will, also wrote in support of her 1892 application, and later married her. Her first novel, published under the name 'Jeanie Gwynne Bettany', was *The House of Rimmon: A Black Country Story* (1885), a three-decker about the appalling effects on the younger generation of an upbringing by a Pharisaical, money-grubbing Puritan father. After her second marriage she published sometimes as 'J. G. Kernahan'; her bibliography includes some forty-five volumes of fiction, rattling romances with implausible plots, some of which were serials for *Temple Bar and Argosy.* In *The Mystery of Magdalen* (1906) a Russian girl steals a baby to avenge herself for the betrayal of her father to the secret police. She marries an Englishman without explaining her past; in the end they make it up. *Ashes of Passion* (1909) is about a vain actress married to a good man. Kernahan was keen on bird-watching. Her son George Kernahan Gwynne Bettany wrote detective stories 1931–51.

KERNAHAN, [John] Coulson (1858–1943) married Mrs Coulson *Kernahan. Born in Ilfracombe, the son of a biblical scholar, he was educated at home and at St Albans School, and became a journalist and miscellaneous author. He worked as a reader at Ward, Lock & Co, from 1889, succeeding his wife's former husband as chief literary adviser in 1891; while there he discovered the work of Joseph *Hocking. His first book was *A Dead Man's Diary* (1890), published serially in *Lippincott's Magazine*, of which he was the

British editor. His religious works, *God and the Ant* (1895) and *The Child, the Wise Man and the Devil* (1896), had combined sales exceeding 100,000. Like W. P. *Drury, William *Le Queux, *Kipling, and others, he was associated with the campaign for rearmament led by Field Marshal Earl Roberts (1832–1914); his book *An Author in the Territorials* (1908) emphasizes the superiority of military life to sport as a training for young men. *The Red Peril* (1908) is an *invasion scare novel about the mutual hatred of Britain and Germany. He had some reputation as a poet, being included in A. H. Miles, *The Poets and the Poetry of the Century* (1898). He assisted Frederick Locker-Lampson (1821–1895) in compiling a once-popular anthology, *Lyra Elegantiarum* (1891). Several of his later works are memoirs of writers he had known; *Celebrities: Little Stories about Famous Folk* (1923) is an example; he also wrote against spiritualism and its proponents, including Arthur Conan *Doyle. His sister Mary Kernahan was a contributor to magazines and author of nonsense verse.

KERNAHAN, J. G.: See Mrs Coulson *Kernahan.

KERR, Lady Amabel: Amabel Frederica Henrietta COWPER (d. 1906) married (1873) Walter Talbot KERR (1839–1927). Daughter of the 6th Earl Cowper, she married Lord Walter Kerr, a naval officer of a Roman Catholic family, and converted—an experience described in *Unravelled Convictions* (1878). Thereafter she published hagiographies, children's books, and two novels. *The Whole Difference* (1902) is about the Protestant members of a family oppressing their long-suffering Catholic relations; the heroine converts her lover.

Kim, Rudyard *Kipling, 1901, Macmillan. An enduringly popular tale woven, with some assistance from Kipling's father, out of the 'vague notion of an Irish boy, born in India and mixed up with native life'. Kimball O'Hara, orphaned son of a soldier serving in an Irish regiment in India, lives on the streets of Lahore, where he is known as 'Little Friend of all the World'. He attaches himself as *chela*, or companion, to a Tibetan lama in search of the River of the Arrow. A picaresque tale unfolds of adventures on the great road of life. Eventually, they stumble across Kim's father's old regiment. Kim is adopted by the regiment and sent, unwillingly, to school, although in the holidays he is reunited with his lama, who has not yet found the River of the Arrow. A split develops in his loyalties when Colonel Creighton, of the Ethnological Survey, recognizes his potential as a spy, and apprentices him to a trusted Indian agent, Hurree Babu. He proves himself by capturing the papers of two Russian spies at work in the Himalayas. The lama does find his river, but he has already, in practice if not in theory, lost his *chela* to the interests of the British Empire. Much the same might be said of the narrative itself, which, after savouring with unprecedented vigour and subtlety the life of the bazaar and the open road, dwindles into a *spy thriller comparable to John *Buchan's *The* Half-Hearted* (1900).

KING, Maude Egerton: Maude Egerton HINE (1867–1927) married (1887) Joseph KING (1860–1943). She was the youngest of the fourteen children of the water-colour painter Henry George Hine (1811–1895); two of her brothers followed his profession. She married a barrister and MP; together they worked to revive rural crafts; founding a weaving industry in Haselmere, where they lived, in 1894. Much of the designing was done by Godfrey Blount, who was married to her sister Ethel. She was Honorary Secretary of the Peasant Arts Guild for some years. In 1910 she started, with her husband's cousin Greville *MacDonald, a monthly magazine called the *Vineyard*, to which Maurice *Hewlett, G. K. *Chesterton, Lord *Dunsany, Ernest *Rhys, Katharine *Tynan, and Allen *Clarke contributed. Her verse and prose has the same emphasis on country life and the woman's sphere. *The Country Heart* (1911) consists of stories collected from magazines such as the *Pall Mall* and the *Century*; it contains her best-known work, 'The Conversion of Miss Caroline Eden', about an Anglican spinster who becomes Congregationalist and eventually is driven mad by realization of the evil of the world. *The Archdeacon's Family* (1909), published as by 'Maud Egerton King', describes several members of a family growing up and dealing with sexual and religious problems. In the foreword to a translation (1912) of *The Forest Farm*, by the Austrian novelist of peasant life Peter Rosegger, she castigates 'earnest women who have slammed the front door on their nearest and dearest stay-at-home duties and pleasures, to go questing after problematical rights'.

King of Alsander, The, James Elroy *Flecker, 1914, Max Goschen. The hero, Norman Price, is the bookish son of an enterprising grocer in the backwater village of Blaindon. 'All the works that glow with dark frenzy, or with diabolical Rembrandt fires, whose authors died nameless deaths or were burnt for magic, all the fantastic tales about new countries on the other side of mountains, or happy islands in limitless seas, all stories of the moon or stars were his especial delight and continual joy.' The arrival in the shop of a mysterious old man dressed in a Norfolk jacket, a cricketing shirt, grey flannel trousers, and brown boots with pointed toes, who demands tobacco and expatiates upon the dullness of Blaindon, inspires Norman to travel. He eventually arrives at the phantom city of Alsander, whose dim ruler, Andrea, last of a decadent line, has been usurped by his regent, Duke Vorza. Norman pursues an affair with his landlady's daughter, Peronella. The clandestine Association for the Advancement of Alsander plots to install him, *Prisoner of Zenda*-style, on the throne. Norman is about to decline the honour when the Association's leader, the androgynous Arnolfo, reveals himself to be the Princess Ianthe, Andrea's cousin, who is in love with Norman. Ianthe masterminds a coup. Peronella, spurned by Norman at his coronation, leads an assault on the palace during which Duke Vorza, who has conspired with her, is killed; she disappears, leaving Norman to rule Alsander with Ianthe as his queen. The novel might be said to constitute the swan song, on the eve of the First World War, of *Ruritanian romance. A preface characterizes it as the kind of tale a poet might tell, devoid of social realism and political commentary; and in a strange coda the old man returns to Blaindon to offer Norman's friend and erstwhile companion John Gaffekin a vision of limitless imagination. Yet Norman himself is very much his father's son. Whereas Duke Vorza wants to keep Alsander 'untouched by the world', Norman improves roads and drains, and establishes an aeroplane service. This is a ruritanian romance whose hero belongs to a social comedy by Arnold *Bennett or H. G. *Wells. 'Well, there's something to be said for being awake and something to be said for modernity.'

KINROSS, Albert (1870–1929) was born in Hampstead, the son of a West India merchant; his mother was Danish. He went to boarding-school in Brighton and then to a day-school in London. Aged 16 he became a clerk, then briefly worked for his father before going to Basle aged 18. He spent the next four years working abroad, where his most successful job was one in Bavaria writing the rhymes inside Christmas cards for the English market; there he determined to become a writer. After his return to England he spent some years living in and near Cambridge before going to London with his first novel and became London correspondent of the *Boston Evening Transcript* (1896–8), existing with the help of an allowance from his father. Next he was associate editor of the **Outlook* (1898–1900) and drama critic of the *Morning Post* (1901–3) He was also art critic of *Academy*, a correspondent during the Russo-Japanese War and the Russian revolt of 1905–6. Then he managed to get a job writing serials for a Chicago magazine, and retired to the country for the next seven years to write fiction full-time and to play as much cricket as possible. He was a member of the Authors team which included Conan *Doyle, *Hornung, and *Wodehouse. In the First World War he served in France, Salonika, Egypt, and Palestine, rose to the rank of captain, and started the *Balkan News* (1916) and the *Palestine News* (1918) for the troops. Afterwards he suffered from shell-shock. His fictional line was fluent romance: in *An Opera and Lady Grasmere* (1899) Merceron, a composer who is to save English music, chooses between Art and Life (first one, then the other) and finally gets both when beautiful Lady Grasmere says she wants to help him in his work. *The Torch: A Novel of the Nineties* (1923) is about setting up a new weekly, and contains humorous sketches of typical journalists of the period: it presumably draws on Kinross's experiences on the *Outlook*. He died suddenly of pneumonia, leaving unfinished an autobiography (1930), mostly about cricket.

KIPLING, [Joseph] Rudyard (1865–1936) married (1892) Caroline Starr BALESTIER (1862–1939). Born in Bombay, the son of a designer and museum official, he was educated at the United Service College, Westward Ho!. Both parents were the children of Methodist ministers; they themselves were Anglican. Of his mother's sisters Georgiana Macdonald (1840–1920) married Sir Edward Burne-Jones (1833–1898); Agnes Macdonald (1843–1906) married Sir Edward Poynter

(1836–1919); and Louisa Macdonald (1845–1925) wrote novels and was the mother of the prime minister Stanley Baldwin (1867–1947). It would be a mistake however, to suppose that at the outset of his career Kipling was surrounded by prosperous and powerful connections. It was certainly important to his development that through his aunts he had contacts with the world of Pre-Raphaelite art and design, but his parents were neither rich nor influential. As was normal for all Anglo-Indian children whose parents could possibly afford it, he and his sister Trix were sent home to live in England. From December 1871 to April 1877 they did not see their parents and lived with a retired marine captain and his wife and son in Southsea, an unhappy episode which inspired the story 'Baa Baa Black Sheep' (1888). In 1878 Kipling was sent to the United Services College, which had been set up a few years before, mainly in order to prepare pupils cheaply for the military colleges at Sandhurst and Woolwich. The headmaster, Cormell Price, was an old friend of Burne-Jones's, cultivated, liberal, and pacifist, who is portrayed as the Head in *Stalky & Co* (1899). Although at first he was bullied, Kipling came to be happy at the school; he was not considered academic enough to try for a scholarship to Oxford or Cambridge and his parents could not afford to send him there without one. So in September 1882, nearly 17, he sailed for India to become assistant editor of the *Civil and Military Gazette*, published in Lahore. Here, in 1885, he was initiated into freemasonry, a subject which was to resurface in his twentieth-century fiction, figuring the necessity of ritual and the brotherhood of men of different races and classes. From 1886 he began to publish in the *Gazette* the stories which were collected as *Plain Tales from the Hills* (Calcutta 1888). This was followed by other volumes of stories of Anglo-Indian life, published, first in the Indian Railway Library, then in England and America, with immense success. In 1887 he was moved to the sister paper, the *Pioneer*, published in Allahabad. In 1889 he left for Europe via America; he was to return only once, for a short visit in 1891. He arrived in London in October 1889 already famous; there was a *Times* leader about his work in March 1890. A semi-engagement to an American, Caroline Taylor, was succeeded by a renewed passion for Violet 'Flo' Garrard, whom he had known since childhood, who wanted to become a painter. His novel *The Light That Failed* (1891) no doubt draws on the bitterness he felt at her preferring her work to his love. The strains of this period led to a breakdown in October 1890. It was at this time that Kipling met Wolcott Balestier (1861–91), the English agent for the American publisher Lovell Inc. They collaborated on *The Naulahka: A Story of East and West* (1892) and Wolcott introduced Kipling to his elder sister, Carrie. In August 1891 Kipling went on a trip via South Africa, New Zealand, Australia, and Ceylon to his parents, reaching Lahore in December. Hearing of Wolcott's death from typhoid and Carrie's request for his return, he left before Christmas, and married her in January 1892, a week after his arrival in England. Together they travelled to America to visit her relations, then went to Japan, where the failure of Kipling's bank meant they had to beat a hasty retreat back to Brattleboro', Vermont and the Balestiers. There they began to build a house called Naulakha [*sic*] on an idiosyncratic plan to protect Kipling from autograph hunters. The Vermont years, 1893–5, were productive ones; there his beloved eldest daughter Josephine was born, there he wrote *The Jungle Book* and *The Second Jungle Book* (1894, 1895) and 'The Mary Gloster' (1894), and there he began work on **Kim* (1901), drawing on his early, abandoned project for a novel of low life in Lahore, *Mother Maturin*. But by summer 1896 local unpopularity and rows with the Balestiers had made life impossible and they returned to England. In early 1899 they went back for a visit; Kipling and Josephine fell ill in New York. He nearly died, she did; the tragedy was compounded by a siege by journalists and publicity of the most hideous kind. Neither of the Kiplings ever returned to the USA and both henceforward had a pathological desire for privacy. After five years at Rottingdean, Sussex, they moved to the much remoter Bateman's in 1902. In the stories in **Actions and Reactions* (1909) and **Puck of Pook's Hill* (1906) and its sequel, **Rewards and Fairies* (1910), Kipling made an imaginative world of the Sussex countryside, people, and history, such as he had made out of India, but never out of America. From 1900 to 1908 they spent the winters in South Africa, where Cecil Rhodes (1853–1902) gave them a house, an experience which affected Kipling's political thought and gave settings to several of the stories in **Traffics and Discoveries* (1904) and **Just So*

Stories (1902). Acknowledged since the impact of 'Recessional' and 'The White Man's Burden', as the poet of imperialism, Kipling was prominent among the writers who supported the formation of the National Defence League (1906) by Field Marshal Earl Roberts (1832–1914). The First World War, long anticipated, gave rise to stories both at the time, such as 'Mary Postgate' (1915) and long afterwards, such as 'The Gardener' (1926). In tribute to his son John, killed in action in 1915, he wrote *The Irish Guards in Wartime* (1923), in researching which he was brought, more than most non-combatants, in touch with the detail of trench warfare. In 1907 he was awarded the Nobel prize for Literature. A rather enigmatic autobiography, *Something of Myself* (1937), was published posthumously. There is a biography by Angus Wilson (1977).

Kipps: *The Story of a Simple Soul*, H. G. *Wells, 1905, Macmillan. Artie Kipps is rescued from the drudgery of a draper's shop in Folkestone by the intervention of James Chitterlow, an aspiring playwright, who knocks him down with his bicycle, and then produces an advertisement in an old newspaper enabling him to claim a large legacy. Kipps's new wealth, minus a substantial investment in the play Chitterlow is writing, introduces him into Folkestone society, where, with the help of Chester Coote, a house agent, he embarks upon a programme of self-improvement. The programme includes the snobbish but impoverished Helen Walsingham. Kipps, however, does not enjoy the social round, and, when he rediscovers his childhood sweetheart, Ann Pornick, now a domestic servant, he decides to marry her. By this time, however, Helen's brother has speculated with and lost a considerable part of Kipps's fortune, and has to flee the country. Kipps buys a bookshop with what remains. But help is once more at hand in the shape of Chitterlow, whose play has been an unexpected success. The royalties will keep the Kippses, and their son, in the modest comfort they have always aspired to. The story was originally part of a more ambitious project, 'The Wealth of Mr Waddy', a social panorama on a Dickensian scale. 'A whole introductory book was written before Kipps himself came upon the scene . . . But it became clear to the writer by the time he had brought Kipps and Chitterlow together that he had planned his task upon too colossal a scale . . . Now books are meant to be read, and there is no interest in writing them unless you believe they will get to readers. So "Kipps" was clipped off short to the dimensions of a practicable book.' Also clipped off short was the bitter tone of parts of the original. Kipps makes his way through a treacherous but not fundamentally evil world with patience and dignity. As in Arnold *Bennett's social comedies, the hero's resilience finds a parallel in the ingenuity of the plotting. Henry *James was not the only reader to find himself lost in amazement at the 'diversity' of Wells's genius: 'what am I to say about Kipps, but that he is not so much a masterpiece as a mere born gem—you having, I know not how, taken a header straight down into mysterious depths of observation and knowledge.'

Kitty Tailleur, May *Sinclair, 1908, Archibald Constable. Sympathetic study of a 'fallen woman'. Thirty-five-year-old Robert Lucy, a gentle, decent widower whose wife died five years before in giving birth to their second daughter, is holidaying with his sister, Jane, amid the 'refined publicity' of the Cliff Hotel at 'Southbourne'. They cannot quite understand why their fellow-guests should so ostentatiously shun a new arrival, Kitty Tailleur, a charming and glamorous widow. Even more puzzling is the decision of Mrs Tailleur's companion, Miss Keating, to leave her. Robert Lucy rides gallantly to her social rescue, and within ten days they are engaged. Kitty becomes fast friends with Jane, and proves a great success with Robert's daughters. However, the applecart is definitively upset by the appearance of Wilfrid Marston, a civil servant and man of the world, who has been Kitty's lover and who wants her back. Even more damning is the fact that she was never in fact married to Tailleur, and that there have been a number of other men between Tailleur and Marston. In desperation, Kitty finds the courage to confess everything to Robert; although they love each other, they agree that they can never marry. Kitty, having discovered a decent man, will not return to an indecent one, and throws herself off the cliff. The novel, which is talkative, claustrophobic, and much concerned with the legacy of the past, rather resembles the plays of Henrik Ibsen (1828–1906).

KLICKMANN, Flora (d. 1958) married (1913) E. HENDERSON-SMITH (d. 1937). After beginning work on the *Windsor Magazine* (which ran

1895–1939) she became editor of the *Girl's Own Paper* from 1908 to 1930 (from 1928 the *Woman's Magazine and Girl's Own Paper*). In that capacity she was technically and perhaps actually editor of a large quantity of books of advice and instruction on subjects including needlework, cookery, etiquette, and the language of flowers, for instance *Artistic Crochet* (1914) and *The Lure of the Pen: A Book for Would-Be Authors* (1919). Constance *Smedley, a contributor, observes in her memoirs that she rescued the paper 'from Victorianism and brought [it] into line with the best traditions of modern journalism'. Smedley says that Klickmann gave organ recitals at the Albert Hall. She also published fiction for both children and adults until 1932, and non-fiction about her house, The Flower Patch, near Tintern in Wales. In *The Ambitions of Jenny Ingram: A True Story of Modern London Life* (1907) a girl comes to London from Wales to become a novelist. Rejection after rejection leads to her being discovered starving by her childhood sweetheart, who marries her. Published in the *Leisure Hour* Monthly Library at sixpence, it offers graphic detail about the miserable lives of single women trying to earn a living, no doubt drawing on first-hand experience though also influenced noticeably by George *Gissing's *New Grub Street* (1891).

L

Ladies Whose Bright Eyes: *A Romance*, Ford Madox *Hueffer, 1911, Constable. Mr Sorrell, publisher of travel books, returns to London from New York with Mrs Lee-Egerton, who has entrusted him with the Tamworth-Egerton crucifix, a family heirloom dating back to the fourteenth century (he has lent money to her son, Jack). A train crash sends him back in time to the fourteenth century, where he is the slave of dead Sir Stanley Egerton. Here, too, he finds the crucifix, which is the cross of St Joseph of Arimathea, made from the money of usurers driven out of the Temple by Christ, in his possession. Does it rightfully belong to the local convent, to Lady Blanche, cousin of the Knight of Egerton of Tamworth, or to Lady Dionissia, his wife? Lady Blanche tries to seduce Sorrell, but he has fallen in love with Dionissia. Sorrell defends the latter's castle against Hugh of Fitz-Greville, and is knighted. Dionissia defeats Blanche in a joust, and then Blanche's husband. The Knight of Egerton kills Sorrell, and is in turn killed by Dionissia. Sorrell wakes up in hospital. Research reveals that Dionissia had a child by an unknown father, and that the child is the ancestor of Jack Lee-Egerton. Sorrell returns to the scene of the accident, and of his previous incarnation, where he finds Dionissia, who has come forward in time to meet him. Hueffer's attempt to divorce Elsie *Martindale and marry Violet *Hunt lies behind the novel's time-travelling.

Lady and Her Husband, A, Amber *Reeves, 1914, William Heinemann. The lady is Mary Heyham, and her husband, James, owns a company, Imperial Refreshments Limited, which runs a chain of extremely successful teashops. When her daughter, Rosemary, announces that she is going to be married, Mary feels at a loose end. Rosemary, a socialist, manages to interest her mother in the working conditions of waitresses in the Imperial teashops, and, with the help of a freelance secretary, Miss Percival, she launches an inquiry. The energetic and well-informed Miss Percival opens her eyes not only to poverty and squalor but also to the subordination of women. She determines to leave home in order to campaign more effectively on behalf of working women. 'She was not a fine lady, she did not care for a fine lady's life. She was an ordinary middle-class woman, who preferred doing practical work to being kept in the house to be beautiful and mysterious and tender and all the rest of it to any man with half an hour to spare.' But she misses her husband, and returns to him at the end, once he has agreed that she may continue her campaign for improved working conditions. The book ends on an ambiguous note. Mary has triumphed, has transformed herself. But James has decided to exploit her achievements by running for Parliament on his (newly acquired) reputation as a model employer. It has been suggested that *A Lady and Her Husband* had some influence on H. G. *Wells's *The *Wife of Sir Isaac Harman* (1914), which also features a magnate and his investigative wife.

Lady Molly of Scotland Yard, Baroness *Orczy, 1910, Cassell. Lady Molly combines aspects of Arthur Conan *Doyle's Sherlock Holmes and Orczy's most famous creation, the Scarlet Pimpernel. Like Holmes, she has a faithful companion who records her achievements and is consistently outpaced by her speed of thought (Orczy insists rather more emphatically than Doyle upon social hierarchy, upgrading the detective to aristocratic status and downgrading the amanuensis, Mary Granard, to an ex-maid). Like the Pimpernel, she has many 'smart friends' who do not realize she is a detective, and switches from gaiety to silent self-possession as soon as a serious matter engages her attention. The book includes twelve separate cases, with *illustrations by Cyrus Cuneo (d. 1916). In the last story, Lady Molly is reunited with her adored and adoring husband, who has been imprisoned for a crime he did not commit, and thereafter severs her connection with the police.

Entirely orthodox in its social and sexual attitudes, the stories do at least allow Lady Molly to score off her male colleagues, and Mary Granard to love her intelligent friend from a respectful distance.

Lady of the Barge, The, W. W. *Jacobs, 1902, George Bell. Mostly comic or comic-sensational tales of artisanal or petit bourgeois life, some featuring Jacobs's stock-in-trade bargees and old salts. Interestingly, the two *crime stories, 'The Well' and 'In the Library', have, as though the genre demanded it, discordantly upper-class settings and protagonists: in both cases, male couples, one of whom tries to murder the other. But the best story in the collection is a much-anthologized *horror story, 'The Monkey's Paw'. The White family (ageing father and mother, and a teenage son, Herbert) occupy Laburnum Villa, in the London suburbs. An old acquaintance of Mr White's, Sergeant-Major Morris, comes out for the evening. One product of his twenty-one years in India is a monkey's paw with a spell on it which will allow three separate men to have three separate wishes fulfilled. Morris reluctantly hands the paw over to Mr White, whose first wish, facetiously undertaken, is for £200 to clear the mortgage on Laburnum Villa. Next day, news comes that Herbert has been crushed to death in some machinery, and that his firm has offered £200 in compensation. Desperate to see her son, Mrs White prevails on her husband to wish him alive. In the middle of the night, there is a thunderous pounding at the door. Mrs White rushes to admit Herbert. But Mr White, knowing that Herbert was hideously disfigured in death, has his third and final wish: *not* to see his son alive again.

Lady on the Drawingroom Floor, The, M. E. *Coleridge, 1906, Edward Arnold. The novel is set in a *suburban lodging-house. Lucilla, a middle-aged woman with a fearsome collection of pets, lives on the floor above Oliver, a shy, bookish, lame, middle-aged solicitor, consoling him by her melodic renditions of Chopin. Lucilla's 19-year-old niece, Kitty, moves in with her for a while, then marries and emigrates to Australia: her passage has reminded Lucilla and Oliver of their lost youth. The opening pages of the novel are distinctly arch, but the interest deepens as Oliver, the narrator, gradually reveals more of himself. His life has taken its shape from emotions arrested brutally twenty years before: hero-worship of Gordon of Khartoum, and of an unnamed soldier friend who, like Gordon, died in Africa in the service of the Empire; love for a young woman whom he renounced when his father went bankrupt and then, the morning after Gordon's death in Khartoum, committed suicide. The way in which the narrator's personality seeps almost unannounced into the narrative gives it a modern feel. The conclusion, however, reverts to melodrama. Lucilla turns out to be the love of Oliver's life, whose letter swearing eternal love he had mislaid. Once he has fallen in love with her all over again, in her new identity as the lady on the drawing-room floor, she can reveal herself.

Lady Rose's Daughter, Mrs Humphry *Ward, 1903, Smith, Elder. After the success in America of her previous novel, *Eleanor* (1900), Mrs Ward moved fast to secure increased advances from both her British and her American publisher (£5,000 from Smith, Elder; £2,400 from Harper's, plus £2,400 for the American serialization). The new novel, begun (in July 1901) as 'A Woman of Title', became (in October) 'Lady Henry's Companion', before finally emerging as *Lady Rose's Daughter*: something of a departure, in fact, since her previous novels had all had as their title the hero's or heroine's unadorned name. Reginald Smith read the manuscript in a restaurant in Boulogne in January 1903 and was moved to tears. 'When the hardened publisher is touched,' he coaxed, 'surely the far larger public will respond.' And they did: 20,000 copies in Britain within a month of publication, 113,000 in America before the end of the year. The novel is set in a rather hazy Victorian England, 'many years ago'. Powerful, cranky Lady Henry Seathwaite runs a Wednesday afternoon salon in London. Almost blind, she has entrusted the management of it to a young companion, Julie Le Breton, whose origins are mysterious: she is in fact the illegitimate daughter of Lady Rose Delaney, who deserted her military husband for an artist. Trouble erupts when Julie dares to hold a 'Wednesday' against Lady Henry's express wishes. The old lady rises from her sickbed and bursts in upon the amazed company. The second half of the novel concerns the gradual disclosure of Julie's birth and its effect on her relations with her two suitors: the adventurer Captain Warkworth and Jacob Delafield, heir to the dukedom of Chudleigh and disciple of Tolstoy. Warkworth dies nobly in Africa and Julie accepts Delafield's proposal, without great enthusiasm. She is reconciled with an agreeably unregenerate Lady Henry. The plot is derived from French history. In eighteenth-century Paris the hostess Madame du Deffand (1697–1780) introduced Julie de Lespinasse (1732–1776) into society under a contract of silence as to her origins (she was the illegitimate daughter of du Deffand's brother and his mother-in-law). Julie fell out with her patroness, then eclipsed her, but eventually committed suicide. Mrs Ward later regretted her imposition of a happy ending. The novel expresses her belief that women should exercise political power indirectly, through the salon rather than the vote, and introduces a preoccupation with the ambitions and frustrations of powerful matriarchs. Her biographer points out that in the autumn of 1903 she took upon herself full responsibility for the future career of her 27-year-old son, hitherto a dismal failure.

Lair of the Giant Worm, The, Bram *Stoker, 1911, William Rider. An occult tale featuring a half-mad mesmerist, a devilish black man, a dove-like girl, and a lady who is being dunned for debt and is really a gigantic, ageless serpent. As in the hugely successful *Dracula* (1897), Stoker assembles a group of ordinary people and confronts them with the extraordinary. This time, the hero, Adam Salton, is not a solicitor, like Jonathan Harker, but a young Australian pioneer summoned home by his great-uncle, a wealthy landowner whose estate lies in the west of England, in the ancient kingdom of Mercia; he immediately demonstrates his practical turn of mind by offering to repair a coach. As in *Dracula*, there are also two young women, Mimi and Lilla Watford, and a wise old bird, Sir Nathaniel de Salis. One of the villains, Edgar Caswall, a 'cold, selfish, dominant' man, has just returned from Africa to the family seat at Castle Regis, bringing with him a servant, Oolanga, an 'unsoftened savage' whose face reveals 'all the hideous possibilities of a lost, devil-ridden child of the forest and the swamp—the lowest and most loathsome of all created things which were in some form ostensibly human'. Next to Caswall's estate lies that of Lady Arabella March, a woman notable for sinuous white hands, a fine figure, a voice 'so soft that the dominant note was of sibilation', and a pair of large green spectacles. Lady Arabella is badly in debt, and consequently becomes very attentive to Caswall, who, however, has begun to exercise his hypnotic powers on the beautiful Lilla Watford. Indeed, his psychic dominance, intensified by the influence of Lady Arabella, proves too strong for Lilla, and she dies. Lady Arabella, meanwhile, has been revealed as a manifestation of the dragon which inhabits a deep pit in the centre of her estate (a pit which has already swallowed the inquisitive Oolanga, who imagines himself to be her proper mate). Adam Salton manages to pack the pit with dynamite, and it blows up during a thunderstorm, spreading fragments of 'rent and torn flesh and fat' far and wide, and taking with it the nearby Castle Regis.

Lake, The, George *Moore, 1905, William Heinemann. Originally planned as a companion story to those in *The *Untilled Field* (1903), *The Lake* grew in length until it became a separate work. At the beginning of the novel, Father Oliver Gogarty walks beside Lough Carra, neglecting both his studies and his parishioners. As a young man Gogarty had rejected marriage, not because he disliked women, but because he believed marriage would entail monotony, stasis. The priesthood, by contrast, had seemed to offer, in the aspirations of 'saints who by renouncement of animal life had contrived to steal up to the last bounds, where they could see the eternal life that lies beyond the grave', an opportunity for adventure. In the seminary at Maynooth, he had sought glimpses of the eternal life through rigid diets and scourging. As he grows older, and undertakes the duties of a working priest, he comes to see such renunciations in a different light. However, he still reacts with severity when he finds that Rose Leicester, the local schoolteacher, is pregnant, and drives her out of the parish. Remorse for this act occupies the first part of the novel. Gogarty is both relieved and chastened when a London priest writes to him, informing him that Rose is alive and well, and reproving him for his harshness. The rest of the novel intersperses Gogarty's meditative rambles around the lake with a prolonged exchange of letters between him and Rose. He thinks he is falling in love with her, but realizes that he has instead begun to follow 'an idea, an abstraction, an opinion; he was separating himself, and for ever, from his native land and his past life, and his quest was, alas! not her, but—He was following what? Life?'

In general, the novel was well received. Reviewers much preferred its lyrical descriptions of the Irish landscape to the naturalism of Moore's earlier books. James *Joyce made fun of the conclusion, which describes Gogarty's faun-like buttocks glistening in the moonlight as he prepares to bathe one last time in the lake. Indeed, Gogarty is a comic character; though it is hard to be sure that Moore knew this. It has been suggested that Gerald *O'Donovan was the model for Gogarty.

LANCASTER, G. B., *pseud.*: Edith Joan LYTTLETON (1874–1945). Born in Tasmania to a well-off, upper-middle-class family, and brought up in Canterbury, New Zealand, from 1878, she reacted against the restricted reading of her childhood by revelling in adventure stories by men (including *Kipling) on *Empire themes and writing in that male-dominated genre. Her early work, for instance *A Spur to Smite* (1905) and *The Tracks We Tread* (1907), dealt with the isolation of colonists on sheep stations in the South Island. She shared Kipling's interest in the codes and rituals which shore up the identity of men under psychological pressure in an alien environment. Other Edwardian fiction includes the Australian story *Jim of the Ranges* (1910); *The Honourable Peggy* (1911), a fictionalized guidebook to Britain, in the mode of A. N. and C. N. *Williamson, which has a Canadian hero; *The Altar Stairs* (1908), set in the south Pacific; and *The Law-Bringers* (1913), whose heroes are Mounties, struggling with romantic and ethical problems against a backdrop of the Canadian wilderness. Later, in *Pageant* (1933), *Promenade* (1938), and *Grand Parade* (1943), Lyttleton attempted historical *family sagas charting the colonial experience in Tasmania, New Zealand, and Canada. In 1909 she left New Zealand, and travelled widely in England, Canada, Cuba, and Australia; unusually for a New Zealand writer, she contrived to have her books published in the US. She died in England.

LANE, Mrs John: Annie Philippine EICHBERG (1853–1927) married, first, Tyler Batcheller KING, and, secondly (1898), John LANE (1854–1925). The American wife of the important *publisher, she translated from the German and was the author of *Kitwyk* (1903), a series of arch comic sketches set in a provincial Dutch village, and *Talk of the Town* (1911). *According to Maria* (1910) is a social satire about a worldly middle-aged woman; it was followed by the sequels *Maria Again* (1915), and *War: Phases According to Maria* (1917).

LANG, Andrew (1844–1912) married (1875) Leonora Blanche ALLEYNE. Born at Selkirk, where his father was sheriff-clerk, he was educated at Selkirk Grammar School, Edinburgh Academy, St Andrews University, and Balliol College, Oxford. He became a fellow of Merton College in 1868, but left Oxford on his marriage. Thereafter he became an immensely prolific journalist and man of letters, legendary for his ability to turn out copy, verse and prose, fiction and non-fiction, in any place or situation, regardless of interruption. He wrote leaders in the *Daily News* which Richard *Le Gallienne described as 'fairy tales written by an erudite Puck'; he collected folklore and wrote fairy tales, translated the *Odyssey* and the poems of Theocritus, and contributed largely to the ninth edition of the *Encyclopaedia Britannica*. The contents of his famous series of collections of traditional fairy-tales, beginning with *The Blue Fairy Book* (1889), were often translated and edited by his wife, who was a considerable linguist. He was a friend of R. L. Stevenson (1850–1894) and consistently defended romance in fiction rather than realism. He published, for instance, a notoriously unfavourable review of *Tess of the D'Urbervilles* in the *New Review* (Feb. 1892) and cited R. L. Stevenson (1850–94) as having agreed with him: 'he said that he would die by my side, in the last ditch, proclaiming it the worst fiction in the world.' Lang also attacked George *Moore and Henry *James. He was a friend and admirer of Rider *Haggard, of whom he published a parody, *He* (1887). Not only as a reviewer, but as adviser to the publisher Longmans, he had great influence on English fiction; Conan *Doyle and the young Stanley J. *Weyman were published by Longman and supported by Lang. Lang's grandfather had been a friend of Walter Scott (1771–1832), and Lang produced a lavish annotated edition of the Waverley novels as well as promoting *historical romance whenever possible. The works of original fiction which he himself produced, which make up a tiny proportion of his vast bibliography, are mostly in this vein. Stevenson and he once planned a detective story called *Where Is Rose?* which was never written. *A Monk of Fife* (1896) is an historical novel about Joan of Arc. He collaborated with A. E. W. *Mason on

Parson Kelly (1900), about the Bishop's Plot of 1722, which drew on his lifelong interest in Jacobitism. His last novel was *The Disentanglers* (1902), a humorous fantasy about escape from marriage. The title-story of *The Valet's Tragedy, and Other Studies in Secret History* (1903) is a solution to the problem of the Man in the Iron Mask; *Historical Mysteries* (1904) is a similar collection. Days before his death he published *A History of English Literature From Beowulf to Swinburne* (1912), on which Henry James commented: 'The extraordinary inexpensiveness and childishness and impertinence of this gave to my sense the measure of a whole side of Lang... His extraordinary *voulu* Scotch provincialism crowns it and rounds it off; really making one at moments ask with what kind of an innermost intelligence such inanities and follies were compatible.' Lang was a founder and first President of the Psychical Research Society (1911).

LANGBRIDGE, Frederick (1849–1922) married (1878) Jane WILSON. Born in Birmingham, he was educated at King Edward VI's School, Birmingham, St Alban Hall, and Merton College, Oxford. He was ordained (1876) to the curacy of St George's, Kendal; three years later he went to Ireland and worked in Derry and Limerick. From 1882 he was Rector of St John's, Limerick. He was made a canon of St Munchins's in Limerick cathedral in 1906. He published some twelve volumes of verse, several plays, books for boys and children, and several novels. Both *The Calling of the Weir* (1902) and *Mack the Miser* (1907) are mildly humorous, sentimental, and improving tales of Protestant middle-class life in County Limerick. Other works include *Love Has No Pity* (1901) and *The Madcaps: A Story for Girls* (1903). He also published two comic novels in 1889 under the pseudonym 'Alfred Fitzmaurice King'. Rosamond *Langbridge was his daughter.

LANGBRIDGE, Rosamond [Grant] (1880–1964) married J. S. *FLETCHER. Born in Donegal, daughter of the Revd Frederick *Langbridge, she was brought up and educated privately in Limerick. Langbridge contributed fiction and articles to the *Manchester Guardian*. She specialized in *marriage problem novels of a mildly racy kind. *The Flame and the Flood* (1903), which appeared in the Fisher Unwin 'First Novel Library', concerns 'amorous passages' between a vulgar professional pianist who is false to his wife and a hysterical heroine who is false to a blind husband. In *The Stars Beyond* (1907) Verity Ambershine, for whom 'one's husband represents a passing mood, one's children fleeting emotions', leaves her entirely admirable husband shortly before the birth of the their first child, and eventually ends up in the same London lodging-house where he now lives with his new wife. *The Ambush of Young Days* (1906) is also set in a lodging-house, this time one occupied by a cross-section of young independent women. *Imperial Richenda: A Fantastic Comedy* (1908) is set in an Irish hotel where the heroine takes a job as a waitress. Langbridge published in all eight volumes of fiction between 1903 and 1929, a volume of verse (1902), and *Charlotte Brontë: A Psychological Study* (1929).

LANGTRY, Lillie: Emilie Charlotte LE BRETON (1853–1929) married first, (1874), Edward LANGTRY (d. 1897) and, secondly (1899), Hugo Gerald DE BATHE (1871–1940), who succeeded (1907) as 5th Baronet. Born in Jersey, daughter of a Church of England clergyman, she became after her first marriage a famous beauty and, in the 1870s, mistress of the future King Edward VII. After her husband's bankruptcy, the breakdown of her marriage, and the birth of an illegitimate daughter, she went on the stage in 1881, later touring America with some success. She published one novel, *All at Sea* (1909), a comedy set on board ship, in which an ultimately devoted couple, Lord and Lady Vernham, cross the Atlantic on the same liner, but as single people occupying separate cabins; and some unreliable memoirs (1925).

Last Hope, The, Henry Seton *Merriman, 1904, Smith, Elder. The story is set in France during the period between the establishment of the Second Republic in 1848 and Louis Bonaparte's *coup d'état* in December 1851. The 'last hope' in question is both the (supposed) son of the Dauphin, who had himself been spirited away from the Terror in 1794 and deposited in the Suffolk village of Carlingford, and the name of the merchantman on which (ignorant of his royal inheritance) he serves under the name of Loo Barebone. Two Royalists, the doddery Marquis de Gemosac and the mildly sinister Dormer Colville, track Barebone down and persuade him to leave Carlingford, and the appealing Miriam Liston, to pursue his claim in France. Colville manages to conceal from his fellow-

Royalists the strong possibility that Barebone may in fact be the illegitimate son of the Comte d'Artois, afterwards Charles X: he has royal blood, in short, but possibly not of the best vintage. There is thus some tension between the person Barebone knows himself to be and the person his adherents believe him to be (and by their belief make him). He tells the truth to the Marquis de Gemosac's daughter, Juliette, with whom he has been linked; she reminds him of another truth, that his professions of love are empty. Meanwhile John Turner, an English banker in the service of the French Republic, gets wind of the conspiracy and disrupts it by kidnapping Barebone and then trying to bribe him, and by sequestering the bulk of the conspirators' funds. Just as it seems that the masquerade may prevail, against all odds, Bonaparte's seizure of power puts an end to it, thus freeing Barebone to return to England and to Miriam.

LAW, John, *pseud.*: Margaret Elise HARKNESS (1854–?1923). One of five children of a Church of England clergyman, the Revd Robert Harkness, Rector of St Giles, Wimborne, she went to school at Stirling House, Bournemouth, with Beatrice Webb (1858–1953), who was her second cousin. She trained from 1877 as a nurse at Westminster Hospital, worked as a dispenser at Guy's Hospital, and then took up social work in the East End, earning her living by preparing studies of ancient Egyptian and Assyrian life in the British Museum. Webb wrote in her diary in 1883: 'It's extraordinary the improvement in Margaret Harkness since she has given herself up to work. When I first remember her at St Giles she was an hysterical egotistical girl with wretched health and still worse spirits. Her clerical and conventional parents tried to repress her extraordinary activity of mind, causing a state of morbid sensibility and fermentation which gave an almost permanent twist to her nature. Now that she has broken loose from all ties, supporting herself by literary piecework... she is blossoming out...' In her social work she met Friedrich Engels (1820–95), who admired her first novel *A City Girl: A Realistic Story* (1887), and also made friends with Eleanor Marx (1855–98) and Olive Schreiner (1855–1920). *Out of Work* (1888) is a tragedy about a young carpenter who comes to London to find work and dies of starvation, exposure, and heartbreak; it hints at the danger of revolution. The bitter documentary realism is enlivened with satire at the expense of religious hypocrisy, especially Methodism. In 1889 she seems to have been involved with the dock strike (though Webb's diary implies that she may have exaggerated her own importance); certainly she was a friend of trade union leaders. But in October 1890 she wrote an article in the *Pall Mall Gazette* denouncing socialism and proclaiming her enthusiasm for the Salvation Army, and shortly afterwards left England for Australia and India. She must have returned to Europe before 1917 when she was nursing in France; although her death date is usually given as 1921, the Salvation Army think she died in Florence in 1923. **George Eastmont, Wanderer* (1905) is dedicated to the memory of Cardinal Manning, 'with whom the author was associated during the Great Dock Strike of 1889'. Some works published by 'John Law' in India are sometimes (but not in the *British Library Catalogue*) attributed to her; they include *The Horoscope* (1915), a novel about the life and spiritual aspirations of an upper-class Sinhalese family in Ceylon under colonial rule, and *Modern Hyderabad* (1914), a hack guidebook. The pseudonym probably derives from her great-grandfather, G. H. Law (1761–1845), Bishop of Bath and Wells and brother of Lord Ellenborough, Lord Chief Justice, (1750–1818), or from John Law of Lauriston (1671–1729), French finance minister and fiscal reformer, a distant relation to whom she dedicated *Out of Work*.

LAWRENCE, C[harles] E[dward] (1870–1940) married ——. 'To call me C. E. Lawrence is—well!—' wrote the young D. H. *Lawrence to Walter *de la Mare (11 Apr. 1912). His namesake was born in Thurston, Yorkshire, the son of a schoolmaster and organist, brought up in Dover and educated privately. He went to work at 16, but studied meanwhile at the City of London College, of which he later became a governor. He worked as a publisher's reader for John Murray from 1897, and reviewed for the *Daily Chronicle*. He was co-editor of the *Quarterly Review* from 1922. His first two novels were *Pilgrimage* (1907), a medieval tale about Luke, a swineherd's son, who regards religion as a monkish tyranny and the chivalric code as a mask for brutal feudalism; and *Much Ado About Something* (1909), in which the fairies descend on London, putting golden thoughts into the heads of rich and poor alike.

The Arnold Lip: A Sort of Comedy (1913) is an arch domestic comedy about a self-satisfied *suburban family. He also wrote two plays.

LAWRENCE, D[avid] H[erbert] (1885–1930) married (1914) Emma Maria Frieda Johanna WEEKLEY née von RICHTOFEN (1879–1956). The son of a coalminer and a former schoolmistress, the sickly youngest of four children, he was born at Eastwood, near Nottingham, and educated at Nottingham High School (having won a scholarship), then (after a brief period as a clerk) at the British School, Eastwood (where he was a pupil teacher), and University College, Nottingham. At the age of 20 he gained a teacher's certificate from the last institution, and went to teach at Davidson Road School, Croydon. He remained a teacher from October 1908 until 1912. There he read avidly: 'I have read much modern work since I came here, Joseph *Conrad, and Björnsterne Björnsterne, *Wells, Tolstoi [1828–1910]. I love modern work,' he wrote in March 1909. Jessie Chambers (1887–1944), a fellow pupil-teacher to whom Lawrence was unofficially engaged until November 1910, sent some of his poems to Ford Madox *Hueffer of the **English Review* in 1909. Hueffer introduced him to literary circles. 'Last Sunday I went up to lunch with Ford Madox Hueffer,' he wrote to another friend in November 1909, 'and with Violet *Hunt ... a fairly well-known novelist. They were both delightful. Hueffer took me to tea at Ernest *Rhys' ... He is very nice indeed, and so is his wife, Grace *Rhys. After tea we went on to call on H. G. Wells ... He is a funny little chap ... [O]n Tuesday ... at the Reform Club ... Elizabeth *Martindale ... and Mary *Cholmondeley were there—and Ezra Pound ... He is jolly nice.' Although his subsequent career was far from easy, it is striking how quickly he was acknowledged as a major writer by many authorities, including the influential Edward Garnett (1868–1937). Walter *de la Mare and Gilbert *Cannan were close friends of his. The death of his mother in December 1910 cut his most important tie to Nottingham, and the success of *The *White Peacock* (1911) secured his position as a writer: he soon afterwards resigned his teaching job. It was followed by *The *Trespasser* (1912), which was also warmly reviewed. **Sons and Lovers* (1913) dealt with some of the emotional material from his childhood and youth. In May 1912 he went abroad for the first time, eloping, after six weeks' acquaintance, with the wife of the professor of French at University College, Nottingham. They travelled in Germany, Austria, and Italy, before returning to England, where they married, in summer 1914. *The *Prussian Officer* (1914) was the first of several collections of his short stories. In the early part of the First World War he lived in London, and on account of his poor health was twice rejected for war service. The prosecution of *The Rainbow* (1915) for obscenity was a severe blow to him both morally and financially; and the Lawrences retreated to remote west Cornwall, where her German birth and his eccentricity led to their being regarded with suspicion. Their close friends 'Katherine *Mansfield' and J. M. Murry (1889–1957) briefly settled with them in 1915. There he worked on *Women in Love* (New York, 1920) until in October 1917 they were ordered not to settle in any restricted area. They moved house several times before leaving England for good in 1919, travelling first to Italy, where *Aaron's Rod* (1922) is partly set. Early in 1922 he left Italy for Ceylon, Australia, and California. He lived at Taos, New Mexico, and in Mexico (which inspired *The Plumed Serpent*, 1926), and travelled in the United States and back again to Europe in 1924 before malaria forced him to return to Europe in 1925, where he lived mostly in Italy and the south of France. These wanderings resulted in several powerful travel books, including *Etruscan Places* (1932). His last novel, *Lady Chatterley's Lover* (Florence, 1928), failed for many years to find an English publisher willing to risk prosecution for obscenity. He died at Vence, in the south of France. The innovative quality of his fiction, especially in its treatment of sexuality, was early recognized; the enthusiastic support of F. R. Leavis (1895–1978), whose first study was published in the year of Lawrence's death, was especially influential in establishing him among the major twentieth-century novelists.

LAWSON, Henry [Hertzberg] (1867–1922) married (1896) Bertha Marie Louise BREDT (1876–1957). Born in a tent on a gold field at Grenfell, New South Wales, of an Australian mother and a Norwegian father called Larsen, the eldest child of an unhappy marriage, he took responsibility at an early age and felt isolated from other children. From the age of 9 he attended Eurunderee Public School, but in that year he began to be affected by the deafness which, worsening, compounded his psychological alienation. After three years at school he began work as a builder; in 1883 he moved to Sydney, where he was apprenticed to a coach-painter and attended night-school. From the late 1880s he published verse and prose of a republican flavour, some in a paper, the *Republican*, run by his mother. He also wrote short stories, including 'The Drover's Wife'. In 1892 he began a journey inland into drought-stricken western New South Wales which furnished material for many more stories, published in such collections as *While the Billy Boils* (1896). His wife came, as he did, from a family of socialists and political agitators. But despite increasing fame Lawson's periods of employment were still episodic and he was apt to relapse into alcoholism. In 1897 the Lawsons moved briefly to New Zealand, where he worked as a teacher of Maoris, but the experiment was unsuccessful and he returned to Sydney and his old ways. He entered an inebriates' home in November 1898, which effected a temporary cure. In April 1900 he set off for England with his wife and two children, where he was enthusiastically supported by Edward Garnett (1868–1937), and published *Joe Wilson and His Mates* (1901), a series of sketches narrated by a bushman, describing his courtship and married life. The autobiographical element in the characterization of the weak, rather mournful Wilson has often been commented on. *Children of the Bush* (1902), published in Australia as *Send Round the Hat*, was also the product of his English trip. However, the country did not suit him; Bertha Lawson became mentally ill and they returned to Sydney in 1902. He attempted suicide and in the following year she obtained a judicial separation. Although he continued to publish both verse and prose, the quality of his work declined and from thenceforward the story of his life becomes a pathetic chronicle of madness and alcoholism, punctuated by periods in prison for failing to pay maintenance to his children.

LEAF, A., *pseud.*: see Lord Ernest *Hamilton.

LE BRETON, John, *pseud.*: M. Harte POTTS and Thomas Murray FORD (b. 1854). According to the *British Library Catalogue*, these writers jointly published eight novels 1897–1912 and wrote plays of which the most successful was a comic sketch about a charwoman called *A Sister to Assist'Er* (1912). Ford also published nineteen novels as 'Thomas Le Breton' from 1904, including racing novels and a comic series about a charwoman called Mrs May, and, under his own name, more racing novels, children's fiction, and *Memoirs of a Poor Devil* (1926). In the latter he states that he was born in Dalston, eldest of nine children of an agent for Continental wine growers, and was educated at private schools and a grammar school before joining his uncle's shipbroking business at 16, later working as a stevedore supervising the loading of cargo in the docks, an experience he subsequently drew on in fiction. He became a journalist when he lost his job after a takeover, working on sporting news and managing *Golden Gates*, a periodical owned by 'John Strange *Winter' and a vehicle for her serials. His first serious novel *Miss Tudor* (1897), written with his wife, exposed the use of the casting-couch by music hall agents; he published it at his own expense, made a profit, and entered into correspondence with W. E. Gladstone (1809–1898). *The Church and Thisbe Gray* (1908) is about the experiences of a woman artist who takes a cottage in rural Cornwall and finds a servant-girl persecuted by the vicar for wanting to marry her deceased sister's husband. Ford also wrote stories for *Pearson's Magazine*. There is much detail about the life of a journalist and art editor of the period, and opinions on life in general: 'If ever we had a Dictator... and we need such an autocrat badly, I would choose King George first, Lord Rothermere next, and after them Mr. [Ramsay] Macdonald, and I am sure that... we should be infinitely better governed.' Like so many of his contemporaries, Ford published a book, *Arm and Prepare* (1907), warning of the danger from Germany (see *invasion scare stories). Potts is not mentioned in Ford's autobiography, and he implies that he was sole author of *A Sister to Assist'Er.* The only collaborator he does acknowledge is an unnamed wife; presumably she was Potts.

LEE, Revd Albert: Albert LEE (1852–1935), MVO, married, first, Emily Hanney WEBSTER (d. 1929) and, secondly, Minnie Anne THOMPSON. After education in Bristol and Westminster, and at Illinois University, Lee qualified as a Congregationalist minister, serving successively at Tockholes (1879–82), Gomersall (1882–93), and Windsor (1893–1906). He was the author of books for boys, *historical fiction, and maritime and military history from 1897 to 1925, including *Hunting an Anarchist: An Adventure With Bomb-Makers* (1910). *The Baronet in Corduroy* (1903) is set in early eighteenth-century London: a beautiful heiress marries a hopeless, drunken rake, thinks him dead, and marries again; Mrs Hodgson *Burnett's *A Lady of Quality* (1896) is an obvious influence. He lived in Windsor after retiring, preached in nearby villages, and worked as a Recorder in the Royal Archives at Windsor Castle until 1930. He died in a nursing-home there. He also wrote as 'Lindon Romaine'.

LEE, Vernon, *pseud.*: Violet PAGET (1856–1935). Born near Boulogne, she was the daughter of a lady of private means, who already had a child, Eugene *Lee-Hamilton, and her second husband, who had been Eugene's tutor and who, although he had at one time been an engineer, was unemployed and dependent on his wife. Paget spent her childhood travelling in Europe with her mother and half-brother; her tyrannical mother's hatred of society and anti-religious views cutting them off from ordinary upper-middle-class expatriate society. They lived in Germany, in Nice, and, from 1868, a good deal in Rome. After Eugene became an invalid in 1873 they lived in or near Florence, until 1889 they moved to the Villa Il Palmerino at Maiano, where Violet Paget lived until her death. Although she had a haphazard education from a series of German and Swiss governesses, she read widely from an early age and her first literary experiments gave her a reputation for brilliance and erudition extraordinary in one so young. She was much influenced by friendship with the mother of John Sargent (1856–1925), the painter. Paget did not visit England until 1881, when she went to stay with the family of her friend the poet Mary Robinson (1857–1944); she usually returned each year thereafter. Her *Studies of the Eighteenth Century in Italy* (1880) was acclaimed for its scholarship; Browning paid tribute to *Euphorion* (1884) in *Asolando* (1889). Much of her early non-fiction is art criticism or aesthetics; as early as *Belcaro* (1881) she attacked the influential opinion of John Ruskin, and proclaimed herself a formalist rather than a moralist. In the late 1880s she made friends with Clementina Anstruther-Thomson, with whom she collaborated on several books on the psychology and physiology of aesthetics, a subject which increasingly interested her. Like a number of Paget's other friendships with women, their association ended in disappointment for her. Her fiction, which she did not regard as her most important work, includes *Ottilie: An Eighteenth-Century Idyll* (1883); *Miss Brown: A Novel* (1884), which was a caricature of English aesthetic society dedicated to Henry *James; *Hauntings: Fantastic Stories* (1890); *Vanitas: Polite Stories* (1892), which contains, in the story 'Lady Tal', a caricature of Henry James; *Penelope Brandling: A Tale of the Welsh Coast in the Eighteenth Century* (1903), whose heroine discovers her husband's family are wreckers; *Pope Jacynth and Other Fantastic Tales* (1904), six stories set in different periods, and all but one in Italy, whose fantastic qualities reviewers associated less with Edgar Allan Poe (1809–49) than with the more sceptical and ironic Anatole France (1844–1924); and **Louis Norbert: A Two-Fold Romance* (1914), in which modern characters become embroiled in a late seventeenth-century intrigue. The last idea had a considerable currency in this period (see under *fantasy). The stories collected in *For Maurice: Five Unlikely Stories* (1927) had all been written by 1913. During the *Boer War, the Italo-Turkish war of 1911, and the First World War (which she spent in Britain) she openly expressed her pacifist views in such a way as to lose some friends and admirers. She was a keen but non-militant suffragist. There is a biography by Peter Gunn (1964).

LEE-HAMILTON, E[ugene] J[acob] (1845–1907) married (1898) Annie E. *HOLDSWORTH. Born in London but educated in France and Germany, Lee-Hamilton went to Oriel College, Oxford in 1864, where he won a scholarship but which he left without a degree. He was then a diplomat until 1873 when he became an invalid (he finally resigned from the diplomatic service in 1875). For twenty years he lived with his mother and half-sister 'Vernon *Lee', lying on his back but well enough to be the centre of a brilliant social circle in Florence and to compose verse, published in such collections as *Gods, Saints, & Men* (1880) and *Apollo and Marsyas* (1884). It was he who told Henry *James of Captain Silsbee's attempts to wheedle some of the papers of Lord Byron (1788–1824) out of 'Claire' Clairmont (1798–1879), and thus provided the germ of *The Aspern Papers* (1888). In 1896, after his mother's funeral, he announced he was leaving the Villa Il Palmerino, and travelled to England and then went to stay with Edith Wharton (1862–1937), an admirer of his verse, in America. He returned to England, where he married, and published a translation of the *Inferno of Dante* (1265–1321). He and his wife published a volume of verse together in 1899. His short married life was blighted by the death in infancy of his only daughter, commemorated in a volume of sonnets, *Mimma Bella: In Memory of a Little Life* (1908). By this date he was estranged from his half-sister. As well as six volumes of verse he published two novels. *The Lord of the Dark Red Star: Being the Story of the Supernatural Influences in the Life of an Italian Despot of the Thirteenth Century* (1903) is set, like *Sordello* (1840) by Robert Browning (1812–89), in the time of Ezelin da Romano ('to me the sight of pain is like strong wine') and is a study of total evil. In *The Romance of the Fountain* (1905) some Spaniards search for the elixir of youth in seventeenth-century South America, and die there.

LE GALLIENNE, Richard: Richard Thomas GALLIENNE (1866–1947), who changed his surname (1887) to LE GALLIENNE, married, first (1891), Mildred LEE (d. 1894), secondly (1897), Julie NØRREGARD (divorced 1901), and, thirdly (1911), Irma HINTON PERRY née ——. Born in Liverpool, the son of a brewery manager, he was educated at Liverpool College. He was then articled to a firm of chartered accountants, where he spent seven years. In 1888, finding the work distasteful and bad for his health (he had asthma) and encouraged by the success of his first volume of poems, he went to London and became a professional writer. From 1891, as 'Log-Roller', he was the literary critic of the *Star*, while G. B. Shaw (1856–1950) was its music critic as 'Corno di Bassetto'; Le Gallienne also became a reader for the Bodley Head and a contributor to the *Yellow Book*. Both his verse and his literary criticism caught the taste of the 1890s. Grant *Richards thought him excessively generous as a reviewer. Le Gallienne, like Conan *Doyle and several other writers of the time, lived at Hindhead in Surrey; after the breakup of his second marriage he went to live in America in 1901, later moving to France, where he died. His first novel was *The Quest of the Golden Girl: A Romance* (1896); *Young Lives* (1899) was an autobiographical novel which describes his blissful first marriage to a Liverpool waitress. *The Life Romantic* (1901) recounts the emotional adventures of Pagan Wasteneys, a rich young man who 'had taken to women as some men take to dominoes' after being disappointed in his love for a woman who wants to be alone, and eventually marries instead an emancipated bookbinder. *Painted Shadows* (1908) is a collection of smartly witty short stories, including 'The Youth of Lady Constantia', about a middle-aged woman who buys eternal youth and falls in love with a young man, and 'The Woman in Possession', about a sensible woman whose husband is a poet who flirts with other women. He wrote about the London literary world of the 1890s in *The Romantic '90s* (1925) and published studies of *Meredith and *Kipling.

LEGGE, A[rthur] E[dward] J[ohn] (1863–1934) married Lucy Isabel WALKER née HOGG (d. 1940). Son of an army officer who later became a Church of England clergyman, he is said to have suffered much at St Mark's School, Windsor, and Haileybury. He later became secretary to Viscount Hambleden (1868–1928). He served in the First World War in the Worcestershire Regiment and was wounded at Salonika in 1916. He was author of ten volumes of verse from 1895 and of four volumes of fiction 1898–1923. *The Ford* (1905) is about an aristocratic family's *rapprochement* with some vulgar neighbours. *Cavaliers* (1936) is a rather touching account of his personal philosophy, introduced by a short biographical sketch by his friend the painter Henry Tonks (1862–1937), which mentions Legge's regret that his poetry was not more widely read. After his death a correspondent wrote to the *Times* (31 May 1934) expressing the view that posterity would choose Legge's poem 'Pilgrim Jester' 'as representative of the best of the early twentieth century, when the drab and lame ugliness of what passes for poetry to-day is mercifully forgotten'. Margaret *Legge was his sister.

LEGGE, Margaret (1872–1957), sister of A. E. J. *Legge, daughter of the Hon. and Revd George Barrington Legge, was educated at home, by a governess, and at the Slade School of Fine Art, where she was a contemporary and friend of Gwen John (1876–1939). She envied her brothers their formal education. She published seven novels betweeen 1912 and 1929, which are similar to May *Sinclair's in their concern with the straitened lives of middle-class women. The *Daily Telegraph* said that 'all who are thinking of present-day Feminism' should read *A Semi-Detached Marriage* (1912), since the author was 'perfectly fair to both sides'. 'Here is a novel which may be classed among the problematical,' the *Daily Chronicle* advised, 'and which yet, strange to say, has nothing disagreeable in it.' A woman is torn between her husband and the women's movement, leaves him and falls in love with the letters she receives from 'A Dreamer' who turns out to be the husband after all. But Legge's second and third novels were darker in tone. *The Price of Stephen Bonynge* (1913) concerns the relationship between the visionary young painter of the title and a puritanical governess turned model, Louie Hopkins. After several misunderstandings and separations, he trains as a carpenter and furniture designer, pays off his debts, and asks her to marry him. She agrees, but dies suddenly, leaving him distraught. *The Rebellion of Esther* (1914) concerns the second of three sisters, children of a tyrannical father and diffident mother, who has some talent as a writer and is rescued from the family home by an aunt who runs a bohemian household in London and the Guild of Good Help. Esther meets artists and suffragettes, and becomes engaged briefly to a rising MP who turns out to have a 'history'. She finds an equally brief happiness with another man, but they decide not to marry because they both have dependants (Esther's two other sisters have married, leaving their mother at the mercy of their father's rages). Legge's later novels deal with psychic phenomena. She had independent means and travelled widely in Italy and Brazil.

LEIGHTON, Marie CONNOR: See Mrs Robert *Leighton.

LEIGHTON, Mrs Robert: Marie Flora Barbara CONNOR (1869–1941) married (1889) Robert *LEIGHTON. Born at Clifton, Gloucestershire, daughter of an extravagant army officer of Irish family, she was educated at Marquise, in the Pas-de-Calais, and at Tunbridge Wells. After a brief tour as an actress with Wilson Barrett (1846–1904), she published, aged 16, her first novel, *Beauty's Queen* (1884). She sent poems to *Young Folks*, met its editor, Robert Leighton, and eloped with him to Scotland. Her earlier books include *historical fiction and modern romance, but by the twentieth century she had settled down to churning out thrillers in large quantities. From 1891 she and her husband worked for Lord Northcliffe (1865–1922); he is depicted in her novel *A Napoleon of the Press* (1900). Her daughter, the engraver Clare Leighton (1899–1986), writes in her biography (1948): 'My mother and father were both writers. My mother wrote . . . melodramatic serials . . . and my father wrote boys' adventure stories. The entire household revolved around my mother's writing, for it was the large sums of money she earned that supported us. My father's work was not supposed to matter nearly as much, because he earned far less.' Leighton later quarrelled with Northcliffe, and the sale of her serials was hit by the outbreak of the First World War, after which she ceased to produce much fiction. Her son Roland (d. 1915) was engaged to Vera Brittain (1896–1970) who wrote about him in *Testament of Youth* (1933); Leighton wrote a memoir of him, *Boy of My Heart* (1917). She published more than sixty volumes of fiction, mostly potboiling *crime stories, some of which are distinguished by having female heroines, for instance *The Bride of Dutton Market* (1911), *Joan Mar, Detective* (1910), and *Lucile Dare, Detective* (1919). She wrote *Convict 413L* (1910), *Convict 100* (1920), and, with her husband, *Convict 99: A True Story of Penal Servitude* (1898), which was her greatest success, and which originally appeared serially for a year in *Answers*, the orange-coloured weekly she and Northcliffe founded. Grant *Richards, who published it in volume form, commented that, though it was 'extraordinarily successful' as a serial, and was 'used again and again, in one paper after another', it never 'attracted anything like as large a public in book-form'. *Convict 413L* is characteristically frantic. By page 30, Lady Honeywood has received a letter from her husband saying that he is going to kill her lover, Gartney, and that she should kill herself. Honeywood, meanwhile, has gone to the lovers' rendezvous, The Red Lodge, near Richmond, where Gartney, finding a revolver in the garden, shoots him dead, the murder being witnessed by two burglars hidden behind the summer-house. There are a further 289 pages. Leighton was a passionate admirer of the works of '*Ouida' and a suffragist. She sometimes published as 'Marie Connor Leighton'.

LEIGHTON, Robert (1858–1934) married (1889) Mrs Robert *Leighton. Born in Ayr, the son of Robert Leighton (1822–1869), poet and seed merchant, he was educated in Liverpool. Aged 14 he joined the *Porcupine* newspaper in Liverpool; he came to London in 1879 and was editor of *Young Folks*. He was editor of the Bristol *Observer* (1886–7) and first literary editor of the *Daily Mail* (1896). With his wife he also wrote serials for them, but most of his own fiction consists of adventure stories for boys set on prairie and pirate ship: it includes *Cap'n Nat's Treasure: A Tale of Old Liverpool* (1902). He also wrote boys' public-school stories, Westerns, and *historical romances like *In the Land of Ju-Ju: A Tale of Benin* (1903) and *Hurrah! For the Spanish Main: A Tale of Drake's Third Voyage to Darien* (1904). He was an authority on the breeding of dogs, especially Great Danes. He was deaf enough to be able to write in the room in which his wife dictated to her secretary. Brought up as a Unitarian, he was converted by her to Roman Catholicism after the First World War.

LEITH, Mrs Disney: Mary Charlotte Julia GORDON (d. 1926) married (1865) Robert William Disney LEITH (1819–1892). The daughter of a baronet, she married a general in the army who had lost an arm at the battle of Mooltan (1849). She published from 1864 translations of Icelandic, verse, and children's fiction, illustrating her books with her own drawings. When she was 70 years old she bathed in the Arctic sea from the shores of Iceland. She was a cousin of A. C. Swinburne (1837–1909), of whom she published a memoir (1917); her *The Children of the Chapel* (1864) incorporates a little play, *The Pilgrimage of Pleasure*, written by him. Her adult fiction includes *A Black Martinmas* (1912), about a Scots girl who falls in love with a widower with small children, and marries him just before his death, and its sequel, *Lachlan's Widow* (1913).

Leonora: *A Novel*, Arnold *Bennett, 1903, Chatto & Windus. The heroine is the beautiful, serene wife of John Stanway, a selfish, deceitful earthenware manufacturer. Stanway, who has been speculating wildly, is on the verge of bankruptcy. His last hope of solvency disappears when his wealthy uncle leaves a considerable fortune to someone else. He deteriorates rapidly, and commits suicide. Leonora, meanwhile, has fallen in love with Arthur Twemlow, son of Stanway's partner, and eventually marries him, despite her 'characteristic quality of supineness'. Bennett was virtually alone among contemporary writers in regarding supineness as a heroic quality. The best moment in an uneven book is Leonora's vigil at her husband's bedside. 'She saw that nothing is so subtly influential as constant uninterrupted familiarity, nothing so binding, and perhaps nothing so sacred. It was a trifle that they had not loved. They had lived.'

LEPPER, John Heron (b. 1878). Born in Belfast, he was educated in Scotland and at Trinity College, Dublin, and became a barrister in northern Ireland. After 1914 he lived in London. He was involved in Irish nationalist politics and wrote *historical novels, many set in Ireland. *Captain Harry: A Tale of the Parliamentary Wars* (1909) and *The Narrative of Frank Maxwell Concerning the Strange Events that Happened to him in the Summer of the Year of Our Lord, 1641, and the Important Persons with whom he had Dealings* (1907), both published in Dublin, are careful with their historical settings and fairly even-handed in their political messages. *A Tory in Arms* (1916) is set in 1715 and deals with the hardships of Catholics in the north of Ireland. *The North-East Corner* (1917) is set in early nineteenth-century Belfast. Lepper also published books on freemasonry and Rosicrucianism and translations from French and German.

LE QUEUX, William [Tufnell] (1864–1927). Born in Châteauroux, France, of a French father who was a draper's assistant, and an English mother, he was educated in London and near Genoa. He studied art in Paris but then became a journalist in London in the 1880s, editing *Gossip* and *Piccadilly*. He was foreign editor of the *Globe* (1891–3) and it was then that he gathered the material about diplomatic affairs which was the staple of his fiction. He became a full-time novelist in 1893. He travelled widely in North Africa, the Balkans, the Arctic, and the Sudan 1907–9, source of much material used in his fiction. He was a collector of medieval manuscripts and seals and a self-proclaimed expert on the secret service. His earliest novel was *Guilty Bonds* (1891) which was banned in Czarist Russia; there are more than 200 later novels, some published posthumously, as well as volumes of short stories and sensational books about contemporary history such as *German Atrocities: A Record of Shameless Deeds* (1914), *German Spies in England: An Exposure* (1915), and *Rasputin, the Rascal Monk* (1917). A sinister, anti-Semitic, and right-wing figure, he was associated, like W. P. *Drury, *Kipling, and other writers, with the rearmament movement led by the 1st Earl Roberts

(1832–1914); he wrote two of the best-known *invasion scare stories, *The Great War in England in 1897* (1894) and *The *Invasion of 1910 With a Full Account of the Siege of London* (1906). He was assisted in writing the latter by H. W. Wilson (1866–1940), a journalist specialising in naval topics. Le Queux's *œuvre* includes occult and *crime novels as well as the *spy thrillers in the development of which he is so important, such as *The Man from Downing Street: A Mystery* (1904), *Secrets of the Foreign Office: Describing the Doings of Duckworth Drew, of the Secret Service* (1903), and **Spies of the Kaiser* (1909). *Treasure of Israel* (1910) is about the discovery of a coded message in the Talmud detailing the whereabouts of the treasure of the Temple of Solomon; rival good and bad gangs race to the site, and there is a romance sub-plot involving a young journalist. He was a friend of George R. *Sims. Wolff's copy of *The Hunchback of Westminster* (1904) bore an inscription from Luisa Gemma Le Queux, possibly a daughter or wife, although the *Dictionary of National Biography: Missing Persons* (1993) states that he was unmarried. He died in Switzerland, where he had been living.

Letters from Queer Street: *Being Some of the Correspondence of the Late Mr John Mason* J. H. M. *Abbott, 1908, Adam & Charles Black. In this down-and-out-in-London story in the tradition of Jack London (1876–1916) and, later, George Orwell (1903–50), John Mason, an Australian and a gentleman, an ex-sailor who fought in the *Boer War, falls badly into debt, and is forced to walk the streets. He eventually dies of tuberculosis, immediately after he has miraculously been rescued from destitution by a Boer, Jan Potgeister. The novel, which takes the form of Mason's letters to a friend in Australia, is melodramatic, snobbish, and anti-Semitic, but includes a number of vivid low-life scenes of the kind that were to remain central to the genre: visits to a pawnshop and to the Cornwall Café, a pick-up joint; nights in jail and in a doss-house.

LETTS, Winifred M[abel] (1882–1972) married (1926) William Henry Foster VERSCHOYLE (1859–1943). Daughter of a Church of England clergyman, she was brought up in Manchester, with holidays near Dublin, and was educated at St Anne's, Abbotts Bromley, and Alexandra College, Dublin. She wrote plays which were performed at the Abbey Theatre, Dublin, verse, and fiction for children and adults. *Waste Castle* (1907), her first book, was a story for girls; the heroine of the children's book *Naughty Sophia* (1912) is a little archduchess who is hidden by faithful peasants during a revolution and thus purged of her arrogance. *Diana Dethroned* (1909) is set in the region of the River Ouse, in Huntingdonshire; Diana, alias Phoebe Lankester, is heir to Hernlea, and courted first by a headstrong genius, Robin Daynant, and then by a distant Australian cousin, Hugh Lankester. *Christina's Son* (1915) focuses on mother love. She also published some impressionistic memoirs (1933).

LEVERSON, Ada: Ada Esther BEDDINGTON (1862–1933) married (1881) Ernest David LEVERSON (*c.*1850–1922). Daughter of a prosperous wool merchant, she was brought up in London and educated by governesses. At 19 she married against his wish and was soon unhappy; her only son died as a baby, and when Ernest emigrated to Canada in the early twentieth century she did not accompany him. A smart London literary hostess in the 1890s and 1900s, she was at one time close to George *Moore. Her first stories were published in *Black and White* in 1892. She published parodies of Oscar Wilde (1854–1900), *Beerbohm, and *Kipling in *Punch* (1893), and stories in the *Yellow Book*. She also wrote a column in the *Referee* (1903–5) as well as novels of manners which deal wittily with unhappy marriages, love affairs, and social pressures. *The Twelfth Hour* (1907) is a mild, well-judged comedy of manners involving a group of (more or less idle) young things: Lady Chetwode, her brother, Savile, a handsome 16-year-old schoolboy, and her sister, Sylvia, who is in love with Frank Woodville, secretary to their father, Sir James Crofton. The action, such as it is, involves the engagement of Frank and Sylvia, and the petering-out of various minor flirtations. See also **Love's Shadow* (1908) and *The *Limit* (1911). Leverson contributed to the **English Review*. She was one of Oscar Wilde's most loyal friends; he stayed with her during his trial when no hotel would have him; he christened her 'the Sphinx'. She was a famous wit: 'I suppose you often go to *The Mikado*, Mr. Waley?' she said to the great Sinophile Arthur Waley (1889–1966). In later years she spent much time abroad in Italy, especially with the Sitwells, and figures as an aged Wilde bore in the biography of Reginald

*Turner. Leverson appears as a character in *The Apes of God* (1930) by Wyndham Lewis (1884–1957). There is a biography by her daughter Violet Wyndham (1963) and a study of her fiction by Charles Burkhart (1973). Her sister Violet (1876–1962) was married to Sydney Schiff (1868–1944), author of *Concessions* (1913), a novel published under his own name, and of other fiction from 1916 as 'Stephen Hudson'. He owned the periodical *Art and Letters*. The Schiffs both translated from French and they were close friends of Marcel Proust (1871–1922).

LEVETT-YEATS, S[idney Kilner Levett] married (1906) Mildred EAGLES. The son of an official in the Indian Civil Service, he worked in its Post Office department from 1878, and became Accountant-General for Post Office and Telegraphs in 1910. He wrote *historical romances in his leisure moments. He states in the preface to *The Honour of Savelli* (1895), a romance set in sixteenth-century Italy, that he had not read 'Mr. Stanley *Weyman's brilliant novel, "A Gentleman of France"' at the time the book was written, a disclaimer which indicates the tendency of his work. *The Lord Protector* (1902) is set during the period of the Commonwealth, shortly after the execution of Charles I, at Coombe Royal, house of Lady Dorothy Capel. *Orrain* (1904) is set in sixteenth-century France, in the court circle of Diane de Poitiers, mistress of Henri II. *The Chevalier D'Auriac* (1897) and *The Traitor's Way* (1901) are both set during the sixteenth-century French wars of religion. He published eight volumes of fiction 1893–1904, and was a member of the Savage Club.

LE VOLEUR, *pseud.*: see under Rosa Nouchette *Carey.

LEWIS, Caroline: see under Harold *Begbie.

LEYS, John K[irkwood] (1847–1909) married, first, Mary King MUNSIE, and, secondly, Helen HOLLIGAN. Born in Glasgow, son of a Lanarkshire clergyman, he was educated at Glasgow High School and Glasgow University. He was called to the Bar (1874) and practised as a barrister in Newcastle-upon-Tyne on the Northern Circuit. He contributed to the **Cornhill Magazine* and **Temple Bar*, and published some twenty volumes of fiction between 1875 and 1919, including *A Wolf in Sheep's Clothing* (1905), in which two sinister Italian murderers exert a stranglehold on a respectable English family, but are eventually worsted.

Life Everlasting, The: *A Reality of Romance*, 'Marie *Corelli', 1911, Methuen. One of Corelli's later, (even more) mystical novels which barely takes the trouble to be a novel at all. It is preceded by a thirty-three-page 'Author's Prologue' in which Corelli attacks the materialism of modern life, urges the reader to develop his or her 'psychic forces' (forces envisaged as a kind of spiritual radioactivity), and offers in passing a favourable review of her own career as a writer. The narrator, a 'psychist', is invited to join an atheistic American plutocrat called Morton Harland and his invalid daughter on a yachting cruise off the coast of Scotland. There they encounter an old friend of Harland's, Rafel Santoris, a psychic superman who sails the seas in a mysteriously self-propelling yacht. Santoris and the narrator, who have met before many times in previous lives, fall in love. She prepares herself for him by undergoing rites of spiritual initiation at a monastery on the Bay of Biscay. Harland and his daughter remain unconverted, and die or marry miserably.

Limit, The, Ada *Leverson, 1911, Grant Richards. Valentia Wyburn, a woman whose 'pagan and spiritual' beauty has raised her above mere loveliness, is the focus of rivalry between her husband, Romer, and Harry de Freyne, a charming, heartless painter. Romer has a genius for love, Harry for lovemaking. There is the usual Leverson quota of minor characters and petering-out flirtations. To distract attention from his affair with Valentia, Harry agrees to marry the unconventional but wealthy Alec Walmer. However, Romer overhears him promising Valentia that he does not really love Alec, and forces him to break his engagement; this will not only save Alec from a loveless marriage but keep Valentia happy. He insists that Valentia should not be told about his own role in the matter. Harry, thinking to humiliate Romer, tells Valentia exactly what has happened. She is repelled by his conduct and forced to recognize that a genius for love is worth more than a genius for lovemaking.

LINDSAY, Harry: Harry Lindsay HUDSON (d. 1926) married Sarah Elizabeth ROSSON. Born in Belfast, of Yorkshire parents, he spent his early life in Liverpool, where he became a schoolteacher.

He was the first editor of the *Methodist Weekly*; he wrote serial stories for the *Liverpool Weekly Courier*. His first novel was *Rhoda Roberts: A Welsh Mining Story* (1895); it was followed by *Methodist Idylls* (1897) and *The Story of Leah* (1902). He published in all thirteen volumes of fiction 1895–1904. Of *The Jacobite*, the *Morning Leader* commented, 'Mr Lindsay has caught the cheerful clink of sword and sabre, the pleasant click of the ready trigger, and the sound of the rushing of armed men. . . . This is the sort of story that serves to restore one's faith in the chivalry of human nature.' In the sentimental and historically implausible *Gypsy Roy: A Story of Early Methodism* (1904), a gypsy boy marries a squire's daughter after converting to Methodism. *Mab* (1900) is a shipwrecked baby adopted by two Methodists who becomes an actress, goes blind, writes a successful novel, and recovers her sight in childbirth.

LINDSAY, Mayne published six volumes of fiction in the period, including *The Antipodeans: A Romance* (1904), a volume of Indian stories entitled *The Valley of Sapphires*, and *Prophet Peter: A Study in Delusions* (1902) which concerns a religious enthusiast gifted with second sight and a passionate hatred of suffering and cruelty, but no great knowledge of human nature, his own or other people's. His mixture of strengths and weaknesses is contrasted with the unrestrained egotism of a rascally vagabond on one hand and the self-sacrifice of an East End clergyman on the other. In the novel's most striking scene, rich and poor alike follow Prophet Peter up onto the downs to be fed with manna from heaven. Wolff suggests that this author may have been Australian.

literary agents. In his good-natured 1932 study *Authors and the Book Trade*, Frank *Swinnerton notes that 'Fifty years ago the agent did not exist', whereas 'now there are very few authors of any standing who do not employ one or other of the leading agents here and in the United States. Authors have never been more prosperous than they are now; the relations of authors with publishers have never been more friendly, and I believe I am right in saying that most publishers would rather deal in business matters with an agent than with an author.' Swinnerton, who worked in publishing most of his life as a reader and editor, saw the agent as 'the proper intermediary between authors and their financial partners, between authors and editors, and between authors and their best selves'. From a publisher's point of view, he thought, 'Authors are better hidden. If they come out they should keep away from publishers and editors, who grow sick of the sight of them.' For Swinnerton, in short, the agent was a necessary part of the publishing business, and tensions in the three-way relationship between author, agent, and publisher were more likely to be between agent and author than between agent and publisher: 'The majority of authors are in the habit of discounting the labour of the agent, and of taking all credit for their own success.'

This account of the literary agent as the publisher's friend deliberately ignores the ways in which most publishers had, in fact, at least up to the beginning of the First World War, opposed the very idea of literary agency. The argument that the literary agent was essentially 'a parasite' on the publishing trade was put most forcefully by William Heinemann (1863–1920) in an article in the *Athenaeum* in 1893. He accused the agent of destroying the personal trust and commitment between author and publisher, and of taking false credit (and payment) for books' success, success which was, in reality, an effect of authors' talent and publishers' hard work. Heinemann is, here, being as disingenuous as Swinnerton; the latter does, after all, make clear that 'the bond of author and agent' is money. The rise of the literary agent, in other words, was a result of the new possibilities of literary money-making that became apparent in the last decades of the nineteenth century. These opportunities followed the development of a mass reading public and a vastly increased demand for books and magazines, but were ultimately dependent on changes in copyright legislation (such as the USA 1891 Copyright Act, which at last gave British authors American copyright protection). Writers' need for someone to handle their business affairs became more pressing with every new form of 'secondary' right in their work—serial and second serial rights, translation rights, foreign rights, American rights, syndication rights, collected-edition rights, illustrated-edition rights, dramatic rights, and, soon, film rights and broadcasting rights. And, notwithstanding Heinemann's bluff assertions, authors certainly could not expect publishers—who were accustomed to buying copyrights outright—to exploit authors' secondary rights for them.

The first modern literary agent, Alexander Pollock Watt (1834–1914), started his business in the mid-1870s, acting for his friend George Macdonald (1824–1905); by the end of the century he represented a number of shrewd and successful writers including Grant Allen (1848–99), Walter *Besant, Arthur Conan *Doyle, Rider *Haggard, Thomas Hardy (1840–1928), and Rudyard *Kipling. Watt saw himself as freeing authors from what Besant had called 'the intolerable trouble of haggling and bargaining', for which service he charged 10 per cent of his authors' earnings (a rate which remains standard). According to James Hepburn in *The Author's Empty Purse: The Rise of the Literary Agent* (London, 1968), Watt's 'main activities consisted in placing works of authors, executing contracts, collecting royalties, and valuing literary property. By the nineties or earlier he was arranging sales to American magazines.' He remained pretty much alone in his trade until 1896, when James Brand Pinker (1863–1922) opened an agency (claiming to be more interested than Watt in unknown writers). The American agent Curtis Brown (1866–1945) opened his London office in 1899, and these three agencies dominated the field throughout the Edwardian period. Another well-known agent was William Morris Colles (1855–1926) of the Authors' Syndicate, which began in association with the Society of Authors.

The value of agents to authors cannot be doubted. Arnold *Bennett, for example, went to Pinker's agency in 1901 when he was earning £2 10*s.* per 1,000 words; over the next twenty years Pinker pushed this rate up to at least £100 per 1,000 words. And it is not surprising that publishers were hostile. What was at stake was not really the 'sacred bond' between publisher and author, but the distribution of a book's earnings, as agents pushed up authors' royalty rates from 10 per cent to 15 per cent, and even to 25 per cent for the bestselling writers (Hall *Caine's agent reportedly negotiated a rate of 33 per cent). There were obviously bad agents and fraudulent agents: Arthur Addison Bright committed suicide in 1906 after swindling J. M. *Barrie out of £16,000; A. M. Burghes and his son were convicted of fraud in 1912. But by then it was clear that if authors were foolish to expect publishers to look after their financial interests, the business of exploiting copyrights had become too complicated (and time-consuming) for authors to handle themselves (even if they continued to resent agents taking 10 per cent of those deals they did arrange without help). In this respect the Edwardian period marked the transition between the Victorian era, when publishers were still, in some respects, simply mediators between authors and printers, and the contemporary mass audience, multi-media publishing business. By the 1920s, as Swinnerton suggests, agents had become necessary to the smooth running of the publishing industry—publishers, as well as authors, relied upon their expertise. See also *publishers.

LITTLE, Mrs Archibald: Alicia Helen Neva BEWICKE (d. 1926) married (1886) Archibald John LITTLE (1838–1908). Born in Madeira, she was married to a merchant who travelled widely in China between 1859 and 1907. Mrs Little states in *Who's Who* that she founded and organised the 'Tien Tsu Hui, or Anti-foot-binding Society of China'. She was Vice-President of the Women's Conference at Shanghai in 1900. Her publications included editions of her husband's writings on China, fiction and non-fiction about China, journalism, and novels, including one, *Mother Darling* (1885), 'written to establish the rights of mothers to their own children'. *Flirts and Flirts, or, A Season at Ryde* (1868) was her earliest work. In *A Marriage in China* (1899) a British consul wants to marry a missionary but has the problem of two children by a Chinese mistress. The *Times* obituarist (6 Aug. 1926) commented that it 'attracted a good deal of attention in the Far East, owing to the identification of some of its characters with well-known residents, despite her energetic disclaimers'. Other works are *Out in China!* (1902) and *A Millionaire's Courtship* (1906), in which a good-looking, modest millionaire who distributes cheques for £500 as though they were 'little bits of paper' plans to develop the Chinese market, and falls in love with the long-legged daughter of the Consul-General, whom she worships, and whose high reputation as a wit raises hopes which are not fulfilled. Little is described by Harry *Furniss in *Some Victorian Women* (1922).

LITTLE, M[aude] (b. 1890) was of Irish family but lived in Glasgow and later in Edinburgh. After publishing her first article in the *Humane Review* in 1908 she wrote four volumes of fiction 1911–15. *The Children's Bread: A Romance* (1912), Tony Legrand sets out to take revenge on his mother's betrayer, an artist called Heyman. But he has the wrong man (the real seducer was Arthur Penthurst, now Sir Arthur and a successful doctor), and is reconciled with Heyman. *A Woman on the Threshold* (1911) discusses the problem of reconciling literary genius with the feminine role. Little also contributed to the *Humanitarian*; she was a member of the London Quill Club.

Little Nugget, The, P. G. *Wodehouse, 1913, Methuen. Mrs Elmer Ford, recently divorced from an American millionaire, is in London where her son Ogden, of whom the father has been given custody, is studying. Her friend Cynthia lures Ogden away from his tutor; the millionaire's private secretary recovers him. Cynthia's fiancé, Peter Burns, gets a job at Ogden's school, and takes over as narrator. Ogden, the much-prized nugget of the title, turns out to be an arrogant little horror. Burns, aided by a secretary, Audrey Sheridan, takes on a gang of kidnappers. The kidnappers get Ogden, and Burns gets Audrey (Cynthia has fallen in love with someone else). The novel originated as a parody of Wilkie Collins (1824–1889), but the awfulness of Ogden, who also features in *Piccadilly Jim* (1917), casts a certain gloom over it.

Little Princess, A: *Being the Whole Story of Sara Crewe Now Told for the First Time*, Frances Hodgson *Burnett, 1905, Frederick Warne. This is the extended version of a story first published as *Sara Crewe, or, What Happened at Miss Minchin's* (1888). Motherless, pampered, 7-year-old Sara is sent back home from India by her father to enter a Seminary for Young Ladies. She finds herself, with her doll, Emily, and her French maid, Mariette, in the custody of Miss Minchin and Miss Amelia. Fluent in French, she becomes Miss Minchin's show pupil, and befriends fat Ermengarde St John. Neither her talents nor her father's wealth seem likely to spoil her: she pretends she is a princess in order to sustain the virtues she associates with royalty. She is particularly kind to the young scullery maid, Becky, giving her food and telling her stories. However, news arrives that her father has died of fever, and moreover died penniless, defrauded by his profligate partner. Miss Minchin keeps her on as a maidservant and assistant teacher, living in hungry squalor in the attic, where she teams up with a rat and imagines she is in the Bastille. Most of the girls she once befriended now ignore her. Carrisford, an Englishman returned from India, moves in next door with his servant and his servant's monkey. Every day something new in the way of furniture or food appears in Sara's room. Carrisford is her father's ex-partner, now wealthy again, and determined to redeem himself by providing for her. A beggar child whom she had helped even when she had virtually nothing herself also finds happiness.

LOCKE, W[illiam] J[ohn] (1863–1930) married (1911) Aimée Maxwell HEATH. Born at Demerara, British Guiana, of English parents, Locke was the son of a banker in Barbados. In 1864 the family went to Trinidad, and Locke was educated at Queen's Royal College there and at St John's College, Cambridge (1881–4), where he read mathematics. He became a schoolmaster at Glenalmond (1891–1897), which he disliked, and then Secretary to the Royal Institute of British Architects (1897–1907), which had decided to appoint a layman who would be unhampered by professional associations. He published novels from 1895 but *The *Morals of Marcus Ordeyne* (1905), his ninth, drawing partly on his Glenalmond experience, was successful enough to allow him to give up his job. As well as producing novels, sometimes two a year, including *The *Beloved Vagabond* (1907), he wrote plays and dramatizations of his own fiction, which were lucrative. His method of writing was to settle down at his desk at 9 p.m. and write up to 800 words, not more. After the First World War his health broke down, partly as a result of his exertions on behalf of convalescent private soldiers and Belgian refugees, and he retired to Cannes, where he died of tuberculosis which had been diagnosed as early as 1890. An appreciation in the *Times* (19 May 1930) notes: 'He specialised in a line of delightfully improbable heroes—children of nature, flamboyant or grotesque but never commonplace, tender and headstrong but always lovable, among whom we particularly recall Pujol.' *The Joyous Adventures of Aristide Pujol* (1912) is a facetious comedy about a Provençal adventurer.

Lodger, The, Mrs Belloc *Lowndes, 1913, Methuen. Robert and Ellen Bunting, a respectable but poverty-stricken lower-middle-class couple, are desperate to find a lodger to occupy untenanted rooms in their house off the Marylebone Road. The sinister, gentlemanly, Bible-reading Mr Sleuth seems like a godsend.

He may have strange habits, but he pays on the nail. Gradually it dawns on them that Mr Sleuth's strange habits—the hatred of women, the nocturnal prowls, 'experiments' which involve the disposal of evidence—coincide with a series of brutal murders committed at first in the East End and then in their own area (and clearly based on the still unsolved Jack the Ripper murders of 1888). The more they learn about the murders, either from the newspapers or from a young detective who is courting their daughter, the more convinced they become of Mr Sleuth's guilt. But self-interest, and a curious fellowship with the man who shares their house, keep them from betraying him. Mr Sleuth gives himself away during a visit to Madame Tussaud's, but escapes through an emergency exit and disappears. The murders promptly cease. Riveting in its attention both to the material circumstances of sensational crime and to the psychological complicity of witnesses like the Buntings, *The Lodger* drew praise from, among others, Gertrude Stein (1874–1946) and Ernest Hemingway (1899–1961). In one of its most striking passages, Lowndes attributes Mrs Bunting's refusal to betray Mr Sleuth to the subordination of women. 'So far, perhaps because she is subject rather than citizen, her duty as a component part of civilised society weighs but lightly on woman's shoulders.' The *Westminster Gazette* commented: 'Mrs Belloc-Lowndes is almost persuaded into a side-track on the Franchise question.'

Lonely Plough, The, Constance *Holme, 1914, Mills & Boon. Lanty Lancaster is land agent for the benevolent but ineffectual Lord Bluecaster, overseeing, as his father had done before him, every conceivable aspect of the latter's Westmorland estate. As the novel opens, he is trying to broker a marriage between the son and daughter of two farming families, the Whinnerahs and the Dockerays. The settled routines of this quasi-feudal world are disrupted by two external, modernizing forces, one good, the other evil. Hamer Shaw, a Lancashire businessman who has tired of suburbia, is made welcome because of his shrewdness and generosity; Lancaster falls in love with his daughter, Dandy. Bracken Holliday, on the other hand, although born of good farming stock, has become embittered and estranged by his social aspirations. 'The grey, old-world atmosphere had foiled this meretricious gentility as an ancient manor-wall a flaring poster.' Holliday proclaims the imminent demise of the Lugg, a sea-wall built by Lancaster's father, and it is indeed destroyed by a freak storm, taking the Whinnerays with it. Lancaster has the strength of mind to survive the catastrophe, and prove himself a fit mate for the faithful Dandy. Introducing the 1931 'World's Classics' edition of the novel, Holme pointed out that it had been written 'at almost the last moment of the old order of things'; hence, no doubt, its enduring attraction.

LONG, George published six novels, 1905–8. In *Valhalla: A Novel* (1906), a deluge destroys all of civilization except for Britain, which is thus transformed into a 'Valhalla' in which 'everywhere, on all sides, the spirits worked for the good of the two surviving human beings'. *In the Days of Marlborough* (1908) is a run-of-the-mill *historical romance which introduces, as one reviewer put it, 'highwaymen, duelling, and other features of the time, not omitting its easy morality'.

Longest Journey, The, E. M. *Forster, 1907, William Blackwood. The novel incorporates two separate plots which just happen to coincide at a place called *suburbia. In the first, sensitive Rickie Elliot's marriage to suburban Agnes Pembroke merely confirms the fatality of his physical disablement (hereditary lameness). Together, like a couple in one of the New Woman novels of the 1890s, they produce a horribly crippled daughter, who soon dies. Thereafter Rickie 'deteriorates'. A second plot crosses this downward spiral. Rickie's race will die out, but his half-brother Stephen Wonham, the product of a more eugenic union with a staunch yeoman farmer, may yet flourish. Distanced genetically from Rickie, Stephen belongs to a different blood-line, a different plot. The genetic distance is also a moral and emotional distance. Agnes Pembroke, who has already drained the life out of Rickie, regards Stephen as a monster. 'He was illicit, abnormal, worse than a man diseased.' Forster defends Stephen's abnormality against suburban convention, because he believes that it alone will preserve the race.

LONGMAN, V. I. In Longman's *Harvest* (1913) Hasil Lathom, daughter of an English father and Indian mother, is orphaned at the age of 18, and comes to England to live with an uncle and aunt. She studies at St Frideswide's, Oxford. Her fiancé, Adrian Harding, breaks off the engagement when he discovers that her mother was Indian. The Harding family, earnestly discussing the consequences of a mixed marriage, reminded the **Times Literary Supplement*'s reviewer of John *Galsworthy's novels, especially *The *Country House* (1907). Hasil marries a priggish young parson, Clemente, on the rebound, gives birth to a child who dies, and drowns herself. Longman's only other publications seem to have been a novel and a translation in the 1930s.

Longman's Magazine (1882–1905). A monthly, costing 6*d*. (and unillustrated) it was set up in 1882 and contained primarily fiction. The first number sold 74,000 copies. Like its main competitors (the *Argosy*, **Temple Bar*, and the **Cornhill*), which cost twice as much, *Longman's* aimed to be a versatile, non-controversial family magazine and to capture a mass market. Throughout the twenty-three years of the magazine's publication it distanced itself from politics and religion. But it contains a fair amount of social history, travel writing, and sport. As the magazine's chief literary adviser, Andrew *Lang displayed an unusual ability to tailor his material to the general reader. His department was known as 'At the Sign of the Ship' and became a household word in middle-class homes. Lang drew writers like *Kipling, Rider *Haggard, Walter *Besant, and R. L. Stevenson (1850–1894) to Longman's. From 1900 on it lost its edge, engaging mainly minor novelists such as Arthur W. *Marchmont and L. B. *Walford. The advent of the new illustrated papers such as Newnes's **Strand* accelerated its demise.

Loot of Cities, The: *Being the Adventures of a Millionaire in Search of Joy*, Arnold *Bennett, 1905, Alston Rivers. Tales concerning the escapades of Cecil Thorold, American millionaire. First he kidnaps Bruce Bowring, Managing Director of the Consolidated Mining and Investment Corporation, whose gains are nothing if not ill-gotten, and blackmails him for £50,000. He lets Bowring go and burns the money. His aim is to impress his journalist friend Miss Eve Fincastle, who has witnessed the episode from hiding. Then he depresses the price of Dry Goods Trust shares by faking the disappearance of the company's President, Simeon Rainshore. Rainshore reappears, the price recovers, and Thorold nets a few million which he donates to Vaux Lowry, the impoverished suitor of Rainshore's daughter. The third adventure involves the recovery of a wealthy actress's bracelet, the fourth the solution of a hotel mystery in Algiers. Thorold proposes to Eve Fincastle, and is accepted. A final kidnapping wins them box seats at the Paris opera.

Lord Jim, Joseph *Conrad, 1900, Blackwood. The story of the handsome, idealistic English gentleman who disgraces himself by leaping overboard was based on that of Augustus Podmore Williams, whom Conrad had probably met. Williams was Chief Officer of the *Jedda*, which set out from Singapore with 900 Moslem pilgrims in 1880. In heavy weather the ship began to take on water, and captain, crew and passengers all panicked. Williams lowered a lifeboat for the captain and officers, was pushed overboard for his pains by angry pilgrims, and hauled into the lifeboat. When the boat reached Aden, the Captain reported that the *Jedda* had sunk. It was towed into port the following day. The incident ended Williams's career. He became a ship's chandler's water-clerk and married a native girl. The same sort of thing happens to Jim, although Conrad provides rather more by way of extenuating circumstance: the *Patna*, Jim's ship, is barely seaworthy in the first place, and crewed by a gang of renegades. The consequences, however, are roughly the same. Condemned by the court of inquiry, loathing himself for his violation of an all-important code of conduct, Jim moves restlessly from job to job in search of anonymity. At this point, his story is taken up by a sympathetic observer, Marlow, who, with the help of a worldly-wise entomologizing trader, Stein, finds him a more secure job in a remote trading station in Patusan. Patusan transforms him into a romantic hero, Lord Jim. Routing the Arab trader, Sherif Ali, and successfully defying the authority of the villainous Rajah Allang, he restores peace to the community, and to himself, and marries Jewel, the stepdaughter of his corrupt predecessor. However, his new-found serenity is rudely disrupted by the arrival of the freebooting Gentleman Brown. Jim promises Chief Doramin that Brown will leave peacefully. Brown does leave, but not peacefully; he kills Doramin's son. Jim offers Doramin his own life in reparation. He dies honourably. The first four chapters of the novel, which cover Jim's early life and the *Patna* débâcle, and which Conrad offered to *Blackwood's* as a short story in 1898, are recounted by an omniscient narrator. Chapters 5–35 are Marlow's after-dinner narration, and the remainder is pieced together by him from the testimonies of various participants and sent to a member of his after-dinner audience. The break between Chapters 4 and 5 has been said to represent the break between the kind of objective telling which was supposedly the aim of most Victorian novelists and a proto-modernist preoccupation with the relativity of point of view. Equally abrupt, and possibly more damaging, is the division of the novel into a closely observed account of the psychological consequences of a single indiscretion and a florid adventure story involving melodramatic villains and jewel-like native women. In a letter to Edward Garnett (12 Nov. 1900), Conrad described this division as the book's 'plague spot'.

LORIMER, Norma [Octavia] (1864–1948). Born in Auchterarder, Perthshire, she was brought up on the Isle of Man and educated at Castletown High School. In the early 1890s she was working as secretary to Douglas *Sladen, with whom she collaborated on *Queer Things about Sicily* (1905). She became a contributor to the *Girl's Own Paper* and author of many travel books and twenty-six rather sentimental novels from *A Sweet Disorder* (1896) to *Where Ignorance Is Bliss* (1938). She travelled widely in America, Asia and Italy. *Catherine Sterling* (1903) is about a woman who has lived with a man unable to marry her because of a mad wife; in *On Etna: A Romance of Brigand Life* (1904) the heroine is kidnapped by the Mafia and falls in love with their leader. Lorimer hit her stride with *A Wife Out of Egypt* (1913), whose heroine is a Christian Syrian woman engaged first to a handsome, empty-headed young Englishman whose class and prejudices make union impossible, and then to another Englishman of finer mind and wider experience; her brother marries the first Englishman's sister. *The Pagan Woman* (1907) found the exotic closer to home: two women of sharply contrasted temperaments keep house for their lodger, an antiquary engaged on work on the local burial mounds. 'Passion spins the plot,' remarked one reviewer.

Lost World, The: *Being an Account of the Recent Amazing Adventures of Professor George E. Challenger, Lord John Roxton, Professor Summerlee, and Mr. E. D. Malone of the 'Daily Gazette'*, A. Conan *Doyle, 1912, Hodder & Stoughton. In order to impress his girlfriend, Gladys Hungerton, a young Irish journalist, Edward Malone, agrees to accompany the hugely brilliant and bad-tempered Professor George Edward Challenger on an expedition to map a 'lost world' in central South America. Also on board are Roxton, a sportsman and traveller, Summerlee, an acidic older scientist, Zambo, a faithful black Hercules, two treacherous 'half-breeds', and a scattering of docile but timid 'Indians'. After various scrapes, and the discovery of a thicket full of skeletons, the white explorers finally penetrate the gigantic extinct volcano which houses a recapitulation of the history of life on the planet: dinosaurs, mammals, ape-men (the 'missing link'), a 'primitive' tribe of near-pygmies. There are glimpses of a splendidly noxious pterodactyl-pit, comic exchanges between the 'pepperpot' professors, and a battle between savages and ape-men during which Malone and Roxton speed up evolution in this corner of the world by shooting large numbers of the latter. If there is a serious undertone, it has to do with the virtues of a manliness constantly renewed by adventure. 'We're all gettin' a deal too soft and dull and comfy,' drawls Lord John. Gladys, however, seems refreshingly immune to gung-ho adventurism. Malone arrives home to find her married to a diminutive solicitor's clerk.

Louis Norbert: *A Two-Fold Romance*, 'Vernon *Lee', 1914, John Lane. In a graveyard in Pisa, glamorous middle-aged Lady Venetia Hammond comes across a marble tablet commemorating Louis Norbert (d. 1984), whose portrait hangs in Lady Venetia's family home, Arthington Manor. Aided by a pedantic (and nameless) young archaeologist who is in love with her, she sets out to unravel the mystery surrounding Norbert's origins and early death: the archaeologist investigates in the Pisan archives, she in the Muniment Room at Arthington, where she is nursing her sick brother. The hypothesis she develops is that Norbert was the product of a secret marriage between Louis XIV and Marie Mancini, niece of Cardinal Mazarin; and that, spirited away by Mazarin's agents, he was brought up in England by Sir Anthony Thesiger, Lady Venetia's ancestor, and eventually killed in a duel while travelling in Italy. The novel, which takes the form of an exchange of letters and telegrams between Lady Venetia and the archaeologist, turns on the ambiguous power of *fantasy. Imaginative sympathy enables Lady Venetia to formulate a hypothesis which the archaeologist's scientific scepticism cannot dislodge. But it also draws her into a mild infatuation with the archaeologist, which reproduces Norbert's own secret romantic history, and which she eventually breaks by agreeing to marry a man her own age. The archaeologist's reference to Lady Venetia's friend Henry *James may suggest one source of inspiration for the novel.

Love and His Mask, Ménie Muriel *Dowie, 1901, William Heinemann. The novel is set during the *Boer War. Widowed Leslie Rose writes to Major-General the Hon. B. de L. Riddington, of the South African Field Force, without revealing her identity. She believes that a manly man and a womanly woman can only communicate properly if they remain unknown to each other. Her letters reveal her (and presumably Dowie's) philosophy of life. However, the situation becomes complicated when Riddington is invalided home, and they meet. Riddington falls in love with Leslie, without realising that she was his mysterious correspondent. She, meanwhile, has begun to fall in love with Toby Tollemache, a previously worthless youth of whom the war has made a man. Toby serves with distinction on Riddington's staff, earning the older man's paternal love. Leslie chooses Toby, and Riddington returns to South Africa and the solitariness of hyper-masculinity; he will be missed chiefly by the almost equally masculine Lady Sarah Dorminster, the most interesting character in the book. The heroine of Dowie's most successful novel, *Gallia* (1895), had chosen a husband on genetic rather than passionate grounds. Here, war serves the function of eugenics, shaping a man of exactly the right degree of masculinity for a woman of exactly the right degree of femininity.

Love and Mr Lewisham, H. G. *Wells, 1900, Harper. At the beginning of the novel, Lewisham is an 18-year-old schoolmaster at Whortley Preparatory School, in Sussex, 'called "Mr" to distinguish him from the bigger boys'. He is talented, ambitious, and sexually susceptible, especially to the relatively sophisticated and cosmopolitan Ethel Henderson. Ethel's father, Chaffery, is a fraudulent medium who robs his clients and deceives his wife. Lewisham successfully pursues his studies in London and begins to make a career for himself as a writer, despite the distraction represented by another aspiring intellectual, Miss Heydinger. He meets Ethel again after a three-year gap, realizes that she is the victim of an unscrupulous father, and courts and marries her. Domesticity and fatherhood ensue. *Love and Mr Lewisham* seemed a surprising sequel to the scientific romances which had made Wells's name in the 1890s. He himself described it as 'sedulously polished'. 'It was consciously a work of art; it was designed to be very clear, simple, graceful and human. It was not a very successful book, no critic discovered any sort of beauty or technical ability in it, and it was some years before the writer could return, in **Kipps* (1905) and **Tono-Bungay* (1909), to his attack on the novel proper.'

Love in a Mist, Olive *Birrell, 1900, Smith, Elder. This conventional romance was given a new(ish) twist by the fact that the man, Keith Hamilton, is a wealthy capitalist and the woman, Sibylla, is the daughter of an aristocrat, Wargrave Lincoln, who has blown his inheritance on socialistic experiments and now lives in comparative poverty. Lincoln is portrayed unsympathetically as an idealist whose worship of an abstraction has blinded him to the needs of his children (there is also a son, Pippin); though he does experience a deathbed repentance. The plot is mechanical, but before it takes hold there is enough time for explorations of the psychology of idealism, and of the new identities being forged by independent working women. Hilda Forrester, a young woman of great ambition and limited talent, leaves home to establish herself in London as an artist (she hires Sibylla as a model). A £500 legacy eases the task. 'We, of this generation', she tells Sibylla, 'must be content to incur obloquy if we develop our natures as we ought. I am glad you are trying to be independent.' She attempts to nurture Sibylla's independence by inviting her to share a flat in Bloomsbury, very much the territory of single working women, with herself and a journalist friend, Dorothy Edge. Hilda and Dorothy, who know life through books, are as ignorant of its necessities and urgencies as Wargrave Lincoln. William Hudson, a prototype of E. M. *Forster's self-taught clerk, Leonard Bast, in **Howards End* (1910), fares little better. He loves

Sibylla, but is doomed to lose her to a stronger (and richer) man.

Love's Shadow, Ada *Leverson, 1908, Grant Richards. First of a trilogy of novels—the others are *Tenterhooks* (1912) and *Love at Second Sight* (1916)—chronicling the marriage of Edith and Bruce Ottley. It begins with Edith and Bruce married for three years and established in a 'very new, very small, very white flat in Knightsbridge—exactly like thousands of other new, small, white flats'. The first thing we hear is Bruce imploring Edith not to make him late for the office (he is a clerk at the Foreign Office). Bruce is a humourless bore and hypochondriac based on Leverson's husband, Ernest, a gambler and speculator whom she married when she was 19. Edith's only answer to his tyranny is a waspish sense of humour, and friendship with Hyacinth Verney, a woman capable of provoking 'the most intense devotion' in people of both sexes, including her cousin and guardian, Sir Charles Cannon, and her companion, Anne Yeo, a spinster who customarily dresses in a mackintosh, golf-cap, and dogskin riding-gloves. Hyacinth is in love with Cecil Reeve, a young man about town, who is in love with Eugenia Raymond, a widow ten years his senior. When Lord Selsey, his uncle and mentor, proposes to Eugenia and is accepted, Cecil marries Hyacinth. She cannot quite believe his protestations, and suspects a continuing intrigue with Eugenia. Eugenia, alerted to Hyacinth's fears by Anne Yeo, resolves the matter by taking her husband off for a long holiday abroad. Meanwhile, Bruce has turned his attention to amateur theatricals, and amateur actresses, while Edith has found an admirer in Bruce's uncouth but amiable colleague F. J. Raggett, Secretary to the Legitimist Society ('I shall request him to keep his secret societies to himself,' Bruce remarks huffily). None of these flirtations amounts to anything very much, and the tone of the novel is light, but both the main plotlines involve the bullying of women by morally and intellectually inferior men.

LOW, Ivy [Thérèse] (1889–1977) married (1916) Maxim Maximovich LITVINOV (1876–1951). Brought up in London, the daughter of Alice *Herbert and of a philologist who translated the novels of Björnstjerne Björnson (1832–1910), she was educated at a boarding-school in Tynemouth, and at Maida Vale High School, and became a clerk in the Prudential Assurance Company in 1908. The historian and journalist, Sir Sidney Low (1857–1932) was her uncle; they were of Hungarian Jewish descent, originally called Loewe. She was a friend of Viola *Meynell, and frequented her parents' literary parties. H. G. *Wells, who had been a great friend of her father's, encouraged her work, and she published articles on slum conditions in the *Manchester Guardian*. Her first two novels were the autobiographical *Growing Pains* (1913), about the development of a young middle-class girl, and *The Questing Beast* (1914), partly set in the Prudential, whose central character is an unconventional, sexually emancipated Jewish woman writer. She married a prominent Bolshevik , and, after two years' separation as he plunged into the revolution, went to Estonia (where he had been appointed ambassador) in 1920 with their two children. In Moscow she found herself unable to write another novel until, hypnotized by a visiting German professor, she wrote *His Master's Voice: A Detective Story* (1930), which deals with the tension between the District Procurator and an officer of the OGPU. She was an enthusiastic proponent of Basic English and during the Stalinist purges of the 1930s went and taught it in Sverdlovsk in the Urals, perhaps partly for safety; she returned to Moscow on Litvinov's fall from power in 1939. He, who spent ten years in Britain as a printer, clerk, commercial traveller, and teacher of Russian, was the first diplomatic representative of the Soviet Republic in Britain in 1917, Foreign Minister (1930–1939), and Russian Ambassador in Washington (1941–1943). Low also published a volume of short stories, *She Knew She Was Right* (1971). She translated fiction and non-fiction from Russian to English 1931–1975, sometimes with her daughter, Tatiana Litvinov. She spent a year in England in 1960, and returned finally in 1972 to live in Hove, where she died. There is a biography by John Carswell (1983).

LOWE, Charles (1848–1931) married Blanche Fitzhardinge LYE (d. 1924). Born at Balconnel, Forfarshire, he was educated at Brechin Grammar School and the universities of Edinburgh (where he contributed poetry to a student magazine edited by R. L. Stevenson, 1850–1894) and Jena. He entered Gray's Inn in 1874, but before being called to the Bar joined the *Times*, where he was first foreign sub-editor, then, for thirteen years from 1878, Berlin correspondent. Dismissed in 1891 by the new assistant manager, C. F. Moberly Bell (1847–1911), he brought an unsuccessful charge for wrongful dismissal against the *Times*, and came back to London. He wrote biographies of Bismarck, Tzar Alexander III, Edward VII, and Kaiser William II, as well as a few *historical novels including *A Lindsay's Love: A Tale of the Tuileries and the Siege of Paris* (1905), a priggish tale of the adventures of a young Scot who wants to become a journalist but ends by inheriting a fortune and buying an estate, *The Prince's Pranks* (1909), and a volume of reminiscences (1927).

Lowest Rung, The, Mary *Cholmondeley, 1908, John Murray. Four short stories, with a preface describing some of the perils of authorship, including male condescension and complete strangers who accuse you of maligning their aunts and uncles. In the title-story a highly-strung, exaggeratedly precious female writer shelters a woman who has been reduced to vagrancy by her dependence on morphia but who, now that she has touched bottom, behaves selflessly. 'The Hand on the Latch' is set on the American prairie during the Civil War. Again, a woman shelters a vagrant, this time a wounded soldier. At first she suspects him of meaning to rob her, but in the end he helps her to kill an intruder who turns out to be her own husband in disguise. 'Saint Luke's Summer' is the story of a man who emigrates to Australia to make his fortune and returns twenty-five years later to marry his childhood sweetheart, at last freed by the death of her invalid father. A sensitive man, despite his outback appearance, he soon realizes that the romance she has woven around him in his absence is more important to her than his presence, and departs without pressing his suit further. In 'The Understudy', a playwright rehearsing one of her plays recognizes in an understudy a man she had abandoned ten years before, and subsequently written the play about. She still loves him, but discovers that he has taken to drink, and so will not give herself to him. The leading lady, however, does, and thereby finds happiness.

LOWIS, Cecil [Champain] (1866–1948) married Sarah Josselyn MAN. Born in Bengal, he was educated at Newton College, Devon, at Göttingen Gymnasium, and at Corpus Christi College, Cambridge. He joined the Indian Civil Service and rose to become Commissioner and Superintendant of Ethnography in Burma; he retired in 1912. He was lent to the Egyptian government in order to supervise the 1907 census there. His first novel was *The Treasury Officer's Wooing* (1899), a witty novel about a white official in Burma, a strong silent man who falls in love; it was followed by fifteen other volumes of fiction to 1936, including *The Machinations of the Myo-ok* (1903), comic sketches about a Burmese mayor, related by another white official.

LOWNDES, Mrs BELLOC: Marie Adelaide Julie Elizabeth Renée BELLOC (1868–1947) married (1896) Frederick Sawrey Archibald LOWNDES (1868–1940). She was the daughter of a French father and an English mother, Bessie Rayner Parkes (1829–1925), who had worked for the emancipation of women, and was educated at Mayfield Convent. Along with Grant *Richards, she worked for W. T. Stead (1849–1912) when he started the *Review of Reviews* in 1890. Hilaire *Belloc was her brother; her husband worked on the *Times*, but she did not publish her first fiction, the sketches *The Philosophy of a Marquise*, until 1899, though she had edited *Life and Letters of Charlotte Elizabeth, Princess Palatine* (1889) and *Pages from the Journal and Correspondence of Edmund and Jules de Goncourt* (1894). The most powerful character in *The Heart of Penelope* (1904), the philanthropic Lord Wantley, who in true mid-Victorian fashion combines liberalism abroad with autocratic pride and narrowness at home, is dead before the story starts. It is he who prevented his daughter, Penelope, from marrying David Winfrith, son of an impoverished clergyman. On the rebound, she has married another rich elderly philanthropist, Melancthon Robinson, whose early death leaves her free for sentimental adventures, culminating in a passionate affair with a married man which has a tragic end but a brighter sequel, in the shape of Penelope's cousin, the young Lord Wantley. Wantley's abilities have gone to waste for lack of direction. Reinvigorated by Penelope's simplicity and directness, he will in turn reinvigorate the Victorian liberal tradition. **Barbara Rebell* (1905) is also about the tendency of one generation to repeat the mistakes made by another. *Studies in Wives* (1909) is in fact as much about husbands as wives, but still struck the **Times Literary Supplement*'s reviewer as yet another product of 'what (alas!) we are all learning to call "feminism"'. Lowndes's best-known work, *The *Lodger* (1912), which sold a million copies in twenty years, was the first of a series of *crime novels, mostly reconstructions of real-life murders, such as *The End of Her Honeymoon* (1914) in which a three-week bride loses her husband in Paris. The heroine of *The Red Cross Barge* (1916) is a French nurse who impresses a German doctor with her heroism. Other fiction includes *Love and Hatred* (1917), *The Lonely House* (1920), and *The Terriford Mystery* (1924). In the 1930s she also became a successful playwright. She published a series of memoirs, full of anecdotes of the Edwardian literary world, which are given special charm by her sense of being, as a Frenchwoman, an outsider: *I, Too, Have Lived in Arcadia: A Record of Love and of Childhood* (1942), *The Merry Wives of Westminster* (1946), *A Passing World* (1948), and *Where Love and Friendship Dwelt* (1943).

LUBBOCK, [Alfred] Basil (1876–1944) married (1912) Dorothy Mary THYNNE née WARNER (d. 1944). Educated at Eton College, he went to Canada in the gold rush in 1897, and came home round Cape Horn as an ordinary seaman. This was the experience which informed such fiction as *Jack Derringer: A Tale of Deep Water* (1906), set on a 'Yankee hell-ship' with much unconvincing dialect. The first hundred pages or so read like an essay about life at sea; then Lubbock remembers that it is a novel and adds a villain and a heroine. In the second part the hero falls overboard and has some adventures in the company of a cowboy before settling down with his pure woman. *Deep Sea Warriors* (1909) is similar. Lubbock later fought in the *Boer War and the First World War, in which he won the MC, and published a number of non-fictional works about maritime history. He was a keen yachtsman. The writer Percy Lubbock (1879–1965) was his first cousin.

LUCAS, E[dward] V[errall] (1868–1938), CH (1932), married (1897) Florence Elizabeth Gertrude GRIFFIN. Born in Eltham, the son of a Quaker insurance agent, he went to eleven schools before being apprenticed, aged 16, to a bookseller. At 18 he got a job on the *Sussex Daily News*. In 1892, with the help of £200 given him by an uncle, he went to lectures at University College London given by W. P. Ker (1855–1923). In 1893 he got a job on the *Globe*. He was also a contributor to *Punch* for many years. He was commissioned by Methuen, the *publishers, to write about Charles Lamb (1775–1834) in 1900; their association grew until he became of the firm in 1924. His long bibliography includes thirty volumes of light essays as well as travel books, anthologies, children's books, and biographies. His most characteristic novels, *Listener's Lure: An Oblique Narration* (1906) and *Over Bemerton's: An Easy-Going Chronicle* (1908) feature middle-aged men who, after delays and setbacks, marry younger women. In the former, Haberton, a Boswell scholar, despatches his ward, Edith Graham, to London and himself to Algiers: on his return, he finds that she is content to have him as he is, bookish and garden-loving. It is as though Lucy Honeychurch, in E. M. *Forster's *A *Room with a View* (1908), had wanted Mr Emerson rather than his son George. *London Lavender* (1912) is a collection of chatty sketches—somewhere between fiction and essay. *The Slowcoach: A Story of Roadside Adventure* (1910) is about the adventures of four children who are given a caravan by an anonymous benefactor; it contrasts with *The *Caravaners* by *'Elizabeth'. *Sir Pulteney: A Fantasy* (1910), published as 'E. D. Ward', is the story of a man whose job is to dissuade would-be suicides from entering a field which has been released from gravity. *The War of the Wenuses* (1898), written with C. L. Graves (1856–1944), was a parody of H. G. *Wells's *The War of the Worlds* (1897), in which men are exterminated by an invasion of beautiful extraterrestrial females. Lucas's fiction is full of digs at modern art and modern ideas.

LUCAS, Reginald [Jaffray] (1865–1914). Fifth son of a baronet, Lucas was educated at Eton College and Trinity College, Cambridge. After serving in the army he was Conservative Unionist MP for Portsmouth (1895–1906). He was keen on racing, suffered severely from indigestion, and committed suicide in his rooms in Albany, shooting himself because he was unable to endure any longer the agonies of tuberculosis. He wrote history books and also fiction, which tended to be in the reflective mode popularized by George *Gissing's *The *Private Papers of Henry Ryecroft* (1903), though less melancholic than its original. In *The Cheerful Day* (1911) the reflections are those of a well-to-do bachelor of cultivated taste in country society; in *The Measure of Our Days* (1913) they take the form of a series of letters addressed to his tutor at Eton by the eldest son of a marquess, also a bachelor, who is not very good at anything and completely outshone by a brilliant younger brother, but an honest and public-spirited fellow all the same, and quietly humorous. In the latter case they range across politics, love, modern manners, and food: the autobiographer holds that it is disgusting to eat soup at lunchtime. Lucas was the author of one other novel in the period, *When All the World Is Young* (1908).

LURGAN, Lester, *pseud.*: see 'May *Wynne'.

LYALL, David, *pseud.*: see Annie S. *Swan.

LYALL, Edna, *pseud.*: Ada Ellen BAYLY (1857–1903). Born and educated in Brighton, she was the daughter of a Unitarian barrister. A strong advocate of women's suffrage, she actively campaigned for the Women's Liberal Association. Perhaps it was the rather uneasy mixture of liberalism and religious conservatism that led her to publish her eighteen novels under a pseudonym. The first, *Won by Waiting* (1879), was not a success. *Donovan: A Modern Englishman* (1882) portrays an MP's struggle to embrace Christianity by overcoming his atheistic tendencies. W. E. Gladstone (1809–98), then Prime Minister, was so struck by Donovan Farrant's inner turmoil that he wrote personally to Bayly. Despite such interest the novel did not sell well (only 320 copies in its first edition). In *We Two* (1884) Bayly again depicts a bid to break free from the clutches of atheism. *In Golden Days* (1885), a *historical novel set in the seventeenth century, is considered one of her most accomplished works. *The Hinderers: A Story of the Present Time* (1902) sets out Lyall's opposition to the *Boer War, which she believed to be the unnecessary result of faint-heartedness on the part of the British Government. The recurrent theme of her novels—the struggle between faith and freedom—most definitely struck a chord in late Victorian Britain. Her writings were attacked by some religious publications such as the *Church Quarterly* for not representing the religious community in a sympathetic light. This onslaught is not borne out by an objective reading of her works. As her obituary in the *Times* (8 Feb. 1903) puts it, 'the whole tendency [of her work] was to advocate Christianity shown in its best, fairest and most tolerant [form]'. Later examples from a steady output include *To Right a Wrong* (1893), *Doreen: The Story of a Singer* (1894), *In Spite of All* (1901), and a children's book, *The Burges Letters: A Record of Child-Life in the Sixties* (1902). She was a devoutly religious woman, and used the royalties from her publications to donate a peal of bells to St Saviour's Church in Eastbourne, where she died after a long period of ill health.

LYONS, A[lbert Michael] Neil (1880–1940). Born in Kimberley, South Africa, he was educated at Bedford Grammar School and in Hanover, Germany. Having tried to become first a solicitor then an accountant he became, at 18, a journalist writing on military subjects. He contributed to many periodicals including the **English Review*. His thirteen volumes of fiction 1902–1937 are light stuff; the best-known is **Cottage Pie* (1911). He also wrote plays. *Clara: Some Scattered Chapters in the Life of a Hussy* (1912) is a collection of facetious sketches about low life in London, mostly in Cockney dialect; the heroine is a golden-hearted soap-seller. He published a biography (1910) of Robert *Blatchford.

LYSAGHT, S[idney] R[oyse] (1856–1941) married (1886) Kathrine CLARKE (d. 1953). A wealthy ironmaster in Bristol, of Irish parentage, he wrote verse as well as fiction. His wife was active in the Irish independence movement. *Her Majesty's Rebels* (1907) is prefaced by a note that, despite the resemblance of the hero's career to that of C. S. Parnell (1846–91), the character is not based on him. The career of Nationalist politician Michael Desmond, son of an impoverished family of Catholic gentry, is ruined by the accusation of adultery. The book expresses the view that the Anglo-Irish gentry would do better to throw in their lot with the Nationalists than to trust in perfidious English politicians. The historian Edward MacLysaght (1887–1986) was his son.

M

MAARTENS, Maarten, *pseud.*: Joost Marius Willem SCHWARTZ (1858–1915), who changed his surname (1889) to van der POORTEN SCHWARTZ, married (1883) Anna von VOLLENHOVEN (*c.*1862–*c.*1924). Born in Amsterdam, the son of a German Jewish doctor who was converted to Presbyterianism, he was educated in England, where the family lived (1864–70), then, after his father's death when he was 12, at the Amsterdam Gymnasium, the Koenigliches Gymnasium, Bonn, and the University of Utrecht, where he studied law. He suffered from ill health, as did his wife, who was his first cousin, and they therefore lived partly on the Riviera, as well as quietly near Doorn in Holland; he felt underrated in his native land. His first novel was the anonymous *The Black Box Murder* (1889); the first under his pseudonym was *The Sin of Joost Avelingh* (1889), which hinges on a questionable neglect of a dying uncle; Schwartz published sixteen other volumes of fiction, and left several unpublished manuscripts. *Some Women I Have Known* (1901) is a collection of short stories: the first about a German duchess whose appallingly dull and restricted life is enlivened briefly when she falls in love with her son's tutor; 'Mrs Russell' is a philanthropist who neglects her husband; 'Madame de Parfondrieu' forces her daughter-in-law to suicide rather than have her son understand she is unfaithful. *The Woman's Victory and Other Stories* (1906) also focus repeatedly on uncongenial marriages, with an undercurrent of more or less random hatred for Napoleon Bonaparte (1769–1821) and for modern financiers. *The New Religion* (1907) is a satire on medical quackery whose dedication reads: 'For those who are sick—for those who believe they are sick'. The scheming Dr Russell diagnoses a 'general debility' in the heroine, Mrs Lomas, and packs her off to a sanatorium in the Vaudois Alps run by an even greater fraud, Dr Vouvray, who promotes a 'Return to Nature'. Russell eventually redeems himself, and marries Mrs Lomas. *The Price of Lis Doris* (1909) is the story of the life of a Dutch painter who is forced to let another man take credit for his work; out of renunciation and sacrifice come art and honour. Schwartz's last novel was *Eve: An Incident of Paradise Regained* (1912), in which the heroine marries a dull older man in order to escape from her joylessly hedonistic family, commits adultery, tells her husband the truth, and frees him by retiring into a convent with her blind illegitimate baby. Schwartz also wrote verse. There is a biography by W. van Maanen (1928). J. *Morgan-de-Groot is another, lesser, example of a Dutch novelist writing in English.

McAULAY, Allan, *pseud.*: Charlotte STEWART (1863–1918) was born in Assam, India, where her father, of an ancient Scots family, was an officer in the Indian army. She was an only child and educated at home. Stewart collaborated on two novels with the American novelist Kate Douglas Wiggin (1856–1923) and Mary and Jane *Findlater. *An Affair at the Inn* (1904) is an international comedy related from the points of view of four of the participants, with each author responsible for a point of view. Kate Wiggin described the world as seen by the sprightly American heroine, Virginia Pomeroy; Mary Findlater undertook Mrs MacGill, a stodgy lady from Tunbridge Wells, Jane Findlater, her companion, Miss Cecilia Eversham, and Stewart herself Sir Archibald Mackenzie, a motorist, who woos and wins Virginia. In *Robinetta* (1911), a rich young American woman visits her old-fashioned English aunt. On her own Stewart published six volumes of fiction between 1900 and 1912. *Black Mary* (1901) is a sad story of disappointment nobly borne by a partly West Indian girl in Scotland; *Beggars and Sorners* (1912) is a *historical romance about Jacobite intrigue in eighteenth-century Amsterdam.

MACAULAY, [Emilie] R[ose] (1881–1958), DBE (1958), was born at Rugby, where her father was a schoolmaster. He was a cousin of the historian Lord Macaulay (1800–59) and her mother was the daughter of a biblical scholar.

She was brought up partly in Italy, and educated by her parents; when they returned to England in 1894 she went to Oxford High School and then (1900–3) to Somerville College, Oxford where she read history. Her first novel, *Abbots Verney* (1906), is about the heir to an ancient line, torn betweeen his respectable grandfather and his cardsharp father. He is attracted by his father but eventually reconciled with his grandfather and his heritage. She had published six more novels by 1914 including *The Secret River* (1909), about a young poet who has a sacramental rather than mystical love for nature, and a narrow-minded wife, whose return after a period of separation both imprisons and humanizes him; and *The Making of a Bigot* (1914), whose hero, Eddy Oliver, finally realises that his indiscriminate enthusiasms are a form of moral paralysis, and converts to prejudice. But her reputation and impact on the literary world was made during the 1920s and 1930s when she published a series of brilliantly witty satirical novels including *Potterism* (1920), about the detrimental effects of the popular press, and *Told by an Idiot* (1923). In 1918, while working in the Ministry of Information, she began an affair with Gerald *O'Donovan, a married man; until his death she was estranged from the Church of England, which she subsequently rejoined. This experience informs her last, bestselling novel, *The Towers of Trebizond* (1956). An edited version of her correspondence with the Revd Father Hamilton Johnson on religious and other issues was published as *Letters to a Friend* 1950–1952 (1961) and *Last Letters to a Friend* (1962). She also wrote three volumes of verse, essays, a study of E. M. *Forster (1938) and several travel books. There are biographies by Constance Babington Smith (1972) and Jane Emery (1991).

McCARTHY, Justin (1830–1912) married (1855) Charlotte ALLMAN (d. 1879). Born in Cork, son of a justice's clerk, he supported his family by journalism from the age of 17, and in his early years was associated with the Young Ireland movement. In 1854 he moved from the *Cork Examiner* to the *Northern Daily Times* in Liverpool, then in 1859 to London and the *Morning Star.* He devoted much energy to the promotion of Home Rule for Ireland, while working as a novelist, historian, journalist, and from 1879 to 1900 as an MP. His most famous and successful book was *A History of Our Own Times from the Accession of Queen Victoria to the Berlin Congress* (1879); there were many later revised editions. He was publishing fiction as early as *Paul Massie* (1866) and *Con Amore* (1869). He retired from Parliament to Folkestone in 1900, blind and ill, and his last novels such as *Mononia* (1901) and *Julian Revelstone: A Romance* (1909) were dictated. The former is set in south-west Ireland during a rising in 1848, and events are shown from a Catholic and nationalist point of view. The latter concerns the heir of an ancient English family who returns from America a wealthy man and visits his old home disguised as his own business agent; his reforming ideas shock his landlord neighbours, especially when he starts wooing the daughter of one of them. McCarthy also wrote fiction in colllaboration with Mrs Campbell *Praed. He published several volumes of autobiography: *Reminiscences* (1899), *The Story of an Irishman* (1904), and *Irish Recollections* (1911).

McCARTHY, Justin [Huntly] (1860–1936) married, first (1894), Marie Cecilia LOFTUS (1876–1943) (divorced 1899) and, secondly (1908), Loullie KILLICK. The only son of Justin *McCarthy, senior, he was educated at University College School and University College London. He wrote political studies and more than thirty novels and collections of short stories, some of which reflected his interest in Home Rule and the Irish problem, for instance *Lily Lass* (1889), about the Young Ireland movement. *The Illustrious O'Hagan* (1906), whose principal characters are two Irish adventurers wandering Europe, *The O'Flynn* (1910), whose hero is a soldier of fortune in the late seventeenth century, and *The Fair Irish Maid* (1911), set in early nineteenth-century London, make a more frivolous use of Irish characters. Like his father he was a Nationalist MP, 1884–92. One noteworthy production was *The Fate of Fenella* (1892) one of the collaborations popular at the turn of the century, written by McCarthy, 'Helen *Mathers', and the unusually large number of twenty-two other writers; it was translated into Polish. He also wrote verse, but his main work was in the theatre. His first wife, Cissie Loftus, was an actress and mimic who published a few songs and stories.

MacDONALD, Greville [Matheson] (1856–1944) married Phoebe WINN (d. 1927). Eldest son and fourth child of the novelist and children's writer, George MacDonald (1824–1905), of whom he published a biography (1924), he was born in Manchester and educated at King's College School, London, and at King's College Hospital Medical School. Increasingly deaf from childhood, less clever than his sisters, and unhappy at school, he discovered in himself a talent for science. He became a specialist in diseases of the nose and throat at the Throat Hospital, Golden Square (where he married the Matron), and then at King's College Hospital. He was also the author of fiction for children and adults including the series of fairy tales about a farming family on the Sussex Downs: *The Magic Crook, or, The Stolen Baby* (1911), *Trystie's Quest, or, Kit, King of the Pigwidgeons* (1912), and *Jack and Jill: A Fairy Tale* (1913). Resigning from King's before the First World War because of his deafness, he retired to Haslemere, where he was associated with Maude Egerton *King, whose husband was his cousin, and the Peasant Arts Guild, which is discussed at length in *Reminiscences of a Specialist* (1932).

McDONNELL, Randal William (1870–) married (*c.*1910) Mary HAMILTON. Born in Dublin, son of a QC, and educated at Armagh Royal School and Trinity College, Dublin, he became an engineer; he was for some time an assistant librarian in Archbishop Marsh's Library, St Patrick's Cathedral, Dublin, and a reviewer for the *Freeman's Journal*. He was also a magistrate and a local government inspector. He was the author of *How to Become a Locomotive Engineer* (1899), verse, and four *historical novels about Ireland: *Ardnaree: The Story of an English Girl in Connaught Told by Herself* (1911), *Kathleen Mavourneen: A Memory of the Great Rebellion* (1898), *My Sword for Patrick Sarsfield: A Story of the Jacobite War in Ireland* (1907), and *When Cromwell Came to Drogheda: A Memory of 1649* (1906).

MACFALL, [Chambers] Haldane [Cooke] (1860–1928) married Mabel PLUMRIDGE. The son of an army doctor, he was educated at Norwich Grammar School and the Royal Military College, Sandhurst. He served in Jamaica and West Africa between 1885 and 1892, and began to contribute impressions of colonial life to the *Graphic*; he was forced to retire as a lieutenant after contracting 'Yellow Jack' fever in Sierra Leone. In the First World War he rejoined and reached the rank of major. His range was wide; he published, among other works, a study (1928) of Aubrey Beardsley (1872–98) and other art-historical works, military studies, and *Ibsen: The Man, His Art & His Significance* (1903). His idiosyncratic and remarkable novels include *The Wooings of Jezebel Pettyfer* (1898), a picaresque novel set in the West Indies (which is dedicated to his stepmother, 'Sarah *Grand'); *The *Masterfolk* (1903); *Rouge* (1906), written with Dion Clayton *Calthrop; and *The Three Students* (1926), set in eleventh-century Persia. He painted, exhibiting at the Royal Academy, designed and decorated books, and was called 'the Marie *Corelli of art criticism'. MacFall was given a Civil List pension in 1914 for services to literature. He died after an operation.

MACGILL, Patrick (1891–1963) married (1915) Margaret GIBBONS. Born in Glenties, Co. Donegal, he was educated at a National School, and at 14 published verse in the *Derby Journal*. Soon afterwards he set out with 10s in his pocket and worked as a labourer. He was later a platelayer on the Caledonian Railway. In 1911 he worked on the *Daily Express*; in 1912–14 in the library of Windsor Castle (perhaps on Erse manuscripts). The popularity of his poems *Songs of a Navvy* (1911) and *Songs of the Dead End* (1912), and of the autobiographical novel **Children of the Dead End: The Autobiography of a Navvy* (1914), which sold 10,000 copies in fifteen days, transformed his life. He was the author of later fiction to 1937, much of it set in Donegal. During the First World War he fought in the London Irish Rifles, described in *The Amateur Army* (1915) and other works. His wife, who also published fiction 1916–36, was a niece of the American Cardinal James Gibbons (1834–1921) and lived in Hendon. MacGill's subsequent career is extremely obscure. He also wrote as 'John O'Gorman'. He published several of his early works himself.

MACHEN, Arthur: Arthur Llewelyn JONES (1863–1947), after 1874 JONES-MACHEN, married, first (1887), Amelia HOGG (*c.*1850–99), and, secondly (1903), Dorothie Purefoy HUDLESTON (d. 1947). Born in Caerleon-on-Usk, only child of a Church of England clergyman, and educated at Hereford Cathedral School, he failed to enter the Royal College of Surgeons and became an impoverished journalist in London in 1881. In 1887 he made friends with the mystic A. E. Waite (1857–1942), a lifelong friend. He worked as a publisher's clerk and tutor, catalogued occult books, and also did translations, most notably of Casanova's *Memoirs* (1894). It was his interest in the supernatural which gave distinction to his original works: 'Literature, as I see it, is the attempt to describe the indescribable.' These include *The Great God Pan* (1894), about a woman possessed by the devil; *The Three Impostors* (1895), which suffered from the unpopularity of 'decadent' writing at the time of the Wilde scandal; and the semi-autobiographical *The *Hill of Dreams* (1907). The latter was completed as early as 1897 and serialized. In *Hieroglyphics: A Note upon Ecstasy in Literature* (1902) he described what for him was the central idea of his work: 'rapture, beauty, adoration, wonder, awe, mystery, sense of the unknown, desire for the unknown . . .' After the death of his first wife from cancer Machen became a member of the Order of the Golden Dawn; in 1901 he joined the Shakespearian repertory company run by Sir Frank Benson (1858–1939) and married a fellow-actor. He also wrote much journalism from this period and had less time for original work. From 1910 to 1921 he worked on the *Evening News*, where he published the story 'The Bowmen' (Sept. 1914) which gave rise to the very widely credited legend of the Angels of Mons. His *The Angels of Mons, The Bowmen, and Other Legends of the War* (1915) was answered by Harold *Begbie, who argued the case for the supernatural. *The *House of Souls* (1906) was a collection of novellas and tales. Despite a revival of interest in his work during the 1920s Machen was badly off for much of his life: an appeal raised money for him in 1943; his work is often concerned with the writer's dilemma, on the one hand wanting money and needing public recognition and on the other trying to evolve a personal and private vision: 'Art and Life are two different spheres.' For all the difficulties of his life, he has always had a circle of admirers, and his work has had considerable influence on horror fiction in Britain and America. He lived from 1929 until his death at Amersham, Buckinghamshire, dying shortly after his wife in a nursing-home in Beaconsfield. He published the memoirs *Far Off Things* (1922), *Things Near and Far* (1923), and *The London Adventure* (1924), and there is a biography by Aidan Reynolds and William Charlton (1963).

MACHRAY, Robert (1857–1946) married (1886) Kathleen Beatrice VANKOUGHNET. Born at Fyvie, Aberdeenshire, he was educated at Cambridge University and became a Church of England clergyman. His uncle, Robert Machray (1831–1904), of whom he published (1909) a biography, was Archbishop of Rupert's Land, and Primate of Canada. Under his patronage, the younger Machray became a professor of ecclesiastical history at St John's College, Manitoba, and a canon of Winnipeg Cathedral. However, he resigned to become a writer. He was at one time on the committee of the Authors' Club. He became war editor of the *Daily Mail* but had to resign in 1905 because of his health. In 1906, and again in 1911, 1912, and 1913, he applied for relief to the Royal Literary Fund, suffering from severe osteoarthritis. He published twelve novels between 1902 and 1915, specializing in rather simple-minded mysteries: *The Mystery of Lincoln's Inn* (1903) features a defaulting solicitor; *The Private Detective* (1906) is about the unmasking of an impostor: *The Disappearance of Lady Diana* (1909) occurs on the eve of her marriage to Lawrence Dundas, apparently in consequence of a letter from an old lover, Major Gartside. After the First World War and during the Second, he published a number of serious works on Balkan and East European issues.

MACK, Louise: Mary Louisa MACK (1870–1935) married, first (1896), John Percy CREED (d. 1914), and, secondly (1924), Allen Illingworth LAYLAND (*c.*1891–1932). Born in Hobart, Tasmania, eldest of thirteen children of a Wesleyan minister, she was educated by her mother and a governess and at Sydney Girls' High School. Her experience at school provided the background for several of her novels. She worked as a columnist on the Sydney *Bulletin* from 1898; then in 1901 she went to London, without her husband, an Irish barrister. She published fourteen romantic novels 1896–1914 including *An Australian Girl in London* (1902), a winsome epistolary novel ending in romance, *Teens: A Story of Australian Schoolgirls* (1903), and *In A White Palace* (1910), in which a woman ex-convict becomes secretary to her accuser (who is now blind), vindicates herself, and marries him. *The Music Makers* (1914) is also about a false accusation: in this case a woman composer is supposed to have stolen a friend's opera. She worked as a journalist and serial writer for the Harmsworth Press. She spent six years living in Florence, where she edited the *Italian Gazette* (1904–1907). During the First World War she was a war correspondent, which she wrote about in *A Woman's*

Experiences in the Great War (1915). In 1916 she went back to Australia to raise money for the Red Cross. She seems to have acquired an illegitimate child by the time of her marriage to a New Zealand soldier in 1924. Her sister Amy Mack (1876–1939) was a children's writer and also came to England, where she worked in the ministry of munitions during the First World War.

MACKENZIE, [Edward Montague] Compton (1883–1972), Kt. (1952), married, first (1905), Faith STONE (*c*.1878–1960), secondly (1962), Christina MacSWEEN (*c*.1909–63), and, thirdly (1965), her sister Lilian MacSWEEN (*c*.1918–). Born at West Hartlepool, the son and grandson of actors whose surname was Mackenzie but who acted under the name Compton, he was the eldest of five children; the actress Fay Compton (1894–1978) was his sister. Mackenzie was educated at St Paul's School, London, and at Magdalen College, Oxford, where he read history. He married the sister of his best friend, Christopher *Stone, who later worked on Mackenzie's magazine the *Gramophone* (1923–). His first novel *The Passionate Elopement* (1911), an eighteenth-century pastiche, was successful; **Carnival*, which followed a year later, was second in the bestseller lists only to *The *Scarlet Pimpernel*, and the Cockney phrases of its heroine became fashionable slang. He got the idea for **Sinister Street* (1913, 1914) from an engraving of a nightmarish street he had seen while renting a flat from Muirhead and Gertrude *Bone; this autobiographical account of unhappy childhood and the sexual curiosity of an adolescent caused much debate, being banned by Boots and W. H. Smith from their circulating libraries, praised by Henry *James, Max *Beerbohm, and F. M. *Hueffer; while at Eton College the young 'George Orwell' (1903–50) stole the copy the young Cyril Connolly (1903–74) kept hidden by his bed. During the First World War Mackenzie served in the Dardanelles campaign, and then worked in Greece for the secret service; he was later to be charged under the Official Secrets Act for indiscretion in his account of this period in *Greek Memories* (1933). He had converted to Roman Catholicism in 1914, in which year he settled on the isle of Capri where he met Norman *Douglas, Somerset *Maugham, D. H. *Lawrence, and others, depicted in *Vestal Fire* (1927) and *Extraordinary Women* (1928). After the war he left for the Channel Islands; later, in 1928, he became a Scottish Nationalist and moved to Barra in the Hebrides, about which he wrote the very successful novel *Whisky Galore* (1947). Though many of his later novels are potboilers (he was extravagant and often in financial straits), his early work was distinctive, innovative, and widely influential. He and his first wife long led separate lives: after her death he began the task of composing his immense autobiography *My Life and Times* (10 vols., 1963–71), with the help of his second wife (who had been his secretary and mistress since the 1920s) and his third wife, the latter's sister, who had to decipher a manuscript which his approaching blindness had made almost illegible.

MACKIE, John (1858–1939). Born in Stirlingshire, younger son of a family of landed gentry, he emigrated to Australia in 1882, travelled there and in the East, went to North America in 1888, joined the Mounties, and, later, served with Brabant's Horse in the *Boer War, where he fought at the battle and siege of Wepender and the battle of Belfast. He wrote *The Bush Mystery, or, The Lost Explorer* (1912), *The Rising of the Red Man: A Romance of the Louis Riel Rebellion* (1904), and other volumes of colonial fiction for boys.

McLAREN, Amy was the author of ten novels 1903–29, of which the first was *From a Davos Balcony* (1903), an epistolary novel; the Scots heroine, nursing her aunt in Switzerland, meets a man with a mad wife, who conveniently shoots herself by the time of the last letter. The heroine of *Through Other Eyes* (1914) dislikes her stepmother and is taught a lesson when she dies leaving twin sons. *Bawbee Jock* (1910), McLaren's most popular work, is a treacly Highland idyll: an heiress marries an impoverished laird without telling him she is rich. The author lived at Biggar, Lanarkshire, and wrote for the *People's Friend* and the *Glasgow Herald*.

MACLAREN, Ian, *pseud.*: John WATSON (1850–1907) married (1878) Jane Burnie FERGUSON. Watson was born in Manningtree, Essex, of Scots parents, his mother being Gaelic-speaking. His family moved to Perth in 1854 when his father, a Scottish civil servant, was been appointed Receiver-General for Taxes in Scotland. In 1866, after attending Perth Grammar School and Stirling High School, Watson matriculated at

Edinburgh University. He graduated in 1870 and went to New College, Edinburgh to train for the Presbyterian Church. Watson was licensed by the Free Church of Scotland in 1874. His first ministry was at Logiealmond in Perthshire (the 'Drumtochty' of his later stories); three years later (1880) he moved to Liverpool to Sefton Park Presbyterian Church. He stayed there until 1905. He was a popular minister and played a leading role in the establishment of Liverpool University. Watson was encouraged to produce sketches of Scottish life by W. R. Nicoll (1851–1923), editor of the *Expositor*. He began writing novels under the name Maclaren, his mother's maiden name, towards the turn of the century. Titles include the tremendously successful *Beside the Bonnie Brier Bush* (1894), *The Days of Auld Land Syne* (1895), *Kate Carnegie and Those Ministers* (1897), which many consider his most accomplished work, *Young Barbarians* (1901), *His Majesty Baby* (1902), *St Jude's* (1907), which consisted of episodes in the life of a Glasgow minister, and *Graham of Claverhouse* (1908). Watson was a renowned public orator and was invited to do 'preaching' tours of the United States. He gave the Lyman Breecher Lecture at Yale University in 1896. On his third trip he fell ill and died at Mount Pleasant, Iowa; his body was returned to Liverpool for burial. He also wrote several theological works under his own name. In his day Watson had a large following both in Britain and abroad. Both Queen Victoria and W. E. Gladstone were admirers of his publications. Yet the great sentimentality of his fiction definitely places him in the Kailyard school. His chief merit was his ability to record rural dialects with reasonable competence, but he lacked skill in connecting sketches to form a unified work. Frederick *Watson was his son.

MACLEOD, Fiona, *pseud.*: William SHARP (1855–1905) married (1884) Elizabeth Amelia SHARP (1856–1932). Although born in Paisley, William Sharp spent some of his childhood in the Scottish highlands. He is reputed to have run away on three different occasions as a child, so strong was his desire for a solitary communion with Nature. The most memorable and extended of these excursions was Sharp's summer spent in a gypsy community. He attended Glasgow Academy and went on to matriculate at the city's university. His discontented college life was followed by an even more unhappy spell as a law clerk. In 1876 Sharp's father died; his family decided that he ought to go to Australia to improve his health (consumption was suspected). He returned, unimpressed by the continent, to take up a job at a bank (1878). He had trouble holding down jobs and eventually decided to try his hand at literature. The Pre-Raphaelites were a great early influence, and, like Hall *Caine, Sharp was much indebted to the help and encouragement of Dante Gabriel Rossetti (1828–82). Sharp married his first cousin in 1884, the year he became the art critic for the *Glasgow Herald*. He wrote several biographies for Eric Robertson's 'Great Writers' series during the late 1880s, and edited the 'Canterbury Poets' series. His own early poetical works, such as *Earth's Voices* (1884), concerned 'Mother Nature and her inner mysteries'. Other verse collections include *Romantic Ballads and Poems of Phantasy* (1888), and *Sospiri di Roma* (1891). He also published several adventure stories for boys. His later novels include *The Gypsy Christ* (1895), *Wives in Exile* (1896), and *Silence Farm* (1899), a semi-autobiographical work. He also published an anthology of Celtic poetry, *Lyra Celtica* (1896), edited with his wife, and an edition (1896) of the Ossianic poems of James Macpherson (1736–96). His first publication as 'Fiona Macleod' was *Pharais: A Romance of the Isles* (1894); it came close on the heels of *The Celtic Twilight* (1893) by W. B. Yeats (1865–1939). To say that 'Fiona Macleod' was Sharp's pseudonym is misleading; it has been suggested that *alter ego* would be more precise. The strain of sustaining his own identity whilst secretly masquerading as Fiona Macleod all but caused a nervous breakdown in the late 1890s. Yeats wrote rather bitterly of Sharp's propensity to invent or evade: 'the facts of life disturbed him and were forgotten'. Sharp's diligent publicization of his 'cousin's' work included a bogus entry for her in *Who's Who*. Only after his death (he had diabetes) did the truth of their relationship emerge publicly. The 'ancestral memories' published by the nostalgic Miss Macleod demonstrate the mix of mysticism and romanticism typical of the 'Celtic Twilight'. These works include *The Mountain Lover* (1895), *The Sin Eater* (1895), *Green Fire* (1896), *The Laughter of Peterkin* (1897), *By Sundown Shores: Studies in Spiritual History* (1900), *Winged Destiny: Studies in the Spiritual History of the Gaels* (1904), the nature essays *Where The Forest Murmurs* (1906), and *A Little Book of Nature*

(1909), selections of her work chosen by Elizabeth Sharp. 'Fiona Macleod' also produced the plays *The House of Usna* (1903) and *The Immortal Hour* (1908). A few days after Sharp's death in Sicily, a hostile obituary in the *Times* (15 Dec. 1905) criticized the work of 'Fiona Macleod': 'If [her writings] represent the Celt of the Western Islands as endowed with the imagination and feelings of a poet, they also portray him as a maudlin and inefficient nincompoop. Also they are too liberal of "word-painting" and many of the descriptions of natural scenery are quite kaleidoscopic in their colouring.' Sharp's works in his own name are grudgingly praised as being 'if not very virile ... at least interesting and finely wrought'. Perhaps there were too many reputations still smarting after the revelations that followed Sharp's death and the simultaneous demise of 'Fiona Macleod'.

MacMAHON, Ella (d. 1956) was the daughter of a Church of England clergyman, chaplain to the Lord Lieutenant of Ireland, and was educated at home. She converted to Roman Catholicism, and her first publications were translations of the writings of St Francis de Sales (1884) and St Theresa de Jesus (1885). She went on to publish more than twenty volumes of fiction between 1889 and 1928, several of which deal with adultery and marital intrigue. Scrope Cuthford, the hero of *Such As Have Erred* (1902), marries a beautiful tobacconist while still a student at Trinity College Dublin; she has a past, and something of a future. After she has left him, he becomes Secretary to the British Ambassador at Rome, and, after a gap of ten years, meets another woman, Honor Beresford of the house of Bawn, who is handsome, pure, and above all genteel. In *The Court of Conscience* (1908) Audrey Dennison, the daughter of disreputable parents, marries Warren Mildmay, a rising politician, without taking the trouble to check his marital history. In *The Divine Folly* (1913), Blanche Adeane discovers that her friend Elma Fancourt has been having an affair with her husband, Sir Lawrence. There are two other main characters, St John Adeane and Ruth Frere. The story concerns the relations between these four, Blanche remaining dour and aloof throughout. *The Job* (1914) is the account of a baronet's struggles to improve his Irish estate despite the fecklessness of the inhabitants and the distractions of a love affair. MacMahon lived in England, worked as a civil servant during the First World War, later contributed to the BBC, and was given a Civil List pension for services to literature.

McMANUS, L[ottie]: Charlotte Elizabeth McMANUS (*c*.1850–1941). Born in Co. Mayo, third of seventeen children of a sugar-planter, she was educated by a governess and at Torquay. In *White Light and Flame: Memories of the Irish Literary Revival and the Anglo-Irish War* (1929) she describes how, in her 40s, in about 1894, while living in England, she began to have doubts about the British Empire, in which she, a Protestant daughter of the Anglo-Irish gentry, had been brought up to believe. She read George Stokes's *Ireland and the Celtic Church* (1886) and *Ireland and the Anglo-Norman Church* (1889), and the novels of Standish O'Grady (1846–1928), learnt Irish and joined the Gaelic League. She was opposed to the *Boer War, and wrote a column in the *Irish Emerald*. She moved back to Mayo and collected folklore. Her novels, published *c*.1894–1922, include *In Sarsfield's Days: A Tale of the Siege of Limerick* (1906), which she later dramatized, and *Nuala: The Story of a Perilous Quest* (1908) whose heroine, the heiress of the O'Donnells, has to rescue their ancestral book, the Cathach, against the background of the Napoleonic wars. The latter was translated into Erse (1954).

MacMANUS, Seumas: James MacMANUS (1869–1960) married, first (1901), Anna JOHNSTON (1866–1902) and, secondly (1911) Catalina Violante PAEZ. Born at Mountcharles, Co. Donegal, son of a peasant farmer, he became a National School teacher aged 17 at the school he had himself attended, then a journalist, poet, and novelist. Much of his work was published in America, where he lived half the year. He was the author of many volumes of tales of Irish life and folklore including *Through the Turf Smoke: Love, Lore and Laughter of Old Ireland* (1899), *Yourself and the Neighbours* (1914), *Doctor Kilgannon* (1907), comic sketches related by a doctor, and the series *Irish Nights* (1903–). His first wife was moderately well known as a Celtic Twilight poet under the name 'Ethna Carbery'. *The Rocky Road to Dublin* (1938) is an autobiography, published in New York in 1947.

MACNAMARA, Rachel Swete (d. 1947). Born in Ennis, Co. Clare, she lived in Cork, where her father was manager of the Munster and Leinster

Bank. She travelled abroad and settled in London, but her novels continued to have Irish settings. She was the author of about sixty volumes of fiction, which find an opportunity in impossible dilemmas and *exotic locations for a (comparatively) lurid frankness about sexual yearning. In *Trance* (1908), Aline Outram, wife of a doctor in a provincial town, has lain in a coma for twenty years, while the heroine, Felicity, looks after him faithfully, thus sacrificing the love of a great literary man who admires her poems. The heroine of *The Awakening* (1914), published in America as *The Torch of Life*, marries a vigorous, passionate man who is crippled on their wedding day, and thereafter seeks consolation in the full if passive enjoyment of her beauty; when, after ten years of misery, he dies, she is awakened by a casual lover, and finds happiness with an old friend of her husband who has always loved her. Exotic locations include Venice, in *The Sibyl of Venice* (1908), six stories about Pia la Strega, a wise woman who dispenses charms and love-potions; and Egypt, in *Seed of Fire* (1910), about a half-French half-English woman, sister of an archaeologist working in Egypt, who falls in love with a young Arab, and in *The Fringe of the Desert* (1913), which concerns an affair between Hesper Deltravers Marlowe, a 35-year-old Irish woman, and Igor Ivors, a famous pianist, who is weak but charming. Altogether less fiery in setting and mood is *Spinners in Silence* (1911), about Lutie Basenal, the unsophisticated daughter of a bookish recluse living on the coast of Ireland. Macnamara kept up this rate of production until *Cuckoo* (1948). Many of her novels were published in the '*People's Friend* Library'. She died in Bayswater, London.

MACNAUGHTAN, S[arah Broom] (1864–1916). Born in Scotland, one of eight children of an upper-middle-class family in Renfrewshire, and educated by German and English governesses, she travelled in the Americas, the Near East and India. She nursed during the Boer and First World Wars and was the author of fourteen volumes of intelligent, humorous, mildly feminist fiction, often set in high society, between 1898 and 1916. *The Fortune of Christina M'Nab* (1901) begins with a woman breaking off her engagement to an electrical engineer because she inherits £18,000 a year, and ends with her breaking off her engagement to a duke to return to him. *The Gift* (1904) is the story of a woman who has had an unhappy childhood, grows up full of religious aspirations, does social work, cannot marry the man who loves her, and embarrassingly declares her love for a celibate priest. *The Expensive Miss Du Cane* (1907) a country-house story in which the unconventional but scrupulously well-bred (the two qualities together constituting her expensiveness) heroine very nearly finds a husband worthy of her. *The Three Miss Graemes* (1908) are Scots girls living on an ancestral island off the west coast of Scotland with their widowed father, whose mad jealousy of a beautiful wife had tragic consequences. He has since gambled away the family estate, and when he dies his daughters throw themselves on the mercy of their aunt, Lady Parfield, a good-hearted, businesslike, popular woman with a thriving establishment in London. Macnaughtan also published *My Canadian Memories* (1920), *My War Experiences in Two Continents* (1919), and *A Woman's Diary of the War* (1915). Reviewers commented on her interesting treatment of older women characters. *Us Four* (1909) is some autobiographical sketches about her childhood; they contain little detail.

MACQUOID, Katherine S.: Katherine Sarah THOMAS (1824–1917) married (1851) Thomas Robert MACQUOID (d. 1912). Born in Kentish Town and educated at home, she published more than fifty volumes of fiction, including children's books and ghost stories, and also wrote a number of travel books about France. She published in periodicals from 1859. Her husband, a painter, illustrated several of her books. Her earliest works, such as *A Bad Beginning: A Story of a French Marriage* (1862), *Chesterford and Some of Its People* (1863), *By the Sea* (1864), and *Hester Kirton* (1864), were published anonymously. Her later works include *His Heart's Desire: A Romance (1903)*, a *historical romance, *A Village Chronicle* (1905), reprinted from the *Illustrated London News*, which is a series of anodyne or melodramatic sketches of rural life, and *Captain Dallington* (1907), about a highwayman. Her brand of pure fiction was becoming old-fashioned by the Edwardian period and she made seven applications to the Royal Literary Fund between 1894 and 1915, when old, ill, but still working. She also received a Civil List pension of £120. She was the mother of the furniture historian Percy Macquoid (1852–1925), who illustrated some of her books.

MAGNAY, Sir William, Bt.: William MAGNAY (1855–1917) who succeeded (1871) as 2nd Baronet, married (1879) Margaret Susannah SOULSBY (d. 1950). Son of a Lord Mayor of London, he published twenty-six volumes of romantic fiction 1897–1918. These include *Count Zarka* (1903), a *Ruritanian thriller in the manner of E. Phillips *Oppenheim, in which Galabin, of the Austrian secret service, is sent hiking in the Carpathian mountains to look for Prince Roel of Rapsberg, kept in an iron mask by the sinister Zarka. Other works include a number of run-of-the-mill thrillers: *The Master Spirit* (1906), in which Paul Gastineau, KC, MP, crippled and supposed dead, renews his career through the person of a young barrister and politician, Herriard (there is also an old murder mystery to unravel); *The Mystery of the Unicorn* (1907), in which Sir Francis Cardale of Gabriels may or may not be the man he says he is; *The Red Stain* (1908), which opens with the late arrival of the inscrutable Captain Grendon at a party at Standerton Court, and the non-arrival of Harry Vyne-Miller of Danes Abbey. *A Poached Peerage* (1909) is a farcical tale of exchanged identity. Lord Quorn, just home from Australia, meets a runaway criminal, Peckover, who is about to poison himself in despair, in the coffee-room of the Quorn Arms. Quorn drinks the drugged wine and Peckover appropriates the title, which is subsequently bought by a millionaire. Magnay only published fiction.

Maid of Mystery, A, L. T. *Meade, 1904, F. V. White. After her mother's sudden death, Alice Brabazon is educated at a convent in Rouen. John Brabazon, her handsome father, whom she adores, communicates with her by way of a sinister man of the world, Blyth St John, who seems to have Brabazon in his power, and who has already singled Alice out as his future wife. Returning to England, Alice encounters Gerard Hamilton, the brother of a Rouen schoolmate, an Englishman 'straight through and through', and a magnetic older woman, Lady Grace Darnley, who is in love with her father. Lady Grace is mugged in the maze at Belfield Park, the Brabazon home, and her priceless jewels are stolen. Gerard proposes to Alice, is accepted, but then has an interview with her father which results in his abrupt and unexplained departure for Canada. Blyth St John presses his suit on Alice, and, despite her aversion to him, she accepts, because her father wishes it. Her father is to marry Lady Grace. The first marriage takes place, but is not consummated, because St John is called away on business. Alice's apprehension, her brief glimpse of freedom, is well rendered. But Meade, suddenly losing patience, rushes the story to a conclusion. St John and Brabazon are exposed as the leaders of a gang of burglars. The former is shot by the police, the latter disappears with Lady Grace, who has presumably forgiven him for mugging her and stealing her jewels (which, as her husband, he now owns).

Maker of History, The, E. Phillips *Oppenheim, 1905, Ward Lock. In the opening chapter, 'An Accidental Spy', Guy Stanton,—'just a good-looking, clean-minded, high-spirited young fellow, full of beans, and needing the bit every now and then'—stumbles across a secret meeting between the Kaiser and the Czar in a forest on the German border. A page of a secret treaty, which floats out of a window and lands close to his hiding-place, reveals that they are coordinating an attack on Britain. Stanton, who cannot speak the lingo and is in any case too full of beans to be interested in politics, becomes the focus of deadly intrigue. The French get hold of him before the Germans, but will not admit it to anyone. Sir George Duncombe, a friend of a friend, who has fallen in love with a photograph of Stanton's sister, herself a captive by this time, eventually tracks him down. The fatal page persuades the French government to ally itself with Britain rather than Russia, and the new alliance proves strong enough to avert war. The Anglo-French alliance of 1904 enabled Oppenheim to produce a narrative based not, as in his previous novels, on the intervention of a secret society, but on political awakening. What connects the protagonists now is not membership of an order or clan, but their status as amateurs. Like the heroes of several early *spy stories, they are all 'accidental spies'. Stanton, the callow tourist, receives a political education; Duncombe, galvanized by the photograph, passes into 'the shadows of the complex life'; his assistant, a journalist, learns how to reconcile patriotism with the desire for a scoop. One of the French kidnappers, a 'drug-sodden degenerate', goes over to the enemy; but another, who has always posed as a 'decadent', turns out all right. The ruling classes on both sides of the Channel have woken up to their responsibilities. The French leader concludes: 'We amateurs have justified our existence.'

Making of a Marchioness, The, Frances Hodgson *Burnett, 1901, Smith, Elder. Emily Fox-Seton is a genteel, impoverished odd-job woman ('one of the new ways women have found of making a living'). The Marquess of Walderhurst marries her because she is cheerful and unselfish, and she adapts effortlessly to her new role. His heir, Alec Osborn, returns to England with an Anglo-Indian wife and Walderhurst goes abroad on a diplomatic mission. When Emily becomes pregnant Alec makes several attempts to procure a miscarriage or murder her, with the help of his wife's devoted Indian maid, Ameerah. But his wife, herself pregnant, warns Emily, who goes into hiding in London. Walderhurst returns to find Emily dying in childbirth, having saved his son and heir 'through superhuman endurance'; he drags her back from death by the force of his love for her. Meanwhile the Osborns return to India with an ugly female baby, and Alec is murdered by Ameerah in revenge for his sadistic ill-treatment of his wife. The novel combines Victorian domestic melodrama with an Edwardian interest in the emotional and practical predicaments of women.

MALET, Lucas, *pseud.*: Mary St Leger KINGSLEY (1852–1931) married (1876) William HARRISON (d. 1897). Born at Eversley, Hampshire, she was the daughter of the novelist and social reformer the Revd Charles Kingsley (1819–75), niece of the novelist Henry Kingsley (1830–76) and cousin of the travel writer Mary Kingsley (1862–1900). She trained at the Slade School of Fine Art but abandoned painting on her marriage to a friend and former curate of her father's, who was soon afterwards appointed rector of Clovelly, Devon, in the area in which her father's novel *Westward Ho!* (1855) is set, where she lived for many years. Her first novel was *Mrs Lorimer: A Sketch in Black and White* (1882). Her fiction is written in a rather elaborate style, with epigrammatic dialogue, much emphasis on philosophical problems, and an atmosphere of highbrow worldliness; we are to imagine her characters are at the epicentre of literary, artistic, and political life. The hero of *Adrian Savage* (1911) is editor of a fortnightly review in Paris and loves a beautiful, warm Parisian; he is loved by his plain, repressed cousin Joanna, whose environment is a wholly different one, middle-class, English, Dissenting, and respectable. See also *The *History of Sir Richard Calmady* (1907) and *The *Far Horizon* (1906). Her most popular novel was *The Wages of Sin* (1891); her last novel, *The Private Life of Mr Justice Syme* (1932), was completed by Gabrielle Vallings, her cousin and adopted daughter. Her marriage, which was childless and unhappy, had ended in separation some time before her husband's death, and she and Vallings travelled widely on the Continent. She became a Roman Catholic in 1902. She applied to the Royal Literary Fund in 1917, citing her slowness of production and the difficulties caused by the First World War.

Manalive, G. K. *Chesterton, 1912, Thomas Nelson. 'Mr Chesterton', a reviewer announced, 'writes stories on the assumption that the only sane men are the apparent lunatics, and the only serious people the apparent practical jokers; and, proceeding thence by an absolutely logical process, he produes a harlequinade in which moral and spiritual meanings are conveyed by knockabout artists.' The knockabout in question here, Innocent Smith, arrives over the garden wall of a Swiss Cottage boarding-house, preceded distantly by a telegram to one of the lodgers which reads 'Man found alive with two legs', and immediately by his panama hat, the victim of a violent gust of wind, a large green umbrella, and a gladstone bag. He thereafter stirs up the clientele of 'young but listless folk': Diana Duke, the landlady's practical niece; Rosamund Hunt, popular but inaccessible; Arthur Inglewood, good-looking, insignificant, an amateur photographer and cyclist; Michael Moon, a flippant journalist with a fondness for low company; Moon's drinking companion, Moses Gould, a Jew with 'negro vitality'; and Dr Herbert Warner, a prosperous young doctor who is only visiting the establishment, as is Rosamund's friend Mary Gray. Smith 'had somehow made a giant stride from babyhood to manhood, and missed that crisis in youth when most of us grow old'. After a few warm-up practical jokes, he proposes to Mary Gray, fires shots at Warner, and is arrested by Warner's accomplice, Cyrus Pym, a Criminal Specialist from America. Pym identifies Smith as a criminal genius who, in the disguise of 'a good man a little cracked', has committed robbery, murder, desertion, and polygamy. In the second half of the book, Smith clears his name in front of a kangeroo court set up in the boarding-house. He is a man who likes to remind himself of the value of familiar experience by approaching it from an unfamiliar angle. To that end, he has burgled himself, shot holes in his friend's top hat, gone all the way around the world in order to arrive at his own home, and left his wife about at various boarding-houses in order to begin courting her again each time he meets her. He has broken the conventions, but kept the Commandments. Suitably stirred by the episode, Michael proposes to Rosamund, and Arthur to Diana. The book was described as just about everything from a 'literary romp' and 'metaphysical extravaganza' to an abject failure of nerve and taste. Rebecca West (1892–1983) called it an 'intoxicating and delicious fairy tale', but protested about its didacticism and its glorification of the inglorious: she might have preferred, one suspects, a hero who kept the conventions but broke the commandments.

Man of Property, The, John *Galsworthy, 1906, William Heinemann. The first volume of the best-known and most ambitious of all Edwardian *family sagas (the next volume, *In Chancery*, was not published until 1920). It opens with a party given by 'old Jolyon' Forsyte in honour of the engagement of his granddaughter, June, to the architect Philip Bosinney. The older members of the family (James, Swithin, Timothy) represent the cautious vigour of Victorian values: they have handsome homes near Hyde Park from which they keep an eye on their investments and their spinster sisters. Second-generation Forsytes like George, a bachelor horse-fancier, and Winifred, wife of the cheerfully disreputable Montague Dartie, show a tendency to kick over the traces. One of the few family members not at the party is young Jolyon, June's father, an artist, who was disowned by his father, old Jolyon, when he left his wife for another woman. Definitely in attendance is Soames Forsyte, dubbed the 'man of property' by old Jolyon, a wealthy lawyer and art collector whose most prized possession is his beautiful wife, Irene. That evening, moved by the occasion, old Jolyon seeks his son out at his club. The reconciliation is subsequently cemented when he visits him at home. Soames has commissioned Bosinney to design a country house for him at Robin Hill. The visionary Bosinney manages both to exceed his budget, much to Soames's disgust, and to begin a liaison with Irene, thus alienating June. Soames, by now with reason to be jealous of Bosinney, as well as angry about the cost of his house, decides to sue him. June falls ill. Soames, taunted by a friend about Bosinney's friendship with his wife, bursts into Irene's bedroom and rapes her. When Irene tells him about the rape, Bosinney wanders the streets in a distraught state and is knocked down and killed. Soames's case against him comes to court the next day, and Soames wins. He returns home to find Irene huddled 'like a bird that is shot and dying'. He moves to Brighton, without every occupying his new house, or becoming aware of the consequences of his jealousy.

Man Who Was Thursday, The: *A Nightmare*, G. K. *Chesterton, 1908, J. W. Arrowsmith. Lucian Gregory rules unopposed over the artists' community of Saffron Park until the arrival of Gabriel Syme, who opposes his own reverence for law, order, and respectability to Gregory's anarchism. Gregory responds by promising Syme an evening's entertainment he will never forget, and must never reveal to anyone. He takes him to a meeting of the Council of the New Anarchists, whose seven members are all named after days of the week. Syme, who is in fact a police detective, and whose reverence for law and order constitutes a rebellion against a family of rebels, puts himself forward for the vacant position of Thursday, and is promptly elected to the General Council of the Anarchists of Europe. His fears for his own safety and for the safety of the world are not eased when the President announces that there's a traitor among them. He fingers his revolver. However, the traitor unmasked is Gogol, supposedly a Polish anarchist, but in fact also a detective. One by one, the members of the Council reveal themselves as detectives. Together, they confront the President, who announces, 'I'm the man in the dark room, who made you all policemen' and leaps over the balcony. A chase ensues, by cab, fire-engine, elephant, and balloon, which concludes with the President inviting his pursuers to a lavish fancy-dress party where they must wear disguises which reveal their true selves. Syme attends as a poet who 'seeks always to make the light in special shapes, to split it up into sun and star'. The point of the exercise has been to enable the participants to find out who they really are. Gregory, whose anarchism is the authentic article, accuses them of playing games; Syme defends the authenticity of their experience. Syme awakes to find that it was all a dream, and that he is now strolling with Gregory as though they were old friends. 'Mr Chesterton has something of [Robert Louis] Stevenson's faculty of squeezing romance out of the commonplace, and he adds something fresh and boyish which is all his own,' the *Westminster Gazette* reported. The *Aberdeen Free Press* compared the book to Stevenson's *The Dynamiter* rewritten by George Bernard Shaw. Gilbert *Cannan thought it an attack on eclecticism which was itself too eclectic for comfort, but others discerned an allegory behind the nonsense. Chesterton himself later explained that the brutal but 'cryptically benevolent' Sunday stood for Nature, not God.

MANN, Mary E.: Mary E. RACKHAM (1848–1929) married Fairman Joseph MANN. Daughter of a merchant in Norwich, she published more than forty volumes of fiction to 1917, many of them set in Norfolk. Her early fiction was anonymously published in the early 1880s; the first seems to have been *The Parish of Hilby: A Simple Story of A Quiet Place*. Her Edwardian fiction includes *Among the Syringas* (1901), which appeared with the motto 'Who's born a woman is born a fool', *Rose at Honeypot* (1906), about a love affair between a married woman and a gamekeeper, *The Sheep and the Goats* (1907), about a flirt who after various trials marries a clergyman, and *Astray in Arcady* (1910), a series of letters from a country village. Wolff records, rather surprisingly, that she and M. E. *Braddon expressed admiration for each other's works.

MANSFIELD, Charlotte (1881–1936) married (1909) W. R. MANSFIELD. She published thirteen novels and a book of travel in southern Africa. Her first publication was a volume of verse (1899); the next *Torn Lace* (1904), whose heroine is an Italian prostitute who dies receiving the wound intended for the man she loves, an English painter. *The Girl and the Gods* (1906) is a lush and absurd Pygmalion or Frankenstein tale in which a doctor and a millionaire create a beautiful girl whose entry into London society is the vehicle for social satire and celebration of spiritualism. The heroine of *Love and A Woman* (1909) is having an affair with a married man who obligingly dies so that she can marry her cousin, who has always loved her. It may be autobiographical. In 1909 Mansfield set out from the Cape to Cairo, and became seriously ill; in October she married a civil engineer, who became a colonel in the war, and later a handwriting expert. She came with her husband to England during the war to speak against naturalized Germans, and began work on her memoirs, but illness forced her to stop. *Strings* (1920) is an occult *horror novel about a sinister violin. Mansfield was a Fellow of the Royal Geographical Society.

MANSFIELD, Katherine, *pseud.*: Kathleen BEAUCHAMP (1888–1923) married, first (1909), George BOWDEN (1877–1975) (divorced 1918) and, secondly (1918), John Middleton MURRY (1889–1957). Born at Wellington, New Zealand, daughter of a banker who was a first cousin to *'Elizabeth', she was educated at Wellington Girls' High School, Miss Swainson's School, Wellington, and in England at Queen's College, Harley Street (1903–6), where she met her lifelong friend Ida Baker (1888–1978). Back in New Zealand she contributed some stories to the *Native Companion*. In 1908 she persuaded her parents to let her return to England to study music, where she arrived in August, and began an affair with a violinist, Garnet Trowell (1889–1947). The only one of her fictions to be published in volume form before the First World War, **In A German Pension* (1911), draws on her experience of boarding-house life in Bavaria, where she miscarried Trowell's child in August 1909; most of the sketches had originally appeared in the **New Age*. In March 1909 she had married Bowden, a musician she scarcely knew, and left him the same evening, returning to him only once briefly, in the following year. She lived with Murry from 1912, writing for *Rhythm* and the **Blue Review* which he edited. She had a brief affair with the novelist Francis Carco (1886–1958) in February 1915. She was much affected by the death of her only brother, Leslie (1894–1915). Mansfield's grief led her to rework the experiences of her childhood in New Zealand: these stories are now regarded as her finest. She and Murry spent the summer of 1916 in Cornwall with D. H. *Lawrence and his wife. In 1917 tuberculosis was diagnosed and much of the rest of her short life was spent abroad. She died in the Institute for the Harmonious Development of Man near Fontainebleau, founded by G. I. Gurdjieff (1872–1949), where she had gone in search of spiritual and physical equilibrium. Her major works are *Prelude* (1918), the original longer version of which was published as *The Aloe* (1930); *Bliss and Other Stories* (1920); *The Garden-Party and Other Stories* (1922); *The Dove's Nest and Other Stories* (1923); and *Something Childish and Other Stories* (1924). Her *Journal* (1927) and *Letters* (1928) were edited by Murry.

MARCHANT, Bessie (1862–1941) married (1889) Jabez Ambrose COMFORT. Born in Kent, she published more than 100 children's books set in foreign parts, especially Canada and the Americas, although there seems to be no evidence that she travelled very far from home. Her husband was a Church of England clergyman and she lived at Charlbury, Oxfordshire. Her works, in which young heroes and heroines display grit and win through, include *Athabasca Bill: A Tale of the Far West* (1906), *A Countess from Canada: A Story of Life in the Backwoods* (1911), *A Girl of the Northland* (1913), *A Girl of the Fortunate Isles* (1907), *Hope's Tryst: A Story of the Siberian Frontier* (1905), and *A Girl and a Caravan: The Story of Irma's Quest in Persia* (1915).

MARCHMONT, Arthur W[illiams] (1852–1923) married (1892) ——. Born in Southgate, Middlesex, son of a Church of England clergyman, he was educated at Pembroke College, Oxford, and at Lincoln's Inn. He became a journalist, and was editor successively of the *North Eastern Daily Gazette* and the *Lancashire Daily Post*. He devoted himself to fiction from 1894 and was the author of nearly fifty novels of various sorts, including *crime fiction like *A Millionaire Girl* (1908) and *Miser Hoadley's Secret* (1904), and *Ruritanian romances like *A Dash for the Throne* (1899), *For Love or Crown* (1901), and *When I Was Czar* (1903), in which an American citizen, Harper C. Denver, who bears an extraordinary resemblance to the Czar, becomes an instrument of Russian diplomacy; he marries a princess and, crying 'Bully for you', bears her off to New York. Marchmont's most popular work seems to have been *By Snare of Love* (1904), in which an American and an Englishman pit themselves against the evil Turkish government in Constantinople.

Margaret Holroyd, *or, The Pioneers*, Annie S. *Swan, 1910, Hodder & Stoughton. The suffrage movement was perhaps a surprising topic for a writer whose sentimental romances constantly emphasized the seriousness of domestic responsibilities. To tackle it, Swan dispensed entirely with the traditional wedlock plot of popular fiction, describing instead a varied group of women in their relations to the campaign for the vote. The book opens in 'an old family home, the cradle of an honourable race', with Margaret Holroyd, the last of that race, looking out over a 'fair and typical English scene'. She is put out because her male servants can vote in the local by-election while she cannot. She resolves to do something about it, and moves to London to join the suffrage movement led by Mrs Cecil Field. The focus then shifts to a succession of women (and some men) who have joined the Cause: spinsters Julia and Emily Cartmell, who are inspired by their young niece to make up for wasted time; Rhoda Chard, daughter of a bullying unemployed carpenter, who becomes a stirring speaker despite her lack of education and 'atrocious' accent; Joyce Mainwaring, whose wholehearted offer of help is declined on account of her family commitments (her father is an invalid); Sara Cummings, who abandons campaigning, but not her convictions, to safeguard her husband's political career; Sybil Wheatley, who is sacked by her employer, Mrs Rosenbaum, because she devotes too much time to the movement, but marries a sympathetic politician; and Mr Marriott, an Egyptologist, who late in life finds happiness with 'a woman who had lost none of her womanly and wifely qualities through enthusiasm for the new era'. The novel confronts honestly the difficulties of political commitment, and of the representation of those difficulties in a genre traditionally associated with private rather than public life. But there can be no mistake about its fundamental conservatism: Margaret Holroyd resigns from the movement because she objects strongly to its militant tactics, while Mrs Cecil Field also resigns when she realizes that her political activism has deprived her son of a mother.

MARNAN, Basil was the author of *A Daughter of the Veldt* (1901), in which an innocent young South African girl is seduced and has a child by a worldly Anglican parson; *The Resident Magistrate* (1902), about the rise to respectability in South Africa of the son of a Fenian traitor; and *A Fair Freebooter* (1902), in which a magistrate's secretary masterminds a series of cattle raids, steals the jewels of a raja, and eventually escapes justice. Internal evidence indicates that he was a South African and perhaps a Roman Catholic.

Marriage, H. G. *Wells, 1912, Macmillan. The third of a series of discussion novels about relations between the sexes, following **Ann Veronica* (1909) and *The *New Machiavelli* (1911). Marjorie Pope, daughter of a coach-builder who went bankrupt when he refused to modernize his factory and make motor cars, is a beautiful and independently minded young woman who is studying science at university. When she returns home to visit her family, her suitor, the middle-aged and extremely unmagnetic Mr Magnet, proposes; she rejects him, knowing that marriage will mean little more than the role of society hostess. He persists, however, and she accepts him—and immediately begins to regret her decision. Whereupon a plane crash-lands on the front lawn. Out of the wreckage steps a former teacher, Trafford, who falls in love with her and encourages her to pursue a career. She disengages herself from Magnet, and moves to London. Mr Pope orders Trafford from his house, and disowns Marjorie, who reacts by eloping with Trafford to Italy. After a decent interval, they return to London society. Marriage, and the birth of a child, begin to have a damaging effect on Trafford's research. The marriage founders, but is rekindled during a holiday in Switzerland. Trafford abandons his research, and applies his hard-won knowledge to the manufacture of rubber. After seven years he has become a wealthy man, and this, together with the birth of a second son, reconciles him to his parents-in-law. A second holiday, this time in Labrador, involving canoes and caribou, further reinvigorates their love, and persuades them to rededicate their lives to nobler aims than rubber and dinner parties. The novel drew a brilliant review from Rebecca West (1892–1983), in which she described Wells as 'the Old Maid among novelists' ('even the sex obsession which lay clotted on *Ann Veronica* and *The New Machiavelli* like cold white sauce was merely Old Maids' mania, the reaction towards the flesh of a mind too long absorbed in airships and colloids'); and a lugubrious damning with faint praise from Henry *James: 'I live with you and in you and (almost cannibal-like) on you, on you H. G. W., to the sacrifice of your Marjories and your Traffords, and whoever may be of their company... I see you "behave" all along, much more than I see them even when they behave.'

Marriage of William Ashe, The, Mrs Humphry *Ward, 1905, Smith, Elder. The main characters, William Ashe and his wife Kitty, are based on William Lamb (1779–1848) and his wife, Caroline (1785–1828). But, as in a number of Mary Ward's Edwardian novels, by far the strongest presence is Ashe's ambitious mother, Lady Tranmore, who wants above all to get her son into Parliament and into marriage. In fact, Ashe makes a disastrous marriage to Kitty Bristol, a young woman possessed of great beauty and 'bad blood'. As he ascends the Liberal party hierarchy to the post of Home Secretary, Kitty becomes more and more of a liability. A physically handicapped child is born, whom she rejects. At the very moment when he stands on the threshold of the premiership itself, she not only throws herself at the caddish Geoffrey Cliffe, but publishes a scandalous *roman à clef* which divulges Cabinet secrets. The marriage reaches crisis point during a visit to Venice. Scorning her husband's kindliness, Kitty runs off with Cliffe to take part in a Balkan uprising against the Turks. She finally dies at Simplon, in Switzerland, after earning Ashe's forgiveness. The novel's strength is its depiction of *political life, and it is sometimes regarded as Mary Ward's last significant work of fiction.

marriage problem novels. George *Meredith's suggestion that all marriage contracts should be reviewed after a period of ten years, and only extended if they were still to the satisfaction of both parties, indicates not only that in the Edwardian period writers did not hesitate to offer social and political commentary, but that the institution of marriage, assaulted in so many of the New Woman novels of the 1890s, was once again, after a brief respite, back on the agenda. The problem remained the same, but the solutions proposed, indeed the tone of the inquiry, were different. 'Quite suddenly the time for defensive experimentation appeared to be over,' Peter Keating observes, 'and attention began to switch to a close analysis of the proven results of those experiments. It could now be assumed that there was no such thing as normal or orthodox sexuality; no single generally acceptable pattern for family life; no one kind of sexuality that was attributable to all women and all men.' A distinction needs to be made between an attention to marital relations which differed only in degree (of frankness, of elaboration) from that evident in Victorian fiction, not in kind, and the emergence of a distinct genre, the 'marriage problem' or 'sex problem' novel, whose emphasis was as much polemical as literary. Henry *James's later novels are marriage problem novels in the first sense, but not in the second. Among Arnold *Bennett's novels, *The *Old Wives' Tale* (1908) and *These Twain* (1916) are marriage problem novels, while *Leonora* (1903) and *Whom God Hath Joined* (1906) are 'marriage problem' novels. Novels which offered a close analysis, in Keating's terms, of the proven results of sexual and marital experiment would include: *The Pastor's Wife* by '*Elizabeth' (1914); Hall *Caine's *The Woman Thou Gavest Me* (1913); C. A. *Dawson-Scott's *The Agony Column* (1909); Mabel *Dearmer's *The Alien Sisters* (1908); Hugh *de Sélincourt's *A Boy's Marriage* (1907); Florence *Farr's *The Solemnization of Jacklin* (1912); Lady Angela *Forbes's *The Broken Commandment* (1910); Lady Helen *Forbes's *The Polar Star* (1911); C. Gasquoigne *Hartley's *The Weaver's Shuttle* (1905); Agnes Grozier *Herbertson's *The Plowers: A Novel* (1906); Maurice *Hewlett's *Half-way House* (1908), *Open Country* (1909), and *Rest Harrow* (1910); Sheila *Kaye-Smith's *Spell Land* (1910); Rosamond *Langbridge's *The Flame and the Flood* (1903); Ada *Leverson's **Love's Shadow* (1908), *The Limit* (1911), and *Tenterhooks* (1912); Mrs Belloc *Lowndes's *Studies in Wives* (1909); John *Masefield's *The Street of Today* (1911); Somerset *Maugham's **Mrs Craddock* (1902); *Saba Macdonald* by *'Rita' (1906); Eden *Phillpotts' *Demeter's Daughter* (1911); Anne Douglas *Sedgwick's *Amabel Challice* (1908); Lady *Troubridge's *The House of Cards* (1908); *The Yoke* (1907) by 'Hubert *Wales'; L. B. *Walford's *The Enlightenment of Olivia* (1907); H. G. *Wells's **Marriage* (1912) and *The *Passionate Friends* (1913). The characteristic note of these novels is the combination of a lofty tone with a plot verging on the sensational. The 'marriage problem' writers who contrived most successfully to avoid priggishness on the one hand and exploitation on the other are 'Elizabeth', Ada Leverson, and Somerset Maugham. But it is worth noting that there was a powerful *feminist slant to a number of other contributions to the genre. In a preface to Maud Churton *Braby's **Downward* (1910) which connects the 'marriage problem' novel of the 1900s to the New Woman novel of the 1890s, Edward Garnett argued that the former, 'even when it is not good art, is a document, a piece of polemics, a special diagnosis of a state of social unrest of a vast class of women who are placed in a radically false situation to men by the defects of our social organization'. Examples of 'special diagnosis' would include: Annesley *Kenealy's *The Poodle-Woman: A Story of 'Restitution of Conjugal Rights'* (1913); Gladys *Mendl's *The Straight Road* (1911); Amber *Reeves's *A *Lady and Her Husband* (1914); Olivia *Shakespear's *Uncle Hilary* (1910); and May *Sinclair's *The *Helpmate* (1907). One group of marriage problem novels, including some of the above, as well as Herbert *Flowerdew's *The Woman's View: A Novel About Marriage* (1903), Stephen *Torre's *The Blot* (1909), Douglas *Sladen's *The Unholy Estate* (1912), and William *de Morgan's *It Can Never Happen Again* (1909), is concerned with the complexity of the laws relating to marriage and divorce and the consequent human difficulties. And some writers looked at marriage problems and divorce law reform from a reactionary point of view, for example Mrs Humphry *Ward in *Daphne* (1909).

MARRIOTT, Charles (1869–1957) married, first (1892), Dora M. M'LOUGHLIN (d. 1917) and, secondly (1919), Bessie WIGAN (d. 1949). Born in Bristol, son of a brewer, he was educated privately and at an art and technical school in South Kensington, before qualifying as a pharmacist. His career was an unusual one. From 1889 to 1901 he was the dispenser and photographer at the County Asylum, Rainhill. He published fiction from 1901 and was art critic of the *Times* (1924–40). He lived for some time at St Ives in Cornwall, where some of his fiction is set, and where he was friends with Mrs Havelock *Ellis and Mrs Alfred *Sidgwick. He was clearly thought of as a writer whose combination of a self-consciously literary style and a liking for social and aesthetic theory with mildly incendiary subject-matter might enable him to bridge the increasing gap between up-market and down-market readerships. The result, however, is a certain confusion of aim and effect centred on a recurring preoccupation with unconsummated sexual love. The hero of Marriott's first novel, *The Column* (1901), returns to the English countryside with a Doric column and a half-Greek daughter who at the end, still an outsider, commits suicide. *The House on the Sands* (1903) is a novel of ideas about an MP, his sister, her lover (a poet), and a couple of relapsed socialists who live together platonically. Their discussions of the *Boer War, state ownership of industry, sex and *marriage, and imperialism end in tragedy. *Genevra* (1904) concerns a missed opportunity: the heroine, a mature woman, hesitates while her lover's passion fades and he becomes absorbed once more in his work. The heroine of *The Lapse of Vivien Eady* (1906) loves a Cornish farmer, Humphrey Stott, with her heart, and Selwyn Harper, a priggish schoolteacher, with her head. This time, for once, the opportunity is seized, as it very definitely is not in *The Wondrous Wife* (1907): a womanly woman, Margaret Lisle, separated from her feebly unfaithful husband, loves and is loved by a manly man, Fawcett, an engineer, but decides that her husband needs her more. *Now!* (1910) and *The Dewpond* (1912) are novels of ideas, at once sympathetic to and sceptical of socialism, the former featuring a Cornish simple-life cult called Morrisonism. *The Catfish* (1913) concerns a passion which is in some strange way perfected even though it never comes to fruition: a shy, imaginative young man defies expectation by establishing a shop in Bristol and marrying, not the only woman in the world who understands him, but a motherly type who guesses at and is glad of what she cannot share. The artist-hero of **Subsoil* (1913) articulates the question raised by Marriott's own career: he believes that in art the qualities of execution which appeal to the virtuoso and the connoisseur are precisely those which separate it from life. 'I'm trying to get down to what quite ordinary people feel about things,' he claims, a little desperately, in the middle of an immense swirling discussion of social and aesthetic theory. Marriott's art criticism includes *Eric Gill as Carver* (1929) and *Laura Knight: A Book of Drawings* (1923). He translated from Italian and Portuguese. Hugh *Walpole began a friendship with him by writing to praise his novels, which influenced his own, and was encouraged in his career as a novelist by Marriott's advice.

MARSH, Richard (*c.*1857–1915). He is supposed to have begun writing for boys' magazines at the age of 12, and was the author of more than seventy volumes of sensational and romantic fiction, some of which, like *The Death Whistle* (1903), struck reviewers as decidedly gruesome. The opening of *A Woman Perfected* (1907) is characteristically blunt: 'Donald Lindsay was prostrated by a stroke of apoplexy on Thursday, April 3.' Lindsay's missing wealth is tracked down by his daughter Nora and her bosom friend Elaine. Other works in the period include *A Drama of the Telephone and Other Tales* (1911) and *Violet Forster's Lover* (1912). He wrote in *Who's Who*: 'Recreations; he loved them all—cricket, football, golf, cycling, billiards, chess, bridge, motoring, and a dozen more; a clumsy but enthusiastic student of whatever made for proficiency in the fine art of doing nothing.' His great success was *The Beetle* (1897) which originally appeared in *Answers*, and which was included by Graham and Hugh Greene in *Victorian Villainies* (1984), the cream of their collection of early thrillers; the latter comments in his introduction that it looks 'from the laconic accounts in the newspapers of the time' as if 'some mystery hung around his death'. He contributed to the **Cornhill*. He died of heart failure aged 58, according to the *Times* (11 Aug. 1915).

MARSHALL, Archibald: Arthur Hammond MARSHALL (1866–1934) married (1902) Helen May BANKS née POLLARD. The son of a Nonconformist businessman, he was educated at Highgate School, and at Trinity College, Cambridge. He became a journalist. Under his own name he published one novel, *Lord Stirling's Son* (1895). He founded the publishing company Alston Rivers when he was unable to publish his second novel, *The House of Merrilees* (1905); during his two years there the firm also published F. M. *Hueffer's *The *Fifth Queen*. He left to work for Lord Northcliffe (1865–1922) on the short-lived **Books* (1906–7); later he was foreign correspondent of the *Daily Mail* and, during the First World War, Paris correspondent of the *Daily News*. *Peter Binney, Undergraduate* (1905) was a comedy about an elderly undergraduate; *The Squire's Daughter* (1909) was the first of a long series of rather predictable Trollopian novels about class and religious differences in the English provinces: Cicely rebels against the narrowness of a life in which the men have all the fun, and elopes with and is rescued from a famous explorer whose many qualities do not include that of being a gentleman. Other similar works are *The Honour of the Clintons* (1913) and *Roding Rectory* (1914), about the conflict between Church and Dissent in a country parish. *Richard Baldock: An Account of Some Episodes in His Childhood, Youth and Early Manhood, and of the Advice that was Freely Offered to Him* (1906) is, as the title suggests, a jovial *Bildungsroman*. The two crucial episodes in young Baldock's life are Dickensian or *Wellsian in emphasis: when he is 13, and living in a sombre vicarage in the New Forest with his tyrannical father, he is invited to visit Paradine Park, seat of a wealthy widowed aunt who has vague intentions of making him her heir, but loses out to a scheming rival; at the age of 18 he has to decide whether to go to Oxford or throw in his lot with a pushy, vulgar, well-intentioned ex-schoolfellow who plans to enter the book trade. Marshall also published *The Terrors, and Other Stories* (1913). He collaborated with Compton *Mackenzie on *Gramophone Nights* (1923) and with H. A. *Vachell on *Mr Allen* (1926). He published an autobiography, *Out and About: Random Reminiscences* (1933), in which he makes resentful comments about the inaccuracy of the account in Hueffer's *Return to Yesterday* (1931) of Marshall himself, Henry *James, and Hueffer's contribution to *Books*.

MARSHALL, [Emma] Beatrice (1861–1944) completed *Cross Purposes* (1899) and *The Parson's Daughter* (1899), the last novels of her mother, Emma Marshall (1830–1899), of whom she also published a biography (1900). Born at Wells, Somerset, setting of several of her mother's decorous novels for young girls, Beatrice Marshall was one of eight children. After Emma Marshall died, the publishers Seeley, who had published her fiction for thirty years, gave the daughter £60 per novel for innocent *historical novels for the young in her mother's style, including *The Siege of York: A Story of the Days of Thomas, Lord Fairfax* (1902), *Old Blackfriars: A Story of the Days of Sir A. Van Dyck* (1901), and *His Most Dear Ladye: A Story of Mary, Countess of Pembroke, Sister of Sir Philip Sidney* (1906). When they gave up publishing fiction in 1906 Beatrice Marshall was desperate. In 1909, 1916, and 1917 she applied to the Royal Literary Fund. She also published several translations from German and contributed an article entitled 'Nietzsche and Richard Wagner' to the *Fortnightly Review* (June 1898).

MARTINDALE, Elizabeth (1876–1949) married (1894) F. M. *HUEFFER (1873–1939). Elsie Hueffer was the author of one undistinguished novel, *Margaret Hever* (1909), about a triangular relationship between a remarkable young girl, an aged historian, and his unconventional young cousin. The book is much indebted to *Middlemarch* (1871–2) by George Eliot (1819–80). In the end, *contre* Eliot, the heroine chooses the historian.

MASEFIELD, John [Edward] (1878–1967), OM (1935), married (1903) Constance DE LA CHEROIS CROMMELIN (1867–1960). Born at Ledbury, Herefordshire, third of six children of a solicitor, he was educated at the King's School, Warwick. He spent a very happy childhood, especially before his mother died when he was six and a half. His father died, after a year confined to a hospital with mental illness, in 1891, and the children lived with an uncle and aunt. Masefield was taken away from the King's School for financial reasons, aged 13, and sent to train for the Merchant Navy on HMS *Conway*, moored in the Mersey. He left in 1894 as an apprentice to the White Star Line on *Gilcruix*, sailing to Chile with a cargo of compressed coal dust. He became ill and was returned home as a Distressed British Seaman, again went to sea in 1895, and jumped ship in New York, determined to be a writer. He worked as a barman and in a carpet factory before returning to England, in poor health, in 1897. There he resumed contact with his family, worked as a clerk, and slowly began to contribute to **Outlook* and other periodicals. With the fashion for down-and-out memoirs like those of Bart *Kennedy and W. H. *Davies, he published autobiographical sketches in the *Speaker* (see the **Nation*) in 1902, but his break was the success of *Salt-Water Ballads* (1902). After his marriage to a schoolmistress, who had some money and was a first cousin of May *Crommelin, he briefly, in 1904, took a job on the staff of the *Manchester Guardian*. As well as verse and stories he wrote history books and edited anthologies and volumes of verse and prose for his publisher, Grant *Richards. He was also much preoccupied with writing plays; *The Campden Wonder* was first performed in 1907 and *The Tragedy of Nan* in 1908. His early fiction includes the sea stories and sketches of *A Mainsail Haul* (1905), mostly comic and *fantastic in tone, one of which concerns a Spanish sailor called Don Alfonso and his love of 'licker', another a skipper who becomes a pirate, another a man who buys a monkey in Panama and is surprised by the creature's sudden loquacity when he threatens to throw it overboard; *Captain Margaret* (1908), a romance of the Spanish Main; **Multitude and Solitude* (1909); and *Lost Endeavour* (1910), a story for boys.

During 1909–10 Masefield had an intense relationship with Elizabeth *Robins (then nearly 50), and became an enthusiastic supporter of women's suffrage. When she withdrew he became depressed; *The Street of Today* (1911) is a pessimistic *marriage problem novel. The hero, Lionel Heseltine, is Masefield's mouthpiece for a violent epigramatic assault, rather in the manner of H. G. *Wells, on the purposeless materialism of the modern world: science, and the formation of a scientific élite, is civilization's only hope. But Heseltine's idealism fades. He ends up editing a magazine called *Snip Snap*, and is bogged down in a miserable marriage. However, in the early part of that year he began to write *The Everlasting Mercy*, a narrative poem about the redemption of a blasphemous, drunken Herefordshire man, which was published to acclaim in the **English Review* in October 1911, and had an immediate impact on contemporary poetry. He was never poor or obscure again. During the First World War he worked for the Red Cross in France and at Gallipoli, lectured in America, and was commissioned officially to write a poem about the Battle of the Somme. Subsequently he lived (until 1933) at Boar's Hill near Oxford, where the great popular success of both his prose and his verse allowed him to be generous to younger writers and to produce verse dramas. After a few years in Gloucestershire the Masefields went to live near Abingdon. He travelled widely, and became enthusiastic about ballet. He succeeded as Poet Laureate in 1930, and in that capacity survived to write a poem on the assassination of John F. Kennedy (1917–63). There is an autobiography, *So Long to Learn* (1952), and a biography by Constance Babington Smith (1978).

MASON, A[lfred] E[dward] W[oodley] (1865–1948). Born in Camberwell, son of a chartered accountant, he was educated at Dulwich College and Trinity College, Oxford (1884–8). Success in the OUDS led to his becoming an actor until 1894 (his first employer was Compton *Mackenzie's father and he acted with Florence *Farr in the first production of *Arms and the Man*, 1894). Oswald *Crawfurd, as editor of *Black and White*, published his first story in January 1895, and told him to write a book: Mason produced *A Romance of Wastdale* (1895), whose hero murders his best friend who has seduced his fiancée, and then the popular *The Courtship of Morrice Buckler* (1896), a *historical adventure story in *Weyman's manner, drawing on Mason's years of acting in eighteenth-century plays. He continued in the vein of historical romance with *Parson Kelly* (1900), written with that devotee of the form, Andrew *Lang, and with *Clementina* (1901), the story of the escape of the princess who married the Old Pretender. *Miranda of the Balcony* (1899) and Mason's best-known novel, *The *Four Feathers* (1902), were still of tales of romantic adventure, but transported into the modern world. The latter drew on travels in Egypt and Sudan in 1901. *The *Broken Road* (1907), which drew on research undertaken for political reasons in India in 1906–7, shares a theme with Hugh *Clifford's 'Sally: A Study'; it exposes race consciousness by contrasting the treatment of an Indian prince at school in England with his treatment by the British in India. The book is said to have been responsible for changing the rule that Indians could not win the Victoria Cross. **At the Villa Rose* (1910) was the first of a successful series of detective stories about Inspector Hanaud. Mason was Liberal MP for Coventry from 1906 to 1910 (he used his election experience in *The Turnstile*, 1912) and during the First World War he worked for the secret service in Spain, Morocco, and Mexico; in the last, looking for radio stations in a neutral country, he remembered the villain of *The *Hound of the Baskervilles* and assumed the disguise of a lepidopterist. He was a friend of *Barrie, 'Anthony *Hope', and E. V. *Lucas, and collaborated with 'Ian *Hay' on *A Present from Margate* (1934). After the First World War his income was augmented with profits from film versions of his novels; he earned as much as £10,000 p.a. at his peak, and by the end of his life was still earning £6,000 p.a. He also wrote several plays and many of his works were dramatized for the stage. He refused a knighthood.

There is a biography by Roger Lancelyn Green (1952).

MASSON, Rosaline [Orme] (d. 1949). She was the youngest daughter of David Masson (1822–1907), professor of English literature at University College London (1853–65) and professor of rhetoric and English literature at the University of Edinburgh (1865–95). She was a friend of R. L. Stevenson (1850–1894), the author of several books on Edinburgh and Scotland and of six volumes of fiction 1893–1911, including what now seem like sub-*Wodehousean farces: *In Our Town* (1901), and *Our By-Election* (1908), in which Lord Harry Calthrop impersonates his uncle, Theophilus, a candidate at the Chucklebury by-election, who has been kidnapped by the other side and hidden on a yacht. She also edited several anthologies.

Masterfolk, The, Haldane *Macfall, 1903, William Heinemann. The story opens in the editorial office of a struggling weekly review, where Oliver Baddlesmere, the fair-haired, precocious, 14-year-old son of the editor and proprietor, is offering one of his father's employees, Netherby Gomme, some literary-critical advice. A saga of Bohemian life unfolds. Oliver, or 'Noll', marries his childhood sweetheart, Betty Modeyne, daughter of a drunken major, despite the damage this alliance may do to his (fairly remote) chances of inheriting Lord Wyntwarde's title and fortune. They move to Paris, where Noll neglects his wife, who decides that she is an obstacle to his self-expression and leaves him. He falls in with a group of anarchists who preach a Nietzschean amoralism. He must learn to steer a path between asceticism and sensual indulgence. By the time he has learnt his lesson, both Lord Wyntwarde and his son are dead, one in a brawl, the other after a stroke. He returns to England, fame and fortune—and Betty, who has given birth to their first child. The novel is dedicated to George *Meredith, and is one of the few in the period to attempt a Meredithian style as well as subject-matter.

Matador of the Five Towns, The, Arnold *Bennett, 1912, Methuen. Short stories about everyday life in the Five Towns (Bursley, Hanbridge, Knype, Longshaw, Turnhill) gathered under two headings: 'Tragic' and 'Frolic'. The title story concerns the captain of the Knype football team, whose wife dies in childbirth, prompting him to renounce the game for ever. In 'The Heroism of Thomas Chadwick', a tram conductor returns a gold purse left on his tram to its owner, but in the process tells a small lie which costs him his job. In 'The Widow of the Balcony' Stephen Cheswardine, a toilet-seat-maker, buys his wife a new house but refuses to appease her vanity by adding a balcony. Other stories involve a peculiar honeymoon, a fair in Bursley, a day in the life of a dentist, and the secret history of the Ebag family, who were once virtually the rulers of Oldcaste, a borough on the edge of the Five Towns. The title of 'Catching the Train' sums up the story itself, and Bennett's resolute matter-of-factness throughout the collection.

MATHERS, Helen, *pseud.*: Ellen Buckingham MATHEWS (1850–1920) married (1875) Henry Albert REEVES (d. 1914). Born at Crewkerne, Somerset, one of twelve children of a landowner, she was educated at a governess's training school at Chantry, near Frome, Somerset. Her first novel *Comin' Thro' the Rye* (1875), which she published as 'H. B. M', was an immensely popular melodrama; the early scenes, an autobiographical account of childhood in a large family with a tyrannical father, are the most compelling. She was editor of the *Burlington Magazine*. Despite the great success of her early novels, her later life was very sad: her only son (who collaborated anonymously on some of her late works, including *Tally Ho!*, 1906) died in 1907; she herself, deaf since a teenage illness, became very rheumatic; and her husband, a physician, became an invalid and unable to earn any money. In 1909 she applied to the Royal Literary Fund and the Royal Bounty Fund for relief. According to her obituary in the *Times* (13 Mar. 1920), she announced her retirement from authorship in that year. Most of her last works are collections of short stories; many were probably written earlier. They include *Venus Victrix and Other Stories* (1902) and *The New Lady Teazle and Other Stories* (1903).

MAUD, Constance E[lizabeth] (*c.*1860–1929). One of seven children of a Church of England clergyman, she was brought up at New Milverton in Warwickshire and educated partly in France and Germany; she often used this experience in fiction and non-fiction. She translated the memoirs (1907) of Mistral. Many of her books, such as *Angélique* (1912), *A Daughter of France* (1908), in which a wife returns to her husband, *Felicity in France* (1906), and *An English Girl in Paris* (1902), are novels of French life, but **No Surrender* (1911) is a suffragette novel, which, like **Suffragette Sally* (1911) by 'G. *Colmore', clearly draws on the real-life case of Lady Constance Lytton (1869–1923) and contrasts the upper-class feminist with a range of other suffragettes. Maud also published on music and contributed to **Temple Bar*. She died in Chelsea.

MAUDE, Frederic Natusch (1854–1933) married (1876) Mary Emily BOOTT. Educated at Wellington College and the Royal Military Academy, Woolwich, he entered the Royal Engineers in 1873 and rose to the rank of colonel. He was a prolific military historian, and the author of one anonymous novel, *The New Battle of Dorking* (1900), an *invasion scare story on the model of *The Battle of Dorking* (1871) by Sir George Chesney (1830–95). For Maude the enemy is a Franco-Russian alliance; but he allows them to be defeated by the British army before they reach London.

Maudie: *Revelations of Life in London*, The *'Chatty' Club, 1909. This pornographic novel features Charlie Osmond, once of Eton and Oxford, and an imaginative courtesan, Maudie ('She has a few hundreds a year, a detestation of suburbia, and no morals'). The studio of Maudie's Thames-side mansion is decorated with pornographic versions of biblical stories: 'everything in history of a picturesquely indelicate tendency was utilised.' The telephone, still something of a novelty, puts in an ingenious appearance: Maudie rides Osmond while he is speaking on the telephone to his valet. 'Suits he asked for, collars, shirts, etc., boots and ties, and at the hats he spent violently.' No doubt he had also 'spent' pretty violently on the hats. Maudie runs a studio-brothel near the Barbican which features child models procured by Osmond. The newspapers get to hear about it, and the couple flee the country. The novel has been attributed to George *Bacchus, who may also have been responsible for **Pleasure Bound 'Afloat'*.

MAUGHAM, W[illiam] Somerset (1874–1965), CH (1954), married (1917) Gwendoline Maude Syrie WELLCOME née BARNARDO (1879–1955) (divorced 1928). He was born at the British embassy in Paris, the son of a solicitor who was legal adviser to the embassy. His mother died when he was 8; his father when he was 10. He was educated at the King's School, Canterbury, Heidelberg University, and at St Thomas's Hospital Medical School, but never practised as a doctor. His first language was French. His first novel, *Liza of Lambeth* (1897), a modish study of low life in London encountered as a medical student, was popular enough to encourage him to take up a literary career. He and Laurence *Housman edited an anthology in the style of the *Yellow Book*, called the *Venture* (1903, 1905), which had contributions from *Hueffer and *Joyce but died after two issues. His main achievement before the First World War was not in fiction, but, after the success of *Lady Frederick* (1907), in drama. A number of the novels he published in the period might also be described as light comedies, for example *Flirtation* (1904) or *The Bishop's Apron: A Study in the Origins of a Great Family* (1906), in which the Hon. and Revd Theodore Spratte, Canon of Tercanbury and Vicar of St Gregory's, South Kensington, secures Lord Wroxham for his daughter, and an heiress and the bishopric of Sheffield for himself. But Maugham's ironic treatment of sexual morality in *The *Hero* (1901), about a soldier's return from the *Boer War, and in **Mrs Craddock* (1902) and *The Merry-Go-Round* (1904), both of which feature a sharp spinster called Miss Ley whose motto is 'Never sin; but if you sin, never repent; and, above all, if you repent, never, never confess', achieves considerable depth. Maugham's theme of the reckless search for experience is given a Faustian twist in *The Magician* (1908), about an evil-genius vivisector. *The Explorer* (1908) does for exploration what *The Hero* had done for military heroism. In 1911 he stopped writing plays to concentrate on an autobiographical novel, influenced by Samuel *Butler, which became *Of Human Bondage* (1915), one of his finest works. After a period working for the Red Cross in France he was sent, in 1915, by the Intelligence department to Geneva; in 1917 he went to Russia. Some of his experiences were drawn on in the immensely popular short stories which he later published, as were his travels in the Far East which began with a trip to research *The Moon and Sixpence* (1919) in 1916. His wife was the daughter of Dr. Barnardo (1845–1905); a daughter was born in 1915; in 1916 Maugham was cited in her divorce from the philanthropist and chemist Henry Wellcome (1853–1936), but their subsequent marriage was unsuccessful. Maugham travelled and lived from 1916 with Gerald Haxton (1892–1944), whom he had met in 1914 while working for the Red Cross in France. Haxton, probably as a result of having been prosecuted for but acquitted of gross indecency in a London hotel in 1916, had been declared an undesirable alien, a fact which influenced Maugham's decision to live in the south of France from 1928. During the Second World War, doing propaganda work in the US, he studied Vedanta in California. After Haxton's death Maugham lived with Alan Searle (1904–85). Towards the end of his life, suffering from intermittent senile dementia and paranoia, he engaged in litigation with his daughter over money and over his proposal to adopt Searle as his son, and an autobiography, *Looking Back*, attacking his wife, was serialized in the *Sunday Express* in 1962, although both his English and American publishers refused to publish it. There is a biography by Ted Morgan (1980).

Maurice Guest, 'Henry Handel *Richardson', 1909, William Heinemann. Richly detailed story of obsession and despair among music students at Leipzig in the 1890s. On his first day in the city, Maurice Guest, who is studying the piano, encounters the plain, forthright Madeleine Wade. His erratic but enduring friendship with her frames his violent passion for the indolent, sensuous Louise Dufrayer. Louise is the mistress of a talented violinist, Eugen Schilsky, and, although immediately fascinated by her, Maurice consoles himself with Ephie Cayhill, a pretty, plump, childlike American who is staying in Leipzig with her mother and her formidable elder sister, Johanna. Schilsky, however, also has his eye on Ephie, and a scandal ensues, resulting in his departure, and hers. Maurice consoles Louise, and, after an exhausting round of concerts, balls, skating parties, and broken engagements, seduces her, or is seduced by her. They live together. Maurice, however, has been forced to come to terms with his own mediocrity. He is also becoming painfully aware of Louise's promiscuous past. One evening, Heinz Krafft, a fellow-student, reveals that he, too, has been her lover, before and during her relationship with Maurice. In a fury, Maurice beats her up. Krafft leaves town, and an abandoned mistress, Avery Hill, commits suicide in despair. Letters arrive from Krafft, revealing yet further depravities. Maurice discovers that Schilsky, now a rising young composer, has returned to Leipzig. Louise leaves him, and, buying a gun, he walks out into the country and shoots himself. As the novel ends, Schilsky is famous, and married to Louise; but there is a suggestion that she has already betrayed him, or may yet betray him. The novel's strength is its ability to convey the intensity of Maurice's obsession from within and yet not disregard the spectacle he makes of himself in other people's eyes. It is not much interested in his abilities as a musician.

Max Carrados, 'Ernest *Bramah', 1914, Methuen. In the opening episode, 'The Coin of Dionysius', Louis Carlyle, a private detective, appeals for help to an amateur numismatist, whom he is surprised to recognize as an old acquaintance, Max Wynn, who since their last meeting has been blinded but has also inherited (on the condition that he takes his benefactor's name) enough money to secure his independence. Carrados solves Carlyle's case without leaving his armchair. 'The Knight's Cross Signal Problem' concerns a train crash which has cost twenty-seven lives. Carrados clears the engine-driver's name and exposes the true culprit, an Indian who has been speculating on the stock market. In 'The Tragedy at Brookbend Cottage' he foils a husband's elaborate plan to electrocute his wife, but cannot prevent the affair ending badly. Other cases involve the obligatory pearl necklace, a murder in 'Oakshire', a burglar called Harry the Actor who becomes a salvationist and returns the loot, and Carlyle's niece, Mrs Bellmark (her garden turns out to contain money buried by the previous owner, who thought it might come in handy in the afterlife, and whose former servants have subsequently shown a suspicious interest in the place). The stories are light-hearted in tone. But Carrados's blindness does immerse him, frighteningly at times, in the world his brilliant deductions are supposed to clarify and regulate. The final episode finds him trapped in a room with three villains, and managing to even the odds by fusing the lights.

MAXWELL, Gerald [Melbourne] (1862–?) married ——. He was the eldest of the children of M. E. *Braddon, and brother of W. B. *Maxwell. In 1881 he spent a year at Trinity College, Cambridge, and then went for two years to the universities of Würzburg and Hanover in Germany, before becoming an actor. But in 1887 he collapsed with a nervous illness on tour in Cincinnati, Ohio. He later became dramatic critic of the *Court Journal*, as well as author of some works of military topography, and also wrote fiction, which was sensational with an overlay of the macabre. *The Miracle Worker* (1906) involves a German grand duke and his wife, a famous doctor, and the famous doctor's pupil, who serves with the Royal Afghans, and whose life is ruled by two young women, a self-sacrificing nurse and a music-hall performer turned criminal: the miracle of the title is an operation carried out by the famous doctor on the latter's brain, which successfully alters her personality. It was followed by *The Fear of Life* (1908) and *The Last Lord Avanley* (1909), about a family with a past (the worst of the lot kept savage beasts on the estate and went in for orgies and experiments): the present earl, though personally amiable and cultivated, was born with the face of a beast. *By Right Divine* (1911) turns up some unpleasantness in high society in Prussia (a Berlin gambling-hell is closed down, a beautiful woman flogged). Conrad von Altsperg, a young lawyer from an ancient Hanoverian family, believes at the outset in the new German empire and its creator, Otto von Bismarck (1815–98), but then falls in with Ida von Lindenau, also from an ancient Hanoverian family, and reverts to legitimist principles: the novel contrasts brutal Prussian officialdom with the afterglow of Hanoverian feudalism in a way that was becoming increasingly fashionable. Maxwell published one further novel after the First World War. He married after his mother's death, and is known to have had a keen interest in freemasonry. R. L. Wolff suggests, in his biography of Braddon, that Maxwell may have suffered from mental illness in later life. In Douglas *Sladen's memoirs there is a story of Braddon complaining, when W. B. *Maxwell was fighting in the First World War, 'Oh, why didn't they take that other son, who never does anything except play golf and give advice.'

MAXWELL, W[illiam] B[abington] (1866–1938) married Sydney Brabazon MOORE. He was one of the five illegitimate children of M. E. *Braddon, and her publisher, John Maxwell, who married her in 1874, after the death of his first wife. He was brought up in Richmond, Middlesex, with the five children of his father's first marriage. As a boy of 14 he persuaded his parents to let him leave his day school in Richmond and train as a painter at the school run by George *Calderon's father in St John's Wood, London. He was given by his father the annual *The Mistletoe Bough* on his twenty-first birthday. His mother was editor and contributed a story to each issue, but the format was old-fashioned and the annual was soon abandoned. He acted as his mother's secretary and manager after his father's death, and went on living in her house in Richmond after his marriage, although his wife and her mother-in-law are supposed to have had domestic disagreements. During the First World War, in which he fought on the Western Front, his mother died, and afterwards they moved to London, where Maxwell became Chairman of the Society of Authors, Chairman of the National Book Council, a member of the Council of the Royal Society of Literature, and of the Committee of the Royal Literary Fund. His first publication in volume form was *Tales of the Thames* (1892); the second, *The Countess of Maybury* (1901), a collection of sketches in the manner of 'Anthony *Hope', originally contributed to the *World*. At first, his Edwardian publications continued in the same vein of lightweight satire of London society: the title of two collections of short stories, *Fabulous Fancies* (1903) and *Odd Lengths* (1907), are indicative. *The Ragged Messenger* (1904) contrasts West End and East End by allowing a philanthropist to come into an immense fortune. Thereafter, however, sexual obsession and betrayal became his main theme. In *The Guarded Flame* (1906), erotic passion disrupts the sober working lives of an ageing rationalist philosopher, his young wife, his even younger niece, and his secretary. In *The Rest Cure* (1910) John Barnard, a self-made man, marries Lady Edith Morville, but neglects her shamefully. She has an affair, and an illegitimate child, which dies. Meanwhile, he breaks down from overwork. Grace Fielding, his managing clerk, who adores him, informs his wife, who returns remorsefully to find him a changed man. He forgives her on his deathbed. Maxwell's most sensational novel in this vein, *The *Devil's Garden* (1913), caused quite a stir. But his output was reasonably varied. *Seymour Charlton* (1909) is a rambling, Thackerayan story about a younger son who unexpectedly inherits a title, a fortune and a political career, but only after he has engaged himself to the daughter of a disreputable furniture dealer. It encompasses three distinct social groups: the hero's political chiefs and associates; his wife's impossible relations; and a coterie of swindling businessmen who use him as the titled figurehead for their company-promoting schemes. *General Mallock's Shadow* (1912), by contrast, is a **Four Feathers*-style tale about a general in the Indian army who is wrongly accused of cowardice and retires in disgrace to Yorkshire, where he lives with his two daughters, and eventually redeems himself in the eyes of the world when his house is attacked by starving strikers and he organizes stout resistance. After a slow start, Maxwell became very prolific; he published a gossipy autobiography, *Time Gathered* (1937). Like his brother Gerald *Maxwell, he was a Freemason.

MAYNE, Ethel Colburn (1870–1941) was brought up and educated in Ireland, where her father was an officer in the Royal Irish Constabulary and then a Resident Magistrate. She published her first story in the *Yellow Book* as 'Frances E. Huntly' in 1895, and became a journalist and reviewer in periodicals including the *Daily News* and the *Daily Chronicle*. She published many translations from German, French, and Russian including Margarete Boehme, *The Department Store* (1911), and wrote extensively on Byron and his circle. She published fiction from 1898 which often exposes the restrictiveness of domesticity for women. The thrusting red-haired heroine of *Jessie Vandeleur* (1902) steals the work of a discarded lover and passes it off as her own in order to impress her new lover, a distinguished novelist. *The Fourth Ship* (1908) is prefaced by a coy parable. 'There are three ships that we all watch for—the golden-sailed Love; the ship with white sails called The Little Child; the Success, with rosy sails. For some of us all come home; for some, one or the other; for some, again, none of the three comes home. But there is a fourth ship that comes for all of us, and it has black sails...' But the narrative itself, set in the 1850s and the 1890s and told from the point of view of a woman for whom none of the first three ships comes in, is made of sterner stuff. Josie Lawrence, the youngest of three daughters living in a backwater rectory in the heart of Ireland with their father, a well-connected and bad-tempered widower, is courted by a young police officer and man of the world, Philip Maryon. However, he is swept off his feet by a beautiful and enterprising visitor, Millicent North. After their marriage, Josie goes to live with them, and thus has a ringside seat when Millicent's ships come in. For her, nothing goes right. Her father remarries, and dies. Her sisters dwindle into spinsterdom, constantly reproving her for her 'unheard of' determination to earn a living. In the book's final section, we see her visiting the now numerous Maryon family, a brisk little old lady and, in the eyes of one of Millicent's daughters, a pioneer of the emancipation of women. As this summary reveals, Mayne's *feminist preoccupations were close to those of her friend May *Sinclair. She also published *Gold Lace: A Study of Girlhood* (1913), about the relations between Irish girls and English officers in a garrison town, and a collection of stories, *Things That No One Tells* (1910). The heroine of *One of Our Grandmothers* (1916) wants to be a professional pianist, but finds that the middle-class world of 1860 provides scant opportunities.

Mayor of Troy, The, *'Q', 1906, Methuen. A comic and picaresque *historical romance set in a small Cornish seaport in the early years of the nineteenth century. The Mayor of Troy is Major Solomon Hymen, whose household includes Cai Tamblyn, an eccentric little man of uncertain age, Scipio, a black servant, Miss Marty, a poor relative, and Lavinia, a slavey. His impressive progress down the main street, in full uniform, indicates a satisfactory present and a brilliant future. Further glory beckons when the Troy Gallants, a volunteer company formed to combat a possible French invasion, take on the Looe Diehards, their counterparts in the next village down the coast. The troop exercise is an ambiguous triumph for Hymen, but one of his dimmer men, thinking that the French have really landed, fires the supply dump. Things go from bad to worse when Hymen attends a performance at the local theatre, and is pressganged by the navy. Taken prisoner by the French, he does not return home until 1814, to find that his great rival, Dr Hansombody, has been elected as Mayor, taken over his house, and married Miss Marty. In addition, he has one leg fewer than he set out with. Undeterred, he exhumes the money he had buried in his garden and sets out to see the world. The novel is dedicated to Kenneth *Grahame. 'Q' himself was Mayor of Fowey in 1937–8.

MAYOR, F[lora] M[acdonald] (1872–1932) Born in Kingston-on-Thames, she was educated at Surbiton High School and Newnham College, Cambridge. She had a twin sister, Alice. Her mother had translated the Icelandic sagas into English; her father was a Church of England clergyman who was Professor of Classics and, later, of Moral Philosophy, at King's College, London. She published a volume of stories, *Mrs Hammond's Children* (1901), as 'Mary Strafford', under which name she also tried to become an actress. In 1903 she became engaged to an old friend, Ernest Shepherd, an architect with an appointment in India, who died there months later. She continued to write to him for a year after she knew he was dead, and the experience was shattering for her. Her first novel under her own name, *The *Third Miss Symons* (1913), appeared with a preface by John *Masefield. Later works are *Miss Browne's Friend*, about the relationship between a middle-class woman and a prostitute, published serially in the *Free Church Suffrage Times* in 1914–15; *The Rector's Daughter* (1924), her major work, published by the Hogarth Press and admired by Virginia Woolf (1882–1941), a delicate exploration of the restricted and frustrated life of a spinster; *The Squire's Daughter* (1929); and *The Room Opposite and Other Tales of Mystery and Imagination* (1935). Her fiction explores the transition from an old world of security and self-abnegation for middle-class women to a new world offering certain kinds of freedom: Mayor exposes the problems of both cultures as well as the difficulty of readjustment.

MEADE, L. T.: Elizabeth Thomasina MEADE (1844–1914) married (1879) Alfred Toulmin SMITH. Born at Bandon, Co. Cork, the daughter of a Church of Ireland clergyman, she was educated by governesses. She published her first novel at 17. After the death of her mother and her father's remarriage she went to live in England in 1874. In early years she lived with a doctor and his wife, and these friends encouraged her to write an exposure of the outpatient system at the London teaching hospitals, which bore harshly on the poor: this was *Great St Benedict's* (1876) her third novel. It may have been through this medical connection that she met the obscure figure 'Robert *Eustace' with whom she published five volumes of science fiction (1898–1902); she also collaborated with 'Clifford Halifax M. D.' (i.e. Edgar Beaumont) on six volumes of crime stories including *Stories from the Diary of a Doctor* in two volumes (1894, 1896). In the 1870s she wrote many of the 'waif' novels which were popular in the period. And of course, famously, she was a prolific author of books for girls, of which one of the most successful was *A World of Girls: The Story of a School* (1886); many of these, for instance *The Rebel of the School* (1902), fit the 'tomboy tamed' pattern (compare Mrs George de Horne *Vaizey and Angela *Brazil). She had other lines in desert-island fiction and crime novels. In 1900 she made a trip to the Far East to gather material. She married a solicitor and they lived in Dulwich, retiring to Oxford shortly before her death. Meade's bibliography exhausts the most enthusiastic investigators. In each of the genres she worked in she produced more than enough for several ordinary writers; whether she wrote every word herself it is not possible to say. She seems to have averaged ten or more books a year throughout the Edwardian period. 1904, for example, saw, in addition to several school stories: *A *Maid of Mystery*, a *crime story; *At the Back of the World*, a romance set on the south-west coast of Ireland; *Castle Poverty*, about a well-bred girl who finds employment as a companion in a vulgar parvenu family; *Nurse Charlotte*, another tale of genteel poverty; *Silenced*, a collection of six stories told to a philanthropic doctor by his patients; and *The Lady Cake-Maker*, about a confectionery business which numbers among its clients a homicidal maniac with a charming manner. One of the school stories, *The Adventures of Miranda*, drove a reviewer to remark that this was the second of Meade's books to appear in one week, with another announced in the press. A sampling of her output for 1909 reveals that a part at least of her secret lay in recycling familiar Victorian motifs: in *Brother or Husband*, Sir Austen Grave insists on marrying his deceased wife's sister; in *The Fountain of Beauty*, an oriental jewel originally stolen from the Shah of Persia is stolen once again from the Englishwoman who has inherited it; in *I Will Sing a New Song*, an organist marries his pupil, and subsequent trials include a murder mystery; in *Wild Heather*, the young heroine leaves her maiden aunt's care for London society, is courted by a wealthy, middle-aged peer, but marries for love; *The Stormy Petrel* is a *historical romance about the Irish potato famine which gives considerable space to the sufferings of the peasantry and their hatred of the English. One indication of the nature and extent of Meade's reputation is that the publisher should have appended to *The Sorceress of the Strand* (1903), in which Dixon Druce grapples with the murderous intrigues of the innocent-seeming Madame Sara, a list of Guy *Boothby's novels. Meade also published a novel, *Under the Dragon Throne* (1897), with Robert Kennaway Douglas, Keeper of Oriental Printed Books and Manuscripts in the British Museum.

MENDL, Gladys: Gladys Henrietta RAPHAEL (1884–1946) married, first (1902) Louis MENDL (divorced) and, secondly (1913), Harry Leslie SCHUETZE. Born in London, she was educated by governesses, and spent much of her childhood ill in bed. Her health improved as she grew up and she was trained as a pianist and singer (she was taught the piano by the husband of E. Maria *Albanesi), but, still not strong enough to perform, she became a writer. Her first marriage, to a corn merchant, was unhappy and short-lived. She joined the WSPU and became a suffragette and a friend of Olive Schreiner and 'Vernon *Lee'. Her disagreeable experiences in England during the First World War as a result of her second husband's German blood are described in her novel *Mrs Fischer's War* (1930), which, like all her fiction after her second marriage, was published under the name 'Henrietta Leslie'. Her early works as 'Gladys Mendl' are *The Roundabout* (1911), about the friendship between two women art students, one of whom has money and marries a drunken painter, *The Straight Road* (1911), about a wife repelled by but faithful to her hard sensual husband, and *Parentage* (1913), about the struggles of a boy with his over-protective parents.

MEREDITH, George (1828–1909), OM (1905), married, first (1849), Mary Ellen NICOLLS née PEACOCK (*c*.1820–61) and, secondly (1864), Marie VULLIAMY (d. 1886). Now the least read of the great Victorian novelists, Meredith was born at Portsmouth, where his grandfather owned a naval outfitter's establishment. His mother died when he was 5. He was educated at St Paul's Church School, Southsea, and later in Germany (1842–4). In 1844 he was articled to a London solicitor, but soon turned to journalism, at the same time publishing poems and essays in literary journals. With his first wife, the widowed daughter of Thomas Love Peacock (1785–1866), he lived a semi-bohemian, and ultimately wretched, life at Weybridge, in Surrey: the misery is reflected in his sonnet sequence, *Modern Love* (1862). His wife abandoned him in 1858, and soon afterwards died herself, abandoned in her turn by her lover, the painter Henry Wallis. He achieved recognition as a novelist with *The Ordeal of Richard Feverel* (1859) and *Evan Harrington* (1860). In 1862 he became a reader for the publishers Chapman & Hall, a position he was to hold for many years, and which enabled him to assist young writers like George *Gissing, Olive Schreiner (1855–1920), and Thomas Hardy (1840–1928). After his second marriage he moved, in 1867, to Flint Cottage, Box Hill, Surrey, where he lived until his death. Novels like *Beauchamp's Career* (1875) and *The Egoist* (1876) earned him a formidable reputation as a literary stylist, but scant popular success. The title of *The Tragic Comedians* (1880), based on the career of the philosopher and political economist Ferdinand Lassalle (1825–64), provides a clue to the scope of his concerns, and to his characteristic tone. *Diana of the Crossways* (1885), *One of Our Conquerors* (1891), and *The Amazing Marriage* (1895) were *feminist in tendency. He was severely crippled with a spinal complaint in later years. By this time, he had earned the friendship and (sometimes equivocal) admiration of many prominent men and women of letters, including Hardy, Gissing, Robert Louis Stevenson (1850–94), Leslie Stephen (1832–1904), Edmund Gosse (1849–1928), Oscar Wilde (1854–1900), J. M. *Barrie, Arthur Conan *Doyle, and Henry *James. James described Meredith's by now well-honed performance as the Sage of Box Hill: 'he remained for me always a charming, a quite splendid and rather strange, Exhibition, so content itself to *be* one, all genially and glitteringly, but all exclusively, that I simply sat before him till the curtain fell, and then came again when I felt I should find it up.' Meredith survived into the Edwardian period as a 'Exhibition', a literary presence and one that was not only genial and glittering but in its way potent, provocative, uncompromised. An address on his 70th birthday was signed by thirty of the great and good, that on his 80th by 250: there was also a letter from fourteen American authors, and telegrams from Edward VII (1841–1910) and President Theodore Roosevelt (1858–1919). Critical studies published in the period include: Walter

C. Jerrold, *George Meredith: An Essay towards Appreciation* (1902); George M. Trevelyan, *The Poetry and Philosophy of George Meredith* (1906); Elmer J. Bailey, *The Novels of George Meredith* (1907); M. Sturge Henderson *George Meredith: Novelist, Poet, Reformer* (1907); Richard Curle, *Aspects of George Meredith* (1908); M. Buxton Forman (ed.), *George Meredith: Some Early Appreciations* (1909); James Moffatt, *George Meredith: A Primer to the Novels* (1909); Bertram Dobell, *The Laureate of Pessimism* (1910); J. McKechnie, *Meredith's Allegory, The Shaving of Shagpat, Interpreted* (1910); Constantin Photiades, *George Meredith: sa vie, son imagination, son art, sa doctrine* (1910); and J. A. Hammerton (ed.), *George Meredith: His Life and Art in Anecdote and Criticism* (1911). Meredith's writing combined two purposes which were shortly to diverge so emphatically that they might be said to constitute thereafter separate cultural traditions. On the one hand, he constantly refined a literary manner which anticipates in its oblique ironies the later novels of Henry James, and in its proliferating inventiveness the work of James *Joyce: a manner which, in true Modernist fashion, precluded any possibility of a mass readership. On the other hand, his fiction was strenuously and explicitly polemical in its commitment to causes and campaigns: not only the emancipation of women, but national defence, and the development of a concept of national identity which would fully assimilate racial and cultural differences. The last is the subject of the incomplete **Celt and Saxon*, published posthumously in 1910. The vigour with which Meredith expounded his social and political philosophy led journalists as well as writers to the door of Flint Cottage. He was passionately opposed to the *Boer War; and later achieved tremendous notoriety by proposing that all marriage contracts should be reviewed after a period of ten years and only extended if they were still to the satisfaction of both parties. When illness prevented him from attending a demonstration against the House of Lords, he sent his gardener instead. His warnings about the degeneracy of the ruling classes were echoed tendentiously by many bestselling writers (see *invasion scare stories, *spy fiction), and more subtly by literary polemicists like H. G. *Wells. Remington, the hero of Wells's *The *New Machiavelli* (1911) describes *One of Our Conquerors* as 'one of the books that have made me'. He regards it as a warning, subsequently endorsed by the far from heartening outcome of the Boer War, of the 'gigantic changes' gathering against Britain on the Continent, changes hitherto obscured in his mind by Rudyard *Kipling's emphasis on *Empire. Remington has also come to understand through his own experience that Meredith was right to stress the connection between the personal and the political. 'A people that will not valiantly face and understand and admit love and passion can understand nothing whatever.' On the whole, Meredith did not receive the ultimate tribute of imitation (though see Haldane *Macfall's, *The *Masterfolk*, 1903; John Collis *Snaith's *Broke of Covenden*, 1904; and George *Gissing's *Our Friend the Charlatan*, 1901). But there can be no doubt about the effect of his presence. 'They say this or that is Meredithian,' he remarked shortly before his death. 'I have become an adjective.'

MEREDITH, Isabel, *pseud.*: Olivia Frances Madox ROSSETTI (1875–1960), who married (1897) Antonio AGRESTI; and her sister Helen Maria Madox ROSSETTI (1879–1969), who married (1903) Gastone ANGELI (d. 1904). The daughters of W. M. Rossetti (1829–1919), civil servant and authority on Italian art and literature, nieces of Christina (1830–94) and Dante Gabriel Rossetti (1828–82), cousins of Ford Madox *Hueffer, they were brought up eccentrically and progressively and educated at home. In June 1891 when Olivia, called Olive, was nearly 16 and Helen 11, they founded *The Torch: A Journal of International Socialism* (from 1894 *The Torch: A Revolutionary Journal of Anarchist-Communism*; from 1896 *The Torch of Anarchy: A Monthly Revolutionary Journal*), at first reproduced hectographically from manuscript, which they continued to edit until 1896: it collapsed in the following year. Their experiences in London anarchist circles are embodied in the novel they published under this pseudonym: *A Girl Among the Anarchists* (1903), with a preface by Morley *Roberts (who contributed to the *Torch*), affirming, 'I know what she has written to be true.' Their heroine, a girl brought up unconventionally by a chemist father, falls in with a group of anarchists, with whom she runs a paper called the *Tocsin*. Later the sisters were interested in Fascism. Olivia, who lived in Italy after her marriage, broadcast in English in its support alongside Ezra Pound (1885–1972), worked as an interpreter in the League of Nations, and was an assistant to David Lubin in the precursor of the United Nations Food and Agriculture Organization.

MERRICK, Leonard: Leonard MILLER (1864–1939) who changed his name by deed poll to MERRICK and married (1894) Hope BUTLER-WILKINS (d. 1917). Born in London, of Jewish family, and educated privately, at Brighton College, he travelled in South Africa as a young man and became first an actor and then a playwright and novelist under the name Leonard Merrick. His first novel was *Mr Bazalgette's Legacy* (1888). Fiction in this period includes *When Love Flies Out of the Window* (1902), **Conrad in Quest of His Youth* (1903), and *Whispers about Women* (1906). The title-story of *All the World Wondered and Other Stories* (1911) is about knowing true love when you find it; a playwright is jilted by an actress and later marries her niece. *The House of Lynch* (1907) has a similar theme: a poor English artist who loves the daughter of an unscrupulous American millionaire whose money they refuse to live on; after some upsets and a separation she learns to economize and gives the money away and he becomes famous. A collected edition of his novels with prefaces by other writers, including Maurice *Hewlett and H. G. *Wells, was published in twelve volumes 1918–19. His wife was the author of the novel *When a Girl's Engaged* (1905).

MERRIMAN, Henry Seton, *pseud*.: Hugh Stowell SCOTT (1862–1903) married (1889) Ethel Frances HALL. Born in Newcastle upon Tyne, son of a wealthy ship-owner, he was educated at Loretto School and then in Wiesbaden and Vevey. In 1885 he became an underwriting member at Lloyds of London. Scott adopted his pseudonym to appease his parents, who were embarrassed by their son's literary ambitions. In 1892, encouraged by James Payn (1830–98), he devoted himself to writing full-time. Novels with colonial settings, such as *With Edged Tools* (1894) and *Flotsam* (1896), allowed Scott to explore situations that would to his mind not be acceptable in Britain: friendships between a working man and an aristocrat, or entrepreneurial flair in a 'worker'. For Scott colonial life was more fluid; the rigid rules (as he saw them) did not apply. *The Sowers* (1896) his greatest success, ran to thirty editions; it portrays the efforts of a Russian nobleman and his adviser to provide education and health care to the peasants on a Russian estate. The process is delineated as necessarily slow and gradual and so while the author indulges in talk of selfless acts of service to the community little is actually done to alter the status quo. In *The Sowers* Scott writes about the sort of reform that is acceptable to him, minimal intervention leading to minimal improvement—the main object of intervention being the avoidance of political revolt. In *The Slave of the Lamp* (1892) and *The *Last Hope* (1904) the insurrectionists are themselves the vestiges of earlier, more conservative regimes. Yet even these potential usurpers of power are defeated and authorially condemned. Most of Scott's Edwardian novels concern the thwarting of uprisings and military campaigns. *The Velvet Glove* (1901) portrays the intrigue and turmoil during the Carlist agitation during the early 1870s (see also *In Kedar's Tents*, 1897). *The Vultures* (1902) features an unsuccessful Polish revolt after the assassination of Tsar Alexander II in Russia. *Barlasch of the Guard* (1903) is set in Danzig and depicts the intrigue in the city during Napoleon's attempt to take Moscow. Scott uses the political intrigue to reveal the moral fibre of his characters—their loyalty, their honour, and their ability to love. His conservatism led him to take a dim view of capitalism; accumulation of wealth was, as he saw it, a back-door method of wresting power and status from their proper owners, the upper classes. In *The Isle of Unrest* (1900) Colonel Gilbert is an engineer in the French army stationed on Corsica during the late 1860s, who uses a family blood feud to cover up the underhand nature of his business speculations. Scott shared with his friend Stanley J. *Weyman a love of travel, and conscientiously researched details of plot and setting. His best works are an extension of the tradition of Alexandre Dumas *père* (1803–70). He died at his home in Woodbridge following an operation to remove an infected appendix. He also collaborated with his sister-in-law 'S. G. *Tallentyre'.

MERRY, Andrew, *pseud*.: Mildred Henrietta Gordon DILL (1867–1932) married (1889) Jonathan Charles DARBY (1855–1943). Daughter of a Brighton doctor of Irish family, she married an Irishman and went to live at the Leap Castle in County Offaly. S. J. Brown observes: 'Never in the criticisms of her literary work has it been suggested that the pen-name hid a woman.' Although she belonged to the Protestant landowning class, her novels about Ireland were sympathetic to the hardships of the Catholic peasantry. Her first book, *An April Fool* (1898), was followed by *The Green Country* (1902), *'Paddy-Risky': Irish Realities of To-Day* (1903), *The Hunger: Being Realities of the Famine Years in Ireland 1845 to 1848* (1903), and *'Anthropoid Apes': A Modern Novel* (1909), a heavy-handed satire on the worldly heartlessness of the upper class and the suffering of the brutalized poor.

MEYNELL, Viola (1886–1956) married (1922) John DALLYN. She was one of the eight children of the journalist and biographer Wilfrid Meynell (1852–1948) and the poet Alice Meynell (1847–1922), of each of whom she published a memoir. The painter Lady Butler (1846–1933) was her mother's sister. Meynell was brought up in Roman Catholic literary circles and began to publish when very young. Much of her fiction is sentimental, sub-Hardyan emotional entanglements in rural settings. In *Cross-in-Hand Farm* (1911) a farmer's daughter gives up her solicitor fiancé to a friend who really loves him; *Lot Barrow* (1913) is about a servant girl growing up and falling in love. Other titles are *Martha Vine: A Love Story of Simple Life* (1910) and *Modern Lovers* (1914). She also wrote biographies.

MIDDLEMASS, Jean: Mary Jane MIDDLEMASS (1834–1919). Born in London, of an affluent Scots family, she was well educated at home, and began to publish her harmless sentimental melodramas for young women after her parents died when she was in her 30s. In later life she was handicapped by poor sight. She published some forty volumes from 1872 to 1906: her last publications include *Ruth Anstey* (1904) and *A Veneered Scamp* (1906). In *A Woman's Calvary* (1903), Betty, a distressed gentlewoman reduced to earning her living by sewing, meets an earl's daughter whose disgraced brother (exiled accused of killing Betty's sister) is proved innocent and marries her.

MIDDLETON, Richard Barham (1882–1911). Born in Staines, Middlesex, son of an engineer, he was educated at four public schools, including St Paul's School and Merchant Taylors' School, before becoming an insurance clerk for six years. In 1907 he left, and thereafter starved as an indigent writer, contributing to the **English Review* and other papers, and associating with *Chesterton, *Belloc, and *Machen. He went to live, for the sake of economy, in Brussels, where he poisoned himself with chloroform. None of his work appeared in volume form before his death. Machen wrote a preface for *The Ghost Ship and Other Stories* (1912), in which he praised Middleton for recognizing that 'true delight arises from the contemplation of mystery'. The title-story concerns a ship full of ghostly pirates which comes to rest in a turnip-field on the edge of a village situated halfway between London and Portsmouth: the pirates simply want to conscript the local ghosts, but the village halfwit stows away as a cabin-boy, and returns a couple of years later tattooed from head to foot and trailing a rusty cutlass. Of the mysteries contemplated in the volume's other stories, the only ones which have any substance are those arising out of the literary life. 'The Story of a Book' concerns a successful novelist who feels that after all his great work was a failure. The protagonist of 'The Biography of a Superman' has 'drawn from the mental confusion of the darker German philosophers an image of the perfect man—an image differing only in inessentials from the idol worshipped by the Imperialists as "efficiency"', but is himself a poor lonely devil who has no idea what makes people happy. There is also *The Day Before Yesterday* (1912), *Monologues* (1913), *Poems and Songs* (1912). Frank *Harris published an obituary in *Rhythm* and Henry Savage a biography (1922) and an edition of his letters (1929).

Mike: *A Public School Story*, P. G. *Wodehouse, 1909, Adam & Charles Black. 'It was a morning in the middle of April, and the Jackson family were consequently breakfasting in comparative silence. The cricket season had not begun, and except during the cricket season they were in the habit of devoting their powerful minds at breakfast almost exclusively to the task of victualling against the labours of the day.' The three grown-up Jacksons play first-class cricket, and Mike hopes to follow in their footsteps after a suitably cricket-intensive education at the Wrykyn school. His arrival there is announced by the comment that there are few better things in life than a public-school summer term. What follows is the standard fare of public-school fiction: picnics, town v. gown rows, cricket matches. The one topic not likely to be touched on in a chapter entitled 'An Expert Examination' is academic achievement. Indeed, Mike fails so comprehensively to learn anything that he is moved by his irate father to another (and non-cricketing) school, Sedleigh, where he becomes friendly with a refugee from Eton, Psmith ('There are too many Smiths, and I don't care for Smythe. My father's content to worry along in the old-fashioned way, but I've decided to strike out a fresh line. I shall found a new dynasty'). Dandyish, obtrusively socialist, effortlessly superior, Psmith is the first of Wodehouse's great comic characters. *Enter Psmith* was the title given to the second half of the novel when it was reissued in two volumes in 1935. Mike persuades the Sedleigh authorities to take cricket more seriously, and leads his team to triumph over the Wrykyn in the final chapter.

MITFORD, Bertram (1855–1914) married Zima Helen EBDEN (1854–1915). A younger son of the Mitford family of Mitford Castle, Northumberland, he emigrated to South Africa. He was an FRGS, and the author of some travel books and non-fiction about Africa, and of more than forty volumes of melodramatic adventure fiction, popular with boys, mostly set in South Africa, including *Aletta: A Tale of the Boer Invasion* (1900), *John Ames, Native Commissioner: A Romance of the Matabele Rising* (1900), *The Sirdar's Oath: A Tale of the North-West Frontier* (1904), and *Forging the Blades: A Tale of the Zulu Rebellion* (1908). His first book (1882) was a verse account of the Zulu wars.

MITFORD, C. Guise was author of nine novels 1900–15. *In Love in Lilac-Land* (1910), Vernon, a writer staying in the eponymous village, observes the chivalric devotion of two ageing bachelor housemates, Captain Carter and Major Magnus, for their mutual childhood sweetheart, Miss Penelope Wise. Other works include *The Wooing of Martha* (1911).

MITTON, G[eraldine] E[dith] (d. 1955) married (1920) James George SCOTT (1851–1935), KCIE (1901). The third daughter of a Church of England clergyman who ran a school in Durham, she contributed to several volumes of Walter *Besant's survey of London and edited many of the guide books published by A. & C. Black. She married, as his third wife, a retired colonial civil servant in Burma, who had formerly been a journalist, of whom she published a memoir, *Scott of the Shan Hills* (1936). She wrote travel books, including *A Bachelor Girl in Burma* (1907), children's textbooks, biographies including *Jane Austen and Her Times* (1905) and *Captain Cook* (1927), and fiction such as *A Bachelor Girl in London* (1898), *The Gifts of Enemies* (1900), and *The Opportunist* (1902), a novel of love and betrayal in London political circles. She also wrote three volumes of fiction (1922–4) with her husband.

MOLESWORTH, Mrs: Mary Louisa STEWART (1839–1921) married (1861) Richard MOLESWORTH (1836–1900). She was born in Rotterdam, Holland. Her family returned to Britain to settle in Manchester in 1841 and, apart from a year spent in Switzerland, she was educated at home. She married an army officer. The four adult novels that she published between 1869 and 1874 under the pseudonym 'Ennis Graham' were soon forgotten; her children's books were popular, numerous, and influential. She began to write for children at the suggestion of her friend, the painter Sir Noel Paton (1821–1901). Her popularity enabled her (for a while) to support her husband, who had been injured in the Crimea, and their seven children (two of whom died young). In 1878 she separated from him and went abroad, returning five years later in 1883. Macmillan published one of her works each Christmas, illustrated by the leading artists of the day. Her output was prolific—over 100 titles in all. The quirky mixture of *fantasy and realism in some of her works bears comparison with 'Lewis Carroll' (1832–98), George Macdonald (1824–1905), E. *Nesbit, and C. S. Lewis (1898–1963). Indeed, a warm obituary in the *Times* (21 July 1921) thought Nesbit her only rival: she 'had a way with her, a fragrance of thought which children instinctively recognize, and adults consciously enjoy.' The most notable amongst many with enduring appeal are *The Cuckoo Clock* (1877), *The Tapestry Room: A Child's Romance* (1879), *The Adventures of Herr Baby* (1881), *Peterkin* (1902), *The Little Guest* (1907), and *The Story of a Year* (1910).

MONKHOUSE, Allan Noble (1858–1936) married, first (1893), Lucy DOWIE (d. 1894) and, secondly (1902), Elizabeth Dorothy PEARSON. Born in Barnard Castle, Durham, he was privately educated, and worked in the cotton industry before working for the *Manchester Guardian* as both 'cotton expert' and book and theatre reviewer (*Books and Plays*, 1894, is a collection of reviews). His novels, mostly about Manchester life, include *A Deliverance* (1898), *Love in a Life* (1903),

Dying Fires (1912), and *Men and Ghosts* (1919). They share a tone of restrained and ironic reflection on life in a provincial town. *Mary Broome* (1911) is a comic complication of the standard theme of the maidservant seduced by the master; *The Education of Mr Surrage* (1912) drew its humour from the confrontation between provincial respectability and the odd world of artists. Monkhouse also wrote plays, attracted by the Manchester Gaiety Theatre's belief in the dramatic value of the ordinary and commonplace. His first wife was a sister of Ménie Muriel *Dowie.

MONTAGUE, Charles Edward (1867–1928) married (1898) Madeline SCOTT. Born in Ealing, son of an apostate Irish Roman Catholic priest, he was educated at the City of London School and Balliol College, Oxford. He joined the *Manchester Guardian* in 1890, eventually becoming assistant editor and chief leader writer, establishing the paper's reputation for stylishness, and marrying the only daughter of its editor, C. P. Scott (1846–1932). His first novel, *A Hind Let Loose* (1910), was a comedy set in the world of the provincial press; it was followed by *The Morning's War* (1913). When the First World War broke out, Montague dyed his hair and volunteered (aged 47), and was sent to the front. His disillusioned and bitter pieces for the *Guardian* were the basis of two books (*Disenchantment*, 1922, and *Right Off the Map*, 1927), and in this period he also published a collection of short stories, *Fiery Particles* (1923). *Dramatic Values* (1911) is a collection of theatre criticism. He also published, with Mrs Humphry, *Ward *William Thomas Arnold* (1907). There is a biography by Oliver Elton (1929).

MONTGOMERY, Florence [Sophia]: (1843–1923). It was George Whyte-Melville (1821–78) who first persuaded Montgomery, second of the six daughters (she had three brothers) of an admiral and baronet, to publish the stories that she had created to amuse her younger sisters. Most of her work was written for children; morals figure prominently. She was willing and able to see life from a child's perspective—a trait she shares with E. *Nesbit. She once confided a propensity 'to side, as it were, with the children against the parents'. Montgomery's publications include *Thrown Together* (1872), *Herbert Manners and Other Tales* (1880), *Colonel Norton* (1895), *Prejudged* (1900), a romantic tale of love abroad for adults, *An Unshared Secret and Other Stories* (1903), and *Behind the Scenes in a School Room* (1914), which describes the experiences of a young governess. However, much her most popular work was the tearjerking early children's book (though it was also much read by adults), *Misunderstood* (1869), which had run to eighteen editions by 1882; a little boy's father doesn't appreciate him but realizes his mistake after the child dies.

MONTGOMERY, K. L., *pseud.*: Kathleen MONTGOMERY (?1863–1960); and her sister Letitia MONTGOMERY (d. 1930). Born in Dublin, they were educated in England and lived in Oxford. Their first novel was *The Cardinal's Pawn* (1903); others include *The Ark of the Curse* (1906), an *historical romance about Cagots in France under Henry IV, culminating in a dramatic scene in which the heroine buys the hero in an Algerian slave market, *Colonel Kate* (1908), is set in eighteenth-century Scotland, and *The Gate-Openers* (1912). They also did translations.

MONTGOMERY, L[ucy] M[aud] (1874–1942), OBE (1935), married (1911) Ewan MACDONALD. The author of a classic of girls' fiction was born at Clifton, Prince Edward Island, Canada. When she was 2 her mother died, her father went west, and she went to live with her elderly maternal grandparents on a remote farm. She was educated at Prince of Wales College, Charlottetown, and Dalhousie University, and qualified as a teacher. She worked as a schoolteacher 1894–8, but on her grandfather's death in the latter year she had to return to look after her grandmother, and began to write stories and articles. After the death of the grandmother, she married a Presbyterian clergyman and left Prince Edward Island. Her first novel, published after several rejections, was *Anne of Green Gables* (1908), in which a red-haired, romantic, unwanted orphan, adopted rather grudgingly by an elderly brother and sister, endears herself to a remote Canadian community by, among other things, saving the life of a baby dying of croup. It gave rise to many sequels, in which Anne qualifies as a teacher, marries a doctor, and brings up a family. While it clearly draws on personal experience, it has debts to earlier novels for girls, especially to *What Katy Did* (1872) by 'Susan Coolidge' (1835–1905) and *Rebecca of Sunnybrook Farm* (1903) by Kate Douglas Wiggin (1856–1923). There is a study of Montgomery (1975) by Mollie Gillen.

Monthly Review, The (1900–7). Founded by the Conservative publisher John Murray (1851–1928) as a vehicle for the editorship of the Liberal writer Henry *Newbolt, its aim was to produce a setting for cultured, political but non-partisan argument. Newbolt's editorial control, though, gave the magazine a distinct Liberal feel, until he resigned in 1904. The *Monthly Review* published a regular book review section, 'On the Line', featuring such authors as Roger Fry (1866–1934) and Arthur Symons (1865–1945), short stories (Walter *de la Mare's early work was published here), and poetry by, among others, W. B. Yeats (1865–1939) and Robert Bridges (1844–1930). But despite its obvious literary quality, the *Monthly Review* was never able to reach an adequate circulation.

MONTRESOR, F[rances] F[rederica] (1843–1934). Born at Walmer, Kent, the daughter of a senior naval officer, she was educated at home and wrote intelligent romantic fiction in a didactic, dramatically charged style. Her publications include *The One Who Looked On* (1895), *False Coin or True* (1896), *At the Cross-Roads* (1897), *The Alien: A Story of Middle Age* (1901), whose heroine, Esther Mordaunt, is brought up by an elderly cousin. When the old lady's son comes back from the dead Esther fights for his rights; he turns out to be an impostor but an illegitimate son. He leaves her, but asks her to bring up his daughter. The heroine of *A Fish Out of Water* (1908), Anne Burns, is the temperamental opposite of the family she lives with, the clever, cultured, easygoing Leslies. Becky Sharp, in Thackeray's *Vanity Fair* (1848), was presumably the model for the engaging, imperious, triumphant Barbara in *Through the Chrysalis* (1910). Montresor gave the theme of the rebellious daughter an ingenious twist in *The Strictly Trained Mother* (1913), a quiet satirical comedy about the elderly, bullied mother of two strong-minded daughters who conspires with a suffragette granddaughter to escape from them.

MOORE, Dorothea [Mary] (1881–1933). Daughter of a Church of England clergyman, she was brought up at Kingston Deverill, Wiltshire, and educated at Godolphin School, Salisbury and Cheltenham Ladies' College. She was an actress 1911–12 and served as a VAD in the First World War. She was author of more than sixty children's books from 1902: some, like *A Brave Little Royalist* (1913) and *A Nest of Malignants* (1919), set during the English Civil War and firmly on the side of the King; others, such as *A Plucky School-Girl* (1908), school stories in the mould of Angela *Brazil. She was a Girl Guide Commissioner, and published, in *Terry the Girl-Guide* (1912), the first guiding novel. She also wrote a few plays. She was a supporter of the Primrose League and a member of the Women Writers' Club.

MOORE, F[rancis] Frankfort (1855–1931) married, first, Grace BALCOMBE (d. 1901) and, secondly, Dorothea HATTON. Moore was born in Limerick, Ireland, and educated at the Royal Academical Institution, Belfast and by a private tutor. He was an inveterate traveller; Africa, India, the West Indies, and South America, were among his ports of call; this is reflected in the wide variety of backdrops for his stories: New Guinea, the North Pacific, the Caribbean, and the American prairies are a few of the locations featured in his work. He was employed as a journalist on the *Belfast Newsletter* from 1876 to 1892. Moore was a prolific author of light popular fiction, specializing in sea yarns and romances. *The Artful Miss Dill* (1906) is the story, set in Venezuela and England, of the manipulations, romantic and otherwise, benevolent and otherwise, practised by the heroine, daughter of a shady 'diplomatist' who has served various South American presidents and patriots. The **Times Literary Supplement* described *The Ulsterman: A Story of Today* (1914) as 'a vision of grim forces as rugged as the Covenanters' native sea-scarred rocks, arrayed for the defence of what they believe to be their rights'. *The Jessamy Bride* (1897) was a bestseller. He also wrote several plays, and biographies of Oliver Goldsmith (?1730–74) and Frances Burney (1752–1840). *The Common Sense Collector* (1910) is a guide to purchasing and displaying antique furniture. He also published *A Garden of Peace: A Medley in Quietude* (1919) under the pseudonym 'F. Littlemore'. Moore was considered an expert on the history of eighteenth-century England: the *Times* (12 May 1931) calls him 'steeped in the memoirs and reminiscences of the period'.

MOORE, George [Augustus] (1852–1933) was the eldest son of a family of Catholic gentry; his father was MP for Mayo 1847–57 and 1868–70, and during the earlier period a leader of the campaign for tenant-right and a brilliant orator. Moore was educated at Oscott College, Birmingham, and was saved by his father's death in 1870 from a military career. He inherited the estate, and as soon as he was 21 moved to Paris to study painting. However, following a meeting with Émile Zola (1840–1902), he became determined to bring 'naturalism' in fiction to England, though his earliest works were plays and poetry. Moore returned to England in 1880, (as his money began to run out) and became a professional writer. His first realist novel, *A Modern Lover* (1883), is an account of the French art scene translated into an English setting; it was produced as a standard three-decker and proved to be commercially unsuccessful, as it offended the circulating libraries (for the rest of the decade Moore led the attack on the libraries and their stifling control of British reading habits). Moore published his next book, *A Mummer's Wife* (1885), as a single volume. This work showed even more clearly the effect of Zola's theories, in its story of a shopkeeper's wife who elopes with an actor and her consequent degeneration into debt, drink, and death. Both books marked a break from the Victorian novel in form and content, and both reflected Moore's determination to introduce European ideas into British literary and artistic culture. His autobiography, *Confessions of a Young Man* (1888), championed French Impressionism and Symbolism, a mission he also pursued as a journalist, for example as art critic of the *Speaker* in 1892–7. Moore was equally contemptuous of the British theatre, and was one of the founders of the Independent Theatre, opened in London to bring the new European plays of Henrik Ibsen (1828–1906) and August Strindberg (1849–1912) to English theatregoers. He continued to develop an English realist tradition in such novels as *Esther Waters* (1894), an enormous critical success, which applied the technique to a broader range of society. W. H. Smith refused to stock the book in its circulating library, and this gave rise to a campaign against such censorship led by Conan *Doyle. Moore treated a broad range of issues, including the nature of religious belief, in *Evelyn Innes* (1898) and its sequel, **Sister Teresa* (1901), both of which refer to his unsuccessful romance with 'John Oliver *Hobbes'.

In 1900 Moore moved back to his native Ireland and turned his attention to Irish literature, writing the short stories for translation into Irish that appeared as *An T-Ur-Gort* (1902) and *The *Untilled Field* (1903), and developing a new interest in 'oral narrative'. He was also involved, somewhat unhappily, with W. B. Yeats (1865–1939) and the Irish Literary Theatre. Moore returned to England in 1911, giving up on the Irish literary scene and becoming instead, an English man of letters, writing his autobiography (which appeared in three parts: *Ave*, 1911, *Salve*, 1912, and *Vale*, 1914), collecting his criticism (*Avowals*, 1917, and *Conversations in Ebury Street*, 1924), and continuing his interests in folklore and the theatre. From the mid-1890s he had a close relationship with Lady Cunard (1872–1948). His importance as a writer rests on his earlier achievements in challenging the conventions and restraints of Victorian art and literature. See also *The *Lake* (1905). His correspondence has been edited by Helmut E. Gerber (1968, 1988).

MOORE, Leslie published sixteen volumes of fiction, including several children's books and two whimsical contemporary tales: *Aunt Olive in Bohemia, or, The Intrusions of a Fairy Godmother* (1913), about a plain maiden lady of 60 who, after a starved and solitary life, becomes wealthy and, following her father's tradition, takes one of seven studios in a Chelsea courtyard and becomes a benefactress to the young men who occupy the other six; and *The Peacock Feather: A Romance* (1913), about a delightful ex-convict who wanders the countryside with the eponymous feather in his hat, and writes a novel called *Robin Adair*, which earns him a well-to-do penfriend in whose neighbourhood he eventually settles, without revealing his authorship.

Morals of Marcus Ordeyne, The, W. J. *Locke, 1905, John Lane. Locke's ninth published book, but his first real commercial success, was both a bestselling novel and, quickly, a popular stage play. Locke's fictional formula did not vary much over his entire output: an open-hearted hero takes on the sins of others and is obliged in consequence to live a ramshackle, bohemian life (without the reader ever forgetting that he, the hero, is really a gentleman). For some reason (perhaps because of its sexual undertones), this version of the story hit a big public chord. Sir Marcus Ordeyne, recluse, book collector, *soi-disant* philosopher, and, like Locke himself (if rather implausibly) an ex-maths teacher, meets a lost and helpless child on the Thames embankment one night. Carlotta (even more implausibly), having been rescued from a harem in Alexandria, has now been abandoned in London by her rescuer. Sir Marcus takes pity on her, adopts her, and devotes himself to her upbringing and social education. After various tribulations (and the usual vagrancy) they marry. Locke specialized in the picaresque—the deliberately eccentric characters and inconsequential, conversational, narrative are self-consciously Dickensian—to which he brought a touch of ironic, self-proclaimed 'French' realism. The effect is a rather unpleasant false innocence, and his books have survived less well than other Edwardian bestsellers, despite their reputation at the time.

MORDAUNT, Elinor, Elenor, or Eleanor, *pseud.*: Evelyn Mary CLOWES (1872–1942) married, first (1898), Maurice WIEHE (divorced) and, secondly, (perhaps 1933), Robert Rawnsley BOWLES. Born into a family of Nottinghamshire landed gentry, brought up near Cheltenham with her six brothers and much younger sister, she moved at 13 to Oxfordshire with the rest of the family, to the circle later depicted in her first novel, *The Garden of Contentment* (1902). She went in 1897 to Mauritius as companion to a cousin, promptly married a local planter, was unhappy, and contracted malaria. She later claimed to have buried two children in Mauritius, and to have been ordered back to England and lain two years in bed. *The Garden of Contentment* was her attempt to capture the memory of England while lying in her sickbed. In 1902 Clowes travelled to Australia, a voyage described in her second novel, *The Ship of Solace* (1911). She bore a son in Australia in about 1903, whom she supported partly by writing, partly by decorative painting and gardening, and returned to England in 1908. A later (and much steamier) novel, *The Cost of It* (1912), concerns the son of a wealthy, cynical, dissolute baronet who discovers that his abandoned mother, a 'Creole', is still living, in miserable poverty, in the sugar-producing Crown colony of 'Monteracine'. He casts off his father and devotes himself to his mother. In Monteracine, he meets an Englishwoman of his own class and marries her, the close of the book concentrating, as the **Times Literary Supplement* put it, 'on the tragic anxieties as to the issue of their union'. *The Island* (1914) includes sixteen stories about English people living in the tropics, and about the dangers of miscegenation. *Lu of the Ranges* (1913) is a grimmish tale about a young woman who as a child was saved from starvation by an itinerant aesthete, and later works as a dancer in order to support the child she has by him; she eventually buys a farm, where he comes to die. Other equally colourful novels include *Tropic Heat* (1911); *Bellamy* (1914), about a charlatan revivalist and a Staffordshire mill-girl; *The Family* (1915); and *The Park Wall* (1916), a semi-autobiographical account of the difficulties of a divorced woman, which was favourably reviewed by Virginia Woolf (1882–1941). Her 1917 application to the Royal Literary Fund stated that she had had no support from her husband for fourteen years, and had been earning about £350 a year by writing, but was in difficulty because of the war, and because of a recent abdominal operation, writer's cramp, and neuritis. Clowes continued to travel, going round the world in 1923 for the *Daily News* on sailing and cargo boats: her experiences *en voyage* are treated in her novels as well as in her travel writing. Her novel *Gin and Bitters* (1931) was written, as 'A. Riposte', as a riposte to W. Somerset *Maugham's attack on Thomas Hardy (1840–1928) and Hugh *Walpole in *Cakes and Ale* (1930); she is said to have been a friend of Hardy's widow. Maugham successfully sued her for libel in October 1931. Her autobiography, *Sinaboda*, was published in 1937. Most accounts of her career are inaccurate, and the evidence tends to suggest that she was a shameless liar.

MORGAN-DE-GROOT, J.: Began by writing novels in his native Holland: *Daï* (1894), which was written as 'Karel Ridóro', *Bouton de Rose* (1895), and *De Loutering van Giuseppe Botall* (1901) were all published in Amsterdam. It seems that he began by translating his fiction into English himself and then, perhaps in imitation of the successful novelist 'Maarten *Maartens', took to composing novels in what the *Bookman's review of *The Bar Sinister* (1906) called 'the English of good journalism'. That novel is about a Dutch boy who discovers that he is illegitimate and leaves Holland. The plot hinges on the complexity of Dutch law, which permits the legitimation of children whose parents married after their birth. Morgan-de-Groot published thirteen volumes of English fiction with Dutch local colour in London between 1898 and 1926.

MORRISON, Arthur (1863–1945) married (1892) Elizabeth Adelaide THATCHER. Unlike Charles Dickens (1812–70), George *Gissing, and Rudyard *Kipling, Morrison was born into the slums he wrote about. Born in Poplar, the son of an engine-fitter, he spent most of his life in London's notorious East End. He worked for a while as a clerk at Walter *Besant's 'People's Palace' in Mile End and was later appointed sub-editor of the [People's] *Palace Journal*. When it ran into financial difficulties in 1890 Morrison moved to the West End of London, took a job on an evening newspaper, and then worked free-lance until his retirement in 1913. His literary career began when *Macmillan's Magazine* published his short story 'A Street' in 1891. W. E. Henley (1849–1903), of the *National Observer*, encouraged Morrison to write further graphic, sympathetic, yet humorous portrayals of London's slum life. His emphasis was on the dreary monotony of the slum-dwellers' lives. Morrison wanted the reading public to be aware of the true nature of such people's existence. Morrison collected fourteen of these portraits in his *Tales of Mean Street* (1894). The collection strikes the same chord as Kipling in 'The Record of Badalia Herodsfoot' and *Maugham in *Liza of Lambeth* (1897)—all assert the respectability and dignity of people living hand to mouth. Indeed, he was criticized for his detachment, his failure to take a personal moral stance. He countered by claiming that his critics wanted him to 'weep obscenely in the public gaze. In other words that I shall do their weeping for them, as a sort of emotional bedesman.' In *A Child of the Jago* (1896) Morrison detachedly depicts the corrupting force of a violent criminal environment upon a young man. *To London Town* (1899) is again about East London but portrays a more affluent side of life. His *The *Hole in the Wall* (1902) is a dramatic and evocative novella that captures the corruption and brutality of life on the Thames waterfront. Morrison explores the friction between a young boy's innocence and the squalor of his surroundings. The narrative is conducted partly through the eyes of the boy and partly by an impartial observer. It is this work that Morrison's obituary in the *Times* (5 Dec. 1945) singles out as his best: 'a sustained effort, crowded with exciting incident, full of well-rounded character studies... told with compelling quietness and objectivity'. **Cunning Murrell* (1900) is set on the coast of Essex. *Divers Vanities* (1905) and *Green Ginger* (1909) are collections of short stories. Other works include a string of *crime stories: *Martin Hewitt, Investigator* (1894), *Chronicles of Martin Hewitt* (1895), *The Adventures of Martin Hewitt* (1896), and *The Red Triangle* (1903). Hewitt is a down-to-earth character dealing with more mundane crimes than Conan *Doyle's Sherlock Holmes, making him a distinctive figure in the history of detective fiction. *The Dorrington Deed Box* (1897) and *The Green Eye of Goona: Stories of a Case of Tokay* (1904) are more detective stories. Morrison also collaborated on a few plays including *That Brute Simmons* (1904) with Herbert C. Sargeant, *A Stroke of Business* (1907) with Horace W. C. *Newte, and *The Dumb Cake* (1907) with Richard *Pryce. Morrison amassed superb collections of both European and oriental art and published *The Painters of Japan* (1911); his collection was acquired by the British Museum in 1913. He and his wife had one son, who died as a result of injuries in the First World War. He himself died at Chalfont St Peter in Buckinghamshire.

MORTLAKE, G. N., *pseud*.: Marie Charlotte Carmichael STOPES (1880–1958) married, first (1911), Reginald Ruggles GATES (1882–1962) (annulled 1916) and, secondly (1918), Humphrey Verdon ROE (1878–1949). Daughter of a feminist writer, Charlotte Carmichael (1841–1929), and a palaeontologist, she was educated at St George's High School, Edinburgh, North London Collegiate School, University College London, and Munich University. Her first novel, *The Love-Letters of a Japanese* (1911), draws on her experience in 1907–8 at the Imperial University in Tokyo, where she went as a young lecturer in palaeobotany at Manchester University and had an emotional relationship with Kenjiro Fujii. She is best known, however, for her books promoting family planning and openness about sexuality, including *Married Love* (1918) and *Radiant Motherhood* (1920). A later novel, *Love's Creation* (1928), was published as 'Marie Carmichael'.

Mr Apollo: *A Just Possible Story*, Ford Madox *Hueffer, 1908, Methuen. The Greek god, Phoebus Apollo, returns to earth in human form to inquire 'into the nature of mortal man', and discovers a general lack of faith and purpose in modern life, an empty materialism, even among such supposed religious figures as the evangelical missionary the Reverend Mr Todd. The central drama of the book is the battle between Apollo and the atheist, Clarges, for the soul of the scientifically minded sceptic, Alfred Milne, who eventually sees the light literally (Apollo destroys the city slums that prevent the sun from reaching him) and figuratively, as Milne comes to believe in God. This is a novel of ideas in which the critique of materialism and scientism is more convincing than the defence of religion—the relationship of Apollo to Christianity or Roman Catholicism is never clear.

Mr Clutterbuck's Election, Hilaire *Belloc, 1908, Eveleigh Nash. This is the story of a financier who acquires, partly through prudence, partly through luck, a fortune, a Surrey mansion, several motor cars, and political ambitions—both the latter being driven at breakneck pace by his young Irish secretary, Charlie Fitzgerald. Mr Clutterbuck's election is declared null, but he gets his knighthood anyway. Set in 1911, the novel envisages a degree of female suffrage, but is otherwise too cynical about the political process to be informative. Furthermore, Belloc loses interest in his hero halfway through, and has to summon up a one-dimensional anti-Semite and a comic detective to keep the story going.

Mr Fleight, Ford Madox *Hueffer, 1913, Howard Latimer. One of several novels by Hueffer which pairs a lazy Englishman with a stupid Englishman. Mr Blood, the lazy Englishman, sits at the window of his club on Derby Day, calculating the proportion of mechanical to horse-drawn vehicles on the Embankment. At the end of the novel he sits at the same window on Christmas Day, doing the same thing. In between, he has masterminded the successful election campaign and engagement of the stupid Englishman, Mr Fleight. His promotion of Mr Fleight does not redeem him, or revitalize him or Mr Fleight; they are, respectively, as lazy and as stupid at the end of the novel as they were at the beginning. Mr Blood is a monster, an anachronism whose violence (he is rumoured to have strangled his groom) throws into doubt his claims to represent the virtues of the landed gentry. His aversion to modern politics is expressed in apocalyptic terms. Mr Fleight is an equally unlikely representative of Englishness. The son of a Jewish soap-manufacturer, he survives in the course of the campaign a formidable amount of racial violence and abuse, some of it from Mr Blood. And yet, like his mentor and occasional tormentor, he is fundamentally decent. Hueffer's achievement was to incorporate a monster and an alien into his representation of Englishness, without compromising it or them. He subsequently adopted the persona of Mr Blood in some of his polemical writings, much to the disgust of Ezra Pound (1885–1972), who had little patience with the nuances of fogeydom.

Mr Perrin and Mr Traill: *A Tragi-comedy*, Hugh *Walpole, 1911, Mills & Boon. The third of Hugh Walpole's published novels was also his first attempt to follow H. G. *Wells's advice 'that we had had enough of romantic nonsense and that novels must deal with real people and be afraid of nothing'. Drawing on Walpole's own unhappy experience of schoolmastering, *Mr Perrin and Mr Traill* is a small-scale but entirely convincing account of the claustrophobia of a minor public school, of the petty tyrannies and humiliations suffered by boys and staff alike, and of the destructive effect on the masters and their wives of their overall sense of failure. Archie Traill, young, attractive, a rugby blue, arrives at Moffatt's School in Cornwall to take up his first post as a junior school master; Vincent Perrin has been at the school with ever-increasing sourness and despair for more than twenty years. His jealousy of Traill's youth and optimism becomes a form of madness when Traill gets engaged to Isabel Desart, whose polite friendliness to him Perrin had fantasized as love. Just before the engagement is announced, Perrin attacks Traill in the masters' common room, thinking that Traill has stolen his umbrella. The school immediately splits into rival camps. Perrin lapses into paranoia. He plans obsessively to kill Traill, and on the last morning of term follows him along a coastal path. When Traill reasons with him, he draws a knife, and Traill, startled, falls over the edge of the cliff. Perrin, stricken by remorse, rescues him from the incoming tide, but is himself drowned in the process.

Mrs Craddock, W. Somerset *Maugham, 1902, William Heinemann. The novel was written in 1900 and turned down by publisher after publisher on the grounds that it was too daring. Eventually Heinemann read it himself and agreed to publish it, subject to the removal of the more shocking passages. Bertha Ley, last representative of decayed Kentish gentry, makes the kind of 'eugenic' marriage with a strapping tenant farmer which was the mainstay of New Woman fiction in the 1890s. At first, the marriage is passionate, but Edward Craddock's innate vulgarity aligns him with the petit bourgeois community, rather than with Bertha. A *Forsterian trip to Italy, and a brief, inconsequential affair with a younger man, Gerald Vaudrey, keep her true to her nature. Edward is killed in a hunting accident, leaving Bertha free, if melancholy.

MUDDOCK, James Edward Preston: see 'Dick *Donovan'.

MULHOLLAND, Clara: see under Lady *Gilbert.

Multitude and Solitude, John *Masefield, 1909, Grant Richards. The novel opens with writer Roger Naldrett at the first night of his new play, *The Roman Matron*, which is not well received. The result is a sleepless night spent thinking about his two idols: the enigmatic and tubercular John O'Neill, who is about to leave for Spain; and enigmatic and Irish Ottalie Fawcett. Roger is an idealist: 'he blamed the world for its vulgarity, and dreariness, and savagery.' Obsessed by Ottalie, he goes to the library to look her up in *Who's Who*, then sets off for Ireland, only to find that she has drowned two days before his arrival. He attends the funeral, and is told that she loved him, but thought he was too impressionable, too selfish, and too wrapped up in art. Back in London, he keeps coming across articles about sleeping sickness, and then meets a friend of Ottalie's, Lionel, a doctor, who gives him further information about the disease. He begins to believe that Ottalie is speaking to him from beyond the grave, urging him to abandon art and devote himself to science. Lionel has studied the epidemiology of sleeping sickness in Africa, and he takes Roger with him on his next expedition, whose purpose is to test a new antidote, atoxyl (Masefield is quite specific about the medical details). They pass through whole villages ravaged by the disease. Their provisions are raided, and their supply of atoxyl stolen. Lionel contracts a fever which will become sleeping sickness unless the antidote is applied. At first Roger, overwhelmed by his responsibilities, retreats into a dream world. Then he pulls himself together, and makes a serum from the blood of wild animals, himself falling sick in the process. The serum triumphs, curing them and their African patients. Returning to civilization, they discover that the serum has already been developed by the Japanese and the Germans. On a pilgrimage to Ottalie's old home, Roger has a redeeming vision. 'The world is just coming to see that science is not a substitute for religion, but religion of a very deep and austere kind.' Science, in short, is a new weapon in the age-old struggle against base human nature.

MUNRO, Neil (1863–1930) was born on a farm near Inverary in Argyll, and it appears from recent research that he was the illegitimate son of a servant girl, the daughter of a former crofter, and subsequently concealed his illegitimacy and date of birth. After leaving Church Square Public School he worked for five years in the office of the Sheriff Clerk of Argyll. During this period he taught himself shorthand, and in 1881 he managed to escape from the depopulated highlands by getting himself a job as a journalist in Glasgow. In 1894 he moved to the *Glasgow Evening News*. His newspaper pieces were all written under the pseudonym 'Mr Incognito'. He retired from journalism to write fiction in 1902, but went back to the *Evening News* during the First World War, serving as its editor from 1918 until 1927; during his term there it was one of the most progressive and well-run evening papers in Britain. Munro's experience of the poverty of the modern highlands, his nostalgia for the lost communities prior to the clearances, and his journalist's knowledge of modern Glasgow provide the three main strands in his fiction. Some of his early works, such as *The Lost Pibroch and Other Sheiling Stories* (1896) and *Gilian the Dreamer* (1899), were heavily influenced by the mysticism and romanticism of the 'Celtic Twilight' movement. *John Splendid* (1898) and *The New Road* (1914), *historical romances, exude a more Stevensonian air. Munro's more realistic works about Glasgow life are now little read. His other works include *Doom Castle: (A Romance)* (1901); *The Shoes of Fortune* (1901); *Children of the Tempest: A Tale of the Outer Isles* (1903), which originally appeared in *Blackwood's; The Daft Days* (1907), about a girl from Chicago who comes to live with her uncle, a Scottish lawyer, and his two sisters, and goes on the stage; and *Fancy Farm* (1910), about the strange inhabitants of a Scottish estate, including a poet, author of *Harebell and Honey*, who becomes a shipbuilder. He also published non-fiction and verse and edited selections of the works of Robert Burns (1759–1896) and Leonard *Merrick. *The Brave Days* (1931) contains an essay on Munro by George Blake.

Hugh *Walpole considered Munro 'one of Scotland's few great novelists'. His best works are generally considered to be *John Splendid* and *Gilian the Dreamer.* A sympathetic *Times* obituary (23 Dec. 1930) concludes that 'his writing was graphic without any straining after effect, and its charm lay chiefly in its straightforwardness'. Sadly, Munro is best known for his humorous, but perhaps rather trivial, dialect tales about the crew of a Clyde steamer, published in the *Glasgow Evening News* from 1905 under the pseudonym 'Hugh Foulis', and collected in *The *Vital Spark and Her Queer Crew* (1906), *In Highland Harbours with Para Handy* (1911), and *Hurricane Jack of the Vital Spark* (1923). The only official recognition of Munro's work was the LL D. awarded by Glasgow University in 1908. He died at home in Helensburgh, Dumbartonshire. Five years later Blackwoods published *The Works of Neil Munro* in nine volumes; and a monument was unveiled at Glen Aray by R. B. Cunninghame *Graham, who described Munro as 'the apostolic successor of Sir Walter Scott'.

MURRAY, David Christie (1847–1907) married, first (1871), Sophie HARRIS and, secondly (*c.*1879), Alice ——. Born at West Bromwich, Staffordshire, son of a printer, he was educated privately there, worked for his father from the age of 12, and began his career as a reporter on the *Birmingham Morning News*. He spent a year as a private in the 4th Royal Irish Dragoon Guards in 1865–6. In 1871 he worked as parliamentary reporter for the *Daily News*, and he was correspondent of the *Times* and the *Scotsman* during the Russo-Turkish war of 1877–8. His fiction is overwhelmingly Victorian in theme and tone. *Demos Awakes* (1908) faithfully recapitulates the 'Condition of England' novels of the 1840s: when Robeson and Macdonald, porcelain manufacturers, mistreat their workers, political agitators make mischief; rioting and vitriol throwing ensue, until young Alan Macdonald brings about a reconciliation. *A Woman in Armour* (1908) is an old-fashioned tale of Nihilism of the kind popular in the 1880s: a successful cellist is mixed up with a gang of revolutionaries and speaks nobly against terrorism. He was also the author of *My Contemporaries in Fiction* (1897) and collaborated on several novels with Henry Herman (1832–94). He lived for some time in Wales, and was an enthusiastic Dreyfusard. Murray has a long file in the archives of the Royal Literary Fund; he first applied in 1893, because of a bankruptcy and nervous breakdown which had reduced his income from £2,700 to £30 in a year. After his death there were a series of applications from Marion Christie Murray, a New Zealander, whom he had not married since he was unable to divorce his second wife (described as a dipsomaniac). 'I rather fancy that he has two relicts,' wrote Maurice *Hewlett, 'but if I could induce the committee to have charity for No. 2., who has babies, I would be as eloquent as I knew how.'

Mystery of Dr Fu Manchu, The, 'Sax *Rohmer', 1913, Methuen. The first of a series of bestselling thrillers which pit the boundlessly evil and intelligent Chinaman against ultra-English Nayland Smith ('a tall, lean man, with his square-cut, clean-shaven face sun-baked to the hue of coffee'). Fu Manchu has arrived in London to dispose of anyone likely to stand in the way of his plans for world domination. His assassination techniques include a scorpion which homes in on a particular scent (Smith eventually pulps it with 'one straight, true blow of the golf club'). The story is told by Smith's friend Dr Petrie, who falls in love with, and is saved from tight corners by, Fu Manchu's Arab slavegirl, Karamaneh. The parallel with Holmes and Watson is strong enough to require disavowal ('"Don't imagine, Petrie," said Smith, "that I am trying to lead you blindfolded in order later to dazzle you with my perspicacity"'). But Rohmer has crossed Conan *Doyle with *Kipling and M. P. *Shiel: his Moriarty is an incarnation of the Yellow Peril, a catalyst of bitter conflict between East and West, an impresario of 'race drama'. The most powerful descriptions are of Fu Manchu's various haunts, footholds the East has established in the West: an opium den off the Ratcliff Highway, a house near Windsor, a hulk moored in the Thames estuary. As Smith and Petrie pursue him from one haunt to another, he comes to seem less like an oriental Moriarty than an oriental Count Dracula.

My Brilliant Career, Miles *Franklin, 1901, Blackwood. Franklin claimed that her first, semi-autobiographical novel, written when she was only sixteen, was 'conceived and tossed off in a matter of weeks': it has a devil-may-care spontaneity of manner entirely appropriate to its tomboy heroine, Sybylla Melvyn. Sybylla lives with her drunken, selfish father and strict mother in the small and utterly stagnant outback town of Possum Gully. Gifted, adventurous, and plain, she bitterly resents the restrictions placed on her by the family's poverty and philistinism, and by traditional notions of femininity. Freedom beckons when she is sent to stay with her cultured grandmother and aunt at their home in Caddagat, and meets Harold Beecham, the handsome and wealthy owner of Five-Bob Downs. Sybylla, a world-class eavesdropper, overhears Beecham confessing his love for her to her aunt, and is dismayed by his patronizing attitude. Although she is attracted to him, she fears that marriage will put an end to her literary ambitions. However, when he loses his fortune, she promises to marry him when she is 21. The prospect is ruined when her father's drinking lands him in debt, and she has to leave the paradisial Caddagat and begin a new life as governess to the unbelievably dirty and vulgar M'Swat children. Close to breakdown, she returns to Possum Gully. In the meantime, her younger and prettier sister, Gertie, has taken her place at Caddagat and, or so her letters home would suggest, in Beecham's heart. But Beecham has remained faithful to her and, his fortunes restored by a legacy, rides over to Possum Gully to propose again. Although deeply torn, she still fears that marriage will enslave her, and refuses him. The novel ends with Sybylla's defiantly Whitmanesque address to her fellow Australians. 'Ah, my sunburnt brothers!—sons of toil and of Australia! I love and respect you well, for you are brave and good and true.'... Publication made Franklin famous. Distressed, it is said, by criticism of the novel's 'embittered and egotistical mood' from Havelock Ellis (1859–1939), she subsequently withdrew it from publication, and it remained out of print between 1901 and 1966. Ellis also described it, quite rightly, as a 'vivid and sincere book'. A sequel, *My Career Goes Bung*, was published in 1946.

N

NAPIER of MAGDALA, Lady: Eva Maria Louisa MACDONALD (1846–1930) married, first (1873), Henry Algernon LANGHAM (1850–1874) and, secondly (1885), Robert William NAPIER (1845–1921), who succeeded (1890) as 2nd Baron NAPIER of MAGDALA and CARYNGTON. Eldest of six surviving children of the 4th Baron Macdonald, who had had to prove his elder brothers illegitimate to inherit his title and estates, she published eight volumes of fiction of uneven quality between 1905 and 1916, all but the first issued by John Murray. Her speciality was the moral contamination of innocent young women by their worldly elders. The heroine of *Fiona* (1909) falls under the spell of the fast Lady Buscarlet, and is rescued from a whale by a devoted admirer—the whale being by some way the best thing in the book. In *To the Third and Fourth Generations* (1913), a variant of the *family saga formula, the experienced Hildegarde Mauleverer contracts a loveless marriage with a marquess, and forces her innocent daughter into the same with a Russian prince. The Countess of *Cromartie was Napier's niece.

NAPIER, [Jane] Rosamond (1879–1976) married (1914) Henry Staveley LAWRENCE (d. 1949), KCSI (1926). Youngest of the six children of an army officer, she married her deceased sister's widower, an official in the Indian Civil Service. *The Heart of a Gypsy* (1909) was the first of seven novels to 1938; a great surgeon falls in love with a gypsy who dies because she cannot bear common life. Death also terminates the passion which flowers in *The Faithful Failure* (1910) between a Catholic artist and another childish, brilliant, unconventional heroine, who will marry his cousin instead afterwards. *Indian Embers* (1949) is a volume of memoirs of her married life.

Napoleon of Notting Hill, The, G. K. *Chesterton, 1904, John Lane. Chesterton's first novel is a *fantasy set in 1984. There have been no wars for five years. England has become a nation of shopkeepers, presided over by a zealous bureaucracy. The monarch is elected by an alphabetical system, and one day the task falls to Auberon Quin, an eccentric antiquary. One day, when he is strolling through Notting Hill, a small boy, Adam Wayne, prods him with a wooden sword and announces, 'I'm the King of the Castle', which suggests to Quin that it might be fun to treat the modern suburbs of London as though they were medieval cities. Ten years later, Adam Wayne is provost of Notting Hill. To him the mock-feudal ceremonies devised by Quin are reality. When a business consortium proposes to build a highway through the centre of his fiefdom, he raises an army in its defence. Quin witnesses the conflict in the guise of a war correspondent. Wayne proves victorious, but his doctrines have taken root throughout the city, provoking imitation patriotisms, and another war. This time Wayne is the only survivor. As he and Quin stand among the corpses, Quin explains that he was simply playing a 'vulgar practical joke'; Wayne replies that the joke has poeticized modern life. The two march off together. The book is dedicated to Hilaire *Belloc. It was very warmly received.

Nation, The, (1890–1921) began life in 1890 as the *Speaker*, a paper for the radical, anti-imperialist wing of the Liberal Party. From 1899 to 1907 it was edited by the historian J. L. Hammond (1872–1949), with Desmond MacCarthy (1877–1952) as literary editor. He brought Lytton Strachey (1880–1932) to the arts pages, and also published work by James *Joyce, G. K. *Chesterton, and J. M. Synge (1871–1909). In 1907 the magazine was reorganized. Its title was changed to the *Nation*, and Hammond was replaced by Henry William Massingham (1860–1924), ex-editor of the *Daily Chronicle*. MacCarthy also left, but the magazine (which now had Leonard *Woolf on its staff) continued to attract distinguished contributors. In 1921 the *Nation* merged with the **Athenaeum*, operating for a while as a double magazine until it too was merged, with the *New Statesman* in 1931.

Nebuly Coat, The, John Meade *Falkner, 1903, Edward Arnold. Priggish, fallible Edward Westray, deputy to the eminent architect Sir George Farquhar, builder of institutes, railway stations, and churches, arrives in Cullerne, a sleepy provincial town, to supervise the restoration of Cullerne Minster. He finds the church in a dilapidated state, and is particularly concerned by an ominous crack in the arch supporting the tower. At the centre of the great window at the end of the transept sits the coat of arms of the local magnates, the Blandamer family: 'barry nebuly of six, argent and vert' (i. e. six undulating bars in silver and green). 'It has been stamped for good or evil on this church, and on this town, for centuries,' the melancholic organist, Mr Sharnall, tells Westray, 'and every tavern loafer will talk to you about the "nebuly coat" as if it was a thing he wore.' Westray lodges in a converted pub run by Miss Euphemia Joliffe and her niece, Anastasia. Anastasia's mother died in childbirth; her father, Martin, a farmer's son who believed himself to be a Blandamer kept out of his rights, largely neglected her in favour of his genealogical obsession, and died unmourned. The present Lord Blandamer, a handsome, forceful, dispassionate man in his early 40s, returns to Cullerne for the first time in twenty years (he had quarrelled violently with his grandfather), and begins to show an interest in the Minster, and in Anastasia. Sharnall, who has for a long time been studying the papers left by Martin Joliffe, is found dead in the organ loft. Westray proposes to Anastasia, and is rejected contemptuously. Blandamer proposes, learns that her father was illegitimate, is not dissuaded, and marries. A question remains as to his motive, since he does not love her. Westray, having got over his disappointment, returns to Cullerne, finds alternative lodgings, and begins to study Joliffe's papers. In the frame of a picture which had hung in his old room, and which he has purchased, he finds the authentic marriage certificate of Martin's parents. This proves that Martin was indeed a Blandamer, and that the present Lord Blandamer is an impostor who has cynically married Anastasia in order to cover the traces of his imposture. Westray reveals his knowledge to Blandamer, but agrees to keep it secret. After a violent storm, the church tower finally collapses, and Blandamer dies saving Westray's life. The novel is remarkable for its taut narrative, and its lack of sentimentality. Hugh *Walpole reported that the 'Cathedral set' were 'shocked to their skins' by its depiction of ecclesiastical squabbles.

NESBIT, E[dith] (1858–1924) married, first (1880), Herbert BLAND (d. 1914) and, secondly (1917), Thomas Terry TUCKER. She was the daughter of the head of an agricultural college in Kennington who died when she was 4, leaving her mother to run the college. Later the family travelled in France and Germany because of the tuberculosis of her sister Mary, who died in 1871. They then went to live in Kent, in a house which inspired several of Nesbit's later books, and later, after a financial crisis, in Islington. Pregnant with her first child, she married Bland, whose brush-manufacturing business soon after failed. He also had a son by another woman, continued his affair with her, and afterwards had an affair with their housekeeper, whose two children were brought up by Nesbit as her own. From this point she supported the family by writing journalism, children's fiction, and verse. She was poetry critic of the **Athenaeum* in the 1890s and editor of *Neolith* (1907–8). Her earliest publications in volume form are verse; she and Bland published the novel *The Prophet's Mantle* (1889), about socialism and anarchism, together as 'Fabian Bland'. *Doggy Tales* (1895) and *Pussy Tales* (1895) were early collections of children's stories. Success finally came with the popularity of *The Story of the Treasure Seekers* (1899), which describes the attempts of the motherless Bastables to restore the family fortunes; sequels were *The Wouldbegoods* (1901), *The New Treasure Seekers* (1904), and *Oswald Bastable and Others* (1905). Recounted by Oswald Bastable (who never admits his authorship), they show Edwardian London from the point of view of middle-class children whose experience comes largely from books, not all of which they understand (of Mrs Humphry *Ward, for instance, Oswald comments, 'I don't suppose you have ever heard of her, though she writes books that some people like very much. But perhaps they are her friends.'). *The Enchanted Castle* (1907) is a more than usually frightening version of the danger of granted wishes. Kathleen, Jimmy, and Gerald have been left at school on holiday. In the park of the castle lie large stone dinosaurs from Crystal Palace and statues of the classical gods. The children put on a play, making the audience out of cloakroom detritus, and then, in ways that are soon beyond their control, discover that they have brought everyone to life, including, most horribly, the Ugly-Wuglies, the umbrella and coathanger audience they had made themselves. Other children's books are the fantasies about the Psammead: *Five Children and It* (1902), *The Phoenix and the Carpet* (1904), and *The *Story of the Amulet* (1906); *The *Railway Children* (1906), a powerful story on her favourite theme of a dispossessed middle-class family restored to respectability and prosperity; and *The House of Arden* (1908). She also published volumes of short stories and novels for adults. Many of the former are *horror stories like those in *Grim Tales* (1893) and *Fear* (1910). The protagonists of *The *Red House* (1902) also appear in *The New Treasure Seekers*. Other adult novels are *The Incomplete Amorist* (1906), in which a clergyman's stepdaughter leaves a dull life for Paris and the life of an art student, which she samples before returning to 'gardens, scenery, the simple life, lofty ideals, cathedrals, and Walt Whitman'; *Daphne in Fitzroy Street* (1909), whose heroine escapes with her little sister from her horrible suburban family to bohemian London and Paris; and *Dormant* (1911), in which a woman put in a trance in 1861 awakes in the modern world. Nesbit and Bland were founder members of the Fabian Society (1884) and prominent in literary and bohemian circles. She occasionally published in periodicals as 'E. Bland'. She applied to the Royal Literary Fund after his death and received a Civil List pension in 1915. There is a biography by Julia Briggs (1987).

NEUMAN, B[erman] Paul (b. 1853). Little is known about this writer except that he was evidently interested in social reform and published eighteen volumes of fiction between 1892 and 1917. Neuman's career as a novelist got off to a strong start with *The Greatness of Josiah Porlick* (1904), a story in the manner of Arnold *Bennett about a provincial shopkeeper's assistant who ends up with a fortune he is reluctant to abandon by dying: the selfish, bullying hero believes himself to be a just and pious man, but a fatal disease tests him beyond endurance, and he dies in a convincing welter of rage, terror, and penitence. Neuman had another success in this manner with the more humorous and *Wellsian *Troddles* (1912), whose hero, a coarse, tyrannical London tailor, is determined that his two sons shall rise in the world: which they do, becoming Mr Justice Troddles and Dr Richard Troddles, MD. *Dominy's Dollars* (1908) also features a self-made man. The hero, an intelligent Jewish boy, is taken off the streets of New York by three philanthropists, a doctor, a musician, and a financier, who invite him to choose between the different salvations they have to offer. He becomes a timber king, sacrificing all other needs in the pursuit of wealth and power. Neuman's other novels were more formulaic. *Spoils of Victory* (1906) and *The Lone Heights* (1911) are predictable tales of literary life. *Simon Brandin* (1912) concerns the machinations of Russian revolutionaries in London, orchestrated by the hero, a wealthy financier and himself a Russian Jew. In *Open Sesame* (1913), the machinations are those of another financier, Mr Gaye, of Acacia Road, St John's Wood, and Will Porteous, a faith healer, founder of the Church of the Gifts. But Neuman never abandoned his interest in social problems. *Chignett Street: A Provided School* (1914) is a collection of stories, reprinted from the *Westminster Gazette*, intended to describe state elementary schools in fiction on the lines of boys' public-school stories. However, it seems better adapted to inform an adult audience than entertain a juvenile one. Neuman's several non-fictional works include *The Boys' Club in Theory and Practice* (1900).

New Age, The, *A Weekly Record of Culture, Social Service, and Literary Life*, [after 1895] *The New Age: A Journal for Thinkers and Workers*, [after 1907] *The New Age: An Independent Socialist Review of Politics, Literature and Art* (1894–1938). Founded by Frederick A. Atkins (1864–1929) as a successor to the *Young Man*, it had an earnestly Christian tone, captured in its subtitle. In 1895 a new editor, A. E. Fletcher (1841–1915), changed this, bringing to the fore the tension between the magazine's Christian Liberalism (G. K. *Chesterton was now a regular contributor) and its Fabianism. In 1898, under a new editor, Arthur Compton-Rickett (1869–1937), it became unashamedly Fabian, and in the 1900s, under Joseph Clayton (1868–1943) and A. R. Orage (1873–1934), who bought the magazine in 1907, the *New Age* moved away from Victorian values altogether to combine literary and social criticism. Under Orage's editorship, in particular, the magazine not only attracted such contributors as T. E. Hulme (1883–1917), Ezra Pound (1885–1972),

W. B. Yeats (1865–1939), and Arnold *Bennett (the articles collected as *Books and Persons* first appeared there) but also in its illustrations and criticism placed itself firmly on the side of modernism as well as of state socialism, to become one of the most important sources of intellectual and literary argument of its time (among other things, introducing to the British reader the ideas of Sigmund Freud, 1856–1939). But it is generally agreed that Orage achieved his most lasting success as an editor before 1918. From 1908 he increased the literary bias of the magazine. Bennett became the fiction critic; drama was analysed by William Archer (1856–1924), and Ashley Dukes (1885–1959); and poetry by F. S. Flint (1885–1960). Bennett's column, 'Books and Persons', appeared pseudonymously as by 'Jacob Tonson', and introduced the works of the new French writers Anatole France (1844–1922), Rémy de Gourmont (1858–1915), and Paul Valéry (1871–1945), and the Russians Anton Chekhov (1860–1904) and Fyodor Dostoevsky (1821–81). Ashley Dukes's reviews of Continental dramatists were later published separately as one of the first critiques in English of modern continental dramatists. F. S. Flint introduced T. E. Hulme to the magazine and subsequently Ezra Pound. In July 1907 Hulme reviewed the philosophical works of William James (1842–1910) and Henri Bergson (1859–1941). The heyday of the *New Age* was, however, from 1911 to 1914. Under the pseudonyms 'B. H. Dias' and 'William Atheling', Ezra Pound acted as art and music critic. His translation of 'The Seafarer' appeared in the issue for 30 November 1911. He later published other translations, including the famous translations of Cavalcanti. Whilst promoting imagism, the *New Age* readily acknowledged the importance of post-impressionism in art. Orage published sketches by Pablo Picasso (1881–1973), and work by Auguste Herbin (1882–1960). He also published some of the first critical essays about their work by John Middleton Murry (1889–1957) and Walter Sickert (1860–1942). Later, the magazine first parodied Filippo Marinetti (1876–1944) but then became a platform for futurism. The vitality of the resulting debates was lost when Orage fell under the influence of the social credit movement and the mysticism of G. I. Gurdjieff (1872–1949). Orage left the magazine in 1922 to join the Gurdjieff Institute near Fontainebleau where 'Katherine *Mansfield' was to die in the following year. It ceased publication in 1938.

NEWBOLT, Henry [John] (1862–1938), Kt. (1915), CH (1922), married (1889) Margaret Edina DUCKWORTH (1867–1960). Newbolt was born at Bilton, Staffordshire, and educated at Caistor Grammar School in Lincolnshire, Clifton College, Bristol (where he held a scholarship and which influenced him profoundly), and Corpus Christi, Oxford, where he gained a first-class classics degree. He qualified as a barrister in 1887 and practised for the next twelve years. His first novel was the anonymous *A Fair Death* (1882), but it was not until the publication of 'Drake's Drum' in the *St James's Gazette* in the following year that Newbolt received wide acclaim. Robert Bridges (1844–1930) said of it: 'It isn't given to man to write anything better,' and helped to produce *Admirals All* (1897), the volume of Newbolt ballads which included 'Drake's Drum'. The book was a runaway best seller which ran to twenty-one editions in two years. Newbolt likened these popular ballads to the work of A. E. Housman (1859–1936) and *Kipling, describing them as 'poems of vivid sentiment written in vivid metre'. The collection included 'He Fell Among Thieves' and 'Vitaï Lampada' (whose refrain: 'Play up, play up, and play the game!' was chanted by soldiers in the *Boer War to stir flagging spirits). *The Island Race* (1898) was another collection of poems steeped with imperialistic fervour. Together, these two volumes assured Newbolt a popularity rivalled only by Kipling's, and he retired from the Bar in 1899 to devote more time to his writing. The *publisher John Murray made him editor of the *Monthly Review* in 1900, with a brief to revive interest in poetry; he held the post until 1904, when Murray took issue with his use of the periodical as a political platform. One significant feature of his editorship was the introduction of the work of Walter *de la Mare. Other contributors during his tenure include W. B. Yeats (1865–1939), Robert Bridges (1844–1930), *'Q', Alice *Meynell (1847–1922), and Roger Fry (1866–1934). Newbolt's *The *Old Country* (1906) is one of several novels of this period in which historical and modern characters are mysteriously bonded (compare fiction by William Hope *Hodgson, 'Vernon *Lee', Norman *Douglas). Connected in theme and characters is *The New June* (1909), a *historical romance about young knights following Richard the Lionheart who treat jousting as cricket and talk like public schoolboys about the choice between duty to man and duty to God. *The Twymans: A Tale of Youth* (1911) is semi-autobiographical. During the First World War he was Controller of Wireless and Cables, and he later produced *A Naval History of the War* 1914–1918 (5 vols., 1920–31). Newbolt's complex of ideas about *Empire and Englishness led him to champion the cause of English literature as a subject for serious academic study. His literary criticism includes *A New Study of English Poetry* (1917), *Studies Green and Grey* (1926), and critical introductions to anthologies containing works by such authors as T. S. Eliot (1888–1965), Ezra Pound (1885–1972), D. H. *Lawrence, and Edith Sitwell (1887–1964). In his inaugural lecture as the Royal Society of Literature's Professor of Poetry Newbolt discussed poetry and its place in the early twentieth century. Poetry, he said, was 'alternately glorified and neglected', but he argued that 'the present era is not really an age of prose, it is an age of re-building'. His reputation today is, however, clouded by ideological considerations; his celebration of the public-school spirit and its expansion to nationalistic fervour are now outmoded. Yet Newbolt was neither unaware of nor unsympathetic to the changing literary scene of his time, and was an early admirer of the works of Wilfred Owen (1893–1918) and Siegfried Sassoon (1886–1967). *My World as in My Time* (1932) is an autobiography.

New Machiavelli, The, H. G. *Wells, 1911, John Lane. One of what Wells called his 'prig novels', *The New Machiavelli* is the autobiographical record of Richard Remington's rise from shabby-genteel childhood to parliamentary eminence, followed by the ruin of his career through his involvement with a woman. The book contains large chunks of political discussion, but does extend Wells's range of characters across the social spectrum. Remington, a radical idealist (in battle with 'the rule of thumb world',) is slowly disillusioned by the English political system, by his colleagues' pettiness and futility, and by a politics that delivers only botched cities and jerry-built suburbs. As a reformer, though, he faces as much hostility from the general public as from the political establishment, and, linking political blindness to sexual repression, Wells shows that Remington's defeat by his enemies is inevitable once he has deserted his wife for a mistress. Like **Ann Veronica* (1909), the book arose in the context of Wells's bitter parting from the Fabian Group.

NEWTE, Horace W[ykeham] C[an] (1870–1949) married (1898) Vera Irene von RASCH. Born at Melksham, Wiltshire, he was educated at Christ's Hospital, and intended for the navy, but became a journalist, playwright, and author of thirty volumes of fiction between 1907 and 1930, including *The Master Beast: Being a True Account of the Ruthless Tyranny Inflicted on the British People by Socialism, AD. 1888–2020* (1907), a sanguinary reversal of *News from Nowhere* (1891) by William Morris (1834–96), in which a young man of liberal views awakes in 2020 AD in a state socialist dystopia; *The Socialist Countess: A Story of To-Day* (1911), in which a man returns from twenty years making his fortune in the East to find his childhood sweetheart a widow with a ridiculous and insincere enthusiasm for socialism, who is appalled when her daughter falls in love with a motor mechanic; and *A 'Young Lady': A Study in Selectness* (1913), which is about a typist who becomes impatient with the atmosphere of lower-middle-class pretension in which she lives, and abandons her fiancé to run away with another man. In Newte's fiction women like having men to make up their minds for them. Some, however, at least have minds to be made up. The heroine of *The Cuckoo Lamb* (1914), Jane Alma Inkerman Gibbs, is a soldier's daughter born, like the 'cuckoo lamb', out of season: she pursues a literary calling while employed as a domestic drudge, and her encounters with the usual crowd of cranks and decadents provide occasions for the development of aesthetic and sociological theories.

Nine to Six-Thirty, 'W. Pett *Ridge', 1910, Methuen. Barbara Harrison rebels against her bullying family and establishes an independent life in London, eventually becoming engaged and reconciled to her family. In London she finds employment as a clerk in a travel agency, War-nett's World-Wide Wanderings, which expands and then goes bust; and as a clerk, and eventually manager, with a firm of process engravers. The success of her career remains in doubt right up until the last moment; and while it remains in doubt there can be no salvation through marriage. She makes it clear that she will continue to work after she is married. The suffragette Jane Collings, who used to live in the same suburban street as Barbara Harrison, represents another alternative: a fulfilment which Barbara respects, even if she does not want it for herself. *Nine to Six-Thirty* is marred by sentimentality and facetiousness, particularly where babies are concerned, but it is a better novel than Wells's **Ann Veronica* (1909), because it gives *suburbia a chance.

Nineteenth Century and After, The, (1877–1972) was founded in 1877 by James Knowles (1831–1908), former editor of the *Contemporary Review*, as the *Nineteenth Century*, but changed its title on 1 January 1901 (eventually, in 1951, becoming the *Twentieth Century*). The magazine focused on national and international affairs, with particular attention being paid to British colonial and imperialist policy, while also featuring literary, historical, and religious debate. The magazine remained successful in attracting prominent figures to write for it (W. E. Gladstone, 1809–98, and Alfred, Lord Tennyson, 1809–92, had been regular contributors to early issues) and this formed the basis of its continuing sales success.

NISBET, Hume (1849–1923) married Blanch——. Born in Stirling, Scotland, in his mid-teens Nisbet set sail for Australia, where he travelled extensively. He returned to Scotland when he was 23 and took up the position of art master at Watt College, Edinburgh. After resigning in 1885 Nisbet worked for *Cassell's* in Australia and New Guinea, and soon decided to turn his attention to writing full-time. His works are adventure stories which reflect his peregrinations in earlier life. In 1891 *A Colonial Tramp: Travels & Adventures in Australia and New Guinea* appeared. He also illustrated books such as R. B. W. Noel, *Livingstone in Africa* (1885). Nisbet published forty-six romances; the best-remembered is *'Bail-Up!': A Romance of Bushrangers and Blacks* (1890). Other novels include *A Bush Girl's Romance* (1894), *The Great Secret: A Tale of Tomorrow* (1895), and *In Sheep's Clothing* (1900), a romance set in Australia, *The Empire Makers* (1900), an adventure story against the backdrop of the *Boer War, and *The Losing Game: An Australian Tragedy* (1901). He also produced verse, collected in *Poetic And Dramatic Works* (1905), volumes of short stories, and several works on art and painting technique. His recreations, according to *Who's Who*, were 'travelling and studying Nature and Humanity'.

NIVEN, Frederick [John] (1878–1944) married (1911) Mary Pauline THORNE-QUELCH. Born in Valparaiso, Chile, son of a muslin manufacturer, he was educated at Hutcheson's Grammar School, Glasgow, and at Glasgow School of Art, and became a librarian in Scotland before going to the Canadian West at the age of 20. On his return he wrote about the life of logging camps in the Glasgow *Weekly Herald* and became a journalist until the success of his first novel, *The Lost Cabin Mine* (1908), enabled him to give up his staff job to write freelance. He visited Canada again in 1912. Like many other writers in this book, he worked in the Ministry of Information during the First World War, after which he went with his wife to live in Nelson, British Columbia. His thirty-odd volumes of fiction 1910–1944 draw on his extensive travels, especially in Canada and the Americas. They include *A Wilderness of Monkeys* (1911), in which a writer called Bliss Henry escapes from the pressures of Fleet Street to the moorland town of Solway; *Ellen Adair* (1913), the naturalistic tale of the fall of an Edinburgh shopgirl whom we leave on the streets of London; *The Porcelain Lady* (1914), about the relations between the young men and women working on a great newspaper; and *Justice of the Peace* (1914), in which the son of a prosperous Glasgow silk weaver becomes an artist, contrasts the puritanical suffragist mother with the generous artist's model wife. The *Pall Mall Gazette* thought it 'unmistakeably big'; the *Spectator* called it 'powerful, engrossing, disquieting'. The hero of *Cinderella of Skookum Creek* (1916) has gone West to grow tomatoes, where he finds a half-educated girl to love; he becomes a famous writer.

NOBLE, Edward (1857–1941) married (1885) Alice WILLCOX (d. 1922). He was the son of a doctor and was educated privately. In *Who's Who* he wrote, 'Twenty odd years wandering, on the seven seas—in sailing and tramp and mail ship; dabbling in engineering, in paint, in work that is unclassified as well as in that which generally is understood to be part and parcel of the business known as sailorising, both ashore and afloat.' He also published eighteen volumes of fiction, many nautical, between 1905 and 1928, including *The Lady Navigators and Incidentally the Man with the Nubbly Brow* (1905), *Fisherman's Gat:*

A Story of the Thames Estuary (1906), and *Dust from the Loom: A Romance of Two Atacamas* (1914), in which a captain in the merchant navy woos a Chilean girl while trying to import copper.

NOMAD, *pseud.*: Adele Crafton SMITH published a volume of verse (1899) and six volumes of fiction from 1882. She thought of herself as a Victorian writer, explaining in *The Woman Decides* (1912) that she had decided to resume her career only because she felt that 'the present style of story-telling' fell short of the 'interesting form and method' which had produced masterpieces like *East Lynne* (1861) by Mrs Henry Wood (1814–1887) and *Uncle Tom's Cabin* (1852) by Harriet Beecher Stowe (1811–96). The novel concerns family complications in country society, mostly to do with the deceased wife's sister question. Her last two novels were *Reminiscences of a Prima Donna* (1912) and *A Strange Will and Its Consequences* (1913).

NORMAN, Mrs George, *pseud.*: Melesina Mary MACKENZIE married G. BLOUNT. Born to an upper-middle-class Roman Catholic family, she was educated at the convent of the Sacred Heart and at the English Convent at Bruges, before returning to a life of polite inaction. After marriage she began to contribute to the *Westminster Gazette*. She published eleven volumes of equally polite fiction 1908–29. The heroine of *Delphine Carfrey* (1911) has £40,000 a year and a tender heart, and politely pursues John Owen, an artist. The **Times Literary Supplement* described *The Silver Dress* (1912), whose clever, well-bred, innocent heroine finds love late in life, as 'a novel which should win a large audience among those who do not want problems'. Mackenzie also published a hagiography and contributed to such periodicals as the *Daily Mail* and the *Tatler*. Her sister Margaret Mackenzie, an actress and poet, discovered *The Young Visiters* (1919) by Daisy Ashford (1881–1972), who had been a friend of theirs from childhood, and showed it to Frank *Swinnerton of Chatto & Windus. After it became a bestseller, according to R. M. Malcolmson's biography of Ashford, Margaret and 'Siney' Mackenzie meanly kept Ashford to her promise of letting them dramatize the novel even when it meant refusing *Barrie's offer to do so. Their play was produced in 1920.

NORRIS, W[illiam] E[dward] (1847–1925) married (1871) Frances Isobel BALLENDEN (d. 1881). Son of the Chief Justice of Ceylon, he was born in London and educated at Eton College. He travelled abroad, abandoned the idea of joining the diplomatic service, qualified as a barrister in 1874, and eventually chose to follow a literary career. He was a friend of Henry *James, although James was not an admirer of Norris's work. His numerous publications were mainly comic society novels of love and romance, untaxingly fortified with a sprinkling of political theory. 'I have no personal liking for what is called the modern realistic school of fiction, because I don't see the good of it,' he observed to Helen Black. 'One does not go to a novel for information as to the uglier facts of existence.' Norris's brand of fiction proved extremely popular and he made a decent living from his work. In *The Flower of the Flock* (1900) a charming American widow solves the financial problems of an English banking family by marrying an expensive young officer. *Nature's Comedian* (1904) concerns a man of facile gifts who plays many parts (lover of an ingenuous girl, rising politician attracted to a woman of the world) without believing, or succeeding, in any of them. His brother, a clergyman, gets the ingenuous Lilian, and turns out to be a genius. The bronzed and manly Captain Desborough gets the political career and the woman of the world. The comedian's only successes are on the stage and in the heart of a dilapidated actress. It all ends tragically when, playing the part of a hero, he rushes into a burning theatre to rescue a straggler and is himself burnt to death. The epitaph pronounced on him is that he was 'a great comedian up to the very last'. *Barham of Beltana* (1905) is a rich Tasmanian, son of a convict, travelling in Europe with a son and a daughter, who is dismayed to have them swept up by an impoverished upper-class brother and sister from the family his father was transported for robbing. *Harry and Ursula: A Story with Two Sides to it* (1907) concerns the misunderstandings between two exceptionally dim individuals who become rich without really meaning to and finally realize that they love each other; the two sides to the story are presented alternately. *The Perjurer* (1909) is about gambling, and *Not Guilty* (1910) about a man who is tried for murder and acquitted in circumstances which leave a stain on his character: he has spent the evening in question in the company of Agatha Campion, a lady with hazel eyes and a stately figure whose reputation he wishes to preserve; he takes himself off to Australia. The *Times* review of *The Triumph of Sara* (1920) observed: 'Mr W. E. Norris is a novelist whom age does not wither—not because he is endowed with infinite variety, but rather because he has set himself certain useful limits within which he has acquired a perfect mastery of method.'

Nostromo: *A Tale of the Seaboard*, Joseph *Conrad, 1904, Harper. An Englishman, Charles Gould, owns a silver mine in Sulaco, in the South American republic of Costaguana, which is plagued by civil war. In order to protect his silver from the rebels, Gould entrusts it to a journalist, Martin Decoud, who in turn recruits the Capataz de Cargadores, Giovanni Batista Fidanza, or 'Nostromo', a local hero, to help him. Their ship is damaged in a collision and they are compelled to hide the silver on a nearby island. Shocked by these events, Decoud's usual scepticism turns to madness, and he drowns himself, weighted down with silver. Back in Sulaco, Nostromo realizes that he has run unnecessary risks and, although neither a selfish nor a greedy man, decides to profit from the risks by making out that the silver was lost, and burying it, after peace returns to Costaguana, on the small island where his fiancée Linda lives with her father, Giorgio Viola, the lighthouse-keeper. The economic interests represented by Gould have assumed control of the country. Nostromo grows rich slowly, drawing on the hidden treasure. But his wealth becomes a corrosive obsession. He is really in love with Linda's sister, Giselle, but before he can do anything about it, he is shot by their father, who mistakes him for a common thief or seducer. Decoud believes in nothing. Nostromo believes at first in nothing, then in one thing only, the silver. Gould believes in one thing only, the silver; although he survives and prospers, his obsession destroys his marriage. There does not appear to be a middle way between too much faith and too little. Conrad's most ambitious novel, which attempts to describe the forces which shape collective as well as individual destinies, is also one of his most consistently ironic. Much of the story is told by an impossibly garrulous old sea captain and self-appointed tour guide. Arnold *Bennett told Conrad that he thought it 'the finest novel of this generation (bar none).'

No Surrender, Constance *Maud, 1911, Gerald Duckworth. Like a number of other suffragette novels, including Annie *Swan's *Margaret Holroyd* (1910), this takes the opportunity of the campaign for the vote to describe a group of women in relation to each other rather than to the opposite sex. The defining scene takes place in prison. 'In a small bare cell about eight feet by six, the furniture of which consisted of one wooden stool, five women were crowded together. Five women of widely different type, age, class, and education, united by only one bond, but that sufficiently strong to break down all the ordinary barriers created by such differences, and place them at once on the footing of comrades and sisters. It was such a bond as united the early Christians crowded together behind the bars of the Coliseum cells awaiting their turn to fight and to die for the faith that was in them.' The women then explain how they came to join the movement. One of them subsequently ends up in a punishment cell being force-fed. The final chapter, 'The Passing of the Women', describes a suffragette procession. The novel is dedicated to the feminist campaigner Charlotte Despard (1844–1939).

O

O'BRIEN, Mrs William: see under George *Raffalovich.

O'BYRNE, Dermot, *pseud.*: Arnold Edward Trevor BAX (1883–1953), Kt. (1937), married (1911) Elsa Luisa SOBRINO. He was born in Streatham, of musical parents, and educated at home, at the Hampstead Conservatoire, and the Royal Academy of Music. In 1902 he read 'The Wanderings of Oisin' by W. B. Yeats (1865–1939); he wrote of this experience: 'in a moment the Celt within me was revealed.' As well as using a Celtic idiom in his music, for instance in the tone poem 'In the Faery Hills' (1910), he published volumes of pseudonymous fiction in this vein: *Children of the Hills: Tales and Sketches of Western Ireland in the Old Time and the Present Day* (1913), *The Sisters and Green Magic* (1912), and *Wrack and Other Stories* (1918). These *fantasies, many set in Donegal, are full of evocations of wild landscape and emphasis on peasant superstition. *Seafoam and Firelight* (1909) is a pamphlet of Yeatsian verse. Later his music became Nordic rather than Celtic in flavour but he published no more fiction. He was Master of the King's (later the Queen's) Musick from 1942 until his death. The dramatist and poet Clifford Bax (1886–1962) was his brother.

Odette d'Antrevernes, Arthur *Firbank, 1905, Elkin Matthews. Two impressionistic tales. The title-piece, set in the Château of Lynes on the banks of the Loire, concerns two revelatory moments in the life of young Odette, who lives there with her aunt (her parents drowned on the way back from India). She overhears her old nurse telling another servant how her aunt's husband was killed in a duel, a month after their marriage. Then she prevents a fallen woman from throwing herself into the river: 'she realized for the first time, that life was cruel, that life was sad, that beyond the beautiful garden in which she dwelt, many millions of people were struggling to live, and sometimes in the struggle for life one failed—like the poor woman by the river bank.' In 'A Study in Temperament' Lady Agnes Charteris, wearing 'a long, clinging gown that coiled about her like a dusky snake', awaits the arrival of a poetess, her sister-in-law, and perhaps her husband ('but then there is something so very early Victorian in seeing one's husband, except, of course, sometimes at meals'). The poetess, Miss Hester Q. Tail, appears. So do the sister-in-law and her daughter, the daughter looking fashionably older than the mother. So does Lord Sevenoaks, a passionate admirer. Lady Agnes considers whether she should run away with him, but self-absorption looks to be winning out at the end.

O'DONOVAN, Gerald: Jeremiah O'DONOVAN (1871–1942) married (1910) Florence Emily Beryl VERSCHOYLE (1886–1968). Born and brought up in Ireland, he was educated in parochial schools in Galway, Cork, and Sligo, and at Maynooth College, which he entered in 1889. He became a Roman Catholic priest, and was in charge of the parish of Loughrea, Galway 1897–1904, where he energetically promoted the causes of temperance, the Gaelic League, the cooperative movement, and the decoration of St Brendan's Cathedral with Irish craftsmanship. He was supposed to be the model for the priest in George *Moore's *The *Lake*. But though he was a national figure he made himself unpopular with his superiors, was suspended in 1904, became bankrupt, and, after a period of uncertainty and depression, was appointed subwarden of Toynbee Hall, a missionary settlement in the East End of London. He left this job in 1911 (because his wife, an upper-class Protestant with some money, found living in the settlement impossible) and worked as a reviewer and in publishing while writing novels. The first of these were *Father Ralph* (1913), a highly autobiographical novel about the education and eventual unfrocking of a young Catholic priest, with much emphasis on the cynicism and hypocrisy of the Catholic establishment; and *Waiting* (1914), in which an idealistic, nationalist, National Schoolmaster who wants to marry a

Protestant woman is frustrated in his political ambitions by the malevolence of his parish priest. He published four later novels, the last in 1922. During the First World War he became head of the Italian section of the Department for Propaganda in Enemy Countries of the Ministry of Information. There he met Rose *Macaulay, who also worked in the Italian section, and began an affair which lasted until his death. From 1938 until his health failed from the cancer which killed him, he was working for the welfare of Czech refugees.

Old Country, The: *A Romance*, Henry *Newbolt, 1906, Smith, Elder. The story begins in the present day, with a country-house party at Gardenleigh. Young Stephen Bulmer, a 'fearless spirit-venturer', author of *The Uplands of the Future*, is strongly attracted to Aubrey Earnshaw, daughter of Gardenleigh's owner and herself a believer in tradition. While reading a book she has lent him about the history of the house, Bulmer slips back into the fourteenth century, to find Aubrey, also a person of more than one incarnation, and her uncle, Sir Henry Marland, worrying about the fate of Ralph Tremur, a college friend of Sir Henry's eldest son, Edmund, who has become a priest. We begin to worry about him too when we learn that he has a promising student called John Wyclif. Grandison, Bishop of Exeter, and Tremur's deadly foe, is on his way to Gardenleigh to excommunicate the heretic. Stephen takes to Ralph, and he remains an advocate of free thought until the very end, when, after many complications, including the Battle of Poitiers, the sentence of excommunication is passed, and he returns to the twentieth century. That Aubrey willingly accompanies him, even though her spiritual home is in the fourteenth century, is a sign that he has learnt to respect tradition. 'I offer no solution to this mystery of Time,' Newbolt wrote in his dedication of the book to the Right Reverend Cosmo Lang, Bishop of Stepney, 'but I have ventured to suggest that it is one worth thinking about, if only that we may be less prone to forget the sympathy we owe to the brave and ardent spirits who hoped our hopes before us, and who belong to a past which can never be truly spoken of as dead.'

Old Wives' Tale, The: *A Novel*, Arnold *Bennett, 1908, Chapman & Hall. Bennett began writing the novel on 8 October 1907, and finished it with his usual dispatch well within the year, on 30 August 1908. It is the story of two sisters, Constance and Sophia Baines, whose father keeps a draper's shop in the main square of Bursley, one of the 'Five Towns'. Baines is incapacitated by a stroke, and responsibility for managing the shop devolves onto the reliable and apparently colourless Samuel Povey. On her father's death, Constance inherits the shop, and marries Samuel. They have a dim and unappreciative son, Cyril. Samuel comes briefly alive when his cousin Daniel is accused of murdering his drunken, sluttish wife, and sentenced to death. Samuel campaigns, unsuccessfully, for a reprieve, and the strain kills him, too. Sophia has long since left the scene, eloping to Paris with a glib commercial traveller, Gerald Scales. Paris arouses her in a way Bursley never did, but not to the point where she loses sight of the longer term. Gerald rapidly runs through their small stock of money, but she has kept some back, and, when he leaves her, she puts it to good use. She not only survives the siege of Paris, in 1870, but prospers and, after the defeat of the Commune, buys the Pension Frensham, in the *rue Lord Byron*. She has lost touch with her family, but a native of Bursley appears at the Pension Frensham, and betrays her. Worn out by hard work, she returns home, to spend the rest of her days with her equally dejected sister. Gerald Scales, meanwhile, has come to a sordid end, and the sight of his corpse stimulates in Sophia a recognition which comes to a number of Bennett's more thoughtful characters. 'Sophia then experienced a pure and primitive emotion, uncoloured by any moral or religious quality. She was not sorry that Gerald had wasted his life, nor that he was a shame to his years and to her. The manner of his life was of no importance. What affected her was that he had once been young, and that he had grown old, and was now dead. That was all.'

OLLIVANT, Alfred (1874–1927) married (1914) Hilda WIGRAM (d. 1959). The son of an army officer, he was educated at Rugby School and the Royal Military College, Sandhurst. He was briefly in the Royal Artillery (1893–8) before a riding accident forced him to retire. Much his best-known work is his first, *Owd Bob, the Grey Dog of Kenmuir* (1898), a powerful and tragic tale of sheepdog trials in Cumbria, which soon was regarded, as animal stories are apt to be, as a children's book. But Ollivant also published thirteen other volumes of fiction, mostly for adults, and sometimes concerned with social problems. In *The Taming of John Blunt* (1911), a hard-bitten socialist journalist sent to investigate a rich autocratic spinster, Lady Rachel Carmelite, of Scar Hall, Cumberland, finds her the ideal landowner (he himself turns out to be of more than respectable origins). *The Royal Road: Being the Story of the Life, Death, and Resurrection of Edward Hankey of London* (1912), dedicated to Beatrice Webb (1858–1943), contains extensive criticism of the system of poor relief. Hankey, who operates a splitting machine at a leather factory, is guided onto the straight and narrow by a slum-doctor and his sister (notable for her sturdy figure, her pince-nez and 'short workmanlike skirt'). He marries happily, and has a child. Then he contracts tuberculosis, and is forced to leave the factory. A lodger steals the money he has put by, and the authorities prove totally unsympathetic. He and his wife attempt to drown themselves, but are prevented by the doctor, who cannot, however, cure the tuberculosis. Ollivant was a member of the Fabian Society.

ONIONS, [George] Oliver (1873–1961), who changed his name (1918) to George OLIVER, married (1909) Berta *RUCK. Born in Bradford, of working-class parents, he studied at the National Arts Training Schools (later the Royal College of Art), from where he went to Paris on a scholarship in 1897. He became an illustrator and draughtsman for the Harmsworth group of newspapers and periodicals before taking to literature around the turn of the century. He contributed many short stories to *Country Life* and other periodicals. *The Compleat Bachelor* (1900), his first novel, consists of sketches concerning a permanent bachelor, Rollo Butterfield, very much in the line of Sam Carter, in *The Dolly Dialogues* by 'Anthony *Hope' (1894) and Vanderbank in Henry *James's *The Awkward Age* (1899). The sketches offer suave reflections on the social round. The twist is that this bachelor proves to be less permanent than his predecessors, and becomes engaged to the only woman he knows who understands his jokes. Onions's pen turned to many different genres, including in this period *Admiral Eddy* (1907), a children's book about a little boy and his boat, and *Back o' the Moon and Other Stories* (1906), long regional tales of peasant life. The title of *Draw in Your Stool* (1909) is presumably meant to indicate examples of the storyteller's ancient but still magnetic art. The contents, however, are miscellaneous and dreary: Roman Gaul, bull-fighting, a fishing village, an ecclesiastical sculptor. *Good Boy Seldom: A Romance of Advertisement* (1911) is a facetious satire on the rise to prosperity and disillusionment of James Wace. Onions's later works include several others with an anti-advertising, anti-big-business theme, and **Widdershins* (1911), a collection of ghost stories. His obituarist in the *Times* (10 Apr. 1961) commented 'He wrote with difficulty, even with anguish'; he suffered intermittently from depression. His wife, a far more consistently prolific novelist, was no doubt the mainstay of the household finances.

Open Window (1910–11). A new illustrated monthly calling itself 'imaginative rather than controversial', appeared in London in October 1910. A 'little magazine' (before this designation was common) in its physical format (6″ × 4 1/2″) its editor and publisher was Vivian Locke Ellis. As a practitioner himself, Ellis sought actively to promote the arts in the pages of his magazine. The poetry of Walter *de la Mare, W. H. *Davies, James *Stephens, and John Drinkwater (1882–1937) was published, as were the plays of Lord *Dunsany, Gilbert *Cannan, and Hugh *de Sélincourt, with E. M. *Forster and Frank *Swinnerton contributing stories. In December 1910 'Katherine *Mansfield' shifted her alliance from the *New Age* to *Open Window* with 'A Fairy Story'. Of equal importance were the many artists whose work featured: these included Jack Butler Yeats (d. 1957), Auguste Rodin (1840–1917), Charles March Gere (1869–1957), long associated with William Morris, and Sir Charles John Holmes (1868–1936), landscape painter and art critic and director of the National Portrait Gallery and the National Gallery. The frontispiece for Volume 2 was produced by Muirhead Bone (see Gertrude *Bone). Ellis produced only two volumes of *Open Window*, of 390 and 370 pages, with publication lasting only one year. It was not particularly avant-garde, yet achieved lasting recognition.

OPENSHAW, Mary (d. 1928) married Edward Arthur BINSTEAD. Brought up in Kendal, Westmorland, she was educated privately and at the Manor House, Brondesbury Park. She was a journalist and published eight volumes of fiction 1908–24, some *historical, some modern, including *The Cross of Honour* (1910), set in Poland and France under Napoleon; *Sunshine: The Story of a Pure Heart* (1914), a saccharine tale of a destitute girl who marries a decaying widower and then, widowed herself, is prevented from marrying her true love, a doctor, until his worldly French wife dies of dissipation; and *Little Grey Girl*, a story about a Quaker which reminded the Standard reviewer of *Cranford*. She was Honorary Secretary of the Society of Women Journalists (1917–27) and of the Femina Vie Heureuse and Bookman Prizes Committee.

OPPENHEIM, E[dward] Phillips (1866–1946) married (1892) Elsie Clara HOPKINS (d. 1946). Born in London, the son of a leather merchant, he was educated at Wyggeston Grammar School, Leicester, but left aged 16 because of a family financial crisis. His first novel, *Expiation* (1887), was published with his father's money; his second did not appear for another seven years. He continued to work in the family firm, often travelling on the Continent and in America, while publishing stories in the *Sheffield Weekly Telegraph* and becoming an increasingly popular author of thrillers. Some have described Oppenheim's *Mysterious Mr Sabin* (1898) as the first *spy novel. Mr Sabin is the prototype of the millionaire would-be Mr Fixits of twentieth-century *crime fiction: he wants to restore the French monarchy with the help of his scientific inventions, which he will give to the Germans so that they can conquer the British. At about the age of 40 Oppenheim sold the firm and took to writing full-time. Much of his vast output (more than 160 volumes of fiction) was dictated to a secretary. Like *Le Queux, *Childers, and others he wrote fiction warning of the danger from Germany: *A *Maker of History* (1905) turns on a plot for a joint Russian-German invasion. See also *The *Secret* (1907). Like many of his fellow-authors he spent the First World War in the Ministry of Information. In 1922 he left England to live on the Riviera (Mecca to many of his characters), perhaps influenced by the prospect of paying tax on the profits of his most successful novel, *The Great Impersonation* (1920). There he lived ostentatiously, even for that frivolous world, and conducted a very public series of love affairs. In the 1920s many of his novels were first published in America in serial form, an arrangement immensely lucrative for Oppenheim: *Collier's*, for example, paid 20,000 dollars to publish *The Treasure House of Martin Hews* (1929). In 1935 he moved his domicile to Guernsey to avoid the French tax authorities, but then bought another house in France, to which he foolishly returned after the outbreak of war; he and his wife managed to escape to Portugal and arrived in England in 1941. In 1945 they were refused permission to return to Guernsey. Oppenheim, probably in an attempt to evade English death duties, chartered a small yacht to take him and his almost senile wife to their house in Guernsey, until recently the local headquarters of the Luftwaffe, where they both soon died.

Oppenheim published many orthodox detective stories, such as, *Slane's Long Shots* (1930), some futuristic novels, such as *The Wrath to Come* (1924), and four plays, but his most distinctive and characteristic works are thrillers about international diplomacy and the secret service in which the hero or heroine works to save civilization, whether from Germans, Bolsheviks, or mad megalomaniacs. Like John *Buchan, he was excited by the thought that the destinies of nations are shaped by a handful of powerful men, some wicked, some benevolent; like many of his imitators and followers, he let the reader identify with the ordinary man caught up in epoch-making events. Not for him, however, the rather later emphasis on the dull and squalid side of intelligence work: his novels take place in casinos, ballrooms, ocean liners, grand hotels, wagons-lits, and embassies; his characters are American millionaires, Russian princes, English aristocrats, and his heroines are invariably fascinating and seductive. Never again was international diplomacy to seem so glamorous and so romantic. Between 1908 and 1912 he published five novels as 'Anthony Partridge' which subsequently appeared under his own name. There is a biography by Ronald Standish (1957) and an autobiography (1941).

ORCZY, Baroness: Emma Magdalena Rosalia Marie Josepha Barbara ORCZY (1865–1947) married (1894) Henry George Montague Maclean BARSTOW (d. 1943). Born in Tarna-Ors, Hungary, to a landowner who became a musician after the peasants on his estate rose up and burned the farm buildings in protest at his innovations, she was educated at convents in Brussels and Paris. When she was 15 her parents came to London; she studied art at the West London School and at Heatherley's, where she met her future husband, who illustrated four volumes of her translations of Hungarian fairy tales, published in 1895. Her first novel was *The Emperor's Candlesticks* (1899); her first success the series of stories about an old man solving crimes in the corner of cheap restaurant, which first appeared in the *Royal Magazine* in 1901 and which were collected in *The Case of Miss Elliott* (1905), *The Old Man in the Corner* (1909), and *Unravelled Knots* (1925). These pioneered the idea of the armchair detective. *By the Gods Beloved* (1905) is a sadistic *Haggardesque fantasy about the discovery of a lost race in the Egyptian desert. The detective stories of **Lady Molly of Scotland Yard* (1910) are also of some interest to historians of the genre but have not worn well. Baroness Orczy's great claim to fame, of course, is the series inaugurated with *The *Scarlet Pimpernel* (1905), which romanticizes the aristocratic victims of the French Revolution. This began life as a novel written in 1902, but was rejected by twelve publishers and not published until after the successful production of a dramatized version written with her husband. The play, the novel, and later the film proved to have immense and enduring success, and her subsequent fiction (with a few exceptions such as the detective stories of *Skin o' My Tooth*, 1928) was *historical romance in the same vein, including no fewer than nine sequels to *The Scarlet Pimpernel*. See, for example, *The *Tangled Skein* (1907), **Beau Brocade: A Romance* (1908), and **Petticoat Government* (1910). Orczy inherited her father's Hungarian estate, but went to live in Monte Carlo after the First World War. Marooned there during the Second World War, she later returned to England, dying in London. Her only child, John Barstow (b. 1899), published fiction as 'John Blakeney'.

OUIDA, *pseud.*: Marie Louise RAMÉ (1839–1908) who took the surname DE LA RAMÉE. Born in Bury St Edmunds to an English mother and a French father, a schoolteacher, who was often absent during her childhood, she moved to London with her mother in 1857 and began to publish stories in *Bentley's Miscellany*. The success of her novels permitted her to pretend that she was an aristocratic beauty as many of her heroines were, and to live in luxury and ostentation surrounded by sycophants. *Under Two Flags* (1867), her bestseller about an English gentleman who is forced by seeming dishonour to join the French Foreign Legion, was to provide a model for many later romances, including A. E. W. *Mason's *The *Four Feathers* and P. C. *Wren's *Beau Geste* (1924). But 'Ouida' 's popularity began to fall off towards the end of the century and her novels began to express a rather more jaundiced view of high society, dwelling especially on the corrupting influence of nouveaux riches and the increasing materialism and extravagance of high society: this is the theme of *Moths* (1880) and *The Massareenes* (1897). Her last works include *The Waters of Edera* (1900), in which Italian peasants unite in a futile but noble struggle against the government; *Street Dust and Other Stories* (1901), which again emphasizes painfully the hunger and destitution of the Italian poor; and the unfinished, posthumously published novel *Helianthus* (1908), set in an imaginary European country: a young prince who is the focus of hope of reform falls in love with a girl from a revolutionary nationalist family. The dangers of Prussian militarism are heavily emphasized. Indeed, the novel is less a narrative than a diatribe against the degeneracy of the modern world. 'Ouida' lived in Italy from 1871. Always unwise, in old age she became eccentric and fanatical, for example on the subjects of anti-vivisection and anti-female suffrage; towards the end of her life, poverty-stricken and animal-mad, she was preserved from starvation by a Civil List pension. There is a biography by Monica Stirling (1957).

Our Friend the Charlatan, George *Gissing, 1901, Chapman & Hall. The charlatan is Dyce Lashmar, son of a morbidly critical country clergyman and his vulgar wife. His egotism (several reviewers compared him to Sir Willoughby Patterne, the hero of George *Meredith's *The Egoist*) encourages him to leave the straight and narrow path as rapidly as possible. He is not malicious; he just lets things go. 'His ideal was honesty, even as he had a strong prejudice in favour of personal cleanliness. But occasionally he shirked the cold tub; and, in the same way, he found it difficult at times to tell the truth.' Lashmar makes his way in life by borrowing ideas: most notably the 'bio-sociological' theory developed by Jean Izoulet in *La Cité moderne*.

From borrowing ideas, it is a short step to borrowing money and influence, mostly from women: the tyrannical philanthropist Lady Ogram; her secretary, Constance Bride, who pledges herself to Lashmar in obedience to Lady Ogram; her great-niece, the emancipated May Tomalin. Lashmar ends up, a bitterly disappointed man, in a marriage which is clearly somewhat beneath his original expectations. But there is no connotation of tragedy. For this is Gissing's most consistently humorous (and Meredithian) novel.

Outlook for Men and Women, The, (1889–1928). This weekly newspaper began as the *New Review,* edited by the owner Archibald Grove (d. 1920) and until 1898 by W. E. Henley (1849–1903). It changed its name to the *Outlook* in February 1898. It consisted of signed articles on politics, literature, and general subjects. L. Allen *Harker began her career by publishing stories in it. Albert *Kinross was assistant editor 1898–1900 and his *The Torch: A Novel of the Nineties* (1923), which is about a literary weekly, is probably based on his experiences then. Filson *Young became its editor in 1904. Edwin Oliver (d. 1950) was assistant editor 1900–06 and editor 1910–17; he was supported by the owner, the Conservative politician Walter Guinness (1880–1944), in the row over the paper's exposure of the Marconi scandal of 1912.

OXENHAM, Elsie J., *pseud.*: Elsie Jeannette DUNKERLEY (*c.*1879–1960). Born in Southport, Lancashire, she was the daughter of 'John *Oxenham'. Her earliest books include *Goblin Island* (1907), *The Conquest of Christina* (1909), *The Girl Who Wouldn't Make Friends* (1909), *A Holiday Queen* (1910), and *Mistress Nanciebel* (1910), but much her best-known books are fifty or so books in the Abbey series, which began with *Girls of the Hamlet Club* (1914) and only ended in 1959, which show Dunkerley's deep interest in the work of the English Folk Dance and Song Society, and include a portrait of its leader, Cecil J. Sharp (1859–1924), brother of Evelyn *Sharp. She was also, like Dorothea *Moore, interested in the Girl Guide Movement; and she was a Guardian in the Camp Fire Association, founded in America to help women and girls appreciate the poetry of home life.

OXENHAM, John, *pseud.*: William Arthur DUNKERLEY (1852–1941) married (1877) Margery ANDERSON (d. 1925). Born in Manchester, son of a wholesale grocer, he was educated at Old Trafford School and Victoria University, Manchester. His parents were pious Congregationalists; his father was a deacon. He joined his father's business, and went to Brittany to organize the importation of fresh food into England. After his marriage there was an interval in the US, then a period in Southport until 1881, when, grocery proving unremunerative, Dunkerley, with Robert *Barr, moved to Bedford Park, London, and began to run the English end of the *Detroit Free Press*. Next, with Barr and Jerome K. *Jerome, he started the **Idler*; later still he was manager of To-day. His first fiction was a serial for the *Detroit Free Press*, published as 'Julian Ross'; he then adopted the name 'John Oxenham' (from *Westward Ho!*, 1855, by Charles Kingsley, 1819–1875) and took very elaborate measures to conceal his real identity even from his fellow-editors. When he was earning enough as a writer to be able to lose his regular salary and still support a wife and six children, he left Fleet Street. The first novel he published in volume form was *God's Prisoner* (1898); later works include *Barbe of Grand Bayou* (1903) and *Bondman Free* (1903), in which a convict unfairly dogged by his past finds refuge and understanding in the household of the judge who once condemned him. Dunkerley was fascinated by islands, and did a good deal for the tourist trade in Sark by publishing novels set there, including *A Maid of the Silver Sea* (1910). In 1913 he published a volume of verse, *Bees in Amber*, which proved a bestseller; he wrote more verse and also prose non-fiction about the First World War. Another landmark in his career was the publication in 1925 of his *The Hidden Years*, a life of Jesus Christ (compare M. P. *Shiel, Hall *Caine, 'Deas *Cromarty', Forrest *Reid), which was followed by other books on the same topic. There is a memoir by his daughter Erica (1942) and a biography by Olive Parr (1943). 'Elsie J. *Oxenham' was his daughter.

PAGE, Gertrude (1873–1922) married George Alexander DOBBIN. Brought up in Bedfordshire, Page emigrated in about 1900 to Salisbury, Rhodesia, with her husband. There, according to the *Times* (3 Apr. 1922) 'she saw much of the service asked by life of overstrained women in a new country'. The title and subtitle of her first novel, *Love in the Wilderness: The Story of Another African Farm* (1907), stake a firm claim to the fictional territory she was to explore for most of her career. The romance (an English girl goes out to an English family in Rhodesia and stirs passion in two men, with tragic consequences) is feeble: but it does provide the opportunity for a detailed description of Rhodesian life and landscape which challenges comparison with the original *Story of an African Farm* (1883) by Olive Schreiner (1855–1920). In *The Silent Rancher* (1909) another English girl, Evelyn Harcourt, goes out to Rhodesia to marry the elderly and offensive General Sir Henry Mahon, falls in love with the supposedly woman-hating Silent Rancher, Metcalf, and is able to disentangle herself from the one and marry the other with the help of an ebullient divorcée, Mrs Leven. One review of the novel characterizes Page as a 'public-spirited Dolf *Wyllarde', 'for she deals with the same outposts of civilization as that daring lady, but instead of employing them chiefly as picturesque backgrounds for lawless passion and bitter regrets, she displays to her puppets (who are by no means sexless) high ideals of colonization'. Page repeated the formula most successfully in *'Where Strange Roads Go Down'* (1913), in which another young bride-elect sets off for Rhodesia, and this time falls in with a mature, well-bred man of the world, variously described as a 'Rhodesian Sir Galahad' and a 'Rhodesian Don Juan' on the boat out. She is eventually rescued by the older and wiser Mrs Lathom, known as 'Joe', who describes the strains imposed on women by life in the outposts: 'Not one in fifty realises the truth until she gets here. Probably they struggle and whine for a bit, then they go with the tide. Those who have plenty or spirit or religion or something of that sort come up smiling. Those who haven't become mere torpid drudges; or they find a solution in having a lover and I'm sure I don't blame them.' Page also produced a number of blander novels, some set in Rhodesia, like *Jill's Rhodesian Philosophy, or, The Dam Farm* (1910) and *The Rhodesian* (1912), and some in England, like *The Great Splendour* (1912) and *The Pathway* (1914). *Paddy-the-Next-Best-Thing* (1908) is a 'wild Irish girl' novel (Page's husband was from Armagh), in the vein of Mrs George de Horne *Vaizey's *Pixie O'Shaughnessy* (1903): the heroine's father describes her as the next best thing to a boy, and she herself becomes the next best thing to a national hero, namely, the mother of one. During the First World War the Dobbins came to England and lectured on Rhodesia; she is known to have supported women's suffrage and opposed forced recruitment of African workers.

PAIN, Barry [Eric Odell] (1864–1928) married (1892) Amelia Nina Anna LEHMANN (d. 1920). Born in Cambridge, where his father owned a drapery, he was educated at Sedbergh School (where he edited the school magazine) and at Corpus Christi College, Cambridge, where he read classics and edited *Granta*. After four years service as an army coach at Guildford, he travelled to London (1890) to take up journalism as a career, and worked for the *Daily Chronicle* and *Black and White*. *In a Canadian Canoe* (1891) was a collection of articles he had written during his student days for the *Granta*. Pain was then asked to submit articles to the **Cornhill Magazine* by its editor, James Payn (1830–1898). Other humorous publications followed: *Stories and Interludes* (1892), *Playthings and Parodies* (1893), and *The Octave of Claudius* (1897). In 1897 he took over from Jerome K. *Jerome as editor of *To-day*. *Eliza* (1900) was the first of a series of books in the tradition of *The Diary of a Nobody* (1892, by George, 1847–1912, and Weedon Grossmith, 1854–1919), supposedly written by an office worker, which cast a satirical eye on *suburban life in general and on his eminently practical wife in particular. It was followed by *Eliza's Husband* (1903); *Eliza Getting On* (1911), in which her husband has also 'got on' to the extent of 'on many occasions practically representing the firm', and they have a greenhouse of their own, and a baby; *Exit Eliza* (1912), in which Mr Bagshawe takes her husband into partnership and the firm begins to demand all his attention; and *Eliza's Son* (1913), which is the autobiography of their son Ernest, a monstrously mean little prig. Pain continued to produce works in the same vein: *Mrs Murphy* (1913) is the discourses of a charwoman who describes herself as 'a hard-working woman, and Church of England if asked'; *Edwards: The Confessions of a Jobbing Gardener* (1915) employs the same formula. *An Exchange of Souls* (1911), on the other hand, is about a scientist who succeeds in exchanging souls with his fiancée. *Robinson Crusoe's Return* (1907) has Crusoe in Edwardian Britain. Pain had a wide range of interests: gemmology, theology, the occult, the literature of the day, and sketching. He wrote some reasonably successful mystery stories such as *The Memoirs of Constantine Dix* (1905), about a philanthropic lay preacher who is also a professional thief, and occult tales such as *The Shadow of the Unseen* (1907). Both the latter and *The Luck of Norman Dale* (1908) were written with James *Blyth. It is possible that Blyth contributed the tragic note to these stories (*The Shadow* is set on the gloomy Norfolk marshlands, and concerns the bitter feud between the family of the heroine, Linda Merle, and the frightening Judith Jennis, who owns a gigantic goat called Bel), and Pain the comic note. Pain's penchant for parody is evident in several works, notably *Another Englishwoman's Love-Letters* (1901), (see *An *Englishwoman's Love-Letters*), *Marge Askinfort* (1920), a joke at the expense of Margot Asquith (1864–1945), and *If Summer Don't* (1922), which poked fun at A. S. M. *Hutchinson's bestseller *If Winter Comes* (1921). Other publications include collections of short stories such as *Nothing Serious* (1901), *Deals* (1904), and *The New Gulliver and Other Stories* (1912). *First Lessons in Story Writing* (1907) is a booklet written for the London Correspondence College, and *The Short Story* (1916) was published in the 'Art and Craft of Letters' series. In 1914 Pain co-wrote *The White Elephant*, a musical hall sketch, with Charles Eddy. There were a number of collections of his humorous writing. In the opening years of the Edwardian era Pain was the leading humorous writer in Britain: his obituary in the *Times* (7 May 1928) mentioned 'a quality of wistfulness, almost sadness, which distinguished his work from that which aimed merely at the farcical'. His wife, who also published fiction, was the daughter of the painter Rudolf Lehmann (1819–1905); Violet *Tweedale and Ménie Muriel *Dowie were her cousins.

Pall Mall Magazine (1893–1914). This monthly magazine was launched by the American millionaire William Waldorf Astor (1848–1919; author of fiction including *Pharoah's Daughter and Other Stories*, 1900), allegedly because his contributions to the *Pall Mall Gazette* (which he also owned) had been turned down by its editor. It was edited by Conservative politicians Sir Douglas Straight (1844–1914) and Lord Frederick Hamilton (1856–1928). It attracted short story writers such as *Wells, R. L. Stevenson (1850–94), *Kipling, Thomas Hardy (1840–1928), and E. *Nesbit, poets such as A. C. Swinburne (1837–1909), Kipling, and Paul Verlaine (1844–96), illustrators such as Aubrey Beardsley (1872–98) and Lawrence Alma-Tadema (1836–1912), and novelists such as *Meredith and *Besant simply by its exceptionally high rates of pay (reflecting Astor's wealth rather than magazine sales). By the end of the decade, though, the magazine was more dependent on popular writers such as H. Rider *Haggard and more philistine in its concerns (sport). George R. Halkett (1855–1918), who edited the magazine 1901–5, restored its literary standards, serializing *Conrad's **Typhoon* and attracting Jack London (1876–1916) as a regular contributor, but did not boost its sales. Thereafter, under a series of anonymous editors, the magazine continued to attract reputable contributors (in 1913 publishing *Chesterton's 'Wisdom of Father Brown', for example, and a new poet, Rupert Brooke, 1887–1915, alongside work by Kipling and Compton *Mackenzie) but without any sense of literary direction. In 1912 C. A. *Dawson-Scott asked what kind of stories were most acceptable and was told: 'The stories should preferably have a strong love interest, and the scenes should be laid in the British Isles, or, if abroad, the characters should be English. You should keep clear of all reference to religion, the more serious sort of sex questions, drunkenness and politics. The stories should of course all have a happy ending and be entirely wholesome throughout. Very little space should be wasted on local colour.' In 1914 Astor sold the magazine to the *publisher Eveleigh Nash, who merged it with *Nash's Magazine* after the outbreak of war.

PANTON, Mrs J. E.: Jane Ellen FRITH (1848–1923) married (1869) James PANTON. Daughter of the painter W. P. Frith (1819–1909) and sister of Walter *Frith, she was born in London and worked from 1882 as a journalist on domestic subjects, and author of advice books such as *Homes of Taste: Economical Hints* (1890), *Within Four Walls: A Handbook for Invalids* (1893), and *Suburban Residences and How To Circumvent Them* (1896). She also wrote novels, of which *Leaves from a Life* (1908) ran to five editions in its first year. Other works include *A Cannibal Crusader: An Allegory for the Times* (1908), in which the pretences of respectable society are exposed by the arrival in its midst of a man born and raised on a remote island, *Leaves from a Garden* (1910), *In Garret and Kitchen: Hints for the Lean Year* (1920), and three volumes of autobiography. Mrs Panton died at home in Taviton Street, London.

PARKER, Eric [Frederick Moore Searle] (1870–1955) married (1902) Ruth Margaret MESSEL (d. 1933). Born in Barnet, north London, the son of a solicitor, he went to Eton College as a King's Scholar and read classics at Merton College, Oxford. After a stint of teaching Parker decided to pursue a career in journalism. He contributed to the *Spectator* and the *St James's Gazette* (which he edited 1900–2). His great passion for the sporting, outdoor life gradually led him to concentrate on that theme; he edited the *Country Gentleman* and *Land and Water* between 1902 and 1907 and contributed to the *Gamekeeper* (which he edited 1908–10) and the *Field*. He was shooting editor (1911–37) and then editor-in-chief (1930–1937) of the *Field*. Parker also illustrated A. R. Collett's *British Inland Birds* (1906) and published a long string of books on shooting, fishing, cricket, and dogs, and a memoir (1924) of his friend Hesketh *Prichard. He was also an editor of 'The Lonsdale Library' and produced an *Anthology to the Bible* in 1939. His first novel, *The *Sinner and the Problem* (1901), was hugely successful and ran to two reprints within three months of its publication. Its theme—the vicissitudes of childhood experience—is again explored in *The Promise of Arden* (1911). He served in the First World War in the Queen's Royal West Surrey Regiment. There is an autobiography, *Memory Looks Forward* (1937).

PARKER, [Horatio] Gilbert [George] (1862–1932) created (1915) 1st Baronet, married (1895) Amy Eliza VAN TINE (d. 1925). Born at Camden East, Ontario, Canada, the son of an emigrant from Ireland, he was educated in the Normal School, Ottawa, and Trinity College, Toronto. He became a schoolteacher at 17, then for a short time trained as a clergyman. He travelled to Australia and Europe in the 1880s and began to write fiction about the Canadian wilderness, although his personal experience of the plains was rather limited. His *historical fiction about the opening up of the American continent by European explorers, such as *The Trail of the Sword* (1894) and *When Valmond came to Pontiac* (1895), found an eager market. *The Battle of the Strong* (1898) is set in Jersey during the French Revolution. Parker was elected Conservative Imperialist MP for Gravesend in 1900 and held the seat until 1918. In *Donovan Pasha* (1902), a collection of short stories, Parker turned his attention from Canada and Australia to a more contentious frontier: Egypt. Donovan Pasha and Fielding Bey bear the white man's administrative burden. The stories are, virtually without exception, second-hand *Kipling. 'A weird picture of change moving across the face of the unchangeable,' the *Daily Chronicle* commented. *A Ladder of Swords: A Tale of Love, Laughter and Tears* (1907) is an Elizabethan swashbuckler set during the period of the Earl of Leicester's disgrace and banishment to Kenilworth: the love and tears are produced by the heroine, a Huguenot maiden who comes to court to plead for her lover's life, which Catherine de Medici has demanded of Elizabeth; the laughter by a pirate called Buonespoir and a genial giant called Raoul Lemprière. *The Weavers: A Tale of England and Egypt of Fifty Years Ago* (1907) alludes in fairly obvious fashion to the story of General Gordon of Khartoum (1833–1885). David Claridge, of Quaker birth and belief, rises to a position of supreme importance under Prince Kaid, leads an expedition into the Sudan, and is surrounded: he turns out to be the elder brother of Lord Eglington, who in Parliament opposes plans to relieve him. *The Judgment House* (1913) is a contemporary story about finance and soldiering. Rudyard Byng, a millionaire, marries a woman who yearns, before and after the wedding, for other men. 'It's little time for dreaming we get in these sodden days,' Byng laments, 'but it's only dreams that do the world's work and our own work in the end.' Here, the world's work includes plans for a Cape-to-Cairo railroad and the *Boer War, while one's own work appears to amount to getting a grip on one's wayward wife. *Northern Lights* (1909) is a volume of stories, *The Going of the White Swan* (1912) a romance. The Imperial Edition of his works was published in twenty-three volumes (1912–23).

PARKES, W. Kineton (1865–1938) married (1889) ——. Born in Warwickshire and educated at King Edward VI's Grammar School, Birmingham and Mason College, Birmingham, he was interested in arts and crafts, editing several journals on that subject and contributing to the *Architectural Review.* His fiction is mostly potboiling, with an undertone of earnestness. *Life's Desert Way* (1907) is about a child of nature, literature, and religion who comes to London and falls in socially and sexually with bohemian circles. *Love à la Mode* (1907) is a collection of stories involving a lot of vapid talk on the subject, *Potiphar's Wife* (1908) a tale of Derbyshire farmers a generation or two before, and *The Altar of Moloch* (1911) an account of the musical temperament. *The Money Hunt: A Comedy of Country Houses* (1914) concerns the stir caused among unintellectual country squires by the arrival in their midst of a beautiful young heiress to a manufacturing fortune. Parkes's major achievement is **Hardware: A Novel in Four Books* (1914), a record of the social, political, commercial, and municipal development of the Midland town of Metlingham. If the novel's subject recalls Arnold *Bennett, its form, which imitates the fragmentation of urban experience by subdividing its four books into forty chapters and its forty chapters into nearly 300 sections, might be said to anticipate aspects of James *Joyce's *Ulysses* (1922). Parkes also published various works on art and art history and literature, and a last novel, *Windylow* (1915).

PARTRIDGE, Anthony, *pseud.*: see E. Phillips *Oppenheim.

Passionate Friends, The: *A Novel*, H. G. *Wells, 1913, Macmillan. Another of Wells's 'prig novels' and his only 'tragedy', *Passionate Friends* portrays a punctilious and dull English gentleman through his memoirs. Stephen Stratton, a rector's son, is devotedly in love with Lady Mary, who chooses to marry a middle-aged plutocrat, with the proviso that she should retain her independence. Stratton wins distinction in the *Boer War and returns to England to become Lady Mary's lover. When their affair is discovered his hopes for a political career are ruined. He goes abroad to study labour problems and wanders in the Far East and the USA. Meanwhile Lady Mary's frustrations drive her to suicide. A small story placed in a wide range of settings and given world history as its backdrop.

PATERNOSTER, G[eorge] Sidney (d. 1925) married Beatrice Marie ——. He was a member of the staff of the *Times* and the author of a book about the Putomayo atrocities (1913). His eight volumes of fiction are lightweight, even when, as in *Gutter Tragedies* (1903), he handles the seamy side of criminal life. *The Motor Pirate* (1903) is about a modern Dick Turpin, and also ends tragically. *The Lady of the Blue Motor* (1907) takes to the road again, this time for a cosmopolitan romantic adventure. *The Great Gift* (1909) is about an honest businessman who works his way up to become a cabinet minister.

PATERSON, Arthur [Henry] (1862–1928) married (1894) Mary M'CALLUM. A doctor's son, he was born at Bowdon, Cheshire, and educated at University College School, London. He then travelled the world, sampling life in the Wild West ofAmerica; sheep-farming in New Mexico (1877–9) and farming in Kansas (1879–80). These experiences were later drawn upon in his fiction. He returned to Britain in the early 1880s and worked his way up to deputy manager of a merchant's office in Birkenhead (1881–4). Paterson was a great friend and admirer of Sir Walter *Besant and shared his political concerns; he became keenly interested in many aspects of social welfare and was District Secretary for the Charity Organization Society (1885–1896), Secretary for the Social Welfare Association for London (from 1910), and Secretary of the National Alliance of Employers and Employed in 1917. Paterson wrote a series of articles concerning the administration of charity for the *Times* which were collected and published during 1908. His novel *John Glynn* (1907) explores social welfare issues and is in quite a different vein to his usual (Western) adventure stories. Examples of this genre are *The Better Man* (1890), *A Partner from the West* (1892), *A Man of his Word* (1895), and

A Son of the Plains (1895). Other novels include *The Gospel Writ in Steel* (1898) and *The King's Agent* (1902), a *historical romance featuring the 1st Duke of Marlborough. Paterson's works were popular and described in his *Times* obituary (18 Jan. 1928) as 'carefully and conscientiously written' and worthy of 'their measure of success'. Paterson also wrote a play, *Colonel Cromwell: An Historical Drama* (1900), based on his (1899) biography of Cromwell. His non-fiction includes *The Homes of Tennyson* (1905), written with his artist sister Helen Allingham (1848–1926), *Administration of Charity* (1908), *The Metropolitan Police* (1909), and *George Eliot's Family Life and Letters* (1928). Paterson was made a Grand Scribe of the Order of Crusaders in 1923. He died at home in Hampstead, north London. The poet William Allingham (1824–89) was his brother-in-law.

PATERSON, W. R.: see 'Benjamin *Swift'.

Pathway of the Pioneer, The: *Nous Autres*, 'Dolf *Wyllarde,' 1906, Methuen. The focus of the story is an informal society, 'Nous Autres', whose members represent 'the professions open to women of no deliberate training, some education, and too much delicacy for the fight before them'. There had in fact been a 'Pioneer Club' for emancipated women in the 1890s; its emblem was a silver axe, for hewing a path through the thickets of prejudice. Nous Autres include a freelance journalist, an actress, a typist and shorthand clerk, a Post Office clerk, a music teacher, and a musician who plays in the Ladies' Catgut Band. These women have been worn down, numbed, and defeminized by anxiety. Like Francis *Gribble in *The *Pillar of Cloud*, Wyllarde switches impartially between the different members of the group. But she seems to have greater faith than he did in the resilience of workaday women, and in their willingness to rely on themselves and on each other. Her collective biography imagines such women as captives in a wilderness of debilitating routine, as pioneers who have sacrificed themselves for a cause whose eventual triumph they will not live to see.

PATTERSON, John Edward (1866–1919) married (1902) Ida Harrylynn PITTENDREIGH. Brought up in the north of England, son of a colliery official, he lost his mother when he was 4, was unhappily shunted between various relations, and ran away to sea. After travelling widely, he was crippled by rheumatism, got work as a lawyer's clerk in Cardiff, and began to publish verse and prose. His first novel was *The Bridge of Llangasty* (1900). His fiction tends to the Hardy-esque, with the sea playing the part of Egdon Heath in *Watchers by the Shore* (1909) and *Love like the Sea* (1911). In *Tillers of the Soil* (1911) Abe Shuttleworth, a shrewd but impulsive Yorkshire farmer, decides to clear himself of a past darkened by his wife's suicide and his wife's companion's infanticide and suicide, by moving to Hall Farm, near Chelmsford, where he does battle with the soil, the Great Eastern Railway, and local apathy. There is slander, sharp practice, incendiarism, and murder before he admits defeat and emigrates to Canada. But the tone of the novel is closer to Henry Fielding than to Hardy. Before the success of *Fishers of the Sea* (1908) put a stop to the rejection of his manuscripts, he planned a series of seven novels, each exhibiting 'a certain phase of our industrial and commercial life'. A book conceived as 'Workers at the Forge' was eventually telescoped into a proposed sequel, 'Makers of the Law', and appeared as *The Story of Stephen Compton* (1913). The hero rises (on one leg only, as it happens) from the Lancashire cotton-mills to become Leader of the Labour party, and the first 'Lib.-Lab.' prime minister: abandoning along the way his true love from the cotton-mills and a cool adventuress who marries him in order to divert him into Conservatism. There is a sub-plot promoting divorce law reform. He published several volumes of autobiography such as *My Vagabondage: Being the Intimate Autobiography of a Nature's Nomad* (1911), *Sea-Pie* (1915), and *Epistles from Deep Seas* (1915), which detail his struggle with great hardships.

Patrician, The, John *Galsworthy, 1911, William Heinemann. Lord Miltoun, eldest son and heir of the patrician Caradoc family, and Conservative idealist, has grand political ambitions but falls in love with Audrey Noel, the estranged wife of a clergyman who lives on the estate. Meanwhile Barbara, Miltoun's younger sister, is interested in Charles Coutier, a friend of Mrs Noel, who stands as Liberal in the local election. Miltoun wins and enters Parliament, but, torn between love and politics, falls dangerously ill. Barbara fetches Audrey Noel to nurse him, but he remains torn between aristocratic obligations, political principles, and love and eventually she leaves England. Meanwhile, similarly torn between his pride, reforming zeal, and love for Barbara, Coutier departs for Persia. The invaders have been seen off; the Caradoc patrician tradition can continue.

PEACOCK, Major Ferdinand: Ferdinand Mansel PEACOCK (1861–1908) married (1899) Emma LANYON. The son of a Church of England clergyman, Peacock was born in Wiltshire, and educated at Marlborough School and the Royal Military College, Sandhurst. He joined the 1st Battalion of the Somerset Light Infantry (1882) and was decorated for gallantry during the Burma Campaign (1885–1887). He was again decorated after serving in South Africa 1899–1902. He retired in 1904. Peacock's novels all owe something to his eventful military life. They include *A Change of Weapons* (1895), *A Soldier and a Maid* (1890), *Sword Flashes* (1895), *A Curl'd Darling* (1896), *Our Master Tony* (1908), and *When the War is O'er* (1912), which features a lovable major who serves in India and South Africa, and eventually retires to a village in Wiltshire.

PEARCE, Charles E. (d. 1924). A journalist who was editor of the *South London Press* (1878–82), he began his fictional career in 1896, contributing serials to the weekly *Answers* (Mrs Robert *Leighton was another contributor). He claimed in *Who's Who* to have published upwards of seventy by 1910. He specialized in Indian romances such as *Love Besieged: A Romance of the Residency in Lucknow* (1909) and *Red Revenge: A Romance of Cawnpore* (1911). *The Bungalow under the Lake* (1910) is the home of Jeffrey Holt, who plans to free himself from his objectionable wife by pretended death at the hands of Dr Bernard Vivien: but the unscrupulous doctor wants the wife and her fortune for himself. Pearce also had a line in popular biographies, such as *The Amazing Duchess: Being the Romantic History of Elizabeth Chudleigh* (1911), *The Beloved Princess: Princess Charlotte of Wales* (1911), *'Polly Peachum': Being the Story of Lavinia Fenton (Duchess of Bolton)* (1913), *The Jolly Duchess: Harriot Mellon* (1915), *Madame Vestris and Her Times* (1923), *Ned Kelly the Bushranger* (1921), and *Sims Reeves* (1924).

PEARD, Frances Mary (1835–1923). Born in Exminster, Devon, she was the daughter of a naval officer. Peard wrote children's books for both boys and girls and fiction for adults, all drawing on her travels abroad, especially in India. Her fiction for adults includes *The Rose Garden* (1872), *Donna Teresa* (1899), and *Number One and Number Two* (1900). *The Ring from Jaipur* (1904) is rather more sober than its title, which suggests jewels and Far Eastern temples: an empty-headed Anglo-Indian wife tires of India and goes home to England, but eventually returns to her post and is reconciled with her husband. The theme—the harshness of conditions in India for women of a less than steely temperament—is comparable to that of Maud *Diver's *The *Great Amulet* (1908), but the treatment less sensational. In *The Flying Months* (1909) the heroine, Cordelia, travels in Italy and India as companion to the volatile Nesta Hastings, and is courted by an old friend, John Elliott, who has come to India to solve the mystery of his parentage. Peard died, an invalid and almost blind, at home in Torquay.

PEARSE, Revd Mark Guy: Mark Guy PEARSE (1842–1930) married (1866) Mary Jane COOPER (d. 1914). He was born at Camborne, Cornwall; his father, also named Mark Guy Pearse, was a Wesleyan Methodist in the tin-mining business, who moved to London and then the Isle of Wight after his son was an adult, and was the author of a number of religious works. The younger was educated at the Revd Mr Butlin's, Camborne, a Moravian school at Zeist in the Netherlands, and the Wesleyan College, Sheffield. His father then articled him to a doctor in Liskeard, and he became a medical student at St Bartholomew's Hospital, London, before deciding instead to become a minister, after which he went to Didsbury College, Manchester, and was ordained in 1863. After working in various parts of the country and suffering a nervous breakdown followed by a period of recuperation in Cornwall, he worked from 1887 at the West London Wesleyan Mission with the Revd Hugh Price Hughes (1847–1902). A Christian Socialist, he had an important influence at this time on the suffragist Emmeline Pethick-Lawrence (1867–1954), who also worked with Hughes. Pearse retired from the Mission in 1903 but continued, health permitting, to lecture up and down the country. Aside from his work for the Church, Pearse produced wholesome fiction for younger readers and wrote some very popular works, many set in Cornwall, including *Rob Rat: A Story of Barge Life* (1888), *Gold and Incense: A West Country Story* (1895), *The Story of a Roman Soldier* (1899), and *A Bit of Shamrock* (1902). *Wounds of the World* (1912) and *A Village Down West* (1924) are collections of short stories. The characteristic note is struck in the preface to a volume of verse, *West Country Songs* (1902), in which Pearse wrote of his regret at the decline of Cornish dialect: 'I have sought to recall the Cornwall that I knew, and that I love with a love that grows with the years. I have tried to recall something of its humour, for the Western Celt carries ever a great laugh in his heart; something of its pathos, for its humour lies hard by the fountain of tears; its quaintness, something too of its religion; and by no means least, its love, for that is the music of their life.' Pearse died at home in north London.

Pearson's Magazine (1896–1939) was published monthly. Launched by Cyril Arthur Pearson (1866–1921), who had already created a newspaper, *Pearson's Weekly*, and was to launch an American *Pearson's Magazine* in 1899, it was aimed at the new reading public, using all the new marketing devices of advertising, cover design, newsagent incentives, reader competitions, etc., while playing on readers' interest in self-improvement and the lives of the already successful, the rich, and the royal. Short stories and serials were included among the articles on 'How to Become Rich' and the illustrations explaining science. The emphasis was on male and female romance. Baroness *Orczy and Ethel M. *Dell were introduced to their public in *Pearson's*, and established writers such as *Kipling, Max *Pemberton, and Rafael *Sabatini were also featured.

PEASE, Howard (b. 1863) married (1887) Margaret KYNASTON. He came from a family of industrialists with interests in the railway business, was educated at Balliol College, Oxford, and was a landowner and magistrate in Northumberland, a Fellow of the Society of Antiquaries, and editor of the *Northern Counties Magazine*. His fiction includes *Tales of Northumbria* (1899), *The Burning Cresset: A Story of the Last Rising of the North* (1908), and *With the Warden of the Marches, or, The Vow by the 'Nine Stane Rig': A Romance of Liddesdale and the Middle March* (1909). *Magnus Sinclair* (1904) is a carefully researched story about Cromwell and the Great Rebellion, with footnotes. *Of Mistress Eve* (1906) is a sequel, set in the period of the Protectorate and the Restoration, which shifts the scene northwards to the strongholds of a powerful Borders lady. As well as some earlier and later fiction he published a history (1913) of the Lord Wardens of the Marches of England and Scotland and one (1924) of the Northumberland Hussars Yeomanry. He is not to be confused with Howard Pease (b. 1894), author of nautical thrillers, who was American.

PEER, A., *pseud.*: He specialized in lurid and frantic tales set on the bohemian fringes of high society which sail as close to the wind as they possibly can. The title of *The Hazard of the Die* (1909) is indicative, as is that of *To Justify the Means* (1910), about a young peer trapped into marriage by an absinthe-drinking adventuress. Indeed, the standard formula, as seen in *Theo* (1911) or *The Ordeal of Silence* (1912), involves the introduction of an innocent young man or woman, usually from Ireland, into the London fast set. It is sometimes given a comic twist: in *A Wife Imperative* (1911), for example, a *Ruritanian tale of Geoffroy Vallance's forced marriage and life as the reigning Duke of Waldenstein, or in *The Decoy Duck* (1913), in which the convent-bred daughter of an Irish squire who lives by gambling is wooed and won by the heir of a great English county family. *The Oyster* (1914), about a woman of fashion in need of money who sells her baby to another in need of a child, is more brutal. Later novels are *Three Persons* (1915), *In the Year of Waiting* (1916), and *Philippa's Pride* (1916), in which a man bets he can marry an heiress and does; she finds out and they are estranged before being reconciled on the last page; the background is the Irish land agitation. All were published by John Long.

PEMBERTON, Max (1863–1950), Kt. (1928). Pemberton, the son of a Black Country foundry owner, was born in Edgbaston, Birmingham, and educated at Merchant Taylors' School in Hertfordshire, before reading law at Caius College, Cambridge. He graduated in 1884 and, failing to get a teaching job, took up a career in journalism. Pemberton's first novel was *The Diary of a Scoundrel* (1891); he wrote the phenomenally successful *The Iron Pirate* (his first best-seller) while editor (1892–3) of *Chums*, a boys' paper published by Cassell. From 1896 to 1906 Pemberton edited *Cassell's Magazine*. He also had a long association with Northcliffe Newspapers—he was director of the group and wrote a memoir (1922) of Lord Northcliffe (1865–1922), a friend of his since youth. Together they founded the London School of Journalism in 1920. His fictional works are predominantly adventure fantasies which proved immensely popular. Of particular interest is *Two Women* (1914), one of the very few early (pre- *Buchan) *spy stories to feature a (supposed) British agent operating in Germany. Based on an actual case, it describes the imprisonment of Reggie Ainsworth in a German fortress on a charge of espionage. Ainsworth bribes his way out, but by that time Pemberton seems more interested in the developing romance between a lord and an adventuress: Reggie ends up with the other of the two women. Other works include *The Iron Pirate* (1893) and its sequel, *Black Iron* (1911), *Jewel Mysteries That I Have Known* (1894), *The Garden of Swords* (1899), *Feci* (1900), *Pro Patria* (1901), an *invasion scare story about the danger of the French digging a Channel Tunnel, and *The House Under the Sea* (1902). In *Dr. Xavier* (1903) actress Esther Venn fails to be taken on at the Casino Theatre, but then encounters the mysterious Doctor and ends up, by a *Ruritanian twist, as Princess of the State of Cadi. In *Mid the Thick Arrows* (1905), a millionaire marries an earl's daughter, only to find himself hampered by a youthful *mésalliance*. *The Show Girl* (1909) is an epistolary novel featuring a circus waif called Mimi who is rescued, educated, and courted by Gastonard, a Parisian art student who is due to inherit a fortune: she is not what she seems. Pemberton also wrote a string of light plays and a couple of revues. The epitome of the professional writer, he could happily and proficiently write to order. With George R. *Sims and A. Conan *Doyle, he was a member of a dining club, Our Society, which discussed fictional and real crime. He died at his home in South Kensington, London. His reminiscences, *Sixty Years Ago and After*, appeared in 1936.

PENDERED, Mary Lucy (1858–1940). Her twenty-odd volumes of fiction between 1893 and 1936 are mostly coy pastoral tales with self-revelatory titles, such as *Daisy the Minx: A Diversion* (1911) or *Phyllida Flouts Me* (1913). *Musk of Roses: From the Ego Book of Delia Wycombe* (1903) is the narrative in diary form of the life of a flirtatious farmer's wife. *At Lavender Cottage* (1912) describes the late-flowering passion of a rural spinster who has already been softened up by the arrival of a young nephew. *The Lily Magic* (1913) of 16-year-old Amaryllis wins over an entire villageful of moaners, louts, and skinflints. Pendered also published biographies and nature studies. She seems to have been a Quaker.

PENNY, F. E.: Fanny Emily FARR (1847–1939) married (1877) Frank PENNY (d. 1928). Born at Covehithe, Suffolk, daughter of a Church of England clergyman, she was brought up in Norfolk and educated at Queen's College, Harley Street. On marriage to another clergyman who had a chaplaincy in Madras she moved to India, where she lived until 1901, when her husband retired to Ealing. She was encouraged to write by Mrs B. M. *Croker, whom she met at the hill-station, Wellington, where Frank Penny was chaplain. She also wrote for the *Madras Mail*. India provided her with the background for forty-four volumes of fiction starting with *Fickle Fortune in Ceylon* (1887), published as by F. E. F. P. Her last novel appeared in the year of her death. *The Outcaste* (1912) concerns the miseries to which an Indian educated in England is subjected when he returns home and refuses to resume his caste or renounce his Christianity. Several of her other novels hinge on the tension for westernized and Christianized Indians, between 'civilized' values and sensual and sinister oriental forces. Penny was an enthusiast for Girl Guiding.

PENROSE, Mrs H. H.: Mary Elizabeth LEWIS (b. 1860) married H. H. PENROSE. Born at Kinsale, Ireland, to a Protestant family, she was educated at Rochelle School, Cork, and Trinity College, Dublin, where she took honours in German and English literature. She contributed fiction to magazines including **Temple Bar* and the *Windsor Magazine* and published seventeen volumes of fiction 1898–1915. The hero of *Denis Trench* (1911) discovers that his father is not dead but has become a Roman Catholic priest: *Burnt Flax* (1914) is about the Land League agitation. Her other novels aim a little too heavy-handedly at lightness of touch. *Charles the Great: A Very Light Comedy* (1912) is about a vain and feeble idiot who poses as a genius, gets someone else to write a brilliant novel for which he takes the credit, and is exposed. *The Brat: A Trifle* (1913) concerns three brattish children who torment their ageing governess, Miss Watts, and are finally checked, not by their mother, a naval officer's grass widow, but Miss Watts's saintly young niece—although not before they have severely provoked a fierce old admiral who is staying in their village, and who turns out to be the governess's long-lost love. *Something Impossible* (1914) is an identity exchange comedy: Dr Marks is convinced that his wife cannot possibly love a man as ugly as himself. His friend Laking gives him an Indian charm, an ivory cow, which allows the possessor one wish. On his way home one day, Marks notices the handsome Captain Darlington, inadvertently exclaims 'By Jove! I wish I were like that fellow!', and becomes him: much to the confusion of his wife, and of the Captain himself, who seeks professional advice from his double.

PERRIN, A.: Alice ROBINSON (1867–1934) married (1886) Charles PERRIN (d. 1931). She was the daughter of a general serving in India; her *Times* obituary (15 Feb. 1934) comments 'she came of old "John Company stock"'. She was educated in England and married an engineer in the Indian Public Works Department who later worked for the London Water Board and the Ministry of Health. Her experiences travelling with him provided the background for the series of novels and tales of Anglo-Indian life, beginning with *Into Temptation* (1894). *The Waters of Destruction* (1905) was originally printed in the *Times*. She was strong on the dangers of miscegenation. Other works include *East of Suez* (1901) and the seventeen short stories of *Red Records* (1906), which are mostly occult and tragic: the *Kiplingesque 'Moore' concerns the muffled cry heard at midnight by an army chaplain staying at a remote resthouse. **Idolatry* (1909) is a cut above average. Perrin and her husband returned to Britain at the turn of the century and retired to Switzerland in about 1925; she died at Vevey.

PETERSON, Margaret [Ann] (1883–1933) married (1915) A. O. FISHER. Daughter of a professor of Sanskrit at Elphinstone College, Bombay, she was brought up in India and educated at home. She came to London in 1910, but married a colonial civil servant. She published a volume of verse (1915) and forty-five volumes of fiction between 1913 and 1934. Peterson's first novel, *The Lure of the Little Drum* (1913), won a prize of 250 guineas put up by the publisher, Andrew Melrose ('Agnes E. *Jacomb' started her career by winning the same prize; several publishers ran such competitions in this period). The judges were Joseph *Conrad, Mary *Cholmondeley, and W. J. *Locke, and they chose a book whose subject-matter is more arresting than its technique: a cruel and sensuous Indian prince lures a young Englishwoman away from her husband and abandons her when his desire begins to fade. Peterson returned to the subject of interracial attraction in *Tony Bellew* (1914), whose hero, in appearance and manner a white man, discovers that he is the product of a liaison between an Indian woman and a highly placed Civil Servant. There is a vivid description of a nurse's life in a civilian hospital in India which gives one some idea of what the distinguished judges might have seen in Petersen's writing. She also published as 'Glint Green'.

Petticoat Government, Baroness *Orczy, 1910, Hutchinson. At the court of Louis XV, where Madame de Pompadour (1721–1764) rules supreme, the search is on for a new Minister of Finance. Pompadour's candidate is the pliable Henry Dewhyrst, Marquis of Eglington, whose wealthy father came over with the exiled James II. Having risked life and fortune for the old Pretender, Eglington, an apparently weak and diffident man ruled by his mother, now serves Louis XV and distances himself from the Young Pretender, who is about to set off for Scotland. He is opposed by Gaston de Stainville, ambitious admirer of the Prime Minister's daughter, Lydie d'Aumont, herself, for sentimental reasons, a staunch supporter of Charles Edward Stuart. Finding out that Stainville has married secretly, Lydie decides not only to back Eglington but to marry him, and to exert influence through him. She thinks him 'weak and unmanly', and imagines that he thinks her 'hard and unfeminine', although he is clearly in love with her. When the Pretender's expedition fails, Lydie wants to send a boat to pick him up. The Duke of Cumberland has offered Louis fifteen million *livres* for the Pretender's person, and tries to persuade Lydie to reveal his whereabouts. While she temporizes, Eglington's dormant loyalty, and an English contempt for a German monarch and his corrupt French ally, is aroused. When Stainville tricks Lydie into appointing him her agent, Eglington once again risks life and fortune to foil Louis's treachery and redeem his wife's honour. Stainville almost kills him in a duel, but he is reconciled with Lydie, who has learnt to love him, and they abandon their French estates and retire to Sussex. The 'obtrusive domination' of women like Pompadour has always been 'obnoxious and abhorrent' to Lydie's mind, 'proud of its femininity, gentle in the consciousness of its strength'. The rekindling of Eglington's patriotism also rekindles his masculinity, putting an end to petticoat government.

PHILIPS, F[rancis] C[harles] (1849–1921) married, first, Maria JONES, and, secondly, Eva Maude Mary KEVILL-DAVIES (d. *c.*1901) The son of a Church of England clergyman, Philips was born in Brighton and educated at Brighton College and the Royal Military College, Sandhurst. He graduated in 1868 and joined the Queen's Own Regiment. but resigned his commission in 1871 to go on the stage under the name 'Fairlie'. He became an actor-manager, but in 1880 began to study law. He was called to the Bar in 1884, and practised on the South Wales circuit. He also wrote plays, novels, and journalism. Philips's first novel *As in a Looking Glass* (1885) caused a great stir—its melodramatic death-scene set the tenor and the pattern of much of his later work. Sarah Bernhardt starred in a stage version. His other publications include *A Woman of the World's Advice* (1901), *The Matrimonial Country and Other Stories* (1910), a collection which varies from the bitterness of the French conte to the banality of the English magazine story, and *The Wicked Miss Keane* (1911). One notable work is the baldly titled *A Question of Colour* (1895), a frank treatment of love and racial prejudice. Philips frequently collaborated with other writers on plays and novels. His autobiography, *My Varied Life*, was published in 1914; it is rather unrevealing of his personal life but goes into interesting detail about the financial side of his theatrical and legal careers.

PHILLIPPS-WOLLEY, Clive: Clive Long Oldnall PHILLIPPS (1854–1918), Kt. (1914), changed his name (1876) to PHILLIPPS-WOLLEY and married (1879) Jane FENWICK. Educated at Rossall School, Lancashire, he was was vice-consul in Kerch in the Crimea 1873–6. After changing his name on inheriting the Wolley estates at Woodhall, Shropshire, he studied law, was called to the Bar in 1884, and practised until 1896, when he accepted an administrative post in British Columbia. He travelled widely: an expedition to the Caucasus gave rise to his *Sport in Crimea and the Caucasus* (1881). His novels were written as a hobby and often dealt with his own favourite pastimes such as shooting and hunting. They include *Savage Svanetia* (1883), *Snap: A Legend of the Lone Mountain* (1890), *Gold, Gold in Cariboo* (1894), *One of the Broken Brigade* (1897), and *The Chicamon Store* (1900), a story of adventures in Alaska and the Yukon. *Songs of an English Esau* (1902) was followed by *Songs from a Young Man's Land* (1920). Phillips-Wolley also wrote non-fiction including *The Trottings of a Tenderfoot* (1884) about Canada, and *Big Game Shooting* (1894). He twice stood unsuccessfully as Conservative candidate for Parliament. He died in British Columbia.

PHILLPOTTS, Eden (1862–1960) married first (1892), Emily TOPHAM (d. 1928), and, secondly (1929), Lucy Robina Joyce WEBB. Born at Mt Aboo, India, son of an officer in the Indian Army, he was educated at Mannamead School, Plymouth. He went to London in 1880 and worked for the next ten years as a clerk in the Sun Fire Insurance Office, studying at first in the evenings to become an actor, before realizing his own ineptitude. He began to write fiction, and eventually left insurance for the job of assistant editor of *Black and White*. He is one of the most prominent *regional novelists of the period: *Children of the Mist* (1898), the first of an ambitious 'Dartmoor Cycle', was dedicated to R. D. Blackmore (1825–1900), who with Thomas Hardy (1840–1928) was the main influence on his work. *Sons of the Morning* followed in 1900, and thereafter his Dartmoor fiction took one of three forms: *historical melodrama, contemporary melodrama of a Hardyesque or Nietzschean tone, and flatter studies of highly localized provincial life. *The American Prisoner* (1904) is set in a Dartmoor prison during the American War of Independence, and confirmed in reviewers the feeling that Phillpotts was a writer of unusual ability who refused to allow literary decorum to get in the way of self-expression. One spoke of it as a book possible only 'where in literature no law reigns, but every man does that which is right in his own eyes, and books commend themselves less by obedience to any standard of taste than by vigorously flaunting their authors' personalities'. Another historical romance published in the same year, *The Farm of the Dagger* (1904), which also involves American (and French) prisoners of war, did little to contradict this impression. The contemporary romances transpose Hardy to Devon. *The*

*Secret Woman (1905) is a study in landscape which also includes a devoted wife who discovers, from the torn fragments of a letter, that her husband has a lover young enough to be his daughter. *The Portreeve* (1906) is a pious, fiery, self-made man brought to a miserable end through the malicious persecutions of a woman whom he has rejected, and who will stop at nothing to revenge herself on him. *The Whirlwind* (1907) is the passion which overwhelms a stupid and volcanic rustic when he discovers that his wife has been unfaithful and goes striding across the moor to kill her. *The Virgin in Judgment* (1908) is the hero's sister, who comes to live with him after his marriage, and terrifies his wife into suicide by misconstruing her innocent friendship with an old lover. The 'immense and far-flung arc' of *The Beacon* (1911) rather outshines the heroine, who arrives from London to work as a barmaid at the Oxenham Arms in South Zeal, and eventually returns home broken-hearted. *Demeter's Daughter* (1911) is a rural *marriage problem novel. Phillpotts became extremely sensitive to the charge that he had emulated Hardy a little too closely both in his pessimism and in his subordination of character to setting. In a 'foreword' to *Widecombe Fair* (1913), a medley of salty village gossip punctuated by lengthy descriptive passages, he invoked Nietzsche to argue that he had always tried 'to say "yea" to life even in its most difficult problems, and to display a will to life rejoicing at its own vitality in the sacrifice of its highest types'. Admitting that he found the 'phenomena of man's environment' as interesting as 'man himself', he envisaged a time when novelists would find ways to express animal and even geological life, thus finally demonstrating the transitoriness of the human race. His most notable study of a provincial backwater, in which hardly anything happens at all, is *The Haven* (1909), set in a Devon fishing village, about an unhappy marriage which neither improves nor deteriorates. Phillpotts must sometimes have longed to get away from all this, and did so in the cosmopolitan stories collected in *The Folk Afield* (1907). He also wrote as 'Harrington Hext', and his postwar work includes many *crime novels.

PICKTHALL, Marmaduke [William] (1875–1936) married Muriel SMITH. The son of a Church of England clergyman in Suffolk, he was educated at Harrow School. He became a dedicated orientalist as a young man, and spent three years in the Middle East, where he learnt Arabic and became a Muslim. His experiences were first described in a series of articles written for the **New Age*, later published as *With the Turk in War-Time* (1914). After serving in the First World War, Pickthall edited the *Bombay Chronicle* (1920–4) and then the *Hyderabad Quarterly Review* and *Islamic Culture* for the Nizam of Hyderabad. He served in the Nizam's Educational Service from 1925. Like Robert *Hichens and A. E. W. *Mason, Pickthall set some of his novels in England, and some in *exotic, and usually oriental, settings. Unlike them, he developed two entirely different styles of writing, so that the English novels and the oriental novels do not seem to have been written by the same writer. The English novels are curiously ornate, almost *Meredithian, in manner, and very derivative. *Enid* (1904), a thin romance set in fashionable West End society, is nearly redeemed by a supporting cast of lively degenerates which includes Lord Elmsdale, who married a servant-girl, and Mrs Garland, who married her groom. *Myopes* (1907), set in London and a Swiss hotel, is even thinner. The oriental tales, by contrast, are adventurous in theme, and not so convoluted in manner. *Said the Fisherman* (1903) concerns a Syrian Arab who travels to London and returns home with his mind unhinged by the experience. *The House of Islam* (1906) is set in the highlands of Gilead and in Jerusalem, in mosques, wine-shops and bazaars, and describes the dilemmas of a saintly sheikh surrounded by ambitious schemers. *The Children of the Nile* (1908) is set in Egypt at the time of Arabi's revolt: a clever, cowardly, impressionable, amoral youth, Marbruk, a rich man's son with a smattering of European education, falls into the hands of a succession of rogues and charlatans, but always emerges more or less unscathed by the sole expedient of placing his trust in Allah. *The Valley of the Kings* (1909) is the almost *Forsterian tale of a young Arab passionately devoted to an English artist, and of the end of their friendship. *The Veiled Women* (1913) is set in a harem in the Sudan, and contrasts the cheerful earthiness of the sultan's four Circassian wives, who regard him as an incidental nuisance, with the rigid etiquette of an English governess who marries his charming son. Rejected by the English authorities of the occupation, she realizes her insignificance in the scheme of things and surrenders herself wholeheartedly to Islam. **Brendle* (1905) is perhaps the most vivid and least ornate of Pickthall's English tales. He also published *Knights of Araby* (1917) and *Oriental Encounters* (1918).

Pigs in Clover, 'Frank *Danby', 1903, William Heinemann. Sensational but nuanced story about the relations between the declining landed interest and new money in the period leading up to the Jameson raid of 1896. As the novel opens, Stephen Hayward's wife, an older woman, has just died giving birth to a daughter, Aline. He is not much moved by her death, having dedicated himself, with the steadfast encouragement of his sister, Constantia, to a political career, and the restoration of his family fortunes. Aline contracts an ill-advised marriage to a disreputable jockey, who is fortunately killed in a riding accident, but not before Hayward has tried to buy him off with money borrowed from a Jewish multi-millionaire, Karl Althaus, who has made his fortune in the South African goldfields. Karl and his womanizing brother, Louis, become involved in politics, on the imperialist side, and with the same woman, a successful novelist, Joan de Groot. Karl proposes to Joan, and is rejected; Louis, hoping to secure a farm owned by her invalid husband, seduces her. Establishing himself as Karl's agent in London, Louis cuts a swathe through fashionable society, while all the time keeping the now pregnant Joan in a suburban cottage, and, in the hope of securing Hayward's influence, courting Aline. Louis marries Aline, and Karl, once the political crisis has receded, begins to unravel his brother's villainy. He tracks Joan down in the East End of London (her son by Louis has died) and takes her under his protection. But although she respects him fervently, she still desires Louis, and, torn between obligation and need, takes an overdose of opium. While contemptuous of the 'pigs in clover'—the (largely Jewish) plutocracy—the novel deplores anti-Semitism. 'It is the misfortune of the Jews that one of their community cannot misbehave without earning opprobrium for their whole body.'

PINKERTON, Thomas A. published nineteen volumes of fiction from 1880 to 1909, and *The New Medea: A Drama in Blank Verse* (1905). He specialized in whimsical *fantasies such as *No Rates and Taxes: A Romance of Five Worlds* (1902), a series of reports transmitted to a professor on Venus by a man banished to Mars, and *Valdora* (1907), a *Ruritanian romance whose hero describes his championing of a tiny Italian State and its hereditary Princess in letters to his sister. *The Adoption of Rhodope: A Chronicle of Thames* (1909) might just as well have been set on Mars, or in Ruritania. Two children, Rhodope and Orion, escape from their wretched guardians in Scotland, and finally, about halfway through the book, reach the Thames, where they are taken in by a famous novelist, Mrs Trefusis.

Pip: *A Romance of Youth*, 'Ian *Hay', 1907, William Blackwood. The book follows Pip from kindergarten to prep and public school. Pip is an orphan (his school is his family) and a brilliant cricketer, but the book's only real drama concerns his relationship with Linklater, a bully whom Pip saves from himself at the cost of a broken collar-bone; the boys become friends over Linklater's sickbed. A light, often funny school story, but most interesting now for its unselfconscious statement of the public school (the officer and gentleman) ethos of a male society: 'in which brains, as such, count for nothing, birth has no part, and wealth is simply disregarded; where genuine ability occasionally gains a precious footing, and then only by disguising itself as something else, but to which muscles, swiftness of foot, and general ability to manipulate a ball with greater dexterity than one's neighbour is received unquestioningly, joyfully, proudly.' The conclusion, in which Pip plays a game of golf with a woman on condition she marries him if she loses, connects it with John Collis *Snaith's cricketing novel *Willow the King* (1899); we see romance defusing the threat of the new female athleticism, as both women really want to lose.

PITCAIRN, J. J.: see under R. Austin *Freeman.

PLATTS, W[illiam] Carter (1864–1944) married (1889) Ellen SAVILE. Born in Huddersfield and educated at Huddersfield College, he went into the woollen trade but became a journalist in about 1890. Subsequently he published many books on fishing, humorous books, and fiction. His main line was in *suburban comedy. *The Whims of Erasmus* (1902) features the high-spirited Tuttleburys, *Up To-morrow, or, Mr Chumson's Experiments* (1903) a mad inventor, and *Bunkumelli* (1904) a humorous ex-circus-proprietor. Characteristic is *Timmins of Crickleton* (1908), whose hero has all sorts of ideas about pike fishing, music machines, and other subjects. *The Million Heiress and John* (1910) sends Linda Hillbrun, daughter of a Colorado cattle baron, off to England in pursuit of John Williamson, whom she once repulsed insultingly but now wants back. Other books with an Anglo-American flavour include *Flush Times and Scimp in the Wild West* (1903) and *The Crickleton Chronicles, or, The Cowboy's Courtship* (1903).

Pleasure Bound 'Afloat': *The Extraordinary Adventures of a Party of Travellers*, 1908, The 'Chatty' Club. This pornographic novel is about a group of upper-class English and American hedonists crossing the ocean. In the sequel, *Pleasure Bound 'Ashore'*, the same gang hijacks a yacht for the same purpose. There is a sub-plot involving German preparations to invade Britain. The German navy has constructed twelve battleships at a secret base on a Pacific island. The hedonists, all patriots at heart, decide to suspend flagellation and buggery long enough to capture the ships, thereby placing the Royal Navy in a 'position of unapproachable supremacy'. The convergence of plot and sub-plot demonstrates the similarity between the secret worlds created by late Victorian pornography on one hand, and Edwardian *spy fiction on the other. Both novels have been attributed to George *Bacchus.

political fiction. If the Victorian era constitutes the golden age of British political fiction, then the Edwardian era must be regarded as distinctly silver, even bronze-ish. Mid-Victorian political novels have a 'collective presence', as Christopher Harvie puts it in his study of the genre (1991). Taken together, they establish a politically saturated geography: metropolis, industrial regions, market towns, hunting counties, Celtic fringe, railway lines, country houses and estates, coastal resorts, and urban slums. That geography gave events like the lockout, the election address, and even the capture of a poacher, allegorical status. The Edwardian political novel, while it never achieved a comparable presence, adapted the geography and devised new allegories. The high politics rendered by Anthony Trollope (1815–82), George *Meredith and others, which tempered élitism with an emphasis on social reconciliation, continued to be a subject for writers such as S. *Baring-Gould, May *Bateman, Mrs Hugh *Bell, Hilaire *Belloc, Marguerite *Bryant, B. M. *Butt, George *Calderon, John *Galsworthy, Philip *Gibbs, 'Maxwell *Gray', Ford Madox *Hueffer, C. F. *Keary, David Christie *Murray, Violet *Tweedale, and Mrs Humphry *Ward. H. G. *Wells's **Tono-Bungay* (1908) and *The *New Machiavelli* (1911), aiming at Dickensian breadth, ponder the political decline of the country-house system and the precarious emergence of a new intellectual (and specifically scientific) élite. It has been argued that the Liberal victory at the general election of 1906 turned the attention of writers like Galsworthy, Wells, and E. M. *Forster to the 'condition of England' question first framed in the 1840s. High politics also provided a familiar context for an unfamiliar problem: the militant campaign for female suffrage (see *feminist fiction). Political novelists became increasingly preoccupied with the role of national and racial identity in the creation of community (an issue examined to memorable effect by George Eliot, 1819–80, in *Daniel Deronda*, 1874–6). Meredith's later novels have much to say about such matters; his last, unfinished and published posthumously in 1910, declares its preoccupation with national identity in its title, **Celt and Saxon*. Israel *Zangwill brought Eliot's theme up to date in *The Mantle of Elijah* (1900), but thereafter found drama a better vehicle than the novel for his promotion of Zionism. Class politics did, however, persist: in the industrial novels of Ethel *Carnie, Allen *Clarke, Joseph *Keating, D. H. *Lawrence, Alfred *Ollivant, W. Kineton *Parkes, John Edward *Patterson, Constance *Smedley, and 'Robert *Tressall'; and in stories of proletarian vagabondage such as Patrick *MacGill's **Children of the Dead End* (1914). By the end of the 1890s the brief phase of the slum novel was over. The East End of London remained an automatic point of reference in many novels, but the portrayal of proletarian and *lumpen*-proletarian life became increasingly light-hearted. Symptomatic of the new mood was the instant success of William *de Morgan's genial, old-fashioned romances. Charles Dickens (1812–70), not the French realist Émile Zola (1840–1902), was the model. In an address to the Boz Club, William Pett *Ridge claimed that Dickens had revealed the 'romance' and the 'cheerfulness' in the lives of 'hard-up people.' Some writers, he went on, described the poor as though they were 'gibbering apes'. But such 'naturalism' was outmoded. 'The reading public knows better; it knows that the Dickens view is the right view.' Ridge, like Edwin *Pugh and W. W. *Jacobs, was proud to be considered a disciple of Dickens. Emollient portrayals of working-class life are to be found in the fiction of A. St John *Adcock, Phyllis *Bottome, 'James *Cassidy', Eleanor Hughes *Gibb, 'Robert *Halifax', A. Neil *Lyons, and Barry *Pain, among others: here, and elsewhere, the slum was beginning to be displaced as a focus of attention by the *suburb. More significant, on the whole, than the direct expression of political ideology in polemical or diagnostic fiction was its indirect expression in popular fiction. Both feminism and Irish nationalism, for example, further coloured a number of already colourful *historical romances. Conservative ideology shaped many tales of international conspiracy. The shift of emphasis is apparent in *Falconet*, the unfinished last novel of Benjamin Disraeli (1804–81), published in the *Times* in 1905: a mysterious stranger, whose aim appears to be global revolution, lays bare the frailty of the established order. In Edwardian thrillers (see *spy fiction) from Guy *Boothby's *A Cabinet Secret* (1901) to John *Buchan's *The Thirty-Nine Steps* (1915), mysterious strangers materialize terrifyingly at the very centre of government itself. High politics provided a setting for criminal behaviour of one kind or another in novels by 'Orme *Agnus', T. T. *Dahle, Sara Jeannette *Duncan, Mrs *Hamilton, Muriel *Hine, John Edward *Patterson, K. C. *Thurston, and others.

POLLARD, Eliza Frances published forty volumes of fiction, mostly historical adventure for girls or boys, from 1864 to 1911, including *A Daughter of France: A Story of Acadia* (1900), *The Last of the Cliffords* (1903), *A Girl of the Eighteenth Century* (1906), *For the Emperor* (1909), and *A New England Maid: A Tale of the American Rebellion* (1911).

Pothunters, The, P. G. *Wodehouse, 1902, Adam & Charles Black. Wodehouse's first published book, a story of the disruptive effects of the theft of the school sports cups on the boys of St Austin's College. Thin on plot and characterization (it is difficult to tell one boy from another), the book already shows Wodehouse's gift for scenes of farcical misunderstanding and, in particular, for esoteric slang-driven dialogue. The closed world of the boys' boarding-school, with its rituals, its clear-cut value system, and its suspicion of outsiders (grown-ups, women, the worldly-wise), all given elaborate linguistic expression, was to be the model for all Wodehouse's subsequent fantasies of upper-class English life.

POTTER, [Helen] Beatrix (1866–1943) married (1913) William HEELIS. She was the daughter of a barrister who did not practise; both her parents came from rich, cotton-spinning, Dissenting Lancashire families. Brought up in London, and educated by governesses at home, she began drawing at an early age. A dull childhood was only enlivened by pets and summer holidays in Scotland and the Lake District, where she and her father were enthusiastic photographers. In 1890 she sold some of her work for Christmas card designs, but had her sketches and a booklet turned down by various publishers, including Frederick Warne. She therefore paid herself for the publication of *The *Tale of Peter Rabbit* (1900) and *The Tailor of Gloucester* (1902). Based on illustrated letters Potter had sent to the children of her former governess, the books' appeal was immediate, and Warne contracted her for these and several more. Twenty-two appeared between 1901 and 1913 (with only one title, *The Tale of Little Pig Robinson*, 1930, appearing later), and Potter used the money to buy a farm in the Lake District, devoting the rest of her life to the breeding of sheep. At 39 she became engaged, despite her parents' opposition, to Norman Warne, but he died after a few months. She later married her solicitor. The enduring success of Potter's tales reflects her success in integrating animal and human characteristics in her protagonists, in Pigling Bland, Samuel Whiskers, Mrs Tiggy-winkle, Jeremy Fisher, Tom Kitten, Jemima Puddle-duck, and Mrs Tittlemouse—their middle-class world is completely familiar from Edwardian children's books, and yet they are also clearly, through Potter's observational skills as a natural history painter, animals, and always likely to behave accordingly. There is a biography by Margaret Lane (1946).

PRAED, Mrs Campbell: Rosa Caroline MURRAY-PRIOR (1851–1935) married (1872) Arthur Campbell Bulkley MACKWORTH-PRAED (1846–1901). She was born at Bromelton, in Queensland, of which State her father was for many years Postmaster General. The first native-born Australian poet, Charles Harpur (1817–68), was her mother's uncle. Responsibility for her education was shared by her mother and the family governess. Murray-Prior began writing at an early age. *The Life of Charlotte Brontë* (1857) by Elizabeth Gaskell (1810–65) was a great inspiration to her, living as she did in the Australian bushlands. In her youth she spent many hours in the Ladies' Gallery at the State Legislature, which gave her a lifelong interest in politics and its machinations. After an unsuccessful attempt at cattle-ranching she and her husband, who was a nephew of the poet Winthrop Mackworth Praed (1802–39), left for England in 1876; he went into the family business and she began to write pieces for publication. Praed was encouraged by George *Meredith during his days as a reader at Chapman & Hall. Her first novel, *An Australian Heroine* (1880), drew on her early married life and was rapidly followed by *Policy and Passion: A Novel of Australian Life* (1881), and *Nadine: The Study of a Woman* (1882). The latter two caused a stir because they acknowledged the existence of women's sexual impulses. Issues concerning women are a vital element in her work. She looked to the root cause of what many of her contemporaries were calling 'women's neuroses' and implied a psychosexual foundation for them. She collaborated with Justin *McCarthy on the political novels *The Right Honourable* (1886), *The Ladies' Gallery* (1888), and *The Rebel Rose* (1888). In 1899 Praed met the medium and mystic Nancy Hayward (1864–1927), who intensified Praed's already keen interest in spiritualism, expressed in such books as *The Brother of the Shadow* (1886) and *The Soul of Countess Adrian* (1891). She left her husband to live with Hayward, and several of her publications after 1900 have mystical, or mystical-sexual, themes: *The Insane Root* (1902); *Nyria* (1904), an exposition of esoteric Buddhism, based on the supposed reincarnation in her companion Nancy of a Roman slave called Nyria; and *The Body of His Desire: A Romance of the Soul* (1912), about a devoted Anglican clergyman erotically haunted by a dream woman who eventually takes the shape of an ancient Egyptian and recognizes him as Thaan, priest of Amen Ra. Other stories deliver the sex without the mysticism. *Some Loves and a Life: A Study of a Neurotic Woman* (1904) features the philanderings of Mrs Van Rennen, wife of a South African millionaire, with a sculptor who soon takes up with someone else, and an aristocratic clergyman who assures her that his 'first horror' at falling in love with her 'seems to have given place to a conviction of ultimate good'. *By Their Fruits* (1908) follows the fortunes of twin sisters, Aglaia Pascaline and Pascaline Aglaia, one saintly, the other vain and egotistical; the latter, a scientist's wife, goes to the bad; complications ensue when her lookalike sister appears on the scene. Praed also published *My Australian Girlhood: Sketches and Impressions of Bush Life* (1902) and other memoirs. *Our Book of Memories* (1912) is an edition of McCarthy's letters to her. Praed brought a rich variety of experience to her writing: her early life in Australia was a lasting inspiration to her and her association with Oscar Wilde (1854–1900), Conan *Doyle, Ellen Terry (1847–1928), and others provided lavish models for her fictional characters. Praed's work has, until recently, been neglected by Australian critics, being regarded as too British.

PRESCOTT, E. Livingston: Edith Katherine SPICER-JAY (d. 1901). The daughter of a barrister, she was educated by tutors; little else is known about her, except that she was an enthusiastic supporter of military charities. Under this pseudonym she published seventeen novels about military life, starting with *The Apotheosis of Mr. Tyrawley* (1896). She was honorary Lady Superintendent of the London Soldiers' Home and Guards' Home. Her publishers seem to have cashed in after her death. 1903 saw the publication of *Donny's Captain*, about a young boy's friendship with a soldier who has a past; *Dragooning a Dragoon*, about the reform of a conceited tyro, the proceeds of which went to the British Home and Hospital for Incurables, Chelsea; *Knit by Felony*, about the reform of a cynical young thief under the influence of the sturdy Unitarian who was the scapegoat for his crime; and *Most Secret Tribunal*, another book which belies its melodramatic title, about the penance undergone by an Englishman who believes that he has killed a high-ranking Indian. 1904 saw the publication of two further novels, *Queen's Own Traitors and With Cords of Love*. It seems likely that there is some connection with 'L. Parry *Truscott', but little is known of either author.

Prester John, John *Buchan, 1910, Thomas Nelson. A boys' adventure story drawing extensively on Buchan's gift for setting his hide-and-seek scenes in convincing natural settings. David Crawford, son of the Kirkcaple manse, has to make his own way in life when his father dies, and takes a job as assistant storekeeper in

Blaauwildebeestefontein in the Transvaal. There he finds himself in the midst of a native uprising, led by the heroic figure of the Revd John Laputa and resting on the legend of the African prince Prester John. Crawford (with the assistance of master spy, Captain Arcoll) thwarts the uprising, and makes his fortune from his discovery of Prester John's treasures. The novel is typical in its colonial attitudes—John Laputa is a noble figure in comparison with the treacherous and shifty Portuguese, Henriques, but doomed to defeat, nevertheless, by racial inferiority. Crawford learns 'the meaning of the white man's duty. He has to take all risks, recking nothing of his life or his fortunes, and well content to find his reward in the fulfilment of his task. That is the difference between white and black, the gift of responsibility, the power of being in a little way a king...'

PREVOST, Francis, *pseud.*: Henry Francis Prevost BATTERSBY (1862–1949) married (1909) Frances Muriel SAUNDERS. The son of a major-general in the army, he was educated at Westminster School before attending both the Royal Military Academy, Woolwich and the Royal Military College, Sandhurst. He graduated from Sandhurst with distinction and took up a lieutenant's commission with the Royal Irish Rifles, before leaving to become a journalist. He was wounded whilst acting as the *Boer War correspondent for the *Morning Post* (1899–1900), and also reported from Somaliland in 1902. Battersby was a special correspondent on the Prince of Wales's Indian Tour of 1905–1906, which he described in *Under Indian Eyes* (1906), with photographs by the author. He was wounded while reporting for the *Morning Post* from France in 1915–16, and gassed while *Reuters* correspondent on the British Front in 1918. He also contributed articles to the *Edinburgh Review*, the *New Review*, the **Nineteenth Century*, and the *National Review.* Battersby was a keen sportsman and was sports correspondent (specializing in hockey) for several papers. His fiction normally took the form of short stories. Titles written under the pseudonym 'Francis Prevost' include *Rust of Gold* (1895), *False Dawn* (1897), *The Plague of the Heart* (1902), and two volumes of verse, *Meliot* (1886) and *Fires of Green Wood* (1887). As H. Battersby he published more verse (1920), novels including *The Avenging Hour* (1906), *The Last Resort* (1912), *The Silence of Men, and The Lure of Romance* (1914). He and Vladimir Tchertkoff published (1893) a translation of Tolstoy's *Christ's Christianity.* Battersby travelled widely (to Russia, Central Asia, India, the Far East and all over Europe). In later life Battersby became interested in psychic phenomena; he wrote *Man Outside Himself: The Facts of Etheric Projection* (1942) and collected and arranged a series of pieces under the title *Psychic Certainties* (1930).

PRICHARD, Kate O'B. and H. V.: Kate O'Brien RYALL (1852–1953), who married Hesketh Brodrick PRICHARD (d. 1876), and her son Hesketh Vernon HESKETH PRICHARD (1876–1922), DSO (1918), MC, married (1908) Elizabeth GRIMSTON (1885–1975). Prichard was born at Jhansi, India, after the death of his father, an officer in the Indian army; his mother brought him home in 1877. He was at Fettes School, Edinburgh (1888–94) and then travelled in Spain and Portugal. Although he started to read law at Edinburgh University, Prichard did not finish the course but instead travelled extensively (South America, Canada, Newfoundland, Haiti) and took every opportunity to indulge in big-game hunting. He became a Fellow of the Royal Geographical Society and led a an expedition to Patagonia (1900–1). Enormously tall, he was a talented amateur cricketer, playing for Hampshire and the Gentlemen of England and leading an MCC team to America in 1907. He was aide-de-camp to the Lord Lieutenant of Ireland in 1907. In 1910 he headed an expedition to protect grey seals from a brutal cull. A famously good shot, he taught marksmanship during the First World War; his experiences during this period are recorded in *Sniping in France*. Prichard was decorated for his contribution to the war effort but did not fully recover his health after the war; he died of blood-poisoning. His mother outlived him for many years. From January 1898 they published together a series of stories, drawing on his Iberian travels, about 'Don Q.' in the *Badminton Magazine*. The eponymous hero—a Hispanic Robin Hood—became an immensely popular cult figure (Douglas Fairbanks, Senior, later successfully portrayed Don Q. on screen). Their other works include *A Modern Mercenary* (1899), *Karadac, Count of Gerzy* (1901), a *historical novel set in the Channel Islands, *Roving Hearts* (1903), *The Chronicles of Don Q.* (1904), *The New Chronicles of Don Q.* (1906), and *The Cahusac Mystery* (1912). He and Mrs Prichard also published fiction as 'E. and H. Heron', including *Tammer's Duel* (1898) and *Ghost Stories* (1916). Prichard's obituary calls their association 'a partnership to which we do not recall any literary parallel'. He also wrote travel books like *Through the Heart of Patagonia* (1902) and *Through Trackless Labrador* (1911) and one novel on his own, *November Joe, Detective of the Woods* (1913). E. W. *Hornung is supposed to have based Raffles on Prichard.

PRIOR, James, *pseud.*: James Prior KIRK (1850–1922) was the son of a Notttinghamshire tradesman. As a boy Kirk was not permitted to read novels—his father was a strict disciplinarian who kept a sharp eye on his son's moral education. The only book not banned was *The Bible in Spain* (1843) by George Borrow (1803–1881), which his parents assumed to be an evangelical work. At the age of 15 Kirk discovered the novels of Walter Scott (1771–1832) and Charles Dickens (1812–70). He later worked in a solicitor's office and in his free time wrote novels with a strong regional flavour. Prior was a conscientious writer whose attention to detail often drove him to scour the countryside to verify information for his work. John *Buchan is one of those who compared his work to that of Thomas Hardy (1840–1928)—he thought Prior's countryfolk especially well drawn. Buchan enthusiastically reviewed *Fortuna Chance* (1910), and its plot, with its mixture of journeying and adventures, is echoed in many of Buchan's own works. However, it was as a Nottinghamshire novelist that Prior first became known. *Hyssop* (1904), about a family in the tradesman class, is characteristic. The emphasis of its opening chapters is on the squabbles, jealousies, and sudden affections which punctuate normal family life. But the narrative takes a different turn with the arrival of Eva, a grown woman with the innocence and charm of a child who has lost her memory in a train accident. Eva's memory is restored by the intervention of a spiritualistic tailor. Before the accident, she had been a prostitute and an alcoholic; she now reverts to her former self, and is eventually purged by the 'hyssop' of hard work. D. H. *Lawrence was introduced to Prior's novels by Edward Garnett (1868–1937). 'What a curious man James Prior is!' he wrote to Garnett on 13 December 1911. 'I did not know him, and he so near home. I was very much interested. But what curious, highly flavoured stuff!' On 3 January 1912 Lawrence recorded a conversation with the publisher William Heinemann (1863–1920), during which Heinemann said, 'We had a fellow from your way—a James Prior—did some Sherwood Forest novels. Very good, I thought—but went quite dead, quite dead.' Lawrence gloomily imagined himself going 'quite dead, quite dead' in Heinemann's hands. *Forest Folk* (1901) was the first of the Sherwood novels.

Private Papers of Henry Ryecroft, The, George *Gissing, 1903, Archibald Constable. A defeated literary man comes in for a legacy and settles down in the country to enjoy life in his own restrained way, observing nature and ruminating on books, people, and himself, on art and science, on religion and democracy. He is determined (like Gissing himself towards the end of his life) to get the most he can out of small pleasures after the years of struggle. Reviewers were not slow to point out the autobiographical element. On the whole they were well disposed to the crotchety patriotism which seems to be Ryecroft's primary note, and critical acclaim was followed by a measure of popular success Gissing had scarcely known before. The **Athenaeum* drew attention to what may have been the cause of the book's success, as well as a possible defect. 'Mr Gissing has been content, to all seeming, to tread pedestrian streets, grey roads, dull alleys, and to breathe the poisonous air of the great city without a murmur. In this book he astonishes by flinging up his arms and inhaling the country breezes. He can think of nothing but of his release.' The sense of release is palpable, but also a little feverish. More recently the critical tendency has been to argue that the feverishness is carefully calculated, and the characterization of Ryecroft ironic throughout. Relevant here is a sentence from the first draft of the Preface 'I need not hesitate to express my opinion that Ryecroft ought never to have taken to professional authorship at all.'

Prodigal Son, The, Hall *Caine, 1904, William Heinemann. A retelling of the story of the prodigal son, set in Iceland, with a simpler sense of justice than the biblical version and a typically elaborate Caine plot. Stephen Magnussen, the Governor-General of Iceland, has two sons, big, slow, noble Magnus and mercurial, musical, irresponsible Oscar. Magnusson's best friend, Factor Neilsen, the chief merchant of the country, has two daughters, the sweet Thora and Helga, who is now living with her mother in Denmark. Magnus loves Thora and they are betrothed, confirming their families' social and economic ties. Shortly before the betrothal ceremony, Oscar returns from Oxford, Thora realizes she loves him, and Magnus sacrifices himself to her happiness, taking on the blame for breaking their tie. He is exiled to a distant family farm; Oscar takes his place as Thora's betrothed. Thora invites Helga to come and share her happiness, but as soon as she arrives she enchants Oscar with her sophistication and understanding of his musical talent. Oscar and Thora are married, but Helga is already part of his life and accompanies the couple on their honeymoon. Back in Iceland she confronts her sister with Oscar's true feelings, and the shocked Thora gives premature birth to a daughter, Elin. Helga persuades Oscar to let her take the child, as Thora is 'unstable'; Thora, with Magnus's help, gets the child back but dies from the strain. Oscar's father and father-in-law discover that he has forged their signatures on a cheque paying off gambling debts run up by him and Helga on the honeymoon trip. His father meets the debt by mortgaging Magnus's farm; he and the Factor fall out irrevocably and a shamed Oscar is cast out. In exile he meets up with Helga who helps him with his musical career until, in another casino crisis, he is compelled to fake his own death. In Iceland his father is voted out of office and his father-in-law's business collapses. Both men die; Magnus, burdened with the family debts, takes charge of his mother and Elin on his desolate farm. The years pass. Under a new name Oscar has become Iceland's most famous composer and is returning to his fatherland. Magnus's farm is to be sold and Oscar intends to buy it for him, but also tries to convince Elin to come and live with him. She rejects both his money and his love, insisting that Magnus is her true father. Oscar realizes that he cannot undo the past and leaves without revealing his identity. He dies in an avalanche, having left the money for the farm under Elin's pillow.

PROTHERO, John Keith, *pseud.*: Ada Elizabeth JONES (1886–1962) married (1917) Cecil Edward CHESTERTON (1879–1918). Born into a family of newspaper folk, she wrote journalism under the name 'Sheridan Jones'. The serialized version of her novel *Motley & Tinsel: A Story of the Stage* (1911) was the subject of a libel action based on the name of one of the characters. When the story appeared in book form, Prothero substituted the names of well-known fellow-authors, with their permission, as a protest against the state of the law. Thus Jess 'shook her head—and, glancing up, she recognised the face of George R. *Sims'. She published no other fiction in the period. Her husband, the younger brother of G. K. *Chesterton, worked on **Outlook* and started the *Eye Witness*, later the *New Witness*. She was assistant editor of the latter and wrote the dramatic criticism. In 1925 she lived as a down-and-out researching her book *In Darkest London*; afterwards she founded the Cecil Houses for homeless women in her husband's memory.

PROTHERO-LEWIS, Helen married James J. G. PUGH. She was the author of twenty-one volumes of sentimental romantic fiction 1890–1928. In *Thraldom* (1903) a vicar's daughter has an unkind stepmother to whom she is reconciled when she restores a long-lost son deserted by the stepmother as a baby.

PROWSE, Richard Orton (1862–1949) was born at Woodbridge in East Anglia, the son of a Church of England clergyman, and educated at Cheltenham College and Balliol College, Oxford. Prowse was fortunate to have enough private income to live modestly whilst pursuing his literary career. Henry *James was a formative influence and Prowse was a lifelong admirer of his work. Yet Prowse was very independent by nature and his work has a unique timbre. His novels deal with serious and complicated subjects. Titles include *The Poison of the Asps* (1892), *A Fatal Reservation* (1895), and *Proud Ashes* (1934). *Voysey* (1901) is a psychological study which Sutherland describes as a 'sordidly realistic study of adultery'; *James Hurd* (1913) is again a psychological study, this time exploring the subject of euthanasia; *A Gift of the Dusk* (1920) describes life inside a sanatorium and was much praised by 'Katherine *Mansfield'; *The Prophet's Wife* (1929) is generally regarded as his most accomplished novel. His obituary in the *Times* (27 May 1949) concludes that Prowse was a 'novelist for the discriminating reader rather than the multitudes'. He also wrote an awkward Ibsenesque play, *Ina*, which was produced by the Stage Society in 1904.

Prussian Officer, The, D. H. *Lawrence, 1914, Gerald Duckworth. Lawrence's first collection of stories consists of twelve explorations of the shape and effect of intense emotion. The title-tale concerns the sadistic relationship between a German officer and his orderly, and shows how a sudden rush of feeling, physical rather than mental, can throw a man into violence. In 'Daughters of the Vicar', the most substantial story here, one sister ignores her physical distaste and lack of feeling to marry a man who can rescue her from poverty; the other defies class convention to marry a collier. In 'Shadow in the Rose Garden' a wife tells her husband of her premarital affair with a man she has just met again, now insane. In 'The Shades of Spring', the emotional dilettante Syson, dallying with a woman in the country, is discomfited by the stubborn sexuality of her new lover, a young gamekeeper. A review in the **Outlook* evoked in its discussion of the title-story the new context provided by the outbreak of the First World War. 'True, the gentleman in question kicks his servant's thighs with the same vigour the German officer has brought to bear on the bombardment of unfortified places, on the massacring of helpless civilians, on the violation of women, and the destruction of those things of beauty which have made the world's holidays. But a subtle savagery is at work in this particular case of bullying that we should find very far to seek in the purely brutish methods which characterize Germany's more collective inhumanities.'

PRYCE, Daisy Hugh. This writer published ten novels 1896–1914, including *Deyncourt of Deyncourt* (1907), a predictable tale of inheritance and babies swapped at birth. *Hill Magic* (1914) is set in a Welsh village. The hero, a man whose high ideals are not shared or even understood by his widowed mother, takes in a foundling girl against her wishes. There is also a rascally land agent and a cynical squire.

PRYCE, Richard (1864–1942). Born in Boulogne, France, the son of an army officer, he went to school at Leamington in Warwickshire, and lived most of his bachelor life in London's West End. He began, like Kenneth *Grahame, as a junior clerk in the Bank of England. His first novel was *An Evil Spirit* (1887). *The Successor* (1904) concerns the rippingly aristocratic third Lady Alton, who is much given to saying 'No fear' and 'Not likely' but who, like her two predecessors, fails to bear Lord Alton a child during his lifetime. This failure arouses his widowed sister-in-law's hopes for her son, Edmund; but after Lord Alton's death a daughter called Gundred is born, who in the end marries Edmund anyway. *Christopher* (1911) is the story of Christopher Herrick, set in Boulogne, Cheltenham, London, and Herrickswood, the family estate, and his hopeless love for Cora, daughter of the forbiddingly remote Mrs St Jemison. Discouraged by the lack of public interest in his work, though reviews were warm, Pryce had more or less given up writing fiction by the outbreak of the First World War. The plays that he wrote were mainly adaptations or based on plots by other writers; they include: *The Dumb Cake* (1907—co-written with Arthur *Morrison), *Little Mrs Cummin* (1909) and *The Visit* (1909), based on stories by Mary E. *Mann, **Helen With the High Hand* (1914) from *Bennett's novel, and *The Old House* (1920) from the story by Mrs *Dudeney. Sadleir writes with regret at this early end to a promising career: 'In this country, despite laudatory reviews, [Pryce] never had the success he deserved.'

PRYDE, Anthony, *pseud.*: see A. R. *Weekes and R. K. *Weekes.

Psmith in the City, P. G. *Wodehouse, 1910, Adam & Charles Black. Mike Jackson, who would rather be playing cricket for the 'Varsity, is compelled by the state of family finances to work for the New Asiatic Bank; Psmith's father is tickled by the idea of Commerce and despatches his dandyish, monocled son to work at the same establishment. With Psmith's languid, disconcerting help, Mike survives the tedium of clerical work until the cricket season proper starts, when he gives it all up to score a century for Middlesex at Lords. An uneasy blend of school story (Mike's sporting triumphs) and farce (Psmith's various dealings with Mr Bickersdyke, the bank's manager), the central, sometimes tense, schoolfriend relationship between dull but decent Mike and clever but affected Psmith was to be better reworked for the purposes of adult comedy in the Jeeves and Wooster stories.

publishers. During 1900–14 British fiction publishing, like the rest of the industry, was in the process of transition in response to technological advances and the expansion of the market. Moreover, fiction sales had very recently been revolutionized by the move, from 1894–5, away from a first edition in three volumes at 31*s.* 6*d.* to one in a single volume at 6*s*. This change, initiated by the influential circulating libraries, was partly a response to the increased volume of fiction being published, but it coincided with a literary reaction against the density and long-windedness of much mid-Victorian fiction. At the same time the proliferating magazines of the 1890s favoured stories, rather than portions of longer works, and the existence of this lucrative market gave rise to many of the volumes of short stories which bulk large in Edwardian fiction. It was not only that the new novel became cheaper, it ceased to be a luxury item; smaller and more convenient to handle, it could be read by a larger proportion of a wider variety of people in all sorts of different places.

As the price of the new novel went down the financial transactions between author and publisher were also being transformed. Both the foundation of the Society of Authors in 1884 and the rise of the *literary agent reflected the increasing desire on the part of writers, including novelists, to enfranchise themselves from their perceived oppression by publishers. The Society, whose membership went up dramatically from 1889, encouraged its members not to sell their work outright to a publisher but to agree a percentage of sales, or 'royalty'. Without going into the complex cultural and commercial issues involved in the tension between writer and publisher, it should be emphasized that the professionalization of authorship met the the development of the mass fiction market. All subsidiary rights to fiction, serial (including syndication) rights, colonial rights, foreign rights, translation rights, dramatization rights, and film rights became increasingly important during this period, and as they did so magnified the potential earning power of the bestsellers and had a consequent impact on the public status of the novelist, whose power to reach a public outside the British middle class was enormously enhanced. The copyright situation both at home and abroad changed during this period. Many European countries signed the Berne Convention (1887) guaranteeing national copyrights to foreign authors. For British authors the problem had always been America: the Chace Act of 1891 gave foreign authors some powers to register American copyright in their works. The Edwardian period saw the opening up of this vast market to British writers, to the point that bestselling authors like Hall *Caine and Mrs Humphry *Ward might make the bulk of their profits from America. In Britain the Copyright Act of 1911 extended an author's rights in his works to fifty years after the year of his death (from forty-two years after publication or seven years after his death). Tillotson's Fiction Bureau, of Bolton, developed the syndication of fiction in provincial newspapers in the 1870s; it was still flourishing in the Edwardian period, but was dealt a severe blow by the outbreak of the First World War, and petered out in 1935. Not only hacks like Dora *Russell but such writers as Arnold *Bennett and Philip *Gibbs sold the firm fiction; and the phenomenon had some literary influence in promoting the local reputations of *regional writers. In all its myriad forms from the six shilling new novel down to the penny Sunday newspaper serial, fiction was reaching a vast public.

Publishers, like authors, sought in this period to professionalize themselves and obtain the benefits of combination: the Publishers' Association was set up in 1896. One of its earliest and most enduring achievements, initiated by Frederick Macmillan (1851–1936), was the Net Book Agreement of 1900, whereby books were sold to bookshops at varying discounts by the publisher, but retailed at a fixed price. The first challenge came from the so-called Book War of 1906–8. In 1905 the *Times*, a famous but old-fashioned paper under pressure from the new journalism of the Harmsworth and Pearson presses, founded the Times Book Club, to which all its annual subscribers automatically belonged. As well as being able to borrow books by mail order, they would be able to buy ex-library stock at a discount. This plan, derived from the American book trade, directly challenged the Net Book Agreement, since it enabled readers to buy almost new books much more cheaply. In October 1906 the Publishers' Association resolved not to supply the *Times* with books either for sale or for review. After two years of war the paper was sold, and in 1908, Lord Northcliffe (1865–1922), the paper's new owner, signed the Agreement: the publishers had won. By 1914 more than two-thirds of new books were sold net. A side effect was that the move to a royalty system was encouraged by the Net Book Agreement, since it was easier to determine a percentage of a fixed price.

Many firms profited from this booming market. Publishers varied a good deal in style, generosity, enthusiasm for literary fiction, and prosperity. In 1911 D. H. *Lawrence advised a friend of a would-be translator: 'If she wants to do fiction, she'd better try Wm Heinemann or Methuen—or if it's anything racy, John Long; if it's essays, Duckworth or Martin Secker or Dent; if it's Drama—well, drama's a bit risky; if it's philosophy... then "The Open Court" or Macmillan.'

The sample of more than 300 volumes of fiction which we have summarized in this book, which favours works of literary merit and works by well-known popular writers, tends to confirm the value of Lawrence's recommendation: Methuen and Heinemann published more of them than any other publishers; the imprint of one or the other is on roughly a fifth of our choice of Edwardian fiction. The firm started in 1890 by William Heinemann (1863–1920) quickly moved into making a profit out of the new 6*s*. novels; they were Hall Caine's publishers, and sold around 400,000 copies of *The Manxman* (1894) in the one-volume format: a key event in the fall of the three-decker. They published Lawrence's *The White Peacock* (1911), though they turned down **Sons and Lovers* (1913) with the qualified support of Walter *de la Mare, then their reader. They published a wide variety of other fiction including works by E. F. *Benson, William *De Morgan, Flora Annie *Steel, Mrs Henry *Dudeney, Ethel *Voynich, and Israel *Zangwill. Of German family and partly educated there, Heinemann was cosmopolitan and forward-looking: he started an 'International Library' of modern foreign fiction, represented Britain in the International Publishers' Congress in 1913, and did important work for the reform of the international copyright situation; he was also a pillar of the Publishers' Association. Methuen & Co., founded in 1889 by Sir Algernon Methuen (né Stedman, 1856–1924), a former schoolmaster, published several bestsellers by 'Marie *Corelli'. They also published Arnold Bennett after he left Chatto & Windus, several of *Conrad's novels including **Chance* (1913), the bestselling *The *Garden of Allah* (1904) by Robert *Hichens, and several late works of Henry *James including *The *Ambassadors* (1903) and *The *Golden Bowl* (1904). Methuen's 'Library of Fiction', founded in 1899, was a sixpenny series of paperbacks of new novels. E. V. *Lucas was a reader for and later a director of the firm.

Far less reputable, but a very significant publisher of fiction in this period, was the firm of John Long. It was taken over by Hutchinson after the First World War, surviving as an imprint of that firm until the 1970s; regrettably, since its archives, which might have yielded much useful information about the lower end of the fiction market in the Edwardian period, presumably went up in smoke with the rest of the Hutchinson records during the bombing of Paternoster Row on the night of 29–30 December 1940. John Long published **Anna Lombard* (1901), by 'Victoria *Cross', the salacious works of 'A *Peer' and 'Lady X', and several steamy novels by Gertie de S. Wentworth-James, 'Lucas *Cleeve', 'Florence *Warden', and Mrs Stanley *Wrench, as well as *The *Yoke* (1907) by 'Hubert *Wales', which the firm was prosecuted for selling. At the same time John Long published perfectly respectable books by Victor L. *Whitechurch, 'Austin *Clare', Lady Helen *Forbes, and other novelists. Nor were they the only dealers in sex novels; similar work was published by other firms such as Greening & Co., Everett & Co., Digby, Long & Co., and A. M. Gardner.

Of the other firms mentioned by Lawrence, some did publish fiction. His *The *Trespasser* (1912), *Sons and Lovers* (1913), and *The *Prussian Officer* (1914) were published by Duckworth, the firm founded in 1898 by Gerald Duckworth (1871–1934), half-brother of Virginia Woolf (1882–1941). He also published the exceedingly popular novels of Elinor *Glyn, and employed the distinguished critic Edward Garnett (1868–1937) as reader from 1901 to 1920. Duckworth published many plays, including *Galsworthy's (though his fiction was published by Heinemann). Martin Secker (1882–1978) founded his firm in 1910, and published several of the works of the new young novelists fashionable just before the First World War: Hugh *Walpole's *The *Duchess of Wrexe* and *Fortitude*, Gilbert Cannan's **Round the Corner*, Compton *Mackenzie's **Carnival* and **Sinister Street* (1913–14), and Oliver Onions's **Widdershins* (1911). He also published the highbrow but unsuccessful periodicals **Rhythm* and the **Blue Review*. During the First World War he was briefly joined as a partner by Rafael *Sabatini, some of whose fiction he also published. In 1920 he succeeded in his ambition of becoming Lawrence's publisher. The firm founded in 1888 by J. M. Dent (1849–1926) is most famous for its 'Everyman Library' series of shilling reprints of great literature, edited by Ernest *Rhys; its self-improving ethos was important to autodidacts including the young D. H. Lawrence. The 'Wayfarers' Library', founded in 1913, was the equivalent for modern literature. But except that Dent published a few of Conrad's works and employed Frank *Swinnerton, it did not have much impact on modern fiction. Macmillan & Co. had been founded in Cambridge in 1850; by the twentieth century it was a large London general publisher and still a family business, run by Frederick Macmillan. He published *Kipling, Maurice *Hewlett, and many but not all of the novels of H. G. *Wells. 'I think you're out of touch with the contemporary movement in literature . . . On the other hand, you are solid and sound and sane,' wrote Wells.

New, or fairly new, publishers were particularly adept at profiting from the demise of the three-decker. One notorious innovator was John Lane (1854–1925) of the Bodley Head, forever associated with the *Yellow Book*, who published *Keynotes* (1893) by 'George *Egerton and started the 'Keynotes' series of modish novels. On his own after 1894, his activities were supported by the literary advice and the capital provided by his American wife, Mrs John *Lane. Lane published the novels of the *Yellow Book*'s editor Henry *Harland, and other fiction tending towards the *fantastic and precious: for example Stephen *Reynolds's *The *Holy Mountain* (1910), *The *Chronicles of Clovis* (1911) and *The *Unbearable Bassington* (1911) by *'Saki', and **Louis Norbert* (1914) by 'Vernon *Lee'. The idea of selling avant-garde fiction in quaintly named series was taken up by Thomas Fisher Unwin (1848–1935), who had left Hodder & Stoughton to found his own firm in 1882. His paper-bound 'Pseudonym Library' launched the careers of 'John Oliver *Hobbes' and John Galsworthy (writing as 'John Sinjohn'); other series were the 'First Novel Library' and the 'Autonym Library'. Unwin was a liberal and free-trader, an opponent of the *Boer War, and sympathetic to female suffrage. He employed Edward Garnett and G. K. *Chesterton as readers. But he also published Ethel M. *Dell, whose first novel, *The *Way of an Eagle* (1912), won a prize in a competition for young writers; at one point her novels accounted for half the firm's sales. One of the most distinguished of all fiction lists of this period is that of the small and always rather precarious firm founded by Grant *Richards in 1897, which had the honour of publishing Samuel *Butler's *The *Way of All Flesh* (1903), Arthur *Machen's *The *Hill of Dreams* (1907), James *Joyce's **Dubliners* (1914), and *The *Ragged-Trousered Philanthropists* (1914) by 'Robert *Tressall'. Herbert Jenkins (d. 1923) was himself, like Richards, the author of some fiction (*Bindle*, 1916); he started his firm in 1912 and published Patrick *MacGill's **Children of the Dead End* (1914). Another new publisher with literary interests was Mrs Humphry Ward's cousin Edward Arnold (1857–1942), who founded his firm in 1890: he published many textbooks as well as fiction, and Mrs Hugh *Bell wrote both for him. He published Forrest *Reid's *The *Bracknels* (1911), J. Meade *Falkner's *The *Nebuly Coat*, Walter de la Mare's *The *Return*, M. R. *James's *Ghost Stories of an Antiquary*, and M. E. *Coleridge's *The *Lady on the Drawingroom Floor*; he also took over from Blackwood the publication of E. M. *Forster's novels from *A *Room with a View* (1908) onwards. Frank Sidgwick (d. 1939) founded Sidgwick and Jackson in 1908 with R. B. Jackson and the bibliographer R. B. McKerrow (1872–1940); his cousin A. C. *Benson was a shareholder. They published the novels of Sidgwick's sister Ethel *Sidgwick, E. M. Forster's *The *Celestial Omnibus* (1911), and J. D. *Beresford's *The *Early History of Jacob Stahl* (1911). They also had a very distinguished poetry list, including works by John *Masefield and the bestselling poems of Rupert Brooke (1887–1915), and published a feminist magazine, the *Englishwoman*.

Of course, by no means all new publishers were markedly highbrow. The firm of Mills & Boon was founded in 1908, and did not begin to concentrate exclusively on romance until the 1930s. In the Edwardian period it had a general list, publishing Hugh *Walpole's **Mr Perrin and Mr Traill* (1911) and Constance *Holme's first two novels, as well as writers like May *Wynne and Sophie *Cole, who fit in better with its current image. Hutchinson & Co. (founded 1887) were expanding quickly at this date, and published much fiction as well as the *Lady's Realm* and works of popular reference which came out in parts. Mrs *Belloc Lowndes was one of their authors, as were '*Rita', G. B. *Stern, and W. B. *Maxwell. In 1904 they took over Hurst & Blackett (founded 1853), one of several firms which had made a good thing out of the three-decker but were floundering slightly in the new age: Charles *Marriott's **Subsoil* (1913) and William *Le Queux's **Spies of the Kaiser* (1909) appeared under the Hurst & Blackett imprint. One of their best salesmen was Stanley Paul, who left in 1906 to found his own firm, which became a subsidiary of Hutchinson in 1928. During his independent period he started a 'Sixpenny Novels' series and also a Votes for Women series (he published suffragist novels by both Annesley *Kenealy and 'G. *Colmore'). The firm of Archibald Constable was new, though it bore an old name, having been founded in London in 1890 by a descendant of the famous Scots publishers; by the twentieth century one of the partners was George *Meredith's son W. M. Meredith (1865–1937), who acted as his father's agent and brought the firm his father's books from 1895; from 1912 Michael Sadleir (1888–1957), the great expert on Victorian fiction, worked there. Constable published several works by George *Gissing, May *Sinclair, and Walter de la Mare. One of their literary advisers, J. M. Eveleigh Nash (1873–1956), left to start his own business in 1902 and *Nash's Magazine* in 1909. He discovered Algernon *Blackwood and published several early works of Hilaire *Belloc.

Among longer-established firms still powerful in the fiction market the great Victorian firm of Smith, Elder & Co. were prominent. Their chairman Reginald Smith (1857–1916) loyally supported Mrs Humphry Ward when she was no longer a bestseller. Several of the other novelists they published also appealed, by the twentieth century, to old-fashioned, romantic and/or conservative tastes: 'F. *Anstey', 'Henry Seton *Merriman', '*Elizabeth', A. E. W. *Mason, Frances Hodgson *Burnett, Henry *Newbolt, Stanley J. *Weyman, the sisters *Findlater. Chapman & Hall (founded 1830) had also lost by this date some of the lustre of the Dickens era; Oswald *Crawfurd was its chairman in the late 1890s and enlisted several new writers; he was followed more successfully by Arthur Waugh (1866–1943), managing director from 1902, and the firm published a number of popular Edwardian novelists including Desmond *Coke and 'Keble *Howard', and also five of Arnold Bennett's works 1907–10. Cassell & Co. (founded 1848), a large business which ran many periodicals including *Cassell's Magazine*, began the period in decline under the management of Sir T. Wemyss Reid (1842–1905), who gave Mrs Henry *Dudeney her start; its revival under Sir W. Newman Flower (1879–1964, author of the novel *Red Harvest*, 1913), began from 1913. Cassell's Edwardian fiction includes G. K. *Chesterton's *The Innocence of Father Brown* (1911) and *The Wisdom of Father Brown* (1914) and works by H. Rider *Haggard and Baroness *Orczy. Chatto & Windus (founded 1873) published eleven volumes of Arnold Bennett's fiction between 1902 and 1907, and Fr. *Rolfe's **Hadrian the Seventh* (1904); it also ran a series of cheap paperback novels printed in double columns. Ward, Lock, & Bowden (founded 1854) were a large publisher of fiction with important branches in Australia and North America; they published the *Windsor Magazine*, a vehicle for popular fiction, and also works by Edgar *Wallace, H. Rider Haggard, E. Phillips *Oppenheim, and Guy *Boothby. Hodder & Stoughton (founded 1868) had early on specialized in Nonconformist theology; Sir William Robertson Nicoll (1851–1923), editor of the *British Weekly* and the **Bookman* and a powerful figure in the firm and in British literary life from the 1880s, oversaw the firm's move into magazine and fiction publishing. They published A. Conan Doyle's **Red Eve* (1911); and Harold *Begbie's *Broken Earthenware* (1909) was one of their bestsellers. Since the death of John Murray III (1808–92) his firm (founded 1768) had relaxed his rule of not publishing fiction; by 1900 fiction was the largest section on its list, and its imprint is on both Horace Annesley *Vachell's sentimental bestseller *The *Hill* (1905), Conan Doyle's *The *Adventures of Brigadier Gerard* (1903), and E. Lacon *Watson's *Barker's* (1910), one of the few novels of the period set in a publisher's office. The even older firm of Longman, Green & Co. (founded 1724), which had branches in New York and Bombay, were advised by Andrew *Lang, and published Winston Spencer *Churchill's **Savrola* (1900).

The above were all based in London. Of fiction publishers elsewhere in Britain the more important firms were Scots. The **Bookman* noted in 1911 that 'Messrs. Blackwood seem to have rather specialized in the novel of

Anglo-Indian life'. The Edinburgh firm published the reactionary *A Derelict Empire* (1912) by 'Mark *Time', the works of 'Sydney Carlyon *Grier' and Maud *Diver, as well as Hugh *Clifford and Miles *Franklin, who wrote about other parts of the *Empire. They also published, unsurprisingly, the works of Scots writers, including some by John *Buchan, Neil *Munro, and 'Ian *Hay'; and they published E. M. Forster's first two novels. Thomas Nelson & Sons (founded 1858), also of Edinburgh, mass publishers of fiction with an international business, employed Buchan as a literary adviser from 1906 and they published his **Prester John* (1910). They also published H. G. Wells's *The Country of the Blind and Other Stories* (1911), Hilaire Belloc's *The *Girondin*, and G. K. Chesterton's **Manalive* (1912). In 1908 they attempted to transform the fiction market with a cheap series of hardback novels at *7d.* each, a project made possible by new machinery; they were defeated by an alliance of the Society of Authors and the Publishers' Association, who united in defence of the *6s.* novel and prevented Nelson's including any fiction less than two years old. Adam & Charles Black (founded 1807) which had deserted Edinburgh for London as recently as 1891, were the publishers of the *Survey of London* undertaken by Walter *Besant with the help of G. E. *Mitton; they published some fiction including works by Douglas *Sladen, first editor of their *Who's Who*, with an emphasis on children's books, including P. G. *Wodehouse's early school stories. William Collins and Sons, a Glasgow firm, were also moving into children's fiction, and employed Herbert *Hayens to enlarge their list, which came to include Geo. Manville *Fenn and Bessie *Marchant. In provincial England the Bristol firm of J. W. Arrowsmith should be mentioned; it grew out of a printing business run by James Williams Arrowsmith (d. 1913), who depended on his own tastes and had a knack of picking bestsellers: he published *The Prisoner of Zenda* (1894) by 'Anthony *Hope', Jerome K. *Jerome's *Three Men in a Boat* (1889), and G. K. Chesterton's *The *Man Who Was Thursday* (1908). A few American publishers had London branches. G. P. Putnam's Sons, for instance, was a New York firm which had maintained a London office from at least 1883; from 1906 it was run by Constant Huntington, whose first big success was Florence L. *Barclay's *The *Rosary* (1909). The Open Court, which Lawrence mentions, was the English arm of a Chicago publisher. But these were unusual cases.

Between the fall of the three-decker and the outbreak of the First World War were twenty years in which fiction was perhaps the most important sector of the leisure industry. With the war came paper shortage which damaged many businesses, and war news, which occupied the literary pages of periodicals. Afterwards the films and the radio challenged the popular novel more and more for the attention of the public. Just as the themes and assumptions of the pre-war novel seemed infinitely old hat in 1920, so the circumstances of its circulation were never quite the same again.

Puck of Pook's Hill, Rudyard *Kipling, 1906, Macmillan. This children's book is among the clearest statements of Kipling's understanding of his English heritage. Dan and Una live in the Sussex weald and are already intimately familiar with its fields and woods and streams, having learned their wood and nature craft from local countrymen such as Hobden the hedger. Their knowledge of English history, though, is limited to a few school facts until one day, performing their own outdoor version of *A Midsummer Night's Dream*, on 'a large old fairy Ring of darkened grass', they summon up Puck, 'the oldest Old Thing in England'. 'I came into England with Oak, Ash and Thorn, and when Oak, Ash and Thorn are gone I shall go too.' The children 'take seizin' from Puck (clods of earth cut from the magic circle) and are thus enabled to take rightful possession of 'all Old England'—'You shall see What you shall see and you shall hear What you shall hear, though it shall have happened these thousand year...' A variety of characters come forth to tell their stories, most notably a centurion of the 30th Legion; Sir Richard Dalyngridge, a Norman knight; and Kadmiel, a Jewish physician from the reign of King John. The children do not just listen; they interrupt and interpret and question. This is not simply a dramatized history lesson: it is Kipling's attempt to integrate a sense of landscape with an understanding of the human forces that shaped it, to display the continuity and importance of the English language (with Shakespeare at its heart), and to suggest that Englishness was embedded here even before the English arrived.

PUGH, Edwin [William] (1874–1930) married —. He was born in St Marylebone, London. His mother was a wardrobe mistress at Covent Garden, while his father played in the orchestra. He was educated at a board school before going to work at 13 in an iron factory; later he worked in a solicitor's office. Pugh experienced the low life of London first-hand, later distilling his observations into fictional form. Heinemann published *A Street in Suburbia* in 1895; *A Man of Straw* followed in 1896. The joint success of these two books led Pugh to devote himself full-time to his writing. *The Fruits of the Vine* (1904), like *The Heritage* (1901), written with Godfrey Burchett, is about alcoholism. The hero, Gideon Bolsover, dictates his autobiography to a friend and collaborator. Born in the gutter, with a hereditary tendency to alcoholism, Bolsover was nurtured by a devout mother. He describes his miserable experiences at school and in employment, his subsequent success as a writer, and his love affairs with a giddy woman of the world and a working-class girl. Unable to resist the force of heredity, he goes into a decline, but eventually wins through. *The Broken Honeymoon* (1908) is another late example of English 'naturalism'. It describes the unhappy marriage of a solicitor's clerk and a schoolmistress: their honeymoon at a cheap watering-place, their interminable quarrels. But Pugh also published novels in a lighter vein. *The Purple Head* (1905) is a sensational mystery set in south-west England; it has a lovable heroine, a Quasimodo-like villain with a memorable mother, and a detective called Sprottle. *The Proof of the Pudding* (1913) features Miss Creamwise, an impostor called Wease, and the sinister Captain Stiffidge, who meets a picturesque end. Pugh also wrote several books about London; these include *The City of a World: A Book about London and the Londoner* (1912), and *The Cockney At Home: Stories and Studies of London Life and Character*. Pugh was a great admirer of Dickens and published *Charles Dickens: The Apostle of the People* (1908). A volume of essays entitled *Slings and Arrows* appeared in 1917. Pugh found himself sadly out of step with the atmosphere of the Edwardian era; he did not regain the brief success that he had during the 1890s, applying to the Royal Literary Fund four times between 1902 and 1916. In 1914 he was supporting his mother and a sister deserted by her husband. 'He has not been one of those people who give themselves airs,' wrote Arthur Waugh (1866–1943) 'and consider that some forms of hack-work are beneath their dignity.' 'His was a unique experience, and he wrote of it with a unique pen,' recalled W. E. Henley (1849–1903). He was one of several writers who found to their cost that the vogue for fiction about lower-middle-class life was short-lived. His autobiography, *The World Is My Oyster*, was published in 1924.

Purple Cloud, The, M. P. *Shiel, 1901, Chatto & Windus. This vivid, futuristic tale of the destruction of the world by a gigantic poison-cloud takes the form of a notebook sent to the author by an old friend, Dr Arthur Lister Browne, who realizes that he is about to die. One of Browne's patients, Miss Mary Wilson, is a time-traveller, and dictates under hypnosis the contents of a journal kept, twenty-five years in the future, by another doctor, Adam Jeffson. An American multi-millionaire and 'king of faddists', Charles P. Stickney, has bequeathed 175 million dollars to the first man to reach the North Pole. A ship, the *Boreal*, is equipped for the purpose, and Jeffson's Lucrezia Borgia-like fiancée, the Countess Clodagh, obtains for him the post of medical officer by poisoning the present incumbent. 'Be first—for Me,' she murmurs. Getting into the spirit of things, Jeffson murders two further members of the expedition and steals a march on the rest. Arriving at the Pole, he discovers a pillar of ice surrounded by a mysteriously fluctuating lake which seems to him 'the substance of a living creature'. Returning, after many adventures, to the *Boreal*, he finds it a ghost-ship, the crew all dead or missing. Sailing south, he encounters trawlers, then liners, each a graveyard. In fact, the world is a graveyard. He spends the next few months travelling the length and breadth of Britain, searching without success for survivors. He is a Robinson Crusoe cast away on a global desert island. After seventeen years he at last finds, in the ruins of Constantinople, a mate: a young woman who was little more than a baby, and captive in an airtight cellar, when the poison-cloud passed over. After coyness on an epic scale, they marry, and embark on the arduous task of repopulating the world. The novel works rather well, because it combines primal *fantasies—not only the Crusoe-esque rebuilding of civilization, but a vision of innocent sexuality comparable to H. de Vere *Stacpoole's *The *Blue Lagoon* (1908)—with a meticulous interest in the day-to-day business of survival.

Q

Q, *pseud.*: Arthur Thomas QUILLER-COUCH (1863–1944), Kt. (1910), married (1889) Louisa Amelia HICKS (d. 1948). Born in Bodmin, Cornwall, the son of a doctor, he was educated at Newton Abbot College, Clifton College, Bristol, and Trinity College, Oxford, where he was a classical scholar. For one year (1886–7) he stayed on as a lecturer in classics; then he left for London and a career as a journalist until 1892. He was associated with the Liberal weekly the *Speaker* from its foundation in 1890 until 1899, but after a breakdown he went to live permanently in 1892 at Fowey in Cornwall, the seaside town which, as 'Troy', figured largely in his fiction from *The Astonishing History of Troy Town* (1888) onwards. There he earned his living partly by editing anthologies, of which the most important is *The Oxford Book of English Verse* (1900), which sold half a million copies in his lifetime and, with its avowed preference for the lyrical over the epigrammatic, shaped the view of English literature for at least two generations of readers. Partly because of his services to Liberalism as a journalist and in Cornwall, he was appointed King Edward VII Professor of English Literature in the University of Cambridge in 1912; by 1917 he had succeeded in establishing an independent honours school of English literature in the university. His fiction is always nostalgic and often historical romance. His first novel was *Dead Man's Rock* (1887); other fiction includes *Hetty Wesley* (1903), dedicated to Andrew *Lang, which is about the founders of Methodism, drawing largely on their family letters; *Shining Ferry* (1905), a saga of a Cornish banking family; *The *Mayor of Troy* (1906); *True Tilda* (1909), another Fowey idyll; and *In Powder and Crinoline: Old Fairy Tales Retold* (1913).

Queen's Quair, The, or, *The Six Years' Tragedy*, Maurice *Hewlett, 1904, Macmillan. The novel opens with the 19-year-old Mary Stuart, a widow of two months and still living in France. Reminded by her brother, Lord James Stuart, that she is Queen of Scotland, she arrives to find her kingdom a hotbed of intrigue. Duels and clan brawls erupt around her. The characters are appropriately larger than life: the florid Earl of Bothwell, his handsome page, Jean-Marie-Baptiste Des-Essars, Mary's true love and author of a book of revealing memoirs, John Knox of the 'flinty-edged brain', and a supporting cast of vivid ladies-in-waiting. Hewlett's manner—'At that hour, I know, her thought was piercingly of France, and the sun, and the peasant girls laughing to each other half across the breezy fields'—narrowly avoids jauntiness. A 'quair' is a *cahier*, a quire, a little book: the title indicates that the narrative will unfold the Queen's intimate experiences. 'What others have guessed at, building surmise upon surmise, she knew; for what they did, she suffered.'

Queer Lady Judas, '*Rita', 1905, Hutchinson. 'This is a book OF WOMEN, FOR WOMEN, BY A WOMAN. They may hate it for its truth, but each and all in their "looking glass" hours will acknowledge that it is true. For his own sake and for sake of some cherished illusions, no "mere man" should be bold enough to read it.' Cécile de Marsac, English widow of a Parisian *roué*, arrives in London to establish herself, under the name of Madame Beaudelet, as a beautician and *masseuse*. Her first client, the spectacularly ugly Lady Judith Vanderbyl, turns out to be Lady Judas, famous *modiste*. Lady Judith provides Cécile with the necessary capital and facilities to expand her business. She has, however, an ulterior motive. The beautiful Countess of Ripley, the ultimate 'sex exponent', has driven Lady Judith's son Bernard to his death, and she wants revenge. She proposes that Cécile should disfigure the Countess with an acidic lotion prepared by her. Cécile refuses. Lady Judith drops her, but promptly falls sick, and has to undergo major surgery. Cécile rushes to her side. After a final apocalyptic public lecture to her ex-clients, in which she demonstrates the futility of the beautician's art, she becomes Lady Judith's permanent companion. Meanwhile, the Countess of Ripley has been to Paris for a miracle face-lift which will restore her beauty temporarily, at the cost of long-term damage. There is a sub-plot concerning a chemist's daughter addicted to morphia. *Queer Lady Judas* is the liveliest of this author's social satires, by virtue of the narrative and metaphorical opportunities which the role of beautician provides.

QUILLER-COUCH, Mabel was the sister of '*Q' and published children's fiction and non-fiction, much of which was set in her native Cornwall: it includes *The Carroll Girls, or, How the Sisters Helped* (1906), *Kitty Trenire* (1909), and *On Windy-cross Moor* (1910).

RAFFALOVICH, George (b. 1880) studied at the university of Nancy, and was naturalized a British subject in 1910. He was author of *The Deuce and All* (1910), a collection of twelve *fantastic tales, *The History of a Soul* (1911), and other fiction and non-fiction, some in French. His collection *The Deuce and All* (1910) is prefaced by an essay 'The Essence of Short Story', which argues that it is an exercise in symphonic form, and includes 'Drones', a stilted tale of conflict between a young man of bourgeois family and an emancipated woman. *Planetary Journeys* (1908) mostly consists of affected parables: 'The Dream of a French Capitalist' is an ironic tale of a bourgeois who has a momentary urge to philanthropy. Some of Raffalovich's work was published by Aleister Crowley (1875–1947), whose magazine the *Equinox* (1909–13) he is supposed to have helped to finance. He was member of a family of rich Russian Jewish bankers, resident in Paris, other members of which also wrote. His cousin Sophie Raffalovich (1860–1960), who married in 1890 the Irish Nationalist William O'Brien (1852–1928), published, as Mrs William O'Brien, fiction including *Rosette* (1907), the story of a governess who becomes a Catholic and then a nun. Her brother Marc-André Raffalovich (1864–1934), lover of the poet John Gray (1866–1934), was author of *A Willing Exile* (1890), a satire on the Wilde circle.

Ragged-Trousered Philanthropists, The: *Being the Story of Twelve Months in Hell, Told by One of the Damned* 'Robert *Tressall', 1914, Grant Richards. A novel of working-class life from a socialist point of view. The hero, Frank Owen, works for an exploitative decorating firm, Rushton & Co., in Brighton. The first twenty-six chapters describe in intricate detail the refurbishment and decoration of a house belonging to the local capitalist, Mr Sweater. The men are driven ferociously by the foreman, Hunter, whose only concern is profit; they live in constant fear of dismissal. Hunter is driven in turn by Rushton, who is driven by the pressures of competition. The result is a skimped and botched job, and an atmosphere of intimidation and mutual suspicion. The solutions proposed by 'Tressall' are class solidarity and socialist policies. Political allegiance will provide a more solid basis for individual identity, combating the fear, and the sense of worthlessness, induced by sweating. Frank Owen, the main character and the author's spokesman, is so engrossed in socialism that he has no time to dwell on his family's poverty. But most of his workmates find allegiance hard work. Their anxiety is deep-rooted enough, palpable enough, to make one doubt the ability of political allegiance to reform people or societies. Owen tries to explain to them that the workers are the subjects rather than the objects of philanthropy; their labour costs employers so little that it might almost be said to represent a donation to an unworthy cause. But they remain sceptical. Owen, a highly skilled decorator, agrees to decorate a drawing-room in the house in 'Moorish' style, even though the preparatory work will have to be done in his own time, with little prospect of financial reward. His 'intense desire' to do the job is fuelled by fear that it may at any moment be abandoned. The wholly private satisfaction he derives from it does as much as his commitment to socialism to create, or confirm, an identity; it gives him a status apart from his workmates. Of course, the pleasure of manual labour conscientiously performed was an article of faith with many British socialists, notably William Morris (1834–1896). But the vivid description of everyday driving and skimping make it seem like a fantasy verging on narcissism. 'Tressall' meant every last didactic word of his book, but also insisted that it was 'not a treatise or essay, but a novel'. He used the form of the novel to dramatize the unnecessary and destructive anxiety at the heart of working-class experience before the establishment of trade unions and the welfare state. Although his focus is on the group of decorators, he provided an incisive portrait of a corrupt and complacent provincial town.

Railway Children, The, E. *Nesbit, 1906, Wells Gardner. This story was originally serialized in the *London Magazine* in 1905. Roberta, Peter, and Phyllis live with their perfect parents and their dog, James. Peter's toy engine explodes. Their father disappears without explanation, and the rest of the family retires to the country, and relatively impoverished circumstances. They learn to love trains. Every morning they wave to an elderly gentleman on the Green Dragon, whose destination is the city where they think their father must be. When their mother falls sick, they ask their friend to buy medicine, on the understanding that Peter will pay him back when he grows up. The man leaves a hamper full of food and medicine, and an obliging note (much to the distress of their mother). Various railway adventures ensue, including the prevention of a serious accident and the discovery of an exiled Russian writer. They ask their elderly friend, who has at least heard of the writer, to help them find his family, which he does. They also ask him to prove the innocence of their father, who, it turns out, has been imprisoned for selling secrets to the Russians. They in their turn rescue an injured schoolboy who is their friend's grandson. In gratitude, he persuades all the passengers to wave to the children as the train passes through the station. Their father returns home.

RAINE, Allen, *pseud.*: Anne Adaliza EVANS (1836–1908) married (1872) Beynon PUDDICOMBE (d. 1906). A solicitor's daughter, she was born at Newcastle Emlyn, Cardiganshire, and could speak Welsh. She was educated privately by a Unitarian minister in Cheltenham, and at school in Southfields, near Wimbledon. In her youth she met both Charles Dickens (1812–70) and 'George Eliot' (1819–80). Her husband worked in a bank in the City of London, and after her marriage she lived first near Croydon, then at Winchmore Hill until 1900, returning to Wales only for summer holidays; her writing seems to have been a reaction to this move from Wales. She won a prize at the National Eisteddfod of 1894 with one of her short stories. In 1897 she published *A Welsh Singer*. Other titles include *Garthowen: A Story of a Welsh Homestead* (1900), *A Welsh Witch* (1902), *Hearts of Wales: An Old Romance* (1905), *Queen of the Rushes: A Tale of the Welsh Revival* (1905), and *Where Billows Roll: A Tale of the Welsh Coast* (1909). In 1900 her husband retired owing to mental illness, and they returned to Cardiganshire. In *All in a Month* (1908) she used her experience of her husband's madness; in the posthumously published *Under the Thatch* (1910) that of the cancer which killed her. Daniel Lleufer Thomas in the *Dictionary of National Biography* states that her total sales outside America were more than two million copies; he writes disapprovingly of the 'prim simple and even child-like dialogue of characters in such faulty English as the uncritical might assume Cardiganshire fishermen to speak'. Ernest *Rhys was another who criticized her picture of Welsh life.

RALLI, Constantine: Constantine SCARAMANGA-RALLI (1854–1934) married Julia Townsend BURNETT née LAWRENCE. He was born in London; both his parents were members of a rich family of Greek origin, bankers specializing in the Indian trade. He was educated at Harrow School and Brasenose College, Oxford, and became a banker. He lived in Hampshire, was a Justice of the Peace, Vice-President of the Allotments and Small Holdings Association, a Liberal, an enthusiast for compulsory military service, and the author of five novels 1904–11, including *Vanessa: A Romance of the New Century and the New World* (1904), which is set in New York in a future when three millionaires control everything, until the populace rises against them, and *The Strange Story of Falconer Thring* (1907), a story of bigamy and murder, interspersed with violent battle scenes in South Africa.

RAMSAY, Rina. Her seven novels 1897–1926 are romances with frequent hunting interludes. In *The Key of the Door* (1908), General Rankin, the popular hero of African campaigns, returns home to be confronted by a woman claiming to be his wife. *The Straw* (1909) is about a marriage which has turned sour, and features by way of comic relief two ingenuous experimental farmers known as 'the Babes'.

RAMSEY, Olivia published nine novels 1909–14. *Two Men and a Governess* (1912) is a comic variant of *Ruritanian romance: a governess taking up a position in the cathedral town of Abbotsfordum has the choice of becoming the Countess of Glenderwent or mistress of the King of Salvia, a Balkan state.

RANDAL, John published four novels, all in this period, of which *Aunt Bethia's Button* (1903), an 'extravaganza of modern life', turns on the fate of the family jewels, and is gently satirical of clerical and upper-class society. *Sweetest Solace* (1906) is set in the cathedral town of Whilborough, where the two Misses Francis from Australia settle as schoolmistresses, and vastly improve themselves through marriage.

RAWSON, Maud Stepney: Alice Maud FIFE married William Stepney RAWSON (d. 1932). Daughter of a general in the army, she married a scientist and amateur musician; her *Labourer's Comedy* (1965) is about the predicament of a married woman forced to earn her living as a journalist, and is supposed to have been based on personal experience. She was the author of eighteen novels, mostly *historical romances, between 1900–25, including *A Lady of the Regency* (1901), whose heroine is a neglected young girl who falls in love at the time of the Queen Caroline affair, and *Journeyman Love* (1902), a tale of a young man's sentimental education, set in early nineteenth-century Paris, contrasting mercantile and artistic values, written in an awkward, pretentious style. She also published *Bess of Hardwick and Her Circle* (1910) and *Penelope Rich and Her Circle* (1911).

RAYMOND, Walter (1852–1931) married (1878) Mary Elizabeth JOHNSTON. He was educated privately, ran a glove-making business, and lived in Taunton. Ernest *Rhys commented that 'when he sat by the fire [he]... turned himself into an old Wessex farmer with round, humorous face and voice to match.... In his writing... he was rarely as good as in his oral tale-telling. One misses the voice and the touches that give life to a story.... His struggle to provide for his family by his pen intrigued us the more because his struggle was so like ours.' He wrote West Country idylls, including *Fortune's Darling* (1901), *Good Souls of Cider-Land* (1901), *The Revenues of the Wicked* (1911), a *historical romance set in the early nineteenth century, about the love of a lawyer's clerk for a farmer's daughter, and books about crafts and local studies such as *Somerset and Her Folk Movement* (1921) and *Under the Spreading Chestnut Tree: A Volume of Rural Lore and Anecdote* (1928). He also wrote as 'Tom Cobbleigh'.

Rebel Women, Evelyn *Sharp, 1910, A. C. Fifield. Stories and sketches, many told in the first person, about the suffrage movement. The cover shows a prison gate burst open, with the book's title on a banner unfurled above it. Several sketches have to do with everyday political activism: 'Filling the War Chest', 'At a Street Corner', 'The Crank of All the Ages', 'Patrolling the Gutter', 'The Black Spot of the Constituency', 'Votes for Women—Forward!' Others describe acts of defiance and protest, either in public ('The Women at the Gate', 'To the Prison While the Sun Shines', 'Shaking Hands with the Middle Ages'), or in private ('The Conversion of Penelope's Mother', 'The Person Who Cannot Escape', 'The Daughter Who Stays at Home'). The heroine of the final story, 'The Game that Wasn't Cricket', is allowed to take part in a game of slum cricket, and triumphantly breaks the rules.

Red Eve, H. Rider *Haggard, 1911, Hodder & Stoughton. It is 1346. In Cathay, Murgh, the harbinger of death, has been spreading pestilence among the 'hundreds of millions of cold-faced yellow men'. In Dunwich, on the Suffolk coast, Hugh de Cressi meets his cousin Eve Clavering at a rendezvous in the marshes. The two families, one representing trade, the other the landed interest, have long been engaged in a bitter feud. Now Eve is to be married to Sir Edmund Acour, Count of Noyon, Seigneur of Cattrina. They plan to elope, accompanied by Hugh's faithful retainer, Grey Dick, a fabulously skilled archer. However, they are intercepted by the Claverings, and Hugh kills Eve's brother John, in a fair fight. They take refuge with Father Andrew Arnold, who reveals that Acour is a French spy, and tells them of a vision of death received during a visit to Murgh's temple in Cathay. Hugh and Dick ride off to inform King Edward. Meanwhile, Eve is lured from sanctuary and married to Acour while in a drugged stupor. Acour escapes to France. Hugh pursues him across the battlefield of Crécy to Venice, where they witness the arrival of Murgh's galley, bearing the Black Death, to Avignon, and then to a final encounter in Dunwich which fulfils Father Andrew's vision. Hugh and Eve are reunited. The novel embeds modern anxieties about the *invasion of England and the Yellow Peril in a characteristically rapid and violent *historical romance.

Red House, The, E. *Nesbit, 1902, Methuen. Newly-weds Len and Chloe inherit a house in the country and £200 a year from Chloe's uncle James. Interior decoration takes up a good deal of their time. One night they hear what sounds like blood dripping and think it is a ghost (the roof leaks). Then the ghost finishes a story Len is writing, and does it much better than he ever could. They think it must be their friend Yolande. They rent one of their cottages to Mr Prosser, but he is no gardener and leaves dirty washing draped everywhere. Yolande finds them a new tenant, and persuades their original London servant, Mary, to return to them, with her new husband. During a party, Yolande turns up with a strange man, both of them dripping blood. The blood is the red paint she put out to trap a thief. The stranger is the new tenant. Len's stories continue to be finished on time, without his help, as are Chloe's drawings. The children of the Bastable family (from Nesbit's earlier novels) ask to be allowed to explore the grounds, and their presence makes Chloe want a child of her own. Yolande marries the new tenant. Len and Chloe have a child. It turns out that they have been finishing each other's work.

Red Thumb Mark, The, R. Austin *Freeman, 1907, Collingwood. The arrival on the scene of the only convincing scientific investigator in early *crime fiction. The achievements of handsome, impassive Dr John Evelyn Thorndyke, medical jurist of King's Bench Walk, London, are described by his admiring friend and companion, Christopher Jervis, MD. Reuben Hornby, clerk to a dealer in precious metals, is accused of stealing a packet of diamonds from his employer's safe, the main evidence being his thumb print in blood on a piece of paper found inside the safe. Juliet Gibson, a friend of Hornby who believes passionately in his innocence, throws suspicion in the direction of his brother, Walter, also an employee of the firm. The bulk of the story is concerned with a series of fiendishly cunning assassination attempts on Thorndyke which include a bullet with a hypodermic needle inside and a poisoned cigar. Surviving these, he has no difficulty in proving that the thumb print is a forgery, and Walter the likely culprit. Reuben is exonerated, and Jervis proposes to Juliet Gibson. In a preface, Freeman claimed that he had written the story to draw attention to 'certain popular misapprehensions on the subject of finger-prints and their evidential value'.

REEVES, Amber (1887–1981) married (1909) George Rivers BLANCO WHITE (1883–1966). She was the daughter of William Pember Reeves (1857–1932), poet, Agent-General for New Zealand in London, and later first Director of the London School of Economics; her mother was a member of the Fabian Women's Group. Reeves was educated at Kensington High School and Newnham College, Cambridge, where she gained a first class degree in moral sciences, and at the London School of Economics. Her affair with H. G. *Wells caused a great scandal in progressive circles in 1909, and was a source for his novel **Ann Veronica* (dedicated to their child, Anna Jane, born in December 1909). Pregnant with his daughter, she married a barrister, but for some time continued to see Wells. There is an extensive discussion of the brouhaha and its effect on the Fabian Society, and on Wells's psychology, in Anthony West, *H. G. Wells* (1984). Reeves worked in the Civil Service during the First World War, an experience evoked in her novel *Give and Take* (1923). After the war she lectured at Morley College and elsewhere. Her publications include effective *feminist novels such as *A *Lady and Her Husband* (1914) and *Helen in Love* (1916), non-fiction on ethics and banking, *Worry in Women* (1941), and contributions to the *Dictionary of National Biography*.

Reflections of Ambrosine, The, Elinor *Glyn, 1902, Gerald Duckworth. Blue-blooded Ambrosine Athelstan has been brought up in haughty impoverishment by her grandmother. Their landlord is a wealthy and amiable young man called Augustus Gurrage (the contrast between surnames says it all), who reveals his essential vulgarity by using phrases like 'snug little crib' and 'beastly hard luck'. Realizing that she does not have long to live, the grandmother instructs Ambrosine to accept Augustus's proposal of marriage. The couple do the round of country houses, where Ambrosine is further humiliated by her husband's coarseness and appalled by the routine promiscuity. Augustus takes to drink and a mistress, Lady Grenellen. Ambrosine, Augustus, and Lady Grenellen are due to visit the immensely handsome and well-bred Sir Anthony Thornhirst, with whom Ambrosine is in love. A fog delays the others, and Ambrosine is left unattended to resist her desire for Sir Anthony

(Lady Grenellen, elsewhere, presumably does no such thing). Augustus enlists for the *Boer War, and dies in a typically vulgar way, from measles, thus freeing Ambrosine to marry Sir Anthony. One final (minor) complication involves Sir Anthony's ex-lover, Lady Tilchester, by whom he has had a child. Sir Anthony is the archetypal Glyn hero: rich, elegant, cultured, brave, a fine shot, a good man to hounds, and very conspicuously idle. It is the unspeakable Augustus, one might note, who fights for his country.

Regent, The: *A Five Towns Story of Adventure in London*, Arnold *Bennett, 1913, Methuen. Edward Henry Machin, the hero of *The *Card*, now 43 long married, and balding, still lives in Bursley in a house equipped with all the latest gadgets. He is bored. When he is offered the chance to buy into a new music-hall venture in London, he leaps at the chance. Episodes in posh London hotels ensue (he has trouble with artichokes). Soon he is in control of the enterprise, and a new theatre rises from the ground just off Piccadilly. Meanwhile he falls in with the beautiful Elsie April, doyenne of the Azure Society, to which the 'spiritual aristocracy' of London all belong. Attending an intellectual verse drama, *The Orient Pearl*, by Carlo Trent, put on by the Society, Machin falls asleep. To cover his confusion, and ingratiate himself with Elsie, he agrees to make the play the first production at his new theatre, the Regent. His flirtation with Elsie ends with the arrival of his wife and three children from Bursley. *The Orient Pearl* does not prove a great popular success. In order to boost it, Machin sails to New York, intercepts a suffragette who is halfway through a world tour, shows her how to achieve the third arrest she requires for maximum publicity, and in return obtains her agreement to appear in his play, which is soon breaking box-office records for verse drama. Once he has made his profit, Machin rents the theatre to a musical comedy syndicate, and goes home. The stunts are entertaining (and the book itself is of course a stunt on Bennett's part), but Machin's second appearance is on the whole less incisive than his first.

Reginald, *'Saki', 1904, Methuen. These fifteen comic sketches first appeared in the *Westminster Gazette*. Reginald is a man about town whose preoccupations rise to the level of worrying whether 'an apricot tie would have gone better with the lilac waistcoat'. He gives his views on Christmas presents (no more 'George, Prince of Wales' prayer-books), writes a peace poem, stage-manages the church choir's annual outing (a Bacchanalian procession involving tin whistles), discusses the ways in which people enter restaurants, tells the story of a woman whose desire to tell the truth led her to accuse the cook of drunkenness ('The cook was a good cook, as cooks go; and as cooks go she went'). And so on. During a meditation on tariffs, Reginald proposes the export of people who 'impress on you that you ought to take life seriously': a sentiment which might serve as the book's epigraph.

regional fiction. In the 1870s and 1880s, perhaps as a reaction against the increasingly urban (and eventually suburban) lives lived by an increasing number of people, a readership emerged for stories, often nostalgic in tone, of provincial life: the west of England romances of R. D. Blackmore (1825–1900), the Wessex novels of Thomas Hardy (1840–1928), and the Edinburgh tales of Robert Louis Stevenson (1850–94). Hardy contributed enthusiastically to the commercialization, in exhibitions, guidebooks, and picture postcards, of the Wessex his novels had created. The Edwardian period saw a further development and diversification of the vogue for regional fiction; the syndication of fiction in provincial newspapers may have had some influence in promoting the trend. Writers were dividing up the map of Britain amongst themselves, declared an essay in *Literature* in 1898, each claiming a parish or two as his or her own, and threatening literary trespassers with 'all the terrors of the Society of Authors'. Among the most often-claimed areas of the country were the Channel Islands (E. Gallienne *Robin, 'John *Oxenham'), Cheshire (Mrs Leith *Adams, C. L. *Antrobus), Cornwall (Mrs Havelock *Ellis, J. Henry *Harris, Jessie Leckie *Herbertson, Joseph *Hocking, Mark Guy *Pearse, '*Q', Mabel *Quiller-Couch, Hugh *Walpole), Cumberland (William Gershom *Collingwood, Alfred *Ollivant), Devon (S. *Baring-Gould, Edith C. M. *Dart, George *Gissing, Eden *Phillpotts, Stephen *Reynolds, M. P. *Willcocks), Dorset ('Orme *Agnus', Walter *Raymond, Wilkinson *Sherren, 'John *Trevena'), the Isle of Man (Hall *Caine), Kent (Mrs A. E. *Aldington), Lancashire ('John *Ackworth', Frances Hodgson *Burnett, Ethel

*Carnie, Allen *Clarke, Allan Noble *Monkhouse), Northumberland ('Austin *Clare', R. H. *Forster, Howard *Pease, Dora *Russell), Nottinghamshire (W. Bourne *Cooke, D. H. *Lawrence, 'James *Prior'), Norfolk (James *Blyth, H. Rider *Haggard), Somerset (Walter *Raymond), Staffordshire (Rhoda *Broughton), Suffolk (M. *Betham-Edwards, Kate *Horn), Sussex (Mrs Henry *Dudeney, Maude *Goldring, Sheila *Kaye-Smith, Rudyard *Kipling, A. Neil *Lyons, Greville *MacDonald), Westmorland (Constance *Holme), and Yorkshire ('Deas *Cromarty', J. S. *Fletcher, R. Murray *Gilchrist, Algernon *Gissing, J. Keighley *Snowden). Two striking features of the English regional fiction of the period are on the one hand the tendency, evident in Alfred *Austin's **Haunts of Ancient Peace* (1902), to see the inhabitants of the rural areas of the southern counties as an epitome of the essential and enduring virtues of Englishness; and on the other hand the tendency, evident in *Gracechurch* (1913) by 'John *Ayscough' and Arthur *Morrison's **Cunning Murrell* (1900), to concentrate on a particular (small, isolated) community. But it must also be said that two of the greatest writers of the period, Arnold *Bennett and D. H. Lawrence, chose to write in far from nostalgic terms about the industrialized Midlands, about modernity. The 'Kailyard' (Scots dialect for 'cabbage-patch') school of the 1890s (J. M. *Barrie, 'Ian *Maclaren', S. R. *Crockett) had presented a predominantly whimsical view of Scottish (usually lowland) rural life, and met a spectacularly grim retort in *The *House with the Green Shutters* by 'George *Douglas' (1901) and J. MacDougall *Hay's *Gillespie* (1914). Brown detested the 'sentimental slop' of the Kailyarders. A balance was struck between the two extremes in the novels Neil *Munro published as 'Hugh Foulis'. There was no Welsh equivalent to the Kailyard and its detractors (though see S. Baring-Gould's *In Dewisland* (1904), E. P. and John *Finnemore's *From a Welsh Hillside* (1923), Joseph *Keating's **Son of Judith: A Tale of the Welsh Mining Valleys* (1901), Daisy Hugh *Pryce's *Hill Magic* (1914), Mrs Fred *Reynolds's *St. David of the Dust* (1908), romances by 'Allen *Raine' and Ernest *Rhys, and, above all, the work of Arthur *Machen). But the increasing complexity and bitterness of Irish politics in the late Victorian and Edwardian periods does seem to have encouraged a remarkable surge of literary activity, not only among the promoters of an Irish Renaissance in poetry and drama but among novelists of widely differing aims and abilities. A list of writers born or domiciled in Ireland who wrote about Irish subjects would include Deborah *Alcock, Jane *Barlow, 'George A. *Birmingham', Shan F. *Bullock, Dorothea *Conyers, Robert *Cromie, Alice *Dease, Edmund *Downey, Lord *Dunsany, Charlotte *Eccles, Stephen *Foreman, 'M. E. *Francis', Lady *Gilbert, 'Sarah *Grand', Catherine J. *Hamilton, 'M. *Hamilton', H. A. *Hinkson, S. R. *Keightley, W. Patrick *Kelly, Frederick *Langbridge, John Heron *Lepper, Winifred M. *Letts, S. R. *Lysaght, Justin H. *M'Carthy, Randall William *McDonnell, Ella *MacMahon, L. *McManus, Seamus *MacManus, Ethel Colburn *Mayne, F. Frankfort *Moore, George *Moore, Mrs H. H. *Penrose, P. A. *Sheehan, E. Œ. *Somerville and 'Martin Ross', James *Stephens, Katharine *Tynan, and, of course, James *Joyce. Overall, the increasing prestige of regional fiction, the sheer availability of different areas and localities, is indicated by the way in which 'M. E. Francis' varied the settings of her novels from the Ireland of her youth to the Lancashire of her married life and to the Dorset of her retirement. What *Literature* had termed the 'current passion for local colour' was strongly reinforced by the work of essayists such as Richard Jefferies (1848–1887), 'George Bourne' (i.e. George Sturt, 1863–1927), W. H. *Hudson, and Edward *Thomas.

REID, Forrest (1875–1947) was born in Belfast, the thirteenth and seventh surviving child of a Presbyterian middle-class family; his father had lost a fortune during the American Civil War and died when Reid was very young. At the age of 6 he was bereft of his beloved nurse; his memoirs describe his subsequent need for a feminine warmth he did not find in his mother or sisters. He was educated at the Royal Academical Institution, Belfast, and then, after a period as an apprentice in the tea trade, his mother's death enabled him to go to Christ's College, Cambridge, where he read medieval and modern languages. After graduating in 1908 he returned to Belfast to write. *The Kingdom of Twilight* (1904) had been published, during his tea-trade period, in T. Fisher Unwin's 'First Novel Library'; 'I detest this book' he later wrote, but Henry

*James sent him an encouraging letter about it. Reid dedicated *The Garden God: A Tale of Two Boys* (1905), a lyrical tale of platonic homosexual love, to James, regarding himself as his pupil, and received in return a letter 'troubled, astonished, disillusioned'. While at Cambridge he planned novels based on the lives of William Beckford (1759–1844) and Thomas Chatterton (1752–1770), and, like several of his contemporaries, made 'notes for a purely imaginative Life of Christ' (compare Hall *Caine, 'Deas *Cromarty', 'John *Oxenham', M. P. *Shiel, Mrs Humphry *Ward). After graduation he wrote *The *Bracknels* (1911; issued in a revised version as *Denis Bracknel*, 1947), which he sent to the *publisher Edward Arnold on the grounds that they had published *The *Return* by Walter *de la Mare, of whom he was a great admirer and later a friend, and on whose work he published a book. **Following Darkness* (1912) (revised as *Peter Waring*, 1937) was dedicated to E. M. *Forster. *The Gentle Lover: A Comedy of Middle Age* (1913) was intended to be 'light and gay'. De la Mare wrote of Reid (in a preface to Russell Burlingham's 1953 study) that he was 'in everything that he cared for most . . . an unflagging devotee—from old woodcuts to Championship croquet, to street cricket, bull-dogs, story-technique, and, via Wagner, to Italian Opera'. He was a close friend of Forster who, in an essay of 1919 reprinted in *Abinger Harvest* (1936), identified the characteristic note of Reid's fiction thus: 'There is squalor and there is beauty, and both of them are haunted.' *Apostate* (1926) and *Private Road* (1940) are intimate autobiographical sketches. There is a biography by B. Taylor (1980).

Return, The, Walter *de la Mare, 1910, Edward Arnold. Strolling in Widdestone churchyard, dull, languid Arthur Lawford pauses beside the grave of Nicholas Sabatier, a Hugenot refugee whose tombstone reveals that he committed suicide in 1739. Lawford returns home a (literally) different man. He has assumed Sabatier's physical form and manner while remaining in other respects himself. The first few chapters describe, with lucid plausibility, the response of his sympathetic but unimaginative wife, Sheila, and the vicar, kindly, bespectacled Mr Bethany, to this distressing transformation. His behaviour begins to change. He insults a pompous friend, Mr Danton. Sheila leaves him, taking with her their 16-year-old daughter, Alice. On a second visit to Widdestone, Lawford encounters a mysterious stranger at Sabatier's grave. This is the reclusive Mr Herbert, who soon becomes a firm friend, and invites Lawford to stay with him and his sister, Grisel. Herbert possesses a book written by Sabatier, which reveals him to have been a libertine. Lawford falls in love with Grisel, and, aided by her, is able to repel Sabatier's efforts to possess him body and soul. He begins to resume his old form and manner. But he cannot resume his old self. He has imagined and experienced too much. Returning home, he overhears Sheila discussing him with Danton and other acquaintances, and realizes how little they have understood about his 'change'. We leave him resolved to remain with Sheila, for Alice's sake, but needing some time for reflection.

Return of Sherlock Holmes, The, A. Conan *Doyle, 1905, George Newnes. In 1893, Sherlock Holmes appeared to have solved his last crime by tumbling off the Reichenbach Falls in the arms of Professor Moriarty. Eventually, after eight years, public demand persuaded Doyle to resuscitate him. The thirteen stories in *The Return* appeared in the **Strand Magazine* between October 1903 and December 1904 and in *Collier's Weekly* between September 1903 and January 1905. Holmes reappears during 'The Empty House', setting up a wax dummy of himself in a window to lure the villain. Most of the stories follow the successful formula of the locked-room mystery, with Watson (and the reader) following respectfully in Holmes's hermeneutic wake. Like its predecessors, the volume contains its full quota of crushed skulls and slit throats, not to mention a man pinned to the wall by a harpoon ('Black Peter'). The most interesting development, no doubt provoked by the increasing popularity of a new genre, the *spy thriller, sees Holmes recovering a stolen document which, if published, would draw Britain into a European war ('The Second Stain').

Rewards and Fairies, Rudyard *Kipling, 1910, Macmillan. This sequel to **Puck of Pook's Hill* (1906) also consists of stories interspersed with poems. Two children, Dan and Una, meet Puck, the last survivor of the fairies, on Midsummer's Eve, and he conjures up figures from history or legend. In this volume, the figures include Elizabeth I; various solid English artisans; a smuggler who travels to America and joins the Seneca tribe; Wilfrid, Archbishop of York, who is rescued from shipwreck by a seal; Nick Culpeper, a physician and astrologer seeking a cure for the plague; Simon Cheyneys, a Rye shipbuilder and companion of Sir Frances Drake (?1540–96); and Sir Richard Dalyngridge, a Norman knight. Kipling described *Rewards and Fairies* as a 'balance' to, as well as a 'seal' upon, some aspects of his '"Imperialistic" output'. Its subject is Englishness, but an Englishness constantly reinvigorated by contact with a sturdy and adventurous past.

REYNOLDS, Mrs Baillie: Gertrude M. ROBINS (d. 1939) married (1890) Louis Baillie REYNOLDS. Born at Teddington, the daughter of a barrister, she married a stockbroker and was the author of more than fifty volumes of fiction between 1886 and 1939. An interview in the *Bookman (September 1907) states that she began telling ghost stories to her brother, who retailed them to the dormitory at his boarding-school; she and her sister started a magazine; and she contributed to the *Family Herald* as a teenager. Her first novel was accepted by Bentley, the first publisher to whom she offered it. She was in the habit of working at her typewriter for four hours each morning, and aimed to interest the ordinary person and hold before him a high standard of conduct and endeavour. Her fiction includes *The Man Who Won* (1905), about a South African girl who eventually marries the boy who has always loved her (in the meantime he has become a millionaire); *A Dull Girl's Destiny* (1907), which turns out to be marriage to a brilliant scientist and explorer and recognition as a great novelist; *The Girl From Nowhere* (1910), in which a disgraced younger son saves a strange girl from suicide and redeems himself; and *The Notorious Miss Lisle* (1911), about a woman who has lost her reputation in a divorce case, and marries a man without telling him, who eventually vindicates her. She also published widely in magazines and was President of the Society of Women Journalists in 1913 and Chair of the Writers' Club in 1911, 1919, and 1929.

REYNOLDS, Mrs Fred: Amy Dora ——(d. 1957) married Frederick REYNOLDS. She published a volume of verse (1890) and then more than forty volumes of fiction between 1895 and 1935. Her novels are sentimental and jocose, and she had a habit of identifying characters by epithet rather than name. Thus the hero of *The Man With the Wooden Face* (1903), who is not in fact a freak but a modern English peer, has to contend, in the Welsh mountains, with the Little Teacher, the Effective Girl, the Boy, the Artist, the Brown-Eyed Girl, the Widow, the Medical, and so forth; while *The Idyll of an Idler: Being Some Adventures of a Caravan in Cornwall* (1910) records domesticities of a gypsy and whimsical nature involving the Madcap, the Monkey, Mother ('Muz'), the Bear, Uncle Freddy, and the Bashful Boy (a dog). In *St David of the Dust* (1908), a mystical Welsh boy generally regarded as an imbecile grows up to be a prophet and bard, but meets a tragic end. She claimed to have lived in a fisherman's cottage at Land's End for two years to research *The Horseshoe* (1911). Later she lived at Baslow, Derbyshire, and at Grange-over-Sands, where she died. She was a client of the *literary agent Curtis Brown.

REYNOLDS, Stephen (1881–1919) was born at Devizes, Wiltshire, son of a landowner with whom he later quarrelled bitterly. He was educated at the College, Devizes, All Saints School, Bloxham, Manchester University (he read chemistry), and the École des Mines, Paris. After leaving the last institution to work on the *Weekly Critical Review*, he went to Sidmouth, Devon, for a fortnight's holiday, and, instead of returning to Paris, bought a fishing-boat. This was followed by a period in his home town of Devizes, recovering from a nervous breakdown; after this he returned to Sidmouth to live and work as a fisherman, and later as a spokesman for the working-class point of view in politics and fishery affairs. His line was to celebrate the strength of the working-class community and deplore intervention (including elementary education) while trying to give fishermen more power in negotiations with middlemen: 'Economically, I'm socialistic, and socially I'm high Tory.' He worked intermittently as a journalist and in early 1909 was very briefly a sub-editor on the **English Review*, but he detested London. Because of this F. M. *Hueffer used to exercise Reynolds's Great Dane in the city. Hueffer called Reynolds's early death 'the greatest loss that has befallen English literature for many years'. He contributed to **Books* during Archibald *Marshall's editorship, to the *Speaker* (see The **Nation*) and to the **New Age*. *The *Holy Mountain* (1910) is a *fantastic tale which portrays a thinly disguised Devizes. This was written before, but published after, *A Poor Man's House* (1909), a non-fictional account of the home life of his friends the Woolleys, which shot to supprising success on publication: Reynolds became a cult figure, and '*Elizabeth' even came down to Sidmouth and went out fishing with him and Bob Woolley. *How 'Twas: Short Stories and Small Travels* was published in 1912. The edition of his letters by Harold Wright (1923) reveals Reynolds's touchy, sentimental, fanatical character. Reynolds died of Spanish 'flu which became pneumonia, compounded, his friends thought, by overwork as Inspector of Fisheries for the south-western area during the First World War. 'The only thing I find fault with in Reynolds', wrote D. H. *Lawrence, apropos of *Alongshore* (1910), 'is that he swanks his acquaintance with the longshoremen so hugely. He writes "de haut en bas" like any old salt talking to a clerk . . . except that he's the clerk himself, carefully got up as the salt.'

RHODES, Kathlyn [Mary] (d. 1962) was born at Thirsk, Yorkshire, youngest of the three daughters of a brewer, and educated by governesses and at schools at Old Southgate and Scarborough. She began her career with a contribution to the *Family Herald*. After her first modest success she decided, attracted by the novels of Robert *Hichens, to go to Egypt to get some local colour. It turned out to be a good idea, and of her fifty-odd volumes of fiction between 1899 and 1954, many are romances in *exotic settings. *The Lure of the Desert* (1916) was probably her best-known book: but her other works include *A Desert Cain and Other Stories* (1922), *Desert Justice* (1913), *Desert Lovers* (1922), *Desert Nocturne* (1939), *Under Desert Stars* (1921), *The Relentless Desert* (1920), *A Daughter in the Desert* (1940), *It Happened in Cairo* (1944), *The Will of Allah* (1908), and *Allah's Gift* (1933). She had sidelines in books for girls such as *Schoolgirl Honour* (1912), and *crime stories. She lived in Scarborough with her mother and sister until 1914; thereafter in Staines. *December Brings Me Roses: A Book of Memories* (1950) is an autobiography. Her eldest sister, Hylda Ball, née Rhodes, published nine volumes of fiction of which the first is *A Vase of Clay* (1914).

RHYS, Ernest [Percival] (1859–1946) married (1891) Grace *RHYS. Born in Islington, London, son of a bookseller's assistant who later became a wine merchant, he was brought up in Carmarthen, where he learned Welsh from his nurse, and in Newcastle on Tyne. He was educated at Bishop's Stortford grammar school for two years, and at a day school in Newcastle, and worked briefly as an engineer in the north of England before becoming a full-time writer in 1885, soon afterwards editing the 'Camelot' series of early prose writers for Walter Scott, the Newcastle publisher. A struggling, hard-working literary journalist with exceptionally high standards, he was the author of many literary essays, biographies, verse, and fiction including *The Whistling Maid* (1900), a densely archaic romance of medieval Wales, whose heroine wanders the countryside, piping, dressed as a pageboy, and *The Man at Odds: A Story of the Welsh Coast and the Severn Sea* (1904), about smugglers in the days of George II. In an application (1896) to the Royal Literary Fund he observed, 'I have been preparing materials for a book on Dafydd ap Gwilym, the great mediaeval poet of Wales, but though I hope to find a publisher for this work, Celtic Literature, in my experience, produces no royalties.' In the end Edward Garnett (1868–1937) persuaded Fisher Unwin to take the translations of Dafydd. In order to provide his wife and five children with bread and butter Rhys took on, in 1906, the task of editing 'Everyman's Library' for the *publisher J. M. Dent, which by the time of his death included 983 volumes; Frank *Swinnerton was one of his clerks. Like Richard *Le Gallienne, he was a member of the Rhymers' Club and contributed to its anthologies, and he was also a member of the Council of the PEN Club. He published the autobiographies *Everyman Remembers* and *Wales England Wed* (1940).

RHYS, Grace: Grace LITTLE (1865–1929) married (1891) Ernest *RHYS. Born at Boyle, Co. Roscommon, daughter of a landowner who gambled away his fortune, she was well educated by governesses, and came to London with her sisters when she grew up to earn her living by teaching. She had frail health which was affected by childbearing and the uncertainties of her husband's profession. She began to write after marriage; Ernest Rhys describes them working together in the British Museum Library. Her first novel was *Mary Dominic* (1898). She set many of her novels in Ireland, but *The Wooing of Sheila* (1901) is set in Wales, and the hero is a child of an unhappy marriage whose happiness is restored by Sheila. *The Charming of Estercel* (1913) is set in Elizabethan Ireland, and *The Bride* (1909) marries a sculptor in London. She also published *The Diverted Village: A Holiday Book* (1903), *The Prince of Lisnover* (1904), and other tales and collections, many aimed at children.

RICHARDS, [Franklin Thomas] Grant (1872–1948) married, first (1898), Elisina —— (divorced) and, secondly (1915), Maria Magdalena de CSANADY. The son of a Fellow of Trinity College, Oxford, he was born in Glasgow and educated at the City of London School, which he left aged 15 for Hamilton, Adams, & Co., wholesale booksellers; while there he started to work as a journalist. Two years later he went to work for W. T. Stead (1849–1912) on the new *Review of Reviews*, where Mrs *Belloc Lowndes also had a job. The novelist Grant Allen (1848–99), who was married to his mother's sister, introduced him to literary circles. On the strength of £1,400 of borrowed capital he started a *publishing company in 1897, and soon signed up Leonard *Merrick, Hugh *Clifford, and 'Nathaniel *Gubbins'. He was *Chesterton's first publisher (*The Wild Knight*); in 1898 he took over the publication of *A Shropshire Lad* by A. E. Housman (1859–1936), who would accept no royalty; he was a friend and supporter of Theodore Dreiser (1871–1945); E. V. *Lucas read manuscripts for him. He paid great attention to the printing and binding of his books, and was also a collector of modern painting. In 1905 he went bankrupt and the firm's assets were sold (his 'World's Classics' series, for example, were bought by Oxford University Press). With his first wife as the nominal head he started another publishing firm, moved his office, and engaged as a reader Filson *Young, whose novels he also published. Young encouraged Richards to publish **Dubliners*. In the late 1920s Richards again went bankrupt and lost control of the publishing firm. Richards himself was author of nine novels to 1935, of which the earliest are *Caviare* (1912), an epigrammatic comedy about a spoilt Englishman in Paris who falls in love with an American millionaire's daughter, and *Valentine* (1913). The hero of the latter is an architect's son and man about town. During the first half of the book he reads newspapers in his father's office, fobs off creditors, falls in love, diverts himself pleasantly in London and Paris, and tries to increase his income by betting. But despite his languid manner he badly wants to become an architect, and in the second half he begins to work in secret on his father's big commission, a 'Palace of Empire', whose fatal flaw he discovers after his father's sudden death, and just in time. Much valuable information about the literary world of the period is recorded in Richards's *Memories of a Misspent Youth* (1932) and its sequel, *Author Hunting by An Old Literary Sportsman* (1934).

RICHARDS, H. Grahame (b. 1885) was (in 1917) Acting British Consul General for Mexico. He translated from French and was author of eight volumes of fiction 1911–1920, including *Lucrezia Borgia's One Love* (1912) and *'Through the Ages Beloved': A Romance of Japan* (1914). In *The Garden of Dreams* (1913) Lord Bellingham falls in love with a Arab girl in Tunis, but they both must die.

RICHARDSON, Henry Handel, *pseud.*: Ethel Florence Lindesay RICHARDSON (1870–1946) married (1895) George John ROBERTSON (d. 1933). Born in Melbourne, Australia, the daughter of an Irish doctor and an Englishwoman who worked as a postmistress, she was educated at the Presbyterian Ladies' College in Melbourne, a disagreeable experience evoked in her novel *The *Getting of Wisdom* (1910). Her father's finances collapsed when she was a small child; he died insane in 1879. In 1888 she and her family went to Leipzig so that she could study music. Disappointed in her desire to become a concert pianist, she turned to writing: her earliest publications were translations from German and critical articles. Her first novel, **Maurice Guest* (1908), is a frank and sometimes morbid account of the unconventional lives led by young musicians, which she published under a male pseudonym because she did not want it read as a woman's novel. In Leipzig she married, and there she lived until 1904, when her husband became professor of German at London University. After his death she retired to Sussex with a woman friend. A trilogy, *The Fortunes of Richard Mahony* (1917–1929), sets the marriage of a couple like her parents against the background of the expansion of nineteenth-century Australia; it was written after her only return visit to her homeland for six weeks in 1912. Recent research has emphasized the extent to which it is based on her father's career. Her last novel was *The*

Young Cosima (1939). There is an unfinished autobiography (1948) and a biography by Dorothy Green (1973).

Riddle of the Sands, The, Erskine *Childers, 1903, Smith, Elder. Carruthers—'a young man of condition and fashion', who knows the right people, belongs to the right clubs, and has a 'safe, possibly a brilliant, future in the Foreign Office'—is finding it hard to endure the emptiness of the London Season in September. His job bores him, and he can't quite believe that his friends miss him as much as they say they do. Then he receives a letter from his college friend, Davies, who invites him for a spot of duck-shooting in the Baltic. 'Yachting in the Baltic in September! The very idea made one shudder.' Still, he accepts, and begins to benefit almost immediately. The change of scene supplies him with a 'solid background of resignation', which is called for when the spartan Davies shows him the tiny yacht. An early-morning swim removes 'yet another crust of discontent and self-conceit', as does his subsequent initiation into the mysteries of sailing and navigation. Childers describes all this in intricate, vivid detail, because, although there is not yet a storm or a Hun in sight, the real adventure—the regeneration of Carruthers—has begun. Davies is a staunch patriot who believes that Germany is preparing for war, and that British complacency may well ensure defeat. Government will continue to ignore the danger unless roused into action by 'civilian agitators' like himself. When they discover the identity of the treacherous Dollman, German master-spy, Carruthers, the Civil Servant, wants to return to England and inform the Admiralty or Scotland Yard. Davies, the civilian agitator, believes that the authorities will do nothing, and persuades him that they must settle the matter themselves. Just as the 'peevish dandy' has been transformed into an outdoorsman, so the Civil Servant now joins the agitators. The narrative turns as much on the second as on the first of these transformations. Like a great deal of contemporary British *spy fiction, *The Riddle of the Sands* is unashamedly xenophobic; but the intricacy of the conception and the lucid detail make it a classic of the genre.

RIDGE, W[illiam] Pett (1857–1930) married (1909) Olga HENTSCHEL. Born at Chartham and educated at Marden, both in Kent, he became a clerk in the Civil Service, and later in the Continental goods office of a railway. He came to London in 1880. As a railway clerk he went to evening classes at the Birkbeck Institution for adult education, where he began to contribute to newspapers. When he found himself earning three times as much from writing as from clerking, he gave up his job. Most of the late nineteenth-century writers who opened up the life of the lower-middle classes to fictional investigation try for a poignant or sordid note: Ridge, one of the most successful practitioners of this mode, took a humorous line. Although he was was one of the best-known English popular novelists, he never (unlike several contemporaries) managed to sell books in quantity in the US. The Society of Authors, acting on his behalf, sued the *English Illustrated Magazine* for publishing a story ostensibly by W. Pett Ridge. Edgar *Jepson, Barry *Pain, and Jerome K. *Jerome gave evidence for the prosecution and he was awarded £150 damages. He published more than sixty volumes of fiction between 1895 and 1930 including *A Clever Wife*, his first novel, *Mord Em'ly* (1898), an early success, **Nine to Six-Thirty* (1910), *Erb* (1903), *Mrs Galer's Business* (1905), *Sixty-nine Birnam Road* (1908), about the difficulties of a *suburban housewife with a successful husband and a dishonest brother, and the autobiographies *A Story Teller: Forty Years in London* (1923) and *I Like to Remember* (1925). His first book, *Eighteen of Them: Singular Stories* (1894), was published as 'Warwick Simpson'; he also wrote some short stories in periodicals under that name. He started a Babies' Home and Day Nursery in Hoxton in about 1907, was a prison visitor, and supporter of several London colleges.

RIDLEY, Alice: Alice DAVENPORT (1860–1945) married (1882) Edward RIDLEY (1843–1928), Kt. (1897). Daughter of a landowner and MP, she was married to a High Court judge. Her first novel *The Story of Aline* (1897) was praised by Andrew *Lang. Some time after its publication she made friends with Mrs Belloc *Lowndes, who described her as 'closer and dearer to [me] than any human being, except [my] husband and children'. Her four novels in this period include *A Daughter of Jael* (1904), in which a horrible, tyrannical old squire is murdered by his granddaughter so that he should not ruin her brother's life as he had ruined her father's; she is then tempted to kill the woman who threatens her marriage.

RITA, *pseud.*: Eliza Margaret Jane GOLLAN (1856–1938) married, first (1872), Karl Otto Edmund BOOTH or von BOOTH, and, secondly, W. Desmond HUMPHREYS. Born at Gollanfield, Inverness, Scotland, she went with her family to Australia as a small child, spending about five years in Sydney. She received her education in a rather haphazard, second-hand fashion from her brother's tutor. The grief of a broken engagement led her to start writing shortly before her 20th birthday. Her first marriage, strenuously opposed by her family, to a German composer of popular music was a disaster; after her second marriage to an Irishman she settled for some years at Youghal, Co. Cork. Desmond Humphreys did not work and later became an invalid whom she had to support. Her considerable output of romantic fiction mainly targeted female library subscribers. Many of her works take the form of diaries and journals, making them in part confessionals. Her most noteworthy work is *Sheba* (1889), a largely autobiographical story of a wild young Australian girl's progress to womanhood. *A Husband of No Importance* (1894) (*A Woman of No Importance*, by Oscar Wilde, 1854–1900, opened in 1893) is an attack upon the New Woman novel; it is the story of a woman who neglects her husband and devotes herself full-time to literature. In 1903 she published the tremendously successful social satire **Souls*, which made her famous, although 'only in the Park had I visioned the notorious Lady A, or the twice-divorced Countess of B, or any other of the queer set whose pursuit of secret vices had been exposed by open scandals'. *Saba Macdonald* (1906) draws upon the bitter experiences of her first marriage. Other works (from a very large output) include *Vivienne* (1877), *The Silent Woman* (1904), **Queer Lady Judas* (1905), *A Man of No Importance* (1907), *The House Called Harrish* (1909), *A Grey Life* (1913), *Jill, All Alone* (1914), and *The Philanthropic Burglar* (1919). Like many writers she found her income much reduced by the First World War, during which she twice applied to the Royal Literary Fund; some details of her struggles with publishers' rapacity are given in *Recollections of a Literary Life* (1936), to which Philip *Gibbs contributed a foreword describing Humphreys as 'a born story-teller'. She also wrote several plays and was an enthusiastic theatre-goer, 'rarely missing a first night performance when in town'. She was the favourite novelist of Queen Mary (1867–1953), who requested a special leather-bound set of Humphreys's work for her private library. In later life she became a keen follower of Madame Blavatsky (1831–91) and ardently devoted to the tenets of Theosophy. She was a founder of the Writer's Club for Women. She died at home in Combe Down, near Bath. The pseudonym may have been an abbreviation of her second Christian name: she signed her letters 'Rita L. Humphreys'.

Robert Orange: *Being a continuation of the History of Robert Orange M. P. and a Sequel to the School for Saints*, 'John Oliver *Hobbes', 1900, T. Fisher Unwin. Bored, unfulfilled Lady Sara, who dislikes being a woman, decides that she also dislikes her suitor, the Duke of Marshire. She is in love with Robert Orange, son of a French émigré. Her best friend, Viscountess Pensée Fitz Rewes, arrives with the news that Robert is to marry Mrs Brigit Parflete, an Alberian Archduchess, whose husband is thought to have committed suicide. Pensée herself is in love with Beauclerk Reckage, ambitious and unpopular leader of a High Church, High Tory society called the 'Bond of Association'. Reckage is to marry Agnes Carillon, who in turn is in love with David Rennes, a painter. Orange, however, begins to wonder whether Brigit, an aspiring actress, is not a little too racy for his taste; when it transpires that Parflete is in fact still alive, they agree to part. Sara refuses Marshire. Agnes elopes with Rennes. Reckage wants Orange out of the political and romantic way, and suggests that he become a Jesuit. Brigit pursues her theatrical career, with great success. Reckage proposes to Sara but is turned down, then thrown from his horse and killed. A rumour starts that Brigit was seen entering Orange's house, which could mean ruin for him; in fact, it was Sara. Even so, the incident persuades Orange to go and see Brigit perform. He realises that he loves her, and that their love is doomed. Mr Parflete dies (really, this time), but Robert is already on his way to Rome, and Brigit keeps the news to herself. Sara becomes a Carmelite nun. The novel consistently parallels emotional and political unfulfilment.

Robert Thorne: *The Story of a London Clerk*, Shan F. *Bullock, 1907, T. Werner Laurie. First-person narrative of a sickly child who would dearly like to grow up to be a clerk, even though his fantasizing father would prefer something rather more manly. Moving to London, Robert passes his examinations and gets a job in a tax office. He falls in love with Nell Willard, sister of his lazy friend, Bertie, who has failed his examinations. His sister dies, and his brother emigrates to New Zealand. Nell's tyrannical father, an alcoholic, dies, and they marry. Bertie moves into their house in suburban Dulwich, and becomes a reformed character. Robert has achieved success without sacrificing his integrity, but cannot help feeling that life has passed him by: perhaps his father was right. After a holiday spent on a Hampshire farm ('here at last were real men and women'), the Thornes decide to emigrate to New Zealand.

ROBERTS, Charles G[eorge] D[ouglas] (1860–1943), Kt. (1935), married (1880) Mary Isabel FENETY (d. 1930). Born at Douglas, New Brunswick, son of a Church of England clergyman, he was educated at Fredericton Collegiate School and the University of New Brunswick. He became a schoolmaster, then a journalist, editing the Toronto *Week* from 1880, and professor at King's College, Nova Scotia. He is important in Canadian literary history as the author of *Orion and Other Poems* (1880), which made him almost the first Canadian author to obtain worldwide reputation and influence; he was also a tireless promoter and encourager of Canadian literature. At the beginning of the First World War he enlisted as a trooper in the Legion of Frontiersmen. He published numerous works on Canadian exploration and natural history, verse, travel books, and fiction. *The Kindred of the Wild* (1902) is the best known of his many animal stories. *Barbara Ladd* (1902), begins with a girl escaping from an uncongenial aunt in New England in 1769; it sold 80,000 copies in the US alone. His brother Theodore Goodridge Roberts (1877–1953) was also the author of Canadian *historical romances; the poet Bliss Carman (1861–1929) was their cousin.

ROBERTS, Morley (1857–1942) married (1896) Alice HAMLYN née SELOUS (d. 1911). Born in London, son of a tax inspector, he was educated at Bedford School and Owens College, Manchester, where he met George *Gissing. In 1876 he went to Australia, where he worked on the railways and on farms. Thereafter he was at various times a clerk in the Civil Service and a ranch-hand or railwayman or sailor in North and Central America, Africa, and the South Seas. These experiences furnish his literary productions: he was the author of plays, verse, books on the sociology of nutrition and on cancer, travel books, and more than sixty volumes of fiction from 1887, including the melodramatic and influential fictionalized account of Gissing's life, *The Private Life of Henry Maitland: A Record Dictated by J. H.* (1912). In this he describes the quixotic youth stealing to help the prostitute he loves, his poverty in America, his miserable life as a hack writer and teacher with an alcoholic wife in London lodgings, his opinions on contemporary literature and literary life, his odd attitude to women, loathing of imperialism, disastrous second marriage, and last idyll with his French translator. The book shares with Roberts's other fiction the theme of correction of Victorian prudery and hypocrisy about sex and divorce. *The Idlers* (1905) is about the emotional education of a young squire, whose sensible fiancée forgives his infidelity. *Taken by Assault* (1901) is a *Boer War novel. *The Degradation of Geoffrey Alwith* (1908) is about a painter who sacrifices his art in the hope of marrying a cold and unworthy woman, succumbs to Addison's Disease, and ends by dying in the arms of a golden-hearted prostitute. *The Promotion of the Admiral and Other Sea Comedies* (1903) and *Captain Ballam of the 'Cormorant' and Other Sea Comedies* (1905) are works in a genre popular in their time (compare C. J. Cutcliffe *Hyne). *Bianca's Caprice and Other Stories* (1904) show competence in a variety of moods. He also wrote Westerns and *A Tramp's Note-Book* (1904). He was a friend of W. H. *Hudson of whom he published a biography (1924). He was awarded a Civil List pension. There is a biography (1961) by Storm Jameson.

ROBIN, E. Gallienne wrote novels about the Channel Islands, including *Jeannette of Jersey* (1900), *Jacquine of the Hut: A Sark Story* (1911), and *Christine, A Guernsey Girl* (1912), and collaborated on a guide to the Channel Islands. The fiction is on the whole predictable, featuring old customs and primitive passions. But *Christine* has an unexpected and quite attractive nastiness: a disagreeable young woman who runs an eating-house blackmails another whose unfortunate secret she happens to know.

ROBINS, Elizabeth (1862–1952) married (1885) George Richmond PARKES (d. 1887). Born in Louisville, Kentucky, eldest of eight children of a banker, she was educated at Putnam Female Seminary and Vassar College. Her mother was a former opera singer who eventually went mad; her father became bankrupt when she was a teenager. She ran away from Vassar to go on the stage, and married another actor who committed suicide shortly afterwards. She came to London in 1888 and played a major part in bringing the plays of Henrik Ibsen (1828–1906) to a British public, with sufficient success to be able to support her mother and put her brothers through college. Always an advocate of practical measures to help the emancipation of women, she took on the production of plays, and was a founder of the Actresses' Franchise League, and a member of the WSPU. Her early novels, *George Mandeville's Husband* (1894), *The New Moon* (1894), *Milly's Story* (1895), and *The Open Question* (1899), appeared under the pseudonym 'C. E. Raimond': they dealt with problems of marriage and female education and artistic aspirations; the last is concerned with eugenics, and draws on her family background in the American South. Her twentieth-century fiction appeared under her own name, sometimes with the pseudonym in brackets. It includes her most famous work *The *Convert* (1907), a novelized version of her very successful play *Votes for Women!* (1907). *The Magnetic North* (1904) was based on a visit to her brother Raymond, a temperance crusader, in the Klondike, and deals with the lives of miners and Eskimos in the Gold Rush. *A Dark Lantern: A Story With a Prologue* (1905), has a heroine who declines a morganatic marriage to a German prince, only to take a rest cure and marry her tyrannical doctor, with whom she finally achieves a successful marriage. The analysis of power relations in the doctor–patient relationship is of special interest (compare 'G. *Colmore'). *'Come and Find Me!'* (1908) shows the cramping of women's lives against a background of California and Alaska; *The Florentine Frame* (1909), begins with a teenage girl being instructed in feminine decorum by her mother, who afterwards gives up the man she loves (who loves her too) to the daughter; *'Where Are You Going To . . . ?'* (1913; published in the US as *My Little Sister*) is a novel about the white slave trade: the issue was current and reinforced by publicity surrounding the 1912 Criminal Law Amendment (White Slavery) bill, and was used by the WSPU as part of their moral crusade. The story of the abduction of two girls at Victoria Station was supposed to have been told Robins by Amber *Reeves's mother. Cicely *Hamilton's dramatization was refused a licence in 1914. Robins also wrote *Ibsen and the Actress* (1928) and several books on female suffrage. She was a friend of Mrs Hugh *Bell, who produced Ibsen plays with her and with whom she collaborated on the play *Alan's Wife* (1893). During the First World War she and Beatrice *Harraden ran a library in a hospital. She was one of the group of feminists who founded *Time and Tide* in 1920. After the First World War she spent more and more time with Dr Octavia Wilberforce (1888–1963), with whom she founded a rest home for suffragettes and women medical students. *Both Sides of the Curtain* (1940) is a disappointingly incoherent account of her early stage career. There is a bibliography by Sue Thomas (1994).

ROHMER, Sax, *pseud.*: Arthur Henry WARD (1883–1959), who changed his name (*c.*1901) to Arthur Sarsfield WARD and later used the name Sax ROHMER, married (1909) Rose Elizabeth KNOX. Born in Birmingham of Irish parents, Ward became a journalist who wrote about the East End of London, including Limehouse, where there was then a large Chinese community, which the works of A. Conan *Doyle, Edgar *Wallace, and M. P. *Shiel were opening up to *crime fiction. Ward's first published story, however, was 'The Mysterious Mummy', published in *Pearson's Weekly* in 1903, about the theft of a mummy from a museum, and drew on his teenage obsession with ancient Egypt, also expressed in the stories of *Brood of the Witch-Queen* (published serially, 1914; in volume form, 1918). From 1905 he often used the pen-name 'Sax Rohmer' which he eventually adopted in real life. His non-fiction *The Romance of Sorcery* (1914) also reflects his interest in the occult. But fame and fortune were to come from his invention of Dr Fu Manchu, who first appeared in a story, 'The Zayat Kiss', published in the *Story-Teller* (Oct. 1912), the first of a series of adventures collected in volume form in *The *Mystery of Dr Fu Manchu* (1913). Here we have, not Shiel's obsessive fear of oriental nationalism and militarism, but a master-criminal who focuses racist fear of the mysterious East. On the proceeds Ward and his wife visited Egypt. *The Sins of Severac Bablon* (1914) is about a Jewish leader of ancient lineage who punishes Jewish criminals. Ward worked for military intelligence in both World Wars. The increasing importance of the American market for his fiction led to visits to the USA from 1919; and he went to live in New York City in 1947, but returned to London shortly before his death. He also wrote as 'Michael Furey'.

ROLFE, Fr.: Frederick William ROLFE (1860–1913), who also called himself 'Frederick William Serafino Austin Lewis Mary ROLFE' and 'Baron CORVO'. Born in London, the son of a piano-maker who had sunk to being a tuner, he left school at 14 and became a teacher. He converted to Roman Catholicism in 1885 and worked as a tutor and schoolmaster until entering the seminary of St Mary's, Oscott, in 1887; he was then expelled from the Scots College in Rome in May 1890 after five months. About this time he made friends with the Duchessa Sforza-Cesarini, an English widow and Catholic convert, who agreed to finance him. At the end of the year he returned to England and settled in Christchurch, Dorset, under the name of 'Baron Corvo', but by the following year the money had ceased to arrive from Rome. Rolfe worked intermittently at painting and photography, and in 1895 went to Holywell in Wales, where he painted and wrote stories, published in the *Yellow Book*, and articles in the local paper outlining in lurid terms his grievances against the Church and his former friends. In 1898 he was the subject of attacks in two Aberdeen newspapers, reprinted in the *Catholic Times*. He arrived destitute in London in 1899, where John Lane agreed to publish the Toto stories from the *Yellow Book* in volume form. (*In His Own Image* came out in 1901.) In 1899 Grant *Richards commissioned *Chronicles of the House of Borgia* (1901). In 1902 Rolfe was given £50 by the Royal Literary Fund. In 1903 his festering resentment gave rise to his novel **Hadrian the Seventh*, in which the central character is an idealized version of himself and the lesser characters vindictive versions of his acquaintances. It was published in 1904, under the name 'Fr. Rolfe', an ambiguous style which implied that he was Father Rolfe, the priest he had never become, although 'Fr.' could also have been short for 'Frederick'. The novel was not a success and did nothing to improve Rolfe's finances, and he got hackwork writing Agricultural and Pastoral Prospects of South Africa, which, since he then engaged in an acrimonious and unsuccessful lawsuit with his employers, led him further into debt. He published *Don Tarquinio* in 1905. Collaboration with R. H. *Benson on a life of St Thomas à Becket was stopped by the Roman hierarchy, much to Rolfe's disgust. In 1908 he went to Venice on holiday, and there he stayed, writing and, as before, making friends, sponging off them, then quarrelling with them. The novel *The Weird of the Wanderer: Being the Papyrus Records of Some Incidents in One of the Previous Lives of Mr Nicholas Crabbe* (1912), written with the help of Harry Pirie-Gordon (1883–?), draws on Rolfe's experiences in literary London in the early twentieth century. A sequel, *The Desire and Pursuit of the Whole* (1934), is a highly coloured version of his Venice period, written in Venice 1909–10. It was also at this time that Rolfe wrote the pornographic letters to Masson Fox (printed in the periodical *Art & Literature* in 1965) and contemplated writing novels of homosexual pornography. In 1910 Rolfe slackened his correspondence with his friends, and took to living in an open boat, in which situation he wrote *Hubert's Arthur* (1935). But in 1912 his debts were paid with the help of the Revd Justus Serjeant, and he agreed to the publication of *The Weird of the Wanderer* (postponed because any profits would have gone to his former lawyers). He began to live in a palace on the Grand Canal, with a gondola; it was in this surprising prosperity that he died. The justly celebrated biography by A. J. A. Symons, *The Quest for Corvo* (1934), is supplemented by Donald Weeks, *Corvo* (1971), which contains a bibliography.

Romance: A Novel, Joseph *Conrad and Ford Madox *Hueffer, 1903, Smith, Elder. Swashbuckler narrated by young John Kemp, who gets involved in the smuggling operations run by a Spanish cousin-in-law, Carlos Riego, and accompanies him to Jamaica, where Kemp assaults an admiral and is kidnapped by pirates. Escape, aided by the beautiful Seraphina, and further capture follow. It turns out that his captor is Riego, who wants Kemp to marry Seraphina, to save her from a villainous associate, O'Brien. After Riego's death things turn nasty: tornadoes, fusillades, manhunts, Havana, wrongful arrest. Accused of piracy, Kemp is shipped back to England, but manages to prove his innocence. He is finally reunited with Seraphina, having learnt that 'suffering is the lot of man.'

Room With A View, A, E. M. *Forster, 1908, Edward Arnold. Lucy Honeychurch arrives in Florence with her companion, Miss Bartlett, only to find that they have not been given rooms with a view at their pensione. When their stubbornly unconventional neighbours, Mr. Emerson and his son George, offer to swap, the arrangement provokes an enduring clash between middle-class inhibition and a sunburnt, vaguely Italianate paganism. The other inmates of the Pensione Bertolini include the clergyman Mr Beebe and the sensational novelist Miss Lavish. Lucy's primness is unsettled first by witnessing a street murder, and then by an impulsive embrace from George in a field of violets. Miss Bartlett promptly removes her charge from Italian sex and violence. The two return to Summer Street, in Surrey, where Lucy becomes engaged to the dilettante Cecil Vyse. Meanwhile George and his father have rented a nearby house called Windy Corner. Lucy, Cecil, and Mrs Honeychurch come across George, Freddy Honeychurch (Lucy's brother), and Mr Beebe bathing nude in a pool in the forest. Further embarrassments ensue when Cecil mockingly reads aloud a passage from Miss Lavish's latest novel, which happens to describe an impulsive embrace in a field of violets. The memory stirs George, who declares his love. Lucy eventually escapes from this 'muddle' with assistance from Mr Emerson and (surprisingly) Miss Bartlett, but none from the previously sympathetic Mr Beebe. She and George marry, and return to the Pensione Bertolini.

Rosa Amorosa: *The Love Letters of a Woman*, 'George *Egerton', 1901, Grant Richards. The supposed author of the letters claims that there are only two things of 'vital importance' in life, love and laughter, and that the British are far too suspicious of both. The letters span a year during which she is separated from her (Russian) lover. They enable her to reminisce, celebrate, and philosophize. He is a musician playing on her soul, 'setting all the strings a-quiver'. He is the 'book-marker' wedged in the 'most golden pages' in her 'special volume of life'. Women, she feels, should not hanker after the vote, but cultivate their femininity, their 'intenser soul-life'. The book ends as she sets off for Russia. A final letter to the 'editor' reveals that they plan to live in China, where her lover will act as interpreter and commercial agent for a railway.

Rosary, The, Florence L. *Barclay, 1909, G. P. Putnam's Sons. Jane Champion is part Jane Eyre, part champion golfer. She rejects beautiful, artistic Garth Dalmain, with his lilac shirts and red socks, because he seems unmanly, a 'mere boy'. But the rejection makes her wonder whether she herself is not too manly. The refusal, rather than disavowing, her femininity, at first defers and then recreates it. Dalmain goes blind. Nursing him in disguise, Jane nurses her own femininity, learning that she need not disguise it, until, a woman at last, she declares her love. However, the free fall, the delirium of self-concealment, is severely curtailed by Dalmain's steadily increasing remasculinization. 'The sense of manhood and master; the right of control, the joy of possession, arose within him. Even in his blindness, he was the stronger.' Written in 1905, while Barclay was recovering from stress caused by an overlong bicycle ride, *The Rosary* was sensationally successful in Britain and America, and was reputed to have sold over a million copies by the time of her death in 1921.

ROSS, Adrian, *pseud.*: Arthur Reed ROPES (1859–1933) married (1901) Ethel WOOD. Born in Lewisham, London, son of a Russian merchant, he was educated at Priory House School, Clapton, Mill Hill School, City of London School, and King's College, Cambridge, where he was a Scholar. He was a Fellow of King's College 1884–1890, lecturing in history; subsequently, under his pseudonym, he was the author of many songs and complete libretti for comic operas, and, under his own name, of history books *c.*1900–30. His novel *The Hole of the Pit* (1914), dedicated to M. R. *James, is an effectively spooky *historical tale, whose hero, a Roundhead, tries to rescue his Cavalier cousin and a sinister Italian woman from a castle surrounded by a marsh.

ROSS, Martin, *pseud.*: see 'E. Œ. *Somerville and Martin Ross'.

Round the Corner: *Being the Life and Death of Francis Christopher Folyat, Bachelor of Divinity and Father of a Large Family*, Gilbert *Cannan, 1913, Martin Secker. The Folyat family has always prepared its sons for the army, the navy, or the

Church. In the current generation, William has entered the army, and Peter the navy, while the mild-mannered Francis draws the short straw and, after studying at the University of Dublin, takes a curacy in south Devon. He sees religion as hard work, and literature as a release from it. He falls in love with Miss Martha Brett, marries her, and fathers ten children, two of whom die young. Although he manages to place his son Frederic in a solicitor's office, he finds it hard to support his apparently endless offspring. The family moves to the north of England, which Martha finds too coarse for her taste. Francis develops an enemy in the shape of the editor of the *Pendle News*, Flynn, who accuses him of Mariolatry. The controversy breaks friendships and windows. Meanwhile two of his daughters, Mary and Annette, fail to find husbands; one of his sons falls off a roof and dies; and another, Serge, a gifted painter, returns from Africa in time to remark that for his parents life is always just around the corner. One daughter, Gertrude, becomes engaged to a local man, Bennett Lawrie; another, Annette, is fired from her post as a governess for bathing naked in the presence of her pupil. She moves back home and finds work as a servant. Frederic gets a woman of a lower class, Annie Lipsett, pregnant. Martha arranges for Frederic to marry the wealthy Jessie Clibran Bell, while Serge, unknown to the family, looks after Annie. Bennett Lawrie realizes that he loves Annette, not Gertrude. Francis, who is beginning to feel that he has failed his children, visits Annie to apologise for Frederic's conduct. Annette and Bennett marry, become parents, and live in happy poverty. Minna, the beauty of the family, marries Basil Haslam, a friend of Frederic. Gertrude marries Streeten Folyat, a distant relation and a fop (a triumph for Martha). Mary marries the 51-year-old father of her ex-pupil. However, Frederic's marriage to Jessie has begun to disintegrate: he blames her for his shattered dreams. He visits Annie, who refuses to see him. Serge has taken his place. Frederic, now bankrupt as well as humiliated in love, shoots himself. Francis reverts haplessly to asceticism. He and Martha return to Devon, 'a place of sleep, of tranquil sleep attended by pleasant dreams of roses and blue water and warm figs ripening in the sunlight mellowed by the soft, moist air'. The novel, one of the *family sagas much favoured by Edwardian readers, became momentarily notorious when the Circulating Libraries Association, in a fit of self-censorship, withdrew it from the shelves. Its offence conceivably lay either in the scene where Annette bathes naked in her charge's presence, or in a later scene where a young man emerges from the undergrowth to find her swinging naked from a tree (a similar interest in nude bathing was to prove the downfall of D. H. *Lawrence's *The Rainbow* in 1915).

ROWLANDS, Effie Adelaide: see E. Maria *Albanesi.

RUCK, Berta: Amy Roberta RUCK (1878–1978) married (1909) Oliver *ONIONS. Born at Murree, India, eldest of eight children of a Welsh-speaking army officer, who later became Chief Constable of Carnarvonshire, and an English mother, and brought up in Wales, she was educated at St Winifred's School, Bangor, and trained as an artist at Lambeth School of Art, the Slade School of Art, and at Calorossi's in Paris. She was a voracious reader in childhood. While at the Slade she met Oliver Onions, who asked her to do an illustration for the **Idler*; later, hard up in Paris, she offered them a story. At Calorossi's she had made friends with E. *Nesbit's daughter Iris Bland; Nesbit helped Ruck in her early literary career. After marriage to Onions and the birth of two sons, the first of her stories reached volume form as *His Official Fiancée* (1914), a cheerful romance about a businessman who needs to seem engaged and persuades his secretary to pretend for 25 *s.* a week which she wants to pay her brother's debts. Eventually, of course, they fall in love. It was followed by more than 150 other volumes of fiction. *A Story-Teller Tells the Truth: Reminiscences and Notes* (1935), *A Smile for the Past* (1959), and *A Trickle of Welsh Blood* (1967) are autobiographical. The poet Frances Cornford (1886–1960) was her first cousin.

Ruritanian romance. The vogue for this subgenre of romantic fiction began with *The Prisoner of Zenda* (1894) by 'Anthony *Hope'. Rudolf Rassendyll, an upright but aimless Englishman visiting the imaginary Middle European country of Ruritania on the eve of the coronation of King Rudolf (to whom he bears an uncanny resemblance), becomes involved in political intrigue. When the King is kidnapped by his villainous half-brother, Duke Michael, Rassendyll impersonates him successfully at the coronation, then rescues him, and falls in love with his intended bride, Princess Flavia. Flavia renounces him for her duties as Queen, and he returns disconsolately to England. A second model, more stylish though less influential, was *Prince Otto* (1885) by Robert Louis Stevenson (1850–94). The hero is the irresponsible ruler of a German statelet, Grunewald, whose belated attempts to reform himself and his government are foiled by revolution. A republic is declared, and the Prince and Princess retire, contentedly enough, to the woods. Hope's narrative concentrates on the moral and emotional regeneration of its ultra-English hero, Stevenson's allows more room for wry politico-philosophical reflection. Between them, they can be said to have inspired *Admonition* (1903) by 'John *Ayscough', E. F. *Benson's *Princess Sophia* (1900), Winston *Churchill's martial **Savrola* (1900), J. S. *Clouston's facetious *Tales of King Fido* (1909), Tom *Gallon's *The Kingdom of Hate* (1899), Samuel *Gordon's *The Queen's Quandary* (1903), Beatrice *Heron-Maxwell's *The Queen Regent* (1903), William *Holt-White's *The Man Who Stole the Earth* (1909), Sir William *Magnay's *Count Zarka* (1903), Arthur W. *Marchmont's *For Love or Crown* (1901) and *When I Was Czar* (1903), Thomas A. *Pinkerton's *Valdora* (1907), *The Tragic Prince* (1912) by 'Anthony *Pryde', Olivia *Ramsey's *Two Men and a Governess* (1912), *The Kingmakers* (1907) by 'Oliver *Sandys', Bram *Stoker's occult *The Lady of the Shroud* (1909), H. B. Marriott *Watson's *Alise of Astra* (1910), and A. R. and R. K. *Weekes's *The Tragic Prince* (1912). Hope might be said to have imitated himself in *Sophy of Kravonia* (1906). Ruritania provided writers with a territory which was at once familiar and unfamiliar, European yet exotic, where magical transformations might occur and political experiments succeed or fail. At times, for example in Magnay's *Count Zarka* (1903), Ruritanian romance intersected with the kind of *spy fiction written by E. Phillips *Oppenheim and others which featured tortuous diplomacy in exotic locations. *Helianthus* (1908) by '*Ouida', set in an imaginary European country, warns in strong terms against the threat of German militarism. The most commercially successful Edwardian adaptation of the genre was Elinor *Glyn's **Three Weeks* (1907), in which another upright but aimless young Englishman is regenerated by an encounter with a Princess. This time, though, the regeneration, which takes place on a tiger-skin rug in a hotel in Geneva, is sexual as well as emotional. Distant echoes of Ruritania can be heard as far afield as George *Meredith's astringent **Celt and Saxon* (1910).

RUSSELL, Dora (b. 1830). Born at Willington, Northumberland, she supported herself from about 1870 by writing serial fiction for Tillotson's newspaper syndicate. She told Black that she had been brought up in prosperity, with ponies and governesses, but that financial disaster led her to earn her living from her pen. In 1898, in failing health, she applied to the Royal Literary Fund for help. At that time she was living in London. Her first book was *The Miner's Oath* (1872), originally published in the *Newcastle Weekly Chronicle*. The *British Library Catalogue* lists thirty-seven volumes of fiction 1874–1907, including *The Curate of Royston* (1906), in which an enthusiastic young clergyman takes pity on a poor lonely widow who turns out to be the victim of a seducer, marries her, and lives happily ever after; and *The Marriage of Colonel Lee and Other Stories* (1906). She is not to be confused with the feminist writer Dora Winifred Russell (1894–1986), née Black, second wife of Bertrand Russell (1872–1970).

RUSSELL, W[illiam] Clark (1844–1911) married (1868) Alexandrina HENRY. Born in New York, son of a singer and composer, he was educated at private schools in Winchester and Boulogne, before joining the Merchant Navy at the age of 13. Aged 21 he began to earn his living writing; he was for some time on the *Newcastle Daily Chronicle*, and later wrote for the *Daily Telegraph* as 'Seafarer'. In the 1870s he published two novels as 'Eliza Rhyl Davies' and five as 'Sydney Mostyn'. Under his own name he was the successful author of much fiction and non-fiction mostly about the sea, including *An Atlantic Tragedy and Other Stories* (1905), and *Rose Island: The Strange Story of a Love Adventure at Sea* (1900).

S

SABATINI, Rafael (1875–1950) married, first (1905), Ruth Goad DIXON (divorced 1932) and, secondly Christine DIXON née——. Born at Jesi, Italy, of an Italian father and English mother, brought up there, and educated in Portugal and Switzerland, he was obsessed with history as a child. Sabatini arrived in Britain to pursue a business career, but the successful publication of *The Tavern Knight* (1904) enabled him to become a full-time writer, specializing in swashbuckling historical romances. During the First World War he was briefly a partner in the publishing firm of Martin Secker. He was naturalized a British citizen in 1918. Thereafter he ransacked European history for themes and settings. *The Tavern Knight* is set in England during the English Civil War, *The Trampling of the Lilies* (1906) in Revolutionary France, *Love-at-Arms* (1907) in medieval Italy, and *Anthony Wilding* (1910) in England during Monmouth's rebellion. *The Shame of Motley* (1908) is 'the memoir of certain transactions in the life of Lazarro Biancomonte of Biancomonte, sometime Fool of the Court of Pesaro'. Biancomonte seeks revenge on the Duke of Pesaro, to whose court he is sent by Cesare Borgia, on a commission of a Borgian character. The South Sea Bubble of 1720 and Jacobite intrigue form the background to *The Lion's Skin* (1911): the son of a French woman by an English peer is brought up to avenge her memory but finds that he cannot bring himself to betray his father. Sabatini's melodramatic costume dramas adapted brilliantly to the cinema, and the cheap reprints of his novels were often illustrated with stills from the films. For example, *The Seahawk* (1915), perhaps his best-known work, includes a photograph of a chained, fainting blonde whose dress has been torn off her shoulders being eyed by three sinister bearded orientals, captioned: 'Her skin was white as milk, her eyes two darkest sapphires, her head of a coppery golden that seemed to glow like metal as the sunlight caught it'. The use of historical settings to license the inclusion of titillating scenes of sexual violence is characteristic of Sabatini's work, and not at all an unusual feature of historical fiction of this period. Sabatini also wrote non-fictional history including *The Life of Cesare Borgia* (1912) and *Torquemada and the Spanish Inquisition* (1914). He lived in Herefordshire towards the end of his life, but died while spending the winter in Switzerland.

Sacred and Profane Love: *A Novel in Three Episodes*, Arnold *Bennett, 1905, Chatto & Windus. This determinedly risqué and (presumably) tongue-in-cheek imitation of a contemporary *marriage problem novel is narrated by a woman novelist, Carlotta Peel, and comprises three episodes. In the first, an adolescent Carlotta is seduced by a pianist, Diaz, who is visiting the Five Towns. In the second, now a successful novelist, she is about to elope with her publisher when his wife commits suicide, thus ending the affair. In the third, she meets Diaz again in Paris; he has gone to seed and is drinking heavily, but under her influence his career recovers. The novel concludes with Carlotta's death from appendicitis. One of the best moments is her spirited skirmish with another novelist, Mrs Sardis, who has attacked the immorality of her work, and who is clearly based on Mrs Humphry *Ward.

Sacred Fount, The, Henry *James, 1901, Methuen. The unnamed narrator spends a country-house weekend trying obsessively to uncover the supposed emotional secrets of his fellow-guests. Or, in the words of Rebecca West (1892–1983), 'a weekend visitor spends more intellectual force than Kant can have used on *The Critique of Pure Reason*, in an unsuccessful attempt to discover whether there exists between certain of his fellow-guests a relationship not more interesting among these vacuous people than it is among sparrows'. The novel's starting-point is the relationship between the Brissendens: an older woman has married a younger man; he has aged and she has been rejuvenated by sipping at the 'sacred fount' of his youth. Another guest, once stupid, has, it seems, become clever, and so the narrator, assuming this is the effect of an affair, looks for a woman once clever and now stupid. This search, tedious in itself, is made interesting by James's portrait of a man who is stubbornly unable to 'read' the people around him, and who becomes more and more preoccupied with his own emotional sensitivity and the follies of his own imagination.

ST AUBYN, Alan, *pseud.*: Frances L. BRIDGES (d. 1920) married Matthew MARSHALL. Born in Surrey and educated in Essex and Cambridge, she was the daughter of a solicitor and playwright, George Bramstone Bridges. She took her pseudonym from the name of her husband's house near Tiverton, Devon. Bridges worked as a journalist, and then, when over 40, began a series of flimsy novels of Cambridge college life, interspersed with the odd Wessex idyll. *The Ordeal of Sara* (1904) concerns the life and loves of a student at Newnham, *The Harp of Life* (1908), the influence of Catholicism on two Cambridge students. *Purple Heather: A Story of Exmoor* (1907) is a story of the Devon hunting set: Sir Richard Hartopp, master of hounds, and his wife; the parson's daughters, and the rich suitor of one of them; Captain Downe, who brings his artist wife to a cottage on the moor and then makes love to Lady Hartopp. Bridges also turned out comic melodramas like *A Coronation Necklace* (1905), in which Gilbert Festing, a young man about town engaged to an heiress, manages to leave the eponymous necklace in a cab. She wrote two improving children's books: *The Trivial Round: A Confirmation Story for Girls* (1902) and *The Squire's Children, or, Footprints: A Story for Sunday Schools* (1908). She was also a keen antiquarian and archaeologist, author of a book on early embroidery, a member of the Cambridge Antiquarian Society, and member and subsequently president of the Somerset Archaeological Society.

ST LEGER, Evelyn, *pseud.*: Evelyn St Leger SAVILE (1861–1944) married (1895) Joseph Randolph RANDOLPH (1867–1936). Daughter of a lawyer, she was married to a county court judge, and wrote romances of an unusual and enterprising kind, with an emphasis on self-sacrifice. *Diaries of Three Women of the Last Century* (1907) concerns three generations: the Hon. Mace Diana Allspice, who runs off to Gretna Green from a state ball in 1821, and lives to be a great-aunt; her niece, who marries, and goes out to nurse in the Crimean War; and the latter's daughter, a modern young woman. *Dapper* (1908) is about the son of Sir Humphrey Cheyne, who belies a langorous upbringing and outlook by committing himself to missionary work, during which he meets a martyr's end. The heroine of *The Blackberry Pickers* (1912) is a devoted maternal woman who believes passionately in an unstable but clever man and does her best to bolster him up during their long engagement by sheer force of personality.

SAKI, *pseud.*: Hector Hugh MUNRO (1870–1916) was born at Akyab, Burma (where his father was a police officer). His mother died when he was 2, and he and an elder brother and sister were brought up in Devon by their grandmother and two quarrelling and tyrannical maiden aunts. He was a delicate child, and was 15 before he could be sent away to Bedford Grammar School. His father retired two years later, and the family travelled widely in Europe. He began his career in 1893 by following his father and brother into the Burma police, but he resigned after fifteen months owing to illness, and after convalescing in Devon went to London, got a ticket to read in the British Museum library, and wrote *The Rise of the Russian Empire* (1900). From 1900 he contributed political satires to the *Westminster Gazette* (published anonymously as *The Westminster Alice*, 1902), and from 1902 to 1908 served as a foreign correspondent for the *Morning Post* in the Balkans, Eastern Europe, Russia, and Paris. As 'Saki' he published the story collections *Reginald* (1906), *Reginald in Russia and Other Stories* (1910), *The *Chronicles of Clovis* (1912), and **Beasts and Superbeasts* (1914); and the novels *The *Unbearable Bassington* (1912) and *When William Came* (1913). Munro sent a copy of the latter to Field-Marshal Earl Roberts (1832–1914), advocate of rearmament and instigator of many *invasion scare writers, who wrote in thanks: 'I... must tell you... how thoroughly I approve the moral it teaches.' Munro told a friend, 'I have always looked forward to the romance of a European war', and enlisted in 1914; he was killed in action in 1916, leaving two books to be posthumously published: *The Toys of Peace* (1919) and *The Square Egg* (1924), which seem more serious in their satire. As a story writer Munro specialized in twists and paradox, but he was also elegantly nasty, and his light-hearted tone is belied by a recurring sense of cruelty and the grotesque, especially where children's views are involved (a reflection of the unhappy time with his aunts). A biography by A. J. Langguth (1981) reads Munro's character and work in the light of his homosexuality; for lack of evidence the discussion is largely speculative.

Sanders of the River, Edgar *Wallace, 1911, Ward Lock. Bestselling *Empire fiction. Commissioner Sanders has made West Central Africa 'his own land', largely by dint of not standing for any nonsense. 'When he saw a dead leaf on the plant of civilization, he plucked it off, or a weed growing with his "flowers", he pulled it up, not stopping to consider the weed's equal right to life.' This Darwinian horticulture involves settling 'palavers', putting down rebellions, and generally discomfiting philanthropists, social theorists, and padres. The drama here is not the drama of exploration, as in *Haggard, or the drama of self-discovery, as in *Kipling and *Conrad, but the drama of authority vindicated. Sanders may occasionally have to endure captivity, even the prospect of torture, but usually his mere presence is enough to make potentates quail, culprits confess, and red-faced young Englishmen abandon their native mistresses. The lethal directness of Wallace's writing matches that of his hero's actions.

SANDYS, Oliver, *pseud.*: Marguerite Florence JERVIS (1894–1964) married, first (1911), Armiger BARCLAY or BARCYNSKY (d. 1930) and, secondly (1933), Caradoc EVANS (1879–1945). Daughter of an officer in the Indian medical service, 'who wasn't very fond of me because I wasn't a boy', she was born in Burma, and sent home to English schools at 5. After several hopeless schools she went to the Royal Academy of Dramatic Art, before becoming a journalist as an alternative to going home without a job. After her marriage to an older writer of Polish birth she became a prolific author of romantic melodramas under various pseudonyms. He made her write serials which were published either over his name or as collaboration between them. When they parted they disputed rights to the several names. She lived with another man until about the time of Barclay's death, when she fell in love with Evans, a journalist and novelist. As 'Oliver Sandys' she published more than sixty romantic novels to 1955 of which the first are *The Woman in the Firelight* (1911) and *Chicane* (1912), which earned the moral disapproval of the critics by portraying a young women who apprentices herself to Lady Weybridge, a high-class gambler and thief. Jervis might perhaps be thought of as the female equivalent to 'A *Peer'. She also published as 'Armiger Barclay' three collaborations with her husband, of which the first is *The Activities of Lavie Jutt* (1911), and three other novels, including *The Worsleys* (1906), about a parlourmaid who marries an MP, to the disgust of his family, but turns out to be just as good as him anyway, and *The Kingmakers* (1907), a *Ruritanian romance about the heir to the throne of Sergia. *The Worsleys* was rapidly dramatized: indeed, it was written more or less as a play, in set-piece scenes or 'situations'. As 'Countess Helene Barcynska' she published fifty novels between 1916 and 1954. She published *Full and Frank: The Private Life of a Woman Novelist* (1941), a biography of her second husband (1946), and, by way of sequel to it a journal dealing with her widowhood, *Unbroken Thread: An Intimate Journal* (1948), in which she affirms her belief in spiritualism.

SAUNDERS, Margaret BAILLIE: Margaret Elsie CROWTHER (1873–1949) married (1901) Frederick BAILLIE-SAUNDERS (d. 1941). Born in Scarborough, a solicitor's daughter, she was educated at Haddo House School, Scarborough, and married a Church of England clergyman. Her first novel, *Saints in Society* (1902), was published in T. Fisher Unwin's 'First Novel Library'; she wrote another forty-four volumes of fiction and a study of Dickens as a social reformer (1905). Her own work, rather like Dickens's, relishes contrasts between high and low life. *The Mayoress's Wooing* (1908) distantly anticipates in some respects H. G. *Wells's **Tono-Bungay* (1909). Sir William Chatto, Mayor of London, has made his fortune out of Mother's Good-Night Calming Elixir, a potion sometimes held responsible for considerable infant mortality. His niece, Sadie, wooes Dr Jason, whose crusade against the Elixir is impeded but not halted by the discovery that he is Chatto's son. The heroine of *Litany Lane* (1909) is a slum girl married to but separated from a man of fashion, who becomes the rage in the London drawing-rooms as a dancer and mimic. Three men pursue her, 'one for her charms, one for her mind, and one for her soul'—the latter being the priest who runs a brotherhood of craftsmen and slum workers in Litany Lane, East London. In *Lady Q* (1912), Anna Flavian, a convict, finds a dead woman on the marshland to the east of London, and steals her clothes; she eventually marries the dead woman's father. *The Belfry* (1914) was published shortly after the outbreak of the First World War, and its Belgian setting no doubt added a certain topical interest. Lucy Briarwell marries a distinguished but drunken husband in order to escape from her Forsyte-ish family. When he ill-treats her and then goes mad, she thinks about a nunnery, but decides to travel instead, ending up in Flanders, where she becomes the inspiration of a selfish dramatic genius and stars in his smash-hit play, *The Belfry*. She finds temporary happiness with the genius, but when her husband suddenly recovers has to choose between the two men. This writer's surname appears as both Baillie Saunders and Baillie-Saunders.

SAVI, Ethel: Ethel Winifred BRYNING (1865–1954) married (1884) John Angelo Henry SAVI (d. 1909). Born in India, of English and American parents, she spent the first twelve years of her marriage in rural Bengal, at Udhua Nullah on the Ganges. In India she published stories for English and Indian periodicals, but she began to write novels only after retiring to England in 1909. She published more than eighty novels to 1955, of which the earliest is a predictable romance, *The Reproof of Chance* (1910), about a 37-year-old guardian who falls in love with his 16-year-old niece, but cannot admit it, and has to suffer while she flirts unconsciously with him and marries another (it all turns out for the best). Savi's great revelation, as a writer, appears to have been Bengal. *The Daughter-in-Law* (1913) concerns an Englishwoman married and enslaved to a wealthy Bengali, and her escape. In the even more *exotic *Baba and the Black Sheep* (1914), the wild and handsome son of Sir Henry and Lady Fulton, of Farnborough Towers, in Kent, leads a 'perfectly gorgeous' bohemian life among theatre people until implicated in a notorious tragedy which obliges him to take advantage of his own reported death and bury himself in a remote rural district of Bengal. There he encounters young Jean Farlow, who lives alone on the large estate left to her by her father, and is known as Miss Baba to her devoted servants. Savi published an autobiography *My Own Story* (1947).

Savrola: *A Tale of the Revolution in Laurania*, Winston Spencer *Churchill, 1900, Longmans Green. Written in 1897, and published in serial form in *Macmillan's Magazine* in 1899, this *Ruritanian (or Lauranian) romance is dedicated to the officers of the IVth (Queen's Own) Hussars. The story opens on the day of a great parade (a squadron of lancers in attendance) in the capital of Laurania. In the five years since the end of a bitter civil war, the country, once a republic, has been ruled by a brutal dictator, Antonio Molara. Savrola, a brilliant soldier with a reputation for philosophy, especially on the subject of polo, has formed a revolutionary party to restore Laurania's 'ancient liberties'. He falls in love with Lucile, the President's wife. She learns of the planned uprising, but does not betray him to her husband. Molara surprises Savrola with Lucile, but their personal antagonism is overtaken by events, as revolution breaks out, aided by British gunboats. Molara appears on the palace steps to surrender, but is shot by Karl Kreutze, leader of the socialist faction and of a mysterious secret society. Although Kreutze himself perishes, his faction triumphs, and Savrola is forced to flee to the frontier with Lucile. However, an epilogue records that 'after the tumults had subsided the hearts of the people turned again to the illustrious exile who had won them freedom, and whom they had deserted in the hour of victory'. The real sign that everything has turned out for the best is the dispatch of the Lancers' polo team to England to defeat the Amalgamated Millionaires in the final match for the Open Cup. The plot creaks, but Churchill evidently took considerable pride in the military details, of which there are many.

Scarlet Pimpernel, The, Baroness *Orczy, 1905, Greening. The bestselling story of the League of the Scarlet Pimpernel, a band of young English gentlemen, dedicated to the rescue of innocent aristocratic victims of the French Revolution and subsequent Reign of Terror. Their leader, Sir Percy Blakeney, continually outwits the enemy (personified by the cunning intellectual, Chauvelin) not simply through plain courage but also by his use of disguise and his sheer insouciance. Blakeney similarly disguises his identity from his society friends in England (and even, for a while, from his wife), thus establishing a model (which would be widely used by detective and spy story writers) of the effete and ineffectual aristocrat who is, in reality, a dashing, ingenious, and determined man of action. Not surprisingly, *The Scarlet Pimpernel* inspired several sequels and has been regularly adapted for stage, screen, and television.

SCHIFF, Sidney: see under Ada *Leverson.

SCHWARTZ, Joost van der POORTEN: see 'Maarten *Maartens'.

science fiction. The aged George *Meredith talked to G. K. *Chesterton once about the books he had *not* written. According to Chesterton, 'He asked me to write one of the stories for him, as he would have asked the milkman, if he had been talking to the milkman. It was a splendid and frantic story, a sort of astronomical farce, all about a man who was rushing up to the Royal Society with the only possible way of avoiding an earth-destroying comet; and it showed how even on this huge errand the man was tripped up by his own weaknesses and vanities; how he lost a train by trifling or was put in gaol for brawling.' Meredith had for some time been nurturing a story about a 'Don Quixote of the Future', a wealthy young man who infuriates everyone with his schemes for improving the race. When Chesterton declined to write it, Meredith summoned H. G. *Wells, by then the author both of futuristic tales like *The War of the Worlds* (1898) and of schemes for improving the world like *Anticipations* (1902). Wells also declined, though he might be said to have attempted the subject in *In the Days of the Comet* (1906), as might 'George *Griffith', to even more sensational effect, in *The World Peril of 1910* (1907), in which a comet hurtling towards the earth is deflected in the nick of time by a projectile fired from a gigantic cannon. Science fiction was very much in vogue in the Edwardian period, both among bestselling writers and among those of more metaphysical or sociological habit: the latter tending to emphasize, as Meredith had, the very recognizable human failings which are likely to persist even in a world otherwise changed out of recognition. The genre became both purposeful and respectable in the 1870s. Sir George Chesney's *The Battle of Dorking* (1871) was the first of innumerable *invasion scare stories which, while purporting to deal with scientific fact rather than fiction, frequently outstripped the actual pace of technological progress (partly, it may be, under the influence of the romances of Jules Verne (1828–1905), widely translated for British magazines, and emulated by writers like Fred T. *Jane and W. Patrick *Kelly). See, for example: *The Stolen Submarine* (1904) by 'George Griffith'; *With Airship and Submarine* (1908) by 'Harry *Collingwood'; Rudyard *Kipling, 'With the Night Mail', in **Actions and Reactions* (1909); H. G. Wells, *The *War in the Air* (1908). Self-evidently fantastic are the stories of global cataclysm, like M. P. *Shiel's *The *Purple Cloud* (1901) and Arthur Conan *Doyle's *The Poison Belt* (1913), and the stories of alien invasion, like J. Henry *Harris's *A Romance in Radium* (1906), where the alien invader is entirely benevolent. Another potent model was *The Coming Race* (1871) by Edward Bulwer-Lytton (1803–73), which imagines a lost underground civilization based on 'vril', a source of infinitely renewable electrical power (the 'Vril-ya' also have ray guns and ESP). Wells's *The *First Men in the Moon* (1901) and *The *Food of the Gods* (1904), and Frederic *Carrel's eugenicist *2010* (1914) are in this tradition.

Sea Lady, The: *A Tissue of Moonshine*, H. G. *Wells, 1902, Methuen. A mermaid comes ashore at Folkestone during a family bathing party and asks to be allowed to live with them for a while, as an ordinary mortal human. It turns out that the sea lady is really in pursuit of Harry Chatteris, a beautiful young man she once saw in the South Seas, who is now engaged to a friend of the family, the earnest Adeline Glendower. Offering him 'better dreams' than those of being a Liberal MP and social reformer, the mermaid persuades Chatteris to accompany her back into the sea. A slight fantasy that partly satirizes middle-class social niceties (what is 'correct behaviour' in a mermaid?), partly draws on Wells's ability to ground a fantasy (in the witty discussion, for example, of the mermaid's reading habits, dependent on the books thrown from ships at sea), and partly gives him a way of portraying a sexually aggressive and determined woman.

Secret, The, E. Phillips *Oppenheim, 1907, Ward Lock. J. Hardross Courage, man of letters and accomplished cricketer, gets implicated in a scheme to restore the French monarchy, this time backed innocently by some American millionaires whose wives want to become titled ladies and, less innocently, by the Germans, who plan to invade Britain after the forts protecting London have been put out of action by a fifth column masquerading as the German Waiters' Union. Courage, who had previously found life 'a tame thing', becomes a new man. Inspired by encounters with a smouldering lady of fortune, Adèle Van Hoyt, he infiltrates the Waiters' Union and uncovers the conspiracy. The authorities refuse to believe him, so he forms an alliance with the scaremongering press, the main platform during the pre-war years for those who felt that the politicians would continue to ignore their warnings. He takes his story to the editor of the *Daily Oracle*, who prints it even though his office is under siege by heavily armed German waiters.

Secret Agent, The: *A Simple Tale*, Joseph *Conrad, 1907, Methuen. Dedicated to H. G. *Wells. Verloc, a spy in the pay of the Russian Embassy, who has dodged along comfortably for years without doing much, is suddenly sent for, and told by the Embassy that he must do something for his money; it is suggested that he instigate some crime which will rouse British opinion and the London police. In terror of losing his job, he incites his half-witted brother-in-law, Stevie, to blow up Greenwich Observatory. Stevie stumbles at the crucial moment and blows himself to pieces. Verloc's wife, Winnie, discovers what has happened, stabs Verloc to death in a fit of frenzy, and then, flying from justice, is robbed and deserted by the anarchist, Ossipon, and throws herself from a cross-Channel steamer. Throughout this grim comedy of anarchism Conrad elevates the subterranean world of terrorism out of thriller and melodrama to the plane of realistic psychology. Subtitled *A Simple Tale*, the novel is partly intended to remind readers how simple men really are, and how narrow a gulf exists between the maker of bombs and the ordinary contented citizen. One can discern both the influence of Émile Zola (1840–1902) and, in the English tradition, of Wilkie Collins (1824–89): Verloc is directly in line from Count Fosco in *The Woman in White* (1860). In *The Secret Agent* the emphasis is on the monotonous domestic existence of the spy, and on the character of his wife and their relationship. What is striking about the novel is the sense of appallingly futile tragedy, and the author's refusal to take sides or express emotion, beyond a grave irony and/or melancholy. In the end, the novel is more a portrait gallery than a story, however, and apart from the murder of Verloc (one of the most intensely dramatic murders in fiction) the characters (anarchists, diplomats, policemen, and stodgy middle-class English) are less convincing in their actions than in their meditations. There are occasional overlong digressions (for example, the departure of Winnie's mother on her way to the workhouse). One of the greatest achievements of the novel is its evocation of London, seen through the eyes of the alien anarchists.

Secret Garden, The, Frances Hodgson *Burnett, 1911, William Heinemann. This is one of the finest and best-loved children's books. When Mary Lennox is 9 her parents die in a cholera epidemic and she is sent to live with her reclusive uncle at Misselthwaite Manor in Yorkshire. She has been brought up lonely and bad-tempered in India, and there seems little reason for her to change her selfish and irritable ways. But her discovery of a secret garden, and her friendship with the housemaid, Martha Sowerby, and her brother, Dickon, who helps her bring the garden back to order, enable her to grow too. Meanwhile, she has heard weeping at night and discovers Colin, the son of the house, introverted and bedridden in a wing of the house she is forbidden to visit. An awkward friendship develops, until she smuggles him into the garden too, while his pride is turned from a bitter self-pity into a means of self-cure. He too becomes interested in the natural world and thus, through exercise in the open air, healthier and saner.

Secret Woman, The, Eden *Phillpotts, 1905, Methuen. A story of desire and betrayal in and between two Dartmoor farming families. Anthony and Ann Redvers have two sons, the restless, introspective Jesse and the stolid, single-minded Michael. Joseph Westaway, a widower, has two daughters: 28-year-old Barbara, handsome but careworn, and 20-year-old Salome, a 'natural creature'. His farm has one unusual feature: a fence constructed out of dummies used for target practice on the Dartmoor firing-ranges. As the novel opens, Jesse is courting Salome, without success, while Joseph and Barbara set off to visit William Arscott, a quarry-owner, with a view to a loan of £300. Ann

Redvers, returning from a visit to her sick mother, discovers by chance a note written by her husband to an unknown correspondent, arranging a nocturnal rendezvous on nearby Halstock Hill. She reflects that in twenty years of marriage they have never kept any secrets from each other, and decides, out of amusement and curiosity, to witness the unlikely meeting. She finds her husband making passionate love to another woman, and, overwhelmed by horror, does not stop even to identify the woman. She knows that she will never be able to forgive him, and, like the notorious heroine of Mary *Braddon's *Lady Audley's Secret* (1862), though for a very different reason, pushes him down a well. Her sons are present at the time: Michael, who sides unequivocally with his mother, wants to conceal the crime; Jesse is not so sure. A verdict of death by misadventure is recorded. Jesse's anger and remorse induce pneumonia, and an extremely colourful delirium. Barbara Westaway, desperate to redeem her father's debt, offers to marry Arscott, but then withdraws when he makes it plain that he will not allow marriage to interfere with business. Jesse recovers, proposes again to Salome, and is accepted. However, her reluctance to name the day eventually provokes a shattering mutual confession. Jesse reveals that Anthony was murdered by Ann, Salome that she was Anthony's lover. Jesse commits suicide. Ann confesses to the crime, is convicted of manslaughter, and sentenced to twenty years' penal servitude. Ann and Salome are reconciled in loss. The success of the novel depends on the plausibility of the genetic and moral resilience which characterizes Ann Redvers, and which distinguishes her in the author's mind from such as the heroine of *Lady Audley's Secret*. 'The strength of the race', she tells Salome, 'be stronger than the ills of the race—stronger than sin—stronger than death.'

SEDGWICK, Anne Douglas (1873–1935) married (1908) Basil DE SÉLINCOURT (b. 1876). American-born, she came to England with her family at the age of 9, and spent most of her life in England and France, where she went as an 18-year-old to study painting. She married, rather suddenly and quietly (possibly because he had been married before), de Sélincourt, a critic, and lived at Chipping Norton in Gloucestershire for the rest of her life. She was deeply interested in philosophy. Her first published novel, *The Dull Miss Archinard* (1898), was based on a story she had told her sisters. Subsequent novels aim at cosmopolitanism. In *The Rescue* (1902) an exquisite Englishwoman elopes with a handsome, disreputable French painter who dies leaving her, at the age of 47, after years of degradation, in miserable poverty. To make matters worse, her daughter has inherited her father's rakish looks and character. A 30-year-old Englishman, who has fallen in love with a photograph of her as she was at 19, searches her out, is not disabused by the original, and takes it upon himself to reclaim her daughter. *Franklin Kane* (1910), also set in Paris, contrasts a warm-hearted American couple with a pair of English gold-diggers. Sedgwick was much exercised by the idea (and the evil effects) of genius. In *Tante* (1911) Mercedes Okraska, part-Polish, part-Italian, part-American, but all pianist, manages to subjugate those around her with the exception of her niece, Karen Woodruff, and the indomitable philistine barrister who marries Karen. In *The Encounter* (1914) Persis Fennamy, a shallow, heartless American woman, tours Europe in search of high intellectual experience. Friedrich Nietzsche (1844–1900) appears in the guise of the philosopher Ludwig Wehlitz, whose first speech definitively gives the game away: 'Tolstoi would lead the world into a nest of maggots where the weak cling together and find sustainment in loathsome unity... We strong ones turn from him laughing.' Sedgwick also wrote a *'marriage problem' novel, *Amabel Channice* (1908), whose heroine leaves her husband and raises a child born out of wedlock on her own. Her letters, effusive, strong on literary tastes, short on biographical detail, were edited by her husband (1936). Hugh *de Sélincourt was her brother-in-law.

Sequence 1905–1912, The, Elinor *Glyn, 1913, Gerald Duckworth. The novel returns to the subject-matter (English country-house life) and the narrative method (first-person) of Glyn's early novels. Guinevere Bohun, married off at the age of 16 to a bullying elderly general, and virtually imprisoned by him in their fortress-like mansion, Redwood Moat, falls in love for the first time at the age of 30 with a neighbour, Sir Hugh Dremont. For years she struggles with her conscience, rejecting the cynical advice of her sister, Letitia, to act like any other wife and have an affair. She finally yields while her husband is away on a military mission, but immediately regrets her decision, breaking off the relationship. Hugh's longing for a son to inherit his title and estates leads him to marry Lady Kathleen Catesby, a ruthless gold-digger who turns out to be not only an octoroon but the lover of her selfish and conceited son, Algernon. A few days after the marriage General Bohun dies, leaving Guinevere a free woman. The concluding chapters are set in Cowes, where Algernon and Kathleen ram the Chequers Buoy in their motor boat and take their secret with them to the bottom of the sea. The novel was too dark in tone to be successful with the public: 'vapid philandering', the **Times Literary Supplement* called it.

SERGEANT, [Emily Frances] Adeline (1851–1904). Born at Ashbourne in Derbyshire, she was the daughter of a Methodist minister. Her mother, born Jane Hall, published wholesome tales for youngsters under the pseudonym 'Adeline' (which Emily herself later adopted). She went to school in Weston-super-Mare before attending Laleham School in Clapham, south London, and Queen's College, Harley Street, graduating with first-class honours. Sergeant began work as a governess to support herself and wrote novels in her free time. By 1884 her novels were successful enough to allow her wholly to devote herself to a literary career. Sergeant lived in Dundee from 1885 to 1887, working for the *People's Friend*. In the late 1880s she became interested in Fabianism and the plight of London's poor. Her output was truly prodigious—as many as seven publications a year (the first of which was a volume of verse published at 15). *Esther Dennison* (1889) describes the loneliness of the single working woman in London. *The Story of a Penitent Soul* (1892) is a novel written in journal form which reveals the miserable life of a discontented churchman. *The Work of Oliver Byrd* (1902) concerns two rivals for the affections of a young editor: the well-to-do Eleanor Denbigh, who takes up writing as a hobby but becomes increasingly preoccupied with the London poor, and Avis Rignold, talented and impoverished, who publishes under the male pseudonym of 'Oliver Byrd'. The devices of conventional domestic melodrama (poison phial, burnt manuscript) are used to highlight the conflicting demands made on women, and the difficulties of independence. Sergeant's subsequent fiction tends to assemble odd families, or odd surrogate families: *Beneath the Veil* (1903) features an orphaned girl living in an isolated grange with her worldly, scheming half-sister; *Accused and Accuser* (1904) concerns an heiress, Nina Davenant, her companion, Miss Eleanor West, and her elderly guardian, Dr Kelvedon; in *The Coming of the Randolphs* (1906) Colonel Underwood, who already has a son and daughter by a previous marriage, takes on a new wife and her large family. Although none of her novels has stood the test of time, the best display the skills of a solid professional writer; her portrayal of provincial middle-class life is worthy of note. For many years Sergeant acted as fiction adviser for R. Bentley & Sons. She converted to Catholicism at the turn of the century, and died in Bournemouth. Her obituary in the *Times* (6 Dec. 1904) emphasizes her favouring of quantity over quality: '[She] would have made a greater reputation, and have left a more considered name in English fiction had she lived before the days of stenographers and typewriters.'

Set of Six, A, Joseph *Conrad, 1908, Methuen. On the cover, the six stories are described as 'A Romantic Tale, An Ironic Tale, An Indignant Tale, A Desperate Tale, A Military Tale, A Pathetic Tale'. But these categories ultimately make little sense, as each one could fit into a number of the groupings. The finest story in the collection is undoubtedly 'The Duel', a lengthy reconstruction of a legendary tale of two French officers of the Napoleonic period who repeatedly duel over minor points of honour. They begin fighting as lieutenants, and meet at intervals to try and kill each other until they are generals. By contrast, 'The Brute' is an elaborately empty pub anecdote about an ill-fated ship, who kills somebody every voyage she makes, until she finally runs aground off the Cape. The other four stories reveal the same grim humour and minute attention to detail as 'The Duel' and 'The Brute', but they are also more straightforward studies in brutality. These stories also share another characteristically Conradian theme: implicit but unrecognized complicity in an irrational fate. The characters get caught up in a deadly chain, which ensnares the innocent, and condemns them to a life of torture. 'Il Conde' is a character study of a Neapolitan aristocrat, repeatedly held up by the same gentleman mugger, and uncertain how to react; 'Gaspar Ruiz' tells of a simple strong-man South American guerilla leader repeatedly switching from the republican to the Spanish royalist sides in the endless brutal confusions of the Chilean war of independence. He dies absurdly splayed across a canon; 'An Anarchist' concerns an innocent young French mechanic, who gets drunk in the company of some anarchists and shouts out their watchwords, as though he were himself one of them. He is is convicted as an anarchist, imprisoned, and then sent off to a French penal colony in South America, blunders into the middle of a riot, commits murder in order to escape, finally escapes, but ends up practically a slave on a colonial ranch; 'The Informer' tells of a London revolutionary group with an upper-class patroness. When she discovers her anarchist lover is a police informer, he commits suicide, and she withdraws from the group. None of the stories in *A Set of Six* gives much sense of the internal life of the characters: the reader is left to work from external evidence.

SHAKESPEAR, O.: Olivia TUCKER (1863–1938) married (1885) Henry Hope SHAKESPEAR (1849–1923). Daughter of a major-general in the Indian army, she was married to a solicitor. She was a first cousin of the poet Lionel Johnson (1867–1902), who introduced her to W. B. Yeats (1865–1939) with whom she had an affair in 1896 (and who later married her brother's stepdaughter). She and Yeats seem to have contemplated eloping together. His poem 'After Long Silence' is addressed to her: 'Bodily decrepitude is wisdom; young / We loved each other and were ignorant.' In 1909 she met Ezra Pound (1885–1972) and, after a protracted engagement and some opposition from the Shakespears (possibly because of Olivia's jealousy), her only child, Dorothy, (1886–1973) married him in 1914. Her own fiction is of the *marriage problem class. The most valuable source of information on her career is John Harwood's (1989) study of her relationship with Yeats, who suggests that her fiction was influenced by that of her friend 'John Oliver *Hobbes'. Her last novel, **Uncle Hilary* (1910), is generally regarded as her best.

SHARP, Evelyn [Jane] (1869–1955) married (1933) Henry Woodd NEVINSON (1856–1941). Suffragette and children's author, she came from a large middle-class family (Cecil J. Sharp, 1859–1924, the collector of folk songs, was her eldest brother; their father was a slate merchant) and was educated at the progressive Kensington Private School. Frustrated in her desire to go to university, Sharp decided early that she wanted to be a writer, and in 1894, aged 24, took a job as a daily governess and took a room of her own in London. Within a year she had published stories in the *Yellow Book*; a novel, *At the Relton Arms*, appeared in 1895. Sharp's most successful books were written for children, such as *The Making of a Schoolgirl* (1897), *The Youngest Girl in School* (1901), and *The Hill That Fell Down* (1909), as well as numerous fairy tales, some of which were illustrated by her friend Mabel *Dearmer. In 1903 her father died and she spent a year looking after her mother, which meant that she lost her pupils and afterwards depended wholly on her earnings from journalism. She was an active suffragette, joining the WSPU in 1906, becoming assistant editor of *Votes for Women* in 1912, and working for the *Daily Herald* 1918–23. She was imprisoned in Holloway twice, and the second time was on hunger strike. Through the suffrage movement she became friends with 'G. *Colmore', Beatrice *Harraden, and Elizabeth *Robins. The lives of suffragists are treated in the stories of **Rebel Women* (1910). *Nicolete* (1907) tells the story of an artistic young girl of an improvident family, nearly forced into an unwelcome marriage, who is left a fortune on condition she does not marry: 'It ought to make it easier to be a great artist.' She ends, however, by choosing life instead of art, in the shape of an idealistic social reformer, coupled with a plan for utopian state socialist reorganization. Sharp was pacifist: she continued suffrage agitation during the First World War, refused to pay income tax, and helped found the Women's International League for Peace and Freedom. In the 1920s she did social work and famine relief work in Germany and Russia; later she was interested in adolescents in the East End of London, and worked for the Labour Party and the NCCL. She wrote the libretto for the opera *The Poisoned Kiss* (1936) by Ralph Vaughan Williams (1872–1958). She published an excellent autobiography, *Unfinished Adventure* (1933), which comments humorously on the *Yellow Book* circle. She is not to be confused with Dame Evelyn Adelaide Sharp (1903–85), the Civil Servant.

SHEEHAN, P[atrick] A[ugustine] (1852–1913). Born at Mallow, Co. Cork, he attended St Colman's College in Fermoy and Maynooth College before his ordination in 1875. Apart from a short spell of missionary work in Exeter and Plymouth (1875–77), Sheehan lived most of his life in Ireland. During 1877–95 he was curate in both Mallow and Queenstown. In 1895 Sheehan moved to be priest in Doneraile, Co. Cork, where he was to settle for the rest of his life. He was appointed Canon of Cloyne in 1903. Sheehan started to submit articles to periodicals during 1881. His publications include the very well-received *Geoffrey Austin, Student* (1895); its sequel, *The Triumph of Failure* (1899), was Sheehan's own favourite among his works. *My New Curate* (1899) was first serialized in the *American Ecclesiastical Review* and proved very popular in the United States. His obituary in the *Times* (7 Oct. 1913) declared that it revealed him to be 'a master of singularly pure, cultured, and lucid English style, and as one of the select band of writers able to picture not only sympathetically but truly the Irish peasant'. *Luke Delmege* (1901) was also serialized in the *Review* before publication in England. His novels veer between sober realism and melodrama, often in proportion to the Irishness of the subject-matter. *Lisheen, or, The Test of the Spirits* (1907), for example, concerns a young Irish landlord, Robert Maxwell, who lives for a year as a labourer among labourers; it includes some convincing Irish peasants, but also a society woman, a sentimental cynic, an ill-omened wedding present, a vengeful Hindu girl, and concealed leprosy. *Miriam Lucas* (1912) is set in Dublin and Glendarragh, and, less persuasively, New York; *The Blindness of Doctor Gray* (1909) in an Irish village. Sheehan also wrote *historical romances. The action of *The Queen's Fillet* (1911) takes place during the French Revolution: Maurice de Brignon buys the fillet worn by Marie Antoinette on her way to the guillotine and uses it twenty-two years later to save his daughter's life. *The Graves at Kilmorna: A Story of '67* (1915) reveals a vein of Irish nationalism in Sheehan's work. Collections of his verse, his sermons, and his essays and lectures were also published, and there are biographies by Herman T. Heuser (1917) and the Revd Francis Boyle (1927).

SHERARD, Robert H[arborough]: Robert Harborough Sherard KENNEDY (1861–1943), who changed his surname to SHERARD (1881) and married, first (1887), Marthe LIPSKA (divorced 1906), secondly (1908), Irene HERVEY (1868–1922), formerly OSGOOD (divorced 1915), and, thirdly (1928), Alice Muriel FIDDIAN. Sherard was born in Putney, London. His father, the Revd Bennet Sherard Calcraft Kennedy, a Church of England clergyman, was an illegitimate son of Robert Sherard, 6th and last Earl of Harborough (1797–1859). His mother, Jane Stanley Wordsworth, was a granddaughter of the poet. Sherard was educated in Italy, Germany, and Guernsey, and briefly at New College, Oxford. After a momentous row with his father Sherard dropped the 'Kennedy' from his name and moved to Naples. He started his writing career in Paris with a novel, *Bartered Honour* (1883), and his only volume of verse, *Whispers* (1884), which is dedicated to Oscar Wilde (1856–1900), about whom he later wrote *Oscar Wilde: The Story of an Unhappy Friendship* (1902). While living in Paris Sherard contributed first-rate interviews and vignettes of Parisian life to the *Pall Mall Gazette*, the *Westminster Gazette*, the *Daily Graphic*, the **Idler*, the **Bookman*, and **Pearson's*, as well as to two American newspapers, the *Morning Journal* and the *World*. He also wrote two biographies of French writers whom he had befriended: *Émile Zola* (1893) and *Alphonse Daudet* (1894). Sherard moved back to Britain in 1895 and published a series of undercover investigations of the social conditions of the poor in Britain and Ireland, published as *The White Slaves of England* (1897), *The Cry of the Poor* (1901), *The Closed Door* (1902), and *The Child Slaves of Britain* (1905). After his recovery from depression Sherard wrote a series of memoirs of his stay in France and another Wilde biography (1906). *After The Fault* (1907) is a cogent and revealing novel which stands out from his usual brand of unimpressive mystery thriller, and was inspired by the breakdown of his first marriage. After a second unhappy marriage Sherard struggled to make a living, and his poor health (he was syphilitic) and alcoholism laid him low. His application to the Royal Literary Fund during the First World War includes a sensational account of his life, including a description of the duel which ended his first marriage to an 'improvident & flighty Polish lady' and the allegation that his second wife forced him to write novels which she then published as 'Irene Osgood'. *The Real Oscar Wilde* (1917) was the only work of note published until his biography of Guy de Maupassant in 1926, for which he was awarded the French *Légion d'Honneur* 1929. The self-effacingly entitled *Memoirs of a Mug* appeared in 1941. Sherard was an intelligent, well-educated man, and although his pieces seem rather verbose and emotional by today's standards, he was a greatly respected journalist in his heyday. Unfortunately his reputation has been permanently dented by unsympathetic treatment by some of Wilde's biographers—notably Hesketh Pearson and Richard Ellmann. He died at Grange Road in Ealing, North London, leaving his widow £50.

SHERREN, Wilkinson (b. 1875) was born in Dorset and became a journalist. He was an author with literary pretensions, the tone of whose work varies from whimsy to polemic. In the first category are the Wessex peasant tales collected in *A Rustic Dreamer and Other Stories* (1903). *The Chronicles of Berthold Darnley* (1907) is the first-person narrative of the life of a consumptive musician who falls in love and loses his reason: the second part of the novel reproduces his writings in the asylum. *Two Girls and a Mannikin* (1911) chronicles the relations between Reuben Rashley, a weak, fanatical Methodist who abandons his faith when his mother dies, and Ruth and Hermione, the daughters of Farmer Batinshaw. The heroine of *Windfrint Virgin* (1912) comes to London from Dorset to earn a living, and falls in with Wentworth Williams, an eccentric writer and lecturer, and manager of the Friend-in-Need Bureau: she marries the seafaring Tim Squebb instead. There is a sympathetic portrait of a suffragette, Miss Rhodes. *The Marriage Tie* (1914) is overtly polemical, a *marriage problem novel concerned with the illegitimacy laws. Sherren also published *Tumult: A Wessex Love Story* (1910), as well as hagiography and a bibliography of Thomas Hardy's fiction (1902). He also wrote as 'Nicholas Fay'.

SHIEL, M[atthew] P[hipps] (1865–1947) married, first (1898), Carolina Garcia GOMEZ and, secondly (*c*.1918) Mrs Gerald JEWSON. Shiel was born at Plymouth, Monserrat, in the West Indies, son of a Methodist minister of Irish and African descent. He went to Harrison College, Barbados, before coming to King's College, London, to study classics. Shiel also attended St Bartholomew's Hospital to read medicine but he only stayed six months, taking no degree. During the 1890s he was a peripheral figure in the circle of Oscar Wilde (1854–1900). Arthur *Machen was a friend and came to his first wedding. The only two jobs that Shiel admitted to having were a brief spell as an interpreter at international medical conference in 1891 (where he became associated with Florence Nightingale, 1820–1910) and in the Censor's Office translating German letters in the First World War. He also spent two years teaching mathematics at a Derbyshire school (he listed his recreations in *Who's Who* as 'mathematics and mountaineering'). He sometimes claimed to have been crowned King of Redonda by his father, and bequeathed his throne to the poet John Gawsworth (1912–70). One of the works which made his name in the 1890s was *Prince Zaleski* (1895), No. 7 in John Lane's 'Keynote' series, which contains three exotic detective/fantasy stories much indebted to the work of Edgar Allen Poe (1809–49). Shiel once said that he 'wrote some books under different influences Poe's, Carlyle's and Job's...' *Stones in the Fire* (1896) includes his best-known fantasy story 'Xelucha'—which owes much to Poe's 'The Fall of the House of Usher' and 'Ligeia'. *The Yellow Danger* (1899), his most popular book, serves as a vivid illustration of the extent of Western concerns about the emergence of power in the Far East. This is the first of several publications that have xenophobic traits; Shiel has been credited with inventing the phrase 'yellow peril'. He also wrote *historical romances such as *The Man Stealers* (1900) which concerns a French counter-plot to capture the 1st Duke of Wellington to compensate for Napoleon's incarceration on Elba. Shiel's first true work of *science fiction was *The Lord of the Sea* (1901), whose protagonist, a 'Jewish Napoleon', finds a diamond-encrusted meteorite; the wealth and power the discovery brings enable him to build a spectacular floating fortress. *The *Purple Cloud* (1901) is a powerful tale which was loosely adapted into a successful film. Its theme anticipates that of Arthur Conan *Doyle's *The Poison Belt* (1913). In *The Isle of Lies* (1909) Hannibal Lepsius, who has been brought up on a remote island and taught to decipher the inscription on an Egyptian stela, becomes in some mysterious way a sensational figure in Parisian society, where he appears with a 'retinue', and is then lured to the sinister Château Egmond in Brittany. In *The Dragon* (1913), an *invasion story, Li Ku Yu, an evil Chinaman known as Sky Blue to the hero, Teddy Reeks, persuades the Japanese to sell their navy to their Germans at a reduced price. Reeks, however, is Edward, Prince of Wales, in Cockney disguise, and he saves the day. The *Times Literary Supplement* identified the rococco style of the latter as a form of 'Euphuism'; adventure yarns are usually of a monosyllabic tendency. Shiel and Louis *Tracy wrote a series of detective stories as 'Gordon Holmes': *An American Emperor* (1897), *The Late Tenant* (1907), *By Force of Circumstance* (1910), and *The House of Silence* (1911).

Shiel's work within the Edwardian era is typified by themes of external threat and destruction. His later publications demonstrate a marked shift away from these preoccupations to more philosophical ones; he was much influenced by the work of Friedrich Nietzsche (1844–1900). Yet there is always a richness and exuberance in his quirky prose style that many find offputting. Shiel was described by Hugh *Walpole as 'a flaming genius'; he has also been called 'gorgeously mad', and he did gradually decline into a rather sad, xenophobic figure. He applied to the Royal Literary Fund in 1914, stating that he was going blind, had three children, the youngest four months old, and that his annual income had declined from about £2,000 at the turn of the century to about £150. Sutherland says that he died 'a religious maniac'. His last work, *Jesus*, has never been published. Shiel was granted a Civil List Pension in 1935 that was increased during 1938. He died in Chichester, Sussex. His *Times* obituary (20 Feb. 1947) describes him as 'a master of *fantasy, less widely known than he deserves'.

SHORE, W. Teignmouth (d. 1932) was the son of a Church of England clergyman and royal chaplain. He was educated at Westminster School and Oxford, became a journalist, and was the author of several accounts of murder trials, cookery books, *Charles Dickens and His Friends* (1909), and six novels. Some of his fiction is humorous: *The Talking Master: An Irresponsibility* (1904), about Fred Cross, who teaches elocution to Eben Riley, a millionaire provision merchant, and his family; *Oh! My Uncle: Being Some Fun with an Undercurrent* (1912). More characteristic, perhaps, are novels dealing with the shabbier or seamier side of life, where the 'undercurrent' rises to the surface. *The Pest* (1908) is about a clergyman's daughter, herself married to a clergyman, who becomes the mistress of an idealizing artist, and subsequently carries on down the slippery slope. *Above All Things* (1909) deals with young journalists living in Vincent Square, Westminster, and *Creature of Clay* (1911) with a down-at-heel clerk who degenerates when he fails to find employment, and dies, and the kindly doctor who looks set to marry his heroic widow. Shore also published *A Soul's Awakening* (1908). He was probably a relation (perhaps a brother?) of Florence Teignmouth Shore, who, as 'Priscilla Craven', published five novels between 1909 and 1913, including *Love and the Lodger* (1909), a suburban comedy about a lodger with a bullying landlady who has a brave, coughing little girl called Lilac, and *Circe's Daughter* (1913), about Claudia (whose mother is fast), who marries the wrong man; he becomes a tiresome invalid and then conveniently dies.

SHORTER, Dora SIGERSON: Dora Mary SIGERSON (1866–1918) married (1896) Clement King SHORTER (1857–1926). The Irish nationalist daughter of a Dublin doctor, she published Celtic Twilight verse from 1894, and also fiction. *The Country-House Party* (1905) is a collection of stories recounted by the various members of a literary house party. *The Father Confessor: Stories of Death and Danger* (1900) are eerie tales of fear and the supernatural. In *Through Wintry Terrors* (1907) a penniless artist takes pity on a girl thrown out by her drunken father, lends her his room for the night, and is made to marry her; they struggle with poverty, part, and are reconciled. Some of her fiction, such as *The Story and Song of Black Roderick* (1906), a tale of ancient Ireland couched in archaic language, appeared under her maiden name. Her husband was a prominent figure in London journalism, editor of the *Illustrated London News* (1891–1900), the *Sketch* (1893–1900), and the *Sphere* (1900–26), and an expert on the novels and lives of Charlotte (1816–55), Emily (1818–48), and Anne Brontë (1820–49).

Shuttle, The, Frances Hodgson *Burnett, 1907, William Heinemann. Reuben Vanderpoel, American multi-millionaire, has two daughters, the prettily passive Rosalie, whose bath is rumoured to be made of Carrara marble, and the beautiful, intrepid, resourceful Bettina. Rosalie marries a degenerate Englishman of title, Sir Nigel Anstruthers, and returns to England to live with him at his dilapidated family seat, Stornham Court. They have a son, Ughtred. After spending some time in Europe, Bettina visits Stornham Court and is revolted by Sir Nigel's treatment of her sister. Under her guidance, both Rosalie and the estate begin to recover. Sir Nigel returns from a trip abroad, and begins to make love to Bettina. Meanwhile, fever has broken out in the village owned by a neighbour, James Hubert John Fergus Saltyre, 15th Earl of Mount Dunstan, whom Bettina had first met on the steamer from America, when he came to her aid during a collision with another ship. Unlike the thoroughly decadent Sir Nigel, Dunstan is a First Man, a natural-born pioneer, a Viking: he has spent some time ranching in the American West. The fever is overcome, thanks to the medical supplies purchased by Betty, and to Dunstan's 'almost military supervision of and command over his villagers'. After a number of confrontations and revelations, Sir Nigel contracts fever and dies, leaving Dunstan to create a better-founded Anglo-American union with Bettina and with her father's millions.

SIDGWICK, Mrs Alfred: Cecily Wilhelmine ULLMANN (*c.*1855–1934) married (1883) Alfred SIDGWICK (1850–1943). Born in Islington, London, of German Jewish family, she was the daughter of a merchant. She converted to Christianity after her marriage to a philosopher (he was a cousin of the better-known philosopher Henry Sidgwick, 1838–1900, and of Ethel *Sidgwick's father). They lived in Manchester, where he was Professor of Logic, from 1886 at Skipton-in-Craven, and later in London and Cornwall. In *Lamorna* (1912) a young woman in fashionable London society is seduced by a married man but subsequently marries the excellent fellow to whom she was already engaged; her cousin, Lamorna, and Lamorna's fiancé, a painter, know the truth but do not tell; someone else, however, does. *Below Stairs* (1912) is a lightweight comedy about a servant girl with an impossible mistress which includes one or two unusual characters, including a gentleman cook, and a German Fräulein. From about 1907 the Sidgwicks lived at St Buryan in Cornwall, and Cornish settings and characters are common in her later works, which are mostly light social comedy. Mrs Sidgwick's non-fiction includes her first book, *Caroline Schlegel and Her Friends* (1889), and *Home Life in Germany* (1908). A few early works were published under the name 'Mrs Andrew Dean'.

SIDGWICK, Ethel (1877–1970) was born in Rugby, educated at Oxford High School, and brought up in intellectual circles. Daughter of a classical scholar, she was first cousin to the *Benson brothers and was the author of a biography of her aunt by marriage, Eleanor Sidgwick (1845–1936), principal of Newnham College, Cambridge, and wife of the philosopher Henry Sidgwick (1838–1900). Her brother Frank Sidgwick (d. 1939) founded the publishers Sidgwick & Jackson, and published his sister's novels. Mrs Alfred *Sidgwick was married to a cousin of Ethel's father. Ethel Sidgwick wrote a dozen novels between 1910 and 1926, starting with *Promise* (1910), most of which were lightly critical stories of upper-class life in England, France, and Ireland, with a clear eye for national cultural traits. *Promise* is described in the preface thus: 'The central figure of the book is a young musical genius, half English, half French, and the author's aim is to illustrate by means of incidents in his life the futility of all attempts to control artistic impulse. The five divisions of the story show how the Child of Promise is affected by the various persons with whom he is brought into contact.' The Child of Promise is Antoine, the second son of James Edgell, an English railway engineer, and his wife Henriette, née Lemaure, the beautiful, spoilt daughter of a famous French violinist. The focus of the story is divided between Antoine and his less gifted but more sympathetic elder brother, Philip, and most of the action takes place in English schools and country houses. 'We are left to hope that the life of this English Jean Christophe [hero of a sequence of novels by Romain Rolland (1866–1944), translated by Gilbert *Cannan 1910–13] will continue through at least another volume,' the *Spectator* declared, 'filled with people as variegated and attractive as those to whom we are introduced here.' *Succession: A Comedy of the Generations* (1913) duly followed, thus identifying the sequence as a *family saga of the kind favoured by Rolland and Cannan,among others. The sequel transfers the action to Paris, where Antoine studies music and Philip medicine. *Le Gentleman* (1911) is an 'idyll' of the Latin quarter in Paris: art student Alexander Ferguson is torn between shallow, merciless (English) Meysie Lampeter and calm, practical, self-sacrificing (French) Gilberte. She also wrote plays for children, beginning with her (1909) adaptation of *The Rose and the Ring* by W. M. Thackeray (1811–1863).

SIGERSON, Dora: see Dora Sigerson *Shorter.

SILBERRAD, U[na] L[ucy] (1872–1955). She was born at Buckhurst Hill, Essex, eldest daughter and second child in a large family; her father, a merchant, was of noble German descent, and her mother was partly Spanish. She published more than forty volumes of fiction between 1897 and 1939. Silberrad specialized in *historical and contemporary fiction in East Anglian settings. *The Wedding of the Lady of Lovell and Other Matches of Tobiah's Making* (1905) and *The Second Book of Tobiah* (1906) are set in the seventeenth century, and concern the various courtships and intrigues masterminded by a sturdy, woman-hating Dissenter. In *Curayl* (1906), the denunciatory clergyman who preaches a hellfire sermon in Chapter 1 turns out to be an adventurous layman performing a part, and describing his performance in slangy letters to a friend; but he does have to contend with an epidemic of typhus. In *Cuddy Yarborough's Daughter* (1914) Sam Bailey, a cheerful and long-suffering colonial Civil Servant, returns to England on leave and goes to visit his old friend Cuddy Yarborough, who lives in a dilapidated country house on the East Anglian coast with his 10-year-old daughter, Violet Jane. Maud, Sam's old love, has long since forgotten him, and married Sir Edward Lassiter. After her father's sudden death, Violet goes to live with Maud, whom she dislikes intensely; complications ensue, but her essential good nature is triumphantly vindicated. Silberrad also published *The Affairs of John Bolsover* (1911).

SIMS, George R. (1847–1922) married (1901) Florence WYKES. Born in London and educated at Hanwell Military College and Bonn University, he returned home to work in his father's successful cabinet-making business until 1874. In the mid-1870s, while working for his father, Sims started to write poetry and review theatre for the *Weekly Dispatch* and *Fun*. He also edited *One and All*. In 1877 Sims moved to the *Sunday Referee* and started his very successful 'Mustard and Cress' column as 'Dagonet' which he continued to his death. The sentimental ballads were collected as *The Dagonet Ballads* (1881) and sales reached 100,000 within a year. *Ballads of Babylon* (1880) and *The Lifeboat* (1883) ran to many editions. Routledge brought out a combined edition of these ballads in 1903, and continued demand led to a seventh impression in 1914. Sims also wrote lurid reports of London's slum areas for the *Pictorial World* and the *Daily News* during 1883. His descriptions of the life of London's poor in the latter led to the establishment of a Royal Commission to investigate and solve the problems. Research for his articles inspired him to write short stories in the style of Arthur *Morrison, such as *Zeph and Other Stories* (1882) and *Tales of Today* (1889). Some of Sims's other London-related publications (both fiction and non-fiction) include *How the Poor Live* (1883), which was reproduced from the *Pictorial World* articles; *Biographs of Babylon: Life-Pictures of London's Moving Scenes* (1902), *The Black Stain* (1907), a harrowing account of the sufferings of London babies at the hands of baby farmers and drunken parents; *London By Night* (1906); and *Behind the Veil* (1913).

He was a successful dramatist: *Lights O'London* (first performed in 1881) was said to have earned him £72,000 by 1894, and he was reputed to be making £20,000 a year in dramatist's fees by the turn of the century. His libretto for *The Golden Ring* (first performed in 1883) put him in the first rank of English light-opera librettists. During the 1890s Sims was author or co-author of more than twenty West End productions, but his great success was petering out by the end of the nineteenth century. He still featured in the theatrical life of the Edwardian period, although mainly in reruns of his most popular pieces. He did publish *The Dandy Fifth: An English Military Comic Opera* (1901), and collaborated in several of the Christmas pantomimes staged at Drury Lane. Like A. Conan *Doyle, he campaigned against false imprisonment; in 1904 he proved that Adolf Beck, a Norwegian, had been wrongly convicted of fraud. He also wrote *crime fiction (e. g. *Dorcas Dene, Detective*, 1897); humorous domestic sketches (e.g. *The Young Mrs Caudle*, 1904, or *Memoirs of a Mother-in-Law*, 1913); and contrasts between high life and low life in London (e.g. *In London's Heart*, 1900; *The *Devil in London*, 1908; 'A Shilling a Night', 'The Motor Car of Santa Claus', and 'The Spitalfields Weaver', in *Joyce Pleasantry and Other Stories*, 1908). Sims paints an interesting picture of life in the theatre in *Without the Limelight: Theatrical Life As It Is* (1900) and he published *My Life: Sixty Years' Recollections of*

Bohemian London (1917). The *Times* obituary (5 Sept. 1922) called him 'a born journalist, with essential flair added to shrewd common sense, imagination, wide sympathies, a vivid interest in every side of life, and a most ardent patriotism'.

SINCLAIR, May: Mary Amelia St Clair SINCLAIR (1863–1946) was the sixth child but the only daughter of a Liverpool shipowner who was bankrupted. Her parents consequently separated; her father, an alcoholic, died in 1881, her mother in 1901, and May, who through her 20s and 30s had to look after her sick brothers, was financially dependent on relatives. She was educated at home, except for a year at Cheltenham Ladies' College under Dorothea Beale (1831–1906), where her interest in philosophy was encouraged (her first essay on idealism, a lifelong interest, appeared in the *New World* in 1893). In 1886 she published, as 'Julian Sinclair', *Nakiketas and Other Poems*. Her first two novels, *Audrey Craven* (1897) and *Mr & Mrs Nevill Tyson* (1898) were social problem novels with a psychological sophistication which pointed both to her subsequent interest in the thought of Sigmund Freud (1856–1939) and to her later novels exploring the plight of women in unacceptable sexual, domestic, or intellectual relationships in such novels as *The *Helpmate* (1907), *The *Judgement of Eve* (1907), **Kitty Tailleur* (1908), and *The *Creators* (1910). Her first popular success, *The *Divine Fire* (1904), was the fairy tale of a London poet who must renounce commercial success for integrity; Sinclair continued her own success with *The *Three Sisters* (1914), the fictional version of *The Three Brontës* (1912), in which Sinclair claimed Charlotte (1816–55), Emily (1818–48), and Anne Brontë (1820–49) for feminism, and *The Tree of Heaven* (1917). The interest of Sinclair's fiction lies in the complexity of her own thought. She was an active suffragette, writing *Feminism* for the Women Writers' Suffrage League in 1912. She was the first woman elected to the Aristotelian Society, in recognition of *A Defence of Idealism* (1917). She was a champion of modernism, as in her essays on *T. S. Eliot* (1917) and *Dorothy Richardson* (1918). In the latter she appropriated for literary criticism the philosophical term 'stream of consciousness', which was to become such a cliché in the analysis of modernist narrative technique. She took an early interest in the implications of Freud's ideas for fiction, putting the combination of psychoanalytic character studies and modernist narrative devices to different ends in *Mary Olivier: A Life* (1919), the study of the rejection of a daughter by a mother, and *The Life and Death of Harriet Frean* (1920), a drab life described in a plain style. She died of Parkinson's disease, her last novel having been published in 1927.

Sinister Street, Compton *Mackenzie, 2 vols., 1913–14, Martin Secker. The first volume was originally published as *Youth's Encounter*, the second as *Sinister Street*. They tell the (semi-autobiographical) story of Michael and Stella Fane, illegitimate children of rich parents. *Sinister Street* focuses on the upbringing of Michael Fane, the first volume covering his childhood (seen convincingly from a child's standpoint) and public schooling at St James' School (a thinly disguised St Paul's); the second his undergraduate years at Oxford, and in particular his journey through Soho in search of a woman who once attracted him and who has now become a prostitute. This is a coming-of-age story in which the hero, 'handicapped by a public school and university education', does so belatedly and painfully.

SINJOHN, John, *pseud.*: see John *Galsworthy.

Sinner and the Problem, The, Eric *Parker, 1901, Macmillan. Bestselling story told by a painter convalescing after the breakdown induced, it turns out, by the collapse of his marriage. He goes to stay with a friend who runs a boarding-school for boys. The characters have epithets rather than names. The Sinner and the Problem are pupils. The Publican is their enemy, an embryonic usurer. The Chief Butler teaches mathematics, the Other Man classics. The painter makes friends with the Sinner and the Problem, reprimands the Publican, is confided in by the Chief Butler and the Other Man, and falls in love with the Lady of the Lake, who owns a house nearby. For the modern reader, the only mystery is the book's success. It is quite extraordinarily thin. But the mixture of (childhood) idyll and facetiousness, with occasional dark hints of tragedy, was one Edwardian readers found hard to resist.

Sister Theresa, George *Moore, 1901, T. Fisher Unwin. This is the second volume of a single work, of which the first was *Evelyn Innes* (1898). Daughter of a music master, Evelyn teaches the viola da gamba, but secretly longs to develop her voice. Sir Owen Asher, rich music-lover, offers to take her abroad for training. She goes off with him, to return to England six years later a famous prima donna. She now becomes fascinated by an Irish poet and mystic, but the shock of having two lovers throws her off balance. She attempts suicide but finds peace in a convent in Wimbledon, where she becomes a postulant. In the event she does not take the veil but refuses to marry her lover either, and settles in the country to a life of good works. In this novel Moore was echoing the contemporary interest in the opposition of art and reality, spirit and flesh. Like *Evelyn Innes, Sister Theresa* is a sensitive exploration of the artistic and religious pathology of creativity. The account of life in the convent allowed Moore to explore the religious impulse more fully, but with less creativity of touch than in *Evelyn Innes. Sister Theresa* ends with Evelyn disappointed by her bid for individual and artistic freedom, but finally at peace, but with the reader probably sharing the view of the priest quoted by W. B. Yeats (1865–1939), who remarked of the novel: 'Everything is there of the convent except the religious life.'

SLADEN, Douglas [Brooke Wheelton] (1856–1947) married, first (1880), Margaret Isabel MUIRHEAD (d. 1919) and, secondly (1920), Christian Dorothea DUTHIE. Born in London, the son of a solicitor, he was educated at Temple Grove, Cheltenham College, and Trinity College, Oxford (where he was a scholar and was awarded a first in history). He went to Australia after graduating, and studied law at Melbourne University. While in Australia, he abandoned the project of a legal and political career, married, and became the first Professor of History at the University of Sydney. His career as a freelance writer began when he became the first person to introduce to British readers popular Australian poets, most importantly Adam Lindsay Gordon (1833–70), of whom he wrote several studies. Returning to Britain, he engaged Norma *Lorimer as a companion/nanny—his first wife having suffered a kind of stroke in childbirth, which affected her mentally. Lorimer, who became his secretary, hostess, and collaborator, encouraged the family to travel. He published a great many travel books and fiction drawing on foreign experience, including *A Japanese Marriage* (1895) and its sequel, *Playing the Game: A Story of Japan* (1905). *A Sicilian Marriage* (1906) has an advertisement pasted on the front cover, in which a nobleman travelling in Sicily seeks a governess for his little boy: the governess whom we are to imagine answering the advertisement is one of the heroines, the other being a Sicilian beauty, who marries; there are also brigands and American tourists involved. But Egypt seems to have been the *exotic location which really caught Sladen's imagination. *The Tragedy of the Pyramids: A Romance of Army Life in Egypt* (1909) is described as a 'counterblast' to Hall *Caine's *The White Prophet*, which Sladen criticized in a lengthy preface: his own novel, he wrote, would provide a different view of the British army and administration in Egypt, a different picture of the 'Egyptian Mutiny' which both Caine and he thought inevitable if 'certain follies' continued. In his version, the 'Mutiny' is engineered by an American millionaire. The equally polemical *The Unholy Estate: A Romance of Military Life and a Protest against the Divorce Laws for Women* (1912), a *marriage problem novel, is set largely in Welsh county society, with Egyptian interludes. Sladen also published as 'Rose Mullion'. He was the first editor of *Who's Who*. There is an enthusiastic description of the literary parties given by the Sladens in their flat near Addison Road in Grant *Richards's *Memories of a Misspent Youth 1872–1896* (1932); Israel *Zangwill and Jerome K. *Jerome were habitués. *My Long Life* (1939) is an autobiography, with many anecdotes of literary life.

SLATER, Francis Carey: see under 'Francis *Bancroft'.

SMEDLEY, [Anne] Constance (1881–1941) married (1909) Maxwell Ashby ARMFIELD (1881–1972). The daughter of a chartered accountant, she was born in Birmingham and educated at King Edward VI High School for Girls and Birmingham School of Art. Beginning her career as an illustrator in the late 1880s, she moved to London and developed a strong interest in the theatre; she was the author of several plays. She was a Christian Scientist, a pacifist, disabled, and the founder of the international Lyceum Clubs for women. She published more than twenty volumes of fiction between 1903 and 1932, ponderous social-problem novels and mildly cynical studies of the position of women. The latter category includes *An April Princess* (1903), about an unconventional, flirtatious, slightly shrewish young woman, her admirers, and her intellectual aunt, and *The June Princess* (1909), whose heroine wants to found an International Society to bring women of different nationalities together (she discusses the matter with the Enchantress, the Pierrot, the Fairy Godfather, the Stranger, the Attache, and others). *Conflict* (1907), about the business and social worlds, and their respective codes of conduct, is more substantial. The primary conflict is between two Birmingham iron foundries, Cuvier's, whose owner is honourable in his business dealings, but also a cynical hedonist, and Berryfield's, whose owner dies, leaving the business to his extremely capable private secretary, Mary van Heyten. Mary collapses from overwork, and recuperates in the London house of her uncle and aunt, Tom and Susan Ellestree, where she meets Cuvier, who is making love to Mrs Ellestree with every prospect of success. A crisis threatens the reputation of Berryfield's and the very existence of Cuvier's. Mary rescues both firms, and Mrs Ellestree from the lascivious Cuvier. She herself pairs off with Hayden Cobb, a secretary at Cuvier's. Her brother, Ferroll, a pagan vagabond, seems to have strayed in from one of Smedley's 'Princess' novels; he and his like were soon to disappear from the author's increasingly moralistic tales. In her memoirs Smedley mentions that the novel was influenced by her horror at the breakup of Richard *Le Gallienne's second marriage, the consequent separation of his daughters by his first and second wives, and the divorce soon afterwards of his sister Esther from her husband, James Welch. *Service: A Domestic Novel* (1910) is, as the reviewers pointed out, like a variation on a theme from the novels of Charlotte M. Yonge (1823–1901): a sweetly charitable, countrified maidservant arrives in a large family where the parents are distinguished by the rigidity of their prejudices and the children by their sentimental radicalism, and puts both parties to shame. *The Emotions of Martha* (1911) is a cautionary tale about restless young women written for the Religious Tract Society. *Commoners' Rights* (1912) is partly about the social problem indicated in the title, the ownership of common land, and partly about the strained relations between a husband and wife from different walks of life. Smedley was married to a symbolist designer and painter, who illustrated several of her books, and, sharing her pacifist views, designed *The Ballet of the Nations* (1915) by 'Vernon *Lee'. *Crusaders* (1929) is an autobiography with valuable and humorous accounts of many literary figures of her day. She published a feminist tract, *Woman: A Few Shrieks* (1907), under the pseudonym 'X'.

Smiths of Surbiton, The: *A Comedy Without a Plot*, 'Keble *Howard', 1906, Chapman & Hall. Archetypal *suburban fiction. Howard has no scruples about defining his newly-weds, Ralph and Enid Smith, in economic and social terms. Ralph is 32, tending to plumpness, an Englishman to the core. He earns £350 per annum as a clerk in an insurance office. Edith, younger and taller than her husband, 'carried herself well, knew how to buy and how to wear clothes, had studied the piano at the Royal College of Music, sang a little, and regarded her mother with a dutiful toleration'. The comedy does indeed have no plot. We learn about Ralph's bad habits, and their neighbour, Miss Snow, a Tennyson 'monomaniac' who has changed the name of her house to Locksley Lodge. The narrative carries us forward to the point, twenty-three years later, when their son, George Harry Nelson, has left for South Africa, to advance the development of the colonies, their daughter, Phyllis Enid, has become engaged to a journalist, and they themselves have moved into a larger and more pretentious house, Valley View. In the preface to a sequel, *The Smiths of Valley View: Being Further Adventures of the Smiths of Surbiton* (1909), Howard protested about the snobbery with which suburban stories were still received.

SNAITH, John Collis (1876–1936) married Madeline ARMSTRONG (d. 1931). Born in Nottingham, son of a paper merchant, he was educated at the Misses Hipkin's School and at the High Pavement School. Aged 13 he joined the Midland Railway as a clerk, devoting his spare time to reading history and playing cricket, at which he was very accomplished. His first novel, *Mistress Dorothy Marvin* (1895), had some success, and both his writing and his cricket were encouraged by J. M. *Barrie, for whose team, the Allahakbarries, he played for many years. In 1897–8 he went to University College, Nottingham, for a year. Charles Tennyson's (1953) memoir calls Snaith's knowledge of cricket 'encyclopaedic'; he is portrayed in *Hornung's *Fathers of Men* (1912). Snaith's work might be described as a succession of experiments in a variety of literary modes. It demonstrates the lengths to which an Edwardian novelist of modest ability might go in order establish a presence and identify a readership. Snaith began by writing *historical romances. *Mistress Dorothy Marvin* (1896) was followed by *Fierceheart the Soldier* (1897) and *Lady Barbarity* (1899). He supplemented these with exercises in light comedy such as *Willow the King* (1899), a cricketing tale, and *William Jordan, Junior* (1908), a *suburban tale in the style of W. Pett *Ridge. On the whole, though, his Edwardian novels show greater ambition. *Broke of Covenden* (1904) is an exercise in *Meredithian tragicomedy which describes the failure of Edmund William Aubrey Carysfort Baigent Broke, Esq., a country squire of immemorial ancestry and pride blessed with with an heir to his name and six healthy daughters, to adapt to the modern world. The most interesting characters are Delia, the daughter who is 'different', and Mrs Broke, who rebels against her husband but through diplomacy saves something from the wreck of his fortunes. *Henry Northcote* (1906) is a study of a morbid temperament in the style of Honoré de Balzac (1799–1850) or R. L. Stevenson (1850–94). Snaith suffered a complete mental breakdown at this time, and his subsequent work never quite achieved the same level of intensity. *Araminta* (1909) is Snaith's attempt to appear as the new Thackeray. The Countess of Crewkerne, an elderly tyrant, adopts her niece, Araminta, an empty-headed and -hearted girl with a 'daffodil-coloured mane', in order to stimulate rivalry between two ageing roués: the Duke of Brancaster, known as 'Gobo' on account of his tendency to gobble like a turkey, a hideous and vulgar widower of 59; and the Earl of Cheriton, who is 65, wears corsets and a wig, dyes his moustache, and paints his face. Araminta has promised herself to a young painter. But when Cheriton wins the auction for her hand by offering a larger settlement she is relinquished by the painter, without too much distress on either side. A few months later, a bedraggled Cheriton calls at the painter's studio with Araminta and a cheque for £10,000 and washes his hands of the whole business. *The Principal Girl* (1912) is lighter in tone. Philip, heir to Lord Shelmerdine of Potterhamworth, a new peer, chooses as his wife an actress whose family proceed to act his disapproving parents off the social stage. *The Coming* (1917) placed Christ's Second Coming in contemporary England. There is a sympathetic study of Snaith in Sir Charles B. L. Tennyson' *Life's All a Fragment* (1953).

SNOWDEN, J[ames] Keighley (1860–1947) married (1884) Agnes Wallace CRAWFORD. Brought up in the West Riding of Yorkshire, he was the author of some fourteen volumes of fiction from 1893. *Barbara West* (1901) is a story of provincial journalism in the 1880s. *Hate of Evil* (1907) is the bizarre and entertaining story of an ardent young clergyman who, to atone for a youthful folly, pledges himself to penury in a small northern hillside parish; his neighbour, Mrs Howard, mistress of Netherfell Hall, worships him; he loves, and betrays, his charwoman, without losing Mrs Howard's regard. *King Jack* (1914) is a *historical romance, set in the Yorkshire dales in the early nineteenth century, about a famous outlaw and poacher. A preface to *The Weaver's Web* (1932), a reprint of *The Web of an Old Weaver* (1896), has an introduction by his kinsman, the politician Philip Snowden (1864–1937), who writes of his 'anxiety to see preserved the characteristics of a people which, I am afraid, are rapidly changing under the influence of modern transport and the uniformity of an education system imposed by a central authority'.

SOMERVILLE, E. Œ. and **ROSS,** Martin, *pseud.*: Edith Anna Œnone SOMERVILLE (1858–1949) and Violet Florence MARTIN (1862–1915). Somerville was born in Corfu, eldest of eight children of an army officer who retired in 1859 to Drishane House, Skibbereen, where she spent much of the rest of her life. She was educated at home and, briefly, at Alexandra College, Dublin, and trained as a painter in London, Dusseldorf, and Paris, scraping together the money to spend a few months in the studios each year. She then tried to establish herself as an illustrator. Her second cousin Violet Martin was born at Ross House, Galway, youngest daughter of an impoverished landowner of ancient lineage, after whose death when she was 10 the family left to live in Dublin. Both her nostalgia for the big house of her childhood and her knowledge of the life of middle-class Protestant townsfolk were to be crucial to the collaborative fiction of the two cousins. Her eldest brother, Robert Martin (1846–1905), was boycotted and therefore lived in London earning a living as a playwright and lyricist; his connections in the literary world helped them to sell their work. In 1886 the cousins met for the first time, and soon afterwards began to collaborate on fiction and non-fiction, journalism, and travel writing, sometimes with illustrations by Somerville. Their first novels together, *An Irish Cousin* (1889) (which was first published under the names 'Geilles Herring' and 'Martin Ross') and *Naboth's Vineyard* (1891), were fictions of Anglo-Irish life. Martin wrote to Somerville in 1889 of their plan to use their relations and friends for gain: 'Let us take Carbery [the area round Skibbereen] and grind its bones to make our bread.' *The Real Charlotte* (1894), probably their best book, evokes the sexual and social tensions among a group of middle- and upper-class people in the Irish countryside: the frustrated spinster, her pretty, vulgar cousin from Dublin, the *fin-de-race* landowner, and his caddish agent. *Some Experiences of an Irish R.M.* (1899), which brought together twelve stories first published in the *Badminton Magazine* in 1898, is an affectionate celebration of the eccentricities of the declining Irish gentry class. Later stories were collected in *Further Experiences of an Irish R.M.* (1908) and *In Mr Knox's Country* (1915). **Dan Russel the Fox* (1911) lacks the same conviction. After Martin's death, which had been preceded by a long period of ill health since a hunting accident in 1898, Somerville continued writing novels, including, most successfully, her study of the final demise of the Anglo-Irish gentry, *The Big House of Inver* (1925). Her belief in spiritualism (already apparent in *In Mr Knox's Country*) led her to continue to put Martin' s pseudonym on the title-pages of posthumous works; however some critics point to a decline in the quality of the work all the same. Somerville was Master of the West Carbery foxhounds and President of the Munster Women's Franchise League; the literary critic Nevill Coghill (1899–1980) was her nephew.

Son of Judith: *A Tale of the Welsh Mining Valleys*, Joseph *Keating, 1900, George Allen. This is a novel about mining, but more powerfully about escape from the mines and self-improvement. Howel Morris, illegitimate son of Judith, is singled out by his dress and appearance, and by his intensity, from his zombie-like workmates, who despise him for his ambition. He must overcome not only their hostility, but his mother's efforts to shape him into an instrument of vengeance against his own father, Griffith Meredith, who seduced and abandoned her. When he refuses to kill his father, she does the job herself; the doomed elders topple into a ravine. Morris's resolution wins him the love of a middle-class woman, Morwen Rhys. His new identity has thus erased both family and class. The plot is unfalteringly melodramatic, but the descriptions of the mine and the miners have real force.

Sons and Lovers, D. H. *Lawrence, 1913, Gerald Duckworth. Lawrence's third published novel is his most straightforwardly autobiographical work. It is partly the story of his mother's married life and his own 'strange obsession' with her, as Jessie Chambers, Miriam in the novel, put it, and partly the story of the self-discovery of an artist, and the ways in which Lawrence's own discontent with provincial commerce, his longing for something more generous, came to be given aesthetic form. Paul Morel is the second son of Walter Morel, a Nottinghamshire miner. Paul's mother, Gertrude, is a sensitive and intellectual woman, daughter of puritanical middle-class parents, who married Walter out of an intense physical fascination. Their marriage has soured: she despises his coarseness and drunken brutality; he resents her fastidiousness. She thus concentrates her love and dreams on her four children, and is determined, in particular, that her three sons will not be like their father. Her ambition becomes focused on Paul when William (who has moved to London) dies of pneumonia, and the book concerns the complications of Paul's resulting feelings for his mother after he leaves school, goes to work as a clerk in Nottingham, and begins to gain confidence and success as an artist. He first falls in love with Miriam Leivers, but is unsympathetic to her romantic desire to sacrifice herself to his needs and starts a passionate affair with a fellow-worker, Clara Dawes, a married woman with feminist ideas. He is unable to give himself fully to her either, and when Mrs Morel contracts cancer, Clara's love seems a distraction. After his mother's death (which he hastens with a dose of morphine), Paul finally rejects life with either Miriam or Clara (who returns to her husband, Baxter, for whom Paul has formed an odd affection) and the idea of joining his mother in the darkness. *Sons and Lovers* was attacked on publication for its sexual frankness, and is the most naturalistic of Lawrence's work in its detailed descriptions of working-class domesticity, its inside experience of a mining community and landscape, its unsentimental picture of a bad marriage. But the novel remains remarkable as much for its psychological as its social realism, for Lawrence's close attention to the nuances of feeling (the Morel children's attitudes to their father, for example, or the emotional uncertainties of Paul's adolescence), and for his understanding of how love becomes possession and how intimacy leads to distance.

Sorcery Shop, The: *An Impossible Romance*, Robert *Blatchford, 1907, Clarion Press. In his 'Author's Note', Blatchford discusses some of the minor difficulties attending utopian romance (details of architecture, technology and costume) and then goes on to state that his purpose is 'to dispel ignorance and diffuse knowledge'. The romance begins in the smoking-room of the Directorate Club, otherwise known as 'Guinea Pigs', where Major-General Sir Frederick Manningtree Storm, Conservative MP for South Loomshire, and Mr Samuel Jorkle, Liberal MP for Shantytown East, unite in condemning Socialism. Their denunciations are interrupted by a mild-mannered elderly gentleman, Mr Nathaniel Fry, who is a wizard, and promptly arranges a little time-travel, via a magical lift and a black pool called the Ink Well. The 'paradise regained' he conducts them to is a republic whose inhabitants neither smoke, nor drink, nor eat meat. There are no laws, but monogamy is the custom, and motherhood is sacred. Prosperity is guaranteed by the elimination of waste and luxury. Sir William Blackstone, Sir Edward Coke, and Sir Frederick Pollock are quoted in support of the argument that land is public property. When the time-travellers return to present-day London, General Storm finds himself moved for the first time by the spectacle of unemployment, and donates several guineas to a startled workman.

Souls: *A Comedy of Intentions*, *'Rita', 1903, Hutchinson. Satirical assault on the corruption of high society which describes the struggle for power within a 'Cult' dedicated to 'the most wonderful emotions' and to a 'standard of moral and unintelligible purity'. The cult's leader, the Honorable Mrs Vanderdecken, is trying to promote, and in some unspecified way corrupt, her latest protégée, a beautiful German singer called Zara Eberhardt. Her plans are thwarted by the introduction into the charmed circle of an ebullient Irishwoman, Mrs Brady, who manages to prise Zara away from her, and in the process detach her closest ally, the Marchioness of Beaude sart. A talented but idle painter, Basil Warrender, falls in love with Mrs Brady, thus demonstrating that true emotions flourish even in the falsest of circumstances. The novel also deplores 'the manner in which high-born and apparently exclusive Society ladies have permitted themselves to be patronised by those who furnish Society news to a certain class of journals'. The novel was a success, and established Rita's reputation as a satirist, though it has less bite than the later **Queer Lady Judas* (1905).

SOUTAR, Andrew (1879–1941) published more than fifty novels between 1909 and 1940. He early established a large following for his serials in the important American periodical market. His fiction includes *Broken Ladders* (1912), a *political novel about an upper-class woman who is gradually broken by her husband, an unscrupulous Labour politician; and *Magpie House* (1913). In later years Soutar wrote many filmscripts. *My Sporting Life* (1934) is a series of memories of boxing, racing, golf, and other sports in the Far East, Europe, and America. He states there that he was brought up among racing people and fought in Russia in 1919. It is a fallacy, he says in a preface, that being a novelist necessarily involves 'long hair, musing and dreaming': 'I have found greater joy in conversation with a professional pugilist or jockey or footballer than with self-styled "intellectualist" politician or idealist.'

Spanish Gold, 'George A. *Birmingham', 1908, Methuen. A familiar enough plot—a competitive search for buried treasure (Spanish gold coins left from an Armada shipwreck off the west coast of Ireland) between the good Revd J. J. Meldon and the evil Sir Giles Buckley—is made unusually entertaining by the Irish setting (which gives plenty of opportunity for misunderstandings between the locals and the treasure-seekers) and, in particular, by the garrulous, ingenious, and unscrupulous character of J. J. Meldon. The book is more successful as a comedy (culminating in Meldon's confrontation with the Irish Chief Secretary, the Rt. Hon. Eustace Willoughby) than as an adventure.

Speaker, The: see *The *Nation*.

Spectator, The: was founded in 1818 as a liberal journal of politics and religion. It was taken over in 1861 by Meredith Townsend (1831–1911), who brought in Richard Holt Hutton (1826–97), editor of the *National Review,* as his co-editor. Together they established the magazine as an influential voice of Victorian moral purpose. The *Spectator* was thus sceptical of both the cultural and the scientific movements of the 1880s and 1890s, when it was taken to be the voice of dull Victorian sobriety. Hutton died in 1897 and was succeeded by John St Loe Strachey (1860–1927), the assistant editor, who remained editor until 1915. He focused the magazine on issues of economics, history, and politics, while retaining a strong ethical approach, turning the *Spectator* into a watchdog of state corruption (and doubling its circulation in the process).

SPEIGHT, T[homas] W[ilkinson] (1830–1915) married —— [a widower by 1910] was born in Liverpool of Cumberland family. He went to a foundation school in Kendal, Cumbria. Speight worked for the Midland Railway Company for forty years (retiring in 1887 with a pension of £98). He began to publish fiction in *Household Words* in 1856; he later wrote for *All the Year Round, Chambers,* the *Graphic,* and *Belgravia.* He specialized in lurid, sensational works, with the occasional foray into *historical romance: reviewers likened him to M. E. *Braddon and Wilkie Collins (1824–89). He was the author of the *Gentleman's Annual* from 1885–1892; each issue contained a complete novel. His Edwardian novels tend towards the sensational, with the odd diversion, as in *On the Fringe* (1912), into the occult. In *As It Was Written* (1902), an anarchist German shoemaker emigrates to America and becomes a millionaire; he eventually marries a peer's daughter who during the course of the novel has murdered two previous husbands. Emigration is also a theme in *The Sport of Chance* (1903), which opens with its three heroines on the deck of a liner bound from Sydney to London. In *The Plotters* (1905), the heir to a baronet's estates is wounded in Africa and loses his memory; the plotters plot to prove him dead. In *Price of a Secret: A Story of Temptation* (1908), three brothers inherit in turn a large estate, and with it a secret which tempts each of them to different effect according to their different characters. Speight also wrote plays. He applied to the Royal Literary Fund four times between 1890 and 1914.

Spies of the Kaiser: *Plotting the Downfall of England,* William *Le Queux, 1909, Hurst & Blackett. Two layabout lawyers, Ray Raymond and John James Jacox, combine to expose a network of German spies controlled by Herman Hartmann, a flabby, sardonic German Jew masquerading as a moneylender. (Le Queux tended to concentrate his prejudices for maximum effect.) First published in *Cassell's Magazine* in 1908, the stores created a major stir. Dozens of people wrote to Le Queux claiming to have recognized German spies. He passed the letters on to the War Office, where they provided the head of the counter-intelligence section, Lt.-Col. James Edmonds (1861–1956), with ammunition for his own campaign against official indifference to the German threat. In March 1909 the Cabinet established a subcommittee to examine the question, which accepted the claim that there were large numbers of spies roaming the country and recommended that the Official Secrets Act of 1889 should be strengthened and a regular secret service established. In the novel Raymond uncovers a German plan to land at Weybourne in Norfolk; and Capt. Vernon Kell (1873–1942), appointed in 1909 the first head of MI5, took his summer holiday on this section of coast in 1914, to uncover any German activities.

spy fiction. The problem with the formula for *invasion scare stories devised by Sir George Chesney (1830–95) in *The Battle of Dorking* (1871), and endlessly reworked ever since, was that it was altogether *too* cautionary. The British always lost. What was needed was a moral and political regeneration without the bitter fruit of humiliating defeat but the germ of victory. Fortunately, however, invasion had its acknowledged preliminaries. The theorists agreed that its success would depend on secret preparations. There would be no invasion, in short, without spies. Stories like William *Le Queux's *The *Invasion of 1910* (1906) or Walter *Wood's *The Enemy in Our Midst* (1906) assumed a vast army of 'advance agents' disguised as waiters, clerks, bakers, hairdressers, and the like. 'Every registered alien was an authority on the topography and resources of the district in which he dwelt,' Wood reports. Spy fever swept the nation. The positivist philosopher Frederic *Harrison wrote to the *Times* on 17 July 1908 to warn that the German army had been 'trained for sudden transmarine descent on a coast; and for this end every road, well, bridge, and smithy in the east of England and Scotland has been docketed in the German War Office.' Questions were asked in the House of Commons. One MP wanted to know about 'the military men from a foreign nation who had been resident for the last two years on and off in the neighbourhood of Epping, and who had been sketching and photographing the whole district and communicating their information directly to their own country'. The much-harassed Secretary of State for War, R. B. Haldane (1856–1928), replied that they could get all the information they needed by looking at a map. In 1916, Le Queux was to claim that before the First World War German agents had 'ranked among the leaders of social and commercial life, and among the sweepings and outcasts of great communities'—some of them had even been 'on golfing terms with the rulers of Great Britain'. If writers were to exploit spy fever for political and commercial ends, they had to devise a new kind of hero: one who would adequately represent a nation which, although sunk in decadence, was still sound at heart, and likely to respond to the scent of battle. They found that hero in the amateur agent or accidental spy, the sleepy young Englishman whose complacency is shattered when he stumbles across some fiendish plot. Contending with the unsportsmanlike conduct of his enemies and the disbelief of his friends, he learns what it is like to be an outsider; the rite of passage regenerates him morally, while the evidence he has accumulated provokes a political awakening (in this respect, spy fiction is the domestic equivalent of *Ruritanian romance). The narrative of moral and political regeneration shaped the mainstream of Edwardian spy fiction from Erskine *Childers' *The *Riddle of the Sands* (1903) through the ultra-sensational tales of Le Queux and E. Phillips *Oppenheim to John *Buchan's *The Thirty-Nine Steps* (1915). Max *Pemberton's *Two Women* (1914) is one of the very few novels to concern a (supposed) British spy operating in Germany.

STABLES, [William] Gordon (1840–1910) married (1874) Theresa Elizabeth Williams McCORMACK. Born at Aberchirder, Banffshire, Scotland, the son of a wine merchant, he attended Aberdeen Grammar School and Aberdeen University, where he read medicine until 1857. He qualified as a physician, joined the Royal Navy as a ship's surgeon, and served at sea from 1863 until the early 1870s, when ill health forced him to resign his commission. After a spell of cruising around (as a member of the merchant navy) Stables settled down at Twyford, Berkshire, and churned out adventure stories for boys. The essence of these tales was described in Stables' obituary in the *Times* (12 May 1910): 'stirring incidents were frequent and the atmosphere was always breezy and healthy.' He was one of the early pioneers of caravanning and from 1886 onwards made annual tours with his caravan. He even lived in it for a while, and recorded his experiences in *The Cruise of the Land Yacht 'Wanderer', or, 1,300 Miles in My Caravan* (1886). Stables also served as the wandering secretary of the Sea Birds Protection Society. His non-fictional works include a string of popular medical books like *The People's ABC Guide To Health* (1902), publications for boys such as *A Boy's Book of Battleships* (1909), and a long list of titles concerning animals (particularly domestic pets) and animal welfare. He died at his home, The Jungle, Twyford.

STACPOOLE, H[enry] de Vere (1863–1951) married, first, Mrs H. de Vere *STACPOOLE and, secondly (1938), her sister Florence ROBSON. Henry Stacpoole was born at Kingstown, Co. Dublin, the son of a Church of Ireland clergyman who ran a school. As a child he travelled widely with his mother, who had been born in Canada. He went to Malvern College before going to London to read medicine at St George's and St Mary's Hospitals (graduating in 1891). His interest in literature was aroused by his reading of Carlyle and the German philosophers and poets. He took up a post as a ship's doctor and travelled the world with the Royal Navy. In the 1890s he became a friend of 'John Oliver *Hobbes' and members of the *Yellow Book* circle, whose influence can be seen in early works like *Death, the Knight, and the Lady* (1897). Fiction such as *The Bourgeois* (1901) and *Garryowen: The Romance of a Race Horse* (1903) did not immediately make money, and in 1904 he applied to the Royal Literary Fund, stating that he suffered from recurrent sciatica and nervous depression, and that whereas he had formerly made an income of about £150 from his writing he was now finding it difficult to work. His situation, however, was transformed by the two exotic novels which brought him popular success: *The Crimson Azaleas* (1907), set in Japan, where two Scottish businessmen bring up a young Japanese girl and one of the them becomes involved with an old flame, now married; and the bestselling desert island romance, *The *Blue Lagoon* (1908). He spent his later life at Chelmsford, Essex, and at Bonchurch, Isle of Wight, a wealthy and successful author. *The Ship of Coral* (1911) was an attempt to repeat the desert island formula. Two French sailors, Gaspard the Provençal and Yves the Breton, shipwrecked on a remote coral reef, discover the remains of a galleon on the sea-floor. Gaspard murders Yves, enters into an alliance with the captain of the ship which rescues him, falls in love with a woman in St Pierre, on Martinique, returns to the reef, is betrayed by his rescuer, watches the latter's ship sink in a hurricane, is rescued again, and returns to St Pierre a rich man, only to find the town buried under a mound of volcanic ash. Stacpoole also wrote *historical romances such as *The Street of the Flute-Player* (1912), which is set in Athens in the fifth century BC (Socrates and Aristophanes both appear), and on the whole more interested in the setting than in the Greek hero and Egyptian-Persian heroine; as well as some verse and translations of the poems of both François Villon (b. 1431) and Sappho (*fl.* 650 BC). His own works have been translated into many languages including Dutch, Swedish, French, and Italian. Stacpoole sometimes used the pseudonym 'Tyler De Saix', for example for *The Vulture's Prey* (1909). Stacpoole published two volumes of autobiography: *Mice and Men: 1863–1942* (1942) and *More Mice and Men* (1945). He died in hospital at Shanklin, Isle of Wight. Stacpoole's informative obituary in the *Times* (13 Apr. 1951) considers the chief merit of his work to lie in 'the reflected light and colour of his tropical seascapes and landfalls' and in his ability to communicate 'a genuine delight and wonder'.

STACPOOLE, Mrs H. de Vere: Margaret Ann ROBSON (d. 1934) married H. de Vere *STACPOOLE. The heroine of *Monte Carlo: A Novel* (1913) is a clergyman's daughter who commits social suicide by eloping to Paris with an artist, and who, once they are established in Monte Carlo with a French theatrical company, sickens of the life and of her good-natured, bohemian husband. There is also an Englishman in the Austrian secret service who has hair's-breadth escapes and acts as honest broker between husband and wife. *London, 1913* (1914) satirizes the worlds of finance and journalism. Mrs Stacpoole also published *The Battle of Flowers* (1916).

STAHLMANN, J. I.: see under Mrs Hugh *Fraser.

STANTON, Coralie, *pseud.*: Alice Cecil Seymour KEAY (b. 1877) married (1901) Heath *HOSKEN. Born in London and educated in Paris and Heidelburg, she married a journalist. Together the two Hoskens published, as 'Heath Hosken and Coralie Stanton', twenty-nine volumes of sensational fiction between 1904 and 1933; among the most popular were *Miriam Lemaire, Money Lender* (1906), the narrative of the triumphs of a social vampire told by one of the few men who knew her well but did not shoot himself; *The Love that Kills* (1909), a *crime story about the double life and mysterious disappearance of Lord Queste, the most popular prime minister the country has ever known; and *Raven, V. C.* (1913), in which the eponymous hero, reputedly a woman-hater, grapples on the north-west frontier of India with the troubles fomented by a treacherous ally, while the high-minded heroine, Hersee Roland, grapples with the scheming Cuckoo Hayle for the General's affections. As 'Coralie Stanton' she also published eleven romances alone between 1928 and 1935. It is likely that others were serialized but never published in volume form.

STEEL, Flora Annie: Flora Annie WEBSTER (1847–1929) married (1867) Henry William STEEL (d. 1923). Born at Harrow-on-the-Hill and brought up in Scotland, where her father was Sheriff-Clerk of Forfar, she was educated at home, at school, and in Brussels. She married an official in the Indian Civil Service and lived in Punjab for twenty-two years, playing an active role in local education and being appointed the first Inspectress of Girls' Schools in 1884. She taught herself Punjabi, and translated folk tales into English verse. Her *Wide-Awake Stories*, published in India in 1884 with illustrations by *Kipling's father, appeared in England as *Tales of the Punjab* (1896). Steel returned to England in 1889 and began her career as a writer of novels and stories about India. Her big success was *On the Face of the Waters* (1896), a *historical romance about the 'Indian Mutiny', which characteristically combines enthusiasm for Indian mysticism and wisdom with faith in imperial paternalist values. *In the Permanent Way* (1897) she claimed had been communicated to her by the apparition of an Indian railway official named Nathaniel James Craddock. *A Prince of Dreamers* (1908) and *King Errant* (1912) celebrate the achievements of the Great Moguls both in their own terms and as an anticipation of the British Raj. In *Mistress of Men* (1917), Steel uses the supposed mystery and spirituality of the East as an *exotic romantic flavouring. Steel was a novelist with an obviously colonialist sensibility in her ambiguous admiration for Indian mores. On the death of her husband in 1923 she turned to philosophy, writing *The Curse of Eve* (1929), in which sex is shown to be the cause of all evil, and published an autobiography, *The Garden of Fidelity* (1929). As well as being involved while in India in the education and emancipation of women, she supported the movement for women's suffrage in Britain.

STEPHENS, James (1882–1950) married (1919) Millicent Josephine GARDINER. A self-taught, undersized child of the Dublin slums, (less than 4 ft. 6 in. as an adult) brought up in a Protestant orphanage, James Stephens started writing poetry, with the encouragement of 'Æ' (George Russell, 1867–1935), who helped him to publish *Insurrections* (1909) and *The Lonely God and Other Poems* (1909). Stephens's first novel, *The Charwoman's Daughter* (1912), describes life in the miserable Dublin tenement where 16-year-old Mary Makebelieve lives with her widowed mother. Mrs Makebelieve, a dressmaker until she could stand the arrogance of her customers no longer, now goes out charring, while her daughter, mysteriously protected from hardship, wanders the city streets and parks. Mary attracts a suitor, the gigantic, authoritative, immensely desirable, and anonymous Policeman. But she remains loyal to her puny but spirited young man who lodges with her neighbour. Mrs Makebelieve inherits the vast fortune which one of her brothers has made in America. Mary's mother and young man are both heroic in their resilience and their hatred of oppression. But the novel's scant regard for the conventions of realism indicates the direction in which Stephens was moving: make-believe. His name was made by his prose *fantasies, *The *Crock of Gold* (1912) and *The Demi-Gods* (1914). The latter is a donkey-and-cart Irish pilgrimage undertaken by a lovable rogue, Patsy MacCann, his roguish daughter, Mary, a red-haired drab called Eileen Ni Cooley, and a trio of 'big, buck angels', Finaun, Caellia, and Art. Mary falls in love with the latter. Stephens also worked as a journalist and was committed to the nationalist cause, as reflected in his account of *The Insurrection in Dublin* (1916) and by his interest in the Gaelic revival and Irish folklore—his collection of *Irish Folk Tales* appeared in 1920. He also published two collections of short stories, *Here are the Ladies* (1913) and *In the Land of Youth* (1924). He was awarded a Civil List Pension in 1942.

STERN, G. B.: Gladys Bertha STERN (1890–1973), who changed her name to Gladys Bronwyn STERN, married (1919) Geoffrey Lisle HOLDSWORTH (divorced). Born in London to Jewish parents, she was educated at Notting Hill High School, the Royal Academy of Dramatic Art, and in Germany and Switzerland. Her first two novels were *Pantomime* (1914) and *'See-Saw'* (1914), both of which are about young actresses choosing between career and domesticity, portraying bohemian societies in which weak men are supported by women but she is best known for the saga, partly drawing on her knowledge of her own family, about the Europe-wide vicissitudes of the matriarchal Rakonitz family: *Children of No Man's Land* (1919), *Tents of Israel* (1923), *A Deputy Was King* (1926), *Mosaic* (1930), and *The Young Matriarch* (1942). She became a Roman Catholic in 1947. She was a close friend of Somerset *Maugham, and collaborated with Sheila *Kaye-Smith on two books about Jane Austen (1775–1817): she was known by friends as 'Peter'. She published six volumes of autobiography.

STEUART, John A[lexander] (1861–1932) married Annie Maude CRAIG. Born in Perthshire, he worked in a bank before travelling to Ireland and then settling in the USA. He gained journalistic experience in the States and then crossed the Pacific Ocean, eventually returning to London at the end of the 1880s. His Victorian publications include *A Millionaire's Daughter* (1888) and *The Minister of State* (1898). His Edwardian fiction tends to be Scottish and/or Anglo-American in emphasis. In *The Son of Gad* (1902), a proud young soldier, Captain Mclean, finds his ancestral highland domain in the hands of a villainous stranger, and wins it back by marrying the stranger's daughter. The novel, whose supporting cast includes two plutocratic Americans, a railroad boss and a congressman, was intended to illustrate 'the community of interest and sentiment which is fast Americanizing England and Anglicizing America'. In *The Rebel Wooing* (1905) Eric Methven, pastor of the West Kirk in Portfotherington, is torn between duty to his patron, Adam Braidwood, a hard-headed shipowner, and his love for Braidwood's daughter, Helen, who is a convert to grace. Methven's growing fame as a revivalist sends him to London and church politics. The bitter struggle between Montrose and Argyle provides the background to *The Red Reaper* (1905), a *historical romance with a full quota of Scottish brawls. *The Wages of Pleasure* (1906), by contrast, concerns the venality of fashionable Anglo-American high society: there is a suicide, and a scandal at the Eupatrids Club when a lady member is arrested. In *Faces in the Mist* (1909) an American millionaire plays the highlander while his wife schemes to catch Lord Benbreck for their daughter, Pamela, who loves, instead, young Chisholm. Chisholm is already Benbreck's sworn enemy; his chance comes when he rescues Pamela from brigands in the Syrian desert. *The Hebrew* (1903) is something of a departure, an East End slum novel in the tradition of *Gissing and *Morrison, except that its emphasis is less on the hero's consciousness than on his hideous environment. In its outrage at the existence of poverty and its scepticism about the reforming efforts of clergymen and American millionaires, it owes much to Charles Dickens (1812–70). The Hebrew, the **Times Literary Supplement* reported, 'is too unctuously wicked, his agent is at least up to the level of a Quilp, and their joint inhumanity is driven home with an iteration that recalls Mr Carker's teeth'. Steuart also wrote two biographical studies of R. L. Stevenson (1850–94), and was editor of the *Publishers' Circular* (1896–1900).

STEVENS, E[thel May] S[tefana] (1879–1972) married (1910) Edwin Mortimer DROWER (1880–1951), KBE (1941). Daughter of a Church of England clergyman, she had published the first of her novels at the time of her marriage to a solicitor practising in Cairo, who later became an advocate in the Sudan, and later still a government adviser on Iraq. Stevens published extensively on the Near and Middle East, starting with fiction and travel pieces, and later concentrating more on translation and more academic studies; her special interest was the Mandaean culture of Iraq and Iran. Her early fictions are mildly racy romances with domestic or *exotic settings. Part I of *The Veil: A Romance of Tunisia* (1909) concerns a French officer and the girl, Mabrouka, he helps to escape from the clutches of Si Ismael, Sheikh of Silga; in Part II, which takes place nineteen years later, Si Ismael and Mabrouka both reappear, the latter now a spy, and there is a new hero in the shape of a young Sicilian who has come out to Tunis to join his uncle. *The Earthen Drum* (1911) contains eight stories about the East, one an allegory, designed to show that hearts beat 'to the same measure' in harem and ballroom alike. *The Mountain of God* (1911) treats a favourite topic of exotic novelists, the love between a Western woman and an Eastern man. *The Long Engagement* (1912) is set in the seaport of Southminster, where the rector's son, a schoolmaster, is lengthily engaged to a colonel's daughter. That Stevens thought of the West as a place of slow complication and of the East as a place of rapid disclosure is confirmed by *The Lure* (1912), in which a young woman journalist falls in love with the editor of a society journal, whose villainies finally unravel during adventures in Egypt. *Sarah Eden* (1914) was her most ambitious work to date. It concerns a religious enthusiast who marries her dead sister's fiancé to prevent him from going to the bad, is left with a young daughter when he too dies, and decides to found a religious community in Jerusalem. Being unorthodox, her sect is not well received, and the liveliest part of the novel is a chronicle of religious disputes and rivalries. There are some impressive Russian pilgrims.

STEVENSON, Philip L. (d. *c.*1920) was the author of six volumes of fiction, five in this period; they are *historical romances in the *Weyman style and include *The Rose of Dauphiny, or, The Adventures of the Sieur de Roquelaure in the French Wars of Religion* (1909), in which the hero, although a Huguenot at heart, is committed by birth and destiny to offer his sword to the kings of France; he is also torn between his cousin Gillonne, heartless maid of honour to the Queen of Navarre, and habituée of a corrupt and decadent court, and Diane, daughter of the Huguenot leader Montbrun, who shows her mettle in a cavalry skirmish. Stevenson's nephew, the journalist Claud Cockburn (1904–81), discusses his fiction and the Edwardian historical romance in

Bestseller (1972), and in *I Claud* (1967) describes him as 'a half-pay Major of Hussars whse hands had been partially paralysed as a result of some accident at polo'. According to Cockburn, he was possessed of a lurid imagination and given to fantasizing about the invasion of Britain, but his fiction lacked the vitality of his anecdotes: 'It was unfortunate from a financial point of view that he had a loving reverence for French history, which he supposed the library subscribers shared.' Despite his injury he rejoined the army and served in the First World War, retiring as an honorary major in January 1917.

STOCKLEY, Cynthia: Lilian Julia WEBB (1877–1936) married, first, Philip George Watts STOCKLEY and, secondly H. E. PELHAM BROWNE. Born in South Africa, she came to London in 1898 and went on the stage, before publishing her thirteen volumes of fiction 1903–1933, of which the first was *Virginia of the Rhodesians* (1903), sketches of white settler life in Africa, with much emphasis on extramarital intrigue, recounted by a witty, sophisticated, fast young woman who finally finds a man who can control her, and the most popular *Poppy: The Story of a South African Girl* (1910). Stockley became a Roman Catholic.

STOKER, Bram: Abraham STOKER (1847–1912) married (1878) Florence Anne Lemon BALCOMBE (1858–1937). Born in Dublin, the son of a government clerk, he was educated at a private school and at Trinity College, Dublin (1866–70), where he read mathematics. As a young child he was an invalid, and heard many Irish folk and fairy tales from his mother. By the time he went to university he was already writing horror stories, though he did not sell anything until 'The Chain of Destiny' in 1875. His wife jilted the young Oscar Wilde (1854–1900) in order to marry him. In 1878 he left the Petty Sessions Clerks department (from where he had contributed unpaid dramatic reviews to the *Dublin Mail*) to become the manager of the Lyceum Theatre company in London, owned by Sir Henry Irving (1838–1905). Irving's death meant that he lost his job, and he had a paralytic stroke in 1906, followed by a nervous breakdown. He applied to the Royal Literary Fund shortly before his death, of Bright's disease and syphilis. His selection of fairy tales, *Under the Sunset*, appeared in 1882, and his first novel was *The Snake's Pass* (1890). His best-known book, *Dracula*, appeared in 1897, but Stoker found it hard to repeat its enormous success. *The Mystery of the Sea* (1902) is set in Aberdeen in 1898, but has to do with a great Spanish treasure bequeathed by the Pope for the subjugation of England at the time of the Armada; there are haughty Spaniards, sea-caves, secret passages, ruined chapels, and a complicated cipher whose use is illustrated by means of appendices full of tables and a specimen dotted page. *Punch* detected echoes of *The Count of Monte Cristo* (1844–5) by Alexandre Dumas *père* (1802–70) and of *Treasure Island* (1883) by R. L. Stevenson (1850–94). Thereafter, Stoker rang the generic changes. *The *Jewel of the Seven Stars* (1903) is an occult tale, as is *The *Lair of the Giant Worm* (1911), which features a half-mad mesmerist, a devilish black man, a dove-like girl, and a lady who is being dunned for debt and is really a gigantic, ageless worm. *Lady Athlyne* (1908) is Anglo-American, and follows the romance between an American heiress, Joy Ogilvie, and the dashing lord who saves her life in New York and is eventually united with her in a 'pythonic embrace' at a Scottish hotel. *The Lady of the Shroud* (1909) is *Ruritanian and occult. Roger Melton, a millionaire with a financial stake in the Balkan State of the Blue Mountains, leaves his interest to his nephew, Rupert, a traveller interested in psychic phenomena, who has gone missing. Roger starts ten travel magazines in the hope that news of Rupert will break. Rupert eventually shows up, inherits his estate, and plunges into Blue Mountains politics. The lady of the shroud visits him by night, and becomes the Queen Consort. Like *Dracula*, the novel takes the form of a collection of documents.

STONE, Christopher [Reynolds] (1882–1965) married (1908) Alice CHINNERY née WILSON. The youngest of ten children of a schoolmaster, he was educated at home until he was 12, and then at Summerfields School, Eton College (where he was a King's Scholar), and Christ Church, Oxford. His fiction includes *The Noise of Life* (1910), about a great poet addicted to opium who is redeemed by son and daughter-in-law after his worldly wife has tried to murder him, *The Shoe of a Horse* (1912), a *Ruritanian romance, and *Letters to an Eton Boy* (1913), whose hero is described through the letters written to him by others. He also published verse and an autobiography, *Christopher Stone Speaking* (1933), in which he mentions that his eight novels brought him little money. He worked on the magazine the *Gramophone* (1923–) founded by his brother-in-law Compton *Mackenzie and also broadcast (introducing records) on the BBC.

Story of the Amulet, The, E. *Nesbit, 1906, T. Fisher Unwin. This is the second book about Cyril, Anthea, Robert, and Jane (who also feature in *The Phoenix and the Carpet*, 1904) and the Psammead, the crotchety sand fairy they found in a gravel-pit (see *Five Children and It*, 1902). This time the children find the creature in a pet-shop in Camden Town, and it is therefore grateful (rather than aggrieved) to be found. The Psammead (as previously agreed) will no longer grant the children their wishes, but does still advise them on the use of magic. Following its advice they buy an oddly shaped red stone in a curio shop. It is half an ancient amulet; find the other half and they can achieve their 'heart's desire' (the return of their mother and father). The search takes them into the past (prehistoric Egypt, Babylon, Atlantis, Roman Britain, Tyre) and, briefly, the future (a utopian—Fabian?—London), and increasingly involves the bemused learned gentleman from upstairs. A mix of history and *fantasy, like other Nesbit books it is most enjoyable for its account of how a distinctive and determined group of middle-class children refuse to be awed by their remarkable adventures.

STRAFFORD, Mary, *pseud.*: see F. M. *Mayor.

STRAIN, E. H.: Euphans Helen McNAUGHTON (d. 1934) married John STRAIN (d. 1931). Born at Auchinleck in Ayrshire, she married an eminent civil engineer and travelled extensively with him. They were friendly with Robert Louis Stevenson (1850–94), and a visit to him in the South Seas is described in her travel pieces for the *Scotsman. A Man's Foes* (1895) is an *historical novel about the siege of Londonderry. In *Laura's Legacy* (1903), foundling Eve enters Lady Laura's life, and that of her nephew, Hugh Barclay, at a particularly desolate moment: since Eve writes a play and Hugh manages a theatre, it all turns out for the best. *A Prophet's Reward* (1908) is a densely idiomatic historical romance about eighteenth-century Scottish politics. *Elmslie's Drag Net* (1900) is a collection of short stories. An obituary in the *Times* (20 Mar. 1934) describes her as 'deeply religious, and with a Spartan sense of duty'.

Strand, The, was published monthly from January 1891 to March 1950. Created by *Tit-Bits* publisher, George Newnes (1851–1910), the *Strand* was intended to entertain the newly educated middle class with a mix of humour, drama, and realism, a combination of fiction and illustration, adventure and biography, with a blend of imperialist swagger and domestic self-deprecation. Under the forty-year editorship of H. Greenhaugh Smith (d. 1935) the *Strand* was remarkably successful (the first issue sold 300,000 copies and issue sales thereafter regularly reached half a million) and attracted not only popular writers (introducing Sherlock Holmes to the nation) but also regular contributions from such literary professionals as Rudyard *Kipling, Somerset *Maugham, and H. G. *Wells.

STRANG, Herbert, *pseud.*: George Herbert ELY (1866–1958) married Margaret ASHWORTH; and C. James L'ESTRANGE (1867–1947) married Maude L'ESTRANGE. Under this pseudonym, and sometimes in collaboration with John Aston, George Lawrence, and Richard Stead, these authors published fiction (*historical, adventure), textbooks, and non-fiction for both boys and girls. Both writers were employed by the Oxford University Press from 1920, who thereafter became their publishers, but earlier works had been published mostly by Blackie and Hodder & Stoughton. Ely also did some translation from the French early in his career. Titles include *The Adventures of Harry Rochester: A Tale of the Days of Marlborough and Eugene* (1906), *Brown of Moukden: A Story of the Russo-Japanese War* (1906), *The Cruise of the Gyro-Car* (1911), and *The Air Patrol: A Story of the North-West Frontier* (1913). The *British Library Catalogue* offers no clues, however, to the identity of 'Mrs Herbert Strang' who sometimes collaborated with 'Herbert Strang'—for instance in editing 'The Golden Treasure Books' series from 1931 —but also was the editor of a large quantity of fiction and non-fiction for girls and small children, such as *The Violet Book for Girls* (1914).

STRAUS, Ralph (1882–1950). Born in Manchester, he was educated at Harrow School and Pembroke College, Cambridge, where he studied biology. However, his publications were distinctly in the field of arts. He was interested in bibliography, and wrote biographies of *John Baskerville* (1907), *Robert Dodsley* (1910), and *The*

Unspeakable Curll (1927); he was a member of a society of bibliophiles, the Sette of Odd Volumes (among whom he was known as 'Brother Scribbler') and had a private press, on which he printed, among other works, an edition of the works of Petronius (d. AD 66). As a novelist his main line was social comedy, often featuring clever, bookish heroes who are forced to cope with the real world. *The Man Apart* (1906) is the bleak tale of a young man who distinguishes himself at Cambridge, but whose unconventional opinions bring him, in a not wholly specified way, to a miserable end. Marching to *The Little God's Drum* (1908) are a celebrated novelist and an improbable peer who goes in for aeroplanes and East End clubs, and remains a bachelor at the end. *The Scandalous Mr Waldo* (1909) is the diary of Henry Waldo, son of a great criminal lawyer, who lives with his father on amicable terms tempered by sarcasm: the diarist's relationship with his father (Henry is a bibliophile, and his *Eminent Libraries of Medieval Europe* is reviewed unfavourably by his father in the *Athenaeum*) is much more interesting than those he subsequently forms with three very different women. *The Prison Without a Wall* (1912) is St Mary's College, Cambridge, one of whose inmates, a Professor of History, author of a famous social history of Rome, is released in order to manage his family estate. *The Orley Tradition* (1914) represents a change of emphasis, in that the tradition in question is not associated with mental agility: the dim hero, an athlete nearly killed in an accident, has nothing to amuse him except an adventuress, from whom he is eventually rescued by a sensible girl; Mrs Damson, owner of the local village shop, acts as chorus. *The Dust Which Is God* (1907) is a futuristic dream-vision, in which a zoologist is afforded a glimpse of the race evolving towards perfection. He also wrote as 'Robert Erstone Forbes'.

Street of Adventure, The, Philip *Gibbs, 1909, William Heinemann. Francis Luttrell, son of a provincial rector, just down from university and at a loose end, is given an introduction by one Philip Gibbs to the editor of the *Liberal*. Amazingly, the editor gives him a job, and he enters Fleet Street at the very bottom of the ladder. The bulk of the story is a vivid description of the life of a young and inexperienced journalist. Luttrell's colleagues include a legendary foreign correspondent, a crime reporter who keeps a (more or less) reformed prostitute, a drama critic with a secret taste for *Meredith, an all-purpose dandy and social butterfly, and a pair of intrepid women journalists. The paper eventually folds. By this time Luttrell has fallen in love with one of the woman journalists, Kitty Halstead, and begun to write novels. They think of marrying, and leaving Fleet Street, but journalism is a habit neither can kick. They both find employment at other newspapers, and remain single. The strength of the novel lies in its local knowledge (the opening description of Luttrell's approach to the editor is excellent), and in its ultimate refusal of the conventions of the wedlock plot.

STUART, Esmé, *pseud.*: Amélie Claire LeROY (1851–1934). Born in Paris, she was brought up in England from the age of 5 or 6. She moved to Winchester in her 20s, and became, like C. R. *Coleridge, a member of the circle of the Anglo-Catholic novelist and children's writer Charlotte M. Yonge (1823–1901) who lived nearby. With Yonge and others she collaborated on *Astray* (1886) (though Coleridge states that the main author was LeRoy's lifelong friend Mary Bramston, 1841–1912). Like Yonge and Coleridge she was a keen supporter of the Girls' Friendly Society and other charitable works. She was the author of more than sixty volumes of fiction, mostly for children and young women, some of it *historical, much of it whimsical, from 1876, including *The Strength of Straw* (1900), *Christalla: An Unknown Quantity* (1900), *For Love and Ransom* (1905), *Mona: A Manx Idyll* (1905), and *A Charming Girl* (1907). The latter is characteristic: Veronica Curryer inspires in every man she meets the belief that she is 'one of God's angels': one admirer dies of it, the others all think they are engaged to her. Her most popular work seems to have been a series beginning with *Harum Scarum: A Poor Relation* (1896).

STUART, Henry Longan (1875–1928). Stuart grew up in the London Irish community and travelled to America as a young man. On returning to Europe he began a career in journalism, interrupted by service in the British army in the First World War. After the Armistice he pursued his newspaper career in the USA, where he settled. He was contemporary fiction reviewer for the *New York Times Book Review*, and translated such poets as Blaise Cendrars (1887–1961), but his central commitment was Catholicism rather than literature. He wrote editorials for the Catholic magazine, the *Commonweal*, and both his published novels deal with problems of belief. *Weeping Cross: An Unworldly Story* (1908) is a *historical romance in the form of the autobiography of Father Fitzsimon, who is present at the massacre by 'Indians' of settlers at Long Meadow, Massachusetts, in 1652, which was said to have been incited by Catholic priests. In *Fenella* (1911), the Hon. and Revd Nigel Barbour marries, to put an end to baseless gossip, the daughter of a Cornish farmer, who, after her husband's death, lets to paying guests the greater part of the mansion he has left her. Their daughter, Fenella, is toughened but not corrupted by these surroundings. She falls in love with Paul Ingram, a writer and wanderer. When he breaks off the affair, she flirts ostentatiously with Sir Brian Lumsden, a sporting Stock Exchange baronet who owns a musichall, in order to win him back. The character of Althea Rees is based on the Catholic convert novelist 'John Oliver *Hobbes'.

Studies in Wives, Mrs Belloc *Lowndes, 1909, William Heinemann. Six short stories about marital conflict. 'Althea's Opportunity' is the greatest service she does her bullying husband: carrying his corpse home when he dies in his mistress's drawing-room—she is then able to respond with a good conscience to her admirer's warmth and competence. 'Mr Jarvice's Wife' concerns a husband's response to his son's involvement with a woman accused of murdering her husband, 'Shameful Behaviour!' a husband's enduring passion for his turbulent ex-wife. In 'The Decree Made Absolute', the decree which would free a man from his unfaithful wife, is made absolute by her death a few minutes before it is made absolute by the courts. Lowndes's main emphasis is on (the dangers of) social and sexual innovation. In 'A Very Modern Instance', a husband discovers that his wife has been accepting money from an admirer. In 'According to Meredith', a man living with a woman in the kind of free union advocated by George *Meredith is driven mad when she leaves him for another man who has promised to marry her, and shoots her lover before slitting his own throat.

STURGIS, Howard [Overing] (1855–1920) was the brother of Julian *Sturgis, and was educated at Eton College and Trinity College, Cambridge. He inherited a private income from his father, a banker, and lived near Windsor with a friend, William Haynes Smith, called 'the Babe', where he devoted himself to Society, literature, and embroidery, in which last he was very expert. He was the author of three novels: *Tim* (1891), *All That Was Possible* (1895), and **Belchamber* (1904), an account of the predicament of a sensitive aristocrat. The last was reprinted in 1935 with an elegant introduction by E. M. *Forster, who wrote of 'this brilliant, sensitive and neglected writer'. Sturgis was a friend of Henry *James, who began one letter, 'You have the art of writing letters which make those who already adore you to the verge of dementia slide over the dizzy edge and fairly sit raving their passion.'

STURGIS, Julian [Russell] (1848–1904) married (1883) Mary Maude BERESFORD. Born in Boston, Massachusetts, Sturgis came to Britain with his family aged seven months. He was educated at Eton College and Balliol College, Oxford, where he read classics. There he proved to be an excellent amateur oarsman, and graduated MA in 1875. He qualified as a barrister in 1876 and was naturalized a British citizen in 1877. He travelled in Turkey in 1878 and in the US in 1880. His first novel was *John-A-Dreams* (1878), and his gently humorous fiction became very popular. In his last novel, *Stephen Calinari* (1901), a rich, wayward young man at Oxford in the 1870s intends to have a brilliant political career, but settles for true love. Sturgis also published *Count Julian: A Spanish Tragedy in Verse* (1893) and *A Book of Song* (1894); and wrote opera libretti, including those for *Ivanhoe* (1891) by Sir Arthur Sullivan (1842–1900) and *Much Ado About Nothing* (1901) by Sir Charles Stanford (1852–1924). Sturgis also published a critique of a statement by Arthur Balfour (1848–1930) on the economic implications of insular free trade: *The Prime Minister's Pamphlet: A Study and Some Thoughts* (1903). Howard *Sturgis was his brother.

Subsoil, Charles *Marriott, 1913, Hurst & Blackett. Intelligent, well-intentioned study of an artist, Hugh Sutherland, who is deeply troubled by art's subservience either to Society or to an increasingly commercialized bohemia, and who travels to Cornwall in order (as his obliging fiancée, Sylvia Bradley, an industrialist's daughter, puts it) to 'touch earth'. There he meets

John Henry Rosewall, the corrupt agent of the local landowner, and his wife, Loveday, whose moral 'breadth' and 'simplicity' impress him greatly. Returning to London, he finds less time for Sylvia, more for a burgeoning arts and crafts movement. When her husband is killed in a motoring accident, Loveday settles in London, where, released at last from the yoke of marriage, she adds adventurousness to her list of admirable qualities. Sylvia and Hugh separate. Hugh proposes to Loveday, but she wishes to remain a friend only, and a partner in a workshop established for the design and manufacture of posters, furniture, and textiles. Sylvia, meanwhile, becomes engaged to a young man who had been one of Loveday's (apparently chaste) adventures. Her father involves Hugh in a project to create a polytechnic in suburban London. The novel is reticent about sex, but good on class, which it regards as a matter of geological strata which incorporate faults, dips, upcrops, and 'infiltrations'.

suburban life. In *London: A Social History* (1994) Roy Porter observes that the growth of suburbia in the second half of the nineteenth century 'marked the end of the old London and the birth of the new'. And not only London, of course. Boosted by railway expansion and the advent of the motor car, suburbia also spread out from the major industrial centres and the coastal resorts. 'It was a radical departure,' Porter continues, 'the moment when, for hundreds of thousands, the allure of urban living finally faded.' In 1909, the Liberal politician C. F. G. Masterman (1873–1927) spoke of the inhabitants of the new suburbs as 'practically the product of the past half century'. 'They form a homogeneous civilization—detached, self-centred, unostentatious ... It is a life of Security; a life of Sedentary occupation; a life of Respectability.' While the population of the central areas of London grew undramatically between 1881 and 1911, that of the 'outer ring' surged from 936,000 to 2,730,000. Suburbia was as tribal as the slums which had attracted the attention of writers during the 1890s, as tempting to the cultural anthropologist; more so, perhaps, since the new tribe was composed of avid novel-readers. The result was a flourishing genre of fiction, taking its tone from *Three Men in a Boat* (1889) by Jerome K. *Jerome and *The Diary of a Nobody* (1892) by George (1847–1912) and Weedon Grossmith (1854–1919). The philanthropic Lady Harman, in H. G. *Wells's *The Wife of Sir Isaac Harman* (1917), who wants inside information about suburbia, is advised to read George *Gissing, Edwin *Pugh, and Frank *Swinnerton. Other writers she might have consulted with profit include 'R. *Andom', Alice and Claude *Askew, J. D. *Beresford, Arthur M. *Binstead, Shan F. *Bullock, Sophie *Cole, William *De Morgan, D. *Gerard, Mrs Harold E. *Gorst, 'Keble *Howard', Edgar *Jepson, Lucas *Malet, Leonard *Merrick, B. Paul *Neuman, Barry *Pain, W. Carter *Platts, W. Pett *Ridge, W. Teignmouth *Shore, John Collis *Snaith, Edward *Thomas, Hugh *Walpole, Percy *White, 'John Strange *Winter', and Leonard *Woolf. John Ruskin (1819–1900) put the objection to suburbia pithily when he alluded to 'those gloomy rows of formalised minuteness, alike without difference and without fellowship, as solitary as similar'. Suburbia permitted neither individuality nor community. It denied the vision fostered by romanticism and embedded in nineteenth-century social theory, of a society united by common human bonds but differentiated according to individual capacities and desires. In E. M. *Forster's **Howards End* (1910), Mrs Munt, alighting at Hilton on her way to rescue Helen Schlegel from the Wilcoxes, wonders which 'country' the station will open into, Suburbia or England, executive comfort or 'local life' and 'personal intercourse'. On the whole, writers like Forster, George *Gissing, John *Galsworthy, and H. G. Wells, at least in **Ann Veronica* (1909), shared Ruskin's view of suburbia. Its uniformity could be regarded as benevolent, or as petty and destructive. The real challenge was to see in it something other than uniformity. Pre-eminent among the few books which rose to the challenge are Arnold *Bennett's **Clayhanger* (1910) and The **Card* (1911), G. K. *Chesterton's *The *Napoleon of Notting Hill* (1904), Henry *James's 'Mora Montravers', in *The *Finer Grain* (1910), Mrs Belloc *Lowndes's *The *Lodger* (1913), Malet's *The *Far Horizon* (1906), Ridge's **From Nine to Six-Thirty* (1910), some of the stories collected in Gissing's **The House of Cobwebs* (1906), and Arthur *Machen's 'A Fragment of Life', in *The *House of Souls* (1905).

Suffragette Sally, 'G. *Colmore', 1911, Stanley Paul. On the whole the suffrage campaign made for better plays than novels. But in this novel 'G. Colmore' extended the tradition of collective biography (cf. *The *Pathway of the Pioneer*) in a novel which reveals an intimate knowledge of the WSPU and its tactics. It follows the destinies of three representative militants: the Cockney serving-maid, Sally Simmonds; the provincial, middle-class Edith Carstairs; and Lady Geraldine Hill, who is clearly based on Lady Constance Lytton (1869–1923), who, imprisoned as a suffragette and released because of her rank, disguised herself as a working woman and was re-arrested and force-fed. The final chapter of *Suffragette Sally* is left blank, with a note stating that the story cannot be concluded because the issue of votes for women is still in the balance: so much for narrative closure. And yet there is closure of an orthodox kind. The inherent bias of the genre towards the middle classes, and particularly the middle classes in love, gradually declares itself. The author's attitude towards Lady Geraldine is frankly adulatory; her attitude towards Sally Simmonds faintly patronizing. The main thrust of the narrative is provided by Edith Carstairs's conversion to militancy, her deepening commitment measured by changes in the way she feels about her two admirers: Cyril Race, a member of the Liberal Cabinet who puts his own career ahead of support for women, and Robbie Colquhoun, a dull country squire who is won over to the cause and seals his conversion by punching Race on the nose. *Suffragette Sally* is both collective biography—a new, politicized form—and domestic romance.

SUTCLIFFE, Halliwell (1870–1932) married (1904) —— COTTRELL. Brought up in Yorkshire, he was educated there and at King's College, Cambridge, and was a full-time writer from 1893. His main line was bleak-moors-and-bad-weather romances such as *Shameless Wayne: A Romance of the Last Feud of Wayne and Ratcliffe* (1900), *Through Sorrow's Gates: A Tale of the Lonely Heath* (1904), *Red o' the Feud* (1905), and *Priscilla of the Good Intent: A Romance of the Grey Fells* (1909). Reviewers thought that he had transposed R. D. Blackmore's (1825–1900) successful combination of rugged landscapes with theatrical plots from a southern to a northern setting. But Sutcliffe also developed a second string of *Gissing-with-a-smile rural meditations. In *An Episode in Arcady* (1898) and *A Bachelor in Arcady* (1906), a cultured writer describes his country life, his garden, and his neighbours. By the time of *A Benedick in Arcady* (1906) he has married the squire's daughter. Many of his novels went into several editions.

SUTHERLAND, Duchess of: see under Lady Angela *Forbes.

SUTHERLAND, Joan, *pseud.*: Joan Maisie COLLINGS (1890–1947) married (1914) Richard KELLY. She published more than forty volumes of fiction to 1948, specializing in frontier tales featuring cool, brusque Englishmen with impossible names whose qualities of leadership fail them in the boudoir. Her first novel, *Cavanagh of Kultann* (1911), set the pattern. It was followed by *The Dawn* (1912), about a rising politician and imperial secret agent with an unsympathetic wife who is redeemed by another woman, and *The Hidden Road* (1913), about a heroic expedition to Lhasa which separates the hero from his fiancée. *Cophetua's Son* (1914) changes the scene from the north-west frontier of India to the marble quarries of Carrara, though the cast is much the same. Sutherland's other novel in the period is *Beyond the Shadow* (1914).

SWAIN, E[dmund] G[ill] (1861–1938) was educated at Manchester Grammar School and at Cambridge, and became chaplain and proctor of King's College, Cambridge. He was a literary disciple of M. R. *James, and published a volume of short stories in that vein entitled *The Stoneground Ghost Tales* (1912). He was subsequently Librarian and, later, Precentor of Peterborough Cathedral.

SWAN, Annie S[hepherd] (1859–1943) married (1883) James Burnett SMITH (d. 1927). A farmer's daughter, she was born at Mountskip, near Gorebridge, Midlothian, and educated at Queen's Street Ladies' College in Edinburgh and at home by governesses. Swan made her literary debut with pieces for *The Woman at Home*. She submitted monthly articles for a number of years that were 'full of sound sense and sympathetic knowledge', and she edited the periodical from 1893–1917. In 1883 she married a physician. Towards the end of the 1890s she produced the *Annie S. Swan Penny Stories*, a penny weekly (and from 1924 also *The Annie Swan Annual*). Mrs Burnett Smith became a popular lecturer for the cause of Temperance. During the First World War she worked for the Ministry of Food, as well as visiting soldiers' camps at home and abroad and working in munitions factories. Her husband served with the Black Watch and their family home in Hertford Heath, Herts., was bombed by Zeppelins.

Unfortunately, Swan is best remembered for the romantic formula stories that she churned out in the twentieth century (over 250 of them were published). Of more interest, however, is earlier work such as *Ups and Downs* (1878), *Aldersyde* (1883), which is a Border story in the Oliphant vein, *Carlowrie* (1884), *Gates of Eden* (1886), and *Who Shall We Serve?* (1891). Many consider *A Divided House* (1885) to be her most accomplished work. Swan's later publications, which continue to insist above all on the seriousness of domestic responsibilities, include: *Mary Garth. A Clydeside Romance* (1904); *Love, The Master Key* (1905); *Christian's Cross, or, Tested but True* (1905); *A Mask of Gold: The Mystery of the Meadows* (1906), about a rascally doctor who attempts to steal an old lady's money, and the unjustly suspected heroine who clears herself in the end; *Nancy Nicolson, or, Who Shall Be Heir?* (1906), about Scottish life and character; *Love Unlocks the Door* (1907), which features Miss Oliphant, a motherly spinster who keeps a baby-linen warehouse and distributes 'the quick sympathy and commonsense of the woman who had been able to live the solitary existence and yet keep herself in touch with life at every point'; *Anne Hyde, Travelling Companion* (1908), whose heroine earns her living for a while and then marries an American millionaire (she uses part of his fortune to combat the 'less desirable aspects' of American society; *The Inheritance* (1909), about a young social reformer who is to inherit a fortune on the condition that he marry the splendid girl who has long been his 'chum', but who falls in love with someone else instead; *The Magic of Love* (1909), a similar tale about a man whose father wants him to marry for money, and when he refuses drives him to enlist in the army and seek a glorious death in South Africa; and *Love's Miracle* (1910), about an ingenuous youth who appals his parents by marrying a chorus girl, who wins them round while he is seeking his fortune in the Klondike. The increasing emphasis on generational conflict is striking. **Margaret Holroyd, or, The Pioneers* (1910), a suffragette novel, is an interesting departure. Swan's *Times* obituary (19 June 1943) describes her typical subject as 'domestic life running upon the most correct and wholesome lines'. She is the favourite novelist of William Morel's dim and pretentious sweetheart, Lily, in D. H. *Lawrence's **Sons and Lovers* (1913). She describes her career in *My Life* (1934), and there is also an edition of her *Letters* (1945) by Mildred Nicholl. Swan also published over eighty titles under the pseudonym 'David Lyall' including *Another Man's Money* (1902), *The Bells of Portknockie* (1902), and *The Ships of Mon Desir* (1910). She died at Aldersyde, Gullane, East Lothian.

SWIFT, Benjamin, *pseud.*: William Romaine PATERSON (1871–?1935). He published fourteen volumes of fiction under this pseudonym, 1896–1923. Swift's novels treat unusual and sometimes macabre subjects, and their tone fluctuates wildly from farce to sustained social criticism. *Nude Souls* (1900) is more daring in title than content. *Sordon* (1902) is about euthanasia, while *Ludus Amoris* (1902) is a farcical extravaganza about a poet and a horse-dealer which incorporates a lengthy account of the treatment and cure of cancer. *In Piccadilly* (1903) is even more ambitious, featuring a Scottish laird who is enslaved in his dotage by his moneylending valet; the laird's heir, whose white knees gleam beneath his kilt; a woman who has married a man for his title; a husband driven to murderous designs by jealousy; and an 'explosive' unknown quantity. The satire is mostly light, but it too has explosive moments. The upper classes are denounced as 'a kind of parasite behind whom lies the blood and plunder of empires', and there is a vivid scene of prostitution in Piccadilly itself. *Gossip* (1905), which is set in Sussex, concerns the conflicting claims of twin brothers to a baronetcy. The hero of *The Death Man* (1908) is about a public executioner: a girl is murdered, and the wrong man hanged. Swift's other novel in the period is *Lady of the Night* (1912). He published some religious works and two novels (1911, 1917) under his own name.

SWINNERTON, Frank [Arthur] (1884–1982) married, first (1919), —— and, secondly (1924) Mary Dorothy BENNETT (d. 1980). Born in London, the son of a copperplate engraver, Swinnerton had a happy childhood although his education was spasmodic owing to poverty and ill health. Aged 15 he joined the staff of the *Scottish Cyclist* magazine, but then in 1901 became clerk-receptionist at J. M. Dent, where he remained for six years; this was followed by twenty-five years working for Chatto & Windus, where his greatest publishing success, by his own account, was the highly profitable 'discovery' of *The Young Visiters*, (1919) by Daisy Ashford (1881–1972). Swinnerton was a significant figure in the London literary world, writing the 'Simon Pure' column for the *Bookman (collected as *A London Bookman*, 1928), reviewing books for the *Observer* and the *Evening News*, and publishing an early study of George *Gissing (1912). He befriended many writers, and remembered them with affection in his useful study of *The Georgian Literary Scene* (1935). Swinnerton's novels have not retained their charm so well. Titles include *The Merry Heart* (1909), *The Young Idea* (1910), *The Casement* (1911), *The Happy Family* (1911), *On the Staircase* (1914), *The Chaste Wife* (1916), *Shops and Houses* (1918), *September* (1919), and his biggest seller, *Nocturne* (1917). The 'merry heart' belongs to a clerk who lives with his public-spirited wife in *suburban Hertfordshire. The 'young idea' is that of a group of young people who share a house in London. His elder brother Philip Swinnerton was a black-and-white engraver.

Swoop!, The, *Or, How Clarence Saved England*, P. G. *Wodehouse, 1909, Alston Rivers. 'It may be thought by some', Wodehouse announced in his preface, 'that in the pages which follow I have painted in too lurid colours the horrors of a foreign invasion of England. Realism in art, it may be argued, can be carried too far. I prefer to think that the majority of my readers will acquit me of a desire to be unduly sensational. It is necessary that England should be roused to a sense of her peril, and only by setting down without flinching the probable results of an invasion can this be done.' Wodehouse manages to satirize both the sluggishness of the English middle classes, and the hysterical tone of the *invasion scare propaganda which was self-importantly designed to arouse them from their torpor. 'SURREY DOING BADLY/GERMAN ARMY LANDS IN ENGLAND,' the posters announce. One of the few to take the second headline more seriously than the first is Clarence MacAndrew Chugwater, boy scout extraordinary. The Germans have landed on the Essex coast, the Russians at Yarmouth, the Mad Mullah at Portsmouth, the Swiss navy to the west of the bathing-machines at Lyme Regis, the Chinese at the pictureseque Welsh watering-place of Lllgxtplll, the Young Turks at Scarborough, and a small but determined band of warriors from the island of Bollygolla at Margate. 'In sporting circles the chief interest centred on the race to London. The papers showed the positions of the various armies each morning in their Runners and Betting columns; six to four on the Germans was freely offered, but found no takers.' The Chinese lose their way near Llanfairpwlgwnngogogoch, but the other powers reach and take London. Before long, however, they fall out over the respective merits of their leaders as music-hall turns, fight each other to a standstill, and are rounded up by Clarence and his cohorts armed with catapults and hockey sticks.

SYRETT, Jerrard: see under Netta *Syrett.

SYRETT, Netta: Janet SYRETT (d. 1943). Eldest daughter of ten in a well-off London family, she was educated at the North London Collegiate School for Girls, where she boarded in the house of the headmistress, Frances Buss (1827–1894), whom she found violent and neurotic, an experience described in her novel *The Victorians* (1915), and at the Training College for Women Teachers, Cambridge, described in her novel *The God of Chance* (1920). The novelist Grant Allen (1848–1899), a friend of her family, introduced her to literary circles and persuaded her that God did not exist. She taught at Swansea High School for a short time before moving to London to live with her four sisters and teach at the Polytechnic Institute for Girls, where she made friends with a fellow-teacher, Mabel Beardsley, sister of Aubrey (1874–98), through whom she met bohemians and contributed to the *Yellow Book*. While still teaching she began to write plays for children. She edited a periodical called *The Dream Garden* (1905–) and published some fifty volumes of fiction, including some children's fiction. *Nobody's Fault* (1896) appeared in the 'Keynote' Series. Her fiction is *feminist, with a strong dash of sensation. *Rosanne* (1902) sets the tone: the heroine, daughter of a model with a hereditary tendency to undisciplined passion, ruins the happy marriage of an old childhood friend. Narrow lives and thwarted ambition form the subject of the stories collected in *Women and Circumstance* (1906). *Olivia L. Carew* (1910), set in New England and Italy, describes the troubled but eventually happy marriage between a New England woman ambitious for a brilliant career and a rather colourless Englishman. The *Three Women* (1912) are Phyllida and Katherine, business partners in a curio shop in Mayfair, and the 'fast' Rosamund, who carries off Phyllida's fiancé. *The Jam Queen* (1914) imagines economic rather than sexual independence for women. The heroine is a self-made millionaire from Houndsditch. 'A great name and a great fortune are two distinct things, my child,' she explains. 'Jam endures.' After this, though, the novel rather peters out. Syrett published an autobiography (1939). Her youngest brother Jerrard Syrett (d. 1926), who was mentally ill and lived as a remittance man in Italy, published *A Household Saint* (1911) and two later novels.

T

Tale of Peter Rabbit, The, Beatrix Potter, 1902, Frederick Warne. (There was also a privately printed edition in 1901.) The first and one of the most powerful of Potter's series of tales of animals for small children, illustrated with her own watercolours facing each page, it is not the only example of a piece of Edwardian fiction which gives the reader the opportunity of vicarious rebellion against authority while emphasizing the penalties of transgression. Peter, unlike his docile sisters Flopsy, Mopsy, and Cotton-tail, disobeys their mother's injunction not to stray into the kitchen garden. As a result he commits such major nursery crimes as theft, losing his clothes, and over-eating, and, after narrowly escaping death at the hands of the sinister gardener Mr MacGregor, runs home to the domestic hearth, where his virtuous sisters are rewarded with a delicious supper which he is denied. *The Tale of Benjamin Bunny* (1904) is a sequel.

TALLENTYRE, S. G., *pseud.*: Evelyn Beatrice HALL (1868–1956). She collaborated with her brother-in-law 'Henry Seton *Merriman' on *From Wisdom Court* (1893) and helped his widow to edit his collected works. She published translations from the French, biographical studies of French subjects such as *The Friends of Voltaire* (1906), and novels including *Early-Victorian: A Village Chronicle* (1910), about heartbreak and restricted lives in a remote village, the similar *Love Laughs Last* (1919), and *Matthew Hargraves* (1914), whose hero comes to regret his cold, loveless marriage.

Tangled Skein, The, Baroness *Orczy, 1907, Greening. It is 1553, and the emissaries of Philip of Spain are trying to arrange a marriage with Queen Mary, against bitter opposition from the defenders of Protestant England, who hope that Mary will marry Robert d'Esclade, the Duke of Wessex, with whom she is deeply in love. Wessex, however, has been engaged since he was a very young man to a woman he has never met, Lady Ursula Glynde, and does not feel inclined to break his father's pledge. At East Moseley Fair, Wessex intervenes to save Lady Ursula from the impertinent attentions of Don Miguel, Marquis de Suarez, envoy of His Most Catholic Majesty, and then Mirrab, a fortune-teller, from the attentions of a mob which would like to burn her as a witch. Meanwhile, the wily Cardinal Moreno, Philip's chief emissary, has earned the Queen's displeasure, and decides to restore himself to favour by separating Wessex from Lady Ursula. Recognizing in Mirrab a likeness to Lady Ursula, he and Don Miguel get her drunk and arrange for her to be found in a compromising position by Wessex. Furious at the way she has been used, Mirrab stabs Don Miguel to death with Wessex's dagger. The Queen tells Moreno that if he can prove Wessex innocent, she will agree to marry Philip. At Moreno's prompting, Lady Ursula agrees to confess to the crime, at once saving the man she loves and condemning herself in his eyes. Mirrab, however, does the decent thing, and confesses in her turn, thus allowing Wessex to marry Lady Ursula. Moreno is sent home in disgrace.

TEARLE, Christian, *pseud.*: Edward Tyrrell JAQUES (d. 1919) married Margaret ——. Admitted as a solicitor in August 1880, he joined the family firm of Jaques & Co. He published a guide book, a volume of verse, and four novels, of which *The Vice-Chancellor's Ward* (1903) and *A Legal Practitioner: Being Certain of My Own Experiences* (1907) are set in the legal world.

Temple Bar: *A London Magazine for Town and Country Readers* (1860–1906). This monthly shilling magazine was first published in December 1860 by John Maxwell, who set out to rival the **Cornhill*. It was edited by the novelist G. A. Sala (1828–98) and each issue ran to 144 pages, containing mostly serialized fiction, half a dozen short stories, three or four poems, and six or seven miscellaneous articles dealing with politics, religion, history, or geography, interspersed with moral essays, all aimed at the Victorian upper middle classes. The subjects range from book reviews to discussion of lunatic asylums and workhouses. M. E. *Braddon, Maxwell's wife, published some of her early work in the magazine before he sold it to Sala in 1862. In January 1866 Richard Bentley (1794–1871) bought *Temple Bar* from Sala and appointed his son George (1828–95) as editor. Until his death the magazine was steadily successful, with a stable circulation of 13,000. The emphasis was still heavily on serialized fiction; current affairs were discussed only in passing. The magazine was dominated by stories and novels by some of the most popular mid-Victorian writers. He was succeeded by his son Richard Bentley (1854–1936), but in 1898 Bentley & Son, including the journal, was sold to Macmillan & Co., and it ceased publication in 1906. The failure of *Temple Bar* following George Bentley's death was largely due to the fact that the serialized fiction became increasingly inferior (including, for example, work by Egerton *Castle and Frances Mary *Peard). Never much concerned with current affairs, *Temple Bar*'s wholesale inability to adapt itself to the modern age was also a contributory factor.

Temporal Power: *A Study in Supremacy*, 'Marie *Corelli', 1902, Methuen. A novel attacking socialism, which in its first week sold the entire first edition of 120,000 copies and 50,000 of a second edition—a bookselling record for a *6s.* volume. The hero of the story is a contemporary king who rules over an unnamed Christian country. The king is married to a beautiful but cold consort and they have three sons. Suddenly aware that he is not doing his duty to his people, the king resolves to go amongst them and see things for himself. He joins a society of socialists, vetoes one declaration of war, and thwarts a Jesuit conspiracy, during which an attempt is made on his life, an attempt foiled by a beautiful working-class woman who receives the knife-thrust in his place. One of the main themes of the book is the secret marriage of prince and pleb (the king's eldest son Humphrey to the beautiful Gloria), and Humphrey's refusal to abandon Gloria when the king insists he make a speedy alliance with a princess of a neighbouring state. The book ends with the abdication and death of the king, his son and Gloria sailing to happier climes. Publication was immediately followed by a heated correspondence between Marie Corelli and the editor of the *Review of Reviews*, who accused her of casting slurs on Queen Alexandra (1844–1925), in the character of the cold queen, and on Joseph Chamberlain (1836–1914) in the character of Carl Perousse. There was also a four-page critique of the novel in the *Review of Reviews* claiming that *Temporal Power* was a covert tract for the guidance of the King. The reasons for the book's success are obscure. *Temporal Power* is conspicuously overwritten, replete with purple passages, and its author's voice is evident throughout vehemently declaring its opinions.

Terrible Tomboy, A, Angela *Brazil, 1904, Hodder & Stoughton. Peggy Vaughan lives in an old abbey with her elder sister, younger brother, kind aunt, and gentleman-farmer father. A tomboy, she goes to the local high school and suffers from the condescension of richer girls despite her ancient birth. She makes friends with a jolly American boy with whom she builds an irrigation system in his aunt's garden, and gets lost in a cave with rising water with her little brother. When her aunt marries a long-lost lover, Peggy resolves to be more domesticated and feminine. Meanwhile the aunt writes to her sister Lilian, a housekeeper at 16: 'There are plenty of "blue" Girton girls in the world who do not seem to me to be of much use to anyone except themselves, while as the "little mother" of your home you are filling a place that is the sphere of every true woman.' Peggy beats up a boy who bullies her little brother at school. The abbey is threatened by a mortgagee—a wicked distiller and father of two school enemies of Peggy's—but fortunately discover a chestful of medieval books which save the old home from desecration by *nouveaux riches*. This disjointed early work lacks the emphasis on the school itself and the importance of its values which is such a feature of most of Brazil's fiction, but several key themes (the healthiness of tomboyish girls and postponed feminization, as opposed to the unhealthiness of precocious internalization of adult values, and the superiority of birth to money) are already present.

Third Miss Symons, The, F. M. *Mayor, 1913, Sidgwick & Jackson. In his preface to the novel, John *Masefield identified its subject as the life of an umarried 'idle' or 'surplus' woman of the mid-Victorian era. Henrietta Symons is the third child in a family of six. Plain, and quickly disappointed in love, she consoles herself with *Jane Eyre* and *Villette* by Charlotte Brontë (1816–55). Her brothers are successful in their professions, her sisters in marriage. When her mother dies, she assumes the management of her father's house. When he remarries, she finds herself at a loose end. 'If she had led a half-occupied life as keeper of her father's house, she now learnt the art of getting through a day in which she did absolutely nothing.' She spends her middle age shifting from *pension* to *pension*, returns home to grow increasingly bitter, quarrel with a feminist niece, and die at the age of 63. 'She has done nothing but live and been nothing but alive,' Masefield commented, 'both to such passive purpose that the ceasing is pitiful; and it is by pushing on to this end, instead of shirking it, and by marking the last tragical fact which puts a dignity upon even the meanest being, that Miss Mayor raises her story above the plane of social criticism, and keeps it sincere.' The novel's subject and its sparse form anticipate May *Sinclair's *The Life and Death of Harriet Frean* (1922).

THOMAS, [Philip] Edward (1878–1917) married (1899) Helen NOBLE. Born in Lambeth, South London, of Welsh parents (his father was a clerk in the Board of Trade), he was educated at several schools, including, from 16, St Paul's School, and Lincoln College, Oxford. Marrying young, he supported himself with great difficulty by reviewing and writing, for very little money, a vast number of miscellaneous books for a variety of publishers, including biographies and topographical works. He suffered from depression for much of his adult life. Like many reviewers and journalists he was hit financially by the outbreak of the First World War. He enlisted in the Artists' Rifles in 1915, transferred to the Royal Garrison Artillery, and was killed at Arras. Before joining the army he had started, encouraged by Robert Frost (1874–1963), to focus his energies on writing poetry; it is for this, not for rural idylls like *Light and Twilight* (1911), let alone for his sole work of fiction, *The Happy-Go-Lucky Morgans* (1913), about the imaginative world of a large Welsh family living in suburban Balham, that he is now remembered.

THORNE, Guy, *pseud.*: see Ranger *Gull.

Three Sisters, The, May *Sinclair, 1914, Hutchinson. This grim and intermittently powerful story about the oppression of women was much influenced by Sinclair's study of the lives of Charlotte Brontë (1816–55) and her sisters Emily (1818–48) and Anne (1820–49). James Cartaret, the stern, repressed vicar of a remote Yorkshire parish, has three daughters who have resigned themselves to spinsterhood until the arrival of Steven Rowcliffe, a young doctor. All three fall in love with him. He is attracted to robust, independent Gwendolen. Sickly Alice becomes even more sickly, and gives up. Homely, stubborn Mary marries him. Alice, meanwhile, has married Jim Greatorex, a local farmer and congenital drunkard; under her benign if wispy influence he reforms. Cartaret has a stroke, and is nursed by Gwendolen; his sudden weakness subdues her more effectively than any display of strength, Rowcliffe continues to look for his 'shining moment' with Gwendolen, but, in the *Jamesian manner, keeps missing it, failing to recognize it. What destroys her, in the end, is the patriarchs' failure to know themselves.

Three Weeks, Elinor *Glyn, 1907, Gerald Duckworth. When his 'episode' begins, Paul Verdayne is an average upper-class English youth. He courts his dog rather more fervently than his girlfriend, a parson's daughter with large red hands. He is a reluctant traveller: Paris bores him, Versailles is 'beastly rot'. One day he is sitting in his Swiss hotel, reading the sports pages, when a woman walks by. He is besotted. Fortunately she has brought with her a tiger-skin rug, on which a famous initiation soon takes place. The woman turns out to be the Queen of a remote East European state. Eventually she is murdered by her jealous husband, but not before she has given birth to Paul's son, who will rule in her place. The politics which convert this awakening into an absolute value are quite explicit. 'You must not just drift, my Paul, like so many of your countrymen do,' coaxes the Queen. 'You must help to stem the tide of your nation's decadence, and be a strong man.' The tiger-skin rug awakens him politically as well as sexually. When he returns to England, he becomes a leader, a figure of authority: 'the three weeks of his lady's influence had changed the inner man beyond all recognition.' Since his son will rule in Eastern Europe, he can even be said to have extended the British Empire. The book's runaway success transformed Glyn from the mildly celebrated author of coy society novels into a national icon. It had a hostile reception, particularly from the *Daily Telegraph*, which referred to the seduction of Paul as 'the most unedifying study of the spider and the fly. Then follows a laborious description of their experiences, concerning which the less said, the better.' It is thought to have sold two million copies worldwide by 1916. Glyn turned the novel into a play, and into an enormously successful film, for Metro-Goldwyn-Mayer, in 1923. One scene, where she lies sprawled langorously on her tiger-skin rug, tested the continuity writer's powers to the limit. 'Better than describe this scene,' he wrote, 'I will simply mention that Mrs Glyn will enact it for Mr Crossland on the set.' The novel gave rise to a parody, *Too Weak* (1907) by 'Ellova Gryn' (i.e. Montague Eliot, 1870–1960, from 1942 8th Earl of St Germans).

THURSTON, E[rnest] Temple (1870–1933) married, first (1901), K. C. *THURSTON, secondly (1911) Joan Katherine CANN (divorced 1924), and, thirdly (1925), Emily Frances COWLIN. Born at Halesworth, Suffolk, he was brought up in Maidstone until, aged 10, he moved with his family to the south of Ireland. He was educated at Carlisle Grammar School and Queen's College, Cork, and then, at 15, joined his father's brewery business. In his spare time he wrote verse, which was published in the *Cork Examiner*, and eventually he went to London to try to become a writer, though in fact he earned his living as an analyst in a Bermondsey yeast factory and as a journalist. He was eventually the author of more than thirty popular novels, some verse and several plays. His most successful books include *The Apple of Eden* (1905), written when he was 17, which argues against the celibacy of the Roman Catholic priesthood, *The Evolution of Katherine* (1907), and *The City of Beautiful Nonsense* (1909). *Traffic* (1906) is the story of an Irish Catholic woman, separated from her husband, who becomes a prostitute because she is unable to get a divorce.

THURSTON, K. C.: Katherine Cecil MADDEN (1875–1911) married (1901) Ernest Temple *THURSTON. Born at Wood's Gift, Cork, the only child of a banker who was Nationalist mayor of Cork, she was educated at home. Her career as a writer began after marriage. She was author of six novels 1903–10. **John Chilcote, M.P.* was much her most popular work (Brown states that it was estimated to have sold 200,000 copies in America alone). *The Gambler* (1905), a study of an upper-middle-class Protestant Irishwoman, set in Ireland, Venice, and London. The heroine of *The Fly on the Wheel* (1908) commits suicide because of an affair with a married man. Thurston died while in the process of divorcing her husband, apparently of a seizure in a hotel in Cork, though Brown implies that she committed suicide.

TIBBITS, Mrs Annie O.: Annie Olive BRAZIER married Charles John TIBBITS (1861–1935). She was the author of fourteen sixpenny novels of which the first is *Marquess Splendid* (1910), whose hero is a rake who saves a girl of 12 from the streets and subsequently marries her and reforms, and the last is dated 1927. Her husband was a journalist, assistant to Lord Northcliffe (1865–1922), and editor of the *Weekly Dispatch* (1895–1903); his *Marriage Making and Breaking* (1911) is a non-fictional contribution to the contemporary debate on divorce law reform: see also *Marriage problem novels.

TIDDEMAN, L[izzie] E[llen] (d. 1937) Born in London, she published more than seventy volumes of fiction, mostly children's books, such as *Next-Door Gwennie* (1910) and *All About Me: The Story of a Seven-Year-Old* (1910) between 1887 and 1931.

TIME, *Mark, pseud.*: Henry Crossly IRWIN (1848–1924). The author of the imperialist scare story *A *Derelict Empire* (1912) was a retired Indian Civil Servant. His father is described as 'Henry Irwin of Banda, East Indies'. The younger Irwin was educated at Blackheath Proprietary School, matriculated at St Edmund Hall, Oxford in 1866, and was a scholar of Queen's College 1867–71. In the latter year he joined the Bengal Civil Service, and rose to become Deputy Commissioner of Oudh, retiring in 1896. He published, as 'H. C. Irwin', *A Man of Honour* (1896), a tale of a young officer in the Indian army in the 1850s, who loves a brother officer's wife but is too high-minded to marry her even after she is widowed; and of With *Sword and Pen: A Story of India in the Fifties* (1904), in which a young officer behaves very well in the Mutiny despite the best efforts of a sinister old Begum. He also wrote *The Garden of India, or, Chapters on Oudh History and Affairs* (1880).

Times Literary Supplement, The, (1902–) was first published on 17 January, as a free supplement to the *Times*. It was not originally conceived as a permanent feature, but as a one of a number of occasional supplements, in this instance intended to carry the reviews of books crowded out of the newspaper by the reports of parliamentary debates. However, it continued to appear after Parliament adjourned on 27 March. It cost a penny extra by 1904, and in 1914 became a separate journal. The editor was first, briefly, J. R. Thursfield (1840–1923), and then, from the autumn of 1902 until 1937, Bruce Richmond (1871–1964). During the Book War of 1906–7 (see *publishers) reviews of some books carried notices that they were not supplied to the Times Book Club on trade terms. As well as reviewing books—including a wide range of fiction—the journal carried articles on drama and art, and the early issues contain a fierce correspondence about inaccuracy in the *Dictionary of National Biography*. It employed many novelists to write both anonymous reviews and signed pieces; these included in its early days A. C. *Benson, John *Buchan, George *Calderon, M. E. *Coleridge, Walter *de la Mare, George *Gissing, E. V. *Lucas, *'Q', and E. Œ. *Somerville. Noteworthy are two guarded articles on modern novelists which appeared in March and April 1914 entitled 'The Younger Generation', in which Henry *James responded to the work of Gilbert *Cannan, Somerset *Maugham, and D. H. *Lawrence, among others.

TIPPETT, Mrs Henry: Isabel Clementine Binny KEMP (1880–1969) married Henry William TIPPETT (1859–1944). Daughter of a Civil Servant in the Exchequer and Audit department, she trained as a nurse. A cousin of Charlotte Despard (1844–1939) she became, like her, a vegetarian, a feminist, a pacifist, a political radical, and author of progressive novels, and was a member of Despard's Women's Freedom League, and of the Labour party. She was imprisoned for suffrage agitation in 1911. Her husband was a prosperous retired lawyer; they lived in Suffolk, then, during the 1920s, in France, then in Gloucestershire. She was the author of eight novels of a moderately emancipated kind (New Woman heroines, *marriage problem plots), published at her husband's expense between 1909 and 1922. In *The Power of the Petticoat* (1911), set in Rome, a prince commits suicide for a woman's love, and asks a priest to convert her, with the consequence that he falls in love with her and she with him; the heroine of *Green Girl* (1913), an ex-art student, finds married life restrictive. In the 1950s Tippett went to live with her son, the composer Sir Michael Tippett (b. 1905), who observes in his autobiography (1991), that her 'quirks (such as mixing laxatives into everyone's food, even when there were guests) and her readiness to flare up into moral argument often made life . . . quite taxing.'

TODD, Margaret [Georgina] (1859–1918). Born in Scotland, and educated at Edinburgh and Glasgow University classes for women, in Berlin, and at the Edinburgh School of Medicine for Women, she qualified as a doctor in Brussels in 1894 and practised at the Edinburgh Hospital for Women and Children. Later she lived in London. In the 1890s she published two novels as 'Graham Travers' and a volume of stories under her own name. Her two twentieth-century novels also appeared under her own name. *The Way of Escape* (1902) is a gloomy tale of a heroine whose only escape from her shame is death; *Growth* (1906) is set among students in contemporary Edinburgh.

Tommy and Grizel, J. M. *Barrie, 1900, Cassell. This is a sequel to *Sentimental Tommy* (1896), which had described Tommy Sandys's boyhood years in working-class London and his relocation to Scotland. Now 16, Tommy has come south again (bringing with him his 12-year-old sister, Elspeth) to act as amanuensis for a successful but indolent hack writer, O. P. Pym. Tommy is a mixture of shrewdness and sentiment. Before long he is virtually writing Pym's stories for him, grafting immense didactic passages onto otherwise formulaic romances. Removed from the stories, the didactic passages become the bestselling *Letters to a Young Man About to be Married*. A minor celebrity at the age of 22, Tommy returns to 'Thrums' (i.e. Kirriemuir), his mother's native village, and to his elusive, sarcastic childhood sweetheart, Grizel, a prostitute's daughter who has been brought up by a benevolent doctor. Tommy believes that he is in love with Grizel, proposes to her, and then discovers that he is not. He returns to London, where his second book, *Unrequited Love*, shortly appears: 'something new in literature, a story that was yet not a story, told in the form of essays which were no mere essays'. Grizel pursues him to London, and then to the Continent, where he has gone in pursuit of the seductive Lady Pippinworth. She suffers a breakdown. Full of remorse, Tommy marries her, and nurses her back to health. But he still does not love her, and is soon ludicrously killed while climbing a wall in pursuit once again of Lady Pippinworth. The secret of Tommy's success in literature and failure in life is that he knows nothing at all about women. An insistent emphasis on the gap between appearance and reality makes this, for all its wry humour, a bitter book.

Tono-Bungay, H. G. *Wells, 1908, Macmillan. The autobiography of George Ponderevo, whose early life is modelled on that of Wells. The narrative is interspersed with digressions, reflections, monologues, and essays. George Ponderevo is apprenticed to his Uncle Teddy, a chemist in a small neighbouring town. When his uncle, who has successfully launched a patent medicine on the market, offers him a share in the business, George accepts, although he is aware that his uncle is a charlatan and that the drug is a quack remedy: 'a nothing coated in advertisements'. For seven years George is caught up in the rise and fall of 'Tono-Bungay' and in his uncle's fraudulent business empire. Meanwhile, he is divorced by his wife, has an affair with a magnificent 'eupeptic' typewriting girl, and with a Lady Beatrice. The novel ends with George bitter and solitary, patiently building and testing a destroyer. *Tono-Bungay* is a brilliant depiction of the modern city and modern man, of modern life and character. In the rise and fall of 'Tono-Bungay', Wells has depicted almost every aspect of modern society, and in particular the most negative aspects of the business world (commerce and advertising). Despite George's amorous adventures, as so often in Wells, the love scenes involve little more than crude physical attraction, and the best passages in the novel are those written in contemplation of the city.

TORRE, Stephen was the author of *The Blot* (1909), a *roman à thèse*; the blot is that which smirches the law of England because of the legal necessity of proving adultery to gain divorce. Watson Romandy, a brilliant young barrister, has parted from his wife, whom he married too young, and loves a pure young American girl. He defends a novelist from the charge of murdering his mistress, full of fellow-feeling for another man cut off from domestic life. Approached by a friend of his wife who wants to find out whether Romandy is likely to commit adultery, he sends some married friends to stay in a Brighton hotel in his name and thus gains a divorce without committing the least impropriety, and is enabled to marry the woman he loves to universal approbation. The book is written rather stiltedly, evidently by an amateur. Although it is the laws of England which are attacked many scenes and characters are American. No other work by this writer seems to have been published in either England or America, and the name may be a pseudonym.

TOWNSHEND, Dorothea: Letitia Jane Dorothea BAKER (c.1853–1930) married (1881) Richard Baxter TOWNSEND (1846–1923), who changed his name to TOWNSHEND. The daughter of a Church of England clergyman and landowner in Gloucestershire, she wrote biographies and children's books including *The Children of Nugentstown and their Dealings with the Sidhe* (1911), in which the Nugent family fortunes are saved through the intervention of the fairies, and *The Faery of Lisbawn* (1900), in which the children of an English settler in Elizabethan Ireland make friends with the dispossessed landowner, who saves their lives. Her husband was educated at Repton School, Trinity College, Cambridge, and Wadham College, Oxford. He was at various times a tutor at the last institution and a miner and rancher in the west of the United States. He also published a translation of Tacitus, several books for boys, and the novels *Lone Pine* (1899) and *A Girl from Mexico* (1914), a Western about an Englishman, learned in the classics, ranching among desperadoes and falling hopelessly in love with a beautiful Spaniard. Husband and wife collaborated on *The Bride of A Day* (1905), whose heroine is a Navajo Indian brought up as a slave in Mexico, who marries an Englishman. He and Dorothea's brother, William Meath Baker (1857–1935), are the subjects of two of the Enigma Variations by Sir Edward Elgar (1857–1934).

TOWNSHEND, R. B.: see under Dorothea *Townshend.

TRACY, Louis (1863–1928) married ——. Born in Liverpool, he was educated privately in Yorkshire and in France. In 1884 he joined the *Northern Echo* in Darlington; he later worked on newspapers in Cardiff (1886), Allahabad (1889), and (1894) on the *Evening News* and the *Sun* in London, in which he had a financial interest. After publishing *What I Saw In India: The Adventures of a Globetrotter* (1892) he went on to write more than sixty popular novels from 1896, mostly thrillers, with some *historical novels set in India. *The Terms of Surrender* (1914) is a Western; the hero's girl is pinched by a sinister millionaire; which is the father of her namesake daughter? *Karl Grier: The Strange Story of a Man With a Sixth Sense* (1906) is a *science fiction fantasy whose hero can see and hear what is happening and can control other people's minds, especially in sunlight. Other self-explanatory titles are *The Invaders: A Story of Britain's Peril* (1901) and *The Red Year: A Story of the Indian Mutiny* (1908). During the First World War Tracy worked in propaganda for the Ministry of Information in the USA. Back in England after the war he was on the editorial staff of the *Times* and the *Daily Mail*. For his collaborative work as 'Gordon Holmes' see under M. P. *Shiel.

Traffics and Discoveries, Rudyard *Kipling, 1904, Macmillan. Short stories, mostly South African or technological in emphasis, and accompanying poems. 'The Captive', 'A Sahib's War', and 'The Comprehensions of Private Copper' reproduce the flavour of Kipling's early stories about the lower ranks in the context of the *Boer War. The same knowing narrator who recorded the yarns of Mulvaney and his cronies in India reappears to authenticate the tale told by a Portuguese stowaway in 'The Bonds of Discipline'. 'Wireless' concerns the testing of a Marconi set. While the assembled audience waits for transmission to begin, the consumptive Mr Shaynor, who has just taken some medicine, recites the poems of John Keats (1795–1821), which he has never read.

TRAFFORD-TAUNTON, Mrs Winefride contributed to the *Lady's Realm* and published seven novels 1901–12 including *Marked With a Cipher* (1901) about a petted heir who discovers he is illegitimate and penniless, *The Doom of the House of Marsaniac* (1905), and *Silent Dominion* (1903).

Trent's Last Case, E. C. *Bentley, 1913, Thomas Nelson. According to Bentley, *Trent's Last Case* was intended to be 'not so much a detective story as an exposure of detective stories'. It arose, like a number of Edwardian *crime stories, out of dissatisfaction at the eccentricity and superhuman powers of the great detective created by Arthur Conan *Doyle. 'It should be possible, I thought, to write a detective story in which the detective was recognizable as a human being, and was not quite so much the "heavy" sleuth.' An economical opening chapter sketches the history of Sigsbee Manderson, an American millionaire. 'Forcible, cold, and unerring, in all he did he ministered to the national lust for magnitude'. Governments and stock exchanges are trembling at rumours that 'the life had departed from one cold heart vowed to the service of greed'. Manderson has indeed been found dead in the grounds of his country house, White Gables. Sir James Molloy, editor of the *Record*, commissions Philip Trent, an artist with a gift for investigation, to work alongside Inspector Murch of Scotland Yard in the search for the killer. Awaiting him at the scene of the crime are his old friend Nathaniel Burton Cupples, a retired banker and member of the London Positivist Society, and Cupples's niece, Mabel, Manderson's widow. Working his way through the usual suspects (butler, secretaries, French maid), Trent arrives at the grim conclusion that Mabel, with whom he has fallen in love, is implicated in the murder. Unable to confide in Murch, Cupples, or Molloy, he retires to the Continent and a commission as roving reporter. Returning after a while to London, he encounters Mabel, who clearly returns his feelings, and admits his suspicions to her. Reviewing the evidence yet again, he is forced to admit that the man he thought guilty, Marlowe, one of Manderson's secretaries, is in fact innocent. He has failed completely. The Manderson case must have been 'revenge on the part of some American black-hand gang'. A final twist reveals that the culprit was the benevolent Cupples, who killed Manderson in self-defence. Dumbfounded, Trent resolves that this will be his last case. Bentley's achievement was to give his detective a life outside detection.

Trespasser, The, D. H. *Lawrence, 1912, Gerald Duckworth. Lawrence's second novel, a story of adulterous love in the fashionable *'marriage problem' genre, was based on the experiences of his friend Helen Corke. Siegmund, a violinist and a married man, falls in love with his student, Helena. They go away together for a rhapsodic holiday on the Isle of Wight. But the idyll does not last. Siegmund runs into an enigmatic 'Stranger' who speaks bitterly of women's destructiveness. Helena is consumed with guilt. Siegmund returns to London, to his wife, Beatrice, and their children. But he cannot conceal his indifference, and the marriage deteriorates rapidly. This section, in its depiction of his family's silent criticism of him, his love of his youngest children, and the way their mother turns them against him, is the most impressive in the book. Siegmund contracts a fever, falls into depression, and hangs himself. There is a curious comic description of Beatrice's subsequent life as a lodging-house keeper. The novel ends a year after the holiday on the Isle of Wight. Another man has fallen in love with Helena. But she only wants 'rest and warmth'. Lawrence received significant help with the book, and the awkward 'Stranger' chapter in particular, from Edward Garnett (1868–1937), Duckworth's reader. He corrected the proofs in April 1912. By the time it was published, in May, he had resolved to elope with Frieda Weekley. Early in 1913, he told Ford Madox *Hueffer that he now thought the book 'a bit messy'. 'But whether it injures my reputation or not, it has brought me enough money to carry me—so modestly, as you may guess—through a winter here on the Lake Garda. One must publish to live.'

TRESSALL, Robert, *pseud.*: Robert NOONAN (1870–1911) married (1891) Elizabeth HARTEL (b. *c.*1873). Born in Dublin, he seems to have been an illegitimate son of a Resident Magistrate, formerly an Inspector in the Royal Irish Constabulary, named Samuel Croker, who was Protestant, middle-class, married, educated, and fairly prosperous. His mother was a Catholic named Mary Noonan. Little is known about his upbringing, but it seems that he was the youngest of several children and that the death of the father brought his education to an end, leaving him less well-educated than his siblings. He was apprenticed to a builder and decorator at about 16, and next appears in Johannesburg, where he married and his daughter Kathleen was born in 1892. The marriage soon ended—whether because his wife died or because she left him is not clear. In South Africa he seems to have achieved his greatest prosperity as a skilled craftsman. He moved in radical circles and was pro-Boer; on the eve of the outbreak of the *Boer War he left for Cape Town and in September 1901 he returned to England with his daughter, his sister, and her son. They went to live in Hastings, where another sister was living, and he began to work for a series of builder's firms as a painter, signwriter, and decorator. There in 1906 he was a founder member of the Hastings branch of the Social Democratic Federation. About 1907 he began to write a long novel based on his experiences in Hastings, and in 1910 tried to get it published. The handwritten manuscript, however, was refused. His chest trouble was getting increasingly bad; he was often out of work. He therefore decided to emigrate to Canada, and went to Liverpool, where he was admitted, in November, to the Royal Liverpool Infirmary, a former workhouse, and died in February. The manuscript remained with his only daughter, Kathleen, who worked as a nanny for a family in North Finchley. While there she mentioned it to Jessie Pope (d. 1941) a contributor to *Punch*, who was their next-door neighbour After having it turned down by Constable, Pope offered it to Grant *Richards, who eventually agreed to buy the copyright from Kathleen for £25; Jessie Pope was paid a similar sum for cutting it down by half and altering the ending. *The *Ragged-Trousered Philanthropists* appeared in April 1914, priced at 6*s*.; an American edition appeared later the same year. The first edition sold 1,752 in England, 1,650 in the colonies. During the war, an even shorter cheap edition came out and circulated much more widely. An edition from the original manuscript was published in 1955. The pseudonym was taken from the trestle used by paperhangers, and was spelt by Noonan himself 'Tressell'. But until 1955 all editions of his work, and consequently all critical references, appeared under the name 'Tressall'. There is a biography by Frederick C. Ball (1973).

TREVENA, John, *pseud.*: Ernest George HENHAM (b. 1870) lived at Verwood, Dorset, and was the author of nineteen novels, mostly with West Country settings, some of which are historical and make play with archaic language, others in dialect. They belong to that school of regionalist fiction satirized by Stella Gibbons (1902–89) in *Cold Comfort Farm* (1932). Of *Furze the Cruel* (1907), the *Bystander*'s reviewer wrote 'It smacks of the open air, of flesh and of real red blood' and the **Bookman* hoped that it 'might exercise a decidedly bracing effect on English fiction'. Set on Dartmoor, it forms a 'moorland trilogy' with *Heather* (1908) and *Granite* (1909). Other works include *Bracken* (1910), *Wintering Hay* (1912), and *Raindrops* (1920).

Triumphs of Eugene Valmont, The, Robert *Barr, 1906, Hurst & Blackett. First-person narrative told by a comic French detective who must be reckoned a distant precursor of Hercule Poirot (in the novels by Agatha Christie, 1890–1972). He is dismissed from the service of the French government when he mistakes a perfectly legal if somewhat unorthodox purchase at auction for theft, and ends up arresting a celebrated English detective by mistake. Thereafter, he establishes himself in London. Disguised as Professor Paul Ducharne, a teacher of the French language and man of advanced opinions, he infiltrates a terrorist society, travels to Paris, and substitutes an elaborate firework for the bomb which is to be hurled at Edward VII. Other cases involve theft and forgery, and the release of Lord Reginald Rantremly, who has been imprisoned in a secret chamber by his father after contracting an unsuitable marriage. Valmont's exploits keep their distance from, while emulating, those of Arthur Conan *Doyle's Sherlock Holmes. At one point, he opposes Thomas Edison's (1847–1931) faith in patience and hard work to the prevalent idea that the detective 'arrives at his solutions in a dramatic way'—Sherlock Holmes-fashion—through following clues invisible to the ordinary man:' and promptly solves the mystery he is currently engaged on by following a clue invisible to ordinary men. He, too, like Holmes, has a plodding Scotland Yard counterpart, Spenser Hale. One story, about a jewel-thief who marries an heiress, reflects the contemporary vogue, inspired by E. W. *Hornung's Raffles stories, for charismatic gentleman-bounders.

TROUBRIDGE, Lady: Laura GURNEY (*c.*1865–1946) married (1893) Thomas Herbert Cochrane TROUBRIDGE (1860–1938), who succeeded (1867) as 4th Baronet. Her mother was a niece of the photographer Julia Margaret Cameron (1815–1879); her father came from a family of Norfolk bankers and landowners, and lost his fortune when she was a child, so that she was brought up partly by relations, including the feminist journalist and temperance campaigner Lady Henry Somerset (1851–1921). Her husband, a stockbroker, was her first cousin. She published more than thirty volumes of fiction from 1897, two books on etiquette, and *Memories and Reflections* (1925). Her fiction includes *The House of Cards* (1908), a *marriage problem novel, *The Woman Who Forgot: A Modern Love Story* (1910), in which amnesia leads to bigamy, *Body and Soul* (1911), about the reformation of a rake by a pure young girl, *The Unguarded Hour* (1913), about the seduction of a flirt, who is allowed to be happy in the end, and *This Man and This Woman* (1914), about the difficulties of early married life. Troubridge is not to be confused with her husband's sister-in-law, Lady Troubridge (d. 1963), the translator, and lover of Radclyffe Hall (1880–1943).

TROWBRIDGE, W[illiam] R[utherford] H[ayes]. This writer's *A Girl of the Multitude* (1902), an *historical romance set during the French Revolution, was published pseudonymously as 'by the author of *The Letters of Her Mother to Elizabeth*'. He was also the author of a social satire, *A Dazzling Reprobate* (1906), and other fiction and non-fiction, including historical biographies.

TRUSCOTT, L. Parry, *pseud.*: Katherine Edith SPICER-JAY (?1869–1915) married Basil HARGRAVE. Little is known about this writer, who lived at Ditchling, Sussex, contributed to *Punch*, the *Glasgow Herald*, and the *Evening Standard*, and published her first novel, *As A Tree Falls* (1903) in T. Fisher Unwin's 'Pseudonym Library'. She also wrote *The Poet and Penelope* (1902), a novel of frivolous high society, whose heroine refuses the poet at first because she does not understand his verse, and nine later novels to 1915. It seems likely that Hargrave had some connection with Edith Katherine Spicer-Jay (d. 1901), who published seventeen novels about military life as 'E. Livingston *Prescott'.

TURLEY, Charles, *pseud.*: Charles Turley SMITH (1868–1940) was the son of the squire of Sedgeberrow, Gloucestershire and was educated at Cheltenham College and Exeter College, Oxford. After university he settled in Broadway, Gloucestershire, and earned his living tutoring and writing books for boys. Later he had a line in biographies of explorers. He subsequently moved to London and then, having weak health, to Mullion in Cornwall, where he played much golf. He reviewed books for *Punch* and also worked as a publisher's reader. His most successful book, *Godfrey Marten, Schoolboy* (1902), was based on his own schooldays. In *Dear Turley* (1942, ed. Eleanor Adlard), a collection of tributes by his friends, A. A. Milne (1882–1956) wrote that 'he remained all his life the very nicest sort of public school boy, and at the same time the simplest and most delightful English gentleman'. He was a friend of J. M. *Barrie, and like A. E. W. *Mason, Maurice *Hewlett, and E. V. *Lucas, played cricket for his team, the Allahakbarries.

TURNER, Reginald (1869 or 1870–1938) is best known as one of the most faithful friends of Oscar Wilde (1854–1900). He inherited, aged 10, an income of £100 p. a. from Lionel Lawson (d. 1879), whose nephew, the 1st Lord Burnham (1833–1916), became his guardian. One or other of these men, co-proprietors of the *Daily Telegraph*, was probably his father; he did not know his mother. He was sent to school in Hove and then to Hurstpierpoint College and Merton College, Oxford, where he met Max *Beerbohm, who became his greatest friend. He read for the Bar and met Oscar Wilde (1856–1900). It was while staying in the same Egyptian hotel as Turner and Lord Alfred Douglas (1870–1945) that Robert *Hichens got enough material about Wilde to furnish *The Green Carnation* (1894). He joined the exodus of homosexuals to the Continent after Wilde's arrest in April 1895; in France he wrote his first story, 'A Chef-d'Œuvre' which was published in the *Yellow Book* in October 1896, about a writer who dies when his masterpiece is rejected. By the late 1890s Turner was back in London, on the permanent staff of the *Telegraph*, writing a gossip column called 'London Day by Day', until 1900. He was present when Wilde died in Paris in 1900. He travelled extensively, eventually settling in Italy during the First World War, and becoming a prominent member of the Florentine expatriate circle, portrayed as Algy Constable in D. H. *Lawrence's *Aaron's Rod* (1922). Turner's first novel, *Cynthia's Damages* (1901), had a heroine based on Cissie Loftus, wife of Justin *MacCarthy Junior. Later novels, such as *Comedy of Progress* (1902), have Wildean epigrams and high-society settings. *Peace on Earth* (1905) was published by Alston Rivers, then owned by Archibald *Marshall: it concerns the experience of the illegitimate posthumous son of a dancer, and was dedicated 'To My Mother'. *Comedy of Progress* (1905) is a Fleet Street satire; the central character is probably based on Lord Northcliffe (1865–1922). *Count Florio and Phyllis K* (1910) takes the international theme as its subject. *King Philip the Gay* (1911) is a parody of a *Ruritanian romance. There is an interesting biography of Turner by Stanley Weintraub (1965).

TWEEDALE, Violet: Violet CHAMBERS (1862–1936) married (1891) Clarens TWEEDALE. Born and brought up in Edinburgh, the daughter of a publisher, she was, like Ménie Muriel *Dowie and Barry *Pain's wife, a granddaughter of Robert Chambers (1802–1871), the author of *Vestiges of the Natural History of Creation* (1844). The eldest daughter of a large family, she was educated haphazardly, and was proofreading *Chambers's Journal* at the age of 16. On her father's death in 1888 she came to London, where she worked as a journalist by day and ran a night shelter in the East End. She was a suffragist and socialist; these themes appear in her thirty-three volumes of fiction 1895–1938, which include *The Honeycomb of Life* (1902), *Hypocrites and Sinners* (1910), and *A Reaper of the Whirlwind* (1911), about hereditary insanity. She became increasingly interested in spiritualism, which she wrote about in *Ghosts I Have Seen and Other Psychic Experiences* (1919); she also wrote ghost stories.

'Twixt Land and Sea, Joseph *Conrad, 1912, J. M. Dent. Three Indian Ocean stories which draw on memories of Conrad's time in the merchant navy. 'A Smile of Fortune' is a story of entrapment. Jacobus, storekeeper on a small tropical island, has a wealthy brother to whom he has not spoken for eighteen years. The brothers were partners, but Jacobus left his wife for a circus woman, whom he has since established in his house, and by whom he has a daughter. Jacobus invites a ship's captain with whom he wishes to do business to the house. His daughter, Alice, is so rude to the Captain that he falls madly in love with her, and is seduced by her. Jacobus uses the Captain's infatuation to secure his business, offloading onto him a potato mountain, which he himself manages to sell on at an inflated price: the 'smile of fortune'. Even so, seafaring has lost its charm. 'The Secret Sharer' was first published in *Harper's Magazine* in 1911. A ship's captain in the Gulf of Siam fishes a naked man out of the sea. This is Leggatt, who has killed a man in a fit of anger, and meant to drown himself. Recognising Leggatt as his double, the Captain hides him in his cabin, and, when the crew become suspicious, smuggles him ashore. 'Freya of the Seven Isles' concerns a Dane called Nielsen, who has bought himself a retirement island in the Malayan archipelago, and his beautiful daughter. Jasper Allen, owner of the brig *Bonito*, and Heemskirk, a Dutch naval officer, are both in love with Freya. Jasper and Freya agree to elope as soon as she comes of age. But Heemskirk has been spying on them, and uses his authority to detain the *Bonito*. Encountering Nielsen some time after these events, the narrator learns that Freya has fallen sick. The old man tries to convince him that she never loved Jasper.

TYNAN, Katharine (1861–1931) married (1893) H. A. *HINKSON. Born in Dublin, daughter of a Catholic and Nationalist cattle trader, she was educated at a Dominican convent in Drogheda. Her eyesight was affected by childhood measles. She published verse from 1878 and novels from 1895. After her marriage to a Protestant, whom she converted to her own faith, she lived in England until he was appointed Resident Magistrate in Mayo in 1911. Her fiction is fairly light, cheerful, and romantic, and she produced it in great quantity to support her family, while continuing to write poetry, which was widely admired in the Irish Literary Revival circles of which she was a prominent member. Her application to the Royal Literary Fund indicates that her writing largely supported the family. Brown comments that 'she has made a specialty of broken-down gentlefolk, and often introduces Quakers into her stories'. Some of her fiction appeared under the imprint of the Catholic Truth Society. The heroine of *A Girl of Galway* (1900) lives with her miserly old grandfather in Connemara, and sees nobody except his wicked agent; the *Three Fair Maids* (1900) are distressed gentlewomen who open a boarding-house and thus secure husbands; *A King's Woman* (1902) is set in 1798, and recounted by a Quaker woman, loyal to the King; *Her Ladyship* (1907) is the story of a great heiress: it follows the female philanthropist model not uncommon in late Victorian fiction (compare, for instance, *Besant's *All Sorts and Conditions of Men*, 1882). Her sister Nora Tynan O'Mahony also published verse, journalism, and fiction including *Una's Enterprise* (1907).

Typhoon *and Other Stories*, Joseph *Conrad, 1903, William Heinemann. Dedicated to R. B. Cunninghame *Graham, the volume contains two novellas, 'Typhoon' and 'Falk', and two short stories, 'Amy Foster' and 'To-morrow'. 'Typhoon', the centrepiece, first appeared in the *Pall Mall Magazine* for January–March 1902. Jukes, chief mate of the steamer *Nan-Shana*, tries to suggest to his captain, MacWhirr, a man who has 'just enough imagination to carry him through each successive day, and no more', that they should alter course in order to avoid an impending typhoon. The typhoon proves unexpectedly fierce, but MacWhirr, by refusing to take it seriously, steers his ship through it and safely into port. While it rages, the Chinese coolies below deck riot. To control them, MacWhirr orders the confiscation of their money. Eventually, he redistributes the money in equal shares, on the grounds that 'you couldn't tell one man's dollars from another's'. Conrad described 'Typhoon' as a 'pendant' to an earlier sea-story, *The Nigger of the 'Narcissus'* (1898), but its interest in the complexity of a simple mind connects it to his later studies in psychological abnormality. 'Falk' is more of a pendant to *Heart of Darkness* (see **Youth and Other Stories*), in that it has a Marlow-like narrator and contrasts narrow bourgeois routine with the depth and intensity of primal experience. The atavistic Falk desires the massive, silent, niece of the captain of the *Diana*, and seizes the ship in order to obtain her. His dark (Kurtz-like) secret is that he once ate man's flesh in order to survive. 'Amy Foster' concerns the miserable life of Yanko Goorall, a Pole from the eastern Carpathians in Austria who is the sole survivor from a shipwreck off the Kent coast. The only person to make him welcome is a simple peasant girl, but even she becomes repelled by his strange ways, and his desire to instruct their child in his native tongue. The main cause of his isolation is language: he 'could talk to no one, and had no hope of ever understanding anybody.' 'To-morrow' is a pot-boiler which Conrad later turned into a play, *One Day More*, possibly in collaboration with Ford Madox *Hueffer. The stories were well received, usually as romances in the manner of *Kipling or R. L. Stevenson (1850–1894). One reviewer, however, observed that for Conrad character was 'an essentially individual creation, separate from, comparatively untouched by ordinary human relationship'.

TYTLER, Sarah, *pseud.*: Henrietta KEDDIE (1827–1914). Born at Cupar, Fife, she earned her living as a writer and teacher from the age of 22. Much of her later life was spent keeping a boarding-house in Oxford. She was the author of more than seventy volumes of fiction, some of it historical, mostly aimed at young girls, from 1865, and of improving non-fiction including a biography of Queen Victoria. Her works in this period include *Logan's Loyalty* (1900), whose heroine is the child of a baronet and a peasant girl, which causes problems resolved in romance, *Jean Kerr of Craigneil* (1900) and *The Machinations of Janet* (1903), which are both about girls who become heiresses, and *The Girls of Inverbarns* (1906), about old maids. Keddie applied to the Royal Literary Fund five times between 1894 and 1913; its archives preserve a letter of 1902 to her agent A. P. Watt (d. 1914) which indicates some of the pressures on old-fashioned writers of this period: 'I am still I am thankful to say willing and happy to work five hours a day and if prices had continued what they were twenty or thirty years ago, I could have managed without assistance; but not only do the young writers push out the old, which is but right and proper, in addition the market you know is so flooded with American, Canadian and Australian— even South African books that there is less chance for the old writers'. *Three Generations* (1911) is non-fiction about her own family.

U

Unbearable Bassington, The, '*Saki', 1912, John Lane. Young, merry, attractive, and utterly selfish Comus Bassington has, in his mother Francesca's words, 'all the charm and advantages that a boy could want to help him on on the world', but, 'behind it all there is the fatal damning gift of utter hopelessness'. Against the brittle, epigrammatic background of London's social and political night-life, the tragedy of Francesca and Comus is played out. He fails to win the hand of heiress, Elaine de Frey (who, despairing of Comus's inability even to pay lip-service to the niceties of courtship, weds instead the equally selfish but emotionally more astute MP Courtenay Youghal), and has to make his way in colonial service in West Africa, where he dies. She struggles to keep up appearances—all she has. The tone of the novel, at once flippant and serious, is as uneasy as the central characters.

Uncle Hilary, *O. Shakespear, 1910, Methuen. The emphasis of the novel is not so much on wise and tolerant Uncle Hilary as on his ward, and eventually wife, Rosamund Colston. Rosamund has been brought up to believe that love is 'the one essential thing in the world'—for a woman, that is. Her desire for desire is fulfilled when she meets a dashing soldier, Colonel Henry. They marry and settle in India. However, Colonel Henry soon becomes absorbed in his work, leaving his wife to reflect that men and women have very different views of marriage: 'a man seeks love as a rest from his activity, a quiet harbour; to a woman love is the activity, into which she comes from a state of quiescence, of expectation.' It turns out that the marriage is invalid, because the dashing colonel was once married to Rosamund's mother. Now pregnant, she returns to London, where Uncle Hilary offers to marry her to protect her reputation and give her child a name. He explains that their marriage will be no more than a 'form', and that Colonel Henry remains her real husband. The baby dies, but Hilary and Rosamund, intellectually and spiritually compatible, and without romantic expectations, find increasing pleasure in each other's company. Although Rosamund now thinks of marriage as an 'arrangement', she is not yet altogether purged of romantic feeling. She goes off to live with Colonel Henry in a remote seaside cottage, 'free from conventions', with Hilary's blessing. 'Love is the worst slavery that exists,' Hilary tells her: 'not only sexual love, but any love: it is the most persistent of the illusions.' Sure enough, Colonel Henry, finding himself without occupation, is soon bored and restless. Rosamund realizes that passion is insufficient for women as well as men. She arranges for Colonel Henry to return to India without her, and resumes her contented relationship with Uncle Hilary. Like many Edwardian '*marriage problem' novels, *Uncle Hilary* deals with such matters as bigamy, divorce, and the marriage laws. But its main theme is the danger of romance itself.

Under Western Eyes, Joseph *Conrad, 1911, Methuen. The story of Razumov is told by an elderly English teacher of languages, drawing on Razumov's diaries and his own memories. Razumov's routine student life in St Petersburg is disrupterd by the arrival in his flat of Victor Haldin, a fellow-student and revolutionary idealist who has just assassinated a minister of state. Although Razumov agrees to hide him, he is still loyal to the Tzar and instead turns Haldin in, only to find that from the police perspective he himself is now a suspect figure. He is sent by them to Geneva, as a secret agent, where he discovers that he is something of a hero to the exiles, and particularly to Haldin's young sister, Natalia, thanks to Haldin's enthusiastic letters about him. Guilty about Haldin, and repelled by the cynicism of the revolutionary groups, he confesses the truth to Natalia (whom by now he loves) and to the revolutionaries. They burst his eardrums, and unable to hear he is hit by a tram and dies.

UNDERHILL, Evelyn (1875–1941) married (1907) Hubert Stuart MOORE. Born in Wolverhampton, only child of a barrister, she was educated at a school in Folkestone and at King's College for Women, London, to which she returned as an honorary Fellow in 1913, and as a Fellow in 1927. Attracted to Roman Catholicism, she became a devout Anglican and, later, in the 1930s, interested in the Greek Orthodox Church. She was a disciple of the Catholic theologian Baron Friedrich von Hügel (1852–1925). In 1921 she became Upton Lecturer in the Philosophy of Religion at Manchester College, Oxford. Her most successful book, *Mysticism: A Study of the Nature and Development of Man's Spiritual Consciousness*, appeared in 1911 (followed twenty years later by *Consciousness*, 1930), but she also wrote poetry (*Immanence: A Book of Verses*, 1912; *Theophanies: A Book of Verses*, 1916), and novels which combine mysticism with an interest in the question of social reform. *Grey World: A Novel* (1904) concerns a slum child who dies in an infirmary and is reborn into an intensely middle-class family, with memories of the grey world he passed through after death. In *The Lost Word* (1907) Paul Vickery, an imaginative youth brought up in the shadow of an ancient English cathedral, encounters a more intense and focused religiosity at Oxford. An Oxford friend who is the heir to Feltham's Embrocation commissions him to design a church for working people which will recreate the spirit of medievalism in the modern suburbs. Protestantism and sanitation are the objects of mild scorn throughout. In *The Column of Dust* (1909) a spirit (the eponymous column) takes up residence in the mind of Constance Tyrrel, a 'vagrant of the invisible' who dabbles in Black Art after hours at the Kensington bookshop where she works. The major revelation, concerning a niece who is in fact a daughter, has little to do with the invasive column. There is an engaging mystic who has built himself a chapel in the Welsh hills, where he keeps the Holy Grail. There is a biography of Underhill by Margaret Cropper (1958).

Untilled Field, The, George *Moore, 1903, T. Fisher Unwin. These stories were written to be translated into Irish (the Irish version came out a year earlier). They are deliberately artless and avoid the exaggeration and narrative twist of the usual 'Irish story'. 'So On He Fares' is the tale of a little boy who runs away from a mother who dislikes him. Visiting her in the afterlife he finds she still dislikes him as much as ever. 'The Exile' is the plain tale of a girl who loves the brother of the man who had loved her. 'The Window' is the story of Biddy M'Hales, a peasant woman who uses her life savings to have a child window dedicated to her. In 'The Wild Goose' Ned Carmody decides in a fit of Irish idealism that he must abandon his wife and children and enlist with the Boers when the wild geese flying south give the signal.

UPWARD, Allen (1863–1926). Born in Worcester, into a family of Plymouth Brethren, he was educated at Great Yarmouth Grammar School and the Royal University of Ireland (where he won the Brooke Scholarship and the O'Hagan Prize for Oratory). His subsequent career is a complex one, with several disparate strands. He was called to the Bar in 1889, having won two scholarships at the Middle Temple. During 1895 he stood unsuccessfully as parliamentary candidate for Merthyr Tydfil; the same year saw the start of his 'International Spy' series of articles for **Pearson's* which ran until 1905. He also fought as a volunteer during the Greco-Turkish War in 1897, and was British Resident in Nigeria in 1901. In 1914 he volunteered to be Scout Master General at the Front. Two years later he was back in Britain, acting as headmaster at Inverness College. Upward was also a Fellow of the Royal Anthropological Institute and a corresponding member of the Parnassos Philological Society of Athens. His non-fiction is of the most various kinds. *The New Word* (1907) was an open letter to the Swedish Academy in Stockholm on the meaning of the word 'idealist'; and *The Divine Mystery* (1913), an account of 'the growth of religion from the primitive type of thunder-maker to the idea of the messiah' made him a Vorticist guru. Ezra Pound (1885–1972) praised him for championing the 'cause of the sensitive'—the prophet or artist who is ahead of his or her time. For these last two works he hoped to be awarded the Nobel prize for Literature, and Pound thought that his suicide might have been from disappointment. Upward contributed articles on the occult to the **New Age* and imagist verse to the avant-garde magazine *Poetry.* In his spare time he wrote popular fiction for money, of whose success he was rather ashamed; they were *crime novels which exploited the mystery surrounding sensational public events like the prosecution of Alfred Dreyfus (1859–1935) or Kaiser Wilhelm II's telegram to Paulus Kruger (1825–1904). His interest in espionage fuelled one of his most successful works, *The Secret History of Today: Being Revelations of a Diplomatic Spy* (1904), about a diplomatic spy who is a master of disguise. *The Discovery of the Dead* (1910) is an occult tale: a quasi-scientific account of experiments of Karl Lucke, who discovers new possibilities in human vision, including 'necromorphs', or the shapes of the dead. *Lord Alistair's Rebellion* (1909) expresses his élitist views, which anticipate the withdrawal of modernist writers from the mainstream of popular culture: it is the story of a man who wants to set up a sanatorium for geniuses but is foiled by society. Upward committed suicide by shooting himself.

URQUHART, M., *pseud.*: Maryon Urquhart GREEN was the author of six volumes of fiction 1905–1910, including *Our Lady of the Mists: A Tragedy in Commonplace* (1905), about the sufferings of a strict mother at the hands of an unhelpful husband and unsympathetic children, *A Romance of Memory* (1907), whose heroine has visions, *The Island of Souls: Being a Sensational Fairy-Tale* (1910), and *The Fool of Faery* (1910).

V

VACHELL, Horace Annesley (1861–1955) married (1889) Lydie PHILLIPS (d. 1895). Born at Sydenham, eldest son of a former landowner, he was brought up partly near Winchester, which he often visited, and was educated at Harrow School and the Royal Military College, Sandhurst. He then served briefly in the Rifle Brigade before going to California, where he married and went into partnership with his father-in-law in a land company. His wife died in childbirth in 1895, in which year his first novel, *Judge Ketchum's Romance*, was published in New York. Vachell soon afterwards returned to England and became a full-time writer, living in some style near Bath with the help of a private income. Amiable and snobbish, he was the author of more than sixty popular novels from 1895. His most famous work *The *Hill: A Romance of Friendship* (1905) is, like *Newbolt's 'Vitaï Lampada', a potent and sentimental idealization of the ethos of male imperialist institutions. Its far less powerful sequel *John Verney* (1911), substitutes a woman, Harry Desmond's sister, for Desmond, the innocent aristocrat whom it is Verney's duty to save from corruption by the modern, nouveau riche, sensual Scaife. *Quinneys* (1914), a novel about the antiques trade, was popular enough to be dramatized and to give rise to three sequels. Vachell also published the following volumes of autobiography and memoirs: *Fellow-Travellers* (1923), *My Vagabondage* (1936), *Distant Fields: A Writer's Autobiography* (1937), *Now Came Still Evening On* (1946), *Twilight Grey* (1948), *In Sober Livery* (1949), *Methuselah's Diary* (1950), and *More From Methuselah* (1951).

VAIZEY, Mrs George de Horne: Jessie BELL (1857–1917) married, first, Henry MANSERGH and, secondly (1899), George de Horne VAIZEY (d. 1927). Born in Liverpool, one of seven children of an insurance broker, she was the author of *Pixie O'Shaughnessy* (1903), about the irruption of an untamed child from an impoverished Irish castle into a respectable English girls' school, which was one of the most popular of all the many 'tomboy tamed' books for girls published in this period, and its sequels, *More About Pixie* (1903) and *The Love Affairs of Pixie* (1914). Pixie's good-heartedness and absolute truthfulness impress the other girls, while in turn she learns tidiness, ladylike manners, and 'the hundred and one restrictions and obligations of society which come as second nature to most girls'. *Pixie* was originally serialized in the *Girl's Own Paper* in 1900, and many of Vaizey's stories first appeared there. Her favourite among her own books was *Salt of Life* (1915), a saga of a move from Scotland to London based on the experience of her own family. Her second husband was also an insurance broker.

VALLINGS, [Edward] Harold (1857–1927) married Charlotte E. ——. Born at Barrackpore, Calcutta, and educated at Tonbridge School (1866–74) and the Royal Military College, Sandhurst (where he came first in the final exam), he went into the the 16th Bedfordshire Regiment. After two years, however, he retired, suffering from a spinal complaint, and became an army coach. He made enough money from writing and teaching to marry, but had a nervous breakdown after the birth of his children. He was the author of fourteen volumes of fiction 1888–1912, but he did not find literature remunerative; the Royal Literary Fund, to whom he applied in 1914 and 1918, were told in the latter year that 'he is very *very* badly off, and to help pay the rent of 2 small rooms his wife cooks for the landlady'. His works include *The Lady Mary of Tavistock* (1908), an historical romance set in Devon in 1630 and much embellished with dialect and archaism.

VANE, Derek, *pseud.*: Blanche Eaton —— (d. 1939) married —— BACK. She was the author under her pseudonym of twenty volumes of fiction between 1893 and 1933, including *The Paradise of Fools* (1913), her most successful book, in which a woman thinks her husband has died during a quarrel in which he hit his head. She contributed to the *Daily Mail* and other periodicals.

VASE, Gillan, *pseud.*: Elizabeth PALMER or PALMER PACHT (1841–1921) married (1880) Richard NEWTON. Born at Falmouth in Cornwall, the daughter of a shopkeeper who died when she was 2, she was brought up in England and Germany and married a bristle-manufacturer from Manchester. Not much is known about her life, but it seems possible that she was adopted by a German family. A peculiar and occasional novelist, she was the author of three volumes of fiction: a sequel (1878) to *Edwin Drood* (1870) by Charles Dickens (1812–1870), *Through Love to Life* (1889), and *Under the Linden* (1900), the story of the life and death of twin sisters, set in the stifling atmosphere of a small German town, lays much emphasis on the thwarting and deforming effects of bad families and bad marriages. She died in Devon.

Vicissitudes of Evangeline, The, Elinor *Glyn, 1905, Gerald Duckworth. Twenty-year-old, red-haired, green-eyed Evangeline is determined to become an adventuress (she is the granddaughter of a housemaid), but rather pre-empts the necessary cynicism by falling in love with Lord Robert Vavasour. Her staid relatives deplore her nightgown, but she is befriended by Lady Verningham, who likes her innocence. Unfortunately, Lady Verningham is Lord Robert's 'special friend'. And there is a further difficulty: Lord Robert is heir to his half-brother's dukedom and fortune, and the Duke will not have anything to do with a housemaid's granddaughter. However, Evangeline charms the Duke, while Lord Robert charmingly explains Lady Verningham away. 'If the story, as supposed to be told by the girl herself in journal form, did not make so consistently entertaining reading, thanks to the rather daring naiveté of its heroine,' the *Sunday Times* commented, 'one might be tempted to wax eloquent of Mrs Glyn's new book as a significant product of the times, as an illustration of the deplorable selfishness, the moral apathy, the ruthless search for pleasure of "smart" society.'

Village in the Jungle, The, L. S. *Woolf, 1913, Edward Arnold. The story of a half-crazed Ceylonese hunter-outcast, Silindu, and his two daughters, Hinnihami and Punchi Menika, one courted by a representative of ancient tradition, the other by a representative of the modern world. Punchirala, a witch-doctor, desires Hinnihami, and puts a spell on Silindu which will only be lifted if she succumbs. The marriage proves disastrous, resulting in the deaths of husband and wife, and of their only daughter. Punchi Menika marries the strapping but dim Babun. However, she is desired by Fernando, a trader from Colombo who settles in the village. Fernando conspires with Silindu's perpetually hostile and scheming brother-in-law Babehami, the village headman, to frame Babun for a robbery and have him thrown in jail. Silindu kills them both. Babun's innocence is no help to him, and he dies in jail. Two years later, Silindu too is dead, and the village abandoned. Punchi Menika lives on alone in her father's house, becoming, like him, a hunter-outcast. 'She had returned to the jungle; it had taken her back; she lived as he had done, understanding it, loving it, fearing it.' The novel finds an emblem for intense (and, one suspects, highly subjective) melancholy in the villagers' fatalism and the jungle's effortless reabsorption of their efforts to cultivate the land. It is one of the very few European novels about colonial territories to relegate Europeans to walk-on parts.

Viper of Milan, The: *A Romance of Lombardy,* Marjorie *Bowen, 1906, Alston Rivers. The author's first novel is a *historical romance set in Lombardy in 1360. Duke Gian Galeazzo Maria Visconti, the Viper of Milan, has conquered Verona, driving out its ruler, Mastino della Scala, and taking prisoner his wife, Isotta. We first encounter Mastino, in disguise, reconnoitring the approaches to Milan, where he takes up with two young Florentines, 19-year-old Tomaso and 10-year-old Vittore, who thereafter provide youthful readers with a counterpoint to political commentary. The narrative is wholeheartedly Gothic, with treacherous acts involving secret passages and poisoned gauntlets. Defeated eventually by Visconti's guile, Mastino agrees to exchange the cities he has recaptured for his wife's freedom. His army surrenders, but Isotta is dead on arrival. Thirsting for revenge, Mastino breaks into Visconti's palace, bearing Isotta's corpse, but is overwhelmed by the guard. Visconti's secretary, appalled by his master's villainy, stabs him to death. In his introduction to the 1963 Penguin reprint, Graham Greene wrote that he read it aged 14 and 'It was as if I had been supplied once and for all with a subject.... Human nature is not black and white but black and grey. I read all that in *The Viper of Milan* and I looked round and I saw that it was so.... I think it was Miss Bowen's apparent zest that made me want to write. One could not read her without believing that to write was to live and to enjoy.'

Visits of Elizabeth, The, Elinor *Glyn, 1900, Gerald Duckworth. The bulk of the book consists of Elizabeth's letters to her mother describing with ingenuous frankness the experiences of her first 'season', and of unchaperoned country house parties in particular. When Sir Dennis sits beside her on the sofa one evening, calls her a perfect darling, complains that he never gets the chance to talk to her alone, and adds that it will be all right if she would only drop her glove outside her bedroom door, Elizabeth asks him, in the middle of a sudden silence, why? Such plot as there is concerns her growing attraction to Harry, Marquis of Valmond, who gets his face slapped for an early impertinence, but in the end proves irresistible. Elizabeth's letters, based on a diary in which Glyn had recorded her own experiences, were published anonymously in the fashionable magazine *The World* in 1899, and caused something of a stir. Glyn expanded them for publication in book form by adding material from a journal she had kept of a visit to France. She felt that she should now publish under her own name, and consulted the celebrated hostess Lady Warwick, who agreed, adding: 'Elinor Glyn sounds like a *nom-de-plume* anyway.' The book was a critical and popular success. **Elizabeth Visits America* (1909) is a sequel.

Vital Spark and Her Queer Crew, The, 'Hugh *Foulis', 1906, Blackwood. This series of short dialect sketches, all but three of which were originally published in the *Glasgow Evening News* from January 1905 chronicles the journeys and adventures of the crew of a small cargo ship plying its trade in the waters of the Western Isles. These light-hearted tales centre around the characters and attitudes of the crew, and of the ship's opportunistic captain, Para Handy. In 'Para Handy's Apprentice', the crew conspires with the ship's owner to discourage his son Alick from running away to sea. In 'The Malingerer', the Tar is tricked into resuming his duties. 'Dougie's Family' is about a running joke the crew have, teasing the mate about his ten children. They hear his wife has had another, and prepare to mock, but when it turns out she has had twins their ribaldry turns to sympathy. In 'Lodgers on a House-Boat' the crew foil the attempt of a large, noisy family to squat on board the *Vital Spark*. 'Para Handy's Wedding', which was written to provide the volume of tales with some sorely needed sense of narrative closure, tells how Para Handy marries Mary, a widow who owns a cake-shop, merely in order that a bridal cake should not be wasted.

VIVIAN, E[velyn] Charles: Charles Henry VIVIAN (1882–1947). He worked at various times on the **English Review, Land and Water,* and *Flying,* and was author of some sixty crime novels. As a young man he travelled in South Africa, and may have fought in the *Boer War. His publications in this period include *With the Royal Army Medical Corps At the Front* (1914) and the novels *The Woman Tempted Me: A Story of a Selfish Man* (1909) and *Wandering of Desire* (1910), but most of his works are later. He was a very popular novelist after the First World War, and published eight novels between 1923 and 1931 as 'Charles Cannell', and a series of occult tales as 'Jack Mann'.

VOYNICH, Ethel: Ethel Lilian BOOLE (1864–1960) married (1891) HABDANK-WOYNICZ (1865–1930), who changed his name to Wilfrid Michael VOYNICH. Born in Cork, the daughter of a mathematician and a feminist philosopher, she worked as a governess before marrying a Pole who had been imprisoned in Siberia as a revolutionary nationalist, on whose experience she drew in her fiction. For Arnold Kettle, 'Almost the whole of the interest of her work can be traced... to the impact of the values and experiences of a powerful and heroic revolutionary movement upon a sensitive and aspiring young woman... It is rather as though Dorothea Casaubon's Will Ladislaw had been a real live revolutionary Polish emigré instead of a milk-and-water idealised aesthete.' Voynich translated from Russian and French. Of her novels *The Gadfly* (1897) was the greatest success, a tale of revolutionaries in the Risorgimento, praised by Fr. *Rolfe but not by *Conrad, who wrote: 'I don't ever remember reading a book I disliked so much.' It is said to have been widely read in the Labour movement. The hero of *Jack Raymond* (1901) is an orphan boy in the care of a sadistic uncle who is adopted by a schoolfriend's mother; the schoolfriend, a great musician, seduces his sister. The substitute mother is a Pole whose experience of Russian justice makes her believe Jack's account of his treatment 'she had lived outside the pale of men's mercy, and her unsheltered eyes had seen the naked sores of the world.' This link between private and public experience of oppression, and the emphasis on violence, is what gives Voynich's work its idiosyncratic power. *Olive Latham* (1904) is a harrowing story of Russian prisons. *An Interrupted Friendship* (1910), is set in early nineteenth-century France, in which a young man goes on an expedition to South America to raise money for an operation on his crippled sister, and meets a broken white man, the Gadfly of the earlier book, who saves his life and becomes his greatest friend. The characteristic confrontation in Voynich's fiction is that between idealism and everyday life, between revolutionaries and pragmatists, between those who are driven and those who have to pick up the pieces. The Voynichs emigrated to the USA in 1916. In later life she concentrated her energies on music, writing only one more novel, *Put Off Thy Shoes* (1946).

VYNNE, Nora: Eleanor Susannah VYNNE (1864–1914). Born in London and educated at home in Norfolk, she came to London after her father's death and worked as a journalist and novelist. She applied to the Royal Literary Fund in 1901 after a physical breakdown, and in 1914 after a cancer operation in 1913. On the second occasion she produced a letter of support from H. G. *Wells, who described *A Man and His Womankind* (1895) rather temperately as 'a quite distinguished piece of fiction'. Her other works, published from 1893, include *The Pieces of Silver* (1911), whose heroine is a feminist journalist and political campaigner, and *So It Is With the Damsel* (1913), which is about the white slave trade (the theme interested other feminists, including Elizabeth *Robins). She collaborated with Helen Blackburn on *Women Under the Factory Act* (1903).

WAINEMAN, Paul, *pseud.*: Sylvia BORGSTROM married —— MACDOUGALL. She was author of seven novels 1902–15, including *By a Finnish Lake* (1903), in which a pastor's wife in remote Finland, unhappy and childless, has a brief summer affair which gives her a child and reconciles her to her husband, and *A Roman Picture* (1914), in which an aristocratic Italian girl, penniless and proud, sells jewels to nurse her stubborn father, and eventually marries a rich banker. What freshness her fiction possesses comes from the depiction of Finnish countryside and social life.

WALES, Hubert, *pseud.*: William PIGOTT (1870–1943) married, first (1895), Beatrice MACFARLANE (d. 1923) and, secondly (1932), Dora DRINAN. Born in Lincolnshire, he was educated at Oundle School and Harrow School, studied law, and practised as a solicitor from 1894. He started writing stories and was soon able to pursue this career exclusively. His novels reflected his interest in the unseen (he was an active member of the Society for Psychical Research) and were daring versions of the '*marriage problem' novel. They include *Mr and Mrs Villiers* (1906), *The *Yoke* (1907), which was his most successful book, *Hilary Thornton* (1909), *The Wife of Colonel Hughes* (1910), *The Spinster* (1912), and *The Thirty Days* (1915). In *Cynthia in the Wilderness* (1907), Harvey, Cynthia's husband, reveres her spirit and is consistently unfaithful to her body. She meets a man who appreciates both and they become lovers. However, the increasingly brutish Harvey catches them in the act and beats her lover over the head with a golf-club. The lover survives. Meanwhile one of Cynthia's friends has self-sacrificingly poisoned Harvey. Cynthia returns from the wilderness to marry her lover. It says much about the seriousness with which Wales took himself, and which appears to have surrounded the whole 'marriage problem' question, that he should also have published a book of essays, *The Purpose: Reflections and Digressions* (1913), with titles like 'On Thinking', 'On Being', 'On Death', and (inevitably) 'On Sex'. The following quotation gives the flavour of the latter: 'For my part, I daresay no more than this: love has so immense a claim that, if it is reciprocal and consummate, other interests can be called upon to give way to it. It should have, I think, something of the privilege of the fire-engine: useful, lumbering vehicles should pull to the side at its approach, the ordinary rule of the road should lose its effect.'

WALFORD, L. B.: Lucy Bethia COLQUHOUN (1845–1915) married (1869) Alfred Saunders WALFORD (d. 1907). She was born at Portobello, near Edinburgh, the youngest daughter of a family of nine. Her father, John Colquhoun (1805–85), an army officer and the younger son of a baronet, was a well-known writer on sport; the novelist Catherine Sinclair (1800–64) was his half-aunt. Lucy Colquhoun received an excellent education at home supervised by governesses, with tutors in specialist subjects. An avid reader from a very early age, she was greatly influenced by the works of Jane Austen (1775–1817) and Charlotte M. Yonge (1823–1901). She began to write secretly after her marriage, and submitted work to *Blackwood's* and later contributed to the *World* and the New York *Critic*. Her first novel was *Mr Smith: A Part of His Life* (1874). *Charlotte* (1901) is the story of the destruction by society of a poor, beautiful, talented, upper-class girl who fails to make a successful marriage and is corrupted by materialism and ruined by scandal. Both theme and setting recall the works of '*Ouida', Henry *James, and Edith Wharton (1862–1937). Later novels reveal a preoccupation, perhaps derived from Yonge, with large families. *Stay-at-Homes* (1903) concerns the Maynard daughters, who find country life intolerably dull; the eldest, Beatrice, decides she must see the world. The most interesting character is a charming middle-aged schemer, Miss Adam, who disguises herself as Beatrice's companion in order to detach the young man Beatrice is in love with from the attentions of Mrs William Curle, a clever outsider with social ambitions and a 'past' (she was once a street singer). *Leonore Stubbs* (1908) is a love story featuring a peppery old general and his four daughters. *The Enlightenment of Olivia* (1907) is a '*marriage problem' novel: Olivia, who is married to a wealthy businessman, Willie Seaford, contracts a friendship with the self-serving Professor Ambrose, an Oxford don: the ensuing remorse, confession and 'enlightenment' as to a wife's duties are observed by an elderly couple, Colonel and Lady Thatcher, perhaps modelled on the Assinghams in Henry *James's *The *Golden Bowl* (1904). *David and Jonathan on the Riviera* (1914) concerns a Scots minister, his well-to-do friend, and his butler, Jeems, who are comprehensively gulled by the colourful Baron and Baroness Pozzi and the even more colourful Madame Petowska. Walford's other notable publications are: *Twelve English Authoresses* (1892), *Memories of Victorian London* (1912), and *Recollections of a Scottish Novelist* (1914). Her husband was the manager of Wrigley's, the paper-manufacturers.

WALKER, William S[ylvester] (1846–1926) married, first, —— and, secondly, ——. Born in Australia, son of the founder of the Royal Sydney Yacht Squadron, he was educated at Sydney Grammar School and Worcester College, Oxford. He subsequently farmed in Australia and New Zealand and mined diamonds in South Africa. Later he lived in Argyllshire. He published ten volumes of fiction, mostly Australian, between 1898 and 1915. *The Silver Queen: A Tale of the Northern Territory* (1908) is representative.

WALKEY, S[amuel] published sixteen volumes of adventure fiction between 1897 and 1935, including *With Redskins on the Warpath* (1901) and *Yo-ho! for the Spanish Main: A Story of Adventure among Pirates* (1910).

WALLACE, [Richard Horatio] Edgar (1875–1932) married first (1901), Ivy Maud CALDECOTT (d. 1926) (divorced 1918), and, secondly (1921) Ethel Violet KING (d. 1933). A phenomenon of twentieth-century publishing, he was author of at least 100 thrillers, thirty plays, three autobiographies, and a history of the First World War. Born in Greenwich, he was the illegitimate child of an actress and dresser, Marie Richards, and of an actor, Richard Horatio Edgar, who was the son of her employer. His mother concealed his birth from her friends, and he was brought up by a Billingsgate fish-porter and his wife named Freeman, and educated at a Board school in Peckham. When he was 2 his mother proposed taking him away from the Freemans (who had ten children) but they indignantly insisted on keeping him, unsubsidized. From the age of 12 he worked at various menial jobs before enlisting in the army in 1893. He served for six years and was sent to South Africa, where he drifted into journalism, acting as Reuters and *Daily Mail* correspondent in the *Boer War from 1899 to 1902. He was a reporter on the *Daily Mail* from his return to England to 1907, then worked on the *Standard* until 1910. He wrote much journalism about horse-racing, and started two racing papers. Despite his vast earnings he died in debt, including £20,000 in unpaid tax. His big break was his first novel *The *Four Just Men* (1906), probably his best book, and the launching-pad for a career as one of the bestselling writers ever. He put his hand to everything that could be loosely called adventure stories for men, whether imperialist fantasy (as in his tales of **Sanders of the River*) or domestic murder (as in his detective stories featuring J. G. Reeder, beginning with *Room 13*, 1924). Though his name will be forever associated with thrillers, and he originated many stock devices of the genre, his bibliography also includes *Smithy* (1905), about soldiers, and *The Duke in the Suburbs* (1909), an arch *Wodehousian comedy about the impact of a duke on a street of pretentious middle-class people, which ends with the duke saving the heroine from Moroccan brigands. Wallace died in Hollywood, where he was writing film scripts. There is a biography (1938) by his daughter-in-law Margaret Lane.

WALLACE, Helen was the daughter of a Scots clergyman. She published, as 'Gordon Roy', three novels between 1889 and 1892, and then, under her own name, nine novels between 1900 and 1913, including *To Pleasure Madame* (1907), a farrago of melodrama about cousins who are left an estate on condition they marry; they are first too high-minded to do so and then prevented by his marriage, and then, when his wife runs away, are prevented from marrying by her.

Wallet of Kai Lung, The, 'Ernest *Bramah', 1900, Grant *Richards. This was the first of a popular series of books in which Chinese storyteller, Kai Lung, entertains passers-by in a variety of circumstances (the first story, 'The Transmutation of Ling', is told to defer Kai Lung's execution by a brigand). The stories have a veneer of oriental detail but feature an entirely mythical China of mandarins and bureacrats and elaborate caste relations (inspired, it seems, more by Chinese art than by Chinese travel) and are written in an elaborately fake formal style (most obvious in 'The Confession of Kai Lung', which features the work of the legendary author Lo Kuan: 'Friends, Chinamen, labourers who are engaged in agricultural pursuits, entrust to this person your acute and well-educated ears . . .'). Many of the stories feature naïve or opportunist young men who end up rich, respected, and married despite an accumulation of social obstacles. This volume (which now seems very heavy-handed) also covers, more entertainingly, the invention of multiplication and the art of picture-making.

WALPOLE, Hugh [Seymour] (1884–1941) Kt. (1937). Born in Auckland, New Zealand, where his father, later Bishop of Edinburgh, was a Church of England clergyman, he was educated at a private school at Marlow, where he was bullied and miserable, at the King's School, Canterbury, from 1898, when his parents went to live in Durham, as a day-boy at Durham School, where he was taught by 'Ian *Hay', and at Emmanuel College, Cambridge, from which he graduated in 1906. A fanciful, lonely little boy, longing for affection and popularity, whose parents lived first in New Zealand and later in America, he read much fiction from an early age and also wrote: his earliest surviving historical romance is dated 1897. At Cambridge he wrote two novels, of which one, a Cornish story, influenced by Charles *Marriott, was eventually published as *The Wooden Horse* (1909) and is about a man who returns home after twenty years in New Zealand to reclaim his ancestral home, and thereafter combines New World energy with Old World wisdom. A brief period of social work in Liverpool changed Walpole's mind about becoming a clergyman, and he travelled, briefly acting as tutor to the children of '*Elizabeth' in 1907, and taught at Epsom College. He then determined to make a living as a writer, something he barely did until he persuaded the *Evening Standard* to give him regular book reviews. During the First World War he went to Moscow as a journalist; there he wrote a study of *Conrad, and worked with the Red Cross (he was awarded the St George's Cross for stretcher-bearing at the battle of Maidan), an experience he used in *The Dark Forest* (1916). He was sent back to produce official propaganda in 1916. He was increasingly successful and prominent in the literary world after the war, though his sales were not matched by the esteem of literary critics. He settled in Cumberland in 1924, in which year he met Harold Cheevers (b. 1893), a police constable who became his 'secretary-chauffeur-friend and ROCK!' until his death. In 1930 he was hurt by the portrayal of him as the social-climbing literary man Alroy Kear in Somerset *Maugham's *Cakes and Ale*: 'Read on with increasing horror. Unmistakeable portrait of myself. Never slept.' Despite this he urged Maugham to have the attack on it by 'Elinor *Mordaunt' banned. He went to Hollywood to write for the films in 1934–5 and found the emancipation from literary rivalry liberating: 'No one here cares a hang abut the relative merits of English writers!' He suffered from diabetes, and his experiences in the Blitz may have hastened his death. Most of his vast collection of books, pictures, and manuscripts was dispersed after his death. *Maradick at Forty* (1910) is a *suburban comedy of manners with melodramatic interludes. Dull Maradick has a dull, pretty wife. Stirred by the love affairs of others, he falls in love himself, for a while. There is an Italianate villain who enjoys twisting necks (rabbits, human beings), and much emphasis on the spirit of place: summer nights and rustling Cornish tides. 'It isn't written *at all*, darling Hugh—by which I mean you have . . . never got expression *tight* and in close quarters (of discrimination, of specification) with its subject,' wrote Henry *James to the author. It was followed by **Mr Perrin and Mr Traill*, whose appearance and popularity led to a break in relations between Walpole and his former colleagues at Epsom College. After he had disentangled himself from a contract with Mills & Boon by dashing off a *crime novel, *The Prelude to Adventure* (1912), in six weeks, he wrote **Fortitude* (1913), the first of his novels to achieve popular success. Walpole also turned his hand to school stories (*Jeremy*, 1919; *Jeremy and Hamlet*, 1923; *Jeremy at Crale*, 1927), *historical romance (the Herries Chronicle, beginning with *Rogue Herries*, 1930, and *Judith Paris*, 1931), social novels (*The Duchess of Wrexe*, 1914); and horror (*Portrait* *of a Man with Red Hair*, 1925). He wrote critical studies of *Conrad (1916), James Branch Cabell (1879–1958) (1926), and Anthony Trollope (1815–82) (1928)—he wrote a Trollopian novel, *The Cathedral* (1922). Frank *Swinnerton judged Walpole the paradigm of the professional writer in the early twentieth century (more so than *Bennett or *Galsworthy), partly because of his willingness to turn his hand to anything; partly, according to Swinnerton, because his desire to be liked was greater than his desire to write well. He was a great friend of Henry *James, whom he emulated in publishing the Cumberland edition (30 vols., 1934–40) of his own works, complete with authorial prefaces, and who is supposed to have portrayed him as Hugh Crimble in *The Outcry* (1911). Though he has sometimes been seen as an archetypal middlebrow, Walpole was a supporter and friend of many important writers throughout his life, and an omnivorous but discerning critic of fiction. Of James's notorious essay 'The Younger Generation' in the **Times Literary Supplement* (14 Mar. 1914), which praised *The Duchess of Wrexe*, if in rather obscure terms, Walpole wrote to his *literary agent that he thought it 'all wrong. Anyone who prefers Edith Wharton to **Chance*, and **Sinister Street* to **Sons and Lovers*! Also no mention of E. M. *Forster, who can put the rest of us in his pocket.' There is a biography (1952) by Rupert Hart-Davis.

Wanderer's Necklace, The, H. Rider *Haggard, 1914, Cassell. In this Viking saga, the wise fool Olaf steals (in order to win the beautiful Iduna) a magical necklace and a magical sword from the burial mound of the Wanderer, a long-dead ancestor (and, we are led to suppose, a previous incarnation). No sooner has Iduna gained possession of the necklace than she flees with Olaf's foster-brother, Steinar. Olaf's father and older brother and Iduna's father are killed in a great sea-battle, and Steinar taken prisoner. Steinar is sacrificed to Odin, and in revenge Olaf smashes the statue of Odin to pieces. He flees the wrath of Odin's priests, having recovered the Wanderer's necklace from Iduna. The scene shifts to Byzantium, where Olaf, now 35 and battle-scarred, is captain of the Northern Guard of the Empress Irene, widow of Leo the Fourth, and joint ruler of the Eastern Empire with her son, Constantine. Olaf becomes a convert to Christianity. During his public acceptance as a Christian in the Cathedral of St Sophia, he sees in the crowd a beautiful face which he recalls from his incarnation as the Wanderer, and which belongs to Heliodore, daughter of Magas, Prince of Egypt. Maddened by jealousy, Irene orders him to be put to death, but the Norsemen among the palace guard rebel, capturing her in her turn. She offers Olaf the Empire, and herself, but he has pledged himself to Heliodore. He is tried for treason and condemned to death. Irene visits him in his cell and, when he once again refuses her, has his eyes put out. The Norsemen rebel, free Olaf, and open the city gates to Constantine. The scene shifts to Egypt, where Olaf has travelled in search of Heliodore, whom he discovers hiding in the Valley of Dead Kings. After further adventures, they marry and retire to Lesbos. Constantine, tiring of Irene's intrigues, sends her to Olaf to be blinded in her turn. He refuses and, knowing that his refusal will be interpreted as treason, sets sail with Heliodore for the land of his birth.

War in the Air, The, *and particularly How Mr. Bert Smallways Fared While it Lasted*, H. G. *Wells, 1908, George Bell. A scientific romance forecasting total war which now reads less like science fiction than realism. The book depicts global warfare and aerial bombardment with remarkable foresight, but also repays reading as a highly enjoyable adventure story. If follows the adventures of Bert Smallways, a former bicycle dealer who is accidentally carried from Britain to Germany in a balloon. Briefly mistaken for the inventor of a coveted flying-machine, Bert is taken to the United States aboard an invading German airship fleet. The Chinese and Japanese intervene in the conflict, and soon a world war and the collapse of industrial civilisation are under way. After shooting the German leader, Prince Karl Albert, at Niagara Falls, Bert makes his way back to Britain and is reunited with his sweetheart Edna. As a witness to key events, Bert provides a subjective view to which Wells is able to add clarification and polemic, balancing the particular and the general as he criticizes the Edwardian arms race and its likely outcome. The novel is deliberately peopled by contemporary English characters, and an eye-witness narrator, Bert Smallways, who has an aggressive cockney common sense: 'there was us in Europe, all at sixes and sevens with our silly flags and our silly newspapers raggin' us up against each other and keepin 'us apart.' Smallways partly represents the ordinary person trapped in the struggle for world domination, but by pitching his humour against the potential horror of total war, Wells preserves a gleam of hope for the future (and provides another prophetic image: the joking Cockney survivors of the Blitz). A sort of extravaganza, *The War in the Air* is also a realistic description of the lowest and poorest side of social life.

WARD, E.: see E. *Everett-Green.

WARD, E. D. *pseud.*: see E. V. *Lucas.

WARD, Mrs Humphry: Mary Augusta ARNOLD (1851–1920) married (1872) Thomas Humphry WARD (1845–1926). Born in Hobart Town, Tasmania, she was the daughter of a school inspector who lost his job on converting to Roman Catholicism when she was 5, though he returned to the Church of England in 1865. She was educated at three different English boarding-schools, and lived after 1865 in Oxford, where she married a Brasenose don, until 1881, when he began working for the *Times* and they moved to London. Her Oxford years are evoked in the late novel *Lady Connie* (1916). Ward started writing in 1870, placing 'The Westmoreland Story' in *Churchman's Companion*, and quickly becoming a regular writer and reviewer for a range of weekly and monthly magazines, always with a reforming or reproving point to make. Granddaughter of Thomas Arnold of Rugby (1795–1842) and niece of Matthew Arnold (1822–88), she shared with them a strong sense of moral purpose—all her novels were designed to serve an argument. That many of them grappled with the relationship between religious conviction and social action and explored the consequences of doubt undoubtedly reflected Ward's own unhappy experience of living through her father's various conversions. The most famous of these books was her second novel, *Robert Elsmere* (1888), the story of an Anglican clergyman who loses his faith, which became an extraordinary bestseller (with an unsuccessful sequel, *The Case of Richard Meyne*, 1911, in which the modernist movement in the Anglican Church is led by the lover of Elsmere's daughter). *Helbeck of Bannisdale* (1898) is a tragedy about the conflict between religion and love in the relationship between a backward-looking Catholic squire and a modern, agnostic girl. Her chief preoccupation in her later novels was the position of women. She campaigned vigorously for women's education, but never lost the belief, expressed in novels like *Eleanor* (1900), that women must subordinate desire to duty, and she wrote numerous novels, like *The *Marriage of William Ashe* (1905) and *Daphne* (1909), in which transgressing women are punished. The latter links suffrage agitation and divorce law reform as attacks on the family: a rich American woman divorces her English husband and ruins his life and that of their daughter. *Eltham House* (1915) is another, more sympathetic novel on the divorce theme. *Eleanor*, the story of a triangular relationship between a brilliant politician, the intellectual woman who loves him, and a beautiful American, was deliberately written so as to be suitable for dramatization: Ward was envious of the large sums earned by such other bestselling writers as J. M. *Barrie and Hall *Caine for dramatized versions of their novels, but her own novels had always been driven by ideas and arguments rather than situation. The play was written in collaboration with Julian *Sturgis, but it was not a success, and nor were her subsequent theatrical ventures. **Lady Rose's Daughter* (1903) is another novel of plot rather than debate, and expresses the view that women rule best through influence rather than political action. A number of novels more or less based on historical figures reinforced this point. *The Marriage of William Ashe* transposes to Edwardian England the career of Lady Caroline Lamb (1785–1828), the flighty wife of an ambitious politician. *Fenwick's Career* (1906) fictionalized the myth of the career of the painter George Romney (1734–1802), on whom Ward's art critic husband was the expert: following ambition to London he conceals the existence of his wife, only to be reconciled to her long afterwards. Ward was in a difficult position during the Book War (see *publishers), with a husband working for the *Times* and a publisher, Reginald Smith, stern in defence of the Net Book Agreement. *Diana Mallory* (1908) is about the marriage of another politician: can he marry a murderess's daughter? The increasing importance of serial and volume sales in the USA, and Ward's increasing enthusiasm for the Empire, prompted a visit to North America in 1908 and the composition of *Canadian Born* (1910), in which an upper-class Englishwoman marries a backwoodsman. But by 1910 she was increasingly out of touch with both her British and American publics, and worrying about money, partly because of her son's gambling—in *The *Coryston Family* (1913) the dominating mother of three sons is disappointed in them all. Suffering from insomnia, eczema, and gynaecological problems, addicted to opiates, Ward's continued output was extraordinary, but the quality markedly declined. In 1908 Ward became a leader of the Women's Anti-Suffrage League; *Delia Blanchflower* (1915) describes the follies and ultimately the conversion of a suffragette; its author and subject had so little appeal that it was hard to persuade an American publisher to buy it at all. She did propaganda work during the First World War, in the shape of *England's Effort* (1916) and *Towards the Goal* (1917). Only the necessity of writing novels to keep up her standard of living prevented her from embarking on another project: like 'Deas *Cromarty', Hall *Caine, Forrest *Reid, 'John *Oxenham', and M. P. *Shiel, she harboured a desire to write a life of Christ. *A Writer's Recollections* (1918) is the most significant of her late works. There is a biography (1990) by John Sutherland.

WARD, Mrs Wilfrid: Josephine Mary HOPE (1864–1932) married (1887) Wilfrid Philip WARD (1856–1916). The daughter of upper-class English Roman Catholics, she was the author of eleven volumes of fiction depicting that world, quiet, ironical tales of passionate devotion and suffering for the Faith, between 1899 and 1932. Daughter of a barrister who was a Catholic convert, she was brought up partly at Abbotsford (her father's first wife had been granddaughter of Walter Scott, 1771–1832). Both her parents were dead by the time she was 8, and she was educated in strictly Catholic fashion while living with her grandmother, the Duchess of Norfolk. Her husband, who was also a child of a convert of the Tractarian era, became an influential writer on theology and biographer. Like Evelyn *Underhill, the Wards were closely associated with Baron von Hügel (1852–1925). *Out of Due Time* (1906) is told by its heroine, torn between her fiancé, a progressive Catholic theologian, and the man she loves, who is engaged to the former's sister. She marries her true love and brother and sister lead separate, saintly lives. In *The Job Secretary: An Impression* (1911), an author engages a secretary whose life turns out to be the novel he is writing, and *Great Possessions* (1909). *One Poor Scruple* (1899) hinges on a Catholic widow's desire to marry a divorced man. As well as writing fiction she worked as a reviewer for the *Spectator*. There is an interesting study by her daughter, Maisie Ward, *The Wilfrid Wards and the Transition* (1934).

WARDEN, Florence, *pseud.*: Florence Alice PRICE (1857–1929) married (1887) George Edward JAMES. A stockbroker's daughter, she was born at Hanworth, Middlesex, and went to school in Brighton and then in France before becoming a finishing governess. She was an actress in her mid-20s (1880–1885) and had some success as a writer, but by the twentieth century she was badly off: bankruptcy threatened in 1909. She applied to the Royal Literary Fund in 1909, 1911, 1912, and 1914. In 1909 she stated that for the last two years she had written a million words a year. She thought she had been cheated by her literary agent. In 1911 her stock in the market was so low that she had to sell a novel of 80,000 words for £10. Her many romances include *At the World's Mercy* (1884) and *From Stage to Peerage: An Autobiography* (1911). James specialized in courtship and marital dilemmas. The girl in whose heart we are to interest ourselves in *The Heart of a Girl* (1903) could be Agatha Reith, whom Lord Jerrall loves, or Tamar Thwaite, the 'country lass' who loves him, or Emmeline Whelton, to whom he is engaged. In *Blindman's Marriage* (1907) the heroine marries Lord Burmarsh to escape from a convent, even though she loves a man who is wanted (in the police sense) by her husband. In *Who Was Lady Thorne?* (1904) Sir Michael Thorne's first wife turns up after the behaviour of his second wife has driven him to drink. In Chapter 1 of *The Financier's Wife* (1906) Theodora Wye appeals to a great financier, Mr Dixon, to intercede on behalf of her ruined father; by the end of the second chapter they are married and Dixon has seen in Bond Street his first wife, who he thought was dead. The hero of *Mad Sir Geoffrey* (1907) becomes reckless after the flight of his treacherous wife, and fills his house with bad company; Hetty Devayne compromises herself in order to scold him, and to protect her reputatation they feign an engagement, which matures into romance. In *The Adventures of a Pretty Woman* (1909) Margaret Carbullan, bored by life in her uncle's dull household, amuses herself by championing Sir Cory Casterton, who has been accused not only of murder, but of stealing her pearls. *Abbots Moat* (1913), for a change, is a shocker about a gang of thieves. James also wrote lightweight plays such as *A Patched Up Affair* (1900) and *Parlez-Vous Français?* (1906).

WARDEN, Gertrude married J. Wilton JONES. She published over thirty volumes of fiction between *c.*1890 and 1915, including *The Nut-Browne Mayd: A Riviera Mystery* (1907) and *The World, the Flesh and the Casino* (1909); her early stories appeared in such serials as *The Family Story-Teller and The Young Ladies' Journal Butterfly Series of Complete Stories*. She collaborated with 'Robert *Eustace' on *The Stolen Pearl* (1903) and with Harold Edward Gorst (see under Mrs Harold *Gorst) on *Compromised* (1905).

WARDLE, Jane, *pseud.*: see Oliver Madox *Hueffer.

Watcher by the Threshold, The, John *Buchan, 1902, William Blackwood. Five Scottish tales, four of them exploring the supernatural. In 'No-Man's-Land' the narrator, a Celtic scholar, is driven mad by his discovery of surviving Picts (and Pictish practices) in an isolated highland glen. In 'The Far Island' the hero, an apparently straightforward English public-school man, is also the descendant of ancient north-west Scotland lairds and is slowly taken over by his inherited vision. In 'The Watcher by the Threshold' a solid Highlands landlord is possessed by Satan. In 'The Outgoing of the Tide' a young couple resist the devil's sexual temptation, but are doomed to death anyway. In 'Fontainebleau' the hero is briefly smitten by love but comes to accept his essential loneliness and, like many of Buchan's heroes, applies his Scottish self-sufficiency and mystical union with nature to colonial service.

WATSON, E[dmund Henry] LACON (1865–1948) married (1896) Ruth DARLING. Born at Sharnford, Leicestershire, son of a Church of England clergyman, he was educated at Winchester College, where he was a scholar, and Caius College, Cambridge, where he read classics. He then became a schoolmaster for seven years, before coming to London in 1894 to earn his living by his pen. He was on the staff of *Literature* and published in periodicals such as the *Westminster Review* and the **Pall Mall Magazine*. His work includes bookish essays, verse, a collection of comic sketches about marriage published as *Benedictine* (1898), and a first novel, *Christopher Deane* (1902), drawing on his experiences at public school and university. The **Bookman* (Apr. 1902) observed of this work: 'it has been affirmed that it contains the best boat-race in fiction, rivalling, if not surpassing [that] in "Ravenshoe".' (*Ravenshoe*, 1862, is by Henry Kingsley, 1830–76.) *Barker's* (1910) is dedicated to Horace Annesley *Vachell; it is the story of the attempted revival of a publishing firm, which involves the launch of a new literary magazine, and is narrated by a middle-aged and self-deprecating bachelor who finds romance at the end. Watson's other fiction includes *The Happy Elopement* (1909) and *Perdita Finds Herself* (1944). *I Look Back Over Seventy Years* (1938) is an autobiography.

WATSON, Frederick (1885–1935) married (1911) Hilda JONES. Younger son of 'Ian *Maclaren', he was educated at Sedbergh School, Edinburgh University, and Emmanuel College, Cambridge, before becoming a partner in the publishers Nisbet & Co. He published fiction between 1912 and 1924 including *The Ghost Rock, or, White Man's Gold* (1912) and *Shallows* (1913), a *historical novel about the Young Pretender, and founded the *Cripple*, a magazine devoted to the cause of handicapped children. He was also a journalist, and the biographer of the hunting novelist R. S. Surtees (1805–94). He and his wife were joint masters of the Tanatside hunt: they lived in Dorset. In emulation of his father he published some of his work under the pseudonyms 'John Ferguson' and 'Ian Ferguson'.

WATSON, H[enry] B[rereton] Marriott (1863–1921) married Rosamund —— (d. 1911). Born at Caulfield, Melbourne, he moved with his family to New Zealand during his early childhood; his father had been offered a position at St John's Church in Christchurch. There he attended Christchurch Grammar School and Canterbury College. He set sail for Britain in 1885 and started his journalistic career in 1887. He worked on the *National Observer* under W. E. Henley (1849–1903) and he was assistant editor at both *Black and White* and the *Pall Mall Gazette*. As a novelist Watson tried out a number of popular genres. *Captain Fortune* (1904) and *Twisted Eglantine* (1905) are *historical romances. The former is set in Cornwall at the time of the Great Rebellion. The latter is a Regency tale. Sir Piers Blakiston, a beau with an iron will, abducts Barbara

Garraway, daughter of a Hampshire squire; she is eventually rescued by a true-hearted soldier, Gilbert Faversham, who deserts his regiment on the eve on the attack on Flushing in response to her appeal. The stories collected in *Alarums and Excursions* (1903) are set in Georgian and early Victorian times. The narrator of *The Castle by the Sea* (1909) rents the eponymous castle for the summer, only to discover that the feckless owner has been mysteriously concealed somewhere about the premises; there are secret chambers and smuggling caves, and heroines called Christobel and Perdita. *Alise of Astra* (1910) is a *Ruritanian fantasy about a semi-independent state on the Rhine. *Godfrey Merivale* (1902) is perhaps Watson's most serious Edwardian novel, Thackerayan in point of view, *Meredithian in style. Godfrey Merivale, the impoverished, scholarly descendant of the Merivales of Pontract, has to earn his living as a journalist until, in due course, he inherits the title (the various heirs who come before him having been disposed of in a single hectic chapter). Grant *Richards remembered that Watson 'used to sail very close to the wind in his short stories, and I heard that legal notice might be taken of their flourishes', and wrote of him as a distinguished member of the school encouraged by W. E. Henley (1849–1903): 'I do not exaggerate the intellectual thrill that one could get from the pages that Henley so nobly, petulantly and truculently controlled.' Like many writers he was hit financially by the outbreak of the First World War, and applied to the Royal Literary Fund in 1914.

Way of All Flesh, The, Samuel *Butler, 1903, Grant Richards. Butler attacks the pieties and tyrannies of Victorian domestic convention by tracing the oppressive relations of fathers to sons through the lineage of the Pontifex family, from John Pontifex, village carpenter, through George Pontifex, religious publisher, and Theobald Pontifex, Evangelical parson, to Ernest Pontifex, pushed as his father was before him into ordination. Things go wrong when, as a curate, Ernest accuses a respectable woman of prostitution and is gaoled for six months, coming out of prison disgraced but capable now of ridding himself of the burden of family, faith, and class. In pursuit of a different kind of life he makes a foolish marriage to Ellen, a former maidservant at the rectory. Ernest is freed from this new domestic millstone by the discovery that Ellen is already married; he inherits a fortune from an aunt and devotes the rest of his life to literature, having farmed out his own children to avoid further expression of Pontifex paternal oppression.

Way of an Eagle, The, Ethel M. *Dell, 1912, T. Fisher Unwin. Nick Ratcliffe, a young subaltern, rescues Muriel Roscoe, little more than a child, during an uprising on the north-west frontier of India. She becomes engaged to him through a sense of obligation, but then withdraws. He releases her, confident that he can win her back. Small and repulsive, one-armed but iron-willed, he is ruthless, and this appals, then fascinates, and finally conquers Muriel. Somehow he has 'kindled' within her the 'undying flame'. 'Against her will, in spite of her utmost resistance, he had done this thing.' Muriel has become a woman, and discovered sexual difference, through masochism alone; indeed she has discovered it *as* masochism. The Edwardian romance of womanhood squared assertion with submission, deferral with deference. The novel, Dell's first, was a bestseller which established the pattern of her work.

WEBLING, Peggy (b. *c*.1870–2) was the daughter of a jeweller and silversmith, and brought up in Bayswater. After being given a part in a play put on by Justin *McCarthy (senior), and his children, she and some of her five sisters gave public recitations, which were very popular. In this way they attracted the attention of John Ruskin (1819–1900), who petted them and wrote to them, and of whom she published a brief memoir. She spent some time in Canada as a young girl. Though they never regained the success of their childhood, three of the sisters continued to perform as adults in this period. Peggy began to work as a journalist, interviewing actors, and published fiction including *Blue Jay* (1906), about an acrobat, and *The Story of Virginia Perfect* (1909), a saccharine tale about the ennobling love between a beautiful Cockney girl and a successful illustrator. *Peggy* (n.d.) is an impressionistic autobiography, with some amusing descriptions of the rigours of touring in Canada and the USA. She published some Canadian fiction as 'Arthur Weston'.

WEEKES, A[gnes] R[ussell] (1880–1940) and WEEKES, R[ose] K[irkpatrick] (1874–1956). The younger sister, Agnes, spent much of this period taking University of London examinations while studying at home. She matriculated in June 1898, and was awarded a first-class degree in English and French in 1907, and an MA in English in 1910. Her first novel was *Yarborough the Premier* (1904); it was followed by thirteen later novels to 1932, including *Faith Unfaithful* (1910), in which Dodo Carminow, a poor parson's daughter, becomes engaged in a moment of coquetry to Charles Auburn, son of a hateful but wealthy baronet, and subsequently falls in love with him; the crucial scene occurs when she visits him in gaol the day before he is due to be hanged for murder. Her sister Rose Weekes's first novel was *Love in Chief* (1904); it was followed by nine other novels to 1934, including *The Fall of the Cards* (1905), *Fellow Prisoners* (1911), and *Seaborne of the Bonnet Shop* (1914). Together the two sisters wrote *The Tragic Prince* (1912), which concerns the disputed succession to the throne of the *Ruritanian princedom of Neuberg, and eighteen later novels between 1923 and 1942. *The Purple Pearl* (1923), by both sisters, and *The Secret Room* (1929), by Agnes alone, were published under the pseudonym 'Anthony Pryde'. The *British Library Catalogue* states that *Prisoners of War* (1899), which was published under the pseudonym 'A. Boyson Weekes', was written by Agnes in collaboration, but with whom is not known. The sisters lived together at Slindon in Sussex.

WELLS, H[erbert] G[eorge] (1866–1946) married, first (1891), Isabel Mary WELLS (divorced 1895) and, secondly (1895), Amy Catherine ROBBINS (d. 1927). Born at Bromley, Kent, he was educated at Morley's Academy, Bromley, Midhurst Grammar School, and the Normal School of Science, South Kensington. During Wells's childhood, his father, a former professional cricketer, was failing as a small shopkeeper in Bromley. He struggled for education while serving apprenticeships in a draper's and a chemist's shop. In 1884 he won a scholarship to the Normal School of Science, and he was awarded a first-class degree in zoology by London University in 1890. His early career was as a teacher; after his second marriage he earned his living by writing, among his early works are textbooks in biology and geography. With the encouragement of Frank *Harris, editor of the *Saturday Review*, he started submitting stories and features. His first marriage, to his cousin, was short-lived, and he eloped with Catherine in 1893. All these events of his early life are comprehensively described in his fiction. And his life once he had entered the literary world and joined (in 1903) the Fabian Society also provided material. His row with fellow-Fabians, the rights and wrongs of which, complicated as they were by personal feeling and sexual scandal, are now hard to disentangle, had an impact on *The *New Machiavelli*. His notorious series of affairs, especially those with Dorothy Richardson (1873–1957) in 1905–7, with E. *Nesbit's adopted daughter, Rosamond Bland in 1908, with Amber *Reeves in 1909, with '*Elizabeth' in 1913, and with Rebecca West (1892–1983) from 1913 to 1923, fed into fiction which treated, as seriously and extensively as that of any of his contemporaries, the relationships between men and women in the age of birth control, female emancipation, and universal suffrage. Wells's early novels and stories were *science fiction; he extrapolated from present scientific and technological knowledge to imagine possible future worlds. Such stories were not simply written as entertainments, but also worked as science education, and enabled Wells to extrapolate likely social futures too, and, in particular, to put science on the side of socialism. Books in this mode include *The Time Machine: An Invention* (1895), *The Wonderful Visit* (1895), *The Stolen Bacillus and Other Stories* (1895), *The Island of Dr Moreau* (1896), *The Invisible Man* (1897), *The War of the Worlds* (1898), *Tales of Space and Time* (1899), *When the Sleeper Wakes* (1899), *The *First Men on the Moon* (1901), **In the Days of the Comet* (1906), *The *War in the Air* (1908), and *The Shape of Things to Come* (1933). These remain classics of science fiction, defining the field formally in terms of the integration of science and the imagination, the attention to detail, the understanding that culture is changed by technology (and vice versa), the seriousness of purpose. Wells was particularly adept at using the short story form (and the story was, at that time, the basic currency of the literary professional, given the demand from magazine editors). But he was, at the same time, developing a different interest, in realist novels of lower-middle-class life, drawing on his own experience, but also using comic techniques familiar in such magazines as *Punch*. Beginning with *Wheels of Chance* (1896), and **Love and Mr Lewisham* (1900), these novels include Wells's most valued works: **Kipps*: *The*

Story of a Simple Soul (1905), **Ann Veronica* (1909), **Tono-Bungay* (1909), *The *History of Mr Polly* (1910), *Mr Britling Sees It Through* (1916). In these books Wells integrated his social purposes into the novel form itself, into its characterization and narrative. In other books (*A Modern Utopia*, 1905; *The New Machiavelli*, 1911; **Marriage*, 1912) the social arguments rather swamp the characters, or else (*The *Wife of Sir Isaac Harman*, 1914; *Bealby: A Holiday*, 1915; *The World of William Clissold*, 1926) are of lighter weight. But whatever his imaginative capacity as a novelist, Wells retained his faith in the power of reason and the value of education. *Anticipation* (1908) is an early example of futurology serving the goal of political instruction. *The Outline of History* (1920) and *The Science of Life* (1929–30), which was written with his son G. P. Wells (1901–1985) and Julian Huxley (1887–1975), were ambitious attempts to popularize knowledge. From 1918 Wells was involved with the League of Nations and with the disarmament movement. He reflected on his life and ambitions in his autobiography, *Experiments in Autobiography: Discoveries and Conclusions of a Very Ordinary Brain* (1934). His second wife, known as 'Jane', was the author, as Catherine Wells, of some fiction after the First World War. Aspects of Wells's life are still the matter of sometimes acrimonious dispute in studies of him and his associates; of his biographies that by David C. Smith (1986) is helpful.

See also *The *Sea Lady*, *The *Food of the Gods*, *The *Country of the Blind* and *Other Stories* and *The *Passionate Friends*.

WEMYSS, Mrs George: Mary LUTYENS (b. 1868) married George WEMYSS. Eldest daughter among fourteen children (she had eight elder brothers) of an army officer and animal painter, she married a rich army officer. She was the sister of the architect Sir Edwin Lutyens (1869–1944), whose daughter records in his biography (1980) that Wemyss loved children, but had none of her own. Her fiction is much concerned with children, although only *All About All of Us* (1911) and *Things We Thought Of* (1911), fictionalized accounts of her own childhood, are actually addressed to children. *The Professional Aunt* (1910), for example, is an adult novel about children; her fiction also includes drawing-room comedy like *A Lost Interest* (1912).

WENTWORTH, Patricia, *pseud.*: Dora Amy ELLES (1878–1961) married, first, George F. DILLON (d. 1906) and, secondly (1920), George Oliver TURNBULL. Born in Mussoorie, India, daughter of an officer in the Indian army, and educated at Blackheath High School, she began to write *historical novels after being widowed for the first time, although she had published serially before; like *Kipling she began by appearing in the Lahore *Civil and Military Gazette*. Both her husbands were army officers. Her first novel was *A Marriage Under the Terror* (1910). After her second marriage she became the very prolific author of *crime stories, including thirty-two featuring Miss Maud Silver, the governess turned private eye, who first appeared in *Grey Mask* (1928). She also published three volumes of verse.

WENTWORTH-JAMES, Gertie de S.: Gertie de S. WENTWORTH married —— JAMES. For a conjectural attribution to this writer of *Confidences* (1903), see under Maud Churton *Braby. She was author of about fifty-five smartly witty novels, self-consciously progressive especially about sex, published between 1908 and 1929. Her romances about upper-class adolescents are rather in the manner of 'Victoria *Cross'. Characteristic in many ways, including the colourful title, is *Red Love* (1908) about the amours of a professional dancer. The title refers to the hero's emotional state. 'There was nothing tender, nothing protective, nothing reverential about the passion which Linda Henniman inspired.' The heroine of *Pink Purity* (1909) is a 14-year-old who looks and behaves like an 18-year-old, thus straddling the 'dangerous period' in a woman's life that the steamier novelists liked to dwell on. A Jewish millionaire pays her an allowance so that he can make love to her married sister, who does not, in the end, succumb. *Crimson Caresses* (1918) even features a romantic novelist who pays off her husband's blackmailing former wife by writing novels such as *The Flaming Fires and A Sin in the Making*. The latter is described as 'forcedly erotic' and the publisher pays her £45 for it, expecting to sell 80,000 copies. *Scarlet Kiss: The Story of a Degenerate Woman Who Drifted* (1910) is about the 30ish editor of a women's magazine who gets married cynically but falls in love. The title-page of *The Child Market* (1918) acknowledges the help of Dr Cooper of the Twilight Sleep Nursing Home, Streatham. Marthe makes her fiancé promise not to have children (babies revolt her). He then disappears to make his fortune in Africa. But all her friends think the English population must be regenerated after the First World War. She nearly decides to have a baby by the man she loves, but decides that illegitimacy is such a stigma that she must return to her husband to have the baby. But meanwhile he has a had a baby by a less fastidious woman, and they arrange a divorce so she can marry the lover. *The Television Girl* (1928) is a futuristic novel about an osteopath who falls in love with a girl he sees on the screen of his telephone when he gets a wrong number. Osteopathy is promoted in Wentworth-James's fiction.

WERNER, Alice: see under Lillias Campbell *Davidson.

WESTRUP, Margaret married (1910) W. Sydney STACEY. Her husband was a painter and they lived in Cornwall. She was the author of eight volumes of fiction in this period, some for children, including *Elizabeth's Children* (1903) and *Helen Alliston* (1904), both published anonymously, and *Elizabeth in Retreat* (1912).

WEYMAN, Stanley J[ohn] (1855–1928) married (1895) Charlotte PANTING. He was born at Ludlow, Shropshire, where he attended the local school; he then went to Shrewsbury Grammar School and Christ Church, Oxford. He graduated with a second in modern history in 1877 and followed his solicitor father into the law, qualifying as a barrister in 1881 and practising for eight years. However, he was of too nervous a disposition to excel in such an adversarial profession. James Payn (1830–98) of the **Cornhill* accepted several short stories and suggested he try his hand at novels. Weyman specialized in *historical romances, which were tremendously popular with younger readers. *A Gentleman of France* (1893) was his first popular success. The typical Weyman hero is humble, unsure of himself, impecunious, and no longer young, but also immensely brave and certain to get the girl in the end. *Under the Red Robe* (1896), the tale of a spy who is reformed by true love, was later dramatized and performed at the Haymarket, London. Weyman's Edwardian romances are notable for his strenuous efforts to seek out less hackneyed historical episodes. *The Long Night* (1903), for example, concerns Charles Emanuel of Savoy's attempt to storm Geneva in 1602. A Syndic, Philibert Blondel, who is mortally sick, betrays the city in exchange for the recipe for an elixir. *The Wild Geese* (1908) is set in early eighteenth-century Ireland. The hero, Captain John Sullivan, is a mercenary who has earned an honourable position in the service of the King of Sweden. Out of a sense of duty, he returns to Ireland to act as trustee to two young kinsfolk, the McMurrough of Morristown, in Kerry, and the McMurrough's sister, Flavia. He finds himself caught up a futile uprising led by the McMurrough. Loathed by all and sundry as a Protestant and a supporter of the Hanoverian succession, he foils the plot, and then boldly resumes his position among the plotters in order to rescue Flavia from her increasingly unscrupulous brother. She reluctantly falls in love with him. But Weyman also resumed his favourite setting: *ancien régime* France. *The Abbess of Vlaye* (1904) is set in the time of Henry of Navarre, in a town on the border of the Périgord. The villainous, one-eyed Captain of Vlaye terrorizes the surrounding countryside, and is loved by the Abbess; she gradually conquers his poisonous rage, and with that the interest of the novel declines. Justice is eventually restored by the rather uninspiring Duc de Joyeuse. Henry of Navarre also appears in some of the stories collected in *In King's Byways* (1902), this time in the midst of Jesuit plotters. Others stories are set in Paris at the time of the Revolution, and in Victorian London. In *Starvecrow Farm* (1905), high-born Henrietta Damer elopes with an agitator who has survived the Peterloo massacre and committed murder. When he abandons her, she is jailed twice, rescues a child kidnapped by a Radical gang, and falls in love with the wooden Captain Clyne, a middle-aged naval martinet. Perhaps the best of the Edwardian romances is **Chippinge* (1906). The Stories in *Laid Up in Lavender* (1907) have contemporary settings. Weyman's *Collected Novels* were published in 1911. Weyman and his wife settled at Plas Llanrhydd, Wales, for the last thirty years of his life, where he became a Justice of the Peace and was closely connected with the Welsh Church.

When It Was Dark: *The Story of a Great Conspiracy*, 'Guy *Thorne', 1903, Greening. Basil Gortre, the strong-minded, sensitive curate of St Thomas's, an outpost of 'chilly, dour Christianity' at Walktown, Lancashire, is about to leave to take up a curacy in London, where he will share rooms in Lincoln's Inn with an old college friend, Harold Spence, a journalist on the *Daily Wire.* Gortre is engaged to Helena Byars, the vicar's statuesque daughter. Before he leaves, he encounters Constantine Schuabe, a north-country millionaire of Jewish descent who seems to him the epitome of modern materialism. 'The curse of indifferentism is over the land,' Gortre laments. The scene switches to London, where Professor Robert Llwellyn, a leading authority on the Holy Land antiquities, works late in his office at the British Museum. Llwellyn is a worried man: he owes Schuabe £14,000, and his mistress, Gertrude Hunt, a Cockney actress, makes constant demands on him. Schuabe, by now revealed as the devil incarnate, blackmails him into travelling to Jerusalem and planting faked archaeological evidence which would prove that Christ never rose from the dead and that Christianity is therefore a lie. The plan works like a dream. The discrediting of Christianity causes mass anarchy and a global crime-wave. Gortre, however, has penetrated the conspiracy and, with the help of Spence and the *Daily Wire,* and a repentant Gertrude, exposes the conspirators. Llewellyn collapses and dies. An epilogue, set five years later, shows us Spence editing the *Daily Wire,* Schuabe in a lunatic asylum, and Gortre, now married to Helena, preaching a sermon on Christ's resurrection in a no longer chilly and dour St Thomas's. The novel's massive success can probably be attributed to its assault on 'indifferentism' and its espousal of absolute moral and spiritual values.

Where Angels Fear to Tread, E. M. *Forster, 1905, William Blackwood. Lilia Herriton, a widow in her 30s, is encouraged by her brother-in-law Philip to spend a year in Italy. She agrees, travelling with a younger neighbour, Caroline Abbott. News then reaches the Herritons that Lilia is to marry again. Philip is sent to stop her, but arrives too late—Lilia has married Gino Carella, a younger man and the son of a dentist. When Lilia dies in childbirth, her mother sends Philip back to Italy, this time to rescue her grandchild. He travels with his sister Harriet, and Caroline Abbott, who, guilty at her part in the story, is now determined to adopt the baby for herself. On arrival they discover that Gino is a devoted father, and Philip and Caroline give up on the project. Harriet perseveres, stealing the baby and fleeing in a carriage. It is involved in an accident and the baby is killed. Gino attacks Philip and the English retreat from Italy. On the way home Philip realises he has fallen in love with Caroline but she is now in love with Gino.

WHISHAW, Frederick J. translated several of the novels of F. M. Dostoevsky (1821–1881) and published verse (1878, 1879) and more than sixty volumes of fiction between 1895 and 1914, some of which are straightforward boys' books, such as *Gubbins Minor and Some Other Fellows: A Story of School Life* (1897) and *The Competitors: A Tale of Upton House School* (1906); some are set in Africa, like *The White Witch of the Matabele* (1897); but most have Russian settings, for instance *The Lion Cub: A Story of Peter the Great* (1902), *Near the Tsar, Near Death* (1903), *A Grand Duke of Russia* (1905), *A Russian Coward* (1906), and *A Russian Judas* (1911). He also published *Out of Doors in Tsar-Land: A Record of the Seeings and Doings of a Wanderer in Russia* (1893) and *A Hunter's Log in Russia* (1900)

WHISTLER, Charles Watts (1856–1913) married (1886) Georgiana Rosalie Shapter STRANGE. Born in Hastings, the son of a Church of England clergyman, he was educated at Merchant Taylors' School, St Thomas's Hospital Medical School, and Emmanuel College, Cambridge. He first worked as a surgeon in Suffolk (1881–84) and then, after a period as an army surgeon, was ordained. He became rector of Elton (1887–95), vicar of Stockland, Somerset (1895–1909), and rector of Cheselbourne, Dorset (1909–). As well as many works on genealogy and history he published some fourteen volumes of fiction, mostly *historical fiction for the young set in pre-Conquest England, including *Havelok the Dane: A Legend of Old Grimsby and Lincoln* (1900), *A Prince of Cornwall: A Story of Glastonbury and the West in the Days of Ina of Wessex* (1904), and *Dragon Osmund: A Story of Athelstan and Brunanburgh* (1914).

WHITBY, Beatrice [Janie] (d. 1931) married Philip HICKS. Born in Ottery St Mary, Devon, daughter of a doctor, she was educated at home and in Hamburg, and married another doctor. *The Awakening of Mary Fenwick* (1889), her first published novel, was a success; it is about an heiress who realizes she has been married for her money. It was followed by fourteen other volumes of intelligent, very mildly *feminist fiction between 1889 and 1911, including *The Result of an Accident* (1908), which focuses on the effect on a solicitor's wife and two elder daughters of his fecklessness and paralysis; *Foggy Fancies and Other Stories* (1903) and *The Whirligig of Time* (1906), about a family in rural Devon with a spendthrift father, who are shaken up when he marries a brisk New Woman who doesn't understand them; she is compared unfavourably to her helpmeet stepdaughters.

WHITE, Percy (1852–1938) married (1888) Constance COOPER (d. 1916). Born in London, the son of a doctor, he was educated privately and taught English literature at the University of Cairo (1911–1924). During the First World War he was an interpreter in the Royal Navy and then worked in RAF intelligence. He was the author of a long series of popular novels beginning with *Mr Bailey-Martin* (1893). *The Triumph of Mrs St George* (1904) concerns an adventuress who sets up as Madame Artemis, clairvoyant, and on the basis of a few lucky hits captures London society. Colonel Foulerton falls in love with her, and learns her secret. She takes poison, and is canonized. *Love and the Poor Suitor* (1908) is a mildly satirical *suburban romance. When Maurice Norman, of Dante Studios, Oak Row, Fulham, the well-bred but impoverished illustrator of 'Lucy's Lovers', a serial currently running in the *Lady's Week*, secures the Secretaryship of the Society for the Prevention of Public Vandalism, at £350 a year, with some leisure for art, he is able to marry Sonia Owen, a rector's daughter from the seaside town of Chailport. They settle at Eglington Mansions in Hammersmith. When Maurice subsequently loses the Secretaryship, his best man, Lionel Musgrave, a wealthy artist and minor rake who imagines himself in love with Sonia, offers to act as their Maecenas. Although Musgrave turns a legacy of £2,000 into £12,000 by a daring speculation, Sonia has little trouble rebuffing him. White lived at Roquebrune, in the south of France.

WHITE, Roma, *pseud.*: Blanche ORAM (1866–1930) married (1897) Charles WINDER. Born in Bury, Lancashire, she started her writing career as a journalist, and wrote novels under a pseudonym adapted from her own name; the first was *Punchinello's Romance* (1892), an odd mix of fairy tale and progressive politics, in which an oppressed orphan girl becomes a radical woman, defending rioting mill girls from the police, uncovering the true story of her mother's 'fall', and living happily ever after. Oram's output continued to be generically various, covering fairy tales (*Moonbeams and Brownies*, 1892), *historical romance (*The Changeling of Brandlesome*, 1894), a melodrama of theatre life (*A Stolen Mask*, 1896), contemporary adventure (*Island of Seven Shadows*, 1898), oriental romance (*Backsheesh* 1902; *Moods and Winds of Araby*, 1906), and, later, domestic tragedies (*Trespassers in Paradise*, 1928, and *The Sin-Offering*, 1930). She also wrote a successful gardening book, *Town and Country: A Book of Suburban Gardening* (1900). A few works were published under her married name.

WHITECHURCH, Victor L[orenzo] (1868–1933) married Florence PARTRIDGE. The son of a Church of England clergyman, he was educated at Chichester Grammar School, Chichester Theological College, and Durham University. He was ordained in 1891 and served in several parishes, retiring as an honorary canon of Christ Church, Oxford. He was collector of *Thrilling Stories of the Railway* (1912), and published about twenty-four volumes of fiction from 1903 to 1933 and some theological works. His best-known novel, *The Canon in Residence* (1904), is a gentle comedy about a clergyman who has his dog-collar stolen on holiday in Switzerland, and, jolted out of his groove, becomes a bit of a radical on his return to a cathedral close. *The Canon's Dilemma and Other Stories* (1909) and *Off the Main Road: A Village Comedy* (1911) are similar.

WHITEING, Richard (1840–1928) married (1869) Helen HARRIS. Born in Museum Street, London, the son of a civil servant working at Somerset House, his childhood was disrupted by the death of his mother. Whiteing lived near the Strand with his father for a few years and attended school at Bromley-by-Bow. He then spent several years with a foster-family in St John's Wood. He was tutored by a French refugee and then attended art classes, where he met John Ruskin (1819–1900) and F. J. Furnivall (1825–1910). The latter is portrayed in Whiteing's novel *Ring in the New* (1906). Whiteing was an apprentice engraver (with Benjamin Wyon, 1802–58) before switching to journalism in 1866. He began to write a series of social/political articles for the *Evening Star* which were collected and published as *Mr Sprouts: His Opinions* (1867). He was Paris correspondent for the *Manchester Guardian* and for *World* (London and New York). He was also a leader-writer for the *Morning Star* (under Justin *McCarthy Senior) and was on the editorial staff of both the *Manchester Guardian* and the *Daily News* during his successful journalistic career. He gave up journalism when he resigned from the *Daily News* in 1899, but his novel-writing continued. His best-remembered work is *No 5 John Street* (1899)—a graphic portrayal of London life which was made into a film in 1919. Grant *Richards, its publisher, called it 'my first considerable commercial success'. Other works are *The Island* (1888), *The Yellow Van* (1903), *All Moonshine* (1907), a collection of essays called *Little People* (1908), and an autobiography *My Harvest* (1915). *The Yellow Van* is Anglo-American. An American schoolmarm marries a Duke and becomes involved in the travails of the local village radical, who has been cruelly treated by the agents of her estimable husband. The Duchess and her brother think of rural England as a museum. Whiteing thought otherwise, and turned his novel into a tract about the persistence of feudalism. The yellow van of the title distributes incendiary literature concerning the rural labourer and his relation to the land he tills. *All Moonshine* is a dream-vision in which all the kingdoms and nations of the earth are quartered on the Isle of Wight, thus enabling the heroine and her sentimental guardian to visit them at will. The moonshine aspect is somewhat tempered by scenes of battlefield carnage which recall Stephen Crane's (1871–1900) *The Red Badge of Courage* (1895). In 1876 Whiteing published *The Democracy* under the pseudonym 'Whyte Thorne'. His wife, Helen, wrote under the pseudonym 'ALB'. Whiteing lived for some time with another woman, the journalist and children's writer Alice Corkran (d. 1916). He was granted a Civil List pension of £100 in 1910; he also got £50 a year from the Author's Society, which he nobly resigned on receiving a legacy, but later had to renew. He applied to the Royal Literary Fund in 1909 and 1913.

WHITELAW, David (1876–1971). Trained as a painter at Heatherley's and in Paris, he moved from designing book covers to composing serial romances. His first novel was *Mc Stodger's Affinity* (1896); his eighth, *The Little Hour of Peter Wells* (1913), is about a clerk whose life is transformed by finding a dead pierrot in Covent Garden market. In later life Whitelaw became an inventor of games (including Lexicon and Monarchy), wrote plays for stage and television, and was editor of the *London Magazine*.

White Peacock, The, D. H. *Lawrence, 1911, William Heinemann. 'To think that *my* son should have written such a story' was the initial comment of Lawrence's mother on the first version of *The White Peacock*, or 'Laetitia', as it was then called, written between April 1906 and June 1907. In 'Laetitia' the heroine, in the manner of contemporary sensational fiction, becomes pregnant by one man and then marries another. The pregnancy and the deceitful marriage did not survive into the published version, but the problem they articulate—the difficulty of finding the right partner in life—certainly did. As the novel opens, Lettie Beardsall, intelligent, forceful, sexually timid but eager to exercise power, an emancipated woman ('she read all things that dealt with modern women'), is divided between Leslie Tempest, a mine-owner's son, passionate but refined, painfully self-conscious, and George Saxton, a farmer's son, charismatic but strangely passive. The story is told by Lettie's brother, the bookish Cyril. Their father, Frank Beardsall, left his wife, Lettice, eighteen years previously, and returns for one last look at his family before his squalid death. Cyril cultivates the Tempests' gamekeeper, Annable, an incorrigible materialist and nihilist, whose respect he earns by taking an interest in the maggots at work in a dead rabbit. Annable was once a curate, and married to a fashionable heiress; their marriage, passionate at first, deteriorated when she 'began to get souly'. She is the peacock of the title ('A woman to the end, I tell you, all vanity and screech and defilement'); a *white* peacock because innocent in her pride. Shortly after, Annable is found dead, buried under a rockfall. Lettie finally opts for Leslie and respectability, while George consoles himself with his voluptuous cousin, Meg, barmaid at the Ram Inn. The group begins to break up. George's sister, Emily, becomes a schoolteacher in Nottingham. Cyril moves to London. Leslie becomes a prominent local figure, inheriting his father's business and house and becoming an MP. Emily, who had at one time seemed destined for Cyril, marries a farmer, Tom Renshaw. George, however, goes into a decline. He drinks heavily, and mistreats his wife. But it is the destruction of his physical beauty which seems to affect Cyril most. 'Like a tree that is falling, going soft and pale and rotten, clammy with small fungi, he stood leaning against the gate, while the dim afternoon drifted with a flow of thick sweet sunshine past him, not touching him.' Yet Cyril himself, the perpetual observer, is perhaps the saddest case of all. 'Last year in Mexico,' Lawrence wrote in 1925, 'I reread *The White Peacock* for the first time in fifteen years. It seemed strange and far off and as if written by somebody else... And then I'd come on something that showed I may have changed in style or form, but I haven't changed fundamentally. '

White Plumes of Navarre, The: *A Romance of the Wars of Religion*, S. R. *Crockett, 1906, Religious Tract Society. Set in mid-sixteenth-century France and Spain against the complicated background of the plotting and counter-plotting of the Catholic League, the Huguenots, the French, and the Spanish royalists, the romance is between Claire Agnew, daughter of Scottish Protestant diplomat, Francis Agnew, and a high-born young Frenchman, John d'Albert. The plot complications are provided by Valentine La Nina, Jesuit agent and secret daughter of Philip II of Spain, who loves John but saves him for Claire; and John Stirling, fanatical Calvinist and master spy, who, disguised as a fool, Jean-aux-Choux (Cabbage Jock), loves Claire but saves her for John.

White Prophet, The, Hall *Caine, 1909, William Heinemann. Ambitious and complicated romance which seeks to explore through the intricacies of personal allegiance the justice and scope of British rule in Egypt. A ceremonial replay of the Battle of Omdurman provokes murmurings against the Consul-General, Lord Nuneham, who has consistently sought to Europeanize Egypt and to suppress Moslem fundamentalism. (The model for Nuneham is the 1st Earl of Cromer, 1841–1917, autocratic Consul-General from 1883 to 1907, who once wrote that the Egyptians 'should be permitted to govern themselves after the fashion in which Europeans think they ought to be governed'.) Nuneham sends his son, Colonel Gordon Lord (named after Gordon of Khartoum, 1833–85), to Alexandria to arrest Ishmael Ameer, a holy man who is thought to be stirring up trouble. Lord, however, discovers that Ishmael Ameer has been campaigning not so much against the British as against the materialism of the modern world, and declines to arrest him. Returning to Cairo, he is ordered to close down the university, a hotbed of dissent, and again refuses. This second refusal results in his disgrace, and in the loss of his fiancée, the 'well grown, splendidly developed' Helena Graves, daughter of the general commanding the British army in Egypt. General Graves suffers from a weak heart, and expires, shortly after a visit from Ishmael Ameer, during a struggle with Lord, whom he has insulted and humiliated. Ishmael Ameer, whose aims are spiritual rather than political, retires to Khartoum, whither he is followed by Lord, now a sympathizer, and by Helena, who thinks he has murdered her father, and seeks to revenge herself by gaining his confidence and then betraying him. Ishmael Ameer and Helena become, spiritually, man and wife. When an opportunity arises to capture the British high command and take Cairo, Ishmael Ameer sends Lord on ahead as his envoy, in the disguise of a Bedouin sheikh, and himself follows after with an increasingly belligerent army of followers and Helena. He is now, under the double influence of his vast fame and his desire for Helena, a changed man. Helena has already betrayed his plan to Lord Nuneham, who allows it to proceed, with a view to teaching him and his fellow-conspirators a lesson. Lord believes that the only way to avoid bloodshed is to sacrifice himself. He is arrested, tried, and sentenced to death. A royal pardon is obtained, and he is promoted to commanding officer of the British army in Egypt. Ishmael Ameer, realizing that Helena loves Lord, releases her from her bonds. Lord Nuneham resigns: the days of autocratic rule are over. Douglas *Sladen described *The Tragedy of the Pyramids: A Romance of Army Life in Egypt* (1909) as a 'counterblast' to *The White Prophet*, which he criticized in a lengthy preface.

Whom God Hath Joined, Arnold *Bennett, 1906, John Nutt. The double plot concerns two Five Towns adulteries. Laurence Ridware discovers that his wife Phyllis has been sleeping with a local schoolmaster to whom she had once been engaged. Meanwhile his boss, Charles Fearns, is caught sleeping, under his own roof, with his children's French governess. The development of the two cases is followed from the point of view of the two protagonists, and leads inexorably towards the hypocritical bear-baiting of the London divorce courts. Ridware, though a solicitor, is tripped up by a point of law (and by his wife's urbane lies). Fearns's daughter, Annunciata, the chief witness against him, breaks down in court, whereupon his wife abandons the case, and they are reconciled, though his philandering continues. Bennett's customary stoicism incorporates without difficulty a passionate protest against the divorce laws.

Widdershins, Oliver *Onions, 1911, Martin Secker. Several of this collection of ghost stories focus on the ghost as (destructive) artistic muse. In 'The Beckoning Fair One' a writer is driven mad by a jealous presence who haunts his writing after he moves into a deserted house; in 'Benlian' a sculptor 'puts himself, body and soul' into his work; in 'Hic Jacet', the narrator, creator of the popular detective, Martin Renard, tries vainly to write the life of his friend, Michael Andriaovsky, a painter who refused commercial compromise. Other stories feature, more familiarly, a ghost ship, a ghost house, a man dogged by something always following and sometimes passing painfully through him, and an office girl possessed by Bacchic spirits.

Wife of Altamont, The, Violet *Hunt, 1910, William Heinemann. When Altamont murders Sir Joris Vere, whose illegitimate son he is, and is sent to gaol, Betsey, his childless wife, takes his mistress, Ada Cox, and her two children to live with her. Ernest Vere, nephew and heir of Sir Joris, meets Betsey at the funeral of Altamont's mother and takes her off to dinner at the Albemarle. Altamont kills himself in prison, and Vere, who is supposed to marry Lady Dobrée de Saye, takes Betsey to the Continent. On her return she retires, with Ada Cox and her children, to Vere's country estate, where she occupies the keep, while Lady Dobrée and a party of friends install themselves in the house. Vere marries Betsey, while Lady Dobrée pairs off with Lee Brice, author of an improper novel called *Red Corpuscles*.

Wife of Sir Isaac Harman, The, H. G. *Wells, 1914, Macmillan. Eighteen-year-old Ellen Sawbridge achieves an ambitious marriage to the founder and proprietor of the International Bread Shops. The figure of the lonely young woman who is the wife of the much older multi-millionaire is a familiar Wellsian motif; and here, as elsewhere she (Ellen) seeks release in a casual affair, in this instance with the novelist Mr Brumley. But she does not commit adultery. Instead, Ellen eventually finds an outlet in militant suffragism and spends a month in gaol as a result of her political activities. Her husband bullies her into a resumption of her former duties but gives her enough freedom to indulge in large-scale social service. At the end of the novel she is finally released by his death. The story is throughout subordinated to long and poorly focused discussion of the management, and conception in principle, of the International Bread shops. In this story Wells also examines the status of the female employee in general, and particularly in connection with their board and lodging outside business hours.

Will Warburton: *A Romance of Real Life*, George *Gissing, 1905, Archibald Constable. Will Warburton, a generous, humane young sugar merchant, whose greatest pleasure in life is helping others, loses his and his family's money when his partner speculates in a City investment that goes wrong, and is obliged to become a grocer, a move he keeps secret from family and friends. The most significant of the latter are Norbert Franks, an artist who decides he has spent too long a time being poor for his painting and so turns his hand with great success to popular themes and society portraits; Rosamund Elvan, who breaks off her engagement to Franks when she thinks he is sacrificing his art to her material needs but eventually marries him anyway; and Bertha Cross, a humorous pragmatist who makes her living as a book illustrator. Warburton briefly, madly, thinks himself in love with Rosamund but comes to realise the value of Bertha, who is happy to be a grocer's wife. A slight, good-natured novel, in which the minor characters (such as Bertha's mother) are more memorable than the principals, and the incidental descriptions of grocering and the servant's lot more illuminating than the big themes of art and commerce, pride and love.

WILLCOCKS, M[ary] P[atricia] [Susan] (1869–1952) lived in Exeter, where she befriended 'Francis *Bancroft' and Edith C. M. *Dart. She published sixteen volumes of fiction between 1905 and 1936, translations of two novels by Anatole France (1844–1924), several biographies, and *Between the Old World and the New: Being Studies in Literary Personality from Goethe and Balzac to*

Anatole France and Thomas Hardy (1925), an interesting attempt to relate the history of imaginative literature to the progress of the human race which she sees as a consequence of evolution. Willcocks's first novel, *Widdicombe* (1905), is a Hardyesque tale of the parallel romances of two sisters, Silphine and Rosemary Rosdew, who live with their uncle in a West Country town. Old-fashioned Rosemary ('she must be counted among the half-developed women of today') marries the squire's son. Thoroughly modern, thoroughly developed Silphine falls in love with a socialist; when he won't have her, she takes up with another man in order to win him back. The later and far more confident **Wings of Desire* (1912) also features two sisters. Wilmot Quick, the heroine of *Wingless Victory* (1907), 'somewhat like a wild strawberry, for she had the knack of gathering but the daintiest perfection from food and air', does not believe in love. But she comes to love the man she had married for convenience, Dr Tony Borlace, and successfully fights off an earthier rival, Johanna Buckingham. *A Man of Genius: A Story of the Judgment of Paris* (1908) rewrites *Jude the Obscure* (1895) by Thomas Hardy (1840–1928). Ambrose Velly rises from obscurity to become a successful architect. He is torn between the passionate, superstitious Thyrza Braund and the educated Damaris Westway. Damaris eventually returns him to Thyrza, finding spiritual consolation in his masterpiece, an oratory. In *The Way Up* (1910) Michael Strode cuts himself adrift from the support of a rich uncle to work in an iron foundry and 'pick, pick, pick like a navvy at the false foundations of our society, trying to build a better'. He marries a social butterfly, Alise, whose wealth enables him to buy a foundry, where he will put his socialistic ideas into practice. Alise, however, cannot stand the life. Waiving her right to her fortune, she bravely abandons him and their young son. He ends up with a 'worthier' woman.

WILLIAMSON, C. N. and A. M.: Charles Norris WILLIAMSON (1859–1920) married (1895) Alice Muriel LIVINGSTON (1869–1933). Alice Livingston was born into an upper-class American family and grew up in New York State. She began writing stories as a child and had published some in America before she visited England armed with a letter (from a journalist cousin and namesake of hers) to Williamson, who introduced her to Alfred Harmsworth, later Lord Northcliffe (1865–1922), who commissioned a serial, and other editors. Charles Williamson had been educated at London University, his parents wishing him to become an engineer, and though he became a journalist he had enough knowledge of mechanics to be interested in the early motor car. In order to get married she asked Harmsworth to take six serials simultaneously: 'I can write seven thousand words a day.' They did not begin to collaborate until their big success, *The Lightning Conductor: The Strange Adventures of a Motor-Car* (1902), 'edited by C. N. and A. M. Williamson', which was based on a series of articles he had been commissioned to write about taking a car through France. When the editor changed his mind she turned the work into a novel in a series of letters, whose hero, an English gentleman, poses as a chauffeur to escort an American heiress around France and Italy. According to her memoirs, *The Inky Way* (1931), she always wrote the story, while he provided the topographical detail, though at the time they claimed that he wrote the man's letters, she the woman's. The Williamsons specialized in tales of travels in England and Europe, part travelogues, part romances, embellished with posed photographs of hero, heroine and motor car, often taken on their own travels. The motifs of disguise and transatlantic marriage recur frequently. In *My Friend the Chauffeur* (1905), for example, an American widow makes her daughter pretend to be a child to conceal her own age; they travel to Dalmatia before all is revealed and the girl marries an English baronet. *The Golden Silence* (1910) is their most geographically ambitious work. An American woman, Victoria Ray, sets off into the Algerian desert to find her sister, who married an Arab sheikh and has not been seen for ten years. The books made the Williamsons rich enough to live in style on the Riviera. After his death she became interested in spiritualism and claimed to be still in touch with him. She committed suicide in a hotel in Bath. She also published much fiction anonymously and under several pseudonyms.

WILSON, Theodora Wilson (d. 1941). Born in Kendal, in the Lake District, she was educated at Stramongate School there, at Croydon High School, and abroad. She was the author of fiction for both children and adults, and of books of biblical exegesis. *T'Bacca Queen* (1901), is set in musical circles in Germany and 'Moorshire' or Yorkshire, and contrasts two girl cousins, one an heiress, the other illegitimate and working-class; each ends marrying happily in her station. In *Sarah the Valiant* (1907), also set partly among music students in Germany, an orphan brother and sister triumph over their villainous uncle and guardian. Other works include *Ursula Raven* (1905), *Bess of Hardendale* (1908), and *The Bargain: A Story of Love* (1909)

WILSON-FOX, Alice: Alice Theodora RAIKES (1863–1943) married (1889) William Arthur WILSON-FOX (1861–1909). The daughter of a Welsh landowner and MP, she was married to a barrister who was a civil servant in the Board of Trade, and published novels, stories, and tracts from 1905, including *A Regular Madam* (1912), set in New France, Canada, and *Hearts and Coronets* (1910), in which a little orphan girl makes friends in a railway accident with some other children and it turns out that she and not their father is the rightful heir to a peerage.

Wind in the Willows, The, Kenneth *Grahame, 1908, Methuen. This is a celebration of the English riverside through the characters of Mole, Water Rat, and Badger, whose humanization seems to confirm their natural forms and habitations—Rat's love of the river, Mole's shyness and simplicity, Badger's gruffness and solidity—while giving their adventures familiarity. These adventures concern Mr Toad, and how his love of motor cars leads him to theft, trial, imprisonment, escape, and a battle to drive the hooligans of the Wild Wood out of Toad Hall. *The Wind in the Willows* is a classic children's book for its integration of the Toad drama and comedy with a continuing sense of the mystery and grace of the countryside and its creatures.

Wings of Desire, M. P. *Willcocks, 1912, John Lane. The heroines are two sisters, Sara and Anne, one married to a famous author, Archer Bellew, who has effectively put an end to her promising career as a concert pianist, the other single, training to be a doctor, and much involved in public-health work (which seems to mean inspecting drains in Liverpool). When the book opens, both are staying with their well-to-do 'parasite' father, Vin Hereford, at his home in a Cornish seaport. Both are chafing under parental, and in Sara's case marital, constraint. Sara is falling in love with a dull sea-captain, Billy Knyvett, while Anne has decided on a marriage of more or less convenience with the equally colourless Peter Westlake, who runs a mission hall for seamen. When Archer Bellew reappears, he begins an affair with the youthful Sally Woodruffe, whose sinister mother is trying to marry her off to one of two local dignitaries. In order to get the men chosen by her heroines out of the way while they decide what to do, Willcocks packs them into a yacht and sends them, as so many (male) authors had sent *their* heroes, on a wild-goose chase after buried treasure in the South Seas. The men seem reluctant to cast off, but are firmly instructed as to their duty and sent about their business by Knyvett's mother, a formidable woman who prepares herself for the task by reading up on 'erotic morbidity' at the local library. Knyvett and Westlake return none the richer, but somewhat the wiser, and a little more interesting. Anne settles for Westlake, while Sara not only contemplates with equanimity the prospect of divorce but resumes her career as a pianist. Meanwhile an independently minded painter, Margaret Rossiter, who was once in love with Archer, decides that she would prefer the single (and creative) life to a resumption of the affair. Overall, though, the book's feminism lies less in the futures it sketches for its heroines than in the mischief it makes with genre.

Wings of the Dove, The, Henry *James, 1902, Archibald Constable. This is a novel of two contrasting heroines and their opposing, overlapping hopes of love and life. Kate Croy, a 'handsome', 'dazzling' young Englishwoman, is in love with Merton Densher, an impoverished journalist, of whom her family disapprove. Her aunt, Maud Lowder, is trying to arrange a good marriage for her; her sister, Maria, supports the suit of Lord Mark. Milly Theale, an open-hearted American heiress, is dying of a mystery illness, and comes to Europe with her friend Susan Shepherd Stringham, through whom she meets Mrs Lowder and her circle, becoming particularly friendly with Kate, who accompanies her to her medical consultation with Sir Luke Stett. He advises Milly to enjoy her remaining life to the full, and suggests she take a palazzo in Venice for the winter. Milly has also met Densher (in New York) but now learns (from Maria) of his love for Kate. On his return to London, though, he continues to pay Milly court, encouraged in this by Kate, who hopes that he will marry Milly (making her happy in her last days) and inherit her fortune, so that he and Kate can then wed. Milly falls in love with Densher but Lord Mark, who has been rejected by her, tells Milly of Densher's continuing relationship with Kate, which Densher cannot deny. Milly's health worsens and she dies, leaving Densher the money on which to marry Kate. He is only willing to do so, though, without the legacy; Kate will only marry him with it—she realizes that he now loves Milly's memory. Kate and Densher agree to part. The story is mostly told indirectly, in a reflection of Milly's own situation: she is both the centre of the drama and ignorant of it; in her fatal sickness she determines everyone else's actions without herself being able to do anything about it.

WINTER, John Strange, *pseud.*: Henrietta Eliza Vaughan PALMER (1856–1911) married (1884) Arthur STANNARD (d. 1912). She was born in York, where her father, a former army officer, was the rector of St Margaret's. She attended Bootham House School, York. She first published fiction in the *Family Herald* (April 1874) under the pseudonym 'Violet Whyte'. In 1881 she began, as 'John Strange Winter', a series of military tales: her *Times* obituary (15 Dec. 1911) quotes the opinion of John Ruskin (1819–1900) that she was 'the author to whom we owe the most finished and faithful rendering ever yet given of the character of the British soldier'. Many readers believed 'Winter' to be a man; a prison warder is supposed to have asked Oscar Wilde (1854–1900) what he thought of him: '"A charming person" says Oscar, "but a lady you know, not a man. Not a great stylist, perhaps, but a good, simple storyteller." "Thank you, Sir, I did not know he was a lady, Sir."' After his release from prison he continued to be friendly with the Stannards. In *How to Publish* (1898), Leopold Wagner advised young writers to begin by establishing 'a reputation in the magazines for a special kind of story', and added: 'Mr *Kipling is identified with Indian life, Mrs Stannard ('John Strange Winter') with cavalry life, Mr G. R. *Sims with London life (of a sort), while Mr Anthony *Hope, Mr *Machen, and others are all specialists in fiction.' Her best received work was *Bootles' Baby: A Story of the Scarlet Lancers* (1885). Her Edwardian output was vast and in fact reasonably diverse. Of the three novels she published in 1902, for example, *A Blaze of Glory* concerns military life up to and including the *Boer War, *Marty* the marriage of a Colonial Office clerk to the daughter of a second-hand clothes dealer, and *Uncle Charles* the marriage of a mildly adventurous young woman to a mildly bohemian artist. According to the **Times Literary Supplement*, which apparently kept the score, *Marty* was her seventy-ninth novel. But there was to be no resting on laurels. *The Little Vanities of Mrs Whitaker* (1904) was her eighty-seventh. Mrs Whitaker believes that her husband, who is 'something in the city', has been unfaithful to her. Herself *suburban yet emancipated, she remains faithful to him, until it is revealed that he has behaved honourably throughout. The Whitakers have a pair of fashionably independent daughters, Maudie and Julia. The social aspects of military life continued to feature strongly in Mrs Stannard's fiction, as in *A Simple Gentleman* (1906), but not to the exclusion of other themes. When the heroine of *The Heart of Maureen* (1910) loses her memory after a mysterious and murderous attack, an innocent man is accused; he eventually earns both his freedom and her heart. In *The Luck of the Napiers* (1911), a solicitor wants to buy a rundown family estate because he has discovered that there is coal beneath it; the heir steps in to retrieve it with a fortune won in the American West. She married a civil engineer, one of whose sisters was married to the journalist G. A. Sala (1828–96). Stannard was the first president of the Writer's Club in 1892, president of the Society of Women Journalists 1901–3, and a Fellow of the Royal Society of Literature. In later life she had hopes of making her fortune selling skin cream. Her obituarist noted that her 'preparations for the toilet were almost as much liked as her stories'. She applied to the Royal Literary Fund in 1908 and, unsuccessfully, in 1911, the second time in great distress because an accident outside a Tube Station in London opened up the scar from a mastectomy she had had in 1900; she died soon afterwards.

Wisdom of Father Brown, The, G. K. *Chesterton, 1914, Cassell. The second collection of Father Brown stories employs the by now familiar formula, with the uniquely dishevelled priest solving crimes by his ability to get under the skins of the criminals. The opening story, 'The Absence of Mr Glass', is less about a crime (it turns out that none has been committed) than about his rivalry with Dr Orion Hood, an 'eminent criminologist and specialist in certain moral disorders', whose scientific theories mask a spectacular ignorance of human nature. In characteristic Chestertonian fashion, the most *exotic settings and circumstances tend to conceal an entirely home-grown villainy, whose home-grownness is its exoticism. Thus the Italian bandit who rules 'The Paradise of Thieves', and whom we first see dressed in futurist style (tweeds of piebald check, a pink tie, protruberant yellow boots), is in fact an actor from Birmingham. Even the political intrigue of the *Ruritanian principality of Heiligwaldenstein yields, in 'The Fairy Tale of Father Brown', to the priest's common sense. Here, as in several of these stories, Father Brown is accompanied by his friend Flambeau, ex-criminal and ex-detective, whose formidable swordstick, the emblem of melodrama, constrasts with his own realistically shabby umbrella.

Wise Virgins, The: *A Story of Words, Opinions, and a Few Emotions*, L. S. *Woolf, 1914, Edward Arnold. Begun in September 1912 and completed by the end of the following year, Woolf's second novel is part *roman à clef*, part antidote to the sentimentality of E. M. *Forster's early novels about romantic escapes from suburbia. Widowed Mrs Garland lives in a red-brick villa in a London suburb with her four virgin daughters, the youngest of whom, Gwen, finds her discontent crystallized by the arrival of a Jewish couple, the Davises, and their son, Harry. Harry, an aspiring artist, becomes intimate with a well-to-do bohemian family, the Lawrences. Mr Lawrence is modelled on Leslie Stephen (1832–1904), Katharine Lawrence on Vanessa Stephen (1879–1961), and Camilla Lawrence on Virginia Stephen (1882–1941), whom Woolf had married in 1912. Their pretentious friend, Arthur Woodhouse, is an acid portrait of Vanessa's husband, Clive Bell (1881–1964). The Lawrences' world, which involves 'interminable talk and silences in very comfortable armchairs', both attracts and repels Harry, as he endures the garden and river parties of suburban life. After a weekend of more than usually interminable talk and silences, he proposes to the flawless and remote Camilla, and is rejected. When the Davises and Garlands holiday in the same Eastbourne hotel, Gwen seduces Harry. Although he does not love her, he feels compelled to marry her, and breaks with Camilla, who seems to be regretting her hasty rejection of him. 'My second novel was published simultaneously with the outbreak of war,' Woolf recalled. 'The war killed it dead and my total earnings from it were £20. His wife read it for the first time on 31 January 1915. 'My opinion is that it's a remarkable book; very bad in parts; first rate in others.'

With Kitchener in the Sudan, G. A. *Henty, 1903, Blackie. In this adventure story for boys, Gregory Hartley, educated at Harrow and Cambridge, is disinherited by his father for marrying a governess. Under the name Gregory Hilliard he takes a clerk's job in Alexandria, and becomes attached to the Egyptian army as an interpreter. He is reported missing in battle and presumed dead. His wife remains in Egypt and brings up their son, also Gregory, in his father's image. When he is 16 she dies, and young Gregory, determined to discover what happened to his father, offers his services to Lord Kitchener (he is fluent in Arabic and Sudanese languages). With the devoted assistance of his servant, Zaki, Gregory performs gallant deeds for the British army (usually in the disguise of a dervish) as it defeats the Mahdist uprising. He also comes to learn his father's fate, and discovers that he is now heir to the family estate. He returns to England to take up his duties as the Marquis of Langdale. This is standard Henty fare—plenty of military action rooted, somewhat confusingly, in real historical events, with the warriors on both sides invariably showing courage in action, stamina on the march, and dignity in defeat.

Within the Tides: *Tales*, Joseph *Conrad, 1915, J. M. Dent. The most substantial of these four stories is 'The Planter of Malata', in which the lonely, laconic planter, Renouard, falls in love with Felicia Moorsam, who is searching for her fiancé, who fled east accused of a financial crime of which he has now been exonerated. In 'The Partner', the narrator is told in a pub a tale of fraud and murder in the English Channel. 'The Inn of the Two Witches' is a story of the Napoleonic wars, of sailors ashore in Spain and the horrors of a decrepit inn. 'Because of the Dollars' tells how a good man in an eastern port foils a robbery from his steamer but in so doing loses his wife. None of the stories is particularly revealing of character or place; each is concerned with how stories come to be told, by whom, for what reasons.

WODEHOUSE, P[elham] G[renville] (1881–1975), KBE (1975), married (1914) Ethel ROWLEY née NEWTON (d. 1984). Born in London, the son of a Hong Kong magistrate and a sister of Mary *Deane, Wodehouse was sent home to England aged 2 because of the climate (like Cicely *Hamilton and *Kipling) and had an unstable childhood with various relations. 'I know I was writing stories when I was five,' he told the *Paris Review.* 'I don't remember what I did before that. Just loafed, I suppose.' He was educated in Guernsey and (1894–1900) at Dulwich College, south London, where he was happy. Because his father would not send both him and his elder brother to Oxford, he left school to work briefly and unsuccessfully in a bank. He was already selling stories to the boys' magazine, *The Captain*, edited by R. S. Warren *Bell. Wodehouse left the bank to become a full-time writer in 1903, being assigned a regular column, 'By the Way', in the London *Globe*. In 1909, as his career as a comic writer blossomed, he went to the USA for a year, and thereafter spent at least half of every year there, writing lyrics for Broadway shows, working in particular with Jerome Kern (1885–1945). Meanwhile, he had moved from England to France, finally settling in 1934 in Le Touquet, in northern France, where he was captured and interned by the invading German army in the Second World War. Following his release in 1941 he indiscreetly made some broadcasts from Berlin to America. The fact that he had done so (rather than the innocently comic content of the talks) made him deeply unpopular in Britain, and after the war he moved to the United States, becoming an American citizen in 1955. He was eventually knighted shortly before his death. Although Wodehouse continued writing stories, lyrics and plays throughout his long life, his basic comic style, the highly wrought mimicry of the upper-class stutter and drawl, and his basic comic characters—from Psmith to Bertie Wooster and Jeeves (who first appeared in 'Extricating Young Gussie' in *The Man with Two Left Feet*, 1917)—were established by the end of the First World War. The basic formula is present in such early works as *Love Among the Chickens* (1906), *A Gentleman of Leisure* (1910), and *The *Little Nugget* (1913). The Wodehouse world (which readily adapted to the stage, as in Wodehouse's collaborations with 'Ian *Hay'), the world of London clubs such as the Drones, of country houses such as Blandings Castle, of irascible peers and awesome aunts, of bold women (often American) in pursuit of enfeebled young men, was less a satire of the Edwardian upper class at play than a fantasy version of it, a fantasy with particular appeal to Americans. What makes Wodehouse a great comic artist, though, is not the world he imagines or the people that inhabit it, but the style. He was, above all, a highly skilled linguistic technician (hence his success as a Broadway lyricist). His very earliest publications were stories of public-school life, with familiar plots of dishonour and sporting prowess: *The *Pothunters* (1902), *A Prefect's Uncle* (1903), *Tales of St Austin's* (1903), *The Gold Bat* (1904), *The Head of Kay's* (1905), *The White Feather* (1907) and **Mike*: *A Public School Story* (1909). In the last of these Wodehouse introduced the character of Psmith, who soon outstripped dull, athletic Mike as hero and foreshadowed the triumph of the frivolous over the authorities which was to be the characteristic dynamic of Wodehouse's fiction; he also appeared in *Psmith in the City: A Sequel to Mike* (1910), *Psmith Journalist* (1915), which includes, rather surprisingly, an exposé of New York slum landlords, and *Leave it to Psmith* (1924). In these early years Wodehouse also published sketches, a children's book, and a parody of the popular *invasion scare stories: *The *Swoop!, or, How Clarence Saved England: A Tale of the Great Invasion* (1909).

WOOD, Walter (1866–1961) married, first, M. A. BAKER (d. 1907) and, secondly (1910), Edith J. BERRY. Born in Bradford, he was educated at Borough West School. He worked briefly in the wool trade, and then for ten years on the *Yorkshire Observer*. He was editor (1913–1946) of *Toilers of the Deep: The Magazine of the Royal National Mission to Deep Sea Fishermen*. He was a prolific author of fact and fiction for boys, including *Men of the North Sea: Tales of the Dogger Bank* (1904); *The Enemy in Our Midst: The Story of a Raid on England* (1906), an *invasion scare story; *Peter the Powder-Boy: A Tale of the Days of Nelson* (1912); and *Grant, the Grenadier: His Adventures in the Fighting Fifth in the Peninsula* (1912).

WOODS, Margaret: Margaret Louisa BRADLEY (1856–1945) married (1879) Henry George WOODS (1842–1915). Born at Rugby, daughter of a Church of England clergyman, later Dean of Westminster, she was married to another clergyman and classical scholar who became president of Trinity College, Oxford. She was a friend of Henry *James. Her fiction, which in its day was regarded with high respect, includes *A Village Tragedy* (1887); *Sons of the Sword: A Romance of the Peninsular War* (1901); *The King's Revoke: An Episode in the Life of Patrick Dillon* (1905), a better than average *historical romance, set in early nineteenth-century Spain, whose hero masquerades as a woman and in other disguises in order to save from French captivity the Spanish king who has feet of clay; and *The Invader* (1907), in which a young woman student at Oxford in the 1880s, clever, earnest, and progressive, in love with her tutor, strangely resembles a flighty great-great-grandmother. Hypnotized by a friend, she becomes, intermittently, her ancestress, fascinates the tutor, gets her first, marries him, has a baby, nearly has a lover, and finally commits suicide to rid herself of the double. Her several volumes of verse were assembled in *Collected Poems* (1914).

WOOD-SEYS, R[oland] A[lexander] (1854–1919). Born at Stourbridge, Worcestershire, Wood-Seys travelled widely from 1876. He worked in London 1884–96 as a reviewer and publisher's reader. In 1897 he settled in California and grew olives. He wrote nine novels as 'Paul Cushing' from 1885, of which the last is *God's Lad: A Novel* (1900) in which the English hero and heroine separately make their fortunes in America; it ends in California. Under his own name he published *The Honourable Derek: A Novel* (1910) and *The Device of the Black Fox* (1911), both of which are set in America and England, celebrate quaint English villages, and are characterized by a great snobbishness about titles and high society and written in a knowing and pretentious style. In the former, the aristocratic English hero falls in love with a beautiful married American; in the latter an American millionaire hears of a penniless English earl and resolves to endow him with riches and marry him to his daughter.

WOOLF, L[eonard] S[idney] (1880–1969) married (1912) Adeline Virginia STEPHEN (1882–1941). Born in London, second son of the nine children of a Jewish barrister who died in 1892, he was educated at St Paul's School and Trinity College, Cambridge, where he read classics and belonged the select club, the Apostles. He was in the colonial service in Ceylon from 1904 until 1911. He left, partly to marry, partly because he was politically disillusioned with imperialism. In 1913 he joined the Fabian Society. His work as a political journalist and socialist thinker resulted in such works as *International Government* (1916) and *Co-operation and the Future of Industry* (1919). In 1915 he moved with his wife to Hogarth House, Richmond, where in 1917 they founded the Hogarth Press. He worked for the Labour Party as an adviser on international affairs, and stood unsuccessfully as Labour candidate for the Combined Universities in 1922. Literary historians will probably always remember him less for his own fiction than for his support, perhaps sometimes misguided but always devoted, of his wife, especially during her mental breakdowns during the First and Second World Wars. His published fiction consists of *The *Village in the Jungle* (1913), *The *Wise Virgins* (1914), and *Stories of the East* (1921). He was the translator of several works of Russian literature, including *The Note-Books of Anton Tchekhov* (1921) and, with D. H. *Lawrence, *The Gentleman from San Francisco and Other Stories* (1922) by I. A. Bunin (1870–1953). He also edited his wife's *A Haunted House and Other Short Stories* (1943) and *A Writer's Diary* (1953).

Workaday Woman, The, Violet *Hunt, 1906, T. Werner Laurie. Caroline Courtenay, the narrator, a hired companion, is paired with Jehane Bruce, a writer. Jehane is 'a worker like myself', and 'one of those women who ought to have been a man.' Her role, like that of a number of minor characters in contemporary fiction, from Hilda Forester in Olive *Birrell's **Love in a Mist* (1900) to Mary Datchet in *Night and Day* (1919) by Virginia Woolf (1882–1941), is to embody an unromantic independence which the heroine admires, but does not in the end want for herself. Bruce throws Bohemian parties in her Bloomsbury flat at which the relations of the sexes are 'a little altered', and the women gain character at the expense of the men. Caroline becomes engaged to charming, feckless Colonel Lisbon. 'Well, well, women must work and men must—play, I suppose.' Hunt, however, contrives a particularly ripe form of disgrace for Lisbon, leaving Caroline independent and alone. The plight of single working women also drew notable reponses from Francis *Gribble and 'Dolf *Wyllarde'.

WREN, P. C.: Percy WREN (1875–1941), who changed his name to Percival WREN and then to Percival Christopher WREN, married ——. Born in Deptford, son of a schoolmaster, he was educated at West Kent School and at the Delegacy of Non-Collegiate Students, Oxford. He graduated in 1898, worked as a schoolmaster and in other jobs, and joined the Indian Educational Service in 1903, where he served in Karachi and Bombay, before retiring, after several periods of sick leave, in 1917. His first volume of fiction was *Dew and Mildew: Semi-Detached Stories from Karabad, India* (1912): there are twenty-five of them, and they robustly defend the robustness of Anglo-Indian life against metropolitan decadence (one features a Mr Buggin, MP for 'Jewsditch'). *Father Gregory, or, Lures and Failures: A Tale of Hindostan* (1913) features a saintly priest and goings-on in a club for decayed and declassed gentlemen. Wren's career did not take off until the publication of *Beau Geste* (1924) and a switch of scene from India to Arabia. *Beau Geste* was sufficiently successful (being immediately adapted for stage and film) to serve him as a model for most of the rest of his output which consisted, in essence, of adventure stories for boys that stood in a direct line of descent from the adventure stories of *Empire of the 1890s, with the same emphasis on dramatic scenes, simple characters, and with a strong undercurrent of racism.

WRENCH, Mrs STANLEY: Violet Louise GIBBS (1880–1966) married (1902) William STANLEY WRENCH (d. 1951). She published several cookery books and, between 1908 and 1938, nineteen novels including *Love's Fool: The Confessions of a Magdalen* (1908), a steamy account of the amorous adventures of a vicar's daughter whose career as a kept woman begins when she makes a surprise visit to her fiancé in India and meets instead the Indian woman with whom he lives, and *Burnt Wings* (1909), whose heroine forgives her husband and adopts his illegitimate child. Some of her short stories for magazines and early fiction were written in collaboration with her husband. She also wrote as 'Mollie Stanley Wrench'. Her daughter Margaret Stanley Wrench (1916–74) was a poet.

WYLIE, I[da] A[lexa] R[oss] (1885–1959). Born in Melbourne, she was brought up in England. Her mother died when she was a baby, and her father, a Scots barrister, left her to her own devices from an early age. Her education thus worked backwards: she began by teaching herself, using her father's library and travelling alone in Europe from the age of 10; she went to finishing school in Belgium at 14, and to Cheltenham Ladies, College at 17. At 19 she went to study in Karlsrühe, where she began publishing stories in English magazines. She remained in Germany until 1911, putting the experience to good use in her fiction, for example in *The Germans* (1909) and *In Different Keys* (1911). On returning to England she became active in the suffrage movement, finally moving to the USA after the First World War, where she remained popular as a writer of short stories. The heroine of *The Paupers of Portman Square* (1913), Cecilia, a country parson's daughter, marries Heathcote St John on the strength of £12,000 a year and a stylish house in Portman Square. St John's fortune dwindles, and he is reduced to driving a cab. They are on the point of selling their only child for an allowance of £5,000 a year when a spirit intervenes to redeem them, and they begin to fall in love. Wylie's stories were collected in such volumes as *Happy Endings* (1915) and the aptly named *Armchair Stories* (1916). She published an autobiography, *My Life with George* (1940).

WYLLARDE, Dolf, *pseud.*: Dorothy Margarette Selby LOWNDES (d. 1950) was educated at King's College, London, and trained as a journalist. She published two volumes of verse (1911, 1920) and more than forty volumes of fiction between 1897 and 1939, including *As Ye Have Sown* (1906), *The *Pathway of the Pioneer: Nous Autres* (1906), *Rose-White Youth* (1908), *Tropical Tales and Others* (1909), and *The Unofficial Honeymoon* (1911). Lowndes's output intriguingly includes both *exotic tales and more serious examinations of the predicament of single women. Little is known about her life, and she may have adopted her pseudonym for everyday purposes. She left nearly £50,000, which suggests a prosperous background, though it is just possible that she might have earned the money from writing her popular romantic novels.

WYNNE, May, *pseud.*: Mabel Winifred KNOWLES (1875–1949). Born in Streatham, London, she was educated at home and worked in a Church of England mission in the East End of London. She also published nearly two hundred volumes of fiction from 1903, most of which (especially after the First World War) is fiction for children of various ages of a formulaic kind, including school stories and animal stories. But she did publish adult fiction to 1945; early examples include *Ronald Lindsay* (1905), *The Goal* (1907), and *The Hero of Urbino* (1914). In *The Red Fleur-de-Lys* (1912), a dashing Irishman rescues a girl cousin during the French Revolution; the situation is complicated by a gang of violent, aristocratic terrorists, who offer an interesting contrast to the invariably gallant aristocratic Scarlet Pimpernel gang in the novels of Baroness *Orczy. Between 1910 and 1913 Wynne wrote six novels as 'Lester Lurgan', including *Bohemian Blood* (1910).

X, Lady, *pseud.* was the author of two sex novels, *Diary of My Honeymoon* (1910) and *Decree Nisi* (1911). These are both narrated by the heroine, an innocent young girl; married off in the first book to a lecherous old baronet and rescued by a young lawyer. In the second book she is married to the lawyer, and they get mixed up in a divorce case, but it turns out that he is only professionally involved, and that, once again, she is too pure to be affected by the corruption and scandal which are the real point of the books.

Y

YARDLEY, Maud H. was the author of eight volumes of fiction to 1919, of which the most popular was her well-plotted first novel, *Sinless* (1906), in which a man returns from India after ten years to meet his wife, with another man identically circumstanced, meets the wrong one in the fog at Charing Cross station, and spends the night with her by mistake. By the end they have contrived to shake off their other halves and are living happily ever after. Other works include *A Man's Life Is Different, or, The Sleeping Flame* (1914), which also deals with adulterous love.

Yoke, The, 'Hubert *Wales', 1907, John Long. Angelica Jenour, still a virgin at 40, realizes that her 20-year-old ward, Maurice, is awakening sexually. She fears that he will resort to prostitutes. A friend of his contracts venereal disease and commits suicide; she decides she will save Maurice from a similar fate, and herself from the 'yoke' of repression, by becoming his lover. After educating him in love, and in 'racial health', she passes him on to his future wife. *The Yoke* was suppressed after a vigorous campaign by the National Vigilance Association, which denounced it as 'immoral garbage'.

YOLLAND, E. published seven novels between 1896 and 1912, including *The Struggle for the Crown: A Romance of the Seventeenth Century* (1912), a book for girls, recounted in the first person by a lady-in-waiting to the Winter Queen.

YORKE, Curtis, *pseud.*: Susan Rowley LONG (d. 1930) married John W. RICHMOND LEE. Born in Glasgow, she married a mining engineer. She published more than fifty cheerful, lightweight romances of which most went into several editions, from 1888. Of *Delphine* (1904) the *Times* commented: 'There is always a charm about Curtis Yorke's books, partly because she has the gift of natural, sympathetic dialogue; and it is not absent from this story of the wayward, elfish, French girl.' In *Queer Little Jane* (1912), an orphaned upper-class girl, bullied at home, runs away to Canada with a little dog and after various adventures comes back with a rich husband whom she has nursed back from the dead. *Dangerous Dorothy* (1912) travels to Spain with her uncle to inspect some mines and finds true love in the shape of the manager who then turns out to be an earl. Lee died in Kensington.

YOUNG, E[mily] H[ilda] (1880–1949) married (1902) J. A. H. DANIELL (d. 1917). Born in Northumberland, daughter of a ship-broker, she was educated at Gateshead Grammar School and Penhros College. She wrote her first three novels while living in Bristol with her husband, a solicitor who was killed during the First World War. These are *A Corn of Wheat* (1910), about a clergyman's sister who gets pregnant, marries a draper, and eventually leaves him to work in an orphanage; *Yonder* (1912), about two middle-class families, one urban, one rural, whose aspirations are cramped by poverty and handicapped by drink and weakness; and *Moon Fires* (1916). There is much emphasis on mystic communion with nature and on spiritual affinity between people. Subsequently Young lived in London and, after 1940, in Wiltshire, in a *ménage à trois* with Ralph Henderson, headmaster of Alleyn's School. Her best-known fictions—*William* (1925), *The Vicar's Daughter* (1928), and *Miss Mole* (1930), which won the James Tait Black Memorial prize—draw on these earlier books in their precise depiction of domestic life and understanding of the seismic effects on middle-class families of small changes of emotion.

YOUNG, [Alexander Bell] Filson (1876–1938) married (1918) Vera RAWNSLEY. Born in Ireland, son of a Church of Ireland clergyman, he worked for the *Manchester Guardian* as correspondent during the *Boer War, and subsequently in London as a journalist. He was literary editor of the *Daily Mail* (1903–4), editor of the **Outlook* (1904), editor of the *Saturday Review* (1921–24), and an adviser to the BBC from 1926. His first novel, *The Sands of Pleasure*

(1905), was a success, according to his publisher, Grant *Richards; it is about a Parisian cocotte called Toni and the English lighthouse engineer who has a brief affair with her before she returns to her profession. Young's other fiction includes *The Lover's Hours* (1907). He worked as a reader for Richards, and encouraged him to publish *Joyce's *Dubliners* (1914) He also published non-fiction about true crime, travel, motoring, and broadcasting.

YOUNG, F[lorence] E[thel] Mills (1875–1954) was the author of more than fifty novels to 1941. Many of her early works were about the English in South Africa: they include *The Purple Mists* (1914), in which a doctor marries an ignorant girl brought up on the veld. She runs away with another man and has a crippled baby before, on the last page, the doctor realizes they love each other. *The War of the Sexes* (1905) is a futuristic fantasy in which only one man is left in England, and has to seek refuge with a female fellow-scientist to avoid the ravening horde of women harassing him. He wakes up to realize this is only a dream, and decides he loves his scientist friend.

YOUNG, Eric BRETT: see under Francis Brett *Young.

YOUNG, Francis BRETT (1884–1954) married (1908) Jessica HANKINSON. Born at Halesowen, the son and grandson of doctors, he was educated at Epsom College and Birmingham University Medical School, and practised as a GP in Devon from 1907 to 1914, taking two years out to serve as a ship's doctor on a Britain to Japan run. During the First World War he served with the Royal Army Medical Corps in East Africa, eventually catching malaria and returning to England no longer fit to practise. He lived and wrote in Anacapri, before returning to his native Worcestershire in 1938. His novels mostly reflected his interests and experiences—medicine, the sea, war—while overlaying these rather sober topics with a distinctive poetic romanticism. His novels include *Undergrowth* (1913), written with his brother, Eric Brett Young; *Deep Sea* (1914), a West Country tragedy, dedicated to 'Pierre Loti' (1850–1923), about a crippled fisherman, his embittered wife, and their lodger's pathetic wife; and *The Iron Age* (1916). Brett Young had a considerable reputation and commercial success during the 1930s. He also published verse from 1917. He died in South Africa, where he had retired on medical advice after the Second World War.

YOUNG, Stuart: John Moray STUART-YOUNG. As a youth of 15, he wrote Oscar Wilde a fan letter and briefly became, in 1894, a friend. He later published (as J. M. Stuart-Young) a little volume of their correspondence, with his own poetry: *Osrac the Self-Sufficient* (1905). He lived at Conakry, West Africa, and published, as 'Stuart Young', fiction and non-fiction set there, including the novel *Merely a Negress: A West African Story* (1904), in which an Englishman marries a 'nearly white' Liberian girl, treats her badly, and eventually realizes her virtues and lives happily ever after.

Youth: *A Narrative and Two Other Stories*, Joseph *Conrad, 1902, Blackwood. The centrepiece of the volume is a novella, 'Heart of Darkness', first published in *Blackwood's Magazine* in 1899, and subsequently the most discussed of all Conrad's works. It is a story told during the course of a single evening on board a yawl moored off Gravesend, in the Thames Estuary. The narrator is a well-travelled sailor, Marlow, and his audience four men who embody respectability but also share the 'bond of the sea'. Marlow describes how he obtained the captaincy of a steamboat in the service of a company trading, we infer, in ivory, in the Belgian Congo. Thirty miles upriver, at the end of its first navigable stretch, he encounters, amidst scenes of routine brutality and wastefulness, an unflappable and faultlessly dressed accountant, who casually mentions a man called Kurtz, a 'first-class' agent in charge of a trading-post in the interior. After tramping for fifteen days through the jungle, Marlow arrives at the next navigable stretch of river, only to find that his steamboat has sunk. While he awaits the rivets which will enable him to repair it, he learns more about Kurtz, who is evidently a remarkable man as well as a first-class agent, a 'special being'. From now on, his purpose is a 'talk with Kurtz'. Proceeding upriver with a gang of carpetbaggers known as the Eldorado Exploring Expedition, dispersing cannibal attackers with blasts of the steam whistle, Marlow finally reaches the Inner Station. Kurtz is dying of fever. Before he dies, he shows Marlow a report he has written for the International Society for the Suppression of Savage Customs, an eloquent defence of the civilizing effects of colonialism on the last page of which he has scrawled a chilling postscript: 'Exterminate the brutes!' Kurtz, it seems, has gone native. Installed as a god-king, he has abandoned all moral restraint. Kurtz's last words ('The horror! The horror!') expose the heart of darkness; though Marlow gives Kurtz's fiancée a different and more elevating account of his death. 'All Europe contributed to the making of Kurtz', and the consequences of what Europe has made are revealed to us indirectly, through their impact on Marlow. In 'Youth', Marlow tells a similar audience of his first voyage to the East, as second mate of a decrepit cargo-boat, the *Judea*, carrying coal to Bangkok. A fierce storm almost sinks her, then the cargo catches fire. As the crew abandons ship, Marlow youthfully resolves that the boat he commands will be the first to reach Java. 'And this is how I see the East. I have seen its secret places and have looked into its very soul; but now I see it always from a small boat, a high outline of mountains, blue and afar in the morning; like faint mist at noon; a jagged wall of purple at sunset.' The story recalls Conrad's first voyage as second mate, on the *Palestine*, also bound for Bangkok with a cargo of coal which caught fire. 'The End of the Tether', is about an ancient mariner, Captain Whalley, who, realizing that he is going blind and that his career is over, chooses to go down with his ship. This has sometimes been related to Conrad's feeling that he was himself at the end of his literary tether.

Youth's Encounter: see under *Sinister Street*.

Z

ZACK, *pseud.*: Gwendoline KEATS (d. 1910). She was the author of five volumes of fiction from 1898, including *The Roman Road* (1903), a collection of three stories, in the first of which an heiress chooses a waster rather than his more virtuous brother, *Tales of Dunstable Weir* (1901), and *The White Cottage* (1901), a Hardyesque Devon tragedy about Luce Myrtle's choice between respectable Mark and the village n'er-do-well, Ben Lupin, with whom she eventually runs away. *Conrad noticed that her *On Trial* (1899) and his **Lord Jim* shared a preoccupation with cowardice. Keats, who also wrote plays, did not publish anything under her own name.

ZANGWILL, Edith Ayrton: Edith Chaplin AYRTON (1875–1945) married (1903) Israel *ZANGWILL. She was the daughter of the distinguished physicist and electrical engineer W. E. Ayrton (1947–1908) and his first wife, Matilda Chaplin (1846–1883), who was a pioneer in the campaign to enable women to qualify as physicians, and who died young of tuberculosis. Educated at Bedford College, she became, like her Jewish stepmother, a suffragist; her marriage to Zangwill, which caused a good deal of controversy among his Jewish friends, coincided with his decision to become a Zionist activist. She published humorous novels with a subtext about social reform and the plight of women. They include *The Barbarous Babes: Being the Memoirs of Molly* (1904); *The First Mrs Mollivar* (1905), in which a woman marries her widowed old flame, and finds the house haunted by the malevolent spirit of his first wife; and *Teresa* (1909), in which a gauche young girl brought up in unnatural innocence and high ideals marries the wrong man because he seems more moral. The nervous breakdown which immediately preceded Israel Zangwill's death is described in her novel *The House* (1928).

ZANGWILL, Israel (1864–1926) married (1903) Edith *ZANGWILL. The son of a Russian refugee, Zangwill was born in London and educated in Bristol, at the Jews' Free School, Spitalfields, London, and at London University. His first book, *Motza Kleis* (1881), written with Louis Cowen, was simply a sketch of market-day in London's Jewish ghetto, from which Zangwill himself came, as the son of Eastern European immigrants; their second collaboration, *The Premier and the Painter* (1888), written as 'J. Freeman Bell', was a satire of British political and cultural life. Zangwill's first books under his own name, *The Bachelors' Club* (1891) and *The Old Maids' Club* (1892), were lightly humorous (Zangwill became a regular contributor to the **Idler*). In 1891 he collaborated with Eleanor Marx Aveling (1855–1898) on *'A Doll's House' Repaired*, a parody in response to British critics of the play, and published the serial version of his locked-room mystery, *The Big Bow Mystery. The Children of the Ghetto* (1892) is his best-known book: a detailed examination of Jewish life in Britain, reflecting Zangwill's faith in realism, his refusal to impose a false order. Zangwill continued to chronicle the dilemmas, the illusions and disillusions of London's Jewish community in the stories and sketches collected as *Ghetto Tragedies* (1893), *Dreamers of the Ghetto* (1898), and **Ghetto Comedies* (1907); he continued to understand the humour of the situation, as in *The King of the Schnorrers: Grotesques and Fantasies*, serialised in the *Idler* in 1894, and he continued to explore the dilemmas of the artist in society, whether in fiction, for instance in *The Master* (1894), or in his critical essays, collected as *Without Prejudice* (1896) and *Italian Fantasies* (1910). He was also increasingly involved in politics, as a supporter of women's suffrage, pacifism, and as an early Zionist. He was interested in the theatre, which, following his *political novel, *The Mantle of Elijah* (1900), he found a better vehicle for his social concerns than fiction, writing such plays as *The Melting Pot* (1909), *The War God* (1911), and *The Next Religion* (1912). His political speeches and writings were collected as *The War for the World* (1916), *The Voice of Jersalem* (1920), and *Watchman: What of the Night?* (1923). There is a biography by Josep H. Udelson.

Zuleika Dobson, *or, An Oxford Love Story,* Max *Beerbohm, 1911, William Heinemann. An undergraduate epic and comic fantasy in which the startlingly beautiful Zuleika Dobson enchants and ultimately destroys the entire student body of Oxford. On a visit to her grandfather, the Warden of Judas College, Zuleika causes devastation among the undergraduates. They all fall in love with her, but she announces that she would only be interested in a man who does not 'bow down to her', and therefore rejects the marriage proposal offered by the besotted dandyish Duke of Dorset. The Duke asserts that he will, instead, lay down his life for Zuleika and drown himself in the Isis at the end of the annual boat races. After a series of delays and interludes, he does indeed commit suicide. He is followed into the river by the entire undergraduate population except for one man, physically unable to do so it. Zuleika Dobson, meanwhile, now Oxford has palled, is calmly studying the train timetable to Cambridge. *Zuleika Dobson*'s absurdist plot is marred by the intrusive tragedy of mass suicide, the sentimental realism of Katie Batch, the landlady's daughter, and the awkward Americanisms attributed to the Rhodes scholar, Mr Abimelech V. Oliver. However, the novel is memorable for its remarkable stylistic surface, the allusive intricacies of its prose, and its lyrical evocation of an Oxford skewed by satire.